Joseph Conrad lived a life that was as fantastic as any of his fiction. Born in Poland on December 3, 1857, he died in England on August 3, 1924. This native of the European interior spent his youth at sea, and although relatively ignorant of the English language until the age of twenty, he ultimately became one of the greatest of English novelists and stylists. Conrad's parents were aristocrats, ardent patriots who died when he was a child as a result of their revolutionary activities. He went to sea at sixteen, taught himself English and, after diligent study, gradually worked his way up until he passed his master's examination and was given command of merchant ships in the Orient and on the Congo. At the age of thirty-two he decided to try his hand at writing, left the sea, married, and became the father of two sons. Although his work won the admiration of critics, sales were small, and debts and poor health plagued Conrad for many years. He was a nervous, introverted, gloomy man for whom writing was an agony, but he was rich in friends who appreciated his genius, among them Henry James, Stephen Crane, and Ford Madox Ford. Although the ocean and the mysterious lands that border it are often the setting for his books, the truth of human experience is his theme, depicted with vigor, rhythm, and passionate contemplation of reality.

Linda Dryden is Lecturer in Cultural Studies at Napier University, Edinburgh. She has published various articles on Conrad in such journals as *The Conradian* and *Conradiana*, and is the author of *Joseph Conrad and the Imperial Romance* (Macmillan, 2000). Dr. Dryden's other interests include literary and cultural studies. She is currently editing a collection of essays on popular culture and writing a book on Robert Louis Stevenson, Oscar Wilde, and H. G. Wells.

·LORD JIM·

Joseph Conrad

With a New Introduction by
LINDA DRYDEN

With an Updated Bibliography

Ⓒ

A SIGNET CLASSIC

SIGNET CLASSIC
Published by New American Library, a division of
Penguin Putnam Inc., 375 Hudson Street,
New York, New York, 10014, U.S.A.
Penguin Books Ltd, 27 Wrights Lane,
London W8 5TZ, England
Penguin Books Australia Ltd, Ringwood,
Victoria, Australia
Penguin Books Canada Ltd, 10 Alcorn Avenue,
Toronto, Ontario, Canada M4V 3B2
Penguin Books (N.Z.) Ltd, 182–190 Wairau Road,
Auckland 10, New Zealand

Penguin Books Ltd, Registered Offices:
Harmondsworth, Middlesex, England

Published by Signet Classic, an imprint of New American Library,
a division of Penguin Putnam Inc.

First Signet Classic Printing (Dryden Introduction), July 2000
10 9 8 7

 REGISTERED TRADEMARK—MARCA REGISTRADA

Printed in the United States of America

Introduction

Joseph Conrad published his first novel, *Almayer's Folly*, in 1895 (the same year that Hardy turned from fiction to poetry after publishing his last great novel, *Jude the Obscure*). Nearly five short years later, with the serialization of *Heart of Darkness* (in *Blackwood's Edinburgh Magazine*, Feb.–Mar. 1899),* Conrad ushered in a new era: the era of literary modernism.

Writing at the *fin de siècle*, Conrad saw little cause for optimism. Therefore his modernism is characterized by an extreme skepticism of the assumptions of the past century, resulting in a subversion of romantic idealism. As Cedric Watts says, Conrad "stands at the intersection of the late Victorian and the early modernist cultural phases; he is both romantic and anti-romantic, both conservative and subversive."† At the century's end Conrad undertakes a serious reassessment of the values of the nineteenth century and suggests a deep unease about an unchallenged acceptance of them.

Coming immediately after *Heart of Darkness*, *Lord Jim* is another expression of Conrad's modernist unease. If Conrad endures nostalgically in the popular imagination as a writer of sea stories, *Heart of Darkness* proves that his fiction is about much more than shipboard adventures. Furthermore, *Lord Jim* is a novel that explores deep psychological issues concerning its eponymous hero, Jim, its main narrator, Marlow, and many of the novel's minor characters. Of *Lord Jim*'s forty-five chapters, only chapters one and two, and possibly Jim's narrative of the *Patna* desertion

---

*In *Blackwood's Magazine* it was titled *The Heart of Darkness*.
†Cedric Watts, *A Preface to Conrad* (New York: Longman, 1982), 46.

in chapters seven through twelve, deal almost exclusively with
events at sea. Yet even these latter chapters are punctuated with
observations and anecdotes from Marlow that lend to them an
ironic philosophical tone that reaches beyond mere storytelling
into profound issues of human experience. As Conrad says in his
Author's Note to *Almayer's Folly*:

> I am content to sympathize with common mortals, no mat-
> ter where they live; in houses or in tents, in the streets
> under a fog, or in the forests behind the dark line of dismal
> mangroves that fringe the vast solitude of the sea. . . . Their
> hearts—like ours—must endure the load of gifts from
> Heaven: the curse of facts and the blessing of illusions, the
> bitterness of our wisdom and the deceptive consolation of
> our folly.

In *Lord Jim*, as in most, if not all, of his fiction, Conrad is concerned with themes that touch upon the hopes and aspirations,
the delusions and self-deceptions, the successes and failures of
individuals everywhere.

The year 2000 marks the centenary of the publication of *Lord
Jim* in novel form. It began serialization in *Blackwood's Edinburgh Magazine* in October 1899, five months after the last in-
stallment of *Heart of Darkness*. On July 6, 1899, Conrad had
sent thirty-one manuscript pages to *Blackwood's* and was expecting to complete the story by the end of July. He had intended
to subtitle it "A Sketch." By December this "sketch" had reached
40,000 words and was continuing to expand. Conrad finally concluded the novel at six a.m. on the morning of July 14, 1900; the
"Sketch" had become "A Tale." The creative process had been so
prolonged that while completing the serial for the magazine
Conrad was simultaneously correcting page proofs of the novel
version for *Blackwood's*.

Early reviews of *Lord Jim* were so favorable that Conrad described himself to William Blackwood as "the spoiled child of
the critics." His first two novels, *Almayer's Folly* and *An Outcast*

of the Islands (1896), had been mistaken by some commentators for imperial romance, but with the publication of *Lord Jim* Conrad began to be regarded as a serious author: he was compared to Henry James, esteemed by Conrad as the greatest living writer in English. Nevertheless, *Lord Jim* does feature some of the preoccupations of Conrad's early novels, notably *An Outcast of the Islands.* Jim, like Willems in *An Outcast*, is exiled from his preferred society and is forced to retreat to a remote Malay community. Betrayal and retribution, thwarted ambition and self-delusion are key themes in both novels. Yet, while *An Outcast* has as its flawed hero a Dutchman, Willems, *Lord Jim* focuses on the blond, blue-eyed son of an English country parson. Marlow, the crusty English mariner who benevolently "adopts" Jim is wont to speculate on his appearance and dubious status as "one of us," an English gentleman and a member of the genteel English classes. Conrad's increasing concern with English moral and social values is thus signaled.

Jim's history is told in two distinct parts: the events leading up to his commission aboard the *Patna*, the events on the *Patna*, the official inquiry into those events, and Jim's subsequent attempts to rehabilitate himself constitute the first half of the novel; Jim's history in Patusan, the Malay community to which he is exiled, forms the second half of the novel. Marlow's account of his consultation with Stein, a Bavarian butterfly collector and erstwhile imperial adventurer, lies at the center of the novel, spanning and connecting these two discrete parts. This apparent disjointed narrative structure has been the subject of much critical comment on *Lord Jim* and has led critics to regard the novel as deeply flawed. The tortuous composition of the story and Conrad's inability to reach closure tend to reinforce this view. Yet, despite the fact that it appears to be a modernist tale in the first half and a romantic adventure in the second, the novel's overarching themes lend a unity and logic to the story that are not always acknowledged.

Jim's romantic aspirations are integral to both halves of the novel, but Conrad's modernist skepticism serves as a unifying narrative trait. Jim's jump from the *Patna* destroys his illusion of romantic heroism aboard ship, and the subsequent revoking of his mariner's certificate amounts to more than public disgrace: it destroys Brierly's belief in the value system that underpins his own self-image. As Marlow says of Jim, "if this sort can go wrong like that. . . ." Jim seems to epitomize the stoic team player and future imperial officer that the Rugby school of *Tom Brown's Schooldays* (1857) creates: he is symbolic of England's ideal imperial son who proves English superiority at sea, on the battlefield, and in the Empire. Yet his desertion of the *Patna*, the result of an instinct for self-preservation that overrides all of his training and breeding as an English gentleman-hero, is the incontrovertible proof that Jim is not "good enough." What destroys Brierly is that Jim is proof too that no one is "good enough" to live up to the stringent ideal of manhood established in the public schools and training centers for those imperial officers who would be representatives of England abroad and in the colonies.

Jim's choice of a life at sea was never a carefully considered career choice based on aptitude, suitability, and temperament. In the opening pages of the novel we are told that nothing more than a "course of light holiday literature" was the impetus for his declared vocation. Immediately the romance themes that dominate the second half of the novel are laid bare. Jim fancies himself as a "hero in a book"; he chooses his vocation after reading sea-faring adventure stories: Ballantyne's *The Coral Island* (1857) or Marryat's *Masterman Ready* (1841) could well have constituted his holiday reading material. With his English country parsonage background and schoolboy idiom—his speech is peppered with expressions like "Jove," "bally," and "Honour bright!"—Jim may even have modeled himself on Hughes's hero Tom Brown. Certainly the name, Jim, like Tom Brown, suggests a typical English boy, and the fact that Jim is given no surname emphasizes his apparent status as such. Jim aspires to romantic heroism whether it is on the deck of the *Patna* plying the eastern seas or as the leader designate of Malay and Bugis villagers in

Patusan. The first line of the novel, however, warns us of Jim's shortcomings: "He was an inch, perhaps two, under six feet. . . ." No genuine hero this: he does not even meet the required, symbolic six feet, and his subsequent history bears out this significant shortfall.

The first half of *Lord Jim*, in particular the fate of the *Patna*, is loosely based on the scandalous real-life story of the desertion of the *Jeddah* and its 953 Muslim passengers on its voyage from Singapore to Jeddah in 1880. Along with several officers and Muslim leaders, the captain and his wife escaped from the leaking boat with the aid of its first mate, Augustine Podmore Williams. Like the *Patna*, the *Jeddah* limped into port, and the subsequent scandal resulted in questions being raised in the House of Commons. Williams, generally regarded as the inspiration for Jim, eventually overcame the disgrace and managed to remain in Singapore society. Jim, of course, is unequal to the public ridicule after the trial and "jumps" from one situation to another, always aided by Marlow. Jim does in fact thrive in his various roles for a while: the good-natured boyish readiness and enthusiasm that endear him to Marlow make him almost indispensable to a series of employers. When the disgraceful truth, however, threatens to overwhelm his newly constructed, fragile reputation, Jim "deserts" his "post" again and again, baffling his employers. With nowhere left to turn (he cannot go home to his country parson father), Jim is finally provided with "the very thing" as Stein's proxy in Patusan.

In creating Jim, what Conrad adds to the story of Augustine Podmore Williams is an "exalted egotism" based on a "shadowy ideal of conduct," all of which are engendered by a nineteenth-century English sense of what constitutes a romantic hero and an imperial adventurer. It is because Jim so nearly fulfills the requirements of such an ideal that Marlow is fascinated and unable to let the illusion be completely destroyed:

> He was a youngster of the sort you like to see about you; of the sort you like to imagine yourself to have been; of the

sort whose appearance claims the fellowship of these illusions you had thought gone out, extinct, cold, and which, as
if rekindled at the approach of another flame, give a flutter
deep, deep down somewhere, give a flutter of light . . . of
heat!

Jim thus awakens Marlow's own youthful dreams of illusory romantic possibilities, and, despite his gruff, tetchy cynicism, Marlow sets about trying to provide Jim with the right conditions for
his romantic ego-ideal to survive and flourish.

There is often a tendency to mistake Marlow's words and
opinions for Conrad's own; but it must be remembered that
within the stories he relates, Marlow is a character in his own
right and one who interacts with the other characters. We are told
that "many times, in distant parts of the world, Marlow showed
himself willing to remember Jim, to remember him at length, in
detail, and audibly." The bulk of Jim's story, chapters five to
thirty-five, is told by Marlow probably "after dinner, on a verandah draped in motionless foliage and crowned with flowers, in
the deep dusk speckled by fiery cigar-ends." Jim's story is difficult to understand and it seems as if, by telling it over and over
again, Marlow is himself trying to make sense of it. Thus Marlow's role contributes to the many symbolic layers of the narrative. Jim is at once En-gland's (perceived) ideal imperial son, but
also the adopted son of Marlow and of a series of father figures.
The "privileged man" is chosen to receive the final pages of
Jim's story because he "alone showed an interest in him that survived the telling of his story." That shared interest binds Marlow
and his chosen reader in the perplexity of what, ultimately, to
make of Jim's fate.

At the center of the novel, between Jim's failures in the "real"
world and the exotic, romantic adventure of Patusan, stands
Stein, variously described by critics as a kind of Merlin figure, a
wizard, a latter-day Prospero, and a holy man. Stein has also
been an imperial adventurer. His history is deliberately told in
the idiom of romantic adventure; but, like Marlow, Stein too has

grown resigned to disillusionment. He lives a cloistered existence watching over the frozen corpses of his glorious past, glass-mounted rare species of butterflies; but Jim arouses Stein's interest, and he sets about finding a solution to Jim's dilemma of "how to be." Stein utters some of the most enigmatic words in Conrad's fiction; the exact meaning of his speech that begins a "man that is born falls into a dream" has been much discussed, argued over, and interpreted. Yet, ultimately what Stein is striving to articulate is a strategy for survival, for holding one's own in an indifferent universe. Recognizing the essential paradox of Jim's situation—his romantic nature is both "very bad" and "very good"—Stein suggests Patusan as the ideal location for Jim to live up to his ideal self-image as the romantic hero. In Patusan Jim can escape the moral complexities of the world of commerce and industry and immerse himself in a pre-civilized community that bears more than a passing resemblance to the people and locations of popular romantic fiction.

The Patusan episode of *Lord Jim* is often regarded as the most flawed in the novel, lending to it a disjointed structure and fracturing its coherence. It is almost certain that in the early stages of composition Conrad had no intention of the novel developing beyond the *Patna* Inquiry. However, he clearly conceived of other possibilities for Jim and these are explored to their inevitable conclusion through the Patusan adventure. Even the population of Patusan seems to be the result of a romantic imagination: speaking of Doramin, his motherly, "witch-like" wife and their son, Dain Waris, a type of "noble savage" with a civilized mind, Jim says they are "like people in a book" who are "well worth seeing." The whole scenario seems to conform to the stereotype and formula of imperial romance: Jim has a faithful servant, Tamb' Itam; Jewel is the beautiful native girl-woman whose devotion saves his life; he defeats the wicked Sherif Ali and effectively becomes ruler of the community; Cornelius is the repulsive spineless villain; and Jim himself has the Anglo-Saxon good looks and immaculate white uniform of the English imperial officer. It seems as if finally Jim has found a sanctuary from the real world of irresolvable dilemmas.

Lord Jim, however, is a modernist tale in which nothing can be taken for granted, no "truths" relied upon, and no romantic closure assumed. The arrival of "Gentleman" Brown heralds the end of romantic wish-fulfillment; but Brown is more than an agent of demonic retribution: he is Jim's callous, vindictive nemesis and an emissary from the world of actuality to remind both Jim and the reader that the "Never-never land" of Patusan is a mirage constituted partly by Jim's (and perhaps Stein's) romantic yearnings. Having infiltrated the heart of this seeming paradise, Brown, in an effort to break out of the deadlock he has created, appeals to the "white man" in Jim, to his English sense of fair play, and to their common racial identity. Relying on the simple rules of romance, Jim assumes that Brown will "play the game" and leave peacefully, if allowed: "there was no reason to doubt the story, whose truth seemed warranted by the rough frankness, by a sort of virile sincerity in accepting the morality and consequences of his acts." It is another error of judgement: Brown is as false as his assumed title, "Gentleman," but Jim's reliance on the myths of romantic fiction blind him to the truth of the man's nature.

Brown's betrayal plunges Jim's fragile utopia back into the turmoil from which he had rescued it. Jim is forced again to accept his failure to live up to his self-imposed romantic ideal. Whatever course of action he now takes would be a betrayal: placing himself in Doramin's hands betrays Jewel; but denying Doramin just retribution would compromise Jim's own "shadowy ideal of conduct." This violent rendering asunder of the romantic idyll of Patusan serves to unite, however tenuously, the two halves of the novel. Conrad returns the narrative to its modernist uncertainty by leaving Marlow's question, "Is he satisfied—quite, now, I wonder?" unanswered. Jim's brief success as an imperial adventurer in Patusan has been shattered by the intrusion of a reality from which it seems he could never finally escape, however far into the romantic East he may retreat.

Conrad's meaning is, as ever, notoriously difficult to pin down. Marlow's narrative with its rambling asides and unanswered questions contributes to this slippage of meaning. Famously, in *Heart of Darkness*, Marlow's storytelling is compared to the "yarns of other seamen" that "have a direct simplicity, the whole meaning of which lies within the shell of a cracked nut":

> But Marlow was not typical (if his propensity to spin yarns be excepted), and to him the meaning of an episode was not inside like a kernel but outside, enveloping the tale which brought it out only as a glow brings out a haze, in the likeness of one of these misty halos that sometimes are made visible by the spectral illumination of moonshine.

In writing this Conrad seems acutely aware of the tendency of his own narratives to defy easy analysis. He seems conscious, too, of the fact that his tales are no ordinary sea stories. If, in the spirit of Marlow, we continue to revisit Jim's story, it may in part be due to the resistance of the narrative to crystallize its purpose. It may also be ascribed to the fact that one hundred years after its publication we, like Marlow, and like Conrad, are still compelled to try to decipher the all too human impulses that motivate a man like Lord Jim.

—LINDA DRYDEN
February 2000

Author's Note

When this novel first appeared in book form a notion got about that I had been bolted away with. Some reviewers maintained that the work starting as a short story had got beyond the writer's control. One or two discovered internal evidence of the fact, which seemed to amuse them. They pointed out the limitations of the narrative form. They argued that no man could have been expected to talk all that time, and other men to listen so long. It was not, they said, very credible.

After thinking it over for something like sixteen years I am not so sure about that. Men have been known, both in the tropics and in the temperate zone, to sit up half the night "swapping yarns." This, however, is but one yarn, yet with interruptions affording some measure of relief; and in regard to the listeners' endurance, the postulate must be accepted that the story *was* interesting. It is the necessary preliminary assumption. If I hadn't believed that it *was* interesting I could never have begun to write it. As to the mere physical possibility we all know that some speeches in Parliament have taken nearer six than three hours in delivery; whereas all that part of the book which is Marlow's narrative can be read through aloud, I should say, in less than three hours. Besides—though I have kept strictly all such significant details out of the tale— we may presume that there must have been refreshments on that night, a glass of mineral water of some sort to help the narrator on.

But, seriously, the truth of the matter is, that my first thought was a short story, concerned only with the pilgrim ship episode; nothing more. And that was a legitimate conception. After writing a few pages, however, I became for some reason discontented and I laid them aside for a time. I didn't take them out of the drawer till the late Mr. William Blackwood suggested I should give something again to his magazine.

It was only then that I perceived that the pilgrim ship episode was a good starting-point for a free and wandering tale; that it was an event, too, which could conceivably colour the whole "sentiment of existence" in a simple and sensitive character. But all these preliminary moods and stirrings of spirit were rather obscure at the time, and they do not appear clearer to me now after the lapse of so many years.

The few pages I had laid aside were not without their weight in the choice of subject. But the whole was re-written deliberately. When I sat down to it I knew it would be a long book, though I didn't foresee that it would spread itself over thirteen numbers of "Maga."

I have been asked at times whether this was not the book of mine I liked best. I am a great foe of favouritism in public life, in private life, and even in the delicate relationship of an author to his works. As a matter of principle I will have no favourites; but I don't go so far as to feel grieved and annoyed by the preference some people give to my Lord Jim. I won't even say that I "fail to understand. . . ." No! But once I had occasion to be puzzled and surprised.

A friend of mine returning from Italy had talked with a lady there who did not like the book. I regretted that, of course, but what surprised me was the ground of her dislike. "You know," she said, "it is all so morbid."

The pronouncement gave me food for an hour's anxious thought. Finally I arrived at the conclusion that, making due allowances for the subject itself being rather foreign to women's normal sensibilities, the lady could not have been an Italian. I wonder whether she was European at all? In any case, no Latin temperament would have perceived anything morbid in the acute consciousness of lost honour. Such a consciousness may be wrong, or it may be right, or it may be condemned as artificial; and, perhaps, my Jim is not a type of wide commonness. But I can safely assure my readers that he is not the product of coldly perverted thinking. He's not a figure of Northern Mists either. One sunny morning in the commonplace surroundings of an Eastern roadstead, I saw his form pass by—appealing—significant—under a cloud—perfectly silent. Which is as it should be. It was for me, with all the sympathy of which I was capable, to seek fit words for his meaning. He was "one of us."

J.C.

June, 1917.

·LORD JIM·

Lord Jim

Chapter One

H<small>E WAS</small> an inch, perhaps two, under six feet, powerfully built, and he advanced straight at you with a slight stoop of the shoulders, head forward, and a fixed from-under stare which made you think of a charging bull. His voice was deep, loud, and his manner displayed a kind of dogged self-assertion which had nothing aggressive in it. It seemed a necessity, and it was directed apparently as much at himself as at anybody else. He was spotlessly neat, apparelled in immaculate white from shoes to hat, and in the various Eastern ports where he got his living as ship-chandler's water-clerk he was very popular.

A water-clerk need not pass an examination in anything under the sun, but he must have Ability in the abstract and demonstrate it practically. His work consists in racing under sail, steam, or oars against other water-clerks for any ship about to anchor, greeting her captain cheerily, forcing upon him a card—the business card of the ship-chandler—and on his first visit on shore piloting him firmly but without ostentation to a vast, cavern-like shop which is full of things that are eaten and drunk on board ship; where you can get everything to make her seaworthy and beautiful, from a set of chain-hooks for her cable to a book of gold-leaf for the carvings of her stern; and where her commander is received like a brother by a ship-chandler he has never seen before. There is a cool parlour, easy-chairs, bottles, cigars, writing implements, a copy of harbour regulations, and a warmth of welcome that melts the salt of a three months' passage out of a seaman's heart. The connection thus begun is kept up, as long as the ship remains in harbour, by the daily visits of the water-clerk. To the captain he is faithful like a friend and attentive like a son, with the patience of Job, the unselfish devotion of a woman, and the jollity of a boon companion. Later on the bill is sent in. It is a beautiful and humane occupation. Therefore good water-clerks are scarce. When a water-clerk who possesses Ability in the abstract has also the advantage of having been brought up to the sea, he is worth to his employer a lot of money and some humouring. Jim had always good wages and as much humouring as would have bought the fidelity of a fiend. Nevertheless, with black ingratitude he would throw up the job suddenly and depart. To his employers the reasons he gave were obviously inadequate. They said "Confounded fool!" as soon as his back was turned. This was their criticism on his exquisite sensibility.

To the white men in the waterside business and to the captains of ships he was just Jim—nothing more. He had, of course, another name, but he was anxious that it should not be pronounced. His incognito, which had as many holes as a sieve, was not meant to hide a personality but a fact. When the fact broke through the incognito he would leave suddenly the seaport where he happened to be at the time and go to another—generally farther east. He kept to seaports because he was a seaman in exile from the sea, and had Ability in the abstract, which is good for no other work but that of a water-clerk. He retreated in good order towards the rising sun, and the fact followed him casually but inevitably. Thus in the course of years he was known successively in Bombay, in Calcutta, in Rangoon, in Penang, in Batavia—and in each of these halting-places was just Jim the water-clerk. Afterwards, when his keen perception of the Intolerable drove him away for good from seaports and white men, even into the virgin forest, the Malays of the jungle village, where he had elected to conceal his deplorable faculty, added a word to the monosyllable of his incognito. They called him Tuan Jim: as one might say—Lord Jim.

Originally he came from a parsonage. Many commanders of fine merchant-ships come from these abodes of piety and peace. Jim's father possessed such certain knowledge of the Unknowable as made for the righteousness of people in cottages without disturbing the ease of mind of those whom an unerring Providence enables to live in mansions. The little church on a hill had the mossy greyness of a rock seen through a ragged screen of leaves. It had stood there for centuries, but the trees around probably remembered the laying of the first stone. Below, the red front of the rectory gleamed with a warm tint in the midst of grass-plots, flower-beds, and fir-trees, with an orchard at the back, a paved stable-yard to the left, and the sloping glass of greenhouses tacked along a wall of bricks. The living had belonged to the family for generations; but Jim was one of five sons, and when after a course of light holiday literature his vocation for the sea had declared itself, he was sent at once to a "training-ship for officers of the mercantile marine."

He learned there a little trigonometry and how to cross top-gallant yards. He was generally liked. He had the third place in navigation and pulled stroke in the first cutter. Having a steady head with an excellent physique, he was very smart aloft. His station was in the fore-top, and often from there he looked down, with the contempt of a man destined to shine in the midst of dangers, at the peaceful multitude of roofs cut in two by the brown tide of the stream, while scattered on the outskirts of the surrounding plain the factory chimneys rose perpendicular against a grimy sky, each slender like a pencil, and belching out smoke like a volcano. He could see the big ships departing, the broad-beamed ferries constantly on the move, the little boats floating far below his feet, with the hazy splendour of the sea in the distance, and the hope of a stirring life in the world of adventure.

On the lower deck in the babel of two hundred voices he would forget himself, and beforehand live in his mind the sea-life of light literature. He saw himself saving people from sinking ships, cutting away masts in a hurricane, swimming through a surf with a line; or as a lonely castaway, barefooted and half naked, walking on uncovered reefs in search of shell-fish to stave off starvation. He confronted savages on tropical shores, quelled mutinies on the high seas, and in a small boat upon the ocean kept the hearts of despairing men—always an example of devotion to duty, and as unflinching as a hero in a book.

"Something's up. Come along."

He leaped to his feet. The boys were streaming up the ladders. Above could be heard a great scurrying about and shouting, and when he got through the hatchway he stood still—as if confounded.

It was the dusk of a winter's day. The gale had freshened since noon, stopping the traffic on the river and now blew with the strength of a hurricane in fitful bursts that boomed like salvoes of great guns firing over the ocean. The rain slanted in sheets that flicked and subsided, and between whiles Jim had threatening glimpses of the tumbling tide, the small craft jumbled and tossing along the shore, the motionless buildings in the driving mist, the broad ferry-boats pitching ponderously at anchor, the vast landing-stages heaving up and down and smothered in sprays. The next gust seemed to blow all this away. The air was full of flying water. There was a fierce purpose in the gale, a furious earnestness in the screech of the wind, in the brutal tumult of earth and sky, that seemed directed at him, and made him hold his breath in awe. He stood still. It seemed to him he was whirled around.

He was jostled. "Man the cutter!" Boys rushed past him. A coaster running in for shelter had crashed through a schooner at anchor, and one of the ship's instructors had seen the accident. A mob of boys clambered on the rails, clustered around the davits. "Collision. Just ahead of us. Mr. Symons saw it." A push made him stagger against the mizzen-mast, and he caught hold of a rope. The old training-ship chained to her moorings quivered all over, bowing gently head to wind, and with her scanty rigging humming in a deep bass the breathless song of her youth at sea. "Lower away!" He saw the boat, manned, drop swiftly below the rail, and rushed after her. He heard a splash. "Let go; clear the falls!" He leaned over. The river alongside seethed in frothy streaks. The cutter could be seen in the falling darkness under the spell of tide and wind, that for a moment held her bound, and tossing abreast of the ship. A yelling voice in her reached him faintly: "Keep stroke, you

young whelps, if you want to save anybody! Keep stroke!"
And suddenly she lifted high her bow, and, leaping with raised
oars over a wave, broke the spell cast upon her by the wind and
tide.

Jim felt his shoulder gripped firmly. "Too late, youngster."
The captain of the ship laid a restraining hand on that boy, who
seemed on the point of leaping overboard, and Jim looked up
with the pain of conscious defeat in his eyes. The captain
smiled sympathetically. "Better luck next time. This will teach
you to be smart."

A shrill cheer greeted the cutter. She came dancing back half
full of water, and with two exhausted men washing about on
her bottom boards. The tumult and the menace of wind and sea
now appeared very contemptible to Jim, increasing the regret
of his awe at their inefficient menace. Now he knew what to
think of it. It seemed to him he cared nothing for the gale. He
could affront greater perils. He would do so—better than anybody. Not a particle of fear was left. Nevertheless he brooded
apart that evening while the bowman of the cutter—a boy with
a face like a girl's and big grey eyes—was the hero of the
lower deck. Eager questioners crowded round him. He narrated: "I just saw his head bobbing, and I dashed my boat-hook
in the water. It caught in his breeches and I nearly went overboard, as I thought I would, only old Symons let go the tiller
and grabbed my legs—the boat nearly swamped. Old Symons
is a fine old chap. I don't mind a bit him being grumpy with us.
He swore at me all the time he held my leg, but that was only
his way of telling me to stick to the boat-hook. Old Symons is
awfully excitable—isn't he? No—not the little fair chap—the
other, the big one with a beard. When we pulled him in he
groaned, 'Oh, my leg! oh, my leg!' turned up his eyes. Fancy
such a big chap fainting like a girl. Would any of you fellows
faint for a jab with a boat-hook?—I wouldn't. It went into his
leg so far." He showed the boat-hook, which he had carried
below for the purpose and produced a sensation. "No, silly! It
was not his flesh that held him—his breeches did. Lots of
blood, of course."

Jim thought it a pitiful display of vanity. The gale had ministered to a heroism as spurious as its own pretence of terror. He felt angry with the brutal tumult of earth and sky for taking him unawares and checking unfairly a generous readiness for narrow escapes. Otherwise he was rather glad he had not gone into the cutter, since a lower achievement had served the turn. He had enlarged his knowledge more than those who had done the work. When all men flinched, then—he felt sure—he alone would know how to deal with the spurious menace of wind and seas. He knew what to think of it. Seen dispassionately, it seemed contemptible. He could detect no trace of emotion in himself, and the final effect of a staggering event was that, unnoticed and apart from the noisy crowd of boys, he exulted with fresh certitude in his avidity for adventure, and in a sense of many-sided courage.

Chapter Two

AFTER TWO years of training he went to sea, and entering the regions so well known to his imagination, found them strangely barren of adventure. He made many voyages. He knew the magic monotony of existence between sky and water: he had to bear the criticism of men, the exactions of the sea, and the prosaic severity of the daily task that gives bread—but whose only reward is in the perfect love of the work. This reward eluded him. Yet he could not go back, because there is nothing more enticing, disenchanting, and enslaving than the life at sea. Besides, his prospects were good. He was gentlemanly, steady, tractable, with a thorough knowledge of his duties; and in time, when yet very young, he became chief mate of a fine ship, without ever having been tested by those events of the sea that show in the light of day the inner worth of a man, the edge of his temper, and the fibre of his stuff; that reveal the quality of his resistance and the secret truth of his pretences, not only to others but also to himself.

Only once in all that time he had again the glimpse of the earnestness of the anger of the sea. That truth is not so often made apparent as people might think. There are many shades in the danger of adventures and gales, and it is only now and then that there appears on the face of facts a sinister violence of intention—that indefinable something which forces it upon the mind and the heart of a man, that this complication of accidents or these elemental furies are coming at him with a purpose of malice, with a strength beyond control, with an unbridled cruelty that means to tear out of him his hope and his fear, the pain of his fatigue and his longing for rest: which means to smash, to destroy, to annihilate all he has seen, known, loved, enjoyed, or hated; all that is priceless and necessary—the sunshine, the memories, the future,—which means to sweep the whole precious world utterly away from his sight by the simple and appalling act of taking his life.

Jim, disabled by a falling spar at the beginning of a week of which his Scottish captain used to say afterwards, "Man! it's a pairfect meeracle to me how she lived through it!" spent many days stretched on his back, dazed, battered, hopeless, and tormented as if at the bottom of an abyss of unrest. He did not care what the end would be, and in his lucid moments overvalued his indifference. The danger, when not seen, has the imperfect vagueness of human thought. The fear grows shadowy; and Imagination, the enemy of men, the father of all terrors, unstimulated sinks to rest in the dulness of exhausted emotion. Jim saw nothing but the disorder of his tossed cabin. He lay there battened down in the midst of a small devastation, and felt secretly glad he had not to go on deck. But now and again an uncontrollable rush of anguish would grip him bodily, make him gasp and writhe under the blankets, and then the unintelligent brutality of an existence liable to the agony of such sensations filled him with a despairing desire to escape at any cost. The fine weather returned, and he thought no more about it.

His lameness, however, persisted, and when the ship arrived at an Eastern port he had to go to the hospital. His recovery was slow, and he was left behind.

There were only two other patients in the white men's ward:

the purser of a gunboat, who had broken his leg falling down a
hatchway; and a kind of railway contractor from a neighbouring province, afflicted by some mysterious tropical disease,
who held the doctor for an ass, and indulged in secret de-
baucheries of patent medicine which his Tamil servant used to
smuggle in with unwearied devotion. They told each other the
story of their lives, played cards a little, or, yawning and in pyjamas, lounged through the day in easy-chairs without saying a
word. The hospital stood on a hill, and a gentle breeze entering
through the windows, always flung wide open, brought into the
bare room the softness of the sky, the languor of the earth, the
bewitching breath of the Eastern waters. There were perfumes
in it, suggestions of infinite repose, the gift of endless dreams.
Jim looked every day over the thickets of gardens, beyond the
roofs of the town, over the fronds of palms growing on the
shore, at that roadstead which is a thoroughfare to the East,—
at the roadstead dotted by garlanded islets, lighted by festal
sunshine, its ships like toys, its brilliant activity resembling a
holiday pageant, with the eternal serenity of the Eastern sky
overhead and the smiling peace of the Eastern seas possessing
the space as far as the horizon.

　　Directly he could walk without a stick, he descended into
the town to look for some opportunity to get home. Nothing
offered just then, and, while waiting, he associated naturally
with the men of his calling in the port. These were of two
kinds. Some, very few and seen there but seldom, led mysterious lives, had preserved an undefaced energy with the temper
of buccaneers and the eyes of dreamers. They appeared to live
in a crazy maze of plans, hopes, dangers, enterprises, ahead of
civilisation, in the dark places of the sea, and their death was
the only event of their fantastic existence that seemed to have
a reasonable certitude of achievement. The majority were men
who, like himself, thrown there by some accident, had remained as officers of country ships. They had now a horror of
the home service, with its harder conditions, severer view of
duty, and the hazard of stormy oceans. They were attuned to
the eternal peace of Eastern sky and sea. They loved short pas-
sages, good deck-chairs, large native crews, and the distinction

of being white. They shuddered at the thought of hard work, and led precariously easy lives, always on the verge of dismissal, always on the verge of engagement, serving Chinamen, Arabs, half-castes—would have served the devil himself had he made it easy enough. They talked everlastingly of turns of luck: how So-and-so got charge of a boat on the coast of China—a soft thing; how this one had an easy billet in Japan somewhere, and that one was doing well in the Siamese navy; and in all they said—in their actions, in their looks, in their persons—could be detected the soft spot, the place of decay, the determination to lounge safely through existence.

To Jim that gossiping crowd, viewed as seamen, seemed at first more unsubstantial than so many shadows. But at length he found a fascination in the sight of those men, in their appearance of doing so well on such a small allowance of danger and toil. In time, beside the original disdain there grew up slowly another sentiment; and suddenly, giving up the idea of going home, he took a berth as chief mate of the *Patna*.

The *Patna* was a local steamer as old as the hills, lean like a greyhound, and eaten up with rust worse than a condemned water-tank. She was owned by a Chinaman, chartered by an Arab, and commanded by a sort of renegade New South Wales German, very anxious to curse publicly his native country, but who, apparently on the strength of Bismarck's victorious policy, brutalised all those he was not afraid of, and wore a "blood-and-iron" air, combined with a purple nose and a red moustache. After she had been painted outside and whitewashed inside, eight hundred pilgrims (more or less) were driven on board of her as she lay with steam up alongside a wooden jetty.

They streamed aboard over three gangways, they streamed in urged by faith and the hope of paradise, they streamed in with a continuous tramp and shuffle of bare feet, without a word, a murmur, or a look back; and when clear of confining rails spread on all sides over the deck, flowed forward and aft, overflowed down the yawning hatchways, filled the inner recesses of the ship—like water filling a cistern, like water flowing into crevices and crannies, like water rising silently even

with the rim. Eight hundred men and women with faith and
hopes, with affections and memories, they had collected there,
coming from north and south and from the outskirts of the
East, after treading the jungle paths, descending the rivers,
coasting in praus along the swallows, crossing in small canoes
from island to island, passing through suffering, meeting
strange sights, beset by strange fears, upheld by one desire.
They came from solitary huts in the wilderness, and populous
campongs, from villages by the sea. At the call of an idea they
had left their forests, their clearings, the protection of their
rulers, their prosperity, their poverty, the surroundings of their
youth and the graves of their fathers. They came covered with
dust, with sweat, with grime, with rags—the strong men at the
head of family parties, the lean old men pressing forward without hope of return; young boys with fearless eyes glancing curiously, shy little girls with tumbled long hair; the timid
women muffled up and clasping to their breasts, wrapped in
loose ends of soiled head-cloths, their sleeping babies, the unconscious pilgrims of an exacting belief.

"Look at dese cattle," said the German skipper to his new
chief mate.

An Arab, the leader of that pious voyage, came last. He
walked slowly aboard, handsome and grave in his white gown
and large turban. A string of servants followed, loaded with his
luggage; the *Patna* cast off and backed away from the wharf.

She was headed between two small islets, crossed obliquely
the anchoring-ground of sailing-ships, swung through half a
circle in the shadow of a hill, then ranged close to a ledge of
foaming reefs. The Arab standing up aft, recited aloud the
prayer of travellers by sea. He invoked the favour of the Most
High upon that journey, implored His blessings on men's toil
and on the secret purposes of their hearts; the steamer pounded
in the dusk the calm water of the Strait; and far astern of the
pilgrim ship a screw-pile lighthouse, planted by unbelievers on
a treacherous shoal, seemed to wink at her its eye of flame, as
if in derision of her errand of faith.

She cleared the Strait, crossed the bay, continued on her way
through the "One-degree" passage. She held on straight for the

Red Sea under a serene sky, under a sky scorching and un-
clouded, enveloped in a fulgor of sunshine that killed all
thought, oppressed the heart, withered all impulses of strength
and energy. And under the sinister splendour of that sky the
sea, blue and profound, remained still, without a stir, without a
ripple, without a wrinkle—viscous, stagnant, dead. The *Patna*,
with a slight hiss, passed over that plain luminous and smooth,
unrolled a black ribbon of smoke across the sky, left behind
her on the water a white ribbon of foam that vanished at once,
like the phantom of a track drawn upon a lifeless sea by the
phantom of a steamer.

Every morning the sun, as if keeping pace in his revolutions
with the progress of the pilgrimage, emerged with a silent
burst of light exactly at the same distance astern of the ship,
caught up with her at noon, pouring the concentrated fire of his
rays on the pious purposes of the men, glided past on his descent, and sank mysteriously into the sea evening after
evening, preserving the same distance ahead of her advancing
bows. The five whites on board lived amidships, isolated from
the human cargo. The awnings covered the deck with a white
roof from stem to stern, and a faint hum, a low murmur of sad
voices, alone revealed the presence of a crowd of people upon
the great blaze of the ocean. Such were the days, still, hot,
heavy, disappearing one by one into the past, as if falling into
an abyss for ever open in the wake of the ship; and the ship,
lonely under a wisp of smoke, held on her steadfast way black
and smouldering in a luminous immensity, as if scorched by a
flame flicked at her from a heaven without pity.

The nights descended on her like a benediction.

Chapter Three

A MARVELLOUS stillness pervaded the world, and the stars,
together with the serenity of their rays, seemed to shed

upon the earth the assurance of everlasting security. The young
moon recurved, and shining low in the west, was like a slender
shaving thrown up from a bar of gold, and the Arabian Sea
smooth and cool to the eye like a sheet of ice, extended its perfect level to the perfect circle of a dark horizon. The propeller
turned without a check, as though its beat had been part of the
scheme of a safe universe; and on each side of the *Patna* two
deep folds of water, permanent and sombre on the unwrinkled
shimmer, enclosed within their straight and diverging ridges a
few white swirls of foam bursting in a low hiss, a few
wavelets, a few ripples, a few undulations that, left behind, agitated the surface of the sea for an instant after the passage of
the ship, subsided splashing gently, calmed down at last into
the circular stillness of water and sky with the black speck of the
moving hull remaining everlastingly in its centre.

Jim on the bridge was penetrated by the great certitude of
unbounded safety and peace that could be read on the silent aspect of nature like the certitude of fostering love upon the
placid tenderness of a mother's face. Below the roof of
awnings, surrendered to the wisdom of white men and to their
courage, trusting the power of their unbelief and the iron shell
of their fire-ship, the pilgrims of an exacting faith slept on
mats, on blankets, on bare planks, on every deck in all the dark
corners, wrapped in dyed cloths, muffled in soiled rags, with
their heads resting on small bundles, with their faces pressed to
bent forearms: the men, the women, the children; the old with
the young, the decrepit with the lusty—all equal before sleep,
death's brother.

A draught of air, fanned from forward by the speed of the
ship, passed steadily through the long gloom between the high
bulwarks, swept over the rows of prone bodies; a few dim
flames in the globe-lamps were hung short here and there
under the ridge-poles, and in the blurred circles of light thrown
down and trembling slightly to the unceasing vibration of the
ship appeared a chin upturned, two closed eyelids, a dark hand
with silver rings, a meagre limb draped in a torn covering, a
head bent back, a naked foot, a throat bared and stretched as if
offering itself to the knife. The well-to-do had made for their

families shelters with heavy boxes and dusty mats; the poor reposed side by side with all they had on earth tied up in a rag under their heads; the lone old men slept, with drawn-up legs, upon their prayer-carpets, with their hands over their ears and one elbow on each side of the face; a father, his shoulders up and his knees under his forehead, dozed dejectedly by a boy who slept on his back with tousled hair and one arm commandingly extended; a woman covered from head to foot, like a corpse, with a piece of white sheeting, had a naked child in the hollow of each arm; the Arabs' belongings, piled right aft, made a heavy mound of broken outlines, with a cargo-lamp swung above, and a great confusion of vague forms behind: gleams of paunchy brass pots, the foot-rest of a deck-chair, blades of spears, the straight scabbard of an old sword leaning against a heap of pillows, the spout of a tin coffee-pot. The patent log on the taffrail periodically rang a single tinkling stroke for every mile traversed on an errand of faith. Above the mass of sleepers a faint and patient sigh at times floated, the exhalation of a troubled dream; and short metallic clangs bursting out suddenly in the depths of the ship, the harsh scrape of a shovel, the violent slam of a furnace-door, exploded brutally, as if the men handling the mysterious things below had their breasts full of fierce anger: while the slim high hull of the steamer went on evenly ahead, without a sway of her bare masts, cleaving continuously the great calm of the waters under the inaccessible serenity of the sky.

Jim paced athwart, and his footsteps in the vast silence were loud to his own ears, as if echoed by the watchful stars: his eyes roaming about the line of the horizon, seemed to gaze hungrily into the unattainable, and did not see the shadow of the coming event. The only shadow on the sea was the shadow of the black smoke pouring heavily from the funnel its immense streamer, whose end was constantly dissolving in the air. Two Malays, silent and almost motionless, steered, one on each side of the wheel, whose brass rim shone fragmentarily in the oval of light thrown out by the binnacle. Now and then a hand, with black fingers alternately letting go and catching hold of revolving spokes, appeared in the illumined part; the links of wheel-chains ground heavily in the grooves of the bar-rel. Jim would glance at the compass, would glance around the unattainable horizon, would stretch himself till his joints cracked with a leisurely twist of the body, in the very excess of well-being; and, as if made audacious by the invincible aspect of the peace, he felt he cared for nothing that could happen to him to the end of his days. From time to time he glanced idly at a chart pegged out with four drawing-pins on a low three-legged table abaft the steering-gear case. The sheet of paper portraying the depths of the sea presented a shiny surface under the light of a bull's-eye lamp lashed to a stanchion, a surface as level and smooth as the glimmering surface of the waters. Parallel rulers with a pair of dividers reposed on it; the ship's position at last noon was marked with a small black cross, and the straight pencil-line drawn firmly as far as Perim figured the course of the ship—the path of souls towards the holy place, the promise of salvation, the reward of eternal life—while the pencil with its sharp end touching the Somali coast lay round and still like a naked ship's spar floating in the pool of a sheltered dock. "How steady she goes," thought Jim with wonder, with something like gratitude for this high peace of sea and sky. At such times his thoughts would be full of val-orous deeds: he loved these dreams and the success of his imaginary achievements. They were the best parts of life, its secret truth, its hidden reality. They had a gorgeous virility, the charm of vagueness, they passed before him with a heroic tread; they carried his soul away with them and made it drunk with the divine philtre of an unbounded confidence in itself. There was nothing he could not face. He was so pleased with the idea that he smiled, keeping perfunctorily his eyes ahead; and when he happened to glance back he saw the white streak of the wake drawn as straight by the ship's keel upon the sea as the black line drawn by the pencil upon the chart.

The ash-buckets racketed, clanking up and down the stoke-hold ventilators, and this tin-pot clatter warned him the end of his watch was near. He sighed with content, with regret as well at having to part from that serenity which fostered the adven-turous freedom of his thoughts. He was a little sleepy, too, and

felt a pleasurable languor running through every limb as
though all the blood in his body had turned to warm milk. His
skipper had come up noiselessly, in pyjamas and with his
sleeping-jacket flung wide open. Red of face, only half awake,
the left eye partly closed, the right staring stupid and glassy, he
hung his big head over the chart and scratched his ribs sleepily.
There was something obscene in the sight of his naked flesh.
His bared breast glistened soft and greasy as though he had
sweated out his fat in his sleep. He pronounced a professional
remark in a voice harsh and dead, resembling the rasping
sound of a wood-file on the edge of a plank; the fold of his
double chin hung like a bag triced up close under the hinge of
his jaw. Jim started, and his answer was full of deference; but
the odious and fleshy figure, as though seen for the first time
in a revealing moment, fixed itself in his memory for ever as
the incarnation of everything vile and base that lurks in the
world we love: in our own hearts we trust for our salvation in
the men that surround us, in the sights that fill our eyes, in the
sounds that fill our ears, and in the air that fills our lungs.

The thin gold shaving of the moon floating slowly downwards had lost itself on the darkened surface of the waters, and
the eternity beyond the sky seemed to come down nearer to the
earth, with the augmented glitter of the stars, with the more
profound sombreness in the lustre of the half-transparent dome
covering the flat disc of an opaque sea. The ship moved so
smoothly that her onward motion was imperceptible to the
senses of men, as though she had been a crowded planet speed-
ing through the dark spaces of ether behind the swarm of suns,
in the appalling and calm solitudes awaiting the breath of future creations. "Hot is no name for it down below," said a
voice.

Jim smiled without looking round. The skipper presented an
unmoved breadth of back: it was the renegade's trick to appear
pointedly unaware of your existence unless it suited his purpose to turn at you with a devouring glare before he let loose a
torrent of foamy, abusive jargon that came like a gush from a
sewer. Now he emitted only a sulky grunt; the second engineer
at the head of the bridge-ladder, kneading with damp palms a

dirty sweat-rag, unabashed, continued the tale of his complaints. The sailors had a good time of it up here, and what was the use of them in the world he would be blowed if he could see. The poor devils of engineers had to get the ship along anyhow, and they could very well do the rest too; by gosh they— "Shut up," growled the German solidly. "Oh yes! Shut up—and when anything goes wrong you fly to us, don't you?" went on the other. He was more than half cooked, he expected; but anyway, now he did not mind how much he sinned, because these last three days he had passed through a fine course of training for the place where the bad boys go when they die—b'gosh, he had—besides being made jolly well deaf by the blasted racket below. The durned, compound, surface-condensing, rotten scrap-heap rattled and banged down there like an old deck-winch, only more so; and what made him risk his life every night and day that God made amongst the refuse of a breaking-up yard flying round at fifty-seven revolutions, was more than *he* could tell. He must have been born reckless, b'gosh. He . . . "Where did you get drink?" inquired the German, very savage, but motionless in the light of the binnacle, like a clumsy effigy of a man cut out of a block of fat. Jim went on smiling at the retreating horizon; his heart was full of generous impulses, and his thought was contemplating his own superiority. "Drink!" repeated the engineer with amiable scorn: he was hanging on with both hands to the rail, a shadowy figure with flexible legs. "Not from you, captain. You're far too mean, b'gosh. You would let a good man die sooner than give him a drop of shnaps. That's what you Germans call economy. Penny wise, pound foolish." He became sentimental. The chief had given him a four-finger nip about ten o'clock—"only one, s'elp me!"—good old chief; but as to getting the old fraud out of his bunk—a five-ton crane couldn't do it. Not it. Not tonight anyhow. He was sleeping sweetly like a little child, with a bottle of prime brandy under his pillow. From the thick throat of the commander of the *Patna* came a low rumble, on which the sound of the word *schwein* fluttered high and low like a capricious feather in a faint stir of air. He and the chief engineer had been cronies for

a good few years—serving the same jovial, crafty, old Chinaman, with horn-rimmed goggles and strings of red silk plaited
into the venerable grey hairs of his pigtail. The quay-side opinion in the *Patna's* home-port was that these two in the way of
brazen peculation "Had done together pretty well everything
you can think of." Outwardly they were badly matched: one
dull-eyed, malevolent, and of soft fleshy curves; the other lean,
all hollows, with a head long and bony like the head of an old
horse, with sunken cheeks, with sunken temples, with an indifferent glazed glance of sunken eyes. He had been stranded out
East somewhere—in Canton, or Shanghai, or perhaps in Yoko-
hama; he probably did not care to remember himself the exact
locality, nor yet the cause of his shipwreck. He had been, in
mercy to his youth, kicked quietly out of his ship twenty years
ago or more, and it might have been so much worse for him
that the memory of the episode had in it hardly a trace of misfortune. Then, steam navigation expanding in these seas and
men of his craft being scarce at first, he had "got on" after a
sort. He was eager to let strangers know in a dismal mumble
that he was "an old stager out here." When he moved a skeleton seemed to sway loose in his clothes; his walk was mere
wandering, and he was given to wander thus around the engine-
room skylight, smoking, without relish, doctored tobacco in a
brass bowl at the end of a cherrywood stem four feet long, with
the imbecile gravity of a thinker evolving a system of philoso-
phy from the hazy glimpse of a truth. He was usually anything
but free with his private store of liquor; but on that night he
had departed from his principles, so that his second, a weak-
headed child of Wapping, what with the unexpectedness of the
treat and the strength of the stuff, had become very happy,
cheeky, and talkative. The fury of the New South Wales German was extreme; he puffed like an exhaust-pipe, and Jim,
faintly amused by the scene, was impatient for the time when
he could get below: the last ten minutes of the watch were irri-
tating like a gun that hangs fire; those men did not belong to
the world of heroic adventure; they weren't bad chaps though.
Even the skipper himself . . . His gorge rose at the mass of
panting flesh from which issued gurgling mutters, a cloudy

trickle of filthy expressions; but he was too pleasurably languid to dislike actively this or any other thing. The quality
of these men did not matter; he rubbed shoulders with them,
but they could not touch him; he shared the air they breathed,
but he was different . . . Would the skipper go for the engineer? . . . The life was easy and he too sure of himself—too
sure of himself to . . . The line dividing his meditation from a
surreptitious doze on his feet was thinner than a thread in a spi-
der's web.

The second engineer was coming by easy transition to the
consideration of his finances and of his courage.

"Who's drunk? I? No, no, captain! That won't do. You ought
to know by this time the chief ain't free-hearted enough to
make a sparrow drunk, b'gosh. I've never been the worse for
liquor in my life; the stuff ain't made yet that would make *me*
drunk. I could drink liquid fire against your whisky peg for
peg, b'gosh, and keep as cool as a cucumber. If I thought I was
drunk I would jump overboard—do away with myself, b'gosh.
I would! Straight! And I won't go off the bridge. Where do you
expect me to take the air on a night like this, eh? On deck
amongst that vermin down there? Likely—ain't it! And I am
not afraid of anything you can do."

The German lifted two heavy fists to heaven and shook
them a little without a word.

"I don't know what fear is," pursued the engineer, with the
enthusiasm of sincere conviction. "I am not afraid of doing all
the bloomin' work in this rotten hooker, b'gosh! And a jolly
good thing for you that there are some of us about the world
that aren't afraid of their lives, or where would you be—you
and this old thing here with her plates like brown paper—
brown paper, s'elp me? It's all very fine for you—you get a
power of pieces out of her one way and another; but what
about me—what do I get? A measly hundred and fifty dollars a
month and find yourself. I wish to ask you respectfully—respectfully, mind—who wouldn't chuck a dratted job like this?
'Tain't safe, s'elp me, it ain't! Only I am one of them fearless
fellows. . . . "

He let go the rail and made ample gestures as if demonstrat-

ing in the air the shape and extent of his valour; his thin voice
darted in prolonged squeaks upon the sea, he tiptoed back and
forth for the better emphasis of utterance, and suddenly
pitched down head-first as though he had been clubbed from
behind. He said "Damn!" as he tumbled; an instant of silence
followed upon his screeching: Jim and the skipper staggered
forward by common accord, and catching themselves up, stood
very stiff and still gazing, amazed, at the undisturbed level of
the sea. Then they looked upwards at the stars.

What had happened? The wheezy thump of the engines
went on. Had the earth been checked in her course. They could
not understand; and suddenly the calm sea, the sky without a
cloud, appeared formidably insecure in their immobility, as if
posed on the brow of yawning destruction. The engineer re-
bounded vertically full length and collapsed again into a vague
heap. This heap said "What's that?" in the muffled accents of
profound grief. A faint noise as of thunder, of thunder infinitely remote, less than a sound, hardly more than a vibration,
passed slowly, and the ship quivered in response, as if the
thunder had growled deep down in the water. The eyes of the
two Malays at the wheel glittered towards the white men, but
their dark hands remained closed on the spokes. The sharp hull
driving on its way seemed to rise a few inches in succession
through its whole length, as though it had become pliable, and
settled down again rigidly to its work of cleaving the smooth
surface of the sea. Its quivering stopped, and the faint noise of
thunder ceased all at once, as though the ship had steamed
across a narrow belt of vibrating water and of humming air.

Chapter Four

A MONTH or so afterwards, when Jim, in answer to pointed
questions, tried to tell honestly the truth of this experience, he said, speaking of the ship: "We went over whatever it

was as easy as a snake crawling over a stick." The illustration
was good: the questions were aiming at facts, and the official
Inquiry was being held in the police court of an Eastern port.
He stood elevated in the witness-box, with burning cheeks in a
cool lofty room: the big framework of punkahs moved gently
to and fro high above his head, and from below many eyes
were looking at him out of dark faces, out of white faces, out
of red faces, out of faces attentive, spellbound, as if all these
people sitting in orderly rows upon narrow benches had been
enslaved by the fascination of his voice. It was very loud, it
rang startling in his own ears, it was the only sound audible in
the world, for the terribly distinct questions that extorted his
answer seemed to shape themselves in anguish and pain within
his breast,—came to him poignant and silent like the terrible
questioning of one's conscience. Outside the court the sun
blazed—within was the wind of great punkahs that made you
shiver, the shame that made you burn, the attentive eyes whose
glance stabbed. The face of the presiding magistrate, clean
shaved and impassible, looked at him deadly pale between the
red faces of the two nautical assessors. The light of a broad
window under the ceiling fell from above on the heads and
shoulders of the three men, and they were fiercely distinct in
the half-light of the big court-room where the audience seemed
composed of staring shadows. They wanted facts. Facts! They
demanded facts from him, as if facts could explain anything!

"After you had concluded you had collided with something
floating awash, say a water-logged wreck, you were ordered
by your captain to go forward and ascertain if there was any
damage done. Did you think it likely from the force of the
blow?" asked the assessor sitting to the left. He had a thin
horseshoe beard, salient cheek-bones and with both elbows on
the desk clasped his rugged hands before his face, looking at
Jim with thoughtful blue eyes; the other a heavy, scornful man,
thrown back in his seat, his left arm extended full length,
drummed delicately with his fingertips on a blotting-pad: in
the middle the magistrate upright in the roomy arm-chair, his
head inclined slightly on the shoulder, had his arms crossed on

his breast and a few flowers in a glass vase by the side of his inkstand.

"I did not," said Jim. "I was told to call no one and to make no noise for fear of creating a panic. I thought the precaution reasonable. I took one of the lamps that were hung under the awnings and went forward. After opening the forepeak hatch I heard splashing in there. I lowered then the lamp the whole drift of its lanyard, and saw the forepeak was more than half full of water already. I knew then there must be a big hole below the waterline." He paused.

"Yes," said the big assessor, with a dreamy smile at the blotting-pad; his fingers played incessantly, touching the paper without noise.

"I did not think of danger just then. I might have been a little startled: all this happened in such a quiet way and so very suddenly. I knew there was no other bulkhead in the ship but the collision bulkhead separating the forepeak from the fore-hold. I went back to tell the captain. I came upon the second engineer getting up at the foot of the bridge-ladder: he seemed dazed, and told me he thought his left arm was broken; he had slipped on the top step when getting down while I was forward. He exclaimed, 'My God! That rotten bulkhead'll give way in a minute, and the damned thing will go down under us like a lump of lead.' He pushed me away with his right arm and ran before me up the ladder, shouting as he climbed. His left arm hung by his side. I followed up in time to see the captain rush at him and knock him down flat on his back. He did not strike him again: he stood bending over him and speaking angrily but quite low. I fancy he was asking him why the devil he didn't go and stop the engines, instead of making a row about it on deck. I heard him say, 'Get up! Run! fly!' He swore also. The engineer slid down the starboard ladder and bolted round the skylight to the engine-room companion which was on the port-side. He moaned as he ran. . . ."

He spoke slowly; he remembered swiftly and with extreme vividness; he could have reproduced like an echo the moaning of the engineer for the better information of these men who wanted facts. After his first feeling of revolt he had come

round to the view that only a meticulous precision of statement
would bring out the true horror behind the appalling face of
things. The facts those men were so eager to know had been
visible, tangible, open to the senses, occupying their place in
space and time, requiring for their existence a fourteen-hundred-
ton steamer and twenty-seven minutes by the watch; they made
a whole that had features, shades of expression, a complicated
aspect that could be remembered by the eye, and something
else besides, something invisible, a directing spirit of perdition
that dwelt within, like a malevolent soul in a detestable body.
He was anxious to make this clear. This had not been a common affair, everything in it had been of the utmost importance,
and fortunately he remembered everything. He wanted to go
on talking for truth's sake, perhaps for his own sake also; and
while his utterance was deliberate, his mind positively flew
round and round the serried circle of facts that had surged up
all about him to cut him off from the rest of his kind: it was
like a creature that, finding itself imprisoned within an enclosure of high stakes, dashes round and round, distracted in the
night, trying to find a weak spot, a crevice, a place to scale,
some opening through which it may squeeze itself and escape.
This awful activity of mind made him hesitate at times in his
speech. . . .

"The captain kept on moving here and there on the bridge;
he seemed calm enough, only he stumbled several times; and
once as I stood speaking to him he walked right into me as
though he had been stone-blind. He made no definite answer to
what I had to tell. He mumbled to himself; all I heard of it were
a few words that sounded like 'confounded steam!' and 'infernal steam!'—something about steam. I thought . . ."

He was becoming irrelevant; a question to the point cut
short his speech, like a pang of pain, and he felt extremely discouraged and weary. He was coming to that, he was coming to
that—and now, checked brutally, he had to answer by yes or
no. He answered truthfully by a curt "Yes, I did"; and fair of
face, big of frame, with young, gloomy eyes, he held his shoulders upright above the box while his soul writhed within him.
He was made to answer another question so much to the point

and so useless, then waited again. His mouth was tastelessly dry, as though he had been eating dust, then salt and bitter as after a drink of sea-water. He wiped his damp forehead, passed his tongue over parched lips, felt a shiver run down his back. The big assessor had dropped his eyelids, and drummed on without a sound, careless and mournful; the eyes of the other above the sunburnt, clasped fingers seemed to glow with kindliness; the magistrate had swayed forward; his pale face hovered near the flowers, and then dropping sideways over the arm of his chair, he rested his temple in the palm of his hand. The wind of the punkahs eddied down on the heads, on the dark-faced natives wound about in voluminous draperies, on the Europeans sitting together very hot and in drill suits that seemed to fit them as close as their skins, and holding their round pith hats on their knees; while gliding along the walls the court peons, buttoned tight in long white coats, flitted rapidly to and fro, running on bare toes, red-sashed, red turban on head, as noiseless as ghosts, and on the alert like so many retrievers.

Jim's eyes, wandering in the intervals of his answers, rested upon a white man who sat apart from the others, with his face worn and clouded, but with quiet eyes that glanced straight, interested and clear. Jim answered another question and was tempted to cry out, "What's the good of this! what's the good!" He tapped with his foot slightly, bit his lip, and looked away over the heads. He met the eyes of the white man. The glance directed at him was not the fascinated stare of the others. It was an act of intelligent volition. Jim between two questions forgot himself so far as to find leisure for a thought. This fellow—ran the thought—looks at me as though he could see somebody or something past my shoulder. He had come across that man before—in the street perhaps. He was positive he had never spoken to him. For days, for many days, he had spoken to no one, but had held silent, incoherent, and endless converse with himself, like a prisoner alone in his cell or like a wayfarer lost in a wilderness. At present he was answering questions that did not matter though they had a purpose, but he doubted whether he would ever again speak out as long as he lived. The sound of his own truthful statements confirmed his deliberate opinion that speech was of no use to him any longer. That man there seemed to be aware of his hopeless difficulty. Jim looked at him, then turned away resolutely, as after a final parting.

And later on, many times, in distant parts of the world, Marlow showed himself willing to remember him at length, in detail and audibly.

Perhaps it would be after dinner, on a verandah draped in motionless foliage and crowned with flowers, in the deep dusk speckled by fiery cigar-ends. The elongated bulk of each canechair harboured a silent listener. Now and then a small red glow would move abruptly, and expanding light up the fingers of a languid hand, part of a face in profound repose, or flash a crimson gleam into a pair of pensive eyes overshadowed by a fragment of an unruffled forehead; and with the very first word uttered Marlow's body, extended at rest in the seat, would become very still, as though his spirit had winged its way back into the lapse of time and were speaking through his lips from the past.

Chapter Five

"OH YES. I attended the inquiry," he would say, "and to this day I haven't left off wondering why I went. I am willing to believe each of us has a guardian angel, if you fellows will concede to me that each of us has a familiar devil as well. I want you to own up, because I don't like to feel exceptional in any way, and I know I have him—the devil, I mean. I haven't seen him, of course, but I go upon circumstantial evidence. He is there right enough, and, being malicious, he lets me in for that kind of thing. What kind of thing, you ask? Why, the inquiry thing, the yellow-dog thing—you wouldn't think a mangy, native tyke would be allowed to trip up people in the verandah of a magistrate's court, would you?—the kind of thing that by devious, unexpected, truly diabolical ways causes me to run up against men with soft spots, with hard spots, with hidden plague spots, by Jove! and loosens their tongues at the sight of me for their infernal confidences; as though, forsooth, I had no confidences to make to myself, as though—God help me!—I didn't have enough confidential information about myself to harrow my own soul till the end of my appointed time. And what I have done to be thus favoured I want to know. I declare I am as full of my own concerns as the next man, and I have as much memory as the average pilgrim in this valley, so you see I am not particularly fit to be a receptacle of confessions. Then why? Can't tell—unless it be to make time pass away after dinner. Charley, my dear chap, your dinner was extremely good, and in consequence these men here look upon a quiet rubber as a tumultuous occupation. They wallow in your good chairs and think to themselves, 'Hang exertion. Let that Marlow talk.'

"Talk! So be it. And it's easy enough to talk of Master Jim, after a good spread, two hundred feet above the sea-level, with a box of decent cigars handy, on a blessed evening of freshness and starlight that would make the best of us forget we are only on sufferance here and got to pick our every irremediable step, trusting we shall manage yet to go out decently in the end—but not so sure of it after all—and with dashed little help to expect from those we touch elbows with right and left. Of course there are men here and there to whom the whole of life is like an after-dinner hour with a cigar; easy, pleasant, empty, perhaps enlivened by some fable of strife to be forgotten before the end is told—before the end is told—even if there happens to be any end to it.

"My eyes met his for the first time at that inquiry. You must know that everybody connected in any way with the sea was there, because the affair had been notorious for days, ever since that mysterious cable message came from Aden to start us all cackling. I say mysterious, because it was so in a sense though it contained a naked fact, about as naked and ugly as a fact can well be. The whole waterside talked of nothing else. First thing in the morning as I was dressing in my state-room,

I would hear through the bulkhead my Parsee Dubash jabbering about the *Patna* with the steward, while he drank a cup of tea, by favour, in the pantry. No sooner on shore I would meet some acquaintance, and the first remark would be, 'Did you ever hear of anything to beat this?' and according to his kind the man would smile cynically, or look sad, or let out a swear or two. Complete strangers would accost each other familiarly, just for the sake of easing their minds on the subject: every confounded loafer in the town came in for a harvest of drinks over this affair: you heard of it in the harbour office, at every ship-broker's, at your agent's, from whites, from natives, from half-castes, from the very boatmen squatting half-naked on the stone steps as you went up—by Jove! There was some indignation, not a few jokes, and no end of discussions as to what had become of them, you know. This went on for a couple of weeks or more, and the opinion that whatever was mysterious in this affair would turn out to be tragic as well, began to prevail, when one fine morning, as I was standing in the shade by the steps of the harbour office, I perceived four men walking towards me along the quay. I wondered for a while where that queer lot had sprung from, and suddenly, I may say, I shouted to myself, 'Here they are!'

"There they were, sure enough, three of them as large as life, and one much larger of girth than any living man has a right to be, just landed with a good breakfast inside of them from an outward-bound Dale Line steamer that had come in about an hour after sunrise. There could be no mistake; I spotted the jolly skipper of the *Patna* at the first glance: the fattest man in the whole blessed tropical belt clear round that good old earth of ours. Moreover, nine months or so before, I had come across him in Samarang. His steamer was loading in the Roads, and he was abusing the tyrannical institutions of the German empire, and soaking himself in beer all day long and day after day in De Jongh's back-shop, till De Jongh, who charged a guilder for every bottle without as much as the quiver of an eyelid, would beckon me aside, and, with his little leathery face all puckered up, declare confidentially, 'Business is business, but this man, captain, he make me very sick. Tfui!'

"I was looking at him from the shade. He was hurrying on a little in advance, and the sunlight beating on him brought out his bulk in a startling way. He made me think of a trained baby elephant walking on hind-legs. He was extravagantly gorgeous too—got up in a soiled sleeping-suit, bright green and deep orange vertical stripes, with a pair of ragged straw slippers on his bare feet, and somebody's cast-off pith hat, very dirty and two sizes too small for him, tied up with a manilla rope-yarn on the top of his big head. You understand a man like that hasn't the ghost of a chance when it comes to borrowing clothes. Very well. On he came in hot haste, without a look right or left, passed within three feet of me, and in the innocence of his heart went on pelting upstairs in the harbour office to make his deposition, or report, or whatever you like to call it.

"It appears he addressed himself in the first instance to the principal shipping-master. Archie Ruthvel had just come in, and, as his story goes, was about to begin his arduous day by giving a dressing-down to his chief clerk. Some of you might have known him—an obliging little Portuguese half-caste with a miserably skinny neck, and always on the hop to get something from the shipmasters in the way of eatables—a piece of salt pork, a bag of biscuits, a few potatoes, or what not. One voyage, I recollect, I tipped him a live sheep out of the remnant of my sea-stock: not that I wanted him to do anything for me—he couldn't, you know—but because his childlike belief in the sacred right to perquisites quite touched my heart. It was so strong as to be almost beautiful. The race—the two races rather—and the climate . . . However, never mind. I know where I have a friend for life.

"Well, Ruthvel says he was giving him a severe lecture—on official morality, I suppose—when he heard a kind of subdued commotion at his back, and turning his head he saw, in his own words, something round and enormous, resembling a sixteen-hundred-weight sugar-hogshead wrapped in a striped flannelette, up-ended in the middle of the large floor space in the office. He declares he was so taken aback that for quite an appreciable time he did not realize the thing was alive, and sat still wondering for what purpose and by what means that object had been transported in front of his desk. The archway from the ante-room was crowded with punkah-pullers, sweepers, police peons, the coxswain and crew of the harbour steam-launch, all craning their necks and almost climbing on each other's backs. Quite a riot. By that time the fellow had managed to tug and jerk his hat clear of his head, and advanced with slight bows at Ruthvel, who told me the sight was so discomposing that for some time he listened quite unable to make out what that apparition wanted. It spoke in a voice harsh and lugubrious but intrepid, and little by little it dawned upon Archie that this was a development of the *Patna* case. He says that as soon as he understood who it was before him he felt quite unwell—Archie is so sympathetic and easily upset—but pulled himself together and shouted 'Stop! I can't listen to you. You must go to the Master Attendant. I can't possibly listen to you. Captain Elliot is the man you want to see. This way, this way.' He jumped up, ran round that long counter, pulled, shoved: the other let him, surprised but obedient at first, and only at the door of the private office some sort of animal instinct made him hang back and snort like a frightened bullock. 'Look here! what's up? Let go! Look here!' Archie flung open the door without knocking. 'The master of the *Patna,* sir,' he shouts. 'Go in, captain.' He saw the old man lift his head from some writing so sharp that his nose-nippers fell off, banged the door to, and fled to his desk, where he had some papers waiting for his signature: but he says the row that burst out in there was so awful that he couldn't collect his senses sufficiently to remember the spelling of his own name. Archie's the most sensitive shipping-master in the two hemispheres. He declares he felt as though he had thrown a man to a hungry lion. No doubt the noise was great. I heard it down below, and I have every reason to believe it was heard clear across the Esplanade as far as the band-stand. Old father Elliot had a great stock of words and could shout—and didn't mind who he shouted at either. He would have shouted at the Viceroy himself. As he used to tell me: 'I am as high as I can get; my pension is safe. I've a few pounds laid by, and if they don't like my notions of duty I would just as soon go home as not. I am an old man, and I have always spoken my mind. All I care for now is to see my girls married before I die.' He was a little crazy on that point. His three daughters were awfully nice, though they resemble him amazingly, and on the mornings he woke up with a gloomy view of their matrimonial prospects the office would read it in his eye and tremble, because, they said, he was sure to have somebody for breakfast. However, that morning he did not eat the renegade, but, if I may be allowed to carry on the metaphor, chewed him up very small, so to speak, and—ah! ejected him again.

"Thus in a very few moments I saw his monstrous bulk descend in haste and stand still on the outer steps. He had stopped close to me for the purpose of profound meditation: his large purple cheeks quivered. He was biting his thumb, and after a while noticed me with a sidelong vexed look. The other three chaps that had landed with him made a little group waiting at some distance. There was a sallow-faced, mean little chap with his arm in a sling, and a long individual in a blue flannel coat, as dry as a chip and no stouter than a broomstick, with drooping grey moustaches, who looked about him with an air of jaunty imbecility. The third was an upstanding, broad-shouldered youth, with his hands in his pockets, turning his back on the other two who appeared to be talking together earnestly. He stared across the empty Esplanade. A ramshackle gharry, all dust and venetian blinds, pulled up short opposite the group, and the driver, throwing up his right foot over his knee, gave himself up to the critical examination of his toes. The young chap, making no movement, not even stirring his head, just stared into the sunshine. This was my first view of Jim. He looked as unconcerned and unapproachable as only the young can look. There he stood, clean-limbed, clean-faced, firm on his feet, as promising a boy as the sun ever shone on; and, looking at him, knowing all he knew and a little more too, I was as angry as though I had detected him trying to get something out of me by false pretences. He had no business to look so sound. I thought to myself—well, if this sort can go wrong like that . . . and I felt as though I could fling down my hat and dance on it from sheer mortification, as I once saw the skipper of an Italian barque do because his duffer of a mate got into a mess with his anchors when making a flying moor in a road-stead full of ships. I asked myself, seeing him there apparently so much at ease—is he silly? is he callous? He seemed ready to start whistling a tune. And note, I did not care a rap about the behaviour of the other two. Their persons somehow fitted the tale that was public property, and was going to be the subject of an official inquiry. 'That old mad rogue upstairs called me a hound,' said the captain of the *Patna*. I can't tell whether he recognized me—I rather think he did; but at any rate our glances met. He glared—I smiled; hound was the very mildest epithet that had reached me through the open window. 'Did he?' I said from some strange inability to hold my tongue. He nodded, bit his thumb again, swore under his breath: then lifting his head and looking at me with sullen and passionate impudence—'Bah! the Pacific is big, my friendt. You damned Englishmen can do your worst; I know where there's plenty room for a man like me: I am well aguaindt in Apia, in Honolulu, in . . .' He paused reflectively, while without effort I could depict to myself the sort of people he was 'aguaindt' with in those places. I won't make a secret of it that I had been 'aguaindt' with not a few of that sort myself. There are times when a man must act as though life were equally sweet in any company. I've known such a time, and, what's more I shan't now pretend to pull a long face over my necessity, because a good many of that bad company from want of moral—moral—what shall I say?—posture, or from some other equally profound cause, were twice as instructive and twenty times more amusing than the usual respectable thief of commerce you fellows ask to sit at your table without any real necessity—from habit, from cowardice, from good-nature, from a hundred sneaking and inadequate reasons.

"'You Englishmen are all rogues,' went on my patriotic Flensborg or Stettin Australian. I really don't recollect now what decent little port on the shores of the Baltic was defiled by being the nest of that precious bird. 'What are you to

shout? Eh? You tell me? You no better than other people, and
that old rogue he make Gottam fuss with me.' His thick carcass trembled on its legs that were like a pair of pillars; it
trembled from head to foot. 'That's what you English always
make—make a tam' fuss—for any little thing, because I was
not born in your tam' country. Take away my certificate. Take
it. I don't want the certificate. A man like me don't want your
verfluchte certificate. I shpit on it.' He spat. 'I vill an Ameri-
gan citizen begome,' he cried, fretting and fuming and shuffling his feet as if to free his ankles from some invisible and
mysterious grasp that would not let him get away from that
spot. He made himself so warm that the top of his bullet head
positively smoked. Nothing mysterious prevented me from
going away: curiosity is the most obvious of sentiments, and
it held me there to see the effect of a full information upon
that young fellow who, hands in pockets, and turning his back
upon the sidewalk, gazed across the grass-plots of the Esplanade at the yellow portico of the Malabar Hotel with the air
of a man about to go for a walk as soon as his friend is ready.
That's how he looked, and it was odious. I waited to see him
overwhelmed, confounded, pierced through and through,
squirming like an impaled beetle—and I was half afraid to see
it too—if you understand what I mean. Nothing more awful
than to watch a man who has been found out, not in a crime
but in a more than criminal weakness. The commonest sort of
fortitude prevents us from becoming criminals in a legal
sense; it is from weakness unknown, but perhaps suspected,
as in some parts of the world you suspect a deadly snake in
every bush—from weakness that may lie hidden, watched or
unwatched, prayed against or manfully scorned, repressed or
maybe ignored more than half a lifetime, not one of us is safe.
We are snared into doing things for which we get called
names, and things for which we get hanged, and yet the spirit
may well survive—survive the condemnations, survive the
halter, by Jove! And there are things—they look small enough
sometimes too—by which some of us are totally and completely undone. I watched the youngster there. I liked his appearance; I knew his appearance; he came from the right

place; he was one of us. He stood there for all the parentage of
his kind, for men and women by no means clever or amusing,
but whose very existence is based upon honest faith, and upon
the instinct of courage. I don't mean military courage, or civil
courage, or any special kind of courage. I mean just that in-
born ability to look temptations straight in the face—a readiness unintellectual enough, goodness knows, but without
pose—a power of resistance, don't you see, ungracious if you
like, but priceless—an unthinking and blessed stiffness before
the outward and inward terrors, before the might of nature,
and the seductive corruption of men—backed by a faith invulnerable to the strength of facts, to the contagion of example, to the solicitation of ideas. Hang ideas! They are tramps,
vagabonds, knocking at the back-door of your mind, each taking a little of your substance, each carrying away some crumb
of that belief in a few simple notions you must cling to if you
want to live decently and would like to die easy!

"This has nothing to do with Jim, directly; only he was outwardly so typical of that good, stupid kind we like to feel
marching right and left of us in life, and of the kind that is not
disturbed by the vagaries of intelligence and the perversions
of—of nerves, let us say. He was the kind of fellow you would,
on the strength of his looks, leave in charge of the deck—figuratively and professionally speaking. I say I would, and I ought
to know. Haven't I turned out youngsters enough in my time,
for the service of the Red Rag, to the craft of the sea, to the
craft whose whole secret could be expressed in one short sentence, and yet must be driven afresh every day into young
heads till it becomes the component part of every waking
thought—till it is present in every dream of their young sleep!
The sea has been good to me, but when I remember all these
boys that passed through my hands, some grown up now and
some drowned by this time, but all good stuff for the sea, I
don't think I have done badly by it either. Were I to go home
to-morrow, I bet that before two days passed over my head
some sunburnt young chief mate would overtake me at some
dock gateway or other, and a fresh deep voice speaking above
my hat would ask: 'Don't you remember me, sir? Why! little

So-and-so. Such and such a ship. It was my first voyage.' And I would remember a bewildered little shaver, no higher than the back of this chair, with a mother and perhaps a big sister on the quay, very quiet but too upset to wave their handkerchiefs at the ship that glides out gently between the pier-heads: or perhaps some decent middle-aged father who had come early with his boy to see him off, and stays all the morning because he is interested in the windlass apparently, and stays too long, and has got to scramble ashore at last with no time at all to say good-bye. The mud pilot on the poop sings out to me in a drawl, 'Hold her with the check line for a moment, Mister Mate. There's a gentleman wants to get ashore. . . . Up with you, sir. Nearly got carried off to Talcahuano, didn't you? Now's your time; easy does it. . . . All right. Slack away again forward there.' The tugs, smoking like the pit of perdition, get hold and churn the old river into fury; the gentleman ashore is dusting his knees—the benevolent steward has shied his umbrella after him. All very proper. He has offered his bit of sacrifice to the sea, and now he may go home pretending he thinks nothing of it; and the little willing victim shall be very sea-sick before next morning. By-and-by, when he has learned all the little mysteries and the one great secret of the craft, he shall be fit to live or die as the sea may decree; and the man who had taken a hand in this fool game, in which the sea wins every toss, will be pleased to have his back slapped by a heavy young hand, and to hear a cheery sea-puppy voice: 'Do you remember me, sir? The little So-and-so.'

"I tell you this is good; it tells you that once in your life at least you had gone the right way to work. I have been thus slapped, and I have winced, for the slap was heavy, and I have glowed all day long and gone to bed feeling less lonely in the world by virtue of that hearty thump. Don't I remember the little So-and-so's! I tell you I ought to know the right kind of looks. I would have trusted the deck to that youngster on the strength of a single glance, and gone to sleep with both eyes—and, by Jove! it wouldn't have been safe. There are depths of horror in that thought. He looked as genuine as a new sovereign, but there was some infernal alloy in his metal. How much? The least thing—the least drop of something rare and accursed; the least drop!—but he made you—standing there with his don't-care-hang air—he made you wonder whether perchance he were nothing more rare than brass.

"I couldn't believe it. I tell you I wanted to see him squirm for the honour of the craft. The other two no-account chaps spotted their captain, and began to move slowly towards us. They chatted together as they strolled, and I did not care any more than if they had not been visible to the naked eye. They grinned at each other—might have been exchanging jokes, for all I know. I saw that with one of them it was the case of a broken arm; and as to the long individual with grey moustaches he was the chief engineer, and in various ways a pretty notorious personality. They were nobodies. They approached. The skipper gazed in an inanimate way between his feet: he seemed to be swollen to an unnatural size by some awful disease, by the mysterious action of an unknown poison. He lifted his head, saw the two before him waiting, opened his mouth with an extraordinary, sneering contortion of his puffed face—to speak to them, I suppose—and then a thought seemed to strike him. His thick, purplish lips came together without a sound, he went off in a resolute waddle to the gharry and began to jerk at the door-handle with such a blind brutality of impatience that I expected to see the whole concern overturned on its side, pony and all. The driver, shaken out of his meditation over the sole of his foot, displayed at once all the signs of intense terror, and held with both hands, looking round from his box at this vast carcass forcing its way into his conveyance. The little machine shook and rocked tumultuously, and the crimson nape of that lowered neck, the size of those straining thighs, the immense heaving of that dingy, striped green-and-orange back, the whole burrowing effort of that gaudy and sordid mass troubled one's sense of probability with a droll and fearsome effect, like one of those grotesque and distinct visions that scare and fascinate one in a fever. He disappeared. I half expected the roof to split in two, the little box on wheels to burst open in the manner of a ripe cotton-pod—but it only sank with a click of flattened springs, and suddenly one venetian blind rattled down. His shoulders reappeared, jammed in the small opening; his head hung out, distended and tossing like a captive balloon, perspiring, furious, spluttering. He reached for the gharry-wallah with vicious flourishes of a fist as dumpy and red as a lump of raw meat. He roared at him to be off, to go on. Where? Into the Pacific, perhaps. The driver lashed; the pony snorted, reared once, and darted off at a gallop. Where? To Apia? to Honolulu? He had 6,000 miles of tropical belt to disport himself in, and I did not hear the precise address. A snorting pony snatched him into 'ewigkeit' in the twinkling of an eye, and I never saw him again; and, what's more, I don't know of anybody that ever had a glimpse of him after he departed from my knowledge sitting inside a ramshackle little gharry that fled round the corner in a white smother of dust. He departed, disappeared, vanished, absconded; and absurdly enough it looked as though he had taken that gharry with him, for never again did I come across a sorrel pony with a slit ear and a lackadaisical Tamil driver afflicted by a sore foot. The Pacific is indeed big; but whether he found a place for a display of his talents in it or not, the fact remains he had flown into space like a witch on a broomstick. The little chap with his arm in a sling started to run after the carriage, bleating, 'Captain! I say, Captain! I sa-a-ay!'—but after a few steps stopped short, hung his head, and walked back slowly. At the sharp rattle of the wheels the young fellow spun round where he stood. He made no other movement, no gesture, no sign, and remained facing in the new direction after the gharry had swung out of sight.

"All this happened in much less time than it takes to tell, since I am trying to interpret for you into slow speech the instantaneous effect of visual impressions. Next moment the half-caste clerk, sent by Archie to look a little after the poor castaways of the *Patna*, came upon the scene. He ran out eager and bareheaded, looking right and left, and very full of his mission. It was doomed to be a failure as far as the principal person was concerned, but he approached the others with fussy importance, and, almost immediately, found himself involved in a violent altercation with the chap that carried his arm in a sling and who turned out to be extremely anxious for a row. He wasn't going to be ordered about—'not he, b'gosh.' He wouldn't be terrified with a pack of lies by a cocky half-breed little quill-driver. He was not going to be bullied by 'no object of that sort,' if the story were true 'ever so!' He bawled his wish, his desire, his determination to go to bed. 'If you weren't a Godforsaken Portuguee,' I heard him yell, 'you would know that the hospital is the right place for me.' He pushed the fist of his sound arm under the other's nose; a crowd began to collect; the half-caste, flustered, but doing his best to appear dignified, tried to explain his intentions. I went away without waiting to see the end.

"But it so happened that I had a man in the hospital at the time, and going there to see about him the day before the opening of the Inquiry, I saw in the white men's ward that little chap tossing on his back, with his arm in splints, and quite light-headed. To my great surprise the other one, the long individual with drooping white moustache, had also found his way there. I remembered I had seen him slinking away during the quarrel, in a half prance, half shuffle, and trying very hard not to look scared. He was no stranger to the port, it seems, and in his distress was able to make tracks straight for Mariani's billiard-room and grog-shop near the bazaar. That unspeakable vagabond, Mariani, who had known the man and had ministered to his vices in one or two other places, kissed the ground, in a manner of speaking, before him, and shut him up with a supply of bottles in an upstairs room of his infamous hovel. It appears he was under some hazy apprehension as to his personal safety, and wished to be concealed. However, Mariani told me a long time after (when he came on board one day to dun my steward for the price of some cigars) that he would have done more for him without asking any questions, from gratitude for some unholy favour received very many years ago—as far as I could make out. He thumped twice his brawny chest, rolled enormous black and white eyes glistening with tears: 'Antonio never forget—Antonio never forget!' What was the precise nature of the immoral obligation I never learned, but be it what it may, he had every facility given him to remain under lock and key, with a chair, a table, a mattress

in a corner, and a litter of fallen plaster on the floor, in an irrational state of funk, and keeping up his pecker with such ton-
ics as Mariani dispensed. This lasted till the evening of the
third day, when, after letting out a few horrible screams, he
found himself compelled to seek safety in flight from a legion
of centipedes. He burst the door open, and made one leap for
dear life down the crazy little stairway, landed bodily on Mariani's stomach, picked himself up, and bolted like a rabbit into
the streets. The police plucked him off a garbage-heap in the
early morning. At first he had a notion they were carrying him
off to be hanged, and fought for liberty like a hero, but when I
sat down by his bed he had been very quiet for two days. His
lean bronzed head, with white moustaches, looked fine and
calm on the pillow, like the head of a war-worn soldier with a
child-like soul, had it not been for a hint of spectral alarm that
lurked in the blank glitter of his glance, resembling a nondescript form of a terror crouching silently behind a pane of
glass. He was so extremely calm, that I began to indulge in the
eccentric hope of hearing something explanatory of the famous affair from his point of view. Why I longed to go grub-
bing into the deplorable details of an occurrence which, after
all, concerned me no more than as a member of an obscure
body of men held together by a community of inglorious toil
and by fidelity to a certain standard of conduct, I can't explain.
You may call it an unhealthy curiosity if you like; but I have a
distinct notion I wished to find something. Perhaps, unconsciously, I hoped I would find that something, some profound
and redeeming cause, some merciful explanation, some convincing shadow of an excuse. I see well enough now that I
hoped for the impossible—for the laying of what is the most
obstinate ghost of man's creation, of the uneasy doubt uprising
like a mist, secret and gnawing like a worm, and more chilling
than the certitude of death—the doubt of the sovereign power
enthroned in a fixed standard of conduct. It is the hardest thing
to stumble against; it is the thing that breeds yelling panics and
good little quiet villainies; it's the true shadow of calamity. Did
I believe in a miracle? and why did I desire it so ardently? Was
it for my own sake that I wished to find some shadow of an ex-

cuse for that young fellow whom I had never seen before, but whose appearance alone added a touch of personal concern to the thoughts suggested by the knowledge of his weakness—made it a thing of mystery and terror—like a hint of a destructive fate ready for us all whose youth—in its day—had resembled his youth? I fear that such was the secret motive of my prying. I was, and no mistake, looking for a miracle. The only thing that at this distance of time strikes me as miraculous is the extent of my imbecility. I positively hoped to obtain from that battered and shady invalid some exorcism against the ghost of doubt. I must have been pretty desperate too, for, without a loss of time, after a few indifferent and friendly sentences which he answered with languid readiness, just as any decent sick man would do, I produced the word *Patna* wrapped up in a delicate question as in a wisp of floss silk. I was delicate selfishly; I did not want to startle him; I had no solicitude for him; I was not furious with him and sorry for him; his experience was of no importance, his redemption would have no point for me. He had grown old in minor iniquities, and could no longer inspire aversion or pity. He repeated *Patna*? interrogatively, seemed to make a short effort of memory and said: 'Quite right. I am an old stager out here. I saw her go down.' I made ready to vent my indignation at such a stupid lie, when he added smoothly, 'She was full of reptiles.'

"This made me pause. What did he mean? The unsteady phantom of terror behind his glassy eyes seemed to stand still and look into mine wistfully. 'They turned me out of my bunk in the middle watch to look at her sinking,' he pursued in a reflective tone. His voice sounded alarmingly strong all at once. I was sorry for my folly. There was no snowy-winged coif of a nursing sister to be seen flitting in the perspective of the ward; but away in the middle of a long row of empty iron bedsteads an accident case from some ship in the Roads sat up brown and gaunt with a white bandage set rakishly on the forehead. Suddenly my interesting invalid shot out an arm thin like a tentacle and clawed my shoulder. 'Only my eyes were good enough to see her go, but they saw that she was gone right enough, and

sang out together—like this.' . . . A wolfish howl searched the
very recesses of my soul. 'Oh! make 'im dry up,' whined the
accident case irritably. 'You don't believe me, I suppose,' went
on the other, with an air of ineffable conceit. 'I tell you there
are no such eyes as mine this side of the Persian Gulf. Look
under the bed.'

"Of course I stooped instantly. I defy anybody not to have
done so. 'What can you see?' he asked. 'Nothing,' I said, feeling awfully ashamed of myself. He scrutinised my face with
wild and withering contempt. 'Just so,' he said, 'but if I were
to look I could see—there's no eyes like mine, I tell you.'
Again he clawed, pulling at me downwards in his eagerness to
relieve himself by a confidential communication. 'Millions of
pink toads. There's no eyes like mine. Millions of pink toads.
It's worse than seeing a ship sink. I could look at sinking ships
and smoke my pipe all day long. Why don't they give me back
my pipe? I would get a smoke while I watched these toads. The
ship was full of them. They've got to be watched, you know.'
He winked facetiously. The perspiration dripped on him off my
head, my drill coat clung to my wet back: the afternoon breeze
swept impetuously over the row of bedsteads, the stiff folds of
curtains stirred perpendicularly, rattling on brass rods, the covers of empty beds blew about noiselessly near the bare floor all
along the line, and I shivered to the very marrow. The soft
wind of the tropics played in that naked ward as bleak as a
winter's gale in an old barn at home. 'Don't you let him start
his hollering, mister,' hailed from afar the accident case in a
distressed angry shout that came ringing between the walls
like a quavering call down a tunnel. The clawing hand hauled
at my shoulder; he leered at me knowingly. 'The ship was full
of them, you know, and we had to clear out on the strict Q.T.,'
he whispered, with extreme rapidity. 'All pink. All pink—as
big as mastiffs, with an eye on the top of the head and claws all
around their ugly mouths. Ough! Ough!' Quick jerks as of gal-
vanic shocks disclosed under the flat coverlet the outlines of
meagre and agitated legs; he let go my shoulder and reached
after something in the air; his body trembled tensely like a released harp-string; and while I looked down, the spectral hor-

ror in him broke through his glassy gaze. Instantly his face of
an old soldier, with its noble and calm outlines, became de-
composed before my eyes by the corruption of stealthy cunning, of an abominable caution and of desperate fear. He
restrained a cry—'Ssh! what are they doing now down there?'
he asked, pointing to the floor with fantastic precautions of
voice and gesture, whose meaning, borne upon my mind in a
lurid flash, made me very sick of my cleverness. 'They are all
asleep,' I answered, watching him narrowly. That was it. That's
what he wanted to hear; these were the exact words that could
calm him. He drew a long breath. 'Ssh! Quiet, steady. I am an
old stager out here. I know them brutes. Bash in the head of the
first that stirs. There's too many of them, and she won't swim
more than ten minutes.' He panted again. 'Hurry up,' he yelled
suddenly, and went on in a steady scream: 'They are all
awake—millions of them. They are trampling on me! Wait!
Oh, wait! I'll smash them in heaps like flies. Wait for me!
Help! H-e-elp!' An interminable and sustained howl completed
my discomfiture. I saw in the distance the accident case raise
deplorably both his hands to his bandaged head; a dresser,
aproned to the chin, showed himself in the vista of the ward, as
if seen in the small end of a telescope. I confessed myself
fairly routed, and without more ado, stepping out through one
of the long windows, escaped into the outside gallery. The
howl pursued me like a vengeance. I turned into a deserted
landing, and suddenly all became very still and quiet around
me, and I descended the bare and shiny staircase in a silence
that enabled me to compose my distracted thoughts. Down
below I met one of the resident surgeons who was crossing the
courtyard and stopped me. 'Been to see your man, Captain? I
think we may let him go to-morrow. These fools have no notion of taking care of themselves, though. I say, we've got the
chief engineer of that pilgrim ship here. A curious case. D.T.'s
of the worst kind. He has been drinking hard in that Greek's or
Italian's grog-shop for three days. What can you expect? Four
bottles of that kind of brandy a day, I am told. Wonderful, if
true. Sheeted with boiler-iron inside, I should think. The head,
ah! the head, of course, gone, but the curious part is there's

some sort of method in his raving. I am trying to find out. Most
unusual—that thread of logic in such a delirium. Traditionally
he ought to see snakes, but he doesn't. Good old tradition's at
a discount nowadays. Eh! His—er—visions are batrachian.
Ha! ha! No, seriously, I never remember being so interested in
a case of jim-jams before. He ought to be dead, don't you
know, after such a festive experiment. Oh! he is a tough object.
Four-and-twenty years of the tropics too. You ought really to
take a peep at him. Noble-looking old boozer. Won't you?'

"I had been all along exhibiting the polite signs of interest,
but now assuming an air of regret I murmured of want of time,
and shook hands in a hurry. 'I say,' he cried after me, 'he can't
attend that inquiry. Is his evidence material, you think?'

"'Not in the least,' I called back from the gateway.

Chapter Six

THE AUTHORITIES were evidently of the same opinion. The
inquiry was not adjourned. It was held on the appointed
day to satisfy the law, and it was well attended because of its
human interest, no doubt. There was no incertitude as to
facts—as to the one material fact, I mean. How the *Patna* came
by her hurt it was impossible to find out; the court did not expect to find out; and in the whole audience there was not a man
who cared. Yet, as I've told you, all the sailors in the port attended, and the waterside business was fully represented.
Whether they knew it or not, the interest that drew them there
was purely psychological—the expectation of some essential
disclosure as to the strength, the power, the horror, of human
emotions. Naturally nothing of the kind could be disclosed.
The examination of the only man able and willing to face it
was beating futilely round the well-known fact, and the play of
questions upon it was as instructive as the tapping with a hammer on an iron box, were the object to find out what's inside.

However, an official inquiry could not be any other thing. Its object was not the fundamental why, but the superficial how, of this affair.

"The young chap could have told them, and, though that very thing was the thing that interested the audience, the questions put to him necessarily led him away from what to me, for instance, would have been the only truth worth knowing. You can't expect the constituted authorities to inquire into the state of a man's soul—or is it only of his liver? Their business was to come down upon the consequences, and frankly, a casual police magistrate and two nautical assessors are not much good for anything else. I don't mean to imply these fellow were stupid. The magistrate was very patient. One of the assessors was a sailing-ship skipper with a reddish beard, and of a pious disposition. Brierly was the other. Big Brierly. Some of you must have heard of Big Brierly—the captain of the crack ship of the Blue Star line. That's the man.

"He seemed consumedly bored by the honour thrust upon him. He had never·in his life made a mistake, never had an accident, never a mishap, never a check in his steady rise, and he seemed to be one of those lucky fellows who know nothing of indecision, much less of self-mistrust. At thirty-two he had one of the best commands going in the Eastern trade—and, what's more, he thought a lot of what he had. There was nothing like it in the world, and I suppose if you had asked him point-blank he would have confessed that in his opinion there was not such another commander. The choice had fallen upon the right man. The rest of mankind that did not command the sixteen-knot steel steamer *Ossa* were rather poor creatures. He had saved lives at sea, had rescued ships in distress, had a gold chronometer presented to him by the underwriters, and a pair of binoculars with a suitable inscription from some foreign Government, in commemoration of these services. He was acutely aware of his merits and of his rewards. I liked him well enough, though some I know—meek, friendly men at that—couldn't stand him at any price. I haven't the slightest doubt he considered himself vastly my superior—indeed, had you been Emperor of East and West, you could not have ig-

nored your inferiority in his presence—but I couldn't get up
any real sentiment of offence. He did not despise me for anything I could help, for anything I was—don't you know? I was
a negligible quantity simply because I was not *the* fortunate
man of the earth, not Montague Brierly in command of the
Ossa, not the owner of an inscribed gold chronometer and of
silver-mounted binoculars testifying to the excellence of my
seamanship and to my indomitable pluck; not possessed of an
acute sense of my merits and of my rewards, besides the love
and worship of a black retriever, the most wonderful of its
kind—for never was such a man loved thus by such a dog. No
doubt, to have all this forced upon you was exasperating
enough; but when I reflected that I was associated in these fatal
disadvantages with twelve hundred millions of other more or
less human beings, I found I could bear my share of his good-
natured and contemptuous pity for the sake of something indefinite and attractive in the man. I have never defined to
myself this attraction, but there were moments when I envied
him. The sting of life could do no more to his complacent soul
than the scratch of a pin to the smooth face of a rock. This was
enviable. As I looked at him flanking on one side the unas-
suming pale-faced magistrate who presided at the inquiry, his
self-satisfaction presented to me and to the world a surface as
hard as granite. He committed suicide very soon after.

"No wonder Jim's case bored him, and while I thought with
something akin to fear of the immensity of his contempt for the
young man under examination, he was probably holding silent
inquiry into his own case. The verdict must have been unmiti-
gated guilt, and he took the secret of the evidence with him in
that leap into the sea. If I understand anything of men, the matter was no doubt of the gravest import, one of those trifles that
awaken ideas—start into life some thought with which a man
unused to such a companionship finds it impossible to live. I
am in a position to know that it wasn't money, and it wasn't
drink, and it wasn't woman. He jumped overboard at sea
barely a week after the end of the inquiry, and less than three
days after leaving port on his outward passage; as though on
that exact spot in the midst of waters he had suddenly per-

ceived the gates of the other world flung open wide for his reception.

"Yet it was not a sudden impulse. His grey-headed mate, a first-rate sailor and a nice old chap with strangers, but in his relations with his commander the surliest chief officer I've ever seen, would tell the story with tears in his eyes. It appears that when he came on deck in the morning Brierly had been writing in the chart-room. 'It was ten minutes to four,' he said, 'and the middle watch was not relieved yet of course. He heard my voice on the bridge speaking to the second mate, and called me in. I was loath to go, and that's the truth, Captain Marlow—I couldn't stand poor Captain Brierly, I tell you with shame; we never know what a man is made of. He had been promoted over too many heads, not counting my own, and he had a damnable trick of making you feel small, nothing but by the way he said "Good morning." I never addressed him, sir, but on matters of duty, and then it was as much as I could do to keep a civil tongue in my head.' (He flattered himself there. I often wondered how Brierly could put up with his manners for more than half a voyage.) 'I've a wife and children,' he went on, 'and I had been ten years in the Company, always expecting the next command—more fool I. Says he, just like this: "Come in here, Mr. Jones," in that swagger voice of his— "Come in here, Mr. Jones." In I went. "We'll lay down her position," says he, stooping over the chart, a pair of dividers in hand. By the standing orders, the officer going off duty would have done that at the end of his watch. However, I said nothing, and looked on while he marked off the ship's position with a tiny cross and wrote the date and the time. I can see him this moment writing his neat figures: seventeen, eight, four A.M. The year would be written in red ink at the top of the chart. He never used his charts more than a year, Captain Brierly didn't. I've the chart now. When he had done he stands looking down at the mark he had made and smiling to himself, then looks up at me. "Thirty-two miles more as she goes," says he, "and then we shall be clear, and you may alter the course twenty degrees to the southward."

"'We were passing to the north of the Hector Bank that voyage. I said, "All right, sir," wondering what he was fussing about, since I had to call him before altering the course anyhow. Just then eight bells were struck: we came out on the bridge, and the second mate before going off mentions in the usual way—"Seventy-one on the log." Captain Brierly looks at the compass and then all round. It was dark and clear, and all the stars were out as plain as on a frosty night in high latitudes. Suddenly he says with a sort of a little sigh: "I am going aft, and shall set the log at zero for you myself, so that there can be no mistake. Thirty-two miles more on this course and then you are safe. Let's see—the correction on the log is six per cent. additive; say, then, thirty by the dial to run, and you may come twenty degrees to starboard at once. No use losing any distance—is there?" I had never heard him talk so much at a stretch, and to no purpose as it seemed to me. I said nothing. He went down the ladder, and the dog, that was always at his heels whenever he moved, night or day, followed, sliding nose first, after him. I heard his boot-heels tap, tap on the after-deck, then he stopped and spoke to the dog—"Go back, Rover. On the bridge, boy! Go on—get." Then he calls out to me from the dark, "Shut that dog up in the chart-room, Mr. Jones—will you?"

"'This was the last time I heard his voice, Captain Marlow. These are the last words he spoke in the hearing of any living human being, sir.' At this point the old chap's voice got quite unsteady. 'He was afraid the poor brute would jump after him, don't you see?' he pursued with a quaver. 'Yes, Captain Marlow. He set the log for me; he—would you believe it?—he put a drop of oil in it too. There was the oil-feeder where he left it near by. The boatswain's mate got the hose along aft to wash down at half-past five; by-and-by he knocks off and runs up on the bridge—"Will you please come aft, Mr. Jones," he says. "There's a funny thing. I don't like to touch it." It was Captain Brierly's gold chronometer watch carefully hung under the rail by its chain.

"'As soon as my eyes fell on it something struck me, and I knew, sir. My legs got soft under me. It was as if I had seen him go over; and I could tell how far behind he was left too.

The taffrail-log marked eighteen miles and three-quarters, and four iron belaying-pins were missing round the mainmast. Put them in his pockets to help him down, I suppose: but, Lord! what's four iron pins to a powerful man like Captain Brierly. Maybe his confidence in himself was just shook a bit at the last. That's the only sign of fluster he gave in his whole life, I should think; but I am ready to answer for him, that once over he did not try to swim a stroke, the same as he would have had pluck enough to keep up all day long on the bare chance had he fallen overboard accidentally. Yes, sir. He was second to none—if he said so himself, as I heard him once. He had written two letters in the middle watch, one to the Company and the other to me. He gave me a lot of instructions as to the passage—I had been in the trade before he was out of his time—and no end of hints as to my conduct with our people in Shanghai, so that I should keep the command of the *Ossa*. He wrote like a father would to a favorite son, Captain Marlow, and I was five-and-twenty years his senior and had tasted salt water before he was fairly breeched. In his letter to the owners—it was left open for me to see—he said that he had always done his duty by them—up to that moment—and even now he was not betraying their confidence, since he was leaving the ship to as competent a seaman as could be found—meaning me, sir, meaning me! He told them that if the last act of his life didn't take away all his credit with them, they would give weight to my faithful service and to his warm recommendation, when about to fill the vacancy made by his death. And much more like this, sir. I couldn't believe my eyes. It made me feel queer all over,' went on the old chap to great perturbation, and squashing something in the corner of his eye with the end of a thumb as broad as a spatula. 'You would think, sir, he had jumped overboard only to give an unlucky man a last show to get on. What with the shock of him going in this awful rash way, and thinking myself a made man by that chance, I was nearly off my chump for a week. But no fear. The captain of the *Pelion* was shifted into the *Ossa*—came aboard in Shanghai—a little popinjay, sir, in a grey check suit, with his hair parted in the middle. "Aw—I am—aw—your new captain,

Mister—Mister—aw—Jones." He was drowned in scent—
fairly stunk with it, Captain Marlow. I daresay it was the look
I gave him that made him stammer. He mumbled something
about my natural disappointment—I had better know at once
that his chief officer got the promotion to the *Pelion*—he had
nothing to do with it, of course—supposed the office knew
best—sorry. . . . Says I, "Don't you mind old Jones, sir; damn
his soul, he's used to it." I could see directly I had shocked his
delicate ear, and while we sat at our first tiffin together he
began to find fault in a nasty manner with this and that in the
ship. I never heard such a voice out of a Punch and Judy show.
I set my teeth hard, and glued my eyes to my plate, and held
my peace as long as I could; but at last I had to say something:
up he jumps tiptoeing, ruffling all his pretty plumes, like a little fighting cock. "You'll find you have a different person to
deal with than the late Captain Brierly." "I've found it," says I,
very glum, but pretending to be mighty busy with my steak.
"You are an old ruffian, Mr.—aw—Jones; and what's more,
you are known for an old ruffian in the employ," he squeaks at
me. The damned bottle-washers stood about listening with
their mouths stretched from ear to ear. "I may be a hard case,"
answers I, "but I ain't so far gone as to put up with the sight of
you sitting in Captain Brierly's chair." With that I lay down my
knife and fork. "You would like to sit in it yourself—that's
where the shoe pinches," he sneers. I left the saloon, got my
rags together, and was on the quay with all my dunnage about
my feet before the stevedores had turned to again. Yes.
Adrift—on shore—after ten years service—and with a poor
woman and four children six thousand miles off depending on
my half-pay for every mouthful they ate. Yes, sir! I chucked it
rather than hear Captain Brierly abused. He left me his night-
glasses—here they are; and he wished me to take care of the
dog—here he is. Hallo, Rover, poor boy. Where's the captain,
Rover?' The dog looked up at us with mournful eyes, gave one
desolate bark, and crept under the table.

"All this was taking place, more than two years afterwards,
on board that nautical ruin the *Fire-Queen* this Jones had got
charge of—quite by a funny accident, too—from Matherson—

mad Matherson they generally called him—the same who used to hang out in Haï-phong, you know, before the occupation days. The old chap snuffled on—

"'Ay, sir, Captain Brierly will be remembered here, if there's no other place on earth. I wrote fully to his father and did not get a word in reply—neither Thank you, nor Go to the devil!—nothing! Perhaps they did not want to know.'

"The sight of that watery-eyed old Jones mopping his bald head with a red cotton handkerchief, the sorrowing yelp of the dog, the squalor of that flyblown cuddy which was the only shrine of his memory, threw a veil of inexpressibly mean pathos over Brierly's remembered figure, the posthumous revenge of fate for that belief in his own splendour which had almost cheated his life of its legitimate terrors. Almost! Perhaps wholly. Who can tell what flattering view he had induced himself to take of his own suicide?

"'Why did he commit the rash act, Captain Marlow—can you think?' asked Jones, pressing his palms together. 'Why? It beats me! Why?' He slapped his low and wrinkled forehead. 'If he had been poor and old and in debt—and never a show—or else mad. But he wasn't of the kind that goes mad, not he. You trust me. What a mate don't know about his skipper isn't worth knowing. Young, healthy, well off, no cares. . . . I sit here sometimes thinking, thinking, till my head fairly begins to buzz. There was some reason.'

"'You may depend on it, Captain Jones,' said I, 'it wasn't anything that would have disturbed much either of us two,' I said; and then, as if a light had been flashed into the muddle of his brain, poor old Jones found a last word of amazing profundity. He blew his nose, nodding at me dolefully:

"'Ay, ay! neither you nor I, sir, had ever thought so much of ourselves.'

"Of course the recollection of my last conversation with Brierly is tinged with the knowledge of his end that followed so close upon it. I spoke with him for the last time during the progress of the inquiry. It was after the first adjournment, and he came up with me in the street. He was in a state of irritation, which I noticed with surprise, his usual behaviour when he condescended to converse being perfectly cool, with a trace of amused tolerance, as if the existence of his interlocutor had been a rather good joke. 'They caught me for that inquiry, you see,' he began, and for a while enlarged complainingly upon the inconveniences of daily attendance in court. 'And goodness knows how long it will last. Three days, I suppose.' I heard him out in silence; in my then opinion it was a way as good as another of putting on side. 'What's the use of it? It is the stupidest set out you can imagine,' he pursued, hotly. I remarked that there was no option. He interrupted me with a sort of pent-up violence. 'I feel like a fool all the time.' I looked up at him. This was going very far—for Brierly—when talking of Brierly. He stopped short, and seizing the lapel of my coat, gave it a slight tug. 'Why are we tormenting that young chap?' he asked. This question chimed in so well to the tolling of a certain thought of mine that, with the image of the absconding renegade in my eye, I answered at once, 'Hanged if I know, unless it be that he lets you.' I was astonished to see him fall into line, so to speak, with that utterance, which ought to have been tolerably cryptic. He said angrily, 'Why, yes. Can't he see that wretched skipper of his has cleared out? What does he expect to happen? Nothing can save him. He's done for.' We walked on in silence a few steps. 'Why eat all that dirt?' he exclaimed, with an oriental energy of expression—about the only sort of energy you can find a trace of east of the fiftieth meridian. I wondered greatly at the direction of his thoughts, but now I strongly suspect it was strictly in character: at bottom poor Brierly must have been thinking of himself. I pointed out to him that the skipper of the *Patna* was known to have feathered his nest pretty well, and could procure almost anywhere the means of getting away. With Jim it was otherwise: the Government was keeping him in the Sailors' Home for the time being, and probably he hadn't a penny in his pocket to bless himself with. It costs some money to run away. 'Does it? Not always,' he said, with a bitter laugh, and to some further remark of mine—'Well, then, let him creep twenty feet underground and stay there! By heavens! *I* would.' I don't know why this tone provoked me, and I said, 'There is a kind of courage in facing it out as he does, knowing very well that if he went away no-body would trouble to run after him.' 'Courage be hanged!' growled Brierly. 'That sort of courage is of no use to keep a man straight, and I don't care a snap for such courage. If you were to say it was a kind of cowardice now—of softness. I tell you what, I will put up two hundred rupees if you put up an-other hundred and undertake to make the beggar clear out early to-morrow morning. The fellow's a gentleman if he ain't fit to be touched—he will understand. He must! This infernal pub-licity is too shocking: there he sits while all these confounded natives, serangs, lascars, quartermasters, are giving evidence that's enough to burn a man to ashes with shame. This is abom-inable. Why, Marlow, don't you think, don't you feel, that this is abominable; don't you now—come—as a seaman? If he went away all this would stop at once.' Brierly said these words with a most unusual animation, and made as if to reach after his pocket-book. I restrained him, and declared coldly that the cowardice of these four men did not seem to me a mat-ter of such great importance. 'And you call yourself a seaman, I suppose,' he pronounced, angrily. I said that's what I called myself, and I hoped I was too. He heard me out, and made a gesture with his big arm that seemed to deprive me of my in-dividuality, to push me away into the crowd. 'The worst of it,' he said, 'is that all you fellows have no sense of dignity; you don't think enough of what you are supposed to be.'

"We had been walking slowly meantime, and now stopped opposite the harbour office, in sight of the very spot from which the immense captain of the *Patna* had vanished as ut-terly as a tiny feather blown away in a hurricane. I smiled. Brierly went on: 'This is a disgrace. We've got all kinds amongst us—some anointed scoundrels in the lot; but, hang it, we must preserve professional decency or we become no bet-ter than so many tinkers going about loose. We are trusted. Do you understand?—trusted! Frankly, I don't care a snap for all the pilgrims that ever came out of Asia, but a decent man would not have behaved like this to a full cargo of old rags in bales. We aren't an organized body of men, and the only thing that holds us together is just the name for that kind of decency.

Such an affair destroys one's confidence. A man may go pretty near through his whole sea-life without any call to show a stiff upper lip. But when the call comes . . . Aha! . . . If I . . .'

"He broke off, and in a changed tone, 'I'll give you two hundred rupees now, Marlow, and you just talk to that chap. Confound him! I wish he had never come out here. Fact is, I rather think some of my people know his. The old man's a parson, and I remember now I met him once when staying with my cousin in Essex last year. If I am not mistaken, the old chap seemed rather to fancy his sailor son. Horrible. I can't do it myself—but you . . .'

"Thus, apropos of Jim, I had a glimpse of the real Brierly a few days before he committed his reality and his sham together to the keeping of the sea. Of course I declined to meddle. The tone of his last 'but you' (poor Brierly couldn't help it), that seemed to imply I was no more noticeable than an insect, caused me to look at the proposal with indignation, and on account of that provocation, or for some other reason, I became positive in my mind that the inquiry was a severe punishment to that Jim, and that his facing it—practically of his own free will—was a redeeming feature in his abominable case. I hadn't been so sure of it before. Brierly went off in a huff. At the time his state of mind was more of a mystery to me than it is now.

"Next day, coming into court late, I sat by myself. Of course I could not forget the conversation I had with Brierly, and now I had them both under my eyes. The demeanour of one suggested gloomy impudence and of the other a contemptuous boredom; yet one attitude might not have been truer than the other, and I was aware that one was not true. Brierly was not bored—he was exasperated; and if so, then Jim might not have been impudent. According to my theory he was not. I imagined he was hopeless. Then it was that our glances met. They met, and the look he gave me was discouraging of any intention I might have had to speak to him. Upon either hypothesis—insolence or despair—I felt I could be of no use to him. This was the second day of the proceedings. Very soon after that exchange of glances the inquiry was adjourned again to the next day. The white men began to troop out at once. Jim had been told to stand down some time before, and was able to leave amongst the first. I saw his broad shoulders and his head outlined in the light of the door, and while I made my way slowly out talking with some one—some stranger who had addressed me casually—I could see him from within the court-room resting both elbows on the balustrade of the verandah and turning his back on the small stream of people trickling down the few steps. There was a murmur of voices and a shuffle of boots.

"The next case was that of assault and battery committed upon a money-lender, I believe; and the defendant—a venerable villager with a straight white beard—sat on a mat just outside the door with his sons, daughters, sons-in-law, their wives, and, I should think, half the population of his village besides, squatting or standing around him. A slim dark woman, with part of her back and one black shoulder bared, and with a thin gold ring in her nose, suddenly began to talk in a high-pitched, shrewish tone. The man with me instinctively looked up at her. We were then just through the door, passing behind Jim's burly back.

"Whether those villagers had brought the yellow dog with them, I don't know. Anyhow, a dog was there, weaving himself in and out amongst people's legs in that mute stealthy way native dogs have and my companion stumbled over him. The dog leaped away without a sound; the man, raising his voice a little, said with a slow laugh, 'Look at that wretched cur,' and directly afterwards we became separated by a lot of people pushing in. I stood back for a moment against the wall while the stranger managed to get down the steps and disappeared. I saw Jim spin round. He made a step forward and barred my way. We were alone; he glared at me with an air of stubborn resolution. I became aware I was being held up, so to speak, as if in a wood. The verandah was empty by then, the noise and movement in court had ceased: a great silence fell upon the building, in which, somewhere far within, an oriental voice began to whine abjectly. The dog in the very act of trying to sneak in at the door, sat down hurriedly to hunt for fleas.

"'Did you speak to me?' asked Jim very low, and bending

forward, not so much towards me but at me, if you know what
I mean. I said 'No' at once. Something in the sound of that
quiet tone of his warned me to be on my defence. I watched
him. It was very much like a meeting in a wood, only more uncertain in its issue, since he could possibly want neither my
money nor my life—nothing that I could simply give up or defend with a clear conscience. 'You say you didn't,' he said,
very sombre. 'But I heard.' 'Some mistake,' I protested, utterly
at a loss, and never taking my eyes off him. To watch his face
was like watching a darkening sky before a clap of thunder,
shade upon shade imperceptibly coming on, the gloom growing mysteriously intense in the calm of maturing violence.

"'As far as I know, I haven't opened my lips in your hearing,' I affirmed with perfect truth. I was getting a little angry,
too, at the absurdity of his encounter. It strikes me now I have
never in my life been so near a beating—I mean it literally; a
beating with fists. I suppose I had some hazy prescience of that
eventuality being in the air. Not that he was actively threatening me. On the contrary, he was strangely passive—don't you
know? but he was lowering, and, though not exceptionally big,
he looked generally fit to demolish a wall. The most reassuring
symptom I noticed was a kind of slow and ponderous hesitation, which I took as a tribute to the evident sincerity of my
manner and of my tone. We faced each other. In the court the
assault case was proceeding. I caught the words: 'Well—buf-
falo—stick—in the greatness of my fear. . . .'

"'What did you mean by staring at me all the morning?'
said Jim at last. He looked up and looked down again. 'Did
you expect us all to sit with downcast eyes out of regard for
your susceptibilities?' I retorted sharply. I was not going to
submit meekly to any of his nonsense. He raised his eyes
again, and this time continued to look me straight in the face.
'No. That's all right,' he pronounced with an air of deliberating with himself upon the truth of this statement—'that's all
right. I am going through with that. Only'—and there he
spoke a little faster—'I won't let any man call me names outside this court. There was a fellow with you. You spoke to

him—oh, yes—I know; 'tis all very fine. You spoke to him, but you meant me to hear. . . .'

"I assured him he was under some extraordinary delusion. I had no conception how it came about. 'You thought I would be afraid to resent this,' he said, with just a faint tinge of bitterness. I was interested enough to discern the slightest shades of expression, but I was not in the least enlightened; yet I don't know what in these words, or perhaps just the intonation of that phrase, induced me suddenly to make all possible allowances for him. I ceased to be annoyed at my unexpected predicament. It was some mistake on his part; he was blundering and I had an intuition that the blunder was of an odious, of an unfortunate nature. I was anxious to end this scene on grounds of decency, just as one is anxious to cut short some unprovoked abominable confidence. The funniest part was, that in the midst of all these considerations of the higher order I was conscious of a certain trepidation as to the possibility—nay, likelihood—of this encounter ending in some disreputable brawl which could not possibly be explained, and would make me ridiculous. I did not hanker after a three days' celebrity as the man who got a black eye or something of the sort from the mate of the *Patna*. He, in all probability, did not care what he did, or at any rate would be fully justified in his own eyes. It took no magician to see he was amazingly angry about something, for all his quiet and even torpid demeanor. I don't deny I was extremely desirous to pacify him at all costs, had I only known what to do. But I didn't know, as you may well imagine. It was blackness without a single gleam. We confronted each other in silence. He hung fire for about fifteen seconds, then made a step nearer, and I made ready to ward off a blow, though I don't think I moved a muscle. 'If you were as big as two men and as strong as six,' he said very softly, 'I would tell you what I think of you. You . . .' 'Stop!' I exclaimed. This checked him for a second. 'Before you tell me what you think of me,' I went on, quickly, 'will you kindly tell me what it is I've said or done?' During the pause that ensued he surveyed me with indignation, while I made supernatural efforts of memory, in which I was hindered by the oriental voice within the court-room expostulating with impassioned volubility against a charge of falsehood. Then we spoke almost together. 'I will soon show you I am not,' he said, in a tone suggestive of a crisis. 'I declare I don't know,' I protested earnestly at the same time. He tried to crush me by the scorn of his glance. 'Now that you see I am not afraid you try to crawl out of it,' he said. 'Who's a cur now—hey?' Then, at last, I understood.

"He had been scanning my features as though looking for a place where he would plant his fist. 'I will allow no man,' . . . he mumbled, threateningly. It was, indeed, a hideous mistake; he had given himself away utterly. I can't give you an idea how shocked I was. I suppose he saw some reflection of my feelings in my face, because his expression changed just a little. 'Good God!' I stammered, 'you don't think I . . .' 'But I am sure I've heard,' he persisted, raising his voice for the first time since the beginning of this deplorable scene. Then with a shade of disdain he added, 'It wasn't you, then? Very well; I'll find the other.' 'Don't be a fool,' I cried in exasperation; 'it wasn't that at all.' 'I've heard,' he said again with an unshaken and sombre perseverance.

"There may be those who could have laughed at his pertinacity. I didn't. Oh, I didn't! There had never been a man so mercilessly shown up by his own natural impulse. A single word had stripped him of his discretion—of that discretion which is more necessary to the decencies of our inner being than clothing is to the decorum of our body. 'Don't be a fool,' I repeated. 'But the other man said it, you don't deny that?' he pronounced, distinctly, and looking in my face without flinching. 'No, I don't deny,' said I, returning my gaze. At last his eyes followed downwards the direction of my pointing finger. He appeared at first uncomprehending, then confounded, and at last amazed and scared as though a dog had been a monster and he had never seen a dog before. 'Nobody dreamt of insulting you,' I said.

"He contemplated the wretched animal, that moved no more than an effigy: it sat with ears pricked and its sharp muzzle pointed into the doorway, and suddenly snapped at a fly like a piece of mechanism.

"I looked at him. The red of his fair sunburnt complexion deepened suddenly under the down of his cheeks, invaded his forehead, spread to the roots of his curly hair. His ears became intensely crimson, and even the clear blue of his eyes were darkened many shades by the rush of blood to his head. His lips pouted a little, trembling as though he had been on the point of bursting into tears. I perceived he was incapable of pronouncing a word from the excess of his humiliation. From disappointment too—who knows? Perhaps he looked forward to that hammering he was going to give me for rehabilitation, for appeasement? Who can tell what relief he expected from this chance of a row? He was naïve enough to expect anything; but he had given himself away for nothing in this case. He had been frank with himself—let alone with me—in the wild hope of arriving in that way at some effective refutation, and the stars had been ironically unpropitious. He made an inarticulate noise in his throat like a man imperfectly stunned by a blow on the head. It was pitiful.

"I didn't catch up again with him till well outside the gate. I had even to trot a bit at the last, but when, out of breath at his elbow, I taxed him with running away, he said, 'Never!' and at once turned at bay. I explained I never meant to say he was running away from *me*. 'From no man—from not a single man on earth,' he affirmed with a stubborn mien. I forebore to point out the one obvious exception which would hold good for the bravest of us; I thought he would find out by himself very soon. He looked at me patiently while I was thinking of something to say, but I could find nothing on the spur of the moment, and he began to walk on. I kept up, and anxious not to lose him, I said hurriedly that I couldn't think of leaving him under a false impression of my—of my—I stammered. The stupidity of the phrase appalled me while I was trying to finish it, but the power of sentences has nothing to do with their sense or the logic of their construction. My idiotic mumble seemed to please him. He cut it short by saying, with courteous placidity that argued an immense power of self-control or else a wonderful elasticity of spirits—'Altogether my mistake.' I marvelled greatly at this expression: he might have been alluding to some trifling occurrence. Hadn't he understood its deplorable meaning? 'You may well forgive me,' he continued, and went on a little moodily, 'All these staring people in court seemed such fools that—that it might have been as I supposed.'

"This opened suddenly a new view of him to my wonder. I looked at him curiously and met his unabashed and impenetrable eyes. 'I can't put up with this kind of thing,' he said, very simply, 'and I don't mean to. In court it's different; I've got to stand that—and I can do it too.'

"I don't pretend I understood him. The views he let me have of himself were like those glimpses through the shifting rents in a thick fog—bits of vivid and vanishing detail, giving no connected idea of the general aspect of a country. They fed one's curiosity without satisfying it; they were no good for purposes of orientation. Upon the whole he was misleading. That's how I summed him up to myself after he left me late in the evening. I had been staying at the Malabar House for a few days, and on my pressing invitation he dined with me there."

Chapter Seven

A N OUTWARD-BOUND mail-boat had come in that afternoon, and the big dining-room of the hotel was more than half full of people with a hundred pounds round-the-world tickets in their pockets. There were married couples looking domesticated and bored with each other in the midst of their travels; there were small parties and large parties, and lone individuals dining solemnly or feasting boisterously, but all thinking, conversing, joking, or scowling as was their wont at home; and just as intelligently receptive of new impressions as their trunks upstairs. Henceforth they would be labelled as having passed through this and that place and so would be their luggage. They would cherish this distinction of their persons, and preserve the gummed tickets on their portmanteaus as documentary evidence, as the only permanent trace of their improving enterprise. The dark-faced servants tripped without noise over the vast and polished floor; now and then a girl's laugh would be heard, as innocent and empty as her mind, or, in a sudden hush of crockery, a few words in an affected drawl from some wit embroidering for the benefit of a grinning tableful the last funny story of shipboard scandal. Two nomadic old maids, dressed up to kill, worked acrimoniously through the bill of fare, whispering to each other with faded lips, woodenfaced and bizarre, like two sumptuous scarecrows. A little wine opened Jim's heart and loosened his tongue. His appetite was good, too, I noticed. He seemed to have buried somewhere the opening episode of our acquaintance. It was like a thing of which there would be no more question in this world. And all the time I had before me these blue, boyish eyes looking straight into mine, this young face, these capable shoulders, the open bronzed forehead with a white line under the roots of clustering fair hair, this appearance appealing at sight to all my sympathies: this frank aspect, the artless smile, the youthful seriousness. He was of the right sort; he was one of us. He talked soberly, with a sort of composed unreserve, and with a quiet bearing that might have been the outcome of manly self-control, of impudence, of callousness, of a colossal unconsciousness, of a gigantic deception. Who can tell! From our tone we might have been discussing a third person, a football match, last year's weather. My mind floated in a sea of conjectures till the turn of the conversation enabled me, without being offensive, to remark that, upon the whole, this inquiry must have been pretty trying to him. He darted his arm across the tablecloth, and clutching my hand by the side of my plate, glared fixedly. I was startled. 'It must be awfully hard,' I stammered, confused by this display of speechless feeling. 'It is—hell,' he burst out in a muffled voice.

"This movement and these words caused two well-groomed male globe-trotters at a neighbouring table to look up in alarm from their iced pudding. I rose, and we passed into the front gallery for coffee and cigars.

"On little octagon tables candles burned in glass globes; clumps of stiff-leaved plants separated sets of cosy wicker chairs; and between the pairs of columns, whose reddish shafts caught in a long row the sheen from the tall windows, the night, glittering and sombre, seemed to hang like a splendid drapery. The riding lights of ships winked afar like setting stars, and the hills across the roadstead resembled rounded black masses of arrested thunder-clouds.

"'I couldn't clear out,' Jim began. 'The skipper did—that's all very well for him. I couldn't, and I wouldn't. They all got out of it in one way or another, but it wouldn't do for me.'

"I listened with concentrated attention, not daring to stir in my chair; I wanted to know—and to this day I don't know, I can only guess. He would be confident and depressed all in the same breath, as if some conviction of innate blamelessness had checked the truth writhing within him at every turn. He began by saying, in the tone in which a man would admit his inability to jump a twenty-foot wall, that he could never go home now; and this declaration recalled to my mind what Brierly had said, 'that the old parson in Essex seemed to fancy his sailor son not a little.'

"I can't tell you whether Jim knew he was especially 'fancied,' but the tone of his references to 'my Dad' was calculated to give me a notion that the good old rural dean was about the finest man that ever had been worried by the cares of a large family since the beginning of the world. This, though never stated, was implied with an anxiety that there should be no mistake about it, which was really very true and charming, but added a poignant sense of lives far off to the other elements of the story. 'He has seen it all in the home papers by this time,' said Jim. 'I can never face the poor old chap.' I did not dare to lift my eyes at this till I heard him add, 'I could never explain. He wouldn't understand.' Then I looked up. He was smoking reflectively, and after a moment, rousing himself, began to talk again. He discovered at once a desire that I should not confound him with his partners in—in crime, let us call it. He was not one of them; he was altogether of another sort. I gave no sign of dissent. I had no intention, for the sake of barren truth, to rob him of the smallest particle of any saving grace that would come in his way. I didn't know how much of it he believed himself. I didn't know what he was playing up to—if he was playing up to anything at all—and I suspect he did not know either; for it is my belief no man ever understands quite his own artful dodges to escape from the grim shadow of self-knowledge. I made no sound all the time he was wondering what he had better do after 'that stupid inquiry was over.'

"Apparently he shared Brierly's contemptuous opinion of these proceedings ordained by law. He would not know where to turn, he confessed, clearly thinking aloud rather than talking to me. Certificate gone, career broken, no money to get away, no work that he could obtain as far as he could see. At home he could perhaps get something; but it meant going to his people for help, and that he would not do. He saw nothing for it but ship before the mast—could get perhaps a quartermaster. . . . 'Do you think you would?' I asked, pitilessly. He jumped up, and going to the stone balustrade looked out into the night. In a moment he was back, towering above my chair with his youthful face clouded yet by the pain of a conquered emotion. He had understood very well I did not doubt his ability to steer a ship. In a voice that quavered a bit he asked me, 'Why did I say that? I had been "no end kind" to him. I had not even laughed at him when'—here he began to mumble—'that mistake, you know—made a confounded ass of myself.' I broke in by saying rather warmly that for me such a mistake was not a matter to laugh at. He sat down and drank deliberately some coffee, emptying the small cup to the last drop. 'That does not mean I admit for a moment the cap fitted,' he declared, distinctly. 'No?' I said. 'No,' he affirmed with quiet decision. 'Do you know what *you* would have done? Do you? And you don't think yourself' . . . he gulped something . . . 'you don't think yourself a—a—cur?'

"And with this—upon my honour!—he looked up at me inquisitively. It was a question it appears—a *bona fide* question! However, he didn't wait for an answer. Before I could recover he went on, with his eyes straight before him, as if reading off something written on the body of the night. 'It is all in being

ready. I wasn't; not—not then. I don't want to excuse myself;
but I would like to explain—I would like somebody to understand—somebody—one person at least! You! Why not you?'

"It was solemn, and a little ridiculous, too, as they always
are, those struggles of an individual trying to save from the fire
his idea of what his moral identity should be, this precious notion of a convention, only one of the rules of the game, nothing
more, but all the same so terribly effective by its assumption of
unlimited power over natural instincts, by the awful penalties
of its failure. He began his story quietly enough. On board that
Dale Line steamer that had picked up these four floating in a
boat upon the discreet sunset glow of the sea, they had been
after the first day looked askance upon. The fat skipper told
some story, the others had been silent, and at first it had been
accepted. You don't cross-examine poor castaways you had the
good luck to save, if not from cruel death, then at least from
cruel suffering. Afterwards, with time to think it over, it might
have struck the officers of the *Avondale* that there was 'something fishy' in the affair; but of course they would keep their
doubts to themselves. They had picked up the captain, the
mate, and two engineers of the steamer *Patna* sunk at sea, and
that, very properly, was enough for them. I did not ask Jim
about the nature of his feelings during the ten days he spent on
board. From the way he narrated that part I was at liberty to
infer he was partly stunned by the discovery he had made—the
discovery about himself—and no doubt was at work trying to
explain it away to the only man who was capable of appreciat-
ing all its tremendous magnitude. You must understand he did
not try to minimise its importance. Of that I am sure; and
therein lies his distinction. As to what sensations he experienced when he got ashore and heard the unforeseen conclusion
of the tale in which he had taken such a pitiful part, he told me
nothing of them, and it is difficult to imagine. I wonder
whether he felt the ground cut from under his feet? I wonder?
But no doubt he managed to get a fresh foothold very soon. He
was ashore a whole fortnight waiting in the Sailors' Home, and
as there were six or seven men staying there at the time, I had
heard of him a little. Their languid opinion seemed to be that in

addition to his other shortcomings, he was a sulky brute. He
had passed these days on the verandah, buried in a long chair,
and coming out of his place of sepulture only at meal-times or
late at night, when he wandered on the quays all by himself,
detached from his surroundings, irresolute and silent, like a
ghost without a home to haunt. 'I don't think I've spoken three
words to a living soul in all that time,' he said, making me very
sorry for him; and directly he added, 'One of these fellows
would have been sure to blurt out something I had made up my
mind not to put up with, and I didn't want a row. No! Not then.
I was too—too . . . I had no heart for it.' 'So that bulkhead held
out after all,' I remarked, cheerfully. 'Yes,' he murmured, 'it
held. And yet I swear to you I felt it bulge under my hand.' 'It's
extraordinary what strains old iron will stand sometimes,' I
said. Thrown back in his seat, his legs stiffly out and arms
hanging down, he nodded slightly several times. You could not
conceive a sadder spectacle. Suddenly he lifted his head; he sat
up; he slapped his thigh. 'Ah! what a chance missed! My God!
what a chance missed!' he blazed out, but the ring of the last
'missed' resembled a cry wrung out by pain.

"He was silent again with a still, far-away look of fierce
yearning after that missed distinction, with his nostrils for an
instant dilated, sniffing the intoxicating breath of that wasted
opportunity. If you think I was either surprised or shocked you
do me an injustice in more ways than one! Ah, he was an imaginative beggar! He would give himself away; he would give
himself up. I could see in his glance darted into the night all his
inner being carried on, projected headlong into the fanciful
realm of recklessly heroic aspirations. He had no leisure to regret what he had lost, he was so wholly and naturally concerned for what he had failed to obtain. He was very far away
from me who watched him across three feet of space. With
every instant he was penetrating deeper into the impossible
world of romantic achievements. He got to the heart of it at
last! A strange look of beatitude overspread his features, his
eyes sparkled in the light of the candle burning between us; he
positively smiled! He had penetrated to the very heart—to the
very heart. It was an ecstatic smile that your faces—or mine ei-

ther—will never wear, my dear boys. I whisked him back by
saying, 'If you had stuck to the ship, you mean!'

"He turned upon me, his eyes suddenly amazed and full of
pain, with a bewildered, startled, suffering face, as though he
had tumbled down from a star. Neither you nor I will ever look
like this on any man. He shuddered profoundly, as if a cold
finger-tip had touched his heart. Last of all he sighed.

"I was not in a merciful mood. He provoked one by his con-
tradictory indiscretions. 'It is unfortunate you didn't know
beforehand!' I said with every unkind intention; but the perfid-
ious shaft fell harmless—dropped at his feet like a spent arrow,
as it were, and he did not think of picking it up. Perhaps he had
not even seen it. Presently, lolling at ease, he said, 'Dash it all!
I tell you it bulged. I was holding up my lamp along the angle-
iron in the lower deck when a flake of rust as big as the palm
of my hand fell off the plate, all of itself.' He passed his hand
over his forehead. 'The thing stirred and jumped off like something alive while I was looking at it.' 'That made you feel
pretty bad,' I observed, casually. 'Do you suppose,' he said,
'that I was thinking of myself, with a hundred and sixty people
at my back, all fast asleep in the fore-'tween-deck alone—and
more of them aft; more on the deck—sleeping—knowing
nothing about it—three times as many as there were boats for,
even if there had been time? I expected to see the iron open out
as I stood there and the rush of water going over them as they
lay. . . . What could I do—what?'

"I can easily picture him to myself in the peopled gloom of
the cavernous place, with the light of the bulk-lamp falling on
a small portion of the bulkhead that had the weight of the
ocean on the other side, and the breathing of unconscious
sleepers in his ears. I can see him glaring at the iron, startled
by the falling rust, overburdened by the knowledge of an im-
minent death. This, I gathered, was the second time he had
been sent forward by that skipper of his, who, I rather think,
wanted to keep him away from the bridge. He told me that his
first impulse was to shout and straight away make all those
people leap out of sleep into terror; but such an overwhelming
sense of his helplessness came over him that he was not able

to produce a sound. This is, I suppose, what people mean by
the tongue cleaving to the roof of the mouth. 'Too dry,' was
the concise expression he used in reference to this state. Without a sound, then, he scrambled out on deck through the number one hatch. A wind-sail rigged down there swung against
him accidentally, and he remembered that the light touch of
the canvas on his face nearly knocked him off the hatchway
ladder.

"He confessed that his knees wobbled a good deal as he
stood on the foredeck looking at another sleeping crowd. The
engines having been stopped by that time, the steam was blowing off. Its deep rumble made the whole night vibrate like a
bass string. The ship trembled to it.

"He saw here and there a head lifted off a mat, a vague form
uprise in sitting posture, listen sleepily for a moment, sink
down again into the billowy confusion of boxes, steam-
winches, ventilators. He was aware all these people did not
know enough to take intelligent notice of that strange noise.
The ship of iron, the men with white faces, all the sights, all
the sounds, everything on board to that ignorant and pious
multitude was strange alike, and as trustworthy as it would for
ever remain incomprehensible. It occurred to him that the fact
was fortunate. The idea of it was simply terrible.

"You must remember he believed, as any other man would
have done in his place, that the ship would go down at any
moment; the bulging, rust-eaten plates that kept back the
ocean, fatally must give way, all at once like an undermined
dam, and let in a sudden and overwhelming flood. He stood
still looking at these recumbent bodies, a doomed man aware
of his fate, surveying the silent company of the dead. They
were dead! Nothing could save them! There were boats
enough for half of them perhaps, but there was no time. No
time! No time! It did not seem worth while to open his lips,
to stir hand or foot. Before he could shout three words, or
make three steps, he would be floundering in the sea
whitened awfully by the desperate struggles of human beings, clamorous with the distress of cries for help. There was
no help. He imagined what would happen perfectly; he went

through it all motionless by the hatchway with the lamp in his hand—he went through it to the very last harrowing detail. I think he went through it again while he was telling me these things he could not tell the court.

"'I saw as clearly as I see you now that there was nothing I could do. It seemed to take all life out of my limbs. I thought I might just as well stand where I was and wait. I did not think I had many seconds . . .' Suddenly the steam ceased blowing off. The noise, he remarked, had been distracting, but the silence at once became intolerably oppressive.

"'I thought I would choke before I got drowned,' he said.

"He protested he did not think of saving himself. The only distinct thought formed, vanishing, and reforming in his brain, was: eight hundred people and seven boats; eight hundred people and seven boats.

"'Somebody was speaking aloud inside my head,' he said a little wildly. 'Eight hundred people and seven boats—and no time! Just think of it.' He leaned towards me across the little table, and I tried to avoid his stare. 'Do you think I was afraid of death?' he asked in a voice very fierce and low. He brought down his open hand with a bang that made the coffee-cups dance. 'I am ready to swear I was not—I was not. . . . By God—no!' He hitched himself upright and crossed his arms; his chin fell on his breast.

"The soft clashes of crockery reached us faintly through the high windows. There was a burst of voices, and several men came out in high good-humour into the gallery. They were exchanging jocular reminiscences of the donkeys in Cairo. A pale anxious youth stepping softly on long legs was being chaffed by a strutting and rubicund globe-trotter about his purchases in the bazaar. 'No, really—do you think I've been done to that extent?' he inquired very earnest and deliberate. The band moved away dropping into chairs as they went; matches flared, illuminating for a second faces without the ghost of an expression and the flat glaze of white shirt-fronts; the hum of many conversations animated with the ardour of feasting sounded to me absurd and infinitely remote.

"'Some of the crew were sleeping on the number one hatch within reach of my arm,' began Jim again.

"You must know they kept Kalashee watch in that ship, all hands sleeping through the night, and only the reliefs of quartermasters and look-out men being called. He was tempted to grip and shake the shoulder of the nearest lascar, but he didn't. Something held his arms down along his sides. He was not afraid—oh no! only he just couldn't—that's all. He was not afraid of death perhaps, but I'll tell you what, he was afraid of the emergency. His confounded imagination had evoked for him all the horrors of panic, the trampling rush, the pitiful screams, boats swamped—all the appalling incidents of a disaster at sea he had ever heard of. He might have been resigned to die but I suspect he wanted to die without added terrors, quietly, in a sort of peaceful trance. A certain readiness to perish is not so very rare, but it is seldom that you meet men whose souls, steeled in the impenetrable armour of resolution, are ready to fight a losing battle to the last, the desire of peace waxes stronger as hope declines, till at last it conquers the very desire of life. Which of us here has not observed this, or maybe experienced something of that feeling in his own person—this extreme weariness of emotions, the vanity of effort, the yearning for rest? Those striving with unreasonable forces know it well—the shipwrecked castaways in boats, wanderers lost in a desert, men battling against the unthinking might of nature, or the stupid brutality of crowds."

Chapter Eight

How long he stood stock-still by the hatch expecting every moment to feel the ship dip under his feet and the rush of water to take him at the back and toss him like a chip, I cannot say. Not very long—two minutes perhaps. A couple of men he could not make out began to converse drowsily, and also, he could not tell where, he detected a curious noise of shuffling feet. Above these faint sounds there was that awful stillness preceding a catastrophe, that trying silence of the moment before the crash; then it came into his head that perhaps he would have time to rush along and cut all the lanyards of the grips, so that the boats would float off as the ship went down.

"The *Patna* had a long bridge, and all the boats were up there, four on one side and three on the other—the smallest of them on the port-side and nearly abreast of the steering gear. He assured me, with evident anxiety to be believed, that he had been most careful to keep them ready for instant service. He knew his duty. I dare say he was a good enough mate as far as that went. 'I always believed in being prepared for the worst,' he commented, staring anxiously in my face. I nodded my approval of the sound principle, averting my eyes before the subtle unsoundness of the man.

"He started unsteadily to run. He had to step over legs, avoid stumbling against heads. Suddenly some one caught hold of his coat from below, and a distressed voice spoke under his elbow. The light of the lamp he carried in his right hand fell upon an upturned dark face whose eyes entreated him together with the voice. He had picked up enough of the language to understand the word water, repeated several times in a tone of insistence, of prayer, almost of despair. He gave a jerk to get away, and felt an arm embrace his leg.

" 'The beggar clung to me like a drowning man,' he said, impressively. 'Water, water! What water did he mean? What did he know? As calmly as I could I ordered him to let go. He was stopping me, time was pressing, other men began to stir; I wanted time—time to cut the boats adrift. He got hold of my hand now, and I felt that he would begin to shout. It flashed upon me it was enough to start a panic, and I hauled off with my free arm and slung the lamp in his face. The glass jingled, the light went out, but the blow made him let go, and I ran off—I wanted to get at the boats; I wanted to get at the boats. He leaped after me from behind. I turned on him. He would not keep quiet; he tried to shout; I had half throttled him before I made out what he wanted. He wanted some water—water to drink; they were on strict allowance, you know, and he had with him a young boy I had noticed several times. His child was sick—and thirsty. He had caught sight of me as I passed by, and was begging for a little water. That's all. We were under the bridge, in the dark. He kept on snatching at my wrists; there was no getting rid of him. I dashed into my berth, grabbed my water-bottle, and thrust it into his hands. He vanished. I didn't find out till then how much I was in want of a drink myself.' He leaned on one elbow with a hand over his eyes.

"I felt a creepy sensation all down my backbone; there was something peculiar in all this. The fingers of the hand that shaded his brow trembled slightly. He broke the short silence.

"'These things happen only once to a man and . . . Ah! well! When I got on the bridge at last the beggars were getting one of the boats off the chocks. A boat! I was running up the ladder when a heavy blow fell on my shoulder, just missing my head. It didn't stop me, and the chief engineer—they had got him out of his bunk by then—raised the boat-stretcher again. Somehow I had no mind to be surprised at anything. All this seemed natural—and awful—and awful. I dodged that miserable maniac, lifted him off the deck as though he had been a little child, and he started whispering in my arms: "Don't! don't! I thought you were one of them niggers." I flung him away, he skidded along the bridge and knocked the legs from under the little chap—the second. The skipper, busy about the boat, looked round and came at me head down, growling like a wild beast. I flinched no more than a stone. I was as solid standing there as this,' he tapped lightly with his knuckles the wall beside his chair. 'It was as though I had heard it all, seen it all, gone through it all twenty times already. I wasn't afraid of them. I drew back my fist and he stopped short, muttering—

"'"Ah! it's you. Lend a hand quick."

"'That's what he said. Quick! As if anybody could be quick

enough. "Aren't you going to do something?" I asked. "Yes. Clear out," he snarled over his shoulder.

"'I don't think I understood then what he meant. The other two had picked themselves up by that time, and they rushed together to the boat. They tramped, they wheezed, they shoved, they cursed the boat, the ship, each other—cursed me. All in mutters. I didn't move, I didn't speak. I watched the slant of the ship. She was as still as if landed on the blocks in a dry dock—only she was like this.' He held up his hand, palm under, the tips of the fingers inclined downwards. 'Like this,' he repeated. 'I could see the line of the horizon before me, as clear as a bell, above her stemhead; I could see the water far off there black and sparkling, and still—still as a pond, deadly still, more still than ever sea was before—more still than I could bear to look at. Have you watched a ship floating head down, checked in sinking by a sheet of old iron too rotten to stand being shored up. Have you? Oh yes, shored up? I thought of that—I thought of every mortal thing; but can you shore up a bulkhead in five minutes—or in fifty for that matter? Where was I going to get men that would go down below? And the timber—the timber! Would you have had the courage to swing the maul for the first blow if you had seen that bulkhead? Don't say you would: you had not seen it; nobody would. Hang it—to do a thing like that you must believe there is a chance, one in a thousand, at least, some ghost of a chance; and you would not have believed. Nobody would have believed. You think me a cur for standing there, but what would you have done? What! You can't tell—nobody can tell. One must have time to turn round. What would you have me do? Where was the kindness in making crazy with fright all those people I could not save single-handed—that nothing could save? Look here! As true as I sit on this chair before you . . .'

"He drew quick breaths at every few words and shot quick glances at my face, as though in his anguish he were watchful of the effect. He was not speaking to me, he was only speaking before me, in a dispute with an invisible personality, an antagonistic and inseparable partner of his existence—another pos-

sessor of his soul. These were issues beyond the competency
of a court of inquiry: it was a subtle and momentous quarrel as
to the true essence of life, and did not want a judge. He wanted
an ally, a helper, an accomplice. I felt the risk I ran of being
circumvented, blinded, decoyed, bullied, perhaps, into taking a
definite part in a dispute impossible of decision if one had to
be fair to all the phantoms in possession—to the reputable that
had its claims and to the disreputable that had its exigencies. I
can't explain to you who haven't seen him and who hear his
words only at second hand the mixed nature of my feelings. It
seemed to me I was being made to comprehend the Inconceivable—and I know of nothing to compare with the discomfort
of such a sensation. I was made to look at the convention that
lurks in all truth and on the essential sincerity of falsehood. He
appealed to all sides at once—to the side turned perpetually to
the light of day, and to that side of us which, like the other
hemisphere of the moon, exists stealthily in perpetual darkness, with only a fearful ashy light falling at times on the edge.
He swayed me. I own to it, I own up. The occasion was obscure, insignificant—what you will: a lost youngster, one in a
million—but then he was one of us; an incident as completely
devoid of importance as the flooding of an ant-heap, and yet
the mystery of this attitude got hold of me as though he had
been an individual in the forefront of his kind, as if the obscure
truth involved were momentous enough to affect mankind's
conception of itself. . . ."

Marlow paused to put new life into his expiring cheroot,
seemed to forget all about the story, and abruptly began
again.

"My fault of course. One has no business really to get interested. It's a weakness of mine. His was of another kind. My
weakness consists in not having a discriminating eye for the
incidental—for the externals—no eye for the hod of the rag-
picker or the fine linen of the next man. Next man—that's it. I
have met so many men," he pursued, with momentary sadness—"met them, too, with a certain—certain—impact, let us
say; like this fellow, for instance—and in each case all I could
see was merely the human being. A confounded democratic

quality of vision which may be better than total blindness, but
has been of no advantage to me, I can assure you. Men expect
one to take into account their fine linen. But I never could get
up any enthusiasm about these things. Oh! it's a failing; it's a
failing; and then comes a soft evening; a lot of men too indo-
lent for whist—and a story. . . ."

He paused again to wait for an encouraging remark perhaps,
but nobody spoke; only the host, as if reluctantly performing a
duty, murmured—

"You are so subtle, Marlow."

"Who? I?" said Marlow in a low voice. "Oh, no! But *he*
was; and try as I may for the success of this yarn I am missing
innumerable shades—they were so fine, so difficult to render
in colourless words. Because he complicated matters by being
so simple, too—the simplest poor devil! . . . By Jove! he was
amazing. There he sat telling me that just as I saw him before
my eyes he wouldn't be afraid to face anything—and believing
in it, too. I tell you it was fabulously innocent and it was enormous, enormous! I watched him covertly, just as though I had
suspected him of an intention to take a jolly good rise out of
me. He was confident that, on the square, 'on the square,
mind!' there was nothing he couldn't meet. Ever since he had
been 'so high'—'quite a little chap,' he had been preparing
himself for all the difficulties that can beset one on land and
water. He confessed proudly to this kind of foresight. He had
been elaborating dangers and defences, expecting the worst,
rehearsing his best. He must have led a most exalted existence.
Can you fancy it? A succession of adventures, so much glory,
such a victorious progress! and the deep sense of his sagacity
crowning every day of his inner life. He forgot himself; his
eyes shone; and with every word my heart, searched by the
light of his absurdity, was growing heavier in my breast. I had
no mind to laugh, and lest I should smile I made for myself a
stolid face. He gave signs of irritation.

"'It is always the unexpected that happens,' I said in a pro-
pitiatory tone. My obtuseness provoked him into a contemptuous 'Pshaw!' I suppose he meant that the unexpected couldn't
touch him; nothing less than the unconceivable itself could get

over his perfect state of preparation. He had been taken unawares—and he whispered to himself a malediction upon the
waters and the firmament, upon the ship, upon the men. Everything had betrayed him! He had been tricked into that sort of
high-minded resignation which prevented him lifting as much
as his little finger, while these others who had a very clear perception of the actual necessity were tumbling against each
other and sweating desperately over that boat business. Something had gone wrong there at the last moment. It appears that
in their flurry they had contrived in some mysterious way to
get the sliding bolt of the foremost boat-chock jammed tight,
and forthwith had gone out of the remnants of their minds over
the deadly nature of that accident. It must have been a pretty
sight, the fierce industry of these beggars toiling on a motionless ship that floated quietly in the silence of a world asleep,
fighting against time for the freeing of that boat, grovelling on
all-fours, standing up in despair, tugging, pushing, snarling at
each other venomously, ready to kill, ready to weep, and only
kept from flying at each other's throats by the fear of death that
stood silent behind them like an inflexible and cold-eyed
taskmaster. Oh, yes! It must have been a pretty sight. He saw it
all, he could talk about it with scorn and bitterness; he had a
minute knowledge of it by means of some sixth sense, I con-
clude, because he swore to me he had remained apart without
a glance at them and at the boat—without one single glance.
And I believe him. I should think he was too busy watching the
threatening slant of the ship, the suspended menace discovered
in the midst of the most perfect security—fascinated by the
sword hanging by a hair over his imaginative head.

"Nothing in the world moved before his eyes, and he could
depict to himself without hindrance the sudden swing upwards
of the dark sky-line, the sudden tilt up of the vast plain of the
sea, the swift still rise, the brutal fling, the grasp of the abyss,
the struggle without hope, the starlight closing over his head
for ever like the vault of a tomb—the revolt of his young life—
the black end. He could! By Jove! who couldn't? And you
must remember he was a finished artist in that peculiar way, he
was a gifted poor devil with the faculty of swift and fore-

stalling vision. The sights it showed him had turned him into
cold stone from the soles of his feet to the nape of his neck; but
there was a hot dance of thoughts in his head, a dance of lame,
blind, mute thoughts—a whirl of awful cripples. Didn't I tell
you he confessed himself before me as though I had the power
to bind and to loose? He burrowed deep, deep, in the hope of
my absolution, which would have been of no good to him. This
was one of those cases which no solemn deception can palli-
ate, which no man can help; where his very Maker seems to
abandon a sinner to his own devices.

"He stood on the starboard side of the bridge, as far as he
could get from the struggle for the boat, which went on with
the agitation of madness and the stealthiness of a conspiracy.
The two Malays had meantime remained holding to the wheel.
Just picture to yourselves the actors in that, thank God! unique,
episode of the sea, four beside themselves with fierce and secret exertions, and three looking on in complete immobility,
above the awnings covering the profound ignorance of hundreds of human beings, with their weariness, with their
dreams, with their hopes, arrested, held by an invisible hand on
the brink of annihilation. For that they were so, makes no
doubt to me: given the state of the ship, this was the deadliest
possible description of accident that could happen. These beggars by the boat had every reason to go distracted with funk.
Frankly, had I been there I would not have given as much as a
counterfeit farthing for the ship's chance to keep above water
to the end of each successive second. And still she floated!
These sleeping pilgrims were destined to accomplish their
whole pilgrimage to the bitterness of some other end. It was as
if the Omnipotence whose mercy they confessed had needed
their humble testimony on earth for a while longer, and had
looked down to make a sign, 'Thou shalt not!' to the ocean.
Their escape would trouble me as a prodigiously inexplicable
event, did I not know how tough old iron can be—as tough
sometimes as the spirit of some men we meet now and then,
worn to a shadow and breasting the weight of life. Not the least
wonder of these twenty minutes, to my mind, is the behaviour
of the two helmsmen. They were amongst the native batch of

all sorts brought over from Aden to give evidence at the inquiry. One of them, labouring under intense bashfulness, was very young, and with his smooth, yellow, cherry countenance looked even younger than he was. I remembered perfectly Brierly asking him, through the interpreter, what he thought of it at the time, and the interpreter, after a short colloquy, turning to the court with an important air—

"'He says he thought nothing.'

"The other with patient blinking eyes, a blue cotton handkerchief, faded with much washing, bound with a smart twist over a lot of grey wisps, his face shrunk into grim hollows, his brown skin made darker by a mesh of wrinkles, explained that he had a knowledge of some evil thing befalling the ship, but there had been no order; he could not remember an order; why should he leave the helm? To some further questions he jerked back his spare shoulders, and declared it never came into his mind then that the white men were about to leave the ship through fear of death. He did not believe it now. There might have been secret reasons. He wagged his old chin knowingly. Aha! secret reasons. He was a man of great experience, and he wanted *that* white Tuan to know—he turned towards Brierly, who didn't raise his head—that he had acquired a knowledge of many things by serving white men on the sea for a great number of years—and, suddenly, with shaky excitement he poured upon our spellbound attention a lot of queer-sounding names, names of dead-and-gone skippers, names of forgotten country ships, names of familiar and distorted sound, as if the hand of dumb time had been at work on them for ages. They stopped him at last. A silence fell upon the court,—a silence that remained unbroken for at least a minute, and passed gently into a deep murmur. This episode was *the* sensation of the second day's proceedings—affecting all the audience, affecting everybody except Jim, who was sitting moodily at the end of the first bench, and never looked up at this extraordinary and damning witness that seemed possessed of some mysterious theory of defence.

"So these two lascars stuck to the helm of that ship without steerage-way, where death would have found them if such had

been their destiny. The whites did not give them half a glance,
had probably forgotten their existence. Assuredly Jim did not
remember it. He remembered he could do nothing; he could do
nothing, now he was alone. There was nothing to do but to sink
with the ship. No use making a disturbance about it. Was
there? He waited upstanding, without a sound, stiffened in the
idea of some sort of heroic discretion. The first engineer ran
cautiously across the bridge to tug at his sleeve.

"'Come and help! For God's sake, come and help!'

"He ran back to the boat on the points of his toes, and returned directly to worry at his sleeve, begging and cursing at
the same time.

"'I believe he would have kissed my hands,' said Jim, sav-
agely, 'and next moment, he starts foaming and whispering in
my face. "If I had the time I would like to crack your skull for
you." I pushed him away. Suddenly he caught hold of me
around the neck. Damn him! I hit him. I hit out without looking. "Won't you save your own life—you infernal coward?" he
sobs. Coward! He called me an infernal coward! Ha! ha! ha!
ha! He called me—ha! ha! ha! . . .'

"He had thrown himself back and was shaking with laughter. I had never in my life heard anything so bitter as that
noise. It felt like a blight on all the merriment about donkeys,
pyramids, bazaars, or what not. Along the whole dim length of
the gallery the voices dropped, the pale blotches of faces
turned our way with one accord, and the silence became so
profound that the clear tinkle of a teaspoon falling on the tes-
selated floor of the verandah rang out like a tiny and silvery
scream.

"'You mustn't laugh like this, with all these people about,' I
remonstrated. 'It isn't nice for them, you know.'

"He gave no sign of having heard at first, but after a while,
with a stare that, missing me altogether, seemed to probe the
heart of some awful vision, he muttered carelessly—'Oh!
they'll think I am drunk.'

"And after that you would have thought from his appearance he would never make a sound again. But—no fear! He

could no more stop telling now than he could have stopped living by the mere exertion of his will."

Chapter Nine

I WAS SAYING to myself, "Sink—curse you! Sink!"' These were the words with which he began again. He wanted it over. He was severely left alone, and he formulated in his head this address to the ship in a tone of imprecation, while at the same time he enjoyed the privilege of witnessing scenes—as far as I can judge—of low comedy. They were still at that bolt. The skipper was ordering, 'Get under and try to lift'; and the others naturally shirked. You understand that to be squeezed flat under the keel of a boat wasn't a desirable position to be caught in if the ship went down suddenly. 'Why don't you— you the strongest?' whined the little engineer. "Gott-for-dam! I am too thick,' spluttered the skipper in despair. It was funny enough to make angels weep. They stood idle for a moment, and suddenly the chief engineer rushed again at Jim.

"'Come and help, man! Are you mad to throw your only chance away? Come and help, man! Man! Look there—look!'

"And at last Jim looked astern where the other pointed with maniacal insistence. He saw a silent black squall which had eaten up already one-third of the sky. You know how these squalls come up there about that time of year. First you see a darkening of the horizon—no more; then a cloud rises opaque like a wall. A straight edge of vapour lined with sickly whitish gleams flies up from the southwest, swallowing the stars in whole constellations; its shadow flies over the waters, and confounds sea and sky into one abyss of obscurity. And all is still. No thunder, no wind, no sound; not a flicker of lightning. Then in the tenebrous immensity a livid arch appears; a swell or two like undulations of the very darkness run past, and suddenly, wind and rain strike together with a peculiar impetuosity as if

they had burst through something solid. Such a cloud had
come up while they weren't looking. They had just noticed it,
and were perfectly justified in surmising that if in absolute
stillness there was some chance for the ship to keep afloat a
few minutes longer, the least disturbance of the sea would
make an end of her instantly. Her first nod to the swell that pre-
cedes the burst of such a squall would be also her last, would
become a plunge, would, so to speak, be prolonged into a long
dive, down, down to the bottom. Hence these new capers of
their fright, these new antics in which they displayed their extreme aversion to die.

"'It was black, black,' pursued Jim with moody steadiness.
'It had sneaked upon us from behind. The infernal thing! I suppose there had been at the back of my head some hope yet. I
don't know. But that was all over anyhow. It maddened me to
see myself caught like this. I was angry, as though I had been
trapped. I *was* trapped! The night was hot, too, I remember.
Not a breath of air.'

"He remembered so well that, gasping in the chair, he
seemed to sweat and choke before my eyes. No doubt it maddened him; it knocked him over afresh—in a manner of speaking—but it made him also remember that important purpose
which had sent him rushing on that bridge only to slip clean
out of his mind. He had intended to cut the lifeboats clear of
the ship. He whipped out his knife and went to work slashing
as though he had seen nothing, had heard nothing, had known
of no one on board. They thought him hopelessly wrong-
headed and crazy, but dared not protest noisily against this useless loss of time. When he had done he returned to the very
same spot from which he had started. The chief was there,
ready with a clutch at him to whisper close to his head,
scathingly, as though he wanted to bite his ear—

"'You silly fool! do you think you'll get the ghost of a show
when all that lot of brutes is in the water? Why, they will bat-
ter your head for you from these boats.'

"He wrung his hands, ignored, at Jim's elbow. The skipper
kept up a nervous shuffle in one place and mumbled, 'Hammer! hammer! Mein Gott! Get a hammer.'

"The little engineer whimpered like a child, but broken arm and all, he turned out the least craven of the lot as it seems, and, actually, mustered enough pluck to run an errand to the engine-room. No trifle, it must be owned in fairness to him. Jim told me he darted desperate looks like a cornered man, gave one low wail, and dashed off. He was back instantly clambering, hammer in hand, and without a pause flung himself at the bolt. The others gave up Jim at once and ran off to assist. He heard the tap, tap of the hammer, the sound of the released chock falling over. The boat was clear. Only then he turned to look—only then. But he kept his distance—he kept his distance. He wanted me to know he had kept his distance; that there was nothing in common between him and these men—who had the hammer. Nothing whatever. It is more than probable he thought himself cut off from them by a space that could not be traversed, by an obstacle that could not be overcome, by a chasm without bottom. He was as far as he could get from them—the whole breadth of the ship.

"His feet were glued to that remote spot and his eyes to their indistinct group bowed together and swaying strangely in the common torment of fear. A hand-lamp lashed to a stanchion above a little table rigged up on the bridge—the *Patna* had no chart-room amidships—threw a light on their labouring shoulders, on their arched and bobbing backs. They pushed at the bow of the boat; they pushed out into the night; they pushed, and would no more look back at him. They had given him up as if indeed he had been too far, too hopelessly separated from themselves, to be worth an appealing word, a glance, or a sign. They had no leisure to look back upon his passive heroism, to feel the sting of his abstention. The boat was heavy; they pushed at the bow with no breath to spare for an encouraging word: but the turmoil of terror that had scattered their self-control like chaff before the wind, converted their desperate exertions into a bit of fooling, upon my word fit for knock-about clowns in a farce. They pushed with their hands, with their heads, they pushed for dear life with all the weight of their bodies, they pushed with all the might of their souls—only no sooner had they succeeded in canting the stem clear of

the davit than they would leave off like one man and start a
wild scramble into her. As a natural consequence the boat
would swing in abruptly, driving them back, helpless and
jostling against each other. They would stand nonplussed for a
while, exchanging in fierce whispers all the infamous names
they could call to mind, and go at it again. Three times this occurred. He described it to me with morose thoughtfulness. He
hadn't lost a single movement of that comic business. 'I
loathed them. I hated them. I had to look at all that,' he said
without emphasis, turning upon me a sombrely watchful
glance. 'Was ever there any one so shamefully tried!'

"He took his head in his hands for a moment, like a man
driven to distraction by some unspeakable outrage. These were
things he could not explain to the court—and not even to me;
but I would have been little fitted for the reception of his confidences had I not been able at times to understand the pauses
between the words. In this assault upon his fortitude there was
the jeering intention of a spiteful and vile vengeance; there
was an element of burlesque in his ordeal—a degradation of
funny grimaces in the approach of death or dishonour.

"He related facts which I have not forgotten, but at this distance of time I couldn't recall his very words: I only remember
that he managed wonderfully to convey the brooding rancour
of his mind into the bare recital of events. Twice, he told me,
he shut his eyes in the certitude that the end was upon him already, and twice he had to open them again. Each time he
noted the darkening of the great stillness. The shadow of the
silent cloud had fallen upon the ship from the zenith, and
seemed to have extinguished every sound of her teeming life.
He could no longer hear the voices under the awnings. He told
me that each time he closed his eyes a flash of thought showed
him that crowd of bodies, laid out for death, as plain as daylight. When he opened them, it was to see the dim struggle of
four men fighting like mad with a stubborn boat. 'They would
fall back before it time after time, stand swearing at each other,
and suddenly make another rush in a bunch. . . . Enough to
make you die laughing,' he commented with downcast eyes;
then raising them for a moment to my face with a dismal smile,

'I ought to have a merry life of it, by God! for I shall see that funny sight a good many times yet before I die.' His eyes fell again. 'See and hear. . . . See and hear,' he repeated twice, at long intervals, filled by vacant staring.

"He roused himself.

" 'I made up my mind to keep my eyes shut,' he said, 'and I couldn't. I couldn't, and I don't care who knows it. Let them go through that kind of thing before they talk. Just let them—and do better—that's all. The second time my eyelids flew open and my mouth too. I had felt the ship move. She just dipped her bows—and lifted them gently—and slow! everlastingly slow; and ever so little. She hadn't done that much for days. The cloud had raced ahead, and this first swell seemed to travel upon a sea of lead. There was no life in that stir. It managed, though, to knock over something in my head. What would you have done? You are sure of yourself—aren't you? What would you do if you felt now—this minute—the house here move, just move a little under your chair. Leap! By heavens! you would take one spring from where you sit and land in that clump of bushes yonder.'

"He flung his arms out at the night beyond the stone balustrade. I held my peace. He looked at me very steadily, very severe. There could be no mistake: I was being bullied now, and it behoved me to make no sign lest by a gesture or a word I should be drawn into a fatal admission about myself which would have had some bearing on the case. I was not disposed to take any risk of that sort. Don't forget I had him before me, and really he was too much like one of us not to be dangerous. But if you want to know I don't mind telling you that I did, with a rapid glance, estimate the distance to the mass of denser blackness in the middle of the grass plot before the verandah. He exaggerated. I would have landed short by several feet—and that's the only thing of which I am fairly certain.

"The last moment had come, as he thought, and he did not move. His feet remained glued to the planks as his thoughts were knocking about loose in his head. It was at this moment, too, that he saw one of the men around the boat step backwards

suddenly, clutch at the air with raised arms, totter and collapse.
He didn't exactly fall, he only slid gently into a sitting posture,
all hunched up and with his shoulders propped against the side
of the engine-room skylight. 'That was the donkey-man. A
haggard, white-faced chap with a ragged moustache. Acted
third engineer,' he explained.

"'Dead,' I said. We had heard something of that in court.

"'So they say,' he pronounced with sombre indifference.
'Of course I never knew. Weak heart. The man had been complaining of being out of sorts for some time before. Excitement. Over-exertion. Devil only knows. Ha! ha! ha! It was
easy to see he did not want to die either. Droll, isn't it? May I
be shot if he hadn't been fooled into killing himself! Fooled—
neither more nor less. Fooled into it, by heavens! just as I . . .
Ah! If he had only kept still; if he had only told them to go to
the devil when they came to rush him out of his bunk because
the ship was sinking! If he had only stood by with his hands in
his pockets and called them names!'

"He got up, shook his fist, glared at me, and sat down.

"'A chance missed, eh?' I murmured.

"'Why don't you laugh?' he said. 'A joke hatched in hell.
Weak heart! . . . I wish sometimes mine had been.'

"This irritated me. 'Do you?' I exclaimed with deep-rooted
irony. 'Yes! Can't *you* understand?' he cried. 'I don't know
what more you could wish for,' I said, angrily. He gave me an
utterly uncomprehending glance. This shaft had also gone
wide of the mark, and he was not the man to bother about stray
arrows. Upon my word, he was too unsuspecting; he was not
fair game. I was glad that my missile had been thrown away,—
that he had not even heard the twang of the bow.

"Of course he could not know at the time the man was dead.
The next minute—his last on board—was crowded with a tumult of events and sensations which beat about him like the
sea upon a rock. I use the simile advisedly, because from his
relation I am forced to believe he had preserved through it all
a strange illusion of passiveness, as though he had not acted
but had suffered himself to be handled by the infernal powers
who had selected him for the victim of their practical joke. The

first thing that came to him was the grinding surge of the heavy davits swinging out at last—a jar which seemed to enter his body from the deck through the soles of his feet, and travel up his spine to the crown of his head. Then, the squall being very near now, another and a heavier swell lifted the passive hull in a threatening heave that checked his breath, while his brain and his heart together were pierced as with daggers by panic-stricken screams. 'Let go! For God's sake, let go! Let go! She's going.' Following upon that the boat-falls ripped through the blocks, and a lot of men began to talk in startled tones under the awnings. 'When these beggars did break out, their yelps were enough to wake the dead,' he said. Next after the splashing shock of the boat literally dropped in the water, came the hollow noises of stamping and tumbling in her, mingled with confused shouts; 'Unhook! Unhook! Shove! Unhook! Shove for your life! Here's the squall down on us. . . .' He heard, high above his head, the faint muttering of the wind; he heard below his feet a cry of pain. A lost voice alongside started cursing a swivel hook. The ship began to buzz fore and aft like a disturbed hive, and, as quietly as he was telling me all of this—because just then he was very quiet in attitude, in face, in voice—he went on to say without the slightest warning as it were, 'I stumbled over his legs.'

"This was the first I heard of his having moved at all. I could not restrain a grunt of surprise. Something had started him off at last, but of the exact moment, of the cause that tore him out of his immobility, he knew no more than the uprooted tree knows of the wind that laid it low. All this had come to him: the sounds, the sights, the legs of the dead man—by Jove! The infernal joke was being crammed devilishly down his throat, but—look you—he was not going to admit of any sort of swallowing motion in his gullet. It's extraordinary how he could cast upon you the spirit of his illusion. I listened as if to a tale of black magic at work upon a corpse.

"'He went over sideways, very gently, and this is the last thing I remember seeing on board,' he continued. 'I did not care what he did. It looked as though he were picking himself up: I thought he was picking himself up, of course: I expected him to bolt past me over the rail and rope into the boat there, and a voice as if crying up a shaft called out "George." Then three voices together raised a yell. They came to me separately: one bleated, another screamed, one howled. Ough!'

"He shivered a little, and I beheld him rise slowly as if a steady hand from above had been pulling him out of the chair by his hair. Up, slowly—to his full height, and when his knees had locked stiff the hand let him go, and he swayed a little on his feet. There was a suggestion of awful stillness in his face, in his movements, in his very voice when he said 'They shouted'—and involuntarily I pricked up my ears for the ghost of that shout that would be heard directly through the false effect of silence. 'There were eight hundred people in that ship,' he said, impaling me to the back of my seat with an awful blank stare. 'Eight hundred living people, and they were yelling after the one dead man to come down and be saved. "Jump, George! Jump! Oh, jump!" I stood by with my hand on the davit. I was very quiet. It had come over pitch dark. You could see neither sky nor sea. I heard the boat alongside go bump, bump, and not another sound down there for a while, but the ship under me was full of talking noises. Suddenly the skipper howled, "Mein Gott! The squall! The squall! Shove off!" With the first hiss of rain, and the first gust of wind, they screamed, "Jump, George! We'll catch you! Jump!" The ship began a slow plunge; the rain swept over her like a broken sea; my cap flew off my head; my breath was driven back into my throat. I heard as if I had been on the top of a tower another wild screech, "Geo-o-o-orge! Oh, jump!" She was going down, down, head first under me. . . .'

"He raised his hand deliberately to his face, and made picking motions with his fingers as though he had been bothered with cobwebs, and afterwards he looked into the open palm for quite half a second before he blurted out—

"'I had jumped . . .' He checked himself, averted his gaze. . . . 'It seems,' he added.

"His clear blue eyes turned to me with a piteous stare, and looking at him standing before me, dumbfounded and hurt, I was oppressed by a sad sense of resigned wisdom, mingled with the amused and profound pity of an old man helpless before a childish disaster.

"'Looks like it,' I muttered.

"'I knew nothing about it till I looked up,' he explained, hastily. And that's possible, too. You had to listen to him as you would to a small boy in trouble. He didn't know. It had happened somehow. It would never happen again. He had landed partly on somebody and fallen across a thwart. He felt as though all his ribs on his left side must be broken; then he rolled over, and saw vaguely the ship he had deserted uprising above him, with the red side-light glowing large in the rain like a fire on the brow of a hill seen through a mist. 'She seemed higher than a wall; she loomed like a cliff over the boat. . . . I wished I could die,' he cried. 'There was no going back. It was as if I had jumped into a well—into an everlasting deep hole. . . .'"

Chapter Ten

HE LOCKED his fingers together and tore them apart. Nothing could be more true: he had indeed jumped into an everlasting deep hole. He had tumbled from a height he could never scale again. By that time the boat had gone driving forward past the bows. It was too dark just then for them to see each other, and, moreover, they were blinded and half drowned with rain. He told me it was like being swept by a flood through a cavern. They turned their backs to the squall; the skipper, it seems, got an oar over the stern to keep the boat before it, and for two or three minutes the end of the world had come through a deluge in a pitchy blackness. The sea hissed 'like twenty thousand kettles.' That's his simile, not mine. I fancy there was not much wind after the first gust; and he himself had admitted at the inquiry that the sea never got up that night to any extent. He crouched down in the bows and stole a furtive glance back. He saw just one yellow gleam of the masthead light high up and blurred like a last star ready to dissolve. 'It terrified me to see it still there,' he said. That's what he said. What terrified him was the thought that the drowning was not over yet. No doubt he wanted to be done with that abomination as quickly as possible. Nobody in the boat made a sound. In the dark she seemed to fly, but of course she could not have had much way. Then the shower swept ahead, and the great, distracting, hissing noise followed the rain into distance and died out. There was nothing to be heard then but the slight wash about the boat's sides. Somebody's teeth were chattering violently. A hand touched his back. A faint voice said, 'You there?' Another cried out, shakily, 'She's gone!' and they all stood up together to look astern. They saw no lights. All was black. A thin cold drizzle was driving into their faces. The boat lurched slightly. The teeth chattered faster, stopped, and began again twice before the man could master his shiver sufficiently to say, 'Ju-ju-st in ti-ti-me. . . . Brrr.' He recognised the voice of the chief engineer saying surlily, 'I saw her go down. I happened to turn my head.' The wind had dropped almost completely.

"They watched in the dark with their heads half turned to windward as if expecting to hear cries. At first he was thankful the night had covered up the scene before his eyes, and then to know of it and yet to have seen and heard nothing appeared somehow the culminating-point of an awful misfortune. 'Strange, isn't it?' he murmured, interrupting himself in his disjointed narrative.

"It did not seem so strange to me. He must have had an unconscious conviction that the reality could not be half as bad, not half as anguishing, appalling, and vengeful as the created terror of his imagination. I believe that, in this first moment, his heart was wrung with all the suffering, that his soul knew the accumulated savour of all the fear, all the horror, all the despair of eight hundred human beings pounced upon in the night by a sudden and violent death, else why should he have said, 'It seemed to me that I must jump out of that accursed boat and swim back to see—half a mile—more—any distance—to

the very spot . . . ?' Why this impulse? Do you see the significance? Why back to the very spot? Why not drown alongside—if he meant drowning? why back to the very spot, to
see—as if his imagination had to be soothed by the assurance
that all was over before death could bring relief? I defy any
one of you to offer another explanation. It was one of those
bizarre and exciting glimpses through the fog. It was an extraordinary disclosure. He let it out as the most natural thing one
could say. He fought down that impulse and then he became
conscious of the silence. He mentioned this to me. A silence
of the sea, of the sky, merged into one indefinite immensity
still as death around these saved, palpitating lives. 'You might
have heard a pin drop in the boat,' he said with a queer con-
traction of his lips, like a man trying to master his sensibilities
while relating some extremely moving fact. A silence! God
alone, who had willed him as he was, knows what he made of
it in his heart. 'I don't think any spot on earth could be so
still,' he said. 'You couldn't distinguish the sea from the sky;
there was nothing to see and nothing to hear. Not a glimmer,
not a shape, not a sound. You could have believed that every
bit of dry land had gone to the bottom; that every man on
earth but I and these beggars in the boat had got drowned.' He
leaned over the table with his knuckles propped amongst coffee-cups, liqueur-glasses, cigar-ends. 'I seemed to believe it.
Everything was gone and—all was over . . .' he fetched a deep
sigh . . . 'with me.' "

Marlow sat up abruptly and flung away his cheroot with
force. It made a darting red trail like a toy rocket fired through
the drapery of creepers. Nobody stirred.

"Hey, what do you think of it?" he cried with sudden animation. "Wasn't he true to himself, wasn't he? His saved life
was over for want of ground under his feet, for want of sights
for his eyes, for want of voices in his ears. Annihilation—
hey! And all the time it was only a clouded sky, a sea that
did not break, the air that did not stir. Only a night; only a
silence.

"It lasted for a while, and then they were suddenly and
unanimously moved to make a noise over their escape. 'I knew

from the first she would go.' 'Not a minute too soon.' 'A narrow squeak, b'gosh!' He said nothing, but the breeze that had
dropped came back, a gentle draught freshened steadily, and
the sea joined its murmuring voice to this talkative reaction
succeeding the dumb moments of awe. She was gone! She was
gone! Not a doubt of it. Nobody could have helped. They repeated the same words over and over again as though they
couldn't stop themselves. Never doubted she would go. The
lights were gone. No mistake. The lights were gone. Couldn't
expect anything else. She had to go. . . . He noticed that they
talked as though they had left behind them nothing but an
empty ship. They concluded she would not have been long
when she once started. It seemed to cause them some sort of
satisfaction. They assured each other that she couldn't have
been long about it—'Just shot down like a flat-iron.' The chief
engineer declared that the masthead light at the moment of
sinking seemed to drop 'like a lighted match you throw down.'
At this the second laughed hysterically. 'I am g-g-glad, I am
gla-a-ad.' His teeth went on 'like an electric rattle,' said Jim,
'and all at once he began to cry. He wept and blubbered like a
child, catching his breath and sobbing. "Oh, dear! oh, dear! oh,
dear!" He would be quiet for a while and start suddenly, "Oh,
my poor arm! oh, my poor a-a-a-arm!" I felt I could knock him
down. Some of them sat in the stern-sheets. I could just make
out their shapes. Voices came to me, mumble, mumble, grunt,
grunt. All this seemed very hard to bear. I was cold, too. And I
could do nothing. I thought that if I moved I would have to go
over the side and . . .'

"His hand groped stealthily, came in contact with a
liqueur-glass, and was withdrawn suddenly as if it had
touched a red-hot coal. I pushed the bottle slightly. 'Won't
you have some more?' I asked. He looked at me angrily.
'Don't you think I can tell you what there is to tell without
screwing myself up?' he asked. The squad of globe-trotters
had gone to bed. We were alone but for a vague white form
erect in the shadow, that, being looked at, cringed forward,
hesitated, backed away silently. It was getting late, but I did
not hurry my guest.

"In the midst of his forlorn state he heard his companions begin to abuse some one. 'What kept you from jumping, you lunatic?' said a scolding voice. The chief engineer left the stern-sheets, and could be heard clambering forward as if with hostile intentions against 'the greatest idiot that ever was.' The skipper shouted with rasping effort offensive epithets from where he sat at the oars. He lifted his head at that uproar, and heard the name 'George,' while a hand in the dark struck him on the breast. 'What have you got to say for yourself, you fool?' queried somebody, with a sort of virtuous fury. 'They were after me,' he said. 'They were abusing me—abusing me . . . by the name of George.'

"He paused to stare, tried to smile, turned his eyes away and went on. 'That little second puts his head right under my nose, "Why, it's that blasted mate!" "What!" howls the skipper from the other end of the boat. "No!" shrieks the chief. And he, too, stopped to look at my face.'

"The wind had left the boat suddenly. The rain began to fall again, and the soft, uninterrupted, little mysterious sound with which the sea receives a shower arose on all sides in the night. 'They were too taken aback to say anything more at first,' he narrated steadily, 'and what could I have to say to them?' He faltered for a moment, and made an effort to go on. 'They called me horrible names.' His voice, sinking to a whisper, now and then would leap up suddenly, hardened by the passion of scorn, as though he had been talking of secret abominations. 'Never mind what they called me,' he said, grimly. 'I could hear hate in their voices. A good thing, too. They could not forgive me for being in that boat. They hated it. It made them mad. . . .' He laughed short. . . . 'But it kept me from—Look! I was sitting with my arms crossed, on the gunwale! . . .' He perched himself smartly on the edge of the table and crossed his arms. . . . 'Like this—see? One little tilt backwards and I would have been gone—after the others. One little tilt—the least bit—the least bit.' He frowned, and tapping his forehead with the tip of his middle finger, 'It was there all the time,' he said, impressively. 'All the time—that notion. And the rain—cold, thick, cool as melted snow—

colder—on my thin cotton clothes—I'll never be so cold again in my life, I know. And the sky was black, too—all black. Not a star, not a light anywhere. Nothing outside that confounded boat and those two yapping before me like a couple of mean mongrels at a tree'd thief. Yap! yap! "What you doing here? You're a fine sort! Too much of a bloomin' gentleman to put his hand to it. Come out of your trance, did you? To sneak in? Did you?" Yap! yap! "You ain't fit to live!" Yap! yap! Two of them together trying to out-bark each other. The other would bay from the stern through the rain—couldn't see him—couldn't make out—some of his filthy jargon. Yap! yap! Bow-ow-ow-ow-ow! Yap! yap! It was sweet to hear them; it kept me alive, I tell you. It saved my life. At it they went, as if trying to drive me overboard with the noise! . . . "I wonder you had pluck enough to jump. You ain't wanted here. If I had known who it was, I would have tipped you over—you skunk. What have you done with the other? Where did you get the pluck to jump—you coward? What's to prevent us three from firing you overboard?" . . . They were out of breath; the shower passed away upon the sea. Then nothing. There was nothing round the boat, not even a sound. Wanted to see me overboard, did they? Upon my soul! I think they would have had their wish if they had only kept quiet. Fire me overboard! Would they? "Try," I said. "I would for twopence." "Too good for you," they screeched together. It was so dark that it was only when one or the other of them moved that I was quite sure of seeing him. By heavens! I only wish they had tried.'

"I couldn't help exclaiming, 'What an extraordinary affair.'

"'Not bad—eh?' he said, as if in some sort astounded. 'They pretended to think I had done away with that donkeyman for some reason or other. Why should I? And how the devil was I to know? Didn't I get somehow into that boat? into that boat—I . . .' The muscles round his lips contracted into an unconscious grimace that tore through the mask of his usual expression—something violent, short-lived, and illuminating like a twist of lightning that admits the eye for an instant into the secret convolutions of a cloud. 'I did. I was plainly there

with them—wasn't I? Isn't it awful a man should be driven to
do a thing like that—and be responsible? What did I know
about their George they were howling after? I remembered I
had seen him curled up on the deck. "Murdering coward!" the
chief kept on calling me. He didn't seem able to remember
any other two words. I didn't care, only his noise began to
worry me. "Shut up," I said. At that he collected himself for a
confounded screech. "You killed him. You killed him." "No,"
I shouted, "but I will kill you directly." I jumped up, and he
fell backwards over a thwart with an awful loud thump. I
don't know why. Too dark. Tried to step back, I suppose. I
stood still facing aft, and the wretched little second began to
whine, "You ain't going to hit a chap with a broken arm—and
you call yourself a gentleman, too." I heard a heavy tramp—
one—two—and wheezy grunting. The other beast was coming at me, clattering his oar over the stern. I saw him moving,
big, big—as you see a man in a mist, in a dream. "Come on,"
I cried. I would have tumbled him over like a bale of shak-
ings. He stopped, muttered to himself, and went back. Perhaps
he had heard the wind. I didn't. It was the last heavy gust we
had. He went back to his oar. I was sorry. I would have tried
to—to . . .'

"He opened and closed his curved fingers, and his hands
had an eager and cruel flutter. 'Steady, steady,' I murmured.

"'Eh? What? I am not excited,' he remonstrated, awfully
hurt, and with a convulsive jerk of his elbow knocked over the
cognac-bottle. I started forward, scraping my chair. He
bounced off the table as if a mine had been exploded behind
his back, and half turned before he alighted, crouching on his
feet to show me a startled pair of eyes and a face white about
the nostrils. A look of intense annoyance succeeded. 'Awfully
sorry. How clumsy of me!' he mumbled very vexed, while the
pungent odour of spilt alcohol enveloped us suddenly with an
atmosphere of a low drinking-bout in the cool, pure darkness
of the night. The lights had been put out in the dining-hall; our
candle glimmered solitary in the long gallery, and the columns
had turned black from pediment to capital. On the vivid stars
the high corner of the Harbour Office stood out distinct across

the Esplanade, as though the sombre pile had glided nearer to
see and hear.

"He assumed an air of indifference.

"'I dare say I am less calm now than I was then. I was ready
for anything. These were trifles. . . .'

"'You had a lively time of it in that boat,' I remarked.

"'I was ready,' he repeated. 'After the ship's lights had
gone, anything might have happened in that boat—anything
in the world—and the world no wiser. I felt this, and I was
pleased. It was just dark enough, too. We were like men
walled up quick in a roomy grave. No concern with anything
on earth. Nobody to pass an opinion. Nothing mattered.' For
the third time during this conversation he laughed harshly, but
there was no one about to suspect him of being only drunk.
'No fear, no law, no sounds, no eyes—not even our own, till—
till sunrise at least.'

"I was struck by the suggestive truth of his words. There is
something peculiar in a small boat upon the wide seas. Over
the lives borne from under the shadow of death there seems to
fall the shadow of madness. When your ship fails you, your
whole world seems to fail you; the world that made you, restrained you, has taken care of you. It is as if the souls of men
floating on an abyss and in touch with immensity had been set
free for any excess of heroism, absurdity, or abomination. Of
course, as with belief, thought, love, hate, conviction, or even
the visual aspect of material things, there are as many ship-
wrecks as there are men, and in this one there was something
abject which made the isolation more complete—there was a
villainy of circumstances that cut these men off more completely from the rest of mankind, whose ideal of conduct had
never undergone the trial of a fiendish and appalling joke.
They were exasperated with him for being a half-hearted
shirker: he focussed on them his hatred of the whole thing; he
would have liked to take a signal revenge for the abhorrent opportunity they had put in his way. Trust a boat on the high seas
to bring out the Irrational that lurks at the bottom of every
thought, sentiment, sensation, emotion. It was part of the burlesque meanness pervading that particular disaster at sea that

they did not come to blows. It was all threats, all a terribly effective feint, a sham from beginning to end, planned by the tremendous disdain of the Dark Powers whose real terrors, always on the verge of triumph, are perpetually foiled by the steadfastness of men. I asked, after waiting for a while, 'Well, what happened?' A futile question. I knew too much already to hope for the grace of a single uplifting touch, for the favour of hinted madness, of shadowed horror. 'Nothing,' he said. 'I meant business, but they meant noise only. Nothing happened.'

"And the rising sun found him just as he had jumped up first in the bows of the boat. What a persistence of readiness! He had been holding the tiller in his hand, too, all the night. They had dropped the rudder overboard while attempting to ship it, and I suppose the tiller got kicked forward somehow while they were rushing up and down that boat trying to do all sorts of things at once so as to get clear of the side. It was a long heavy piece of hard wood, and apparently he had been clutching it for six hours or so. If you don't call that being ready! Can you imagine him, silent and on his feet half the night, his face to the gusts of rain, staring at sombre forms, watchful of vague movements, straining his ears to catch rare low murmurs in the stern-sheets! Firmness of courage or effort of fear? What do you think? And the endurance is undeniable, too. Six hours more or less on the defensive; six hours of alert immobility while the boat drove slowly or floated arrested according to the caprice of the wind; while the sea, calmed, slept at last; while the clouds passed above his head; while the sky from an immensity lustreless and black, diminished to a sombre and lustrous vault, scintillated with a greater brilliance, faded to the east, paled at the zenith; while the dark shapes blotting the low stars astern got outlines, relief; became shoulders, heads, faces, features,—confronted him with dreary stares, had dishevelled hair, torn clothes, blinked red eyelids at the white dawn. 'They looked as though they had been knocking about drunk in gutters for a week,' he described graphically; and then he muttered something about the sunrise being of a kind that foretells a calm day. You know that sailor habit of referring to the weather in every connection. And on my side his few mumbled words were enough to make me see the lower limb of the sun clearing the line of the horizon, the tremble of a vast ripple running over all the visible expanse of the sea, as if the waters had shuddered, giving birth to the globe of light, while the last puff of the breeze would stir the air in a sigh of relief.

"'They sat in the stern shoulder to shoulder, with the skipper in the middle, like three dirty owls, and stared at me,' I heard him say with an intention of hate that distilled a corrosive virtue into the commonplace words like a drop of powerful poison falling into a glass of water; but my thoughts dwelt upon that sunrise. I could imagine under the pellucid emptiness of the sky these four men imprisoned in the solitude of the sea, the lonely sun, regardless of the speck of life, ascending the clear curve of the heaven as if to gaze ardently from a greater height at his own splendour reflected in the still ocean. 'They called out to me from aft,' said Jim, 'as though we had been chums together. I heard them. They were begging me to be sensible and drop that "blooming piece of wood." Why *would* I carry on so? They hadn't done me any harm—had they? There had been no harm. . . . No harm!'

"His face crimsoned as though he could not get rid of the air in his lungs.

"'No harm!' he burst out. "I leave it to you. You can understand. Can't you? You see it—don't you? No harm! Good God! What more could they have done? Oh, yes, I know very well— I jumped. Certainly. I jumped! I told you I jumped; but I tell you they were too much for any man. It was their doing as plainly as if they had reached up with a boathook and pulled me over. Can't you see? You must see it. Come. Speak— straight out.'

"His uneasy eyes fastened upon mine, questioned, begged, challenged, entreated. For the life of me I couldn't help murmuring, 'You've been tried.' 'More than is fair,' he caught up, swiftly. 'I wasn't given half a chance—with a gang like that. And now they were friendly—oh, so damnably friendly! Chums, shipmates. All in the same boat. Make the best of it.

They hadn't meant anything. They didn't care a hang for George. George had gone back to his berth for something at the last moment and got caught. The man was a manifest fool. Very sad, of course. . . . Their eyes looked at me; their lips moved; they wagged their heads at the other end of the boat—three of them; they beckoned—to me. Why not? Hadn't I jumped? I said nothing. There are no words for the sort of things I wanted to say. If I had opened my lips just then I would have simply howled like an animal. I was asking myself when I would wake up. They urged me aloud to come aft and hear quietly what the skipper had to say. We were sure to be picked up before the evening—right in the track of all the Canal traffic; there was no smoke to the northwest now.

" 'It gave me an awful shock to see this faint, faint blur, this low trail of brown mist through which you could see the boundary of sea and sky. I called out to them that I could hear very well where I was. The skipper started swearing, as hoarse as a crow. He wasn't going to talk at the top of his voice for *my* accommodation. "Are you afraid they will hear you on shore?" I asked. He glared as if he would have liked to claw me to pieces. The chief engineer advised him to humour me. He said I wasn't right in my head yet. The other rose astern, like a thick pillar of flesh—and talked—talked. . . .'

"Jim remained thoughtful. 'Well?' I said. 'What did I care what story they agreed to make up?' he cried, recklessly. 'They could tell what they jolly well liked. It was their business. I knew the story. Nothing they could make people believe could alter it for me, I let him talk, argue—talk, argue. He went on and on. Suddenly I felt my legs give way under me. I was sick, tired—tired to death. I let fall the tiller, turned my back on them, and sat down on the foremost thwart. I had enough. They called to me to know if I understood—wasn't it true, every word of it? It was true, by God! after their fashion. I did not turn my head. I heard them palavering together. "The silly ass won't say anything." "Oh, he understands well enough." "Let him be; he will be all right." "What can he do?" What could I do? Weren't we all in the same boat? I tried to be deaf. The smoke had disappeared to the northward. It was a dead calm.

They had a drink from the water-breaker, and I drank, too. Afterwards they made a great business of spreading the boat-sail over the gunwales. Would I keep a look-out? They crept under, out of my sight, thank God! I felt weary, weary, done up, as if I hadn't had one hour's sleep since the day I was born. I couldn't see the water for the glitter of the sunshine. From time to time one of them would creep out, stand up to take a look all round, and get under again. I could hear spells of snoring below the sail. Some of them could sleep. One of them at least. I couldn't! All was light, light, and the boat seemed to be falling through it. Now and then I would feel quite surprised to find myself sitting on a thwart. . . .'

"He began to walk with measured steps to and fro before my chair, one hand in his trousers-pocket, his head bent thoughtfully, and his right arm at long intervals raised for a gesture that seemed to put out of his way an invisible intruder.

"'I suppose you think I was going mad,' he began in a changed tone. 'And well you may, if you remember I had lost my cap. The sun crept all the way from east to west over my bare head, but that day I could not come to any harm, I suppose. The sun could not make me mad. . . .' His right arm put aside the idea of madness. . . . 'Neither could it kill me. . . .' Again his arm repulsed a shadow. . . . 'That rested with me.'

"'Did it?' I said, inexpressibly amazed at this new turn, and I looked at him with the same sort of feeling I might be fairly conceived to experience had he, after spinning round on his heel, presented an altogether new face.

"'I didn't get brain fever, I did not drop dead either,' he went on. 'I didn't bother myself at all about the sun over my head. I was thinking as coolly as any man that ever sat thinking in the shade. That greasy beast of a skipper poked his big cropped head from under the canvas and screwed his fish eyes up at me. "Donnerwetter! you will die," he growled, and drew in like a turtle. I had seen him. I had heard him. He didn't interrupt me. I was thinking just then that I wouldn't.'

"He tried to sound my thought with an attentive glance dropped on me in passing. 'Do you mean to say you had been deliberating with yourself whether you would die?' I asked in as impenetrable a tone as I could command. He nodded without stopping. 'Yes, it had come to that as I sat there alone,' he said. He passed on a few steps to the imaginary end of his beat, and when he flung round to come back both his hands were thrust deep into his pockets. He stopped short in front of my chair and looked down. 'Don't you believe it?' he inquired with tense curiosity. I was moved to make a solemn declaration of my readiness to believe implicitly anything he thought fit to tell me."

Chapter Eleven

HE HEARD me out with his head on one side, and I had another glimpse through a rent in the mist in which he moved and had his being. The dim candle spluttered within the ball of glass, and that was all I had to see him by; at his back was the dark night with the clear stars, whose distant glitter disposed in retreating planes lured the eye into the depths of a greater darkness; and yet a mysterious light seemed to show me his boyish head, as if in that moment the youth within him had, for a moment, gleamed, and expired. 'You are an awful good sort to listen like this,' he said. 'It does me good. You don't know what it is to me. You don't' . . . words seemed to fail him. It was a distinct glimpse. He was a youngster of the sort you like to see about you; of the sort you like to imagine yourself to have been; of the sort whose appearance claims the fellowship of these illusions you had thought gone out, extinct, cold, and which, as if rekindled at the approach of another flame, give a flutter deep, deep down somewhere, give a flutter of light . . . of heat! . . . Yes; I had a glimpse of him then . . . and it was not the last of that kind. . . . 'You don't know what it is for a fellow in my position to be believed—make a clean breast of it to an elder man. It is so difficult—so awfully unfair—so hard to understand.'

"The mists were closing again. I don't know how old I appeared to him—and how much wise. Not half as old as I felt just then; not half as uselessly wise as I knew myself to be. Surely in no other craft as in that of the sea do the hearts of those already launched to sink or swim go out so much to the youth on the brink, looking with shining eyes upon that glitter of the vast surface which is only a reflection of his own glances full of fire. There is such magnificent vagueness in the expectations that had driven each of us to sea, such a glorious indefiniteness, such a beautiful greed of adventures that are their own and only reward! What we get—well, we won't talk of that; but can one of us restrain a smile? In no other kind of life is the illusion more wide of reality—in no other is the beginning *all* illusion—the disenchantment more swift—the subjugation more complete. Hadn't we all commenced with the same desire, ended with the same knowledge, carried the memory of the same cherished glamour through the sordid days of imprecation? What wonder that when some heavy prod gets home the bond is found to be close; that besides the fellowship of the craft there is felt the strength of a wider feeling—the feeling that binds a man to a child. He was there before me, believing that age and wisdom can find a remedy against the pain of truth, giving me a glimpse of himself as a young fellow in a scrape that is the very devil of a scrape, the sort of scrape greybeards wag at solemnly while they hide a smile. And he had been deliberating upon death—confound him! He had found *that* to meditate about because he thought he had saved his life, while all its glamour had gone with the ship in the night. What more natural! It was tragic enough and funny enough in all conscience to call aloud for compassion, and in what was I better than the rest of us to refuse him my pity? And even as I looked at him the mists rolled into the rent, and his voice spoke—

"'I was so lost, you know. It was the sort of thing one does not expect to happen to one. It was not like a fight, for instance.'

"'It was not,' I admitted. He appeared changed as if he had suddenly matured.

"'Ah! You were not sure,' I said, and was placated by the sound of a faint sigh that passed between us like the flight of a bird in the night.

"'Well, I wasn't,' he said, courageously. 'It was something like that wretched story they made up. It was not a lie—but it wasn't truth all the same. It was something. . . . One knows a downright lie. There was not the thickness of a sheet of paper between the right and wrong of this affair.'

"'How much more did you want?' I asked; but I think I spoke so low that he did not catch what I said. He had advanced his argument as though life had been a network of paths separated by chasms. His voice sounded reasonable.

"'Suppose I had not—I mean to say, suppose I had stuck to the ship? Well. How much longer? Say a minute—half a minute. Come. In thirty seconds, as it seemed certain then, I would have been overboard; and do you think I would not have laid hold of the first thing that came in my way—oar, life-buoy, grating—anything? Wouldn't you?'

"'And be saved,' I interjected.

"'I would have meant to be,' he retorted. 'And that's more than I meant when I' . . . he shivered as if about to swallow some nauseous drug . . . 'jumped,' he pronounced with a convulsive effort, whose stress, as if propagated by the waves of the air, made my body stir a little in the chair. He fixed me with lowering eyes. 'Don't you believe me?' he cried. 'I swear! . . . Confound it! You got me here to talk, and . . . You must! . . . You said you would believe.' 'Of course I do,' I protested in a matter-of-fact tone which produced a calming effect. 'Forgive me,' he said. 'Of course I wouldn't have talked to you about all this if you had not been a gentleman. I ought to have known . . . I am—I am—a gentleman, too . . .' 'Yes, yes,' I said, hastily. He was looking me squarely in the face and withdrew his gaze slowly. 'Now you understand why I didn't after all . . . didn't go out in that way. I wasn't going to be frightened at what I had done. And, anyhow, if I had stuck to the ship I would have done my best to be saved. Men have been known to float for hours—in the open sea—and be picked up not much the worse for it. I might have lasted it out better than many others. There's nothing the matter with *my* heart.' He withdrew his right fist from his pocket, and the blow he struck on his chest resounded like a muffled detonation in the night.

"'No,' I said. He meditated, with his legs slightly apart and his chin sunk. 'A hair's-breadth,' he muttered. 'Not the breadth of a hair between this and that. And at the time . . .'

"'It is difficult to see a hair at midnight,' I put in, a little viciously I fear. Don't you see what I mean by the solidarity of the craft? I was aggrieved against him, as though he had cheated me—me!—of a splendid opportunity to keep up the illusion of my beginnings, as though he had robbed our common life of the last spark of its glamour. 'And so you cleared out—at once.'

"'Jumped,' he corrected me incisively. 'Jumped—mind!' he repeated, and I wondered at the evident but obscure intention. 'Well, yes! Perhaps I could not see then. But I had plenty of time and any amount of light in that boat. And I could think, too. Nobody would know, of course, but this did not make it any easier for me. You've got to believe that, too. I did not want all this talk. . . . No . . . Yes . . . I won't lie . . . I wanted it: it is the very thing I wanted—there. Do you think you or anybody could have made me if I . . . I am—I am not afraid to tell. And I wasn't afraid to think either. I looked it in the face. I wasn't going to run away. At first—at night, if it hadn't been for these fellows I might have . . . No! by heavens! I was not going to give them that satisfaction. They had done enough. They made up a story, and believed it for all I know. But I knew the truth, and I would live it down—alone, with myself. I wasn't going to give in to such a beastly unfair thing. What did it prove after all? I was confoundedly cut up. Sick of life—to tell you the truth; but what would have been the good to shirk it—in—in—that way? That was not the way. I believe—I believe it would have—it would have ended—nothing.'

He had been walking up and down but with the last word he turned short at me.

"'What do *you* believe?' he asked with violence. A pause ensued, and suddenly I felt myself overcome by a profound and hopeless fatigue, as though his voice had startled me out of a dream of wandering through empty spaces whose immensity had harassed my soul and exhausted my body.

"'. . . Would have ended nothing,' he muttered over me obstinately, after a little while. 'No! the proper thing was to face it out—alone for myself—wait for another chance—find out . . .'"

Chapter Twelve

ALL AROUND everything was still as far as the eye could reach. The mist of his feelings shifted between us, as if disturbed by his struggles, and in the rifts of the immaterial veil he would appear to my staring eyes distinct of form and pregnant with vague appeal like a symbolic figure in a picture. The chill air of the night seemed to lie on my limbs as heavy as a slab of marble.

"'I see,' I murmured, more to prove to myself that I could break my state of numbness than for any other reason.

"'The *Avondale* picked us up just before sunset,' he remarked, moodily. 'Steamed right straight for us. We had only to sit and wait.'

"After a long interval, he said, 'They told their story.' And again there was that oppressive silence. 'Then only I knew what it was I had made up my mind to,' he added.

"'You said nothing,' I whispered.

"'What could I say?' he asked, in the same low tone. . . . 'Shock slight. Stopped the ship. Ascertained the damage. Took measures to get the boats out without creating a panic. As the first boat was lowered ship went down in a squall. Sank like lead. . . . What could be more clear' . . . he hung his head . . . 'and more awful?' His lips quivered while he looked straight into my eyes. 'I had jumped—hadn't I?' he asked, dismayed. 'That's what I had to live down. The story didn't matter.' . . .

He clasped his hands for an instant, glanced right and left into the gloom: 'It was like cheating the dead,' he stammered.

"'And there were no dead,' I said.

"He went away from me at this. That is the only way I can describe it. In a moment I saw his back close to the balustrade. He stood there for some time, as if admiring the purity and the peace of the night. Some flowering-shrub in the garden below spread its powerful scent through the damp air. He returned to me with hasty steps.

"'And that did not matter,' he said, as stubbornly as you please.

"'Perhaps not,' I admitted. I began to have a notion he was too much for me. After all, what did *I* know?

"'Dead or not dead, I could not get clear,' he said. 'I had to live; hadn't I?'

"'Well, yes—if you take it in that way,' I mumbled.

"'I was glad, of course,' he threw out carelessly with his mind fixed on something else. 'The exposure,' he pronounced, slowly, and lifted his head. 'Do you know what was my first thought when I heard? I was relieved. I was relieved to learn that those shouts—did I tell you I heard shouts? No? Well, I did. Shouts for help . . . blown along with the drizzle. Imagination I suppose. And yet I can hardly . . . How stupid. . . . The others did not. I asked them afterwards. They all said No. No? And I was hearing them even then! I might have known—but I didn't think—I only listened. Very faint screams—day after day. Then that little half-caste chap here came up and spoke to me. "The *Patna* . . . French gunboat . . . towed successfully to Aden . . . Investigation . . . Marine Office . . . Sailors' Home . . . arrangements made for your board and lodging!" I walked along with him, and I enjoyed the silence. So there had been no shouting. Imagination. I had to believe him. I could hear nothing any more. I wonder how long I could have stood it. It was getting worse, too . . . I mean—louder.'

"He fell into thought.

"'And I had heard nothing! Well—so be it. But the lights! The lights did go! We did not see them. They were not there. If they had been, I would have swam back—I would have gone

back and shouted along side—I would have begged them to
take me on board. . . . I would have had my chance. . . . You
doubt me? . . . How do you know how I felt? . . . What right
have you to doubt? . . . I very nearly did it as it was—do you
understand?' His voice fell. 'There was not a glimmer—not a
glimmer,' he protested, mournfully. 'Don't you understand that
if there had been, you would not have seen me here? You see
me—and you doubt.'

"I shook my head negatively. This question of the lights
being lost sight of when the boat could not have been more
than a quarter of a mile from the ship was a matter for much
discussion. Jim stuck to it that there was nothing to be seen
after the first shower had cleared away; and the others had affirmed the same thing to the officers of the *Avondale*. Of
course people shook their heads and smiled. One old skipper
who sat near me in court tickled my ear with his white beard to
murmur, 'Of course they would lie.' As a matter of fact nobody
lied; not even the chief engineer with his story of the masthead
light dropping like a match you throw down. Not consciously,
at least. A man with his liver in such a state might very well
have seen a floating spark in the corner of his eye when stealing a hurried glance over his shoulder. They had seen no light
of any sort though they were well within range, and they could
only explain this in one way: the ship had gone down. It was
obvious and comforting. The foreseen fact coming so swiftly
had justified their haste. No wonder they did not cast about for
any other explanation. Yet the true one was very simple, and as
soon as Brierly suggested it the court ceased to bother about
the question. If you remember, the ship had been stopped and
was lying with her head on the course steered through the
night, with her stern canted high and her bows brought low
down in the water through the filling of the fore-compartment.
Being thus out of trim, when the squall struck her a little on the
quarter, she swung head to wind as sharply as though she had
been at anchor. By this change in her position all her lights
were in a very few moments shut off from the boat to leeward.
It may very well be that, had they been seen, they would have
had the effect of a mute appeal—that their glimmer lost in the

darkness of the cloud would have had the mysterious power of
the human glance that can awaken the feelings of remorse and
pity. It would have said, 'I am here—still here' . . . and what
more can the eye of the most forsaken of human beings say?
But she turned her back on them as if in disdain of their fate:
she had swung round, burdened, to glare stubbornly at the new
danger of the open sea which she so strangely survived to end
her days in a breaking-up yard, as if it had been her recorded
fate to die obscurely under the blows of many hammers. What
were the various ends their destiny provided for the pilgrims I
am unable to say; but the immediate future brought, at about
nine o'clock next morning, a French gunboat homeward bound
from Réunion. The report of her commander was public property. He had swept a little out of his course to ascertain what
was the matter with that steamer floating dangerously by the
head upon a still and hazy sea. There was an ensign, union
down, flying at her main gaff (the serang had the sense to make
a signal of distress at daylight); but the cooks were preparing
the food in the cooking-boxes forward as usual. The decks
were packed as close as a sheep-pen: there were people
perched all along the rails, jammed on the bridge in a solid
mass; hundreds of eyes stared, and not a sound was heard
when the gunboat ranged abreast, as if all that multitude of lips
had been sealed by a spell.

"The Frenchman hailed, could get no intelligible reply, and
after ascertaining through his binoculars that the crowd on
deck did not look plague-stricken, decided to send a boat. Two
officers came on board, listened to the serang, tried to talk with
the Arab, couldn't make head or tail of it: but of course the nature of the emergency was obvious enough. They were also
very much struck by discovering a white man, dead and curled
up peacefully on the bridge. '*Fort intrigués par ce cadavre,*' as
I was informed a long time after by an elderly French lieutenant whom I came across one afternoon in Sydney, by the
merest chance, in a sort of café, and who remembered the affair perfectly. Indeed this affair, I may notice in passing, had an
extraordinary power of defying the shortness of memories and
the length of time: it seemed to live, with a sort of uncanny vi-

tality, in the minds of men, on the tips of their tongues. I've
had the questionable pleasure of meeting it often, years afterwards, thousands of miles away, emerging from the remotest
possible talk, coming to the surface of the most distant allusions. Has it not turned up to-night between us? And I am the
only seaman here. I am the only one to whom it is a memory.
And yet it has made its way out! But if two men who, unknown
to each other, knew of this affair met accidentally on any spot
on this earth, the thing would pop up between them as sure as
fate, before they parted. I had never seen that Frenchman before, and at the end of an hour we had done with each other for
life: he did not seem particularly talkative either; he was a
quiet, massive chap in a creased uniform sitting drowsily over
a tumbler half full of some dark liquid. His shoulder-straps
were a bit tarnished, his clean-shaved cheeks were large and
sallow; he looked like a man who would be given to taking
snuff—don't you know? I won't say he did; but the habit
would have fitted that kind of man. It all began by his handing
me a number of *Home News,* which I didn't want, across the
marble table. I said, 'Merci.' We exchanged a few apparently
innocent remarks, and suddenly, before I knew how it had
come about, we were in the midst of it, and he was telling me
how much they had been 'intrigued by that corpse.' It turned
out he had been one of the boarding officers.

"In the establishment where we sat one could get a variety
of foreign drinks which were kept for the visiting naval officers, and he took a sip of the dark medical-looking stuff, which
probably was nothing more nasty than *cassis à l'eau,* and
glancing with one eye into the tumbler, shook his head slightly.
'Impossible de comprendre—vous concevez,' he said, with a
curious mixture of unconcern and thoughtfulness. I could very
easily conceive how impossible it had been for them to understand. Nobody in the gunboat knew enough English to get hold
of the story as told by the serang. There was a good deal of
noise, too, round the two officers. 'They crowded upon us.
There was a circle round that dead man *(autour de ce mort),*'
he described. 'One had to attend to the most pressing. These
people were beginning to agitate themselves—*Parbleu!* A mob

like that—don't you see?' he interjected with philosophic in-
dulgence. As to the bulkhead, he had advised his commander
that the safest thing was to leave it alone, it was so villainous
to look at. They got two hawsers on board promptly *(en toute
hâte)* and took the *Patna* in tow—stern foremost at that—
which, under the circumstances, was not so foolish, since the
rudder was too much out of the water to be of any great use for
steering, and this manœuvre eased the strain on the bulkhead,
whose state, he expounded with stolid glibness, demanded the
greatest care *(éxigeait les plus grands ménagements)*. I could
not help thinking that my new acquaintance must have had a
voice in most of these arrangements: he looked a reliable officer, no longer very active, and he was seamanlike, too, in a
way, though, as he sat there, with his thick fingers clasped
lightly on his stomach, he reminded you of one of those snuffy,
quiet village priests, into whose ears are poured the sins, the
sufferings, the remorse of peasant generations, on whose faces
the placid and simple expression is like a veil thrown over the
mystery of pain and distress. He ought to have had a thread-
bare black *soutane* buttoned smoothly up to his ample chin, instead of a frockcoat with shoulder-straps and brass buttons.
His broad bosom heaved regularly while he went on telling me
that it had been the very devil of a job, as doubtless *(sans
doute)* I could figure to myself in my quality of a seaman *(en
votre qualité de marin)*. At the end of the period he inclined his
body slightly towards me, and, pursing his shaved lips, allowed the air to escape with a gentle hiss. 'Luckily,' he continued, 'the sea was level like this table, and there was no more
wind than there is here.' . . . The place struck me as indeed intolerably stuffy, and very hot; my face burned as though I had
been young enough to be embarrassed and blushing. They had
directed their course, he pursued, to the nearest English port
'*naturellement,*' where their responsibility ceased '*Dieu
merci.*' . . . He blew out his flat cheeks a little. . . . 'Because,
mind you *(notez bien),* all the time of towing we had two quartermasters stationed with axes by the hawsers, to cut us clear
of our tow in case she . . .' He fluttered downwards his heavy
eyelids, making his meaning as plain as possible. . . . 'What

would you! One does what one can *(on fait ce qu'on peut),*' and for a moment he managed to invest his ponderous immobility with an air of resignation. 'Two quartermasters—thirty hours—always there. Two!' he repeated, lifting up his right hand a little, and exhibiting two fingers. This was absolutely the first gesture I saw him make. It gave me the opportunity to 'note' a starred scar on the back of his hand—effect of a gunshot clearly; and, as if my sight had been made more acute by this discovery, I perceived also the seam of an old wound, beginning a little below the temple and going out of sight under the short grey hair at the side of his head—the graze of a spear or the cut of a sabre. He clasped his hands on his stomach again. 'I remained on board that—that—my memory is going *(s'en va). Ah! Patt-nà. C'est bien ça. Patt-nà Merci.* It is droll how one forgets. I stayed on that ship thirty hours. . . .'

"'You did!' I exclaimed. Still gazing at his hands, he pursed his lips a little, but this time made no hissing sound. 'It was judged proper,' he said, lifting his eyebrows dispassionately, 'that one of the officers should remain to keep an eye open *(pour ouvrir l'œil)*' . . . he sighed idly . . . 'and for communicating by signals with the towing ship—do you see?—and so on. For the rest, it was my opinion, too. We made our boats ready to drop over—and I also on that ship took measures. . . . *Enfin!* One has done one's possible. It was a delicate position. Thirty hours. They prepared me some food. As for the wine— go and whistle for it—not a drop.' In some extraordinary way, without any marked change in his inert attitude and in the placid expression of his face, he managed to convey the idea of profound disgust. 'I—you know—when it comes to eating without my glass of wine—I am nowhere.'

"I was afraid he would enlarge upon the grievance, for he didn't stir a limb or twitch a feature, he made one aware how much he was irritated by the recollection. But he seemed to forget all about it. They delivered their charge to the 'port authorities,' as he expressed it. He was struck by the calmness with which it had been received. 'One might have thought they had such a droll find *(drôle de trouvaille)* brought them every day. You are extraordinary—you others,' he commented, with his back propped against the wall, and looking himself as incapable of an emotional display as a sack of meal. There happened to be a man-of-war and an Indian Marine steamer in the harbour at the time, and he did not conceal his admiration of the efficient manner in which the boats of these two ships cleared the *Patna* of her passengers. Indeed his torpid demeanour concealed nothing: it had that mysterious, almost miraculous, power of producing striking effects by means impossible of detection which is the last word of the highest art. 'Twenty-five minutes—watch in hand—twenty-five, no more.' . . . He unclasped and clasped again his fingers without removing his hands from his stomach, and made it infinitely more effective than if he had thrown up his arms to heaven in amazement. . . . 'All that lot *(tout ce monde)* on shore—with their little affairs—nobody left but a guard of seamen *(marins de l'État)* and that interesting corpse *(cet intéressant cadavre).* Twenty-five minutes.' . . . With downcast eyes and his head tilted slightly on one side he seemed to roll knowingly on his tongue the savour of a smart bit of work. He persuaded one without any further demonstration that his approval was eminently worth having, and resuming his hardly interrupted immobility, he went on to inform me that, being under orders to make the best of their way to Toulon, they left in two hours' time, 'so that *(de sorte que)* there are many things in this incident of my life *(dans cet épisode de ma vie)* which have remained obscure.'"

Chapter Thirteen

AFTER THESE words, and without a change of attitude, he, so to speak, submitted himself passively to a state of silence. I kept him company; and suddenly, but not abruptly, as if the appointed time had arrived for his moderate and husky voice to come out of his immobility, he pronounced, *'Mon Dieu!* how

the time passes!' Nothing could have been more commonplace
than his remark; but its utterance coincided for me with a moment of vision. It's extraordinary how we go through life with
eyes half shut, with dull ears, with dormant thoughts. Perhaps
it's just as well; and it may be that it is this very dulness that
makes life to the incalculable majority so supportable and so
welcome. Nevertheless, there can be but few of us who had
never known one of these rare moments of awakening when
we see, hear, understand ever so much—everything—in a
flash—before we fall back again into our agreeable somno-
lence. I raised my eyes when he spoke, and I saw him as
though I had never seen him before. I saw his chin sunk on his
breast, the clumsy folds of his coat, his clasped hands, his motionless pose, so curiously suggestive of his having been simply left there. Time had passed indeed: it had overtaken him
and gone ahead. It had left him hopelessly behind with a few
poor gifts: the iron-grey hair, the heavy fatigue of the tanned
face, two scars, a pair of tarnished shoulder-straps; one of
those steady, reliable men who are the raw material of great
reputations, one of those uncounted lives that are buried without drums and trumpets under the foundations of monumental
successes. 'I am now third lieutenant of the *Victorieuse*' (she
was the flagship of the French Pacific squadron at the time), he
said, detaching his shoulders from the wall a couple of inches
to introduce himself. I bowed slightly on my side of the table,
and told him I commanded a merchant vessel at present anchored in Ruschcutters' Bay. He had 'remarked' her,—a pretty
little craft. He was very civil about it in his impassive way. I
even fancy he went to the length of tilting his head in compli-
ment as he repeated, breathing visibly the while, 'Ah, yes. A
little craft painted black,—very pretty—very pretty *(très co-
quet).*' After a time he twisted his body slowly to face the glass
door on our right. 'A dull town *(triste ville),*' he observed, staring into the street. It was a brilliant day; a southerly buster was
raging, and we could see the passers-by, men and women, buf-
feted by the wind on the sidewalks, the sunlit fronts of the
houses across the road blurred by the tall whirls of dust. 'I descended on shore,' he said, 'to stretch my legs a little, but . . .'

He didn't finish, and sank into the depths of his repose. 'Pray—tell me,' he began, coming up ponderously, 'what was there at the bottom of this affair—precisely *(au juste)*? It is curious. That dead man, for instance—and so on.'

"'There were living men, too,' I said; 'much more curious.'

"'No doubt, no doubt,' he agreed half audibly, then, as if after mature consideration, murmured, 'Evidently.' I made no difficulty in communicating to him what had interested me most in this affair. It seemed as though he had a right to know: hadn't he spent thirty hours on board the *Patna*—had he not taken the succession, so to speak, had he not done 'his possible'? He listened to me, looking more priest-like than ever, and with what—probably on account of his downcast eyes—had the appearance of devout concentration. Once or twice he elevated his eyebrows (but without raising his eyelids), as one would say 'The devil!' Once he calmly exclaimed, 'Ah, bah!' under his breath, and when I had finished he pursed his lips in a deliberate way and emitted a sort of sorrowful whistle.

"In any one else it might have been an evidence of boredom, a sign of indifference; but he, in his occult way, managed to make his immobility appear profoundly responsive, and as full of valuable thoughts as an egg is of meat. What he said at last was nothing more than a 'very interesting,' pronounced politely, and not much above a whisper. Before I got over my disappointment he added, but as if speaking to himself, 'That's it. That *is* it.' His chin seemed to sink lower on his breast, his body to weigh heavier on his seat. I was about to ask him what he meant when a sort of preparatory tremor passed over his whole person, as a faint ripple may be seen upon stagnant water even before the wind is felt. 'And so that poor young man ran away along with the others,' he said, with grave tranquillity.

"I don't know what made me smile: it is the only genuine smile of mine I can remember in connection with Jim's affair. But somehow this simple statement of the matter sounded funny in French. . . . '*S'est enfui avec les autres,*' had said the lieutenant. And suddenly I began to admire the discrimination of the man. He had made out the point at once: He did get hold of the only thing I cared about. I felt as though I were taking professional opinion on the case. His imperturbable and mature calmness was that of an expert in possession of the facts, and to whom one's perplexities are mere child's-play. 'Ah! The young, the young,' he said, indulgently. 'And after all, one does not die of it.' 'Die of what?' I asked, swiftly. 'Of being afraid.' He elucidated his meaning and sipped his drink.

"I perceived that the three last fingers of his wounded hand were stiff and could not move independently of each other, so that he took up his tumbler with an ungainly clutch. 'One is always afraid. One may talk, but . . .' He put down the glass awkwardly. . . . 'The fear, the fear—look you—it is always there.' . . . He touched his breast near a brass button on the very spot where Jim had given a thump to his own when protesting that there was nothing the matter with his heart. I suppose I made some sign of dissent, because he insisted, 'Yes! yes! One talks, one talks; this is all very fine; but at the end of the reckoning one is no cleverer than the next man— and no more brave. Brave! This is always to be seen. I have rolled my hump *(roulé ma bosse),*' he said, using the slang expression with imperturbable seriousness, 'in all parts of the world; I have known brave men—famous ones! *Allez!*' . . . He drank carelessly. . . . 'Brave—you conceive—in the Service— one has got to be—the trade demands it *(le métier veux ça).* Is it not so?' he appealed to me reasonably. *'Eh bien!* Each of them—I say each of them, if he were an honest man—*bien entendu*—would confess that there is a point—there is a point— for the best of us—there is somewhere a point when you let go everything *(vous lachez tout).* And you have got to live with that truth—do you see? Given a certain combination of circumstances, fear is sure to come. Abominable funk *(un trac épouvantable).* And even for those who do not believe this truth there is fear all the same—the fear of themselves. Absolutely so. Trust me. Yes. Yes. . . . At my age one knows what one is talking about—*que diable*?' . . . He had delivered himself of all this as immovably as though he had been the mouthpiece of abstract wisdom, but at this point he heightened the effect of detachment by beginning to twirl his thumbs slowly.

'It's evident—*parbleu!*' he continued; 'for, make up your mind
as much as you like, even a simple headache or a fit of indi-
gestion *(un dérangement d'estomac)* is enough to . . . Take me,
for instance—I have made my proofs. *Eh bien!* I, who am
speaking to you, once . . .'

"He drained his glass and returned to his twirling. 'No, no;
one does not die of it,' he pronounced, finally, and when I
found he did not mean to proceed with the personal anecdote,
I was extremely disappointed; the more so as it was not the sort
of story, you know, one could very well press him for. I sat
silent, and he too, as if nothing could please him better. Even
his thumbs were still now. Suddenly his lips began to move.
'That is so,' he resumed, placidly. 'Man is born a coward
(l'homme est né poltron). It is a difficulty—*parbleu!* It would
be too easy otherwise. But habit—habit—necessity do you
see?—the eye of others—*voilà*. One puts up with it. And then
the example of others who are no better than yourself, and yet
make good countenance. . . .'

"His voice ceased.

"'That young man—you will observe—had none of these
inducements—at least at the moment,' I remarked.

"He raised his eyebrows forgivingly: 'I don't say; I don't
say. The young man in question might have had the best dispositions—the best dispositions,' he repeated, wheezing a little.

"'I am glad to see you take a lenient view,' I said. 'His own
feeling in the matter was—ah!—hopeful, and . . .'

"The shuffle of his feet under the table interrupted me. He
drew up his heavy eyelids. Drew up, I say—no other expression can describe the steady deliberation of the act—and at last
was disclosed completely to me. I was confronted by two narrow grey circlets, like two tiny steel rings around the profound
blackness of the pupils. The sharp glance, coming from that
massive body, gave a notion of extreme efficiency, like a razor-
edge on a battle-axe. 'Pardon,' he said, punctiliously. His right
hand went up, and he swayed forward. 'Allow me . . . I contended that one may get on knowing very well that one's
courage does not come of itself *(ne vient pas tout seul)*.

There's nothing much in that to get upset about. One truth the more ought not to make life impossible. . . . But the honour—the honour, monsieur! . . . The honour . . . that is real—that is! And what life may be worth when' . . . he got on his feet with a ponderous impetuosity, as a startled ox might scramble up from the grass . . . 'when the honour is gone—*ah ça! par exemple*—I can offer no opinion. I can offer no opinion—because—monsieur—I know nothing of it.'

"I had risen, too, and, trying to throw infinite politeness into our attitudes, we faced each other mutely, like two china dogs on a mantelpiece. Hang the fellow! he had pricked the bubble. The blight of futility that lies in wait for men's speeches had fallen upon our conversation, and made it a thing of empty sounds. 'Very well,' I said, with a disconcerted smile, 'but couldn't it reduce itself to not being found out?' He made as if to retort readily, but when he spoke he had changed his mind. 'This, monsieur, is too fine for me—much above me—I don't think about it.' He bowed heavily over his cap, which he held before him by the peak, between the thumb and the forefinger of his wounded hand. I bowed, too. We bowed together: we scraped our feet at each other with much ceremony, while a dirty specimen of a waiter looked on critically, as though he had paid for the performance. 'Serviteur,' said the Frenchman. Another scrape. 'Monsieur' . . . 'Monsieur.' . . . The glass door swung behind his burly back. I saw the southerly buster get hold of him and drive him down wind with his hand to his head, his shoulders braced, and the tails of his coat blown hard against his legs.

"I sat down again alone and discouraged—discouraged about Jim's case. If you wonder that after more than three years it had preserved its actuality, you must know that I had seen him only very lately. I had come straight from Samarang, where I had loaded a cargo for Sydney: an utterly uninteresting bit of business,—what Charley here would call one of my rational transactions—and in Samarang I had seen something of Jim. He was then working for De Jongh, on my recommendation. Water-clerk. 'My representative afloat,' as De Jongh called him. You can't imagine a mode of life more barren of

consolation, less capable of being invested with a spark of
glamour—unless it be the business of an insurance canvasser.
Little Bob Stanton—Charley here knew him well—had gone
through that experience. The same who got drowned afterwards trying to save a lady's-maid in the *Sephora* disaster. A
case of collision on a hazy morning off the Spanish coast you
may remember. All the passengers had been packed tidily into
the boats and shoved clear of the ship when Bob sheered
alongside again and scrambled back on deck to fetch that girl.
How she had been left behind I can't make out; anyhow, she
had gone completely crazy—wouldn't leave the ship—held to
the rail like grim death. The wrestling-match could be seen
plainly from the boats; but poor Bob was the shortest chief
mate in the merchant service, and the woman stood five feet
ten in her shoes and was as strong as a horse, I've been told. So
it went on, pull devil, pull baker, the wretched girl screaming
all the time, and Bob letting out a yell now and then to warn his
boat to keep well clear of the ship. One of the hands told me,
hiding a smile at the recollection, 'It was for all the world, sir,
like a naughty youngster fighting with his mother.' The same
old chap said that 'At the last we could see that Mr. Stanton
had given up hauling at the gal, and just stood by looking at
her, watching like. We thought afterwards he must've been
reckoning that, maybe, the rush of water would tear her away
from the rail by and by and give him a show to save her. We
daren't come alongside for our life; and after a bit the old ship
went down all on a sudden with a lurch to starboard—plop.
The suck in was something awful. We never saw anything
alive or dead come up.' Poor Bob's spell of shore-life had been
one of the complications of a love affair, I believe. He fondly
hoped he had done with the sea for ever, and made sure he had
got hold of all the bliss on earth, but it came to canvassing in
the end. Some cousin of his in Liverpool put him up to it. He
used to tell us his experiences in that line. He made us laugh
till we cried, and, not altogether displeased at the effect, un-
dersized and bearded to the waist like a gnome, he would tip-
toe amongst us and say, 'It's all very well for you beggars to
laugh, but my immortal soul was shrivelled down to the size of

a parched pea after a week of that work.' I don't know how Jim's soul accommodated itself to the new conditions of his life—I was kept too busy in getting him something to do that would keep body and soul together—but I am pretty certain his adventurous fancy was suffering all the pangs of starvation. It had certainly nothing to feed upon in this new calling. It was distressing to see him at it, though he tackled it with a stubborn serenity for which I must give him full credit. I kept my eye on his shabby plodding with a sort of notion that it was a punishment for the heroics of his fancy—an expiation for his craving after more glamour than he could carry. He had loved too well to imagine himself a glorious racehorse, and now he was condemned to toil without honour like a costermonger's donkey. He did it very well. He shut himself in, put his head down, said never a word. Very well; very well indeed—except for certain fantastic and violent outbreaks, on the deplorable occasions when the irrepressible *Patna* case cropped up. Unfortunately that scandal of the Eastern seas would not die out. And this is the reason why I could never feel I had done with Jim for good.

"I sat thinking of him after the French lieutenant had left, not, however, in connection with De Jongh's cool and gloomy backshop, where we had hurriedly shaken hands not very long ago, but as I had seen him years before in the last flickers of the candle, alone with me in the long gallery of the Malabar House, with the chill and the darkness of the night at his back. The respectable sword of his country's law was suspended over his head. To-morrow—or was it today? (midnight had slipped by long before we parted)—the marble-faced police magistrate, after distributing fines and terms of imprisonment in the assault-and-battery case, would take up the awful weapon and smite his bowed neck. Our communion in the night was uncommonly like a last vigil with a condemned man. He was guilty, too. He was guilty—as I had told myself repeatedly, guilty and done for; nevertheless, I wished to spare him the mere detail of a formal execution. I don't pretend to explain the reasons of my desire—I don't think I could; but if you haven't got a sort of notion by this time, then I must have been very obscure in my narrative, or you too sleepy to seize

upon the sense of my words. I don't defend my morality. There
was no morality in the impulse which induced me to lay before
him Brierly's plan of evasion—I may call it—in all its primitive simplicity. There were the rupees—absolutely ready in my
pocket and very much at his service. Oh! a loan; a loan of
course—and if an introduction to a man (in Rangoon) who
could put some work in his way . . . Why! with the greatest
pleasure. I had pen, ink, and paper in my room on the first
floor. And even while I was speaking I was impatient to begin
the letter: day, month, year, 2:30 A.M. . . . for the sake of our
old friendship I ask you to put some work in the way of Mr.
James So-and-so, in whom, &c., &c. . . . I was even ready to
write in that strain about him. If he had not enlisted my sympathies he had done better for himself—he had gone to the
very fount and origin of that sentiment, he had reached the secret sensibility of my egoism. I am concealing nothing from
you, because were I to do so my action would appear more unintelligible than any man's action has the right to be, and—in
the second place—to-morrow you shall forget my sincerity
along with the other lessons of the past. In this transaction, to
speak grossly and precisely, I was the irreproachable man; but
the subtle intentions of my immorality were defeated by the
moral simplicity of the criminal. No doubt he was selfish, too,
but his selfishness had a higher origin, a more lofty aim. I discovered that, say what I would, he was eager to go through the
ceremony of execution; and I didn't say much, for I felt that in
argument his youth would tell against me heavily: he believed
where I had already ceased to doubt. There was something fine
in the wildness of his unexpressed, hardly formulated hope.
'Clear out! Couldn't think of it,' he said, with a shake of the
head. 'I make you an offer for which I neither demand nor expect any sort of gratitude,' I said; 'you shall repay the money
when convenient, and . . .' 'Awfully good of you,' he muttered
without looking up. I watched him narrowly: the future must
have appeared horribly uncertain to him; but he did not falter,
as though indeed there had been nothing wrong with his heart.
I felt angry—not for the first time that night. 'The whole
wretched business,' I said, 'is bitter enough, I should think, for

a man of your kind . . .' 'It is, it is,' he whispered twice, with his eyes fixed on the floor. It was heartrending. He towered above the light, and I could see the down on his cheek, the colour mantling warm under the smooth skin of his face. Believe me or not, I say it was outrageously heartrending. It provoked me to brutality. 'Yes,' I said; 'and allow me to confess that I am totally unable to imagine what advantage you can expect from this licking of the dregs.' 'Advantage!' he murmured out of his stillness. 'I am dashed if I do,' I said, enraged. 'I've been trying to tell you all there is in it,' he went on, slowly, as if meditating something unanswerable. 'But after all, it is *my* trouble.' I opened my mouth to retort, and discovered suddenly that I'd lost all confidence in myself; and it was as if he, too, had given me up, for he mumbled like a man thinking half aloud. 'Went away . . . went into hospitals. . . . Not one of them would face it. . . . They! . . .' He moved his hand slightly to imply disdain. 'But I've got to get over this thing, and I mustn't shirk any of it or . . . I won't shirk any of it.' He was silent. He gazed as though he had been haunted. His unconscious face reflected the passing expressions of scorn, of despair, of resolution,—reflected them in turn, as a magic mirror would reflect the gliding passage of unearthly shapes. He lived surrounded by deceitful ghosts, by austere shades. 'Oh! nonsense, my dear fellow,' I began. He had a movement of impatience. 'You don't seem to understand,' he said, incisively; then looking at me without a wink, 'I may have jumped, but I don't run away.' 'I meant no offence,' I said; and added stupidly, 'Better men than you have found it expedient to run, at times.' He coloured all over, while in my confusion I half-choked myself with my own tongue. 'Perhaps so,' he said at last; 'I am not good enough; I can't afford it. I am bound to fight this thing down—I am fighting it *now*.' I got out of my chair and felt stiff all over. The silence was embarrassing, and to put an end to it I imagined nothing better but to remark, 'I had no idea it was so late,' in an airy tone. . . . 'I daresay you have had enough of this,' he said, brusquely: 'and to tell you the truth'—he began to look round for his hat—'so have I.'

"Well! he had refused this unique offer. He had struck aside my helping hand; he was ready to go now, and beyond the balustrade the night seemed to wait for him very still, as though he had been marked down for its prey. I heard his voice. 'Ah! here it is.' He had found his hat. For a few seconds we hung in the wind. 'What will you do after—after . . .' I asked very low. 'Go to the dogs as likely as not,' he answered in a gruff mutter. I had recovered my wits in a measure, and judged best to take it lightly. 'Pray remember,' I said, 'that I should like very much to see you again before you go.' 'I don't know what's to prevent you. The damned thing won't make me invisible,' he said with intense bitterness—'no such luck.' And then at the moment of taking leave he treated me to a ghastly muddle of dubious stammers and movements, to an awful display of hesitations. God forgive him—me! He had taken it into his fanciful head that I was likely to make some difficulty as to shaking hands. It was too awful for words. I believe I shouted suddenly at him as you would bellow to a man you saw about to walk over a cliff; I remember our voices being raised, the appearance of a miserable grin on his face, a crushing clutch on my hand, a nervous laugh. The candle spluttered out, and the thing was over at last, with a groan that floated up to me in the dark. He got himself away somehow. The night swallowed his form. He was a horrible bungler. Horrible. I heard the quick crunch-crunch of the gravel under his boots. He was running. Absolutely, running, with nowhere to go to. And he was not yet four-and-twenty."

Chapter Fourteen

I SLEPT little, hurried over my breakfast, and after a slight hesitation gave up my early morning visit to my ship. It was really very wrong of me, because, though my chief mate was an excellent man all round, he was the victim of such black imaginings that if he did not get a letter from his wife at the expected time he would go quite distracted with rage and jealousy, lose all grip on the work, quarrel with all hands, and either weep in his cabin or develop such a ferocity of temper as all but drove the crew to the verge of mutiny. The thing had always seemed inexplicable to me: they had been married thirteen years; I had a glimpse of her once, and honestly, I couldn't conceive a man abandoned enough to plunge into sin for the sake of such an un-attractive person. I don't know whether I have not done wrong by refraining from putting that view before poor Selvin: the man made a little hell on earth for himself, and I also suffered indirectly, but some sort of, no doubt, false delicacy prevented me. The marital relations of seamen would make an interesting subject, and I could tell you instances. . . . However, this is not the place, nor the time, and we are concerned with Jim—who was unmarried. If his imaginative conscience or his pride; if all the extravagant ghosts and austere shades that were the disas-trous familiars of his youth would not let him run away from the block, I, who of course can't be suspected of such familiars, was irresistibly impelled to go and see his head roll off. I wended my way towards the court. I didn't hope to be very much impressed or edified, or interested or even frightened—though, as long as there is any life before one, a jolly good fright now and then is a salutary discipline. But neither did I ex-pect to be so awfully depressed. The bitterness of his punish-ment was in its chill and mean atmosphere. The real significance of crime is in its being a breach of faith with the community of mankind, and from that point of view he was no mean traitor, but his execution was a hole-and-corner affair. There was no high scaffolding, no scarlet cloth (did they have scarlet cloth on Tower Hill? They should have had), no awe-stricken multitude to be horrified at his guilt and be moved to tears at his fate—no air of sombre retribution. There was, as I walked along, the clear sunshine, a brilliance too passionate to be consoling, the streets full of jumbled bits of colour like a damaged kaleidoscope: yellow, green, blue, dazzling white, the brown nudity of an undraped shoulder, a bullock-cart with a red canopy, a company of native infantry in a drab body with dark heads marching in dusty laced boots, a native policeman in a

sombre uniform of scanty cut and belted in patent leather, who
looked up at me with orientally pitiful eyes as though his mi-
grating spirit were suffering exceedingly from that unforeseen—what d'ye call 'em?—avatar—incarnation. Under the
shade of a lonely tree in the courtyard, the villagers connected
with the assault case sat in a picturesque group, looking like a
chromo-lithograph of a camp in a book of Eastern travel. One
missed the obligatory thread of smoke in the foreground and
the pack-animals grazing. A blank yellow wall rose behind
overtopping the tree, reflecting the glare. The court-room was
sombre, seemed more vast. High up in the dim space the
punkahs were swaying short to and fro, to and fro. Here and
there a draped figure, dwarfed by the bare walls, remained
without stirring amongst the rows of empty benches, as if absorbed in pious meditation. The plaintiff, who had been beaten,
an obese chocolate-coloured man with shaved head, one fat
breast bare and a bright yellow caste-mark above the bridge of
his nose, sat in pompous immobility; only his eyes glittered,
rolling in the gloom, and the nostrils dilated and collapsed violently as he breathed. Brierly dropped into his seat looking done
up, as though he had spent the night in sprinting on a cinder-
track. The pious sailing-ship skipper appeared excited and
made uneasy movements, as if restraining with difficulty an impulse to stand up and exhort us earnestly to prayer and repentance. The head of the magistrate, delicately pale under the
neatly arranged hair, resembled the head of a hopeless invalid
after he had been washed and brushed and propped up in bed.
He moved aside the vase of flowers—a bunch of purple with a
few pink blossoms on long stalks—and seizing in both hands a
long sheet of bluish paper, ran his eye over it, propped his forearms on the edge of the desk, and began to read aloud in an
even, distinct, and careless voice.

"By Jove! for all my foolishness about scaffolds and heads
rolling off—I assure you it was infinitely worse than a behead-
ing. A heavy sense of finality brooded over all this, unrelieved
by the hope of rest and safety following the fall of the axe.
These proceedings had all the cold vengefulness of a death-
sentence, had all the cruelty of a sentence of exile. This is how

I looked at it that morning—and even now I seem to see an undeniable vestige of truth in that exaggerated view of a common occurrence. You may imagine how strongly I felt this at the time. Perhaps it is for that reason that I could not bring myself to admit the finality. The thing was always with me, I was always eager to take opinion on it, as though it had not been practically settled: individual opinion—international opinion—by Jove! That Frenchman's, for instance. His own country's pronouncement was uttered in the passionless and definite phraseology a machine would use, if machines could speak. The head of the magistrate was half hidden by the paper, his brow was like alabaster.

"There were several questions before the Court. The first as to whether the ship was in every respect fit and seaworthy for the voyage. The court found she was not. The next point, I remember, was, whether up to the time of the accident the ship had been navigated with proper and seamanlike care. They said Yes to that, goodness knows why, and then they declared that there was no evidence to show the exact cause of the accident. A floating derelict probably. I myself remember that a Norwegian barque bound out with a cargo of pitch-pine had been given up as missing about that time, and it was just the sort of craft that would capsize in a squall and float bottom up for months—a kind of maritime ghoul on the prowl to kill ships in the dark. Such wandering corpses are common enough in the North Atlantic, which is haunted by all the terrors of the sea,—fogs, icebergs, dead ships bent upon mischief, and long sinister gales that fasten upon one like a vampire till all the strength and the spirit and even hope are gone, and one feels like the empty shell of a man. But there—in those areas—the incident was rare enough to resemble a special arrangement of a malevolent providence, which, unless it had for its object the killing of a donkeyman and the bringing of worse than death upon Jim, appeared an utterly aimless piece of devilry. This view occurring to me took off my attention. For a time I was aware of the magistrate's voice as a sound merely; but in a moment it shaped itself into distinct words . . . 'in utter disregard of their plain duty,' it said. The next sentence escaped me somehow, and then . . . 'abandoning in the moment of danger the lives and property confided to their charge' . . . went on the voice evenly, and stopped. A pair of eyes under the white forehead shot darkly a glance above the edge of the paper. I looked for Jim hurriedly, as though I had expected him to disappear. He was very still—but he was there. He sat pink and fair and extremely attentive. 'Therefore, . . .' began the voice emphatically. He stared with parted lips, hanging upon the words of the man behind the desk. These came out into the stillness wafted on the wind made by the punkahs, and I, watching for their effect upon him, caught only the fragments of official language. . . . 'The Court . . . Gustav So-and-so master . . . native of Germany . . . James So-and-so . . . mate . . . certificates cancelled.' A silence fell. The magistrate had dropped the paper, and leaning sideways on the arm of his chair, began to talk with Brierly easily. People started to move out; others were pushing in, and I also made for the door. Outside I stood still, and when Jim passed me on his way to the gate, I caught at his arm and detained him. The look he gave discomposed me, as though I had been responsible for his state: he looked at me as if I had been the embodied evil of life. "It's all over,' I stammered. 'Yes,' he said, thickly. 'And now let no man . . .' He jerked his arm out of my grasp. I watched his back as he went away. It was a long street, and he remained in sight for some time. He walked rather slow, and straddled his legs a little, as if he had found it difficult to keep a straight line. Just before I lost him I fancied he staggered a bit.

"'Man overboard,' said a deep voice behind me. Turning round, I saw a fellow I knew slightly, a West Australian; Chester was his name. He, too, had been looking after Jim. He was a man with an immense girth of chest, a rugged, clean-shaved face of mahogany colour, and two blunt tufts of iron-grey, thick wiry hairs on his upper lip. He had been pearler, wrecker, trader, whaler, too, I believe; in his own words—anything and everything a man may be at sea, but a pirate. The Pacific, north and south, was his proper hunting-ground; but he had wandered so far afield looking for a cheap steamer to buy. Lately he had discovered—so he said—a guano island somewhere, but its approaches were dangerous, and the anchorage, such as it was, could not be considered safe, to say the least of it. 'As good as a gold-mine,' he would exclaim. 'Right bang in the middle of the Walpole Reefs, and if it's true enough that you can get no holding-ground anywhere in less than forty fathom, then what of that? There are the hurricanes, too. But it's a first-rate thing. As good as a gold-mine—better! Yet there's not a fool of them that will see it. I can't get a skipper or a shipowner to go near the place. So I made up my mind to cart the blessed stuff myself.' . . . This was what he required a steamer for, and I knew he was just then negotiating enthusiastically with a Parsee firm for an old, brig-rigged, sea-anachronism of ninety horse-power. We had met and spoken together several times. He looked knowingly after Jim. 'Takes it to heart?' he asked scornfully. 'Very much,' I said. 'Then he's no good,' he opined. 'What's all the to-do about? A bit of ass's skin. That never yet made a man. You must see things exactly as they are—if you don't, you may just as well give in at once. You will never do anything in this world. Look at me. I made it a practice never to take anything to heart.' 'Yes,' I said, 'you see things as they are.' 'I wish to see my partner coming along, that's what I wish to see,' he said. 'Know my partner? Old Robinson. Yes; *the* Robinson. Don't *you* know? The notorious Robinson. The man who smuggled more opium and bagged more seals in his time than any loose Johnny now alive. They say he used to board the sealing-schooners up Alaska way when the fog was so thick that the Lord God, He alone, could tell one man from another. Holy-Terror Robinson. That's the man. He is with me in that guano thing. The best chance he ever came across in his life.' He put his lips to my ear. 'Cannibal?—well, they used to give him the name years and years ago. You remember the story? A shipwreck on the west side of Stewart Island; that's right, seven of them got ashore, and it seems they did not get on very well together. Some men are too cantankerous for anything—don't know how to make the best of a bad job—don't see things as they are—as they *are,* my boy! And then what's the consequences? Obvious! Trouble, trouble; as likely as not a knock on the head; and serve 'em right, too. That sort is the most useful when it's dead. The story goes that a boat of Her Majesty's ship *Wolverine* found him kneeling on the kelp, naked as the day he was born, and chanting some psalm-tune or other; light snow was falling at the time. He waited till the boat was an oar's length from the shore, and then up and away. They chased him for an hour up and down the boulders, till a marine flung a stone that took him behind the ear providentially and knocked him senseless. Alone! Of course. But that's like that tale of sealing-schooners; the Lord God knows the right and the wrong of that story. The cutter did not investigate much. They wrapped him in a boat-cloak and took him off as quick as they could, with a dark night coming on, the weather threatening, and the ship firing recall guns every five minutes. Three weeks afterwards he was as well as ever. He didn't allow any fuss that was made on shore to upset him, he just shut his lips tight, and let people screech. It was bad enough to have lost his ship, and all he was worth besides, without paying attention to the hard names they called him. That's the man for me.' He lifted his arm for a signal to some one down the street. 'He's got a little money, so I had to let him into my thing. Had to! It would have been sinful to throw away such a find, and I was cleaned out myself. It cut me to the quick, but I could see the matter just as it was and if I *must* share—thinks I—with any man, then give me Robinson. I left him at breakfast in the hotel to come to court, because I've an idea . . . Ah! Good morning, Captain Robinson. . . . Friend of mine, Captain Robinson.'

"An emaciated patriarch in a suit of white drill, a solah topi with a green-lined rim on a head trembling with age, joined us after crossing the street in a trotting shuffle, and stood propped with both hands on the handle of an umbrella. A white beard with amber streaks hung lumpily down to his waist. He blinked his creased eyelids at me in a bewildered way. 'How do you do? how do you do?' he piped, amiably, and tottered. 'A little deaf,' said Chester aside. 'Did you drag him over six thousand miles to get a cheap steamer?' I asked. 'I would have taken him twice round the world as soon as look at him,' said Chester with immense energy. 'The steamer will be the making of us, my lad. Is it my fault that every skipper and shipowner in the whole of blessed Australasia turns out a blamed fool? Once I talked for three hours to a man in Auckland. "Send a ship," I said, "send a ship. I'll give you half of the first cargo for yourself, free gratis for nothing—just to make a good start." Says he, "I wouldn't do it if there was no other place on earth to send a ship to." Perfect ass, of course. Rocks, currents, no anchorage, sheer cliff to lay to, no insurance company would take the risk, didn't see how he could get loaded under three years. Ass! I nearly went on my knees to him. "But look at the thing as it is," says I. "Damn rocks and hurricanes. Look at it as it is. There's guano there Queensland sugar-planters would fight for—fight for on the quay, I tell you." . . . What can you do with a fool? . . . "That's one of your little jokes, Chester," he says. . . . Joke! I could have wept. Ask Captain Robinson here. . . . And there was another shipowning fellow—a fat chap in a white waistcoat in Wellington, who seemed to think I was up to some swindle or other. "I don't know what sort of fool you're looking for," he says, "but I am busy just now. Good morning." I longed to take him in my two hands and smash him through the window of his own office. But I didn't. I was as mild as a curate. "Think of it," says I. "*Do* think it over. I'll call to-morrow." He grunted something about being "out all day." On the stairs I felt ready to beat my head against the wall from vexation. Captain Robinson here can tell you. It was awful to think of all that lovely stuff lying waste under the sun—stuff that would send the sugar-cane shooting sky-high. The making of Queensland! The making of Queensland! And in Brisbane, where I went to have a last try, they gave me the name of a lunatic. Idiots! The only sensible man I came across was the cabman who drove me about. A broken-down swell he was, I fancy. Hey! Captain Robinson? You remember I told you about my cabby in Brisbane—don't you? The chap had a wonderful eye for things. He saw it all in a jiffy. It was a real pleasure to talk with him. One evening after a devil of a day amongst shipowners I felt so bad that, says I, "I must get drunk. Come along; I must get drunk, or I'll go mad." "I am your man," he says; "go ahead." I don't know what I would have done without him. Hey! Captain Robinson.'

"He poked the ribs of his partner. 'He! he! he!' laughed the Ancient, looked aimlessly down the street, then peered at me doubtfully with sad, dim pupils. . . . 'He! he! he!' . . . He leaned heavier on the umbrella, and dropped his gaze on the ground. I needn't tell you I had tried to get away several times, but Chester had foiled every attempt by simply catching hold of my coat. 'One minute. I've a notion.' 'What's your infernal notion?' I exploded at last. 'If you think I am going in with you . . .' 'No, no, my boy. Too late, if you wanted ever so much. We've got a steamer.' 'You've got the ghost of a steamer,' I said. 'Good enough for a start—there's no superior nonsense about us. Is there, Captain Robinson?' 'No! no! no!' croaked the old man without lifting his eyes, and the senile tremble of his head became almost fierce with determination. 'I understand you know that young chap,' said Chester, with a nod at the street from which Jim had disappeared long ago. 'He's been having grub with you in the Malabar last night—so I was told.'

"I said that was true, and after remarking that he, too, liked to live well and in style, only that, for the present, he had to be saving of every penny—'none too many for the business! Isn't that so, Captain Robinson?'—he squared his shoulders and stroked his dumpy moustache, while the notorious Robinson, coughing at his side, clung more than ever to the handle of the umbrella, and seemed ready to subside passively into a heap of old bones. 'You see, the old chap has all the money,' whispered Chester, confidentially. 'I've been cleaned out trying to engineer the dratted thing. But wait a bit, wait a bit. The good time is coming.' . . . He seemed suddenly astonished at the signs of impatience I gave. 'Oh, crakee!' he cried; 'I am telling you of the biggest thing that ever was, and you . . .' 'I have an appointment,' I pleaded mildly. 'What of that?' he asked with genuine surprise; 'let it wait.' 'That's exactly what I am doing now,' I remarked; 'hadn't you better tell me what it is you want?' 'Buy twenty hotels like that,' he growled to himself; 'and every joker boarding in them, too—twenty times over.' He lifted his head smartly. 'I want that young chap.' 'I don't understand,' I said.

'He's no good, is he?' said Chester, crisply. 'I know nothing about it,' I protested. 'Why, you told me yourself he was taking it to heart,' argued Chester. 'Well, in my opinion a chap who . . . Anyhow, he can't be much good; but then you see I am on the look-out for somebody, and I've just got a thing that will suit him. I'll give him a job on my island.' He nodded significantly. 'I'm going to dump forty coolies there—if I've got to steal 'em. Somebody must work the stuff. Oh! I mean to act square: wooden shed, corrugated-iron roof—I know a man in Hobart who will take my bill at six months for the materials. I do. Honour bright. Then there's the water-supply. I'll have to fly round and get somebody to trust me for half-a-dozen second-hand iron tanks. Catch rain-water, hey? Let him take charge. Make him supreme boss over the coolies. Good idea, isn't it? What do you say?' 'There are whole years when not a drop of rain falls on Walpole,' I said, too amazed to laugh. He bit his lip and seemed bothered. 'Oh, well, I will fix up something for them—or land a supply. Hang it all! That's not the question.'

"I said nothing. I had a rapid vision of Jim perched on a shadowless rock, up to his knees in guano, with the screams of sea-birds in his ears, the incandescent ball of the sun above his head; the empty sky and the empty ocean all aquiver, simmering together in the heat as far as the eye could reach. 'I wouldn't advise my worst enemy . . .' I began. 'What's the matter with you?' cried Chester; 'I mean to give him a good screw—that is, as soon as the thing is set going, of course. It's as easy as falling off a log. Simply nothing to do; two six-shooters in his belt. . . . Surely he wouldn't be afraid of anything forty coolies could do—with two six-shooters and he the only armed man, too! It's much better than it looks. I want you to help me to talk him over.' 'No!' I shouted. Old Robinson lifted his bleared eyes dismally for a moment, Chester looked at me with infinite contempt. 'So you wouldn't advise him?' he uttered, slowly. 'Certainly not,' I answered, as indignant as though he had requested me to help murder somebody; 'moreover, I am sure he wouldn't. He is badly cut up, but he isn't mad as far as I know.' 'He is no earthly good for anything,' Chester mused aloud. 'He would just have done for me. If you only could see a thing as it

is, you would see it's the very thing for him. And besides . . .
Why! it's the most splendid, sure chance' . . . He got angry suddenly. 'I must have a man. There! . . .' He stamped his foot and
smiled unpleasantly. 'Anyhow, I could guarantee the island
wouldn't sink under him—and I believe he is a bit particular on
that point.' 'Good morning,' I said, curtly. He looked at me as
though I had been an incomprehensible fool. . . . 'Must be moving, Captain Robinson,' he yelled suddenly into the old man's
ear. 'These Parsee Johnnies are waiting for us to clinch the bargain.' He took his partner under the arm with a firm grip, swung
him round, and unexpectedly, leered at me over his shoulder. 'I
was trying to do him a kindness,' he asserted with an air and
tone that made my blood boil. 'Thank you for nothing—in his
name,' I rejoined. 'Oh! you are devilish smart,' he sneered; 'but
you are like the rest of them. Too much in the clouds. See what
you will do with him.' 'I don't know that I want to do anything
with him.' 'Don't you?' he spluttered; his grey moustache bris-
tled with anger, and by his side the notorious Robinson,
propped on the umbrella, stood with his back to me, as patient
and still as a worn-out cab-horse. 'I haven't found a guano island,' I said. 'It's my belief you wouldn't know one if you were
led right up to it by the hand,' he riposted quickly; 'and in this
world you've got to see a thing first, before you can make use
of it. Got to see it through and through at that, neither more nor
less.' 'And get others to see it, too,' I insinuated, with a glance
at the bowed back by his side. Chester snorted at me. 'His eyes
are right enough—don't you worry. He ain't a puppy.' 'Oh,
dear, no!' I said. 'Come along, Captain Robinson,' he shouted,
with a sort of bullying deference under the rim of the old man's
hat; the Holy Terror gave a submissive little jump. The ghost of
a steamer was waiting for them. Fortune on that fair isle! They
made a curious pair of Argonauts. Chester strode on leisurely,
well set up, portly, and of conquering mien; the other, long,
wasted, drooping, and hooked to his arm, shuffled his withered
shanks with desperate haste."

Chapter Fifteen

I DID not start in search of Jim at once, only because I had really an appointment which I could not neglect. Then, as ill-luck would have it, in my agent's office I was fastened upon by a fellow fresh from Madagascar with a little scheme for a wonderful piece of business. It had something to do with cattle and cartridges and a Prince Ravonalo something; but the pivot of the whole affair was the stupidity of some admiral—Admiral Pierre, I think. Everything turned on that, and the chap couldn't find words strong enough to express his confidence. He had globular eyes starting out of his head with a fishy glitter, bumps on his forehead, and wore his long hair brushed back without a parting. He had a favourite phrase which he kept on repeating triumphantly, 'The minimum of risk with the maximum of profit is my motto. What?' He made my head ache, spoiled my tiffin, but got his own out of me all right; and as soon as I had shaken him off, I made straight for the water-side. I caught sight of Jim leaning over the parapet of the quay. Three native boatmen quarrelling over five annas were making an awful row at his elbow. He didn't hear me come up, but spun round as if the slight contact of my finger had released a catch. 'I was looking,' he stammered. I don't remember what I said, not much anyhow, but he made no difficulty in following me to the hotel.

"He followed me as manageable as a little child, with an obedient air, with no sort of manifestation, rather as though he had been waiting for me there to come along and carry him off. I need not have been so surprised as I was at his tractability. On all the round earth, which to some seems so big and that others affect to consider as rather smaller than a mustard-seed, he had no place where he could—what shall I say?—where he could withdraw. That's it! Withdraw—be alone with his loneliness. He walked by my side very calm, glancing here and there, and once turned his head to look after a Sidiboy fireman in a cut-away coat and yellowish trousers, whose black face had silky gleams like a lump of anthracite coal. I doubt, however, whether he saw anything, or even remained all the time aware of my companionship, because if I had not edged him to the left here, or pulled him to the right there, I believe he would have gone straight before him in any direction till stopped by a wall or some other obstacle. I steered him into my bedroom, and sat down at once to write letters. This was the only place in the world (unless, perhaps, the Walpole Reef—but that was not so handy) where he could have it out with himself without being bothered by the rest of the universe. The damned thing— as he had expressed it—had not made him invisible, but I be- haved exactly as though he were. No sooner in my chair I bent over my writing-desk like a medieval scribe, and, but for the movement of the hand holding the pen, remained anxiously quiet. I can't say I was frightened; but I certainly kept as still as if there had been something dangerous in the room, that at the first hint of a movement on my part would be provoked to pounce upon me. There was not much in the room—you know how these bed-rooms are—a sort of four-poster bedstead under a mosquito-net, two or three chairs, the table I was writing at, a bare floor. A glass door opened on an upstairs verandah, and he stood with his face to it, having a hard time with all possi- ble privacy. Dusk fell; I lit a candle with the greatest economy of movement and as much prudence as though it were an ille- gal proceeding. There is no doubt that he had a very hard time of it, and so had I, even to the point, I must own, of wishing him to the devil, or on Walpole Reef at least. It occurred to me once or twice that, after all, Chester was, perhaps, the man to deal effectively with such a disaster. That strange idealist had found a practical use for it at once—unerringly, as it were. It was enough to make one suspect that, maybe, he really could see the true aspect of things that appeared mysterious or utterly hopeless to less imaginative persons. I wrote and wrote; I liq- uidated all the arrears of my correspondence, and then went on writing to people who had no reason whatever to expect from me a gossipy letter about nothing at all. At times I stole a side- long glance. He was rooted to the spot, but convulsive shud- ders ran down his back; his shoulders would heave suddenly.

He was fighting, he was fighting—mostly for his breath, as it seemed. The massive shadows, cast all one way from the straight flame of the candle, seemed possessed of gloomy consciousness; the immobility of the furniture had to my furtive eyes an air of attention. I was becoming fanciful in the midst of my industrious scribbling; and though, when the scratching of my pen stopped for a moment, there was complete silence and stillness in the room, I suffered from that profound disturbance and confusion of thought which is caused by a violent and menacing uproar—of a heavy gale at sea, for instance. Some of you may know what I mean,—that mingled anxiety, distress, and irritation with a sort of craven feeling creeping in— not pleasant to acknowledge, but which gives a quite special merit to one's endurance. I don't claim any merit for standing the stress of Jim's emotions; I could take refuge in the letters; I could have written to strangers if necessary. Suddenly, as I was taking up a fresh sheet of notepaper, I heard a low sound, the first sound that, since we had been shut up together, had come to my ears in the dim stillness of the room. I remained with my head down, with my hand arrested. Those who have kept vigil by a sickbed have heard such faint sounds in the stillness of the night watches, sounds wrung from a racked body, from a weary soul. He pushed the glass door with such force that all the panes rang: he stepped out, and I held my breath, straining my ears without knowing what else I expected to hear. He was really taking too much to heart an empty formality which to Chester's rigorous criticism seemed unworthy the notice of a man who could see things as they were. An empty formality; a piece of parchment. Well, well. As to the inaccessible guano deposit, that was another story altogether. One could intelligibly break one's heart over that. A feeble burst of many voices mingled with the tinkle of silver and glass floated up from the dining-room below; through the open door the outer edge of the light from my candle fell on his back faintly; beyond all was black; he stood on the brink of a vast obscurity, like a lonely figure by the shore of a sombre and hopeless ocean. There was the Walpole Reef in it—to be sure—a speck in the dark void, a straw for the drowning man.

My compassion for him took the shape of the thought that I wouldn't have liked his people to see him at that moment. I found it trying myself. His back was no longer shaken by his gasps; he stood straight as an arrow, faintly visible and still; and the meaning of this stillness sank to the bottom of my soul like lead into the water, and made it so heavy that for a second I wished heartily that the only course left open for me were to pay for his funeral. Even the law had done with him. To bury him would have been such an easy kindness! It would have been so much in accordance with the wisdom of life, which consists in putting out of sight all the reminders of our folly, of our weakness, of our mortality; all that makes against our efficiency—the memory of our failures, the hints of our undying fears, the bodies of our dead friends. Perhaps he did take it too much to heart. And if so then—Chester's offer. . . . At this point I took up a fresh sheet and began to write resolutely. There was nothing but myself between him and the dark ocean. I had a sense of responsibility. If I spoke, would that motionless and suffering youth leap into the obscurity—clutch at the straw? I found out how difficult it may be sometimes to make a sound. There is a weird power in a spoken word. And why the devil not? I was asking myself persistently while I drove on with my writing. All at once, on the blank page, under the very point of the pen, the two figures of Chester and his antique partner, very distinct and complete, would dodge into view with stride and gestures, as if reproduced in the field of some optical toy. I would watch them for a while. No! They were too phantasmal and extravagant to enter into any one's fate. And a word carries far—very far—deals destruction through time as the bullets go flying through space. I said nothing; and he, out there with his back to the light, as if bound and gagged by all the invisible foes of man, made no stir and made no sound."

Chapter Sixteen

THE time was coming when I should see him loved, trusted, admired, with a legend of strength and prowess forming round his name as though he had been the stuff of a hero. It's true—I assure you; as true as I'm sitting here talking about him in vain. He, on his side, had that faculty of beholding at a hint the face of his desire and the shape of his dream, without which the earth would know no lover and no adventurer. He captured much honour and an Arcadian happiness (I won't say anything about innocence) in the bush, and it was as good to him as the honour and the Arcadian happiness of the streets to another man. Felicity, felicity—how shall I say it?—is quaffed out of a golden cup in every latitude: the flavour is with you—and you alone, and you can make it as intoxicating as you please. He was of the sort that would drink deep, as you may guess from what went before. I found him, if not exactly intoxicated, then at least flushed with the elixir at his lips. He had not obtained it at once. There had been, as you know, a period of probation amongst infernal ship-chandlers, during which he had suffered and I had worried about—about—my trust—you may call it. I don't know that I am completely reassured now, after beholding him in all his brilliance. That was my last view of him—in a strong light, dominating, and yet in complete accord with his surroundings—with the life of the forests and with his surroundings—with the life of the forests and with the life of men. I own that I was impressed, but I must admit to myself that after all this is not the lasting impression. He was protected by his isolation, alone of his own superior kind, in close touch with Nature, that keeps faith on such easy terms with her lovers. But I cannot fix before my eye the image of his safety. I shall always remember him as seen through the open door of my room, taking, perhaps, too much to heart the mere consequences of his failure. I am pleased, of course, that some good—and even some splendour—came out of my endeavours; but at times it seems to me it would have

been better for my peace of mind if I had not stood between
him and Chester's confoundedly generous offer. I wonder what
his exuberant imagination would have made of Walpole islet—
that most hopelessly forsaken crumb of dry land on the face of
the waters. It is not likely I would ever have heard, for I must
tell you that Chester, after calling at some Australian port to
patch up his brig-rigged sea-anachronism, steamed out into the
Pacific with a crew of twenty-two hands all told, and the only
news having a possible bearing upon the mystery of his fate
was the news of a hurricane which is supposed to have swept
in its course over the Walpole shoals, a month or so afterwards.
Not a vestige of the Argonauts ever turned up; not a sound
came out of the waste. Finis! The Pacific is the most discreet
of live, hot-tempered oceans: the chilly Antarctic can keep a
secret, too, but more in the manner of a grave.

"And there is a sense of blessed finality in such discretion,
which is what we all more or less sincerely are ready to
admit—for what else is it that makes the idea of death supportable? End! Finis! the potent word that exorcises from the
house of life the haunting shadow of fate. This is what—
notwithstanding the testimony of my eyes and his own earnest
assurances—I miss when I look back upon Jim's success.
While there's life there is hope, truly; but there is fear, too. I
don't mean to say that I regret my action, nor will I pretend
that I can't sleep o' nights in consequence; still the idea ob-
trudes itself that he made so much of his disgrace while it is the
guilt alone that matters. He was not—if I may say so—clear to
me. He was not clear. And there is a suspicion he was not clear
to himself either. There were his fine sensibilities, his fine feelings, his fine longings—a sort of sublimated, idealised selfishness. He was—if you allow me to say so—very fine; very
fine—and very unfortunate. A little coarser nature would not
have borne the strain; it would have had to come to terms with
itself—with a sigh, with a grunt, or even with a guffaw; a still
coarser one would have remained invulnerably ignorant and
completely uninteresting.

"But he was too interesting or too unfortunate to be thrown
to the dogs, or even to Chester. I felt this while I sat with my

face over the paper and he fought and gasped, struggling for
his breath in that terrible stealthy way, in my room; I felt it
when he rushed out on the verandah as if to fling himself
over—and didn't; I felt it more and more all the time he remained outside, faintly lighted on the background of night, as
if standing on the shore of a sombre and hopeless sea.

"An abrupt heavy rumble made me lift my head. The noise
seemed to roll away, and suddenly a searching and violent
glare fell on the blind face of the night. The sustained and dazzling flickers seemed to last for an unconscionable time. The
growl of the thunder increased steadily while I looked at him,
distinct and black, planted solidly upon the shores of a sea of
light. At the moment of greatest brilliance the darkness leaped
back with a culminating crash, and he vanished before my dazzled eyes as utterly as though he had been blown to atoms. A
blustering sigh passed; furious hands seemed to tear at the
shrubs, shake the tops of the trees below, slam doors, break
window-panes, all along the front of the building. He stepped
in, closing the door behind him, and found me bending over
the table; my sudden anxiety as to what he would say was very
great, and akin to fright. 'May I have a cigarette?' he asked. I
gave a push to the box without raising my head. 'I want—
want—tobacco,' he muttered. I became extremely buoyant.
'Just a moment,' I grunted, pleasantly. He took a few steps here
and there. 'That's over,' I heard him say. A single distant clap
of thunder came from the sea like a gun of distress. 'The mon-
soon breaks up early this year,' he remarked, conversationally,
somewhere behind me. This encouraged me to turn round,
which I did as soon as I had finished addressing the last envelope. He was smoking greedily in the middle of the room, and
though he heard the stir I made, he remained with his back to
me for a time.

"'Come—I carried it off pretty well,' he said, wheeling suddenly. 'Something's paid off—not much. I wonder what's to
come.' His face did not show any emotion, only it appeared a
little darkened and swollen, as though he had been holding his
breath. He smiled reluctantly as it were, and went on while I
gazed up at him mutely. . . . 'Thank you, though—your

room—jolly convenient—for a chap—badly hipped.' . . . The
rain pattered and swished in the garden; a water-pipe (it must
have had a hole in it) performed just outside the window a par-
ody of blubbering woe with funny sobs and gurgling lamentations, interrupted by jerky spasms of silence. . . . 'A bit of
shelter,' he mumbled and ceased.

"A flash of faded lightning darted in through the black
framework of the windows and ebbed out without any noise. I
was thinking how I had best approach him (I did not want to be
flung off again) when he gave a little laugh. 'No better than a
vagabond now' . . . the end of the cigarette smouldered between his fingers . . . 'without a single—single,' he pronounced slowly; 'and yet . . .' He paused; the rain fell with
redoubled violence. 'Some day one's bound to come upon
some sort of chance to get it all back again. Must!' he whispered, distinctly, glaring at my boots.

"I did not even know what it was he wished so much to regain, what it was he had so terribly missed. It might have been
so much that it was impossible to say. A piece of ass's skin, according to Chester. . . . He looked up at me inquisitively. 'Perhaps. If life's long enough,' I muttered through my teeth with
unreasonable animosity. 'Don't reckon too much on it.'

"'Jove! I feel as if nothing could ever touch me,' he said in
a tone of sombre conviction. 'If this business couldn't knock
me over, then there's no fear of there being not enough time
to—climb out, and . . .' He looked upwards.

"It struck me that it is from such as he that the great army of
waifs and strays is recruited, the army that marches down,
down into all the gutters of the earth. As soon as he left my
room, that 'bit of shelter,' he would take his place in the ranks,
and begin the journey towards the bottomless pit. I at least had
no illusions; but it was I, too, who a moment ago had been so
sure of the power of words, and now was afraid to speak, in the
same way one dares not move for fear of losing a slippery
hold. It is when we try to grapple with another man's intimate
need that we perceive how incomprehensible, wavering, and
misty are the beings that share with us the sight of the stars and
the warmth of the sun. It is as if loneliness were a hard and ab-

solute condition of existence; the envelope of flesh and blood
on which our eyes are fixed melts before the outstretched
hand, and there remains only the capricious, unconsolable, and
elusive spirit that no eye can follow, no hand can grasp. It was
the fear of losing him that kept me silent, for it was borne upon
me suddenly and with unaccountable force that should I let
him slip away into the darkness I would never forgive myself.

"'Well. Thanks—once more. You've been—er—uncommonly—really there's no word to . . . Uncommonly! I don't
know why, I am sure. I am afraid I don't feel as grateful as I
would if the whole thing hadn't been so brutally sprung on me.
Because at bottom . . . you, yourself . . .' He stuttered.

"'Possibly,' I struck in. He frowned.

"'All the same, one is responsible.' He watched me like a hawk.

"'And that's true, too,' I said.

"'Well. I've gone with it to the end, and I don't intend to let
any man cast it in my teeth without—without—resenting it.'
He clenched his fist.

"'There's yourself,' I said with a smile—mirthless enough,
God knows—but he looked at me menacingly. 'That's my business,' he said. An air of indomitable resolution came and went
upon his face like a vain and passing shadow. Next moment he
looked a dear good boy in trouble, as before. He flung away the
cigarette. 'Good-bye,' he said, with the sudden haste of a man
who had lingered too long in view of a pressing bit of work
waiting for him; and then for a second or so he made not the
slightest movement. The downpour fell with the heavy uninterrupted rush of a sweeping flood, with a sound of unchecked
overwhelming fury that called to one's mind the images of col-
lapsing bridges, of uprooted trees, of undermined mountains. No
man could breast the colossal and headlong stream that seemed
to break and swirl against the dim stillness in which we were
precariously sheltered as if on an island. The perforated pipe
gurgled, choked, spat, and splashed in odious ridicule of a swim-
mer fighting for his life. 'It is raining,' I remonstrated, 'and
I . . .' 'Rain or shine,' he began, brusquely, checked himself, and
walked to the window. 'Perfect deluge,' he muttered after a
while; he leaned his forehead on the glass. 'It's dark, too.'

"'Yes, it is very dark,' I said.

"He pivoted on his heels, crossed the room, and had actually opened the door leading into the corridor before I leaped up from my chair. 'Wait,' I cried, 'I want you to . . .' 'I can't dine with you again to-night,' he flung at me, with one leg out of the room already. 'I haven't the slightest intention to ask you,' I shouted. At this he drew back his foot, but remained mistrustfully in the very doorway. I lost no time in entreating him earnestly not to be absurd; to come in and shut the door."

Chapter Seventeen

HE came in at last; but I believe it was mostly the rain that did it; it was falling just then with a devastating violence which quieted down gradually while we talked. His manner was very sober and set; his bearing was that of a naturally taciturn man possessed by an idea. My talk was of the material aspect of his position; it had the sole aim of saving him from the degradation, ruin, and despair that out there close so swiftly upon a friendless, homeless man; I pleaded with him to accept my help; I argued reasonably; and every time I looked up at that absorbed smooth face, so grave and youthful, I had a disturbing sense of being no help but rather an obstacle in some mysterious, inexplicable, impalpable striving of his wounded spirit.

"'I suppose you intend to eat and drink and to sleep under shelter in the usual way,' I remember saying with irritation. 'You say you won't touch the money that is due you.' . . . He came as near as his sort can to making a gesture of horror. (There were three weeks and five days' pay owing him as mate of the *Patna*.) 'Well, that's too little to matter anyhow; but what will you do to-morrow? Where will you turn? You must live . . .' 'That isn't the thing,' was the comment that escaped him under his breath. I ignored it, and went on combating what I assumed to be the scruples of an exaggerated delicacy. 'On every conceivable ground,' I concluded, 'you must let me help you.' 'You can't,' he said very simply and gently, and holding fast to some deep idea which I could detect shimmering like a pool of water in the dark, but which I despaired of ever approaching near enough to fathom. I surveyed his well-proportioned bulk. 'At any rate,' I said, 'I am able to help what I can see of you. I don't pretend to do more.' He shook his head skeptically without looking at me. I got very warm. 'But I can,' I insisted. 'I can do even more. I *am* doing more. I am trusting you . . .' 'The money . . .' he began. 'Upon my word you deserve being told to go to the devil,' I cried, forcing the note of indignation. He was startled, smiled, and I pressed my attack home. 'It isn't a question of money at all. You are too superficial,' I said (and at the same time I was thinking to myself: Well, here goes! And perhaps he is after all). 'Look at the letter I want you to take. I am writing to a man of whom I've never asked a favour, and I am writing about you in terms that one only ventures to use when speaking of an intimate friend. I make myself unreservedly responsible for you. That's what I am doing. And really if you will only reflect a little what that means . . .'

"He lifted his head. The rain had passed away; only the water-pipe went on shedding tears with an absurd drip, drip outside the window. It was very quiet in the room, whose shadows huddled together in corners, away from the still flame of the candle flaring upright in the shape of a dagger; his face after a while seemed suffused by a reflection of a soft light as if the dawn had broken already.

"'Jove!' he gasped out. 'It is noble of you!'

"Had he suddenly put out his tongue at me in derision, I could not have felt more humiliated. I thought to myself—Serve me right for a sneaking humbug. . . . His eyes shone straight into my face, but I perceived it was not a mocking brightness. All at once he sprang into jerky agitation, like one of those flat wooden figures that are worked by a string. His arms went up, then came down with a slap. He became another man altogether. 'And I had never seen,' he shouted; then suddenly bit his lip and frowned. 'What a bally ass I've been,' he cried very slow in an awed tone. . . . 'You are a brick,' he cried next in a muffled

voice. He snatched my hand as though as he had just then seen
it for the first time, and dropped it at once. 'Why! this is what
I—you—I . . .' he stammered, and then with a return of his old
stolid, I may say mulish manner he began heavily, 'I would be a
brute now if I . . .' and then his voice seemed to break. 'That's
all right,' I said. I was almost alarmed by this display of feeling,
through which pierced a strange elation. I had pulled the string
accidentally, as it were; I did not fully understand the working of
the toy. 'I must go now,' he said. 'Jove! You *have* helped me.
Can't sit still. The very thing . . .' He looked at me with puzzled
admiration. 'The very thing . . .'

   "Of course it was the thing. It was ten to one that I had saved
him from starvation—of that peculiar sort that is almost invariably associated with drink. This was all. I had not a single
illusion on that score, but looking at him, I allowed myself to
wonder at the nature of the one he had, within the last three
minutes, so evidently taken into his bosom. I had forced into
his hand the means to carry on decently the serious business of
life, to get food, drink, and shelter of the customary kind while
his wounded spirit, like a bird with a broken wing, might hop
and flutter into some hole to die quietly of inanition there. This
is what I had thrust upon him: a definitely small thing; and—
behold!—by the manner of its reception it loomed in the dim
light of the candle like a big, indistinct, perhaps a dangerous
shadow. 'You don't mind me not saying anything appropriate,'
he burst out. 'There isn't anything one could say. Last night already you had done me no end of good. Listening to me—you
know. I give you my word I've thought more than once the top
of my head would fly off . . .' He darted—positively darted—
here and there, rammed his hands into his pockets, jerked them
out again, flung his cap on his head. I had no idea it was in him
to be so airily brisk. I thought of a dry leaf imprisoned in an
eddy of wind, while a mysterious apprehension, a load of indefinite doubt, weighed me down in my chair. He stood stock-
still, as if struck motionless by a discovery. 'You have given
me confidence,' he declared, soberly. 'Oh! for God's sake, my
dear fellow—don't!' I entreated, as though he had hurt me.
'All right. I'll shut up now and henceforth. Can't prevent me

thinking though. . . . Never mind! . . . I'll show yet . . .' He went to the door in a hurry, paused with his head down, and came back, stepping deliberately. 'I always thought that if a fellow could begin with a clean slate . . . And now you . . . in a measure . . . yes . . . clean slate.' I waved my hand, and he marched out without looking back; the sound of his footfalls died out gradually behind the closed door—the unhesitating tread of a man walking in broad daylight.

"But as to me, left alone with the solitary candle, I remained strangely unenlightened. I was no longer young enough to behold at every turn the magnificence that besets our insignificant footsteps in good and in evil. I smiled to think that, after all, it was yet he, of us two, who had the light. And I felt sad. A clean slate, did he say? As if the initial word of each our destiny were not graven in imperishable characters upon the face of a rock."

Chapter Eighteen

Six months afterwards my friend (he was a cynical, more than middle-aged bachelor, with a reputation for eccentricity, and owned a rice-mill) wrote to me, and judging, from the warmth of my recommendation, that I would like to hear, enlarged a little upon Jim's perfections. These were apparently of a quiet and effective sort. 'Not having been able so far to find more in my heart than a resigned toleration for an individual of my kind, I have lived till now alone in a house that even in this steaming climate could be considered as too big for one man. I have had him to live with me for some time past. It seems I haven't made a mistake.' It seemed to me on reading this letter that my friend had found in his heart more than tolerance for Jim,—that there were the beginnings of active liking. Of course he stated his grounds in a characteristic way. For one thing, Jim kept his freshness in the climate. Had he been a girl—my friend wrote—

one could have said he was blooming—blooming modestly—
like a violet, not like some of these blatant tropical flowers. He
had been in the house for six weeks, and had not as yet at-
tempted to slap him on the back, or address him as 'old boy,' or
try to make him feel a superannuated fossil. He had nothing of
the exasperating young man's chatter. He was good-tempered,
had not much to say for himself, was not clever by any means,
thank goodness—wrote my friend. It appeared, however, that
Jim was clever enough to be quietly appreciative of his wit,
while, on the other hand, he amused him by his naïveness. 'The
dew is yet on him, and since I had the bright idea of giving him
a room in the house and having him at meals I feel less withered
myself. The other day he took it into his head to cross the room
with no other purpose but to open a door for me; and I felt more
in touch with mankind than I had been for years. Ridiculous,
isn't it? Of course I guess there is something—some awful little
scrape—which you know all about—but if I am sure that it is
terribly heinous, I fancy one could manage to forgive it. For my
part, I declare I am unable to imagine him guilty of anything
much worse than robbing an orchard. Is *it* much worse? Perhaps
you ought to have told me; but it is such a long time since we
both turned saints that you may have forgotten we, too, had
sinned in our time? It may be that some day I shall have to ask
you, and then I shall expect to be told. I don't care to question
him myself till I have some idea what it is. Moreover, it's too
soon as yet. Let him open the door a few times more for me. . . .'
Thus my friend. I was trebly pleased—at Jim's shaping so well,
at the tone of the letter, at my own cleverness. Evidently I had
known what I was doing. I had read characters aright, and so on.
And what if something unexpected and wonderful were to come
of it? That evening, reposing in a deck-chair under the shade of
my own poop awning (it was in Hong-Kong harbour), I laid on
Jim's behalf the first stone of a castle in Spain.

"I made a trip to the northward, and when I returned I found
another letter from my friend waiting for me. It was the first
envelope I tore open. 'There are no spoons missing, as far as I
know,' ran the first line; 'I haven't been interested enough to
inquire. He is gone, leaving on the breakfast-table a formal lit-

tle note of apology, which is either silly or heartless. Probably both—and it's all one to me. Allow me to say, lest you should have some more mysterious young men in reserve, that I have shut up shop, definitely and for ever. This is the last eccentricity I shall be guilty of. Do not imagine for a moment that I care a hang; but he is very much regretted at tennis-parties, and for my own sake I've told a plausible lie at the club. . . .' I flung the letter aside and started looking through the batch on my table, till I came upon Jim's handwriting. Would you believe it? One chance in a hundred! But it is always that hundredth chance! That little second engineer of the *Patna* had turned up in a more or less destitute state, and got a temporary job of looking after the machinery of the mill. 'I couldn't stand the familiarity of the little beast,' Jim wrote from a seaport seven hundred miles south of the place where he should have been in clover. 'I am now for the time with Egström & Blake, ship-chandlers, as their—well—runner, to call the thing by its right name. For reference I gave them your name, which they know of course, and if you could write a word in my favour it would be a permanent employment.' I was utterly crushed under the ruins of my castle, but of course I wrote as desired. Before the end of the year my new charter took me that way, and I had an opportunity of seeing him.

"He was still with Egström & Blake, and we met in what they called 'our parlour' opening out of the store. He had that moment come in from boarding a ship, and confronted me head down, ready for a tussle. 'What have you got to say for yourself?' I began as soon as we had shaken hands. 'What I wrote you—nothing more,' he said stubbornly. 'Did the fellow blab—or what?' I asked. He looked up at me with a troubled smile. 'Oh, no! He didn't. He made it a kind of confidential business between us. He was most damnably mysterious whenever I came over to the mill; he would wink at me in a respectful manner—as much as to say, "We know what we know." Infernally fawning and familiar—and that sort of thing.' He threw himself into a chair and stared down his legs. 'One day we happened to be alone and the fellow had the cheek to say, "Well, Mr. James"—I was called Mr. James there as if I had been the son—"here we are together once more. This is better than the old ship—ain't it?" . . . Wasn't it appalling, eh? I looked at him, and he put on a knowing air. "Don't you be uneasy, sir," he says. "I know a gentleman when I see one, and I know how a gentleman feels. I hope, though, you will be keeping me on this job. I had a hard time of it, too, along of that rotten old *Patna* racket." Jove! It was awful. I don't know what I should have said or done if I had not just then heard Mr. Denver calling me in the passage. It was tiffin-time, and we walked together across the yard and through the garden to the bungalow. He began to chaff me in this kindly way . . . I believe he liked me . . .'

"Jim was silent for a while.

"'I know he liked me. That's what made it so hard. Such a splendid man! That morning he slipped his hand under my arm. . . . He, too, was familiar with me.' He burst into a short laugh, and dropped his chin on his breast. 'Pah! When I remembered how that mean little beast had been talking to me,' he began suddenly in a vibrating voice. 'I couldn't bear to think of myself . . . I suppose you know . . .' I nodded. . . . 'More like a father,' he cried; his voice sank. 'I would have had to tell him. I couldn't let it go on—could I?' 'Well?' I murmured, after waiting a while. 'I preferred to go,' he said, slowly; 'this thing must be buried.'

"We could hear in the shop Blake upbraiding Egström in an abusive, strained voice. They had been associated for many years, and every day from the moment the doors were opened to the last minute before closing, Blake, a little man with sleek, jetty hair and unhappy, beady eyes, could be heard rowing his partner incessantly with a sort of scathing and plaintive fury. The sound of that ever-lasting scolding was part of the place like the other fixtures; even strangers would very soon come to disregard it completely unless if be perhaps to mutter 'Nuisance,' or to get up suddenly and shut the door of the 'parlour.' Egström himself, a raw-boned, heavy Scandinavian, with a busy manner and immense blonde whiskers, went on directing his people, checking parcels, making out bills or writing letters at a stand-up desk in the shop, and comported himself in that clatter exactly as though he had been stone-deaf. Now and again he would emit a bothered perfunctory 'Sssh,' which neither produced nor was expected to produce the slightest effect. 'They are very decent to me here,' said Jim. 'Blake's a little cad, but Egström's all right.' He stood up quickly, and walking with measured steps to a tripod telescope standing in the window and pointed at the roadstead, he applied his eye to it. 'There's that ship which had been becalmed outside all the morning has got a breeze now and is coming in,' he remarked, patiently; 'I must go and board.' We shook hands in silence, and he turned to go. 'Jim!' I cried. He looked round with his hand on the lock. 'You—you have thrown away something like a fortune.' He came back to me all the way from the door. 'Such a splendid old chap,' he said. 'How could I? How could I?' His lips twitched. '*Here* it does not matter.' 'Oh! you—you—' I began, and had to cast about for a suitable word, but before I became aware that there was no name that would just do, he was gone. I heard outside Egström's deep gentle voice saying cheerily, 'That's the *Sarah W. Granger,* Jimmy. You must manage to be first aboard'; and directly Blake struck in, screaming after the manner of an outraged cockatoo. 'Tell the captain we've got some of his mail here. That'll fetch him. D'ye hear, Mister What's-your-name?' And there was Jim answering Egström with something boyish in his tone. 'All right. I'll make a race of it.' He seemed to take refuge in the boat-sailing part of that sorry business.

"I did not see him again that trip, but on my next (I had a six months' charter) I went up to the store. Ten yards away from the door Blake's scolding met my ears, and when I came in he gave me a glance of utter wretchedness; Egström, all smiles, advanced, extending a large bony hand. 'Glad to see you, captain. . . . Sssh. . . . Been thinking you were about due back here. What did you say, Sir? . . . Sssh. . . . Oh! him! He has left us. Come into the parlour.' . . . After the slam of the door Blake's strained voice became faint, as the voice of one scolding desperately in a wilderness. . . . 'Put us to a great inconvenience, too. Used us badly—I must say . . .' 'Where's he gone to? Do you know?' I asked. 'No. It's no use asking either,' said

Egström, standing bewhiskered and obliging before me with his arms hanging down his sides clumsily and a thin silver watch-chain looped very low on a rucked-up blue serge waist-coat. 'A man like that don't go anywhere in particular.' I was too concerned at the news to ask for the explanation of that pronouncement, and he went on. 'He left—let's see—the very day a steamer with returning pilgrims from the Red Sea put in here with two blades of her propeller gone. Three weeks ago now.' 'Wasn't there something said about the *Patna* case?' I asked, fearing the worst. He gave a start, and looked at me as if I had been a sorcerer. 'Why, yes! How do you know? Some of them were talking about it here. There was a captain or two, the manager of Vanlo's engineering shop at the harbour, two or three others, and myself. Jim was in here, too, having a sand-wich and a glass of beer; when we are busy—you see, cap-tain—there's no time for a proper tiffin. He was standing by this table eating sandwiches, and the rest of us were round the telescope watching that steamer come in; and by and by Vanlo's manager began to talk about the chief of the *Patna*; he had done some repairs for him once, and from that he went on to tell us what an old ruin she was, and the money that had been made out of her. He came to mention her last voyage, and then we all struck in. Some said one thing, and some another—not much—what you or any other man might say; and there was some laughing. Captain O'Brien of the *Sarah W. Granger,* a large, noisy old man with a stick—he was sitting listening to us in this arm-chair here—he let drive suddenly with his stick at the floor, and roars out, "Skunks!" . . . Made us all jump. Vanlo's manager winks at us and asks, "What's the matter, Captain O'Brien?" "Matter! matter!" the old man began to shout; "what are you Injuns laughing at? It's no laughing mat-ter. It's a disgrace to human natur'—that's what it is. I would despise being seen in the same room with one of those men. Yes, sir?" He seemed to catch my eye like, and I had to speak out of civility. "Skunks!" says I, "of course, Captain O'Brien, and I wouldn't care to have them here myself, so you're quite safe in this room, Captain O'Brien. Have a little something cool to drink." "Dam' your drink, Egström," says he, with a twinkle in his eye; "when I want a drink I will shout for it. I am going to quit. It stinks here now." At this all the others burst out laughing, and out they go after the old man. And then, sir, that blasted Jim he puts down the sandwich he had in his hand and walks round the table to me; there was his glass of beer poured out quite full. "I am off," he says—just like this. "It isn't half-past one yet," says I; "you might snatch a smoke first." I thought he meant it was time for him to go down to his work. When I understood what he was up to, my arms fell— so! Can't get a man like that every day, you know, sir; a regular devil for sailing a boat; ready to go out miles to sea to meet ships in any sort of weather. More than once a captain would come in here full of it and the first thing he would say would be, "That's a reckless sort of a lunatic you've got for water-clerk, Egström. I was feeling my way in at daylight under short canvas when there comes flying out of the mist right under my forefoot a boat half under water, sprays going over the mast-head, two frightened niggers on the bottom boards, a yelling fiend at the tiller. Hey! hey! Ship ahoy! ahoy! Captain! Hey! hey! Egström & Blake's man first to speak to you! Hey! hey! Egström & Blake! Hallo! hey! whoop! Kick the niggers—out reefs—a squall on at the time—shoots ahead whooping and yelling to me to make sail and he would give me a lead in— more like a demon than a man. Never saw a boat handled like that in all my life. Couldn't have been drunk—was he? Such a quiet, soft-spoken, chap, too—blush like a girl when he came on board. . . ." I tell you, Captain Marlow, nobody had a chance against us with a strange ship when Jim was out. The other ship-chandlers just kept their old customers, and . . .'

"Egström appeared overcome with emotion.

"'Why, sir—it seemed as though he wouldn't mind going a hundred miles out to sea in an old shoe to nab a ship for the firm. If the business had been his own and all to make yet, he couldn't have done more in that way. And now . . . all at once . . . like this! Thinks I to myself: "Oho! a rise in the screw—that's the trouble—is it? All right," says I, "no need of all that fuss with me, Jimmy. Just mention your figure. Anything in reason." He looks at me as if he wanted to swallow something that stuck in

his throat. "I can't stop with you." "What's the blooming joke?"
I asks. He shakes his head, and I could see in his eye he was as
good as gone already, sir. So I turned to him and slanged him till
all was blue. "What is it you're running away from?" I asks.
"Who has been getting at you? What scared you? You haven't as
much sense as a rat; they don't clear out from a good ship.
Where do you expect to get a better berth?—you this and you
that." I made him look sick, I can tell you. "This business ain't
going to sink," says I. He gave a big jump. "Good-bye," he says,
nodding at me like a lord; "you ain't half a bad chap, Egström. I
give you my word that if you knew my reasons you wouldn't
care to keep me." "That's the biggest lie you ever told in your
life," says I; "I know my own mind." He made me so mad that I
had to laugh. "Can't you really stop long enough to drink this
glass of beer here, you funny beggar, you?" I don't know what
came over him; he didn't seem able to find the door; something
comical, I can tell you, captain. I drank the beer myself. "Well,
if you're in such a hurry, here's luck to you in your own drink,"
says I; "only, you mark my words, if you keep up this game
you'll very soon find that the earth ain't big enough to hold
you—that's all." He gave me one black look, and out he rushed
with a face fit to scare little children.'

"Egström snorted bitterly, and combed one auburn whisker
with knotty fingers. 'Haven't been able to get a man that was
any good since. It's nothing but worry, worry, worry in business. And where might you have come across him, captain, if
it's fair to ask?'

"'He was the mate of the *Patna* that voyage,' I said, feeling
that I owed some explanation. For a time Egström remained
very still, with his fingers plunged in the hair at the side of his
face, and then exploded. 'And who the devil cares about that?'
'I daresay no one,' I began . . . 'And what the devil is he—anyhow—for to go on like this?' He stuffed suddenly his left
whisker into his mouth and stood amazed. 'Jee!' he exclaimed,
'I told him the earth wouldn't be big enough to hold his caper.'

Chapter Nineteen

I HAVE told you these two episodes at length to show his manner of dealing with himself under the new conditions of his life. There were many others of the sort, more than I could count on the fingers of my two hands.

"They were all equally tinged by a high-minded absurdity of intention which made their futility profound and touching. To fling away your daily bread so as to get your hands free for a grapple with a ghost may be an act of prosaic heroism. Men had done it before (though we who have lived know full well that it is not the haunted soul but the hungry body that makes an outcast), and men who had eaten and meant to eat every day had applauded the creditable folly. He was indeed unfortunate, for all his recklessness could not carry him out from under the shadow. There was always a doubt of his courage. The truth seems to be that it is impossible to lay the ghost of a fact. You can face it or shirk it—and I have come across a man or two who could wink at their familiar shades. Obviously Jim was not of the winking sort; but what I could never make up my mind about was whether his line of conduct amounted to shirking his ghost or to facing him out.

"I strained my mental eyesight only to discover that, as with the complexion of all our actions, the shade of difference was so delicate that it was impossible to say. It might have been flight and it might have been a mode of combat. To the common mind he became known as a rolling stone, because this was the funniest part; he did after a time become perfectly known, and even notorious, within the circle of his wanderings (which had a diameter of, say, three thousand miles), in the same way as an eccentric character is known to a whole countryside. For instance, in Bangkok, where he found employment with Yucker Brothers, charterers and teak merchants, it was almost pathetic to see him go about in sunshine hugging his secret, which was known to the very up-country logs on the river. Schomberg, the keeper of the hotel where he boarded, a hirsute

Alsatian of manly bearing and an irrepressible retailer of all
the scandalous gossip of the place, would, with both elbows on
the table, impart an adorned version of the story to any guest
who cared to imbibe knowledge along with the more costly
liquors. 'And, mind you, the nicest fellow you could meet,'
would be his generous conclusion; 'quite superior.' It says a lot
for the casual crowd that frequented Schomberg's establishment that Jim managed to hang out in Bangkok for a whole six
months. I remarked that people, perfect strangers, took to him
as one takes to a nice child. His manner was reserved, but it
was as though his personal appearance, his hair, his eyes, his
smile, made friends for him wherever he went. And, of course,
he was no fool. I heard Siegmund Yucker (native of Switzer-
land), a gentle creature ravaged by a cruel dyspepsia, and so
frightfully lame that his head swung through a quarter of a circle at every step he took, declare appreciatively that for one so
young he was 'of great gabasidy,' as though it had been a mere
question of cubic contents. 'Why not send him up country?' I
suggested anxiously. (Yucker Brothers had concessions and
teak forests in the interior.) 'If he has capacity, as you say, he
will soon get hold of the work. And physically he is very fit.
His health is always excellent.' 'Ach! It's a great ting in dis
goundry to be vree vrom tispep-shia,' sighed poor Yucker en-
viously, casting a stealthy glance at the pit of his ruined stomach. I left him drumming pensively on his desk and muttering,
'Es ist ein idee. Es ist ein idee.' Unfortunately, that very
evening an unpleasant affair took place in the hotel.

"I don't know that I blame Jim very much, but it was a truly
regrettable incident. It belonged to the lamentable species of
bar-room scuffles, and the other party to it was a cross-eyed
Dane of sorts whose visiting card recited under his misbegot-
ten name: first lieutenant in the Royal Siamese Navy. The fellow, of course, was utterly hopeless at billiards, but did not like
to be beaten, I suppose. He had had enough to drink to turn
nasty after the sixth game, and make some scornful remark at
Jim's expense. Most of the people there didn't hear what was
said, and those who had heard seemed to have had all precise
recollection scared out of them by the appalling nature of the

consequences that immediately ensued. It was very lucky for the Dane that he could swim, because the room opened on a verandah and the Menam flowed below very wide and black. A boat-load of Chinamen, bound, as likely as not, on some thieving expedition, fished out the officer of the King of Siam, and Jim turned up at about midnight on board my ship without a hat. 'Everybody in the room seemed to know,' he said, gasping yet from the contest, as it were. He was rather sorry, on general principles, for what had happened, though in this case there had been, he said, 'no option.' But what dismayed him was to find the nature of his burden as well known to everybody as though he had gone about all that time carrying it on his shoulders. Naturally after this he couldn't remain in the place. He was universally condemned for the brutal violence, so unbecoming a man in his delicate position; some maintained he had been disgracefully drunk at the time; others criticised his want of tact. Even Schomberg was very much annoyed. 'He is a very nice young man,' he said, argumentatively, to me, 'but the lieutenant is a first-rate fellow, too. He dines every night at my *table d'hôte,* you know. And there's a billiard-cue broken. I can't allow that. First thing this morning I went over with my apologies to the lieutenant, and I think I've made it all right for myself; but only think, captain, if everybody started such games! Why, the man might have been drowned! And here I can't run out into the next street and buy a new cue. I've got to write to Europe for them. No, no! A temper like that won't do!' . . . He was extremely sore on the subject.

"This was the worst incident of all in his—his retreat. Nobody could deplore it more than myself; for if, as somebody said hearing him mentioned, 'Oh, yes! I know. He has knocked about a good deal out here,' yet he had somehow avoided being battered and chipped in the process. This last affair, however, made me seriously uneasy, because if his exquisite sensibilities were to go the length of involving him in pothouse shindies, he would lose his name of an inoffensive, if aggravating, fool, and acquire that of a common loafer. For all my confidence in him I could not help reflecting that in such

cases from the name to the thing itself is but a step. I suppose
you will understand that by that time I could not think of washing my hands of him. I took him away from Bangkok in my
ship, and we had a longish passage. It was pitiful to see how he
shrank within himself. A seaman, even if a mere passenger,
takes an interest in a ship, and looks at the sea-life around him
with the critical enjoyment of a painter, for instance, looking at
another man's work. In every sense of the expression he is 'on
deck'; but my Jim, for the most part, skulked down below as
though he had been a stowaway. He infected me so that I
avoided speaking on professional matters, such as would sug-
gest themselves naturally to two sailors during a passage. For
whole days we did not exchange a word; I felt extremely un-
willing to give orders to my officers in his presence. Often,
when alone with him on deck or in the cabin, we didn't know
what to do with our eyes.

"I placed him with De Jongh, as you know, glad enough to
dispose of him in any way, yet persuaded that his position
was now growing intolerable. He had lost some of that elasticity which had enabled him to rebound back into his uncompromising position after every overthrow. One day,
coming ashore, I saw him standing on the quay; the water of
the roadstead and the sea in the offing made one smooth ascending plane, and the outermost ships at anchor seemed to
ride motionless in the sky. He was waiting for his boat, which
was being loaded at our feet with packages of small stores for
some vessel ready to leave. After exchanging greetings, we
remained silent—side by side. 'Jove!' he said, suddenly, 'this
is killing work.'

"He smiled at me; I must say he generally could manage a
smile. I made no reply. I knew very well he was not alluding to
his duties; he had an easy time of it with De Jongh. Nevertheless, as soon as he had spoken I became completely convinced
that the work was killing. I did not even look at him. 'Would
you like,' said I, 'to leave this part of the world altogether; try
California or the West Coast? I'll see what I can do . . .' He interrupted me a little scornfully. 'What difference would it
make?' . . . I felt at once convinced that he was right. It would

make no difference; it was not relief he wanted; I seemed to perceive dimly that what he wanted, what he was, as it were, waiting for, was something not easy to define—something in the nature of an opportunity. I had given him many opportunities, but they had been merely opportunities to earn his bread. Yet what more could any man do? The position struck me as hopeless, and poor Brierly's saying recurred to me, 'Let him creep twenty feet underground and stay there.' Better that, I thought, than this waiting above ground for the impossible. Yet one could not be sure even of that. There and then, before his boat was three oars' lengths away from the quay, I had made up my mind to go and consult Stein in the evening.

"This Stein was a wealthy and respected merchant. His 'house' (because it was a house, Stein & Co., and there was some sort of partner who, as Stein said, 'Looked after the Moluccas') had a large inter-island business, with a lot of trading posts established in the most out-of-the-way places for collecting the produce. His wealth and his respectability were not exactly the reasons why I was anxious to seek his advice. I desired to confide my difficulty to him because he was one of the most trustworthy men I had ever known. The gentle light of a simple unwearied, as it were, and intelligent good-nature illuminated his long hairless face. It had deep downward folds, and was pale as of a man who had always led a sedentary life—which was indeed very far from being the case. His hair was thin, and brushed back from a massive and lofty forehead. One fancied that at twenty he must have looked very much like what he was now at three-score. It was a student's face; only the eyebrows nearly all white, thick and bushy, together with the resolute searching glance that came from under them, were not in accord with his, I may say, learned appearance. He was tall and loose-jointed; his slight stoop, together with an innocent smile, made him appear benevolently ready to lend you his ear; his long arms with pale big hands had rare deliberate gestures of a pointing out, demonstrating kind. I speak of him at length, because under his exterior, and in conjunction with an upright and indulgent nature, this man possessed an intrepidity of spirit and a physical courage that could have been called reckless had it not been like a natural function of the body—say good digestion, for instance—completely unconscious of itself. It is sometimes said of a man that he carries his life in his hand. Such a saying would have been inadequate if applied to him; during the early part of his existence in the East he had been playing ball with it. All this was in the past, but I knew the story of his life and the origin of his fortune. He was also a naturalist of some distinction, or perhaps I should say a learned collector. Entomology was his special study. His collection of *Buprestidoe* and *Longicorns*—beetles all—horrible miniature monsters, looking malevolent in death and immobility, and his cabinet of butterflies, beautiful and hovering under the glass of cases on lifeless wings, had spread his fame far over the earth. The name of this merchant, adventurer, sometime adviser of a Malay sultan (to whom he never alluded otherwise than as 'my poor Mohammed Bonso'), had, on account of a few bushels of dead insects, become known to learned persons in Europe, who could have had no conception, and certainly would not have cared to know anything, of his life or character. I, who knew, considered him an eminently suitable person to receive my confidences about Jim's difficulties as well as my own.

Chapter Twenty

LATE in the evening I entered his study, after traversing an imposing but empty dining-room very dimly lit. The house was silent. I was preceded by an elderly grim Javanese servant in a sort of livery of white jacket and yellow sarong, who, after throwing the door open, exclaimed low, 'O master!' and stepping aside, vanished in a mysterious way as though he had been a ghost only momentarily embodied for that particular service. Stein turned round with the chair, and in the same movement his spectacles seemed to get pushed up on his forehead. He welcomed me in his quiet and humorous voice. Only one corner of the vast room, the corner in which stood his writing-desk, was strongly lighted by a shaded reading-lamp, and the rest of the spacious apartment melted into shapeless gloom like a cavern. Narrow shelves filled with dark boxes of uniform shape and colour ran round the walls, not from floor to ceiling, but in a sombre belt about four feet broad. Catacombs of beetles. Wooden tablets were hung above at irregular intervals. The light reached one of them, and the word *Coleoptera* written in gold letters glittered mysteriously upon a vast dimness. The glass cases containing the collection of butterflies were ranged in three long rows upon slender-legged little tables. One of these cases had been removed from its place and stood on the desk, which was bestrewn with oblong slips of paper blackened with minute handwriting.

"'So you see me—so,' he said. His hand hovered over the case where a butterfly in solitary grandeur spread out dark bronze wings, seven inches or more across with exquisite white veinings and a gorgeous border of yellow spots. 'Only one specimen like this they have in *your* London, and then—no more. To my small native town this my collection I shall bequeath. Something of me. The best.'

"He bent forward in the chair and gazed intently, his chin over the front of the case. I stood at his back. 'Marvellous,' he whispered, and seemed to forget my presence. His history was curious. He had been born in Bavaria, and when a youth of twenty-two had taken an active part in the revolutionary movement of 1848. Heavily compromised, he managed to make his escape, and at first found a refuge with a poor republican watchmaker in Trieste. From there he made his way to Tripoli with a stock of cheap watches to hawk about,—not a very great opening truly, but it turned out lucky enough, because it was there he came upon a Dutch traveller—a rather famous man, I believe, but I don't remember his name. It was that naturalist who, engaging him as a sort of assistant, took him to the East. They travelled in the Archipelago together and separately, collecting insects and birds, for four years or more. Then the naturalist went home, and Stein, having no more

home to go to, remained with an old trader he had come across
in his journeys in the interior of Celebes—if Celebes may be
said to have an interior. This old Scotsman, the only white man
allowed to reside in the country at the time, was a privileged
friend of the chief ruler of Wajo States, who was a woman. I
often heard Stein relate how that chap, who was slightly paralysed on one side, had introduced him to the native court a short
time before another stroke carried him off. He was a heavy
man with a patriarchal white beard, and of imposing stature.
He came into the council-hall where all the rajahs, pangerans,
and headmen were assembled, with the queen, a fat wrinkled
woman (very free in her speech, Stein said), reclining on a
high couch under a canopy. He dragged his leg, thumping with
his stick, and grasped Stein's arm, leading him right up to the
couch. 'Look, queen, and you rajahs, this is my son,' he proclaimed in a stentorian voice. 'I have traded with your fathers,
and when I die he shall trade with you and your sons.'

"By means of this simple formality Stein inherited the
Scotsman's privileged position and all his stock-in-trade, together with a fortified house on the banks of the only naviga-
ble river in the country. Shortly afterwards the old queen, who
was so free in her speech, died, and the country became disturbed by various pretenders to the throne. Stein joined the
party of a younger son, the one of whom thirty years later he
never spoke otherwise but as 'my poor Mohammed Bonso.'
They both became the heroes of innumerable exploits; they
had wonderful adventures, and once stood a siege in the Scotsman's house for a month, with only a score of followers
against a whole army. I believe the natives talk of that war to
this day. Meantime, it seems, Stein never failed to annex on his
own account every butterfly or beetle he could lay hands on.
After some eight years of war, negotiations, false truces, sudden outbreaks, reconciliation, treachery, and so on, and just as
peace seemed at last permanently established, his 'poor Mohammed Bonso' was assassinated at the gate of his own royal
residence while dismounting in the highest spirits on his return
from a successful deer-hunt. This event rendered Stein's position extremely insecure, but he would have stayed perhaps had

it not been that a short time afterwards he lost Mohammed's sister ('my dear wife the princess,' he used to say solemnly), by whom he had had a daughter—mother and child both dying within three days of each other from some infectious fever. He left the country, which this cruel loss had made unbearable to him. Thus ended the first and adventurous part of his existence. What followed was so different that, but for the reality of sorrow which remained with him, this strange part must have resembled a dream. He had a little money; he started life afresh, and in the course of years acquired a considerable fortune. At first he had travelled a good deal amongst the islands, but age had stolen upon him, and of late he seldom left his spacious house three miles out of town, with an extensive garden, and surrounded by stables, offices, and bamboo cottages for his servants and dependants, of whom he had many. He drove in his buggy every morning to town, where he had an office with white and Chinese clerks. He owned a small fleet of schooners and native craft, and dealt in island produce on a large scale. For the rest he lived solitary, but not misanthropic, with his books and his collection, classing and arranging specimens, corresponding with entomologists in Europe, writing up a descriptive catalogue of his treasures. Such was the history of the man whom I had come to consult upon Jim's case without any definite hope. Simply to hear what he would have to say would have been a relief. I was very anxious, but I respected the intense, almost passionate, absorption with which he looked at a butterfly, as though on the bronze sheen of these frail wings, in the white tracings, in the gorgeous markings, he could see other things, an image of something as perishable and defying destruction as these delicate and lifeless tissues displaying a splendour unmarred by death.

"'Marvellous!' he repeated, looking up at me. 'Look! The beauty—but that is nothing—look at that accuracy, the harmony. And so fragile! And so strong! And so exact! This is Nature—the balance of colossal forces. Every star is so—and every blade of grass stands *so*—and the mighty Kosmos in perfect equilibrium produces—this. This wonder; this masterpiece of Nature—the great artist.'

" 'Never heard an entomologist go on like this,' I observed, cheerfully. 'Masterpiece! And what of man?'

" 'Man is amazing, but he is not a masterpiece,' he said, keeping his eyes fixed on the glass case. 'Perhaps the artist was a little mad. Eh? What do you think? Sometimes it seems to me that man is come where he is not wanted, where there is no place for him; for if not, why should he want all the place? Why should he run about here and there making a great noise about himself, talking about the stars, disturbing the blades of grass? . . .'

" 'Catching butterflies,' I chimed in.

"He smiled, threw himself back in his chair, and stretched his legs. 'Sit down,' he said. 'I captured this rare specimen myself one very fine morning. And I had a very big emotion. You don't know what it is for a collector to capture such a rare specimen. You can't know.'

"I smiled at my ease in a rocking-chair. His eyes seemed to look far beyond the wall at which they stared; and he narrated how, one night, a messenger arrived from his 'poor Mohammed,' requiring his presence at the 'residenz'—as he called it—which was distant some nine or ten miles by a bridle-path over a cultivated plain, with patches of forest here and there. Early in the morning he started from his fortified house, after embracing his little Emma, and leaving the 'princess,' his wife, in command. He described how she came with him as far as the gate, walking with one hand on the neck of his horse; she had on a white jacket, gold pins in her hair, and a brown leather belt over her left shoulder with a revolver in it. 'She talked as women will talk,' he said, 'telling me to be careful, and to try to get back before dark, and what a great wickedness it was for me to go alone. We were at war, and the country was not safe; my men were putting up bullet-proof shutters to the house and loading their rifles, and she begged me to have no fear for her. She could defend the house against anybody till I returned. And I laughed with pleasure a little. I liked to see her so brave and young and strong. I, too, was young then. At the gate she caught hold of my hand and gave it one squeeze and fell back. I made my horse stand still outside till I heard the bars of the gate put up behind me. There was a great enemy of

mine, a great noble—and a great rascal, too—roaming with a
band in the neighbourhood. I cantered for four or five miles;
there had been rain in the night, but the mists had gone up,
up—and the face of the earth was clean; it lay smiling to me,
so fresh and innocent—like a little child. Suddenly somebody
fires a volley—twenty shots at least it seemed to me. I hear
bullets sing in my ear, and my hat jumps to the back of my
head. It was a little intrigue, you understand. They got my poor
Mohammed to send for me and then laid that ambush. I see it
all in a minute, and I think— This wants a little management.
My pony snort, jump, and stand and I fall slowly, forward with
my head on his mane. He begins to walk, and with one eye I
could see over his neck a faint cloud of smoke hanging in front
of a clump of bamboos to my left. I think— Aha! my friends,
why you not wait long enough before you shoot? This is not
yet *gelungen*. Oh, no! I get hold of my revolver with my right
hand—quiet—quiet. After all, there were only seven of these
rascals. They get up from the grass and start running with their
sarongs tucked up, waving spears above their heads, and
yelling to each other to look out and catch the horse, because I
was dead. I let them come as close as the door here, and then
bang, bang, bang—take aim each time, too. One more shot I
fire at a man's back, but I miss. Too far already. And then I sit
alone on my horse with the clean earth smiling at me, and there
are the bodies of three men lying on the ground. One was
curled up like a dog, another on his back had an arm over his
eyes as if to keep off the sun, and the third man he draws up his
leg very slowly and makes it with one kick straight again. I
watch him very carefully from my horse, but there is no
more—*bleibt ganz ruhig*—keep still, so. And as I looked at his
face for some sign of life I observed something like a faint
shadow pass over his forehead. It was the shadow of this butterfly. Look at the form of the wing. This species fly high with
a strong flight. I raised my eyes and I saw him fluttering away.
I think— Can it be possible? And then I lost him. I dismounted
and went on very slow, leading my horse and holding my revolver with one hand and my eyes darting up and down and
right and left, everywhere! At last I saw him sitting on a small

heap of dirt ten feet away. At once my heart began to beat quick. I let go my horse, keep my revolver in one hand, and with the other snatch my soft felt hat off my head. One step. Steady. Another step. Flop! I got him! When I got up I shook like a leaf with excitement, and when I opened these beautiful wings and made sure what a rare and so extraordinary perfect specimen I had, my head went round and my legs became so weak with emotion that I had to sit on the ground. I had greatly desired to possess myself of a specimen of that species when collecting for the professor. I took long journeys and underwent great privations; I had dreamed of him in my sleep, and here suddenly I had him in my fingers—for myself! In the words of the poet' (he pronounced it 'boet')—

> So halt' ich's endlich denn in meinen Händen,
> Und nenn' es in gewissem Sinne mein.

He gave to the last word the emphasis of a suddenly lowered voice, and withdrew his eyes slowly from my face. He began to charge a long-stemmed pipe busily and in silence, then, pausing with his thumb on the orifice of the bowl, looked again at me significantly.

"'Yes, my good friend. On that day I had nothing to desire; I had greatly annoyed my principal enemy; I was young, strong; I had friendship; I had the love' (he said 'lof') 'of woman, a child I had, to make my heart very full—and even what I had once dreamed in my sleep had come into my hand, too!'

"He struck a match, which flared violently. His thoughtful placid face twitched once.

"'Friend, wife, child,' he said, slowly, gazing at the small flame—'phoo!' The match was blown out. He sighed and turned again to the glass case. The frail and beautiful wings quivered faintly, as if his breath had for an instant called back to life that gorgeous object of his dreams.

"'The work,' he began, suddenly, pointing to the scattered slips, and in his usual gentle and cheery tone, 'is making great progress. I have been this rare specimen describing. . . . Na! And what is your good news?'

"'To tell the truth, Stein,' I said with an effort that surprised me, 'I came here to describe a specimen. . . .'

"'Butterfly?' he asked, with an unbelieving and humorous eagerness.

"'Nothing so perfect,' I answered, feeling suddenly dispirited with all sorts of doubts. 'A man!'

"'*Ach* so?' he murmured, and his smiling countenance, turned to me, became grave. Then after looking at me for a while he said slowly, 'Well—I am a man, too.'

"Here you have him as he was; he knew how to be so generously encouraging as to make a scrupulous man hesitate on the brink of confidence; but if I did hesitate it was not for long.

"He heard me out, sitting with crossed legs. Sometimes his head would disappear completely in a great eruption of smoke, and a sympathetic growl would come out from the cloud. When I finished he uncrossed his legs, laid down his pipe, leaned forward towards me earnestly with his elbows on the arms of his chair, the tips of his fingers together.

"'I understand very well. He is romantic.'

"He had diagnosed the case for me, and at first I was quite startled to find how simple it was; and indeed our conference resembled so much a medical consultation—Stein, of learned aspect, sitting in an arm-chair before his desk; I, anxious, in another, facing him, but a little to one side—that it seemed natural to ask—

"'What's good for it?'

"He lifted up a long forefinger.

"'There is only one remedy! One thing alone can us from being ourselves cure!' The finger came down on the desk with a smart rap. The case which he had made to look so simple before became if possible still simpler—and altogether hopeless. There was a pause. 'Yes,' said I, 'strictly speaking, the question is not how to get cured, but how to live.'

"He approved with his head, a little sadly as it seemed. '*Ja! ja!* In general, adapting the words of your great poet: That is the question. . . .' He went on nodding sympathetically. . . . 'How to be! *Ach!* How to be.'

"He stood up with the tips of his fingers resting on the desk.

"'We want in so many different ways to be,' he began again. 'This magnificent butterfly finds a little heap of dirt and sits still on it; but man he will never on his heap of mud keep still. He want to be so, and again he want to be so. . . .' He moved his hand up, then down. . . . 'He wants to be a saint, and he wants to be a devil—and every time he shuts his eyes he sees himself as a very fine fellow—so fine as he can never be. . . . In a dream. . . .'

"He lowered the glass lid, the automatic lock clicked sharply, and taking up the case in both hands he bore it religiously away to its place, passing out of the bright circle of the lamp into the ring of fainter light—into shapeless dusk at last. It had an odd effect—as if these few steps had carried him out of this concrete and perplexed world. His tall form, as though robbed of its substance, hovered noiselessly over invisible things with stooping and indefinite movements; his voice, heard in that remoteness where he could be glimpsed mysteriously busy with immaterial cares, was no longer incisive, seemed to roll voluminous and grave—mellowed by distance.

"'And because you not always can keep your eyes shut there comes the real trouble—the heart pain—the world pain. I tell you, my friend, it is not good for you to find you cannot make your dream come true, for the reason that you not strong enough are, or not clever enough. *Ja!* . . . And all the time you are such a fine fellow, too! *Wie? Was? Gott in Himmel!* How can that be? Ha! ha! ha!'

"The shadow prowling amongst the graves of butterflies laughed boisterously.

"'Yes! Very funny this terrible thing is. A man that is born falls into a dream like a man who falls into the sea. If he tries to climb out into the air as inexperienced people endeavour to do, he drowns—*nicht wahr?* . . . No! I tell you! The way is to the destructive element submit yourself, and with the exertions of your hands and feet in the water make the deep, deep sea keep you up. So if you ask me—how to be?'

"His voice leaped up extraordinarily strong, as though away there in the dusk he had been inspired by some whisper of knowledge. 'I will tell you! For that, too, there is only one way.'

"With a hasty swish swish of his slippers he loomed up in the ring of faint light, and suddenly appeared in the bright circle of the lamp. His extended hand aimed at my breast like a pistol; his deep-set eyes seemed to pierce through me, but his twitching lips uttered no word, and the austere exaltation of a certitude seen in the dusk vanished from his face. The hand that had been pointing at my breast fell, and by-and-by, coming a step nearer, he laid it gently on my shoulder. There were things, he said mournfully, that perhaps could never be told, only he had lived so much alone that sometimes he forgot—he forgot. The light had destroyed the assurance which had inspired him in the distant shadows. He sat down and, with both elbows on the desk, rubbed his forehead. 'And yet it is true—it is true. In the destructive element immerse.' . . . He spoke in a subdued tone, without looking at me, one hand on each side of his face. 'That was the way. To follow the dream, and again to follow the dream—and so—*ewig—usque ad finem*. . . .' The whisper of his conviction seemed to open before me a vast and uncertain expanse, as of a crepuscular horizon on a plain at dawn—or was it, perchance, at the coming of the night? One had not the courage to decide; but it was a charming and deceptive light, throwing the impalpable poesy of its dimness over pitfalls—over graves. His life had begun in sacrifice, in enthusiasm for generous ideas; he had travelled very far, on various ways, on strange paths, and whatever he followed it had been without faltering, and therefore without shame and without regret. In so far he was right. That was the way, no doubt. Yet for all that the great plain on which men wander amongst graves and pitfalls remained very desolate under the impalpable poesy of its crepuscular light, overshadowed in the centre, circled with a bright edge as if surrounded by an abyss full of flames. When at last I broke the silence it was to express the opinion that no one could be more romantic than himself.

"He shook his head slowly, and afterwards looked at me with a patient and inquiring glance. It was a shame, he said. There we were sitting and talking like two boys, instead of putting our heads together to find something practical—a practical remedy—for the evil—for the great evil—he repeated,

with a humorous and indulgent smile. For all that, our talk did
not grow more practical. We avoided pronouncing Jim's name
as though we had tried to keep flesh and blood out of our discussion, or he were nothing but an erring spirit, a suffering and
nameless shade. 'Na!' said Stein, rising. 'To-night you sleep
here, and in the morning we shall do something practical—
practical. . . .' He lit a two-branched candlestick and led the
way. We passed through empty dark rooms, escorted by
gleams from the lights Stein carried. They glided along the
waxed floors, sweeping here and there over the polished surface of the table, leaped upon a fragmentary curve of a piece of
furniture, or flashed perpendicularly in and out of distant mir-
rors, while the forms of two men and the flicker of two flames
could be seen for a moment stealing silently across the depths
of a crystalline void. He walked slowly a pace in advance with
stooping courtesy; there was a profound, as it were a listening,
quietude on his face; the long flaxen locks mixed with white
threads were scattered thinly upon his slightly bowed neck.

"'He is romantic—romantic,' he repeated. 'And that is very
bad—very bad. . . . Very good, too," he added. 'But *is he?*' I
queried.

"'*Gewiss,*' he said, and stood still holding up the cande-
labrum, but without looking at me. 'Evident! What is it that by
inward pain makes him know himself? What is it that for you
and me makes him—exist?'

"At that moment it was difficult to believe in Jim's existence—starting from a country parsonage, blurred by crowds of
men as by clouds of dust, silenced by the clashing claims of life
and death in a material world—but his imperishable reality
came to me with a convincing, with an irresistible force! I saw
it vividly, as though in our progress through the lofty silent
rooms amongst fleeting gleams of light and the sudden revela-
tions of human figures stealing with flickering flames within
unfathomable and pellucid depths, we had approached nearer to
absolute Truth, which, like Beauty itself, floats elusive, obscure, half submerged, in the silent still waters of mystery. 'Perhaps he is,' I admitted with a slight laugh, whose unexpectedly
loud reverberation made me lower my voice directly; 'but I am

sure you are.' With his head dropping on his breast and the light held high he began to walk again. 'Well—I exist, too,' he said.

"He preceded me. My eyes followed his movements, but what I did see was not the head of the firm, the welcome guest at afternoon receptions, the correspondent of learned societies, the entertainer of stray naturalists; I saw only the reality of his destiny, which he had known how to follow with unfaltering footsteps, that life begun in humble surroundings, rich in generous enthusiasms, in friendship, love, war—in all the exalted elements of romance. At the door of my room he faced me. 'Yes,' I said, as though carrying on a discussion, 'and amongst other things you dreamed foolishly of a certain butterfly; but when one fine morning your dream came in your way you did not let the splendid opportunity escape. Did you? Whereas he ... .' Stein lifted his hand. 'And do you know how many opportunities I let escape; how many dreams I had lost that had come in my way?' He shook his head regretfully. 'It seems to me that some would have been very fine—if I had made them come true. Do you know how many? Perhaps I myself don't know.' 'Whether his were fine or not,' I said, 'he knows of one which he certainly did not catch.' 'Everybody knows of one or two like that,' said Stein; 'and that is the trouble—the great trouble. . . .'

"He shook hands on the threshold, peered into my room under his raised arm. 'Sleep well. And tomorrow we must do something practical—practical. . . .'

"Though his own room was beyond mine I saw him return the way he came. He was going back to his butterflies."

Chapter Twenty-one

I DON'T suppose any of you had ever heard of Patusan?" Marlow resumed, after a silence occupied in the careful lighting of a cigar. "It does not matter; there's many a heavenly body in the lot crowding upon us of a night that mankind had never

heard of, it being outside the sphere of its activities and of no
earthly importance to anybody but to the astronomers who are
paid to talk learnedly about its composition, weight, path—the
irregularities of its conduct, the aberrations of its light—a sort of
scientific scandal-mongering. Thus with Patusan. It was referred
to knowingly in the inner government circles in Batavia, especially as to its irregularities and aberrations, and it was known
by name to some few, very few, in the mercantile world. Nobody, however, had been there, and I suspect no one desired to
go there in person, just as an astronomer, I should fancy, would
strongly object to being transported into a distant heavenly
body, where, parted from his earthly emoluments, he would be
bewildered by the view of an unfamiliar heavens. However, neither heavenly bodies nor astronomers have anything to do with
Patusan. It was Jim who went there. I only meant you to understand that had Stein arranged to send him into a star of the fifth
magnitude the change could not have been greater. He left his
earthly failings behind him and that sort of reputation he had,
and there was a totally new set of conditions for his imaginative
faculty to work upon. Entirely new, entirely remarkable. And he
got hold of them in a remarkable way.

"Stein was the man who knew more about Patusan than anybody else. More than was known in the government circles I
suspect. I have no doubt he had been there, either in his butterfly-
hunting days or later on, when he tried in his incorrigible way
to season with a pinch of romance the fattening dishes of his
commercial kitchen. There were very few places in the Archipelago he had not seen in the original dusk of their being, before light (and even electric light) had been carried into them
for the sake of better morality and—and—well—the greater
profit, too. It was at breakfast of the morning following our talk
about Jim that he mentioned the place, after I had quoted poor
Brierly's remark: 'Let him creep twenty feet underground and
stay there.' He looked up at me with interested attention, as
though I had been a rare insect. 'This could be done, too,' he remarked, sipping his coffee. 'Bury him in some sort,' I explained. 'One doesn't like to do it of course, but it would be the
best thing, seeing what he is.' 'Yes; he is young,' Stein mused.

'The youngest human being now in existence,' I affirmed. '*Schön.* There's Patusan,' he went on in the same tone. . . 'And the woman is dead now,' he added incomprehensibly.

"Of course I don't know that story; I can only guess that once before Patusan had been used as a grave for some sin, transgression or misfortune. It is impossible to suspect Stein. The only woman that had ever existed for him was the Malay girl he called 'My wife the princess,' or, more rarely in moments of expansion, 'the mother of my Emma.' Who was the woman he had mentioned in connection with Patusan I can't say; but from his allusions I understand she had been an educated and very good-looking Dutch-Malay girl, with a tragic or perhaps only a pitiful history, whose most painful part no doubt was her marriage with a Malacca Portuguese who had been clerk in some commercial house in the Dutch colonies. I gathered from Stein that this man was an unsatisfactory person in more ways than one, all being more or less indefinite and offensive. It was solely for his wife's sake that Stein had appointed him manager of Stein & Co.'s trading post in Patusan; but commercially the arrangement was not a success, at any rate for the firm, and now the woman had died, Stein was disposed to try another agent there. The Portuguese, whose name was Cornelius, considered himself a very deserving but ill-used person, entitled by his abilities to a better position. This man Jim would have to relieve. 'But I don't think he will go away from the place,' remarked Stein. 'That has nothing to do with me. It was only for the sake of the woman that I . . . But as I think there is a daughter left, I shall let him, if he likes to stay, keep the old house'

"Patusan is a remote district of a native-ruled State, and the chief settlement bears the same name. At a point on the river about forty miles from the sea, where the first houses come into view, there can be seen rising above the level of the forests the summits of two steep hills very close together, and separated by what looks like a deep fissure, the cleavage of some mighty stroke. As a matter of fact, the valley between is nothing but a narrow ravine; the appearance from the settlement is of one irregularly conical hill split in two, and with the two halves leaning slightly apart. On the third day after the full, the moon, as seen from the open space in front of Jim's house (he had a very fine house in the native style when I visited him), rose exactly behind these hills, its diffused light at first throwing the two masses into intensely black relief, and then the nearly perfect disc, glowing ruddily, appeared, gliding upwards between the sides of the chasm, till it floated away above the summits, as if escaping from a yawning grave in gentle triumph. 'Wonderful effect,' said Jim by my side. 'Worth seeing. Is it not?'

"And this question was put with a note of personal pride that made me smile, as though he had had a hand in regulating that unique spectacle. He had regulated so many things in Patusan! Things that would have appeared as much beyond his control as the motions of the moon and the stars.

"It was inconceivable. That was the distinctive quality of the part into which Stein and I had tumbled him unwittingly, with no other notion than to get him out of the way; out of his own way, be it understood. That was our main purpose, though, I own, I might have had another motive which had influenced me a little. I was about to go home for a time; and it may be I desired, more than I was aware of myself, to dispose of him—to dispose of him, you understand—before I left. I was going home, and he had come to me from there, with his miserable trouble and his shadowy claim, like a man panting under a burden in a mist. I cannot say I had ever seen him distinctly—not even to this day, after I had my last view of him; but it seemed to me that the less I understood the more I was bound to him in the name of that doubt which is the inseparable part of our knowledge. I did not know so much more about myself. And then, I repeat, I was going home—to that home distant enough for all its hearthstones to be like one hearthstone, by which the humblest of us has the right to sit. We wander in our thousands over the face of the earth, the illustrious and the obscure, earning beyond the seas our fame, our money, or only a crust of bread; but it seems to me that for each of us going home must be like going to render an account. We return to face our superiors, our kindred, our friends—those whom we obey, and those whom we love, but even they who have neither, the most free, lonely, irresponsible and bereft of ties,—even those for whom home holds no dear face, no familiar voice,—even they have to meet the spirit that dwells within the land under its sky, in its air, in its valleys, and on its rises, in its fields, in its waters and in its trees—a mute friend, judge, and inspirer. Say what you like, to get its joy, to breathe its peace, to face its truth, one must return with a clear consciousness. All this may seem to you sheer sentimentalism; and indeed very few of us have the will or the capacity to look consciously under the surface of familiar emotions. There are the girls we love, the men we look up to, the tenderness, the friendships, the opportunities, the pleasures! But the fact remains that you must touch your reward with clean hands, lest it turn to dead leaves, to thorns, in your grasp. I think it is the lonely, without a fireside or an affection they may call their own, those who return not to a dwelling but to the land itself, to meet its disembodied, eternal, and unchangeable spirit—it is those who understand best its severity, its saving power, the grace of its secular right to our fidelity, to our obedience. Yes! few of us understand, but we all feel it though, and I say *all* without exception, because those who do not feel do not count. Each blade of grass has its spot on earth whence it draws its life, its strength; and so is man rooted to the land from which he draws his faith together with his life. I don't know how much Jim understood; but I know he felt, he felt confusedly but powerfully, the demand of some such truth or some such illusion—I don't care how you call it, there is so little difference, and the difference means so little. The thing is that in virtue of his feeling he mattered. He would never go home now. Not he. Never. Had he been capable of picturesque manifestations he would have shuddered at the thought and made you shudder, too. But he was not of that sort, though he was expressive enough in his way. Before the idea of going home he would grow desperately stiff and immovable, with lowered chin and pouted lips, and with those candid blue eyes of his glowering darkly under a frown, as if before something unbearable, as if before something revolting. There was imagination in that hard skull of his, over which the thick clustering hair fitted like a cap. As to me, I have no imagination (I would be more certain about him to-day, if I had), and I do not mean to imply that I figured to myself the spirit of the land uprising above the white cliffs of Dover, to ask me what I—returning with no bones broken, so to speak—had done with my very young brother. I could not make such a mistake. I knew very well he was of those about whom there is no inquiry; I had seen better men go out, disappear, vanish utterly, without provoking a sound of curiosity or sorrow. The spirit of the land, as becomes the ruler of great enterprises, is careless of innumerable lives. Woe to the stragglers! We exist only in so far as we hang together. He had straggled in a way; he had not hung on; but he was aware of it with an intensity that made him touching, just as a man's more intense life makes his death more touching than the death of a tree. I happened to be handy, and I happened to be touched. That's all there is to it. I was concerned as to the way he would go out. It would have hurt me if, for instance, he had taken to drink. The earth is so small that I was afraid of, some day, being waylaid by a blear-eyed, swollen-faced besmirched loafer, with no soles to his canvas shoes, and with a flutter of rags about the elbows, who, on the strength of old acquaintance, would ask for a loan of five dollars. You know the awful jaunty bearing of these scarecrows coming to you from a decent past, the rasping careless voice, the half-averted impudent glances—those meetings more trying to a man who believes in the solidarity of our lives than the sight of an impenitent deathbed to a priest. That, to tell you the truth, was the only danger I could see for him and for me; but I also mistrusted my want of imagination. It might even come to something worse, in some way it was beyond my powers of fancy to foresee. He wouldn't let me forget how imaginative he was, and your imaginative people swing farther in any direction, as if given a longer scope of cable in the uneasy anchorage of life. They do. They take to drink, too. It may be I was belittling him by such a fear. How could I tell? Even Stein could say no more than that he was romantic. I only knew he was one of us. And what business had he to be romantic? I am telling you so much about my own instinctive feelings and be-mused reflections because there remains so little to be told of him. He existed for me, and after all it is only through me that he exists for you. I've led him out by the hand; I have paraded him before you. Were my commonplace fears unjust? I won't say—not even now. You may be able to tell better, since the proverb has it that the onlookers see most of the game. At any rate, they were superfluous. He did not go out, not at all; on the contrary, he came on wonderfully, came on straight as a die and in excellent form, which showed that he could stay as well as spurt. I ought to be delighted, for it is a victory in which I had taken my part; but I am not so pleased as I would have ex-pected to be. I ask myself whether his rush had really carried him out of that mist in which he loomed interesting if not very big, with floating outlines—a straggler yearning inconsolably for his humble place in the ranks. And besides, the last word is not said,—probably shall never be said. Are not our lives too short for that full utterance which through all our stammerings is of course our only and abiding intention? I have given up ex-pecting those last words, whose ring, if they could only be pro-nounced, would shake both heaven and earth. There is never time to say our last word—the last word of our love, of our de-sire, faith, remorse, submission, revolt. The heaven and earth must not be shaken. I suppose—at least, not by us who know so many truths about either. My last words about Jim shall be few. I affirm he had achieved greatness; but the thing would be dwarfed in the telling, or rather in the hearing. Frankly, it is not my words that I mistrust but your minds. I could be eloquent were I not afraid you fellows had starved your imaginations to feed your bodies. I do not mean to be offensive; it is re-spectable to have no illusions—and safe—and profitable—and dull. Yet you, too, in your time must have known the intensity of life, that light of glamour created in the shock of trifles, as amazing as the glow of sparks struck from a cold stone—and as short-lived, alas!"

Chapter Twenty-two

THE conquest of love, honour, men's confidence—the pride
of it, the power of it, are fit materials for a heroic tale;
only our minds are struck by the externals of such a success,
and to Jim's successes there were no externals. Thirty miles of
forest shut it off from the sight of an indifferent world, and the
noise of the white surf along the coast overpowered the voice
of fame. The stream of civilisation, as if divided on a head-
land a hundred miles north of Patusan, branches east and
south-east, leaving its plains and valleys, its old trees and its
old mankind, neglected and isolated, such as an insignificant
and crumbling islet between the two branches of a mighty, devouring stream. You find the name of the country pretty often
in collections of old voyages. The seventeenth-century traders
went there for pepper, because the passion for pepper seemed
to burn like a flame of love in the breast of Dutch and English
adventurers about the time of James the First. Where wouldn't
they go for pepper? For a bag of pepper they would cut each
other's throats without hesitation, and would forswear their
souls, of which they were so careful otherwise: the bizarre obstinacy of that desire made them defy death in a thousand
shapes; the unknown seas, the loathsome and strange dis-
eases; wounds, captivity, hunger, pestilence, and despair. It
made them great! By heavens! it made them heroic; and it
made them pathetic, too, in their craving for trade with the inflexible death levying its toll on young and old. It seems impossible to believe that mere greed could hold men to such a
steadfastness of purpose, to such a blind persistence in endeavour and sacrifice. And indeed those who adventured their
persons and lives risked all they had for a slender reward.
They left their bones to lie bleaching on distant shores, so that
wealth might flow to the living at home. To us, their less tried
successors, they appear magnified, not as agents of trade but
as instruments of a recorded destiny, pushing out into the unknown in obedience to an inward voice, to an impulse beating

in the blood, to a dream of the future. They were wonderful; and it must be owned they were ready for the wonderful. They recorded it complacently in their sufferings, in the aspect of the seas, in the customs of strange nations, in the glory of splendid rulers.

"In Patusan they had found lots of pepper, and had been impressed by the magnificence and the wisdom of the Sultan; but somehow, after a century of checkered intercourse, the country seems to drop gradually out of the trade. Perhaps the pepper had given out. Be it as it may, nobody cares for it now; the glory has departed, the Sultan is an imbecile youth with two thumbs on his left hand and an uncertain and beggarly revenue extorted from a miserable population and stolen from him by his many uncles.

"This of course I have from Stein. He gave me their names and a short sketch of the life and character of each. He was as full of information about native States as an official report, but infinitely more amusing. He *had* to know. He traded in so many, and in some districts—as in Patusan, for instance—his firm was the only one to have an agency by special permit from the Dutch authorities. The Government trusted his discretion, and it was understood that he took all the risks. The men he employed understood that, too, but he made it worth their while apparently. He was perfectly frank with me over the breakfast-table in the morning. As far as he was aware (the last news was thirteen months old, he stated precisely), utter insecurity for life and property was the normal condition. There were in Patusan antagonistic forces, and one of them was Rajah Allang, the worst of the Sultan's uncles, the governor of the river, who did the extorting and the stealing, and ground down to the point of extinction the country-born Malays, who, utterly defenseless, had not even the resource of emigrating,—'for indeed,' as Stein remarked, 'where could they go, and how could they get away?' No doubt they did not even desire to get away. The world (which is circumscribed by lofty impassable mountains) has been given into the hand of the high-born, and *this* Rajah they knew; he was of their own royal house. I had the pleasure of meeting the gentleman later on. He was a dirty, little, used-up old man with evil eyes and a weak mouth, who swallowed an opium pill every two hours, and in defiance of common decency wore his hair uncovered and falling in wild stringy locks about his wizened grimy face. When giving audience he would clamber upon a sort of narrow stage erected in a hall like a ruinous barn with a rotten bamboo floor, through the cracks of which you could see twelve or fifteen feet below the heaps of refuse and garbage of all kinds lying under the house. That is where and how he received us when, accompanied by Jim, I paid him a visit of ceremony. There were about forty people in the room, and perhaps three times as many in the great courtyard below. There was constant movement, coming and going, pushing and murmuring, at our backs. A few youths in gay silks glared from the distance; the majority, slaves and humble dependants, were half naked, in ragged sarongs, dirty with ashes and mud-stains. I had never seen Jim look so grave, so self-possessed, in an impenetrable, impressive way. In the midst of these dark-faced men, his stalwart figure in white apparel, the gleaming clusters of his fair hair, seemed to catch all the sunshine that trickled through the cracks in the closed shutters of that dim hall, with its walls of mats and a roof of thatch. He appeared like a creature not only of another kind but of another essence. Had they not seen him come up in a canoe they might have thought he had descended upon them from the clouds. He did, however, come in a crazy dug-out, sitting (very still and with his knees together, for fear of overturning the thing)—sitting on a tin box—which I had lent him—nursing on his lap a revolver of the Navy pattern—presented by me on parting—which, through an interposition of Providence, or through some wrong-headed notion, that was just like him, or else from sheer instinctive sagacity, he had decided to carry unloaded. That's how he ascended the Patusan river. Nothing could have been more prosaic and more unsafe, more extravagantly casual, more lonely. Strange, this fatality that would cast the complexion of a flight upon all his acts, of impulsive unreflecting desertion—of a jump into the unknown.

"It is precisely the casualness of it that strikes me most. Neither Stein nor I had a clear conception of what might be on the other side when we, metaphorically speaking, took him up and hove him over the wall with scant ceremony. At the moment I merely wished to achieve his disappearance. Stein characteristically enough had a sentimental motive. He had a notion of paying off (in kind, I suppose) the old debt he had never forgotten. Indeed he had been all his life especially friendly to anybody from the British Isles. His late benefactor, it is true, was a Scot—even to the length of being called Alexander M'Neil—and Jim came from a long way south of the Tweed; but at the distance of six or seven thousand miles Great Britain, though never diminished, looks foreshortened enough even to its own children to rob such details of their importance. Stein was excusable, and his hinted intentions were so generous that I begged him most earnestly to keep them secret for a time. I felt that no consideration of personal advantage should be allowed to influence Jim; that not even the risk of such influence should be run. We had to deal with another sort of reality. He wanted a refuge, and a refuge at the cost of danger should be offered him—nothing more.

"Upon every other point I was perfectly frank with him, and I even (as I believed at the time) exaggerated the danger of the undertaking. As a matter of fact I did not do it justice; his first day in Patusan was nearly his last—would have been his last if he had not been so reckless or so hard on himself and had condescended to load that revolver. I remember, as I unfolded our precious scheme for his retreat, how his stubborn but weary resignation was gradually replaced by surprise, interest, wonder, and by boyish eagerness. This was a chance he had been dreaming of. He couldn't think how he merited that I . . . He would be shot if he could see to what he owed . . . And it was Stein, Stein the merchant, who . . . but of course it was me he had to . . . I cut him short. He was not articulate, and his gratitude caused me inexplicable pain. I told him that if he owed this chance to any one especially, it was to an old Scot of whom he had never heard, who had died many years ago, of whom little was remembered besides a roaring voice and a rough sort of honesty. There was really no one to receive his thanks. Stein was passing on to a young man the help he had received in his own young days, and I had done no more than to mention his name. Upon this he coloured, and, twisting a bit of paper in his fingers, he remarked bashfully that I had always trusted him.

"I admitted that such was the case, and added after a pause that I wished he had been able to follow my example. 'You think I don't?' he asked uneasily, and remarked in a mutter that one had to get some sort of show first; then brightening up, and in a loud voice he protested he would give me no occasion to regret my confidence, which—which . . .

"'Do not misapprehend,' I interrupted. 'It is not in your power to make me regret anything.' There would be no regrets; but if there were, it would be altogether my own affair: on the other hand, I wished him to understand clearly that this arrangement, this—this—experiment, was his own doing; he was responsible for it and no one else. 'Why? Why,' he stammered, 'this is the very thing that I . . .' I begged him not to be dense, and he looked more puzzled than ever. He was in a fair way to make life intolerable to himself. . . . 'Do you think so?' he asked, disturbed; but in a moment added confidently, 'I was going on though. Was I not?' It was impossible to be angry with him: I could not help a smile, and told him that in the old days people who went on like this were on the way of becoming hermits in a wilderness. 'Hermits be hanged!' he commented with engaging impulsiveness. Of course he didn't mind a wilderness. . . . 'I was glad of it,' I said. That was where he would be going to. He would find it lively enough, I ventured to promise. 'Yes, yes,' he said, keenly. He had shown a desire, I continued inflexibly, to go out and shut the door after him. . . . 'Did I?' he interrupted in a strange access of gloom that seemed to envelop him from head to foot like the shadow of a passing cloud. He was wonderfully expressive after all. Wonderfully! 'Did I?' he repeated, bitterly. 'You can't say I made much noise about it. And I can keep it up, too— only, confound it! You show me a door.' . . . 'Very well. Pass on,' I struck in. I could make him a solemn promise that it

would be shut behind him with a vengeance. His fate, whatever it was, would be ignored, because the country, for all its
rotten state, was not judged ripe for interference. Once he got
in, it would be for the outside world as though he had never existed. He would have nothing but the soles of his two feet to
stand upon, and he would have first to find his ground at that.
'Never existed—that's it, by Jove!' he murmured to himself.
His eyes, fastened upon my lips, sparkled. If he had thoroughly
understood the conditions, I concluded, he had better jump
into the first gharry he could see and drive on to Stein's house
for his final instructions. He flung out of the room before I had
fairly finished speaking.

Chapter Twenty-three

H E DID not return till next morning. He had been kept to
dinner and for the night. There never had been such a
wonderful man as Mr. Stein. He had in his pocket a letter for
Cornelius ('the Johnnie who's going to get the sack,' he explained with a momentary drop in his elation), and he exhib-
ited with glee a silver ring, such as natives use, worn down
very thin and showing faint traces of chasing.

"This was his introduction to an old chap called Doramin—
one of the principal men out there—a big pot—who had been
Mr. Stein's friend in that country where he had all these adventures. Mr. Stein called him 'war-comrade.' War-comrade
was good. Wasn't it? And didn't Mr. Stein speak English wonderfully well? Said he had learned it in Celebes—of all places!
That was awfully funny. Was it not? He did not speak with an
accent—a twang—did I notice? That chap Doramin had given
him the ring. They had exchanged presents when they parted
for the last time. Sort of promising eternal friendship. He
called it fine—did I not? They had to make a dash for dear life
out of the country when that Mohammed—Mohammed—

What's-his-name had been killed. I knew the story, of course. Seemed a beastly shame, didn't it? . . .

"He ran on like this, forgetting his plate, with a knife and fork in hand (he had found me at tiffin), slightly flushed, and with his eyes darkened many shades, which was with him a sign of excitement. The ring was a sort of credential—('It's like something you read of in books,' he threw in appreciatively) and Doramin would do his best for him. Mr. Stein had said, but he—Jim—had his own opinion about that. Mr. Stein was just the man to look out for such accidents. No matter. Accident or purpose, this would serve his turn immensely. Hoped to goodness the jolly old beggar had not gone off the hooks meantime. Mr. Stein could not tell. There had been no news for more than a year; they were kicking up no end of an all-fired row amongst themselves, and the river was closed. Jolly awkward, this; but, no fear; he would manage to find a crack to get in.

"He impressed, almost frightened, me with his elated rattle. He was voluble like a youngster on the eve of a long holiday with a prospect of delightful scrapes, and such an attitude of mind in a grown man and in this connection had in it something phenomenal, a little mad, dangerous, unsafe. I was on the point of entreating him to take things seriously when he dropped his knife and fork (he had begun eating, or rather swallowing food, as it were, unconsciously), and began a search all round his plate. The ring! The ring! Where the devil . . . Ah! Here it was. . . . He closed his big hand on it, and tried all his pockets one after another. Jove! wouldn't do to lose the thing. He meditated gravely over his fist. Had it? Would hang the bally affair round his neck! And he proceeded to do this immediately, producing a string (which looked like a bit of cotton shoelace) for the purpose. There! That would do the trick! It would be the deuce if . . . He seemed to catch sight of my face for the first time, and it steadied him a little. I probably didn't realize, he said with a naïve gravity, how much importance he attached to that token. It meant a friend; and it is a good thing to have a friend. He knew something about that. He nodded at me expressively, but before my disclaiming gesture

he leaned his head on his hand and for a while sat silent, playing thoughtfully with the bread-crumbs on the cloth. . . . 'Slam
the door—that was jolly well put,' he cried, and jumping up,
began to pace the room, reminding me by the set of the shoulders, the turn of his head, the headlong and uneven stride, of
that night when he had paced thus, confessing, explaining—
what you will—but, in the last instance, living—living before
me, under his own little cloud, with all his unconscious sub-
tlety which could draw consolation from the very source of
sorrow. It was the same mood, the same and different, like a
fickle companion that to-day guiding you on the true path,
with the same eyes, the same step, the same impulse, to-
morrow will lead you hopelessly astray. His tread was assured,
his straying, darkened eyes seemed to search the room for
something. One of his footfalls somehow sounded louder than
the other—the fault of his boots probably—and gave a curious
impression of an invisible halt in his gait. One of his hands was
rammed deep into his trousers-pocket, the other waved suddenly above his head. 'Slam the door!' he shouted. 'I've been
waiting for that. I'll show yet . . . I'll . . . I'm ready for any
confounded thing. . . . I've been dreaming of it . . . Jove! Get
out of this. Jove! This is luck at last. . . . You wait. I'll . . .'

"He tossed his head fearlessly, and I confess that for the first
and last time in our acquaintance I perceived myself unexpectedly to be thoroughly sick of him. Why these vapourings? He
was stumping about the room flourishing his arm absurdly, and
now and then feeling on his breast for the ring under his
clothes. Where was the sense of such exaltation in a man appointed to be a trading-clerk, and in a place where there was no
trade—at that? Why hurl defiance at the universe? This was
not a proper frame of mind to approach any undertaking; an
improper frame of mind not only for him, I said, but for any
man. He stood still over me. Did I think so? he asked, by no
means subdued, and with a smile in which I seemed to detect
suddenly something insolent. But then I am twenty years his
senior. Youth *is* insolent; it is its right—its necessity; it has got
to assert itself, and all assertion in this world of doubts is a defiance, is an insolence. He went off into a far corner, and com-

ing back, he, figuratively speaking, turned to rend me. I spoke like that because I—even I, who had been no end kind to him—even I remembered—remembered—against him—what—what had happened. And what about others—the—the—world? Where's the wonder he wanted to get out, meant to get out, meant to stay out—by heavens! And I talked about proper frames of mind!

"'It is not I or the world who remember,' I shouted. 'It is you—you, who remember.'

"He did not flinch, and went on with heat, 'Forget everything, everybody, everybody.' . . . His voice fell. . . . 'But you,' he added.

"'Yes—me, too—if it would help,' I said, also in a low tone. After this we remained silent and languid for a time as if exhausted. Then he began again, composedly, and told me that Mr. Stein had instructed him to wait for a month or so, to see whether it was possible for him to remain, before he began building a new house for himself, so as to avoid 'vain expense.' He did make use of funny expressions—Stein did. 'Vain expense' was good. . . . Remain? Why! of course. He would hang on. Let him only get in—that's all; he would answer for it he would remain. Never get out. It was easy enough to remain.

"'Don't be foolhardy,' I said, rendered uneasy by his threatening tone. 'If you only live long enough you will want to come back.'

"'Come back to what?' he asked, absently, with his eyes fixed upon the face of a clock on the wall.

"I was silent for a while. 'Is it to be never, then?' I said. 'Never,' he repeated, dreamily, without looking at me, and then flew into sudden activity. 'Jove! Two o'clock, and I sail at four!'

"It was true. A brigantine of Stein's was leaving for the westward that afternoon, and he had been instructed to take his passage in her, only no orders to delay the sailing had been given. I suppose Stein forgot. He made a rush to get his things while I went aboard my ship, where he promised to call on his way to the outer roadster. He turned up accordingly in a great hurry and with a small leather valise in his hand. This wouldn't do, and I offered him an old tin trunk of mine supposed to be water-tight, or at least damp-tight. He effected the transfer by the simple process of shooting out the contents of his valise as you would empty a sack of wheat. I saw three books in the tumble; two small in dark covers, and a thick green-and-gold volume—a half-crown complete Shakespeare. 'You read this?' I asked. 'Yes. Best thing to clear up a fellow,' he said, hastily. I was struck by this appreciation, but there was no time for Shakespearian talk. A heavy revolver and two small boxes of cartridges were lying on the cuddy-table. 'Pray take this,' I said. 'It may help you to remain.' No sooner were these words out of my mouth than I perceived what grim meaning they could bear. 'May help you get in,' I corrected myself, remorsefully. He, however, was not troubled by obscure meanings; he thanked me effusively and bolted out, calling Good-bye over his shoulder. I heard his voice through the ship's side urging his boatmen to give way, and looking out of the sternport I saw the boat rounding under the counter. He sat in her leaning forward, exciting his men with voice and gestures; and as he had kept the revolver in his hand and seemed to be presenting it at their heads, I shall never forget the scared faces of the four Javanese, and the frantic swing of their stroke which snatched that vision from under my eyes. Then turning away, the first thing I saw were the two boxes of cartridges on the cuddy-table. He had forgotten to take them.

"I ordered my gig manned at once; but Jim's rowers, under the impression that their lives hung on a thread while they had that madman in the boat, made such excellent time that before I had traversed half the distance between the two vessels I caught sight of him clambering over the rail, and of his box being passed up. All the brigantine's canvas was loose, her mainsail was set, and the windlass was just beginning to clink as I stepped upon her deck: her master, a dapper little half-caste of forty or so, in a blue flannel suit, with lively eyes, his round face the colour of lemon-peel, and with a thin little black moustache drooping on each side of his thick, dark lips, came forward smirking. He turned out, notwithstanding his self-satisfied and cheery exterior, to be of a careworn temperament. In answer to a remark of mine (while Jim had gone below for a moment) he said, 'Oh, yes. Patusan.' He was going to carry the gentleman to the mouth of the river, but would 'never ascend.' His flowing English seemed to be derived from a dictionary compiled by a lunatic. Had Mr. Stein desired him to 'ascend,' he would have 'reverentially'—(I think he wanted to say respectfully—but devil only knows)—'reverentially made objects for the safety of properties.' If disregarded, he would have presented 'resignation to quit.' Twelve months ago he had made his last voyage there, and though Mr. Cornelius 'propitiated many offertories' to Mr. Rajah Allang and the 'principal populations,' on conditions which made the trade 'a snare and ashes in the mouth,' yet his ship had been fired upon from the woods by 'irresponsive parties' all the way down the river; which causing his crew 'from exposure to limb to remain silent in hidings,' the brigantine was nearly stranded on a sandbank at the bar, where she 'would have been perishable beyond the act of man.' The angry disgust at the recollection, the pride of his fluency, to which he turned an attentive ear, struggled for the possession of his broad simple face. He scowled and beamed at me, and watched with satisfaction the undeniable effect of his phraseology. Dark frowns ran swiftly over the placid sea, and the brigantine, with her fore-topsail to the mast and her main-boom amidships, seemed bewildered amongst the cat's-paws. He told me further, gnashing his teeth, that the Rajah was a 'laughable hyæna' (can't imagine how he got hold of hyænas); while somebody else was many times falser than the 'weapons of a crocodile.' Keeping one eye on the movements of his crew forward, he let loose his volubility—comparing the place to a 'cage of beasts made ravenous by long impenitence.' I fancy he meant impunity. He had no intention, he cried, to 'exhibit himself to be made attached purposefully to robbery.' The long-drawn wails, giving the time for the pull of the men catting the anchor, came to an end, and he lowered his voice. 'Plenty too much enough of Patusan,' he concluded, with energy.

"I heard afterwards he had been so indiscreet as to get himself tied up by the neck with a rattan halter to a post planted in the middle of a mud-hole before the Rajah's house. He spent the best part of a day and a whole night in that unwholesome situation, but there is every reason to believe the thing had been meant as a sort of joke. He brooded for a while over that horrid memory, I suppose, and then addressed in a quarrelsome tone the man coming aft to the helm. When he turned to me again it was to speak judicially, without passion. He would take the gentleman to the mouth of the river at Batu Kring (Patusan town 'being situated internally,' he remarked, 'thirty miles'). But in his eyes, he continued—a tone of bored, weary conviction replacing his previous voluble delivery—the gentleman was already 'in the similitude of a corpse.' 'What? What do you say?' I asked. He assumed a startlingly ferocious demeanour, and imitated to perfection the act of stabbing from behind. 'Already like the body of one deported,' he explained, with the insufferably conceited air of his kind after what they imagine a display of cleverness. Behind him I perceived Jim smiling silently at me and with a raised hand checking the exclamation on my lips.

"Then, while the half-caste, bursting with importance, shouted his orders, while the yards swung creaking and the heavy boom came surging over, Jim and I, alone as it were, to leeward of the mainsail, clasped each other's hands and exchanged the last hurried words. My heart was freed from that dull resentment which had existed side by side with interest in his fate. The absurd chatter of the half-caste had given more reality to the miserable dangers of his path than Stein's careful statements. On that occasion the sort of formality that had been always present in our intercourse vanished from our speech; I believe I called him 'dear boy,' and he tacked on the words 'old man' to some half-uttered expression of gratitude, as though his risk set off against my years had made us more equal in age and in feeling. There was a moment of real and profound intimacy, unexpected and short-lived like a glimpse of some everlasting, of some saving truth. He exerted himself to soothe me as though he had been the more mature of the two. 'All right, all right,' he said, rapidly, and with feeling. 'I promise to take care of myself. Yes; I won't take any risks. Not a single blessed risk. Of course not. I mean to hang out. Don't you worry. Jove! I feel as if nothing could touch me. Why! this is luck from the word Go. I wouldn't spoil such a magnificent chance!' . . . A magnificent chance! Well, it *was* magnificent, but chances are what men make them, and how was I to know? As he had said, even I—even I remembered—his—his misfortunes against him. It was true. And the best thing for him was to go.

"My gig had dropped in the wake of the brigantine, and I saw him aft detached upon the light of the westering sun, raising his cap high above his head. I heard an indistinct shout, 'You—shall—hear—of—me.' Of me, or from me, I don't know which. I think it must have been *of* me. My eyes were too dazzled by the glitter of the sea below his feet to see him clearly; I am fated never to see him clearly; but I can assure you no man could have appeared less 'in the similitude of a corpse,' as that half-caste croaker had put it. I could see the little wretch's face, the shape and colour of a ripe pumpkin, poked out somewhere under Jim's elbow. He, too, raised his arm as if for a downward thrust. *Absit omen!*"

Chapter Twenty-four

THE coast of Patusan (I saw it nearly two years afterwards) is straight and sombre, and faces a misty ocean. Red trails are seen like cataracts of rust streaming under the dark green foliage of bushes and creepers clothing the low cliffs. Swampy plains open out at the mouth of the rivers, with a view of jagged blue peaks beyond the vast forests. In the offing a chain of islands, dark, crumbling shapes, stand out in the everlasting sunlit haze like the remnants of a wall breached by the sea.

"There is a village of fisher-folk at the mouth of the Batu Kring branch of the estuary. The river, which had been closed

so long, was open then, and Stein's little schooner, in which I
had my passage, worked her way up in three tides without
being exposed to a fusillade from 'irresponsive parties.' Such a
state of affairs belonged already to ancient history, if I could
believe the elderly headman of the fishing village, who came
on board to act as a sort of pilot. He talked to me (the second
white man he had ever seen) with confidence, and most of his
talk was about the first white man he had ever seen. He called
him Tuan Jim, and the tone of his references was made remarkable by a strange mixture of familiarity and awe. They, in
the village, were under that lord's special protection, which
showed that Jim bore no grudge. If he had warned me that I
would hear of him it was perfectly true. I was hearing of him.
There was already a story that the tide had turned two hours
before its time to help him on his journey up the river. The
talkative old man himself had steered the canoe and had marvelled at the phenomenon. Moreover, all the glory was in his
family. His son and his son-in-law had paddled; but they were
only youths without experience, who did not notice the speed
of the canoe till he pointed out to them the amazing fact.

   "Jim's coming to that fishing village was a blessing; but to
them, as to many of us, the blessing came heralded by terrors.
So many generations had been released since the last white
man had visited the river that the very tradition had been lost.
The appearance of the being that descended upon them and demanded inflexibly to be taken up to Patusan was discomposing; his insistence was alarming; his generosity more than
suspicious. It was an unheard-of request. There was no prece-
dent. What would the Rajah say to this? What would he do to
them? The best part of the night was spent in consultation; but
the immediate risk from the anger of that strange man seemed
so great that at last a cranky dug-out was got ready. The
women shrieked with grief as it put off. A fearless old hag
cursed the stranger.

   "He sat in it, as I've told you, on his tin box, nursing the unloaded revolver on his lap. He sat with precaution—than
which there is nothing more fatiguing—and thus entered the
land he was destined to fill with the fame of his virtues, from

the blue peaks inland to the white ribbon of surf on the coast.
At the first bend he lost sight of the sea with its laboring waves
for ever rising, sinking, and vanishing to rise again—the very
image of struggling mankind—and faced the immovable
forests rooted deep in the soil, soaring towards the sunshine,
everlasting in the shadowy might of their tradition, like life itself. And his opportunity sat veiled by his side like an Eastern
bride waiting to be uncovered by the hand of the master. He,
too, was the heir of a shadowy and mighty tradition! He told
me, however, that he had never in his life felt so depressed and
tired as in that canoe. All the movement he dared to allow himself was to reach, as it were by stealth, after the shell of half a
cocoa-nut floating between his shoes, and bale some of the
water out with a carefully restrained action. He discovered
how hard the lid of a block-tin case was to sit upon. He had
heroic health; but several times during that journey he experienced fits of giddiness, and between whiles he speculated
hazily as to the size of the blister the sun was raising on his
back. For amusement he tried by looking ahead to decide
whether the muddy object he saw lying on the water's edge
was a log of wood or an alligator. Only very soon he had to
give that up. No fun in it. Always alligator. One of them
flopped into the river and all but capsized the canoe. But this
excitement was over directly. Then in a long empty reach he
was very grateful to a troop of monkeys who came right down
on the bank and made an insulting hullabaloo on his passage.
Such was the way in which he was approaching greatness as
genuine as any man ever achieved. Principally, he longed for
sunset; and meantime his three paddlers were preparing to put
into execution their plan of delivering him up to the Rajah.

"'I suppose I might have been stupid with fatigue, or perhaps I did doze off for a time,' he said. The first thing he knew
was his canoe coming to the bank. He became instantaneously
aware of the forest having been left behind, of the first houses
being visible higher up, of a stockade on his left, and of his
boatmen leaping out together upon a low point of land and taking to their heels. Instinctively he leaped out after them. At
first he thought himself deserted for some inconceivable rea-

son, but he heard excited shouts, a gate swung open, and a lot
of people poured out, making towards him. At the same time a
boat full of armed men appeared on the river and came alongside his empty canoe, thus shutting off his retreat.

"'I was too startled to be quite cool—don't you know? And
if that revolver had been loaded I would have shot somebody—perhaps two, three bodies, and that would have been
the end of me. But it wasn't. . . .' 'Why not?' I asked. 'Well, I
couldn't fight the whole population, and I wasn't coming to
them as if I were afraid of my life,' he said, with just a faint
hint of his stubborn sulkiness in the glance he gave me. I refrained from pointing out to him that they could not have
known the chambers were actually empty. He had to satisfy
himself in his own way. . . .'Anyhow it wasn't,' he repeated,
good-humouredly, 'and so I just stood still and asked them
what was the matter. That seemed to strike them dumb. I saw
some of these thieves going off with my box. That long-
legged old scoundrel Kassim (I'll show him to you to-morrow)
ran out fussing at me about the Rajah wanting to see me. I
said, "All right"; I, too, wanted to see the Rajah, and I simply
walked in through the gate and—and—here I am.' He
laughed, and then with unexpected emphasis, 'and do you
know what's the best in it?' he asked. 'I'll tell you. It's the
knowledge that had I been wiped out it is this place that would
have been the loser.'

"He spoke thus to me before his house on that evening I've
mentioned—after we had watched the moon float away
above the chasm between the hills like an ascending spirit out
of a grave; its sheen descended, cold and pale, like the ghost
of dead sunlight. There is something haunting in the light of
the moon; it has all the dispassionateness of a disembodied
soul, and something of its inconceivable mystery. It is to our
sunshine, which—say what you like—is all we have to live
by, what the echo is to the sound: misleading and confusing
whether the note be mocking or sad. It robs all forms of matter—which, after all, is our domain—of their substance, and
gives a sinister reality to shadows alone. And the shadows
were very real around us, but Jim by my side looked very

stalwart, as though nothing—not even the occult power of moonlight—could rob him of his reality in my eyes. Perhaps, indeed, nothing could touch him since he had survived the assault of the dark powers. All was silent, all was still; even on the river the moonbeams slept as on a pool. It was the moment of high water, a moment of immobility that accentuated the utter isolation of this lost corner of the earth. The houses crowding along the wide shining sweep without ripple or glitter, stepping into the water in a line of jostling, vague, grey, silvery forms mingled with black masses of shadow, were like a spectral herd of shapeless creatures pressing forward to drink in a spectral and lifeless stream. Here and there a red gleam twinkled within the bamboo walls, warm, like a living spark, significant of human affections, of shelter, of repose.

"He confessed to me that he often watched these tiny warm gleams go out one by one, that he loved to see people go to sleep under his eyes, confident in the security of to-morrow. 'Peaceful here, eh?' he asked. He was not eloquent, but there was a deep meaning in the words that followed. 'Look at these houses; there's not one where I am not trusted. Jove! I told you I would hang on. Ask any man, woman or child . . .' He paused. 'Well, I am all right anyhow.'

"I observed quickly that he had found that out in the end. I had been sure of it, I added. He shook his head. 'Were you?' He pressed my arm lightly above the elbow. 'Well, then—you were right.'

"There was elation and pride, there was awe almost, in that low exclamation. 'Jove!' he cried, 'only think what it is to me.' Again he pressed my arm. 'And you asked me whether I thought of leaving. Good God! I! Want to leave! Especially now after what you told me of Mr. Stein's . . . Leave! Why! That's what I was afraid of. It would have been—it would have been harder than dying. No—on my word. Don't laugh. I must feel—every day, every time I open my eyes—that I am trusted—that nobody has a right—don't you know? Leave! For where? What for? To get what?'

"I had told him (indeed it was the main object of my visit) that it was Stein's intention to present him at once with the house and the stock of trading goods, on certain easy conditions which would make the transaction perfectly regular and valid. He began to snort and plunge at first. 'Confound your delicacy!' I shouted. 'It isn't Stein at all. It's giving you what you had made for yourself. And in any case keep your remarks for M'Neil—when you meet him in the other world. I hope it won't happen soon. . . .' He had to give in to my arguments, because all his conquests, the trust, the fame, the friendships, the love—all these things that made him master had made him a captive, too. He looked with an owner's eye at the peace of the evening, at the river, at the houses, at the everlasting life of the forests, at the life of the old mankind, at the secrets of the land, at the pride of his own heart: but it was they that possessed him and made him their own to the innermost thought, to the slightest stir of blood, to his last breath.

"It was something to be proud of. I, too, was proud—for him, if not so certain of the fabulous value of the bargain. It was wonderful. It was not so much of his fearlessness that I thought. It is strange how little account I took of it: as if it had been something too conventional to be at the root of the matter. No. I was more struck by the other gifts he had displayed. He had proved his grasp of the unfamiliar situation, his intellectual alertness in that field of thought. There was his readiness, too! Amazing. And all this had come to him in a manner like keen scent to a well-bred hound. He was not eloquent, but there was a dignity in this constitutional reticence, there was a high seriousness in his stammering. He had still his old trick of stubborn blushing. Now and then, though, a word, a sentence, would escape him that showed how deeply, how solemnly, he felt about that work which had given him the certitude of rehabilitation. That is why he seemed to love the land and the people with a sort of fierce egoism, with a contemptuous tenderness."

Chapter Twenty-five

THIS is where I was prisoner for three days,' he murmured to me (it was on the occasion of our visit to the Rajah), while we were making our way slowly through a kind of awe-struck riot of dependants across Tunku Allang's courtyard. 'Filthy place, isn't it? And I couldn't get anything to eat either, unless I made a row about it, and then it was only a small plate of rice and a fried fish not much bigger than a stickle-back—confound them! Jove! *I've* been hungry prowling inside this stinking enclosure with some of these vagabonds shoving their mugs right under my nose. I had given up that famous revolver of yours at the first demand. Glad to get rid of the bally thing. Look like a fool walking about with an empty shooting-iron in my hand.' At that moment we came into the presence, and he became unflinchingly grave and complimentary with his late captor. Oh! magnificent! I want to laugh when I think of it. But I was impressed, too. The old disreputable Tunku Allang could not help showing his fear (he was no hero, for all the tales of his hot youth he was fond of telling); and at the same time there was a wistful confidence in his manner towards his late prisoner. Note! Even where he would be most hated he was still trusted. Jim—as far as I could follow the conversation—was improving the occasion by the delivery of a lecture. Some poor villagers had been waylaid and robbed while on their way to Doramin's house with a few pieces of gum or beeswax which they wished to exchange for rice. 'It was Doramin who was a thief,' burst out the Rajah. A shaking fury seemed to enter that old frail body. He writhed weirdly on his mat, gesticulating with his hands and feet, tossing the tangled strings of his mop—an impotent incarnation of rage. There were staring eyes and dropping jaws all around us. Jim began to speak. Resolutely, coolly, and for some time he enlarged upon the text that no man should be prevented from getting his food and his children's food honestly. The other sat like a tailor at his board, one palm on each

knee, his head low, and fixing Jim through the grey hair that
fell over his very eyes. When Jim had done there was a great
stillness. Nobody seemed to breathe even; no one made a
sound till the old Rajah sighed faintly, and looking up, with a
toss of his head, said quickly, 'You hear, my people! No more
of these little games.' This decree was received in profound
silence. A rather heavy man, evidently in a position of confidence, with intelligent eyes, a bony, broad, very dark face, and
a cheerily officious manner (I learned later on he was the executioner), presented to us two cups of coffee on a brass tray,
which he took from the hands of an inferior attendant. 'You
needn't drink,' muttered Jim very rapidly. I didn't perceive
the meaning at first, and only looked at him. He took a good
sip and sat composedly, holding the saucer in his left hand. In
a moment I felt excessively annoyed. 'Why the devil,' I whispered, smiling at him amiably, 'do you expose me to such a
stupid risk?' I drank, of course, there was nothing for it,
while he gave no sign, and almost immediately afterwards we
took our leave. While we were going down the courtyard to
our boat, escorted by the intelligent and cheery executioner,
Jim said he was very sorry. It was the barest chance, of
course. Personally he thought nothing of poison. The remotest chance. He was—he assured me—considered to be
infinitely more useful than dangerous, and so . . . 'But the
Rajah is afraid of you abominably. Anybody can see that,' I
argued, with, I own, a certain peevishness, and all the time
watching anxiously for the first twist of some sort of ghastly
colic. I was awfully disgusted. 'If I am to do any good here
and preserve my position,' he said, taking his seat by my side
in the boat, 'I must stand the risk: I take it once every month,
at least. Many people trust me to do that—for them. Afraid of
me! That's just it. Most likely he is afraid of me because I am
not afraid of his coffee.' Then showing me a place on the
north front of the stockade where the pointed tops of several
stakes were broken. 'This is where I leaped over on my third
day in Patusan. They haven't put new stakes there yet. Good
leap, eh?' A moment later we passed the mouth of a muddy
creek. 'This is my second leap. I had a bit of a run and took

this one flying, but fell short. Thought I would leave my skin there. Lost my shoes struggling. And all the time I was thinking to myself how beastly it would be to get a jab with a bally long spear while sticking in the mud like this. I remember how sick I felt wriggling in that slime. I mean really sick—as if I had bitten something rotten.'

"That's how it was—and the opportunity ran by his side, leaped over the gap, floundered in the mud . . . still veiled. The unexpectedness of his coming was the only thing, you understand, that saved him from being at once despatched with krises and flung into the river. They had him, but it was like getting hold of an apparition, a wraith, a portent. What did it mean? What to do with it? Was it too late to conciliate him? Hadn't he better be killed without more delay? But what would happen then? Wretched old Allang went nearly mad with apprehension and through the difficulty of making up his mind. Several times the council was broken up, and the advisers made a break helter-skelter for the door and out on to the verandah. One—it is said—even jumped down to the ground— fifteen feet, I should judge—and broke his leg. The royal governor of Patusan had bizarre mannerisms, and one of them was to introduce boastful rhapsodies into every arduous discussion, when, getting gradually excited, he would end by flying off his perch with a kris in his hand. But, barring such interruptions, the deliberations upon Jim's fate went on night and day.

"Meanwhile he wandered about the courtyard, shunned by some, glared at by others, but watched by all, and practically at the mercy of the first casual ragamuffin with a chopper, in there. He took possession of a small tumbledown shed to sleep in; the effluvia of filth and rotten matter incommoded him greatly: it seems he had not lost his appetite though, because—he told me—he had been hungry all the blessed time. Now and again 'some fussy ass' deputed from the council-room would come out running to him, and in honeyed tones would administer amazing interrogatories: 'Were the Dutch coming to take the country? Would the white man like to go back down the river? What was the object of coming to such

a miserable country? The Rajah wanted to know whether the
white man could repair a watch? They did actually bring out
to him a nickel clock of New England make, and out of sheer
unbearable boredom he busied himself in trying to get the
alarum to work. It was apparently when thus occupied in his
shed that the true perception of his extreme peril dawned upon
him. He dropped the thing—he says—'like a hot potato,' and
walked out hastily, without the slightest idea of what he
would, or indeed could, do. He only knew that the position
was intolerable. He strolled aimlessly beyond a sort of ramshackle little granary on posts, and his eyes fell on the broken
stakes of the palisade; and then—he says—at once, without
any mental process as it were, without any stir of emotion, he
set about his escape as if executing a plan matured for a
month. He walked off carelessly to give himself a good run,
and when he faced about there was some dignitary, with two
spearmen in attendance, close at his elbow ready with a question. He started off 'from under his very nose,' went over 'like
a bird,' and landed on the other side with a fall that jarred all
his bones and seemed to split his head. He picked himself up
instantly. He never thought of anything at the time; all he
could remember—he said—was a great yell; the first houses
of Patusan were before him four hundred yards away; he saw
the creek, and as it were mechanically put on more pace. The
earth seemed fairly to fly backwards under his feet. He took
off from the last dry spot, felt himself flying through the air,
felt himself, without any shock, planted upright in an extremely soft and sticky mudbank. It was only when he tried to
move his legs and found he couldn't that, in his own words,
'he came to himself.' He began to think of the 'bally long
spears.' As a matter of fact, considering that the people inside
the stockade had to run to the gate, then get down to the land-
ing-place, get into boats, and pull round a point of land, he
had more advance than he imagined. Besides, it being low
water, the creek was without water—you couldn't call it
dry—and practically he was safe for a time from everything
but a very long shot perhaps. The higher firm ground was
about six feet in front of him. 'I thought I would have to die

there all the same,' he said. He reached and grabbed desperately with his hands and only succeeded in gathering a horrible cold shiny heap of slime against his breast—up to his very chin. It seemed to him he was burying himself alive, and then he struck out madly, scattering the mud with his fists. It fell on his head, on his face, over his eyes, into his mouth. He told me that he remembered suddenly the courtyard, as you remember a place where you have been very happy years ago. He longed—so he said—to be back there again, mending the clock. Mending the clock—that was the idea. He made efforts, tremendous sobbing, gasping efforts that seemed to burst his eyeballs in their sockets and make him blind, and culminating into one mighty supreme effort in the darkness to crack the earth asunder, to throw it off his limbs—and he felt himself creeping feebly up the bank. He lay full length on the firm ground and saw the light, the sky. Then as a sort of happy thought the notion came to him that he would go to sleep. He will have it that he *did* actually go to sleep; that he slept—perhaps for a minute, perhaps for twenty seconds, or only for one second, but he recollects distinctly the violent convulsive start of awakening. He remained lying still for a while, and then he arose muddy from head to foot and stood there, thinking he was alone of his kind for hundreds of miles, alone, with no help, no sympathy, no pity to expect from any one, like a hunted animal. The first houses were not more than twenty yards from him; and it was the desperate screaming of a frightened woman trying to carry off a child that started him again. He pelted straight on in his socks, beplastered with filth out of all semblance to a human being. He traversed more than half the length of the settlement. The nimbler women fled right and left, the slower men just dropped whatever they had in their hands, and remained petrified with dropping jaws. He was a flying terror. He says he noticed the little children trying to run for life, falling on their little stomachs and kicking. He swerved between two houses up a slope, clambered in desperation over a barricade of felled trees (there wasn't a week without some fight in Patusan at that time), burst through a fence into a maize-patch, where a scared boy flung a stick at him, blundered upon a path, and ran all at once into the arms of several startled men. He just had breath enough to gasp out, 'Doramin! Doramin!' He remembers being half-carried, half-rushed to the top of the slope, and in a vast enclosure with palms and fruit-trees being run up to a large man sitting massively in a chair in the midst of the greatest possible commotion and excitement. He fumbled in mud and clothes to produce the ring, and finding himself suddenly on his back, wondered who had knocked him down. They had simply let him go—don't you know?—but he couldn't stand. At the foot of the slope random shots were fired, and above the roofs of the settlement there rose a dull roar of amazement. But he was safe. Doramin's people were barricading the gate and pouring water down his throat; Doramin's old wife, full of business and commiseration, was issuing shrill orders to her girls. 'The old woman,' he said, softly, 'made a to-do over me as if I had been her own son. They put me into an immense bed—her state bed—and she ran in and out wiping her eyes to give me pats on the back. I must have been a pitiful object. I just lay there like a log for I don't know how long.'

"He seemed to have a great liking for Doramin's old wife. She on her side had taken a motherly fancy to him. She had a round, nut-brown, soft face, all fine wrinkles, large, bright red lips (she chewed betel assiduously), and screwed-up, winking, benevolent eyes. She was constantly in movement, scolding busily and ordering unceasingly a troop of young women with clear brown faces and big grave eyes, her daughters, her servants, her slave-girls. You know how it is in these households: it's generally impossible to tell the difference. She was very spare, and even her ample outer garment, fastened in front with jeweled clasps, had somehow a skimpy effect. Her dark bare feet were thrust into yellow straw slippers of Chinese make. I have seen her myself flitting about with her extremely thick, long, grey hair falling about her shoulders. She uttered homely shrewd sayings, was of noble birth, and was eccentric and arbitrary. In the afternoon she would sit in a very roomy armchair, opposite her husband, gazing steadily through a wide opening in the wall which gave an extensive view of the settlement and the river.

"She invariably tucked up her feet under her, but old Doramin sat squarely, sat imposingly as a mountain sits on a plain. He was only of the *nakhoda* or merchant class, but the respect shown to him and the dignity of his bearing were very striking. He was the chief of the second power in Patusan. The immigrants from Celebes (about sixty families that, with dependants and so on, could muster some one hundred men 'wearing the kris') had elected him years ago for their head. The men of that race are intelligent, enterprising, revengeful, but with a more frank courage than the other Malays, and restless under oppression. They formed the party opposed to the Rajah. Of course the quarrels were for trade. This was the primary cause of faction fights, of the sudden outbreaks that would fill this or that part of the settlement with smoke, flame, the noise of shots and shrieks. Villages were burnt, men were dragged into the Rajah's stockade to be killed or tortured for the crime of trading with anybody else but himself. Only a day or two before Jim's arrival several heads of households in the very fishing village that was afterwards taken under his especial protection had been driven over the cliffs by a party of the Rajah's spearmen, on suspicion of having been collecting edible birds' nests for a Celebes trader. Rajah Allang pretended to be the only trader in his country, and the penalty for the breach of the monopoly was death; but his idea of trading was indistinguishable from the commonest forms of robbery. His cruelty and rapacity had no other bounds than his cowardice, and he was afraid of the organised power of the Celebes men, only—till Jim came—he was not afraid enough to keep quiet. He struck at them through his subjects, and thought himself pathetically in the right. The situation was complicated by a wandering stranger, an Arab half-breed, who, I believe, on purely religious grounds, had incited the tribes in the interior (the bush-folk, as Jim himself called them) to rise, and had established himself in a fortified camp on the summit of one of the twin hills. He hung over the town of Patusan like a hawk over a poultry-yard, but he devastated the open country. Whole villages, deserted, rotted on their blackened posts over the banks of clear streams, dropping piecemeal into the water the grass of their walls, the leaves of their roofs, with a curious effect of natural decay as if they had been a form of vegetation stricken by a blight at its very root. The two parties in Patusan were not sure which one this partisan most desired to plunder. The Rajah intrigued with him feebly. Some of the Bugis settlers, weary with endless insecurity, were half inclined to call him in. The younger spirits amongst them, chaffing, advised to 'get Sherif Ali with his wild men and drive the Rajah Allang out of the country.' Doramin restrained them with difficulty. He was growing old, and, though his influence had not diminished, the situation was getting beyond him. This was the state of affairs when Jim, bolting from the Rajah's stockade, appeared before the chief of the Bugis, produced the ring, and was received, in a manner of speaking, into the heart of the community."

Chapter Twenty-six

DORAMIN was one of the most remarkable men of his race I had ever seen. His bulk for a Malay was immense, but he did not look merely fat; he looked imposing, monumental. This motionless body, clad in rich stuffs, colored silks, gold embroideries; this huge head, enfolded in a red-and-gold head-kerchief; the flat, big, round face, wrinkled, furrowed, with two semicircular heavy folds starting on each side of wide, fierce nostrils, and enclosing a thick-lipped mouth; the throat like a bull; the vast corrugated brow overhanging the staring proud eyes— made a whole that, once seen, can never be forgotten. His impassive repose (he seldom stirred a limb when once he sat down) was like a display of dignity. He was never known to raise his voice. It was a hoarse and powerful murmur, slightly veiled as if heard from a distance. When he walked, two short, sturdy young fellows, naked to the waist, in white sarongs and

with black skull-caps on the backs of their heads, sustained his
elbows; they would ease him down and stand behind his chair
till he wanted to rise, when he would turn his head slowly, as if
with difficulty, to the right and to the left, and then they would
catch him under his armpits and help him up: For all that, there
was nothing of a cripple about him: on the contrary, all his ponderous movements were like manifestations of a mighty deliberate force. It was generally believed he consulted his wife as to
public affairs; but nobody, as far as I know, had ever heard them
exchange a single word. When they sat in state by the wide
opening it was in silence. They could see below them in the de-
clining light the vast expanse of the forest country, a dark sleeping sea of sombre green undulating as far as the violet and
purple range of mountains; the shining sinuosity of the river
like an immense letter S of beaten silver; the brown ribbon of
houses following the sweep of both banks, overtopped by the
twin hills uprising above the nearer tree-tops. They were wonderfully contrasted: she, light, delicate, spare, quick, a little
witch-like, with a touch of motherly fussiness in her repose; he,
facing her, immense and heavy, like a figure of a man roughly
fashioned of stone, with something magnanimous and ruthless
in his immobility. The son of these old people was a most distinguished youth.

"They had him late in life. Perhaps he was not really so
young as he looked. Four- or five-and twenty is not so young
when a man is already father of a family at eighteen. When he
entered the large room, lined and carpeted with fine mats, and
with a high ceiling of white sheeting, where the couple sat in
state surrounded by a most deferential retinue, he would make
his way straight to Doramin, to kiss his hand—which the other
abandoned to him majestically—and then would step across to
stand by his mother's chair. I suppose I may say they idolised
him, but I never caught them giving him an overt glance.
Those, it is true, were public functions. The room was generally thronged. The solemn formality of greetings and leave-
takings, the profound respect expressed in gestures, on the
faces, in the low whispers, is simply indescribable. 'It's well
worth seeing,' Jim had assured me while we were crossing the

river, on our way back. 'They are like people in a book, aren't
they?' he said triumphantly. 'And Dain Waris—their son—is
the best friend (barring you) I ever had. What Mr. Stein would
call a good "war-comrade." I was in luck. Jove! I was in luck
when I tumbled amongst them at my last gasp.' He meditated
with bowed head, then rousing himself he added: ·

"'Of course I didn't go to sleep over it, but . . .' He paused
again. 'It seemed to come to me,' he murmured. 'All at once I
saw what I had to do . . .'

"There was no doubt that it had come to him; and it had
come through the war, too, as is natural, since this power that
came to him was the power to make peace. It is in this sense
alone that might so often *is* right. You must not think he had
seen his way at once. When he arrived the Bugis community
was in a most critical position. 'They were all afraid,' he said to
me—'each man afraid of himself; while I could see as plain as
possible that they must do something at once, if they did not
want to go under one after another, what between the Rajah and
that vagabond Sherif.' But to see that was nothing. When he got
his idea he had to drive it into reluctant minds, through the bulwarks of fear, of selfishness. He drove it in at last. And that was
nothing. He had to devise the means. He devised them—an audacious plan; and his task was only half done. He had to inspire
with his own confidence a lot of people who had hidden and
absurd reasons to hang back; he had to conciliate imbecile jeal-
ousies, and argue away all sorts of senseless mistrusts. Without
the weight of Doramin's authority and his son's fiery enthusiasm, he would have failed. Dain Waris, the distinguished youth,
was the first to believe in him; theirs was one of those strange,
profound, rare friendships between brown and white, in which
the very difference of race seems to draw two human beings
closer by some mystic element of sympathy. Of Dain Waris, his
own people said with pride that he knew how to fight like a
white man. This was true; he had that sort of courage—the
courage in the open, I may say—but he had also a European
mind. You meet them sometimes like that, and are surprised to
discover unexpectedly a familiar turn of thought, an unob-
scured vision, a tenacity of purpose, a touch of altruism. Of

small stature, but admirably well proportioned, Dain Waris had
a proud carriage, a polished, easy bearing, a temperament like a
clear flame. His dusky face, with big black eyes, was in action
expressive, and in repose thoughtful. He was of a silent disposition; a firm glance, an ironic smile, a courteous deliberation
of manner seemed to hint at great reserves of intelligence and
power. Such beings open to the Western eye, so often concerned with mere surfaces, the hidden possibilities of races and
lands over which hangs the mystery of unrecorded ages. He not
only trusted Jim, he understood him, I firmly believe. I speak of
him because he had captivated me. His—if I may say so—his
caustic placidity, and, at the same time, his intelligent sympathy
with Jim's aspirations, appealed to me. I seemed to behold the
very origin of friendship. If Jim took the lead, the other had
captivated his leader. In fact, Jim the leader was a captive in
every sense. The land, the people, the friendship, the love, were
like the jealous guardians of his body. Every day added a link to
the fetters of that strange freedom. I felt convinced of it, as from
day to day I learned more of the story.

"The story! Haven't I heard the story? I've heard it on the
march, in camp (he made me scour the country after invisible
game); I've listened to a good part of it on one of the twin summits, after climbing the last hundred feet or so on my hands
and knees. Our escort (we had volunteer followers from village to village) had camped meantime on a bit of level ground
half-way up the slope, and in the still breathless evening the
smell of wood-smoke reached our nostrils from below with the
penetrating delicacy of some choice scent. Voices also ascended, wonderful in their distinct and immaterial clearness.
Jim sat on the trunk of a felled tree, and pulling out his pipe
began to smoke. A new growth of grass and bushes was spring-
ing up; there were traces of an earthwork under a mass of
thorny twigs. 'It all started from here,' he said, after a long and
meditative silence. On the other hill, two hundred yards across
a sombre precipice, I saw a line of high blackened stakes,
showing here and there ruinously—the remnants of Sherif
Ali's impregnable camp.

"But it had been taken though. That had been his idea. He

had mounted Doramin's old ordnance on the top of that hill;
two rusty iron 7-pounders, a lot of small brass cannon—cur-
rency cannon. But if the brass guns represent wealth, they can
also, when crammed recklessly to the muzzle, send a solid shot
to some little distance. The thing was to get them up there. He
showed me where he had fastened the cables, explained how
he had improvised a rude capstan out of a hollowed log turning
upon a pointed stake, indicated with the bowl of his pipe the
outline of the earthwork. The last hundred feet of the ascent
had been the most difficult. He had made himself responsible
for success on his own head. He had induced the war party to
work hard all night. Big fires lighted at intervals blazed all
down the slopes, 'but up here,' he explained, 'the hoisting
gang had to fly around in the dark.' From the top he saw men
moving on the hillside like ants at work. He himself on that
night had kept on rushing down and climbing up like a squir-
rel, directing, encouraging, watching all along the line. Old
Doramin had himself carried up the hill in his arm-chair. They
put him down on the level place upon the slope, and he sat
there in the light of one of the big fires—'amazing old chap—
real old chieftain,' said Jim, 'with his little fierce eyes—a pair
of immense flintlock pistols on his knees. Magnificent things,
ebony, silver-mounted, with beautiful locks and a caliber like
an old blunderbuss. A present from Stein, it seems—in exchange for that ring, you know. Used to belong to good old
M'Neil. God only knows how *he* came by them. There he sat,
moving neither hand nor foot, a flame of dry bushwood behind
him, and lots of people rushing about, shouting and pulling
around him—the most solemn, imposing old chap you can
imagine. *He* wouldn't have had much chance if Sherif Ali had
let his infernal crew loose at us and stampeded my lot. Eh?
Anyhow, he had come up there to die if anything went wrong.
No mistake! Jove! It thrilled me to see him there—like a rock.
But the Sherif must have thought us mad, and never troubled
to come and see how we got on. Nobody believed it could be
done. Why! I think the very chaps who pulled and shoved and
sweated over it did not believe it could be done! Upon my
word I don't think they did. . . .'

"He stood erect, the smouldering brier-wood in his clutch, with a smile on his lips and a sparkle in his boyish eyes. I sat on the stump of a tree at his feet, and below us stretched the land, the great expanse of the forests, sombre under the sunshine, rolling like a sea, with glints of winding rivers, the grey spots of villages, and here and there a clearing, like an islet of light amongst the dark waves of continuous tree-tops. A brooding gloom lay over this vast and monotonous landscape; the light fell on it as if into an abyss. The land devoured the sunshine; only far off, along the coast, the empty ocean, smooth and polished within the faint haze, seemed to rise up to the sky in a wall of steel.

"And there I was with him, high in the sunshine on the top of that historic hill of his. He dominated the forest, the secular gloom, the old mankind. He was like a figure set up on a pedestal, to represent in his persistent youth the power, and perhaps the virtues, of races that never grow old, that have emerged from the gloom. I don't know why he should always have appeared to me symbolic. Perhaps this is the real cause of my interest in his fate. I don't know whether it was exactly fair to him to remember the incident which had given a new direction to his life, but at that very moment I remembered very distinctly. It was like a shadow in the light."

Chapter Twenty-seven

ALREADY the legend had gifted him with supernatural powers. Yes, it was said, there had been many ropes cunningly disposed, and a strange contrivance that turned by the efforts of many men, and each gun went up tearing slowly through the bushes, like a wild pig rooting its way in the undergrowth, but . . . and the wisest shook their heads. There was something occult in all this, no doubt; for what is the strength of ropes and of men's arms? There is a rebellious soul in things which must

be overcome by powerful charms and incantations. Thus old
Sura—a very respectable householder of Patusan—with whom
I had a quiet chat one evening. However, Sura was a professional sorcerer also, who attended all the rice sowings and reap-
ings for miles around for the purpose of subduing the stubborn
soul of things. This occupation he seemed to think a most arduous one, and perhaps the souls of things are more stubborn than
the souls of men. As to the simple folk of outlying villages, they
believed and said (as the most natural thing in the world) that
Jim had carried the guns up the hill on his back—two at a time.

"This would make Jim stamp his foot in vexation and exclaim with an exasperated little laugh, 'What can you do with
such silly beggars? They will sit up half the night talking bally
rot, and the greater the lie the more they seem to like it.' You
could trace the subtle influence of his surroundings in this irritation. It was part of his captivity. The earnestness of his denials
was amusing, and at last I said, 'My dear fellow, you don't suppose *I* believe this.' He looked at me quite startled. 'Well, no! I
suppose not,' he said, and burst into a Homeric peal of laughter.
'Well, anyhow the guns were there, and went off together at
sunrise. Jove! You should have seen the splinters fly,' he cried.
By his side Dain Waris, listening with a quiet smile, dropped
his eyelids and shuffled his feet a little. It appears that the success in mounting the guns had given Jim's people such a feeling of confidence that he ventured to leave the battery under
charge of two elderly Bugis who had seen some fighting in their
day, and went to join Dain Waris and the storming party who
were concealed in the ravine. In the small hours they began
creeping up, and when two-thirds of the way up, lay in the wet
grass waiting for the appearance of the sun, which was the
agreed signal. He told me with what impatient anguishing emotion he watched the swift coming of the dawn; how, heated with
the work and the climbing, he felt the cold dew chilling his very
bones; how afraid he was he would begin to shiver and shake
like a leaf before the time came for the advance. 'It was the
slowest half-hour in my life,' he declared. Gradually the silent
stockade came out on the sky above him. Men scattered all
down the slope were crouching amongst the dark stones and

dripping bushes. Dain Waris was lying flattened by his side. 'We looked at each other,' Jim said, resting a gentle hand on his friend's shoulder. 'He smiled at me as cheery as you please, and I dared not stir my lips for fear I would break out into a shivering fit. 'Pon my word, it's true! I had been streaming with perspiration when we took cover—so you may imagine . . .' He declared, and I believe him, that he had no fears as to the result. He was only anxious as to his ability to repress these shivers. He didn't bother about the result. He was bound to get to the top of that hill and stay there, whatever might happen. There could be no going back for him. Those people had trusted him implicitly. Him alone! His bare word. . . .

"I remember how, at this point, he paused with his eyes fixed upon me. 'As far as he knew, they never had an occasion to regret it yet,' he said. 'Never. He hoped to God they never would. Meantime—worse luck!—they had got into the habit of taking his word for anything and everything. I could have no idea! Why? Only the other day an old fool he had never seen in his life came from some village miles away to find out if he should divorce his wife. Fact. Solemn word. That's the sort of thing. . . . He wouldn't have believed it. Would I? Squatted on the verandah chewing betel-nut, sighing and spitting all over the place for more than an hour, and as glum as an undertaker before he came out with that dashed conundrum. That's the kind of thing that isn't so sunny as it looks. What was a fellow to say?—Good wife?—Yes. Good wife—old though; started a confounded long story about some brass pots. Been living together for fifteen years—twenty years—could not tell. A long, long time. Good wife. Beat her a little—not much—just a little, when she was young. Had to—for the sake of his honour. Suddenly in her old age she goes and lends three brass pots to her sister's son's wife, and begins to abuse him every day in a loud voice. His enemies jeered at him; his face was utterly blackened. Pots totally lost. Awfully cut up about it. Impossible to fathom a story like that; told him to go home, and promised to come along myself and settle it all. It's all very well to grin, but it was the dashedest nuisance! A day's journey through the forest, another day lost in coaxing a lot of silly villagers to get at the rights of the affair. There was the making of a sanguinary shindy in the thing. Every bally idiot took sides with one family or the other, and one half of the village was ready to go for the other half with anything that came handy. Honour bright! No joke! . . . Instead of attending to their bally crops. Got him the infernal pots back of course— and pacified all hands. No trouble to settle it. Of course not. Could settle the deadliest quarrel in the country by crooking his little finger. The trouble was to get at the truth of anything. Was not sure to this day whether he had been fair to all parties. It worried him. And the talk! Jove! There didn't seem to be any head or tail to it. Rather storm at a twenty-foot-high old stockade any day. Much! Child's play to that other job. Wouldn't take so long either. Well, yes; a funny set out, upon the whole—the fool looked old enough to be his grandfather. But from another point of view it was no joke. His word decided everything—ever since the smashing of Sherif Ali. An awful responsibility,' he repeated. 'No, really—joking apart, had it been three lives instead of three rotten brass pots it would have been the same. . . .'

"Thus he illustrated the moral effect of his victory in war. It was in truth immense. It had led him from strife to peace, and through death into the innermost life of the people; but the gloom of the land spread out under the sunshine preserved its appearance of inscrutable, of secular repose. The sound of his fresh young voice—it's extraordinary how very few signs of wear he showed—floated lightly, and passed away over the unchanged face of the forests like the sound of the big guns on that cold dewy morning when he had no other concern on earth but the proper control of the chills in his body. With the first slant of sun-rays along these immovable tree-tops the summit of one hill wreathed itself, with heavy reports, in white clouds of smoke, and the other burst into an amazing noise of yells, war-cries, shouts of anger, of surprise, of dismay. Jim and Dain Waris were the first to lay their hands on the stakes. The popular story has it that Jim with a touch of one finger had thrown down the gate. He was, of course, anxious to disclaim this achievement. The whole stockade—he would insist on explaining to you—was a poor affair (Sherif Ali trusted mainly to the inaccessible position); and, anyway, the thing had been already knocked to pieces and only hung together by a miracle. He put his shoulder to it like a little fool and went in head over heels. Jove! If it hadn't been for Dain Waris, a pock-marked tattooed vagabond would have pinned him with his spear to a baulk of timber like one of Stein's beetles. The third man in, it seems, had been Tamb' Itam, Jim's own servant. This was a Malay from the north, a stranger who had wandered into Patusan, and had been forcibly detained by Rajah Allang as paddler of one of the state boats. He had made a bolt of it at the first opportunity, and finding a precarious refuge (but very little to eat) among the Bugis settlers, had attached himself to Jim's person. His complexion was very dark, his face flat, his eyes prominent and injected with bile. There was something excessive, almost fanatical, in his devotion to his 'white lord.' He was inseparable from Jim like a morose shadow. On state occasions he would tread on his master's heels, one hand on the haft of his kris, keeping the common people at a distance by his truculent brooding glances. Jim had made him the headman of his establishment, and all Patusan respected and courted him as a person of much influence. At the taking of the stockade he had distinguished himself greatly by the methodical ferocity of his fighting. The storming-party had come on so quick—Jim said—that notwithstanding the panic of the garrison, there was a 'Hot five minutes hand-to-hand inside that stockade, till some bally ass set fire to the shelters of boughs and dry grass, and we all had to clear out for dear life.'

"The rout, it seems, had been complete. Doramin waiting immovably in his chair on the hillside, with the smoke of the guns spreading slowly above his big head, received the news with a deep grunt. When informed that his son was safe and leading the pursuit, he, without another sound, made a mighty effort to rise; his attendants hurried to his help, and held up reverently, he shuffled with great dignity into a bit of shade where he laid himself down to sleep covered entirely with a piece of white sheeting. In Patusan the excitement was intense. Jim told me that from the hill, turning his back on the stockade with its embers, black ashes, and half-consumed corpses, he could see time after time the open spaces between the houses on both sides of the stream fill suddenly with a seething rush of people and get empty in a moment. His ears caught feebly from below the tremendous din of gongs and drums; the wild shouts of the crowd reached him in bursts of faint roaring. A lot of streamers made a flutter as of little white, red, yellow birds amongst the brown ridges of roofs. 'You must have enjoyed it,' I murmured, feeling the stir of sympathetic emotion.

"'It was ... it was immense! Immense!' he cried aloud, flinging his arms open. The sudden movement startled me as though I had seen him bare the secrets of his breast to the sunshine, the brooding forests, to the steely sea. Below us the town reposed in easy curves up on the banks of a stream whose current seemed to sleep. 'Immense!' he repeated for a third time, speaking in a whisper, for himself alone.

"Immense! No doubt it was immense; the seal of success upon his words, the conquered ground for the soles of his feet, the blind trust of men, the belief in himself snatched from the fire, the solitude of his achievement. All this, as I've warned you, gets dwarfed in the telling. I can't with mere words convey to you the impression of his total and utter isolation. I know, of course, he was in every sense alone of his kind there, but the unsuspected qualities of his nature had brought him in such close touch with his surroundings that this isolation seemed only the effect of his power. His loneliness added to his stature. There was nothing within sight to compare him with, as though he had been one of those exceptional men who can be only measured by the greatness of their fame; and his fame, remember, was the greatest thing around for many a day's journey. You would have to paddle, pole, or track a long weary way through the jungle before you passed beyond the reach of its voice. Its voice was not the trumpeting of the disreputable goddess we all know—not blatant—not brazen. It took its tone from stillness and gloom of the land without a past, where his word was the one truth of every passing day. It shared something of the nature of that silence through which it accompanied you into unexplored depths, heard continuously

by your side, penetrating, far-reaching—tinged with wonder
and mystery on the lips of whispering men."

Chapter Twenty-eight

THE defeated Sherif Ali fled the country without making another stand, and when the miserable hunted villagers
began to crawl out of the jungle back to their rotting houses, it
was Jim who, in consultation with Dain Waris, appointed the
headmen. Thus he became the virtual ruler of the land. As to
old Tunku Allang, his fears at first had known no bounds. It is
said that at the intelligence of the successful storming of the
hill he flung himself, face down, on the bamboo floor of his
audience-hall, and lay motionless for a whole night and a
whole day, uttering stifled sounds of such an appalling nature
that no man dared approach his prostrate form nearer than a
spear's length. Already he could see himself driven ignomin-
iously out of Patusan, wandering abandoned, stripped, without
opium, without his women, without followers, a fair game for
the first comer to kill. After Sherif Ali his turn would come,
and who could resist an attack led by such a devil? And indeed
he owed his life and such authority as he still possessed at the
time of my visit to Jim's idea of what was fair alone. The Bugis
had been extremely anxious to pay off old scores, and the impassive old Doramin cherished the hope of yet seeing his son
ruler of Patusan. During one of our interviews he deliberately
allowed me to get a glimpse of this secret ambition. Nothing
could be finer in its way than the dignified wariness of his approaches. He himself—he began by declaring—had used his
strength in his younger days, but now he had grown old and
tired. . . . With his imposing bulk and haughty little eyes darting sagacious, inquisitive glances, he reminded one irresistibly
of a cunning old elephant; the slow rise and fall of his vast
breast went on powerful and regular, like the heave of a calm

208 *Joseph Conrad*

sea. He, too, as he protested, had an unbounded confidence in
Tuan Jim's wisdom. If he could only obtain a promise! One
word would be enough! . . . His breathing silences, the low
rumblings of his voice, recalled the last efforts of a spent thun-
derstorm.

"I tried to put the subject aside. It was difficult, for there
could be no question that Jim had the power; in his new sphere
there did not seem to be anything that was not his to hold or to
give. But that, I repeat, was nothing in comparison with the notion, which occurred to me, while I listened with a show of attention, that he seemed to have come very near at last to
mastering his fate. Doramin was anxious about the future of
the country, and I was struck by the turn he gave to the argument. The land remains where God had put it; but white men—
he said—they come to us and in a little while they go. They go
away. Those they leave behind do not know when to look for
their return. They go to their own land, to their people, and so
this white man, too, would. . . . I don't know what induced me
to commit myself at this point by a vigorous 'No, no.' The
whole extent of this indiscretion became apparent when Doramin, turning full upon me his face, whose expression, fixed
in rugged deep folds, remained unalterable, like a huge brown
mask, said that this was good news indeed, reflectively; and
then wanted to know why.

'His little, motherly witch of a wife sat on my other hand,
with her head covered and her feet tucked up, gazing through
a great shutter-hole. I could only see a straying lock of grey
hair, a high cheek-bone, the slight masticating motion of the
sharp chin. Without removing her eyes from the vast prospect
of forests stretching as far as the hills, she asked me in a pity-
ing voice why was it that he so young had wandered from his
home, coming so far, through so many dangers? Had he no
household there, no kinsmen in his own country? Had he no
old mother, who would always remember his face? . . .

"I was completely unprepared for this. I could only mutter
and shake my head vaguely. Afterwards I am perfectly aware I
cut a very poor figure trying to extricate myself out of this difficulty. From that moment, however, the old *nakhoda* became

taciturn. He was not very pleased, I fear, and evidently I had given him food for thought. Strangely enough, on the evening of that very day (which was my last in Patusan) I was once more confronted with the same question, with the unanswerable why of Jim's fate. And this brings me to the story of his love.

"I suppose you think it is a story that you can imagine for yourselves. We have heard so many such stories, and the majority of us don't believe them to be stories of love at all. For the most part we look upon them as stories of opportunities: episodes of passion at best, or perhaps only of youth and temptation, doomed to forgetfulness in the end, even if they pass through the reality of tenderness and regret. This view mostly is right, and perhaps in this case, too. . . . Yet I don't know. To tell this story is by no means so easy as it should be—were the ordinary standpoint adequate. Apparently it is a story very much like the others: for me, however, there is visible in its background the melancholy figure of a woman, the shadow of a cruel wisdom buried in a lonely grave, looking on wistfully, helplessly, with sealed lips. The grave itself, as I came upon it during an early morning stroll, was a rather shapeless brown mound, with an inlaid neat border of white lumps of coral at the base, and enclosed within a circular fence made of split saplings, with the bark left on. A garland of leaves and flowers was woven about the heads of the slender posts—and the flowers were fresh.

"Thus, whether the shadow is of my imagination or not, I can at all events point out the significant fact of an unforgotten grave. When I tell you besides that Jim with his own hands had worked at the rustic fence, you will perceive directly the difference, the individual side of the story. There is in his espousal of memory and affection belonging to another human being something characteristic of his seriousness. He had a conscience, and it was a romantic conscience. Through her whole life the wife of the unspeakable Cornelius had no other companion, confidante, and friend but her daughter. How the poor woman had come to marry the awful Malacca Portuguese—after the separation from the father of her girl—and how that separation had been brought about, whether by death, which can be sometimes merciful, or by the merciless pressure of conventions, is a mystery to me. From the little which Stein (who knew so many stories) had let drop in my hearing, I am convinced that she was no ordinary woman. Her own father had been a white; a high official; one of the brilliantly endowed men who are not dull enough to nurse a success, and whose careers so often end under a cloud. I suppose she, too, must have lacked the saving dulness—and her career ended in Patusan. Our common fate . . . for where is the man—I mean a real sentient man—who does not remember vaguely having been deserted in the fullness of possession by some one or something more precious than life? . . our common fate fastens upon the women with a peculiar cruelty. It does not punish like a master, but inflicts lingering torment, as if to gratify a secret, unappeasable spite. One would think that, appointed to rule on earth, it seeks to revenge itself upon the beings that come nearest to rising above the trammels of earthly caution; for it is only women who manage to put at times into their love an element just palpable enough to give one a fright—an extraterrestrial touch. I ask myself with wonder—how the world can look to them—whether it has the shape and substance *we* know, the air *we* breathe! Sometimes I fancy it must be a region of unreasonable sublimities seething with the excitement of their adventurous souls, lighted by the glory of all possible risks and renunciations. However, I suspect there are very few women in the world, though of course I am aware of the multitudes of mankind and of the equality of sexes in point of numbers—that is. But I am sure that the mother was as much of a woman as the daughter seemed to be. I cannot help picturing to myself these two, at first the young woman and the child, then the old woman and the young girl, the awful sameness and the swift passage of time, the barrier of forest, the solitude and the turmoil round these two lonely lives, and every word spoken between them penetrated with sad meaning. There must have been confidences, not so much of fact, I suppose, as of innermost feelings—regrets—fears—warnings, no doubt: warnings that the younger did not fully understand till the elder was dead—and Jim came along. Then I am sure she understood much—not everything—the fear mostly, it seems. Jim called her by a word that means precious, in the sense of a precious gem—jewel. Pretty, isn't it? But he was capable of anything. He was equal to his fortune, as he—after all—must have been equal to his misfortune. Jewel he called her; and he would say this as he might have said 'Jane,' don't you know—with a marital, homelike, peaceful effect. I heard the name for the first time ten minutes after I had landed in his courtyard, when, after nearly shaking my arm off, he darted up the steps and began to make a joyous, boyish disturbance at the door under the heavy eaves. 'Jewel! Oh Jewel! Quick! Here's a friend come,' . . . and suddenly peering at me in the dim verandah, he mumbled earnestly, 'You know—this—no confounded nonsense about it—can't tell you how much I owe to her—and so—you understand—I—exactly as if . . .' His hurried, anxious whispers were cut short by the flitting of a white form within the house, a faint exclamation, and a childlike but energetic little face with delicate features and a profound, attentive glance peeped out of the inner gloom, like a bird out of the recess of a nest. I was struck by the name, of course; but it was not till later on that I connected it with an astonishing rumour that had met me on my journey, at a little place on the coast about 230 miles south of Patusan river. Stein's schooner, in which I had my passage, put in there, to collect some produce, and going ashore, I found to my great surprise that the wretched locality could boast of a third-class deputy-assistant resident, a big, fat, greasy, blinking fellow of mixed descent, with turned-out, shiny lips. I found him lying extended on his back in a cane chair, odiously unbuttoned, with a large green leaf of some sort on the top of his steaming head, and another in his hand which he used lazily as a fan. . . . Going to Patusan? Oh, yes. Stein's Trading Company. He knew. Had a permission? No business of his. It was not so bad there now, he remarked negligently, and, he went on drawling, 'There's some sort of white vagabond has got in there, I hear. . . . Eh? What you say? Friend of yours? So! . . . Then it was true there was one of these *verdamte*—What was he up to? Found his way in, the rascal. Eh? I had not been sure. Patusan—they cut throats there—no business of ours.' He interrupted himself to groan. 'Phoo! Almighty! The heat! The heat! Well, then, there might be something in the story, too, after all, and . . .' He shut one of his beastly glassy eyes (the eyelid went on quivering), while he leered at me atrociously with the other. 'Look here,' says he, mysteriously, 'if—do you understand?—if he has really got hold of something fairly good—none of your bits of green glass—understand?—I am a government official—you tell the rascal . . . Eh? What? Friend of yours?' . . He continued wallowing calmly in the chair. . . . 'You said so; that's just it; and I am pleased to give you the hint. I suppose you, too, would like to get something out of it? Don't interrupt. You just tell him I've heard the tale, but to my government I have made no report. Not yet. See? Why make a report? Eh? Tell him to come to me if they let him get alive out of the country. He had better look out for himself. Eh? I promise to ask no questions. On the quiet—you understand? You, too—you shall get something from me. Small commission for the trouble. Don't interrupt. I am a government official, and make no report. That's business. Understand? I know some good people that will buy anything worth having, and can give him more money than the scoundrel ever saw in his life. I know his sort.' He fixed me steadfastly with both his eyes open, while I stood over him utterly amazed and asking myself whether he was mad or drunk. He perspired, puffed, moaning feebly, and scratching himself with such horrible composure that I could not bear the sight long enough to find out. Next day, talking casually with the people of the little native court of the place, I discovered that a story was traveling slowly down the coast about a mysterious white man in Patusan who had got hold of an extraordinary gem—namely, an emerald of an enormous size, and altogether priceless. The emerald seems to appeal more to the Eastern imagination than any other precious stone. The white man had obtained it, I was told, partly by the exercise of his wonderful strength and partly by cunning, from the ruler of a distant country, whence he had fled instantly, arriving in Patusan in utmost distress, but frightening the people by his extreme ferocity, which nothing seemed able to subdue. Most of my informants were of the opinion that the stone was probably unlucky,—like the famous stone of the Sultan of Succadana, which in the old times had brought wars and untold calamities upon that country. Perhaps it was the same stone—one couldn't say. Indeed the story of a fabulously large emerald is as old as the arrival of the first white men in the Archipelago; and the belief in it is so persistent that less than forty years ago there had been an official Dutch inquiry into the truth of it. Such a jewel—it was explained to me by the old fellow from whom I heard most of this amazing Jim-myth—a sort of scribe to the wretched little Rajah of the place—such a jewel, he said, cocking his poor purblind eyes up at me (he was sitting on the cabin floor out of respect), is best preserved by being concealed about the person of a woman. Yet it is not every woman that would do. She must be young—he sighed deeply—and insensible to the seductions of love. He shook his head sceptically. But such a woman seemed to be actually in existence. He had been told of a tall girl, whom the white man treated with great respect and care, and who never went forth from the house unattended. People said the white man could be seen with her almost any day; they walked side by side, openly, he holding her arm under his—pressed to his side—thus—in a most extraordinary way. This might be a lie, he conceded, for it was indeed a strange thing for any one to do: on the other hand, there could be no doubt she wore the white man's jewel concealed upon her bosom."

Chapter Twenty-nine

THIS was the theory of Jim's marital evening walks. I made a third on more than one occasion, unpleasantly aware every time of Cornelius, who nursed the aggrieved sense of his legal paternity, slinking in the neighbourhood with that pecu-

liar twist of his mouth as if he were perpetually on the point of
gnashing his teeth. But do you notice how, three hundred miles
beyond the end of telegraph cables and mail-boat lines, the
haggard utilitarian lies of our civilisation wither and die, to be
replaced by pure exercises of imagination, that have the futility, often the charm, and sometimes the deep hidden truthfulness, of works of art? Romance had singled Jim for its
own—and that was the true part of the story, which otherwise
was all wrong. He did not hide his jewel. In fact, he was extremely proud of it.

"It comes to me now that I had, on the whole, seen very little of her. What I remember best is the even, olive pallor of her
complexion, and the intense blue-black gleams of her hair,
flowing abundantly from under a small crimson cap she wore
far back on her shapely head. Her movements were free, assured, and she blushed a dusky red. While Jim and I were talking, she would come and go with rapid glances at us, leaving
on her passage an impression of grace and charm and a distinct
suggestion of watchfulness. Her manner presented a curious
combination of shyness and audacity. Every pretty smile was
succeeded swiftly by a look of silent, repressed anxiety, as if
put to flight by the recollection of some abiding danger. At
times she would sit down with us and, with her soft cheek dim-
pled by the knuckles of her little hand, she would listen to our
talk; her big clear eyes would remain fastened on our lips, as
though each pronounced word had a visible shape. Her mother
had taught her to read and write; she had learned a good bit of
English from Jim, and she spoke it most amusingly, with his
own clipping, boyish intonation. Her tenderness hovered over
him like a flutter of wings. She lived so completely in his contemplation that she had acquired something of his outward aspect, something that recalled him in her movements, in the
way she stretched her arm, turned her head, directed her
glances. Her vigilant affection had an intensity that made it almost perceptible to the senses; it seemed actually to exist in
the ambient matter of space, to envelop him like a peculiar fragrance, to dwell in the sunshine like a tremulous, subdued, and
impassioned note. I suppose you think that I, too, am romantic,

but it is a mistake. I am relating to you the sober impressions of a bit of youth, of a strange uneasy romance that had come in my way. I observed with interest the work of his—well—good fortune. He was jealously loved, but why she should be jealous, and of what, I could not tell. The land, the people, the forests were her accomplices, guarding him with vigilant accord, with an air of seclusion, of mystery, of invincible possession. There was no appeal, as it were; he was imprisoned within the very freedom of his power, and she, though ready to make a footstool of her head for his feet, guarded her conquest inflexibly—as though he were hard to keep. The very Tamb' Itam, marching on our journeys upon the heels of his white lord, with his head thrown back, truculent and be-weaponed like a janissary, with kris, chopper, and lance (besides carrying Jim's gun); even Tamb' Itam allowed himself to put on airs of uncompromising guardianship, like a surly devoted jailer ready to lay down his life for his captive. On the evenings when we sat up late his silent, indistinct form would pass and repass under the verandah, with noiseless footsteps, or lifting my head I would unexpectedly make him out standing rigidly erect in the shadow. As a general rule he would vanish after a time, without a sound; but when we rose he would spring up close to us as if from the ground, ready for any orders Jim might wish to give. The girl, too, I believe, never went to sleep till we had separated for the night. More than once I saw her and Jim through the window of my room come out together quietly and lean on the rough balustrade—two white forms very close, his arm about her waist, her head on his shoulder. Their soft murmurs reached me, penetrating, tender, with a calm sad note in the stillness of the night, like a self-communion of one being carried on in two tones. Later on, tossing on my bed under the mosquito-net, I was sure to hear slight creakings, faint breathing, a throat cleared cautiously—and I would know that Tamb' Itam was still on the prowl. Though he had (by the favour of the white lord) a house in the compound, had 'taken wife,' and had lately been blessed with a child, I believe that, during my stay at all events, he slept on the verandah every night. It was very difficult to make this faithful and grim retainer talk. Even Jim himself was answered in jerky short sentences, under protest as it were. Talking, he seemed to imply, was no business of his. The longest speech I heard him volunteer was one morning when, suddenly extending his hand towards the courtyard, he pointed at Cornelius and said, 'Here comes the Nazarene.' I don't think he was addressing me, though I stood at his side; his object seemed rather to awaken the indignant attention of the universe. Some muttered allusions, which followed, to dogs and the smell of roast-meat, struck me as singularly felicitous. The courtyard, a large square space, was one torrid glaze of sunshine, and, bathed in intense light, Cornelius was creeping across in full view with an inexpressible effect of stealthiness, of dark and secret slinking. He reminded one of everything that is unsavoury. His slow laborious walk resembled the creeping of a repulsive beetle, the legs alone moving with horrid industry while the body glided evenly. I suppose he made straight enough for the place where he wanted to get to, but his progress with one shoulder carried forward seemed oblique. He was often seen circling slowly amongst the sheds, as if following a scent; passing before the verandah with upward stealthy glances; disappearing without haste round the corner of some hut. That he seemed free of the place demonstrated Jim's absurd carelessness or else his infinite disdain, for Cornelius had played a very dubious part (to say the least of it) in a certain episode which might have ended fatally for Jim. As a matter of fact, it had redounded to his glory. But everything redounded to his glory; and it was the irony of his good fortune that he, who had been too careful of it once, seemed to bear a charmed life.

"You must know he had left Doramin's place very soon after his arrival—much too soon, in fact, for his safety, and of course a long time before the war. In this he was actuated by a sense of duty; he had to look after Stein's business, he said. Hadn't he? To that end, with an utter disregard of his personal safety, he crossed the river and took up his quarters with Cornelius. How the latter had managed to exist through the troubled times I can't say. As Stein's agent, after all, he must have had Doramin's protection in a measure; and in one way or another he had managed to wriggle through all the deadly complications, while I have no doubt that his conduct, whatever line he was forced to take, was marked by that abjectness which was like the stamp of the man. That was his characteristic; he was fundamentally and outwardly abject, as other men are markedly of a generous, distinguished, or venerable appearance. It was the element of his nature which permeated all his acts and passions and emotions; he raged abjectly, smiled abjectly, was abjectly sad; his civilities and his indignation were alike abject. I am sure his love would have been the most abject of sentiments—but can one imagine a loathsome insect in love? And his loathsomeness, too, was abject, so that a simply disgusting person would have appeared noble by his side. He has his place neither in the background nor in the foreground of the story; he is simply seen skulking on its outskirts, enigmatical and unclean, tainting the fragrance of its youth and of its naïveness.

"His position in any case could not have been other than extremely miserable, yet it may very well be that he found some advantages in it. Jim told me he had been received at first with an abject display of the most amicable sentiments. 'The fellow apparently couldn't contain himself for joy,' said Jim with disgust. 'He flew at me every morning to shake both my hands—confound him! but I could never tell whether there would be any breakfast. If I got three meals in two days I considered myself jolly lucky, and he made me sign a chit for ten dollars every week. Said he was sure Mr. Stein did not mean him to keep me for nothing. Well—he kept me on nothing as near as possible. Put it down to the unsettled state of the country, and made as if to tear his hair out, begging my pardon twenty times a day, so that I had at last to entreat him not to worry. It made me sick. Half the roof of his house had fallen in, and the whole place had a mangy look, with wisps of dry grass sticking out and the corners of broken mats flapping on every wall. He did his best to make out that Mr. Stein owed him money on the last three years' trading, but his books were all torn, and some were missing. He tried to hint it was his late wife's fault. Disgusting scoundrel! At last I had to forbid him to mention his late wife

at all. It made Jewel cry. I couldn't discover what became of all
the trade-goods; there was nothing in the store but rats, having
a high old time amongst a litter of brown paper and old sack-
ing. It was argued on every hand that he had a lot of money
buried somewhere, but of course could get nothing out of him.
It was the most miserable existence I led there in that wretched
house. I tried to do my duty by Stein, but I had also other matters to think of. When I escaped to Doramin old Tunku Allang
got frightened and returned all my things. It was done in a
round-about way, and with no end of mystery, through a Chinaman who keeps a small shop here; but as soon as I left the
Bugis quarter and went to live with Cornelius it began to be
said openly that the Rajah had made up his mind to have me
killed before long. Pleasant, wasn't it? And I couldn't see what
there was to prevent him if he really *had* made up his mind.
The worst of it was, I couldn't help feeling I wasn't doing any
good either for Stein or for myself. Oh! it was beastly—the
whole six weeks of it.'"

Chapter Thirty

HE TOLD me further that he didn't know what made him
hang on—but of course we may guess. He sympathised
deeply with the defenceless girl, at the mercy of that 'mean,
cowardly scoundrel.' It appears Cornelius led her an awful life,
stopping only short of actual ill-usage, for which he had not
the pluck, I suppose. He insisted upon her calling him father—
'and with respect, too—with respect,' he would scream, shaking a little yellow fist in her face. 'I am a respectable man, and
what are you? Tell me—what are you? You think I am going to
bring up somebody else's child and not to be treated with respect? You ought to be glad I let you. Come—say Yes, father. . . . No? . . . you wait a bit.' Thereupon he would begin to
abuse the dead woman, till the girl would run off with her

hands to her head. He pursued her, dashing in and out and
round the house and amongst the sheds, would drive her into
some corner, where she would fall on her knees stopping her
ears, and then he would stand at a distance and declaim filthy
denunciations at her back for half an hour at a stretch. 'Your
mother was a devil, a deceitful devil—and you, too, are a
devil,' he would shriek in a final outburst, pick up a bit of dry
earth or a handful of mud (there was plenty of mud around the
house), and fling it into her hair. Sometimes, though, she
would hold out full of scorn, confronting him in silence, her
face sombre and contracted, and only now and then uttering a
word or two that would make the other jump and writhe with
the sting. Jim told me these scenes were terrible. It was indeed
a strange thing to come upon in the wilderness. The endless-
ness of such a subtly cruel situation was appalling—if you
think of it. The respectable Cornelius (Inchi 'Nelyus the
Malays called him, with a grimace that meant many things)
was a much-disappointed man. I don't know what he had expected would be done for him in consideration of his marriage;
but evidently the liberty to steal, and embezzle, and appropriate to himself for many years and in any way that suited him
best, the goods of Stein's Trading Company (Stein kept the
supply up unfalteringly as long as he could get his skippers to
take it there) did not seem to him a fair equivalent for the sacrifice of his honourable name. Jim would have enjoyed exceedingly thrashing Cornelius within an inch of his life; on the
other hand, the scenes were of so painful a character, so abominable, that his impulse would be to get out of earshot, in order
to spare the girl's feelings. They left her agitated, speechless,
clutching her bosom now and then with a stony, desperate face,
and then Jim would lounge up and say unhappily, 'Now—
come—really—what's the use—you must try to eat a bit,' or
give some such mark of sympathy. Cornelius would keep on
slinking through the doorways, across the verandah and back
again, as mute as a fish and with malevolent, mistrustful, un-
derhand glances. 'I can stop his game,' Jim said to her once.
'Just say the word.' And do you know what she answered? She
said—Jim told me impressively—that if she had not been sure

he was intensely wretched himself, she would have found the
courage to kill him with her own hands. 'Just fancy that! The
poor devil of a girl, almost a child, being driven to talk like
that,' he exclaimed in horror. It seemed impossible to save her
not only from that mean rascal but even from herself! It wasn't
that he pitied her so much, he affirmed; it was more than pity;
it was as if he had something on his conscience, while that life
went on. To leave the house would have appeared a base desertion. He had understood at last that there was nothing to expect from a longer stay, neither accounts nor money, nor truth
of any sort, but he stayed on, exasperating Cornelius to the
verge, I won't say of insanity, but almost of courage. Meantime he felt all sorts of dangers gathering obscurely about him.
Doramin had sent over twice a trusty servant to tell him seriously that he could do nothing for his safety unless he would
recross the river again and live amongst the Bugis as at first.
People of every condition used to call, often in the dead of
night, in order to disclose to him plots for his assassination. He
was to be poisoned. He was to be stabbed in the bath-house.
Arrangements were being made to have him shot from a boat
on the river. Each of these informants professed himself to be
his very good friend. It was enough—he told me—to spoil a
fellow's rest for ever. Something of the kind was extremely
possible—nay, probable—but the lying warnings gave him
only the sense of deadly scheming going on all around him, on
all sides, in the dark. Nothing more calculated to shake the best
of nerve. Finally, one night, Cornelius himself, with a great ap-
paratus of alarm and secrecy, unfolded in solemn wheedling
tones a little plan wherein for one hundred dollars—or even for
eighty; let's say eighty—he, Cornelius, would procure a trustworthy man to smuggle Jim out of the river, all safe. There was
nothing else for it now—if Jim cared a pin for his life. What's
eighty dollars? A trifle. An insignificant sum. While he, Cornelius, who had to remain behind, was absolutely courting
death by his proof of devotion to Mr. Stein's young friend. The
sight of his abject grimacing was—Jim told me—very hard to
bear; he clutched at his hair, beat his breast, rocked himself to
and fro with his hands pressed to his stomach, and actually

pretended to shed tears. 'Your blood be on your own head,' he
squeaked at last, and rushed out. It is a curious question how
far Cornelius was sincere in that performance. Jim confessed
to me that he did not sleep a wink after the fellow had gone. He
lay on his back on a thin mat spread over the bamboo flooring,
trying idly to make out the bare rafters and listening to the
rustling in the torn thatch. A star suddenly twinkled through a
hole in the roof. His brain was in a whirl; but, nevertheless, it
was on that very night that he matured his plan for overcoming
Sherif Ali. It had been the thought of all the moments he could
spare from the hopeless investigation into Stein's affairs, but
the notion—he says—came to him then all at once. He could
see, as it were, the guns mounted on the top of the hill. He got
very hot and excited lying there; sleep was out of the question
more than ever. He jumped up and went out barefooted on the
verandah. Walking silently, he came upon the girl, motionless
against the wall, as if on the watch. In his then state of mind it
did not surprise him to see her up, nor yet to hear her ask in an
anxious whisper where Cornelius could be. He simply said he
did not know. She moaned a little, and peered into the *campong*. Everything was very quiet. He was possessed by his new
idea, and so full of it that he could not help telling the girl all
about it at once. She listened, clapped her hands lightly, whispered softly her admiration, but was evidently on the alert all
the time. It seems he had been used to make a confidante of her
all along—and that she on her part could and did give him a lot
of useful hints as to Patusan affairs there is no doubt. He assured me more than once that he had never found himself the
worse for her advice. At any rate, he was proceeding to explain
his plan fully to her there and then, when she pressed his arm
once, and vanished from his side. Then Cornelius appeared
from somewhere, and, perceiving Jim, ducked sideways, as
though he had been shot at, and afterwards stood very still in
the dusk. At last he came forward prudently, like a suspicious
cat. 'There were some fishermen there—with fish,' he said in a
shaky voice. 'To sell fish—you understand.' . . . It must have
been then two o'clock in the morning—a likely time for anybody to hawk fish about!

"Jim, however, let the statement pass, and did not give it a single thought. Other matters occupied his mind, and besides he had neither seen nor heard anything. He contented himself by saying, 'Oh!' absently, got a drink of water out of a pitcher standing there, and leaving Cornelius a prey to some inexplicable emotion—that made him embrace with both arms the worm-eaten rail of the verandah as if his legs had failed—went in again and lay down on his mat to think. By-and-by he heard stealthy footsteps. They stopped. A voice whispered tremulously through the wall, 'Are you asleep?' 'No! What is it?' he answered, briskly, and there was an abrupt movement outside, and then all was still, as if the whisperer had been startled. Extremely annoyed at this, Jim came out impetuously, and Cornelius with a faint shriek fled along the verandah as far as the steps, where he hung on to the broken banister. Very puzzled, Jim called out to him from the distance to know what the devil he meant. 'Have you given your consideration to what I spoke to you about?' asked Cornelius, pronouncing the words with difficulty, like a man in the cold fit of a fever. 'No!' shouted Jim in a passion. 'I did not, and I don't intend to. I am going to live here, in Patusan.' 'You shall d-d-die h-h-here,' answered Cornelius, still shaking violently, and in a sort of expiring voice. The whole performance was so absurd and provoking that Jim didn't know whether he ought to be amused or angry. 'Not till I have seen you tucked away, you bet,' he called out, exasperated yet ready to laugh. Half seriously (being excited with his own thoughts, you know) he went on shouting, 'Nothing can touch me! You can do your damnedest.' Somehow the shadowy Cornelius far off there seemed to be the hateful embodiment of all the annoyances and difficulties he had found in his path. He let himself go—his nerves had been overwrought for days—and called him many pretty names,—swindler, liar, sorry rascal: in fact, carried on in an extraordinary way. He admits he passed all bounds, that he was quite beside himself—defied all Patusan to scare him away—declared he would make them all dance to his own tune yet, and so on, in a menacing, boasting strain. Perfectly bombastic and ridiculous, he said. His ears burned at the bare recollection. Must

have been off his chump in some way. . . . The girl, who was
sitting with us, nodded her little head at me quickly, frowned
faintly, and said, 'I heard him,' with childlike solemnity. He
laughed and blushed. What stopped him at last, he said, was
the silence, the complete deathlike silence, of the indistinct
figure far over there, that seemed to hang collapsed, doubled
over the rail in a weird immobility. He came to his senses, and
ceasing suddenly, wondered greatly at himself. He watched for
a while. Not a stir, not a sound. 'Exactly as if the chap had died
while I had been making all that noise,' he said. He was so
ashamed of himself that he went indoors in a hurry without another word, and flung himself down again. The row seemed to
have done him good though, because he went to sleep for the
rest of the night like a baby. Hadn't slept like that for weeks,
'But *I* didn't sleep,' struck the girl, one elbow on the table and
nursing her cheek. 'I watched.' Her big eyes flashed, rolling a
little, and then she fixed them on my face intently."

Chapter Thirty-one

YOU may imagine with what interest I listened. All these details were perceived to have some significance twenty-
four hours later. In the morning Cornelius made no allusion to
the events of the night. 'I suppose you will come back to my
poor house,' he muttered, surlily, slinking up just as Jim was
entering the canoe to go over to Doramin's *campong*. Jim only
nodded, without looking at him. 'You find it good fun, no
doubt,' muttered the other in a sour tone. Jim spent the day
with the old *nakhoda*, preaching the necessity of vigorous action to the principal men of the Bugis community, who had
been summoned for a big talk. He remembered with pleasure
how very eloquent and persuasive he had been. 'I managed to
put some backbone into them that time, and no mistake,' he
said. Sherif Ali's last raid had swept the outskirts of the settle-

ment, and some women belonging to the town had been carried off to the stockade. Sherif Ali's emissaries had been seen in the marketplace the day before, strutting about haughtily in white cloaks, and boasting of the Rajah's friendship for their master. One of them stood forward in the shade of a tree, and, leaning on the long barrel of a rifle, exhorted the people to prayer and repentance, advising them to kill all the strangers in their midst, some of whom, he said, were infidels and others even worse—children of Satan in the guise of Moslems. It was reported that several of the Rajah's people amongst the listeners had loudly expressed their approbation. The terror amongst the common people was intense. Jim, immensely pleased with his day's work, crossed the river again before sunset.

"As he had got the Bugis irretrievably committed to action and had made himself responsible for success on his own head, he was so elated that in the lightness of his heart he absolutely tried to be civil with Cornelius. But Cornelius became wildly jovial in response, and it was almost more than he could stand, he says, to hear his little squeaks of false laughter, to see him wriggle and blink, and suddenly catch hold of his chin and crouch low over the table with a distracted stare. The girl did not show herself, and Jim retired early. When he rose to say good-night, Cornelius jumped up, knocking his chair over, and ducked out of sight as if to pick up something he had dropped. His good-night came huskily from under the table. Jim was amazed to see him emerge out with a dropping jaw, and staring, stupidly frightened eyes. He clutched the edge of the table. 'What's the matter? Are you unwell?' asked Jim. 'Yes, yes, yes. A great colic in my stomach,' says the other; and it is Jim's opinion that it was perfectly true. If so, it was, in view of his contemplated action, an abject sign of a still imperfect callousness for which he must be given all due credit.

'Be it as it may, Jim's slumbers were disturbed by a dream of heavens like brass resounding with a great voice, which called upon him to Awake! Awake! so loud that, notwithstanding his desperate determination to sleep on, he did wake up in reality. The glare of a red spluttering conflagration going on in mid-air fell on his eyes. Coils of black thick smoke curved round the head of some apparition, some unearthly being, all in white, with a severe, drawn, anxious face. After a second or so he recognised the girl. She was holding a dammar torch at arm's-length aloft, and in a persistent, urgent monotone she was repeating, 'Get up! Get up! Get up!'

"Suddenly, he leaped to his feet; at once she put into his hand a revolver, his own revolver, which had been hanging on a nail, but loaded this time. He gripped it in silence, bewildered, blinking in the light. He wondered what he could do for her.

"She asked rapidly and very low, 'Can you face four men with this?' He laughed while narrating this part at the recollection of his polite alacrity. It seems he made a great display of it. 'Certainly—of course—certainly—command me.' He was not properly awake, and had a notion of being very civil in these extraordinary circumstances, of showing his unquestioning, devoted readiness. She left the room, and he followed her; in the passage they disturbed an old hag who did the casual cooking of the household, though she was so decrepit as to be hardly able to understand human speech. She got up and hobbled behind them, mumbling toothlessly. On the verandah a hammock of sailcloth, belonging to Cornelius, swayed lightly to the touch of Jim's elbow. It was empty.

"The Patusan establishment, like all the posts of Stein's Trading Company, had originally consisted of four buildings. Two of them were represented by two heaps of sticks, broken bamboos, rotten thatch, over which the four corner-posts of hardwood leaned sadly at different angles: the principal storeroom, however, stood yet, facing the agent's house. It was an oblong hut, built of mud and clay: it had at one end a wide door of stout planking, which so far had not come off the hinges, and in one of the side walls there was a square aperture, a sort of window, with three wooden bars. Before descending the few steps the girl turned her face over her shoulder and said quickly, 'You were to be set upon while you slept.' Jim tells me he experienced a sense of deception. It was the old story. He was weary of these attempts upon his life. He had had his fill of these alarms. He was sick of them. He assured me he was angry with the girl for deceiving him. He had followed her under the impression that it was she who wanted his help, and now he had half a mind to turn on his heel and go back in disgust. 'Do you know,' he commented, profoundly, 'I rather think I was not quite myself for whole weeks on end about that time.' 'Oh, yes. You were though,' I couldn't help contradicting.

"But she moved on swiftly, and he followed her into the courtyard. All its fences had fallen in a long time ago; the neighbours' buffaloes would pace in the morning across the open space, snorting profoundly, without haste; the very jungle was invading it already. Jim and the girl stopped in the rank grass. The light in which they stood made a dense blackness all round, and only above their heads there was an opulent glitter of stars. He told me it was a beautiful night—quite cool, with a little stir of breeze from the river. It seems he noticed its friendly beauty. Remember this is a love story I am telling you now. A lovely night that seemed to breathe on them a soft caress. The flame of the torch streamed now and then with a fluttering noise like a flag, and for a time this was the only sound. 'They are in the storeroom waiting,' whispered the girl; 'they are waiting for the signal.' 'Who's to give it?' he asked. She shook the torch, which blazed up after a shower of sparks. 'Only you have been sleeping so restlessly,' she continued in a murmur. 'I watched your sleep, too.' 'You!' he exclaimed, craning his neck to look about him. 'You think I watched on this night only!' she said, with a sort of despairing indignation.

'He says it was as if he had received a blow on the chest. He gasped. He thought he had been an awful brute somehow, and he felt remorseful, touched, happy, elated. This, let me remind you again, is a love story; you can see it by the imbecility, not a repulsive imbecility, the exalted imbecility of these proceedings, this station in torchlight, as if they had come there on purpose to have it out for the edification of concealed murderers. If Sherif Ali's emissaries had been possessed—as Jim remarked—of a pennyworth of spunk, this was the time to make a rush. His heart was thumping—not in fear—but he seemed to hear the grass rustle, and he stepped smartly out of the light.

Something dark, imperfectly seen, flitted rapidly out of sight. He called out in a strong voice, 'Cornelius! O Cornelius!' A profound silence succeeded: his voice did not seem to have carried twenty feet. Again the girl was by his side. 'Fly!' she said. The old woman was coming up; her broken figure hovered in crippled little jumps on the edge of the light; they heard her mumbling, and a light, moaning sigh. 'Fly!' repeated the girl, excitedly. 'They are frightened now—this light—the voices. They know you are awake now—they know you are big, strong, fearless . . .' 'If I am all that,' he began, but she interrupted him. 'Yes—to-night! But what of to-morrow night? Of the next night? Of the night after—of all the many, many nights? Can I be always watching?' A sobbing catch of her breath affected him beyond the power of words.

"He told me that he had never felt so small, so powerless—and as to courage, what was the good of it? he thought. He was so helpless that even flight seemed of no use; and though she kept on whispering, 'Go to Doramin, go to Doramin,' with feverish insistence, he realised that for him there was no refuge from that loneliness which centupled all his dangers except—in her. 'I thought,' he said to me, 'that if I went away from her it would be the end of everything somehow.' Only as they couldn't stop there for ever in the middle of that courtyard, he made up his mind to go and look into the storehouse. He let her follow him without thinking of any protest, as if they had been indissolubly united. 'I am fearless—am I?' he muttered through his teeth. She restrained his arm. 'Wait till you hear my voice,' she said, and, torch in hand, ran lightly round the corner. He remained alone in the darkness, his face to the door; not a sound, not a breath came from the other side. The old hag let out a dreary groan somewhere behind his back. He heard a high-pitched almost screaming call from the girl. 'Now! Push!' he pushed violently; the door swung with a creak and a clatter, disclosing to his intense astonishment the low dungeon-like interior illuminated by a lurid, waving glare. A turmoil of smoke eddied down upon an empty wooden crate in the middle of the floor, a litter of rags and straw tried to soar, but only stirred feebly in the draught. She had thrust the light through the bars of the window. He saw her bare round arm extended and rigid, holding up the torch with the steadiness of an iron bracket. A conical ragged heap of old mats cumbered a distant corner almost to the ceiling, and that was all.

"He explained to me that he was bitterly disappointed at this. His fortitude had been tried by so many warnings, he had been for weeks surrounded by so many hints of danger, that he wanted the relief of some reality, of something tangible that he could meet. 'It would have cleared the air for a couple of hours at least, if you know what I mean,' he said to me. 'Jove! I had been living for days with a stone on my chest.' Now at last he had thought he would get hold of something, and—nothing! Not a trace, not a sign of anybody. He had raised his weapon as the door flew open, but now his arm fell. 'Fire! Defend yourself,' the girl outside cried in an agonising voice. She being in the dark and with her arm thrust in to the shoulder through the small hole, couldn't see what was going on, and she dared not withdraw the torch now to run round. 'There's nobody here!' yelled Jim, contemptuously, but his impulse to burst into a resentful exasperated laugh died without a sound: he had perceived in the very act of turning away that he was exchanging glances with a pair of eyes in the heap of mats. He saw a shifting gleam of whites. 'Come to!' he cried in a fury, a little doubtful, and a dark-faced head, a head without a body, shaped itself in the rubbish, a strangely detached head, that looked at him with a steady scowl. Next moment the whole mound stirred, and with a low grunt a man emerged swiftly, and bounded towards Jim. Behind him the mats as it were jumped and flew, his right arm was raised with a crooked elbow, and the dull blade of a kris protruded from his fist held off, a little above his head. A cloth wound tight round his loins seemed dazzlingly white on his bronze skin; his naked body glistened as if wet.

"Jim noted all this. He told me he was experiencing a feeling of unutterable relief, of vengeful elation. He held his shot, he says, deliberately. He held it for the tenth part of a second, for three strides of the man—an unconscionable time. He held it for the pleasure of saying to himself, That's a dead man! He was absolutely positive and certain. He let him come on because it did not matter. A dead man, anyhow. He noticed the dilated nostrils, the wide eyes, the intent, eager stillness of the face, and then he fired.

"The explosion in that confined space was stunning. He stepped back a pace. He saw the man jerk his head up, fling his arms forward, and drop the kris. He ascertained afterwards that he had shot him through the mouth, a little upwards, the bullet coming out high at the back of the skull. With the impetus of his rush the man drove straight on, his face suddenly gaping disfigured, with his hands open before him gropingly, as though blinded, and landed with terrific violence on his forehead, just short of Jim's bare toes. Jim says he didn't lose the smallest detail of all this. He found himself calm, appeased, without rancour, without uneasiness, as if the death of that man had atoned for everything. The place was getting very full of sooty smoke from the torch, in which the unswaying flame burned blood-red without a flicker. He walked in resolutely, striding over the dead body, and covered with his revolver another naked figure outlined vaguely at the other end. As he was about to pull the trigger, the man threw away with force a short heavy spear, and squatted submissively on his hams, his back to the wall and his clasped hands between his legs. 'You want your life?' Jim said. The other made no sound. 'How many more of you?' asked Jim again. 'Two more, Tuan,' said the man very softly, looking with big fascinated eyes into the muzzle of the revolver. Accordingly two more crawled from under the mats, holding out ostentatiously their empty hands."

Chapter Thirty-two

JIM took up an advantageous position and shepherded them out in a bunch through the doorway: all that time the torch had remained vertical in the grip of a little hand, without so much as a tremble. The three men obeyed him, perfectly mute, moving automatically. He ranged them in a row. 'Link arms!' he ordered. They did so. 'The first who withdraws his arm or turns his head is a dead man,' he said. 'March!' They stepped out together, rigidly; he followed, and at the side the girl, in a trailing white gown, her black hair falling as low as her waist, bore the light. Erect and swaying, she seemed to glide without touching the earth; the only sound was the silky swish and rustle of the long grass. 'Stop!' cried Jim.

"The river-bank was steep; a great freshness ascended, the light fell on the edge of smooth dark water frothing without a ripple; right and left the shapes of the houses ran together below the sharp outlines of the roofs. 'Take my greetings to Sherif Ali—till I come myself,' said Jim. Not one head of the three budged. 'Jump!' he thundered. The three splashes made one splash, a shower flew up, black heads bobbed convulsively, and disappeared; but a great blowing and spluttering went on, growing faint, for they were diving industriously in great fear of a parting shot. Jim turned to the girl, who had been a silent and attentive observer. His heart seemed suddenly to grow too big for his breast and choke him in the hollow of his throat. This probably made him speechless for so long, and after returning his gaze she flung the burning torch with a wide sweep of the arm into the river. The ruddy fiery glare, taking a long flight through the night, sank with a vicious hiss, and the calm soft starlight descended upon them, unchecked.

"He did not tell me what it was he said when at last he recovered his voice. I don't suppose he could be very eloquent. The world was still, the night breathed on them, one of those nights that seemed created for the sheltering of tenderness, and there are moments when our souls, as if freed from their dark envelope, glow with an exquisite sensibility that makes certain silences more lucid than speeches. As to the girl, he told me, 'She broke down a bit. Excitement—don't you know. Reaction. Deucedly tired she must have been—and all that kind of thing. And—and—hang it all—she was fond of me, don't you see. . . . I, too . . . didn't know, of course . . . never entered my head. . . .'

"There he got up and began to walk about in some agitation. 'I—I love her dearly. More than I could tell. Of course one cannot tell. You take a different view of your actions when you come to understand, when you are *made* to understand every day that your existence is necessary—you see, absolutely necessary—to another person. I am made to feel that. Wonderful. But only try to think what her life had been. It is too extravagantly awful! Isn't it? And me finding her here like this—as you may go out for a stroll and come suddenly upon somebody drowning in a lonely dark place. Jove! No time to lose. Well, it is a trust, too . . . I believe I am equal to it. . . .'

"I must tell you the girl had left us to ourselves some time before. He slapped his chest. 'Yes! I feel that, but I believe I am equal to all my luck!' He had the gift of finding a special meaning in everything that happened to him. This was the view he took of his love-affair; it was idyllic, a little solemn, and also true, since his belief had all the unshakable seriousness of youth. Some time after, on another occasion, he said to me, 'I've been only two years here, and now, upon my word, I can't conceive being able to live anywhere else. The very thought of the world outside is enough to give me a fright; because, don't you see,' he continued, with downcast eyes watching the action of his boot busied in squashing thoroughly a tiny bit of dried mud (we were strolling on the river-bank)—'because I have not forgotten why I came here. Not yet!'

"I refrained from looking at him, but I think I heard a short sigh; we took a turn or two in silence. 'Upon my soul and conscience,' he began again, 'if such a thing can be forgotten, then I think I have a right to dismiss it from my mind. Ask any man here' . . . his voice changed. 'Is it not strange,' he went on in a gentle, almost yearning tone, 'that all these people, all these people who would do anything for me, can never be made to understand? Never! If you disbelieve me I could not call them up. It seems hard, somehow. I am stupid, am I not? What more can I want? If you ask them who is brave—who is true—who is just—who is it they would trust with their lives?—they would say, Tuan Jim. And yet they can never know the real, real truth . . .'

"That's what he said to me on my last day with him. I did not let a murmur escape me: I felt he was going to say more, and come no nearer to the root of the matter. The sun, whose concentrated glare dwarfs the earth into a restless mote of dust, had sunk behind the forest, and the diffused light from an opal sky seemed to cast upon a world without shadows and without brilliance the illusion of a calm and pensive greatness. I don't know why, listening to him, I should have noted so distinctly the gradual darkening of the river, of the air; the irresistible slow work of the night settling silently on all the visible forms, effacing the outlines, burying the shapes deeper and deeper, like a steady fall of impalpable black dust.

"'Jove!' he began, abruptly, 'there are days when a fellow is too absurd for anything; only I know I can tell you what I like. I talk about being done with it—with the bally thing at the back of my head. . . . Forgetting.. . . . Hang me if I know! I can think of it quietly. After all, what has it proved? Nothing. I suppose you don't think so. . . .'

"I made a protesting murmur.

"'No matter,' he said. 'I am satisfied . . . nearly. I've got to look only at the face of the first man that comes along, to regain my confidence. They can't be made to understand what is going on in me. What of that? Come! I haven't done so badly.'

"'Not so badly,' I said.

"'But all the same, you wouldn't like to have me aboard your own ship—hey?'

"'Confound you!' I cried. 'Stop this.'

"'Aha! You see,' he cried, crowing, as it were, over me placidly. 'Only,' he went on, 'you just try to tell this to any of them here. They would think you a fool, a liar, or worse. And so I can stand it. I've done a thing or two for them, but this is what they have done for me.'

"'My dear chap,' I cried, 'you shall always remain for them an insoluble mystery.' Thereupon we were silent.

"'Mystery,' he repeated, before looking up. 'Well, then let me always remain here.'

"After the sun had set, the darkness seemed to drive upon us, borne on every faint puff of the breeze. In the middle of a hedged path I saw the arrested, gaunt, watchful, and apparently one-legged silhouette of Tamb' Itam; and across the dusky space my eye detected something white moving to and fro behind the supports of the roof. As soon as Jim, with Tamb' Itam at his heels, had started upon his evening rounds, I went up to the house alone, and, unexpectedly, found myself waylaid by the girl, who had been clearly waiting for this opportunity.

"It is hard to tell you what it was precisely she wanted to wrest from me. Obviously it would be something very simple—the simplest impossibility in the world; as, for instance, the exact description of the form of a cloud. She wanted an assurance, a statement, a promise, an explanation—I don't know how to call it: the thing has no name. It was dark under the projecting roof, and all I could see were the flowing lines of her gown, the pale small oval of her face, with the white flash of her teeth, and, turned towards me, the big sombre orbits of her eyes, where there seemed to be a faint stir, such as you may fancy you can detect when you plunge your gaze to the bottom of an immensely deep well. What is it that moves there? you ask yourself. Is it a blind monster or only a lost gleam from the universe? It occurred to me—don't laugh—that all things being dissimilar, she was more inscrutable in her childish ignorance than the Sphinx propounding childish riddles to wayfarers. She had been carried off to Patusan before her eyes were open. She had grown up there; she had seen nothing, she had known nothing, she had no conception of anything. I ask myself whether she were sure that anything else existed. What notions she may have formed of the outside world is to me inconceivable: all that she knew of its inhabitants were a betrayed woman and a sinister pantaloon. Her lover also came to her from there, gifted with irresistible seductions; but what would become of her if he should return to these inconceivable regions that seemed always to claim back their own? Her mother had warned her of this with tears, before she died. . . .

"She had caught hold of my arm firmly, and as soon as I had stopped she had withdrawn her hand in haste. She was audacious and shrinking. She feared nothing, but she was checked by the profound incertitude and the extreme strangeness—a

brave person groping in the dark. I belonged to this Unknown
that might claim Jim for its own at any moment. I was, as it
were, in the secret of its nature and of its intentions;—the confidant of a threatening mystery:—armed with its power perhaps! I believe she supposed I could with a word whisk Jim
away out of her very arms; it is my sober conviction she went
through agonies of apprehension during my long talks with
Jim; through a real and intolerable anguish that might have
conceivably driven her into plotting my murder, had the fierceness of her soul been equal to the tremendous situation it had
created. This is my impression, and it is all I can give you: the
whole thing dawned gradually upon me, and as it got clearer
and clearer I was overwhelmed by a slow incredulous amazement. She made me believe her, but there is no word that on
my lips could render the effect of the headlong and vehement
whisper, of the soft, passionate tones, of the sudden breathless
pause and the appealing movement of the white arms extended
swiftly. They fell; the ghostly figure swayed like a slender tree
in the wind, the pale oval of the face drooped; it was impossible to distinguish her features, the darkness of the eyes was unfathomable; two wide sleeves uprose in the dark like unfolding
wings, and she stood silent, holding her head in her hands."

Chapter Thirty-three

I WAS immensely touched: her youth, her ignorance, her
pretty beauty, which had the simple charm and the delicate
vigour of a wild-flower, her pathetic pleading, her helplessness, appealed to me with almost the strength of her own unreasonable and natural fear. She feared the unknown as we all
do, and her ignorance made the unknown infinitely vast. I
stood for it, for myself, for you fellows, for all the world that
neither cared for Jim nor needed him in the least. I would have
been ready enough to answer for the indifference of the teem-

ing earth but for the reflection that he, too, belonged to this
mysterious unknown of her fears, and that, however much I
stood for, I did not stand for him. This made me hesitate. A
murmur of hopeless pain unsealed my lips. I began by protesting that I at least had come with no intention to take Jim away.

"Why did I come, then? Afer a slight movement she was as
still as a marble statue in the night. I tried to explain briefly:
friendship, business; if I had any wish in the matter it was
rather to see him stay. . . . 'They always leave us,' she murmured. The breath of sad wisdom from the grave which her
piety wreathed with flowers seemed to pass in a faint sigh. . . .
Nothing, I said, could separate Jim from her.

"It is my firm conviction now; it was my conviction at the
time; it was the only possible conclusion from the facts of the
case. It was not made more certain by her whispering in a tone
in which one speaks to oneself. 'He swore this to me.' 'Did
you ask him?' I said.

"She made a step nearer. 'No. Never!' She had asked him
only to go away. It was that night on the river-bank, after he
had killed the man—after she had flung the torch in the water
because he was looking at her so. There was too much light,
and the danger was over then—for a little time—for a little
time. He said then he would not abandon her to Cornelius. She
had insisted. She wanted him to leave her. He said that he
could not—that it was impossible. He trembled while he said
this. She had felt him tremble. . . . One does not require much
imagination to see the scene, almost to hear their whispers.
She was afraid for him, too. I believe that then she saw in him
only a predestined victim of dangers which she understood
better than himself. Though by nothing but his mere presence
he had mastered her heart, had filled all her thoughts, and had
possessed himself of all her affections, she under-estimated his
chances of success. It is obvious that at about that time everybody was inclined to under-estimate his chances. Strictly
speaking he didn't seem to have any. I know this was Cornelius's view. He confessed that much to me in extenuation of
the shady part he had played in Sherif Ali's plot to do away
with the infidel. Even Sherif Ali himself, as it seems certain

now, had nothing but contempt for the white man. Jim was to
be murdered mainly on religious grounds, I believe. A simple
act of piety (and so far infinitely meritorious), but otherwise
without much importance. In the last part of this opinion Cornelius concurred. 'Honourable sir,' he argued abjectly on the
only occasion he managed to have me to himself—'Honourable sir, how was I to know? Who was he? What could he
do to make people believe him? What did Mr. Stein mean
sending a boy like that to talk big to an old servant? I was
ready to save him for eighty dollars. Only eighty dollars. Why
didn't the fool go? Was I to get stabbed myself for the sake of
a stranger?' He grovelled in spirit before me, with his body
doubled up insinuatingly and his hands hovering about my
knees, as though he were ready to embrace my legs. 'What's
eighty dollars? An insignificant sum to give to a defenceless
old man ruined for life by a deceased she-devil.' Here he wept.
But I anticipate. I didn't that night chance upon Cornelius till I
had had it out with the girl.

"She was unselfish when she urged Jim to leave her, and
even to leave the country. It was his danger that was foremost
in her thoughts—even if she wanted to save herself, too—perhaps unconsciously: but then look at the warning she had, look
at the lesson that could be drawn from every moment of the re-
cently ended life in which all her memories were centred. She
fell at his feet—she told me so—there by the river, in the discreet light of stars which showed nothing except great masses
of silent shadows, indefinite open spaces, and trembling
faintly upon the broad stream made it appear as wide as the
sea. He had lifted her up. He lifted her up, and then she would
struggle no more. Of course not. Strong arms, a tender voice, a
stalwart shoulder to rest her poor lonely little head upon. The
need—the infinite need—of all this for the aching heart, for
the bewildered mind;—the promptings of youth—the necessity of the moment. What would you have? One understands—
unless one is incapable of understanding anything under the
sun. And so she was content to be lifted up—and held. 'You
know—Jove! this is serious—no nonsense in it!' as Jim had
whispered hurriedly with a troubled concerned face on the

threshold of his house. I don't know so much about nonsense, but there was nothing lighthearted in their romance: they came together under the shadow of a life's disaster, like knight and maiden meeting to exchange vows amongst haunted ruins. The starlight was good enough for that story, a light so faint and remote that it cannot resolve shadows into shapes, and show the other shore of a stream. I did look upon the stream that night and from the very place; it rolled silent and as black as Styx: the next day I went away, but I am not likely to forget what it was she wanted to be saved from when she entreated him to leave her while there was time. She told me what it was, calmed—she was now too passionately interested for mere excitement—in a voice as quiet in the obscurity as her white half-lost figure. She told me, 'I didn't want to die weeping.' I thought I had not heard aright.

"'You did not want to die weeping?' I repeated after her. 'Like my mother,' she added readily. The outlines of her white shape did not stir in the least. 'My mother had wept bitterly before she died,' she explained. An inconceivable calmness seemed to have risen from the ground around us, imperceptibly, like the still rise of a flood in the night, obliterating the familiar landmarks of emotions. There came upon me, as though I had felt myself losing my footing in the midst of waters, a sudden dread, the dread of the unknown depths. She went on explaining that, during the last moments, being alone with her mother, she had to leave the side of the couch to go and set her back against the door, in order to keep Cornelius out. He desired to get in, and kept on drumming with both fists, only desisting now and again to shout huskily, 'Let me in! Let me in! Let me in!' In a far corner upon a few mats the moribund woman, already speechless and unable to lift her arm, rolled her head over, and with a feeble movement of her hand seemed to command—'No! No!' and the obedient daughter, setting her shoulders with all her strength against the door, was looking on. 'The tears fell from her eyes—and then she died,' concluded the girl in an imperturbable monotone, which more than anything else, more than the white statuesque immobility of her person, more than mere words could do, troubled my

mind profoundly with the passive, irremediable horror of the
scene. It had the power to drive me out of my conception of existence, out of that shelter each of us makes for himself to
creep under in moments of danger, as a tortoise withdraws
within its shell. For a moment I had a view of a world that
seemed to wear a vast and dismal aspect of disorder, while, in
truth, thanks to our unwearied efforts, it is as sunny an arrangement of small conveniences as the mind of man can conceive.
But still—it was only a moment: I went back into my shell directly. One *must*—don't you know?—though I seemed to have
lost all my words in the chaos of dark thoughts I had contemplated for a second or two beyond the pale. These came back,
too, very soon, for words also belong to the sheltering conception of light and order which is our refuge. I had them ready at
my disposal before she whispered softly, 'He swore he would
never leave me, when we stood there alone! He swore to
me!' . . 'And is it possible that you—you! do not believe him?'
I asked, sincerely reproachful, genuinely shocked. Why couldn't
she believe? Wherefore this craving for incertitude, this clinging to fear, as if incertitude and fear had been the safeguards of
her love. It was monstrous. She should have made for herself a
shelter of inexpugnable peace out of that honest affection. She
had not the knowledge—not the skill perhaps. The night had
come on apace; it had grown pitch-dark where we were, so that
without stirring she had faded like the intangible form of a
wistful and perverse spirit. And suddenly I heard her quiet
whisper again, 'Other men had sworn the same thing.' It was
like a meditative comment on some thoughts full of sadness, of
awe. And she added, still lower if possible, 'My father did.'
She paused the time to draw an inaudible breath. 'Her father,
too.' . . . These were the things she knew! At once I said, 'Ah!
but he is not like that.' This, it seemed, she did not intend to
dispute; but after a time the strange still whisper wandering
dreamily in the air stole into my ears. 'Why is he different? Is
he better? Is he . . .' 'Upon my word of honour,' I broke in, 'I
believe he is.' We subdued our tones to a mysterious pitch.
Amongst the huts of Jim's workmen (they were mostly liber-
ated slaves from the Sherif's stockade) somebody started a

shrill, drawling song. Across the river a big fire (at Doramin's,
I think) made a glowing ball, completely isolated in the night.
'Is he more true?' she murmured. 'Yes,' I said. 'More true than
any other man,' she repeated in lingering accents. 'Nobody
here,' I said, 'would dream of doubting his word—nobody
would dare—except you.'

"I think she made a movement at this. 'More brave,' she
went on in a changed tone. 'Fear shall never drive him away
from you,' I said a little nervously. The song stopped short on
a shrill note, and was succeeded by several voices talking in
the distance. Jim's voice, too. I was struck by her silence.
'What has he been telling you? He has been telling you something?' I asked. There was no answer. 'What is it he told you?'
I insisted.

"'Do you think I can tell you? How am I to know? How am
I to understand?' she cried at last. There was a stir. I believe
she was wringing her hands. 'There is something he can never
forget.'

"'So much the better for you,' I said gloomily.

"'What is it? What is it?' she put an extraordinary force of
appeal into her supplicating tone. 'He says he had been afraid.
How can I believe this? Am I a mad woman to believe this?
You all remember something! You all go back to it. What is it?
You tell me! What is this thing? Is it alive?—is it dead? I hate
it. It is cruel. Has it got a face and a voice—this calamity? Will
he see it—will he hear it? In his sleep perhaps when he cannot
see me—and then arise and go. Ah! I shall never forgive him.
My mother had forgiven—but I, never! Will it be a sign—a
call?'

"It was a wonderful experience. She mistrusted his very
slumbers—and she seemed to think I could tell her why! Thus
a poor mortal seduced by the charm of an apparition might
have tried to wring from another ghost the tremendous secret
of the claim the other world holds over a disembodied soul
astray amongst the passions of this earth. The very ground on
which I stood seemed to melt under my feet. And it was so
simple, too; but if the spirits evoked by our fears and our unrest have ever to vouch for each other's constancy before the

forlorn magicians that we are, then I—I alone of us dwellers in the flesh—have shuddered in the hopeless chill of such a task. A sign, a call! How telling in its expression with her ignorance. A few words! How she came to know them, how she came to pronounce them, I can't imagine. Women find their inspiration in the stress of moments that for us are merely awful, absurd, or futile. To discover that she had a voice at all was enough to strike awe into the heart. Had a spurned stone cried out in pain it could not have appeared a greater and more pitiful miracle. These few sounds wandering in the dark had made their two benighted lives tragic to my mind. It was impossible to make her understand. I chafed silently at my impotence. And Jim, too—poor devil! Who would need him? Who would remember him? He had what he wanted. His very existence probably had been forgotten by this time. They had mastered their fates. They were tragic.

"Her immobility before me was clearly expectant, and my part was to speak for my brother from the realm of forgetful shades. I was deeply moved at my responsibility and at her distress. I would have given anything for the power to soothe her frail soul, tormenting itself in its invincible ignorance like a small bird beating about the cruel wires of a cage. Nothing easier than to say, Have no fear! Nothing more difficult. How does one kill fear, I wonder? How do you shoot a spectre through the heart, slash off its spectral head, take it by its spectral throat? It is an enterprise you rush into while you dream, and are glad to make your escape with wet hair and every limb shaking. The bullet is not run, the blade not forged, the man not born; even the winged words of truth drop at your feet like lumps of lead. You require for such a desperate encounter an enchanted and poisoned shaft dipped in a lie too subtle to be found on earth. An enterprise for a dream, my master!

"I began my exorcism with a heavy heart, with a sort of sullen anger in it, too. Jim's voice, suddenly raised with a stern intonation, carried across the courtyard, reproving the carelessness of some dumb sinner by the river-side. Nothing—I said, speaking in a distinct murmur—there could be nothing in that unknown world she fancied so eager to rob her of her happiness, there was nothing neither living nor dead, there was no face, no voice, no power, that could tear Jim from her side. I drew breath and she whispered softly, 'He told me so.' 'He told you the truth,' I said. 'Nothing,' she sighed out, and abruptly turned upon me with a barely audible intensity of tone: 'Why did you come to us from out there? He speaks of you too often. You make me afraid. Do you—do you want him?' A sort of stealthy fierceness had crept into our hurried mutters. 'I shall never come again,' I said, bitterly. 'And I don't want him. No one wants him.' 'No one,' she repeated in a tone of doubt. 'No one,' I affirmed, feeling myself swayed by some strange excitement. 'You think him strong, wise, courageous, great—why not believe him to be true, too? I shall go to-morrow—and that is the end. You shall never be troubled by a voice from there again. This world you don't know is too big to miss him. You understand? Too big. You've got his heart in your hand. You must feel that. You must know that.' 'Yes, I know that,' she breathed out, hard and still, as a statue might whisper.

"I felt I had done nothing. And what is it that I had wished to do? I am not sure now. At the time I was animated by an inexplicable ardour, as if before some great and necessary task—the influence of the moment upon my mental and emotional state. There are in all our lives such moments, such influences, coming from the outside, as it were, irresistible, incomprehensible—as if brought about by the mysterious conjunctions of the planets. She owned, as I had put it to her, his heart. She had that and everything else—if she could only believe it. What I had to tell her was that in the whole world there was no one who ever would need his heart, his mind, his hand. It was a common fate, and yet it seemed an awful thing to say of any man. She listened without a word, and her stillness now was like the protest of an invincible unbelief. What need she care for the world beyond the forests? I asked. From all the multitudes that peopled the vastness of that unknown there would come, I assured her, as long as he lived, neither a call nor a sign for him. Never. I was carried away. Never! Never! I remember with wonder the sort of dogged fierceness I displayed.

I had the illusion of having got the spectre by the throat at last. Indeed the whole real thing has left behind the detailed and amazing impression of a dream. Why should she fear? She knew him to be strong, true, wise, brave. He was all that. Certainly. He was more. He was great—invincible—and the world did not want him, it had forgotten him, it would not even know him.

"I stopped; the silence over Patusan was profound, and the feeble dry sound of a paddle striking the side of a canoe somewhere in the middle of the river seemed to make it infinite. 'Why?' she murmured. I felt that sort of rage one feels during a hard tussle. The spectre was trying to slip out of my grasp. 'Why?' she repeated louder; 'tell me!' And as I remained confounded, she stamped with her foot like a spoilt child. 'Why? Speak.' 'You want to know?' I asked in a fury. 'Yes!' she cried. 'Because he is not good enough,' I said, brutally. During the moment's pause I noticed the fire on the other shore blaze up, dilating the circle of its glow like an amazed stare, and contract suddenly to a red pin-point. I only knew how close to me she had been when I felt the clutch of her fingers on my forearm. Without raising her voice, she threw into it an infinity of scathing contempt, bitterness, and despair.

" 'This is the very thing he said. . . . You lie!'

"The last two words she cried at me in the native dialect. 'Hear me out!' I entreated; she caught her breath tremulously, flung my arm away. 'Nobody, nobody is good enough,' I began with the greatest eagerness. I could hear the sobbing labour of her breath frightfully quickened. I hung my head. What was the use? Footsteps were approaching; I slipped away without another word. . . ."

Chapter Thirty-four

MARLOW swung his legs out, got up quickly, and staggered a little, as though he had been set down after a rush through space. He leaned his back against the balustrade and faced a disordered array of long cane-chairs. The bodies prone in them seemed startled out of their torpor by his movement. One or two sat up as if alarmed; here and there a cigar glowed yet; Marlow looked at them all with the eyes of a man returning from the excessive remoteness of a dream. A throat was cleared; a calm voice encouraged negligently, "Well."

"Nothing," said Marlow with a slight start. "He had told her—that's all. She did not believe him—nothing more. As to myself, I do not know whether it be just, proper, decent for me to rejoice or to be sorry. For my part, I cannot say what I believed—indeed I don't know to this day, and never shall probably. But what did the poor devil believe himself? Truth shall prevail—don't you know *Magna est veritas et* . . . Yes, when it gets a chance. There is a law, no doubt—and likewise a law regulates your luck in the throwing of dice. It is not Justice the servant of men, but accident, hazard, Fortune—the ally of patient Time—that holds an even and scrupulous balance. Both of us had said the very same thing. Did we both speak the truth—or one of us did—or neither? . . ."

Marlow paused, crossed his arms on his breast, and in a changed tone—

"She said we lied. Poor soul. Well—let's leave it to Chance, whose ally is Time that cannot be hurried, and whose enemy is Death, that will not wait. I had retreated—a little cowed, I must own. I had tried a fall with fear itself and got thrown—of course. I had only succeeded in adding to her anguish the hint of some mysterious collusion, of an inexplicable and incomprehensible conspiracy to keep her for ever in the dark. And it had come easily, naturally, unavoidably, by his act, by her own act! It was as though I had been shown the working of the implacable destiny of which we are the victims—and the tools. It was appalling to think of the girl whom I had left standing there motionless; Jim's footsteps had a fateful sound as he tramped by, without seeing me, in his heavy laced boots. 'What? No lights!' he said in a loud surprised voice. 'What are you doing in the dark—you two?' Next moment he caught sight of her, I suppose. 'Hallo, girl!' he cried, cheerily. 'Hallo, boy!' she answered at once, with amazing pluck.

"This was their usual greeting to each other, and the bit of swagger she would put into her rather high but sweet voice was very droll, pretty, and childlike. It delighted Jim greatly. This was the last occasion on which I heard them exchange this familiar hail, and it struck a chill into my heart. There was the high sweet voice, the pretty effort, the swagger; but it all seemed to die out prematurely, and the playful call sounded like a moan. It was too confoundedly awful. 'What have you done with Marlow?' Jim was asking; and then, 'Gone down—has he? Funny I didn't meet him. . . . You there, Marlow?'

"I didn't answer. I wasn't going in—not yet at any rate. I really couldn't. While he was calling me I was engaged in making my escape through a little gate leading out upon a stretch of newly cleared ground. No; I couldn't face them yet. I walked hastily with lowered head along a trodden path. The ground rose gently, the few big trees had been felled, the undergrowth had been cut down and the grass fired. He had a mind to try a coffee-plantation there. The big hill, rearing its double summit coal-black in the clear yellow glow of the rising moon, seemed to cast its shadow upon the ground prepared for that experiment. He was going to try ever so many experiments; I had admired his energy, his enterprise, and his shrewdness. Nothing on earth seemed less real now than his plans, his energy, and his enthusiasm; and raising my eyes, I saw part of the moon glittering through the brushes at the bottom of the chasm. For a moment it looked as though the smooth disc, falling from its place in the sky upon the earth, had rolled to the bottom of that precipice; its ascending movement was like a leisurely rebound; it disengaged itself from the tangle of twigs; the bare contorted limb of some tree, growing on the slope, made a black crack right across its face. It threw

its level rays afar as if from a cavern, and in this mournful
eclipse-like light the stumps of felled trees uprose very dark,
the heavy shadows fell at my feet on all sides, my own moving
shadow, and across my path the shadow of the solitary grave
perpetually garlanded with flowers. In the darkened moonlight
the interlaced blossoms took on shapes foreign to one's memory and colours indefinable to the eye, as though they had been
special flowers gathered by no man, grown not in this world,
and destined for the use of the dead alone. Their powerful
scent hung in the warm air, making it thick and heavy like the
fumes of incense. The lumps of white coral shone round the
dark mound like a chaplet of bleached skulls, and everything
around was so quiet that when I stood still all sound and all
movements in the world seemed to come to an end.

"It was a great peace, as if the earth had been one grave, and
for a time I stood there thinking mostly of the living who,
buried in remote places out of the knowledge of mankind, still
are fated to share in its tragic or grotesque miseries. In its
noble struggles, too—who knows? The human heart is vast
enough to contain all the world. It is valiant enough to bear the
burden, but where is the courage that would cast it off?

"I suppose I must have fallen into a sentimental mood; I
only know that I stood there long enough for the sense of utter
solitude to get hold of me so completely that all I had lately
seen, all I had heard, and the very human speech itself, seemed
to have passed away out of existence, living only for a while
longer in my memory, as though I had been the last of
mankind. It was a strange a melancholy illusion, evolved half-
consciously like all our illusions, which I suspect only to be visions of remote unattainable truth, seen dimly. This was,
indeed, one of the lost, forgotten, unknown places of the earth;
I had looked under its obscure surface; and I felt that when to-
morrow I had left it for ever, it would slip out of existence, to
live only in my memory till I myself passed into oblivion. I
have that feeling about me now; perhaps it is that feeling
which has incited me to tell you the story, to try to hand over
to you, as it were, its very existence, its reality—the truth disclosed in a moment of illusion.

"Cornelius broke upon it. He bolted out, vermin-like, from the long grass growing in a depression of the ground. I believe his house was rotting somewhere near by, though I've never seen it, not having been far enough in that direction. He ran towards me upon the path; his feet, shod in dirty white shoes, twinkled on the dark earth: he pulled himself up, and began to whine and cringe under a tall stove-pipe hat. His dried-up little carcass was swallowed up, totally lost, in a suit of black broadcloth. That was his costume for holidays and ceremonies, and it reminded me that this was the fourth Sunday I had spent in Patusan. All the time of my stay I had been vaguely aware of his desire to confide in me, if he only could get me all to himself. He hung about with an eager craving look on his sour yellow little face; but his timidity had kept him back as much as my natural reluctance to have anything to do with such an unsavoury creature. He would have succeeded, nevertheless, had he not been so ready to slink off as soon as you looked at him. He would slink off before Jim's severe gaze, before my own, which I tried to make indifferent, even before Tamb' Itam's surly, superior glance. He was perpetually slinking away; whenever seen he was seen moving off deviously, his face over his shoulder, with either a mistrustful snarl or a woe-begone, piteous, mute aspect; but no assumed expression could conceal this innate irremediable abjectness of his nature, any more than an arrangement of clothing can conceal some monstrous deformity of the body.

"I don't know whether it was the demoralisation of my utter defeat in my encounter with a spectre of fear less than an hour ago, but I let him capture me without even a show of resistance. I was doomed to be the recipient of confidences, and to be confronted with unanswerable questions. It was trying; but the contempt, the unreasoned contempt, the man's appearance provoked, made it easier to bear. He couldn't possibly matter. Nothing mattered, since I had made up my mind that Jim, for whom alone I cared, had at last mastered his fate. He had told me he was satisfied . . . nearly. This is going further than most of us dare. I—who have the right to think myself good enough—dare not. Neither does any of you here, I suppose? . . ."

Marlow paused, as if expecting an answer. Nobody spoke.

"Quite right," he began again. "Let no soul know, since the truth can be wrung out of us only by some cruel, little, awful catastrophe. But he is one of us, and he could say he was satisfied . . . nearly. Just fancy this! Nearly satisfied. One could almost envy him his catastrophe. Nearly satisfied. After this nothing could matter. It did not matter who suspected him, who trusted him, who loved him, who hated him—especially as it was Cornelius who hated him.

"Yet after all this was a kind of recognition. You shall judge of a man by his foes as well as by his friends, and this enemy of Jim was such as no decent man would be ashamed to own, without, however, making too much of him. This was the view Jim took, and in which I shared; but Jim disregarded him on general grounds. 'My dear Marlow,' he said, 'I feel that if I go straight nothing can touch me. Indeed I do. Now you have been long enough here to have a good look round—and, frankly, don't you think I am pretty safe? It all depends upon me, and, by Jove! I have lots of confidence in myself. The worst thing he could do would be to kill me, I suppose. I don't think for a moment he would. He couldn't, you know—not if I were myself to hand him a loaded rifle for the purpose, and then turn my back on him. That's the sort of thing he is. And suppose he would—suppose he could? Well—what of that? I didn't come here flying for my life—did I? I came here to set my back against the wall, and I am going to stay here . . .'

" 'Till you are *quite* satisfied,' I struck in.

"We were sitting at the time under the roof in the stern of his boat; twenty paddles flashed like one, ten on a side, striking the water with a single splash, while behind our backs Tamb' Itam dipped silently right and left, and stared right down the river, attentive to keep the long canoe in the greatest strength of the current. Jim bowed his head, and our last talk seemed to flicker out for good. He was seeing me off as far as the mouth of the river. The schooner had left the day before, working down and drifting on the ebb, while I had prolonged my stay overnight. And now he was seeing me off.

"Jim had been a little angry with me for mentioning Cornelius at all. I had not, in truth, said much. The man was too insignificant to be dangerous, though he was as full of hate as he could hold. He had called me 'honourable sir' at every second sentence, and had whined at my elbow as he followed me from the grave of his 'late wife' to the gate of Jim's compound. He declared himself the most unhappy of men, a victim, crushed like a worm; he entreated me to look at him. I wouldn't turn my head to do so; but I could see out of the corner of my eye his obsequious shadow gliding after mine, while the moon, suspended on our right hand, seemed to gloat serenely upon the spectacle. He tried to explain—as I've told you—his share in the events of the memorable night. It was a matter of expediency. How could he know who was going to get the upper hand? 'I would have saved him, honourable sir! I would have saved him for eighty dollars,' he protested in dulcet tones, keeping a pace behind me. 'He has saved himself,' I said, 'and he has forgiven you.' I heard a sort of tittering, and turned upon him; at once he appeared ready to take to his heels. 'What are you laughing at?' I asked, standing still. 'Don't be deceived, honourable sir!' he shrieked, seemingly losing all control over his feelings. '*He* save himself! He knows nothing, honourable sir—nothing whatever. Who is he? What does he want here—the big thief? What does he want here? He throws dust into everybody's eyes; he throws dust into your eyes, honourable sir; but he can't throw dust into my eyes. He is a big fool, honourable sir.' I laughed contemptuously, and, turning on my heel, began to walk on again. He ran up to my elbow and whispered forcibly, "He's no more than a little child here—like a little child—a little child.' Of course I didn't take the slightest notice, and seeing the time pressed, because we were approaching the bamboo fence that glittered over the blackened ground of the clearing, he came to the point. He commenced by being abjectly lachrymose. His great misfortunes had affected his head. He hoped I would kindly forget what nothing but his troubles made him say. He didn't mean anything by it; only the honourable sir did not know what it was to be ruined, broken down, trampled upon. After this introduction he approached the matter near his heart, but in such a rambling, ejaculatory, craven fashion, that for a long time I couldn't make out what he was driving at. He wanted me to intercede with Jim in his favour. It seemed, too, to be some sort of money affair. I heard time and again the words, 'Moderate provision—suitable present.' He seemed to be claiming value for something, and he even went the length of saying with some warmth that life was not worth having if a man were to be robbed of everything. I did not breathe a word, of course, but neither did I stop my ears. The gist of the affair, which became clear to me gradually, was in this, that he regarded himself as entitled to some money in exchange for the girl. He had brought her up. Somebody else's child. Great trouble and pains—old man now—suitable present. If the honourable sir would say a word. . . . I stood still to look at him with curiosity, and fearful lest I should think him extortionate, I suppose, he hastily brought himself to make a concession. In consideration of a 'suitable present' given at once, he would, he declared, be willing to undertake the charge of the girl, 'without any other provision—when the time came for the gentleman to go home.' His little yellow face, all crumpled as though it had been squeezed together, expressed the most anxious, eager avarice. His voice whined coaxingly, 'No more trouble—natural guardian—a sum of money. . . .'

"I stood there and marvelled. That kind of thing, with him, was evidently a vocation. I discovered suddenly in his cringing attitude a sort of assurance, as though he had been all his life dealing in certitudes. He must have thought I was dispassionately considering his proposal, because he became as sweet as honey. 'Every gentleman made a provision when the time came to go home,' he began, insinuatingly. I slammed the little gate. 'In this case, Mr. Cornelius,' I said, 'the time shall never come.' He took a few seconds to gather this in. 'What!' he fairly squealed. 'Why," I continued from my side of the gate, 'haven't you heard him say so himself? He will never go home.' 'Oh! this is too much,' he shouted. He would not ad-

dress me as 'honoured sir' any more. He was very still for a
time, and then without a trace of humility began very low.
'Never go—ah! He—he—he come here devil knows from
where—comes here—devil knows why—to trample on me till
I die—ah—trample' (he stamped softly with both feet), 'trample like this—nobody knows why—till I die. . . .' His voice became quite extinct; he was bothered by a little cough; he came
up close to the fence and told me, dropping onto a confidential
and piteous tone, that he would *not* be trampled upon. 'Patience—patience,' he muttered, striking his breast. I had done
laughing at him, but unexpectedly he treated me to a wild
cracked burst of it. "Ha! ha! ha! We shall see! We shall see!
What! Steal from me? Steal from me everything! Everything!
Everything!' His head drooped on one shoulder, his hands
were hanging before him lightly clasped. One would have
thought he had cherished the girl with surpassing love, that his
spirit had been crushed and his heart broken by the most cruel
of spoliations. Suddenly he lifted his head and shot out an infamous word. 'Like her mother—she is like her deceitful
mother. Exactly. In her face, too. In her face. The devil!' He
leaned his forehead against the fence, and in that position uttered threats and horrible blasphemies in Portuguese in very
weak ejaculations, mingled with miserable plaints and groans,
coming out with a heave of the shoulders as though he had
been overtaken by a deadly fit of sickness. It was an inexpressibly grotesque and vile performance, and I hastened
away. He tried to shout something after me. Some disparage-
ment of Jim, I believe—not too loud though, we were too near
the house. All I heard distinctly was, 'No more than a little
child—a little child.' "

Chapter Thirty-five

BUT next morning, at the first bend of the river shutting off the houses of Patusan, all this dropped out of my sight bodily, and its colour, its design, and its meaning, like a picture created by fancy on a canvas, upon which, after long contemplation, you turn your back for the last time. It remains in the memory motionless, unfaded, with its life arrested, in an unchanging light. There are the ambitions, the fears, the hate, the hopes, and they remain in my mind just as I had seen them—intense and as if for ever suspended in their expression. I had turned away from the picture and was going back to the world where events move, men change, light flickers, life flows in a clear stream, no matter whether over mud or over stones. I wasn't going to dive into it; I would have enough to do to keep my head above the surface. But as to what I was leaving behind, I cannot imagine any alteration. The immense and magnanimous Doramin and his little motherly witch of a wife, gazing together upon the land and nursing secretly their dreams of parental ambition; Tunku Allang, wizened and greatly perplexed; Dain Waris, intelligent and brave, with his faith in Jim, with his firm glance and his ironic friendliness; the girl, absorbed in her frightened, suspicious adoration; Tamb' Itam, surly and faithful; Cornelius, leaning his forehead against the fence under the moonlight—I am certain of them. They exist as if under an enchanter's wand. But the figure round which all these are grouped—that one lives, and I am not certain of him. No magician's wand can immobilise him under my eyes. He is one of us.

"Jim, as I've told you, accompanied me on the first stage of my journey back to the world he had renounced, and the way at times seemed to lead through the very heart of untouched wilderness. The empty reaches sparkled under the high sun; between the high walls of vegetation the heat drowsed upon the water, and the boat, impelled vigorously, cut her way through the air that seemed to have settled dense and warm under the shelter of lofty trees.

"The shadow of the impending separation had already put an immense space between us, and when we spoke it was with an effort, as if to force our low voices across a vast and increasing distance. The boat fairly flew; we sweltered side by side in the stagnant superheated air; the smell of mud, of marsh, the primeval smell of fecund earth, seemed to sting our faces; till suddenly at a bend it was as if a great hand far away had lifted a heavy curtain, had flung open an immense portal. The light itself seemed to stir, the sky above our heads widened, a far-off murmur reached our ears, a freshness enveloped us, filled our lungs, quickened our thoughts, our blood, our regrets—and, straight ahead, the forests sank down against the dark-blue ridge of the sea.

"I breathed deeply, I revelled in the vastness of the opened horizon, in the different atmosphere that seemed to vibrate with a toil of life, with the energy of an impeccable world. This sky and this sea were open to me. The girl was right—there was a sign, a call in them—something to which I responded with every fibre of my being. I let my eyes roam through space, like a man released from bonds who stretches his cramped limbs, runs, leaps, responds to the inspiring elation of freedom. 'This is glorious!' I cried, and then I looked at the sinner by my side. He sat with his head sunk on his breast and said 'Yes,' without raising his eyes, as if afraid to see writ large on the clear sky of the offing the reproach of his romantic conscience.

"I remember the smallest details of that afternoon. We landed on a bit of white beach. It was backed by a low cliff wooded on the brow, draped in creepers to the very foot. Below us the plain of the sea, of a serene and intense blue, stretched with a slight upward tilt to the thread-like horizon drawn at the height of our eyes. Great waves of glitter blew lightly along the pitted dark surface, as swift as feathers chased by the breeze. A chain of islands sat broken and massive facing the wide estuary, displayed in a sheet of pale glassy water reflecting faithfully the contour of the shore. High in the colourless sunshine a solitary bird, all black, hovered, dropping and soaring above the same spot with a slight rocking motion of the wings. A ragged, sooty bunch of flimsy mat hovels was perched over its own inverted image upon a crooked multitude of high piles the colour of ebony. A tiny black canoe put off from amongst them with two tiny men, all black, who toiled exceedingly, striking down at the pale water: and the canoe seemed to slide painfully on a mirror. This bunch of miserable hovels was the fishing village that boasted of the white lord's especial protection, and the two men crossing over were the old headman and his son-in-law. They landed and walked up to us on the white sand lean, dark-brown as if dried in smoke, with ashy patches on the skin of their naked shoulders and breasts. Their heads were bound in dirty but carefully folded handkerchiefs, and the old man began at once to state a complaint, voluble, stretching a lank arm, screwing up at Jim his old bleared eyes confidently. The Rajah's people would not leave them alone; there had been some trouble about a lot of turtles' eggs his people had collected on the islets there—and leaning at arm's-length upon his paddle, he pointed with a brown skinny hand over the sea. Jim listened for a time without looking up, and at last told him gently to wait. He would hear him by-and-by. They withdrew obediently to some little distance, and sat on their heels, with their paddles lying before them on the sand; the silvery gleams in their eyes followed our movements patiently; and the immensity of the outspread sea, the stillness of the coast, passing north and south beyond the limits of my vision, made up one colossal Presence watching us four dwarfs isolated on a strip of glistening sand.

"'The trouble is,' remarked Jim, moodily, 'that for generations these beggars of fishermen in that village there had been considered as the Rajah's personal slaves—and the old rip can't get it into his head that . . .'

"He paused. 'That you have changed all that,' I said.

"'Yes. I've changed all that,' he muttered in a gloomy voice.

"'You had your opportunity,' I pursued.

"'Had I?' he said. 'Well, yes. I suppose so. Yes. I have got back my confidence in myself—a good name—yet sometimes

I wish . . . No! I shall hold what I've got. Can't expect anything more.' He flung his arm out towards the sea. 'Not out there anyhow.' He stamped his foot upon the sand. 'This is my limit, because nothing less will do.'

"We continued pacing the beach. 'Yes, I've changed all that,' he went on, with a sidelong glance at the two patient squatting fishermen; 'but only try to think what it would be if I went away. Jove! can't you see it? Hell loose. No! To-morrow I shall go and take my chance of drinking that silly old Tunku Allang's coffee, and I shall make no end of fuss over these rotten turtles' eggs. No. I can't say—enough. Never. I must go on, go on for ever holding up my end, to feel sure that nothing can touch me. I must stick to their belief in me to feel safe and to—to' . . . He cast about for a word, seemed to look for it on the sea . . . 'to keep in touch with' . . . His voice sank suddenly to a murmur . . . 'with those whom, perhaps, I shall never see any more. With—with—you, for instance.'

"I was profoundly humbled by his words. 'For God's sake,' I said, 'don't set me up, my dear fellow; just look to yourself.' I felt a gratitude, an affection, for that straggler whose eyes had singled me out, keeping my place in the ranks of an insignificant multitude. How little that was to boast of, after all! I turned my burning face away; under the low sun, glowing, darkened and crimson, like an ember snatched from the fire, the sea lay outspread, offering all its immense stillness to the approach of the fiery orb. Twice he was going to speak, but checked himself; at last, as if he had found a formula—

"'I shall be faithful,' he said, quietly. 'I shall be faithful,' he repeated, without looking at me, but for the first time letting his eyes wander upon the waters, whose blueness had changed to a gloomy purple under the fires of sunset. Ah! he was romantic, romantic. I recalled some words of Stein's. . . . 'In the destructive element immerse! . . . To follow the dream, and again to follow the dream—and so—always—*usque ad finem* . . .' He was romantic, but none the less true. Who could tell what forms, what faces, what visions, what forgiveness he could see in the glow of the west! . . . A small boat, leaving the schooner, moved slowly, with a regular beat of two oars, towards the sandbank to take me off. 'And then there's Jewel,' he said, out of the great silence of earth, sky, and sea, which had mastered my very thoughts so that his voice made me start. 'There's Jewel.' 'Yes,' I murmured. 'I need not tell you what she is to me,' he pursued. 'You've seen. In time she will come to understand . . .' 'I hope so,' I interrupted. 'She trusts me, too,' he mused, and then changed his tone. 'When shall we meet next, I wonder?' he said.

"'Never—unless you come out,' I answered, avoiding his glance. He didn't seem to be surprised; he kept very quiet for a while.

"'Good-bye, then,' he said, after a pause. 'Perhaps it's just as well.'

"We shook hands, and I walked to the boat, which waited with her nose on the beach. The schooner, her mainsail set and jib-sheet to windward, curveted on the purple sea; there was a rosy tinge on her sails. 'Will you be going home again soon?' asked Jim, just as I swung my leg over the gunwale. 'In a year or so if I live,' I said. The forefoot grated on the sand, the boat floated, the wet oars flashed and dipped once, twice. Jim, at the water's edge, raised his voice. 'Tell them . . .' he began. I signed to the men to cease rowing, and waited in wonder. Tell who? The half-submerged sun faced him; I cold see its red gleam in his eyes that looked dumbly at me. . . . 'No—nothing,' he said, and with a slight wave of his hand motioned the boat away. I did not look again at the shore till I had clambered on board the schooner.

"By that time the sun had set. The twilight lay over the east, and the coast, turned black, extended infinitely its sombre wall that seemed the very stronghold of the night; the western horizon was one great blaze of gold and crimson in which a big detached cloud floated dark and still, casting a slaty shadow on the water beneath, and I saw Jim on the beach watching the schooner fall off and gather headway.

"The two half-naked fishermen had arisen as soon as I had gone; they were no doubt pouring the plaint of their trifling, miserable, oppressed lives into the ears of the white lord, and no doubt he was listening to it, making it his own, for was it not a part of his luck—the luck 'from the word Go'—the luck to which he had assured me he was so completely equal? They, too, I should think, were in luck, and I was sure their pertinacity would be equal to it. Their dark-skinned bodies vanished on the dark background long before I had lost sight of their protector. He was white from head to foot, and remained persistently visible with the stronghold of the night at his back, the sea at his feet, the opportunity by his side—still veiled. What do you say? Was it still veiled? I don't know. For me that white figure in the stillness of coast and sea seemed to stand at the heart of a vast enigma. The twilight was ebbing fast from the sky above his head, the strip of sand had sunk already under his feet, he himself appeared no bigger than a child—then only a speck, a tiny white speck, that seemed to catch all the light left in a darkened world. . . . And, suddenly, I lost him. . . ."

Chapter Thirty-six

WITH these words Marlow had ended his narrative, and his audience had broken up forthwith, under his abstract, pensive gaze. Men drifted off the verandah in pairs or alone without loss of time, without offering remark, as if the last image of that incomplete story, its incompleteness itself, and the very tone of the speaker, had made discussion vain and comment impossible. Each of them seemed to carry away his own impression, to carry it away with him like a secret; but there was only one man of all these listeners who was ever to hear the last word of the story. It came to him at home, more than two years later, and it came contained in a thick packet addressed in Marlow's upright and angular handwriting.

The privileged man opened the packet, looked in, then, laying it down, went to the window. His rooms were in the highest flat of a lofty building, and his glance could travel afar beyond the clear panes of glass, as though he were looking out

of the lantern of a lighthouse. The slopes of the roofs glistened,
the dark broken ridges succeeded each other without end like
sombre, uncrested waves, and from the depths of the town
under his feet ascended a confused and unceasing mutter. The
spires of churches, numerous, scattered haphazard, uprose like
beacons on a maze of shoals without a channel; the driving
rain mingled with the falling dusk of a winter's evening; and
the booming of a big clock on a tower striking the hour, rolled
past in voluminous, austere bursts of sound, with a shrill vibrating cry at the core. He drew the heavy curtains.

The light of his shaded reading-lamp slept like a sheltered
pool, his footfalls made no sound on the carpet, his wandering
days were over. No more horizons as boundless as hope, no
more twilights within the forests as solemn as temples, in the
hot quest of the Ever-undiscovered Country over the hill,
across the stream, beyond the wave. The hour was striking! No
more! No more!—but the opened packet under the lamp
brought back the sounds, the visions, the very savour of the
past—a multitude of fading faces, a tumult of low voices,
dying away upon the shores of distant seas under a passionate
and unconsoling sunshine. He sighed and sat down to read.

At first he saw three distinct enclosures. A good many pages
closely blackened and pinned together; a loose square sheet of
greyish paper with a few words traced in a handwriting he had
never seen before, and an explanatory letter from Marlow.
From this last fell another letter, yellowed by time and frayed
on the folds. He picked it up and, laying it aside, turned to
Marlow's message, ran swiftly over the opening lines, and,
checking himself, thereafter read on deliberately, like one approaching with slow feet and alert eyes the glimpse of an
undiscovered country.

". . . I don't suppose you've forgotten," went on the letter.
"You alone have showed an interest in him that survived the
telling of his story, though I remember well you would not
admit he had mastered his fate. You prophesied for him the disaster of weariness and of disgust with acquired honour, with
the self-appointed task, with the love sprung from pity and
youth. You had said you knew so well 'that kind of thing,' its

illusory satisfaction, its unavoidable deception. You said also—I call to mind—that 'giving your life up to them' (*them* meaning all of mankind with skins brown, yellow, or black in colour) 'was like selling your soul to a brute.' You contended that 'that kind of thing' was only endurable and enduring when based on a firm conviction in the truth of ideas racially our own, in whose name are established the order, the mortality of an ethical progress. 'We want its strength at our backs,' you had said. 'We want a belief in its necessity and its justice, to make a worthy and conscious sacrifice of our lives. Without it the sacrifice is only forgetfulness, the way of offering is no better than the way to perdition.' In other words, you maintained that we must fight in the ranks or our lives don't count. Possibly! You ought to know—be it said without malice—you who have rushed into one or two places single-handed and came out cleverly, without singeing your wings. The point, however, is that of all mankind Jim had no dealings but with himself, and the question is whether at the last he had not confessed to a faith mightier than the laws of order and progress.

"I affirm nothing. Perhaps you may pronounce—after you've read. There is much truth—after all—in the common expression 'under a cloud.' It is impossible to see him clearly—especially as it is through the eyes of others that we take our last look at him. I have no hesitation in imparting to you all I know of the last episode that, as he used to say, had 'come to him.' One wonders whether this was perhaps that supreme opportunity, that last and satisfying test for which I had always suspected him to be waiting, before he could frame a message to the impeccable world. You remember that when I was leaving him for the last time he had asked whether I would be going home soon, and suddenly cried after me 'Tell them!' . . . I had waited—curious I'll own, and hopeful, too—only to hear him shout, "No. Nothing.' That was all then—and there shall be nothing more; there shall be no message, unless such as each of us can interpret for himself from the language of facts, that are so often more enigmatic than the craftiest arrangement of words. He made, it is true, one more attempt to deliver himself; but that, too, failed, as you may perceive if you look at the

sheet of greyish foolscap enclosed here. He had tried to write;
do you notice the commonplace hand? It is headed 'The Fort,
Patusan.' I suppose he had carried out his intention of making
out of his house a place of defence. It was an excellent plan: a
deep ditch, an earth wall toppled by a palisade, and at the angles guns mounted on platforms to sweep each side of the
square. Doramin had agreed to furnish him the guns; and so
each man of his party would know there was a place of safety,
upon which every faithful partisan could rally in case of some
sudden danger. All this showed his judicious foresight, his
faith in the future. What he called 'my own people'—the liber-
ated captives of the Sherif—were to make a distinct quarter of
Patusan, with their huts and little plots of ground under the
walls of the stronghold. Within he would be an invincible host
in himself. 'The Fort, Patusan.' No date, as you observe. What
is a number and a name to a day of days? It is also impossible
to say whom he had in his mind when he seized the pen:
Stein—myself—the world at large—or was this only the aimless startled cry of a solitary man confronted by his fate? 'An
awful thing has happened,' he wrote before he flung the pen
down for the first time; look at the ink blot resembling the head
of an arrow under these words. After a while he had tried
again, scrawling heavily, as if with a hand of lead, another line.
'I must now at once . . .' The pen had spluttered, and that time
he gave it up. There's nothing more; he had seen a broad gulf
that neither eye nor voice could span. I can understand this. He
was overwhelmed by the inexplicable; he was overwhelmed
by his own personality—the gift of that destiny which he had
done his best to master.

"I send you also an old letter—a very old letter. It was found
carefully preserved in his writing-case. It is from his father,
and by the date you can see he must have received it a few
days before he joined the *Patna*. Thus it must be the last letter
he ever had from home. He had treasured it all these years. The
good old parson fancied his sailor-son. I've looked in at a sentence here and there. There is nothing in it except just affection. He tells his 'dear James' that the last long letter from him
was very 'honest and entertaining.' He would not have him

'judge men harshly or hastily.' There are four pages of it, easy morality and family news. Tom had 'taken orders.' Carrie's husband had 'money losses.' The old chap goes on equably trusting Providence and the established order of the universe, but alive to its small danger and its small mercies. One can almost see him, grey-haired and serene in the inviolable shelter of his book-lined, faded, and comfortable study, where for forty years he had conscientiously gone over and over again the round of his little thoughts about faith and virtue, about the conduct of life and the only proper manner of dying; where he had written so many sermons, where he sits talking to his boy, over there, on the other side of the earth. But what of the distance? Virtue is one all over the world, and there is only one faith, one conceivable conduct of life, one manner of dying. He hopes his 'dear James' will never forget that 'who once gives way to temptation, in the very instant hazards his total depravity and everlasting ruin. Therefore resolve fixedly never, through any possible motives, to do anything which you believe to be wrong.' There is also some news of a favourite dog; and a pony, 'which all you boys used to ride,' had gone blind from old age and had to be shot. The old chap invokes Heaven's blessing; the mother and all the girls then at home send their love. . . . No, there is nothing much in that yellow frayed letter fluttering out of his cherishing grasp after so many years. It was never answered, but who can say what converse he may have held with all these placid, colourless forms of men and women peopling that quiet corner of the world as free of danger or strife as a tomb, and breathing equably the air of undisturbed rectitude. It seems amazing that he should belong to it, he to whom so many things 'had come.' Nothing ever came to them; they would never be taken unawares, and never be called upon to grapple with fate. Here they all are, evoked by the mild gossip of the father, all these brothers and sisters, bone of his bone and flesh of his flesh, gazing with clear unconscious eyes, while I seem to see him, returned at last, no longer a mere white speck at the heart of an immense mystery, but of full stature, standing disregarded amongst their untroubled shapes, with a stern and romantic aspect, but always mute, dark—under a cloud.

"The story of the last events you shall find in the few pages enclosed here. You must admit that it is romantic beyond the wildest dreams of his boyhood, and yet there is to my mind a sort of profound and terrifying logic in it, as if it were our imagination alone that could set loose upon us the might of an overwhelming destiny. The imprudence of our thoughts recoils upon our heads; who toys with the sword shall perish by the sword. This astounding adventure, of which the most astounding part is that it is true, comes on as an unavoidable consequence. Something of the sort had to happen. You repeat this to yourself while you marvel that such a thing could happen in the year of grace before last. But it has happened—and there is no disputing its logic.

"I put it down here for you as though I had been an eyewitness. My information was fragmentary, but I've fitted the pieces together, and there is enough of them to make an intelligible picture. I wonder how he would have related it himself. He has confided so much in me that at times it seems as though he must come in presently and tell the story in his own words, in his careless yet feeling voice, with his offhand manner, a little puzzled, a little bothered, a little hurt, but now and then by a word or a phrase giving one of these glimpses of his very own self that were never any good for purposes of orientation. It's difficult to believe he will never come. I shall never hear his voice again, nor shall I see his smooth tan-and-pink face with a white line on the forehead, and the youthful eyes darkened by excitement to a profound, unfathomable blue."

Chapter Thirty-seven

IT ALL begins with a remarkable exploit of a man called Brown, who stole with complete success a Spanish schooner out of a small bay near Zamboanga. Till I discovered the fellow my information was incomplete, but most unexpectedly I did come upon him a few hours before he gave up his arrogant ghost. Fortunately he was willing and able to talk between the choking fits of asthma, and his racked body writhed with malicious exultation at•the bare thought of Jim. He exulted thus at the idea that he had 'paid out the stuck-up beggar after all.' He gloated over his action. I had to bear the sunken glare of his fierce crow-footed eyes if I wanted to know; and so I bore it, reflecting how much certain forms of evil are akin to madness, derived from intense egoism, inflamed by resistance, tearing the soul to pieces, and giving factitious vigour to the body. The story also reveals unsuspected depths of cunning in the wretched Cornelius, whose abject and intense hate acts like a subtle inspiration, pointing out an unerring way towards revenge.

"'I could see directly I set my eyes on him what sort of a fool he was,' gasped the dying Brown. 'He a man! Hell! He was a hollow sham. As if he couldn't have said straight out, "Hands off my plunder!" blast him! That would have been like a man! Rot his superior soul! He had me there—but he hadn't devil enough in him to make an end of me. Not he! A thing like that letting me off as if I wasn't worth a kick! . . .' Brown struggled desperately for breath. . . . 'Fraud. . . . Letting me off. . . . And so I did make an end of him after all. . . .' He choked again. . . . 'I expect this thing'll kill me, but I shall die easy now. You . . . you hear . . . I don't know your name—I would give you a five-pound note if—if I had it—for the news—or my name's not Brown. . . .' He grinned horribly. . . . 'Gentleman Brown.'

"He said all these things in profound gasps, staring at me with his yellow eyes out of a long, ravaged brown face; he jerked his left arm; a pepper-and-salt matted beard hung almost into his lap; a dirty ragged blanket covered his legs. I had found him out in Bangkok through that busybody Schomberg, the hotelkeeper, who had, confidentially, directed me where to look. It appears that a sort of loafing, fuddled vagabond—a white man living amongst the natives with a Siamese woman—

had considered it a great privilege to give a shelter to the last days of the famous Gentleman Brown. While he was talking to me in the wretched hovel, and, as it were, fighting for every minute of his life, the Siamese woman, with big bare legs and a stupid coarse face, sat in a dark corner chewing betel stolidly. Now and then she would get up for the purpose of shooing a chicken away from the door. The whole hut shook when she walked. An ugly yellow child, naked and pot-bellied like a little heathen god, stood at the foot of the couch, finger in mouth, lost in a profound and calm contemplation of the dying man.

"He talked feverishly; but in the middle of a word, perhaps, an invisible hand would take him by the throat, and he would look at me dumbly with an expression of doubt and anguish. He seemed to fear that I would get tired of waiting and go away, leaving him with his tale untold, with his exultation unexpressed. He died during the night, I believe, but by that time I had nothing more to learn.

"So much as to Brown, for the present.

"Eight months before this, coming into Samarang, I went as usual to see Stein. On the garden side of the house a Malay on the verandah greeted me shyly, and I remembered that I had seen him in Patusan, in Jim's house, amongst other Bugis men who used to come in the evening to talk interminably over their war reminiscences and to discuss State affairs. Jim had pointed him out to me once as a respectable petty trader owning a small seagoing native craft, who had showed himself 'one of the best at the taking of the stockade.' I was not very surprised to see him, since any Patusan trader venturing as far as Samarang would naturally find his way to Stein's house. I returned his greeting and passed on. At the door of Stein's room I came upon another Malay in whom I recognised Tamb' Itam.

"I asked him at once what he was doing there; it occurred to me that Jim might have come on a visit. I own I was pleased and excited at the thought. Tamb' Itam looked as if he did not know what to say. 'Is Tuan Jim inside?' I asked, impatiently. 'No,' he mumbled, hanging his head for a moment, and then with sudden earnestness, 'He would not fight. He would not fight,' he repeated twice. As he seemed unable to say anything else, I pushed him aside and went in.

"Stein, tall and stooping, stood alone in the middle of the room between the rows of butterfly cases. '*Ach!* is it you, my friend?' he said, sadly, peering through his glasses. A drab sack-coat of alpaca hung, unbuttoned, down to his knees. He had a Panama hat on his head, and there were deep furrows on his pale cheeks. 'What's the matter now?' I asked nervously. 'There's Tamb' Itam there. . . .' 'Come and see the girl. Come and see the girl. She is here,' he said, with a half-hearted show of activity. I tried to detain him, but with gentle obstinacy he would take no notice of my eager questions. 'She is here, she is here,' he repeated, in great perturbation. 'They came here two days ago. An old man like me, a stranger—*sehen Sie*—cannot do much. . . . Come this way . . . Young hearts are unforgiving. . . .' I could see he was in utmost distress. . . . 'The strength of life in them, the cruel strength of life. . . .' He mumbled, leading me round the house; I followed him, lost in dismal and angry conjectures. At the door of the drawing-room he barred my way. 'He loved her very much?' he said interrogatively, and I only nodded, feeling so bitterly disappointed that I would not trust myself to speak. 'Very frightful,' he murmured. 'She can't understand me. I am only a strange old man. Perhaps you . . . she knows you. Talk to her. We can't leave it like this. Tell her to forgive him. It was very frightful.' 'No doubt,' I said, exasperated at being in the dark; 'but have *you* forgiven him?' He looked at me queerly. 'You shall hear,' he said, and opening the door, absolutely pushed me in.

'You know Stein's big house and the two immense reception-rooms, uninhabited, clean, full of solitude and of shining things that look as if never beheld by the eye of man? They are cool on the hottest days, and you enter them as you would a scrubbed cave underground. I passed through one, and in the other I saw the girl sitting at the end of a big mahogany table, on which she rested her head, the face hidden in her arms. The waxed floor reflected her dimly as though it had been a sheet of frozen water. The rattan screens were down, and through the strange greenish gloom made by the foliage of the trees outside, a strong wind blew in gusts, swaying the long draperies of windows and doorways. Her white figure seemed shaped in snow; the pendent crystals of a great chandelier clicked above her head like glittering icicles. She looked up and watched my approach. I was chilled as if these vast apartments had been the cold abode of despair.

"She recognised me at once, and as soon as I had stopped, looking down at her: 'He has left me,' she said, quietly; 'you always leave us—for your own ends.' Her face was set. All the heat of life seemed withdrawn within some inaccessible spot in her breast. 'It would have been easy to die with him,' she went on, and made a slight weary gesture as if giving up the incomprehensible. 'He would not! It was like a blindness—and yet it was I who was speaking to him; it was I who stood before his eyes; it was at me that he looked all the time! Ah! you are hard, treacherous, without truth, without compassion. What makes you so wicked? Or is it that you are all mad?'

"I took her hand; it did not respond, and when I dropped it, it hung down to the floor. That indifference, more awful than tears, cries, and reproaches, seemed to defy time and consolation. You felt that nothing you could say would reach the seat of the still and benumbing pain.

"Stein had said, 'You shall hear.' I did hear. I heard it all, listening with amazement, with awe, to the tones of her inflexible weariness. She could not grasp the real sense of what she was telling me and her resentment filled me with pity for her—for him, too. I stood rooted to the spot after she had finished. Leaning on her arm, she stared with hard eyes, and the wind passed in gusts, the crystals kept on clicking in the greenish gloom. She went on whispering to herself: 'And yet he was looking at me! He could see my face, hear my grief! When I used to sit at his feet, with my cheek against his knee and his hand on my head, the curse of cruelty and madness was already within him, waiting for the day. The day came! . . . and before the sun had set he could not see me any more—he was made blind and deaf and without pity, as you all are. He shall have no tears from me. Never, never. Not one tear. I will not! He went away from me as if I had been worse than death. He fled as if driven by some accursed thing he had heard or seen in his sleep. . . .'

"Her steady eyes seemed to strain after the shape of a man torn out of her arms by the strength of a dream. She made no sign to my silent bow. I was glad to escape.

"I saw her once again, the same afternoon. On leaving her I had gone in search of Stein, whom I could not find indoors; and I wandered out, pursued by distressful thoughts, into the gardens, those famous gardens of Stein, in which you can find every plant and tree of tropical lowlands. I followed the course of the canalised stream, and sat for a long time on a shaded bench near the ornamental pond, where some waterfowl with clipped wings were diving and splashing noisily. The branches of casuarina-trees behind me swayed lightly, incessantly, reminding me of the soughing of fir-trees at home.

"This mournful and restless sound was a fit accompaniment to my meditations. She had said he had been driven away from her by a dream,—and there was no answer one could make her—there seemed to be no forgiveness for such a transgression. And yet is not mankind itself, pushing on its blind way, driven by a dream of its greatness and its power upon the dark paths of excessive cruelty and of excessive devotion. And what is the pursuit of truth, after all?

"When I rose to get back to the house I caught sight of Stein's drab coat through a gap in the foliage, and very soon at the turn of the path I came upon him walking with the girl. Her little hand rested on his forearm, and under the broad, flat rim of his Panama hat he bent over her, grey-haired, paternal, with compassionate and chivalrous deference. I stood aside, but they stopped, facing me. His gaze was bent on the ground at his feet; the girl, erect and slight on his arm, stared sombrely beyond my shoulder with black, clear, motionless eyes. '*Schrecklich*,' he murmured. 'Terrible! Terrible! What can one do?' He seemed to be appealing to me, but her youth, the length of the days suspended over her head, appealed to me more; and suddenly, even as I realised that nothing could be said, I found myself pleading his cause for her sake. 'You must forgive him,' I concluded, and my own voice seemed to me

muffled, lost in an irresponsive deaf immensity. 'We all want
to be forgiven,' I added after a while.

"'What have I done?' she asked with her lips only.

"'You always mistrusted him,' I said.

"'He was like the others,' she pronounced slowly.

"'Not like the others,' I protested, but she continued evenly,
without any feeling—

"'He was false.' And suddenly Stein broke in. "No! no! no!
My poor child! . . .' He patted her hand lying passively on his
sleeve. 'No! no! Not false! True! true! true!' He tried to look
into her stony face. 'You don't understand. *Ach!* Why you do
not understand? . . . Terrible,' he said to me. 'Some day she
shall understand.'

"'Will *you* explain?' I asked, looking hard at him. They
moved on.

"I watched them. Her gown trailed on the path, her black
hair fell loose. She walked upright and light by the side of the
tall man, whose long shapeless coat hung in perpendicular
folds from the stooping shoulders, whose feet moved slowly.
They disappeared beyond that spinney (you may remember)
where sixteen different kinds of bamboo grow together, all dis-
tinguishable to the learned eye. For my part, I was fascinated
by the exquisite grace and beauty of that fluted grove, crowned
with pointed leaves and feathery heads, the lightness, the
vigour, the charm as distinct as a voice of that unperplexed
luxuriating life. I remember staying to look at it for a long
time, as one would linger within reach of a consoling whisper.
The sky was pearly grey. It was one of those overcast days so
rare in the tropics, in which memories crowd upon one, memories of other shores, of other faces.

"I drove back to town the same afternoon, taking with me
Tamb' Itam and the other Malay, in whose seagoing craft they
had escaped in the bewilderment, fear, and gloom of the disaster. The shock of it seemed to have changed their natures. It
had turned her passion into stone, and it made the surly taciturn Tamb' Itam almost loquacious. His surliness, too, was
subdued into puzzled humility, as though he had seen the failure of a potent charm in a supreme moment. The Bugis trader,

a shy hesitating man, was very clear in the little he had to say. Both were evidently overawed by a sense of deep inexpressible wonder, by the touch of an inscrutable mystery."

There with Marlow's signature the letter proper ended. The privileged reader screwed up his lamp, and solitary above the billowy roofs of the town, like a lighthouse-keeper above the sea, he turned to the pages of the story.

Chapter Thirty-eight

IT ALL begins, as I've told you, with the man called Brown," ran the opening sentence of Marlow's narrative. "You who have knocked about the Western Pacific must have heard of him. He was the show ruffian on the Australian coast—not that he was often to be seen there, but because he was always trotted out in the stories of lawless life a visitor from home is treated to; and the mildest of these stories which were told about him from Cape York to Eden Bay was more than enough to hang a man if told in the right place. They never failed to let you know, too, that he was supposed to be the son of a baronet. Be it as it may, it is certain he had deserted from a home ship in the early gold-digging days, and in a few years became talked about as the terror of this or that group of islands in Polynesia. He would kidnap natives, he would strip some lonely white trader to the very pyjamas he stood in, and after he had robbed the poor devil, he would as likely as not invite him to fight a duel with shot-guns on the beach—which would have been fair enough as these things go, if the other man hadn't been by that time already half-dead with fright. Brown was a latter-day buccaneer, sorry enough, like his more celebrated prototypes; but what distinguished him from his contemporary brother ruffians, like Bully Hayes or the mellifluous Pease, or that perfumed, Dundreary-whiskered, dandified scoundrel known as Dirty Dick, was the arrogant temper of his misdeeds

and a vehement scorn of mankind at large and for his victims
in particular. The others were merely vulgar and greedy brutes,
but he seemed moved by some complex intention. He would
rob a man as if only to demonstrate his poor opinion of the
creature, and he would bring to the shooting or maiming of
some quiet, unoffending stranger a savage and vengeful
earnestness fit to terrify the most reckless of desperadoes. In
the days of his greatest glory he owned an armed barque,
manned by a mixed crew of Kanakas and runaway whalers,
and boasted, I don't know with what truth, of being financed
on the quiet by a most respectable firm of copra merchants.
Later on he ran off—it was reported—with the wife of a mis-
sionary, a very young girl from Clapham way, who had married the mild, flatfooted fellow in a moment of enthusiasm, and
suddenly transplanted to Melanesia, lost her bearings somehow. It was a dark story. She was ill at the time he carried her
off, and died on board his ship. It is said—as the most wonderful part of the tale—that over her body he gave way to an outburst of sombre and violent grief. His luck left him, too, very
soon after. He lost his ship on some rocks off Malaita, and disappeared for a time as though he had gone down with her. He
is heard of next at Nuka-Hiva, where he bought an old French
schooner out of Government service. What creditable enterprise he might have had in view when he made that purchase I
can't say, but it is evident that what with High Commissioners,
consuls, men-of-war, and international control, the South Seas
were getting too hot to hold gentlemen of his kidney. Clearly
he must have shifted the scene of his operations farther west,
because a year later he plays an incredibly audacious, but not a
very profitable part, in a serio-comic business in Manila Bay,
in which a peculating governor and an absconding treasurer
are the principal figures; thereafter he seems to have hung
around the Philippines in his rotten schooner, battling with an
adverse fortune, till at last, running his appointed course, he
sails into Jim's history, a blind accomplice of the Dark Powers.

"His tale goes that when a Spanish patrol cutter captured
him he was simply trying to run a few guns for the insurgents.
If so, then I can't understand what he was doing off the south

coast of Mindanao. My belief, however, is that he was black-
mailing the native villages along the coast. The principal thing
is that the cutter, throwing a guard on board, made him sail in
company towards Zamboanga. On the way, for some reason or
other, both vessels had to call at one of these new Spanish set-
tlements—which never came to anything in the end—where
there was not only a civil official in charge on shore, but a
good stout coasting schooner lying at anchor in the little bay;
and this craft, in every way much better than his own, Brown
made up his mind to steal.

"He was down on his luck—as he told me himself. The
world he had bullied for twenty years with fierce, aggressive
disdain, had yielded him nothing in the way of material advantage except a small bag of silver dollars, which was concealed
in his cabin so that 'the devil himself couldn't smell it out.'
And that was all—absolutely all. He was tired of his life, and
not afraid of death. But this man, who would stake his existence on a whim with a bitter and jeering recklessness, stood in
mortal fear of imprisonment. He had an unreasoning cold-
sweat, nerve-shaking, blood-to-water-turning sort of horror at
the bare possibility of being locked up—the sort of terror a su-
perstitious man would feel at the thought of being embraced by
a spectre. Therefore the civil official who came on board to
make a preliminary investigation into the capture, investigated
arduously all day long, and only went ashore after dark, muffled up in a cloak, and taking great care not to let Brown's little all clink in its bag. Afterwards, being a man of his word, he
contrived (the very next evening, I believe) to send off the
Government cutter on some urgent bit of special service. As
her commander could not spare a prize crew, he contented
himself by taking away before he left all the sails of Brown's
schooner to the very last rag, and took good care to tow his two
boats on to the beach a couple of miles off.

"But in Brown's crew there was a Solomon Islander, kid-
napped in his youth and devoted to Brown, who was the best
man of the whole gang. That fellow swam off to the coaster—
five hundred yards or so—with the end of a warp made up of
all the running gear unrove for the purpose. The water was

smooth, and the bay dark, 'like the inside of a cow,' as Brown
described it. The Solomon Islander clambered over the bulwarks with the end of the rope in his teeth. The crew of the
coaster—all Tagals—were ashore having a jollification in the
native village. The two shipkeepers left on board woke up suddenly and saw the devil. It had glittering eyes and leaped quick
as lightning about the deck. They fell on their knees, paralysed
with fear, crossing themselves and mumbling prayers. With a
long knife he found in the caboose the Solomon Islander, without interrupting their orisons, stabbed first one, then the other;
with the same knife he set to sawing patiently at the coir cable
till suddenly it parted under the blade with a splash. Then in
the silence of the bay he let out a cautious shout, and Brown's
gang, who meantime had been peering and straining their
hopeful ears in the darkness, began to pull gently at their end
of the warp. In less than five minutes the two schooners came
together with a slight shock and a creak of spars.

"Brown's crowd transferred themselves without losing an
instant, taking with them their firearms and a large supply of
ammunition. They were sixteen in all: two runaway blue-
jackets, a lanky deserter from a Yankee man-of-war, a couple
of simple, blond Scandinavians, a mulatto of sorts, one bland
Chinaman who cooked—and the rest of the nondescript spawn
of the South Seas. None of them cared; Brown bent them to his
will, and Brown, indifferent to gallows, was running away
from the spectre of a Spanish prison. He didn't give them the
time to trans-ship enough provisions; the weather was calm,
the air was charged with dew, and when they cast off the ropes
and set sail to a faint off-shore draught there was no flutter in
the damp canvas; their old schooner seemed to detach itself
gently from the stolen craft and slip away silently, together
with the black mass of the coast, into the night.

"They got clear away. Brown related to me in detail their
passage down the Straits of Macassar. It is a harrowing and
desperate story. They were short of food and water; they
boarded several native craft and got a little from each. With a
stolen ship Brown did not dare to put into any port, of course.
He had no money to buy anything, no papers to show, and no

lie plausible enough to get him out again. An Arab barque,
under the Dutch flag, surprised one night at anchor off Poulo
Laut, yielded a little dirty rice, a bunch of bananas, and a cask
of water; three days of squally misty weather from the north-
east shot the schooner across the Java Sea. The yellow muddy
waves drenched that collection of hungry ruffians. They
sighted mail-boats moving on their appointed routes; passed
well-found home ships with rusty iron sides anchored in the
shallow sea waiting for a change of weather or the turn of the
tide; an English gunboat, white and trim, with two slim masts,
crossed their bows one day in the distance; and on another occasion a Dutch corvette, black and heavily sparred, loomed
upon their quarter, steaming dead slow in the mist. They
slipped through unseen or disregarded, a wan, sallow-faced
band of utter outcasts, enraged with hunger and hunted by fear.
Brown's idea was to make for Madagascar, where he expected,
on grounds not altogether illusory, to sell the schooner in
Tamatave, and no questions asked, or perhaps obtain some
more or less forged papers for her. Yet before he could face the
long passage across the Indian Ocean food was wanted—
water, too.

"Perhaps he had heard of Patusan—or perhaps he just only
happened to see the name written in small letters on the
chart—probably that of a largish village up a river in a native
state, perfectly defenceless, far from the beaten tracks of the
sea and from the ends of submarine cables. He had done that
kind of thing before—in the way of business; and this now was
an absolute necessity, a question of life and death—or rather of
liberty. Of liberty! He was sure to get provisions—bullocks—
rice—sweet-potatoes. The sorry gang licked their chops. A
cargo of produce for the schooner perhaps could be extorted—
and, who knows?—some real ringing coined money! Some of
these chiefs and village headmen can be made to part freely.
He told me he would have roasted their toes rather than be
baulked. I believe him. His men believed him too. They didn't
cheer aloud, being a dumb pack, but made ready wolfishly.

"Luck served him as to weather. A few days of calm would
have brought unmentionable horrors on board that schooner,

but with the help of land and sea breezes, in less than a week after clearing the Sunda Straits, he anchored off the Batu Kring mouth within a pistol-shot of the fishing village.

"Fourteen of them packed into the schooner's long-boat (which was big, having been used for cargo-work) and started up the river, while two remained in charge of the schooner with food enough to keep starvation off for ten days. The tide and wind helped, and early one afternoon the big white boat under a ragged sail shouldered its way before the sea breeze into Patusan Reach, manned by fourteen assorted scarecrows glaring hungrily ahead, and fingering the breech-blocks of cheap rifles. Brown calculated upon the terrifying surprise of his appearance. They sailed in with the last of the flood; the Rajah's stockade gave no sign; the first houses on both sides of the stream seemed deserted. A few canoes were seen up the reach in full flight. Brown was astonished at the size of the place. A profound silence reigned. The wind dropped between the houses; two oars were got out and the boat held on up-stream, the idea being to effect a lodgment in the centre of the town before the inhabitants could think of resistance.

"It seems, however, that the headman of the fishing village at Batu Kring had managed to send off a timely warning. When the long-boat came abreast of the mosque (which Do-ramin had built: a structure with gables and roof finials of carved coral) the open space before it was full of people. A shout went up, and was followed by a clash of gongs all up the river. From a point above two little brass six-pounders were discharged, and the round-shot came skipping down the empty reach, spiriting glittering jets of water in the sunshine. In front of the mosque a shouting lot of men began firing in volleys that whipped athwart the current of the river; an irregular, rolling fusillade was opened on the boat from both banks, and Brown's men replied with a wild, rapid fire. The oars had been got in.

"The turn of the tide at high water comes on very quick in that river, and the boat in midstream, nearly hidden in smoke, began to drift back stern foremost. Along both shores the smoke thickened also, lying below the roofs in a level streak as

you may see a long cloud cutting the slope of a mountain. A tumult of war-cries, the vibrating clang of gongs, the deep snoring of drums, yells of rage, crashes of volley-firing, made an
awful din, in which Brown sat confounded but steady at the
tiller, working himself into a fury of hate and rage against
those people who dared to defend themselves. Two of his men
had been wounded, and he saw his retreat cut off below the
town by some boats that had put off from Tunku Allang's
stockade. There were six of them full of men. While he was
thus beset he perceived the entrance of the narrow creek (the
same which Jim had jumped at low water). It was then brim
full. Steering the long-boat in, they landed, and, to make a long
story short, they established themselves on a little knoll about
900 yards from the stockade, which, in fact, they commanded
from that position. The slopes of the knoll were bare, but there
were a few trees on the summit. They went to work cutting
these down for a breastwork, and were fairly intrenched before
dark; meantime the Rajah's boats remained in the river with
curious neutrality. When the sun set the glare of many brush-
wood blazes lighted on the river-front, and between the double
line of houses on the land side threw into black relief the roofs,
the groups of slender palms, the heavy clumps of fruit-trees.
Brown ordered the grass round his position to be fired; a low
ring of thin flames under the slow, ascending smoke wriggled
rapidly down the slops of the knoll; here and there a dry bush
caught with a tall, vicious roar. The conflagration made a clear
zone of fire for the rifles of the small party, and expired smouldering on the edge of the forests and along the muddy bank of
the creek. A strip of jungle luxuriating in a damp hollow between the knoll and the Rajah's stockade stopped it on that side
with a great crackling and detonations of bursting bamboo
stems. The sky was sombre, velvety, and swarming with stars.
The blackened ground smoked quietly with low creeping
wisps, till a little breeze came on and blew everything away.
Brown expected an attack to be delivered as soon as the tide
had flowed enough again to enable the war-boats which had
cut off his retreat to enter the creek. At any rate he was sure
there would be an attempt to carry off his long-boat, which lay

below the hill, a dark high lump on the feeble sheen of a wet mud-flat. But no move of any sort was made by the boats in the river. Over the stockade and the Rajah's buildings Brown saw their lights on the water. They seemed to be anchored across the stream. Other lights afloat were moving in the reach, crossing and recrossing from side to side. There were also lights twinkling motionless upon the long walls of houses up the reach, as far as the bend, and more still beyond, others isolated inland. The loom of the big fires disclosed buildings, roofs, black piles as far as he could see. It was an immense place. The fourteen desperate invaders lying flat behind the felled trees raised their chins to look over at the stir of that town that seemed to extend up-river for miles and swarm with thousands of angry men. They did not speak to each other. Now and then they would hear a loud yell, or a single shot rang out, fired very far somewhere. But round their position everything was still, dark, silent. They seemed to be forgotten, as if the excitement keeping awake all the population had nothing to do with them, as if they had been dead already."

Chapter Thirty-nine

A LL the events of that night have a great importance, since they brought about a situation which remained unchanged till Jim's return. Jim had been away in the interior for more than a week, and it was Dain Waris who had directed the first repulse. That brave and intelligent youth ('who knew how to fight after the manner of white men') wished to settle the business off-hand, but his people were too much for him. He had not Jim's racial prestige and the reputation of invincible, supernatural power. He was not the visible, tangible incarnation of unfailing truth and of unfailing victory. Beloved, trusted, and admired as he was, he was still one of *them*, while Jim was one of *us*. Moreover, the white man, a tower of strength in himself, was invulnerable, while Dain Waris could be killed. Those unexpressed thoughts guided the opinions of the chief men of the town, who elected to assemble in Jim's fort for deliberation upon the emergency, as if expecting to find wisdom and courage in the dwelling of the absent white man. The shooting of Brown's ruffians was so far good, or lucky, that there had been half-a-dozen casualties amongst the defenders. The wounded were lying on the verandah tended by their womenfolk. The women and children from the lower part of the town had been sent into the fort at the first alarm. There Jewel was in command, very efficient and high-spirited, obeyed by Jim's 'own people,' who, quitting in a body their little settlement under the stockade, had gone in to form the garrison. The refugees crowded round her; and through the whole affair, to the very disastrous last, she showed an extraordinary martial ardour. It was to her that Dain Waris had gone at once at the first intelligence of danger, for you must know that Jim was the only one in Patusan who possessed a store of gunpowder. Stein, with whom he had kept up intimate relations by letters, had obtained from the Dutch Government a special authorisation to export five hundred kegs of it to Patusan. The powder-magazine was a small hut of rough logs covered entirely with earth, and in Jim's absence the girl had the key. In the council, held at eleven o'clock in the evening in Jim's dining-room, she backed up Waris's advice for immediate and vigorous action. I am told that she stood up by the side of Jim's empty chair at the head of the long table and made a warlike impassioned speech, which for the moment extorted murmurs of approbation from the assembled headmen. Old Doramin, who had not showed himself outside his own gate for more than a year, had been brought across with great difficulty. He was, of course, the chief man there. The temper of the council was very unforgiving, and the old man's word would have been decisive; but it is my opinion that, well aware of his son's fiery courage, he dared not pronounce the word. More dilatory counsels prevailed. A certain Haji Saman pointed out at great length that 'these tyrannical and ferocious men had delivered themselves to a certain death in any case. They would stand

fast on their hill and starve, or they would try to regain their
boat and be shot from ambushes across the creek, or they
would break and fly into the forest and perish singly there.' He
argued that by the use of proper stratagems these evil-minded
strangers could be destroyed without the risk of a battle, and
his words had a great weight, especially with the Patusan men
proper. What unsettled the minds of the townsfolk was the failure of the Rajah's boats to act at the decisive moment. It was
the diplomatic Kassim who represented the Rajah at the council. He spoke very little, listened smilingly, very friendly and
impenetrable. During the sitting messengers kept arriving
every few minutes almost, with reports of the invaders' proceedings. Wild and exaggerated rumours were flying: there
was a large ship at the mouth of the river with big guns and
many more men—some white, others with black skins and of
blood-thirsty appearance. They were coming with many more
boats to exterminate every living thing. A sense of near, incomprehensible danger affected the common people. At one
moment there was a panic in the courtyard amongst the
women; shrieking; a rush; children crying—Haji Saman went
out to quiet them. Then a fort sentry fired at something moving
on the river, and nearly killed a villager bringing in his
women-folk in a canoe together with the best of his domestic
utensils and a dozen fowls. This caused more confusion.
Meantime the palaver inside Jim's house went on in the presence of the girl. Doramin sat fierce-faced, heavy, looking at the
speakers in turn, and breathing slow like a bull. He didn't
speak till the last, after Kassim had declared that the Rajah's
boats would be called in because the men were required to defend his master's stockade. Dain Waris in his father's presence,
would offer no opinion, though the girl entreated him in Jim's
name to speak out. She offered him Jim's own men in her anxiety to have these intruders driven out at once. He only shook
his head, after a glance or two at Doramin. Finally, when the
council broke up it had been decided that the houses nearest
the creek should be strongly occupied to obtain the command
of the enemy's boat. The boat itself was not to be interfered
with openly, so that the robbers on the hill should be tempted

to embark, when a well directed fire would kill most of them, no doubt. To cut the escape of those who might survive, and to prevent more of them coming up, Dain Waris was ordered by Doramin to take an armed party of Bugis down the river to a certain spot ten miles below Patusan, and there form a camp on the shore and blockade the stream with the canoes. I don't believe for a moment that Doramin feared the arrival of fresh forces. My opinion is, that his conduct was guided solely by his wish to keep his son out of harm's way. To prevent a rush being made into the town the construction of a stockade was to be commenced at daylight at the end of the street on the left bank. The old *nakhoda* declared his intention to command there himself. A distribution of powder, bullets, and percussion caps was made immediately under the girl's supervision. Several messengers were to be despatched in different directions after Jim, whose exact whereabouts were unknown. These men started at dawn, but before that time Kassim had managed to open communications with the besieged Brown.

"That accomplished diplomatist and confidant of the Rajah, on leaving the fort to go back to his master, took into his boat Cornelius, whom he found slinking mutely amongst the people in the courtyard. Kassim had a little plan of his own and wanted him for an interpreter. Thus it came about that towards morning Brown, reflecting upon the desperate nature of his position, heard from the marshy overgrown hollow an amicable, quavering, strained voice crying—in English—for permission to come up, under a promise of personal safety and on a very important errand. He was overjoyed. If he was spoken to he was no longer a hunted wild beast. These friendly sounds took off at once the awful stress of vigilant watchfulness as of so many blind men not knowing whence the deathblow might come. He pretended a great reluctance. The voice declared itself 'a white man. A poor, ruined, old man who had been living here for years.' A mist, wet and chilly, lay on the slopes of the hill, and after some more shouting from one to the other, Brown called out, 'Come on, then, but alone, mind!' As a matter of fact—he told me, writhing with rage at the recollection of his helplessness—it made no difference. They couldn't see more than a few yards before them, and no treachery could make their position worse. By-and-by Cornelius, in his week-day attire of a ragged dirty shirt and pants, barefooted, with a broken-rimmed pith hat on his head, was made out vaguely, sidling up to the defenses, hesitating, stopping to listen in a peering posture. "Come along! You are safe,' yelled Brown, while his men stared. All their hopes of life became suddenly centred in that dilapidated, mean new-comer, who in profound silence clambered clumsily over a felled tree-trunk, and shiv-ering, with his sour mistrustful face, looked about at the knot of bearded, anxious, sleepless desperadoes.

"Half an hour's confidential talk with Cornelius opened Brown's eyes as to the home affairs of Patusan. He was on the alert at once. There were possibilities, immense possibilities; but before he would talk over Cornelius's proposals he de-manded that some food should be sent up as a guarantee of good faith. Cornelius went off, creeping sluggishly down the hill on the side of the Rajah's palace, and after some delay a few of Tunku Allang's men came up, bringing a scanty supply of rice, chillies, and dried fish. This was immeasurably better than nothing. Later on Cornelius returned accompanying Kas-sim, who stepped out with an air of perfect good-humoured trustfulness, in sandals, and muffled up from neck to ankles in dark-blue sheeting. He shook hands with Brown discreetly, and the three drew aside for a conference. Brown's men, re-covering their confidence, were slapping each other on the back, and cast knowing glances at their captain while they bus-ied themselves with preparations for cooking.

"Kassim disliked Doramin and his Bugis very much, but he hated the new order of things still more. It had occurred to him that these whites, together with the Rajah's followers, could at-tack and defeat the Bugis before Jim's return. Then, he rea-soned, general defection of the townsfolk was sure to follow, and the reign of the white man who protected poor people would be over. Afterwards the new allies could be dealt with. They would have no friends. The fellow was perfectly able to perceive the difference of character, and had seen enough of white men to know that these newcomers were outcasts, men

without country. Brown preserved a stern and inscrutable demeanour. When he first heard Cornelius's voice demanding
admittance, it brought merely the hope of a loophole for escape. In less than an hour other thoughts were seething in his
head. Urged by an extreme necessity, he had come there to
steal food, a few tons of rubber or gum maybe, perhaps a handful of dollars, and had found himself enmeshed by deadly dangers. Now in consequence of these overtures from Kassim he
began to think of stealing the whole country. Some confounded fellow had apparently accomplished something of the
kind—single-handed at that. Couldn't have done it very well
though. Perhaps they could work together—squeeze everything dry and then go out quietly. In the course of his negotiations with Kassim he became aware that he was supposed to
have a big ship with plenty of men outside. Kassim begged
him earnestly to have this big ship with his many guns and
men brought up the river without delay for the Rajah's service.
Brown professed himself willing, and on this basis the negoti-
ation was carried on with mutual distrust. Three times in the
course of the morning the courteous and active Kassim went
down to consult the Rajah and came up busily with his long
stride. Brown, while bargaining, had a sort of grim enjoyment
in thinking of his wretched schooner, with nothing but a heap
of dirt in her hold, that stood for an armed ship, and a Chinaman and a lame ex-beachcomber of Levuka on board, who represented all his many men. In the afternoon he obtained further
doles of food, a promise of some money, and a supply of mats
for his men to make shelters for themselves. They lay down
and snored, protected from the burning sunshine; but Brown,
sitting fully exposed on one of the felled trees, feasted his eyes
upon the view of the town and the river. There was much loot
here. Cornelius, who had made himself at home in the camp,
talked at his elbow, pointing out the localities, imparting advice, giving his own version of Jim's character, and comment-
ing in his own fashion upon the events of the last three years.
Brown, who, apparently indifferent and gazing away, listened
with attention to every word, could not make out clearly what
sort of man this Jim could be. 'What's his name? Jim! Jim!

That's not enough for a man's name.' 'They call him,' said
Cornelius, scornfully, 'Tuan Jim here. As you may say Lord
Jim.' 'What is he? Where does he come from?' inquired
Brown. 'What sort of man is he? Is he an Englishman?' 'Yes,
yes, he's an Englishman. I am an Englishman, too. From
Malacca. He is a fool. All you have to do is to kill him and then
you are king here. Everything belongs to him,' explained Cornelius. 'It strikes me he may be made to share with somebody
before very long,' commented Brown half aloud. 'No, no. The
proper way is to kill him the first chance you get, and then you
can do what you like,' Cornelius would insist earnestly. 'I have
lived for many years here, and I am giving you a friend's advice.'

"In such converse and in gloating over the view of Patusan,
which he had determined in his mind should become his prey,
Brown whiled away most of the afternoon, his men, meantime, resting. On that day Dain Waris's fleet of canoes stole
one by one under the shore farthest from the creek, and went
down to close the river against his retreat. Of this Brown was
not aware, and Kassim, who came up the knoll an hour before
sunset, took good care not to enlighten him. He wanted the
white man's ship to come up the river, and this news, he
feared, would be discouraging. He was very pressing with
Brown to send the 'order,' offering at the same time a trusty
messenger, who for greater secrecy (as he explained) would
make his way by land to the mouth of the river and deliver the
'order' on board. After some reflection Brown judged it expedient to tear a page out of his pocket-book, on which he simply wrote, 'We are getting on. Big job. Detain the man.' The
stolid youth selected by Kassim for that service performed it
faithfully, and was rewarded by being suddenly tipped, head
first, into the schooner's empty hold by the ex-beachcomber
and the Chinaman, who thereupon hastened to put on the
hatches. What became of him afterwards Brown did not say."

Chapter Forty

B ROWN'S object was to gain time by fooling with Kassim's
diplomacy. For doing a real stroke of business he could
not help thinking the white man was the person to work with.
He could not imagine such a chap (who must be confoundedly
clever after all to get hold of the natives like that) refusing a
help that would do away with the necessity for slow, cautious,
risky cheating, that imposed itself as the only possible line of
conduct for a single-handed man. He, Brown, would offer him
the power. No man could hesitate. Everything was in coming
to a clear understanding. Of course they would share. The idea
of there being a fort—all ready to his hand—a real fort, with
artillery (he knew this from Cornelius), excited him. Let him
only once get in and . . . He would impose modest conditions.
Not too low, though. The man was no fool, it seemed. They
would work like brothers till . . . till the time came for a quarrel and a shot that would settle all accounts. With grim impatience of plunder he wished himself to be talking with the man
now. The land already seemed to be his to tear to pieces,
squeeze, and throw away. Meantime Kassim had to be fooled
for the sake of food first—and for a second string. But the
principal thing was to get something to eat from day to day.
Besides, he was not averse to begin fighting on that Rajah's account, and teach a lesson to those people who had received
him with shots. The lust of battle was upon him.

"I am sorry that I can't give you this part of the story, which
of course I have mainly from Brown, in Brown's own words.
There was in the broken, violent speech of that man, unveiling
before me his thoughts with the very hand of Death upon his
throat, an undisguised ruthlessness of purpose, a strange
vengeful attitude towards his own past, and a blind belief in
the righteousness of his will against all mankind, something of
that feeling which could induce the leader of a horde of wandering cut-throats to call himself proudly the Scourge of God.
No doubt the natural senseless ferocity which is the basis of
such a character was exasperated by failure, ill-luck, and the

recent privations, as well as by the desperate position in which
he found himself; but what was most remarkable of all was
this, that while he planned treacherous alliances, had already
settled in his own mind the fate of the white man, and intrigued
in an overbearing, offhand manner with Kassim, one could
perceive that what he had really desired, almost in spite of
himself, was to play havoc with that jungle town which had
defied him, to see it strewn over with corpses and enveloped in
flames. Listening to his pitiless, panting voice, I could imagine
how he must have looked at it from the hillock, peopling it
with images of murder and repine. The part nearest to the creek
wore an abandoned aspect, though as a matter of fact every
house concealed a few armed men on the alert. Suddenly beyond the stretch of waste ground, interspersed with small
patches of low dense bush, excavations, heaps of rubbish, with
trodden paths between, a man, solitary and looking very small,
strolled out into the deserted opening of the street between the
shut-up, dark, lifeless buildings at the end. Perhaps one of the
inhabitants, who had fled to the other bank of the river, coming
back for some object of domestic use. Evidently he supposed
himself quite safe at that distance from the hill on the other
side of the creek. A light stockade, set up hastily, was just
round the turn of the street, full of his friends. He moved
leisurely. Brown saw him, and instantly called to his side the
Yankee deserter, who acted as a sort of second in command.
This lanky, loose-jointed fellow came forward, wooden-faced,
trailing his rifle lazily. When he understood what was wanted
from him a homicidal and conceited smile uncovered his teeth,
making two deep folds down his sallow, leathery cheeks. He
prided himself on being a dead shot. He dropped on one knee,
and taking aim from a steady rest through the unlopped
branches of a felled tree, fired, and at once stood up to look.
The man, far away, turned his head to the report, made another
step forward, seemed to hesitate, and abruptly got down on his
hands and knees. In the silence that fell upon the sharp crack of
the rifle, the dead shot, keeping his eyes fixed upon the quarry,
guessed that 'this there coon's health would never be a source
of anxiety to his friends any more.' The man's limbs were seen

to move rapidly under his body in an endevour to run on all-
fours. In that empty space arose a multitudinous shout of dismay and surprise. The man sank flat, face down, and moved no
more. 'That showed them what we could do,' said Brown to
me. 'Struck the fear of sudden death into them. That was what
we wanted. They were two hundred to one, and this gave them
something to think over for the night. Not one of them had an
idea of such a long shot before. That beggar belonging to the
Rajah scouted down-hill with his eyes hanging out of his
head.'

"As he was telling me this he tried with a shaking hand to
wipe the thin foam on his blue lips. 'Two hundred to one.
Two hundred to one . . . strike terror . . . terror, terror, I tell
you. . . .' His own eyes were starting out of their sockets. He
fell back, clawing the air with skinny fingers, sat up again,
bowed and hairy, glared at me sideways like some man-beast
of folklore, with open mouth in his miserable and awful
agony before he got his speech back after that fit. There are
sights one never forgets.

"Furthermore, to draw the enemy's fire and locate such parties as might have been hiding in the bushes along the creek,
Brown ordered the Solomon Islander to go down to the boat
and bring an oar, as you send a spaniel after a stick into the
water. This failed, and the fellow came back without a single
shot having been fired at him from anywhere. 'There's nobody,' opined some of the men. It is 'unnatural,' remarked the
Yankee. Kassim had gone, by that time, very much impressed,
pleased, too, and also uneasy. Pursuing his tortuous policy, he
had despatched a message to Dain Waris warning him to look
out for the white men's ship, which, he had had information,
was about to come up the river. He minimised its strength and
exhorted him to oppose its passage. This double-dealing answered his purpose, which was to keep the Bugis forces divided and to weaken them by fighting. On the other hand, he
had in the course of that day sent word to the assembled Bugis
chiefs in town, assuring them that he was trying to induce the
invaders to retire; his messages to the fort asked earnestly for
powder for the Rajah's men. It was a long time since Tunku Al-

lang had had ammunition for the score or so of old muskets
rusting in their arm-racks in the audience-hall. The open intercourse between the hill and the palace unsettled all the minds.
It was already time for men to take sides, it began to be said.
There would soon be much bloodshed, and thereafter great
trouble for many people. The social fabric of orderly, peaceful
life, when every man was sure of to-morrow, the edifice raised
by Jim's hands, seemed on that evening ready to collapse into
a ruin reeking with blood. The poorer folk were already taking
to the bush or flying up the river. A good many of the upper
class judged it necessary to go and pay their court to the Rajah.
The Rajah's youths jostled them rudely. Old Tunku Allang, almost out of his mind with fear and indecision, either kept a
sullen silence or abused them violently for daring to come with
empty hands: they departed very much frightened; only old
Doramin kept his countrymen together and pursued his tactics
inflexibly. Enthroned in a big chair behind the improvised
stockade, he issued his orders in a deep veiled rumble, unmoved, like a deaf man, in the flying rumours.

"Dusk fell, hiding first the body of the dead man, which had
been left lying with arms outstretched as if nailed to the
ground, and then the revolving sphere of the night rolled
smoothly over Patusan and came to a rest, showering the glitter of countless worlds upon the earth. Again, in the exposed
part of the town big fires blazed along the only street, revealing from distance to distance upon their glares the falling
straight lines of roofs, the fragments of wattled walls jumbled
in confusion, here and there a whole hut elevated in the glow
upon the vertical black stripes of a group of high piles: and all
this line of dwellings, revealed in patches by the swaying
flames, seemed to flicker tortuously away up-river into the
gloom at the heart of the land. A great silence, in which the
looms of successive fires played without noise, extended into
the darkness at the foot of the hill; but the other bank of the
river, all dark save for a solitary bonfire at the river-front before the fort, sent out into the air an increasing tremor that
might have been the stamping of a multitude of feet, the hum
of many voices, or the fall of an immensely distant waterfall. It

was then, Brown confessed to me, while, turning his back on
his men, he sat looking at it all, that notwithstanding his disdain, his ruthless faith in himself, a feeling came over him that
at last he had run his head against a stone wall. Had his boat
been afloat at the time, he believed he would have tried to steal
away, taking his chances of a long chase down the river and of
starvation at sea. It was very doubtful whether he would have
succeeded in getting away. However, he didn't try this. For another moment he had a passing thought of trying to rush the
town, but he perceived very well that in the end he would find
himself in the lighted street, where they would be shot down
like dogs from the houses. They were two hundred to one—he
thought, while his men, huddling round two heaps of smouldering embers, munched the last of the bananas and roasted the
few yams they owed to Kassim's diplomacy. Cornelius sat
amongst them dozing sulkily.

"Then one of the whites remembered that some tobacco had
been left on the boat, and, encouraged by the impunity of the
Solomon Islander, said he would go to fetch it. At this all the
others shook off their despondency. Brown applied to, said,
'Go, and be d—d to you,' scornfully. He didn't think there was
any danger in going to the creek in the dark. The man threw a
leg over the tree-trunk and disappeared. A moment later he was
heard clambering into the boat and then clambering out. 'I've
got it,' he cried. A flash and a report at the very foot of the hill
followed. 'I am hit,' yelled the man. 'Look out, look out—I am
hit,' and instantly all the rifles went off. The hill squirted fire
and noise into the night like a little volcano, and when Brown
and the Yankee with curses and cuffs stopped the panic-
stricken firing, a profound, weary groan floated up from the
creek, succeeded by a plaint whose heart-rending sadness was
like some poison turning the blood cold in the veins. Then, a
strong voice pronounced several distinct incomprehensible
words somewhere beyond the creek. 'Let no one fire,' shouted
Brown. 'What does it mean?' . . . 'Do you hear on the hill? Do
you hear? Do you hear?' repeated the voice three times. Cornelius translated, and then prompted the answer. 'Speak,' cried
Brown, 'we hear.' Then the voice, declaiming in the sonorous

inflated tone of a herald, and shifting continually on the edge
of the vague waste-land, proclaimed that between the men of
the Bugis nation living in Patusan and the white men on the
hill and those with them, there would be no faith, no compassion, no speech, no peace. A bush rustled; a haphazard volley
rang out. 'Dam' foolishness,' muttered the Yankee, vexedly
grounding the butt. Cornelius translated. The wounded man
below the hill, after crying out twice, 'Take me up! take me
up!' went on complaining in moans. While he had kept on
the blackened earth of the slope and afterwards crouching in
the boat, he had been safe enough. It seems that in his joy at
finding tobacco he forgot himself and jumped out on her off-
side, as it were. The white boat, lying high and dry, showed
him up; the creek was no more than seven yards wide in that
place, and there happened to be a man crouching in the bush on
the other bank.

"He was a Bugis of Tondano only lately come to Patusan,
and a relation of the man shot in the afternoon. That famous
long shot had indeed appalled the beholders. The man in utter
security had been struck down, in full view of his friends,
dropping with a joke on his lips, and they seemed to see in the
act an atrocity which had stirred a bitter rage. That relation of
his, Si-Lapa by name, was then with Doramin in the stockade
only a few feet away. You who know these chaps must admit
that the fellow showed an unusual pluck by volunteering to
carry the message, alone, in the dark. Creeping across the open
ground, he had deviated to the left and found himself opposite
the boat. He was startled when Brown's man shouted. He came
to a sitting position with his gun to his shoulder, and then the
other jumped out, exposing himself, he pulled the trigger and
lodged three jagged slugs point-blank into the poor wretch's
stomach. Then, lying flat on his face, he gave himself up for
dead, while a thin hail of lead chopped and swished the bushes
close on his right hand; afterwards he delivered his speech
shouting, bent double, dodging all the time in cover. With the
last word he leaped sideways, lay close for a while, and afterwards got back to the houses unharmed, having achieved on

that night such a renown as his children will not willingly allow to die.

"And on the hill the forlorn band let the two little heaps of embers go out under their bowed heads. They sat dejected on the ground with compressed lips and downcast eyes, listening to their comrade below. He was a strong man and died hard, with moans now loud, now sinking to a strange confidential note of pain. Sometimes he shrieked, and again, after a period of silence, he could be heard muttering deliriously a long and unintelligible complaint. Never for a moment did he cease.

"'What's the good?' Brown had said unmoved once, seeing the Yankee, who had been swearing under his breath, prepare to go down. 'That's so,' assented the deserter, reluctantly desisting. 'There's no encouragement for wounded men here. Only his voice is calculated to make all the others think too much of the hereafter, cap'n.' 'Water!' cried the wounded man in an extraordinarily clear vigorous voice, and then went off moaning feebly. 'Ay, water. Water will do it,' muttered the other to himself, resignedly. 'Plenty by-and-by. The tide is flowing.'

"At last the tide flowed, silencing the plaint and the cries of pain, and the dawn was near when Brown, sitting with his chin in the palm of his hand before Patusan, as one might stare at the unscalable side of a mountain, heard the brief ringing bark of a brass six-pounder far away in town somewhere. 'What's this?' he asked of Cornelius, who hung about him. Cornelius listened. A muffled roaring shout rolled down-river over the town; a big drum began to throb, and others responded, pulsating and droning. Tiny scattered lights began to twinkle in the dark half of the town, while the part lighted by the loom of fires hummed with a deep and prolonged murmur. 'He has come,' said Cornelius. 'What? Already? Are you sure?' Brown asked. 'Yes! yes! Sure. Listen to the noise.' 'What are they making that row about?' pursued Brown. 'For joy,' snorted Cornelius; 'he is a very great man, but all the same, he knows no more than a child, and so they make a great noise to please him, because they know no better.' 'Look here,' said Brown, 'how is one to get at him?' 'He shall come to talk to you,' Cor-

nelius declared. 'What do you mean? Come down here
strolling as it were?' Cornelius nodded vigorously in the dark.
'Yes. He will come straight here and talk to you. He is just like
a fool. You shall see what a fool he is.' Brown was incredulous.
'You shall see; you shall see,' repeated Cornelius. 'He is not
afraid—not afraid of anything. He will come and order you to
leave his people alone. Everybody must leave his people
alone. He is like a little child. He will come to you straight.'
Alas! he knew Jim well—that 'mean little skunk,' as Brown
called him to me. 'Yes, certainly,' he pursued with ardour, 'and
then, captain, you tell that tall man with a gun to shoot him.
Just you kill him, and you shall frighten everybody so much
that you can do anything you like with them afterwards—get
what you like—go away when you like. Ha! ha! ha! Fine. . . .'
He almost danced with impatience and eagerness; and Brown,
looking over his shoulder at him, could see, shown up by the
pitiless dawn, his men drenched with dew, sitting amongst the
cold ashes and the litter of the camp, haggard, cowed, and in
rags."

Chapter Forty-one

TO THE very last moment, till the full day came upon them
with a spring, the fires on the west bank blazed bright and
clear; and then Brown saw in a knot of coloured figures motionless between the advanced houses a man in European
clothes, in a helmet, all white. 'That's him; look! look!' Cornelius said excitedly. All Brown's men had sprung up and
crowded at his back with lustreless eyes. The group of vivid
colours and dark faces with the white figure in the midst were
observing the knoll. Brown could see naked arms being raised
to shade the eyes and other brown arms pointing. What should
he do? He looked around, and the forests that faced him on all
sides walled the cock-pit of an unequal contest. He looked

once more at his men. A contempt, a weariness, the desire of life, the wish to try for one more chance—for some other grave—struggled in his breast. From the outline the figure presented it seemed to him that the white man there, backed up by all the power of the land, was examining his position through binoculars. Brown jumped up on the log, throwing his arms up, the palms outwards. The coloured group closed round the white man, and fell back twice before he got clear of them, walking slowly alone. Brown remained standing on the log till Jim, appearing and disappearing between the patches of thorny scrub, had nearly reached the creek; then Brown jumped off and went down to meet him on his side.

"They met, I should think, not very far from the place, perhaps on the very spot, where Jim took the second desperate leap of his life—the leap that landed him into the life of Patusan, into the trust, the love, the confidence of the people. They faced each other across the creek, and with steady eyes tried to understand each other before they opened their lips. Their antagonism must have been expressed in their glances; I know that Brown hated Jim at first sight. Whatever hopes he might have had vanished at once. This was not the man he had expected to see. He hated him for this—and in a checked flannel shirt with sleeves cut off at the elbows, grey bearded, with a sunken, sun-blackened face—he cursed in his heart the other's youth and assurance, his clear eyes and his untroubled bearing. That fellow had got in a long way before him! He did not look like a man who would be willing to give anything for assistance. He had all the advantages on his side—possession, security, power, he was on the side of an overwhelming force! He was not hungry and desperate, and he did not seem in the least afraid. And there was something in the very neatness of Jim's clothes, from the white helmet to the canvas leggings and pipe-clayed shoes, which in Brown's sombre irritated eyes seemed to belong to things he had in the very shaping of his life contemned and flouted.

"'Who are you?' asked Jim at last, speaking in his usual voice. "My name's Brown,' answered the other, loudly; 'Captain Brown. What's yours?' and Jim after a little pause went on

quietly, as if he had not heard: 'What made you come here?'
'You want to know,' said Brown bitterly. 'It's easy to tell.
Hunger. And what made you?'

"'The fellow started at this,' said Brown, relating to me the
opening of this strange conversation between those two men,
separated only by the muddy bed of a creek, but standing on
the opposite poles of that conception of life which includes all
mankind—'The fellow started at this and got very red in the
face. Too big to be questioned, I suppose. I told him that if he
looked upon me as a dead man with whom you may take liber-
ties, he himself was not a whit better off really. I had a fellow
up there who had a bead drawn on him all the time, and only
waited for a sign from me. There was nothing to be shocked at
in this. He had come down of his own freewill. "Let us agree,"
said I, "that we are both dead men, and let us talk on that basis,
as equals. We are all equal before death," I said. I admitted I
was there like a rat in a trap, but we had been driven to it, and
even a trapped rat can give a bite. He caught me up in a moment. "Not if you don't go near the trap till the rat is dead." I
told him that sort of game was good enough for these native
friends of his, but I would have thought him too white to serve
even a rat so. Yes, I had wanted to talk with him. Not to beg for
my life, though. My fellows were—well—what they were—
men like himself, anyhow. All we wanted from him was to
come on in the devil's name and have it out. "God d—n it,"
said I, while he stood there as still as a wooden post, "you
don't want to come out here every day with your glasses to
count how many of us are left on our feet. Come. Either bring
your infernal crowd along or let us go out and starve in the
open sea, by God! You have been white once, for all your tall
talk of this being your own people and you being one with
them. Are you? And what the devil do you get for it; what is it
you've found here that is so d—d precious? Hey? You don't
want us to come down here perhaps—do you? You are two
hundred to one. You don't want us to come down into the open.
Ah! I promise you we shall give you some sport before you've
done. You talk about me making a cowardly set upon unoffending people. What's that to me that they are unoffending

when I am starving for next to no offence? But I am not a coward. Don't you be one. Bring them along or, by all the fiends, we shall yet manage to send half your unoffending town to heaven with us in smoke!"'

"He was terrible—relating this to me—this tortured skeleton of a man drawn up together with his face over his knees, upon a miserable bed in that wretched hovel, and lifting his head to look at me with malignant triumph.

"'That's what I told him—I knew what to say,' he began again, feebly at first, but working himself up with incredible speed into a fiery utterance of his scorn. 'We aren't going into the forest to wander like a string of living skeletons dropping one after another for ants to go to work upon us before we are fairly dead. Oh, no! . . .' "You don't déserve a better fate," he said. "And what do you deserve," I shouted at him, "you that I find skulking here with your mouth full of your responsibility, of innocent lives, of your infernal duty? What do you know more of me than I know of you? I came here for food. D'ye hear?—food to fill our bellies. And what did *you* come for? What did you ask for when you came here? We don't ask you for anything but to give us a fight or a clear road to go back whence we came. . . ." "I would fight with you now," says he, pulling at his little moustache. "And I would let you shoot me, and welcome," I said. "This is as good a jumping-off place for me as another. I am sick of my infernal luck. But it would be too easy. There are my men in the same boat—and, by God, I am not the sort to jump out of trouble and leave them in a d—d lurch," I said. He stood thinking for a while and then wanted to know what I had done ("out there," he says, tossing his head down-stream) to be hazed about so. "Have we met to tell each other the story of our lives?" I asked him. "Suppose you begin. No? Well, I am sure I don't want to hear. Keep it to yourself. I know it is no better than mine. I've lived—and so did you though you talk as if you were one of those people that should have wings so as to go about without touching the dirty earth. Well—it is dirty. I haven't got any wings. I am here because I was afraid once in my life. Want to know what of? Of a prison. That scares me, and you may know it—if it's any

good to you. I won't ask you what scared you into this infernal
hole, where you seem to have found pretty pickings. That's
your luck and this is mine—the privilege to beg for the favour
of being shot quickly, or else kicked out to go free and starve
in my own way." ' . . .

"His debilitated body shook with an exultation so vehement,
so assured, and so malicious that it seemed to have driven off
the death waiting for him in that hut. The corpse of his mad
self-love uprose from rags and destitution as from the dark
horrors of a tomb. It is impossible to say how much he lied to
Jim then, how much he lied to me now—and to himself always. Vanity plays lurid tricks with our memory, and the truth
of every passion wants some pretence to make it live. Standing
at the gate of the other world in the guise of a beggar, he had
slapped this world's face, he had spat on it, he had thrown
upon it an immensity of scorn and revolt at the bottom of his
misdeeds. He had overcome them all—men, women, savages,
traders, ruffians, missionaries—and Jim—that beefy-faced
beggar. I did not begrudge him this triumph *in articulo mortis*,
this almost posthumous illusion of having trampled all the
earth under his feet. While he was boasting to me, in his sordid
and repulsive agony, I couldn't help thinking of the chuckling
talk relating to the time of his greatest splendour when, during
a year or more, Gentleman Brown's ship was to be seen, for
many days on end, hovering off an islet befringed with green
upon azure, with the dark dot of the mission-house on a white
beach; while Gentleman Brown, ashore, was casting his spells
over a romantic girl for whom Melanesia had been too much,
and giving hopes of a remarkable conversation to her husband.
The poor man, some time or other, had been heard to express
the intention of winning 'Captain Brown to a better way of
life.' . . . 'Bag Gentleman Brown for Glory'—as a leery-eyed
loafer expressed it once—'just to let them see up above what a
Western Pacific trading skipper looks like.' And this was the
man, too, who had run off with a dying woman, and had shed
tears over her body. 'Carried on like a big baby,' his then mate
was never tired of telling, 'and where the fun came in may I be
kicked to death by diseased Kanakas if *I* know. Why, gents!

she was too far gone when he brought her aboard to know him;
she just lay there on her back in his bunk staring at the beam
with awful shining eyes—and then she died. Dam' bad sort of
fever, I guess. . . .' I remembered all these stories while, wiping his matted lump of a beard with a livid hand, he was telling
me from his noisome couch how he got round, got in, got
home, on the confounded, immaculate, don't-you-touch-me
sort of fellow. He admitted that he couldn't be scared, but there
was a way, 'as broad as a turnpike, to get in and shake his
twopenny soul around and inside out and upside down—by
God!' "

Chapter Forty-two

I DON'T think he could do more than perhaps look upon that
straight path. He seemed to have been puzzled by what he
saw, for he interrupted himself in his narrative more than once
to exclaim, 'He nearly slipped from me there. I could not
make him out. Who was he?' And after glaring at me wildly
he would go on, jubilating and sneering. To me the conversation of these two across the creek appears now as the deadliest
kind of duel on which Fate looked on with her cold-eyed
knowledge of the end. No, he didn't turn Jim's soul inside out,
but I am much mistaken if the spirit so utterly out of his reach
had not been made to taste to the full the bitterness of that
contest. These were the emissaries with whom the world he
had renounced was pursuing him in his retreat. White men
from 'out there' where he did not think himself good enough
to live. This was all that came to him—a menace, a shock, a
danger to his work. I suppose it is this sad, half-resentful,
half-resigned feeling, piercing through the few words Jim said
now and then, that puzzled Brown so much in the reading of
his character. Some great men owe most of their greatness to
the ability of detecting in those they destine for their tools the

exact quality of strength that matters for their work, and
Brown, as though he had been really great, had a satanic gift
of finding out the best and the weakest spot in his victims. He
admitted to me that Jim wasn't of the sort that can be got over
by truckling, and accordingly he took care to show himself as
a man confronting without dismay ill-luck, censure, and disaster. The smuggling of a few guns was no great crime, he
pointed out. As to coming to Patusan, who had the right to say
he hadn't come to beg? The infernal people here let loose at
him from both banks without staying to ask questions. He
made the point brazenly, for, in truth, Dain Waris's energetic
action had prevented the greatest calamities; because Brown
told me distinctly that, perceiving the size of the place, he had
resolved instantly in his mind that as soon as he had gained a
footing he would set fire right and left, and begin by shooting
down everything living in sight, in order to cow and terrify
the population. The disproportion of forces was so great that
this was the only way giving him the slightest chance of at-
taining his ends—he argued in a fit of coughing. But he didn't
tell Jim this. As to the hardships and starvation they had gone
through, these had been very real; it was enough to look at his
band. He made, at the sound of a shrill whistle, all his men appear standing in a row on the logs in full view, so that Jim
could see them. For the killing of the man, it had been done—
well, it had—but was not this war, bloody war—in a corner?
and the fellow had been killed cleanly, shot through the chest,
not like that poor devil of his lying now in the creek. They had
to listen to him dying for six hours, with his entrails torn with
slugs. At any rate this was a life for a life. . . . And all this was
said with the weariness, with the recklessness of a man
spurred on and on by ill-luck till he cares not where he runs.
When he asked Jim, with a sort of brusque despairing frankness, whether he himself—straight now—didn't understand
that when 'it came to saving one's life in the dark, one didn't
care who else went—three, thirty, three hundred people'—it
was as if a demon had been whispering advice in his ear. 'I
made him wince,' boasted Brown to me. 'He very soon left off
coming the righteous over me. He just stood there with noth-

ing to say, and looking as black as thunder—not at me—on the ground.' He asked Jim whether he had nothing fishy in his life to remember that he was so damnedly hard upon a man trying to get out of a deadly hole by the first means that came to hand—and so on, and so on. And there ran through the rough talk a vein of subtle reference to their common blood, an assumption of common experience; a sickening suggestion of common guilt, of secret knowledge that was like a bond of their minds and of their hearts.

"At last Brown threw himself down full length and watched Jim out of the corners of his eyes. Jim on his side of the creek stood thinking and switching his leg. The houses in view were silent, as if a pestilence had swept them clean of every breath of life; but many invisible eyes were turned, from within, upon the two men with the creek between them, a stranded white boat, and the body of the third man half sunk in the mud. On the river canoes were moving again, for Patusan was recovering its belief in the stability of earthly institutions since the return of the white lord. The right bank, the platforms of the houses, the rafts moored along the shores, even the roofs of bathing-huts, were covered with people that, far away out of earshot and almost out of sight, were straining their eyes towards the knoll beyond the Rajah's stockade. Within the wide irregular ring of forests broken in two places by the sheen of the river there was a silence. 'Will you promise to leave the coast?' Jim asked. Brown lifted and let fall his hand, giving everything up as it were—accepting the inevitable. 'And surrender your arms?' Jim went on. Brown sat up and glared across. 'Surrender our arms! Not till you come to take them out of our stiff hands. You think I am gone crazy with funk? Oh, no! That and the rags I stand in is all I have got in the world, besides a few more breech-loaders on board; and I expect to sell the lot in Madagascar, if I ever get so far—begging my way from ship to ship.'

"Jim said nothing to this. At last, throwing away the switch he held in his hand, he said, as if speaking to himself, 'I don't know whether I have the power.' . . . 'You don't know! And you wanted me just now to give up my arms! That's good, too,' cried Brown. 'Suppose they say one thing to you, and do the other thing to me.' He calmed down markedly. 'I daresay you have the power, or what's the meaning of all this talk?' he continued. 'What did you come down here for? To pass the time of day?'

"'Very well,' said Jim, lifting his head suddenly after a long silence. 'You shall have a clear road or else a clear fight.' He turned on his heel and walked away.

"Brown got up at once, but he did not go up the hill till he had seen Jim disappear between the first houses. He never set his eyes on him again. On his way back he met Cornelius slouching down with his head between his shoulders. He stopped before Brown. 'Why didn't you kill him?' he demanded in a sour, discontented voice. 'Because I could do better than that,' Brown said with an amused smile. 'Never! never!' protested Cornelius with energy. 'Couldn't. I have lived here for many years.' Brown looked up at him curiously. There were many sides to the life of that place in arms against him; things he would never find out. Cornelius slunk past dejectedly in the direction of the river. He was now leaving his new friends; he accepted the disappointing course of events with a sulky obstinacy which seemed to draw more togther his little yellow old face; and as he went down he glanced askant here and there, never giving up his fixed idea.

"Henceforth events move fast without a check, flowing from the very hearts of men like a stream from a dark source, and we see Jim amongst them, mostly through Tamb' Itam's eyes. The girl's eyes had watched him, too, but her life is too much entwined with his: there is her passion, her wonder, her anger, and, above all, her fear and her unforgiving love. Of the faithful servant, uncomprehending as the rest of them, it is the fidelity alone that comes into play; a fidelity and a belief in his lord so strong that even amazement is subdued to a sort of saddened acceptance of a mysterious failure. He has eyes only for one figure, and through all the mazes of bewilderment he preserves his air of guardianship, of obedience, of care.

"His master came back from his talk with the white men, walking slowly towards the stockade in the street. Everybody

was rejoiced to see him return, for while he was away every
man had been afraid not only of him being killed, but also of
what would come after Jim went into one of the houses, where
old Doramin had retired, and remained alone for a long time
with the head of the Bugis settlers. No doubt he discussed the
course to follow with him then, but no man was present at the
conversation. Only Tamb' Itam, keeping as close to the door as
he could, heard his master say, 'Yes. I shall let all the people
know that such is my wish; but I spoke to you, O Doramin, before all the others, and alone; for you know my heart as well as
I know yours and its greatest desire. And you know well also
that I have no thought but for the people's good.' Then his
master, lifting the sheeting in the doorway, went out, and he,
Tamb' Itam, had a glimpse of old Doramin within, sitting in
the chair with his hands on his knees, and looking between his
feet. Afterwards he followed his master to the fort, where all
the principal Bugis and Patusan inhabitants had been summoned for a talk. Tamb' Itam himself hoped there would be
some fighting. 'What was it but the taking of another hill?' he
exclaimed regretfully. However, in the town many hoped that
the rapacious strangers would be induced, by the sight of so
many brave men making ready to fight, to go away. It would
be a good thing if they went away. Since Jim's arrival had been
made known before daylight by the gun fired from the fort and
the beating of the big drum there, the fear that had hung over
Patusan had broken and subsided like a wave on a rock, leaving the seething foam of excitement, curiosity, and endless
speculation. Half of the population had been ousted out of their
homes for purposes of defence, and were living in the street on
the left side of the river, crowding round the fort, and in momentary expectation of seeing their abandoned dwellings on
the threatened bank burst into flames. The general anxiety was
to see the matter settled quickly. Food, through Jewel's care,
had been served out to the refugees. Nobody knew what their
white man would do. Some remarked that it was worse than in
Sherif Ali's war. Then many people did not care; now everybody had something to lose. The movements of canoes passing
to and fro between the two parts of the town were watched

with interest. A couple of Bugis war-boats lay anchored in the
middle of the stream to protect the river, and a thread of smoke
stood at the bow of each; the men in them were cooking their
midday rice when Jim, after his interviews with Brown and
Doramin, crossed the river and entered by the water-gate of his
fort. The people inside crowded round him so that he could
hardly make his way to the house. They had not seen him before, because on his arrival during the night he had only exchanged a few words with the girl, who had come down to the
landing-stage for the purpose, and had then gone on at once to
join the chiefs and the fighting men on the other bank. People
shouted greetings after him. One old woman raised a laugh by
pushing her way to the front madly and enjoining him in a
scolding voice to see to it that her two sons, who were with
Doramin, did not come to harm at the hands of the robbers.
Several of the bystanders tried to pull her away, but she struggled and cried, 'Let me go. What is this, O Muslims? This
laughter is unseemly. Are they not cruel, bloodthirsty robbers
bent on killing?' 'Let her be,' said Jim, and as a silence fell
suddenly, he said slowly, 'Everybody shall be safe.' He entered
the house before the great sigh, and the loud murmurs of satisfaction, had died out.

"There's no doubt his mind was made up that Brown should
have his way clear back to the sea. His fate, revolted, was forcing his hand. He had for the first time to affirm his will in the
face of out-spoken opposition. 'There was much talk, and at
first my master was silent,' Tamb' Itam said. 'Darkness came,
and then I lit the candles on the long table. The chiefs sat on
each side, and the lady remained by my master's right hand.'

"When he began to speak the unaccustomed difficulty
seemed only to fix his resolve more immovably. The white
men were now waiting for his answer on the hill. Their chief
had spoken to him in the language of his own people, making
clear many things difficult to explain in any other speech. They
were erring men whom suffering had made blind to right and
wrong. It is true that lives had been lost already, but why lose
more? He declared to his hearers, the assembled heads of the
people, that their welfare was his welfare, their losses his

losses, their mourning his mourning. He looked round at the grave listening faces and told them to remember that they had fought and worked side by side. They knew his courage . . . Here a murmur interrupted him . . . And that he had never deceived them. For many years they had dwelt together. He loved the land and the people living in it with a very great love. He was ready to answer with his life for any harm that should come to them if the white men with beards were allowed to retire. They were evil-doers, but their destiny had been evil, too. Had he ever advised them ill? Had his words ever brought suffering to the people? he asked. He believed that it would be best to let these whites and their followers go with their lives. It would be a small gift. 'I whom you have tried and found always true ask you to let them go.' He turned to Doramin. The old *nakhoda* made no movement. 'Then,' said Jim, 'call in Dain Waris, your son, my friend, for in this business I shall not lead.'"

Chapter Forty-three

TAMB' ITAM behind his chair was thunderstruck. The declaration produced an immense sensation. 'Let them go because this is best in my knowledge which has never deceived you,' Jim insisted. There was a silence. In the darkness of the courtyard could be heard the subdued whispering, shuffling noise of many people. Doramin raised his heavy head and said that there was no more reading of hearts than touching the sky with the hand, but—he consented. The others gave their opinion in turn. 'It is best,' 'Let them go,' and so on. But most of them simply said that they 'believed Tuan Jim.'

"In this simple form of assent to his will lies the whole gist of the situation; their creed, his truth; and the testimony to that faithfulness which made him in his own eyes the equal of the impeccable men who never fall out of the ranks. Stein's words,

'Romantic!—Romantic!' seem to ring over those distances that will never give him up now to a world indifferent to his failing and his virtues, and to that ardent and clinging affection that refuses him the dole of tears in the bewilderment of a great grief and of eternal separation. From the moment the sheer truthfulness of his last three years of life carries the day against the ignorance, the fear, and the anger of men, he appears no longer to me as I saw him last—a white speck catching all the dim light left upon a sombre coast and the darkened sea—but greater and more pitiful in the loneliness of his soul, that remains even for her who loved him best a cruel and insoluble mystery.

"It is evident that he did not mistrust Brown; there was no reason to doubt the story, whose truth seemed warranted by the rough frankness, by a sort of virile sincerity in accepting the morality and the consequences of his acts. But Jim did not know the almost inconceivable egotism of the man which made him, when resisted and foiled in his will, mad with the indignant and revengeful rage of a thwarted autocrat. But if Jim did not mistrust Brown, he was evidently anxious that some misunderstanding should not occur, ending perhaps in collision and bloodshed. It was for this reason that directly the Malay chiefs had gone he asked Jewel to get him something to eat, as he was going out of the fort to take command in the town. On her remonstrating against this on the score of his fatigue, he said that something might happen for which he would never forgive himself. 'I am responsible for every life in the land,' he said. He was moody at first; she served him with her own hands, taking the plates and dishes (of the dinner-service presented him by Stein) from Tamb' Itam. He brightened up after a while; told her she would be again in command of the fort for another night. 'There's no sleep for us, old girl,' he said, 'while our people are in danger.' Later on he said jokingly that she was the best man of them all. 'If you and Dain Waris had done what you wanted, not one of these poor devils would be alive to-day.' 'Are they very bad?' she asked, leaning over his chair. 'Men act badly sometimes without being much worse than others,' he said after some hesitation.

"Tamb' Itam followed his master to the landing-stage out-side the fort. The night was clear, but without a moon, and the middle of the river was dark, while the water under each bank reflected the light of many fires 'as on a night of Ramadan,' Tamb' Itam said. War-boats drifted silently in the dark lane or, anchored, floated motionless with a loud ripple. That night there was much paddling in a canoe and walking at his mas-ter's heels for Tamb' Itam: up and down the street they tramped, where the fires were burning, inland on the outskirts of the town where small parties of men kept guard in the fields. Tuan Jim gave his orders and was obeyed. Last of all they went to the Rajah's stockade, which a detachment of Jim's people manned on that night. The old Rajah had fled early in the morning with most of his women to a small house he had near a jungle village on a tributary stream. Kassim, left behind, had attended the council with his air of diligent activity to explain away the diplomacy of the day before. He was considerably cold-shouldered, but managed to preserve his smiling, quiet alertness, and professed himself highly delighted when Jim told him sternly that he proposed to occupy the stockade on that night with his own men. After the council broke up he was heard outside accosting this and that departing chief, and speaking in a loud, gratified tone of the Rajah's property being protected in the Rajah's absence.

"About ten or so of Jim's men marched in. The stockade commanded the mouth of the creek, and Jim meant to remain there till Brown had passed below. A small fire was lit on the flat, grassy point outside the wall of stakes, and Tamb' Itam placed a little folding-stool for his master. Jim told him to try and sleep. Tamb' Itam got a mat and lay down a little way off; but he could not sleep, though he knew he had to go on an im-portant journey before the night was out. His master walked to and fro before the fire with bowed head and with his hands be-hind his back. His face was sad. Whenever his master ap-proached him Tamb' Itam pretended to sleep, not wishing his master to know he had been watched. At last his master stood still, looking down on him as he lay, and said softly, 'It is time.'

"Tamb' Itam arose directly and made his preparations. His mission was to go down the river, preceding Brown's boat by an hour or more, to tell Dain Waris finally and formally that the whites were to be allowed to pass out unmolested. Jim would not trust anybody else with that service. Before starting Tamb' Itam, more as a matter of form (since his position about Jim made him perfectly known), asked for a token. 'Because, Tuan,' he said, 'the message is important, and these are the very words I carry.' His master first put his hand into one pocket, then into another, and finally took off his forefinger Stein's silver ring, which he habitually wore, and gave it to Tamb' Itam. When Tamb' Itam left on his mission, Brown's camp on the knoll was dark but for a single small glow shining through the branches of one of the trees the white men had cut down.

"Early in the evening Brown had received from Jim a folded piece of paper on which was written, 'You get the clear road. Start as soon as your boat floats on the morning tide. Let your men be careful. The bushes on both sides of the creek and the stockade at the mouth are full of well-armed men. You would have no chance, but I don't believe you want bloodshed.' Brown read it, tore the paper into small pieces, and, turning to Cornelius, who had brought it, said jeeringly, 'Good-bye, my excellent friend.' Cornelius had been in the fort, and had been sneaking around Jim's house during the afternoon. Jim chose him to carry the note because he could speak English, was known to Brown, and was not likely to be shot by some nervous mistake of one of the men as a Malay, approaching in the dusk, perhaps might have been.

"Cornelius didn't go away after delivering the paper. Brown was sitting up over a tiny fire; all the others were lying down. 'I could tell you something you would like to know,' Cornelius mumbled crossly. Brown paid no attention. 'You did not kill him,' went on the other, 'and what do you get for it? You might have had money from the Rajah, besides the loot of all the Bugis houses, and now you get nothing.' 'You had better clear out from here,' growled Brown, without even looking at him. But Cornelius let himself drop by his side and began to whis-

per very fast, touching his elbow from time to time. What he
had to say made Brown sit up at first, with a curse. He had simply informed him of Dain Waris's armed party down the river.
At first Brown saw himself completely sold and betrayed, but
a moment's reflection convinced him that there could be no
treachery intended. He said nothing, and after a while Cornelius remarked, in a tone of complete indifference, that there
was another way out of the river which he knew very well. 'A
good thing to know, too,' said Brown, pricking up his ears; and
Cornelius began to talk of what went on in town and repeated
all that had been said in council, gossiping in an even under-
tone at Brown's ear as you talk amongst sleeping men you do
not wish to wake. 'He thinks he has made me harmless, does
he?' mumbled Brown very low. . . . 'Yes. He is a fool. A little
child. He came here and robbed me,' droned on Cornelius,
'and he made all the people believe him. But if something happened that they did not believe him any more, where would he
be? And the Bugis Dain who is waiting for you down the river
there, captain, is the very man who chased you up here when
you first came.' Brown observed nonchalantly that it would be
just as well to avoid him, and with the same detached, musing
air Cornelius declared himself acquainted with a backwater
broad enough to take Brown's boat past Waris's camp. 'You
will have to be quiet,' he said as an afterthought, 'for in one
place we pass close behind his camp. Very close. They are
camped ashore with their boat hauled up.' 'Oh, we know how
to be as quiet as mice; never fear,' said Brown. Cornelius stip-
ulated that in case he were to pilot Brown out, his canoe should
be towed. 'I'll have to get back quick,' he explained.

"It was two hours before the dawn when word was passed to
the stockade from outlying watches that the white robbers were
coming down to their boat. In a very short time every armed
man from one end of Patusan to the other was on the alert, yet
the banks of the river remained so silent that but for the fires
burning with sudden blurred flares the town might have been
asleep as if in peace-time. A heavy mist lay very low on the
water, making a sort of an illusive grey light that showed nothing. When Brown's long-boat glided out of the creek into the

river, Jim was standing on the low point of land before the
Rajah's stockade—on the very spot where for the first time he
put his foot on Patusan shore. A shadow loomed up, moving in
the greyness, solitary, very bulky, and yet constantly eluding
the eye. A murmur of low talking came out of it. Brown at the
tiller heard Jim speak calmly: 'A clear road. You had better trust
to the current while the fog lasts; but this will lift presently.'
'Yes, presently we shall see clear,' replied Brown.

"The thirty or forty men standing with muskets at ready outside the stockade held their breath. The Bugis owner of the
prau, whom I saw on Stein's verandah, and who was amongst
them, told me that the boat, shaving the low point close,
seemed for a moment to grow big and hang over it like a
mountain. 'If you think it worth your while to wait a day outside,' called out Jim, ' I'll try to send you down something—
bullock, some yams—what I can.' The shadow went on
moving. 'Yes. Do,' said a voice, blank and muffled out of the
fog. Not one of the many attentive listeners understood what
the words meant; and then Brown and his men in their boat
floated away, fading spectrally without the slightest sound.

"Thus Brown, invisible in the mist, goes out of Patusan
elbow to elbow with Cornelius in the stern-sheets of the long-
boat. 'Perhaps you shall get a small bullock,' said Cornelius.
'Oh, yes. Bullock. Yam. You'll get it if *he* said so. He always
speaks the truth. He stole everything I had. I suppose you like
a small bullock better than the loot of many houses.' 'I would
advise you to hold your tongue, or somebody here may fling
you overboard into this damned fog,' said Brown. The boat
seemed to be standing still; nothing could be seen, not even the
river alongside, only the water-dust flew and trickled, con-
densed, down their beards and faces. It was weird, Brown told
me. Every individual man of them felt as though he were adrift
alone in a boat, haunted by an almost imperceptible suspicion
of sighing, muttering ghosts. 'Throw me out, would you? But
I would know where I was,' mumbled Cornelius, surlily. 'I've
lived many years here.' 'Not long enough to see through a fog
like this,' Brown said, lolling back with his arm swinging to
and fro on the useless tiller. 'Yes. Long enough for that,'

snarled Cornelius. 'That's very useful,' commented Brown. 'Am I to believe you could find that backway you spoke of blindfold, like this?' Cornelius grunted. 'Are you too tired to row?' he asked after a silence. 'No, by God!' shouted Brown suddenly. 'Out with your oars there.' There was great knocking in the fog, which after a while settled into a regular grind of invisible sweeps against invisible thole-pins. Otherwise nothing was changed, and but for the slight splash of a dipped blade it was like rowing a balloon car in a cloud, said Brown. Thereafter Cornelius did not open his lips except to ask querulously for somebody to bale out his canoe, which was towing behind the long-boat. Gradually the fog whitened and became luminous ahead. To the left Brown saw a darkness as though he had been looking at the back of the departing night. All at once a big bough covered with leaves appeared above his head, and ends of twigs, dripping and still, curved slenderly close alongside. Cornelius, without a word, took the tiller from his hand."

Chapter Forty-four

I DON'T think they spoke together again. The boat entered a narrow by-channel, where it was pushed by the oar-blades set into crumbling banks, and there was a gloom as if enormous black wings had been outspread above the mist that filled its depth to the summits of the trees. The branches overhead showered big drops through the gloomy fog. At a mutter from Cornelius, Brown ordered his men to load. 'I'll give you a chance to get even with them before we're done, you dismal cripples, you,' he said to his gang. 'Mind you don't throw it away—you hounds.' Low growls answered that speech. Cornelius showed much fussy concern for the safety of his canoe.

"Meantime Tamb' Itam had reached the end of his journey. The fog had delayed him a little, but he had paddled steadily, keeping in touch with the south bank. By-and-by daylight came

like a glow in a ground glass globe. The shores made on each
side of the river a dark smudge, in which one could detect hints
of columnar forms and shadows of twisted branches high up.
The mist was still thick on the water, but a good watch was
being kept, for as Tamb' Itam approached the camp the figures
of two men emerged out of the white vapour, and voices spoke
to him boisterously. He answered, and presently a canoe lay
alongside, and he exchanged news with the paddlers. All was
well. The trouble was over. Then the men in the canoe let go
their grip on the side of his dug-out and incontinently fell out of
sight. He pursued his way till he heard voices coming to him
quietly over the water, and saw, under the now lifting, swirling
mist, the glow of many little fires burning on a sandy stretch,
backed by lofty thin timber and bushes. There again a look-out
was kept, for he was challenged. He shouted his name as the two
last sweeps of his paddle ran his canoe up on the strand. It was a
big camp. Men crouched in many knots under a subdued murmur of early morning talk. Many thin threads of smoke curled
slowly on the white mist. Little shelters, elevated above the
ground, had been built for the chiefs. Muskets were stacked in
small pyramids, and long spears were stuck singly into the sand
near the fires.

"Tamb' Itam, assuming an air of importance, demanded to
be led to Dain Waris. He found the friend of his white lord
lying on a raised couch made of bamboo, and sheltered by a
sort of shed of sticks covered with mats. Dain Waris was
awake, and a bright fire was burning before his sleeping-place,
which resembled a rude shrine. The only son of Nakhoda Doramin answered his greeting kindly. Tamb' Itam began by
handing him the ring which vouched for the truth of the messenger's words. Dain Waris, reclining on his elbow, bade him
speak and tell all the news. Beginning with the consecrated
formula, 'The news is good,' Tamb' Itam delivered Jim's own
words. The white men, departing with the consent of all the
chiefs, were to be allowed to pass down the river. In answer to
a question or two Tamb' Itam then reported the proceedings of
the last council. Dain Waris listened attentively to the end, toy-
ing with the ring which ultimately he slipped on the forefinger

of his right hand. After hearing all he had to say he dismissed Tamb' Itam to have food and rest. Orders for the return in the afternoon were given immediately. Afterwards Dain Waris lay down again, open-eyed, while his personal attendants were preparing his food at the fire, by which Tamb' Itam also sat talking to the men who lounged up to hear the latest intelligence from the town. The sun was eating up the mist. A good watch was kept upon the reach of the main stream where the boat of the whites was expected to appear every moment.

"It was then that Brown took his revenge upon the world which, after twenty years of contemptuous and reckless bullying, refused him the tribute of a common robber's success. It was an act of cold-blooded ferocity, and it consoled him on his deathbed like a memory of an indomitable defiance. Stealthily he landed his men on the other side of the island opposite to the Bugis camp, and led them across. After a short but quite silent scuffle, Cornelius, who had tried to slink away at the moment of landing, resigned himself to show the way where the undergrowth was most sparse. Brown held both his skinny hands together behind his back in the grip of one vast fist, and now and then impelled him forward with a fierce push. Cornelius remained as mute as a fish, abject but faithful to his purpose, whose accomplishment loomed before him dimly. At the edge of the patch of forest Brown's men spread themselves out in cover and waited. The camp was plain from end to end before their eyes, and no one looked their way. Nobody even dreamed that the white men could have any knowledge of the narrow channel at the back of the island. When he judged the moment come, Brown yelled, 'Let them have it,' and fourteen shots rang out like one.

"Tamb' Itam told me the surprise was so great that, except for those who fell dead or wounded, not a soul of them moved for quite an appreciable time after the first discharge. Then a man screamed, and after that scream a great yell of amazement and fear went up from all the throats. A blind panic drove these men in a surging swaying mob to and fro along the shore like a herd of cattle afraid of the water. Some few jumped into the river then, but most of them did so only after the last discharge.

Three times Brown's men fired into the ruck, Brown, the only one in view, cursing and yelling, 'Aim low! aim low!'

"Tamb' Itam says that, as for him, he understood at the first volley what had happened. Though untouched he fell down and lay as if dead, but with his eyes open. At the sound of the first shots Dain Waris, reclining on the couch, jumped up and ran out upon the open shore, just in time to receive a bullet in his forehead at the second discharge. Tamb' Itam saw him fling his arms wide open before he fell. Then, he says, a great fear came upon him—not before. The white men retired as they had come—unseen.

"Thus Brown balanced his account with the evil fortune. Notice that even in this awful outbreak there is a superiority as of a man who carries right—the abstract thing—within the envelope of his common desires. It was not a vulgar and treacherous massacre; it was a lesson, a retribution—a demonstration of some obscure and awful attribute of our nature which, I am afraid, is not so very far under the surface as we like to think.

"Afterwards the whites depart unseen by Tamb' Itam, and seem to vanish from before men's eyes altogether; and the schooner, too, vanishes after the manner of stolen goods. But a story is told of a white long-boat picked up a month later in the Indian Ocean by a cargo-steamer. Two parched, yellow, glassy-eyed, whispering skeletons in her recognised the authority of a third, who declared that his name was Brown. His schooner, he reported, bound south with a cargo of Java sugar, had sprung a bad leak and sank under his feet. He and his companions were the survivors of a crew of six. The two died on board the steamer which rescued them. Brown lived to be seen by me, and I can testify that he had played his part to the last.

"It seems, however, that in going away they had neglected to cast off Cornelius's canoe. Cornelius himself Brown had let go at the beginning of the shooting, with a kick for a parting benediction. Tamb' Itam, after arising from amongst the dead, saw the Nazarene running up and down the shore amongst the corpses and expiring fires. He uttered little cries. Suddenly he rushed to the water, and made frantic efforts to get one of the Bugis boats in the water. 'Afterwards, till he had seen me,' related Tamb' Itam, 'he stood looking at the heavy canoe and scratching his head.' 'What became of him?' I asked. Tamb' Itam, staring at me, made an expressive gesture with his right arm. 'Twice I struck, Tuan,' he said. 'When he beheld me approaching he cast himself violently on the ground and made a great outcry, kicking. He screeched like a frightened hen till he felt the point; then he was still, and lay staring at me while his life went out of his eyes.'

"This done, Tamb' Itam did not tarry. He understood the importance of being the first with the awful news at the fort. There were, of course, many survivors of Dain Waris's party; but in the extremity of panic some had swum across the river, others had bolted into the bush. The fact is that they did not know really who struck that blow—whether more white robbers were not coming, whether they had not already got hold of the whole land. They imagined themselves to be the victims of a vast treachery, and utterly doomed to destruction. It is said that some small parties did not come in till three days afterwards. However, a few tried to make their way back to Patusan at once, and one of the canoes that were patrolling the river that morning was in sight of the camp at the very moment of the attack. It is true that at first the men in her leaped overboard and swam to the opposite bank, but afterwards they returned to their boat and started fearfully upstream. Of these Tamb' Itam had an hour's advance."

Chapter Forty-five

WHEN Tamb' Itam, paddling madly, came into the town-reach, the women, thronging the platforms before the houses, were looking out for the return of Dain Waris's little fleet of boats. The town had a festive air; here and there men, still with spears or guns in their hands, could be seen moving or standing on the shore in groups, Chinamen's shops had been opened early; but the market-place was empty, and a sentry, still posted at the corner of the fort, made out Tamb' Itam, and shouted to those within. The gate was wide open. Tamb' Itam jumped ashore and ran in headlong. The first person he met was the girl coming down from the house.

"Tamb' Itam, disordered, panting, with trembling lips and wild eyes, stood for a time before her as if a sudden spell had been laid on him. Then he broke out very quickly: 'They have killed Dain Waris and many more.' She clapped her hands, and her first words were, 'Shut the gates.' Most of the fortmen had gone back to their houses, but Tamb' Itam hurried on the few who remained for their turn of duty within. The girl stood in the middle of the courtyard, while the others ran about. 'Doramin,' she cried despairingly, as Tamb' Itam passed her. Next time he went by he answered her thought rapidly, 'Yes. But we have all the powder in Patusan.' She caught him by the arm, and, pointing at the house, 'Call him out,' she whispered, trembling.

"Tamb' Itam ran up the steps. His master was sleeping. 'It is I, Tamb' Itam,' he cried at the door, 'with tidings that cannot wait.' He saw Jim turn over on the pillow and open his eyes, and he burst out at once. 'This, Tuan, is a day of evil, an accursed day.' His master raised himself on his elbow to listen— just as Dain Waris had done. And then Tamb' Itam began his tale, trying to relate the story in order, calling Dain Waris Panglima, and saying: 'The Panglima then called out to the chief of his own boatmen, "Give Tamb' Itam something to eat" '— when his master put his feet to the ground and looked at him with such a discomposed face that the words remained in his throat.

"'Speak out,' said Jim. 'Is he dead?' 'May you live long,' cried Tamb' Itam. 'It was a most cruel treachery. He ran out at the first shots and fell. . . .' His master walked to the window and with his fist struck at the shutter. The room was made light; and then in a steady voice, but speaking fast, he began to give him orders to assemble a fleet of boats for immediate pursuit, go to this man, to the other—send messengers; and as he talked he sat down on the bed stooping to lace his boots hurriedly, and suddenly looked up. "Why do you stand here?' he asked very red-faced. 'Waste no time.' Tamb' Itam did not move. 'Forgive me, Tuan, but . . . but,' he began to stammer. 'What?' cried his master aloud, looking terrible, leaning forward with his hands gripping the edge of the bed. 'It is not safe for thy servant to go out amongst the people,' said Tamb' Itam, after hesitating a moment.

"Then Jim understood. He had retreated from one world, for a small matter of an impulsive jump, and now the other, the work of his own hands, had fallen in ruins upon his head. It was not safe for his servant to go out amongst his own people! I believe that in that very moment he had decided to defy the disaster in the only way it occurred to him such a disaster could be defied; but all I know is that, without a word, he came out of his room and sat before the long table, at the head of which he was accustomed to regulate the affairs of his world, proclaiming daily the truth that surely lived in his heart. The dark powers should not rob him twice of his peace. He sat like a stone figure. Tamb' Itam, deferential, hinted at preparations for defence. The girl he loved came in and spoke to him, but he made a sign with his hand, and she was awed by the dumb appeal for silence in it. She went out on the verandah and sat on the threshold, as if to guard him with her body from dangers outside.

"What thoughts passed through his head—what memories? Who can tell? Everything was gone, and he who had been once unfaithful to his trust had lost again all men's confidence. It was then, I believe, he tried to write—to somebody—and gave it up. Loneliness was closing on him. People had trusted him with their lives—only for that; and yet they could never, as he had said, never be made to understand him. Those without did not hear him make a sound. Later, towards the evening, he came to the door and called for Tamb' Itam. 'Well ?' he asked. 'There is much weeping. Much anger, too,' said Tamb' Itam. Jim looked up at him. 'You know,' he murmured. 'Yes, Tuan,' said Tamb' Itam. 'Thy servant does know, and the gates are closed. We shall have to fight.' 'Fight! What for?' he asked. 'For our lives.' 'I have no life,' he said. Tamb' Itam heard a cry from the girl at the door. 'Who knows?' said Tamb' Itam. 'By audacity and cunning we may even escape. There is much fear in men's hearts, too.' He went out, thinking vaguely of boats and of open sea, leaving Jim and the girl together.

"I haven't the heart to set down here such glimpses as she had given me of the hour or more she has passed in there wrestling with him for the possession of her happiness. When he had any hope—what he expected, what he imagined—it is impossible to say. He was inflexible, and with the growing loneliness of his obstinacy his spirit seemed to rise above the ruins of his existence. She cried 'Fight!' into his ear. She could not understand. There was nothing to fight for. He was going to prove his power in another way and conquer the fatal destiny itself. He came out into the courtyard, and behind him, with streaming hair, wild of face, breathless, she staggered out and leaned on the side of the doorway. 'Open the gates,' he ordered. Afterwards, turning to those of his men who were inside, he gave them leave to depart to their homes. 'For how long, Tuan?' asked one of them timidly. 'For all life,' he said, in a sombre tone.

"A hush had fallen upon the town after the outburst of wailing and lamentation that had swept over the river, like a gust of wind from the opened abode of sorrow. But rumors flew in whispers, filling the hearts with consternation and horrible doubts. The robbers were coming back, bringing many others with them, in a great ship, and there would be no refuge in the land for any one. A sense of utter insecurity as during an earthquake pervaded the minds of men, who whispered their suspicions, looking at each other as if in the presence of some awful portent.

"The sun was sinking towards the forests when Dain Waris's body was brought into Doramin's *campong*. Four men carried it in, covered decently with a white sheet which the old mother had sent out down to the gate to meet her son on his return. They laid him at Doramin's feet, and the old man sat still for a long time, one hand on each knee, looking down. The fronds of palms swayed gently, and the foliage of fruit-trees stirred above his head. Every single man of his people was there, fully armed, when the old *nakhoda* at last raised his eyes. He moved them slowly over the crowd, as if seeking for a missing face. Again his chin sank on his breast. The whispers of many men mingled with the slight rustling of the leaves.

"The Malay who had brought Tamb' Itam and the girl to Samarang was there, too. 'Not so angry as many,' he said to me, but struck with a great awe and wonder at the 'suddenness of men's fate, which hangs over their heads like a cloud charged with thunder.' He told me that when Dain Waris's body was uncovered at a sign of Doramin's, he whom they often called the white lord's friend was disclosed lying unchanged with his eyelids a little open as if about to wake. Doramin leaned forward a little more, like one looking for something fallen on the ground. His eyes searched the body from its feet to its head, for the wound maybe. It was in the forehead and small; and there was no word spoken while one of the bystanders, stooping, took off the silver ring from the cold stiff hand. In silence he held it up before Doramin. A murmur of dismay and horror ran through the crowd at the sight of that familiar token. The old *nakhoda* stared at it, and suddenly let out one great fierce cry, deep from the chest, a roar of pain and fury, as mighty as the bellow of a wounded bull, bringing great fear into men's hearts, by the magnitude of his anger and his sorrow that could be plainly discerned without words. There was a great stillness afterwards for a space, while the body was being borne aside by four men. They laid it down under a tree, and on the instant, with one long shriek, all the women of the household began to wail together; they mourned with shrill cries; the sun was setting, and in the intervals of screamed lamentations the high singsong voices of two old men intoning the Koran chanted alone.

"About this time Jim, leaning on a gun-carriage, looked at the river, and turned his back on the house; and the girl, in the doorway, panting as if she had run herself to a standstill, was looking at him across the yard. Tamb' Itam stood not far from his master, waiting patiently for what might happen. All at once Jim, who seemed to be lost in quiet thought, turned to him and said, 'Time to finish this.'

"'Tuan?' said Tamb' Itam, advancing with alacrity. He did not know what his master meant, but as soon as Jim made a movement the girl started, too, and walked down into the open space. It seems that no one else of the people of the house was in sight. She tottered slightly, and about half-way down called out to Jim, who had apparently resumed his peaceful contemplation of the river. He turned around, setting his back against the sun. 'Will you fight?' she cried. 'There is nothing to fight for,' he said; 'nothing is lost.' Saying this he made a step towards her. 'Will you fly?' she cried again. 'There is no escape,' he said, stopping short, and she stood still also, silent, devouring him with her eyes. 'And you shall go?' she said, slowly. He bent his head. 'Ah!' she exclaimed, peering at him as it were, 'you are mad or false. Do you remember the night I prayed you to leave me, and you said that you could not? That it was impossible! Impossible! Do you remember you said you would never leave me? Why? I asked you for no promise. You promised unasked—remember.' 'Enough, poor girl,' he said. 'I should not be worth having.'

"Tamb' Itam said that while they were talking she would laugh loud and senselessly like one under the visitation of God. His master put his hands to his head. He was fully dressed as for every day, but without a hat. She stopped laughing suddenly. 'For the last time,' she cried, menacingly, 'will you defend yourself?' 'Nothing can touch me,' he said in a flicker of superb egoism. Tamb' Itam saw her lean forward where she stood, open her arms, and run at him swiftly. She flung herself upon his breast and clasped him round the neck.

"'Ah! but I shall hold thee thus,' she cried. . . . 'Thou art mine!'

"She sobbed on his shoulder. The sky over Patusan was blood-red, immense, streaming like an open vein. An enormous sun nestled crimson amongst the tree-tops, and the forest below had a black and forbidding face.

"Tamb' Itam tells me that on that evening the aspect of the heavens was angry and frightful. I may well believe it, for I know that on that very day a cyclone passed within sixty miles of the coast, though there was hardly more than a languid stir of air in the place.

"Suddenly Tamb' Itam saw Jim catch her arms, trying to unclasp her hands. She hung on them with her head fallen back; her hair touched the ground. 'Come here!' his master called, and Tamb'Itam helped to ease her down. It was difficult to separate her fingers. Jim, bending over her, looked earnestly upon her face, and all at once ran to the landing-stage. Tamb' Itam followed him, but turning his head, he saw that she had struggled up to her feet. She ran after them a few steps, then fell down heavily on her knees. 'Tuan! Tuan!' called Tamb' Itam, 'look back'; but Jim was already in a canoe, standing up paddle in hand. He did not look back. Tamb' Itam had just time to scramble in after him when the canoe floated clear. The girl was then on her knees, with clasped hands, at the water-gate. She remained thus for a time in a supplicating attitude before she sprang up. 'You are false!' she screamed out after Jim. 'Forgive me,' he cried. 'Never! Never!' she called back.

"Tamb' Itam took the paddle from Jim's hands, it being unseemly that he should sit while his lord paddled. When they reached the other shore his master forbade him to come any farther; but Tamb' Itam did follow him at a distance, walking up the slope to Doramin's *campong.*

"It was beginning to grow dark. Torches twinkled here and there. Those they met seemed awestruck, and stood aside hastily to let Jim pass. The wailing of women came from above. The courtyard was full of armed Bugis with their followers, and of Patusan people.

"I do not know what this gathering really meant. Were these preparations for war, or for vengeance, or to repulse a threatened invasion? Many days elapsed before the people had ceased to look out, quaking, for the return of the white men with long beards and in rags, whose exact relation to their own white man they could never understand. Even for those simple minds poor Jim remains under a cloud.

"Doramin, alone, immense and desolate, sat in his arm-chair with the pair of flintlock pistols on his knees, faced by an armed throng. When Jim appeared, at somebody's exclamation, all the heads turned round together, and then the mass opened right and left, and he walked up a lane of averted glances. Whispers followed him; murmurs: 'He has worked all the evil.' 'He hath a charm.' . . . He heard them—perhaps!

"When he came up into the light of torches the wailing of the women ceased suddenly. Doramin did not lift his head, and Jim stood silent before him for a time. Then he looked to the left, and moved in that direction with measured steps. Dain Waris's mother crouched at the head of the body, and the grey dishevelled hair concealed her face. Jim came up slowly, looked at his dead friend, lifting the sheet, then dropped it without a word. Slowly he walked back.

"'He came! He came!' was running from lip to lip, making a murmur to which he moved. 'He hath taken it upon his own head,' a voice said aloud. He heard this and turned to the crows. 'Yes. Upon my head.' A few people recoiled. Jim waited awhile before Doramin, and then said gently, 'I am come in sorrow.' He waited again. 'I am come ready and un-armed,' he repeated.

"The unwieldy old man, lowering his big forehead like an ox under a yoke, made an effort to rise, clutching at the flint-lock pistols on his knees. From his throat came gurgling, chok-ing, inhuman sounds, and his two attendants helped him from behind. People remarked that the ring which he had dropped on his lap fell and rolled against the foot of the white man, and that poor Jim glanced down at the talisman that had opened for him the door of fame, love, and success within the wall of forests fringed with white foam, within the coast that under the western sun looks like the very stronghold of the night. Do-ramin, struggling to keep his feet, made with his two support-ers a swaying, tottering group; his little eyes stared with an expression of mad pain, of rage, with a ferocious glitter, which the bystanders noticed; and then, while Jim stood stiffened and with bared head in the light of torches, looking him straight in the face, he clung heavily with his left arm round the neck of a bowed youth, and lifting deliberately his right, shot his son's friend through the chest.

'The crowd, which had fallen apart behind Jim as soon as

Doramin had raised his hand, rushed tumultuously forward after the shot. They say that the white man sent right and left at all those faces a proud and unflinching glance. Then with his hand over his lips he fell forward dead.

"And that's the end. He passes away under a cloud, inscrutable at heart, forgotten, unforgiven, and excessively romantic. Not in the wildest days of his boyish visions could he have seen the alluring shape of such an extraordinary success! For it may very well be that in the short moment of his last proud and unflinching glance, he had beheld the face of that opportunity which, like an Eastern bride, had come veiled to his side.

"But we can see him, an obscure conqueror of fame, tearing himself out of the arms of a jealous love at the sign, at the call of his exalted egoism. He goes away from a living woman to celebrate his pitiless wedding with a shadowy ideal of conduct. Is he satisfied—quite, now, I wonder? We ought to know. He is one of us—and have I not stood up once, like an evoked ghost, to answer for his eternal constancy? Was I so very wrong after all? Now he is no more, there are days when the reality of his existence comes to me with an immense, with an overwhelming force; and yet upon my honour there are moments, too, when he passes from my eyes like a disembodied spirit astray amongst the passions of this earth, ready to surrender himself faithfully to the claim of his own world of shades.

"Who knows? He is gone, inscrutable at heart, and the poor girl is leading a sort of soundless, inert life in Stein's house. Stein has aged greatly of late. He feels it himself, and says often that he is 'preparing to leave all this; preparing to leave . . .' while he waves his hand sadly at his butterflies."

September 1899—July 1900

Selected Bibliography

SELECTED BIBLIOGRAPHY

WORKS BY JOSEPH CONRAD

Almayer's Folly, 1895 Novel

An Outcast of the Islands, 1896 Novel

The Nigger of the "Narcissus," 1897 Novel

Tales of Unrest, 1898 Stories

Lord Jim, 1900 Novel

The Inheritors, 1901, with Ford Madox Ford

Heart of Darkness, 1899, 1902 Short Novel (Signet Classic 0-451-52657-0)

"Youth," 1898, 1902 Story (*Youth, a Narrative, and Two Other Stories*, 1902)

Typhoon, 1902 Short Novel

Typhoon and Other Tales, 1903 Stories

Romance, 1903, with Ford Madox Ford

Nostromo, 1904 Novel

The Mirror of the Sea, 1906 Personal impressions

The Secret Agent, 1907 Novel (Signet Classic 0-451-52416-0)

A Set of Six, 1908 Stories

The Secret Sharer, 1910 Short Novel (Signet Classic 0-451-52657-0)

Under Western Eyes, 1911 Novel

'Twixt Land and Sea, 1912 Stories

A Personal Record, 1912 Autobiography

Chance, 1913 Novel

Victory, 1915 Novel

Within the Tides, 1915 Stories

The Shadow-Line, 1917 Short Novel

The Arrow of Gold, 1919 Novel

The Rescue, 1920 Novel

Notes on Life and Letters, 1921 Reminiscences

The Rover, 1923 Novel

The Nature of a Crime, 1924 (written in 1908), with Ford Madox Ford

Suspense, 1925 Novel (incomplete), posthumous

Tales of Hearsay, 1925 Stories

Last Essays, 1926 Essays
The Sisters, 1928 (written in 1896, incomplete)

CRITICISM AND BIOGRAPHY

Batchelor, John. *The Life of Joseph Conrad: A Critical Biography.* Cambridge: Blackwell Publishers, 1993.

Berthoud, Jacques. *Joseph Conrad: The Major Phase.* New York: Cambridge University, 1978.

Billy, Ted. *Critical Essays on Joseph Conrad.* Boston: G.K. Hall & Co., 1987.

Boehmer, Elleke. *Colonial & Postcolonial Literature.* New York: Oxford University, 1995.

Dryden, Linda. *Joseph Conrad and the Imperial Romance.* New York: St. Martin's, 1999.

Erdinast-Vulcan, Daphna. *Joseph Conrad and the Modern Temper.* New York: Oxford University, 1991.

Fincham, Gail and Myrtle Hooper. *Under Postcolonial Eyes: Joseph Conrad After Empire.* Cape Town: University of Cape Town, 1996.

Green, Martin. *Dreams of Adventure, Deeds of Empire.* New York: Basic Books, 1979.

Guerard, Albert J. *Conrad the Novelist.* Cambridge: Harvard University, 1958.

Hampson, Robert. *Joseph Conrad: Betrayal and Identity.* New York: St. Martin's, 1992.

Hunter, Allan. *Joseph Conrad and the Ethics of Darwinism: The challenges of science.* London: Croom Helm, 1983.

Jameson, Fredric. *The Political Unconscious: Narrative as a Socially Symbolic Act.* Ithaca, N.Y.: Cornell University, 1981.

Karl, Frederick R. and Laurence Davies, eds. *The Collected Letters of Joseph Conrad, Volumes I–V.* New York: Cambridge University, 1983.

Kuehn, Robert E., ed. *Twentieth-Century Interpretations of Lord Jim.* Englewood Cliffs, N.J.: Prentice-Hall, 1969.

Najder, Zdzislaw. *Joseph Conrad: A Chronicle.* New York: Cambridge University, 1983.

O'Hanlon, Redmond. *Joseph Conrad and Charles Darwin: The*

influence of scientific thought on Conrad's fiction. Edinburgh: The Salamander Press, 1984.

Parry, Benita. *Conrad and Imperialism: Ideological boundaries and visionary frontiers.* Topsfield, Mass.: Salem Academy/ Merrimack, 1984.

Roussel, Royal. *The Metaphysics of Darkness: A Study in the Unity and Development of Conrad's Fiction.* Baltimore: The Johns Hopkins Press, 1971.

Said, Edward W. *Culture & Imperialism.* New York: Knopf, 1993.

———. *Orientalism: Western Conceptions of the Orient.* New York: Pantheon Books, 1978.

Sherry, Norman. *Conrad's Eastern World.* London: Cambridge University, 1966.

———. *Conrad: The Critical Heritage.* Boston: Routledge & Kegan Paul, 1973.

Tanner, Tony. *Conrad: Lord Jim.* New York: Barron's Educational Studies, 1963.

Thorburn, David. *Conrad's Romanticism.* New Haven: Yale University, 1974.

Watt, Ian P. *Conrad in the Nineteenth Century.* Berkeley: University of California, 1979.

Watts, Cedric. *A Preface to Conrad.* New York: Longman Group Limited, 1982.

———. *Joseph Conrad: A Literary Life.* New York: St. Martin's, 1989.

JOURNALS AND PAPERS

McCracken, Scott. "Reading Masculinity in *Lord Jim.*" *The Conradian* 17:2 (1993), 17–38.

Mongia, Padmini. "Narrative Strategy and Imperialism in Conrad's *Lord Jim.*" *Studies in the Novel* 24 (1992), 173–86.

———. "Ghosts of the Gothic." *The Conradian* 17:2 (1993), 1–16.

Newell, Kenneth B. "The Yellow Dog Incident in Conrad's *Lord Jim.*" *Studies in the Novel* 3 (1977), 26–33.

Saveson, J. E. "Conrad's View of Primitive Peoples in *Lord Jim* and *Heart of Darkness.*" *Modern Fiction Studies* 16 (Summer 1970), 163–83.

A Note on the Text

Joseph Conrad considered the final text of his works to be that printed in the Collected Edition, which was published in both England and America. This Signet Classic edition follows the text of *Lord Jim* as it appeared in the Collected American Edition, published by Doubleday & Company, Inc., 1920.

READ THE TOP 20 SIGNET CLASSICS

Brüder Grimm
Kinder- und Hausmärchen

Brüder Grimm
Kinder- und Hausmärchen

Ausgabe letzter Hand
mit den Originalanmerkungen
der Brüder Grimm

Mit einem Anhang
sämtlicher, nicht in allen Auflagen
veröffentlichter Märchen
und Herkunftsnachweisen herausgegeben
von Heinz Rölleke

Reclam

Brüder Grimm
Kinder- und Hausmärchen

Band 2

Märchen
Nr. 87–200

Kinderlegenden
Nr. 1–10

Anhang
Nr. 1–28

Reclam

RECLAMS UNIVERSAL-BIBLIOTHEK Nr. 3192
1980 Philipp Reclam jun. GmbH & Co. KG,
Siemensstraße 32, 71254 Ditzingen
Druck und Bindung: Eberl & Koesel GmbH & Co. KG,
Am Buchweg 1, 87452 Altusried-Krugzell
Printed in Germany 2022
RECLAM, UNIVERSAL-BIBLIOTHEK und
RECLAMS UNIVERSAL-BIBLIOTHEK sind eingetragene Marken
der Philipp Reclam jun. GmbH & Co. KG, Stuttgart
ISBN 978-3-15-003192-6
www.reclam.de

Inhalt

Kinderlegenden

Anhang

Märchenfrau

Kinder-

und

Hausmärchen

gesammelt

durch

die Brüder Grimm.

Zweiter Band.

Große Ausgabe.

Siebente Auflage.

Göttingen.

Verlag der Dieterichschen Buchhandlung.

1857.

87

Der Arme und der Reiche.

Vor alten Zeiten, als der liebe Gott noch selber auf Erden unter den Menschen wandelte, trug es sich zu, dass er eines Abends müde war und ihn die Nacht überfiel, bevor er zu einer Herberge kommen konnte. Nun standen auf dem Weg vor ihm zwei Häuser einander gegenüber, das eine groß und schön, das andere klein und ärmlich anzusehen, und gehörte das große einem Reichen, das kleine einem armen Manne. Da dachte unser Herr Gott »dem Reichen werde ich nicht beschwerlich fallen: bei ihm will ich übernachten.« Der Reiche, als er an seine Türe klopfen hörte, machte das Fenster auf und fragte den Fremdling was er suche? Der Herr antwortete »ich bitte um ein Nachtlager.« Der Reiche guckte den Wandersmann von Haupt bis zu den Füßen an, und weil der liebe Gott schlichte Kleider trug und nicht aussah wie einer, der viel Geld in der Tasche hat, schüttelte er mit dem Kopf und sprach »ich kann euch nicht aufnehmen, meine Kammern liegen voll Kräuter und Samen, und sollte ich einen jeden beherbergen, der an meiner Türe klopft, so könnte ich selber den Bettelstab in die Hand nehmen. Sucht euch anderswo ein Auskommen.« Schlug damit sein Fenster zu und ließ den lieben Gott stehen. Also kehrte ihm der liebe Gott den Rücken und gieng hinüber zu dem kleinen Haus. Kaum hatte er angeklopft, so klinkte der Arme schon sein Türchen auf und bat den Wandersmann einzutreten. »Bleibt die Nacht über bei mir«, sagte er »es ist schon finster, und heute könnt ihr doch nicht weiter kommen.« Das gefiel dem lieben Gott und er trat zu ihm ein. Die Frau des Armen reichte ihm die Hand, hieß ihn willkommen und sagte er möchte sich's bequem machen und vorlieb nehmen, sie hätten nicht viel, aber was es wäre, gäben sie von Herzen gerne. Dann setzte sie Kartoffeln ans Feuer, und derweil sie kochten, melkte

sie ihre Ziege, damit sie ein wenig Milch dazu hätten. Und
als der Tisch gedeckt war, setzte sich der liebe Gott nieder
und aß mit ihnen, und schmeckte ihm die schlechte Kost
gut, denn es waren vergnügte Gesichter dabei. Nachdem sie
gegessen hatten, und Schlafenszeit war, rief die Frau heimlich ihren Mann und sprach »hör, lieber Mann, wir wollen
uns heute Nacht eine Streu machen, damit der arme Wanderer sich in unser Bett legen und ausruhen kann: er ist den
ganzen Tag über gegangen, da wird einer müde.« »Von
Herzen gern«, antwortete er, »ich will's ihm anbieten«,
gieng zu dem lieben Gott und bat ihn, wenn's ihm recht
wäre, möcht er sich in ihr Bett legen und seine Glieder ordentlich ausruhen. Der liebe Gott wollte den beiden Alten
ihr Lager nicht nehmen, aber sie ließen nicht ab, bis er es
endlich tat und sich in ihr Bett legte: sich selbst aber machten sie eine Streu auf die Erde. Am andern Morgen standen
sie vor Tag schon auf und kochten dem Gast ein Frühstück,
so gut sie es hatten. Als nun die Sonne durchs Fensterlein
schien und der liebe Gott aufgestanden war, aß er wieder
mit ihnen und wollte dann seines Weges ziehen. Als er in
der Türe stand, kehrte er sich um und sprach »weil ihr so
mitleidig und fromm seid, so wünscht euch dreierlei, das
will ich euch erfüllen.« Da sagte der Arme »was soll ich mir
sonst wünschen als die ewige Seligkeit, und dass wir zwei,
so lang wir leben, gesund dabei bleiben und unser notdürf-
tiges tägliches Brot haben; fürs dritte weiß ich mir nichts zu
wünschen.« Der liebe Gott sprach »willst du dir nicht ein
neues Haus für das alte wünschen?« »O ja«, sagte der
Mann, »wenn ich das auch noch erhalten kann, so wär mir's
wohl lieb.« Da erfüllte der Herr ihre Wünsche, verwandelte
ihr altes Haus in ein neues, gab ihnen nochmals seinen Segen und zog weiter.
Es war schon voller Tag, als der Reiche aufstand. Er legte
sich ins Fenster und sah gegenüber ein neues reinliches
Haus mit roten Ziegeln, wo sonst eine alte Hütte gestanden
hatte. Da machte er große Augen, rief seine Frau herbei

und sprach »sag mir, was ist geschehen? Gestern Abend
stand noch die alte elende Hütte, und heute steht da ein
schönes neues Haus. Lauf hinüber und höre wie das gekommen ist.« Die Frau gieng und fragte den Armen aus: er
erzählte ihr »gestern Abend kam ein Wanderer, der suchte
Nachtherberge, und heute Morgen beim Abschied hat er
uns drei Wünsche gewährt, die ewige Seligkeit, Gesundheit
in diesem Leben und das notdürftige tägliche Brot dazu
und zuletzt noch statt unserer alten Hütte ein schönes neues Haus.« Die Frau des Reichen lief eilig zurück und erzählte ihrem Manne wie alles gekommen war. Der Mann
sprach »ich möchte mich zerreißen und zerschlagen: hätt
ich das nur gewusst! der Fremde ist zuvor hier gewesen
und hat bei uns übernachten wollen, ich habe ihn aber abgewiesen.« »Eil dich«, sprach die Frau, »und setze dich auf
dein Pferd, so kannst du den Mann noch einholen, und
dann musst du dir auch drei Wünsche gewähren lassen.«
Der Reiche befolgte den guten Rat, jagte mit seinem Pferd
davon und holte den lieben Gott noch ein. Er redete fein
und lieblich und bat er möcht's nicht übel nehmen, dass er
nicht gleich wäre eingelassen worden, er hätte den Schlüssel
zur Haustüre gesucht, derweil wäre er weggegangen: wenn
er des Weges zurück käme, müsste er bei ihm einkehren.
»Ja«, sprach der liebe Gott, »wenn ich einmal zurückkom-
me, will ich es tun.« Da fragte der Reiche ob er nicht auch
drei Wünsche tun dürfte, wie sein Nachbar? Ja, sagte der
liebe Gott, das dürfte er wohl, es wäre aber nicht gut für
ihn, und er sollte sich lieber nichts wünschen. Der Reiche
meinte er wollte sich schon etwas aussuchen, das zu seinem
Glück gereiche, wenn er nur wüsste, dass es erfüllt würde.
Sprach der liebe Gott »reit heim, und drei Wünsche, die du
tust, die sollen in Erfüllung gehen.«
Nun hatte der Reiche was er verlangte, ritt heimwärts und
fieng an nachzusinnen was er sich wünschen sollte. Wie er
sich so bedachte und die Zügel fallen ließ, fieng das Pferd
an zu springen, so dass er immerfort in seinen Gedanken

gestört wurde und sie gar nicht zusammen bringen konnte.
Er klopfte ihm an den Hals und sagte »sei ruhig, Liese«,
aber das Pferd machte aufs neue Männerchen. Da ward er
zuletzt ärgerlich und rief ganz ungeduldig »so wollt ich,
dass du den Hals zerbrächst!« Wie er das Wort ausgesprochen hatte, plump, fiel er auf die Erde, und lag das Pferd tot
und regte sich nicht mehr; damit war der erste Wunsch erfüllt. Weil er aber von Natur geizig war, wollte er das Sat-
telzeug nicht im Stich lassen, schnitt's ab, hieng's auf seinen
Rücken, und musste nun zu Fuß gehen. »Du hast noch
zwei Wünsche übrig« dachte er und tröstete sich damit.
Wie er nun langsam durch den Sand dahin gieng, und zu
Mittag die Sonne heiß brannte, ward's ihm so warm und
verdrießlich zu Mut: der Sattel drückte ihn auf den Rücken,
auch war ihm noch immer nicht eingefallen, was er sich
wünschen sollte. »Wenn ich mir auch alle Reiche und
Schätze der Welt wünsche«, sprach er zu sich selbst, »so
fällt mir hernach noch allerlei ein, dieses und jenes, das
weiß ich im voraus: ich will's aber so einrichten, dass mir
gar nichts mehr übrig zu wünschen bleibt.« Dann seufzte
er und sprach »ja, wenn ich der bayrische Bauer wäre, der
auch drei Wünsche frei hatte, der wusste sich zu helfen, der
wünschte sich zuerst recht viel Bier, und zweitens so viel
Bier als er trinken könnte, und drittens noch ein Fass Bier
dazu.« Manchmal meinte er jetzt hätte er es gefunden, aber
hernach schien's ihm doch zu wenig. Da kam ihm so in die
Gedanken was es seine Frau jetzt gut hätte, die säße daheim
in einer kühlen Stube und ließe sich's wohl schmecken. Das
ärgerte ihn ordentlich, und ohne dass er's wusste, sprach er
so hin »ich wollte die säße daheim auf dem Sattel, und
könnte nicht herunter, statt dass ich ihn da auf meinem Rücken schleppe.« Und wie das letzte Wort aus seinem Mun-
de kam, so war der Sattel von seinem Rücken verschwunden, und er merkte dass sein zweiter Wunsch auch in Erfüllung gegangen war. Da ward ihm erst recht heiß, er fieng an
zu laufen und wollte sich daheim ganz einsam in seine

Kammer hinsetzen und auf etwas Großes für den letzten
Wunsch sinnen. Wie er aber ankommt und die Stubentür
aufmacht, sitzt da seine Frau mittendrin auf dem Sattel und
kann nicht herunter, jammert und schreit. Da sprach er
»gib dich zufrieden, ich will dir alle Reichtümer der Welt
herbei wünschen, nur bleib da sitzen.« Sie schalt ihn aber
einen Schafskopf und sprach »was helfen mir alle Reichtümer der Welt, wenn ich auf dem Sattel sitze; du hast mich
darauf gewünscht, du musst mir auch wieder herunter helfen.« Er mochte wollen oder nicht, er musste den dritten
Wunsch tun, dass sie vom Sattel ledig wäre und herunter
steigen könnte; und der Wunsch ward alsbald erfüllt. Also
hatte er nichts davon als Ärger, Mühe, Scheltworte und ein
verlorenes Pferd: die Armen aber lebten vergnügt still und
fromm bis an ihr seliges Ende.

88.

Das singende springende Löweneckerchen.

Es war einmal ein Mann, der hatte eine große Reise vor,
und beim Abschied fragte er seine drei Töchter was er ihnen mitbringen sollte. Da wollte die älteste Perlen, die
zweite wollte Diamanten, die dritte aber sprach »lieber Vater, ich wünsche mir ein singendes springendes Löweneckerchen (Lerche).« Der Vater sagte »ja, wenn ich es kriegen kann, sollst du es haben«, küsste alle drei und zog fort.
Als nun die Zeit kam, dass er wieder auf dem Heimweg
war, so hatte er Perlen und Diamanten für die zwei ältesten
gekauft, aber das singende springende Löweneckerchen für
die jüngste hatte er umsonst aller Orten gesucht, und das
tat ihm leid, denn sie war sein liebstes Kind. Da führte ihn
der Weg durch einen Wald, und mitten darin war ein prächtiges Schloss, und nah am Schloss stand ein Baum, ganz

oben auf der Spitze des Baums aber sah er ein Löweneckerchen singen und springen. »Ei, du kommst mir gerade
recht« sagte er ganz vergnügt und rief seinem Diener, er
sollte hinauf steigen und das Tierchen fangen. Wie er aber
zu dem Baum trat, sprang ein Löwe darunter auf, schüttelte
sich und brüllte, dass das Laub an den Bäumen zitterte.
»Wer mir mein singendes springendes Löweneckerchen
stehlen will«, rief er, »den fresse ich auf.« Da sagte der
Mann »ich habe nicht gewusst, dass der Vogel dir gehört:
ich will mein Unrecht wieder gut machen, und mich mit
schwerem Golde loskaufen, lass mir nur das Leben.« Der
Löwe sprach »dich kann nichts retten, als wenn du mir zu
eigen versprichst, was dir daheim zuerst begegnet; willst du
das aber tun, so schenke ich dir das Leben und den Vogel
für deine Tochter obendrein.« Der Mann aber weigerte sich
und sprach »das könnte meine jüngste Tochter sein, die hat
mich am liebsten und läuft mir immer entgegen, wenn ich
nach Haus komme.« Dem Diener aber war angst und er
sagte »muss euch denn gerade eure Tochter begegnen, es
könnte ja auch eine Katze oder ein Hund sein.« Da ließ
sich der Mann überreden, nahm das singende springende
Löweneckerchen und versprach dem Löwen zu eigen was
ihm daheim zuerst begegnen würde.
Wie er daheim anlangte und in sein Haus eintrat, war das
erste, was ihm begegnete, niemand anders als seine jüngste
liebste Tochter: die kam gelaufen, küsste und herzte ihn,
und als sie sah, dass er ein singendes springendes Löweneckerchen mitgebracht hatte, war sie außer sich vor Freude.
Der Vater aber konnte sich nicht freuen, sondern fieng an
zu weinen und sagte »mein liebstes Kind, den kleinen Vogel
habe ich teuer gekauft, ich habe dich dafür einem wilden
Löwen versprechen müssen, und wenn er dich hat, wird er
dich zerreißen und fressen«, und erzählte ihr da alles, wie
es zugegangen war, und bat sie nicht hin zu gehen, es
möchte auch kommen was da wollte. Sie tröstete ihn aber
und sprach »liebster Vater, was ihr versprochen habt muss

auch gehalten werden: ich will hingehen und will den Löwen schon besänftigen, dass ich wieder gesund zu euch komme.« Am andern Morgen ließ sie sich den Weg zeigen, nahm Abschied und gieng getrost in den Wald hinein. Der Löwe aber war ein verzauberter Königssohn, und war bei Tag ein Löwe, und mit ihm wurden alle seine Leute Löwen, in der Nacht aber hatten sie ihre natürliche menschliche Gestalt. Bei ihrer Ankunft ward sie freundlich empfangen und in das Schloss geführt. Als die Nacht kam, war er ein schöner Mann und die Hochzeit ward mit Pracht gefeiert. Sie lebten vergnügt mit einander, wachten in der Nacht und schliefen am Tag. Zu einer Zeit kam er und sagte »morgen ist ein Fest in deines Vaters Haus, weil deine älteste Schwester sich verheiratet, und wenn du Lust hast hinzugehen, so sollen dich meine Löwen hinführen.« Da sagte sie ja, sie möchte gern ihren Vater wiedersehen, fuhr hin und ward von den Löwen begleitet. Da war große Freude, als sie ankam, denn sie hatten alle geglaubt sie wäre von dem Löwen zerrissen worden und schon lange nicht mehr am Leben. Sie erzählte aber wie sie für einen schönen Mann hätte und wie gut es ihr gienge, und blieb bei ihnen so lang die Hochzeit dauerte, dann fuhr sie wieder zurück in den Wald. Wie die zweite Tochter heiratete und sie wieder zur Hochzeit eingeladen war, sprach sie zum Löwen »diesmal will ich nicht allein sein, du musst mitgehen.« Der Löwe aber sagte das wäre zu gefährlich für ihn, denn wenn dort der Strahl eines brennenden Lichts ihn berührte, so würde er in eine Taube verwandelt, und müsste sieben Jahre lang mit den Tauben fliegen. »Ach«, sagte sie, »geh nur mit mir: ich will dich schon hüten und vor allem Licht bewahren.« Also zogen sie zusammen und nahmen auch ihr kleines Kind mit. Sie ließ dort einen Saal mauern, so stark und dick, dass kein Strahl durchdringen konnte, darin sollt er sitzen, wann die Hochzeitslichter angesteckt würden. Die Tür aber war von frischem Holz gemacht, das sprang und bekam einen kleinen Ritz, den kein Mensch bemerkte. Nun

ward die Hochzeit mit Pracht gefeiert, wie aber der Zug
aus der Kirche zurückkam mit den vielen Fackeln und
Lichtern an dem Saal vorbei, da fiel ein haarbreiter Strahl
auf den Königssohn, und wie dieser Strahl ihn berührt hatte, in dem Augenblick war er auch verwandelt, und als sie
hineinkam und ihn suchte, sah sie ihn nicht, aber es saß da
eine weiße Taube. Die Taube sprach zu ihr »sieben Jahr
muss ich in die Welt fortfliegen: alle sieben Schritte aber
will ich einen roten Blutstropfen und eine weiße Feder fallen lassen, die sollen dir den Weg zeigen, und wenn du der
Spur folgst, kannst du mich erlösen.«

Da flog die Taube zur Tür hinaus, und sie folgte ihr nach,
und alle sieben Schritte fiel ein rotes Blutströpfchen und
ein weißes Federchen herab und zeigte ihr den Weg. So
gieng sie immer zu in die weite Welt hinein, und schaute
nicht um sich und ruhte sich nicht, und waren fast die sieben Jahre herum: da freute sie sich und meinte sie wären
bald erlöst, und war noch so weit davon. Einmal, als sie so
fortgieng, fiel kein Federchen mehr und auch kein rotes
Blutströpfchen, und als sie die Augen aufschlug, so war die
Taube verschwunden. Und weil sie dachte »Menschen können dir da nicht helfen«, so stieg sie zur Sonne hinauf und
sagte zu ihr »du scheinst in alle Ritzen und über alle Spitzen, hast du keine weiße Taube fliegen sehen?« »Nein«,
sagte die Sonne, »ich habe keine gesehen, aber da schenk
ich dir ein Kästchen, das mach auf, wenn du in großer Not
bist.« Da dankte sie der Sonne und gieng weiter bis es
Abend war, und der Mond schien, da fragte sie ihn »du
scheinst ja die ganze Nacht und durch alle Felder und Wälder, hast du keine weiße Taube fliegen sehen?« »Nein«, sagte der Mond, »ich habe keine gesehen, aber da schenk ich
dir ein Ei, das zerbrich wenn du in großer Not bist.« Da
dankte sie dem Mond, und gieng weiter, bis der Nachtwind
heran kam und sie anblies: da sprach sie zu ihm »du wehst
ja über alle Bäume und unter allen Blättern weg, hast
du keine weiße Taube fliegen sehen?« »Nein«, sagte der

Nachtwind, »ich habe keine gesehen, aber ich will die drei andern Winde fragen, die haben sie vielleicht gesehen.« Der Ostwind und der Westwind kamen und hatten nichts gesehen, der Südwind aber sprach »die weiße Taube habe ich gesehen, sie ist zum roten Meer geflogen, da ist sie wieder ein Löwe geworden, denn die sieben Jahre sind herum, und der Löwe steht dort im Kampf mit einem Lindwurm, der Lindwurm ist aber eine verzauberte Königstochter.« Da sagte der Nachtwind zu ihr »ich will dir Rat geben, geh zum roten Meer, am rechten Ufer da stehen große Ruten, die zähle, und die eilfte schneid dir ab, und schlag den Lindwurm damit, dann kann ihn der Löwe bezwingen, und beide bekommen auch ihren menschlichen Leib wieder. Hernach schau dich um, und du wirst den Vogel Greif sehen, der am roten Meer sitzt, schwing dich mit deinem Liebsten auf seinen Rücken: der Vogel wird euch übers Meer nach Haus tragen. Da hast du auch eine Nuss, wenn du mitten über dem Meere bist, lass sie herab fallen, alsbald wird sie aufgehen, und ein großer Nussbaum wird aus dem Wasser hervor wachsen, auf dem sich der Greif ausruht: und könnte er nicht ruhen, so wäre er nicht stark genug euch hinüber zu tragen: und wenn du vergisst die Nuss herab zu werfen, so lässt er euch ins Meer fallen.«

Da gieng sie hin und fand alles wie der Nachtwind gesagt hatte. Sie zählte die Ruten am Meer und schnitt die eilfte ab, damit schlug sie den Lindwurm, und der Löwe bezwang ihn: alsbald hatten beide ihren menschlichen Leib wieder. Aber wie die Königstochter, die vorher ein Lindwurm gewesen war, vom Zauber frei war, nahm sie den Jüngling in den Arm, setzte sich auf den Vogel Greif, und führte ihn mit sich fort. Da stand die arme weitgewanderte, und war wieder verlassen, und setzte sich nieder und weinte. Endlich aber ermutigte sie sich und sprach »ich will noch so weit gehen als der Wind weht und so lange als der Hahn kräht, bis ich ihn finde.« Und gieng fort, lange lange Wege, bis sie endlich zu dem Schloss kam, wo beide zusammen lebten: da hörte sie dass bald ein Fest wäre, wo sie Hochzeit mit einander machen wollten. Sie sprach aber »Gott hilft mir noch«, und öffnete das Kästchen, das ihr die Sonne gegeben hatte, da lag ein Kleid darin, so glänzend wie die Sonne selber. Da nahm sie es heraus und zog es an und gieng hinauf in das Schloss, und alle Leute, und die Braut selber, sahen sie mit Verwunderung an; und das Kleid gefiel der Braut so gut, dass sie dachte es könnte ihr Hochzeitskleid geben, und fragte ob es nicht feil wäre? »Nicht für Geld und Gut«, antwortete sie, »aber für Fleisch und Blut.« Die Braut fragte was sie damit meinte. Da sagte sie »lasst mich eine Nacht in der Kammer schlafen, wo der Bräutigam schläft.« Die Braut wollte nicht, und wollte doch gerne das Kleid haben, endlich willigte sie ein, aber der Kammerdiener musste dem Königssohn einen Schlaftrunk geben. Als es nun Nacht war und der Jüngling schon schlief, ward sie in die Kammer geführt. Da setzte sie sich ans Bett und sagte »ich bin dir nachgefolgt sieben Jahre, bin bei Sonne und Mond und bei den vier Winden gewesen, und habe nach dir gefragt, und habe dir geholfen gegen den Lindwurm, willst du mich denn ganz vergessen?« Der Königssohn aber schlief so hart, dass es ihm nur vorkam als rauschte der Wind draußen in den Tannenbäumen. Wie nun der Morgen anbrach, da ward sie wieder hinausgeführt und musste das goldene Kleid hingeben. Und als auch das nichts geholfen hatte, ward sie traurig, gieng hinaus auf eine Wiese, setzte sich da hin und weinte. Und wie sie so saß, da fiel ihr das Ei noch ein, das ihr der Mond gegeben hatte: sie schlug es auf, da kam eine Glucke heraus mit zwölf Küchlein ganz von Gold, die liefen herum und piepten und krochen der Alten wieder unter die Flügel, so dass nichts schöneres auf der Welt zu sehen war. Da stand sie auf, trieb sie auf der Wiese vor sich her, so lange bis die Braut aus dem Fenster sah, und da gefielen ihr die kleinen Küchlein so gut, dass sie gleich herab kam und fragte ob sie nicht feil wären? »Nicht für Geld und Gut, aber für Fleisch und Blut; lasst mich noch eine Nacht in der Kammer schlafen, wo der Bräutigam schläft.« Die Braut sagte »ja«, und wollte sie betrügen wie am vorigen Abend. Als aber der Königssohn zu Bett gieng, fragte er seinen Kammerdiener was das Murmeln und Rauschen in der Nacht gewesen sei. Da erzählte der Kammerdiener alles, dass er ihm einen Schlaftrunk hätte geben müssen, weil ein armes Mädchen heimlich in der Kammer geschlafen hätte, und heute Nacht sollte er ihm wieder einen geben. Sagte der Königssohn »gieß den Trank neben das Bett aus.« Zur Nacht wurde sie wieder hereingeführt, und als sie anfieng zu erzählen wie es ihr traurig ergangen wäre, da erkannte er gleich an der Stimme seine liebe Gemahlin, sprang auf und rief »jetzt bin ich erst recht erlöst, mir ist gewesen wie in einem Traum, denn die fremde Königstochter hatte mich bezaubert, dass ich dich vergessen musste, aber Gott hat noch zu rechter Stunde die Betörung von mir genommen.« Da giengen sie beide in der Nacht heimlich aus dem Schloss, denn sie fürchteten sich vor dem Vater der Königstochter, der ein Zauberer war, und setzten sich auf den Vogel Greif, der trug sie über das rote Meer, und als sie in der Mitte waren, ließ sie die Nuss fallen. Alsbald wuchs ein großer Nussbaum, darauf ruhte sich der Vogel, und dann führte er sie nach Haus, wo sie ihr Kind fanden, das war groß und schön geworden, und sie lebten von nun an vergnügt bis an ihr Ende.

89.

Die Gänsemagd.

Es lebte einmal eine alte Königin, der war ihr Gemahl schon lange Jahre gestorben, und sie hatte eine schöne Tochter. Wie die erwuchs, wurde sie weit über Feld an einen Königssohn versprochen. Als nun die Zeit kam, wo sie vermählt werden sollten und das Kind in das fremde Reich abreisen musste, packte ihr die Alte gar viel köstliches Gerät und Geschmeide ein, Gold und Silber, Becher und Kleinode, kurz alles, was nur zu einem königlichen Brautschatz gehörte, denn sie hatte ihr Kind von Herzen lieb. Auch gab sie ihr eine Kammerjungfer bei, welche mitreiten und die Braut in die Hände des Bräutigams überliefern sollte, und jede bekam ein Pferd zur Reise, aber das Pferd der Königstochter hieß *Falada* und konnte sprechen. Wie nun die Abschiedsstunde da war, begab sich die alte Mutter in ihre Schlafkammer, nahm ein Messerlein und schnitt damit in ihre Finger, dass sie bluteten: darauf hielt sie ein weißes Läppchen unter und ließ drei Tropfen Blut hineinfallen, gab sie der Tochter und sprach »liebes Kind, verwahre sie wohl, sie werden dir unterweges Not tun.«

Also nahmen beide von einander betrübten Abschied: das Läppchen steckte die Königstochter in ihren Busen vor sich, setzte sich aufs Pferd und zog nun fort zu ihrem Bräutigam. Da sie eine Stunde geritten waren, empfand sie heißen Durst und sprach zu ihrer Kammerjungfer »steig ab, und schöpfe mir mit meinem Becher, den du für mich mitgenommen hast, Wasser aus dem Bache, ich möchte gern einmal trinken.« »Wenn ihr Durst habt«, sprach die Kammerjungfer, »so steigt selber ab, legt euch ans Wasser und trinkt, ich mag eure Magd nicht sein.« Da stieg die Königstochter vor großem Durst herunter, neigte sich über das Wasser im Bach und trank, und durfte nicht aus dem goldenen Becher trinken. Da sprach sie »ach Gott!« da antworteten die drei Blutstropfen »wenn das deine Mutter wüsste, das Herz im Leibe tät ihr zerspringen.« Aber die Königsbraut war demütig, sagte nichts und stieg wieder zu Pferd. So ritten sie etliche Meilen weiter fort, aber der Tag war warm, die Sonne stach, und sie durstete bald von neuem. Da sie nun an einen Wasserfluss kamen, rief sie noch einmal ihrer Kammerjungfer »steig ab und gib mir aus meinem Goldbecher zu trinken«, denn sie hatte aller bösen Worte längst vergessen. Die Kammerjungfer sprach aber noch hochmütiger, »wollt ihr trinken, so trinkt allein, ich mag nicht eure Magd sein.« Da stieg die Königstochter hernieder vor großem Durst, legte sich über das fließende Wasser, weinte und sprach »ach Gott!« und die Blutstropfen antworteten wiederum »wenn das deine Mutter wüsste, das Herz im Leibe tät ihr zerspringen.« Und wie sie so trank und sich recht überlehnte, fiel ihr das Läppchen, worin die drei Tropfen waren, aus dem Busen und floss mit dem Wasser fort ohne dass sie es in ihrer großen Angst merkte. Die Kammerjungfer hatte aber zugesehen und freute sich dass sie Gewalt über die Braut bekäme: denn damit, dass diese die Blutstropfen verloren hatte, war sie schwach und machtlos geworden. Als sie nun wieder auf ihr Pferd steigen wollte, das da hieß Falada, sagte die Kammerfrau »auf Falada gehör ich, und auf meinen Gaul gehörst du«; und das musste sie sich gefallen lassen. Dann befahl ihr die Kammerfrau mit harten Worten die königlichen Kleider auszuziehen und ihre schlechten anzulegen, und endlich musste sie sich unter freiem Himmel verschwören dass sie am königlichen Hof keinem Menschen etwas davon sprechen wollte; und wenn sie diesen Eid nicht abgelegt hätte, wäre sie auf der Stelle umgebracht worden. Aber Falada sah das alles an und nahm's wohl in Acht.

Die Kammerfrau stieg nun auf Falada und die wahre Braut auf das schlechte Ross, und so zogen sie weiter, bis sie endlich in dem königlichen Schloss eintrafen. Da war große Freude über ihre Ankunft, und der Königssohn sprang ihnen entgegen, hob die Kammerfrau vom Pferde und meinte sie wäre seine Gemahlin: sie ward die Treppe hinaufgeführt, die wahre Königstochter aber musste unten stehen bleiben. Da schaute der alte König am Fenster, und sah sie im Hof halten und sah wie sie fein war, zart und gar schön: gieng alsbald hin ins königliche Gemach und fragte die Braut nach der, die sie bei sich hätte und da unten im Hofe stände, und wer sie wäre? »Die hab ich mir unterwegs mitge-

nommen zur Gesellschaft; gebt der Magd was zu arbeiten,
dass sie nicht müßig steht.« Aber der alte König hatte keine
Arbeit für sie und wusste nichts, als dass er sagte »da hab
ich so einen kleinen Jungen, der hütet die Gänse, dem mag
sie helfen.« Der Junge hieß *Kürdchen* (Conrädchen), dem
musste die wahre Braut helfen Gänse hüten.

Bald aber sprach die falsche Braut zu dem jungen König
»liebster Gemahl, ich bitte euch tut mir einen Gefallen.« Er
antwortete »das will ich gerne tun.« »Nun so lasst den
Schinder rufen und da dem Pferde, worauf ich hergeritten
bin, den Hals abhauen weil es mich unterweges geärgert
hat.« Eigentlich aber fürchtete sie dass das Pferd sprechen
möchte wie sie mit der Königstochter umgegangen war.
Nun war das so weit geraten, dass es geschehen und der
treue Falada sterben sollte, da kam es auch der rechten Königstochter zu Ohr, und sie versprach dem Schinder heimlich ein Stück Geld, das sie ihm bezahlen wollte, wenn er
ihr einen kleinen Dienst erwiese. In der Stadt war ein großes finsteres Tor, wo sie Abends und Morgens mit den
Gänsen durch musste, unter das finstere Tor möchte er dem
Falada seinen Kopf hinnageln, dass sie ihn doch noch mehr
als einmal sehen könnte. Also versprach das der Schinders-
knecht zu tun, hieb den Kopf ab und nagelte ihn unter das
finstere Tor fest.

Des Morgens früh, da sie und Kürdchen unterm Tor hinaus
trieben, sprach sie im Vorbeigehen

>»o du Falada, da du hangest,«

da antwortete der Kopf

>»o du Jungfer Königin, da du gangest,
> wenn das deine Mutter wüsste,
> ihr Herz tät ihr zerspringen.«

Da zog sie still weiter zur Stadt hinaus, und sie trieben die
Gänse aufs Feld. Und wenn sie auf der Wiese angekommen
war, saß sie nieder und machte ihre Haare auf, die waren ei-
tel Gold, und Kürdchen sah sie und freute sich wie sie
glänzten, und wollte ihr ein paar ausraufen. Da sprach sie

»weh, weh, Windchen,
nimm Kürdchen sein Hütchen,
und lass 'n sich mit jagen,
bis ich mich geflochten und geschnatzt,
und wieder aufgesatzt.«

Und da kam ein so starker Wind, dass er dem Kürdchen sein Hütchen weg wehte über alle Land, und es musste ihm nachlaufen. Bis es wieder kam war sie mit dem Kämmen und Aufsetzen fertig, und er konnte keine Haare kriegen. Da war Kürdchen bös und sprach nicht mit ihr; und so hüteten sie die Gänse bis dass es Abend ward, dann giengen sie nach Haus.

Den andern Morgen, wie sie unter dem finstern Tor hinaus trieben, sprach die Jungfrau

»o du Falada, da du hangest,«

Falada antwortete

»o du Jungfer Königin, da du gangest,
wenn das deine Mutter wüsste,
das Herz tät ihr zerspringen.«

Und in dem Feld setzte sie sich wieder auf die Wiese und fieng an ihr Haar auszukämmen, und Kürdchen lief und wollte danach greifen, da sprach sie schnell

»weh, weh, Windchen,
nimm Kürdchen sein Hütchen,
und lass 'n sich mit jagen,
bis ich mich geflochten und geschnatzt,
und wieder aufgesatzt.«

Da wehte der Wind und wehte ihm das Hütchen vom Kopf weit weg, dass Kürdchen nachlaufen musste; und als es wieder kam, hatte sie längst ihr Haar zurecht, und es konnte keins davon erwischen; und so hüteten sie die Gänse bis es Abend ward.

Abends aber, nachdem sie heim gekommen waren, gieng Kürdchen vor den alten König und sagte »mit dem Mädchen will ich nicht länger Gänse hüten.« »Warum denn?« fragte der alte König. »Ei, das ärgert mich den ganzen Tag.«

Da befahl ihm der alte König zu erzählen wie's ihm denn
mit ihr gienge. Da sagte Kürdchen »Morgens, wenn wir
unter dem finstern Tor mit der Herde durchkommen, so ist
da ein Gaulskopf an der Wand, zu dem redet sie

>   »Falada, da du hangest,«
da antwortet der Kopf

>   »o du Königsjungfer, da du gangest,
>   wenn das deine Mutter wüsste,
>   das Herz tät ihr zerspringen.«

Und so erzählte Kürdchen weiter was auf der Gänsewiese
geschähe, und wie es da dem Hut im Winde nachlaufen
müsste.

Der alte König befahl ihm den nächsten Tag wieder hinaus
zu treiben, und er selbst, wie es Morgen war, setzte sich
hinter das finstere Tor und hörte da wie sie mit dem Haupt
des Falada sprach: und dann gieng er ihr auch nach in das
Feld und barg sich in einem Busch auf der Wiese. Da sah er
nun bald mit seinen eigenen Augen wie die Gänsemagd
und der Gänsejunge die Herde getrieben brachte, und wie
nach einer Weile sie sich setzte und ihre Haare losflocht,
die strahlten von Glanz. Gleich sprach sie wieder

>   »weh, weh, Windchen,
>   fass Kürdchen sein Hütchen,
>   und lass 'n sich mit jagen,
>   bis dass ich mich geflochten und geschnatzt,
>   und wieder aufgesatzt.«

Da kam ein Windstoß und fuhr mit Kürdchens Hut weg,
dass es weit zu laufen hatte, und die Magd kämmte und
flocht ihre Locken still fort, welches der alte König alles
beobachtete. Darauf gieng er unbemerkt zurück, und als
Abends die Gänsemagd heim kam, rief er sie bei Seite, und
fragte warum sie dem allem so täte? »Das darf ich euch
nicht sagen, und darf auch keinem Menschen mein Leid
klagen, denn so hab ich mich unter freiem Himmel ver-
schworen, weil ich sonst um mein Leben gekommen wäre.«
Er drang in sie und ließ ihr keinen Frieden, aber er konnte

nichts aus ihr herausbringen. Da sprach er »wenn du mir
nichts sagen willst, so klag dem Eisenofen da dein Leid«,
und gieng fort. Da kroch sie in den Eisenofen, fieng an zu
jammern und zu weinen, schüttete ihr Herz aus und sprach
»da sitze ich nun von aller Welt verlassen, und bin doch
eine Königstochter, und eine falsche Kammerjungfer hat
mich mit Gewalt dahin gebracht dass ich meine königlichen
Kleider habe ablegen müssen, und hat meinen Platz bei
meinem Bräutigam eingenommen, und ich muss als Gänsemagd gemeine Dienste tun. Wenn das meine Mutter wüsste,
das Herz im Leib tät ihr zerspringen.« Der alte König
stand aber außen an der Ofenröhre, lauerte ihr zu und hörte was sie sprach. Da kam er wieder herein und hieß sie aus
dem Ofen gehen. Da wurden ihr königliche Kleider angetan, und es schien ein Wunder wie sie so schön war. Der
alte König rief seinen Sohn und offenbarte ihm dass er die
falsche Braut hätte: die wäre bloß ein Kammermädchen, die
wahre aber stände hier, als die gewesene Gänsemagd. Der
junge König war herzensfroh, als er ihre Schönheit und Tugend erblickte, und ein großes Mahl wurde angestellt, zu
dem alle Leute und guten Freunde gebeten wurden. Oben-
an saß der Bräutigam, die Königstochter zur einen Seite
und die Kammerjungfer zur andern, aber die Kammerjungfer war verblendet und erkannte jene nicht mehr in dem
glänzenden Schmuck. Als sie nun gegessen und getrunken
hatten, und gutes Muts waren, gab der alte König der Kammerfrau ein Rätsel auf, was eine solche wert wäre, die den
Herrn so und so betrogen hätte, erzählte damit den ganzen
Verlauf und fragte »welches Urteils ist diese würdig?« Da
sprach die falsche Braut »die ist nichts besseres wert, als
dass sie splitternackt ausgezogen und in ein Fass gesteckt
wird, das inwendig mit spitzen Nägeln beschlagen ist: und
zwei weiße Pferde müssen vorgespannt werden, die sie
Gasse auf Gasse ab zu Tode schleifen.« »Das bist du«,
sprach der alte König, »und hast dein eigen Urteil gefunden, und danach soll dir widerfahren.« Und als das Urteil

vollzogen war, vermählte sich der junge König mit seiner
rechten Gemahlin, und beide beherrschten ihr Reich in
Frieden und Seligkeit.

90.

Der junge Riese.

Ein Bauersmann hatte einen Sohn, der war so groß wie ein
Daumen und ward gar nicht größer und wuchs in etlichen
Jahren nicht ein Haarbreit. Einmal wollte der Bauer ins Feld
gehen und pflügen, da sagte der Kleine »Vater, ich will mit
hinaus.« »Du willst mit hinaus?« sprach der Vater, »bleib du
hier, dort bist du zu nichts nutz: du könntest mir auch verloren gehen.« Da fieng der Däumling an zu weinen, und um
Ruhe zu haben, steckte ihn der Vater in die Tasche und
nahm ihn mit. Draußen auf dem Felde holte er ihn wieder
heraus und setzte ihn in eine frische Furche. Wie er da so
saß, kam über den Berg ein großer Riese daher. »Siehst du
dort den großen Butzemann?« sagte der Vater, und wollte
den Kleinen schrecken, damit er artig wäre, »der kommt und
holt dich.« Der Riese aber hatte mit seinen langen Beinen
kaum ein paar Schritte getan, so war er bei der Furche. Er
hob den kleinen Däumling mit zwei Fingern behutsam in
die Höhe, betrachtete ihn und gieng ohne ein Wort zu sprechen, mit ihm fort. Der Vater stand dabei, konnte vor Schrecken keinen Laut hervor bringen und dachte nicht anders als
sein Kind für verloren, also dass er's sein Lebtag nicht wieder mit Augen sehen würde.

Der Riese aber trug es heim und ließ es an seiner Brust saugen, und der Däumling wuchs und ward groß und stark
nach Art der Riesen. Nach Verlauf von zwei Jahren gieng
der Alte mit ihm in den Wald, wollte ihn versuchen und
sprach »zieh dir eine Gerte heraus.« Da war der Knabe
schon so stark, dass er einen jungen Baum mit den Wurzeln

aus der Erde riss. Der Riese aber meinte »das muss besser kommen«, nahm ihn wieder mit, und säugte ihn noch zwei Jahre. Als er ihn versuchte, hatte seine Kraft schon so zugenommen, dass er einen alten Baum aus der Erde brechen konnte. Das war dem Riesen noch immer nicht genug, er säugte ihn abermals zwei Jahre, und als er dann mit ihm in den Wald gieng, und sprach »nun reiß einmal eine ordentliche Gerte aus«, so riss der Junge den dicksten Eichenbaum aus der Erde, dass er krachte, und war ihm nur ein Spaß. »Nun ist's genug«, sprach der Riese, »du hast ausgelernt«, und führte ihn zurück auf den Acker, wo er ihn geholt hatte. Sein Vater stand da hinter dem Pflug, der junge Riese gieng auf ihn zu und sprach »sieht er wohl, Vater, was sein Sohn für ein Mann geworden ist.« Der Bauer erschrak, und sagte »nein, du bist mein Sohn nicht, ich will dich nicht, geh weg von mir.« »Freilich bin ich sein Sohn, lass er mich an die Arbeit, ich kann pflügen so gut als er und noch besser.« »Nein, nein, du bist mein Sohn nicht, du kannst auch nicht pflügen, geh weg von mir.« Weil er sich aber vor dem großen Mann fürchtete, ließ er den Pflug los, trat zurück und setzte sich zur Seite ans Land. Da nahm der Junge das Geschirr und drückte bloß mit einer Hand darauf, aber der Druck war so gewaltig, dass der Pflug tief in die Erde gieng. Der Bauer konnte das nicht mit ansehen und rief ihm zu »wenn du pflügen willst, musst du nicht so gewaltig drücken, das gibt schlechte Arbeit.« Der Junge aber spannte die Pferde aus, zog selber den Pflug und sagte »geh er nur nach Haus, Vater, und lass er die Mutter eine große Schüssel voll Essen kochen; ich will derweil den Acker schon umreißen.« Da gieng der Bauer heim und bestellte das Essen bei seiner Frau: der Junge aber pflügte das Feld, zwei Morgen groß, ganz allein, und dann spannte er sich auch selber vor die Egge und eggte alles mit zwei Eggen zugleich. Wie er fertig war, gieng er in den Wald und riss zwei Eichenbäume aus, legte sie auf die Schultern, und hinten und vorn eine Egge darauf, und hinten und vorn auch ein Pferd, und trug das alles, als wär es ein Bund Stroh, nach seiner Eltern Haus. Wie er in den Hof kam, erkannte ihn seine Mutter nicht und fragte »wer ist der entsetzliche, große Mann?« Der Bauer sagte »das ist unser Sohn.« Sie sprach »nein, unser Sohn ist das nimmermehr, so groß haben wir keinen gehabt, unser war ein kleines Ding.« Sie rief ihm zu »geh fort, wir wollen dich nicht.« Der Junge schwieg still, zog seine Pferde in den Stall, gab ihnen Hafer und Heu, alles wie sich's gehörte. Als er fertig war, gieng er in die Stube, setzte sich auf die Bank und sagte »Mutter, nun hätte ich Lust zu essen, ist's bald fertig?« Da sagte sie »ja« und brachte zwei große große Schüsseln voll herein, daran hätten sie und ihr Mann acht Tage lang satt gehabt. Der Junge aber aß sie allein auf und fragte ob sie nicht mehr vorsetzen könnte? »Nein«, sagte sie, »das ist alles, was wir haben.« »Das war ja nur zum Schmecken, ich muss mehr haben.« Sie getraute nicht ihm zu widerstehen, gieng hin und setzte einen großen Schweinekessel voll übers Feuer, und wie es gar war, trug sie es herein. »Endlich kommen noch ein paar Brocken« sagte er und aß alles hinein; es war aber doch nicht genug seinen Hunger zu stillen. Da sprach er »Vater, ich sehe wohl, bei ihm werd ich nicht satt, will er mir einen Stab von Eisen verschaffen, der stark ist, und den ich vor meinen Knien nicht zerbrechen kann, so will ich fort in die Welt gehen.« Der Bauer war froh, spannte seine zwei Pferde vor den Wagen und holte bei dem Schmied einen Stab so groß und dick, als ihn die zwei Pferde nur fort schaffen konnten. Der Junge nahm ihn vor die Knie und ratsch! brach er ihn wie eine Bohnenstange in der Mitte entzwei und warf ihn weg. Der Vater spannte vier Pferde vor und holte einen Stab so groß und dick, als ihn die vier Pferde fort schaffen konnten. Der Sohn knickte auch diesen vor dem Knie entzwei, warf ihn hin und sprach »Vater, der kann mir nicht helfen, er muss besser vorspannen und einen stärkern Stab holen.« Da spannte der Vater acht Pferde vor und holte einen so groß und dick, als ihn die acht Pfer-

de herbei fahren konnten. Wie der Sohn den in die Hand
nahm, brach er gleich oben ein Stück davon ab und sagte
»Vater, ich sehe er kann mir keinen Stab anschaffen wie ich
ihn brauche, ich will nicht länger bei ihm bleiben.«

Da gieng er fort und gab sich für einen Schmiedegesellen
aus. Er kam in ein Dorf, darin wohnte ein Schmied, der
war ein Geizmann, gönnte keinem Menschen etwas und
wollte alles allein haben; zu dem trat er in die Schmiede
und fragte ob er keinen Gesellen brauchte. »Ja« sagte der
Schmied, sah ihn an und dachte »das ist ein tüchtiger Kerl,
der wird gut vorschlagen und sein Brot verdienen.« Er
fragte »wie viel willst du Lohn haben?« »Gar keinen will
ich haben«, antwortete er, »nur alle vierzehn Tage, wenn
die andern Gesellen ihren Lohn bezahlt kriegen, will ich dir
zwei Streiche geben, die musst du aushalten.« Das war der
Geizmann von Herzen zufrieden und dachte damit viel
Geld zu sparen. Am andern Morgen sollte der fremde Geselle zuerst vorschlagen, wie aber der Meister den glühenden Stab brachte und jener den ersten Schlag tat, so flog das
Eisen von einander und der Amboss sank in die Erde, so
tief, dass sie ihn gar nicht wieder heraus bringen konnten.
Da ward der Geizmann bös und sagte »ei was, dich kann
ich nicht brauchen, du schlägst gar zu grob, was willst du
für den einen Zuschlag haben?« Da sprach er »ich will dir
nur einen ganz kleinen Streich geben, weiter nichts.« Und
hob seinen Fuß auf und gab ihm einen Tritt, dass er über
vier Fuder Heu hinausflog. Darauf suchte er sich den
dicksten Eisenstab aus, der in der Schmiede war, nahm ihn
als einen Stock in die Hand und gieng weiter.

Als er eine Weile gezogen war, kam er zu einem Vorwerk
und fragte den Amtmann ob er keinen Großknecht nötig
hätte. »Ja«, sagte der Amtmann, »ich kann einen brauchen:
du siehst aus wie ein tüchtiger Kerl, der schon was vermag,
wie viel willst du Jahrslohn haben?« Er antwortete wiederum er verlangte gar keinen Lohn, aber alle Jahre wollte er
ihm drei Streiche geben, die müsste er aushalten. Das war

der Amtmann zufrieden, denn er war auch ein Geizhals.
Am andern Morgen, da sollten die Knechte ins Holz fahren, und die andern Knechte waren schon auf, er aber lag
noch im Bett. Da rief ihn einer an »steh auf, es ist Zeit, wir
wollen ins Holz, und du musst mit.« »Ach«, sagte er ganz
grob und trotzig, »geht ihr nur hin, ich komme doch eher
wieder als ihr alle mit einander.« Da giengen die andern
zum Amtmann und erzählten ihm der Großknecht läge
noch im Bett und wollte nicht mit ins Holz fahren. Der
Amtmann sagte sie sollten ihn noch einmal wecken und
heißen die Pferde vorspannen. Der Großknecht sprach aber
wie vorher »geht ihr nur hin, ich komme doch eher wieder
als ihr alle mit einander.« Darauf blieb er noch zwei Stunden liegen, da stieg er endlich aus den Federn, holte sich
aber erst zwei Scheffel voll Erbsen vom Boden, kochte sich
einen Brei und aß den mit guter Ruhe, und wie das alles geschehen war, gieng er hin, spannte die Pferde vor und fuhr
ins Holz. Nicht weit vor dem Holz war ein Hohlweg, wo
er durch musste, da fuhr er den Wagen erst vorwärts, dann
mussten die Pferde stille halten, und er gieng hinter den
Wagen, nahm Bäume und Reisig und machte da eine große
Hucke (Verhack), so dass kein Pferd durchkommen konnte. Wie er nun vors Holz kam, fuhren die andern eben mit
ihren beladenen Wagen heraus und wollten heim, da sprach
er zu ihnen »fahrt nur hin, ich komme doch eher als ihr
nach Haus.« Er fuhr gar nicht weit ins Holz, riss gleich
zwei der allergrößten Bäume aus der Erde, warf sie auf den
Wagen und drehte um. Als er vor der Hucke anlangte, standen die andern noch da und konnten nicht durch. »Seht ihr
wohl«, sprach er, »wärt ihr bei mir geblieben, so wärt ihr
eben so schnell nach Haus gekommen und hättet noch eine
Stunde schlafen können.« Er wollte nun zufahren, aber seine Pferde konnten sich nicht durcharbeiten, da spannte er
sie aus, legte sie oben auf den Wagen, nahm selber die
Deichsel in die Hand, und hüf! zog er alles durch, und das
gieng so leicht als hätt er Federn geladen. Wie er drüben

war, sprach er zu den andern »seht ihr wohl, ich bin schneller hindurch als ihr«, fuhr weiter, und die andern mussten stehen bleiben. In dem Hof aber nahm er einen Baum in die Hand, zeigte ihn dem Amtmann und sagte »ist das nicht ein schönes Klafterstück?« Da sprach der Amtmann zu seiner Frau »der Knecht ist gut; wenn er auch lang schläft, er ist doch eher wieder da als die andern.«

Nun diente er dem Amtmann ein Jahr: wie das herum war, und die andern Knechte ihren Lohn kriegten, sprach er es wäre Zeit, er wollte sich auch seinen Lohn nehmen. Dem Amtmann ward aber angst vor den Streichen, die er kriegen sollte, und bat ihn inständig er möchte sie ihm schenken, lieber wollte er selbst Großknecht werden, und er sollte Amtmann sein. »Nein«, sprach er, »ich will kein Amtmann werden, ich bin Großknecht und will's bleiben, ich will aber austeilen was bedungen ist.« Der Amtmann wollte ihm geben, was er nur verlangte, aber es half nichts, der Großknecht sprach zu allem »nein«. Da wusste sich der Amtmann nicht zu helfen und bat ihn um vierzehn Tage Frist, er wollte sich auf etwas besinnen. Der Großknecht sprach die Frist sollte er haben. Der Amtmann berief alle seine Schreiber zusammen, sie sollten sich bedenken und ihm einen Rat geben. Die Schreiber besannen sich lange, endlich sagten sie vor dem Großknecht wäre niemand seines Lebens sicher, der schlüge einen Menschen wie eine Mücke tot. Er sollte ihn heißen in den Brunnen steigen und ihn reinigen, wenn er unten wäre, wollten sie einen von den Mühlensteinen, die da lägen, herbei rollen und ihm auf den Kopf werfen, dann würde er nicht wieder an des Tages Licht kommen. Der Rat gefiel dem Amtmann, und der Großknecht war bereit in den Brunnen hinab zu steigen. Als er unten auf dem Grund stand, rollten sie den größten Mühlstein hinab, und meinten der Kopf wäre ihm eingeschlagen, aber er rief »jagt die Hühner vom Brunnen weg, die kratzen da oben im Sand und werfen mir die Körner in die Augen, dass ich nicht sehen kann.« Da rief der Amt-

mann »husch! husch!« und tat als scheuchte er die Hühner
weg. Als der Großknecht mit seiner Arbeit fertig war, stieg
er herauf und sagte »seht einmal, ich habe doch ein schönes
Halsband um«, da war es der Mühlenstein, den er um den
Hals trug. Der Großknecht wollte jetzt seinen Lohn nehmen, aber der Amtmann bat wieder um vierzehn Tage Bedenkzeit. Die Schreiber kamen zusammen und gaben den
Rat er sollte den Großknecht in die verwünschte Mühle
schicken um dort in der Nacht Korn zu mahlen: von da
wäre noch kein Mensch Morgens lebendig herausgekom-
men. Der Anschlag gefiel dem Amtmann, er rief den Großknecht noch denselben Abend und hieß ihn acht Malter
Korn in die Mühle fahren und in der Nacht noch mahlen;
sie hätten's nötig. Da gieng der Großknecht auf den Boden
und tat zwei Malter in seine rechte Tasche, zwei in die linke, vier nahm er in einem Quersack halb auf den Rücken,
halb auf die Brust, und gieng also beladen nach der verwünschten Mühle. Der Müller sagte ihm bei Tag könnte er
recht gut da mahlen, aber nicht in der Nacht, da wäre die
Mühle verwünscht, und wer da noch hinein gegangen wäre,
den hätte man am Morgen tot darin gefunden. Er sprach
»ich will schon durchkommen, macht euch nur fort und
legt euch aufs Ohr.« Darauf gieng er in die Mühle und
schüttete das Korn auf. Gegen elf Uhr gieng er in die Mül-
lerstube und setzte sich auf die Bank. Als er ein Weilchen
da gesessen hatte, tat sich auf einmal die Tür auf und kam
eine große große Tafel herein, und auf die Tafel stellte sich
Wein und Braten, und viel gutes Essen, alles von selber,
denn es war niemand da, der's auftrug. Und danach rückten
sich die Stühle herbei, aber es kamen keine Leute, bis auf
einmal sah er Finger, die hantierten mit den Messern und
Gabeln und legten Speisen auf die Teller, aber sonst konnte
er nichts sehen. Da er hungrig war und die Speisen sah, so
setzte er sich auch an die Tafel, aß mit und ließ sich's gut
schmecken. Als er satt war und die andern ihre Schüsseln
auch ganz leer gemacht hatten, da wurden die Lichter auf

einmal alle ausgeputzt, das hörte er deutlich, und wie's nun stockfinster war, so kriegte er so etwas wie eine Ohrfeige ins Gesicht. Da sprach er »wenn noch einmal so etwas kommt, so teil ich auch wieder aus.« Und wie er zum zweiten Mal eine Ohrfeige kriegte, da schlug er gleichfalls mit hinein. Und so gieng das fort die ganze Nacht, er nahm nichts umsonst, sondern gab reichlich zurück und schlug nicht faul um sich herum: bei Tagesanbruch aber hörte alles auf. Wie der Müller aufgestanden war, wollt er nach ihm sehen und verwunderte sich, dass er noch lebte. Da sprach er »ich habe mich satt gegessen, habe Ohrfeigen gekriegt, aber ich habe auch Ohrfeigen ausgeteilt.« Der Müller freute sich und sagte nun wäre die Mühle erlöst, und wollte ihm gern zur Belohnung viel Geld geben. Er sprach aber »Geld will ich nicht, ich habe doch genug.« Dann nahm er sein Mehl auf den Rücken, gieng nach Haus und sagte dem Amtmann er hätte die Sache ausgerichtet und wollte nun seinen bedungenen Lohn haben. Wie der Amtmann das hörte, da ward ihm erst recht angst: er wusste sich nicht zu lassen, gieng in der Stube auf und ab, und die Schweißtropfen liefen ihm von der Stirne herunter. Da machte er das Fenster auf nach frischer Luft, eh er sich's aber versah, hatte ihm der Großknecht einen Tritt gegeben, dass er durchs Fenster in die Luft hinein flog, immer fort, bis ihn niemand mehr sehen konnte. Da sprach der Großknecht zur Frau des Amtmanns »kommt er nicht wieder, so müsst ihr den anderen Streich hinnehmen.« Sie rief »nein, nein, ich kann's nicht aushalten«, und machte das andere Fenster auf, weil ihr die Schweißtropfen die Stirne herunter liefen. Da gab er ihr einen Tritt, dass sie gleichfalls hinaus flog und da sie leichter war, noch viel höher als ihr Mann. Der Mann rief »komm doch zu mir«, sie aber rief »komm du zu mir, ich kann nicht zu dir.« Und sie schwebten da in der Luft, und konnte keins zum andern kommen, und ob sie da noch schweben, das weiß ich nicht; der junge Riese aber nahm seine Eisenstange und gieng weiter.

91.

Dat Erdmänneken.

Et was mal en rik Künig west, de hadde drei Döchter had, de wören alle Dage in den Schlottgoren spazeren gaen, un de Künig, dat was so en Leivhawer von allerhand wackeren Bömen west: un einen, den hadde he so leiv had, dat he denjenigen, de ümme en Appel dervon plückede, hunnerd Klafter unner de Eere verwünschede. Als et nu Hervest was, da worden de Appel an den einen Baume so raut as Blaud. De drei Döchter gungen alle Dage unner den Baum un seihen to ov nig de Wind 'n Appel herunner schlagen hädde, awerst se fannen ir Levedage kienen, un de Baum de satt so vull, dat he breken wull, un de Telgen (Zweige) hungen bis up de Eere. Da gelustede den jungesten Künigskinne gewaldig un et segde to sinen Süstern »use Teite (Vater), de hett us viel to leiv, ase dat he us verwünschen deihe: ik glöve dat he dat nur wegen de frümden Lude dahen hat.« Un indes plücked dat Kind en gans dicken Appel af un sprunk fur sinen Süstern un segde »a, nu schmecket mal, mine lewen Süsterkes, nu hew ik doch min Levedage so wat schones no nig schmecket.« Da beeten de beiden annern Künigsdöchter auch mal in den Appel, un da versünken se alle drei deip unner de Eere, dat kien Haan mer danach krähete.

As et da Middag is, da wull se de Künig do Diske roopen, do sind se nirgends to finnen: he söket se so viel im Schlott un in Goren, awerst he kun se nig finnen. Da werd he so bedröwet un let dat ganse Land upbeien (aufbieten), un wer ünne sine Döchter wier brechte, de sull ene davon tor Fruen hewen. Da gahet so viele junge Lude uwer Feld un söket, dat is gans ut der Wiese (über alle Maßen), denn jeder hadde de drei Kinner geren had, wiil se wören gegen jedermann so fründlig un so schön von Angesichte west. Un et togen auck drei Jägerburschen ut, un ase da wol en acht

Dage rieset hadden, da kummet se up en grot Schlot[t], da woren so hübsche Stoben inne west, un in einen Zimmer is en Disch decket, darup wören so söte Spi[e]sen, de sied noch so warme dat se dampet, awerst in den ganzen Schlott is kien Minsk to hören noch to seihen. Do wartet se noch en halwen Dag, un de Spiesen bliewet immer warme un dampet, bis up et lest, da weret se so hungerig, dat se sik derbie settet un ettet, un macket mit en anner ut, se wüllen up den Schlotte wuhnen bliewen, un wüllen darümme loosen, dat eine in Huse blev un de beiden annern de Dochter söketen; dat doet se auck, un dat Loos dreppet den ölesten. Den annern Dag da gaet de twei jüngesten söken, un de öleste mot to Huse bliewen. Am Middage kümmt der so en klein klein Männeken un hölt um 'n Stükesken Braud ane, da nümmt he von dem Braude, wat he da funnen hädde, un schnitt en Stücke rund umme den Braud weg un will ünne dat giewen, indes dat he et ünne reiket, lett et dat kleine Männeken fallen un segd he sulle dok so gut sin un giewen ün dat Stücke wier. Da will he dat auck doen un bucket sik, mit des nümmt dat Männeken en Stock un päckt ünne bie den Haaren un giwt ünne düete Schläge. Den anneren Dag, da is de tweide to Hus bliewen, da geit et nicks better. Ase de beiden annern da den Avend nah Hus kümmet, da segd de öleste »no, wie hätt et die dann gaen?« »O, et geit mie gans schlechte.« Da klaget se sik enanner ere Naud, awerst den jungesten hadden se nicks davonne sagd, den hadden se gar nig lien (leiden) mogt un hadden ünne jummer den dummen Hans heiten, weil he nig recht van de Weld was. Den dritten Dag, da blivt de jungeste to Hus, da kümmet dat kleine Männeken wier un hölt um en Stücksken Braud an; da he ünne dat giewen hätt, let he et wier fallen un segd he mügte dock so gut sin un reiken ünne dat Stücksken wier. Da segd he to den kleinen Männeken »wat! kannst du dat Stücke nig sulwens wier up nummen, wenn du die de Möhe nig mal um dine dägliche Narunge giewen wust, so bist du auck nich werth, dat du et etest.« Da word dat

Männeken so bös un sehde he möst et doen: he awerst nig
fuhl, nam min lewe Männeken un drosch et duet dör (tüchtig durch). Da schriege dat Männeken so viel un rep »hör
up, hör up, un lat mie geweren, dann will ik die auck seggen wo de Künigsdöchter sied.« Wie he dat hörde, häll hei
up to slaen, un dat Männeken vertelde he wör en Erdmänneken, un sulke wären mehr ase dusend, he mögte man mit
ünne gaen, dann wulle he ünne wiesen wo de Künigsdöchter weren. Da wist he ünne en deipen Born, da is awerst
kien Water inne west. Da segd dat Männeken he wuste
wohl dat et sine Gesellen nig ehrlich mit ünne meinten,
wenn he de Künigskinner erlösen wulle, dann möste he et
alleine doen. De beiden annern Broer wullen wohl auck geren de Künigsdöchter wier hewen, awerst se wullen der
kiene Möge un Gefahr umme doen, he möste so en grauten
Korv nümmen, un möste sik mit sinen Hirschfänger un en
Schelle darinne setten un sik herunter winnen laten: unnen
da wören drei Zimmer, in jeden sette ein Künigskind un
hädde en Drachen mit villen Köppen to lusen, den möste
he de Köppe afschlagen. Ase dat Erdmänneken nu dat alle
sagd hadde, verschwand et. Ase 't Awend is, da kümmet de
beiden annern un fraget wie et ün gaen hädde, da segd he
»o, so wit gud«, un hädde keinen Minsken sehen, ase des
Middags, da wer so ein klein Männeken kummen, de hädde
ün umme en Stücksken Braud biddit, do he et ünne giewen
hädde, hädde dat Männeken et fallen laten un hädde segd
he mögtet ünne doch wier up nümmen, wie he dat nig hadde doen wullt, da hädde et anfangen to puchen, dat hädde
he awerst unrecht verstan un hädde dat Männeken prügelt,
un da hädde et ünne vertellt wo de Künigsdöchter wären.
Da ärgerten sik de beiden so viel, dat se gehl un grön wören. Den annern Morgen da gungen se to haupe an den
Born un mackten Loose, wer sik dat erste in den Korv setten sulle, da feel dat Loos wier den öllesten to, he mot sik
darin setten un de Klingel mitnümmen. Da segd he »wenn
ik klingele, so mutt gi mik nur geschwinne wier herupwin-

nen.« Ase he en bitken herunner is, da klingelte wat, da
winnen se ünne wier heruper: da sett sik de tweide herinne,
de maket ewen sau: nu kümmet dann auck de Riege an den
jungesten, da lät sik awerst gans drinne runner winnen. Ase
he ut den Korve stiegen is, da nümmet he sinen Hirschfänger un geit vor der ersten Doer staen un lustert, da hort he
den Drachen gans lute schnarchen. He macket langsam de
Döre oppen, da sitt da de eine Künigsdochter un häd op
eren Schot niegene (neun) Drachenköppe ligen un luset de.
Da nümmet he sinen Hirschfänger un hogget to, da siet de
niegne Koppe awe. De Künigsdochter sprank up un fäl
ünne um den Hals un drucket un piepete (küsste) ünn so
viel, un nümmet ihr Bruststücke, dat wor von rauen Golle
west, un henget ünne dat umme. Da geit he auck nach der
tweiden Künigsdochter, de häd en Drachen mit sieven
Köppe to lusen un erlöset de auck, so de jungeste, de hadde
en Drachen mit vier Köppen to lusen had, da geit he auck
hinne. Do froget se sich alle so viel, un drucketen un piepe-
ten ohne uphören. Da klingelte he sau harde, bis dat se
owen hört. Da set he de Künigsdöchter ein nach der annern
in den Korv un let se alle drei heruptrecken, wie nu an
ünne de Riege kümmt, da fallet ün de Woore (Worte) von
den Erdmänneken wier bie, dat et sine Gesellen mit ünne
nig gut meinen. Da nümmet he en groten Stein, de da ligt
un legt ün in den Korv, ase de Korv da ungefähr bis in de
Midde herup is, schnien de falsken Broer owen dat Strick
af, dat de Korv mit den Stein up den Grund füll, un meinten he wöre nu daude, up laupet mit de drei Künigsdöchter
wege un latet sik dervan verspreken dat se an ehren Vater
seggen willt dat se beiden se erlöset hädden; da kümmet se
tom Künig, un begert se tor Frugen. Unnerdies geit de jungeste Jägerbursche gans bedröwet in den drei Kammern
herummer un denket dat he nu wull sterwen möste, da süht
he an der Wand 'n Fleutenpipe hangen, da segd he »worümme hengest du da wull, hier kann ja doch keiner lustig
sin?« He bekucket auck de Drachenköppe, un segd »ju

künnt mie nu auck nig helpen.« He geit so mannigmal up
un af spatzeren, dat de Erdboden davon glat werd. Up et
lest, da kriegt he annere Gedanken, da nümmet he de Fleu-
tenpipen van der Wand un blest en Stücksken, up eenmahl
kummet da so viele Erdmännekens, bie jeden Don, den he
däht, kummt eint mehr: da blest he so lange dat Stücksken,
bis det Zimmer stopte vull is. De fraget alle wat sin Begeren
wöre, da segd he he wull geren wier up de E[e]re an Dages
Licht, da fatten sie ünne alle an, an jeden Spir (Faden) Haar,
wat he up sinen Koppe hadde, un sau fleiget se mit ünne
herupper his up de E[e]re. Wie he owen is, geit he glick
nach den Künigsschlott, wo grade de Hochtit mit der einen
Künigsdochter sin sulle, un geit up den Zimmer, wo de Künig mit sinen drei Döchtern is. Wie ünne da de Kinner seihet, da wered se gans beschwämt (ohnmächtig). Da werd
de Künig so böse un let ünne glick in een Gefängnisse setten, weil he meint he hädde den Kinnern en Leid anne
daen. Ase awer de Künigsdöchter wier to sik kummt, da
biddet se so viel he mogte ünne doch wier lose laten. De
Künig fraget se worümme, da segd se dat se dat nig vertellen dorften, awerst de Vaer de segd se sullen et den Owen
(Ofen) vertellen. Da geit he herut un lustert an de Döre un
hört alles. Da lät he de beiden an en Galgen hängen, un den
einen givt he de jungeste Dochter: un da trok ik en Paar
gläserne Schohe an, un da stott ik an en Stein, da segd et
»klink!« da wören se caput.

92.

Der König vom goldenen Berg[e].

Ein Kaufmann, der hatte zwei Kinder, einen Buben und ein
Mädchen, die waren beide noch klein und konnten noch
nicht laufen. Es giengen aber zwei reichbeladene Schiffe

von ihm auf dem Meer, und sein ganzes Vermögen war darin, und wie er meinte dadurch viel Geld zu gewinnen, kam die Nachricht, sie wären versunken. Da war er nun statt eines reichen Mannes ein armer Mann und hatte nichts mehr übrig als einen Acker vor der Stadt. Um sich sein Unglück ein wenig aus den Gedanken zu schlagen, gieng er hinaus auf den Acker, und wie er da so auf und ab ging, stand auf einmal ein kleines schwarzes Männchen neben ihm und fragte warum er so traurig wäre, und was er sich so sehr zu Herzen nähme. Da sprach der Kaufmann »wenn du mir helfen könntest, wollt ich dir es wohl sagen.« »Wer weiß«, antwortete das schwarze Männchen, »vielleicht helf ich dir.« Da erzählte der Kaufmann dass ihm sein ganzer Reichtum auf dem Meer zu Grunde gegangen wäre, und hätte er nichts mehr übrig als diesen Acker. »Bekümmere dich nicht«, sagte das Männchen, »wenn du mir versprichst das, was dir zu Haus am ersten widers Bein stößt, in zwölf Jahren hierher auf den Platz zu bringen, sollst du Geld haben so viel du willst.« Der Kaufmann dachte »was kann das anders sein als mein Hund?« aber an seinen kleinen Jungen dachte er nicht und sagte ja, gab dem schwarzen Mann Handschrift und Siegel darüber und gieng nach Haus.

Als er nach Haus kam, da freute sich sein kleiner Junge so sehr darüber, dass er sich an den Bänken hielt, zu ihm herbei wackelte und ihn an den Beinen fest packte. Da erschrak der Vater, denn es fiel ihm sein Versprechen ein und er wusste nun was er verschrieben hatte: weil er aber immer noch kein Geld in seinen Kisten und Kasten fand, dachte er es wäre nur ein Spaß von dem Männchen gewesen. Einen Monat nachher gieng er auf den Boden und wollte altes Zinn zusammen suchen und verkaufen, da sah er einen großen Haufen Geld liegen. Nun war er wieder guter Dinge, kaufte ein, ward ein größerer Kaufmann als vorher und ließ Gott einen guten Mann sein. Unterdessen ward der Junge groß und dabei klug und gescheit. Je näher aber die zwölf Jahre herbei kamen, je sorgvoller ward der Kaufmann, so

dass man ihm die Angst im Gesicht sehen konnte. Da fragte ihn der Sohn einmal was ihm fehlte: der Vater wollte es
nicht sagen, aber jener hielt so lange an, bis er ihm endlich
sagte er hätte ihn, ohne zu wissen was er verspräche, einem
schwarzen Männchen zugesagt und vieles Geld dafür bekommen. Er hätte seine Handschrift mit Siegel darüber gegeben, und nun müsste er ihn, wenn zwölf Jahre herum
wären, ausliefern. Da sprach der Sohn »o Vater, lasst euch
nicht bang sein, das soll schon gut werden, der Schwarze
hat keine Macht über mich.«

Der Sohn ließ sich von dem Geistlichen segnen, und als die
Stunde kam, giengen sie zusammen hinaus auf den Acker,
und der Sohn machte einen Kreis und stellte sich mit seinem
Vater hinein. Da kam das schwarze Männchen und sprach
zu dem Alten »hast du mitgebracht, was du mir versprochen
hast?« Er schwieg still, aber der Sohn fragte »was willst du
hier?« Da sagte das schwarze Männchen »ich habe mit deinem Vater zu sprechen und nicht mir dir.« Der Sohn antwortete »du hast meinen Vater betrogen und verführt, gib
die Handschrift heraus.« »Nein«, sagte das schwarze Männchen, »mein Recht geb ich nicht auf.« Da redeten sie noch
lange mit einander, endlich wurden sie einig, der Sohn, weil
er nicht dem Erbfeind und nicht mehr seinem Vater zuge-
hörte, sollte sich in ein Schiffchen setzen, das auf einem hin-
abwärts fließenden Wasser stände, und der Vater sollte es
mit seinem eigenen Fuß fortstoßen, und dann sollte der
Sohn dem Wasser überlassen bleiben. Da nahm er Abschied
von seinem Vater, setzte sich in ein Schiffchen, und der Vater
musste es mit seinem eigenen Fuß fortstoßen. Das Schiffchen schlug um, so dass der unterste Teil oben war, die Decke aber im Wasser; und der Vater glaubte, sein Sohn wäre
verloren, gieng heim und trauerte um ihn.

Das Schiffchen aber versank nicht, sondern floss ruhig fort,
und der Jüngling saß sicher darin, und so floss es lange, bis
es endlich an einem unbekannten Ufer festsitzen blieb. Da
stieg er ans Land, sah ein schönes Schloss vor sich liegen

und gieng darauf los. Wie er aber hineintrat, war es verwünscht: er gieng durch alle Zimmer, aber sie waren leer
bis er in die letzte Kammer kam, da lag eine Schlange darin
und ringelte sich. Die Schlange aber war eine verwünschte
Jungfrau, die freute sich, wie sie ihn sah, und sprach zu ihm
»kommst du, mein Erlöser? auf dich habe ich schon zwölf
Jahre gewartet; dies Reich ist verwünscht, und du musst es
erlösen.« »Wie kann ich das?« fragte er. »Heute Nacht
kommen zwölf schwarze Männer, die mit Ketten behangen
sind, die werden dich fragen was du hier machst, da
schweig aber still und gib ihnen keine Antwort, und lass sie
mit dir machen was sie wollen: sie werden dich quälen,
schlagen und stechen, lass alles geschehen, nur rede nicht;
um zwölf Uhr müssen sie wieder fort. Und in der zweiten
Nacht werden wieder zwölf andere kommen, in der dritten
vier und zwanzig, die werden dir den Kopf abhauen: aber
um zwölf Uhr ist ihre Macht vorbei, und wenn du dann
ausgehalten und kein Wörtchen gesprochen hast, so bin ich
erlöst. Ich komme zu dir, und habe in einer Flasche das
Wasser des Lebens, damit bestreiche ich dich, und dann bist
du wieder lebendig und gesund wie zuvor.« Da sprach er
»gerne will ich dich erlösen.« Es geschah nun alles so, wie
sie gesagt hatte: die schwarzen Männer konnten ihm kein
Wort abzwingen, und in der dritten Nacht ward die
Schlange zu einer schönen Königstochter, die kam mit dem
Wasser des Lebens und machte ihn wieder lebendig. Und
dann fiel sie ihm um den Hals und küsste ihn, und war Ju-
bel und Freude im ganzen Schloss. Da wurde ihre Hochzeit
gehalten, und er war König vom *goldenen Berge*.
Also lebten sie vergnügt zusammen, und die Königin gebar
einen schönen Knaben. Acht Jahre waren schon herum, da
fiel ihm sein Vater ein und sein Herz ward bewegt, und er
wünschte ihn einmal heimzusuchen. Die Königin wollte ihn
aber nicht fortlassen und sagte »ich weiß schon dass es mein
Unglück ist«, er ließ ihr aber keine Ruhe bis sie einwilligte.
Beim Abschied gab sie ihm noch einen Wünschring und

sprach »nimm diesen Ring und steck ihn an deinen Finger,
so wirst du alsbald dahin versetzt, wo du dich hinwünschest,
nur musst du mir versprechen dass du ihn nicht gebrauchst,
mich von hier weg zu deinem Vater zu wünschen.« Er versprach ihr das, steckte den Ring an seinen Finger und
wünschte sich heim vor die Stadt, wo sein Vater lebte. Im
Augenblick befand er sich auch dort und wollte in die Stadt:
wie er aber vors Tor kam, wollten ihn die Schildwachen
nicht einlassen, weil er seltsame und doch so reiche und
prächtige Kleider an hatte. Da gieng er auf einen Berg, wo
ein Schäfer hütete, tauschte mit diesem die Kleider und zog
den alten Schäferrock an und gieng also ungestört in die
Stadt ein. Als er zu seinem Vater kam, gab er sich zu erkennen, der aber glaubte nimmermehr dass es sein Sohn wäre
und sagte er hätte zwar einen Sohn gehabt, der wäre aber
längst tot: doch weil er sähe dass er ein armer dürftiger Schäfer wäre, so wollte er ihm einen Teller voll zu essen geben.
Da sprach der Schäfer zu seinen Eltern »ich bin wahrhaftig
euer Sohn, wisst ihr kein Mal an meinem Leibe, woran ihr
mich erkennen könnt?« »Ja«, sagte die Mutter, »unser Sohn
hatte eine Himbeere unter dem rechten Arm.« Er streifte das
Hemd zurück, da sahen sie die Himbeere unter seinem rechten Arm und zweifelten nicht mehr dass es ihr Sohn wäre.
Darauf erzählte er ihnen er wäre König vom goldenen Berge
und eine Königstochter wäre seine Gemahlin, und sie hätten
einen schönen Sohn von sieben Jahren. Da sprach der Vater
»nun und nimmermehr ist das wahr: das ist mir ein schöner
König, der in einem zerlumpten Schäferrock hergeht.« Da
ward der Sohn zornig und drehte, ohne an sein Versprechen
zu denken, den Ring herum und wünschte beide, seine Gemahlin und sein Kind, zu sich. In dem Augenblick waren sie
auch da, aber die Königin, die klagte und weinte, und sagte
er hätte sein Wort gebrochen und hätte sie unglücklich gemacht. Er sagte »ich habe es unachtsam getan und nicht mit
bösem Willen« und redete ihr zu; sie stellte sich auch als
gäbe sie nach, aber sie hatte Böses im Sinn.

Da führte er sie hinaus vor die Stadt auf den Acker und zeigte ihr das Wasser, wo das Schiffchen war abgestoßen worden, und sprach dann »ich bin müde, setze dich nieder, ich will ein wenig auf deinem Schoß schlafen.« Da legte er seinen Kopf auf ihren Schoß und sie lauste ihn ein wenig, bis er einschlief. Als er eingeschlafen war, zog sie erst den Ring von seinem Finger, dann zog sie den Fuß unter ihm weg und ließ nur den Toffel zurück: hierauf nahm sie ihr Kind in den Arm und wünschte sich wieder in ihr Königreich. Als er aufwachte, lag er da ganz verlassen, und seine Gemahlin und das Kind waren fort und der Ring vom Finger auch, nur der Toffel stand noch da zum Wahrzeichen. »Nach Haus zu deinen Eltern kannst du nicht wieder gehen«, dachte er, »die würden sagen, du wärst ein Hexenmeister, du willst aufpacken und gehen bis du in dein Königreich kommst.« Also gieng er fort und kam endlich zu einem Berg, vor dem drei Riesen standen und mit einander stritten, weil sie nicht wussten wie sie ihres Vaters Erbe teilen sollten. Als sie ihn vorbei gehen sahen, riefen sie ihn an und sagten kleine Menschen hätten klugen Sinn, er sollte ihnen die Erbschaft verteilen. Die Erbschaft aber bestand aus einem Degen, wenn einer den in die Hand nahm und sprach »Köpf alle runter, nur meiner nicht«, so lagen alle Köpfe auf der Erde: zweitens aus einem Mantel, wer den anzog, war unsichtbar; drittens aus ein paar Stiefeln, wenn man die angezogen hatte und sich wohin wünschte, so war man im Augenblick da. Er sagte »gebt mir die drei Stücke damit ich probieren könnte ob sie noch in gutem Stande sind.« Da gaben sie ihm den Mantel, und als er ihn umgehängt hatte, war er unsichtbar und war in eine Fliege verwandelt. Dann nahm er wieder seine Gestalt an und sprach »der Mantel ist gut, nun gebt mir das Schwert.« Sie sagten »nein, das geben wir nicht! wenn du sprächst ›Köpf alle runter, nur meiner nicht!‹ so wären unsere Köpfe alle herab und du allein hättest den deinigen noch.« Doch gaben sie es ihm unter der Bedingung dass er's an einem Baum probie-

ren sollte. Das tat er, und das Schwert zerschnitt den
Stamm eines Baums wie einen Strohhalm. Nun wollte er
noch die Stiefeln haben, sie sprachen aber »nein, die geben
wir nicht weg, wenn du sie angezogen hättest und wünsch-
test dich oben auf den Berg, so stünden wir da unten und
hätten nichts.« »Nein«, sprach er, »das will ich nicht tun.«
Da gaben sie ihm auch die Stiefeln. Wie er nun alle drei
Stücke hatte, so dachte er an nichts als an seine Frau und
sein Kind und sprach so vor sich hin »ach wäre ich auf dem
goldenen Berg«, und alsbald verschwand er vor den Augen
der Riesen, und war also ihr Erbe geteilt. Als er nah beim
Schloss war, hörte er Freudengeschrei, Geigen und Flöten,
und die Leute sagten ihm seine Gemahlin feierte ihre
Hochzeit mit einem andern. Da ward er zornig und sprach
»die Falsche, sie hat mich betrogen und mich verlassen, als
ich eingeschlafen war.« Da hieng er seinen Mantel [um] und
gieng unsichtbar ins Schloss hinein. Als er in den Saal eintrat, war da eine große Tafel mit köstlichen Speisen besetzt,
und die Gäste aßen und tranken, lachten und scherzten. Sie
aber saß in der Mitte in prächtigen Kleidern auf einem königlichen Sessel und hatte die Krone auf dem Haupt. Er
stellte sich hinter sie und niemand sah ihn. Wenn sie ihr ein
Stück Fleisch auf den Teller legten, nahm er ihn weg und aß
es: und wenn sie ihr ein Glas Wein einschenkten, nahm er's
weg und trank's aus; sie gaben ihr immer, und sie hatte
doch immer nichts, denn Teller und Glas verschwanden augenblicklich. Da ward sie bestürzt und schämte sie sich,
stand auf und gieng in ihre Kammer und weinte, er aber
gieng hinter ihr her. Da sprach sie »ist denn der Teufel über
mir, oder kam mein Erlöser nie?« Da schlug er ihr ins Angesicht und sagte »kam dein Erlöser nie? er ist über dir, du
Betrügerin. Habe ich das an dir verdient?« Da machte er
sich sichtbar, gieng in den Saal und rief »die Hochzeit ist
aus, der wahre König ist gekommen!« Die Könige, Fürsten
und Räte, die da versammelt waren, höhnten und verlach-
ten ihn: er aber gab kurze Worte und sprach »wollt ihr hin-

aus oder nicht?« Da wollten sie ihn fangen und drangen auf ihn ein, aber er zog sein Schwert und sprach »Köpf alle runter, nur meiner nicht.« Da rollten alle Köpfe zur Erde, und er war allein der Herr und war wieder König vom goldenen Berge.

93.

Die Rabe.

Es war einmal eine Königin, die hatte ein Töchterchen, das war noch klein und musste noch auf dem Arm getragen werden. Zu einer Zeit war das Kind unartig, und die Mutter mochte sagen was sie wollte, es hielt nicht Ruhe. Da ward sie ungeduldig, und weil die Raben so um das Schloss herum flogen, öffnete sie das Fenster und sagte »ich wollte du wärst eine Rabe und flögst fort, so hätt ich Ruhe.« Kaum hatte sie das Wort gesagt, so war das Kind in eine Rabe verwandelt und flog von ihrem Arm zum Fenster hinaus. Sie flog aber in einen dunkeln Wald und blieb lange Zeit darin und die Eltern hörten nichts von ihr. Danach führte einmal einen Mann sein Weg in diesen Wald, der hörte die Rabe rufen und gieng der Stimme nach: und als er näher kam, sprach die Rabe »ich bin eine Königstochter von Geburt und bin verwünscht worden, du aber kannst mich erlösen.« »Was soll ich tun?« fragte er. Sie sagte »geh weiter in den Wald und du wirst ein Haus finden, darin sitzt eine alte Frau, die wird dir Essen und Trinken reichen, aber du darfst nichts nehmen: wenn du etwas issest oder trinkst, so verfällst du in einen Schlaf und kannst du mich nicht erlösen. Im Garten hinter dem Haus ist eine große Lohhucke, darauf sollst du stehen und mich erwarten. Drei Tage lang komm ich jeden Mittag um zwei Uhr zu dir in einem Wagen, der ist erst mit vier weißen Hengsten bespannt, dann mit vier roten und zuletzt mit vier schwarzen, wenn du aber nicht wach bist, sondern schläfst, so werde ich nicht erlöst.« Der Mann versprach alles zu tun, was sie verlangt hatte, die Rabe aber sagte »ach, ich weiß es schon, du wirst mich nicht erlösen, du nimmst etwas von der Frau.« Da versprach der Mann noch einmal er wollte gewiss nichts anrühren weder von dem Essen noch von dem Trinken. Wie er aber in das Haus kam, trat die alte Frau zu ihm und sagte »armer Mann, was seid ihr abgemattet, kommt und erquickt euch, esset und trinkt.« »Nein«, sagte der Mann, »ich will nicht essen und nicht trinken.« Sie ließ ihm aber keine Ruhe und sprach »wenn ihr dann nicht essen wollt, so tut einen Zug aus dem Glas, einmal ist keinmal.« Da ließ er sich überreden und trank. Nachmittags gegen zwei Uhr gieng er hinaus in den Garten auf die Lohhucke und wollte auf die Rabe warten. Wie er da stand, ward er auf einmal so müde, und konnte es nicht überwinden und legte sich ein wenig nieder: doch wollte er nicht einschlafen. Aber kaum hatte er sich hin gestreckt, so fielen ihm die Augen von selber zu, und er schlief ein und schlief so fest dass ihn nichts auf der Welt hätte erwecken können. Um zwei Uhr kam die Rabe mit vier weißen Hengsten gefahren, aber sie war schon in voller Trauer und sprach »ich weiß dass er schläft.« Und als sie in den Garten kam, lag er auch da auf der Lohhucke und schlief. Sie stieg aus dem Wagen, gieng zu ihm und schüttelte ihn und rief ihn an, aber er erwachte nicht. Am andern Tag zur Mittagszeit kam die alte Frau wieder und brachte ihm Essen und Trinken, aber er wollte es nicht annehmen. Doch sie ließ ihm keine Ruhe und redete ihm so lange zu bis er wieder einen Zug aus dem Glase tat. Gegen zwei Uhr gieng er in den Garten auf die Lohhucke und wollte auf die Rabe warten da empfand er auf einmal so große Müdigkeit, dass seine Glieder ihn nicht mehr hielten: er konnte sich nicht helfen, musste sich legen und fiel in tiefen Schlaf. Als die Rabe daher fuhr mit vier braunen Hengsten, war sie schon in voller Trauer und sagte »ich weiß dass er schläft.« Sie gieng zu ihm hin,

aber er lag da im Schlaf und war nicht zu erwecken. Am
andern Tag sagte die alte Frau was das wäre? er äße und
tränke nichts, ob er sterben wollte? Er antwortete »ich will
und darf nicht essen und nicht trinken.« Sie stellte aber die
Schüssel mit Essen und das Glas mit Wein vor ihm hin, und
als der Geruch davon zu ihm aufstieg, so konnte er nicht
widerstehen und tat einen starken Zug. Als die Zeit kam,
gieng er hinaus in den Garten auf die Lohhucke und wartete auf die Königstochter: da ward er noch müder, als die
Tage vorher, legte sich nieder und schlief so fest als wär er
ein Stein. Um zwei Uhr kam die Rabe und hatte vier
schwarze Hengste, und die Kutsche und alles war schwarz.
Sie war aber schon in voller Trauer und sprach »ich weiß
dass er schläft und mich nicht erlösen kann.« Als sie zu ihm
kam, lag er da und schlief fest. Sie rüttelte ihn und rief ihn,
aber sie konnte ihn nicht aufwecken. Da legte sie ein Brot
neben ihn hin, dann ein Stück Fleisch, zum dritten eine Flasche Wein, und er konnte von allem so viel nehmen, als er
wollte, es ward nicht weniger. Danach nahm sie einen goldenen Ring von ihrem Finger, und steckte ihn an seinen
Finger, und war ihr Name eingegraben. Zuletzt legte sie einen Brief hin, darin stand was sie ihm gegeben hatte und
dass es nie all würde, und es stand auch darin »ich sehe
wohl dass du mich hier nicht erlösen kannst, willst du mich
aber noch erlösen, so komm nach dem goldenen Schloss
von Stromberg, es steht in deiner Macht, das weiß ich gewiss.« Und wie sie ihm das alles gegeben hatte, setzte sie
sich in ihren Wagen und fuhr in das goldene Schloss von
Stromberg.
Als der Mann aufwachte und sah dass er geschlafen hatte,
ward er von Herzen traurig und sprach »gewiss nun ist sie
vorbei gefahren und ich habe sie nicht erlöst.« Da fielen
ihm die Dinge in die Augen, die neben ihm lagen, und er
las den Brief darin geschrieben stand wie es zugegangen
war. Also machte er sich auf und gieng fort, und wollte
nach dem goldenen Schloss von Stromberg, aber er wusste

nicht wo es lag. Nun war er schon lange in der Welt herumgegangen, da kam er in einen dunkeln Wald und gieng vierzehn Tage darin fort und konnte sich nicht heraus finden. Da ward es wieder Abend, und er war so müde, dass er sich an einen Busch legte und einschlief. Am andern Tag gieng er weiter und Abends als er sich wieder an einen Busch legen wollte, hörte er ein Heulen und Jammern dass er nicht einschlafen konnte. Und wie die Zeit kam, wo die Leute Lichter anstecken, sah er eins schimmern, machte sich auf und gieng ihm nach: da kam er vor ein Haus, das schien so klein, denn es stand ein großer Riese davor. Da dachte er bei sich »gehst du hinein und der Riese erblickt dich, so ist es leicht um dein Leben geschehen.« Endlich wagte er es und trat heran. Als der Riese ihn sah, sprach er »es ist gut, dass du kommst, ich habe lange nichts gegessen: ich will dich gleich zum Abendbrot verschlucken.« »Lass das lieber sein«, sprach der Mann, »ich lasse mich nicht gerne verschlucken; verlangst du zu essen, so habe ich genug um dich satt zu machen.« »Wenn das wahr ist«, sagte der Riese, »so kannst du ruhig bleiben; ich wollte dich nur verzehren, weil ich nichts anderes habe.« Da giengen sie und setzten sich an den Tisch, und der Mann holte Brot, Wein und Fleisch, das nicht all ward. »Das gefällt mir wohl« sprach der Riese und aß nach Herzenslust. Danach sprach der Mann zu ihm »kannst du mir nicht sagen wo das goldene Schloss von Stromberg ist?« Der Riese sagte »ich will auf meiner Landkarte nachsehen, darauf sind alle Städte, Dörfer und Häuser zu finden.« Er holte die Landkarte, die er in der Stube hatte, und suchte das Schloss, aber es stand nicht darauf. »Es tut nichts«, sprach er, »ich habe oben im Schranke noch größere Landkarten; darauf wollen wir suchen«; aber es war auch vergeblich. Der Mann wollte nun weiter gehen; aber der Riese bat ihn noch ein paar Tage zu warten bis sein Bruder heim käme, der wäre ausgegangen Lebensmittel zu holen. Als der Bruder heim kam, fragten sie nach dem goldenen Schloss von Stromberg, er antworte-

te »wenn ich gegessen habe und satt bin, dann will ich auf
der Karte suchen.« Er stieg dann mit ihnen auf seine Kammer und sie suchten auf seiner Landkarte, konnten es aber
nicht finden: da holte er noch andere alte Karten, und sie
ließen nicht ab, bis sie endlich das goldene Schloss von
Stromberg fanden, aber es war viele tausend Meilen weit
weg. »Wie werde ich nun dahin kommen?« fragte der
Mann. Der Riese sprach »zwei Stunden hab ich Zeit, da
will ich dich bis in die Nähe tragen, dann aber muss ich
wieder nach Haus und das Kind säugen, das wir haben.«
Da trug der Riese den Mann bis etwa hundert Stunden vom
Schloss und sagte »den übrigen Weg kannst du wohl allein
gehen.« Dann kehrte er um, der Mann aber gieng vorwärts
Tag und Nacht, bis er endlich zu dem goldenen Schloss von
Stromberg kam. Es stand aber auf einem gläsernen Berge,
und die verwünschte Jungfrau fuhr in ihrem Wagen um das
Schloss herum und gieng dann hinein. Er freute sich als er
sie erblickte und wollte zu ihr hinauf steigen, aber wie er es
auch anfieng, er rutschte an dem Glas immer wieder herunter. Und als er sah dass er sie nicht erreichen konnte, ward
er ganz betrübt und sprach zu sich selbst »ich will hier unten bleiben und auf sie warten.« Also baute er sich eine
Hütte und saß darin ein ganzes Jahr und sah die Königstochter alle Tage oben fahren, konnte aber nicht zu ihr hinauf kommen.

Da sah er einmal aus seiner Hütte wie drei Räuber sich
schlugen und rief ihnen zu »Gott sei mit euch!« Sie hielten
bei dem Ruf inne, als sie aber niemand sahen, fiengen sie
wieder an sich zu schlagen, und das zwar ganz gefährlich.
Da rief er abermals »Gott sei mit euch!« Sie hörten wieder
auf, guckten sich um, weil sie aber niemand sahen, fuhren
sie auch wieder fort sich zu schlagen. Da rief er zum drittenmal »Gott sei mit euch!« und dachte »du musst sehen
was die drei vorhaben« gieng hin, und fragte warum sie auf
einander losschlügen. Da sagte der eine er hätte einen Stock
gefunden, wenn er damit wider eine Tür schlüge, so sprän-

ge sie auf; der andere sagte er hätte einen Mantel gefunden, wenn er den umhienge, so wär er unsichtbar; der dritte aber sprach er hätte ein Pferd gefangen, damit könnte man überall hin reiten, [auch] auf den gläsernen Berg hinauf. Nun wüssten sie nicht ob sie das in Gemeinschaft behalten oder ob sie sich trennen sollten. Da sprach der Mann »die drei Sachen will ich euch eintauschen: Geld habe ich zwar nicht, aber andere Dinge, die mehr wert sind! doch muss ich vorher eine Probe machen, damit ich sehe ob ihr auch die Wahrheit gesagt habt.« Da ließen sie ihn aufs Pferd sitzen, hiengen ihm den Mantel um und gaben ihm den Stock in die Hand, und wie er das alles hatte, konnten sie ihn nicht mehr sehen. Da gab er ihnen tüchtige Schläge und rief »nun, ihr Bärenhäuter, da habt ihr was euch gebührt: seid ihr zufrieden?« Dann ritt er den Glasberg hinauf und als er oben vor das Schloss kam, war es verschlossen: da schlug er mit dem Stock an das Tor und alsbald sprang es auf. Er trat ein und gieng die Treppe hinauf bis oben in den Saal, da saß die Jungfrau und hatte einen goldenen Kelch mit Wein vor sich. Sie konnte ihn aber nicht sehen, weil er den Mantel um hatte. Und als er vor sie kam, zog er den Ring, den sie ihm gegeben hatte, vom Finger und warf ihn in den Kelch dass es klang. Da rief sie »das ist mein Ring, so muss auch der Mann da sein, der mich erlösen wird.« Sie suchten im ganzen Schloss und fanden ihn nicht, er war aber hinaus gegangen, hatte sich aufs Pferd gesetzt und den Mantel abgeworfen. Wie sie nun vor das Tor kamen, sahen sie ihn und schrien vor Freude. Da stieg er ab und nahm die Königstochter in den Arm: sie aber küsste ihn und sagte »jetzt hast du mich erlöst, und morgen wollen wir unsere Hochzeit feiern.«

94

Die kluge Bauerntochter.

Es war einmal ein armer Bauer, der hatte kein Land, nur ein
kleines Häuschen und eine alleinige Tochter, da sprach die
Tochter »wir sollten den Herrn König um ein Stückchen
Rottland bitten.« Da der König ihre Armut hörte, schenkte
er ihnen auch ein Eckchen Rasen, den hackte sie und ihr
Vater um, und wollten ein wenig Korn und der Art Frucht
darauf säen. Als sie den Acker beinah herum hatten, so fanden sie in der Erde einen Mörsel von purem Gold. »Hör«,
sagte der Vater zu dem Mädchen, »weil unser Herr König
ist so gnädig gewesen und hat uns diesen Acker geschenkt,
so müssen wir ihm den Mörsel dafür geben.« Die Tochter
aber wollt es nicht bewilligen und sagte »Vater, wenn wir
den Mörsel haben und haben den Stößer nicht, dann müssen wir auch den Stößer herbei schaffen, darum schweigt
lieber still.« Er wollte ihr aber nicht gehorchen, nahm den
Mörsel, trug ihn zum Herrn König und sagte den hätte er
gefunden in der Heide, ob er ihn als eine Verehrung annehmen wollte. Der König nahm den Mörsel und fragte ob er
nichts mehr gefunden hätte? »Nein«, antwortete der Bauer.
Da sagte der König er sollte nun auch den Stößer herbeischaffen. Der Bauer sprach den hätten sie nicht gefunden;
aber das half ihm so viel, als hätt er's in den Wind gesagt, er
ward ins Gefängnis gesetzt, und sollte so lange da sitzen,
bis er den Stößer herbeigeschafft hätte. Die Bedienten
mussten ihm täglich Wasser und Brot bringen, was man so
in dem Gefängnis kriegt, da hörten sie, wie der Mann als
fort schrie »ach, hätt ich meiner Tochter gehört! ach, ach,
hätt ich meiner Tochter gehört!« Da giengen die Bedienten
zum König und sprachen das, wie der Gefangene als fort
schrie »ach, hätt ich doch meiner Tochter gehört!« und
wollte nicht essen und nicht trinken. Da befahl er den Bedienten sie sollten den Gefangenen vor ihn bringen, und da

fragte ihn der Herr König warum er also fort schrie »ach, hätt ich meiner Tochter gehört!« »Was hat eure Tochter denn gesagt?« »Ja, sie hat gesprochen ich sollte den Mörsel nicht bringen, sonst müsst ich auch den Stößer schaffen.« »Habt ihr so eine kluge Tochter, so lasst sie einmal herkommen.« Also musste sie vor den König kommen, der fragte sie ob sie denn so klug wäre, und sagte er wollte ihr ein Rätsel aufgeben, wenn sie das treffen könnte, dann wollte er sie heiraten. Da sprach sie gleich ja, sie wollt's erraten. Da sagte der König »komm zu mir, nicht gekleidet, nicht nackend, nicht geritten, nicht gefahren, nicht in dem Weg, nicht außer dem Weg, und wenn du das kannst, will ich dich heiraten.« Da gieng sie hin, und zog sich aus splinternackend, da war sie nicht gekleidet, und nahm ein großes Fischgarn, und setzte sich hinein und wickelte es ganz um sich herum, da war sie nicht nackend: und borgte einen Esel fürs Geld und band dem Esel das Fischgarn an den Schwanz, darin er sie fortschleppen musste, und war das nicht geritten und nicht gefahren: der Esel musste sie aber in der Fahrgleise schleppen, so dass sie nur mit der großen Zehe auf die Erde kam, und war das nicht in dem Weg und nicht außer dem Wege. Und wie sie so daher kam, sagte der König sie hätte das Rätsel getroffen, und es wäre alles erfüllt. Da ließ er ihren Vater los aus dem Gefängnis, und nahm sie bei sich als seine Gemahlin und befahl ihr das ganze königliche Gut an.

Nun waren etliche Jahre herum, als der Herr König einmal auf die Parade zog, da trug es sich zu, dass Bauern mit ihren Wagen vor dem Schloss hielten, die hatten Holz verkauft; etliche hatten Ochsen vorgespannt, und etliche Pferde. Da war ein Bauer, der hatte drei Pferde, davon kriegte eins ein junges Füllchen, das lief weg und legte sich mitten zwischen zwei Ochsen, die vor dem Wagen waren. Als nun die Bauern zusammen kamen, fiengen sie an sich zu zanken, zu schmeißen und zu lärmen, und der Ochsenbauer wollte das Füllchen behalten und sagte die Ochsen hätten's gehabt: und der andere sagte nein, seine Pferde hätten's gehabt, und es wäre sein. Der Zank kam vor den König, und der tat den Ausspruch wo das Füllen gelegen hätte, da sollt es bleiben; und also bekam's der Ochsenbauer, dem's doch nicht gehörte. Da gieng der andere weg, weinte und lamentierte über sein Füllchen. Nun hatte er gehört wie dass die Frau Königin so gnädig wäre, weil sie auch von armen Bauersleuten gekommen wäre: gieng er zu ihr und bat sie ob sie ihm nicht helfen könnte dass er sein Füllchen wieder bekäme. Sagte sie »ja, wenn ihr mir versprecht dass ihr mich nicht verraten wollt, so will ich's euch sagen. Morgen früh, wenn der König auf der Wachtparade ist, so stellt euch hin mitten in die Straße, wo er vorbei kommen muss, nehmt ein großes Fischgarn und tut als fischtet ihr, und fischt also fort und schüttet das Garn aus, als wenn ihr's voll hättet«, und sagte ihm auch was er antworten sollte, wenn er vom König gefragt würde. Also stand der Bauer am andern Tag da und fischte auf einem trockenen Platz. Wie der König vorbei kam und das sah, schickte er seinen Laufer hin, der sollte fragen was der närrische Mann vor hätte. Da gab er zur Antwort »ich fische.« Fragte der Laufer wie er fischen könnte, es wäre ja kein Wasser da. Sagte der Bauer »so gut als zwei Ochsen können ein Füllen kriegen, so gut kann ich auch auf dem trockenen Platz fischen.« Der Laufer gieng hin und brachte dem König die Antwort, da ließ er den Bauer vor sich kommen und sagte ihm das hätte er nicht von sich, von wem er das hätte: und sollt's gleich bekennen. Der Bauer aber wollt's nicht tun und sagte immer Gott bewahr! er hätt es von sich. Sie legten ihn aber auf ein Gebund Stroh und schlugen und drangsalten ihn so lange, bis er's bekannte, dass er's von der Frau Königin hätte. Als der König nach Haus kam, sagte er zu seiner Frau »warum bist du so falsch mit mir, ich will dich nicht mehr zur Gemahlin: deine Zeit ist um, geh wieder hin, woher du kommen bist, in dein Bauernhäuschen.« Doch erlaubte er ihr eins, sie sollte sich das

Liebste und Beste mitnehmen was sie wüsste, und das sollte ihr Abschied sein. Sie sagte »ja, lieber Mann, wenn du's
so befiehlst, will ich es auch tun«, und fiel über ihn her
und küsste ihn und sprach sie wollte Abschied von ihm
nehmen. Dann ließ sie einen starken Schlaftrunk kommen,
Abschied mit ihm zu trinken: der König tat einen großen
Zug, sie aber trank nur ein wenig. Da geriet er bald in einen tiefen Schlaf und als sie das sah, rief sie einen Bedienten und nahm ein schönes weißes Linnentuch und schlug
ihn da hinein, und die Bedienten mussten ihn in einen Wagen vor die Türe tragen, und fuhr sie ihn heim in ihr
Häuschen. Da legte sie ihn in ihr Bettchen, und er schlief
Tag und Nacht in einem fort, und als er aufwachte, sah er
sich um, und sagte »ach Gott, wo bin ich denn?« rief seinen Bedienten, aber es war keiner da. Endlich kam seine
Frau vors Bett und sagte »lieber Herr König, ihr habt mir
befohlen ich sollte das Liebste und Beste aus dem Schloss
mitnehmen, nun hab ich nichts Besseres und Lieberes als
dich, da hab ich dich mitgenommen.« Dem König stiegen
die Tränen in die Augen, und er sagte »liebe Frau, du sollst
mein sein und ich dein«, und nahm sie wieder mit ins königliche Schloss und ließ sich aufs neue mit ihr vermählen;
und werden sie ja wohl noch auf den heutigen Tag leben.

95.

Der alte Hildebrand.

Es war amahl a Baur und a Bäurin, und dö Bäurin, dö hat
der Pfarra im Dorf gern gesegn, und da hat er alleweil
gwunschen, wann er nur amahl an ganzen Tag mit der Bäurin allan recht vergnügt zubringa kunnt, und der Bäurin der
war's halt a recht gwesn. No, da hat er amahl zu der Bäurin
gsagt »hanz, mei liebi Bäurin, hietzt hab i was ausstudiert,

wie wir halt amahl an ganzen Tag recht vergnügt mitanander zubringa kunnten. Wisst's was, ös legt's eng auf'm Mittwoch ins Bett und sagt's engern Mon ös seit's krang, und lamatiert's und übelt's nur recht, und das treibt's fort bis auf'm Sunta, wann i die Predi halt, und da wir (werde) i predigen, dass wer z' Haus a krangs Kind, an krangen Mon, a krangs Weib, an krangen Vader, a krange Muader, a krange Schwester, Bruader, oda wer's sunst nacha is, hat, und der tut a Wollfart auf'm Göckerliberg in Wälischland, wo ma um an Kreuzer an Metzen Lorberbladen kriegt, dem wird's krange Kind, der krange Mon, 's krange Weib, der krange Vader, d' krange Muader, d' krange Schwester, oda wer's sunst nacha is, auf der Stell gsund.«

»Dös wir i schon machen« hat die Bäurin drauf gsagt. No, drauf, auf'm Mittwoch hat sie halt d' Bäurin ins Bett glegt und hat glamatiert und gübelt als wie, und ihr Mon hat ihr alles braucht, was er nur gwisst hat, 's hat aber halt nix gholfn. Wie denn der Sunta kuma is, hat d' Bäurin gsagt »mir is zwar so miserabel als ob i glei verschaden sollt, aber ans möcht i do no vor mein End, i möcht halt in Herrn Pfarra sei Predi hörn, dö er heund halten wird.« »A, mei Kind«, sagt der Baur drauf, »tu du dös nit, du kunntst schlechter wern, wann aufstundst. Schau, es wir i in d' Predi gehn und wir recht acht gebe und wir dir alles wieder derzöhln, was der Herr Pfarra gsagt hat.« »No«, hat d' Bäurin gsagt, »so geh halt und gib recht Acht und derzöhl mir alles, was d' ghört hast.« No, und da is der Baur halt in d' Predi ganga, und da hat der Herr Pfarra also an gfangt zun predigen und hat halt gsagt, wann ans a krangs Kind, an krangen Mon, a krangs Weib, an krangen Vader, a krange Muader, a krange Schwester, Bruader, oda wer's sunst nacha war, z' Haus hät, und der wollt a Wollfart machen auf'm Göckerliberg in Wälischland, wo der Metzen Lorberbladen an Kreuzer kost, dem wird's krange Kind, der krange Mon, 's krange Weib, der krange Vader, d' krange Muader, d' krange Schwester, Bruader, oda wer's sunst na-

cha war, auf der Stell gesund wern, und wer also dö Ras un-
ternehma wollt, der soll nach der Mess zu ihm kuma, da
wird er ihm den Lorbersack gebn und den Kreuzer. Da war
niembd fröher als der Bauer, und nach der Mess is er gleich
zum Pfarra ganga, und der hat ihm also den Lorbersack
gebn und den Kreuzer. Drauf is er nach Haus kuma und
hat schon bei der Haustür eini gschrien »juchesha, liebes
Weib, hietzt is so viel als ob's gsund warst. Der Herr Pfarra
hat heunt predigt, dass wer a krangs Kind, an krangen
Mon, a kranges Weib, an krangen Vader, a krange Muader,
a krange Schwester, Bruader, oda wer's sunst nacha war,
z' Haus hat, und der macht a Wollfart auf'm Göckerliberg
in Wälischland, wo der Metzen Lorberbladen an Kreuzer
kost, dem wird 's krange Kind, der krange Mon, 's krange
Weib, der krange Vader, d' krange Muader, d' krange
Schwester, Bruader, oda wer's sunst nacha war, auf der Stell
gsund; und hietzt hab i mir schon den Lorbersack gholt
vom Herrn Pfarra und den Kreuzer, und wir glei mein
Wanderschaft antreten, dass d' desto ehender gsund wirst«;
und drauf is er fort ganga. Er war aber kam fort, so is die
Bäurin schon auf gwesn, und der Pfarra war a glei do.
Hietz[t] lassen wir aber dö zwa indessen auf der Seiten und
gänga mir mit'n Baur. Der is halt alleweil drauf los ganga,
damit er desto ehender auf'm Göckerliberg kummt, und
wie [er] halt so geht, begegnt ihm sein Gvatter. Sein Gvatter
dös war an Armon (Eiermann), und der is just von Mark
kuma, wo er seine Ar verkauft hat. »Globt seist«, sagt sein
Gvatter, »wo gehst denn so trabi hin, Gvatter?« »In Ewigkeit, Gvatter«, sagt der Baur, »mein Weib is krang worn,
und da hab i heund in Herrn Pfarra sein Predi ghört, und
da hat er predigt, dass wann aner z' Haus an krangs Kind,
an krangen Mon, a krangs Weib, an krangen Vader, a krange Muader, a krange Schwester, Bruader, oda wer's sunst
nacha war, hat, und er macht a Wollfart auf'm Göckerliberg
in Wälischland, wo der Metzen Lorberbladen an Kreuzer
kost, dem wird's krange Kind, der krange Mon, 's krange

Weib, der krange Vader, d' krange Muader, d' krange
Schwester, Bruader, oda wer's sunst nacha war, auf der Stell
gsund, und da hab i mir von Herrn Pfarra den Lorbersack
un den Kreuzer gholt, und hietzt trit i halt mein Wanderschaft an.« »Aber hanz, Gvatter«, hat der Gvatter zum
Baur gsagt, »seit's denn gar so dacket (einfältig), dass so
was glauben könt's? Wisst's was is? der Pfarra möcht gern
mit engern Weib an ganzen Tag allan recht vergnügt zubringa, drum habn's eng den Bärn anbunden, dass ihr en
aus'n Füßen kumts.« »Mein«, hat der Baur gsagt, »so
möcht i do wissen, ob das wahr is.« »No«, hat der Gvatter
gsagt, »wast was, setz di in mein Arkorb eini, so will i di
nach Haus tragn, und da wirst es selber segn.« No, das is
also gschegn, und den Baur hat sein Gvatter in sein Arkorb
eini gsetzt, und der hat 'n nach Haus tragn. Wie's nach
Haus kuma san, holla, da is schon lusti zuganga. Da hat die
Bäurin schon fast alles, was nur in ihren Hof war, abgsto-
chen ghabt, und Krapfen hat's bachen, und der Pfarra war a
schon da und hat a sein Geige mitbracht ghabt. Und da hat
halt der Gvatter anklopft, und d' Bäurin hat gfragt wer
draußen war. »I bin's, Gevatterin«, hat der Gvatter gsagt,
»mei, gebt's mir heund Nacht a Herberg, i hab meini Ar
auf'm Mark nit verkauft, und hietzt muss i's wieder nach
Haus trage, und sö san gar z' schwar, i bring's nit fort, es is
a schon finster.« »Ja, mein Gvatter«, sagt d' Bäurin drauf,
»ös kumts mir recht zur unglegna Zeit. No, weil's halt her
nit anders is, so kömts eina und setzt's eng dort auf d'
Ofenbank.« No hat sie der Gvatter also mit sein Buckelkorb auf d' Ofenbank gsetzt. Der Pfarra aber und d' Bäurin
dö warn halt recht lusti. Endli fangt der Pfarra an und sagt
»hanz, mein liebi Bäurin, ös könnt's ja so schön singa,
singt's mir do ans.« »Ah« sagt die Bäurin, »hietzt kann i nix
mehr singa, ja in mein junge Jahren, da hab i's wohl könna,
aber hietzt is schon vorbei.« »Ei«, sagt wieder der Pfarra,
»singt's do nur a bissl.« No, da fangt die Bäurin an und
singt

>>I hab mein Mon wohl ausgesandt
auf'm Göckerliberg in Wälischland.<<
Drauf singt der Pfarra
>>I wollt er blieb da a ganzes Jahr,
was fragt i nach dem Lorbersack.

Halleluja!<<

Hietzt fangt der Gvatter hinten an und singt (da muss i
aber derzöhln dass der Baur Hildebrand ghassen hat), singt
also der Gvatter
>>Ei du, mein lieber Hildebrand,
was machst du auf der Ofenbank?

Halleluja!<<

Und hietzt singt der Baur in Korb drinna
>>Hietzt kann i das Singa nimmermehr leiden,
hietzt muss i aus mein Buckelkorb steigen.<<
Und steigt aus'n Korb und prügelt den Pfaffen beim Haus
hinaus.

96.

De drei Vügelkens.

Et is wul dusent un meere Jaare hen, da wören hier im Lanne luter kleine Künige, da hed auck einer up den Keuter-
berge wünt (gewohnt), de gink san geren up de Jagd. Ase
nu mal mit sinen Jägern vom Schlotte herruttrok, höen (hüteten) unner den Berge drei Mäkens ire Köge (Kühe), un
wie sei den Künig mit den vielen Lüen (Leuten) seien, so
reip de öllste den annern beden Mäkens to, un weis up
den Künig, >>helo! helo! wenn ik den nig kriege, so will ik
keinen.<< Da antworde de zweide up de annere Side vom
Berge, un weis up den, de dem Künige rechter Hand gink,
>>helo! helo! wenn ik den nig kriege, so will ik keinen.<< da
reip de jüngeste, un weis up den, de linker Hand gink,
>>helo! helo! wenn ik den nig kriege, so will ik keinen.<< Dat

wören averst de beden Ministers. Dat hörde de Künig alles,
un ase von der Jagd heime kummen was, leit he de drei Mäkens to sik kummen un fragete se wat se da gistern am Berge segd hedden. Dat wullen se nig seggen, de Künig frog
awerst de ölleste, ob se ün wol tom Manne hewen wulle?
Da segde se ja, un ere beiden Süstern friggeten de beiden
Ministers, denn se wören alle drei scheun un schir (klar,
schön) von Angesicht, besunnders de Künigin, de hadde
Hare ase Flass.

De beiden Süstern awerst kregen keine Kinner, un ase de
Künig mal verreisen moste, let he se tor Künigin kummen,
um se up to munnern, denn se was grae (gerad) swanger. Se
kreg en kleinen Jungen, de hadde 'n ritsch roen (roten)
Stern mit up de Weld. Da sehden de beiden Süstern, eine
tor annern, se wullen den hübsken Jungen in't Water wer-
pen. Wie se 'n darin worpen hadden (ick glöwe, et is de
Weser west), da flügt 'n Vügelken in de Högte, dat sank

> »tom Daude bereit,
> up wietern Bescheid
> tom Lilienstrus:
> wacker Junge, bist du's?«

Da dat de beiden hörten, kregen se de Angst up'n Lieve, un
makten dat se fort keimen. Wie de Künig na Hus kam, sehden se to üm de Künigin hedde 'n Hund kregen. Da segde
de Künig »wat Gott deiet, dat is wole dahn.«

Et wunde averst 'n Fisker an den Water, de fiskede den
kleinen Jungen wier herut, ase noch ewen lebennig was, un
da sine Fru kene Kinner hadde, foerden (fütterten) s' en up.
Na 'n Jaar was de Künig wier verreist, da krig de Künigin
wier 'n Jungen, den namen de beiden falsken Süstern un
warpen 'n auck in't Water, da flügt dat Vügelken wier in de
Högte un sank

> »tom Daude bereit,
> up wietern Bescheid
> tom Lilienstrus:
> wacker Junge, bist du's?«

Un wie de Künig torügge kam, sehden se to üm, de Künigin hedde wier 'n Hund bekummen, un he segde wier »wat Gott deit, dat is wole dahn.« Awerst de Fisker trok düsen auck ut den Water un foerd 'n up.

Da verreisede de Künig wier, un de Künigin kreg 'n klein Mäken, dat warpen de falsken Süstern auck in't Water. Da flügt dat Vügelken wier in de Högte un sank

»tom Daude bereit,
up wietern Bescheid
tom Lilienstrus:
wacker Mäken, bist du's?«

Un wie de Künig na Hus kam, sehden se to üm, de Künigin hedde ne Katte kregt. Da worde de Künig beuse, un leit sine Fru in't Gefängnis smieten, da hed se lange Jaare in setten.

De Kinner wören unnerdes anewassen, da gink de ölleste mal mit annern Jungens herut to fisken, da wüllt ün de annern Jungens nig twisken sik hewen un segget »du Fündling, gaa du diner Wege.« Da ward he gans bedröwet un frägget de olen Fisker ob dat war wöre? De vertellt ün dat he mal fisked hedde, un hedde ün ut den Water troken (gezogen). Da segd he he wulle furt un sinen Teiten (Vater) söken. De Fisker de biddet 'n he mögde doch bliven, awerst he let sik gar nicht hallen, bis de Fisker et tolest to givt. Da givt he sik un den Weg un geit meere Dage hinner'n anner, endlich kümmt he vor 'n graut allmächtig Water, davor steit ne ole Fru un fiskede. »Guden Dag, Moer«, segde de Junge. »Groten Dank.« »Du süst da wol lange fisken, e du 'n Fisk fängest.« »Un du wol lange söken, e du dinen Teiten findst. Wie wust du der denn da över't Water kummen?« sehde de Fru. »Ja, dat mag Gott witten.« Da nümmt de ole Fru ün up den Rüggen un dragt 'n derdörch, un he söcht lange Tiid un kann sinen Teiten nig finnen. Ase nu wol 'n Jahr veröwer is, da trekt de tweide auck ut un will sinen Broer söken. He kümmt an dat Water, un da geit et ün ewen so, ase sinen Broer. Nu was nur noch de Dochter allein to

Hus, de jammerde so viel na eren Broern, dat se upt lest auck den Fisker bad he mögte se treken laten, se wulle ere Broerkes söken. Da kam se auck bie den grauten Water, da sehde se tor olen Fru »guden Dag, Moer.« »Groten Dank.« »Gott helpe ju bie juen fisken.« Ase de ole Fru dat hörde, da word se ganz fründlich un drog se över't Water un gab er 'n Roe (Rute) un sehde to er »nu gah man jümmer up düsen Wege to, mine Dochter, un wenn du bie einen groten swarten Hund vorbie kummst, so must du still un drist un one to lachen un one ün an to kicken, vorbie gaan. Dann kümmest du an 'n grot open Schlot[t], up'n Süll (Schwelle) most du de Roe fallen laten un stracks dörch dat Schlott an den annern Side wier herut gahen; da is 'n olen Brunnen, darut is 'n groten Boom wassen, daran hänget 'n Vugel im Buer, den nümm af: dann nümm noch 'n Glas Water ut den Brunnen un gaa mit düsen beiden den sülvigen Weg wier torügge: up den Süll nümm de Roe auck wier mit, un wenn du dann wier bie den Hund vorbie kummst, so schlah ün in't Gesicht, awerst sü to dat ü treppest, un dann kumm nur wier to me torügge.« Da fand se et grade so, ase de Fru et sagd hadde, un up den Rückwege da fand se de beiden Broer, de sik de halve Welt durchsöcht hadden. Se gieng[en] tosammen bis wo de swarte Hund an den Weg lag, den schlog se in't Gesicht, da word et 'n schönen Prinz, de geit mit ünen, bis an dat Water. Da stand da noch de ole Fru, de frögede sik ser, da se alle wier da wören, un drog se alle över't Water, un dann gink se auck weg, denn se was nu erlöst. De annern awerst gingen alle na den olen Fisker, un alle wören froh dat se sik wier funnen hadden, den Vügel awerst hüngen se an der Wand.

De tweide Suhn kunne awerst nig to Huse rasten, un nam 'n Flitzebogen un gink up de Jagd. Wie he möe was, nam he sine Flötepipen un mackte 'n Stücksken. De Künig awerst wör auck up de Jagd un hörde dat, da gieng he hin, un wie he den Jungen drap, so sehde he »we hett die verlöwt hier to jagen?« »O, neimes (niemand).« »Wen hörst du

dann to?« »Ik bin den Fisker sin Suhn.« »De hett ja keine
Kinner.« »Wenn du't nig glöwen wust, so kum mit.« Dat
dehe de Künig un frog den Fisker, de vertälle ün alles, un
dat Vügelken an der Wand fing an to singen

»de Möhme (Mutter) sitt allein,
wol in dat Kerkerlein.
o Künig, edeles Blod,
dat sind dine Kinner god.
De falsken Süstern beide
de dehen de Kinnerkes Leide,
wol in des Waters Grund,
wo se de Fisker fund.«

Da erschraken se alle, un de Künig nahm den Vugel, den
Fisker un de drei Kinner mit sik na den Schlotte un leit dat
Gefänknis upschluten un nam sine Fru wier herut, de was
awerst gans kränksch un elennig woren. Da gav er de
Dochter von den Water ut den Brunnen to drinken, da war
se frisk un gesund. De beiden falsken Süstern wören awerst
verbrennt, un de Dochter friggede den Prinzen.

97.

Das Wasser des Lebens.

Es war einmal ein König, der war krank, und niemand
glaubte dass er mit dem Leben davon käme. Er hatte aber
drei Söhne, die waren darüber betrübt, giengen hinunter in
den Schlossgarten und weinten. Da begegnete ihnen ein alter Mann, der fragte sie nach ihrem Kummer. Sie sagten
ihm ihr Vater wäre so krank, dass er wohl sterben würde,
denn es wollte ihm nichts helfen. Da sprach der Alte »ich
weiß noch ein Mittel, das ist das Wasser des Lebens, wenn
er davon trinkt, so wird er wieder gesund: es ist aber
schwer zu finden.« Der älteste sagte »ich will es schon fin-

den«, gieng zum kranken König und bat ihn er möchte ihm
erlauben auszuziehen um das Wasser des Lebens zu suchen,
denn das könnte ihn allein heilen. »Nein«, sprach der König, »die Gefahr dabei ist zu groß, lieber will ich sterben.«
Er bat aber so lange, bis der König einwilligte. Der Prinz
dachte in seinem Herzen »bringe ich das Wasser, so bin ich
meinem Vater der liebste und erbe das Reich.«

Also machte er sich auf, und als er eine Zeitlang fortgeritten war, stand da ein Zwerg auf dem Wege, der rief ihn an
und sprach »wo hinaus so geschwind?« »Dummer Knirps«,
sagte der Prinz ganz stolz, »das brauchst du nicht zu wissen«, und ritt weiter. Das kleine Männchen aber war zornig
geworden und hatte einen bösen Wunsch getan. Der Prinz
geriet bald hernach in eine Bergschlucht, und je weiter er
ritt, je enger taten sich die Berge zusammen, und endlich
ward der Weg so eng, dass er keinen Schritt weiter konnte;
es war nicht möglich das Pferd zu wenden oder aus dem
Sattel zu steigen, und er saß da wie eingesperrt. Der kranke
König wartete lange Zeit auf ihn, aber er kam nicht. Da
sagte der zweite Sohn »Vater, lasst mich ausziehen und das
Wasser suchen«, und dachte bei sich »ist mein Bruder tot,
so fällt das Reich mir zu.« Der König wollt ihn anfangs
auch nicht ziehen lassen, endlich gab er nach. Der Prinz
zog also auf demselben Weg fort, den sein Bruder eingeschlagen hatte, und begegnete auch dem Zwerg, der ihn anhielt und fragte wohin er so eilig wolle. »Kleiner Knirps«,
sagte der Prinz, »das brauchst du nicht zu wissen« und ritt
fort ohne sich weiter umzusehen. Aber der Zwerg verwünschte ihn, und er geriet wie der andere in eine Bergschlucht und konnte nicht vorwärts und rückwärts. So
geht's aber den Hochmütigen.

Als auch der zweite Sohn ausblieb, so erbot sich der jüngste auszuziehen und das Wasser zu holen, und der König
musste ihn endlich ziehen lassen. Als er dem Zwerg begegnete, und dieser fragte wohin er so eilig wolle, so hielt er
an, gab ihm Rede und Antwort und sagte »ich suche das

Wasser des Lebens, denn mein Vater ist sterbenskrank.«
»Weißt du auch wo das zu finden ist?« »Nein« sagte der
Prinz. »Weil du dich betragen hast, wie sich's geziemt, nicht
übermütig wie deine falschen Brüder, so will ich dir Aus-
kunft geben und dir sagen wie du zu dem Wasser des Lebens gelangst. Es quillt aus einem Brunnen in dem Hofe eines verwünschten Schlosses, aber du dringst nicht hinein,
wenn ich dir nicht eine eiserne Rute gebe und zwei Laiber-
chen Brot. Mit der Rute schlag dreimal an das eiserne Tor
des Schlosses, so wird es aufspringen: inwendig liegen zwei
Löwen, die den Rachen aufsperren, wenn du aber jedem
ein Brot hinein wirfst, so werden sie still und dann eile dich
und hol von dem Wasser des Lebens bevor es zwölf
schlägt, sonst schlägt das Tor wieder zu und du bist eingesperrt.« Der Prinz dankte ihm, nahm die Rute und das
Brot, und machte sich auf den Weg. Und als er anlangte,
war alles so, wie der Zwerg gesagt hatte. Das Tor sprang
beim dritten Rutenschlag auf, und als er die Löwen mit
dem Brot gesänftigt hatte, trat er in das Schloss und kam in
einen großen schönen Saal: darin saßen verwünschte Prinzen, denen zog er die Ringe vom Finger, dann lag da ein
Schwert und ein Brot, das nahm er weg. Und weiter kam
er in ein Zimmer, darin stand eine schöne Jungfrau, die freute
sich, als sie ihn sah, küsste ihn und sagte er hätte sie erlöst,
und sollte ihr ganzes Reich haben, und wenn er in einem
Jahr wieder käme, so sollte ihre Hochzeit gefeiert werden.
Dann sagte sie ihm auch, wo der Brunnen wäre mit dem
Lebenswasser, er müsste sich aber eilen und daraus schöpfen eh es zwölf schlüge. Da gieng er weiter und kam endlich in ein Zimmer, wo ein schönes frischgedecktes Bett
stand, und weil er müde war, wollt er erst ein wenig ausruhen. Also legte er sich und schlief ein: als er erwachte,
schlug es drei Viertel auf zwölf. Da sprang er ganz erschrocken auf, lief zu dem Brunnen und schöpfte daraus mit einem Becher, der daneben stand, und eilte dass er fortkam.
Wie er eben zum eisernen Tor hinaus gieng, da schlug's

zwölf, und das Tor schlug so heftig zu, dass es ihm noch ein Stück von der Ferse wegnahm.

Er aber war froh dass er das Wasser des Lebens erlangt hatte, gieng heimwärts und kam wieder an dem Zwerg vorbei. Als dieser das Schwert und das Brot sah, sprach er »damit hast du großes Gut gewonnen, mit dem Schwert kannst du ganze Heere schlagen, das Brot aber wird niemals all.« Der Prinz wollte ohne seine Brüder nicht zu dem Vater nach Haus kommen und sprach »lieber Zwerg, kannst du mir nicht sagen, wo meine zwei Brüder sind? sie sind früher als ich nach dem Wasser des Lebens ausgezogen und sind nicht wiedergekommen.« »Zwischen zwei Bergen stecken sie eingeschlossen«, sprach der Zwerg, »dahin habe ich sie verwünscht, weil sie so übermütig waren.« Da bat der Prinz so lange, bis der Zwerg sie wieder los ließ, aber er warnte ihn und sprach »hüte dich vor ihnen, sie haben ein böses Herz.«

Als seine Brüder kamen, freute er sich und erzählte ihnen wie es ihm ergangen wäre, dass er das Wasser des Lebens gefunden und einen Becher voll mitgenommen und eine schöne Prinzessin erlöst hätte, die wollte ein Jahr lang auf ihn warten, dann sollte Hochzeit gehalten werden, und er bekäme ein großes Reich. Danach ritten sie zusammen fort und gerieten in ein Land, wo Hunger und Krieg war, und der König glaubte schon er müsste verderben, so groß war die Not. Da gieng der Prinz zu ihm und gab ihm das Brot, womit er sein ganzes Reich speiste und sättigte: und dann gab ihm der Prinz auch das Schwert, damit schlug er die Heere seiner Feinde und konnte nun in Ruhe und Frieden leben. Da nahm der Prinz sein Brot und Schwert wieder zurück, und die drei Brüder ritten weiter. Sie kamen aber noch in zwei Länder, wo Hunger und Krieg herrschten, und da gab der Prinz den Königen jedesmal sein Brot und Schwert, und hatte nun drei Reiche gerettet. Und danach setzten sie sich auf ein Schiff, und fuhren übers Meer. Während der Fahrt da sprachen die beiden ältesten unter sich

»der jüngste hat das Wasser des Lebens gefunden und wir nicht, dafür wird ihm unser Vater das Reich geben, das uns gebührt, und er wird unser Glück wegnehmen.« Da wurden sie rachsüchtig und verabredeten mit einander dass sie ihn verderben wollten. Sie warteten bis er einmal fest eingeschlafen war, da gossen sie das Wasser des Lebens aus dem Becher und nahmen es für sich, ihm aber gossen sie bitteres Meerwasser hinein.

Als sie nun daheim ankamen, brachte der jüngste dem kranken König seinen Becher, damit er daraus trinken und gesund werden sollte. Kaum aber hatte er ein wenig von dem bitteren Meerwasser getrunken, so ward er noch kränker als zuvor. Und wie er darüber jammerte, kamen die beiden ältesten Söhne und klagten den jüngsten an er hätte ihn vergiften wollen, sie brächten ihm das rechte Wasser des Lebens und reichten es ihm. Kaum hatte er davon getrunken, so fühlte er seine Krankheit verschwinden, und ward stark und gesund wie in seinen jungen Tagen. Danach giengen die beiden zu dem jüngsten, verspotteten ihn und sagten »du hast zwar das Wasser des Lebens gefunden, aber du hast die Mühe gehabt und wir den Lohn; du hättest klüger sein und die Augen aufbehalten sollen, wir haben dir's genommen während du auf dem Meere eingeschlafen warst, und übers Jahr da holt sich einer von uns die schöne Königstochter. Aber hüte dich dass du nichts davon verrätst, der Vater glaubt dir doch nicht, und wenn du ein einziges Wort sagst, so sollst du noch obendrein dein Leben verlieren, schweigst du aber, so soll dir's geschenkt sein.«

Der alte König war zornig über seinen jüngsten Sohn und glaubte er hätte ihm nach dem Leben getrachtet. Also ließ er den Hof versammeln und das Urteil über ihn sprechen dass er heimlich sollte erschossen werden. Als der Prinz nun einmal auf die Jagd ritt und nichts Böses vermutete, musste des Königs Jäger mitgehen. Draußen, als sie ganz allein im Wald waren, und der Jäger so traurig aussah, sagte der Prinz zu ihm »lieber Jäger, was fehlt dir?« Der Jäger sprach »ich kann's nicht sagen und soll es doch.« Da sprach der Prinz »sage heraus was es ist, ich will dir's verzeihen.« »Ach«, sagte der Jäger, »ich soll euch totschießen, der König hat mir's befohlen.« Da erschrak der Prinz, und sprach »lieber Jäger, lass mich leben, da geb ich dir mein königliches Kleid, gib mir dafür dein schlechtes.« Der Jäger sagte »das will ich gerne tun, ich hätte doch nicht nach euch schießen können.« Da tauschten sie die Kleider, und der Jäger gieng heim, der Prinz aber gieng weiter in den Wald hinein.

Über eine Zeit, da kamen zu dem alten König drei Wagen mit Gold und Edelsteinen für seinen jüngsten Sohn: sie waren aber von den drei Königen geschickt, die mit des Prinzen Schwert die Feinde geschlagen und mit seinem Brot ihr Land ernährt hatten, und die sich dankbar bezeigen wollten. Da dachte der alte König »sollte mein Sohn unschuldig gewesen sein?« und sprach zu seinen Leuten »wäre er noch am Leben, wie tut mir's so leid, dass ich ihn habe töten lassen.« »Er lebt noch«, sprach der Jäger, »ich konnte es nicht übers Herz bringen euern Befehl auszuführen«, und sagte dem König wie es zugegangen war. Da fiel dem König ein Stein von dem Herzen, und er ließ in allen Reichen verkündigen, sein Sohn dürfte wiederkommen und sollte in Gnaden aufgenommen werden.

Die Königstochter aber ließ eine Straße vor ihrem Schloss machen, die war ganz golden und glänzend, und sagte ihren Leuten wer darauf geradeswegs zu ihr geritten käme, das wäre der rechte, und den sollten sie einlassen, wer aber daneben käme, der wäre der rechte nicht, und den sollten sie auch nicht einlassen. Als nun die Zeit bald herum war, dachte der älteste er wollte sich eilen, zur Königstochter gehen und sich für ihren Erlöser ausgeben, da bekäme er sie zur Gemahlin und das Reich daneben. Also ritt er fort, und als er vor das Schloss kam und die schöne goldene Straße sah, dachte er »das wäre jammerschade, wenn du darauf rittest«, lenkte ab und ritt rechts nebenher. Wie er aber vor

das Tor kam, sagten die Leute zu ihm er wäre der rechte
nicht, er sollte wieder fortgehen. Bald darauf machte sich
der zweite Prinz auf, und wie der zur goldenen Straße kam,
und das Pferd den einen Fuß darauf gesetzt hatte, dachte er
»es wäre jammerschade, das könnte etwas abtreten«, lenkte
ab und ritt links nebenher. Wie er aber vor das Tor kam,
sagten die Leute er wäre der rechte nicht, er sollte wieder
fortgehen. Als nun das Jahr ganz herum war, wollte der
dritte aus dem Wald fort zu seiner Liebsten reiten und bei
ihr sein Leid vergessen. Also machte er sich auf, und dachte
immer an sie und wäre gerne schon bei ihr gewesen, und
sah die goldene Straße gar nicht. Da ritt sein Pferd mitten
darüber hin, und als er vor das Tor kam, ward es aufgetan,
und die Königstochter empfieng ihn mit Freuden und sagte
er wär ihr Erlöser und der Herr des Königreichs, und ward
die Hochzeit gehalten mit großer Glückseligkeit. Und als
sie vorbei war, erzählte sie ihm dass sein Vater ihn zu sich
entboten und ihm verziehen hätte. Da ritt er hin und sagte
ihm alles, wie seine Brüder ihn betrogen und er doch dazu
geschwiegen hätte. Der alte König wollte sie strafen, aber
sie hatten sich aufs Meer gesetzt und waren fortgeschifft
und kamen ihr Lebtag nicht wieder.

98.

Doktor Allwissend.

Es war einmal ein armer Bauer Namens *Krebs*, der fuhr mit
zwei Ochsen ein Fuder Holz in die Stadt und verkaufte es
für zwei Taler an einen Doktor. Wie ihm nun das Geld aus-
bezahlt wurde, saß der Doktor gerade zu Tisch: da sah der
Bauer wie er schön aß und trank, und das Herz gieng ihm
danach auf und er wäre auch gern ein Doktor gewesen.
Also blieb er noch ein Weilchen stehen und fragte endlich

ob er nicht auch könnte ein Doktor werden. »O ja«, sagte der Doktor, »das ist bald geschehen.« »Was muss ich tun?« fragte der Bau[e]r. »Erstlich kauf dir ein Abc-Buch, so eins, wo vorn ein Göckelhahn drin ist; zweitens mache deinen Wagen und deine zwei Ochsen zu Geld und schaff dir damit Kleider an, und was sonst zur Doktorei gehört; drittens lass dir ein Schild malen mit den Worten ›ich bin der Doktor Allwissend‹, und lass das oben über deine Haustür nageln.« Der Bauer tat alles, wie's ihm geheißen war. Als er nun ein wenig gedoktert hatte, aber noch nicht viel, ward einem reichen großen Herrn Geld gestohlen. Da ward ihm von dem Doktor Allwissend gesagt, der in dem und dem Dorfe wohnte und auch wissen müsste wo das Geld hingekommen wäre. Also ließ der Herr seinen Wagen anspannen, fuhr hinaus ins Dorf und fragte bei ihm an ob er der Doktor Allwissend wäre? Ja, der wär er. So sollte er mitgehen und das gestohlene Geld wiederschaffen. O ja, aber die Grete, seine Frau, müsste auch mit. Der Herr war das zufrieden, und ließ sie beide in den Wagen sitzen, und sie fuhren zusammen fort. Als sie auf den adligen Hof kamen, war der Tisch gedeckt, da sollte er erst mitessen. Ja, aber seine Frau, die Grete, auch sagte er und setzte sich mit ihr hinter den Tisch. Wie nun der erste Bediente mit einer Schüssel schönem Essen kam, stieß der Bauer seine Frau an und sagte »Grete, das war der erste«, und meinte es wäre derjenige, welcher das erste Essen brächte. Der Bediente aber meinte er hätte damit sagen wollen »das ist der erste Dieb«, und weil er's nun wirklich war, ward ihm angst, und er sagte draußen zu seinen Kameraden »der Doktor weiß alles, wir kommen übel an: er hat gesagt ich wäre der erste.« Der zweite wollte gar nicht herein, er musste aber doch. Wie er nun mit seiner Schüssel herein kam, stieß der Bauer seine Frau an, »Grete, das ist der zweite.« Dem Bedienten ward ebenfalls angst, und er machte dass er hinaus kam. Dem dritten gieng's nicht besser, der Bauer sagte wieder »Grete, das ist der dritte.« Der vierte musste eine verdeckte Schüs-

sel hereintragen, und der Herr sprach zum Doktor er sollte
seine Kunst zeigen und raten was darunter läge; es waren
aber Krebse. Der Bauer sah die Schüssel an, wusste nicht
wie er sich helfen sollte und sprach »ach, ich armer *Krebs*!«
Wie der Herr das hörte, rief er »da, er weiß es, nun weiß er
auch wer das Geld hat.«

Dem Bedienten aber ward gewaltig angst und er blinzelte
den Doktor an, er möchte einmal heraus kommen. Wie er
nun hinaus kam, gestanden sie ihm alle viere sie hätten das
Geld gestohlen: sie wollten's ja gerne heraus geben und ihm
eine schwere Summe dazu, wenn er sie nicht verraten wollte: es ginge ihnen sonst an den Hals. Sie führten ihn auch
hin, wo das Geld versteckt lag. Damit war der Doktor zufrieden, gieng wieder hinein, setzte sich an den Tisch, und
sprach »Herr, nun will ich in meinem Buch suchen wo das
Geld steckt.« Der fünfte Bediente aber kroch in den Ofen
und wollte hören ob der Doktor noch mehr wüsste. Der
saß aber und schlug sein Abc-Buch auf, blätterte hin und
her und suchte den Göckelhahn. Weil er ihn nicht gleich
finden konnte, sprach er »du bist doch darin und musst
auch heraus.« Da glaubte der im Ofen er wäre gemeint,
sprang voller Schrecken heraus und rief »der Mann weiß alles.« Nun zeigte der Doktor Allwissend dem Herrn wo das
Geld lag, sagte aber nicht wer's gestohlen hatte, bekam von
beiden Seiten viel Geld zur Belohnung, und ward ein be-
rühmter Mann.

99.

Der Geist im Glas.

Es war einmal ein armer Holzhacker, der arbeitete vom
Morgen bis in die späte Nacht. Als er sich endlich etwas
Geld zusammengespart hatte, sprach er zu seinem Jungen
»du bist mein einziges Kind, ich will das Geld, das ich mit

saurem Schweiß erworben habe, zu deinem Unterricht anwenden; lernst du etwas rechtschaffenes, so kannst du mich im Alter ernähren, wenn meine Glieder steif geworden sind, und ich daheim sitzen muss.« Da gieng der Junge auf eine hohe Schule und lernte fleißig, so dass ihn seine Lehrer rühmten, und blieb eine Zeit lang dort. Als er ein paar Schulen durchgelernt hatte, doch aber noch nicht in allem vollkommen war, so war das bisschen Armut, das der Vater erworben hatte, drauf gegangen, und er musste wieder zu ihm heim kehren. »Ach«, sprach der Vater betrübt, »ich kann dir nichts mehr geben und kann in der teuern Zeit auch keinen Heller mehr verdienen als das tägliche Brot.« »Lieber Vater«, antwortete der Sohn, »macht euch darüber keine Gedanken, wenn's Gottes Wille also ist, so wird's zu meinem Besten ausschlagen; ich will mich schon drein schicken.« Als der Vater hinaus in den Wald wollte, um etwas am Malterholz (am Zuhauen und Aufrichten) zu verdienen, so sprach der Sohn »ich will mit euch gehen und euch helfen.« »Ja, mein Sohn«, sagte der Vater, »das sollte dir beschwerlich an kommen, du bist an harte Arbeit nicht gewöhnt, du hältst das nicht aus; ich habe auch nur eine Axt und kein Geld übrig, um noch eine zu kaufen.« »Geht nur zum Nachbar«, antwortete der Sohn, »der leiht euch seine Axt so lange, bis ich mir selbst eine verdient habe.«

Da borgte der Vater beim Nachbar eine Axt, und am andern Morgen, bei Anbruch des Tags, giengen sie zusammen hinaus in den Wald. Der Sohn half dem Vater und war ganz munter und frisch dabei. Als nun die Sonne über ihnen stand, sprach der Vater »wir wollen rasten und Mittag halten, hernach geht's noch einmal so gut.« Der Sohn nahm sein Brot in die Hand und sprach »ruht euch nur aus, Vater, ich bin nicht müde, ich will in dem Wald ein wenig auf und abgehen und Vogelnester suchen.« »O du Geck«, sprach der Vater, »was willst du da herum laufen, hernach bist du müde und kannst den Arm nicht mehr aufheben; bleib hier und setze dich zu mir.«

Der Sohn aber gieng in den Wald, aß sein Brot, war ganz
fröhlich und sah in die grünen Zweige hinein, ob er etwa
ein Nest entdecke. So gieng er hin und her, bis er endlich
zu einer großen gefährlichen Eiche kam, die gewiss schon
viele hundert Jahre alt war und die keine fünf Menschen
umspannt hätten. Er blieb stehen und sah sie an und dachte
»es muss doch mancher Vogel sein Nest hinein gebaut haben.« Da däuchte ihn auf einmal als hörte er eine Stimme.
Er horchte und vernahm wie es mit so einem recht dumpfen Ton rief »lass mich heraus, lass mich heraus.« Er sah
sich rings um, konnte aber nichts entdecken, doch es war
ihm als ob die Stimme unten aus der Erde hervor käme. Da
rief er »wo bist du?« Die Stimme antwortete »ich stecke da
unten bei den Eichwurzeln. Lass mich heraus, lass mich
heraus.« Der Schüler fieng an unter dem Baum aufzuräu-
men und bei den Wurzeln zu suchen, bis er endlich in einer
kleinen Höhlung eine Glasflasche entdeckte. Er hob sie in
die Höhe und hielt sie gegen das Licht, da sah er ein Ding,
gleich einem Frosch gestaltet, das sprang darin auf und nieder. »Lass mich heraus, lass mich heraus«, rief's von neuem,
und der Schüler, der an nichts Böses dachte, nahm den
Pfropfen von der Flasche ab. Alsbald stieg ein Geist heraus
und fieng an zu wachsen, und wuchs so schnell, dass er in
wenigen Augenblicken als ein entsetzlicher Kerl, so groß
wie der halbe Baum, vor dem Schüler stand. »Weißt du«,
rief er mit einer fürchterlichen Stimme, »was dein Lohn dafür ist, dass du mich heraus gelassen hast?« »Nein«, antwortete der Schüler ohne Furcht, »wie soll ich das wissen?«
»So will ich dir's sagen«, rief der Geist, »den Hals muss ich
dir dafür brechen.« »Das hättest du mir früher sagen sollen«, antwortete der Schüler, »so hätte ich dich stecken lassen; mein Kopf aber soll vor dir wohl feststehen, da müssen
mehr Leute gefragt werden.« »Mehr Leute hin, mehr Leute
her«, rief der Geist, »deinen verdienten Lohn den sollst du
haben. Denkst du, ich wäre aus Gnade da so lange Zeit eingeschlossen worden, nein, es war zu meiner Strafe; ich bin

der großmächtige Merkurius, wer mich loslässt, dem muss ich den Hals brechen.« »Sachte«, antwortete der Schüler, »so geschwind geht das nicht, erst muss ich auch wissen dass du wirklich in der kleinen Flasche gesessen hast und dass du der rechte Geist bist: kannst du auch wieder hinein, so will ich's glauben, und dann magst du mit mir anfangen was du willst.« Der Geist sprach voll Hochmut »das ist eine geringe Kunst«, zog sich zusammen und machte sich so dünn und klein, wie er anfangs gewesen war, also dass er durch dieselbe Öffnung und durch den Hals der Flasche wieder hinein kroch. Kaum aber war er darin, so drückte der Schüler den abgezogenen Pfropfen wieder auf und warf die Flasche unter die Eichwurzeln an ihren alten Platz, und der Geist war betrogen.

Nun wollte der Schüler zu seinem Vater zurückgehen, aber der Geist rief ganz kläglich »ach, lass mich doch heraus, lass mich doch heraus.« »Nein«, antwortete der Schüler, »zum zweitenmale nicht: wer mir einmal nach dem Leben gestrebt hat, den lass ich nicht los, wenn ich ihn wieder eingefangen habe.« »Wenn du mich frei machst«, rief der Geist, »so will ich dir so viel geben, dass du dein Lebtag genug hast.« »Nein«, antwortete der Schüler, »du würdest mich betriegen wie das erstemal.« »Du verscherzest dein Glück«, sprach der Geist, »ich will dir nichts tun, sondern dich reichlich belohnen.« Der Schüler dachte »ich will's wagen, vielleicht hält er Wort, und anhaben soll er mir doch nichts.« Da nahm er den Pfropfen ab, und der Geist stieg wie das vorigemal heraus, dehnte sich auseinander, und ward groß wie ein Riese. »Nun sollst du deinen Lohn haben«, sprach er, und reichte dem Schüler einen kleinen Lappen, ganz wie ein Pflaster, und sagte »wenn du mit dem einen Ende eine Wunde bestreichst, so heilt sie: und wenn du mit dem andern Ende Stahl und Eisen bestreichst, so wird es in Silber verwandelt.« »Das muss ich erst versuchen«, sprach der Schüler, gieng an einen Baum, ritzte die Rinde mit seiner Axt und bestrich sie mit dem einen Ende

des Pflasters: alsbald schloss sie sich wieder zusammen und
war geheilt. »Nun, es hat seine Richtigkeit«, sprach er zum
Geist, »jetzt können wir uns trennen.« Der Geist dankte
ihm für seine Erlösung, und der Schüler dankte dem Geist
für sein Geschenk und gieng zurück zu seinem Vater.
»Wo bist du herum gelaufen?« sprach der Vater, »warum
hast du die Arbeit vergessen? Ich habe es ja gleich gesagt
dass du nichts zu Stande bringen würdest.« »Gebt euch zufrieden, Vater, ich will's nachholen.« »Ja, nachholen«,
sprach der Vater zornig, »das hat keine Art.« »Habt acht,
Vater, den Baum da will ich gleich umhauen, dass er krachen soll.« Da nahm er sein Pflaster, bestrich die Axt damit
und tat einen gewaltigen Hieb: aber weil das Eisen in Silber
verwandelt war, so legte sich die Schneide um. »Ei, Vater,
seht einmal, was habt ihr mir für eine schlechte Axt gegeben, die ist ganz schief geworden.« Da erschrak der Vater
und sprach »ach, was hast du gemacht! nun muss ich die
Axt bezahlen und weiß nicht womit; das ist der Nutzen,
den ich von deiner Arbeit habe.« »Werdet nicht bös«, antwortete der Sohn, »die Axt will ich schon bezahlen.« »O,
du Dummbart«, rief der Vater, »wovon willst du sie bezahlen? du hast nichts als was ich dir gebe; das sind Studenten-
kniffe, die dir im Kopf stecken, aber vom Holzhacken hast
du keinen Verstand.«
Über ein Weilchen sprach der Schüler »Vater, ich kann
doch nichts mehr arbeiten, wir wollen lieber Feierabend
machen.« »Ei was«, antwortete er, »meinst du ich wollte
die Hände in den Schoß legen wie du? ich muss noch schaffen, du kannst dich aber heim packen.« »Vater, ich bin zum
erstenmal hier in dem Wald, ich weiß den Weg nicht allein,
geh doch mit mir.« Weil sich der Zorn gelegt hatte, so ließ
der Vater sich endlich bereden und gieng mit ihm heim. Da
sprach er zum Sohn »geh und verkauf die verschändete Axt
und sieh zu was du dafür kriegst; das übrige muss ich verdienen, um sie dem Nachbar zu bezahlen.« Der Sohn nahm
die Axt und trug sie in die Stadt zu einem Goldschmied,

der probierte sie, legte sie auf die Waage und sprach »sie ist vierhundert Taler wert, so viel habe ich nicht bar.« Der Schüler sprach »gebt mir was ihr habt, das übrige will ich euch borgen.« Der Goldschmied gab ihm dreihundert Taler und blieb einhundert schuldig. Darauf gieng der Schüler heim und sprach »Vater, ich habe Geld, geht und fragt was der Nachbar für die Axt haben will.« »Das weiß ich schon«, antwortete der Alte, »einen Taler, sechs Groschen.« »So gebt ihm zwei Taler, zwölf Groschen, das ist das Doppelte und ist genug; seht ihr, ich habe Geld im Überfluss«, und gab dem Vater einhundert Taler und sprach »es soll euch niemals fehlen, lebt nach eurer Bequemlichkeit.« »Mein Gott«, sprach der Alte, »wie bist du zu dem Reichtum gekommen?« Da erzählte er ihm wie alles zugegangen wäre und wie er im Vertrauen auf sein Glück einen so reichen Fang getan hätte. Mit dem übrigen Geld aber zog er wieder hin auf die hohe Schule, und lernte weiter, und weil er mit seinem Pflaster alle Wunden heilen konnte, ward er der berühmteste Doktor auf der ganzen Welt.

100.

Des Teufels rußiger Bruder.

Ein abgedankter Soldat hatte nichts zu leben und wusste sich nicht mehr zu helfen. Da gieng er hinaus in den Wald, und als er ein Weilchen gegangen war, begegnete ihm ein kleines Männchen, das war aber der Teufel. Das Männchen sagte zu ihm »was fehlt dir? du siehst ja so trübselig aus.« Da sprach der Soldat »ich habe Hunger aber kein Geld.« Der Teufel sagte »willst du dich bei mir vermieten und mein Knecht sein, so sollst du für dein Lebtag genug haben; sieben Jahre sollst du mir dienen, hernach bist du wieder frei. Aber eins sag ich dir, du darfst dich nicht waschen, nicht kämmen, nicht schnippen, keine Nägel und Haare abschneiden und kein Wasser aus den Augen wischen.« Der Soldat sprach »frisch dran, wenn's nicht anders sein kann«, und gieng mit dem Männchen fort, das führte ihn geradewegs in die Hölle hinein. Dann sagte es ihm was er zu tun hätte: er müsste das Feuer schüren unter den Kesseln, wo die Höllenbraten drin säßen, das Haus rein halten, den Kehrdreck hinter die Türe tragen, und überall auf Ordnung sehen: aber guckte er ein einziges Mal in die Kessel hinein, so würde es ihm schlimm ergehen. Der Soldat sprach »es ist gut, ich will's schon besorgen.« Da gieng nun der alte Teufel wieder hinaus auf seine Wanderung, und der Soldat trat seinen Dienst an, legte Feuer zu, kehrte und trug den Kehrdreck hinter die Türe, alles wie es befohlen war. Wie der alte Teufel wieder kam, sah er nach ob alles geschehen war, zeigte sich zufrieden und gieng zum zweitenmal fort. Der Soldat schaute sich nun einmal recht um, da standen die Kessel rings herum in der Hölle, und war ein gewaltiges Feuer darunter, und es kochte und brutzelte darin. Er hätte für sein Leben gerne hinein geschaut, wenn es ihm der Teufel nicht so streng verboten hätte: endlich konnte er sich nicht mehr anhalten, hob vom ersten Kessel ein klein bisschen den Deckel auf und guckte hinein. Da sah er seinen ehemaligen Unteroffizier darin sitzen: »aha, Vogel«, sprach er, »treff ich dich hier? du hast mich gehabt, jetzt hab ich dich«, ließ geschwind den Deckel fallen, schürte das Feuer und legte noch frisch zu. Danach gieng er zum zweiten Kessel, hob ihn auch ein wenig auf und guckte, da saß sein Fähnrich darin: »aha, Vogel, treff ich dich hier? du hast mich gehabt, jetzt hab ich dich«, machte den Deckel wieder zu und trug noch einen Klotz herbei, der sollte ihm erst recht heiß machen. Nun wollte er auch sehen wer im dritten Kessel säße, da war's gar ein General: »aha, Vogel, treff ich dich hier? du hast mich gehabt, jetzt hab ich dich«, holte den Blasbalg und ließ das Höllenfeuer recht unter ihm flackern. Also tat er sieben Jahr seinen Dienst in der Hölle, wusch sich nicht, kämmte sich nicht, schnippte sich nicht, schnitt sich die Nägel und Haare nicht und wischte sich kein Wasser aus den Augen; und die sieben Jahre waren ihm so kurz, dass er meinte es wäre nur ein halbes Jahr gewesen. Als nun die Zeit vollends herum war, kam der Teufel und sagte »nun, Hans, was hast du gemacht?« »Ich habe das Feuer unter den Kesseln geschürt, ich habe gekehrt und den Kehrdreck hinter die Türe getragen.« »Aber du hast auch in die Kessel geguckt; dein Glück ist, dass du noch Holz zugelegt hast, sonst war dein Leben verloren; jetzt ist deine Zeit herum, willst du wieder heim?« »Ja«, sagte der Soldat, »ich wollt auch gerne sehen was mein Vater daheim macht.« Sprach der Teufel »damit du deinen verdienten Lohn kriegst, geh und raffe dir deinen Ranzen voll Kehrdreck und nimm's mit nach Haus. Du sollst auch gehen ungewaschen und ungekämmt, mit langen Haaren am Kopf und am Bart, mit ungeschnittenen Nägeln und mit trüben Augen, und wenn du gefragt wirst, woher du kämst, sollst du sagen ›Aus der Hölle‹, und wenn du gefragt wirst, wer du wärst, sollst du sagen ›des Teufels rußiger Bruder, und mein König auch.‹« Der Soldat schwieg still und tat was der Teufel sagte, aber er war mit seinem Lohn gar nicht zufrieden.

Sobald er nun wieder oben im Wald war, hob er seinen Ranzen vom Rücken und wollt ihn ausschütten: wie er ihn aber öffnete, so war der Kehrdreck pures Gold geworden. »Das hätte ich mir nicht gedacht« sprach er, war vergnügt und gieng in die Stadt hinein. Vor dem Wirtshaus stand der Wirt, und wie ihn der heran kommen sah, erschrak er, weil Hans so entsetzlich aussah, ärger als eine Vogelscheuche. Er rief ihn an und fragte »woher kommst du?« »Aus der Hölle.« »Wer bist du?« »Dem Teufel sein rußiger Bruder, und mein König auch.« Nun wollte der Wirt ihn nicht einlassen, wie er ihm aber das Gold zeigte, gieng er und klinkte selber die Türe auf. Da ließ sich Hans die beste Stube geben und köstlich aufwarten, aß und trank sich satt, wusch sich

aber nicht und kämmte sich nicht, wie ihm der Teufel geheißen hatte, und legte sich endlich schlafen. Dem Wirt
aber stand der Ranzen voll Gold vor Augen und ließ ihm
keine Ruhe, bis er in der Nacht hinschlich und ihn weg-
stahl.

Wie nun Hans am andern Morgen aufstand, den Wirt bezahlen und weiter gehen wollte, da war sein Ranzen weg.
Er fasste sich aber kurz, dachte, »du bist ohne Schuld unglücklich gewesen«, und kehrte wieder um, geradezu in die
Hölle: da klagte er dem alten Teufel seine Not und bat ihn
um Hülfe. Der Teufel sagte »setze dich, ich will dich waschen, kämmen, schnippen, die Haare und Nägel schneiden
und die Augen auswischen«, und als er mit ihm fertig war,
gab er ihm den Ranzen wieder voll Kehrdreck und sprach
»geh hin, und sage dem Wirt er sollte dir dein Gold wieder
herausgeben, sonst wollt ich kommen und ihn abholen,
und er sollte an deinem Platz das Feuer schüren.« Hans
gieng hinauf und sprach zum Wirt »du hast mein Gold gestohlen, gibst du's nicht wieder, so kommst du in die Hölle
an meinen Platz, und sollst aussehen so gräulich wie ich.«
Da gab ihm der Wirt das Gold und noch mehr dazu, und
bat ihn nur still davon zu sein; und Hans war nun ein reicher Mann.

Hans machte sich auf den Weg heim zu seinem Vater, kaufte sich einen schlechten Linnenkittel auf den Leib, gieng
herum und machte Musik, denn das hatte er bei dem Teufel
in der Hölle gelernt. Es war aber ein alter König im Land,
vor dem musst er spielen, und der geriet darüber in solche
Freude, dass er dem Hans seine älteste Tochter zur Ehe
versprach. Als die aber hörte dass sie so einen gemeinen
Kerl im weißen Kittel heiraten sollte, sprach sie »eh ich das
tät, wollt ich lieber ins tiefste Wasser gehen.« Da gab ihm
der König die jüngste, die wollt's ihrem Vater zu Liebe gerne tun; und also bekam des Teufels rußiger Bruder die Königstochter und als der alte König gestorben war auch das
ganze Reich.

101

Der Bärenhäuter.

Es war einmal ein junger Kerl, der ließ sich als Soldat an-
werben, hielt sich tapfer und war immer der vorderste,
wenn es blaue Bohnen regnete. Solange der Krieg dauerte,
gieng alles gut, aber als Friede geschlossen war, erhielt er
seinen Abschied, und der Hauptmann sagte er könnte gehen wohin er wollte. Seine Eltern waren tot, und er hatte
keine Heimat mehr, da gieng er zu seinen Brüdern und bat
sie möchten ihm so lange Unterhalt geben bis der Krieg
wieder anfienge. Die Brüder aber waren hartherzig und
sagten »was sollen wir mit dir? wir können dich nicht brauchen, sieh zu wie du dich durchschlägst.« Der Soldat hatte
nichts übrig als sein Gewehr, das nahm er auf die Schulter
und wollte in die Welt gehen. Er kam auf eine große Heide,
auf der nichts zu sehen war als ein Ring von Bäumen: darunter setzte er sich ganz traurig nieder und sann über sein
Schicksal nach. »Ich habe kein Geld«, dachte er, »ich habe
nichts gelernt als das Kriegshandwerk, und jetzt weil Friede
geschlossen ist, brauchen sie mich nicht mehr; ich sehe voraus ich muss verhungern.« Auf einmal hörte er ein Brausen,
und wie er sich umblickte, stand ein unbekannter Mann vor
ihm, der einen grünen Rock trug, recht stattlich aussah,
aber einen garstigen Pferdefuß hatte. »Ich weiß schon was
dir fehlt«, sagte der Mann, »Geld und Gut sollst du haben,
so viel du mit aller Gewalt durchbringen kannst, aber ich
muss zuvor wissen ob du dich nicht fürchtest, damit ich
mein Geld nicht umsonst ausgebe.« »Ein Soldat und Furcht,
wie passt das zusammen?« antwortete er, »du kannst mich
auf die Probe stellen.« »Wohlan«, antwortete der Mann,
»schau hinter dich.« Der Soldat kehrte sich um und sah einen großen Bär, der brummend auf ihn zutrabte. »Oho«,
rief der Soldat, »dich will ich an der Nase kitzeln, dass dir
die Lust zum Brummen vergehen soll«, legte an und schoss

den Bär auf die Schnauze, dass er zusammenfiel und sich nicht mehr regte. »Ich sehe wohl«, sagte der Fremde, »dass dir's an Mut nicht fehlt, aber es ist noch eine Bedingung dabei, die musst du erfüllen.« »Wenn mir's an meiner Seligkeit nicht schadet«, antwortete der Soldat, der wohl merkte wen er vor sich hatte, »sonst lass ich mich auf nichts ein.« »Das wirst du selber sehen«, antwortete der Grünrock, »du darfst in den nächsten sieben Jahren dich nicht waschen, dir Bart und Haare nicht kämmen, die Nägel nicht schneiden und kein Vaterunser beten. Dann will ich dir einen Rock und Mantel geben, den musst du in dieser Zeit tragen. Stirbst du in diesen sieben Jahren, so bist du mein, bleibst du aber leben, so bist du frei und bist reich dazu für dein Lebtag.« Der Soldat dachte an die große Not, in der er sich befand, und da er so oft in den Tod gegangen war, wollte er es auch jetzt wagen und willigte ein. Der Teufel zog den grünen Rock aus, reichte ihn dem Soldaten hin und sagte, »wenn du den Rock an deinem Leibe hast und in die Tasche greifst, so wirst du die Hand immer voll Geld haben.« Dann zog er dem Bären die Haut ab und sagte »das soll dein Mantel sein und auch dein Bett, denn darauf musst du schlafen und darfst in kein anderes Bett kommen. Und dieser Tracht wegen sollst du Bärenhäuter heißen.« Hierauf verschwand der Teufel.

Der Soldat zog den Rock an, griff gleich in die Tasche und fand dass die Sache ihre Richtigkeit hatte. Dann hieng er die Bärenhaut um, gieng in die Welt, war guter Dinge und unterließ nichts was ihm wohl und dem Gelde wehe tat. Im ersten Jahr gieng es noch leidlich, aber in dem zweiten sah er schon aus wie ein Ungeheuer. Das Haar bedeckte ihm fast das ganze Gesicht, sein Bart glich einem Stück grobem Filztuch, seine Finger hatten Krallen, und sein Gesicht war so mit Schmutz bedeckt, dass wenn man Kresse hinein gesät hätte, sie aufgegangen wäre. Wer ihn sah, lief fort, weil er aber aller Orten den Armen Geld gab, damit sie für ihn beteten dass er in den sieben Jahren nicht stürbe, und weil er alles gut bezahlte, so erhielt er doch immer noch Herberge. Im vierten Jahr kam er in ein Wirtshaus, da wollte ihn der Wirt nicht aufnehmen und wollte ihm nicht einmal einen Platz im Stall anweisen, weil er fürchtete seine Pferde würden scheu werden. Doch als der Bärenhäuter in die Tasche griff und eine Hand voll Dukaten herausholte, so ließ der Wirt sich erweichen, und gab ihm eine Stube im Hintergebäude; doch musste er versprechen sich nicht sehen zu lassen, damit sein Haus nicht in bösen Ruf käme.

Als der Bärenhäuter Abends allein saß und von Herzen wünschte dass die sieben Jahre herum wären, so hörte er in einem Nebenzimmer ein lautes Jammern. Er hatte ein mitleidiges Herz, öffnete die Türe und erblickte einen alten Mann, der heftig weinte und die Hände über dem Kopf zusammen schlug. Der Bärenhäuter trat näher, aber der Mann sprang auf und wollte entfliehen. Endlich, als er eine menschliche Stimme vernahm, ließ er sich bewegen, und durch freundliches Zureden brachte es der Bärenhäuter dahin, dass er ihm die Ursache seines Kummers offenbarte. Sein Vermögen war nach und nach geschwunden, er und seine Töchter mussten darben, und er war so arm, dass er den Wirt nicht einmal bezahlen konnte und ins Gefängnis sollte gesetzt werden. »Wenn ihr weiter keine Sorgen habt«, sagte der Bärenhäuter, »Geld habe ich genug.« Er ließ den Wirt herbeikommen, bezahlte ihn und steckte dem Unglücklichen noch einen Beutel voll Gold in die Tasche.

Als der alte Mann sich aus seinen Sorgen erlöst sah, wusste er nicht womit er sich dankbar beweisen sollte. »Komm mit mir«, sprach er zu ihm, »meine Töchter sind Wunder von Schönheit, wähle dir eine davon zur Frau. Wenn sie hört was du für mich getan hast, so wird sie sich nicht weigern. Du siehst freilich ein wenig seltsam aus, aber sie wird dich schon wieder in Ordnung bringen.« Dem Bärenhäuter gefiel das wohl und er gieng mit. Als ihn die älteste erblickte, entsetzte sie sich so gewaltig vor seinem Antlitz, dass sie aufschrie und fort lief. Die zweite blieb zwar stehen und betrachtete ihn, von Kopf bis zu Füßen, dann aber sprach sie »wie kann ich einen Mann nehmen, der keine menschliche Gestalt mehr hat? Da gefiel mir der rasierte Bär noch besser, der einmal hier zu sehen war und sich für einen Menschen ausgab, der hatte doch einen Husarenpelz an und weiße Handschuhe. Wenn er nur hässlich wäre, so könnte ich mich an ihn gewöhnen.« Die jüngste aber sprach »lieber Vater, das muss ein guter Mann sein, der euch aus der Not geholfen hat, habt ihr ihm dafür eine Braut versprochen, so muss euer Wort gehalten werden.« Es war Schade, dass das Gesicht des Bärenhäuters von Schmutz und Haaren bedeckt war, sonst hätte man sehen können wie ihm das Herz im Leibe lachte, als er diese Worte hörte. Er nahm einen Ring von seinem Finger, brach ihn entzwei und gab ihr die eine Hälfte, die andere behielt er für sich. In ihre Hälfte aber schrieb er seinen Namen und in seine Hälfte schrieb er ihren Namen und bat sie ihr Stück gut aufzuheben. Hierauf nahm er Abschied und sprach »ich muss noch drei Jahre wandern. Komm ich aber nicht wieder, so bist du frei, weil ich dann tot bin. Bitte aber Gott dass er mir das Leben erhält.«

Die arme Braut kleidete sich ganz schwarz, und wenn sie an ihren Bräutigam dachte, so kamen ihr die Tränen in die Augen. Von ihren Schwestern ward ihr nichts als Hohn und Spott zu Teil. »Nimm dich in Acht«, sagte die älteste, »wenn du ihm die Hand reichst, so schlägt er dir mit der Tatze darauf.« »Hüte dich«, sagte die zweite, »die Bären lieben die Süßigkeit, und wenn du ihm gefällst, so frisst er dich auf.« »Du musst nur immer seinen Willen tun«, hub die älteste wieder an, »sonst fängt er an zu brummen.« Und die zweite fuhr fort »aber die Hochzeit wird lustig sein, Bären die tanzen gut.« Die Braut schwieg still und ließ sich nicht irre machen. Der Bärenhäuter aber zog in der Welt herum, von einem Ort zum andern, tat Gutes, wo er konnte und gab den Armen reichlich, damit sie für ihn beteten. Endlich als der letzte Tag von den sieben Jahren anbrach,

gieng er wieder hinaus auf die Heide, und setzte sich unter
den Ring von Bäumen. Nicht lange, so sauste der Wind,
und der Teufel stand vor ihm und blickte ihn verdrießlich
an; dann warf er ihm den alten Rock hin und verlangte seinen grünen zurück. »So weit sind wir noch nicht«, antwortete der Bärenhäuter, »erst sollst du mich reinigen.« Der
Teufel mochte wollen oder nicht, er musste Wasser holen,
den Bärenhäuter abwaschen, ihm die Haare kämmen, und
die Nägel schneiden. Hierauf sah er wie ein tapferer
Kriegsmann aus, und war viel schöner als je vorher.

Als der Teufel glücklich abgezogen war, so war es dem Bärenhäuter ganz leicht ums Herz. Er gieng in die Stadt, tat
einen prächtigen Sammetrock an, setzte sich in einen Wagen, mit vier Schimmeln bespannt und fuhr zu dem Haus
seiner Braut. Niemand erkannte ihn, der Vater hielt ihn für
einen vornehmen Feldobrist und führte ihn in das Zimmer,
wo seine Töchter saßen. Er musste sich zwischen den beiden ältesten niederlassen: sie schenkten ihm Wein ein, legten ihm die besten Bissen vor und meinten sie hätten keinen schönern Mann auf der Welt gesehen. Die Braut aber
saß in schwarzem Kleide ihm gegenüber, schlug die Augen
nicht auf und sprach kein Wort. Als er endlich den Vater
fragte ob er ihm eine seiner Töchter zur Frau geben wollte,
so sprangen die beiden ältesten auf, liefen in ihre Kammer
und wollten prächtige Kleider anziehen, denn eine jede bil-
dete sich ein sie wäre die Auserwählte. Der Fremde, sobald
er mit seiner Braut allein war, holte den halben Ring hervor
und warf ihn in einen Becher mit Wein, den er ihr über den
Tisch reichte. Sie nahm ihn an, aber als sie getrunken hatte
und den halben Ring auf dem Grund liegen fand, so schlug
ihr das Herz. Sie holte die andere Hälfte, die sie an einem
Band um den Hals trug, hielt sie daran, und es zeigte sich
dass beide Teile vollkommen zu einander passten. Da
sprach er »ich bin dein verlobter Bräutigam, den du als Bärenhäuter gesehen hast, aber durch Gottes Gnade habe ich
meine menschliche Gestalt wieder erhalten, und bin wieder

rein geworden.« Er gieng auf sie zu, umarmte sie und gab
ihr einen Kuss. Indem kamen die beiden Schwestern in vollem Putz herein, und als sie sahen dass der schöne Mann
der jüngsten zu Teil geworden war, und hörten dass das der
Bärenhäuter war, liefen sie voll Zorn und Wut hinaus; die
eine ersäufte sich im Brunnen, die andere erhenkte sich an
einem Baum. Am Abend klopfte jemand an der Türe, und
als der Bräutigam öffnete, so war's der Teufel im grünen
Rock, der sprach »siehst du, nun habe ich zwei Seelen für
deine eine.«

102.

Der Zaunkönig und der Bär.

Zur Sommerszeit giengen einmal der Bär und der Wolf im
Wald spazieren, da hörte der Bär so schönen Gesang von
einem Vogel, und sprach »Bruder Wolf, was ist das für ein
Vogel, der so schön singt?« »Das ist der König der Vögel«,
sagte der Wolf, »vor dem müssen wir uns neigen«, es war
aber der Zaunkönig. »Wenn das ist«, sagte der Bär, »so
möcht ich auch gerne seinen königlichen Palast sehen,
komm und führe mich hin.« »Das geht nicht so, wie du
meinst«, sprach der Wolf, »du musst warten bis die Frau
Königin kommt.« Bald darauf kam die Frau Königin, und
hatte Futter im Schnabel, und der Herr König auch, und
wollten ihre Jungen ätzen. Der Bär wäre gerne nun gleich
hinterdrein gegangen, aber der Wolf hielt ihn am Ärmel
und sagte »nein, du musst warten bis Herr und Frau Königin wieder fort sind.« Also nahmen sie das Loch in Acht,
wo das Nest stand, und trabten wieder ab. Der Bär aber
hatte keine Ruhe, wollte den königlichen Palast sehen, und
gieng nach einer kurzen Weile wieder vor. Da waren König
und Königin richtig ausgeflogen: er guckte hinein und sah
fünf oder sechs Junge, die lagen darin. »Ist das der königli-

che Palast!« rief der Bär, »das ist ein erbärmlicher Palast!
ihr seid auch keine Königskinder, ihr seid unehrliche Kinder.« Wie das die jungen Zaunkönige hörten, wurden sie
gewaltig bös, und schrien »nein, das sind wir nicht, unsere
Eltern sind ehrliche Leute; Bär, das soll ausgemacht werden
mit dir.« Dem Bär und dem Wolf ward angst, sie kehrten
um und setzten sich in ihre Höhlen. Die jungen Zaunkönige aber schrien und lärmten fort, und als ihre Eltern wieder
Futter brachten, sagten sie »wir rühren kein Fliegenbeinchen an, und sollten wir verhungern, bis ihr erst ausgemacht habt ob wir ehrliche Kinder sind oder nicht: der Bär
ist da gewesen, und hat uns gescholten.« Da sagte der alte
König »seid nur ruhig, das soll ausgemacht werden.« Flog
darauf mit der Frau Königin dem Bären vor seine Höhle
und rief hinein »alter Brummbär, warum hast du meine
Kinder gescholten? das soll dir übel bekommen, das wollen
wir in einem blutigen Krieg ausmachen.« Also war dem Bären der Krieg angekündigt, und ward alles vierfüßige Getier
berufen, Ochs, Esel, Rind, Hirsch, Reh, und was die Erde
sonst alles trägt. Der Zaunkönig aber berief alles was in der
Luft fliegt; nicht allein die Vögel groß und klein, sondern
auch die Mücken, Hornissen, Bienen und Fliegen mussten
herbei.
Als nun die Zeit kam, wo der Krieg angehen sollte, da
schickte der Zaunkönig Kundschafter aus, wer der kommandierende General des Feindes wäre. Die Mücke war die
listigste von allen, schwärmte im Wald, wo der Feind sich
versammelte, und setzte sich endlich unter ein Blatt auf den
Baum, wo die Parole ausgegeben wurde. Da stand der Bär,
rief den Fuchs vor sich und sprach »Fuchs, du bist der
schlauste unter allem Getier, du sollst General sein, und uns
anführen.« »Gut«, sagte der Fuchs, »aber was für Zeichen
wollen wir verabreden?« Niemand wusste es. Da sprach
der Fuchs »ich habe einen schönen langen buschigen
Schwanz, der sieht aus fast wie ein roter Federbusch; wenn
ich den Schwanz in die Höhe halte, so geht die Sache gut,

und ihr müsst darauf los marschieren: lass ich ihn aber herunterhängen, so lauft was ihr könnt.« Als die Mücke das gehört hatte, flog sie wieder heim und verriet dem Zaunkönig alles haarklein.

Als der Tag anbrach, wo die Schlacht sollte geliefert werden, hu, da kam das vierfüßige Getier dahergerennt mit Gebraus, dass die Erde zitterte; Zaunkönig mit seiner Armee kam auch durch die Luft daher, die schnurrte, schrie und schwärmte dass einem angst und bange ward; und giengen sie da von beiden Seiten an einander. Der Zaunkönig aber schickte die Hornisse hinab, sie sollte sich dem Fuchs unter den Schwanz setzen und aus Leibeskräften stechen. Wie nun der Fuchs den ersten Stich bekam, zuckte er, dass er das eine Bein aufhob, doch ertrug er's und hielt den Schwanz noch in der Höhe: beim zweiten Stich musst er ihn einen Augenblick herunter lassen: beim dritten aber konnte er sich nicht mehr halten, schrie und nahm den Schwanz zwischen die Beine. Wie das die Tiere sahen, meinten sie alles wäre verloren und fiengen an zu laufen, jeder in seine Höhle: und hatten die Vögel die Schlacht gewonnen.

Da flog der Herr König und die Frau Königin heim zu ihren Kindern, und riefen »Kinder, seid fröhlich, esst und trinkt nach Herzenslust, wir haben den Krieg gewonnen.« Die jungen Zaunkönige aber sagten »noch essen wir nicht, der Bär soll erst vors Nest kommen und Abbitte tun und soll sagen dass wir ehrliche Kinder sind.« Da flog der Zaunkönig vor das Loch des Bären und rief »Brummbär, du sollst vor das Nest zu meinen Kindern gehen und Abbitte tun und sagen dass sie ehrliche Kinder sind, sonst sollen dir die Rippen im Leib zertreten werden.« Da kroch der Bär in der größten Angst hin und tat Abbitte. Jetzt waren die jungen Zaunkönige erst zufrieden, setzten sich zusammen, aßen und tranken und machten sich lustig bis in die späte Nacht hinein.

103.

Der süße Brei.

Es war einmal ein armes frommes Mädchen, das lebte mit seiner Mutter allein, und sie hatten nichts mehr zu essen. Da gieng das Kind hinaus in den Wald, und begegnete ihm da eine alte Frau, die wusste seinen Jammer schon und schenkte ihm ein Töpfchen, zu dem sollt es sagen »Töpfchen koche«, so kochte es guten süßen Hirsenbrei, und wenn es sagte »Töpfchen steh«, so hörte es wieder auf zu kochen. Das Mädchen brachte den Topf seiner Mutter heim, und nun waren sie ihrer Armut und ihres Hungers ledig und aßen süßen Brei so oft sie wollten. Auf eine Zeit war das Mädchen ausgegangen, da sprach die Mutter »Töpfchen koche«, da kocht es, und sie isst sich satt; nun will sie dass das Töpfchen wieder aufhören soll, aber sie weiß das Wort nicht. Also kocht es fort, und der Brei steigt über den Rand hinaus und kocht immer zu, die Küche und das ganze Haus voll, und das zweite Haus und dann die Straße, als wollt's die ganze Welt satt machen, und ist die größte Not, und kein Mensch weiß sich da zu helfen. Endlich, wie nur noch ein einziges Haus übrig ist, da kommt das Kind heim, und spricht nur »Töpfchen steh«, da steht es und hört auf zu kochen; und wer wieder in die Stadt wollte, der musste sich durchessen.

104.

Die klugen Leute.

Eines Tages holte ein Bauer seinen hagebüchnen Stock aus der Ecke und sprach zu seiner Frau »Trine, ich gehe jetzt über Land und komme erst in drei Tagen wieder zurück.

Wenn der Viehhändler in der Zeit bei uns einspricht und
will unsere drei Kühe kaufen, so kannst du sie losschlagen,
aber nicht anders als für zweihundert Taler, geringer nicht,
hörst du.« »Geh nur in Gottes Namen«, antwortete die
Frau, »ich will das schon machen.« »Ja, du!« sprach der
Mann, »du bist als ein kleines Kind einmal auf den Kopf
gefallen, das hängt dir bis auf diese Stunde nach. Aber das
sage ich dir, machst du dummes Zeug, so streiche ich dir
den Rücken blau an, und das ohne Farbe, bloß mit dem
Stock den ich da in der Hand habe, und der Anstrich soll
ein ganzes Jahr halten, darauf kannst du dich verlassen.«
Damit gieng der Mann seiner Wege.
Am andern Morgen kam der Viehhändler, und die Frau
brauchte mit ihm nicht viel Worte zu machen. Als er die
Kühe besehen hatte und den Preis vernahm, sagte er »das
gebe ich gerne, so viel sind sie unter Brüdern wert. Ich will
die Tiere gleich mitnehmen.« Er machte sie von der Kette
los und trieb sie aus dem Stall. Als er eben zum Hoftor hinaus wollte, fasste ihn die Frau am Ärmel und sprach »ihr
müsst mir erst die zweihundert Taler geben sonst kann ich
Euch nicht gehen lassen.« »Richtig«, antwortete der Mann,
»ich habe nur vergessen meine Geldkatze umzuschnallen.
Aber macht Euch keine Sorge, ihr sollt Sicherheit haben,
bis ich zahle. Zwei Kühe nehme ich mit und die dritte lasse
ich Euch zurück, so habt Ihr ein gutes Pfand.« Der Frau
leuchtete das ein, sie ließ den Mann mit seinen Kühen abziehen und dachte »wie wird sich der Hans freuen, wenn er
sieht dass ich es so klug gemacht habe.« Der Bauer kam
den dritten Tag, wie er gesagt hatte, nach Haus und fragte
gleich ob die Kühe verkauft wären. »Freilich, lieber Hans«,
antwortete die Frau, »und wie du gesagt hast, für zweihundert Taler. So viel sind sie kaum wert, aber der Mann nahm
sie ohne Widerrede.« »Wo ist das Geld?« fragte der Bauer.
»Das Geld das habe ich nicht«, antwortete die Frau, »er
hatte gerade seine Geldkatze vergessen, wird's aber bald
bringen; er hat mir ein gutes Pfand zurück gelassen.« »Was

für ein Pfand?« fragte der Mann. »Eine von den drei Kühen, die kriegt er nicht eher, als bis er die andern bezahlt hat. Ich habe es klug gemacht, ich habe die kleinste zurück behalten, die frisst am wenigsten.« Der Mann ward zornig, hob seinen Stock in die Höhe und wollte ihr damit den verheißenen Anstrich geben. Plötzlich ließ er ihn sinken und sagte »du bist die dümmste Gans, die auf Gottes Erdboden herum wackelt, aber du dauerst mich. Ich will auf die Landstraße gehen und drei Tage lang warten, ob ich Jemand finde, der noch einfältiger ist als du bist. Glückt mir's, so sollst du frei sein, finde ich ihn aber nicht, so sollst du deinen wohl verdienten Lohn ohne Abzug erhalten.«

Er gieng hinaus auf die große Straße, setzte sich auf einen Stein und wartete auf die Dinge, die kommen sollten. Da sah er einen Leiterwagen heran fahren, und eine Frau stand mitten darauf, statt auf dem Gebund Stroh zu sitzen, das dabei lag, oder neben den Ochsen zu gehen und sie zu leiten. Der Mann dachte »das ist wohl eine, wie du sie suchst«, sprang auf und lief vor dem Wagen hin und her, wie einer der nicht recht gescheit ist. »Was wollt ihr Gevatter«, sagte die Frau zu ihm, »ich kenne euch nicht, von wo kommt Ihr her?« »Ich bin von dem Himmel gefallen«, antwortete der Mann, »und weiß nicht wie ich wieder hin kommen soll; könnt ihr mich nicht hinauf fahren?« »Nein«, sagte die Frau »ich weiß den Weg nicht. Aber wenn Ihr aus dem Himmel kommt, so könnt Ihr mir wohl sagen wie es meinem Mann geht, der schon seit drei Jahren dort ist: Ihr habt ihn gewiss gesehen?« »Ich habe ihn wohl gesehen, aber es kann nicht allen Menschen gut gehen. Er hütet die Schafe, und das liebe Vieh macht ihm viel zu schaffen, das springt auf die Berge und verirrt sich in der Wildnis, und da muss er hinterher laufen und es wieder zusammen treiben. Abgerissen ist er auch, und die Kleider werden ihm bald vom Leib fallen. Schneider gibt es dort nicht, der heil. Petrus lässt keinen hinein, wie Ihr aus dem Märchen wisst.« »Wer hätte sich das gedacht!« rief die

Frau, »wisst Ihr was? ich will seinen Sonntagsrock holen,
der noch daheim im Schrank hängt, den kann er dort mit
Ehren tragen. Ihr seid so gut und nehmt ihn mit.« »Das
geht nicht wohl«, antwortete der Bauer, »Kleider darf man
nicht in den Himmel bringen, die werden einem vor dem
Tor abgenommen.« »Hört mich an«, sprach die Frau, »ich
habe gestern meinen schönen Weizen verkauft und ein hübsches Geld dafür bekommen, das will ich ihm schicken.
Wenn Ihr den Beutel in die Tasche steckt, so wird's kein
Mensch gewahr.« »Kann's nicht anders sein«, erwiderte der
Bauer, »so will ich Euch wohl den Gefallen tun.« »Bleibt
nur da sitzen«, sagte sie, »ich will heim fahren und den
Beutel holen; ich bin bald wieder hier. Ich setze mich nicht
auf das Bund Stroh, sondern stehe auf dem Wagen, so hat's
das Vieh leichter.« Sie trieb ihre Ochsen an, und der Bauer
dachte »die hat Anlage zur Narrheit, bringt sie das Geld
wirklich, so kann meine Frau von Glück sagen, denn sie
kriegt keine Schläge.« Es dauerte nicht lange, so kam sie gelaufen, brachte das Geld und steckte es ihm selbst in die Tasche. Eh sie weggieng, dankte sie ihm noch tausendmal für
seine Gefälligkeit.
Als die Frau wieder heim kam, so fand sie ihren Sohn, der
aus dem Feld zurück gekehrt war. Sie erzählte ihm was sie
für unerwartete Dinge erfahren hätte und setzte dann hinzu
»ich freue mich recht dass ich Gelegenheit gefunden habe,
meinem armen Mann etwas zu schicken, wer hätte sich
vorgestellt, dass er im Himmel an etwas Mangel leiden
würde?« Der Sohn war in der größten Verwunderung,
»Mutter«, sagte er, »so einer aus dem Himmel kommt nicht
alle Tage, ich will gleich hinaus und sehen dass ich den
Mann noch finde: der muss mir erzählen wie's dort aussieht
und wie's mit der Arbeit geht.« Er sattelte das Pferd und
ritt in aller Hast fort. Er fand den Bauer, der unter einem
Weidenbaum saß und das Geld, das im Beutel war, zählen
wollte. »Habt Ihr nicht den Mann gesehen«, rief ihm der
Junge zu, »der aus dem Himmel gekommen ist?« »Ja«, ant-

wortete der Bauer, »der hat sich wieder auf den Rückweg
gemacht und ist den Berg dort hinauf gegangen, von wo
er's etwas näher hat. Ihr könnt ihn noch einholen, wenn Ihr
scharf reitet.« »Ach«, sagte der Junge, »ich habe mich den
ganzen Tag abgeäschert, und der Ritt hierher hat mich vollends müde gemacht: Ihr kennt den Mann, seid so gut und
setzt Euch auf mein Pferd und überredet ihn dass er hierher
kommt.« »Aha«, meinte der Bauer, »das ist auch einer, der
keinen Docht in seiner Lampe hat.« »Warum sollte ich
Euch den Gefallen nicht tun?« sprach er, stieg auf und ritt
im stärksten Trab fort. Der Junge blieb sitzen bis die Nacht
einbrach, aber der Bauer kam nicht zurück. »Gewiss«,
dachte er »hat der Mann aus dem Himmel große Eile gehabt und nicht umkehren wollen, und der Bauer hat ihm
das Pferd mitgegeben, um es meinem Vater zu bringen.« Er
gieng heim und erzählte seiner Mutter was geschehen war:
das Pferd habe er dem Vater geschickt, damit er nicht immer herum zu laufen brauche. »Du hast wohl getan«, antwortete sie, »du hast noch junge Beine und kannst zu Fuß
gehen.«

Als der Bauer nach Haus gekommen war, stellte er das
Pferd in den Stall neben die verpfändete Kuh, gieng dann
zu seiner Frau und sagte »Trine, das war dein Glück, ich
habe zwei gefunden, die noch einfältigere Narren sind als
du: diesmal kommst du ohne Schläge davon, ich will sie für
eine andere Gelegenheit aufsparen.« Dann zündete er seine
Pfeife an, setzte sich in den Großvaterstuhl und sprach »das
war ein gutes Geschäft, für zwei magere Kühe ein glattes
Pferd und dazu einen großen Beutel voll Geld. Wenn die
Dummheit immer so viel einbrächte, so wollte ich sie gerne
in Ehren halten.« So dachte der Bauer, aber dir sind gewiss
die einfältigen lieber.

105

Märchen von der Unke.

I.

Es war einmal ein kleines Kind, dem gab seine Mutter jeden Nachmittag ein Schüsselchen mit Milch und Weckbrocken, und das Kind setzte sich damit hinaus in den Hof. Wenn es aber anfieng zu essen, so kam die Hausunke aus einer Mauerritze hervor gekrochen, senkte ihr Köpfchen in die Milch und aß mit. Das Kind hatte seine Freude daran, und wenn es mit seinem Schüsselchen da saß, und die Unke kam nicht gleich herbei, so rief es ihr zu

>»Unke, Unke, komm geschwind,
>komm herbei, du kleines Ding,
>sollst dein Bröckchen haben,
>an der Milch dich laben.«

Da kam die Unke gelaufen und ließ es sich gut schmecken. Sie zeigte sich auch dankbar, denn sie brachte dem Kind aus ihrem heimlichen Schatz allerlei schöne Dinge, glänzende Steine, Perlen und goldene Spielsachen. Die Unke trank aber nur Milch und ließ die Brocken liegen. Da nahm das Kind einmal sein Löffelchen, schlug ihr damit sanft auf den Kopf und sagte »Ding, iss auch Brocken.« Die Mutter, die in der Küche stand, hörte dass das Kind mit jemand sprach, und als sie sah dass es mit seinem Löffelchen nach einer Unke schlug, so lief sie mit einem Scheit Holz heraus und tötete das gute Tier.

Von der Zeit an gieng eine Veränderung mit dem Kinde vor. Es war, so lange die Unke mit ihm gegessen hatte, groß und stark geworden, jetzt aber verlor es seine schönen roten Backen und magerte ab. Nicht lange, so fieng in der Nacht der Totenvogel an zu schreien, und das Rotkehlchen sammelte Zweiglein und Blätter zu einem Totenkranz, und bald hernach lag das Kind auf der Bahre.

II.

Ein Waisenkind saß an der Stadtmauer und spann, da sah es eine Unke aus einer Öffnung unten an der Mauer hervor kommen. Geschwind breitete es sein blau seidenes Halstuch neben sich aus, das die Unken gewaltig lieben und auf das sie allein gehen. Alsobald die Unke das erblickte, kehrte sie um, kam wieder und brachte ein kleines goldenes Krönchen getragen, legte es darauf und gieng dann wieder fort. Das Mädchen nahm die Krone auf, sie glitzerte und war von zartem Goldgespinst. Nicht lange, so kam die Unke zum zweitenmal wieder: wie sie aber die Krone nicht mehr sah, kroch sie an die Wand und schlug vor Leid ihr Köpfchen so lange dawider, als sie nur noch Kräfte hatte, bis sie endlich tot da lag. Hätte das Mädchen die Krone liegen lassen, die Unke hätte wohl noch mehr von ihren Schätzen aus der Höhle herbeigetragen.

III.

Unke ruft »huhu, huhu«, Kind spricht »komm herut.« Die Unke kommt hervor, da fragt das Kind nach seinem Schwesterchen »hast du Rotstrümpfchen nicht gesehen?« Unke sagt »ne, ik og nit: wie du denn? huhu, huhu, huhu.«

106.

Der arme Müllerbursch und das Kätzchen.

In einer Mühle lebte ein alter Müller, der hatte weder Frau noch Kinder, und drei Müllerburschen dienten bei ihm. Wie sie nun etliche Jahre bei ihm gewesen waren, sagte er eines Tags zu ihnen »ich bin alt, und will mich hinter den Ofen setzen: zieht aus, und wer mir das beste Pferd nach

Haus bringt, dem will ich die Mühle geben, und er soll
mich dafür bis an meinen Tod verpflegen.« Der dritte von
den Burschen war aber der Kleinknecht, der ward von den
andern für albern gehalten, dem gönnten sie die Mühle
nicht; und er wollte sie hernach nicht einmal. Da zogen alle
drei mit einander aus, und wie sie vor das Dorf kamen, sagten die zwei zu dem albernen Hans »du kannst nur hier
bleiben, du kriegst dein Lebtag keinen Gaul.« Hans aber
gieng doch mit, und als es Nacht war, kamen sie an eine
Höhle, da hinein legten sie sich schlafen. Die zwei Klugen
warteten bis Hans eingeschlafen war, dann stiegen sie auf,
machten sich fort und ließen Hänschen liegen, und meinten's recht fein gemacht zu haben; ja, es wird euch doch
nicht gut gehen! Wie nun die Sonne kam, und Hans aufwachte, lag er in einer tiefen Höhle: er guckte sich überall
um und rief »ach Gott, wo bin ich!« Da erhob er sich und
krappelte die Höhle hinauf, gieng in den Wald und dachte
»ich bin hier ganz allein und verlassen, wie soll ich nun zu
einem Pferd kommen!« Indem er so in Gedanken dahin
gieng, begegnete ihm ein kleines buntes Kätzchen, das
sprach ganz freundlich »Hans, wo willst du hin?« »Ach, ich
kannst mir doch nicht helfen.« »Was dein Begehren ist,
weiß ich wohl«, sprach das Kätzchen, »du willst einen hübschen Gaul haben. Komm mit mir und sei sieben Jahre lang
mein treuer Knecht, so will ich dir einen geben, schöner als
du dein Lebtag einen gesehen hast.« »Nun das ist eine
wunderliche Katze«, dachte Hans, »aber sehen will ich
doch ob das wahr ist was sie sagt.« Da nahm sie ihn mit in
ihr verwünschtes Schlösschen und hatte da lauter Kätzchen, die ihr dienten: die sprangen flink die Treppe auf und
ab, waren lustig und guter Dinge. Abends, als sie sich
zu Tisch setzten, mussten drei Musik machen: eins strich
den Bass, das andere die Geige, das dritte setzte die Trom-
pete an und blies die Backen auf so sehr es nur konnte.
Als sie gegessen hatten, wurde der Tisch weggetragen, und
die Katze sagte »nun komm, Hans, und tanze mit mir.«

»Nein«, antwortete er, »mit einer Miezekatze tanze ich nicht, das habe ich noch niemals getan.« »So bringt ihn ins Bett« sagte sie zu den Kätzchen. Da leuchtete ihm eins in seine Schlafkammer, eins zog ihm die Schuhe aus, eins die Strümpfe und zuletzt blies eins das Licht aus. Am andern Morgen kamen sie wieder und halfen ihm aus dem Bett: eins zog ihm die Strümpfe an, eins band ihm die Strumpf-bänder, eins holte die Schuhe, eins wusch ihn und eins trocknete ihm mit dem Schwanz das Gesicht ab. »Das tut recht sanft« sagte Hans. Er musste aber auch der Katze die-nen und alle Tage Holz klein machen; dazu kriegte er eine Axt von Silber, und die Keile und Säge von Silber, und der Schläger war von Kupfer. Nun, da machte er's klein, blieb da im Haus, hatte sein gutes Essen und Trinken, sah aber niemand als die bunte Katze und ihr Gesinde. Einmal sagte sie zu ihm »geh hin und mähe meine Wiese, und mache das Gras trocken«, und gab ihm von Silber eine Sense und von Gold einen Wetzstein, hieß ihn aber auch alles wieder rich-tig abliefern. Da gieng Hans hin und tat was ihm geheißen war; nach vollbrachter Arbeit trug er Sense, Wetzstein und Heu nach Haus, und fragte ob sie ihm noch nicht seinen Lohn geben wollte. »Nein«, sagte die Katze, »du sollst mir erst noch einerlei tun, da ist Bauholz von Silber, Zimmer-axt, Winkeleisen und was nötig ist, alles von Silber, daraus baue mir erst ein kleines Häuschen.« Da baute Hans das Häuschen fertig und sagte er hätte nun alles getan, und hät-te noch kein Pferd. Doch waren ihm die sieben Jahre her-umgegangen wie ein halbes. Fragte die Katze ob er ihre Pferde sehen wollte? »Ja« sagte Hans. Da machte sie ihm das Häuschen auf, und weil sie die Türe so aufmacht, da stehen zwölf Pferde, ach, die waren gewesen ganz stolz, die hatten geblänkt und gespiegelt, dass sich sein Herz im Lei-be darüber freute. Nun gab sie ihm zu essen und zu trinken und sprach »geh heim, dein Pferd geb ich dir nicht mit: in drei Tagen aber komm ich und bringe dir's nach.« Also machte Hans sich auf, und sie zeigte ihm den Weg zur

Mühle. Sie hatte ihm aber nicht einmal ein neues Kleid gegeben, sondern er musste sein altes lumpiges Kittelchen behalten, das er mitgebracht hatte, und das ihm in den sieben
Jahren überall zu kurz geworden war. Wie er nun heim
kam, so waren die beiden andern Müllerburschen auch wieder da: jeder hatte zwar sein Pferd mitgebracht, aber des einen seins war blind, des andern seins lahm. Sie fragten:
»Hans, wo hast du dein Pferd?« »In drei Tagen wird's
nachkommen.« Da lachten sie und sagten »ja du Hans, wo
willst du ein Pferd herkriegen, das wird was rechtes sein!«
Hans gieng in die Stube, der Müller sagte aber er sollte
nicht an den Tisch kommen, er wäre so zerrissen und zer-
lumpt, man müsste sich schämen, wenn jemand herein
käme. Da gaben sie ihm ein bisschen Essen hinaus, und wie
sie Abends schlafen giengen, wollten ihm die zwei andern
kein Bett geben, und er musste endlich ins Gänseställchen
kriechen und sich auf ein wenig hartes Stroh legen. Am
Morgen, wie er aufwacht, sind schon die drei Tage herum,
und es kommt eine Kutsche mit sechs Pferden, ei, die
glänzten, dass es schön war, und ein Bedienter, der brachte
noch ein siebentes, das war für den armen Müllerbursch.
Aus der Kutsche aber stieg eine prächtige Königstochter
und gieng in die Mühle hinein, und die Königstochter war
das kleine bunte Kätzchen, dem der arme Hans sieben Jahr
gedient hatte. Sie fragte den Müller wo der Mahlbursch, der
Kleinknecht wäre? Da sagte der Müller »den können wir
nicht in die Mühle nehmen, der ist so verrissen und liegt im
Gänsestall.« Da sagte die Königstochter sie sollten ihn
gleich holen. Also holten sie ihn heraus, und er musste sein
Kittelchen zusammenpacken, um sich zu bedecken. Da
schnallte der Bediente prächtige Kleider aus, und musste
ihn waschen und anziehen, und wie er fertig war, konnte
kein König schöner aussehen. Danach verlangte die Jungfrau die Pferde zu sehen, welche die andern Mahlbursche
mitgebracht hatten, eins war blind, das andere lahm. Da
ließ sie den Bedienten das siebente Pferd bringen: wie der

Müller das sah, sprach er so eins wär ihm noch nicht auf
den Hof gekommen; »und das ist für den dritten Mahlbursch« sagte sie. »Da muss er die Mühle haben« sagte der
Müller, die Königstochter aber sprach da wäre das Pferd, er
sollte seine Mühle auch behalten: und nimmt ihren treuen
Hans und setzt ihn in die Kutsche und fährt mit ihm fort.
Sie fahren zuerst nach dem kleinen Häuschen, das er mit
dem silbernen Werkzeug gebaut hat, da ist es ein großes
Schloss, und ist alles darin von Silber und Gold; und da hat
sie ihn geheiratet, und war er reich, so reich, dass er für sein
Lebtag genug hatte. Darum soll keiner sagen, dass wer al-
bern ist, deshalb nichts rechtes werden könne.

107.

Die beiden Wanderer.

Berg und Tal begegnen sich nicht, wohl aber die Menschenkinder, zumal gute und böse. So kam auch einmal ein
Schuster und ein Schneider auf der Wanderschaft zusammen. Der Schneider war ein kleiner hübscher Kerl und war
immer lustig und guter Dinge. Er sah den Schuster von der
andern Seite heran kommen, und da er an seinem Felleisen
merkte was er für ein Handwerk trieb, rief er ihm ein
Spottliedchen zu,

>   »nähe mir die Naht,
>   ziehe mir den Draht,
>   streich ihn rechts und links mit Pech,
>   schlag, schlag mir fest den Zweck.«

Der Schuster aber konnte keinen Spaß vertragen, er verzog
ein Gesicht, als wenn er Essig getrunken hätte, und machte
Miene das Schneiderlein am Kragen zu packen. Der kleine
Kerl fieng aber an zu lachen, reichte ihm seine Flasche und
sprach »es ist nicht bös gemeint, trink einmal und schluck

die Galle hinunter.« Der Schuster tat einen gewaltigen
Schluck, und das Gewitter auf seinem Gesicht fieng an sich
zu verziehen. Er gab dem Schneider die Flasche zurück und
sprach »ich habe ihr ordentlich zugesprochen, man sagt
wohl vom vielen Trinken aber nicht vom großen Durst.
Wollen wir zusammen wandern?« »Mir ist's recht«, antwortete der Schneider, »wenn du nur Lust hast in eine große Stadt zu gehen, wo es nicht an Arbeit fehlt.« »Gerade
dahin wollte ich auch«, antwortete der Schuster, »in einem
kleinen Nest ist nichts zu verdienen, und auf dem Lande
gehen die Leute lieber barfuß.« Sie wanderten also zusammen weiter und setzten immer einen Fuß vor den andern
wie die Wiesel im Schnee.

Zeit genug hatten sie beide, aber wenig zu beißen und zu
brechen. Wenn sie in eine Stadt kamen, so giengen sie umher und grüßten das Handwerk, und weil das Schneiderlein
so frisch und munter aussah und so hübsche rote Backen
hatte, so gab ihm jeder gerne, und wenn das Glück gut war,
so gab ihm die Meistertochter unter der Haustüre auch
noch einen Kuss auf den Weg. Wenn er mit dem Schuster
wieder zusammen traf, so hatte er immer mehr in seinem
Bündel. Der griesgrämige Schuster schnitt ein schiefes Gesicht und meinte »je größer der Schelm, je größer das
Glück.« Aber der Schneider fieng an zu lachen und zu singen, und teilte alles, was er bekam, mit seinem Kameraden.
Klingelten nun ein paar Groschen in seiner Tasche, so ließ
er auftragen, schlug vor Freude auf den Tisch dass die Gläser tanzten, und es hieß bei ihm »leicht verdient und leicht
vertan.«

Als sie eine Zeitlang gewandert waren, kamen sie an einen
großen Wald, durch welchen der Weg nach der Königsstadt
gieng. Es führten aber zwei Fußsteige hindurch, davon war
der eine sieben Tage lang, der andere nur zwei Tage, aber
niemand von ihnen wusste, welcher der kürzere Weg war.
Die zwei Wanderer setzten sich unter einen Eichenbaum
und ratschlagten wie sie sich vorsehen und für wie viel Tage

sie Brot mitnehmen wollten. Der Schuster sagte »man muss weiter denken als man geht, ich will für sieben Tage Brot mit nehmen.« »Was«, sagte der Schneider, »für sieben Tage Brot auf dem Rücken schleppen wie ein Lasttier und sich nicht umschauen? ich halte mich an Gott und kehre mich an nichts. Das Geld, das ich in der Tasche habe, das ist im Sommer so gut als im Winter, aber das Brot wird in der heißen Zeit trocken und obendrein schimmelig. Mein Rock geht auch nicht länger als auf die Knöchel. Warum sollen wir den richtigen Weg nicht finden? Für zwei Tage Brot und damit gut.« Es kaufte sich also ein jeder sein Brot, und dann giengen sie auf gut Glück in den Wald hinein.

In dem Wald war es so still wie in einer Kirche. Kein Wind wehte, kein Bach rauschte, kein Vogel sang, und durch die dichtbelaubten Äste drang kein Sonnenstrahl. Der Schuster sprach kein Wort, ihn drückte das schwere Brot auf dem Rücken, dass ihm der Schweiß über sein verdrießliches und finsteres Gesicht herabfloss. Der Schneider aber war ganz munter, sprang daher, pfiff auf einem Blatt oder sang ein Liedchen, und dachte »Gott im Himmel muss sich freuen dass ich so lustig bin.« Zwei Tage gieng das so fort, aber als er am dritten Tag der Wald kein Ende nehmen wollte, und der Schneider sein Brot aufgegessen hatte, so fiel ihm das Herz doch eine Elle tiefer herab: indessen verlor er nicht den Mut, sondern verließ sich auf Gott und auf sein Glück. Den dritten Tag legte er sich Abends hungrig unter einen Baum und stieg den andern Morgen hungrig wieder auf. So gieng es auch den vierten Tag, und wenn der Schuster sich auf einen umgestürzten Baum setzte, und seine Mahlzeit verzehrte, so blieb dem Schneider nichts als das Zusehen. Bat er um ein Stückchen Brot, so lachte der andere höhnisch und sagte »du bist immer so lustig gewesen, da kannst du auch einmal versuchen wie's tut wenn man unlustig ist: die Vögel die Morgens zu früh singen, die stößt Abends der Habicht«, kurz, er war ohne Barmherzigkeit. Aber am fünften Morgen konnte der arme Schneider nicht mehr aufstehen und vor Mattigkeit kaum ein Wort herausbringen; die Backen waren ihm weiß und die Augen rot. Da sagte der Schuster zu ihm »ich will dir heute ein Stück Brot geben, aber dafür will ich dir dein rechtes Auge ausstechen.« Der unglückliche Schneider, der doch gerne sein Leben erhalten wollte, konnte sich nicht anders helfen: er weinte noch einmal mit beiden Augen und hielt sie dann hin, und der Schuster, der ein Herz von Stein hatte, stach ihm mit einem scharfen Messer das rechte Auge aus. Dem Schneider kam in den Sinn was ihm sonst seine Mutter gesagt hatte, wenn er in der Speisekammer genascht hatte »essen so viel man mag, und leiden was man muss.« Als er sein teuer bezahltes Brot verzehrt hatte, machte er sich wieder auf die Beine, vergaß sein Unglück und tröstete sich damit dass er mit einem Auge noch immer genug sehen könnte. Aber am sechsten Tag meldete sich der Hunger aufs neue und zehrte ihm fast das Herz auf. Er fiel Abends bei einem Baum nieder, und am siebenten Morgen konnte er sich vor Mattigkeit nicht erheben, und der Tod saß ihm im Nacken. Da sagte der Schuster »ich will Barmherzigkeit ausüben und dir nochmals Brot geben; umsonst bekommst du es nicht, ich steche dir dafür das andere Auge noch aus.« Da erkannte der Schneider sein leichtsinniges Leben, bat den lieben Gott um Verzeihung und sprach »tue was du musst, ich will leiden was ich muss; aber bedenke dass unser Herrgott nicht jeden Augenblick richtet und dass eine andere Stunde kommt, wo die böse Tat vergolten wird, die du an mir verübst und die ich nicht an dir verdient habe. Ich habe in guten Tagen mit dir geteilt was ich hatte. Mein Handwerk ist der Art dass Stich muss Stich vertreiben. Wenn ich keine Augen mehr habe, und nicht mehr nähen kann, so muss ich betteln gehen. Lass mich nur, wenn ich blind bin, hier nicht allein liegen, sonst muss ich verschmachten.« Der Schuster aber, der Gott aus seinem Herzen vertrieben hatte, nahm das Messer und stach ihm noch das linke Auge aus. Dann gab er ihm ein Stück Brot zu essen, reichte ihm einen Stock und führte ihn hinter sich her.

Als die Sonne untergieng, kamen sie aus dem Wald, und vor dem Wald auf dem Feld stand ein Galgen. Dahin leitete der Schuster den blinden Schneider, ließ ihn dann liegen und gieng seiner Wege. Vor Müdigkeit, Schmerz und Hunger schlief der Unglückliche ein und schlief die ganze Nacht. Als der Tag dämmerte, erwachte er, wusste aber nicht wo er lag. An dem Galgen hiengen zwei arme Sünder, und auf dem Kopfe eines jeden saß eine Krähe. Da fieng der eine an zu sprechen »Bruder, wachst du?« »Ja, ich wache« antwortete der zweite. »So will ich dir etwas sagen«, fieng der erste wieder an, »der Tau der heute Nacht über uns vom Galgen herabgefallen ist, der gibt jedem, der sich damit wäscht, die Augen wieder. Wenn das die Blinden wüssten, wie mancher könnte sein Gesicht wieder haben, der nicht glaubt dass das möglich sei.« Als der Schneider das hörte, nahm er sein Taschentuch, drückte es auf das Gras, und als es mit dem Tau befeuchtet war, wusch er seine Augenhöhlen damit. Alsbald gieng in Erfüllung was der Gehenkte gesagt hatte, und ein paar frische und gesunde Augen füllten die Höhlen. Es dauerte nicht lange, so sah der Schneider die Sonne hinter den Bergen aufsteigen: vor ihm in der Ebene lag die große Königsstadt mit ihren prächtigen Toren und hundert Türmen, und die goldenen Knöpfe und Kreuze, die auf den Spitzen standen, fiengen an zu glühen. Er unterschied jedes Blatt an den Bäumen, erblickte die Vögel, die vorbei flogen, und die Mücken, die in der Luft tanzten. Er holte eine Nähnadel aus der Tasche, und als er den Zwirn einfädeln konnte, so gut als er es je gekonnt hatte, so sprang sein Herz vor Freude. Er warf sich auf seine Knie, dankte Gott für die erwiesene Gnade und sprach seinen Morgensegen: er vergaß auch nicht für die armen Sünder zu bitten, die da hiengen, wie der Schwengel in der Glocke, und die der Wind aneinander schlug. Dann nahm er seinen Bündel auf den Rücken, vergaß bald das ausgestandene Herzeleid und gieng unter Singen und Pfeifen weiter.

Das erste was ihm begegnete, war ein braunes Füllen, das frei im Felde herumsprang. Er packte es an der Mähne, wollte sich aufschwingen und in die Stadt reiten. Das Füllen aber bat um seine Freiheit: »ich bin noch zu jung«, sprach es, »auch ein leichter Schneider wie du bricht mir den Rücken entzwei, lass mich laufen bis ich stark geworden bin. Es kommt vielleicht eine Zeit, wo ich dir's lohnen kann.« »Lauf hin«, sagte der Schneider, »ich sehe du bist auch so ein Springinsfeld.« Er gab ihm noch einen Hieb mit der Gerte über den Rücken, dass es vor Freude mit den Hinterbeinen ausschlug, über Hecken und Gräben setzte und in das Feld hineinjagte.

Aber das Schneiderlein hatte seit gestern nichts gegessen. »Die Sonne«, sprach er, »füllt mir zwar die Augen, aber das Brot nicht den Mund. Das erste was mir begegnet und halbweg genießbar ist, das muss herhalten.« Indem schritt ein Storch ganz ernsthaft über die Wiese daher. »Halt, halt«, rief der Schneider und packte ihn am Bein, »ich weiß nicht ob du zu genießen bist, aber mein Hunger erlaubt mir keine lange Wahl, ich muss dir den Kopf abschneiden und dich braten.« »Tue das nicht«, antwortete der Storch, »ich bin ein heiliger Vogel, dem niemand ein Leid zufügt, und der den Menschen großen Nutzen bringt. Lässt du mir mein Leben, so kann ich dir's ein andermal vergelten.« »So zieh ab, Vetter Langbein« sagte der Schneider. Der Storch erhob sich, ließ die langen Beine hängen und flog gemächlich fort.

»Was soll daraus werden?« sagte der Schneider zu sich selbst, »mein Hunger wird immer größer und mein Magen immer leerer. Was mir jetzt in den Weg kommt, das ist verloren.« Indem sah er auf einem Teich ein paar junge Enten daher schwimmen. »Ihr kommt ja wie gerufen«, sagte er, packte eine davon, und wollte ihr den Hals umdrehen. Da fieng eine alte Ente, die in dem Schilf steckte, laut an zu kreischen, schwamm mit aufgesperrtem Schnabel herbei und bat ihn flehentlich sich ihrer lieben Kinder zu erbarmen. »Denkst du nicht«, sagte sie, »wie deine Mutter jammern würde, wenn dich einer wegholen und dir den Garaus machen wollte.« »Sei nur still«, sagte der gutmütige Schneider, »du sollst deine Kinder behalten«, und setzte die Gefangene wieder ins Wasser.

Als er sich umkehrte, stand er vor einem alten Baum, der halb hohl war, und sah die wilden Bienen aus- und einfliegen. »Da finde ich gleich den Lohn für meine gute Tat« sagte der Schneider, »der Honig wird mich laben.« Aber der Weisel kam heraus, drohte und sprach »wenn du mein Volk anrührst und mein Nest zerstörst, so sollen dir unsere Stacheln wie zehntausend glühende Nadeln in die Haut fahren. Lässt du uns aber in Ruhe und gehst deiner Wege, so wollen wir dir ein andermal dafür einen Dienst leisten.«

Das Schneiderlein sah dass auch hier nichts anzufangen war. »Drei Schüsseln leer«, sagte er, »und auf der vierten nichts, das ist eine schlechte Mahlzeit.« Er schleppte sich also mit seinem ausgehungerten Magen in die Stadt, und da es eben zu Mittag läutete, so war für ihn im Gasthaus schon gekocht und er konnte sich gleich zu Tisch setzen. Als er satt war, sagte er »nun will ich auch arbeiten.« Er gieng in der Stadt umher, suchte einen Meister und fand auch bald ein gutes Unterkommen. Da er aber sein Handwerk von Grund aus gelernt hatte, so dauerte es nicht lange, er ward berühmt, und jeder wollte seinen neuen Rock von dem kleinen Schneider gemacht haben. Alle Tage nahm sein Ansehen zu. »Ich kann in meiner Kunst nicht weiter kommen«, sprach er, »und doch geht's jeden Tag besser.« Endlich bestellte ihn der König zu seinem Hofschneider.

Aber wie's in der Welt geht. An demselben Tag war sein ehemaliger Kamerad, der Schuster, auch Hofschuster geworden. Als dieser den Schneider erblickte und sah dass er wieder zwei gesunde Augen hatte, so peinigte ihn das Gewissen. »Ehe er Rache an mir nimmt«, dachte er bei sich selbst, »muss ich ihm eine Grube graben.« Wer aber andern eine Grube gräbt, fällt selbst hinein. Abends, als er Feierabend

gemacht hatte, und es dämmerig geworden war, schlich er
sich zu dem König und sagte »Herr König, der Schneider ist
ein übermütiger Mensch, und hat sich vermessen er wollte
die goldene Krone wieder herbei schaffen, die vor alten Zeiten ist verloren gegangen.« »Das sollte mir lieb sein« sprach
der König, ließ den Schneider am andern Morgen vor sich
fordern und befahl ihm die Krone wieder herbeizuschaffen,
oder für immer die Stadt zu verlassen. »Oho«, dachte der
Schneider, »ein Schelm gibt mehr als er hat. Wenn der murr-
köpfige König von mir verlangt was kein Mensch leisten
kann, so will ich nicht warten bis morgen, sondern gleich
heute wieder zur Stadt hinaus wandern.« Er schnürte also
sein Bündel, als er aber aus dem Tor heraus war, so tat es ihm
doch leid dass er sein Glück aufgeben und die Stadt, in der es
ihm so wohl gegangen war, mit dem Rücken ansehen sollte.
Er kam zu dem Teich, wo er mit den Enten Bekanntschaft
gemacht hatte, da saß gerade die Alte, der er ihre Jungen gelassen hatte, am Ufer und putzte sich mit dem Schnabel. Sie
erkannte ihn gleich, und fragte warum er den Kopf so hängen lasse. »Du wirst dich nicht wundern, wenn du hörst was
mir begegnet ist« antwortete der Schneider und erzählte ihr
sein Schicksal. »Wenn's weiter nichts ist«, sagte die Ente, »da
können wir Rat schaffen. Die Krone ist ins Wasser gefallen
und liegt unten auf dem Grund, wie bald haben wir sie wieder heraufgeholt. Breite nur derweil dein Taschentuch ans
Ufer aus.« Sie tauchte mit ihren zwölf Jungen unter, und
nach fünf Minuten war sie wieder oben und saß mitten in
der Krone, die auf ihren Fittigen ruhte, und die zwölf Jungen schwammen rund herum, hatten ihre Schnäbel unterge-
legt und halfen tragen. Sie schwammen ans Land und legten
die Krone auf das Tuch. Du glaubst nicht wie prächtig die
Krone war, wenn die Sonne darauf schien, so glänzte sie wie
hunderttausend Karfunkelsteine. Der Schneider band sein
Tuch mit den vier Zipfeln zusammen und trug sie zum König, der in einer Freude war und dem Schneider eine goldene
Kette um den Hals hieng.

Als der Schuster sah dass der eine Streich misslungen war, so besann er sich auf einen zweiten, trat vor den König und sprach »Herr König, der Schneider ist wieder so übermütig geworden, er vermisst sich das ganze königliche Schloss mit allem was darin ist, los und fest, innen und außen, in Wachs abzubilden.« Der König ließ den Schneider kommen und befahl ihm das ganze königliche Schloss mit allem was darin wäre, los und fest, innen und außen, in Wachs abzubilden und wenn er es nicht zu Stande brächte, oder es fehlte nur ein Nagel an der Wand, so sollte er zeitlebens unter der Erde gefangen sitzen. Der Schneider dachte »es kommt immer ärger, das hält kein Mensch aus«, warf sein Bündel auf den Rücken und wanderte fort. Als er an den hohlen Baum kam, setzte er sich nieder und ließ den Kopf hängen. Die Bienen kamen heraus geflogen, und der Weisel fragte ihn ob er einen steifen Hals hätte, weil er den Kopf so schief hielt. »Ach nein«, antwortete der Schneider, »mich drückt etwas anderes«, und erzählte was der König von ihm gefordert hatte. Die Bienen fiengen an unter einander zu summen und zu brummen, und der Weisel sprach »geh nur wieder nach Haus, komm aber Morgen um diese Zeit wieder und bring ein großes Tuch mit, so wird alles gut gehen.« Da kehrte er wieder um, die Bienen aber flogen nach dem königlichen Schloss, geradezu in die offenen Fenster hinein, krochen in allen Ecken herum und besahen alles aufs genauste. Dann liefen sie zurück und bildeten das Schloss in Wachs nach mit einer solchen Geschwindigkeit, dass man meinte es wüchse einem vor den Augen. Schon am Abend war alles fertig, und als der Schneider am folgenden Morgen kam, so stand das ganze prächtige Gebäude da, und es fehlte kein Nagel an der Wand und keine Ziegel auf dem Dach; dabei war es zart und schneeweiß, und roch süß wie Honig. Der Schneider packte es vorsichtig in sein Tuch und brachte es dem König, der aber konnte sich nicht genug verwundern, stellte es in seinem größten Saal auf und schenkte dem Schneider dafür ein großes steinernes Haus.

Der Schuster aber ließ nicht nach, gieng zum drittenmal zu dem König und sprach »Herr König, dem Schneider ist zu Ohren gekommen dass auf dem Schlosshof kein Wasser springen will, da hat er sich vermessen es solle mitten im Hof mannshoch aufsteigen und hell sein wie Kristall.« Da ließ der König den Schneider herbei holen und sagte »wenn nicht Morgen ein Strahl von Wasser in meinem Hof springt, wie du versprochen hast, so soll dich der Scharfrichter auf demselben Hof um einen Kopf kürzer machen.« Der arme Schneider besann sich nicht lange und eilte zum Tore hinaus, und weil es ihm diesmal ans Leben gehen sollte, so rollten ihm die Tränen über die Backen herab. Indem er so voll Trauer dahin gieng, kam das Füllen herangesprungen, dem er einmal die Freiheit geschenkt hatte, und aus dem ein hübscher Brauner geworden war. »Jetzt kommt die Stunde«, sprach er zu ihm, »wo ich dir deine Guttat vergelten kann. Ich weiß schon was dir fehlt, aber es soll dir bald geholfen werden, sitz nur auf, mein Rücken kann deiner zwei tragen.« Dem Schneider kam das Herz wieder, er sprang in einem Satz auf, und das Pferd rennte in vollem Lauf zur Stadt hinein und geradezu auf den Schlosshof. Da jagte es dreimal rund herum, schnell wie der Blitz und beim drittenmal stürzte es nieder. In dem Augenblick aber krachte es furchtbar: ein Stück Erde sprang in der Mitte des Hofs wie eine Kugel in die Luft und über das Schloss hinaus, und gleich dahinter her erhob sich ein Strahl von Wasser so hoch wie Mann und Pferd, und das Wasser war so rein wie Kristall, und die Sonnenstrahlen fiengen an darauf zu tanzen. Als der König das sah, stand er vor Verwunderung auf, gieng und umarmte das Schneiderlein im Angesicht aller Menschen.

Aber das Glück dauerte nicht lang. Der König hatte Töchter genug, eine immer schöner als die andere, aber keinen Sohn. Da begab sich der boshafte Schuster zum viertenmal zu dem Könige, und sprach »Herr König, der Schneider lässt nicht ab von seinem Übermut. Jetzt hat er sich vermessen, wenn er wolle, so könne er dem Herrn König einen Sohn durch die Lüfte herbei tragen lassen.« Der König ließ den Schneider rufen und sprach »wenn du mir binnen neun Tagen einen Sohn bringen lässt, so sollst du meine älteste Tochter zur Frau haben.« »Der Lohn ist freilich groß«, dachte das Schneiderlein, »da täte man wohl ein übriges, aber die Kirschen hängen mir zu hoch: wenn ich danach steige, so bricht unter mir der Ast, und ich falle herab.« Er gieng nach Haus, setzte sich mit unterschlagenen Beinen auf seinen Arbeitstisch und bedachte sich was zu tun wäre. »Es geht nicht«, rief er endlich aus, »ich will fort, hier kann ich doch nicht in Ruhe leben.« Er schnürte sein Bündel und eilte zum Tore hinaus. Als er auf die Wiesen kam, erblickte er seinen alten Freund, den Storch, der da, wie ein Weltweiser, auf und abgieng, zuweilen still stand, einen Frosch in nähere Betrachtung nahm und ihn endlich verschluckte. Der Storch kam heran und begrüßte ihn. »Ich sehe«, hub er an, »du hast deinen Ranzen auf dem Rücken, warum willst du die Stadt verlassen?« Der Schneider erzählte ihm was der König von ihm verlangt hatte und er nicht erfüllen konnte, und jammerte über sein Missgeschick. »Lass dir darüber keine grauen Haare wachsen«, sagte der Storch, »ich will dir aus der Not helfen. Schon lange bringe ich die Wickelkinder in die Stadt, da kann ich auch einmal einen kleinen Prinzen aus dem Brunnen holen. Geh heim und verhalte dich ruhig. Heut über neun Tage begib dich in das königliche Schloss, da will ich kommen.« Das Schneiderlein gieng nach Haus und war zu rechter Zeit in dem Schloss. Nicht lange, so kam der Storch heran geflogen und klopfte ans Fenster. Der Schneider öffnete ihm, und Vetter Langbein stieg vorsichtig herein und gieng mit gravitätischen Schritten über den glatten Marmorboden; er hatte aber ein Kind im Schnabel, das schön wie ein Engel, und seine Händchen nach der Königin ausstreckte. Er legte es ihr auf den Schoß, und sie herzte und küsste es, und war vor Freude außer sich. Der Storch nahm, bevor er wieder wegflog, seine Reisetasche von der Schulter herab und überreichte sie der Königin. Es steckten Düten darin mit bunten Zuckererbsen, sie wurden unter die kleinen Prinzessinnen verteilt. Die älteste aber erhielt nichts, sondern bekam den lustigen Schneider zum Mann. »Es ist mir geradeso«, sprach der Schneider, »als wenn ich das große Los gewonnen hätte. Meine Mutter hatte doch recht, die sagte immer wer auf Gott vertraut und nur Glück hat, dem kann's nicht fehlen.«

Der Schuster musste die Schuhe machen, in welchen das Schneiderlein auf dem Hochzeitfest tanzte, hernach ward ihm befohlen die Stadt auf immer zu verlassen. Der Weg nach dem Wald führte ihn zu dem Galgen. Von Zorn, Wut und der Hitze des Tages ermüdet, warf er sich nieder. Als er die Augen zumachte und schlafen wollte, stürzten die beiden Krähen von den Köpfen der Gehenkten mit lautem Geschrei herab und hackten ihm die Augen aus. Unsinnig rannte er in den Wald und muss darin verschmachtet sein, denn es hat ihn niemand wieder gesehen oder etwas von ihm gehört.

108.

Hans mein Igel.

Es war einmal ein Bauer, der hatte Geld und Gut genung, aber wie reich er war, so fehlte doch etwas an seinem Glück: er hatte mit seiner Frau keine Kinder. Öfters, wenn er mit den andern Bauern in die Stadt gieng, spotteten sie und fragten warum er keine Kinder hätte. Da ward er endlich zornig, und als er nach Haus kam, sprach er »ich will ein Kind haben, und sollt's ein Igel sein.« Da kriegte seine Frau ein Kind, das war oben ein Igel und unten ein Junge, und als sie das Kind sah, erschrak sie und sprach »siehst du, du hast uns verwünscht.« Da sprach der Mann »was kann das alles helfen, getauft muss der Junge werden, aber wir können keinen Gevatter dazu nehmen.« Die Frau sprach »wir können ihn auch nicht anders taufen als *Hans mein Igel.*« Als er getauft war, sagte der Pfarrer »der kann wegen seiner Stacheln in kein ordentlich Bett kommen.« Da ward hinter dem Ofen ein wenig Stroh zurecht gemacht und Hans mein Igel darauf gelegt. Er konnte auch an der Mutter nicht trinken, denn er hätte sie mit seinen Stacheln gestochen. So lag er da hinter dem Ofen acht Jahre, und sein Vater war ihn müde und dachte wenn er nur stürbe; aber er starb nicht, sondern blieb da liegen. Nun trug es sich zu, dass in der Stadt ein Markt war, und der Bauer wollte hin gehen, da fragte er seine Frau, was er ihr sollte mitbringen. »Ein wenig Fleisch und ein paar Wecke, was zum Haushalt gehört« sprach sie. Darauf fragte er die Magd, die wollte ein paar Toffeln und Zwickelstrümpfe. Endlich sagte er auch »Hans mein Igel, was willst du denn haben?« »Väterchen«, sprach er, »bring mir doch einen Dudelsack mit.« Wie nun der Bauer wieder nach Haus kam, gab er der Frau, was er ihr gekauft hatte, Fleisch und Wecke, dann gab er der Magd die Toffeln und die Zwickelstrümpfe, endlich gieng er hinter den Ofen und gab dem Hans mein Igel den Dudelsack. Und wie Hans mein Igel den Dudelsack hatte, sprach er »Väterchen, geht doch vor die Schmiede und lasst mir meinen Göckelhahn beschlagen, dann will ich fortreiten und will nimmermehr wiederkommen.« Da war der Vater froh dass er ihn los werden sollte, und ließ ihm den Hahn beschlagen, und als er fertig war, setzte sich Hans mein Igel darauf, ritt fort, nahm auch Schweine und Esel mit, die wollt er draußen im Walde hüten. Im Wald aber musste der Hahn mit ihm auf einen hohen Baum fliegen, da saß er und hütete die Esel und Schweine, und saß lange Jahre bis die Herde ganz groß war, und wusste sein Vater nichts von ihm. Wenn er aber auf dem Baum saß, blies er seinen Dudelsack und machte Musik, die war sehr schön. Einmal kam ein König vorbeigefahren, der hatte sich verirrt, und hörte die Musik: da verwunderte er sich darüber und schickte seinen Bedienten hin, er sollte sich einmal umgucken wo die Musik herkäme. Er guckte sich um, sah aber nichts als ein kleines Tier auf dem Baum oben sitzen, das war wie ein Göckelhahn, auf dem ein Igel saß, und der machte die Musik. Da sprach der König zum Bedienten er sollte fragen warum er da säße, und ob er nicht wüsste wo der Weg in sein Königreich gienge. Da stieg Hans mein Igel vom Baum und sprach er wollte den Weg zeigen, wenn der König ihm wollte verschreiben und versprechen, was ihm zuerst begegnete am königlichen Hofe, sobald er nach Haus käme. Da dachte der König »das kann ich leicht tun, Hans mein Igel versteht's doch nicht, und ich kann schreiben was ich will.« Da nahm der König Feder und Dinte und schrieb etwas auf, und als es geschehen war, zeigte ihm Hans mein Igel den Weg, und er kam glücklich nach Haus. Seine Tochter aber, wie sie ihn von weitem sah, war so voll Freuden, dass sie ihm entgegen lief und ihn küsste. Da gedachte er an Hans mein Igel und erzählte ihr wie es ihm gegangen wäre, und dass er einem wunderlichen Tier hätte verschreiben sollen was ihm daheim zuerst begegnen würde, und das Tier hätte auf einem Hahn wie auf einem Pferde gesessen und schöne Musik gemacht; er hätte aber geschrieben es sollt's nicht haben, denn Hans mein Igel könnt es doch nicht lesen. Darüber war die Prinzessin froh und sagte das wäre gut, denn sie wäre doch nimmermehr hingegangen.

Hans mein Igel aber hütete die Esel und Schweine, war immer lustig, saß auf dem Baum und blies auf seinem Dudelsack. Nun geschah es, dass ein anderer König gefahren kam mit seinen Bedienten und Laufern, und hatte sich verirrt, und wusste nicht wieder nach Haus zu kommen, weil der Wald so groß war. Da hörte er gleichfalls die schöne Musik von weitem und sprach zu seinem Laufer was das wohl wäre, er sollte einmal zusehen. Da gieng der Laufer hin unter den Baum und sah den Göckelhahn sitzen und Hans mein Igel oben drauf. Der Laufer fragte ihn was er da oben vorhätte. »Ich hüte meine Esel und Schweine; aber was ist

euer Begehren?« Der Laufer sagte sie hätten sich verirrt
und könnten nicht wieder ins Königreich, ob er ihnen den
Weg nicht zeigen wollte. Da stieg Hans mein Igel mit dem
Hahn vom Baum herunter, und sagte zu dem alten König
er wolle ihm den Weg zeigen, wenn er ihm zu eigen geben
wollte was ihm zu Haus vor seinem königlichen Schlosse
das erste begegnen würde. Der König sagte »ja« und unterschrieb sich dem Hans mein Igel, er sollte es haben. Als das
geschehen war ritt er auf dem Göckelhahn voraus und
zeigte ihm den Weg, und gelangte der König glücklich wieder in sein Reich. Wie er auf den Hof kam, war große Freude darüber. Nun hatte er eine einzige Tochter, die war sehr
schön, die lief ihm entgegen, fiel ihm um den Hals und
küsste ihn und freute sich dass ihr alter Vater wieder kam.
Sie fragte ihn auch wo er so lange in der Welt gewesen
wäre, da erzählte er ihr er hätte sich verirrt und wäre beinahe gar nicht wieder gekommen, aber als er durch einen
großen Wald gefahren wäre, hätte einer, halb wie ein Igel,
halb wie ein Mensch, rittlings auf einem Hahn in einem hohen Baum gesessen, und schöne Musik gemacht, der hätte
ihm fortgeholfen und den Weg gezeigt, er aber hätte ihm
dafür versprochen was ihm am königlichen Hofe zuerst begegnete, und das wäre sie, und das täte ihm nun so leid. Da
versprach sie ihm aber sie wollte gerne mit ihm gehen wann
er käme, ihrem alten Vater zu Liebe.
Hans mein Igel aber hütete seine Schweine, und die
Schweine bekamen wieder Schweine, und wurden ihrer so
viel, dass der ganze Wald voll war. Da wollte Hans mein
Igel nicht länger im Walde leben, und ließ seinem Vater sagen sie sollten alle Ställe im Dorf räumen, denn er käme mit
einer so großen Herde, dass jeder schlachten könnte, der
nur schlachten wollte. Da war sein Vater betrübt, als er das
hörte, denn er dachte Hans mein Igel wäre schon lange gestorben. Hans mein Igel aber setzte sich auf seinen Göckelhahn, trieb die Schweine vor sich her ins Dorf, und ließ
schlachten; hu! da war ein Gemetzel und ein Hacken, dass

man's zwei Stunden weit hören konnte. Danach sagte Hans
mein Igel »Väterchen, lasst mir meinen Göckelhahn noch
einmal vor der Schmiede beschlagen, dann reit ich fort und
komme mein Lebtag nicht wieder.« Da ließ der Vater den
Göckelhahn beschlagen und war froh dass Hans mein Igel
nicht wieder kommen wollte.

Hans mein Igel ritt fort in das erste Königreich, da hatte
der König befohlen wenn einer käme auf einem Hahn geritten, und hätte einen Dudelsack bei sich, dann sollten alle
auf ihn schießen, hauen und stechen, damit er nicht ins
Schloss käme. Als nun Hans mein Igel daher geritten kam,
drangen sie mit den Bajonetten auf ihn ein, aber er gab dem
Hahn die Sporn, flog auf, über das Tor hin vor des Königs
Fenster, ließ sich da nieder, und rief ihm zu er sollt ihm geben was er versprochen hätte, sonst so wollt er ihm und
seiner Tochter das Leben nehmen. Da gab der König seiner
Tochter gute Worte, sie möchte zu ihm hinaus gehen, damit
sie ihm und sich das Leben rettete. Da zog sie sich weiß an,
und ihr Vater gab ihr einen Wagen mit sechs Pferden und
herrliche[n] Bedienten, Geld und Gut. Sie setzte sich ein,
und Hans mein Igel mit seinem Hahn und Dudelsack neben sie, dann nahmen sie Abschied und zogen fort, und der
König dachte er kriegte sie nicht wieder zu sehen. Es gieng
aber anders als er dachte, denn als sie ein Stück Wegs von
der Stadt waren, da zog ihr Hans mein Igel die schönen
Kleider aus, und stach sie mit seiner Igelhaut bis sie ganz
blutig war, sagte »das ist der Lohn für eure Falschheit, geh
hin, ich will dich nicht«, und jagte sie damit nach Haus,
und war sie beschimpft ihr Lebtag.

Hans mein Igel aber ritt weiter auf seinem Göckelhahn und
mit seinem Dudelsack nach dem zweiten Königreich, wo er
dem König auch den Weg gezeigt hatte. Der aber hatte bestellt, wenn einer käme, wie Hans mein Igel, sollten sie das
Gewehr präsentieren, ihn frei hereinführen, Vivat rufen,
und ihn ins königliche Schloss bringen. Wie ihn nun die
Königstochter sah, war sie erschrocken, weil er doch gar zu

wunderlich aussah, sie dachte aber es wäre nicht anders, sie hätte es ihrem Vater versprochen. Da ward Hans mein Igel von ihr bewillkommt, und ward mit ihr vermählt, und er musste mit an die königliche Tafel gehen, und sie setzte sich zu seiner Seite, und sie aßen und tranken. Wie's nun Abend ward, dass sie wollten schlafen gehen, da fürchtete sie sich sehr vor seinen Stacheln: er aber sprach, sie sollte sich nicht fürchten, es geschähe ihr kein Leid, und sagte zu dem alten König, er sollte vier Mann bestellen, die sollten wachen vor der Kammertüre und ein großes Feuer anmachen, und wann er in die Kammer eingienge und sich ins Bett legen wollte, würde er aus seiner Igelshaut herauskriechen und sie vor dem Bett liegen lassen: dann sollten die Männer hurtig herbeispringen und sie ins Feuer werfen, auch dabei bleiben, bis sie vom Feuer verzehrt wäre. Wie die Glocke nun elfe schlug, da gieng er in die Kammer, streifte die Igelshaut ab, und ließ sie vor dem Bette liegen: da kamen die Männer und holten sie geschwind und warfen sie ins Feuer; und als sie das Feuer verzehrt hatte, da war er erlöst, und lag da im Bett ganz als ein Mensch gestaltet, aber er war kohlschwarz wie gebrannt. Der König schickte zu seinem Arzt, der wusch ihn mit guten Salben und balsamierte ihn, da ward er weiß, und war ein schöner junger Herr. Wie das die Königstochter sah, war sie froh, und am andern Morgen stiegen sie mit Freuden auf, aßen und tranken, und ward die Vermählung erst recht gefeiert, und Hans mein Igel bekam das Königreich von dem alten König.

Wie etliche Jahre herum waren, fuhr er mit seiner Gemahlin zu seinem Vater und sagte er wäre sein Sohn; der Vater aber sprach er hätte keinen, er hätte nur einen gehabt, der wäre aber wie ein Igel mit Stacheln geboren worden, und wäre in die Welt gegangen. Da gab er sich zu erkennen, und der alte Vater freute sich und gieng mit ihm in sein Königreich.

Mein Märchen ist aus,
und geht vor Gustchen sein Haus.

109.

Das Totenhemdchen.

Es hatte eine Mutter ein Büblein von sieben Jahren, das war so schön und lieblich, dass es niemand ansehen konnte ohne ihm gut zu sein, und sie hatte es auch lieber als alles auf der Welt. Nun geschah es, dass es plötzlich krank ward, und der liebe Gott es zu sich nahm; darüber konnte sich die Mutter nicht trösten und weinte Tag und Nacht. Bald darauf aber, nachdem es begraben war, zeigte sich das Kind Nachts an den Plätzen, wo es sonst im Leben gesessen und gespielt hatte; weinte die Mutter, so weinte es auch, und wenn der Morgen kam, war es verschwunden. Als aber die Mutter gar nicht aufhören wollte zu weinen, kam es in einer Nacht mit seinem weißen Totenhemdchen, in welchem es in den Sarg gelegt war, und mit dem Kränzchen auf dem Kopf, setzte sich zu ihren Füßen auf das Bett und sprach »ach Mutter, höre doch auf zu weinen, sonst kann ich in meinem Sarge nicht einschlafen, denn mein Totenhemdchen wird nicht trocken von deinen Tränen, die alle darauf fallen.« Da erschrak die Mutter, als sie das hörte, und weinte nicht mehr. Und in der andern Nacht kam das Kindchen wieder, hielt in der Hand ein Lichtchen und sagte »siehst du, nun ist mein Hemdchen bald trocken, und ich habe Ruhe in meinem Grab.« Da befahl die Mutter dem lieben Gott ihr Leid und ertrug es still und geduldig, und das Kind kam nicht wieder, sondern schlief in seinem unterirdischen Bettchen.

110

Der Jude im Dorn.

Es war einmal ein reicher Mann, der hatte einen Knecht, der diente ihm fleißig und redlich, war alle Morgen der erste aus dem Bett und Abends der letzte hinein, und wenn's eine saure Arbeit gab, wo keiner anpacken wollte, so stellte er sich immer zuerst daran. Dabei klagte er nicht, sondern war mit allem zufrieden, und war immer lustig. Als sein Jahr herum war, gab ihm der Herr keinen Lohn und dachte »das ist das gescheitste, so spare ich etwas, und er geht mir nicht weg, sondern bleibt hübsch im Dienst.« Der Knecht schwieg auch still, tat das zweite Jahr wie das erste seine Arbeit, und als er am Ende desselben abermals keinen Lohn bekam, ließ er sich's gefallen und blieb noch länger. Als auch das dritte Jahr herum war, bedachte sich der Herr, griff in die Tasche, holte aber nichts heraus. Da fieng der Knecht endlich an und sprach »Herr, ich habe euch drei Jahre redlich gedient, seid so gut und gebt mir, was mir von Rechtswegen zukommt: ich wollte fort und mich gerne weiter in der Welt umsehen.« Da antwortete der Geizhals »ja, mein lieber Knecht, du hast mir unverdrossen gedient, dafür sollst du mildiglich belohnet werden«, griff abermals in die Tasche und zählte dem Knecht drei Heller einzeln auf, »da hast du für jedes Jahr einen Heller, das ist ein großer und reichlicher Lohn, wie du ihn bei wenigen Herrn empfangen hättest.« Der gute Knecht, der vom Geld wenig verstand, strich sein Kapital ein und dachte »nun hast du vollauf in der Tasche, was willst du sorgen und dich mit schwerer Arbeit länger plagen.«

Da zog er fort, bergauf, bergab, sang und sprang nach Herzenslust. Nun trug es sich zu, als er an ein[em] Buschwerk vorüber kam, dass ein kleines Männchen hervortrat und ihn anrief »wo hinaus, Bruder Lustig? ich sehe du trägst nicht schwer an deinen Sorgen.« »Was soll ich traurig sein«, ant-

wortete der Knecht, »ich habe vollauf, der Lohn von drei
Jahren klingelt in meiner Tasche.« »Wie viel ist denn deines
Schatzes?« fragte ihn das Männchen. »Wie viel? drei bare
Heller, richtig gezählt.« »Höre«, sagte der Zwerg, »ich bin
ein armer bedürftiger Mann, schenke mir deine drei Heller:
ich kann nichts mehr arbeiten, du aber bist jung und kannst
dir dein Brot leicht verdienen.« Und weil der Knecht ein
gutes Herz hatte und Mitleid mit dem Männchen fühlte, so
reichte er ihm seine drei Heller und sprach »in Gottes Namen, es wird mir doch nicht fehlen.« Da sprach das Männchen »weil du dein gutes Herz sehe, so gewähre ich dir
drei Wünsche, für jeden Heller einen, die sollen dir in Erfüllung gehen.« »Aha«, sprach der Knecht, »du bist einer,
der blau pfeifen kann. Wohlan, wenn's doch sein soll, so
wünsche ich mir erstlich ein Vogelrohr, das alles trifft, wonach ich ziele: zweitens eine Fidel, wenn ich darauf streiche, so muss alles tanzen, was den Klang hört: und drittens,
wenn ich an jemand eine Bitte tue, so darf er sie nicht abschlagen.« »Das sollst du alles haben« sprach das Männchen, griff in den Busch, und, denk einer, da lag schon Fidel und Vogelrohr in Bereitschaft, als wenn sie bestellt
wären. Er gab sie dem Knecht und sprach »was du dir immer erbitten wirst, kein Mensch auf der Welt soll dir's abschlagen.«

»Herz, was begehrst du nun?« sprach der Knecht zu sich
selber und zog lustig weiter. Bald darauf begegnete er einem Juden mit einem langen Ziegenbart, der stand und
horchte auf den Gesang eines Vogels, der hoch oben in der
Spitze eines Baumes saß. »Gottes Wunder!« rief er aus, »so
ein kleines Tier hat so eine grausam mächtige Stimme!
wenn's doch mein wäre! wer ihm doch Salz auf den
Schwanz streuen könnte!« »Wenn's weiter nichts ist«,
sprach der Knecht, »der Vogel soll bald herunter sein«, legte an und traf aufs Haar, und der Vogel fiel herab in die
Dornhecken. »Geh, Spitzbub«, sagte er zum Juden, »und
hol dir den Vogel heraus.« »Mein«, sprach der Jude, »lass

der Herr den Bub weg, so kommt ein Hund gelaufen; ich will mir den Vogel auflesèn, weil ihr ihn doch einmal getroffen habt«, legte sich auf die Erde und fieng an sich in den Busch hinein zu arbeiten. Wie er nun mitten in dem Dorn steckte, plagte der Mutwille den guten Knecht, dass er seine Fidel abnahm und anfieng zu geigen. Gleich fieng auch der Jude an die Beine zu heben und in die Höhe zu springen: und je mehr der Knecht strich, desto besser gieng der Tanz. Aber die Dörner zerrissen ihm den schäbigen Rock, kämmten ihm den Ziegenbart und stachen und zwickten ihn am ganzen Leib. »Mein«, rief der Jude, »was soll mir das Geigen! lass der Herr das Geigen, ich begehre nicht zu tanzen.« Aber der Knecht hörte nicht darauf und dachte »du hast die Leute genug geschunden, nun soll dir's die Dornhecke nicht besser machen«, und fieng von neuem an zu geigen, dass der Jude immer höher aufspringen musste, und die Fetzen von seinem Rock an den Stacheln hängen blieben. »Au weih geschrien!« rief der Jude, »geb ich doch dem Herrn, was er verlangt, wenn er nur das Geigen lässt, einen ganzen Beutel mit Gold.« »Wenn du so spendabel bist«, sprach der Knecht, »so will ich wohl mit meiner Musik aufhören, aber das muss ich dir nachrühmen, du machst deinen Tanz noch mit, dass es eine Art hat«, nahm darauf den Beutel und gieng seiner Wege.

Der Jude blieb stehen und sah ihm nach und war still bis der Knecht weit weg und ihm ganz aus den Augen war, dann schrie er aus Leibeskräften, »du miserabler Musikant, du Bierfiedler: wart, wenn ich dich allein erwische! ich will dich jagen, dass du die Schuhsohlen verlieren sollst: du Lump, steck einen Groschen ins Maul, dass du sechs Heller wert bist«, und schimpfte weiter was er nur los bringen konnte. Und als er sich damit etwas zu Gute getan und Luft gemacht hatte, lief er in die Stadt zum Richter. »Herr Richter, au weih geschrien! seht wie mich auf offener Landstraße ein gottloser Mensch beraubt und übel zugerichtet hat: ein Stein auf dem Erdboden möcht sich erbarmen: die

Kleider zerfetzt! der Leib zerstochen und zerkratzt! mein
bisschen Armut samt dem Beutel genommen! lauter Dukaten, ein Stück schöner als das andere: um Gotteswillen,
lasst den Menschen ins Gefängnis werfen.« Sprach der
Richter »war's ein Soldat, der dich mit seinem Säbel so zugerichtet hat?« »Gott bewahr!« sagte der Jude, »einen
nackten Degen hat er nicht gehabt, aber ein Rohr hat er gehabt auf dem Buckel hängen und eine Geige am Hals; der
Bösewicht ist leicht zu erkennen.« Der Richter schickte seine Leute nach ihm aus, die fanden den guten Knecht, der
ganz langsam weiter gezogen war, und fanden auch den
Beutel mit Gold bei ihm. Als er vor Gericht gestellt wurde,
sagte er »ich habe den Juden nicht angerührt und ihm das
Geld nicht genommen, er hat mir's aus freien Stücken ange-
boten, damit ich nur aufhörte zu geigen, weil er meine Musik nicht vertragen konnte.« »Gott bewahr!« schrie der
Jude, »der greift die Lügen wie Fliegen an der Wand.« Aber
der Richter glaubte es auch nicht und sprach »das ist eine
schlechte Entschuldigung, das tut kein Jude«, und verurteilte den guten Knecht, weil er auf offener Straße einen
Raub begangen hätte, zum Galgen. Als er aber abgeführt
ward, schrie ihm noch der Jude zu »du Bärenhäuter, du
Hundemusikant, jetzt kriegst du deinen wohlverdienten
Lohn.« Der Knecht stieg ganz ruhig mit dem Henker die
Leiter hinauf, auf der letzten Sprosse aber drehte er sich um
und sprach zum Richter »gewährt mir noch eine Bitte, eh
ich sterbe.« »Ja«, sprach der Richter, »wenn du nicht um
dein Leben bittest.« »Nicht ums Leben«, antwortete der
Knecht, »ich bitte, lasst mich zu guter Letzt noch einmal
auf meiner Geige spielen.« Der Jude erhob ein Zetterge-
schrei, »um Gotteswillen, erlaubt's nicht, erlaubt's nicht.«
Allein der Richter sprach »warum soll ich ihm die kurze
Freude nicht gönnen: es ist ihm zugestanden, und dabei soll
es sein Bewenden haben.« Auch konnte er es ihm nicht abschlagen wegen der Gabe, die dem Knecht verliehen war.
Der Jude aber rief »au weih! au weih! bindet mich an, bin-

det mich fest.« Da nahm der gute Knecht seine Geige vom Hals, legte sie zurecht, und wie er den ersten Strich tat, fieng alles an zu wabern und zu wanken, der Richter, die Schreiber, und die Gerichtsdiener: und der Strick fiel dem aus der Hand, der den Juden fest binden wollte: beim zweiten Strich hoben alle die Beine, und der Henker ließ den guten Knecht los und machte sich zum Tanze fertig: bei dem dritten Strich sprang alles in die Höhe und fieng an zu tanzen, und der Richter und der Jude waren vorn und sprangen am besten. Bald tanzte alles mit, was auf den Markt aus Neugierde herbei gekommen war, alte und junge, dicke und magere Leute untereinander: sogar die Hunde, die mitgelaufen waren, setzten sich auf die Hinterfüße und hüpften mit. Und je länger er spielte, desto höher sprangen die Tänzer, dass sie sich einander an die Köpfe stießen und anfiengen jämmerlich zu schreien. Endlich rief der Richter ganz außer Atem, »ich schenke dir dein Leben, höre nur auf zu geigen.« Der gute Knecht ließ sich bewegen, setzte die Geige ab, hing sie wieder um den Hals und stieg die Leiter herab. Da trat er zu dem Juden, der auf der Erde lag und nach Atem schnappte, und sagte »Spitzbube, jetzt gesteh wo du das Geld hast, oder ich nehme meine Geige vom Hals und fange wieder an zu spielen.« »Ich hab's gestohlen, ich hab's gestohlen«, schrie er, »du aber hast's redlich verdient.« Da ließ der Richter den Juden zum Galgen führen und als einen Dieb aufhängen.

111.

Der gelernte Jäger.

Es war einmal ein junger Bursch, der hatte die Schlosserhantierung gelernt und sprach zu seinem Vater er wollte jetzt in die Welt gehen und sich versuchen. »Ja«, sagte der

Vater, »das bin ich zufrieden« und gab ihm etwas Geld auf die Reise. Also zog er herum und suchte Arbeit. Auf eine Zeit, da wollt ihm das Schlosserwerk nicht mehr folgen und stand ihm auch nicht mehr an, aber er kriegte Lust zur Jägerei. Da begegnete ihm auf der Wanderschaft ein Jäger in grünem Kleide, der fragte wo er her käme und wo er hin wollte. Er wär ein Schlossergesell, sagte der Bursch, aber das Handwerk gefiele ihm nicht mehr, und hätte Lust zur Jägerei, ob er ihn als Lehrling annehmen wollte. »O ja, wenn du mit mir gehen willst.« Da gieng der junge Bursch mit, vermietete sich etliche Jahre bei ihm und lernte die Jägerei. Danach wollte er sich weiter versuchen, und der Jäger gab ihm nichts zum Lohn als eine Windbüchse, die hatte aber die Eigenschaft, wenn er damit einen Schuss tat, so traf er ohnfehlbar. Da gieng er fort und kam in einen sehr großen Wald, von dem konnte er in einem Tag das Ende nicht finden. Wie's Abend war, setzte er sich auf einen hohen Baum, damit er aus den wilden Tieren käme. Gegen Mitternacht zu, däuchte ihn, schimmerte ein kleines Lichtchen von weitem, da sah er durch die Äste darauf hin und behielt in acht wo es war. Doch nahm er erst noch seinen Hut und warf ihn nach dem Licht zu herunter, dass er danach gehen wollte, wann er herabgestiegen wäre, als nach einem Zeichen. Nun kletterte er herunter, gieng auf seinen Hut los, setzte ihn wieder auf und zog gerades Wegs fort. Je weiter er gieng, je größer ward das Licht, und wie er nahe dabei kam, sah er dass es ein gewaltiges Feuer war, und saßen drei Riesen dabei und hatten einen Ochsen am Spieß und ließen ihn braten. Nun sprach der eine »ich muss doch schmecken ob das Fleisch bald zu essen ist«, riss ein Stück herab und wollt es in den Mund stecken, aber der Jäger schoss es ihm aus der Hand. »Nun ja«, sprach der Riese, »da weht mir der Wind das Stück aus der Hand« und nahm sich ein anderes. Wie er eben anbeißen wollte, schoss es ihm der Jäger abermals weg; da gab der Riese dem, der neben ihm saß, eine Ohrfeige und rief zornig »was reißt du mir mein Stück weg?« »Ich habe es nicht weggerissen«, sprach der andere, »es wird dir's ein Scharfschütz weggeschossen haben.« Der Riese nahm sich das dritte Stück, konnte es aber nicht in der Hand behalten, der Jäger schoss es ihm heraus. Da sprachen die Riesen »das muss ein guter Schütze sein, der den Bissen vor dem Maul wegschießt, so einer wäre uns nützlich«, und riefen laut »komm herbei, du Scharfschütze, setze dich zu uns ans Feuer und iss dich satt, wir wollen dir nichts tun; aber kommst du nicht, und wir holen dich mit Gewalt, so bist du verloren.« Da trat der Bursch herzu und sagte er wäre ein gelernter Jäger, und wonach er mit seiner Büchse ziele, das treffe er auch sicher und gewiss. Da sprachen sie wenn er mit ihnen gehen wollte, sollte er's gut haben, und erzählten ihm vor dem Wald sei ein großes Wasser, dahinter ständ ein Turm, und in dem Turm säß eine schöne Königstochter, die wollten sie gern rauben. »Ja«, sprach er, »die will ich bald geschafft haben.« Sagten sie weiter »es ist aber noch etwas dabei, es liegt ein kleines Hündchen dort, das fängt gleich an zu bellen, wann sich jemand nähert, und sobald das bellt, wacht auch alles am königlichen Hofe auf: und deshalb können wir nicht hinein kommen; unterstehst du dich das Hündchen tot zu schießen?« »Ja«, sprach er, »das ist mir ein kleiner Spaß.« Danach setzte er sich auf ein Schiff und fuhr über das Wasser, und wie er bald beim Land war, kam das Hündlein gelaufen und wollte bellen, aber er kriegte seine Windbüchse und schoss es tot. Wie die Riesen das sahen, freuten sie sich und meinten sie hätten die Königstochter schon gewiss, aber der Jäger wollte erst sehen wie die Sache beschaffen war, und sprach sie sollten haußen bleiben, bis er sie riefe. Da gieng er in das Schloss, und es war mäuschenstill darin, und schlief alles. Wie er das erste Zimmer aufmachte, hieng da ein Säbel an der Wand, der war von purem Silber, und war ein goldener Stern darauf und des Königs Name; daneben aber lag auf einem Tisch ein versiegelter Brief, den brach er auf, und es stand darin wer den Säbel hätte, könnte

alles ums Leben bringen, was ihm vorkäme. Da nahm er
den Säbel von der Wand, hieng ihn um und gieng weiter: da
kam er in das Zimmer, wo die Königstochter lag und
schlief: und sie war so schön, dass er still stand und sie betrachtete und den Atem anhielt. Er dachte bei sich selbst
»wie darf ich eine unschuldige Jungfrau in die Gewalt der
wilden Riesen bringen, die haben Böses im Sinn.« Er
schaute sich weiter um, da standen unter dem Bett ein paar
Pantoffeln, auf dem rechten stand ihres Vaters Name mit
einem Stern und auf dem linken ihr eigener Name mit einem Stern. Sie hatte auch ein großes Halstuch um, von Seide mit Gold ausgestickt, auf der rechten Seite ihres Vaters
Name, auf der linken ihr Name, alles mit goldenen Buch-
staben. Da nahm der Jäger eine Schere und schnitt den
rechten Schlippen ab und tat ihn in seinen Ranzen, und
dann nahm er auch den rechten Pantoffel mit des Königs
Namen und steckte ihn hinein. Nun lag die Jungfrau noch
immer und schlief, und sie war ganz in ihr Hemd einge-
näht: da schnitt er auch ein Stückchen von dem Hemd ab
und steckte es zu dem andern, doch tat er das alles ohne sie
anzurühren. Dann gieng er fort und ließ sie ungestört
schlafen, und als er wieder ans Tor kam, standen die Riesen
noch draußen, warteten auf ihn und dachten er würde die
Königstochter bringen. Er rief ihnen aber zu sie sollten
herein kommen, die Jungfrau wäre schon in seiner Gewalt:
die Türe könnte er ihnen aber nicht aufmachen, aber da
wäre ein Loch, durch welches sie kriechen müssten. Nun
kam der erste näher, da wickelte der Jäger des Riesen Haar
um seine Hand, zog den Kopf herein und hieb ihn mit seinem Säbel in einem Streich ab, und duns (zog) ihn dann
vollends hinein. Dann rief er den zweiten und hieb ihm
gleichfalls das Haupt ab, und endlich auch dem dritten, und
war froh dass er die schöne Jungfrau von ihren Feinden befreit hatte und schnitt ihnen die Zungen aus und steckte sie
in seinen Ranzen. Da dachte er »ich will heim gehen zu
meinem Vater und ihm zeigen was ich schon getan habe,

dann will ich in der Welt herum ziehen; das Glück, das mir
Gott bescheren will, wird mich schon erreichen.«

Der König in dem Schloss aber, als er aufwachte, erblickte er
die drei Riesen, die da tot lagen. Dann gieng er in die Schlafkammer seiner Tochter, weckte sie auf und fragte wer das
wohl gewesen wäre, der die Riesen ums Leben gebracht hätte. Da sagte sie »lieber Vater, ich weiß es nicht, ich habe geschlafen.« Wie sie nun aufstand und ihre Pantoffeln anziehen wollte, da war der rechte weg, und wie sie ihr Halstuch
betrachtete, war es durchschnitten und fehlte der rechte
Schlippen, und wie sie ihr Hemd ansah, war ein Stückchen
heraus. Der König ließ den ganzen Hof zusammen kommen, Soldaten und alles, was da war, und fragte wer seine
Tochter befreit und die Riesen ums Leben gebracht hätte?
Nun hatte er einen Hauptmann, der war einäugig und ein
hässlicher Mensch, der sagte er hätte es getan. Da sprach der
alte König so er das vollbracht hätte, sollte er seine Tochter
auch heiraten. Die Jungfrau aber sagte »lieber Vater, dafür,
dass ich den heiraten soll, will ich lieber in die Welt gehen, so
weit als mich meine Beine tragen.« Da sprach der König
wenn sie den nicht heiraten wollte, sollte sie die königlichen
Kleider ausziehen und Bauernkleider antun und fortgehen;
und sie sollte zu einem Töpfer gehen und einen Handel mit
irdenem Geschirr anfangen. Da tat sie ihre königlichen Kleider aus und gieng zu einem Töpfer und borgte sich einen
Kram irden Werk; sie versprach ihm auch, wenn sie's am
Abend verkauft hätte, wollte sie es bezahlen. Nun sagte der
König sie sollte sich an eine Ecke damit setzen und es verkaufen, dann bestellte er etliche Bauernwagen, die sollten
mitten durchfahren, dass alles in tausend Stücke gienge. Wie
nun die Königstochter ihren Kram auf die Straße hingestellt
hatte, kamen die Wagen und zerbrachen ihn zu lauter Scherben. Sie fieng an zu weinen und sprach »ach Gott, wie will
ich nun dem Töpfer bezahlen.« Der König aber hatte sie damit zwingen wollen den Hauptmann zu heiraten, statt dessen gieng sie wieder zum Töpfer und fragte ihn ob er ihr

noch einmal borgen wollte. Er antwortete nein, sie sollte erst das Vorige bezahlen. Da gieng sie zu ihrem Vater, schrie und jammerte, und sagte sie wollte in die Welt hineingehen. Da sprach er »ich will dir draußen in dem Wald ein Häuschen bauen lassen, darin sollst du dein Lebtag sitzen und für jedermann kochen, du darfst aber kein Geld nehmen.« Als das Häuschen fertig war, ward vor die Türe ein Schild gehängt, darauf stand geschrieben »heute umsonst, morgen für Geld«. Da saß sie lange Zeit, und sprach es sich in der Welt herum, da säße eine Jungfrau, die kochte umsonst, und das stände vor der Türe an einem Schild. Das hörte auch der Jäger und dachte »das wär etwas für dich, du bist doch arm und hast kein Geld.« Er nahm also seine Windbüchse und seinen Ranzen, worin noch alles steckte, was er damals im Schloss als Wahrzeichen mitgenommen hatte, gieng in den Wald und fand auch das Häuschen mit dem Schild »heute umsonst, morgen für Geld«. Er hatte aber den Degen umhängen, womit er den drei Riesen den Kopf abgehauen hatte, trat so in das Häuschen hinein und ließ sich etwas zu essen geben. Er freute sich über das schöne Mädchen, es war aber auch bildschön. Sie fragte wo er her käme und hin wollte, da sagte er »ich reise in der Welt herum.« Da fragte sie ihn wo er den Degen her hätte, da stände ja ihres Vaters Name darauf. Fragte er ob sie des Königs Tochter wäre. »Ja«, antwortete sie. »Mit diesem Säbel«, sprach er, »habe ich drei Riesen den Kopf abgehauen« und holte zum Zeichen ihre Zungen aus dem Ranzen, dann zeigte er ihr auch den Pantoffel, den Schlippen vom Halstuch und das Stück vom Hemd. Da war sie voll Freude und sagte er wäre derjenige der sie erlöst hätte. Darauf giengen sie zusammen zum alten König und holten ihn herbei, und sie führte ihn in ihre Kammer und sagte ihm der Jäger wäre der rechte, der sie von den Riesen erlöst hätte. Und wie der alte König die Wahrzeichen alle sah, da konnte er nicht mehr zweifeln und sagte es wäre ihm lieb dass er wüsste wie alles zugegangen wäre, und er sollte sie nun auch zur Gemahlin haben; darüber freute sich die Jungfrau von Herzen. Darauf kleideten sie ihn, als wenn er ein fremder Herr wäre, und der König ließ ein Gastmahl anstellen. Als sie nun zu Tisch giengen, kam der Hauptmann auf die linke Seite der Königstochter zu sitzen, der Jäger aber auf die rechte: und der Hauptmann meinte das wäre ein fremder Herr und wäre zum Besuch gekommen. Wie sie gegessen und getrunken hatten, sprach der alte König zum Hauptmann er wollte ihm etwas aufgeben, das sollte er erraten: wenn einer spräche er hätte drei Riesen ums Leben gebracht, und er gefragt würde, wo die Zungen der Riesen wären, und er müsste zusehen, und wären keine in ihren Köpfen, wie das zugienge? Da sagte der Hauptmann »sie werden keine gehabt haben.« »Nicht so«, sagte der König, »jedes Getier hat eine Zunge«, und fragte weiter was der wert wäre, dass ihm widerführe? Antwortete der Hauptmann »der gehört in Stücken zerrissen zu werden.« Da sagte der König er hätte sich selber sein Urteil gesprochen, und ward der Hauptmann gefänglich gesetzt und dann in vier Stücke zerrissen, die Königstochter aber mit dem Jäger vermählt. Danach holte er seinen Vater und seine Mutter herbei, und die lebten in Freude bei ihrem Sohn, und nach des alten Königs Tod bekam er das Reich.

112.

Der Dreschflegel vom Himmel.

Es zog einmal ein Bauer mit einem Paar Ochsen zum Pflügen aus. Als er auf den Acker kam, da fiengen den beiden Tieren die Hörner an zu wachsen, wuchsen fort, und als er nach Haus wollte, waren sie so groß, dass er nicht mit zum Tor hinein konnte. Zu gutem Glück kam gerade ein Metzger daher, dem überließ er sie, und schlossen sie den Handel dergestalt, dass er sollte dem Metzger ein Maß Rübsamen bringen, der wollt ihm dann für jedes Korn einen brabanter

Taler aufzählen. Das heiß ich gut verkauft! Der Bauer gieng
nun heim, und trug das Maß Rübsamen auf dem Rücken
herbei; unterwegs verlor er aber aus dem Sack ein Körnchen.
Der Metzger bezahlte ihn wie gehandelt war richtig aus; hätte der Bauer das Korn nicht verloren, so hätte er einen brabanter Taler mehr gehabt. Indessen, wie er wieder des Wegs
zurück kam, war aus dem Korn ein Baum gewachsen, der
reichte bis an den Himmel. Da dachte der Bauer »weil die
Gelegenheit da ist, musst du doch sehen, was die Engel da
droben machen, und ihnen einmal unter die Augen gucken.«
Also stieg er hinauf und sah dass die Engel oben Hafer droschen und schaute das mit an; wie er so schaute, merkte er,
dass der Baum, worauf er stand, anfieng zu wackeln, guckte
hinunter und sah dass ihn eben einer umhauen wollte.
»Wenn du da herab stürztest, das wär ein böses Ding« dachte er, und in der Not wusst er sich nicht besser zu helfen, als
dass er die Spreu vom Hafer nahm, die haufenweis da lag,
und daraus einen Strick drehte: auch griff er nach einer Hacke und einem Dreschflegel, die da herum im Himmel lagen,
und ließ sich auf dem Seil herunter. Er kam aber unten auf
der Erde gerade in ein tiefes tiefes Loch, und da war es ein
rechtes Glück, dass er die Hacke hatte, denn er hackte sich
damit eine Treppe, stieg in die Höhe und brachte den
Dreschflegel zum Wahrzeichen mit, so dass niemand an seiner Erzählung mehr zweifeln konnte.

113.

De beiden Künigeskinner.

Et was mol en Künig west, de hadde en kleinen Jungen kregen, in den sin Teiken (Zeichen) hadde stahn, he sull von einen Hirsch ümmebracht weren, wenn he sestein Johr alt
wäre. Ase he nu so wit anewassen was, do giengen de Jä-

gers mol mit ünne up de Jagd. In den Holte, do kümmt de
Künigssohn bie de anneren denne (von den andern weg),
up einmol süht he do ein grooten Hirsch, den wull he
scheiten, he kunn en awerst nig dreppen; up't lest is de
Hirsch so lange für ünne herut laupen, bis gans ut den Holte, do steiht do up einmol so ein grot lank Mann stad des
Hirsches, de segd »nu dat is gut, dat ik dik hewe; ik hewe
schon sess paar gleserne Schlitschau hinner die caput jaget
un hewe dik nig kriegen könnt.« Do nümmet he ün mit sik
un schlippet em dür ein grot Water bis für en grot Künigsschlott, da mut he mit an 'n Disk un eten wat. Ase se tosammen wat geeten hed, segd de Künig »ik hewe drei
Döchter, bie der öl[l]esten musst du en Nacht waken, von
des Obends niegen Uhr bis Morgen sesse, un ik kumme je-
desmol, wenn de Klocke schlätt, sülwens un rope, un wenn
du mie dann kine Antwort givst, so werst du Morgen ümmebracht, wenn du awerst mie immer Antwort givst, so
salst du se tor Frugge hewen.« Ase do die jungen Lude up
de Schlopkammer kämen, do stund der en steineren Christoffel, do segd de Künigsdochter to emme »um niegen
Uhr kummet min Teite (Vater), alle Stunne bis en dreie
schlätt, wenn he froget, so giwet gi em Antwort statt des
Künigssuhns.« Do nickede de steinerne Christoffel mit den
Koppe gans schwinne un dann jümmer lanksamer, bis he to
leste wier stille stand. Den anneren Morgen, da segd de Künig to emme »du hest dine Sacken gut macket, awerst mine
Dochter kann ik nig hergiewen, du möstest dann en Nacht
bie de tweiden Dochter wacken, dann will ik mie mal drup
bedenken, ob du mine ölleste Dochter tor Frugge hewen
kannst; awerst ik kumme olle Stunne sülwenst, un wenn ik
die rope, so antworte mie, un wenn ik die rope und du antwortest nig, so soll fleiten din Blaud für mie.« Un do gen-
gen de beiden up de Schlopkammer, do stand do noch en
gröteren steineren Christoffel, dato segd de Künigsdochter »wenn min Teite frögt, so antworte du.« Do nickede
de grote steinerne Christoffel wier mit den Koppe gans

schwinne un dann jümmer lanksamer bis he to leste wier
stille stand. Un de Künigssohn legte sik up den Dörsüll
(Türschwelle), legte de Hand unner den Kopp un schläp
inne. Den anneren Morgen seh de Künig to ünne »du hast
dine Sacken twaren gut macket, awerst mine Dochter kann
ik nig hergiewen, du möstest süs bie der jungesten Künigsdochter en Nacht wacken, dann will ik mie bedenken, ob
du mine tweide Dochter tor Frugge hewen kannst; awerst
ik kumme olle Stunne sülwenst un wenn ik die rope, so
antworte mie, un wenn ik die rope un du antwortest nig, so
soll fleiten din Blaud für mie.« Do giengen se wier tohope
(zusammen) up ehre Schlopkammer, do was do noch en
viel grötern un viel längern Christoffel, ase bie de twei ersten. Dato segd de Künigsdochter »wenn min Teite röpet, so
antworte du«, do nickede de grote lange steinerne Christoffel wohl ene halwe Stunne mit den Koppe, bis de Kopp tolest wier stille stand. Un de Künigssohn legte sik up de
Dörsül un schläp inne. Den annern Morgen, do segd de
Künig »du hast twaren gut wacket, awerst ik kann die nau
mine Dochter nig giewen, ik hewe so en groten Wall, wenn
du mie den von hüte Morgen sesse bis Obends sesse afhog-
gest, so will ik mie drup bedenken.« Do dehe (tat d. i. gab)
he ünne en gleserne Exe, en gleseren Kiel un en gleserne
Holthacke midde. Wie he in dat Holt kummen is, do hog-
gete he einmal to, do was de Exe entwei: do nam he den
Kiel un schlett einmal mit de Holthacke daruppe, do is et
so kurt un so klein ase Grutt (Sand). Do was he so bedröwet un glövte nu möste he sterwen, un he geit sitten un
grient (weint). Asset nu Middag is, do segd de Künig »eine
von juck Mäken mott ünne wat to etten bringen.« »Nee«,
segged de beiden öllesten, »wie willt ün nicks bringen, wo
he dat leste bie wacket het, de kann ün auck wat bringen.«
Do mutt de jungeste weg un bringen ünne wat to etten.
Ase in den Walle kummet, do frägt se ün wie et ünne gienge? »Oh« seh he, et gienge ün gans schlechte. Do seh se he
sull herkommen un etten eest en bitken; »nee«, seh he, dat

künne he nig, he möste jo doch sterwen, etten wull he nig
mehr. Do gav se ünne so viel gute Woore, he möchte et
doch versöken: do kümmt he un ett wat. Ase he wat getten
hett, do seh se »ik will die eest en bitken lusen, dann werst
du annerst to Sinnen.« Do se ün luset, do werd he so möhe
un schlöppet in, un do nümmet se ehren Doock un binnet
en Knupp do in, un schlätt ün dreimol up de Eere un segd
»Arweggers, herut!« Do würen gliek so viele Eerdmännekens herfur kummen un hadden froget wat de Künigsdochter befelde. Do seh se »in Tied von drei Stunnen mutt de
grote Wall afhoggen un olle dat Holt in Höpen settet sien.«
Do giengen de Eerdmännekens herum un boen ehre ganse
Verwanschap up, dat se ehnen an de Arweit helpen sullen.
Do fiengen se gliek an, un ase de drei Stunne ümme würen,
do is olles to Enne (zu Ende) west: un do keimen se wier to
der Künigsdochter un sehent ehr. Do nümmet se wier ehren witten Doock un segd »Arweggers, nah Hus!« Do siet
se olle wier wege west. Do de Künigssohn upwacket, so
werd he so frau, do segd se »wenn et nu sesse schloen het,
so kumme nah Hus.« Dat het he auck bevolget, un do frägt
de Künig »hest du den Wall aawe (ab)?« »Jo« segd de Künigssuhn. Ase se do an een Diske sittet, do seh de Künig
»ik kann di nau mine Dochter nie tor Frugge giewen«, he
möste eest nau wat umme se dohen. Do frägt he wat dat
denn sien sulle. »Ik hewe so en grot Dieck«, seh de Künig,
»do most du den annern Morgen hünne un most en utschloen, dat he so blank is ase en Spegel, un et müttet von
ollerhand Fiske dorinne sien.« Den anneren Morgen do gav
ünne de Künig ene gleserne Schute (Schüppe) un segd
»umme sess Uhr mot de Dieck ferrig sien.« Do geit he weg,
ase he bie den Dieck kummet, do stecket he mit de Schute
in de Muhe (Moor, Sumpf), do brack se af: do stecket he
mit de Hacken in de Muhe, un et was wier caput. Do werd
he gans bedröwet. Den Middag brachte de jüngeste Dochter ünne wat to etten, do frägt se wo et ünne gienge? Do
seh de Künigssuhn et gienge ünne gans schlechte, he sull

sienen Kopp wohl missen mutten: »dat Geschirr is mie
wier klein gohen.« »Oh«, seh se, »he sull kummen un etten
eest wat, dann werst du anneren Sinnes.« »Nee«, segd he,
etten kunn he nig, he wer gar to bedröwet. Do givt se ünne
viel gude Woore bis he kummet un ett wat. Do luset se ünn
wier, un he schloppet in: se nümmet von niggen en Doock,
schlett en Knupp do inne un kloppet mit den Knuppe dreimol up de Eere un segd »Arweggers, herut!« Do kummt
gliek so viele Eerdmännekens un froget olle wat ehr Begeren wür. In Tied von drei Stunne mosten seden Dieck gans
utschloen hewen, un he möste so blank sien, dann man sik
inne speigelen künne, un von ollerhand Fiske mosten dorinne sien. Do giengen de Eerdmännekens hünn un boen
ehre Verwanschap up, dat se ünnen helpen sullen; un et is
auck in zwei Stunnen ferrig west. Do kummet se wier un
segged »wie hät dohen, so us befolen is.« Do nümmet de
Künigsdochter den Doock un schlett wier dre[i]mol up de
Eere un segd »Arweggers, to Hus!« Do siet se olle wier
weg. Ase do de Künigssuhn upwacket, do is de Dieck ferrig. Do geit de Künigsdochter auck weg, un segd wenn et
sesse wär, dann sull he nah Hus kummen. Ase he do nah
Hus kummet, do frägt de Künig »hes du den Dieck ferrig?«
»Jo«, seh de Künigssuhn. Dat wür schöne. Do se do wier to
Diske sittet, do seh de Künig »du hast den Dieck twaren
ferrig, awerst ik kann die mine Dochter noch nie giewen,
du most eest nau eins dohen.« »Wat is dat denn?« frögte de
Künigssuhn. He hedde so en grot Berg, do würen luter Dorenbuske anne, de mosten olle afhoggen weren, un bowen
up moste he en grot Schlott buggen, dat moste so wacker
sien, ase 't nu en Menske denken kunne, un olle Ingedömse, de in den Schlott gehorden, de mösten der olle inne sien.
Do he nu den anneren Morgen up steit, do gav ünne de
Künig en gleserne Exen un en gleserne Boren mit: et
mott awerst um sess Uhr ferrig sien. Do he an den eersten
Dorenbuske mit de Exen anhogget, do gieng se so kurt un
so klein dat de Stücker rund um ünne herfloen, un de Bo-

ren kunn he auck nig brucken. Do war he gans bedröwet un toffte (wartete) up sine Leiweste, op de nie keime un ünn ut de Naut hülpe. Ase 't do Middag is, do kummet se un bringet wat to etten: do geit he ehr in de Möte (entgegen) un vertellt ehr olles un ett wat, un lett sik von ehr lusen un schloppet in. Do nümmetse wier den Knupp un schlett domit up de Eere un segd »Arweggers, herut!« Do kummet wier so viel Eerdmännekens un froget wat ehr Begeren wür? Do seh se »in Tied von drei Stunnen müttet ju den gansen Busk afhoggen, un bowen uppe den Berge do mot en Schlott stohen, dat mot so wacker sien, ase 't nu ener denken kann, un olle Ingedömse muttet do inne sien.« Do gienge se hünne un boen ehre Verwanschap up, dat se helpen sullen, un ase de Tied umme was, do was alles ferrig. Do kümmet se to der Künigsdochter un segged dat, un de Künigsdochter nümmet den Doock un schlett dreimol domit up de Eere un segd »Arweggers to Hus!« Do siet se gliek olle wier weg west. Do nu de Künigssuhn upwacket, un olles soh, do was he so frau ase en Vugel in der Luft. Do et do sesse schloen hadde, do giengen se tohaupe nah Hus. Do segd de Künig »is dat Schlott auck ferrig?« »Jo«, seh de Künigssuhn. Ase do to Diske sittet, do segd de Künig »mine jungeste Dochter kann ik nie giewen, befur de twei öllesten frigget het.« Do wor de Künigssuhn un de Künigsdochter gans bedröwet, un de Künigssuhn wuste sik gar nig to bergen (helfen). Do kummet he mol bie Nachte to der Künigsdochter un löppet dermit furt. Ase do en bitken wegsiet, do kicket sik de Dochter mol umme un süht ehren Vader hinner sik. »Oh«, seh se, »wo sul wie dat macken? min Vader is hinner us un will us ummeholen: ik will die grade to 'n Dörenbusk macken un mie tor Rose un ik will mie ümmer midden in den Busk waaren (schützen).« Ase do de Vader an de Stelle kummet, do steit do en Dörenbusk un ene Rose do anne: do will he de Rose afbrecken, do kummet de Dören un stecket ün in de Finger, dat he wier nah Hus gehen mut. Do frägt sine Frugge worumme he se

nig hädde middebrocht. Do seh he he wür der balt bie
west, awerst he hedde se uppen mol ut den Gesichte verloren, un do hädde do en Dörenbusk un ene Rose stohen. Do
seh de Künigin »heddest du ment (nur) de Rose afbrocken,
de Busk hedde sullen wohl kummen.« Do geit he wier weg
un will de Rose herholen. Unnerdes waren awerst de beiden schon wiet öwer Feld, un de Künig löppet der hinner
her. Do kicket sik de Dochter wier umme un süht ehren
Vader kummen: do seh se »Oh, wo sull wie et nu macken?
ik will die grade tor Kerke macken un mie tom Pastoer: do
will ik up de Kanzel stohn un pr[i]edigen.« Ase do de Künig an de Stelle kummet, do steiht do ene Kerke, un up de
Kanzel is en Pastoer un priediget: do hort he de Priedig to
un geit wier nah Hus. Do frägt de Küniginne worumme he
se nig midde brocht hedde, da segd he »nee, ik hewe se so
lange nachlaupen, un as ik glovte ik wer der bold bie, do
steit do en Kerke un up de Kanzel en Pastoer, de priedig-
te.« »Du häddest sullen ment den Pastoer bringen«, seh de
Fru, »de Kerke hädde sullen wohl kummen: dat ik die auck
(wenn ich dich auch) schicke, dat kann nig mer helpen, ik
mut sülwenst hünne gohen.« Ase se do ene Wiele wege is
un de beiden von fern süht, do kicket sik de Künigsdochter
umme un süht ehre Moder kummen un segd »nu si wie un-
glücksk, nu kummet miene Moder sülwenst: ik will die grade tom Dieck macken un mie tom Fisk.« Do de Moder up
de Stelle kummet, do is do en grot Dieck, un in de Midde
sprank en Fisk herumme un kickete mit den Kopp ut den
Water un was gans lustig. Do wull se geren den Fisk
kri[e]gen, awerst se kunn ün gar nig fangen. Do werd se
gans böse un drinket den gansen Dieck ut, dat se den Fisk
kriegen will, awerst do werd se so üwel, dat se sick spiggen
mott un spigget den gansen Dieck wier ut. Do seh se »ik
sehe do wohl dat et olle nig mer helpen kann«: sei mogten
nu wier to ehr kummen. Do gohet se dann auck wier hünne,
un de Küniginne givt der Dochter drei Wallnütte un
segd »do kannst du die mit helpen, wenn du in dine högste

Naud bist.« Un do giengen de jungen Lüde wier tohaupe
weg. Do se do wohl tein Stunne gohen hadden, do kummet
se an dat Schlott, wovon de Künigssuhn was, un dobie was
en Dorp. Ase se do anne keimen, do segd de Künigssuhn
»blief hie, mine Leiweste, ik will eest up dat Schlott gohen,
un dann will ik mit den Wagen un Bedeinten kummen un
will die afholen.« Ase he do up dat Schlott kummet, do
werd se olle so frau dat se den Künigssuhn nu wier hett: do
vertellt he he hedde ene Brut, un de wür ietzt in den Dorpe, se wullen mit den Wagen hintrecken un se holen. Do
spannt se auck gliek an, un viele Bedeinten setten sich up
den Wagen. Ase do de Künigssuhn instiegen wull, do gab
ün sine Moder en Kus, do hadde he alles vergeten, wat
schehen was un auck wat he dohen will. Do befal de Moder
se sullen wier utspannen, un do giengen se olle wier in't
Hus. Dat Mäken awerst sitt im Dorpe un luert un luert un
meint he sull se afholen, et kummet awerst keiner. Do ver-
maiet (vermietet) sik de Künigsdochter in de Muhle, de
hoerde bie dat Schlott, do moste se olle Nohmiddage bie
den Watter sitten un Stunze schüren (Gefäße reinigen). Do
kummet de Küniginne mol von den Schlotte gegohen, un
gohet an den Wat[t]er spazeiern, un seihet dat wackere
Mäken do sitten, do segd se »wat is dat für en wacker Mäken! wat geföllt mie dat gut!« Do kicket se et olle an,
awerst keen Menske hadde et kand. Do geit wohl ene lange
Tied vorbie, dat dat Mäken eerlick un getrugge bie den
Müller deint. Unnerdes hadde de Küniginne ene Frugge für
ehren Suhn socht, de is gans feren ut der Weld west. Ase do
de Brut ankümmet, do söllt se gliek tohaupe giewen weren.
Et laupet so viele Lüde tosamen, de dat olle seihen willt, do
segd dat Mäken to den Müller he mögte ehr doch auck Ver-
löv giewen. Do seh de Müller »ase 't do weg will, do macket e ene van den drei Wallnütten up,
do legt do so en wacker Kleid inne, dat trecket et an un
gienk domie in de Kerke gigen den Altor stohen. Up enmol
kummt de Brut un de Brüme (Bräutigam), un settet sik für

den Altor, un ase de Pastor se do insegnen wull, do kicket
sik de Brut van der Halwe (seitwärts), un süht et do stohen,
do steit se wier up, un segd se wull sik nie giewen loten, bis
se auck so en wacker Kleid hädde, ase de Dame. Do giengen se wier nah Hus un läten de Dame froen ob se dat
Kleid wohl verkofte. Nee, verkaupen dau se't nig, awerst
verdeinen, dat mögte wohl sien. Do fragten se ehr wat se
denn dohen sullen. Do segd se wenn se van Nachte fur dat
Dohr van den Künigssuhn schlapen döffte, dann wull se et
wohl dohen. Do segd se jo, dat sul se menten dohen. Do
muttet de Bedeinten den Künigssuhn en Schlopdrunk ingiewen, un do legt se sik up den Süll un günselt (winselt) de
heile Nacht, se hädde den Wall für ün afhoggen loten, se
hädde de[n] Dieck fur ün utschloen, se hädde dat Schlott
für ün bugget, se hädde ünne ton Dörenbusk macket, dann
wier tor Kerke un tolest tom Dieck, un he hädde se so geschwinne vergeten. De Künigssuhn hadde nicks davon
hört, de Bedeinten awerst würen upwacket un hadden to-
lustert un hadden nie wust wat et sull bedüen. Den anneren
Morgen, ase se upstohen würen, do trock de Brut dat Kleid
an, un fort mit den Brümen nah der Kerke. Unnerdes macket dat wackere Mäken de tweide Wallnutt up, un do is
nau en schöner Kleid inne, dat tüt et wier an un geit domie
in de Kerke gigen den Altor stohen, do geit et dann ewen
wie dat vürge mol. Un dat Mäken liegt wier en Nacht für
den Süll, de nah des Künig[s]suhns Stobe geit, un de Bedeinten süllt ün wier en Schlopdrunk ingiewen; de Bedeinten kummet awerst un giewet ünne wat to wacken, domie
legt he sik to Bedde: un de Müllersmaged fur den Dörsüll
günselt wier so viel un segd wat se dohen hädde. Dat hört
olle de Künigssuhn un werd gans bedröwet, un et föllt
ünne olle wier bie wat vergangen was. Do will he nah ehr
gohen, awerst sine Moder hadde de Dör toschlotten. Den
annern Morgen awerst gieng he gliek to siner Leiwesten un
vertellte ehr olles, wie et mit ünne togangen wür, un se
mögte ünne doch nig beuse sin dat he se so lange vergetten

hädde. Do macket de Künigsdochter de dridde Wallnutt up, do is nau en viel wackerer Kleid inne: dat trecket sie an un fört mit ehrem Brümen nah de Kerke, un do keimen so viele Kinner, de geiwen ünne Blomen un hellen ünne bunte Bänner fur de Föte, un se leiten sik insegnen un hellen ene lustige Hochtied; awerst de falske Moder un Brut mosten weg. Un we dat lest vertellt het, den is de Mund noch wärm.

114.
Vom klugen Schneiderlein.

Es war einmal eine Prinzessin gewaltig stolz: kam ein Freier, so gab sie ihm etwas zu raten auf, und wenn er's nicht erraten konnte, so ward er mit Spott fortgeschickt. Sie ließ auch bekannt machen, wer ihr Rätsel löste, sollte sich mit ihr vermählen, und möchte kommen wer da wollte. Endlich fanden sich auch drei Schneider zusammen, davon meinten die zwei ältesten sie hätten so manchen feinen Stich getan und hätten's getroffen, da könnt's ihnen nicht fehlen, sie müssten's auch hier treffen; der dritte war ein kleiner unnützer Springinsfeld, der nicht einmal sein Handwerk verstand, aber meinte er müsste dabei Glück haben, denn woher sollt's ihm sonst kommen. Da sprachen die zwei andern zu ihm »bleib nur zu Haus, du wirst mit deinem bisschen Verstande nicht weit kommen.« Das Schneiderlein ließ sich aber nicht irre machen und sagte es hätte einmal seinen Kopf darauf gesetzt und wollte sich schon helfen, und gieng dahin als wäre die ganze Welt sein.
Da meldeten sich alle drei bei der Prinzessin und sagten sie sollte ihnen ihre Rätsel vorlegen: es wären die rechten Leute angekommen, die hätten einen feinen Verstand, dass man ihn wohl in eine Nadel fädeln könnte. Da sprach die Prinzessin »ich habe zweierlei Haar auf dem Kopf, von was für

Farben ist das?« »Wenn's weiter nichts ist«, sagte er erste, »es wird schwarz und weiß sein, wie Tuch, das man Kümmel und Salz nennt.« Die Prinzessin sprach »falsch geraten, antworte der zweite.« Da sagte der zweite »ist's nicht schwarz und weiß, so ist's braun und rot, wie meines Herrn Vaters Bratenrock.« »Falsch geraten«, sagte die Prinzessin, »antworte der dritte, dem seh ich's an, der weiß es sicherlich.« Da trat das Schneiderlein keck hervor, und sprach »die Prinzessin hat ein silbernes und ein goldenes Haar auf dem Kopf, und das sind die zweierlei Farben.« Wie die Prinzessin das hörte, ward sie blass, und wäre vor Schrecken beinah hingefallen, denn das Schneiderlein hatte es getroffen, und sie hatte fest geglaubt das würde kein Mensch auf der Welt heraus bringen. Als ihr das Herz wieder kam, sprach sie »damit hast du mich noch nicht gewonnen, du musst noch eins tun, unten im Stall liegt ein Bär, bei dem sollst du die Nacht zubringen; wenn ich dann morgen aufstehe, und du bist noch lebendig, so sollst du mich heiraten.« Sie dachte aber damit wollte sie das Schneiderlein los werden, denn der Bär hatte noch keinen Menschen lebendig gelassen, der ihm unter die Tatzen gekommen war. Das Schneiderlein ließ sich nicht abschrecken, war ganz vergnügt, und sprach »frisch gewagt, ist halb gewonnen.«

Als nun der Abend kam, ward mein Schneiderlein hinunter zum Bären gebracht. Der Bär wollt auch gleich auf den kleinen Kerl los und ihm mit seiner Tatze einen guten Willkommen geben. »Sachte, sachte«, sprach das Schneiderlein, »ich will dich schon zur Ruhe bringen.« Da holte es ganz gemächlich, als hätt es keine Sorgen, welsche Nüsse aus der Tasche, biss sie auf und aß die Kerne. Wie der Bär das sah, kriegte er Lust und wollte auch Nüsse haben. Das Schneiderlein griff in die Tasche und reichte ihm eine Hand voll; es waren aber keine Nüsse sondern Wackersteine. Der Bär steckte sie ins Maul, konnte aber nichts aufbringen, er mochte beißen wie er wollte. »Ei«, dachte er, »was bist du für ein dummer Klotz! kannst nicht einmal die Nüsse aufbeißen« und sprach zum Schneiderlein »mein, beiß mir die Nüsse auf.« »Da siehst du was du für ein Kerl bist«, sprach das Schneiderlein, »hast so ein großes Maul und kannst die kleine Nuss nicht aufbeißen.« Da nahm es die Steine, war hurtig, steckte dafür eine Nuss in den Mund, und knack, war sie entzwei. »Ich muss das Ding noch einmal probieren«, sprach der Bär, »wenn ich's so ansehe, ich mein, ich müsst's auch können.« Da gab ihm das Schneiderlein abermals Wackersteine, und der Bär arbeitete und biss aus allen Leibeskräften hinein. Aber du glaubst auch nicht dass er sie aufgebracht hat. Wie das vorbei war, holte das Schneiderlein eine Violine unter dem Rock hervor und spielte sich ein Stückchen darauf. Als der Bär die Musik vernahm, konnte er es nicht lassen und fieng an zu tanzen, und als er ein Weilchen getanzt hatte, gefiel ihm das Ding so wohl, dass er zum Schneiderlein sprach »hör, ist das Geigen schwer?« »Kinderleicht, siehst du, mit der Linken leg ich die Finger auf und mit der Rechten streich ich mit dem Bogen drauf los, da geht's lustig, hopsasa, vivallalera!« »So Geigen«, sprach der Bär, »das möcht ich auch verstehen, damit ich tanzen könnte, so oft ich Lust hätte. Was meinst du dazu? Willst du mir Unterricht darin geben?« »Von Herzen gern«, sagte das Schneiderlein, »wenn du Geschick dazu hast. Aber weis einmal deine Tatzen her, die sind gewaltig lang, ich muss dir die Nägel ein wenig abschneiden.« Da ward ein Schraubstock herbei geholt, und der Bär legte seine Tatzen darauf, das Schneiderlein aber schraubte sie fest und sprach »nun warte bis ich mit der Schere komme«, ließ den Bären brummen, so viel er wollte, legte sich in die Ecke auf ein Bund Stroh und schlief ein.

Die Prinzessin, als sie am Abend den Bären so gewaltig brummen hörte, glaubte nicht anders, als er brumme vor Freuden und hätte dem Schneider den Garaus gemacht. Am Morgen stand sie ganz unbesorgt und vergnügt auf, wie sie aber nach dem Stall guckt, so steht das Schneiderlein ganz munter davor und ist gesund wie ein Fisch im Wasser. Da konnte sie nun kein Wort mehr dagegen sagen, weil sie's öffentlich versprochen hatte, und der König ließ einen Wagen kommen, darin musste sie mit dem Schneiderlein zur Kirche fahren, und sollte sie da vermählt werden. Wie sie eingestiegen waren, giengen die beiden andern Schneider, die ein falsches Herz hatten und ihm sein Glück nicht gönnten, in den Stall und schraubten den Bären los. Der Bär in voller Wut rannte hinter dem Wagen her. Die Prinzessin hörte ihn schnauben und brummen: es ward ihr angst, und sie rief »ach, der Bär ist hinter uns und will dich holen.« Das Schneiderlein war fix, stellte sich auf den Kopf, streckte die Beine zum Fenster hinaus und rief »siehst du den Schraubstock? wann du nicht gehst, so sollst du wieder hinein.« Wie der Bär das sah, drehte er um und lief fort. Mein Schneiderlein fuhr da ruhig in die Kirche und die Prinzessin ward ihm an die Hand getraut, und lebte er mit ihr vergnügt wie eine Heidlerche. Wer's nicht glaubt, bezahlt einen Taler.

115.

Die klare Sonne bringt's an den Tag.

Ein Schneidergesell reiste in der Welt auf sein Handwerk herum und konnte er einmal keine Arbeit finden, und war die Armut bei ihm so groß, dass er keinen Heller Zehrgeld hatte. In der Zeit begegnete ihm auf dem Weg ein Jude, und da dachte er der hätte viel Geld bei sich und stieß Gott aus seinem Herzen, gieng auf ihn los, und sprach »gib mir dein Geld, oder ich schlag dich tot.« Da sagte der Jude »schenkt mir doch das Leben, Geld hab ich keins und nicht mehr als acht Heller.« Der Schneider aber sprach »du hast doch Geld, und das soll auch heraus«, brauchte Gewalt und schlug ihn so lange bis er nah am Tod war. Und wie der Jude nun sterben wollte, sprach er das letzte Wort »die klare Sonne wird es an den Tag bringen!« und starb damit. Der Schneidergesell griff ihm in die Tasche und suchte nach Geld, er fand aber nicht mehr als die acht Heller, wie der Jude gesagt hatte. Da packte er ihn auf, trug ihn hinter einen Busch und zog weiter auf sein Handwerk. Wie er nun lange Zeit gereist war, kam er in eine Stadt bei einem Meister in Arbeit, der hatte eine schöne Tochter, in die verliebte er sich, und heiratete sie und lebte in einer guten vergnügten Ehe.

Über lang, als sie schon zwei Kinder hatten, starben Schwiegervater und Schwiegermutter, und die jungen Leute hatten den Haushalt allein. Eines Morgens, wie der Mann auf dem Tisch vor dem Fenster saß, brachte ihm die Frau den Kaffee, und als er ihn in die Unterschale ausgegossen hatte und eben trinken wollte da schien die Sonne darauf und der Widerschein blinkte oben an der Wand so hin und her und machte Kringel daran. Da sah der Schneider hinauf und sprach »ja, die will's gern an den Tag bringen und kann's nicht!« Die Frau sprach »ei, lieber Mann, was ist denn das? was meinst du damit?« Er antwortete »das darf ich dir nicht sagen.« Sie aber sprach »wenn du mich lieb hast, musst du mir's sagen« und gab ihm die allerbesten Worte, es sollt's kein Mensch wieder erfahren, und ließ ihm keine Ruhe. Da erzählte er, vor langen Jahren, wie er auf der Wanderschaft ganz abgerissen und ohne Geld gewesen, habe er einen Juden erschlagen, und der Jude habe in der letzten Todesangst die Worte gesprochen »die klare Sonne wird's an den Tag bringen!« Nun hätt's die Sonne eben gern an den Tag bringen wollen, und hätt an der Wand geblinkt und Kringel gemacht, sie hätt's aber nicht gekonnt. Danach bat er sie noch besonders, sie dürfte es niemand sagen, sonst käm er um sein Leben, das versprach sie auch. Als er sich aber zur Arbeit gesetzt hatte, gieng sie zu ihrer Gevatterin und vertraute ihr die Geschichte, sie dürfte sie aber keinem Menschen wieder sagen; ehe aber drei Tage vergiengen, wusste es die ganze Stadt, und der Schneider kam vor das Gericht und ward gerichtet. Da brachte es doch die klare Sonne an den Tag.

116.

Das blaue Licht.

Es war einmal ein Soldat, der hatte dem König lange Jahre treu gedient: als aber der Krieg zu Ende war und der Soldat, der vielen Wunden wegen, die er empfangen hatte, nicht weiter dienen konnte, sprach der König zu ihm »du kannst heim gehen, ich brauche dich nicht mehr: Geld bekommst du weiter nicht, denn Lohn erhält nur der, welcher mir Dienste dafür leistet.« Da wusste der Soldat nicht womit er sein Leben fristen sollte: gieng voll Sorgen fort und gieng den ganzen Tag, bis er Abends in einen Wald kam. Als die Finsternis einbrach, sah er ein Licht, dem näherte er sich und kam zu einem Haus, darin wohnte eine Hexe. »Gib mir doch ein Nachtlager und ein wenig Essen und Trinken«, sprach er zu ihr, »ich verschmachte sonst.« »Oho!« antwortete sie, »wer gibt einem verlaufenen Soldaten etwas? doch will ich barmherzig sein und dich aufnehmen, wenn du tust was ich verlange.« »Was verlangst du?« fragte der Soldat. »Dass du mir morgen meinen Garten umgräbst.« Der Soldat willigte ein und arbeitete den folgenden Tag aus allen Kräften, konnte aber vor Abend nicht fertig werden. »Ich sehe wohl«, sprach die Hexe, »dass du heute nicht weiter kannst: ich will dich noch eine Nacht behalten, dafür sollst du mir morgen ein Fuder Holz spalten und klein machen.« Der Soldat brauchte dazu den ganzen Tag, und Abends machte ihm die Hexe den Vorschlag noch eine Nacht zu bleiben. »Du sollst mir morgen nur eine geringe Arbeit tun, hinter meinem Hause ist ein alter wasserleerer Brunnen, in den ist mir mein Licht gefallen, es brennt blau und verlischt nicht, das sollst du mir wieder herauf holen.« Den andern Tag führte ihn die Alte zu dem Brunnen und ließ ihn in einem Korb hinab. Er fand das blaue Licht und machte ein Zeichen dass sie ihn wieder hinauf ziehen sollte. Sie zog ihn auch in die Höhe, als er aber dem Rand nahe war, reichte sie die Hand hinab und wollte ihm das blaue Licht abnehmen. »Nein«, sagte er und merkte ihre bösen Gedanken, »das Licht gebe ich dir nicht eher, als bis ich mit beiden Füßen auf dem Erdboden stehe.« Da geriet die Hexe in Wut, ließ ihn wieder hinab in den Brunnen fallen und gieng fort.

Der arme Soldat fiel ohne Schaden zu nehmen auf den feuchten Boden, und das blaue Licht brannte fort, aber was konnte ihm das helfen? er sah wohl dass er dem Tod nicht entgehen würde. Er saß eine Weile ganz traurig, da griff er zufällig in seine Tasche und fand seine Tabakspfeife, die noch halb gestopft war. »Das soll dein letztes Vergnügen sein« dachte er, zog sie heraus, zündete sie an dem blauen Licht an und fieng an zu rauchen. Als der Dampf in der Höhle umhergezogen war, stand auf einmal ein kleines schwarzes Männchen vor ihm und fragte »Herr, was befiehlst du?« »Was habe ich dir zu befehlen?« erwiderte der Soldat ganz verwundert. »Ich muss alles tun«, sagte das Männchen, »was du verlangst.« »Gut«, sprach der Soldat, »so hilf mir zuerst aus dem Brunnen.« Das Männchen nahm ihn bei der Hand und führte ihn durch einen unterirdischen Gang, vergaß aber nicht das blaue Licht mitzunehmen. Es zeigte ihm unterwegs die Schätze, welche die Hexe zusammengebracht und da versteckt hatte, und der Soldat nahm so viel Gold als er tragen konnte. Als er oben war, sprach er zu dem Männchenn »nun geh hin, bind die alte Hexe und führe sie vor das Gericht.« Nicht lange, so kam sie auf einem wilden Kater mit furchtbarem Geschrei schnell wie der Wind vorbei geritten, und es dauerte abermals nicht lang, so war das Männchen zurück, »es ist alles ausgerichtet« sprach es, »und die Hexe hängt schon am Galgen.« »Herr, was befiehlst du weiter?« fragte der Kleine. »In dem Augenblick nichts«, antwortete der Soldat, »du kannst nach Haus gehen: sei nur gleich bei der Hand wenn ich dich rufe.« »Es ist nichts nötig«, sprach das Männchen, »als dass du deine Pfeife an dem blauen Licht anzündest,

dann stehe ich gleich vor dir.« Darauf verschwand es vor
seinen Augen.

Der Soldat kehrte in die Stadt zurück, aus der er gekommen war. Er gieng in den besten Gasthof und ließ sich
schöne Kleider machen, dann befahl er dem Wirt ihm ein
Zimmer so prächtig als möglich einzurichten. Als es fertig
war und der Soldat es bezogen hatte, rief er das schwarze
Männchen und sprach »ich habe dem König treu gedient,
er aber hat mich fortgeschickt und mich hungern lassen,
dafür will ich jetzt Rache nehmen.« »Was soll ich tun?«
fragte der Kleine. »Spät Abends wenn die Königstochter im
Bett liegt, so bring sie schlafend hierher, sie soll Mägdedienste bei mir tun.« Das Männchen sprach »für mich ist
das ein leichtes, für dich aber ein gefährliches Ding, wenn
das heraus kommt, wird es dir schlimm ergehen.« Als es
zwölf geschlagen hatte, sprang die Türe auf, und das Männchen trug die Königstochter herein. »Aha, bist du da?« rief
der Soldat, »frisch an die Arbeit! geh, hol den Besen und
kehr die Stube.« Als sie fertig war, hieß er sie zu seinem
Sessel kommen, streckte ihr die Füße entgegen und sprach
»zieh mir die Stiefel aus«, warf sie ihr dann ins Gesicht,
und sie musste sie aufheben, reinigen und glänzend machen. Sie tat aber alles, was er ihr befahl, ohne Wider-
streben, stumm und mit halbgeschlossenen Augen. Bei dem
ersten Hahnschrei trug sie das Männchen wieder in das königliche Schloss und in ihr Bett zurück.

Am andern Morgen, als die Königstochter aufgestanden
war, gieng sie zu ihrem Vater, und erzählte ihm sie hätte einen wunderlichen Traum gehabt, »ich ward durch die Straßen mit Blitzesschnelle fortgetragen und in das Zimmer eines Soldaten gebracht, dem musste ich als Magd dienen und
aufwarten und alle gemeine Arbeit tun, die Stube kehren
und die Stiefel putzen. Es war nur ein Traum, und doch bin
ich so müde, als wenn ich wirklich alles getan hätte.« »Der
Traum könnte wahr gewesen sein«, sprach der König, »ich
will dir einen Rat geben, stecke deine Tasche voll Erbsen

und mache ein klein Loch in die Tasche, wirst du wieder abgeholt, so fallen sie heraus und lassen die Spur auf der Straße.« Als der König so sprach, stand das Männchen unsichtbar dabei und hörte alles mit an. Nachts, als es die schlafende Königstochter wieder durch die Straßen trug, fielen zwar einzelne Erbsen aus der Tasche, aber sie konnten keine Spur machen, denn das listige Männchen hatte vorher in allen Straßen Erbsen verstreut. Die Königstochter aber musste wieder bis zum Hahnenschrei Mägdedienste tun.

Der König schickte am folgenden Morgen seine Leute aus, welche die Spur suchen sollten, aber es war vergeblich, denn in allen Straßen saßen die armen Kinder und lasen Erbsen auf und sagten »es hat heut Nacht Erbsen geregnet.« »Wir müssen etwas anderes aussinnen«, sprach der König, «behalt deine Schuh an, wenn du dich zu Bett legst, und ehe du von dort zurück kehrst, verstecke einen davon; ich will ihn schon finden.« Das schwarze Männchen vernahm den Anschlag, und als der Soldat Abends verlangte er sollte die Königstochter wieder herbei tragen, riet es ihm ab und sagte gegen diese List wüsste es kein Mittel, und wenn der Schuh bei ihm gefunden würde, so könnte es ihm schlimm ergehen. »Tue was ich dir sage« erwiderte der Soldat, und die Königstochter musste auch in der dritten Nacht wie eine Magd arbeiten; sie versteckte aber, ehe sie zurückgetragen wurde, einen Schuh unter das Bett.

Am andern Morgen ließ der König in der ganzen Stadt den Schuh seiner Tochter suchen: er ward bei dem Soldaten gefunden, und der Soldat selbst, der sich auf Bitten des Kleinen zum Tor hinaus gemacht hatte, ward bald eingeholt und ins Gefängnis geworfen. Er hatte sein Bestes bei der Flucht vergessen, das blaue Licht und das Gold, und hatte nur noch einen Dukaten in der Tasche. Als er nun mit Ketten belastet an dem Fenster seines Gefängnisses stand, sah er einen seiner Kameraden vorbeigehen. Er klopfte an die Scheibe, und als er herbeikam, sagte er »sei so gut und hol mir das kleine Bündelchen, das ich in dem Gasthaus habe liegen lassen, ich gebe dir dafür einen Dukaten.« Der Kamerad lief hin, und brachte ihm das Verlangte. Sobald der Soldat wieder allein war, steckte er seine Pfeife an und ließ das schwarze Männchen kommen. »Sei ohne Furcht«, sprach es zu seinem Herrn, »geh hin wo sie dich hinführen und lass alles geschehen, nimm nur das blaue Licht mit.« Am anderen Tag ward Gericht über den Soldaten gehalten, und obgleich er nichts Böses getan hatte, verurteilte ihn der Richter doch zum Tode. Als er nun hinaus geführt wurde, bat er den König um eine letzte Gnade. »Was für eine?« fragte der König. »Dass ich auf dem Weg noch eine Pfeife rauchen darf.« »Du kannst drei rauchen«, antwortete der König, »aber glaube nicht dass ich dir das Leben schenke.« Da zog der Soldat seine Pfeife heraus und zündete sie an dem blauen Licht an, und wie ein paar Ringel von Rauch aufgestiegen waren, so stand schon das Männchen da, hatte einen kleinen Knüppel in der Hand und sprach »was befiehlt mein Herr?« »Schlag mir da die falschen Richter und ihre Häscher zu Boden, und verschone auch den König nicht, der mich so schlecht behandelt hat.« Da fuhr das Männchen wie der Blitz, zickzack, hin und her, und wen es mit seinem Knüppel nur anrührte, der fiel schon zu Boden, und getraute sich nicht mehr zu regen. Dem König ward angst, er legte sich auf das Bitten und um nur das Leben zu behalten gab er dem Soldat das Reich und seine Tochter zur Frau.

117.

Das eigensinnige Kind.

Es war einmal ein Kind eigensinnig und tat nicht was seine Mutter haben wollte. Darum hatte der liebe Gott kein Wohlgefallen an ihm und ließ es krank werden, und kein

Arzt konnte ihm helfen, und in kurzem lag es auf dem To-
tenbettchen. Als es nun ins Grab versenkt und Erde über es
hingedeckt war, so kam auf einmal sein Ärmchen wieder
hervor und reichte in die Höhe, und wenn sie es hineinleg-
ten und frische Erde darüber taten, so half das nicht, und
das Ärmchen kam immer wieder heraus. Da musste die
Mutter selbst zum Grabe gehn und mit der Rute aufs Ärmchen schlagen, und wie sie das getan hatte, zog es sich hinein, und das Kind hatte nun erst Ruhe unter der Erde.

118.

Die drei Feldscherer.

Drei Feldscherer reisten in der Welt, die meinten ihre
Kunst ausgelernt zu haben und kamen in ein Wirtshaus, wo
sie übernachten wollten. Der Wirt fragte wo sie her wären
und hinaus wollten? »Wir ziehen auf unsere Kunst in der
Welt herum.« »Zeigt mir doch einmal, was ihr könnt« sagte
der Wirt. Da sprach der erste er wollte seine Hand abschneiden und morgen früh wieder anheilen: der zweite
sprach er wollte sein Herz ausreißen und morgen früh wieder anheilen: der dritte sprach er wollte seine Augen aussste-
chen und morgen früh wieder einheilen. »Könnt ihr das«,
sprach der Wirt, »so habt ihr ausgelernt.« Sie hatten aber
eine Salbe, was sie damit bestrichen, das heilte zusammen,
und das Fläschchen, wo sie drin war, trugen sie beständig
bei sich. Da schnitten sie Hand Herz und Auge vom Leibe,
wie sie gesagt hatten, legten's zusammen auf einen Teller
und gaben's dem Wirt: der Wirt gab's einem Mädchen, das
sollt's in den Schrank stellen und wohl aufheben. Das Mädchen aber hatte einen heimlichen Schatz, der war ein Soldat. Wie nun der Wirt, die drei Feldscherer und alle Leute
im Haus schliefen, kam der Soldat und wollte was zu essen

haben. Da schloss das Mädchen den Schrank auf und holte ihm etwas, und über der großen Liebe vergaß es die Schranktüre zuzumachen, setzte sich zum Liebsten an Tisch, und sie schwätzten mit einander. Wie es so vergnügt saß und an kein Unglück dachte, kam die Katze hereingeschlichen, fand den Schrank offen, nahm die Hand das Herz und die Augen der drei Feldscherer, und lief damit hinaus. Als nun der Soldat gegessen hatte und das Mädchen das Gerät aufheben und den Schrank zuschließen wollte, da sah es wohl dass der Teller, den ihm der Wirt aufzuheben gegeben hatte, ledig war. Da sagte es erschrocken zu seinem Schatz »ach, was will ich armes Mädchen anfangen! Die Hand ist fort, das Herz und die Augen sind auch fort, wie wird mir's morgen früh ergehen!« »Sei still«, sprach er, »ich will dir aus der Not helfen: es hängt ein Dieb draußen am Galgen, dem will ich die Hand abschneiden; welche Hand war's denn?« »Die rechte.« Da gab ihm das Mädchen ein scharfes Messer, und er gieng hin, schnitt dem armen Sünder die rechte Hand ab und brachte sie herbei. Darauf packte er die Katze und stach ihr die Augen aus; nun fehlte nur noch das Herz. »Habt ihr nicht geschlachtet, und liegt das Schweinefleisch nicht im Keller?« »Ja« sagte das Mädchen. »Nun, das ist gut« sagte der Soldat, gieng hinunter und holte ein Schweineherz. Das Mädchen tat alles zusammen auf den Teller, und stellte ihn in den Schrank, und als ihr Liebster darauf Abschied genommen hatte, legte es sich ruhig ins Bett.

Morgens, als die Feldscherer aufstanden, sagten sie dem Mädchen es sollte ihnen den Teller holen, darauf Hand Herz und Augen lägen. Da brachte es ihn aus dem Schrank, und der erste hielt sich die Diebshand an und bestrich sie mit seiner Salbe, alsbald war sie ihm angewachsen. Der zweite nahm die Katzenaugen und heilte sie ein: der dritte machte das Schweineherz fest. Der Wirt aber stand dabei, bewunderte ihre Kunst und sagte dergleichen hätt er noch nicht gesehen, er wollte sie bei jedermann rühmen und empfehlen. Darauf bezahlten sie ihre Zeche und reisten weiter.

Wie sie so dahin giengen, so blieb der mit dem Schweineherzen gar nicht bei ihnen, sondern wo eine Ecke war, lief er hin und schnüffelte darin herum, wie Schweine tun. Die andern wollten ihn an dem Rockschlippen zurückhalten, aber das half nichts, er riss sich los und lief hin, wo der dickste Unrat lag. Der zweite stellte sich auch wunderlich an, rieb die Augen und sagte zu dem andern »Kamerad, was ist das? das sind meine Augen nicht, ich sehe ja nichts, leite mich doch einer, dass ich nicht falle.« Da giengen sie mit Mühe fort bis zum Abend, wo sie zu einer andern Herberge kamen. Sie traten zusammen in die Wirtsstube, da saß in einer Ecke ein reicher Herr vorm Tisch und zählte Geld. Der mit der Diebshand gieng um ihn herum, zuckte ein paarmal mit dem Arm, endlich, wie der Herr sich umwendete, griff er in den Haufen hinein und nahm eine Hand voll Geld heraus. Der eine sah's und sprach »Kamerad, was machst du? stehlen darfst du nicht, schäm dich!« »Ei«, sagte er, »was kann ich dafür! es zuckt mir in der Hand, ich muss zugreifen, ich mag wollen oder nicht.« Sie legten sich danach schlafen, und wie sie da liegen, ist's so finster, dass man keine Hand vor Augen sehen kann. Auf einmal erwachte der mit den Katzenaugen, weckte die andern und sprach »Brüder, schaut einmal auf, seht ihr die weißen Mäuschen, die da herumlaufen?« Die zwei richteten sich auf, konnten aber nichts sehen. Da sprach er »es ist mit uns nicht richtig, wir haben das Unsrige nicht wieder gekriegt, wir müssen zurück nach dem Wirt, der hat uns betrogen.« Also machten sie sich am andern Morgen dahin auf und sagten dem Wirt sie hätten ihr richtig Werk nicht wieder gekriegt, der eine hätte eine Diebshand, der zweite Katzenaugen, und der dritte ein Schweineherz. Der Wirt sprach daran müsste das Mädchen Schuld sein und wollte es rufen, aber wie das die drei hatte kommen sehen, war es zum Hinterpförtchen fortgelaufen,

und kam nicht wieder. Da sprachen die drei er sollte ihnen
viel Geld geben, sonst ließen sie ihm den roten Hahn
übers Haus fliegen: da gab er was er hatte und nur aufbringen konnte, und die drei zogen damit fort. Es war für
ihr Lebtag genug, sie hätten aber doch lieber ihr richtig
Werk gehabt.

119.

Die sieben Schwaben.

Einmal waren sieben Schwaben beisammen, der erste war
der Herr Schulz, der zweite der Jackli, der dritte der Marli,
der vierte der Jergli, der fünfte der Michal, der sechste der
Hans, der siebente der Veitli; die hatten alle siebene sich
vorgenommen die Welt zu durchziehen, Abenteuer zu suchen und große Taten zu vollbringen. Damit sie aber auch
mit bewaffneter Hand und sicher giengen, sahen sie's für
gut an, dass sie sich zwar nur einen einzigen aber recht
starken und langen Spieß machen ließen. Diesen Spieß fassten sie alle siebene zusammen an, vorn gieng der kühnste
und männlichste, das musste der Herr Schulz sein, und
dann folgten die andern nach der Reihe und der Veitli war
der letzte.
Nun geschah es, als sie im Heumonat eines Tags einen weiten Weg gegangen waren, auch noch ein gut Stück bis in
das Dorf hatten, wo sie über Nacht bleiben mussten, dass
in der Dämmerung auf einer Wiese ein großer Rosskäfer
oder eine Hornisse nicht weit von ihnen hinter einer Staude
vorbeiflog und feindlich brummelte. Der Herr Schulz erschrak, dass er fast den Spieß hätte fallen lassen und ihm
der Angstschweiß am ganzen Leibe ausbrach. »Horcht,
horcht«, rief er seinen Gesellen, »Gott, ich höre eine Trommel!« Der Jackli, der hinter ihm den Spieß hielt und dem

ich weiß nicht was für ein Geruch in die Nase kam, sprach
»etwas ist ohne Zweifel vorhanden, denn ich schmeck das
Pulver und den Zündstrick.« Bei diesen Worten hub der
Herr Schulz an die Flucht zu ergreifen, und sprang im Hui
über einen Zaun, weil er aber gerade auf die Zinken eines
Rechen sprang, der vom Heumachen da liegen geblieben
war, so fuhr ihm der Stiel ins Gesicht und gab ihm einen
ungewaschenen Schlag. »O wei, o wei«, schrie der Herr
Schulz, »nimm mich gefangen, ich ergeb mich, ich ergeb
mich!« Die andern sechs hüpften auch alle einer über den
andern herzu und schrien »gibst du dich, so geb ich mich
auch, gibst du dich, so geb ich mich auch.« Endlich, wie
kein Feind da war, der sie binden und fortführen wollte,
merkten sie dass sie betrogen waren: und damit die Geschichte nicht unter die Leute käme, und sie nicht genarrt
und gespottet würden, verschwuren sie sich unter einander
so lang davon still zu schweigen, bis einer unverhofft das
Maul auftäte.

Hierauf zogen sie weiter. Die zweite Gefährlichkeit, die sie
erlebten, kann aber mit der ersten nicht verglichen werden.
Nach etlichen Tagen trug sie ihr Weg durch ein Brachfeld,
da saß ein Hase in der Sonne und schlief, streckte die Ohren in die Höhe, und hatte die großen gläsernen Augen
starr aufstehen. Da erschraken sie bei dem Anblick des
grausamen und wilden Tieres insgesamt und hielten Rat
was zu tun das wenigst gefährliche wäre. Denn so sie fliehen wollten, war zu besorgen, das Ungeheuer setzte ihnen
nach und verschlänge sie alle mit Haut und Haar. Also
sprachen sie »wir müssen einen großen und gefährlichen
Kampf bestehen, frisch gewagt ist halb gewonnen!« fassten
alle siebene den Spieß an, der Herr Schulz vorn und der
Veitli hinten. Der Herr Schulz wollte den Spieß noch immer anhalten, der Veitli aber war hinten ganz mutig geworden, wollte losbrechen und rief

> »stoß zu in aller Schwabe Name,
> sonst wünsch i, dass ihr möcht erlahme.«

Aber der Hans wusst ihn zu treffen und sprach
>>beim Element, du hascht gut schwätze,
bischt stets der letscht beim Drachehetze.<<
Der Michal rief
>>es wird nit fehle um ei Haar,
so ischt es wohl der Teufel gar.<<
Drauf kam an den Jergli die Reihe der sprach
>>ischt er es nit, so ischt's sei Muter
oder des Teufels Stiefbruder.<<
Der Marli hatte da einen guten Gedanken und sagte zum
Veitli
>>gang, Veitli, gang, gang du voran,
i will dahinte vor di stahn.<<
Der Veitli hörte aber nicht drauf und der Jackli sagte
>>der Schulz, der muss der erschte sei,
denn ihm gebührt die Ehr allei.<<
Da nahm sich der Herr Schulz ein Herz und sprach gravi-
tätisch
>>so zieht denn herzhaft in den Streit,
hieran erkennt man tapfre Leut.<<
Da giengen sie insgesamt auf den Drachen los. Der Herr
Schulz segnete sich und rief Gott um Beistand an: wie aber
das alles nicht helfen wollte und er dem Feind immer näher
kam, schrie er in großer Angst >>hau! hurlehau! hau! hau-
hau!<< Davon erwachte der Has, erschrak und sprang eilig
davon. Als ihn der Herr Schulz so feldflüchtig sah, da rief
er voll Freude
>>potz, Veitli, lueg, lueg, was isch das?
das Ungehüer ischt a Has.<<
Der Schwabenbund suchte aber weiter Abenteuer und kam
an die Mosel, ein mosiges, stilles und tiefes Wasser, darüber
nicht viel Brücken sind, sondern man an mehrern Orten
sich muss in Schiffen überfahren lassen. Weil die sieben
Schwaben dessen unberichtet waren, riefen sie einem
Mann, der jenseits des Wassers seine Arbeit vollbrachte, zu,
wie man doch hinüber kommen könnte? Der Mann ver-

stand wegen der Weite und wegen ihrer Sprache nicht was
sie wollten, und fragte auf sein trierisch »wat? wat?« Da
meinte der Herr Schulz er spräche nicht anders als »wade,
wade durchs Wasser«, und hub an, weil er der Vorderste
war, sich auf den Weg zu machen und in die Mosel hinein-
zugehen. Nicht lang, so versank er in den Schlamm und in
die antreibenden tiefen Wellen, seinen Hut aber jagte der
Wind hinüber an das jenseitige Ufer, und ein Frosch setzte
sich dabei und quakte »wat, wat, wat«. Die sechs andern
hörten das drüben und sprachen »unser Gesell, der Herr
Schulz, ruft uns, kann er hinüber waden, warum wir nicht
auch?« Sprangen darum eilig alle zusammen in das Wasser
und ertranken, also dass ein Frosch ihrer sechse ums Leben
brachte, und niemand von dem Schwabenbund wieder nach
Haus kam.

120.

Die drei Handwerksburschen.

Es waren drei Handwerksbursche, die hatten es verabredet
auf ihrer Wanderung beisammen zu bleiben und immer in
einer Stadt zu arbeiten. Auf eine Zeit aber fanden sie bei ihren Meistern kein Verdienst mehr, so dass sie endlich ganz
abgerissen waren und nichts zu leben hatten. Da sprach der
eine »was sollen wir anfangen? hier bleiben können wir
nicht länger, wir wollen wieder wandern, und wenn wir in
der Stadt, wo wir hin kommen, keine Arbeit finden, so
wollen wir beim Herbergsvater ausmachen dass wir ihm
schreiben wo wir uns aufhalten, und einer vom andern
Nachricht haben kann, und dann wollen wir uns trennen«;
das schien den andern auch das Beste. Sie zogen fort, da
kam ihnen auf dem Weg ein reich gekleideter Mann entgegen, der fragte wer sie wären. »Wir sind Handwerksleute
und suchen Arbeit: wir haben uns bisher zusammen gehal-

ten, wenn wir aber keine mehr finden, so wollen wir uns trennen.« »Das hat keine Not«, sprach der Mann, »wenn ihr tun wollt was ich euch sage, soll's euch an Geld und Arbeit nicht fehlen; ja ihr sollt große Herren werden und in Kutschen fahren.« Der eine sprach »wenn's unserer Seele und Seligkeit nicht schadet, so wollen wir's wohl tun.« »Nein«, antwortete der Mann, »ich habe keinen Teil an euch.« Der andere aber hatte nach seinen Füßen gesehen, und als er da einen Pferdefuß und einen Menschenfuß erblickte, wollte er sich nicht mit ihm einlassen. Der Teufel aber sprach »gebt euch zufrieden, es ist nicht auf euch abgesehen, sondern auf eines anderen Seele, der schon halb mein ist, und dessen Maß nur voll laufen soll.« Weil sie nun sicher waren, willigten sie ein, und der Teufel sagte ihnen was er verlangte, der erste sollte auf jede Frage antworten »wir alle drei«, der zweite »ums Geld«, der dritte »und das war Recht«. Das sollten sie immer hinter einander sagen, weiter aber dürften sie kein Wort sprechen, und überträten sie das Gebot, so wäre gleich alles Geld verschwunden: so lange sie es aber befolgten, sollten ihre Taschen immer voll sein. Zum Anfang gab er ihnen auch gleich so viel als sie tragen konnten, und hieß sie in die Stadt in das und das Wirtshaus gehen. Sie giengen hinein, der Wirt kam ihnen entgegen und fragte »wollt ihr etwas zu essen?« Der erste antwortete »wir alle drei.« »Ja«, sagte der Wirt, »das mein ich auch.« Der zweite »ums Geld.« »Das versteht sich« sagte der Wirt. Der dritte »und das war Recht.« »Ja wohl war's Recht« sagte der Wirt. Es ward ihnen nun gut Essen und Trinken gebracht, und wohl aufgewartet. Nach dem Essen musste die Bezahlung geschehen, da hielt der Wirt dem einen die Rechnung hin, der sprach »wir alle drei«, der zweite »ums Geld«, der dritte »und das war Recht«. »Freilich ist's recht«, sagte der Wirt, »alle drei bezahlen, und ohne Geld kann ich nichts geben.« Sie bezahlten aber noch mehr als er gefordert hatte. Die Gäste sahen das mit an und sprachen »die Leute müssen toll sein.« »Ja, das sind sie auch«,

sagte der Wirt, »sie sind nicht recht klug.« So blieben sie
eine Zeit lang in dem Wirtshaus und sprachen kein ander
Wort als »wir alle drei«, »ums Geld«, »und das war Recht«.
Sie sahen aber, und wussten alles was darin vorgieng. Es
trug sich zu, dass ein großer Kaufmann kam mit vielem
Geld, der sprach »Herr Wirt, heb er mir mein Geld auf, da
sind die drei närrischen Handwerksbursche, die möchten
mir's stehlen.« Das tat der Wirt. Wie er den Mantelsack in
seine Stube trug, fühlte er dass er schwer von Gold war.
Darauf gab er den drei Handwerkern unten ein Lager, der
Kaufmann aber kam oben hin in eine besondere Stube. Als
Mitternacht war und der Wirt dachte sie schliefen alle, kam
er mit seiner Frau, und sie hatten eine Holzaxt und schlugen den reichen Kaufmann tot; nach vollbrachtem Mord
legten sie sich wieder schlafen. Wie's nun Tag war, gab's
großen Lärm, der Kaufmann lag tot im Bett und schwamm
in seinem Blut. Da liefen alle Gäste zusammen, der Wirt
aber sprach »das haben die drei tollen Handwerker getan.«
Die Gäste bestätigten es, und sagten »niemand anders
kann's gewesen sein.« Der Wirt aber ließ sie rufen und sagte zu ihnen »habt ihr den Kaufmann getötet?« »Wir alle
drei« sagte der erste, »ums Geld« der zweite, »und das war
Recht« der dritte. »Da hört ihr's nun«, sprach der Wirt, »sie
gestehen's selber.« Sie wurden also ins Gefängnis gebracht,
und sollten gerichtet werden. Wie sie nun sahen dass es so
ernsthaft gieng, ward ihnen doch angst, aber Nachts kam
der Teufel und sprach »haltet nur noch einen Tag aus, und
verscherzt euer Glück nicht, es soll euch kein Haar ge-
krümmt werden.« Am andern Morgen wurden sie vor Gericht geführt: da sprach der Richter »seid ihr die Mörder?«
»Wir alle drei.« »Warum habt ihr den Kaufmann erschlagen?« »Ums Geld.« »Ihr Bösewichter«, sagte der Richter,
»habt ihr euch nicht der Sünde gescheut?« »Und das war
Recht.« »Sie haben bekannt und sind noch halsstarrig
dazu« sprach der Richter, »führt sie gleich zum Tod.« Also
wurden sie hinausgebracht, und der Wirt musste mit in den

Kreis treten. Wie sie nun von den Henkersknechten gefasst und oben aufs Gerüst geführt wurden, wo der Scharfrichter mit bloßem Schwerte stand, kam auf einmal eine Kutsche mit vier blutroten Füchsen bespannt, und fuhr dass das Feuer aus den Steinen sprang, aus dem Fenster aber winkte einer mit einem weißen Tuche. Da sprach der Scharfrichter »es kommt Gnade«, und ward auch aus dem Wagen »Gnade! Gnade!« gerufen. Da trat der Teufel heraus, als ein sehr vornehmer Herr, prächtig gekleidet und sprach »ihr drei seid unschuldig; ihr dürft nun sprechen, sagt heraus was ihr gesehen und gehört habt.« Da sprach der älteste »wir haben den Kaufmann nicht getötet, der Mörder steht da im Kreis« und deutete auf den Wirt, »zum Wahrzeichen geht hin in seinen Keller, da hängen noch viele andere, die er ums Leben gebracht.« Da schickte der Richter die Henkersknechte hin, die fanden es, wie's gesagt war, und als sie dem Richter das berichtet hatten, ließ er den Wirt hinauf führen und ihm das Haupt abschlagen. Da sprach der Teufel zu den dreien »nun hab ich die Seele, die ich haben wollte, ihr seid aber frei und habt Geld für euer Lebtag.«

121.

Der Königssohn der sich vor nichts fürchtet.

Es war einmal ein Königssohn, dem gefiel's nicht mehr daheim in seines Vaters Haus, und weil er vor nichts Furcht hatte, so dachte er »ich will in die weite Welt gehen, da wird mir Zeit und Weile nicht lang, und ich werde wunderliche Dinge genug sehen.« Also nahm er von seinen Eltern Abschied und gieng fort, immer zu, von Morgen bis Abend, und es war ihm einerlei wo hinaus ihn der Weg führte. Es trug sich zu, dass er vor eines Riesen Haus kam, und weil er müde war, setzte er sich vor die Türe und ruhte. Und als er seine Augen so hin und her gehen ließ, sah er auf dem Hof des Riesen Spielwerk liegen: das waren ein paar mächtige Kugeln und Kegel so groß als ein Mensch. Über ein Weilchen bekam er Lust, stellte die Kegel auf und schob mit den Kugeln danach, schrie und rief wenn die Kegel fielen, und war guter Dinge. Der Riese hörte den Lärm, streckte seinen Kopf zum Fenster heraus und erblickte einen Menschen, der nicht größer war als andere, und doch mit seinen Kegeln spielte. »Würmchen«, rief er, »was kegelst du mit meinen Kegeln? wer hat dir die Stärke dazu gegeben?« Der Königssohn schaute auf, sah den Riesen an und sprach »o du Klotz, du meinst wohl, du hättest allein starke Arme? ich kann alles, wozu ich Lust habe.« Der Riese kam herab, sah dem Kegeln ganz verwundert zu und sprach »Menschenkind, wenn du der Art bist, so geh und hol mir einen Apfel vom Baum des Lebens.« »Was willst du damit?« sprach der Königssohn. »Ich will den Apfel nicht für mich«, antwortete der Riese, »aber ich habe eine Braut, die verlangt danach; ich bin weit in der Welt umher gegangen und kann den Baum nicht finden.« »Ich will ihn schon finden«, sagte der Königssohn, »und ich weiß nicht was mich abhalten soll, den Apfel herunter zu holen.« Der Riese sprach »du meinst wohl das wäre so leicht? der Garten, worin der Baum steht, ist von einem eisernen Gitter umgeben, und vor dem Gitter liegen wilde Tiere, eins neben dem andern, die halten Wache und lassen keinen Menschen hinein.« »Mich werden sie schon einlassen«, sagte der Königssohn. »Ja, gelangst du auch in den Garten und siehst den Apfel am Baum hängen, so ist er doch noch nicht dein: es hängt ein Ring davor, durch den muss einer die Hand stecken, wenn er den Apfel erreichen und abbrechen will, und das ist noch keinem geglückt.« »Mir soll's schon glücken« sprach der Königssohn.

Da nahm er Abschied von dem Riesen, gieng fort über Berg und Tal, durch Felder und Wälder, bis er endlich den Wundergarten fand. Die Tiere lagen rings herum, aber sie hatten die Köpfe gesenkt und schliefen. Sie erwachten auch nicht, als er heran kam, sondern er trat über sie weg, stieg über das Gitter und kam glücklich in den Garten. Da stand mitten inne der Baum des Lebens, und die roten Äpfel leuchteten an den Ästen. Er kletterte an dem Stamm in die Höhe, und wie er nach einem Apfel reichen wollte, sah er einen Ring davor hängen, aber er steckte seine Hand ohne Mühe hindurch und brach den Apfel. Der Ring schloss sich fest an seinen Arm und er fühlte wie auf einmal eine gewaltige Kraft durch seine Adern drang. Als er mit dem Apfel von dem Baum wieder herab gestiegen war, wollte er nicht über das Gitter klettern, sondern fasste das große Tor und brauchte nur einmal daran zu schütteln, so sprang es mit Krachen auf. Da gieng er hinaus, und der Löwe, der davor gelegen hatte, war wach geworden und sprang ihm nach, aber nicht in Wut und Wildheit, sondern er folgte ihm demütig als seinem Herrn.

Der Königssohn brachte dem Riesen den versprochenen Apfel und sprach »siehst du, ich habe ihn ohne Mühe geholt.« Der Riese war froh dass sein Wunsch so bald erfüllt war, eilte zu seiner Braut und gab ihr den Apfel, den sie verlangt hatte. Es war eine schöne und kluge Jungfrau, und da sie den Ring nicht an seinem Arm sah, sprach sie »ich glaube nicht eher dass du den Apfel geholt hast, als bis ich den Ring an deinem Arm erblicke.« Der Riese sagte »ich brauche nur heim zu gehen und ihn zu holen« und meinte es wäre ein leichtes dem schwachen Menschen mit Gewalt weg zu nehmen, was er nicht gutwillig geben wollte. Er forderte also den Ring von ihm, aber der Königssohn weigerte sich. »Wo der Apfel ist muss auch der Ring sein«, sprach der Riese, »gibst du ihn nicht gutwillig, so musst du mit mir darum kämpfen.«

Sie rangen lange Zeit mit einander, aber der Riese konnte dem Königssohn, den die Zauberkraft des Ringes stärkte, nichts anhaben. Da sann der Riese auf eine List und sprach »mir ist warm geworden bei dem Kampf, und dir auch, wir

wollen im Flusse baden und uns abkühlen, eh wir wieder
anfangen.« Der Königssohn, der von Falschheit nichts
wusste, gieng mit ihm zu dem Wasser, streifte mit seinen
Kleidern auch den Ring vom Arm und sprang in den Fluss.
Alsbald griff der Riese nach dem Ring und lief damit fort,
aber der Löwe, der den Diebstahl bemerkt hatte, setzte
dem Riesen nach, riss den Ring ihm aus der Hand und
brachte ihn seinem Herrn zurück. Da stellte sich der Riese
hinter einen Eichbaum, und als der Königssohn beschäftigt
war seine Kleider wieder anzuziehen, überfiel er ihn und
stach ihm beide Augen aus.

Nun stand da der arme Königssohn, war blind und wusste
sich nicht zu helfen. Da kam der Riese wieder herbei, fasste
ihn bei der Hand, wie jemand der ihn leiten wollte, und
führte ihn auf die Spitze eines hohen Felsens. Dann ließ er
ihn stehen, und dachte »noch ein paar Schritte weiter, so
stürzt er sich tot, und ich kann ihm den Ring abziehen.«
Aber der treue Löwe hatte seinen Herrn nicht verlassen,
hielt ihn am Kleide fest und zog ihn allmählig wieder zurück. Als der Riese kam und den Toten berauben wollte,
sah er dass seine List vergeblich gewesen war. »Ist denn ein
so schwaches Menschenkind nicht zu verderben!« sprach er
zornig zu sich selbst, fasste den Königssohn und führte ihn
auf einem andern Weg nochmals zu dem Abgrund: aber der
Löwe, der die böse Absicht merkte, half seinem Herrn
auch hier aus der Gefahr. Als sie nahe zum Rand gekommen waren, ließ der Riese die Hand des Blinden fahren und
wollte ihn allein zurücklassen, aber der Löwe stieß den
Riesen, dass er hinab stürzte und zerschmettert auf den Boden fiel.

Das treue Tier zog seinen Herrn wieder von dem Abgrund
zurück und leitete ihn zu einem Baum, an dem ein klarer
Bach floss. Der Königssohn setzte sich da nieder, der Löwe
aber legte sich und spritzte mit seiner Tatze ihm das Wasser
ins Antlitz. Kaum hatten ein paar Tröpfchen die Augenhöhlen benetzt, so konnte er wieder etwas sehen und be-

merkte ein Vöglein, das flog ganz nah vorbei, stieß sich
aber an einen Baumstamm: hierauf ließ es sich in das Wasser herab und badete sich darin, dann flog es auf, strich
ohne anzustoßen zwischen den Bäumen hin, als hätte es
sein Gesicht wieder bekommen. Da erkannte der Königssohn den Wink Gottes, neigte sich herab zu dem Wasser
und wusch und badete sich darin das Gesicht. Und als er
sich aufrichtete, hatte er seine Augen wieder so hell und
rein, wie sie nie gewesen waren.

Der Königssohn dankte Gott für die große Gnade und zog
mit seinem Löwen weiter in der Welt herum. Nun trug
es sich zu dass er vor ein Schloss kam, welches verwünscht
war. In dem Tor stand eine Jungfrau von schöner Gestalt
und feinem Antlitz, aber sie war ganz schwarz. Sie redete
ihn an und sprach »ach, könntest du mich erlösen aus dem
bösen Zauber, der über mich geworfen ist.« »Was soll ich
tun?« sprach der Königssohn. Die Jungfrau antwortete
»drei Nächte musst du in dem großen Saal des verwünschten Schlosses zubringen, aber es darf keine Furcht in dein
Herz kommen. Wenn sich dich auf das ärgste quälen und du
hältst es aus ohne einen Laut von dir zu geben, so bin ich
erlöst; das Leben dürfen sie dir nicht nehmen.« Da sprach
der Königssohn »ich fürchte mich nicht, ich will's mit Gottes Hülfe versuchen.« Also gieng er fröhlich in das Schloss,
und als es dunkel ward, setzte er sich in den großen Saal
und wartete. Es war aber still bis Mitternacht, da fieng
plötzlich ein großer Lärm an, und aus allen Ecken und
Winkeln kamen kleine Teufel herbei. Sie taten als ob sie ihn
nicht sähen, setzten sich mitten in die Stube, machten ein
Feuer an und fiengen an zu spielen. Wenn einer verlor,
sprach er »es ist nicht richtig, es ist einer da, der nicht zu
uns gehört, der ist Schuld, dass ich verliere.« »Wart ich
komme, du hinter dem Ofen«, sagte ein anderer. Das
Schreien ward immer größer, so dass es niemand ohne
Schrecken hätte anhören können. Der Königssohn blieb
ganz ruhig sitzen und hatte keine Furcht: doch endlich

sprangen die Teufel von der Erde auf und fielen über ihn
her, und es waren so viele, dass er sich ihrer nicht erwehren
konnte. Sie zerrten ihn auf dem Boden herum, zwickten,
stachen, schlugen und quälten ihn, aber er gab keinen Laut
von sich. Gegen Morgen verschwanden sie, und er war so
abgemattet, dass er kaum seine Glieder regen konnte: als
aber der Tag anbrach, da trat die schwarze Jungfrau zu ihm
herein. Sie trug in ihrer Hand eine kleine Flasche, worin
Wasser des Lebens war, damit wusch sie ihn, und alsbald
fühlte er wie alle Schmerzen verschwanden und frische
Kraft in seine Adern drang. Sie sprach »eine Nacht hast du
glücklich ausgehalten, aber noch zwei stehen dir bevor.«
Da gieng sie wieder weg, und im Weggehen bemerkte er
dass ihre Füße weiß geworden waren. In der folgenden
Nacht kamen die Teufel und fiengen ihr Spiel aufs neue an:
sie fielen über den Königssohn her und schlugen ihn viel
härter als in der vorigen Nacht, dass sein Leib voll Wunden
war. Doch da er alles still ertrug, mussten sie von ihm lassen, und als die Morgenröte anbrach, erschien die Jungfrau
und heilte ihn mit dem Lebenswasser. Und als sie weggieng, sah er mit Freuden dass sie schon weiß geworden
war bis zu den Fingerspitzen. Nun hatte er nur noch eine
Nacht auszuhalten, aber die war die schlimmste. Der Teu-
felsspuk kam wieder: »bist du noch da?« schrien sie, »du
sollst gepeinigt werden, dass dir der Atem stehen bleibt.«
Sie stachen und schlugen ihn, warfen ihn hin und her und
zogen ihn an Armen und Beinen, als wollten sie ihn zerreißen: aber er duldete alles und gab keinen Laut von sich.
Endlich verschwanden die Teufel, aber er lag da ohnmächtig und regte sich nicht: er konnte auch nicht die Augen
aufheben, um die Jungfrau zu sehen, die herein kam und
ihn mit dem Wasser des Lebens benetzte und begoss. Aber
auf einmal war er von allen Schmerzen befreit und fühlte
sich frisch und gesund, als wäre er aus einem Schlaf erwacht, und wie er die Augen aufschlug, so sah er die Jungfrau neben sich stehen, die war schneeweiß und schön, wie

der helle Tag. »Steh auf«, sprach sie, »und schwing dein
Schwert dreimal über die Treppe, so ist alles erlöst.« Und
als er das getan hatte, da war das ganze Schloss vom Zauber
befreit, und die Jungfrau war eine reiche Königstochter.
Die Diener kamen und sagten im großen Saale wäre die Tafel schon zubereitet und die Speisen aufgetragen. Da setzten sie sich nieder, aßen und tranken zusammen, und
Abends ward in großen Freuden die Hochzeit gefeiert.

122.

Der Krautesel.

Es war einmal ein junger Jäger, der gieng in den Wald auf
Anstand. Er hatte ein frisches und fröhliches Herz, und als
er daher gieng und auf dem Blatt pfiff, kam ein altes hässli-
ches Mütterchen, das redete ihn an und sprach »guten Tag,
lieber Jäger, du bist wohl lustig und vergnügt, aber ich leide
Hunger und Durst, gib mir doch ein Almosen.« Da dauerte
den Jäger das arme Mütterchen, dass er in seine Tasche griff
und ihr nach seinem Vermögen etwas reichte. Nun wollte
er weiter gehen, aber die alte Frau hielt ihn an, und sprach
»höre, lieber Jäger, was ich dir sage, für dein gutes Herz
will ich dir ein Geschenk machen: geh nur immer deiner
Wege, über ein Weilchen wirst du an einen Baum kommen,
darauf sitzen neun Vögel, die haben einen Mantel in den
Krallen und raufen sich darum. Da lege du deine Büchse an
und schieß mitten drunter: den Mantel werden sie dir wohl
fallen lassen, aber auch einer von den Vögeln wird getroffen sein und tot herab stürzen. Den Mantel nimm mit dir,
es ist ein Wunschmantel, wenn du ihn um die Schultern
wirfst, brauchst du dich nur an einen Ort zu wünschen,
und im Augenblick bist du dort. Aus dem toten Vogel
nimm das Herz heraus, und verschluck es ganz, dann wirst

du allen und jeden Morgen früh beim Aufstehen ein Goldstück unter deinem Kopfkissen finden.«

Der Jäger dankte der weisen Frau und dachte bei sich »schöne Dinge, die sie mir versprochen hat, wenn's nur auch all so einträfe.« Doch, wie er etwa hundert Schritte gegangen war, hörte er über sich in den Ästen ein Geschrei und Gezwitscher, dass er aufschauete: da sah er einen Haufen Vögel, die rissen mit den Schnäbeln und Füßen ein Tuch herum, schrien, zerrten und balgten sich, als wollt's ein jeder allein haben. »Nun«, sprach der Jäger, »das ist wunderlich, es kommt ja gerade so, wie das Mütterchen gesagt hat«, nahm die Büchse von der Schulter, legte an und tat seinen Schuss mitten hinein, dass die Federn herumflogen. Alsbald nahm das Getier mit großem Schreien die Flucht, aber einer fiel tot herab, und der Mantel sank ebenfalls herunter. Da tat der Jäger wie ihm die Alte geheißen hatte, schnitt den Vogel auf, suchte das Herz, schluckte es hinunter und nahm den Mantel mit nach Haus.

Am andern Morgen, als er aufwachte, fiel ihm die Verheißung ein, und er wollte sehen ob sie auch eingetroffen wäre. Wie er aber sein Kopfkissen in die Höhe hob, da schimmerte ihm das Goldstück entgegen und am andern Morgen fand er wieder eins, und so weiter jedesmal, wenn er aufstand. Er sammlete sich einen Haufen Gold, endlich aber dachte er »was hilft mir all mein Gold, wenn ich daheim bleibe? ich will ausziehen und mich in der Welt umsehen.«

Da nahm er von seinen Eltern Abschied, hieng seinen Jägerranzen und seine Flinte um und zog in die Welt. Es trug sich zu, dass er eines Tages durch einen dicken Wald kam, und wie der zu Ende war lag in der Ebene vor ihm ein ansehnliches Schloss. In einem Fenster desselben stand eine Alte mit einer wunderschönen Jungfrau und schaute herab. Die Alte aber war eine Hexe und sprach zu dem Mädchen »dort kommt einer aus dem Wald, der hat einen wunderbaren Schatz im Leib, den müssen wir darum berücken, mein

Herzenstöchterchen: uns steht das besser an als ihm. Er hat ein Vogelherz bei sich, deshalb liegt jeden Morgen ein Goldstück unter seinem Kopfkissen.« Sie erzählt ihr wie es damit beschaffen wäre und wie sie darum zu spielen hätte, und zuletzt drohte sie und sprach mit zornigen Augen »und wenn du mir nicht gehorchst, so bist du unglücklich.« Als nun der Jäger näher kam, erblickte er das Mädchen und sprach zu sich »ich bin nun so lang herumgezogen, ich will einmal ausruhen und in das schöne Schloss einkehren, Geld hab ich ja vollauf.« Eigentlich aber war die Ursache, dass er ein Auge auf das schöne Bild geworfen hatte.

Er trat in das Haus ein, und ward freundlich empfangen und höflich bewirtet. Es dauerte nicht lange, da war er so in das Hexenmädchen verliebt, dass er an nichts anders mehr dachte und nur nach ihren Augen sah, und was sie verlangte, das tat er gerne. Da sprach die Alte »nun müssen wir das Vogelherz haben, er wird nichts spüren, wenn es ihm fehlt.« Sie richteten einen Trank zu, und wie der gekocht war, tat sie ihn in einen Becher und gab ihn dem Mädchen, das musste ihn dem Jäger reichen. Sprach es »nun, mein Liebster, trink mir zu.« Da nahm er den Becher, und wie er den Trank geschluckt hatte, brach er das Herz des Vogels aus dem Leibe. Das Mädchen musste es heimlich fortschaffen und dann selbst verschlucken, denn die Alte wollte es haben. Von nun an fand er kein Gold mehr unter seinem Kopfkissen, sondern es lag unter dem Kissen des Mädchens, wo es die Alte jeden Morgen holte: aber er war so verliebt und vernarrt, dass er an nichts anders dachte, als sich mit dem Mädchen die Zeit zu vertreiben.

Da sprach die alte Hexe »das Vogelherz haben wir, aber den Wunschmantel müssen wir ihm auch abnehmen.« Antwortete das Mädchen »den wollen wir ihm lassen, er hat ja doch seinen Reichtum verloren.« Da ward die Alte bös und sprach »so ein Mantel ist ein wunderbares Ding, das selten auf der Welt gefunden wird, den soll und muss ich haben.« Sie gab dem Mädchen Anschläge und sagte wenn es ihr nicht gehorchte, sollte es ihm schlimm ergehen. Da tat es nach dem Geheiß der Alten, stellte sich einmal ans Fenster und schaute in die weite Gegend, als wäre es ganz traurig. Fragte der Jäger »was stehst du so traurig da?« »Ach, mein Schatz«, gab es zur Antwort, »da gegenüber liegt der Granatenberg, wo die köstlichen Edelsteine wachsen. Ich trage so groß Verlangen danach, dass wenn ich daran denke, ich ganz traurig bin; aber wer kann sie holen! nur die Vögel, die fliegen, kommen hin, ein Mensch nimmermehr.« »Hast du weiter nichts zu klagen«, sagte der Jäger, »den Kummer will ich dir bald vom Herzen nehmen.« Damit fasste er sie unter seinen Mantel und wünschte sich hinüber auf den Granatenberg, und im Augenblick saßen sie auch beide drauf. Da schimmerte das edele Gestein von allen Seiten dass es eine Freude war anzusehen, und sie lasen die schönsten und kostbarsten Stücke zusammen. Nun hatte es aber die Alte durch ihre Hexenkunst bewirkt, dass dem Jäger die Augen schwer wurden. Er sprach zu dem Mädchen »wir wollen ein wenig niedersitzen und ruhen, ich bin so müde, dass ich mich nicht mehr auf den Füßen erhalten kann.« Da setzten sie sich, und er legte sein Haupt in ihren Schoß und schlief ein. Wie er entschlafen war, da band es ihm den Mantel von den Schultern und hieng ihn sich selbst um, las die Granaten und Steine auf und wünschte sich damit nach Haus.

Als aber der Jäger seinen Schlaf ausgetan hatte und aufwachte, sah er dass seine Liebste ihn betrogen und auf dem wilden Gebirg allein gelassen hatte. »Oh«, sprach er, »wie ist die Untreue so groß auf der Welt!« saß da in Sorge und Herzeleid und wusste nicht was er anfangen sollte. Der Berg aber gehörte wilden und ungeheuern Riesen, die darauf wohnten und ihr Wesen trieben, und er saß nicht lange, so sah er ihrer drei daher schreiten. Da legte er sich nieder, als wäre er in tiefen Schlaf versunken. Nun kamen die Riesen herbei, und der erste stieß ihn mit dem Fuß an und sprach »was liegt da für ein Erdwurm und beschaut sich in-

wendig?« Der zweite sprach »tritt ihn tot.« Der dritte aber
sprach verächtlich »das wäre der Mühe wert! lasst ihn nur
leben, hier kann er nicht bleiben, und wenn er höher steigt
bis auf die Bergspitze, so packen ihn die Wolken und tragen ihn fort.« Unter diesem Gespräch giengen sie vorüber,
der Jäger aber hatte auf ihre Worte gemerkt, und sobald sie
fort waren, stand er auf und klimmte den Berggipfel hinauf.
Als er ein Weilchen da gesessen hatte, so schwebte eine
Wolke heran, ergriff ihn, trug ihn fort und zog eine Zeitlang am Himmel her, dann senkte sie sich und ließ sich
über einen großen, rings mit Mauern umgebenen Krautgar-
ten nieder, also dass er zwischen Kohl und Gemüsen sanft
auf den Boden kam.

Da sah der Jäger sich um und sprach »wenn ich nur etwas
zu essen hätte, ich bin so hungrig, und mit dem Weiter-
kommen wird's schwer fallen; aber hier seh ich keinen Apfel und keine Birne und keinerlei Obst, überall nichts als
Krautwerk.« Endlich dachte er »zur Not kann ich von dem
Salat essen, der schmeckt nicht sonderlich, wird mich aber
erfrischen.« Also suchte er sich ein schönes Haupt aus und
aß davon, aber kaum hatte er ein paar Bissen hinab geschluckt, so war ihm so wunderlich zu Mute, und er fühlte
sich ganz verändert. Es wuchsen ihm vier Beine, ein dicker
Kopf und zwei lange Ohren, und er sah mit Schrecken dass
er in einen Esel verwandelt war. Doch weil er dabei immer
noch großen Hunger spürte und ihm der saftige Salat nach
seiner jetzigen Natur gut schmeckte, so aß er mit großer
Gier immer zu. Endlich gelangte er an eine andere Art Salat, aber kaum hatte er etwas davon verschluckt, so fühlte
er aufs neue eine Veränderung, und kehrte in seine menschliche Gestalt zurück.

Nun legte sich der Jäger nieder und schlief seine Müdigkeit
aus. Als er am andern Morgen erwachte, brach er ein
Haupt von dem bösen und eins von dem guten Salat ab und
dachte »das soll mir zu dem Meinigen wieder helfen und
die Treulosigkeit bestrafen.« Dann steckte er die Häupter

zu sich, kletterte über die Mauer und gieng fort, das Schloss seiner Liebsten zu suchen. Als er ein paar Tage herum gestrichen war, fand er es glücklicherweise wieder. Da bräunte er sich schnell sein Gesicht, dass ihn seine eigene Mutter nicht erkannt hätte, gieng in das Schloss und bat um eine Herberge. »Ich bin so müde«, sprach er, »und kann nicht weiter.« Fragte die Hexe »Landsmann, wer seid ihr, und was ist euer Geschäft?« Er antwortete »ich bin ein Bote des Königs und war ausgeschickt den köstlichsten Salat zu suchen, der unter der Sonne wächst. Ich bin auch so glücklich gewesen ihn zu finden und trage ihn bei mir, aber die Sonnenhitze brennt gar zu stark, dass mir das zarte Kraut zu welken droht und ich nicht weiß ob ich es weiter bringen werde.«

Als die Alte von dem köstlichen Salat hörte, ward sie lüstern und sprach »lieber Landsmann, lasst mich doch den wunderbaren Salat versuchen.« »Warum nicht?« antwortete er, »ich habe zwei Häupter mitgebracht und will euch eins geben«, machte seinen Sack auf und reichte ihr das böse hin. Die Hexe dachte an nichts arges und der Mund wässerte ihr so sehr nach dem neuen Gericht, dass sie selbst in die Küche gieng und es zubereitete. Als es fertig war, konnte sie nicht warten, bis es auf dem Tisch stand, sondern sie nahm gleich ein paar Blätter und steckte sie in den Mund, kaum aber waren sie verschluckt, so war auch die menschliche Gestalt verloren, und sie lief als eine Eselin hinab in den Hof. Nun kam die Magd in die Küche, sah den fertigen Salat da stehen und wollte ihn auftragen, unterwegs aber überfiel sie, nach alter Gewohnheit, die Lust zu versuchen, und sie aß ein paar Blätter. Alsbald zeigte sich die Wunderkraft, und sie ward ebenfalls zu einer Eselin und lief hinaus zu der Alten, und die Schüssel mit Salat fiel auf die Erde. Der Bote saß in der Zeit bei dem schönen Mädchen, und als niemand mit dem Salat kam, und es doch auch lüstern danach war, sprach es »ich weiß nicht wo der Salat bleibt.« Da dachte der Jäger »das Kraut wird schon gewirkt haben«

und sprach »ich will nach der Küche gehen und mich er-
kundigen.« Wie er hinab kam, sah er die zwei Eselinnen im
Hof herum laufen, der Salat aber lag auf der Erde. »Schon
recht«, sprach er, »die zwei haben ihr Teil weg« und hob
die übrigen Blätter auf, legte sie auf die Schüssel und brachte sie dem Mädchen. »Ich bring euch selbst das köstliche
Essen«, sprach er, »damit ihr nicht länger zu warten
braucht.« Da aß sie davon und war alsbald wie die übrigen
ihrer menschlichen Gestalt beraubt und lief als eine Eselin
in den Hof.

Nachdem sich der Jäger sein Angesicht gewaschen hatte,
also dass ihn die Verwandelten erkennen konnten, gieng er
hinab in den Hof und sprach »jetzt sollt ihr den Lohn für
eure Untreue empfangen.« Er band sie alle drei an ein Seil
und trieb sie fort, bis er zu einer Mühle kam. Er klopfte an
das Fenster, der Müller steckte den Kopf heraus und fragte
was sein Begehren wäre. »Ich habe drei böse Tiere«, antwortete er, »die ich nicht länger behalten mag. Wollt ihr sie
bei euch nehmen, Futter und Lager geben, und sie halten
wie ich euch sage, so zahl ich dafür was ihr verlangt.«
Sprach der Müller »warum das nicht? wie soll ich sie aber
halten?« Da sagte der Jäger der alten Eselin, und das war
die Hexe, sollte er täglich dreimal Schläge und einmal zu
fressen geben; der jüngern, welche die Magd war, einmal
Schläge und dreimal Futter; und der jüngsten, welche das
Mädchen war, keinmal Schläge und dreimal zu fressen;
denn er konnte es doch nicht über das Herz bringen, dass
das Mädchen sollte geschlagen werden. Darauf gieng er zurück in das Schloss, und was er nötig hatte, das fand er alles
darin.

Nach ein paar Tagen kam der Müller und sprach er müsste
melden dass die alte Eselin, die nur Schläge bekommen hätte und nur einmal zu fressen, gestorben wäre. »Die zwei
andern«, sagte er weiter, »sind zwar nicht gestorben und
kriegen auch dreimal zu fressen, aber sie sind so traurig,
dass es nicht lange mit ihnen dauern kann.« Da erbarmte

sich der Jäger, ließ den Zorn fahren und sprach zum Müller er sollte sie wieder hertreiben. Und wie sie kamen, gab er ihnen von dem guten Salat zu fressen, dass sie wieder zu Menschen wurden. Da fiel das schöne Mädchen vor ihm auf die Knie und sprach »ach, mein Liebster, verzeiht mir was ich Böses an euch getan, meine Mutter hatte mich dazu gezwungen; es ist gegen meinen Willen geschehen, denn ich habe euch von Herzen lieb. Euer Wunschmantel hängt in einem Schrank, und für das Vogelherz will ich einen Brechtrunk einnehmen.« Da ward er anderes Sinnes, und sprach »behalt es nur, es ist doch einerlei, denn ich will dich zu meiner treuen Ehegemahlin annehmen.« Und da ward Hochzeit gehalten, und sie lebten vergnügt mit einander bis an ihren Tod.

123.

Die Alte im Wald.

Es fuhr einmal ein armes Dienstmädchen mit seiner Herrschaft durch einen großen Wald, und als sie mitten darin waren, kamen Räuber aus dem Dickicht hervor und ermordeten wen sie fanden. Da kamen alle mit einander um bis auf das Mädchen, das war in der Angst aus dem Wagen gesprungen und hatte sich hinter einen Baum verborgen. Wie die Räuber mit ihrer Beute fort waren, trat es herbei und sah das große Unglück. Da fieng es an bitterlich zu weinen und sagte »was soll ich armes Mädchen nun anfangen, ich weiß mich nicht aus dem Wald heraus zu finden, keine Menschenseele wohnt darin, so muss ich gewiss verhungern.« Es gieng herum, suchte einen Weg, konnte aber keinen finden. Als es Abend war, setzte es sich unter einen Baum, befahl sich Gott, und wollte da sitzen bleiben und nicht weggehen, möchte geschehen was immer wollte. Als es aber eine Weile da gesessen hatte, kam ein weiß Täub-

chen zu ihm geflogen und hatte ein kleines goldenes
Schlüsselchen im Schnabel. Das Schlüsselchen legte es ihm
in die Hand und sprach »siehst du dort den großen Baum,
daran ist ein kleines Schloss, das schließ mit dem Schlüsselchen auf, so wirst du Speise genug finden und keinen Hunger mehr leiden.« Da gieng es zu dem Baum und schloss
ihn auf und fand Milch in einem kleinen Schüsselchen und
Weißbrot zum Einbrocken dabei, dass es sich satt essen
konnte. Als es satt war, sprach es »jetzt ist es Zeit, wo die
Hühner daheim auffliegen, ich bin so müde, könnt ich
mich doch auch in mein Bett legen.« Da kam das Täubchen
wieder geflogen und brachte ein anderes goldenes Schlüsselchen im Schnabel und sagte »schließ dort den Baum auf,
so wirst du ein Bett finden.« Da schloss es auf und fand ein
schönes weiches Bettchen: da betete es zum lieben Gott, er
möchte es behüten in der Nacht, legte sich und schlief ein.
Am Morgen kam das Täubchen zum drittenmal, brachte
wieder ein Schlüsselchen und sprach »schließ dort den
Baum auf, da wirst du Kleider finden«, und wie es aufschloss, fand es Kleider mit Gold und Edelsteinen besetzt,
so herrlich, wie sie keine Königstochter hat. Also lebte es
da eine Zeit lang und kam das Täubchen alle Tage und
sorgte für alles, was es bedurfte, und war das ein stilles, gutes Leben.

Einmal aber kam das Täubchen und sprach »willst du mir
etwas zu Liebe tun?« »Von Herzen gerne« sagte das Mädchen. Da sprach das Täubchen »ich will dich zu einem kleinen Häuschen führen, da geh hinein, mittendrein am Herd
wird eine alte Frau sitzen und »guten Tag« sagen. Aber gieb
ihr bei Leibe keine Antwort sie mag auch anfangen, was sie
will, sondern geh zu ihrer rechten Hand weiter, da ist eine
Türe, die mach auf, so wirst du in eine Stube kommen, wo
eine Menge von Ringen allerlei Art auf dem Tisch liegt,
darunter sind prächtige mit glitzerigen Steinen, die lass aber
liegen und suche einen schlichten heraus, der auch darunter
sein muss, und bring ihn zu mir her so geschwind du

kannst.« Das Mädchen gieng zu dem Häuschen und trat zu der Türe ein: da saß eine Alte, die machte große Augen wie sie es erblickte und sprach »guten Tag mein Kind.« Es gab ihr aber keine Antwort und gieng auf die Türe zu. »Wo hinaus?« rief sie und fasste es beim Rock und wollte es festhalten, »das ist mein Haus, da darf niemand herein, wenn ich's nicht haben will.« Aber das Mädchen schwieg still, machte sich von ihr los und gieng gerade in die Stube hinein. Da lag nun auf dem Tisch eine übergroße Menge von Ringen, die glitzten und glimmerten ihm vor den Augen: es warf sie herum und suchte nach dem schlichten, konnte ihn aber nicht finden. Wie es so suchte, sah es die Alte, wie sie daher schlich und einen Vogelkäfig in der Hand hatte und damit fort wollte. Da gieng es auf sie zu und nahm ihr den Käfig aus der Hand, und wie es ihn aufhob und hinein sah, saß ein Vogel darin, der hatte den schlichten Ring im Schnabel. Da nahm es den Ring und lief ganz froh damit zum Haus hinaus und dachte das weiße Täubchen würde kommen und den Ring holen, aber es kam nicht. Da lehnte es sich an einen Baum und wollte auf das Täubchen warten, und wie es so stand, da war es als wäre der Baum weich und biegsam und senkte seine Zweige herab. Und auf einmal schlangen sich die Zweige um es herum, und waren zwei Arme, und wie es sich umsah, war der Baum ein schöner Mann, der es umfasste und herzlich küsste und sagte »du hast mich erlöst und aus der Gewalt der Alten befreit, die eine böse Hexe ist. Sie hatte mich in einen Baum verwandelt, und alle Tage ein paar Stunden war ich eine weiße Taube, und so lang sie den Ring besaß, konnte ich meine menschliche Gestalt nicht wieder erhalten.« Da waren auch seine Bedienten und Pferde von dem Zauber frei, der sie auch in Bäume verwandelt hatte, und standen neben ihm. Da fuhren sie fort in sein Reich, denn er war eines Königs Sohn, und sie heirateten sich und lebten glücklich.

124.

Die drei Brüder.

Es war ein Mann, der hatte drei Söhne und weiter nichts im
Vermögen als das Haus, worin er wohnte. Nun hätte jeder
gerne nach seinem Tode das Haus gehabt, dem Vater war
aber einer so lieb als der andere, da wusste er nicht wie er's
anfangen sollte, dass er keinem zu nahe tät; verkaufen wollte er das Haus auch nicht, weil's von seinen Voreltern war,
sonst hätte er das Geld unter sie geteilt. Da fiel ihm endlich
ein Rat ein und er sprach zu seinen Söhnen »geht in die
Welt und versucht euch und lerne jeder sein Handwerk,
wenn ihr dann wiederkommt, wer das beste Meisterstück
macht, der soll das Haus haben.«
Das waren die Söhne zufrieden, und der älteste wollte ein
Hufschmied, der zweite ein Barbier, der dritte aber ein
Fechtmeister werden. Darauf bestimmten sie eine Zeit, wo
sie wieder nach Haus zusammen kommen wollten, und zogen fort. Es traf sich auch, dass jeder einen tüchtigen Meister fand, wo er was rechtschaffenes lernte. Der Schmied
musste des Königs Pferde beschlagen und dachte »nun
kann dir's nicht fehlen, du kriegst das Haus.« Der Barbier
rasierte lauter vornehme Herren und meinte auch das Haus
wäre schon sein. Der Fechtmeister kriegte manchen Hieb,
biss aber die Zähne zusammen und ließ sich's nicht verdrießen, denn er dachte bei sich »fürchtest du dich vor einem
Hieb, so kriegst du das Haus nimmermehr.« Als nun die
gesetzte Zeit herum war, kamen sie bei ihrem Vater wieder
zusammen: sie wussten aber nicht wie sie die beste Gelegenheit finden sollten, ihre Kunst zu zeigen, saßen beisammen und ratschlagten. Wie sie so saßen, kam auf einmal ein Hase übers Feld daher gelaufen. »Ei«, sagte der
Barbier, »der kommt wie gerufen«, nahm Becken und Seife,
schaumte so lange, bis der Hase in die Nähe kam, dann
seifte er ihn in vollem Laufe ein, und rasierte ihm auch in

vollem Laufe ein Stutzbärtchen, und dabei schnitt er ihn nicht und tat ihm an keinem Haare weh. »Das gefällt mir«, sagte der Vater, »wenn sich die andern nicht gewaltig angreifen, so ist das Haus dein.« Es währte nicht lang, so kam ein Herr in einem Wagen daher gerennt in vollem Jagen. »Nun sollt ihr sehen, Vater, was ich kann«, sprach der Hufschmied, sprang dem Wagen nach, riss dem Pferd, das in einem fort jagte, die vier Hufeisen ab und schlug ihm auch im Jagen vier neue wieder an. »Du bist ein ganzer Kerl«, sprach der Vater, »du machst deine Sachen so gut, wie dein Bruder; ich weiß nicht wem ich das Haus geben soll.« Da sprach der dritte »Vater, lasst mich auch einmal gewähren«, und weil es anfing zu regnen, zog er seinen Degen und schwenkte ihn in Kreuzhieben über seinen Kopf, dass kein Tropfen auf ihn fiel: und als der Regen stärker ward, und endlich so stark, als ob man mit Mulden vom Himmel gösse, schwang er den Degen immer schneller und blieb so trocken, als säß er unter Dach und Fach. Wie der Vater das sah, erstaunte er und sprach »du hast das beste Meisterstück gemacht, das Haus ist dein.«

Die beiden andern Brüder waren damit zufrieden, wie sie vorher gelobt hatten, und weil sie sich einander so lieb hatten, blieben sie alle drei zusammen im Haus und trieben ihr Handwerk; und da sie so gut ausgelernt hatten und so geschickt waren, verdienten sie viel Geld. So lebten sie vergnügt bis in ihr Alter zusammen, und als der eine krank ward und starb, grämten sich die zwei andern so sehr darüber, dass sie auch krank wurden und bald starben. Da wurden sie, weil sie so geschickt gewesen waren und sich so lieb gehabt hatten, alle drei zusammen in ein Grab gelegt.

125

Der Teufel und seine Großmutter.

Es war ein großer Krieg, und der König hatte viel Soldaten, gab ihnen aber wenig Sold, so dass sie nicht davon leben konnten. Da taten sich drei zusammen und wollten ausreißen. Einer sprach zum andern »wenn wir erwischt werden, so hängt man uns an den Galgenbaum: wie wollen wir's machen?« Sprach der andere »seht dort das große Kornfeld, wenn wir uns da verstecken, so findet uns kein Mensch: das Heer darf nicht hinein und muss morgen weiter ziehen.« Sie krochen in das Korn, aber das Heer zog nicht weiter, sondern blieb rund herum liegen. Sie saßen zwei Tage und zwei Nächte im Korn und hatten so großen Hunger dass sie beinah gestorben wären: giengen sie aber heraus, so war ihnen der Tod gewiss. Da sprachen sie »was hilft uns unser Ausreißen, wir müssen hier elendig sterben.« Indem kam ein feuriger Drache durch die Luft geflogen, der senkte sich zu ihnen herab und fragte sie warum sie sich da versteckt hätten. Sie antworteten »wir sind drei Soldaten und sind ausgerissen, weil unser Sold gering war: nun müssen wir hier Hungers sterben, wenn wir liegen bleiben, oder wir müssen am Galgen baumeln, wenn wir heraus gehen.« »Wollt ihr mir sieben Jahre dienen«, sagte der Drache, »so will ich euch mitten durchs Heer führen, dass euch niemand erwischen soll.« »Wir haben keine Wahl und müssen's annehmen« antworteten sie. Da packte sie der Drache in seine Klauen, führte sie durch die Luft über das Heer hinweg und setzte sie weit davon wieder auf die Erde; der Drache war aber niemand als der Teufel. Er gab ihnen ein kleines Peitschchen und sprach »peitscht und knallt ihr damit, so wird so viel Geld vor euch herum springen, als ihr verlangt: ihr könnt dann wie große Herrn leben, Pferde halten und in Wagen fahren: nach Verlauf der sieben Jahre aber seid ihr mein eigen.« Dann hielt er ihnen ein Buch vor, in das mussten sie sich alle drei unterschreiben. »Doch will ich euch«, sprach er, »erst noch ein Rätsel aufgeben, könnt ihr das raten, sollt ihr frei sein und aus meiner Gewalt entlassen.« Da flog der Drache von ihnen weg, und sie reisten fort mit ihren Peitschchen, hatten Geld die Fülle, ließen sich Herrenkleider machen und zogen in der Welt herum. Wo sie waren, lebten sie in Freuden und Herrlichkeit, fuhren mit Pferden und Wagen, aßen und tranken, taten aber nichts Böses. Die Zeit verstrich ihnen schnell, und als es mit den sieben Jahren zu Ende gieng, ward zweien gewaltig angst und bang, der dritte aber nahm's auf die leichte Schulter und sprach »Brüder, fürchtet nichts, ich bin nicht auf den Kopf gefallen, ich errate das Rätsel.« Sie giengen hinaus aufs Feld, saßen da und die zwei machten betrübte Gesichter. Da kam eine alte Frau daher, die fragte warum sie so traurig wären. »Ach, was liegt euch daran, ihr könnt uns doch nicht helfen.« »Wer weiß«, antwortete sie, »vertraut mir nur euern Kummer.« Da erzählten sie ihr sie wären des Teufels Diener gewesen, fast sieben Jahre lang, der hätte ihnen Geld wie Heu geschafft, sie hätten sich ihm aber verschrieben, und wären ihm verfallen, wenn sie nach den sieben Jahren nicht ein Rätsel auflösen könnten. Die Alte sprach »soll euch geholfen werden, so muss einer von euch in den Wald gehen, da wird er an eine eingestürzte Felsenwand kommen, die aussieht wie ein Häuschen, in das muss er eintreten, dann wird er Hilfe finden.« Die zwei traurigen dachten »das wird uns doch nicht retten«, und blieben sitzen, der dritte aber, der lustige, machte sich auf und gieng so weit in den Wald, bis er die Felsenhütte fand. In dem Häuschen aber saß eine steinalte Frau, die war des Teufels Großmutter, und fragte ihn woher er käme und was er hier wollte. Er erzählte ihr alles, was geschehen war, und weil er ihr wohl gefiel, hatte sie Erbarmen und sagte sie wollte ihm helfen. Sie hob einen großen Stein auf, der über einem Keller lag, und sagte »da verstecke dich, du kannst alles hören was hier gesprochen wird, sitz nur still und rege dich nicht: wann der Drache kommt, will ich ihn wegen der Rätsel befragen: mir sagt er alles; und dann achte auf das was er antwortet.« Um zwölf Uhr Nachts kam der Drache angeflogen und verlangte sein Essen. Die Großmutter deckte den Tisch und trug Trank und Speise auf, dass er vergnügt war, und sie aßen und tranken zusammen. Da fragte sie ihn im Gespräch wie's den Tag ergangen wäre, und wie viel Seelen er kriegt hätte. »Es wollte mir heute nicht recht glücken«, antwortete er, »aber ich habe drei Soldaten gepackt, die sind mir sicher.« »Ja, drei Soldaten«, sagte sie, »die haben etwas an sich, die können dir noch entkommen.« Sprach der Teufel höhnisch »die sind mein, denen gebe ich noch ein Rätsel auf, das sie nimmermehr raten können.« »Was ist das für ein Rätsel?« fragte sie. »Das will ich dir sagen: in der großen Nordsee liegt eine tote Meerkatze, das soll ihr Braten sein: und von einem Walfisch die Rippe, das soll ihr silberner Löffel sein; und ein alter hohler Pferdefuß, das soll ihr Weinglas sein.« Als der Teufel zu Bett gegangen war, hob die alte Großmutter den Stein auf und ließ den Soldaten heraus. »Hast du auch alles wohl in Acht genommen?« »Ja«, sprach er, »ich weiß genug und will mir schon helfen.« Darauf musste er auf einem andern Weg durchs Fenster heimlich und in aller Eile zu seinen Gesellen zurück gehen. Er erzählte ihnen, wie der Teufel von der alten Großmutter wäre überlistet worden und wie er die Auflösung des Rätsels von ihm vernommen hätte. Da waren sie alle fröhlich und guter Dinge, nahmen die Peitsche und schlugen sich so viel Geld dass es auf der Erde herum sprang. Als die sieben Jahre völlig herum waren, kam der Teufel mit dem Buche, zeigte die Unterschriften und sprach »ich will euch mit in die Hölle nehmen, da sollt ihr eine Mahlzeit haben: könnt ihr mir raten, was ihr für einen Braten werdet zu essen kriegen, so sollt ihr frei und los sein und dürft auch das Peitschchen behalten.« Da fieng der erste Soldat an »in der großen Nordsee liegt eine tote Meerkatze, das wird wohl der Braten sein.« Der Teufel är-

gerte sich, machte »hm! hm! hm!« und fragte den zweiten
»was soll aber euer Löffel sein?« »Von einem Walfisch die
Rippe, das soll unser silberner Löffel sein.« Der Teufel
schnitt ein Gesicht, knurrte wieder dreimal »hm! hm! hm!«
und sprach zum dritten »wisst ihr auch was euer Weinglas
sein soll?« »Ein alter Pferdefuß, das soll unser Weinglas
sein.« Da flog der Teufel mit einem lauten Schrei fort und
hatte keine Gewalt mehr über sie: aber die drei behielten
das Peitschchen, schlugen Geld hervor, so viel sie wollten,
und lebten vergnügt bis an ihr Ende.

126.

Ferenand getrü un Ferenand ungetrü.

Et was mal en Mann un ne Fru west, de hadden so lange se
rick wören kene Kinner, as se awerst arm woren, da kregen
se en kleinen Jungen. Se kunnen awerst kenen Paen dato
kregen, da segde de Mann, he wulle mal na den annern
Ohre (Orte) gahn un tosehn ob he da enen krege. Wie he
so gienk, begegnete ünn en armen Mann, de frog en wo he
hünne wulle, he segde he wulle hünn un tosehn dat he 'n
Paen kriegte, he sie arm, un da wulle ünn ken Minske to
Gevaher stahn. »Oh«, segde de arme Mann, »gi sied arm,
un· ik sie arm, ik will guhe (Euer) Gevaher weren; ik sie
awerst so arm, ik kann dem Kinne nix giwen, gahet hen un
segget de Bähmoer (Wehmutter) se sulle man mit den Kinne na der Kerken kummen.« Ase se nu tohaupe an der Kerken kummet, da is de Bettler schaun darinne, de givt dem
Kinne den Namen *Ferenand getrü*.
Wie he nu ut der Kerken gahet, da segd de Bettler, »nu gahet
man na Hus, ik kann guh (euch) nix giwen un gi süllt mi ok
nix giwen.« De Bähmoer awerst gav he 'n Schlüttel un segd
er se mögt en, wenn se na Hus käme, dem Vaer giwen, de

sull 'n verwahren, bis dat Kind vertein Johr old wöre, dann
sull et up de Heide gahn, da wöre 'n Schlott, dato passte de
Schlüttel, wat darin wöre, dat sulle em hören. Wie dat Kind
nu sewen Johr alt wor, un düet (tüchtig) wassen wor, gienk
et mal spilen mit annern Jungens, da hadde de eine noch
mehr vom Paen kriegt, ase de annere, he awerst kunne nix
seggen, un da grinde he un gienk na Hus un segde tom Vaer
»hewe ik denn gar nix vom Paen kriegt?« »O ja«, segde de
Vaer, »du hest en Schlüttel kriegt, wenn up de Heide 'n
Schlott steit, so gah man hen un schlut et up.« Da gienk he
hen, awerst et was kein Schlott to hören un to sehen. Wier na
sewen Jahren, ase he vertein Johr old is, geit he nochmals
hen, da steit en Schlott darup. Wie he et upschloten het, da is
der nix enne, ase 'n Perd, 'n Schümmel. Da werd de Junge so
vuller Früden dat he dat Perd hadde, dat he sik darup sett un
to sinen Vaer jegd (jagt). »Nu hew ik auck 'n Schümmel, nu
will ik auck reisen« segd he.

Da treckt he weg, un wie he unnerweges is, ligd da ne
Schriffedder up 'n Wegge, he will se eist (erst) upnümmen,
da denkt he awerst wier bie sich »Oh, du süst se auck liggen laten, du findst ja wul, wo du hen kümmst, ne Schriffedder, wenn du eine bruckest.« Wie he so weggeit, do
roppt et hinner üm »Ferenand getrü, nümm se mit.« He süt
sik ümme, süt awerst keinen, da geit he wier torugge un
nümmt se up. Wie he wier ne Wile rien (geritten) is, kümmt
he bie 'n Water vorbie, so ligd da en Fisk am Oewer (Ufer)
un snappet un happet na Luft; so segd he »töv, min lewe
Fisk, ik will die helpen, dat du in't Water kümmst«, un
gript 'n bie 'n Schwans un werpt 'n in't Water. Da steckt de
Fisk den Kopp ut den Water un segd »nu du mie ut den
Kot holpen hest, will ik die ne Flötenpiepen giwen, wenn
du in de Naud bist, so flöte derup, dann will ik die helpen,
un wenn du mal wat in Water hest fallen laten, so flöte
man, so will ik et die herut reicken.« Nu ritt he wege, da
kümmt so 'n Minsk to üm, de frägt 'n wo he hen wull.
»Oh, na den neggsten Ohre.« Wu he dann heite? »Fere-

nand getrü.« »Sü, da hewe wie ja fast den sülwigen Namen, ik heite *Ferenand ungetrü*.« Da trecket se beide na den neggsten Ohre in dat Wertshus.

Nu was et schlimm, dat de Ferenand ungetrü allet wuste wat 'n annerer dacht hadde un doen wulle; dat wust he döre so allerhand slimme Kunste. Et was awerst im Wertshuse so 'n wacker Mäken, dat hadde 'n schier (klares) Angesicht un drog sik so hübsch; dat verleiv sik in den Ferenand getrü, denn et was 'n hübschen Minschen west, un frog 'n wo he hen to wulle. Oh, he wulle so herümmer reisen. Da segd se so sull he doch nur da bliewen, et wöre hier to Lanne 'n Künig, de neime wull geren 'n Bedeenten oder 'n Vorrüter: dabie sulle he in Diensten gahn. He antworde he kunne nig gud so to einen hingahen un been sik an. Da segde dat Mäken »Oh, dat will ik dann schun dauen.« Un so gienk se auck stracks hen na den Künig un sehde ünn se wüste ünn 'n hübschen Bedeenten. Dat was de wol tofreen un leit 'n to sik kummen un wull 'n tom Bedeenten macken. He wull awerst leewer Vorrüter sin, denn wo sin Perd wöre, da möst he auck sin; da mackt 'n de Künig tom Vorrüter. Wie düt de Ferenand ungetrü gewahr wore, da segd he to den Mäken »töv, helpest du den an un mie nig?« »Oh«, segd dat Mäken, »ik will 'n auck anhelpen.« Se dachte »den most du die tom Frünne wahren, denn he is nig to truen.« Se geit alse vorm Künig stahn un beed 'n als Bedeenten an; dat is de Künig tofreen.

Wenn he nu also det Morgens den Heren antrock, da jammerte de jümmer »o wenn ik doch eist mine Leiveste bie mie hädde.« De Ferenand ungetrü was awerst dem Ferenand getrü jümmer uppsettsig, wie asso de Künig mal wier so jammerte, da segd he »Sie haben ja den Vorreiter, den schicken Sie hin, der muss sie herbeischaffen, und wenn er es nicht tut, so muss ihm der Kopf vor die Füße gelegt werden.« Do leit de Künig den Ferenand getrü to sik kummen un sehde üm he hädde da un da ne Leiveste, de sull he ünn herschappen, wenn he dat nig deie, sull he sterwen.

De Ferenand getrü gienk in Stall to sinen Schümmel un
grinde un jammerde. »O wat sin ik 'n unglücksch Min-
schenkind.« Do röppet jeimes hinner üm »Ferdinand getreu, was weinst du?« He süt sik um, süt awerst neimes, un
jammerd jümmer fort »o min lewe Schümmelken, nu mot
ik die verlaten, nu mot ik sterwen.« Do röppet et wier
»Ferdinand getreu, was weinst du?« Do merket he eist dat
dat sin Schümmelken dei, dat Fragen. »Döst du dat, min
Schümmelken, kannst du küren (reden)?« Un segd wier »ik
sull da un da hen, un sull de Brut halen, west du nig wie ik
dat wol anfange?« Do antwoerd dat Schümmelken »gah du
na den Künig un segg wenn he die giwen wulle wat du hewen möstest, so wullest du se ünn schappen: wenn he die 'n
Schipp vull Fleisk un 'n Schipp vull Brod giwen wulle, so
sull et gelingen; da wören grauten Riesen up den Water,
wenn du denen ken Fleisk midde brächtes, so terreit[e]n se
die: un da wören de grauten Vüggel, de pickeden die de
Ogen ut den Koppe, wenn du ken Brod vor se häddest.«
Da lett de Künig alle Slächter im Lanne slachten un alle Be-
cker backen, dat de Schippe vull werdt. Wie se vull sied,
segd dat Schümmelken tom Ferenand getrü »nu gah man
up mie sitten un treck mit mie in't Schipp, wenn dann de
Riesen kümmet, so segg

> still, still, meine lieben Riesechen,
> ich hab euch wohl bedacht,
> ich hab euch was mitgebracht.‹

Un wenn de Vüggel kümmet, so seggst du wier

> still, still, meine lieben Vögelchen,
> ich hab euch wohl bedacht,
> ich hab euch was mitgebracht.‹

Dann doet sie die nix, un wenn du dann bie dat Schlott
kümmst, dann helpet die de Riesen, dann gah up dat
Schlott un nümm 'n Paar Riesen mit, da ligd de Prinzessin
un schlöppet; du darfst se awerst nig upwecken, sonnern de
Riesen mött se mit den Bedde upnümmen un in dat Schipp
dregen.« Und da geschah nun alles, wie das Schimmelchen

gesagt hatte, und den Riesen und den Vögeln gab der Ferenand getrü was er ihnen mitgebracht hatte, dafür wurden die Riesen willig und trugen die Prinzessin in ihrem Bett zum König. Un ase se tom Künig kümmet, segd se se künne nig liwen, se möste ere Schriften hewen, de wören up eren Schlotte liggen bliwen. Da werd de Ferenand getrü up Anstifften det Ferenand ungetrü roopen, un de Künig bedütt ünn he sulle de Schriften van dem Schlotte halen, süst sull he sterwen. Da geit he wier in Stall, un grind un segd »o min lewe Schümmelken, nu sull ik noch 'n mal weg, wie süll wie dat macken?« Da segd de Schümmel se sullen dat Schipp man wier vull laen (laden). Da geht es wieder wie das vorigemal, und die Riesen und die Vögel werden von dem Fleisch gesättigt und besänftigt. Ase se bie dat Schlott kümmet, segd de Schümmel to ünn he sulle man herin gahn, in den Schlapzimmer der Prinzessin, up den Diske da lägen de Schriften. Da geit Ferenand getrü hün un langet se. Ase se up'n Water sind, da let he sine Schriffedder in't Water fallen, da segd de Schümmel »nu kann ik die awerst nig helpen.« Da fällt 'n dat bie mit de Flötepiepen, he fänkt an to flöten, da kümmt de Fisk un het de Fedder im Mule un langet se 'm hen. Nu bringet he de Schriften na dem Schlotte, wo de Hochtid hallen werd.

De Künigin mogte awerst den Künig nig lien, weil he keine Nese hadde, sonnern se mogte den Ferenand getrü geren lien. Wie nu mal alle Herens vom Hove tosammen sied, so segd de Künigin, se könne auck Kunststücke macken, se künne einen den Kopp afhoggen un wier upsetten, et sull nur mant einer versöcken. Da wull awerst kener de eiste sien, da mott Ferenand getrü daran, wier up Anstifften von Ferenand ungetrü, den hogget se den Kopp af un sett 'n ünn auck wier up, et is auck glick wier tau heilt, dat et ut sach ase hädde he 'n roen Faen (Faden) üm 'n Hals. Da segd de Künig to ehr »mein Kind, wo hast du denn das gelernt?« »Ja«, segd se, »die Kunst versteh ich, soll ich es an dir auch einmal versuchen?« »O ja« segd he. Do hogget se

en awerst den Kopp af un sett 'n en nig wier up, se doet as
ob se 'n nig darup kriegen künne, un as ob he nig fest sitten
wulle. Da werd de Künig begrawen, se awerst frigget den
Ferenand getrü.

He ride awerst jümmer sinen Schümmel, un ase he mal darup sat, da segd he to em he sulle mal up ne annere Heide de
he em wist, trecken un da dreimal mit em herumme jagen.
Wie he dat dahen hadde, da geit de Schümmel up de Hin-
nerbeine stahn un verwannelt sik in 'n Künigssuhn.

127.

Der Eisenofen.

Zur Zeit, wo das Wünschen noch geholfen hat, ward ein
Königssohn von einer alten Hexe verwünscht, dass er im
Walde in einem großen Eisenofen sitzen sollte. Da brachte
er viele Jahre zu, und konnte ihn niemand erlösen. Einmal
kam eine Königstochter in den Wald, die hatte sich irre gegangen und konnte ihres Vaters Reich nicht wieder finden:
neun Tage war sie so herum gegangen und stand zuletzt vor
dem eisernen Kasten. Da kam eine Stimme heraus und fragte sie »wo kommst du her, und wo willst du hin?« Sie antwortete »ich habe meines Vaters Königreich verloren und
kann nicht wieder nach Haus kommen.« Da sprach's aus
dem Eisenofen »ich will dir wieder nach Haus verhelfen
und zwar in einer kurzen Zeit, wenn du willst unterschreiben zu tun was ich verlange. Ich bin ein größerer Königssohn als du eine Königstochter, und will dich heiraten.« Da
erschrak sie, und dachte »lieber Gott, was soll ich mit dem
Eisenofen anfangen!« Weil sie aber gerne wieder zu ihrem
Vater heim wollte, unterschrieb sie sich doch zu tun was er
verlangte. Er sprach aber »du sollst wiederkommen, ein
Messer mitbringen und ein Loch in das Eisen schrappen.«

Dann gab er ihr jemand zum Gefährten, der gieng nebenher und sprach nicht: er brachte sie aber in zwei Stunden
nach Haus. Nun war große Freude im Schloss, als die Königstochter wieder kam, und der alte König fiel ihr um den
Hals und küsste sie. Sie war aber sehr betrübt und sprach
»lieber Vater, wie mir's gegangen hat! ich wäre nicht wieder
nach Haus gekommen aus dem großen wilden Walde, wenn
ich nicht wäre bei einen eisernen Ofen gekommen, dem
habe ich mich müssen dafür unterschreiben, dass ich wollte
wieder zu ihm zurück kehren, ihn erlösen und heiraten.«
Da erschrak der alte König so sehr, dass er beinahe in eine
Ohnmacht gefallen wäre, denn er hatte nur die einzige
Tochter. Beratschlagten sich also, sie wollten die Müllerstochter, die schön wäre, an ihre Stelle nehmen; führten die
hinaus, gaben ihr ein Messer und sagten sie sollte an dem
Eisenofen schaben. Sie schrappte auch vier und zwanzig
Stunden lang, konnte aber nicht das geringste herabbrin-
gen. Wie nun der Tag anbrach, rief's in dem Eisenofen
»mich däucht es ist Tag draußen.« Da antwortete sie »das
däucht mich auch, ich meine ich höre meines Vaters Mühle
rappeln.« »So bist du eine Müllerstochter, dann geh gleich
hinaus und lass die Königstochter herkommen.« Da gieng
sie hin und sagte dem alten König der draußen wollte sie
nicht, er wollte seine Tochter. Da erschrak der alte König
und die Tochter weinte. Sie hatten aber noch eine Schweinehirtentochter, die war noch schöner als die Müllerstochter, der wollten sie ein Stück Geld geben, damit sie für die
Königstochter zum eisernen Ofen gienge. Also ward sie
hinausgebracht und musste auch vier und zwanzig Stunden
lang schrappen; sie brachte aber nichts davon. Wie nun der
Tag anbrach, rief's im Ofen »mich däucht es ist Tag draußen.« Da antwortete sie »das däucht mich auch, ich meine
ich höre meines Vaters Hörnchen tüten.« »So bist du eine
Schweinehirtentochter, geh gleich fort und lass die Königstochter kommen: und sag ihr es sollt ihr widerfahren was
ich ihr versprochen hätte, und wenn sie nicht käme, sollte

im ganzen Reich alles zerfallen und einstürzen und kein
Stein auf dem andern bleiben.« Als die Königstochter das
hörte, fieng sie an zu weinen: es war aber nun nicht anders,
sie musste ihr Versprechen halten. Da nahm sie Abschied
von ihrem Vater, steckte ein Messer ein und gieng zu dem
Eisenofen in den Wald hinaus. Wie sie nun angekommen
war, hub sie an zu schrappen und das Eisen gab nach, und
wie zwei Stunden vorbei waren, hatte sie schon ein kleines
Loch geschabt. Da guckte sie hinein und sah einen so schönen Jüngling, ach, der glimmerte in Gold und Edelsteinen,
dass er ihr recht in der Seele gefiel. Nun da schrappte sie
noch weiter fort und machte das Loch so groß, dass er heraus konnte. Da sprach er »du bist mein und ich bin dein,
du bist meine Braut und hast mich erlöst.« Er wollte sie mit
sich in sein Reich führen, aber sie bat sich aus dass sie noch
einmal dürfte zu ihrem Vater gehen, und der Königssohn
erlaubte es ihr, doch sollte sie nicht mehr mit ihrem Vater
sprechen als drei Worte, und dann sollte sie wiederkommen. Also gieng sie heim, sie sprach aber mehr als drei
Worte: da verschwand alsbald der Eisenofen und ward weit
weg gerückt über gläserne Berge und schneidende Schwerter; doch der Königssohn war erlöst, und nicht mehr darin
eingeschlossen. Danach nahm sie Abschied von ihrem Vater
und nahm etwas Geld mit, aber nicht viel, gieng wieder in
den großen Wald und suchte den Eisenofen, allein der war
nicht zu finden. Neun Tage suchte sie, da ward ihr Hunger
so groß, dass sie sich nicht zu helfen wusste, denn sie hatte
nichts mehr zu leben. Und als es Abend ward, setzte sie
sich auf einen kleinen Baum und gedachte darauf die Nacht
hinzubringen, weil sie sich vor den wilden Tieren fürchtete.
Als nun Mitternacht heran kam, sah sie von fern ein kleines
Lichtchen und dachte »ach, da wär ich wohl erlöst«, stieg
vom Baum und gieng dem Lichtchen nach, auf dem Weg
aber betete sie. Da kam sie zu einem kleinen alten Häuschen, und war viel Gras darum gewachsen, und stand ein
kleines Häufchen Holz davor. Dachte sie »ach wo kommst

du hier hin!« guckte durchs Fenster hinein, so sah sie nichts
darin, als dicke und kleine Itschen (Kröten), aber einen
Tisch, schön gedeckt mit Wein und Braten, und Teller und
Becher waren von Silber. Da nahm sie sich das Herz und
klopfte an. Alsbald rief die Dicke

>Jungfer grün und klein,
Hutzelbein,
Hutzelbeins Hündchen,
hutzel hin und her,
lass geschwind sehen wer draußen wär.«

Da kam eine kleine Itsche herbei gegangen und machte ihr
auf. Wie sie eintrat, hießen alle sie willkommen, und sie
musste sich setzen. Sie fragten »wo kommt ihr her? wo wollt
ihr hin?« Da erzählte sie alles, wie es ihr gegangen wäre, und
weil sie das Gebot übertreten hätte, nicht mehr als drei Worte zu sprechen, wäre der Ofen weg samt dem Königssohn:
nun wollte sie so lange suchen und über Berg und Tal wandern, bis sie ihn fände. Da sprach die alte Dicke

>Jungfer grün und klein,
Hutzelbein,
Hutzelbeins Hündchen,
hutzel hin und her,
bring mir die große Schachtel her.«

Da gieng die kleine hin und brachte die Schachtel herbeigetragen. Hernach gaben sie ihr Essen und Trinken, und
brachte[n] sie zu einem schönen gemachten Bett, das war
wie Seide und Sammet, da legte sie sich hinein und schlief
in Gottes Namen. Als der Tag kam, stieg sie auf, und gab
ihr die alte Itsche drei Nadeln aus der großen Schachtel, die
sollte sie mitnehmen; sie würden ihr nötig tun, denn sie
müsste über einen hohen gläsernen Berg und über drei
schneidende Schwerter und über ein großes Wasser: wenn
sie das durchsetzte, würde sie ihren Liebsten wiederkrie-
gen. Nun gab sie hiermit drei Teile (Stücke), die sollte sie
recht in Acht nehmen, nämlich drei große Nadeln, ein
Pflugrad und drei Nüsse. Hiermit reiste sie ab, und wie sie

vor den gläsernen Berg kam, der so glatt war, steckte sie die
drei Nadeln als hinter die Füße und dann wieder vorwärts,
und gelangte so hinüber, und als sie hinüber war, steckte sie
sie an einen Ort, den sie wohl in Acht nahm. Danach kam
sie vor die drei schneidenden Schwerter, da stellte sie sich
auf ihr Pflugrad und rollte hinüber. Endlich kam sie vor ein
großes Wasser, und wie sie übergefahren war, in ein großes
schönes Schloss. Sie gieng hinein und hielt um einen Dienst
an, sie wär eine arme Magd und wollte sich gerne vermieten; sie wusste aber dass der Königssohn drinne war, den
sie erlöst hatte aus dem eisernen Ofen im großen Wald.
Also ward sie angenommen zum Küchenmädchen für geringen Lohn. Nun hatte der Königssohn schon wieder eine
andere an der Seite, die wollte er heiraten, denn er dachte
sie wäre längst gestorben. Abends, wie sie aufgewaschen
hatte und fertig war, fühlte sie in die Tasche und fand die
drei Nüsse, welche ihr die alte Itsche gegeben hatte. Biss
eine auf und wollte den Kern essen, siehe, da war ein stol-
zes königliches Kleid drin. Wie's nun die Braut hörte, kam
sie und hielt um das Kleid an und wollte es kaufen und sagte »es wäre kein Kleid für eine Dienstmagd«. Da sprach sie
nein sie wollt's nicht verkaufen, doch wann sie ihr einerlei
(ein Ding) wollte erlauben, so sollte sie's haben, nämlich
eine Nacht in der Kammer ihres Bräutigams zu schlafen.
Die Braut erlaubt[e] es ihr, weil das Kleid so schön war und
sie noch keins so hatte. Wie's nun Abend war, sagte sie zu
ihrem Bräutigam »das närrische Mädchen will in deiner
Kammer schlafen.« »Wenn du's zufrieden bist, bin ich's
auch« sprach er. Sie gab aber dem Mann ein Glas Wein, in
das sie einen Schlaftrunk getan hatte. Also giengen beide in
die Kammer schlafen, und er schlief so fest, dass sie ihn
nicht erwecken konnte. Sie weinte die ganze Nacht und rief
»ich habe dich erlöst aus dem wilden Wald und aus einem
eisernen Ofen, ich habe dich gesucht und bin gegangen
über einen gläsernen Berg, über drei schneidende Schwerter
und über ein großes Wasser, ehe ich dich gefunden habe,

und willst mich doch nicht hören.« Die Bedienten saßen vor der Stubentüre und hörten wie sie so die ganze Nacht weinte und sagten's am Morgen ihrem Herrn. Und wie sie am andern Abend aufgewaschen hatte, biss sie die zweite Nuss auf, da war noch ein weit schöneres Kleid drin; wie das die Braut sah, wollte sie es auch kaufen. Aber Geld wollte das Mädchen nicht und bat sich aus dass es noch einmal in der Kammer des Bräutigams schlafen dürfte. Die Braut gab ihm aber einen Schlaftrunk, und er schlief so fest, dass er nichts hören konnte. Das Küchenmädchen weinte aber die ganze Nacht, und rief »ich habe dich erlöst aus einem Walde und aus einem eisernen Ofen, ich habe dich gesucht und bin gegangen über einen gläsernen Berg, über drei schneidende Schwerter und über ein großes Wasser, ehe ich dich gefunden habe, und du willst mich doch nicht hören.« Die Bedienten saßen vor der Stubentüre und hörten wie sie so die ganze Nacht weinte, und sagten's am Morgen ihrem Herrn. Und als sie am dritten Abend aufgewaschen hatte, biss sie die dritte Nuss auf, da war ein noch schöneres Kleid drin, das starrte von purem Gold. Wie die Braut das sah, wollte sie es haben, das Mädchen aber gab es nur hin, wenn es zum drittenmal dürfte in der Kammer des Bräutigams schlafen. Der Königssohn aber hütete sich und ließ den Schlaftrunk vorbei laufen. Wie sie nun anfieng zu weinen und zu rufen »liebster Schatz, ich habe dich erlöst aus dem grausamen wilden Walde und aus einem eisernen Ofen«, so sprang der Königssohn auf und sprach »du bist die rechte, du bist mein, und ich bin dein.« Darauf setzte er sich noch in der Nacht mit ihr in einen Wagen, und der falschen Braut nahmen sie die Kleider weg, dass sie nicht aufstehen konnte. Als sie zu dem großen Wasser kamen, da schifften sie hinüber, und vor den drei schneidenden Schwertern, da setzten sie sich aufs Pflugrad, und vor dem gläsernen Berg, da steckten sie die drei Nadeln hinein. So gelangten sie endlich zu dem alten kleinen Häuschen, aber wie sie hineintraten, war's ein großes Schloss: die Itschen

waren alle erlöst und lauter Königskinder und waren in
voller Freude. Da ward Vermählung gehalten, und sie blieben in dem Schloss, das war viel größer als ihres Vaters
Schloss. Weil aber der Alte jammerte dass er allein bleiben
sollte, so fuhren sie weg und holten ihn zu sich, und hatten
zwei Königreiche und lebten in gutem Ehestand.

    Da kam eine Maus,
    Das Märchen war aus.

128.

Die faule Spinnerin.

Auf einem Dorfe lebte ein Mann und eine Frau, und die
Frau war so faul, dass sie immer nichts arbeiten wollte: und
was ihr der Mann zu spinnen gab, das spann sie nicht fertig,
und was sie auch spann, haspelte sie nicht, sondern ließ alles auf dem Klauel gewickelt liegen. Schalt sie nun der
Mann, so war sie mit ihrem Maul doch vornen, und sprach
»ei, wie sollt ich haspeln, da ich keinen Haspel habe, geh du
erst in den Wald und schaff mir einen.« »Wenn's daran
liegt«, sagte der Mann, »so will ich in den Wald gehen und
Haspelholz holen.« Da fürchtete sich die Frau, wenn er das
Holz hätte, dass er daraus einen Haspel machte, und sie ab-
haspeln und dann wieder frisch spinnen müsste. Sie besann
sich ein bisschen, da kam ihr ein guter Einfall, und sie lief
dem Manne heimlich nach in den Wald. Wie er nun auf einen Baum gestiegen war, das Holz auszulesen und zu hau-
en, schlich sie darunter in das Gebüsch, wo er sie nicht sehen konnte und rief hinauf

    »wer Haspelholz haut, der stirbt,
    wer da haspelt, der verdirbt.«

Der Mann horchte, legte die Axt eine Weile nieder und
dachte nach was das wohl zu bedeuten hätte. »Ei was«,

sprach er endlich, »was wird's gewesen sein! es hat dir in
den Ohren geklungen, mache dir keine unnötige Furcht.«
Also ergriff er die Axt von neuem und wollte zuhauen, da
rief's wieder von unten herauf

»wer Haspelholz haut, der stirbt,
wer da haspelt der verdirbt.«

Er hielt ein, kriegte angst und bang und sann dem Ding nach.
Wie aber ein Weilchen vorbei war, kam ihm das Herz wieder,
und er langte zum drittenmal nach der Axt und wollte zuhauen. Aber zum drittenmale rief's und sprach's laut

»wer Haspelholz haut, der stirbt,
wer da haspelt der verdirbt.«

Da hatte er's genug, und alle Lust war ihm vergangen, so
dass er eilends den Baum herunter stieg und sich auf den
Heimweg machte. Die Frau lief, was sie konnte, auf Ne-
benwegen, damit sie eher nach Haus käme. Wie er nun in
die Stube trat, tat sie unschuldig, als wäre nichts vorgefallen, und sagte »nun, bringst du ein gutes Haspelholz?«
»Nein«, sprach er, »ich sehe wohl, es geht mit dem Haspeln
nicht«, erzählte ihr was ihm im Walde begegnet war und
ließ sie von nun an damit in Ruhe.
Bald hernach fieng der Mann doch wieder an sich über die
Unordnung im Hause zu ärgern. »Frau«, sagte er, »es ist
doch eine Schande, dass das gesponnene Garn da auf dem
Klauel liegen bleibt.« »Weißt du was«, sprach sie, »weil wir
doch zu keinem Haspel kommen, so stell dich auf den Boden und ich steh unten, da will ich dir den Klauel hinauf
werfen, und du wirfst ihn herunter, so gibt's doch einen
Strang.« »Ja, das geht«, sagte der Mann. Also taten sie das,
und wie sie fertig waren, sprach er »das Garn ist nun ge-
strängt, nun muss es auch gekocht werden.« Der Frau ward
wieder angst, sie sprach zwar »ja wir wollen's gleich morgen früh kochen«, dachte aber bei sich auf einen neuen
Streich. Frühmorgens stand sie auf, machte Feuer an und
stellte den Kessel bei, allein statt des Garns legte sie einen
Klumpen Werg hinein, und ließ es immer zu kochen. Dar-

auf gieng sie zum Manne, der noch zu Bette lag, und sprach
zu ihm »ich muss einmal ausgehen, steh derweil auf und
sieh nach dem Garn, das im Kessel überm Feuer steht: aber
du musst's bei Zeit tun, gib wohl Acht, denn wo der Hahn
kräht, und du sähest nicht nach, wird das Garn zu Werg.«
Der Mann war bei der Hand und wollte nichts versäumen,
stand eilends auf, so schnell er konnte, und gieng in die
Küche. Wie er aber zum Kessel kam und hinein sah, so erblickte er mit Schrecken nichts als einen Klumpen Werg.
Da schwieg der arme Mann mäuschenstill, dachte er hätt's
versehen und wäre Schuld daran und sprach in Zukunft gar
nicht mehr von Garn und Spinnen. Aber das musst du
selbst sagen, es war eine garstige Frau.

nasty

129.

Die vier kunstreichen Brüder.

Es war ein armer Mann, der hatte vier Söhne, wie die herangewachsen waren, sprach er zu ihnen »liebe Kinder, ihr
müsst jetzt hinaus in die Welt, ich habe nichts, das ich euch
geben könnte; macht euch auf und geht in die Fremde, lernt
ein Handwerk und seht wie ihr euch durchschlagt.« Da ergriffen die vier Brüder den Wanderstab, nahmen Abschied
von ihrem Vater und zogen zusammen zum Tor hinaus. Als
sie eine Zeit lang gewandert waren, kamen sie an einen
Kreuzweg, der nach vier verschiedenen Gegenden führte.
Da sprach der älteste »hier müssen wir uns trennen, aber
heut über vier Jahre wollen wir an dieser Stelle wieder zusammen treffen und in der Zeit unser Glück versuchen.«
Nun gieng jeder seinen Weg, und dem ältesten begegnete
ein Mann, der fragte ihn wo er hinaus wollte und was er
vor hätte. »Ich will ein Handwerk lernen«, antwortete er.
Da sprach der Mann »geh mit mir, und werde ein Dieb.«

»Nein«, antwortete er, »das gilt für kein ehrliches Hand-werk mehr, und das Ende vom Lied ist, dass einer als Schwengel in der Feldglocke gebraucht wird.« »Oh«, sprach der Mann, »vor dem Galgen brauchst du dich nicht zu fürchten: ich will dich bloß lehren wie du holst was sonst kein Mensch kriegen kann, und wo dir niemand auf die Spur kommt.« Da ließ er sich überreden, ward bei dem Manne ein gelernter Dieb und ward so geschickt, dass vor ihm nichts sicher war, was er einmal haben wollte. Der zweite Bruder begegnete einem Mann, der dieselbe Frage an ihn tat, was er in der Welt lernen wollte. »Ich weiß es noch nicht« antwortete er. »So geh mit mir und werde ein Sterngucker: nichts besser als das, es bleibt einem nichts verborgen.« Er ließ sich das gefallen und ward ein so ge-schickter Sterngucker, dass sein Meister, als er ausgelernt hatte und weiter ziehen wollte, ihm ein Fernrohr gab und zu ihm sprach »damit kannst du sehen was auf Erden und am Himmel vorgeht, und kann dir nichts verborgen blei-ben.« Den dritten Bruder nahm ein Jäger in die Lehre und gab ihm in allem, was zur Jägerei gehört, so guten Unter-richt, dass er ein ausgelernter Jäger ward. Der Meister schenkte ihm beim Abschied eine Büchse und sprach »die fehlt nicht, was du damit aufs Korn nimmst, das triffst du sicher.« Der jüngste Bruder begegnete gleichfalls einem Manne, der ihn anredete und nach seinem Vorhaben fragte. »Hast du nicht Lust ein Schneider zu werden?« »Dass ich nicht wüsste«, sprach der Junge, »das Krummsitzen von Morgens bis Abends, das Hin- und Herfegen mit der Na-del und das Bügeleisen will mir nicht in den Sinn.« »Ei was«, antwortete der Mann, »du sprichst wie du's verstehst: bei mir lernst du eine ganz andere Schneiderkunst, die ist anständig und ziemlich, zum Teil sehr ehrenvoll.« Da ließ er sich überreden, gieng mit und lernte die Kunst des Man-nes aus dem Fundament. Beim Abschied gab ihm dieser eine Nadel und sprach »damit kannst du zusammen nähen was dir vorkommt, es sei so weich wie ein Ei oder so hart als Stahl; und es wird ganz zu einem Stück, dass keine Naht mehr zu sehen ist.«

Als die bestimmten vier Jahre herum waren, kamen die vier Brüder zu gleicher Zeit an dem Kreuzwege zusammen, herzten und küssten sich und kehrten heim zu ihrem Vater. »Nun«, sprach dieser ganz vergnügt, »hat euch der Wind wieder zu mir geweht?« Sie erzählten wie es ihnen ergangen war und dass jeder das Seinige gelernt hätte. Nun saßen sie gerade vor dem Haus unter einem großen Baum, da sprach der Vater »jetzt will ich euch auf die Probe stellen und sehen was ihr könnt.« Danach schaute er auf und sagte zu dem zweiten Sohne »oben im Gipfel dieses Baums sitzt zwischen zwei Ästen ein Buchfinkennest, sag mir wie viel Eier liegen darin?« Der Sterngucker nahm sein Glas, schaute hinauf und sagte »fünfe sind's.« Sprach der Vater zum ältesten »hol du die Eier herunter, ohne dass der Vogel, der darauf sitzt und brütet, gestört wird.« Der kunstreiche Dieb stieg hinauf und nahm dem Vöglein, das gar nichts davon merkte und ruhig sitzen blieb, die fünf Eier unter dem Leib weg und brachte sie dem Vater herab. Der Vater nahm sie, legte an jede Ecke des Tisches eins und das fünfte in die Mitte, und sprach zum Jäger »du schießest mir mit einem Schuss die fünf Eier in der Mitte entzwei.« Der Jäger legte seine Büchse an und schoss die Eier, wie es der Vater verlangt hatte, alle fünfe, und zwar in einem Schuss. Der hatte gewiss von dem Pulver das um die Ecke schießt. »Nun kommt die Reihe an dich«, sprach der Vater zu dem vierten Sohn, »du nähst die Eier wieder zusammen und auch die jungen Vöglein, die darin sind, und zwar so, dass ihnen der Schuss nichts schadet.« Der Schneider holte seine Nadel und nähte wie's der Vater verlangt hatte. Als er fertig war, musste der Dieb die Eier wieder auf den Baum ins Nest tragen und dem Vogel, ohne dass er etwas merkte, wieder unter legen. Das Tierchen brütete sie vollends aus, und nach ein paar Tagen krochen die Jungen hervor und hatten da, wo sie vom Schneider zusammengenäht waren, ein rotes Streifchen um den Hals.

»Ja«, sprach der Alte zu seinen Söhnen, »ich muss euch über den grünen Klee loben, ihr habt eure Zeit wohl benutzt und was rechtschaffenes gelernt: ich kann nicht sagen wem von euch der Vorzug gebührt. Wenn ihr nur bald Gelegenheit habt eure Kunst anzuwenden, da wird sich's ausweisen.« Nicht lange danach kam großer Lärm ins Land, die Königstochter wäre von einem Drachen entführt worden. Der König war Tag und Nacht darüber in Sorgen und ließ bekannt machen wer sie zurück brächte, sollte sie zur Gemahlin haben. Die vier Brüder sprachen unter einander »das wäre eine Gelegenheit, wo wir uns könnten sehen lassen« wollten zusammen ausziehen und die Königstochter befreien. »Wo sie ist, will ich bald wissen« sprach der Sterngucker, schaute durch sein Fernrohr und sprach »ich sehe sie schon, sie sitzt weit von hier auf einem Felsen im Meer und neben ihr der Drache, der sie bewacht.« Da gieng er zu dem König und bat um ein Schiff für sich und seine Brüder und fuhr mit ihnen über das Meer bis sie zu dem Felsen hin kamen. Die Königstochter saß da, aber der Drache lag in ihrem Schoß und schlief. Der Jäger sprach »ich darf nicht schießen, ich würde die schöne Jungfrau zugleich töten.« »So will ich mein Heil versuchen« sagte der Dieb, schlich sich heran und stahl sie unter dem Drachen weg, aber so leis und behend, dass das Untier nichts merkte, sondern fortschnarchte. Sie eilten voll Freude mit ihr aufs Schiff und steuerten in die offene See: aber der Drache, der bei seinem Erwachen die Königstochter nicht mehr gefunden hatte, [flog] hinter ihnen her und schnaubte wütend durch die Luft. Als er gerade über dem Schiff schwebte und sich herablassen wollte, legte der Jäger seine Büchse an und schoß ihm mitten ins Herz. Das Untier fiel tot herab, war aber so groß und gewaltig, dass es im Herabfallen das ganze Schiff zertrümmerte. Sie erhaschten glücklich noch ein paar Bretter und schwammen auf dem weiten Meer umher. Da war wieder große Not, aber der Schneider, nicht faul, nahm seine wunderbare Nadel, nähte die Bretter mit ein paar großen Stichen in die Eile zusam-

men, setzte sich darauf, und sammelte alle Stücke des
Schiffs. Dann nähte er auch diese so geschickt zusammen,
dass in kurzer Zeit das Schiff wieder segelfertig war und sie
glücklich heim fahren konnten.

Als der König seine Tochter wieder erblickte, war große
Freude. Er sprach zu den vier Brüdern »einer von euch soll
sie zur Gemahlin haben, aber welcher das ist, macht unter
euch aus.« Da entstand ein heftiger Streit unter ihnen, denn
jeder machte Ansprüche. Der Sterngucker sprach »hätt ich
nicht die Königstochter gesehen, so wären alle eure Künste
umsonst gewesen: darum ist sie mein.« Der Dieb sprach
»was hätte das Sehen geholfen, wenn ich sie nicht unter
dem Drachen weggeholt hätte: darum ist sie mein.« Der Jäger sprach »ihr wärt doch samt der Königstochter von dem
Untier zerrissen worden, hätte es meine Kugel nicht getroffen: darum ist sie mein.« Der Schneider sprach »und hätte
ich euch mit meiner Kunst nicht das Schiff wieder zusam-
mengeflickt, ihr wärt alle jämmerlich ertrunken: darum ist
sie mein.« Da tat der König den Ausspruch »jeder von euch
hat ein gleiches Recht, und weil ein jeder die Jungfrau nicht
haben kann, so soll sie keiner von euch haben, aber ich will
jedem zur Belohnung ein halbes Königreich geben.« Den
Brüdern gefiel diese Entscheidung, und sie sprachen »es ist
besser so, als dass wir uneins werden.« Da erhielt jeder ein
halbes Königreich, und sie lebten mit ihrem Vater in aller
Glückseligkeit, so lange es Gott gefiel.

130.

Einäuglein, Zweiäuglein und Dreiäuglein.

Es war eine Frau, die hatte drei Töchter, davon hieß die älteste *Einäuglein*, weil sie nur ein einziges Auge mitten auf
der Stirn hatte, und die mittelste *Zweiäuglein*, weil sie zwei

Augen hatte wie andere Menschen, und die jüngste *Drei-äuglein*, weil sie drei Augen hatte, und das dritte stand bei ihr gleichfalls mitten auf der Stirne. Darum aber, dass Zwei-äuglein nicht anders aussah als andere Menschenkinder, konnten es die Schwestern und die Mutter nicht leiden. Sie sprachen zu ihm »du mit deinen zwei Augen bist nicht besser als das gemeine Volk, du gehörst nicht zu uns.« Sie stießen es herum und warfen ihm schlechte Kleider hin und gaben ihm nicht mehr zu essen als was sie übrig ließen, und taten ihm Herzeleid an, wo sie nur konnten.

Es trug sich zu, dass Zweiäuglein hinaus ins Feld gehen und die Ziege hüten musste, aber noch ganz hungrig war, weil ihm seine Schwestern so wenig zu essen gegeben hatten. Da setzte es sich auf einen Rain und fieng an zu weinen und so zu weinen, dass zwei Bächlein aus seinen Augen herabflossen. Und wie es in seinem Jammer einmal aufblickte, stand eine Frau neben ihm, die fragte »Zweiäuglein, was weinst du?« Zweiäuglein antwortete »soll ich nicht weinen? weil ich zwei Augen habe wie andre Menschen, so können mich meine Schwestern und meine Mutter nicht leiden, stoßen mich aus einer Ecke in die andere, werfen mir alte Kleider hin und geben mir nichts zu essen als was sie übrig lassen. Heute haben sie mir so wenig gegeben, dass ich noch ganz hungrig bin.« Sprach die weise Frau »Zweiäuglein, trockne dir dein Angesicht, ich will dir etwas sagen, dass du nicht mehr hungern sollst. Sprich nur zu deiner Ziege

>Zicklein, meck,
Tischlein, deck<,

so wird ein sauber gedecktes Tischlein vor dir stehen und das schönste Essen darauf, dass du essen kannst so viel du Lust hast. Und wenn du satt bist und das Tischlein nicht mehr brauchst, so sprich nur

>Zicklein, meck,
Tischlein, weg<,

so wird's vor deinen Augen wieder verschwinden.« Darauf gieng die weise Frau fort. Zweiäuglein aber dachte »ich

muss gleich einmal versuchen ob es wahr ist, was sie gesagt
hat, denn mich hungert gar zu sehr« und sprach

>»Zicklein, meck,

Tischlein, deck«,

und kaum hatte sie die Worte ausgesprochen, so stand da
ein Tischlein mit einem weißen Tüchlein gedeckt, darauf
ein Teller mit Messer und Gabel und silbernem Löffel, die
schönsten Speisen standen rund herum, rauchten und waren noch warm, als wären sie eben aus der Küche gekommen. Da sagte Zweiäuglein das kürzeste Gebet her, das es
wusste, »Herr Gott, sei unser Gast zu aller Zeit, Amen«,
langte zu und ließ sich's wohl schmecken. Und als es satt
war, sprach es, wie die weise Frau gelehrt hatte,

>»Zicklein, meck,

Tischlein, weg.«

Alsbald war das Tischchen und alles, was darauf stand wieder verschwunden. »Das ist ein schöner Haushalt« dachte
Zweiäuglein und war ganz vergnügt und guter Dinge.

Abends, als es mit seiner Ziege heim kam, fand es ein irde-
nes Schüsselchen mit Essen, das ihm die Schwestern hingestellt hatten, aber es rührte nichts an. Am andern Tag zog es
mit seiner Ziege wieder hinaus und ließ die paar Brocken,
die ihm gereicht wurden, liegen. Das erstemal und das
zweitemal beachteten es die Schwestern gar nicht, wie es
aber jedesmal geschah, merkten sie auf und sprachen »es ist
nicht richtig mit dem Zweiäuglein, das lässt jedesmal das
Essen stehen und hat doch sonst alles aufgezehrt, was ihm
gereicht wurde: das muss andere Wege gefunden haben.«
Damit sie aber hinter die Wahrheit kämen, sollte Einäuglein
mitgehen, wenn Zweiäuglein die Ziege auf die Weide trieb,
und sollte achten was es da vor hätte, und ob ihm jemand
etwas Essen und Trinken brächte.

Als nun Zweiäuglein sich wieder aufmachte, trat Einäuglein
zu ihm und sprach »ich will mit ins Feld und sehen dass die
Ziege auch recht gehütet und ins Futter getrieben wird.«
Aber Zweiäuglein merkte was Einäuglein im Sinne hatte

und trieb die Ziege hinaus in hohes Gras und sprach
»komm, Einäuglein, wir wollen uns hinsetzen, ich will dir
was vorsingen.« Einäuglein setzte sich hin und war von
dem ungewohnten Weg und von der Sonnenhitze müde,
und Zweiäuglein sang immer
    »Einäuglein, wachst du?
    Einäuglein, schläfst du?«
Da tat Einäuglein das eine Auge zu und schlief ein. Und als
Zweiäuglein sah dass Einäuglein fest schlief und nichts verraten konnte, sprach es
    »Zicklein, meck,
    Tischlein, deck«,
und setzte sich an sein Tischlein und aß und trank bis es
satt war, dann rief es wieder
    »Zicklein, meck,
    Tischlein, weg«,
und alles war augenblicklich verschwunden. Zweiäuglein
weckte nun Einäuglein und sprach »Einäuglein, du willst hüten und schläfst dabei ein, derweil hätte die Ziege in alle Welt
laufen können; komm, wir wollen nach Haus gehen.« Da
giengen sie nach Haus, und Zweiäuglein ließ wieder sein
Schüsselchen unangerührt stehen, und Einäuglein konnte der
Mutter nicht verraten warum es nicht essen wollte und sagte
zu seiner Entschuldigung »ich war draußen eingeschlafen.«
Am andern Tag sprach die Mutter zu Dreiäuglein »diesmal
sollst du mit gehen und Acht haben ob Zweiäuglein draußen isst und ob ihm jemand Essen und Trinken bringt,
denn essen und trinken muss es heimlich.« Da trat Dreiäuglein zum Zweiäuglein und sprach »ich will mitgehen
und sehen ob auch die Ziege recht gehütet und ins Futter
getrieben wird.« Aber Zweiäuglein merkte was Dreiäuglein
im Sinne hatte und trieb die Ziege hinaus ins hohe Gras
und sprach »wir wollen uns dahin setzen, Dreiäuglein, ich
will dir was vorsingen.« Dreiäuglein setzte sich und war
müde von dem Weg und der Sonnenhitze, und Zweiäuglein
hub wieder das vorige Liedlein an und sang

»Dreiäuglein, wachst du?«

Aber statt dass es nun singen musste

»Dreiäuglein, schläfst du?«

sang es aus Unbedachtsamkeit

»Zweiäuglein, schläfst du?«

und sang immer

»Dreiäuglein, wachst du?

Zweiäuglein, schläfst du?«

Da fielen dem Dreiäuglein seine zwei Augen zu und schliefen, aber das dritte, weil es von dem Sprüchlein nicht angeredet war, schlief nicht ein. Zwar tat es Dreiäuglein zu, aber nur aus List, gleich als schlief es auch damit: doch blinzelte es und konnte alles gar wohl sehen. Und als Zweiäuglein meinte Dreiäuglein schliefe fest, sagte es sein Sprüchlein

»Zicklein, meck,

Tischlein, deck«,

aß und trank nach Herzenslust und hieß dann das Tischlein wieder fortgehen,

»Zicklein, meck,

Tischlein, weg«,

und Dreiäuglein hatte alles mit angesehen. Da kam Zweiäuglein zu ihm, weckte es und sprach »ei, Dreiäuglein, bist du eingeschlafen? du kannst gut hüten! komm, wir wollen heim gehen.« Und als sie nach Haus kamen, aß Zweiäuglein wieder nicht, und Dreiäuglein sprach zur Mutter »ich weiß nun warum das hochmütige Ding nicht isst: wenn sie draußen zur Ziege spricht

›Zicklein, meck,

Tischlein, deck‹,

so steht ein Tischlein vor ihr, das ist mit dem besten Essen besetzt, viel besser als wir's hier haben: und wenn sie satt ist, so spricht sie

›Zicklein, meck,

Tischlein, weg‹,

und alles ist wieder verschwunden; ich habe alles genau mit angesehen. Zwei Augen hatte sie mir mit einem Sprüchlein eingeschläfert, aber das eine auf der Stirne, das war zum Glück wach geblieben.« Da rief die neidische Mutter »willst du's besser haben, als wir? die Lust soll dir vergehen!« Sie holte ein Schlachtmesser und stieß es der Ziege ins Herz, dass sie tot hinfiel.

Als Zweiäuglein das sah, gieng es voll Trauer hinaus, setzte sich auf den Feldrain und weinte seine bitteren Tränen. Da stand auf einmal die weise Frau wieder neben ihm und sprach »Zweiäuglein, was weinst du?« »Soll ich nicht weinen!« antwortete es, »die Ziege, die mir jeden Tag, wenn ich euer Sprüchlein hersagte, den Tisch so schön deckte, ist von meiner Mutter tot gestochen; nun muss ich wieder Hunger und Kummer leiden.« Die weise Frau sprach »Zweiäuglein, ich will dir einen guten Rat erteilen, bitt deine Schwestern dass sie dir das Eingeweide von der geschlachteten Ziege geben und vergrab es vor der Haustür in die Erde, so wird's dein Glück sein.« Da verschwand sie, und Zweiäuglein gieng heim und sprach zu den Schwestern, »liebe Schwestern, gebt mir doch etwas von meiner Ziege, ich verlange nichts Gutes, gebt mir nur das Eingeweide.« Da lachten sie und sprachen »[Das] kannst du haben, wenn du weiter nichts willst.« Und Zweiäuglein nahm das Eingeweide und vergrub's Abends in aller Stille nach dem Rate der weisen Frau vor die Haustüre.

Am andern Morgen, als sie insgesamt erwachten und vor die Haustüre traten, so stand da ein wunderbarer prächtiger Baum, der hatte Blätter von Silber, und Früchte von Gold hiengen dazwischen, dass wohl nichts schöneres und köstlicheres auf der weiten Welt war. Sie wussten aber nicht wie der Baum in der Nacht dahin gekommen war, nur Zweiäuglein merkte, dass er aus den Eingeweiden der Ziege aufgewachsen war, denn er stand gerade da, wo es sie in die Erde begraben hatte. Da sprach die Mutter zu Einäuglein »steig hinauf, mein Kind und brich uns die Früchte von dem Baume ab.« Einäuglein stieg hinauf, aber wie es einen von den goldenen Äpfeln greifen wollte, so fuhr ihm der

Zweig aus den Händen: und das geschah jedesmal, so dass
es keinen einzigen Apfel brechen konnte, es mochte sich
anstellen wie es wollte. Da sprach die Mutter »Dreiäuglein,
steig du hinauf, du kannst mit deinen drei Augen besser um
dich schauen als Einäuglein.« Einäuglein rutschte herunter
und Dreiäuglein stieg hinauf. Aber Dreiäuglein war nicht
geschickter und mochte schauen wie es wollte, die goldenen Äpfel wichen immer zurück. Endlich ward die Mutter
ungeduldig und stieg selbst hinauf, konnte aber so wenig
wie Einäuglein und Dreiäuglein die Frucht fassen und griff
immer in die leere Luft. Da sprach Zweiäuglein »ich will
mich einmal hinaufmachen, vielleicht gelingt mir's eher.«
Die Schwestern riefen zwar »du, mit deinen zwei Augen,
was willst du wohl!« Aber Zweiäuglein stieg hinauf, und
die goldenen Äpfel zogen sich nicht vor ihm zurück, sondern ließen sich von selbst in seine Hand herab, also dass es
einen nach dem andern abpflücken konnte und ein ganzes
Schürzchen voll mit herunter brachte. Die Mutter nahm sie
ihm ab, und statt dass sie, Einäuglein und Dreiäuglein dafür
das arme Zweiäuglein hätten besser behandeln sollen, so
wurden sie nur neidisch dass es allein die Früchte holen
konnte und giengen noch härter mit ihm um.

Es trug sich zu, als sie einmal beisammen an dem Baum
standen, dass ein junger Ritter daher kam. »Geschwind,
Zweiäuglein«, riefen die zwei Schwestern, »kriech unter,
dass wir uns deiner nicht schämen müssen« und stürzten
über das arme Zweiäuglein in aller Eil ein leeres Fass, das
gerade neben dem Baume stand, und schoben die goldenen
Äpfel, die es abgebrochen hatte, auch darunter. Als nun der
Ritter näher kam, war es ein schöner Herr, der hielt still,
bewunderte den prächtigen Baum von Gold und Silber und
sprach zu den beiden Schwestern »wem gehört dieser schöne Baum? wer mir einen Zweig davon gäbe, könnte dafür
verlangen was er wollte.« Da antworteten Einäuglein und
Dreiäuglein der Baum gehörte ihnen zu, und sie wollten
ihm einen Zweig wohl abbrechen. Sie gaben sich auch beide

große Mühe, aber sie waren es nicht im Stande, denn die Zweige und Früchte wichen jedesmal vor ihnen zurück. Da sprach der Ritter »das ist ja wunderlich, dass der Baum euch zugehört und ihr doch nicht Macht habt etwas davon abzubrechen.« Sie blieben dabei, der Baum wäre ihr Eigentum. Indem sie aber so sprachen, rollte Zweiäuglein aus dem Fasse ein paar goldene Äpfel heraus, so dass sie zu den Füßen des Ritters liefen, denn Zweiäuglein war bös dass Einäuglein und Dreiäuglein nicht die Wahrheit sagten. Wie der Ritter die Äpfel sah, erstaunte er und fragte wo sie herkämen. Einäuglein und Dreiäuglein antworteten sie hätten noch eine Schwester, die dürfte sich aber nicht sehen lassen, weil sie nur zwei Augen hätte, wie andere gemeine Menschen. Der Ritter aber verlangte sie zu sehen und rief »Zweiäuglein, komm hervor.« Da kam Zweiäuglein ganz getrost unter dem Fass hervor, und der Ritter war verwundert über seine große Schönheit, und sprach »du, Zweiäuglein, kannst mir gewiss einen Zweig von dem Baum abbrechen.« »Ja«, antwortete Zweiäuglein, »das will ich wohl können, denn der Baum gehört mir.« Und stieg hinauf und brach mit leichter Mühe einen Zweig mit seinen silbernen Blättern und goldenen Früchten ab, und reichte ihn dem Ritter hin. Da sprach der Ritter »Zweiäuglein, was soll ich dir dafür geben?« »Ach«, antwortete Zweiäuglein, »ich leide Hunger und Durst, Kummer und Not vom frühen Morgen bis zum späten Abend: wenn ihr mich mitnehmen und erlösen wollt, so wäre ich glücklich.« Da hob der Ritter das Zweiäuglein auf sein Pferd und brachte es heim auf sein väterliches Schloss: dort gab er ihm schöne Kleider, Essen und Trinken nach Herzenslust, und weil er es so lieb hatte, ließ er sich mit ihm einsegnen, und ward die Hochzeit in großer Freude gehalten.

Wie nun Zweiäuglein so von dem schönen Rittersmann fortgeführt ward, da beneideten die zwei Schwestern ihm erst recht sein Glück. »Der wunderbare Baum bleibt uns doch«, dachten sie, »können wir auch keine Früchte davon brechen, so wird doch jedermann davor stehen bleiben, zu uns kommen und ihn rühmen; wer weiß wo unser Weizen noch blüht!« Aber am andern Morgen war der Baum verschwunden und ihre Hoffnung dahin. Und wie Zweiäuglein zu seinem Kämmerlein hinaussah, so stand er zu seiner großen Freude davor und war ihm also nachgefolgt.

Zweiäuglein lebte lange Zeit vergnügt. Einmal kamen zwei arme Frauen zu ihm auf das Schloss und baten um ein Almosen. Da sah ihnen Zweiäuglein ins Gesicht und erkannte ihre Schwestern Einäuglein und Dreiäuglein, die so in Armut geraten waren, dass sie umherziehen und vor den Türen ihr Brot suchen mussten. Zweiäuglein aber hieß sie willkommen und tat ihnen Gutes und pflegte sie, also dass die beiden von Herzen bereuten was sie ihrer Schwester in der Jugend Böses angetan hatten.

131.

Die schöne Katrinelje und Pif Paf Poltrie.

»Guten Tag, Vater *Hollenthe*.« »Großen Dank, Pif Paf Poltrie.« »Könnt ich wohl eure Tochter kriegen?« »O ja, wenn's die Mutter Malcho (Melk-Kuh), der Bruder Hohenstolz, die Schwester Käsetraut und die schöne Katrinelje will, so kann's geschehen.«

»Wo ist dann die Mutter Malcho?«

»Sie ist im Stall und melkt die Kuh.«

»Guten Tag, Mutter *Malcho*.« »Großen Dank, Pif Paf Poltrie.« »Könnt ich wohl eure Tochter kriegen?« »O ja, wenn's der Vater Hollenthe, der Bruder Hohenstolz, die Schwester Käsetraut und die schöne Katrinelje will, so kann's geschehen.«

»Wo ist dann der Bruder Hohenstolz?«

»Er ist in der Kammer und hackt das Holz.«

»Guten Tag, Bruder *Hohenstolz*.« »Großen Dank, Pif Paf Poltrie.« »Könnt ich wohl eure Schwester kriegen?« »O ja, wenn's der Vater Hollenthe, die Mutter Malcho, die Schwester Käsetraut und die schöne Katrinelje will, so kann's geschehen.«

»Wo ist dann die Schwester Käsetraut?«

»Sie ist im Garten und schneidet das Kraut.«

»Guten Tag, Schwester *Käsetraut*.« »Großen Dank, Pif Paf Poltrie.« »Könnt ich wohl eure Schwester kriegen?« »O ja, wenn's der Vater Hollenthe, die Mutter Malcho, der Bruder Hohenstolz und die schöne Katrinelje will, so kann's geschehen.«

»Wo ist dann die schöne Katrinelje?«

»Sie ist in der Kammer und zählt ihre Pfennige.«

»Guten Tag, schöne *Katrinelje*.« »Großen Dank, Pif Paf Poltrie.« »Willst du wohl mein Schatz sein?« »O ja, wenn's der Vater Hollenthe, die Mutter Malcho, der Bruder Hohenstolz, die Schwester Käsetraut will, so kann's geschehen.«

»Schön Katrinelje, wie viel hast du an Brautschatz?«

»Vierzehn Pfennige bares Geld, drittehalb Groschen Schuld, ein halb Pfund Hutzeln, eine Hand voll Prutzeln, eine Hand voll Wurzeln,

un so der watt:

is dat nig en guden Brutschatt?«

»*Pif Paf Poltrie*, was kannst du für ein Handwerk? bist du ein Schneider?« »Noch viel besser.« »Ein Schuster?« »Noch viel besser.« »Ein Ackersmann?« »Noch viel besser.« »Ein Schreiner?« »Noch viel besser.« »Ein Schmied?« »Noch viel besser.« »Ein Müller?« »Noch viel besser.« »Vielleicht ein Besenbinder?« »Ja, das bin ich: ist das nicht ein schönes Handwerk?«

132

Der Fuchs und das Pferd.

Es hatte ein Bauer ein treues Pferd, das war alt geworden und konnte keine Dienste mehr tun, da wollte ihm sein Herr nichts mehr zu fressen geben und sprach »brauchen kann ich dich freilich nicht mehr, indes mein ich es gut mit dir, zeigst du dich noch so stark, dass du mir einen Löwen hierher bringst, so will ich dich behalten, jetzt aber mach dich fort aus meinem Stall«, und jagte es damit ins weite Feld. Das Pferd war traurig und gieng nach dem Wald zu, dort ein wenig Schutz vor dem Wetter zu suchen. Da begegnete ihm der Fuchs und sprach »was hängst du so den Kopf und gehst so einsam herum?« »Ach«, antwortete das Pferd, »Geiz und Treue wohnen nicht beisammen in einem Haus: mein Herr hat vergessen was ich ihm für Dienste in so vielen Jahren geleistet habe, und weil ich nicht recht mehr ackern kann, will er mir kein Futter mehr geben, und hat mich fortgejagt.« »Ohne allen Trost?« fragte der Fuchs. »Der Trost war schlecht, er hat gesagt wenn ich noch so stark wäre, dass ich ihm einen Löwen brächte, wollt er mich behalten, aber er weiß wohl, dass ich das nicht vermag.« Der Fuchs sprach »da will ich dir helfen, leg dich nur hin, strecke dich aus und rege dich nicht, als wärst du tot.« Das Pferd tat was der Fuchs verlangte, der Fuchs aber gieng zum Löwen, der seine Höhle nicht weit davon hatte und sprach »da draußen liegt ein totes Pferd, komm doch mit hinaus, da kannst du eine fette Mahlzeit halten.« Der Löwe gieng mit und wie sie bei dem Pferd standen, sprach der Fuchs »hier hast du's doch nicht nach deiner Gemächlichkeit, weißt du was? ich will's mit dem Schweif an dich binden, so kannst du's in deine Höhle ziehen und in aller Ruhe verzehren.« Dem Löwen gefiel der Rat, er stellte sich hin und damit ihm der Fuchs das Pferd festknüpfen könnte, hielt er ganz still. Der Fuchs aber band mit des Pferdes

Schweif dem Löwen die Beine zusammen und drehte und schnürte alles so wohl und stark, dass es mit keiner Kraft zu zerreißen war. Als er nun sein Werk vollendet hatte, klopfte er dem Pferd auf die Schulter und sprach »zieh, Schimmel, zieh.« Da sprang das Pferd mit einmal auf und zog den Löwen mit sich fort. Der Löwe fieng an zu brüllen, dass die Vögel in dem ganzen Wald vor Schrecken aufflogen, aber das Pferd ließ ihn brüllen, zog und schleppte ihn über das Feld vor seines Herrn Tür. Wie der Herr das sah, besann er sich eines bessern und sprach zu dem Pferd, »du sollst bei mir bleiben und es gut haben«, und gab ihm satt zu fressen bis es starb.

133.

Die zertanzten Schuhe.

Es war einmal ein König, der hatte zwölf Töchter, eine immer schöner als die andere. Sie schliefen zusammen in einem Saal, wo ihre Betten neben einander standen, und Abends, wenn sie darin lagen, schloss der König die Tür zu und verriegelte sie. Wenn er aber am Morgen die Türe aufschloss, so sah er dass ihre Schuhe zertanzt waren, und niemand konnte herausbringen wie das zugegangen war. Da ließ der König ausrufen wer's könnte ausfindig machen, wo sie in der Nacht tanzten, der sollte sich eine davon zur Frau wählen und nach seinem Tod König sein: wer sich aber meldete und es nach drei Tagen und Nächten nicht heraus brächte, der hätte sein Leben verwirkt. Nicht lange, so meldete sich ein Königssohn und erbot sich das Wagnis zu unternehmen. Er ward wohl aufgenommen, und Abends in ein Zimmer geführt, das an den Schlafsaal stieß. Sein Bett war da aufgeschlagen und er sollte Acht haben wo sie hingiengen und tanzten; und damit sie nichts heimlich treiben

konnten oder zu einem andern Ort hinaus giengen, war
auch die Saaltüre offen gelassen. Dem Königssohn fiel's
aber wie Blei auf die Augen und er schlief ein, und als er
am Morgen aufwachte waren alle zwölfe zum Tanz gewesen, denn ihre Schuhe standen da und hatten Löcher in den
Sohlen. Den zweiten und dritten Abend gieng's nicht anders, und da ward ihm sein Haupt ohne Barmherzigkeit abgeschlagen. Es kamen hernach noch viele und meldeten sich
zu dem Wagestück, sie mussten aber alle ihr Leben lassen.
Nun trug sich's zu, dass ein armer Soldat, der eine Wunde
hatte und nicht mehr dienen konnte, sich auf dem Weg
nach der Stadt befand, wo der König wohnte. Da begegnete
ihm eine alte Frau, die fragte ihn wo er hin wollte. »Ich
weiß selber nicht recht«, sprach er, und setzte im Scherz
hinzu »ich hätte wohl Lust ausfindig zu machen wo die
Königstöchter ihre Schuhe vertanzen, und darnach König
zu werden.« »Das ist so schwer nicht«, sagte die Alte, »du
musst den Wein nicht trinken, der dir Abends gebracht
wird, und musst tun als wärst du fest eingeschlafen.« Darauf gab sie ihm ein Mäntelchen und sprach »wenn du das
umhängst, so bist du unsichtbar und kannst den zwölfen
dann nachschleichen.« Wie der Soldat den guten Rat bekommen hatte, ward's Ernst bei ihm, so dass er ein Herz
fasste, vor den König gieng und sich als Freier meldete. Er
ward so gut aufgenommen wie die andern auch, und wurden ihm königliche Kleider angetan. Abends zur Schlafenszeit ward er in das Vorzimmer geführt, und als er zu Bette
gehen wollte, kam die älteste und brachte ihm einen Becher
Wein: aber er hatte sich einen Schwamm unter das Kinn gebunden, ließ den Wein da hineinlaufen, und trank keinen
Tropfen. Dann legte er sich nieder, und als er ein Weilchen
gelegen hatte, fieng er an zu schnarchen wie im tiefsten
Schlaf. Das hörten die zwölf Königstöchter, lachten, und
die älteste sprach »der hätte auch sein Leben sparen können.« Danach standen sie auf, öffneten Schränke, Kisten
und Kasten, und holten prächtige Kleider heraus: putzten

sich vor den Spiegeln, sprangen herum und freuten sich auf den Tanz. Nur die jüngste sagte »ich weiß nicht, ihr freut euch, aber mir ist so wunderlich zu Mute: gewiss widerfährt uns ein Unglück.« »Du bist eine Schneegans«, sagte die älteste, »die sich immer fürchtet. Hast du vergessen wie viel Königssöhne schon umsonst dagewesen sind? dem Soldaten hätt ich nicht einmal brauchen einen Schlaftrunk zu geben, der Lümmel wäre doch nicht aufgewacht.« Wie sie alle fertig waren, sahen sie erst nach dem Soldaten, aber der hatte die Augen zugetan, rührte und regte sich nicht, und sie glaubten nun ganz sicher zu sein. Da gieng die älteste an ihr Bett und klopfte daran: alsbald sank es in die Erde, und sie stiegen durch die Öffnung hinab, eine nach der andern, die älteste voran. Der Soldat, der alles mit angesehen hatte, zauderte nicht lange, hieng sein Mäntelchen um und stieg hinter der jüngsten mit hinab. Mitten auf der Treppe trat er ihr ein wenig aufs Kleid, da erschrak sie und rief »was ist das? wer hält mich am Kleid?« »Sei nicht so einfältig«, sagte die älteste, »du bist an einem Haken hängen geblieben.« Da giengen sie vollends hinab, und wie sie unten waren, standen sie in einem wunderprächtigen Baumgang, da waren alle Blätter von Silber, und schimmerten und glänzten. Der Soldat dachte »du willst dir ein Wahrzeichen mitnehmen«, und brach einen Zweig davon ab: da fuhr ein gewaltiger Krach aus dem Baume. Die jüngste rief wieder »es ist nicht richtig, habt ihr den Knall gehört?« Die älteste aber sprach »das sind Freudenschüsse, weil wir unsere Prinzen bald erlöst haben.« Sie kamen darauf in einen Baumgang, wo alle Blätter von Gold, und endlich in einen dritten, wo sie klarer Demant waren: von beiden brach er einen Zweig ab, wobei es jedesmal krachte, dass die jüngste vor Schrecken zusammenfuhr: aber die älteste blieb dabei, es wären Freudenschüsse. Sie giengen weiter und kamen zu einem großen Wasser, darauf standen zwölf Schifflein, und in jedem Schifflein saß ein schöner Prinz, die hatten auf die zwölfe gewartet, und jeder nahm eine zu sich, der Soldat aber setzte sich mit der jüngsten ein. Da sprach der Prinz »ich weiß nicht das Schiff ist heute viel schwerer und ich muss aus allen Kräften rudern, wenn ich es fortbringen soll.« »Wovon sollte das kommen«, sprach die jüngste, »als vom warmen Wetter, es ist mir auch so heiß zu Mut.« Jenseits des Wassers aber stand ein schönes hellerleuchtetes Schloss, woraus eine lustige Musik erschallte von Pauken und Trompeten. Sie ruderten hinüber, traten ein, und jeder Prinz tanzte mit seiner Liebsten; der Soldat tanzte aber unsichtbar mit, und wenn eine einen Becher mit Wein hielt, so trank er ihn aus, dass er leer war, wenn sie ihn an den Mund brachte; und der jüngsten ward auch angst darüber, aber die älteste brachte sie immer zum Schweigen. Sie tanzten da bis drei Uhr am andern Morgen, wo alle Schuhe durchgetanzt waren und sie aufhören mussten. Die Prinzen fuhren sie über das Wasser wieder zurück, und der Soldat setzte sich diesmal vornen hin zur ältesten. Am Ufer nahmen sie von ihren Prinzen Abschied und versprachen in der folgenden Nacht wieder zu kommen. Als sie an der Treppe waren, lief der Soldat voraus und legte sich in sein Bett, und als die Zwölf langsam und müde herauf getrippelt kamen, schnarchte er schon wieder so laut, dass sie's alle hören konnten, und sie sprachen »vor dem sind wir sicher.« Da taten sie ihre schönen Kleider aus, brachten sie weg, stellten die zertanzten Schuhe unter das Bett und legten sich nieder. Am andern Morgen wollte der Soldat nichts sagen, sondern das wunderliche Wesen noch mit ansehen, und gieng die zweite und die dritte Nacht wieder mit. Da war alles wie das erstemal, und sie tanzten jedesmal bis die Schuhe entzwei waren. Das drittemal aber nahm er zum Wahrzeichen einen Becher mit. Als die Stunde gekommen war, wo er antworten sollte, steckte er die drei Zweige und den Becher zu sich und gieng vor den König, die Zwölfe aber standen hinter der Türe und horchten was er sagen würde. Als der König die Frage tat »wo haben meine zwölf Töchter ihre Schuhe in der Nacht vertanzt?« so antwortete er »mit zwölf Prinzen in einem unterirdischen Schloss«, berichtete wie es zugegangen war und holte die Wahrzeichen hervor. Da ließ der König seine Töchter kommen und fragte sie ob der Soldat die Wahrheit gesagt hätte, und da sie sahen dass sie verraten waren und Leugnen nichts half, so mussten sie alles eingestehen. Darauf fragte ihn der König welche er zur Frau haben wollte. Er antwortete »ich bin nicht mehr jung, so gebt mir die älteste.« Da ward noch an selbigem Tage die Hochzeit gehalten und ihm das Reich nach des Königs Tode versprochen. Aber die Prinzen wurden auf so viel Tage wieder verwünscht, als sie Nächte mit den Zwölfen getanzt hatten.

134.

Die sechs Diener.

Vor Zeiten lebte eine alte Königin, die war eine Zauberin, und ihre Tochter war das schönste Mädchen unter der Sonne. Die Alte dachte aber auf nichts als wie sie die Menschen ins Verderben locken könnte, und wenn ein Freier kam, so sprach sie wer ihre Tochter haben wollte, müsste zuvor einen Bund (eine Aufgabe) lösen, oder er müsste sterben. Viele waren von der Schönheit der Jungfrau verblendet und wagten es wohl, aber sie konnten nicht vollbringen was die Alte ihnen auflegte, und dann war keine Gnade, sie mussten niederknien, und das Haupt ward ihnen abgeschlagen. Ein Königssohn der hatte auch von der großen Schönheit der Jungfrau gehört und sprach zu seinem Vater »lasst mich hinziehen, ich will um sie werben.« »Nimmermehr«, antwortete der König, »gehst du fort, so gehst du in deinen Tod.« Da legte der Sohn sich nieder und ward sterbenskrank, und lag sieben Jahre lang und kein Arzt konnte ihm helfen. Als der Vater sah dass keine Hoffnung mehr war, sprach er voll Herzenstraurigkeit zu ihm »zieh hin und versuche dein Glück, ich weiß dir sonst nicht zu helfen.« Wie der Sohn das hörte, stand er auf von seinem Lager, ward gesund und machte sich fröhlich auf den Weg.

Es trug sich zu, als er über eine Heide zu reiten kam, dass er von weitem auf der Erde etwas liegen sah wie einen großen Heuhaufen, und wie er sich näherte, konnte er unterscheiden dass es der Bauch eines Menschen war, der sich dahingestreckt hatte; der Bauch aber sah aus wie ein kleiner Berg. Der Dicke, wie er den Reisenden erblickte, richtete sich in die Höhe und sprach »wenn ihr jemand braucht, so nehmt mich in eure Dienste.« Der Königssohn antwortete »was soll ich mit einem so ungefügen Mann anfangen?« »Oh«, sprach der Dicke, »das will nichts sagen, wenn ich mich recht aus einander tue, bin ich noch dreitausendmal so dick.« »Wenn das ist«, sagte der Königssohn, »so kann ich dich brauchen, komm mit mir.« Da gieng der Dicke hinter dem Königssohn her, und über eine Weile fanden sie einen andern, der lag da auf der Erde und hatte das Ohr auf den Rasen gelegt. Fragte der Königssohn »was machst du da?« »Ich horche«, antwortete der Mann. »Wonach horchst du so aufmerksam?« »Ich horche nach dem was eben in der Welt sich zuträgt, denn meinen Ohren entgeht nichts, das Gras sogar hör ich wachsen.« Fragte der Königssohn »sage mir, was hörst du am Hofe der alten Königin, welche die schöne Tochter hat?« Da antwortete er »ich höre das Schwert sausen, das einem Freier den Kopf abschlägt.« Der Königssohn sprach »ich kann dich brauchen, komm mit mir.« Da zogen sie weiter und sahen einmal ein paar Füße da liegen und auch etwas von den Beinen, aber das Ende konnten sie nicht sehen. Als sie eine gute Strecke fortgegangen waren, kamen sie zu dem Leib und endlich auch zu dem Kopf. »Ei«, sprach der Königssohn, »was bist du für ein langer Strick!« »Oh«, antwortete der Lange, »das ist noch gar nichts, wenn ich meine Gliedmaßen erst recht ausstrecke, bin ich noch dreitausendmal so lang, und bin größer als der höchste Berg auf Erden. Ich will euch gerne dienen, wenn ihr mich annehmen wollt.« »Komm mit«, sprach der Königssohn, »ich kann dich brauchen.« Sie zogen weiter und fanden einen am Weg sitzen, der hatte die Augen zugebunden. Sprach der Königssohn zu ihm »hast du blöde Augen, dass du nicht in das Licht sehen kannst?« »Nein«, antwortete der Mann, »ich darf die Binde nicht abnehmen denn was ich mit meinen Augen ansehe, das springt aus einander, so gewaltig ist mein Blick. Kann euch das nützen, so will ich euch gern dienen.« »Komm mit«, antwortete der Königssohn, »ich kann dich brauchen.« Sie zogen weiter und fanden einen Mann, der lag mitten im heißen Sonnenschein und zitterte und fror am ganzen Leibe, so dass ihm kein Glied still stand. »Wie kannst du frieren«, sprach der Königssohn, »und die Sonne scheint so warm?« »Ach«, antwortete der Mann, »meine Natur ist ganz anderer Art, je heißer es ist, desto mehr frier ich, und der Frost dringt mir durch alle Knochen: und je kälter es ist, desto heißer wird mir: mitten im Eis kann ich's vor Hitze, und mitten im Feuer vor Kälte nicht aushalten.« »Du bist ein wunderlicher Kerl«, sprach der Königssohn, »aber wenn du mir dienen willst, so komm mit.« Nun zogen sie weiter und sahen einen Mann stehen, der machte einen langen Hals, schaute sich um und schaute über alle Berge hinaus. Sprach der Königssohn »wonach siehst du so eifrig?« Der Mann antwortete »ich habe so helle Augen, dass ich über alle Wälder und Felder, Täler und Berge hinaus und durch die ganze Welt sehen kann.« Der Königssohn sprach »willst du, so komm mit mir, denn so einer fehlte mir noch.«

Nun zog der Königssohn mit seinen sechs Dienern in die Stadt ein, wo die alte Königin lebte. Er sagte nicht wer er wäre, aber er sprach »wollt ihr mir eure schöne Tochter geben, so will ich vollbringen, was ihr mir auferlegt.« Die Zauberin freute sich dass ein so schöner Jüngling wieder in ihre Netze fiel und sprach »dreimal will ich dir einen Bund auf-

geben, lösest du ihn jedesmal, so sollst du der Herr und Gemahl meiner Tochter werden.« »Was soll das erste sein?«
fragte er. »Dass du mir einen Ring herbei bringst, den ich ins
rote Meer habe fallen lassen.« Da gieng der Königssohn
heim zu seinen Dienern und sprach »der erste Bund ist nicht
leicht, ein Ring soll aus dem roten Meer geholt werden, nun
schafft Rat.« Da sprach der mit den hellen Augen »ich will
sehen wo er liegt«, schaute in das Meer hinab und sagte
»dort hängt er an einem spitzen Stein.« Der Lange trug sie
hin und sprach »ich wollte ihn wohl heraus holen, wenn ich
ihn nur sehen könnte.« »Wenn's weiter nichts ist«, rief der
Dicke, legte sich nieder und hielt seinen Mund ans Wasser:
da fielen die Wellen hinein wie in einen Abgrund, und er
trank das ganze Meer aus, dass es trocken ward wie eine
Wiese. Der Lange bückte sich ein wenig und holte den Ring
mit der Hand heraus. Da war der Königssohn froh als er den
Ring hatte, und brachte ihn der Alten. Sie erstaunte und
sprach »ja, es ist der rechte Ring: den ersten Bund hast du
glücklich gelöst, aber nun kommt der zweite. Siehst du dort
auf der Wiese vor meinem Schlosse, da weiden dreihundert
fette Ochsen, die musst du mit Haut und Haar, Knochen
und Hörnern verzehren: und unten im Keller liegen dreihundert Fässer Wein, die musst du dazu austrinken; und
bleibt von den Ochsen ein Haar und von dem Wein ein
Tröpfchen übrig, so ist mir dein Leben verfallen.« Sprach
der Königssohn »darf ich mir keine Gäste dazu laden? ohne
Gesellschaft schmeckt keine Mahlzeit.« Die Alte lachte bos-
haft und antwortete »einen darfst du dir dazu laden, damit
du Gesellschaft hast, aber weiter keinen.«

Da gieng der Königssohn zu seinen Dienern und sprach zu
dem Dicken »du sollst heute mein Gast sein und dich einmal satt essen.« Da tat sich der Dicke von einander und aß
die dreihundert Ochsen, dass kein Haar übrig blieb, und
fragte ob weiter nichts als das Frühstück da wäre: den Wein
aber trank er gleich aus den Fässern, ohne dass er ein Glas
nötig hatte, und trank den letzten Tropfen vom Nagel her-

unter. Als die Mahlzeit zu Ende war, gieng der Königssohn
zur Alten und sagte ihr der zweite Bund wäre gelöst. Sie
verwunderte sich und sprach »so weit hat's noch keiner gebracht, aber es ist noch ein Bund übrig«, und dachte »du
sollst mir nicht entgehen und wirst deinen Kopf nicht oben
behalten.« »Heut Abend«, sprach sie, »bring ich meine
Tochter zu dir in deine Kammer und du sollst sie mit deinem Arm umschlingen: und wenn ihr da beisammen sitzt,
so hüte dich dass du nicht einschläfst: ich komme Schlag
zwölf Uhr, und ist sie dann nicht mehr in deinen Armen, so
hast du verloren.« Der Königssohn dachte, »der Bund ist
leicht, ich will wohl meine Augen offen behalten«, doch
rief er seine Diener, erzählte ihnen, was die Alte gesagt hatte und sprach »wer weiß, was für eine List dahinter steckt,
Vorsicht ist gut, haltet Wache und sorgt dass die Jungfrau
nicht wieder aus meiner Kammer kommt.« Als die Nacht
einbrach, kam die Alte mit ihrer Tochter und führte sie in
die Arme des Königssohns, und dann schlang sich der Lange um sie beide in einen Kreis, und der Dicke stellte sich
vor die Türe, also dass keine lebendige Seele herein konnte.
Da saßen sie beide, und die Jungfrau sprach kein Wort,
aber der Mond schien durchs Fenster auf ihr Angesicht,
dass er ihre wunderbare Schönheit sehen konnte. Er tat
nichts als sie anschauen, war voll Freude und Liebe, und es
kam keine Müdigkeit in seine Augen. Das dauerte bis elf
Uhr, da warf die Alte einen Zauber über alle, dass sie ein-
schliefen, und in dem Augenblick war auch die Jungfrau
entrückt.
Nun schliefen sie hart bis ein Viertel vor zwölf, da war der
Zauber kraftlos, und sie erwachten alle wieder. »O Jammer
und Unglück«, rief der Königssohn, »nun bin ich verloren!« Die treuen Diener fiengen an zu klagen, aber der
Horcher sprach »seid still, ich will horchen«, da horchte er
einen Augenblick und dann sprach er »sie sitzt in einem
Felsen dreihundert Stunden von hier, und bejammert ihr
Schicksal. Du allein kannst helfen, Langer, wenn du dich

aufrichtest, so bist du mit ein paar Schritten dort.« »Ja«, antwortete der Lange, »aber der mit den scharfen Augen muss mitgehen, damit wir den Felsen wegschaffen.« Da huckte der Lange den mit verbundenen Augen auf, und im Augenblick, wie man eine Hand umwendet waren sie vor dem verwünschten Felsen. Alsbald nahm der Lange dem andern die Binde von den Augen, der sich nur umschaute, so zersprang der Felsen in tausend Stücke. Da nahm der Lange die Jungfrau auf den Arm, trug sie in einem Nu zurück, holte eben so schnell auch noch seinen Kameraden, und eh es zwölfe schlug, saßen sie alle wieder wie vorher und waren munter und guter Dinge. Als es zwölf schlug, kam die alte Zauberin herbei geschlichen, machte ein höhnisches Gesicht, als wollte sie sagen »nun ist er mein«, und glaubte ihre Tochter säße dreihundert Stunden weit im Felsen. Als sie aber ihre Tochter in den Armen des Königssohns erblickte, erschrak sie und sprach »da ist einer, der kann mehr als ich.« Aber sie durfte nichts einwenden und musste ihm die Jungfrau zusagen. Da sprach sie ihr ins Ohr »Schande für dich, dass du gemeinem Volk gehorchen sollst und dir einen Gemahl nicht nach deinem Gefallen wählen darfst.«

Da ward das stolze Herz der Jungfrau mit Zorn erfüllt und sann auf Rache. Sie ließ am andern Morgen dreihundert Malter Holz zusammenfahren und sprach zu dem Königssohn, die drei Bünde wären gelöst, sie würde nicht eher seine Gemahlin werden, bis einer bereit wäre, sich mitten in das Holz zu setzen und das Feuer auszuhalten. Sie dachte keiner seiner Diener würde sich für ihn verbrennen, und aus Liebe zu ihr würde er selber sich hinein setzen, und dann wäre sie frei. Die Diener aber sprachen »wir haben alle etwas getan, nur der Frostige noch nicht, der muss auch daran«, setzten ihn mitten auf den Holzstoß und steckten ihn an. Da begann das Feuer zu brennen und brannte drei Tage, bis alles Holz verzehrt war, und als die Flammen sich legten, stand der Frostige mitten in der Asche, zitterte wie ein Espenlaub und sprach »einen solchen Frost habe ich mein Lebtage nicht ausgehalten, und wenn er länger gedauert hätte, so wäre ich erstarrt.«

Nun war keine Aussicht mehr zu finden, die schöne Jungfrau musste den unbekannten Jüngling zum Gemahl nehmen. Als sie aber nach der Kirche fuhren, sprach die Alte »ich kann die Schande nicht ertragen« und schickte ihr Kriegsvolk nach, das sollte alles niedermachen, was ihm vorkäme, und ihr die Tochter zurück bringen. Der Horcher aber hatte die Ohren gespitzt und die heimlichen Reden der Alten vernommen. »Was fangen wir an?« sprach er zu dem Dicken, aber der wusste Rat, spie einmal oder zweimal hinter dem Wagen einen Teil von dem Meereswasser aus, das er getrunken hatte, da entstand ein großer See, worin die Kriegsvölker stecken blieben und ertranken. Als die Zauberin das vernahm, schickte sie ihre geharnischten Reiter, aber der Horcher hörte das Rasseln ihrer Rüstung und band dem einen die Augen auf, der guckte die Feinde ein bisschen scharf an, da sprangen sie aus einander wie Glas. Nun fuhren sie ungestört weiter, und als die beiden in der Kirche eingesegnet waren, nahmen die sechs Diener ihren Abschied, und sprachen zu ihrem Herrn »eure Wünsche sind erfüllt, ihr habt uns nicht mehr nötig, wir wollen weiter ziehen und unser Glück versuchen.«

Eine halbe Stunde vor dem Schloss war ein Dorf, vor dem hütete ein Schweinehirt seine Herde: wie sie dahin kamen, sprach er zu seiner Frau »weißt du auch recht wer ich bin? ich bin kein Königssohn, sondern ein Schweinehirt, und der mit der Herde dort, das ist mein Vater: wir zwei müssen auch daran und ihm helfen hüten.« Dann stieg er mit ihr in das Wirtshaus ab, und sagte heimlich zu den Wirtsleuten in der Nacht sollten sie ihr die königlichen Kleider wegnehmen. Wie sie nun am Morgen aufwachte, hatte sie nichts anzutun, und die Wirtin gab ihr einen alten Rock und ein paar alte wollene Strümpfe, dabei tat sie noch als wär's ein großes Geschenk und sprach »wenn nicht euer

Mann wäre, hätt ich's euch gar nicht gegeben.« Da glaubte
sie er wäre wirklich ein Schweinehirt und hütete mit ihm
die Herde und dachte »ich habe es verdient mit meinem
Übermut und Stolz.« Das dauerte acht Tage, da konnte sie
es nicht mehr aushalten, denn die Füße waren ihr wund geworden. Da kamen ein paar Leute und fragten ob sie wüsste wer ihr Mann wäre. »Ja«, antwortete sie, »er ist ein
Schweinehirt, und ist eben ausgegangen mit Bändern und
Schnüren einen kleinen Handel zu treiben.« Sie sprachen
aber »kommt einmal mit, wir wollen euch zu ihm hinführen«, und brachten sie ins Schloss hinauf; und wie sie in
den Saal kam, stand da ihr Mann in königlichen Kleidern.
Sie erkannte ihn aber nicht, bis er ihr um den Hals fiel, sie
küsste und sprach »ich habe so viel für dich gelitten, da
hast du auch für mich leiden sollen.« Nun ward erst die
Hochzeit gefeiert, und der's erzählt hat wollte, er wäre
auch dabei gewesen.

135.

Die weiße und die schwarze Braut.

Eine Frau gieng mit ihrer Tochter und Stieftochter über
Feld, Futter zu schneiden. Da kam der liebe Gott als ein armer Mann zu ihnen gegangen und fragte »wo führt der
Weg ins Dorf?« »Wenn ihr ihn wissen wollt«, sprach die
Mutter, »so sucht ihn selber«, und die Tochter setzte hinzu
»habt ihr Sorge dass ihr ihn nicht findet, so nehmt euch einen Wegweiser mit.« Die Stieftochter aber sprach »armer
Mann, ich will dich führen, komm mit mir.« Da zürnte der
liebe Gott über die Mutter und Tochter, wendete ihnen den
Rücken zu und verwünschte sie, dass sie sollten schwarz
werden wie die Nacht und hässlich wie die Sünde. Der armen Stieftochter aber war Gott gnädig und gieng mit ihr,
und als sie nahe am Dorf waren, sprach er einen Segen über

sie und sagte »wähle dir drei Sachen aus, die will ich dir gewähren.« Da sprach das Mädchen »ich möchte gern so schön und rein werden wie die Sonne«; alsbald war sie weiß und schön wie der Tag. »Dann möchte ich einen Geldbeutel haben, der nie leer würde«: den gab ihr der liebe Gott auch, sprach aber »vergiss das Beste nicht.« Sagte sie »ich wünsche mir zum dritten das ewige Himmelreich nach meinem Tode.« Das ward ihr auch gewährt, und also schied der liebe Gott von ihr.

Als die Stiefmutter mit ihrer Tochter nach Hause kam und sah dass sie beide kohlschwarz und hässlich waren, die Stieftochter aber weiß und schön, so stieg die Bosheit in ihrem Herzen noch höher, und sie hatte nichts anders im Sinn als wie sie ihr ein Leid antun könnte. Die Stieftochter aber hatte einen Bruder Namens Reginer, den liebte sie sehr und erzählte ihm alles, was geschehen war. Nun sprach Reginer einmal zu ihr »liebe Schwester, ich will dich abmalen, damit ich dich beständig vor Augen sehe, denn meine Liebe zu dir ist so groß, dass ich dich immer anblicken möchte.« Da antwortete sie »aber ich bitte dich lass niemand das Bild sehen.« Er malte nun seine Schwester ab und hieng das Bild in seiner Stube auf; er wohnte aber in des Königs Schloss, weil er bei ihm Kutscher war. Alle Tage gieng er davor stehen und dankte Gott für das Glück seiner lieben Schwester. Nun war aber gerade dem König, bei dem er diente, seine Gemahlin verstorben, und die war so schön gewesen, dass man keine finden konnte, die ihr gliche, und der König war darüber in tiefer Trauer. Die Hofdiener bemerkten aber dass der Kutscher täglich vor dem schönen Bilde stand, missgönnten's ihm und meldeten es dem König. Da ließ dieser das Bild vor sich bringen, und als er sah dass es in allem seiner verstorbenen Frau glich, nur noch schöner war, so verliebte er sich sterblich hinein. Er ließ den Kutscher vor sich kommen und fragte wen das Bild vorstellte. Der Kutscher sagte es wäre seine Schwester, so entschloss sich der König keine andere als diese zur Gemahlin zu nehmen,

gab ihm Wagen und Pferde und prächtige Goldkleider und
schickte ihn fort, seine erwählte Braut abzuholen. Wie Reginer mit der Botschaft an kam, freute sich seine Schwester,
allein die Schwarze war eifersüchtig über das Glück, ärgerte
sich über alle Maßen und sprach zu ihrer Mutter »was helfen nun all eure Künste, da ihr mir ein solches Glück doch
nicht verschaffen könnt.« »Sei still«, sagte die Alte »ich will
dir's schon zuwenden.« Und durch ihre Hexenkünste trüb-
te sie dem Kutscher die Augen, dass er halb blind war, und
der Weißen verstopfte sie die Ohren, dass sie halb taub war.
Darauf stiegen sie in den Wagen, erst die Braut in den herr-
lichen königlichen Kleidern, dann die Stiefmutter mit ihrer
Tochter, und Reginer saß auf dem Bock, um zu fahren. Wie
sie eine Weile unterwegs waren, rief der Kutscher

>>deck dich zu, mein Schwesterlein,
dass Regen dich nicht nässt,
dass Wind dich nicht bestäubt
dass du fein schön zum König kommst.<<

Die Braut fragte »was sagt mein lieber Bruder?« »Ach«,
sprach die Alte, »er hat gesagt du solltest dein gülden Kleid
ausziehen und es deiner Schwester geben.« Da zog sie's aus
und tat's der Schwarzen an, die gab ihr dafür einen schlechten grauen Kittel. So fuhren sie weiter: über ein Weilchen
rief der Bruder abermals

>>deck dich zu, mein Schwesterlein,
dass Regen dich nicht nässt,
dass Wind dich nicht bestäubt,
und du fein schön zum König kommst.<<

Die Braut fragte »was sagt mein lieber Bruder?« »Ach«,
sprach die Alte, »er hat gesagt, du solltest deine güldene
Haube ab tun und deiner Schwester geben.« Da tat sie die
Haube ab und tat sie der Schwarzen auf und saß im bloßen
Haar. So fuhren sie weiter: wiederum über ein Weilchen
rief der Bruder

>>deck dich zu, mein Schwesterlein,
dass Regen dich nicht nässt,

dass Wind dich nicht bestäubt,
und du fein schön zum König kommst.«
Die Braut fragte »was sagt mein lieber Bruder?« »Ach«,
sprach die Alte, »er hat gesagt du möchtest einmal aus dem
Wagen sehen.« Sie fuhren aber gerade auf einer Brücke
über ein tiefes Wasser. Wie nun die Braut aufstand und aus
dem Wagen sich heraus bückte, da stießen sie die beiden
hinaus, dass sie mitten ins Wasser stürzte. Als sie versunken
war, in demselben Augenblick, stieg eine schneeweiße Ente
aus dem Wasserspiegel hervor und schwamm den Fluss
hinab. Der Bruder hatte gar nichts davon gemerkt und fuhr
den Wagen weiter, bis sie an den Hof kamen. Da brachte er
dem König die Schwarze als seine Schwester und meinte sie
wär's wirklich, weil es ihm trübe vor den Augen war und er
doch die Goldkleider schimmern sah. Der König, wie er
die grundlose Hässlichkeit an seiner vermeinten Braut erblickte, ward sehr bös und befahl den Kutscher in eine
Grube zu werfen, die voll Ottern und Schlangengezücht
war. Die alte Hexe aber wusste den König doch so zu be-
stricken und durch ihre Künste ihm die Augen zu verblen-
den, dass er sie und ihre Tochter behielt, ja dass sie ihm
ganz leidlich vorkam und er sich wirklich mit ihr verheiratete.
Einmal Abends, während die schwarze Braut dem König
auf dem Schoße saß, kam eine weiße Ente zum Gossenstein
in die Küche geschwommen und sagte zum Küchenjungen
      »Jüngelchen, mach Feuer an,
      dass ich meine Federn wärmen kann.«
Das tat der Küchenjunge und machte ihr ein Feuer auf dem
Herd: da kam die Ente und setzte sich daneben, schüttelte
sich und strich sich die Federn mit dem Schnabel zurecht.
Während sie so saß und sich wohltat, fragte sie
      »was macht mein Bruder Reginer?«
Der Küchenjunge antwortete
      »liegt in der Grube gefangen
      bei Ottern und bei Schlangen.«

Fragte sie weiter
>>was macht die schwarze Hexe im Haus?<<
Der Küchenjunge antwortete
>>die sitzt warm
ins Königs Arm.<<
Sagte die Ente
>>dass Gott erbarm!<<
und schwamm den Gossenstein hinaus.

Den folgenden Abend kam sie wieder und tat dieselben Fragen und den dritten Abend noch einmal. Da konnte es der Küchenjunge nicht länger übers Herz bringen, gieng zu dem König und entdeckte ihm alles. Der König aber wollte es selbst sehen, gieng den andern Abend hin, und wie die Ente den Kopf durch den Gossenstein herein streckte, nahm er sein Schwert, und hieb ihr den Hals durch, da ward sie auf einmal zum schönsten Mädchen und glich genau dem Bild, das der Bruder von ihr gemacht hatte. Der König war voll Freuden; und weil sie ganz nass da stand, ließ er köstliche Kleider bringen und ließ sie damit bekleiden. Dann erzählte sie ihm wie sie durch List und Falschheit wäre betrogen und zuletzt in den Fluss hinabgeworfen worden; und ihre erste Bitte war, dass ihr Bruder aus der Schlangenhöhle heraus geholt würde. Und als der König diese Bitte erfüllt hatte, gieng er in die Kammer, wo die alte Hexe saß und fragte >>was verdient die, welche das und das tut?<< und erzählte was geschehen war. Da war sie so verblendet, dass sie nichts merkte und sprach >>die verdient dass man sie nackt auszieht und in ein Fass mit Nägeln legt, und dass man vor das Fass ein Pferd spannt und das Pferd in alle Welt schickt.<< Das geschah alles an ihr und ihrer schwarzen Tochter. Der König aber heiratete die weiße und schöne Braut und belohnte den treuen Bruder, indem er ihn zu einem reichen und angesehenen Mann machte.

136

Der Eisenhans.

Es war einmal ein König, der hatte einen großen Wald bei seinem Schloss, darin lief Wild aller Art herum. Zu einer Zeit schickte er einen Jäger hinaus, der sollte ein Reh schießen, aber er kam nicht wieder. »Vielleicht ist ihm ein Unglück zugestoßen«, sagte der König, und schickte den folgenden Tag zwei andere Jäger hinaus, die sollten ihn aufsuchen, aber die blieben auch weg. Da ließ er am dritten Tag alle seine Jäger kommen und sprach »streift durch den ganzen Wald und lasst nicht ab bis ihr sie alle drei gefunden habt.« Aber auch von diesen kam keiner wieder heim, und von der Meute Hunde, die sie mitgenommen hatten, ließ sich keiner wieder sehen. Von der Zeit an wollte sich niemand mehr in den Wald wagen, und er lag da in tiefer Stille und Einsamkeit, und man sah nur zuweilen einen Adler oder Habicht darüber hin fliegen. Das dauerte viele Jahre, da meldete sich ein fremder Jäger bei dem König, suchte eine Versorgung und erbot sich in den gefährlichen Wald zu gehen. Der König aber wollte seine Einwilligung nicht geben und sprach »es ist nicht geheuer darin, ich fürchte es geht dir nicht besser als den andern, und du kommst nicht wieder heraus.« Der Jäger antwortete »Herr, ich will's auf meine Gefahr wagen: von Furcht weiß ich nichts.«

Der Jäger begab sich also mit seinem Hund in den Wald. Es dauerte nicht lange, so geriet der Hund einem Wild auf die Fährte und wollte hinter ihm her: kaum aber war er ein paar Schritte gelaufen, so stand er vor einem tiefen Pfuhl, konnte nicht weiter und ein nackter Arm streckte sich aus dem Wasser, packte ihn und zog ihn hinab. Als der Jäger das sah, gieng er zurück und holte drei Männer, die mussten mit Eimern kommen und das Wasser ausschöpfen. Als sie auf den Grund sehen konnten, so lag da ein wilder Mann, der braun am Leib war, wie rostiges Eisen, und dem die Haare über das Gesicht bis zu den Knien herab hiengen. Sie banden ihn mit Stricken und führten ihn fort, in das Schloss. Da war große Verwunderung über den wilden Mann, der König aber ließ ihn in einen eisernen Käfig auf seinen Hof setzen und verbot bei Lebensstrafe die Türe des Käfigs zu öffnen, und die Königin musste den Schlüssel selbst in Verwahrung nehmen. Von nun an konnte ein jeder wieder mit Sicherheit in den Wald gehen.

Der König hatte einen Sohn von acht Jahren, der spielte einmal auf dem Hof, und bei dem Spiel fiel ihm sein goldener Ball in den Käfig. Der Knabe lief hin und sprach »gib mir meinen Ball heraus.« »Nicht eher«, antwortete der Mann, »als bis du mir die Türe aufgemacht hast.« »Nein«, sagte der Knabe, »das tue ich nicht, das hat der König verboten«, und lief fort. Am andern Tag kam er wieder und forderte seinen Ball: der wilde Mann sagte »öffne meine Türe«, aber der Knabe wollte nicht. Am dritten Tag war der König auf die Jagd geritten, da kam der Knabe nochmals und sagte »wenn ich auch wollte, ich kann die Türe nicht öffnen, ich habe den Schlüssel nicht.« Da sprach der wilde Mann »er liegt unter dem Kopfkissen deiner Mutter, da kannst du ihn holen.« Der Knabe, der seinen Ball wieder haben wollte, schlug alles Bedenken in den Wind und brachte den Schlüssel herbei. Die Türe gieng schwer auf, und der Knabe klemmte sich den Finger. Als sie offen war, trat der wilde Mann heraus, gab ihm den goldenen Ball und eilte hinweg. Dem Knaben war angst geworden, er schrie und rief ihm nach »ach, wilder Mann, geh nicht fort, sonst bekomme ich Schläge.« Der wilde Mann kehrte um, hob ihn auf, setzte ihn auf seinen Nacken und gieng mit schnellen Schritten in den Wald hinein. Als der König heim kam, bemerkte er den leeren Käfig und fragte die Königin wie das zugegangen wäre. Sie wusste nichts davon, suchte den Schlüssel, aber er war weg. Sie rief den Knaben, aber niemand antwortete. Der König schickte Leute aus, die ihn auf dem Feld suchen sollten, aber sie fanden ihn nicht. Da konnte er leicht erraten was geschehen war, und es herrschte große Trauer an dem königlichen Hof.

Als der wilde Mann wieder in dem finstern Wald angelangt war, so setzte er den Knaben von den Schultern herab und sprach zu ihm »Vater und Mutter siehst du nicht wieder, aber ich will dich bei mir behalten, denn du hast mich befreit, und ich habe Mitleid mit dir. Wenn du alles tust, was ich dir sage, so sollst du's gut haben. Schätze und Gold habe ich genug und mehr als jemand in der Welt.« Er machte dem Knaben ein Lager von Moos, auf dem er einschlief, und am andern Morgen führte ihn der Mann zu einem Brunnen und sprach »siehst du der Goldbrunnen ist hell und klar wie Kristall: du sollst dabei sitzen und acht haben dass nichts hinein fällt, sonst ist er verunehrt. Jeden Abend komme ich und sehe ob du mein Gebot befolgt hast.« Der Knabe setzte sich an den Rand des Brunnens, sah wie manchmal ein goldner Fisch, manchmal eine goldne Schlange sich darin zeigte, und hatte acht dass nichts hinein fiel. Als er so saß, schmerzte ihn einmal der Finger so heftig dass er ihn unwillkürlich in das Wasser steckte. Er zog ihn schnell wieder heraus, sah aber dass er ganz vergoldet war, und wie große Mühe er sich gab das Gold wieder abzuwischen, es war alles vergeblich. Abends kam der Eisenhans zurück, sah den Knaben an und sprach »was ist mit dem Brunnen geschehen?« »Nichts, nichts« antwortete er und hielt den Finger auf den Rücken, dass er ihn nicht sehen sollte. Aber der Mann sagte »du hast den Finger in das Wasser getaucht: diesmal mag's hingehen, aber hüte dich dass du nicht wieder etwas hinein fallen lässt.« Am frühsten Morgen saß er schon bei dem Brunnen und bewachte ihn. Der Finger tat ihm wieder weh und er fuhr damit über seinen Kopf, da fiel unglücklicher Weise ein Haar herab in den Brunnen. Er nahm es schnell heraus, aber es war schon ganz vergoldet! Der Eisenhans kam und wusste schon was geschehen war. »Du hast ein Haar in den Brunnen fallen lassen«, sagte er, »ich will dir's noch einmal nachsehen, aber wenn's zum drittenmal geschieht, so ist der Brunnen entehrt, und du kannst nicht länger bei mir bleiben.« Am dritten Tag saß der Knabe am Brunnen, und bewegte den Finger nicht, wenn er ihm noch so weh tat. Aber die Zeit ward ihm lang, und er betrachtete sein Angesicht, das auf dem Wasserspiegel stand. Und als er sich dabei immer mehr beugte, und sich recht in die Augen sehen wollte, so fielen ihm seine langen Haare von den Schultern herab in das Wasser. Er richtete sich schnell in die Höhe, aber das ganze Haupthaar war schon vergoldet und glänzte wie eine Sonne. Ihr könnt denken wie der arme Knabe erschrak. Er nahm sein Taschentuch und band es um den Kopf, damit es der Mann nicht sehen sollte. Als er kam, wusste er schon alles und sprach »binde das Tuch auf.« Da quollen die goldenen Haare hervor und der Knabe mochte sich entschuldigen, wie er wollte, es half ihm nichts. »Du hast die Probe nicht bestanden und kannst nicht länger hier bleiben. Geh hinaus in die Welt, da wirst du erfahren, wie die Armut tut. Aber weil du kein böses Herz hast und ich's gut mit dir meine, so will ich dir eins erlauben: wenn du in Not gerätst, so geh zu dem Wald und rufe ›Eisenhans‹, dann will ich kommen und dir helfen. Meine Macht ist groß, größer als du denkst, und Gold und Silber habe ich im Überfluss.«

Da verließ der Königssohn den Wald und gieng über gebahnte und ungebahnte Wege immer zu, bis er zuletzt in eine große Stadt kam. Er suchte da Arbeit, aber er konnte keine finden und hatte auch nichts erlernt, womit er sich hätte forthelfen können. Endlich gieng er in das Schloss und fragte ob sie ihn behalten wollten. Die Hofleute wussten nicht wozu sie ihn brauchen sollten, aber sie hatten Wohlgefallen an ihm und hießen ihn bleiben. Zuletzt nahm ihn der Koch in Dienst und sagte er könnte Holz und Wasser tragen und die Asche zusammen kehren. Einmal, als gerade kein anderer zur Hand war, hieß ihn der Koch die Speisen zur königlichen Tafel tragen, da er aber seine goldenen Haare nicht wollte sehen lassen, so behielt er sein Hüt-

chen auf. Dem König war so etwas noch nicht vorgekom-
men, und er sprach »wenn du zur königlichen Tafel
kommst, musst du deinen Hut abziehen.« »Ach Herr«, antwortete er, »ich kann nicht, ich habe einen bösen Grind auf
dem Kopf.« Da ließ der König den Koch herbei rufen,
schalt ihn und fragte wie er einen solchen Jungen hätte in
seinen Dienst nehmen können; er sollte ihn gleich fortja-
gen. Der Koch aber hatte Mitleiden mit ihm und vertauschte ihn mit dem Gärtnerjungen.

Nun musste der Junge im Garten pflanzen und begießen,
hacken und graben, und Wind und böses Wetter über sich
ergehen lassen. Einmal im Sommer als er allein im Garten
arbeitete, war der Tag so heiß dass er sein Hütchen abnahm
und die Luft ihn kühlen sollte. Wie die Sonne auf das Haar
schien, glitzte und blitzte es dass die Strahlen in das Schlaf-
zimmer der Königstochter fielen und sie aufsprang um zu
sehen was das wäre. Da erblickte sie den Jungen und rief
ihn an »Junge, bring mir einen Blumenstrauß.« Er setzte in
aller Eile sein Hütchen auf, brach wilde Feldblumen ab und
band sie zusammen. Als er damit die Treppe hinauf stieg,
begegnete ihm der Gärtner und sprach »wie kannst du der
Königstochter einen Strauß von schlechten Blumen bringen? geschwind hole andere, und suche die schönsten und
seltensten aus.« »Ach nein«, antwortete der Junge, »die wilden riechen kräftiger und werden ihr besser gefallen.« Als
er in ihr Zimmer kam, sprach die Königstochter »nimm
dein Hütchen ab, es ziemt sich nicht dass du ihn vor mir
auf behältst.« Er antwortete wieder »ich darf nicht, ich
habe einen grindigen Kopf.« Sie griff aber nach dem Hütchen und zog es ab, da rollten seine goldenen Haare auf die
Schultern herab, dass es prächtig anzusehen war. Er wollte
fortspringen, aber sie hielt ihn am Arm und gab ihm eine
Hand voll Dukaten. Er gieng damit fort, achtete aber des
Goldes nicht, sondern er brachte es dem Gärtner und
sprach »ich schenke es deinen Kindern, die können damit
spielen.« Den andern Tag rief ihm die Königstochter aber-

mals zu er sollte ihr einen Strauß Feldblumen bringen, und
als er damit eintrat, grapste sie gleich nach seinem Hütchen
und wollte es ihm wegnehmen, aber er hielt es mit beiden
Händen fest. Sie gab ihm wieder eine Hand voll Dukaten,
aber er wollte sie nicht behalten und gab sie dem Gärtner
zum Spielwerk für seine Kinder. Den dritten Tag gieng's
nicht anders, sie konnte ihm sein Hütchen nicht weg nehmen, und er wollte ihr Gold nicht.

Nicht lange danach ward das Land mit Krieg überzogen.
Der König sammelte sein Volk und wusste nicht ob er dem
Feind, der übermächtig war und ein großes Heer hatte, Widerstand leisten könnte. Da sagte der Gärtnerjunge »ich bin
herangewachsen und will mit in den Krieg ziehen, gebt mir
nur ein Pferd.« Die andern lachten und sprachen »wenn
wir fort sind, so suche dir eins: wir wollen dir eins im Stall
zurück lassen.« Als sie ausgezogen waren, gieng er in den
Stall und zog das Pferd heraus; es war an einem Fuß lahm
und hickelte hunkepuus, hunkepuus. Dennoch setzte er
sich auf und ritt fort nach dem dunkeln Wald. Als er an den
Rand desselben gekommen war, rief er dreimal Eisenhans
so laut dass es durch die Bäume schallte. Gleich darauf erschien der wilde Mann und sprach »was verlangst du?«
»Ich verlange ein starkes Ross, denn ich will in den Krieg
ziehen.« »Das sollst du haben und noch mehr als du verlangst.« Dann gieng der wilde Mann in den Wald zurück,
und es dauerte nicht lange, so kam ein Stallknecht aus dem
Wald und führte ein Ross herbei, das schnaubte aus den
Nüstern, und war kaum zu bändigen. Und hinterher folgte
eine große Schar Kriegsvolk, ganz in Eisen gerüstet, und
ihre Schwerter blitzten in der Sonne. Der Jüngling übergab
dem Stallknecht sein dreibeiniges Pferd, bestieg das andere
und ritt vor der Schar her. Als er sich dem Schlachtfeld näherte, war schon ein großer Teil von des Königs Leuten gefallen und es fehlte nicht viel, so mussten die übrigen weichen. Da jagte der Jüngling mit seiner eisernen Schar heran,
fuhr wie ein Wetter über die Feinde und schlug alles nieder

was sich ihm widersetzte. Sie wollten fliehen, aber der Jüngling saß ihnen auf dem Nacken und ließ nicht ab bis kein Mann mehr übrig war. Statt aber zu dem König zurück zu kehren, führte er seine Schar auf Umwegen wieder zu dem Wald und rief den Eisenhans heraus. »Was verlangst du?« fragte der wilde Mann. »Nimm dein Ross und deine Schar zurück und gib mir mein dreibeiniges Pferd wieder.« Es geschah alles, was er verlangte, und [er] ritt auf seinem dreibeinigen Pferd heim. Als der König wieder in sein Schloss kam, gieng ihm seine Tochter entgegen und wünschte ihm Glück zu seinem Sieg. »Ich bin es nicht, der den Sieg davon getragen hat« sprach er »sondern ein fremder Ritter, der mir mit seiner Schar zu Hilfe kam.« Die Tochter wollte wissen wer der fremde Ritter wäre, aber der König wusste es nicht und sagte »er hat die Feinde verfolgt, und ich habe ihn nicht wieder gesehen.« Sie erkundigte sich bei dem Gärtner nach seinem Jungen: der lachte aber und sprach »eben ist er auf seinem dreibeinigen Pferd heim gekommen, und die andern haben gespottet und gerufen ›da kommt unser Hunkepuus wieder an.‹ Sie fragten auch ›hinter welcher Hecke hast du derweil gelegen und geschlafen?‹ Er sprach aber ›ich habe das beste getan, und ohne mich wäre es schlecht gegangen.‹ Da ward er noch mehr ausgelacht.«

Der König sprach zu seiner Tochter »ich will ein großes Fest ansagen lassen, das drei Tage währen soll, und du sollst einen goldenen Apfel werfen: vielleicht kommt der unbekannte herbei.« Als das Fest verkündigt war, gieng der Jüngling hinaus zu dem Wald und rief den Eisenhans. »Was verlangst du?« fragte er. »Dass ich den goldenen Apfel der Königstochter fange.« »Es ist so gut als hättest du ihn schon« sagte Eisenhans, »du sollst auch eine rote Rüstung dazu haben und auf einem stolzen Fuchs reiten.« Als der Tag kam, sprengte der Jüngling heran, stellte sich unter die Ritter und ward von niemand erkannt. Die Königstochter trat hervor und warf den Rittern einen goldenen Apfel zu, aber keiner

fieng ihn als er allein, aber sobald er ihn hatte, jagte er davon.
Am zweiten Tag hatte ihn Eisenhans als weißen Ritter aus-
gerüstet und ihm einen Schimmel gegeben. Abermals fieng
er allein den Apfel, verweilte aber keinen Augenblick, sondern jagte damit fort. Der König ward bös und sprach »das
ist nicht erlaubt, er muss vor mir erscheinen und seinen Namen nennen.« Er gab den Befehl, wenn der Ritter, der den
Apfel gefangen habe, sich wieder davon machte, so sollte
man ihm nachsetzen und wenn er nicht gutwillig zurück
kehrte, auf ihn hauen und stechen. Am dritten Tag erhielt er
vom Eisenhans eine schwarze Rüstung und einen Rappen
und fieng auch wieder den Apfel. Als er aber damit fortjagte,
verfolgten ihn die Leute des Königs und einer kam ihm so
nahe dass er mit der Spitze des Schwerts ihm das Bein ver-
wundete. Er entkam ihnen jedoch, aber sein Pferd sprang so
gewaltig dass der Helm ihm vom Kopf fiel, und sie konnten
sehen dass er goldene Haare hatte. Sie ritten zurück und
meldeten dem König alles.
Am andern Tag fragte die Königstochter den Gärtner nach
seinem Jungen. »Er arbeitet im Garten: der wunderliche
Kauz ist auch bei dem Fest gewesen und erst gestern Abend
wieder gekommen; er hat auch meinen Kindern drei goldene
Äpfel gezeigt, die er gewonnen hat.« Der König ließ ihn vor
sich fordern, und er erschien und hatte wieder sein Hütchen
auf dem Kopf. Aber die Königstochter gieng auf ihn zu und
nahm es ihm ab, und da fielen seine goldenen Haare über die
Schultern, und er war so schön, dass alle erstaunten. »Bist du
der Ritter gewesen, der jeden Tag zu dem Fest gekommen
ist, immer in einer andern Farbe, und der die drei goldenen
Äpfel gefangen hat?« fragte der König. »Ja« antwortete er,
»und da sind die Äpfel«, holte sie aus seiner Tasche und
reichte sie dem König. »Wenn ihr noch mehr Beweise verlangt, so könnt ihr die Wunde sehen, die mir eure Leute geschlagen haben, als sie mich verfolgten. Aber ich bin auch
der Ritter, der euch zum Sieg über die Feinde geholfen hat.«
»Wenn du solche Taten verrichten kannst, so bist du kein

Gärtnerjunge: sage mir, wer ist dein Vater?« »Mein Vater ist
ein mächtiger König und Goldes habe ich die Fülle und so
viel ich nur verlange.« »Ich sehe wohl«, sprach der König,
»ich bin dir Dank schuldig, kann ich dir etwas zu Gefallen
tun?« »Ja« antwortete er, »das könnt ihr wohl, gebt mir eure
Tochter zur Frau.« Da lachte die Jungfrau und sprach »der
macht keine Umstände, aber ich habe schon an seinen goldenen Haaren gesehen dass er kein Gärtnerjunge ist«, gieng
dann hin und küsste ihn. Zu der Vermählung kam sein Vater
und seine Mutter und waren in großer Freude, denn sie hatten schon alle Hoffnung aufgegeben ihren lieben Sohn wieder zu sehen. Und als sie an der Hochzeitstafel saßen, da
schwieg auf einmal die Musik, die Türen giengen auf und ein
stolzer König trat herein mit großem Gefolge. Er gieng auf
den Jüngling zu, umarmte ihn und sprach »ich bin der Eisenhans, und war in einen wilden Mann verwünscht, aber du
hast mich erlöst. Alle Schätze, die ich besitze, die sollen dein
Eigentum sein.«

137.

De drei schwatten Prinzessinnen.

Ostindien was von den Fiend belagert, he wull de Stadt nig
verloeten, he wull ersten seshundert Dahler hebben. Do leiten se dat ut trummen, well de schaffen könne, de soll Börgemester weren. Do was der en armen Fisker, de fiskede up
de See mit sinen Sohn, do kam de Fiend un nam den Sohn
gefangen un gav em doför seshundert Dahler. Do genk de
Vader hen un gav dat de Heerens in de Stadt, un de Fiend
trock av un de Fisker wurde Börgemester. Do word utro-
pen wer nig »Heer Börgemester« segde, de soll an de Galge
richtet weren.
De Sohn de kam de Fiend wier ut de Hände un kam in en
grauten Wold up en haujen Berg. De Berg de dei sick up,

do kam he in en graut verwünsket Schloss, woin Stohle, Diske un Bänke alle schwatt behangen wören. Do queimen drei Prinzessinnen, de gans schwatt antrokken wören, de men en lück (wenig) witt in't Gesicht hädden, de segden to em he soll men nig bange sien, se wullen em nix dohn, he könn eer erlösen. Do seg he je dat wull he gern dohn, wann he men wüste wo he dat macken söll. Do segget se he söll en gans Johr nig met en kühren (sprechen), un söll se auck nig anseihen; wat he gern hebben wull, dat söll he men seggen, wann se Antwort giewen dröften (geben dürften), wullen se et dohn. As he ne Tied lang der west was, sede he he wull asse gern noh sin Vader gohn, da segget se dat söll he men dohn, düssen Buel (Beutel) met Geld söll he met niermen, düsse Klöder soll he antrecken, un in acht Dage möst he der wier sien.

Do werd he upnurmen (aufgehoben), un is glick in Ostindien. Do kann he sin Vader in de Fiskhütte nig mer finden un frög de Luide wo doh de arme Fisker blierwen wöre, do segget se dat möst he nig seggen, dann queim he an de Galge. Do kümmt he bi sin Vader, do seg he »Fisker, wo sin ji do to kummen?« Do seg de »dat möt ji nig seggen, wann dat de Heerens van de Stadt gewahr weeret, kümme ji an de Galge.« He willt ober gar nig loten, he werd noh de Galge bracht. Es he do is, seg he »o mine Heerens, gierwet mie doh Verlöv dat ick noh de olle Fiskhütte gohn mag.« Do tüt he sinen ollen Kiel an, do kümmet he wier noh de Heerens un seg »seih ji et nu wull, sin ick nig en armen Fisker sinen Sohn? in düt Tueg heve ick minen Vader un Moder dat Braud gewunnen.« Do erkennet se en un badden üm Vergiebnüs un niermt en met noh sin Hues, do verteld he alle wü et em gohn hev, dat he wöre in en Wold kummen up en haujen Berg, do hädde sick de Berg updohn, do wöre he in en verwünsket Schloss kummen, wo alles schwatt west wöre, un drei Prinzessinnen wören der an kummen, de wören schwatt west, men en lück witt in't Gesicht. De hädden em segd he söll nig bange sien, he könn eer erlösen.

Do seg sine Moder dat mög wull nig guet sien, he soll ne
gewiehte Wasskeefze met niermen un drüppen (tropfen) eer
gleinig (glühend) Wass in't Gesicht.

He geit wier hen, un do gruelte (graute) em so, un he
drüppde er Wass in't Gesicht, asse se sleipen, un se wören
all halv witt. Do sprüngen alle de drei Prinzessinnen up un
segden »de verfluchte Hund, usse Bloet soll örfer die Rache
schreien, nu is kin Mensk up de Welt geboren un werd geboren, de us erlösen kann, wie hevet noh drei Bröders, de
sind in siewen Ketten anschloeten, de söllt die terreiten.«
Do givt et en Gekriesk in't ganse Schloss, un he sprank noh
ut dat Fenster un terbrack dat Been, un dat Schloss sunk
wier in de Grunde, de Berg was wier to, un nümmes wust
wo et west was.

138.

Knoist un sine dre Sühne.

Twisken Werrel un Soist, do wuhnde 'n Mann, un de hede
Knoist, de hadde dre Sühne, de eene was blind, de annre
was lahm un de dridde was splenternaket. Do giengen se
mol öwer Feld, do sehen se eenen Hasen. De blinne de
schöt en, de lahme de fienk en, de nackede de stack en in de
Tasken. Do käimen se für en groot allmächtig Waater, do
wuren dre Schippe uppe, dat eene dat rann, dat annre dat
sank, dat dridde, do was keen Buoden inne. Wo keen Buoden inne was, do giengen se olle dre inne. Do käimen se an
eenen allmächtig grooten Walle (Wald), do was en groot allmächtig Boom inne, in den Boom was eene allmächtig
groote Kapelle, in de Kapelle was een hageböcken Köster
un en bussboomen Pastoer, de deelden dat Wiggewaater
mit Knuppeln uit.
        Sielig is de Mann,
        de den Wiggewaater entlaupen kann.

139.
Dat Mäken von Brakel.

Et gien mal 'n Mäken von Brakel na de sünt Annen Kapellen uner de Hinnenborg, un weil et gierne 'n Mann heven wulle un ock meinde et wäre süs neimes in de Kapellen, sau sank et

>»O hilge sünte Anne,
help mie doch bald tom Manne.
du kennst 'n ja wull:
he wuhnt var'm Suttmerdore,
hed gele Hore:
du kennst 'n ja wull.«

De Köster stand awerst hünner de Altare un höre dat, da rep he mit ner gans schrögerigen Stimme »du kriggst 'n nig, du kriggst 'n nig.« Dat Mäken awerst meinde dat Marienkinneken, dat bie de Mudder Anne steiht, hedde üm dat to ropen, da wor et beuse un reip »pepperlepep, dumme Blae, halt de Schnuten un lat de Möhme kühren (die Mutter reden).«

140.
Das Hausgesinde.

»Wo wust du henne?« »Nah *Walpe*.« »Ick nah Walpe, du nah Walpe; sam, sam, goh wie dann.«

»Häst du auck 'n Mann? wie hedd din Mann?« »*Cham*.« »Min Mann Cham, din Mann Cham: ick nah Walpe, du nah Walpe; sam, sam, goh wie dann.«

»Häst du auck 'n Kind? wie hedd din Kind?« »*Grind*.« »Min Kind Grind, din Kind Grind: min Mann Cham, din Mann Cham: ick nah Walpe, du nah Walpe; sam, sam, goh wie dann.«

»Häst du auck 'n Weige? wie hedd dine Weige?« »*Hippo-deige.*« »Mine Weige Hippodeige, dine Weige Hippodeige: min Kind Grind, din Kind Grind: min Mann Cham, din Mann Cham: ick nah Walpe, du nah Walpe; sam, sam, goh wie dann.«

»Häst du auck 'n Knecht? wie hedd din Knecht?« »*Machmirsrecht.*« »Min Knecht Machmirsrecht, din Knecht Machmirsrecht: mine Weige Hippodeige, dine Weige Hippodeike: min Kind Grind, din Kind Grind: min Mann Cham, din Mann Cham: ick nah Walpe, du nah Walpe; sam, sam, goh wie dann.«

141.

Das Lämmchen und Fischchen.

Es war einmal ein Brüderchen und Schwesterchen, die hatten sich herzlich lieb. Ihre rechte Mutter war aber tot, und sie hatten eine Stiefmutter, die war ihnen nicht gut und tat ihnen heimlich alles Leid an. Es trug sich zu, dass die zwei mit andern Kindern auf einer Wiese vor dem Haus spielten, und an der Wiese war ein Teich, der gieng bis an die eine Seite vom Haus. Die Kinder liefen da herum, kriegten sich und spielten Abzählens:

»Eneke, Beneke, lat mi liewen,
will die ock min Vügelken giewen.
Vügelken sall mie Strau söken,
Strau will ick den Köseken giewen,
Köseken sall mie Melk giewen,
Melk will ick den Bäcker giewen,
Bäcker sall mie 'n Kocken backen,
Kocken will ick den Kätken giewen,
Kätken sall mie Müse fangen,
Müse will ick in 'n Rauck hangen
un will se anschnien.«

Dabei standen sie in einem Kreis, und auf welchen nun das Wort »anschnien« fiel, der musste fortlaufen und die anderen liefen ihm nach und fiengen ihn. Wie sie so fröhlich dahinsprangen, sah's die Stiefmutter vom Fenster mit an und ärgerte sich. Weil sie aber Hexenkünste verstand, so verwünschte sie beide, das Brüderchen in einen Fisch und das Schwesterchen in ein Lamm. Da schwamm das Fischchen im Teich hin und her, und war traurig, das Lämmchen gieng auf der Wiese hin und her, und war traurig und fraß nicht und rührte kein Hälmchen an. So gieng eine lange Zeit hin, da kamen fremde Gäste auf das Schloss. Die falsche Stiefmutter dachte »jetzt ist die Gelegenheit gut«, rief den Koch, und sprach zu ihm »geh und hol das Lamm von der Wiese und schlacht's, wir haben sonst nichts für die Gäste.« Da gieng der Koch hin und holte das Lämmchen und führte es in die Küche und band ihm die Füßchen; das litt es alles geduldig. Wie er nun sein Messer herausgezogen hatte und auf der Schwelle wetzte, um es abzustechen, sah es, wie ein Fischlein in dem Wasser vor dem Gossenstein hin und her schwamm und zu ihm hinaufblickte. Das war aber das Brüderchen, denn als das Fischchen gesehen hatte wie der Koch das Lämmchen fortführte, war es im Teich mitgeschwommen bis zum Haus. Da rief das Lämmchen hinab

>»ach Brüderchen im tiefen See,
wie tut mir doch mein Herz so weh!
der Koch der wetzt das Messer,
will mir mein Herz durchstechen.«

Das Fischchen antwortete

>»ach Schwesterchen in der Höh,
wie tut mir doch mein Herz so weh
in dieser tiefen See!«

Wie der Koch hörte dass das Lämmchen sprechen konnte und so traurige Worte zu dem Fischchen hinabrief, erschrak er und dachte es müsste kein natürliches Lämmchen sein, sondern wäre von der bösen Frau im Haus verwünscht. Da sprach er »sei ruhig, ich will dich nicht schlachten« nahm ein anderes Tier und bereitete das für die Gäste, und brachte das Lämmchen zu einer guten Bäuerin, der erzählte er alles, was er gesehen und gehört hatte. Die Bäuerin war aber gerade die Amme von dem Schwesterchen gewesen, vermutete gleich wer's sein würde und gieng mit ihm zu einer weisen Frau. Da sprach die weise Frau einen Segen über das Lämmchen und Fischchen, wovon sie ihre menschliche Gestalt wieder bekamen, und danach führte sie beide in einen großen Wald in ein klein Häuschen, wo sie einsam, aber zufrieden und glücklich lebten.

142.

Simeliberg.

Es waren zwei Brüder, einer war reich, der andere arm. Der Reiche aber gab dem Armen nichts, und er musste sich vom Kornhandel kümmerlich ernähren; da gieng es ihm oft so schlecht, dass er für seine Frau und Kinder kein Brot hatte. Einmal fuhr er mit seinem Karren durch den Wald, da erblickte er zur Seite einen großen kahlen Berg, und weil er den noch nie gesehen hatte, hielt er still und betrachtete ihn mit Verwunderung. Wie er so stand, sah er zwölf wilde große Männer daher kommen: weil er nun glaubte das wären Räuber, schob er seinen Karren ins Gebüsch und stieg auf einen Baum und wartete was da geschehen würde. Die zwölf Männer giengen aber vor den Berg und riefen »Berg *Semsi*, Berg *Semsi*, tu dich auf.« Alsbald tat sich der kahle Berg in der Mitte von einander, und die zwölfe giengen hinein, und wie sie drin waren, schloss er sich zu. Über eine kleine Weile aber tat er sich wieder auf, und die Männer kamen heraus und trugen schwere Säcke auf den Rücken, und wie sie alle wieder am Tageslicht waren, sprachen sie »Berg *Semsi*, Berg *Semsi*, tu dich zu.« Da fuhr der Berg zusammen, und war kein Eingang mehr an ihm zu sehen, und die Zwölfe giengen fort. Als sie ihn nun ganz aus den Augen waren, stieg der Arme vom Baum herunter, und war neugierig was wohl im Berge heimliches verborgen wäre. Also gieng er davor und sprach »Berg *Semsi*, Berg *Semsi*, tu dich auf«, und der Berg tat sich auch vor ihm auf. Da trat er hinein, und der ganze Berg war eine Höhle voll Silber und Gold, und hinten lagen große Haufen Perlen und blitzende Edelsteine, wie Korn aufgeschüttet. Der Arme wusste gar nicht was er anfangen sollte, und ob er sich etwas von den Schätzen nehmen dürfte; endlich füllte er sich die Taschen mit Gold, die Perlen und Edelsteine aber ließ er liegen. Als er wieder herauskam, sprach er gleichfalls »Berg *Semsi*, Berg *Semsi*, tu dich zu«, da schloss sich der Berg, und er fuhr mit seinem Karren nach Haus. Nun brauchte er nicht mehr zu sorgen und konnte mit seinem Golde für Frau und Kind Brot und auch Wein dazu kaufen, lebte fröhlich und redlich, gab den Armen und tat jedermann Gutes. Als aber das Geld zu Ende war, gieng er zu seinem Bruder, lieh einen Scheffel und holte sich von neuem; doch rührte er von den großen Schätzen nichts an. Wie er sich zum drittenmal etwas holen wollte, borgte er bei seinem Bruder abermals den Scheffel. Der Reiche war aber schon lange neidisch über sein Vermögen und den schönen Haushalt, den er sich eingerichtet hatte, und konnte nicht begreifen woher der Reichtum käme und was sein Bruder mit dem Scheffel anfienge. Da dachte er eine List aus und bestrich den Boden mit Pech, und wie er das Maß zurück bekam, so war ein Goldstück darin hängen geblieben. Alsbald gieng er zu seinem Bruder und fragte ihn »was hast du mit dem Scheffel gemessen?« »Korn und Gerste« sagte der andere. Da zeigte er ihm das Goldstück und drohte ihm, wenn er nicht die Wahrheit sagte, so wollt er ihn beim Gericht verklagen. Er erzählte ihm nun alles, wie es zugegangen war. Der Reiche aber ließ gleich einen Wagen anspannen, fuhr hinaus, wollte die Gelegenheit besser benutzen und ganz andere Schätze mitbringen. Wie er vor den Berg kam, rief er »Berg *Semsi*, Berg *Semsi*, tu dich auf.« Der Berg tat sich auf, und er gieng hinein. Da lagen die Reichtümer alle vor ihm, und er wusste lange nicht wozu er am ersten greifen sollte, endlich lud er Edelsteine auf so viel er tragen konnte. Er wollte seine Last hinausbringen, weil aber Herz und Sinn ganz voll von den Schätzen waren, hatte er darüber den Namen des Berges vergessen und rief »Berg *Simeli*, Berg *Simeli*, tu dich auf.« Aber das war der rechte Name nicht, und der Berg regte sich nicht und blieb verschlossen. Da ward ihm angst, aber je länger er nachsann, desto mehr verwirrten sich seine Gedanken, und halfen ihm alle Schätze nichts mehr. Am Abend tat sich der Berg auf und die zwölf Räuber kamen herein, und als sie ihn sahen, lachten sie und riefen »Vogel, haben wir dich endlich, meinst du wir hätten's nicht gemerkt dass du zweimal hereingekommen bist, aber wir konnten dich nicht fangen, zum drittenmal sollst du nicht wieder heraus.« Da rief er »ich war's nicht, mein Bruder war's«, aber er mochte bitten um sein Leben und sagen was er wollte, sie schlugen ihm das Haupt ab.

143.

Up Reisen gohn.

Et was emol ne arme Frau, de hadde enen Suhn, de wull so gerne reisen, do seg de Mohr »wu kannst du reisen? wi hebt je gar kien Geld, dat du mitniemen kannst.« Do seg de Suhn »ick will mi gut behelpen, ick will alltied seggen ›Nig viel, nig viel, nig viel.‹«

Do genk he ene gude Tied un sede alltied »nig viel, nig viel, nig viel.« Kam do bi en Trop Fisker un seg »Gott helpe ju! nig viel, nig viel, nig viel.« »Wat segst du, Kerl, nig viel?«

Un asse dat Gören (Garn) uttrocken, kregen se auck nig
viel Fiske. So met enen Stock up de Jungen, un »hest du mi
nig dresken (dreschen) seihn?« »Wat sall ick denn seggen?«
seg de Junge. »Du sallst seggen ›fank vull, fank vull.‹«
Do geit he wier ene ganze Tied un seg »fank vull, fank
vull«, bis he kümmt an enen Galgen, do hebt se en armen
Sünder, den willt se richten. Do seg he »guden Morgen,
fank vull, fank vull.« »Wat segst du, Kerl, fank vull? söllt
der noch mehr leige (leidige, böse) Lude in de Welt sien? is
düt noch nig genog?« He krig wier wat up den Puckel.
»Wat sall ick denn seggen?« »Du sallst seggen ›Gott tröst
de arme Seele.‹«
Der Junge geit wier ene ganze Tied un seg »Gott tröst de
arme Seele!« Do kümmet he an en Grawen, do steit en Fil-
ler (Schinder), de tüt en Perd af. De Junge seg »guden Morgen, Gott tröst de arme Seele!« »Wat segst du, leige Kerl?«
un schleit en met sinen Filhacken üm de Ohren, dat he ut
den Augen nig seihen kann. »Wu sall ick denn seggen?«
»Du sallst seggen ›do ligge du Aas in en Grawen.‹«
Do geit he un seg alltied »do ligge du Aas in en Grawen!
do ligge du Aas in en Grawen!« Nu kümmt he bi enen Wagen vull Lüde, do seg he »guden Morgen, do ligge du Aas
in en Grawen!« Do föllt de Wagen üm in en Grawen, de
Knecht kreg de Pietske un knapt den Jungen, dat he wier to
sine Mohr krupen moste. Un he is sien Lewen nig wier up
reisen gohn.

144.

Das Eselein.

Es lebte einmal ein König und eine Königin, die waren
reich und hatten alles, was sie sich wünschten, nur keine
Kinder. Darüber klagte sie Tag und Nacht und sprach »ich
bin wie ein Acker, auf dem nichts wächst.« Endlich erfüllte

Gott ihre Wünsche: als das Kind aber zur Welt kam, sah's nicht aus wie ein Menschenkind, sondern war ein junges Eselein. Wie die Mutter das erblickte, fieng ihr Jammer und Geschrei erst recht an, sie hätte lieber gar kein Kind gehabt als einen Esel, und sagte man sollt ihn ins Wasser werfen, damit ihn die Fische fräßen. Der König aber sprach »nein, hat Gott ihn gegeben, soll er auch mein Sohn und Erbe sein, nach meinem Tod auf dem königlichen Thron sitzen und die königliche Krone tragen.« Also ward das Eselein aufgezogen, nahm zu, und die Ohren wuchsen ihm auch fein hoch und gerad hinauf. Es war aber sonst fröhlicher Art, sprang herum, spielte und hatte besonders seine Lust an der Musik, so dass es zu einem berühmten Spielmann gieng und sprach »lehre mich deine Kunst, dass ich so gut die Laute schlagen kann als du.« »Ach, liebes Herrlein«, antwortete der Spielmann, »das sollt euch schwer fallen, eure Finger sind nicht allerdings dazu gemacht und gar zu groß; ich sorge die Saiten halten's nicht aus.« Es half keine Ausrede, das Eselein wollte und musste die Laute schlagen, war beharrlich und fleißig, und lernte es am Ende so gut als sein Meister selber. Einmal gieng das junge Herrlein nachdenksam spazieren und kam an einen Brunnen, da schaute es hinein und sah im spiegelhellen Wasser seine Eseleinsgestalt. Darüber war es so betrübt, dass es in die weite Welt gieng und nur einen treuen Gesellen mitnahm. Sie zogen auf und ab, zuletzt kamen sie in ein Reich, wo ein alter König herrschte, der nur eine einzige aber wunderschöne Tochter hatte. Das Eselein sagte »hier wollen wir weilen«, klopfte ans Tor und rief »es ist ein Gast haußen, macht auf, damit er eingehen kann.« Als aber nicht aufgetan ward, setzte er sich hin, nahm seine Laute und schlug sie mit seinen zwei Vorderfüßen aufs lieblichste. Da sperrte der Türhüter gewaltig die Augen auf, lief zum König und sprach »da draußen sitzt ein junges Eselein vor dem Tor, das schlägt die Laute so gut als ein gelernter Meister.« »So lass mir den Musikant hereinkommen« sprach der König. Wie

aber ein Eselein hereintrat, fieng alles an über den Lauten-
schläger zu lachen. Nun sollte das Eselein unten zu den
Knechten gesetzt und gespeist werden, es ward aber unwil-
lig und sprach »ich bin kein gemeines Stalleselein, ich bin
ein vornehmes.« Da sagten sie »wenn du das bist, so setze
dich zu dem Kriegsvolk.« »Nein«, sprach es, »ich will beim
König sitzen.« Der König lachte und sprach in gutem Mut
»ja, es soll so sein, wie du verlangst, Eselein, komm her zu
mir.« Danach fragte er »Eselein, wie gefällt dir meine Tochter?« Das Eselein drehte den Kopf nach ihr, schaute sie an,
nickte und sprach »aus der Maßen wohl, sie ist so schön
wie ich noch keine gesehen habe.« »Nun, so sollst du auch
neben ihr sitzen« sagte der König. »Das ist mir eben recht«
sprach das Eselein und setzte sich an ihre Seite, aß und
trank und wusste sich fein und säuberlich zu betragen. Als
das edle Tierlein eine gute Zeit an des Königs Hof geblieben war, dachte es »was hilft das alles, du musst wieder
heim«, ließ den Kopf traurig hängen, trat vor den König
und verlangte seinen Abschied. Der König hatte es aber
lieb gewonnen und sprach »Eselein, was ist dir? du schaust
ja sauer, wie ein Essigkrug: bleib bei mir, ich will dir geben,
was du verlangst. Willst du Gold?« »Nein« sagte das Eselein und schüttelte mit dem Kopf. »Willst du Kostbarkeiten
und Schmuck?« »Nein.« »Willst du mein halbes Reich?«
»Ach nein.« Da sprach der König »wenn ich nur wüsste
was dich vergnügt machen könnte: willst du meine schöne
Tochter zur Frau?« »Ach ja«, sagte das Eselein, »die möchte ich wohl haben«, war auf einmal ganz lustig und guter
Dinge, denn das war's gerade, was es sich gewünscht hatte.
Also ward eine große und prächtige Hochzeit gehalten.
Abends, wie Braut und Bräutigam in ihr Schlafkämmerlein
geführt wurden, wollte der König wissen ob sich das Eselein auch fein artig und manierlich betrüge, und hieß einem
Diener sich dort verstecken. Wie sie nun beide drinnen waren, schob der Bräutigam den Riegel vor die Türe, blickte
sich um, und wie er glaubte dass sie ganz allein wären, da

warf er auf einmal seine Eselshaut ab und stand da als ein schöner königlicher Jüngling. »Nun siehst du«, sprach er, »wer ich bin, und siehst auch dass ich deiner nicht unwert war.« Da ward die Braut froh, küsste ihn und hatte ihn von Herzen lieb. Als aber der Morgen herankam, sprang er auf, zog seine Tierhaut wieder über, und hätte kein Mensch gedacht was für einer dahinter steckte. Bald kam auch der alte König gegangen, »ei«, rief er, »ist das Eselein schon munter! Du bist wohl recht traurig«, sagte er zu seiner Tochter, »dass du keinen ordentlichen Menschen zum Mann bekommen hast?« »Ach nein, lieber Vater, ich habe ihn so lieb, als wenn er der allerschönste wäre, und will ihn mein Lebtag behalten.« Der König wunderte sich, aber der Diener, der sich versteckt hatte, kam und offenbarte ihm alles. Der König sprach »das ist nimmermehr wahr.« »So wacht selber die folgende Nacht, ihr werdet's mit eigenen Augen sehen, und wisst ihr was, Herr König, nehmt ihm die Haut weg und werft sie ins Feuer, so muss er sich wohl in seiner rechten Gestalt zeigen.« »Dein Rat ist gut« sprach der König, und Abends als sie schliefen, schlich er sich hinein, und wie er zum Bett kam, sah er im Mondschein einen stolzen Jüngling da ruhen, und die Haut lag abgestreift auf der Erde. Da nahm er sie weg und ließ draußen ein gewaltiges Feuer anmachen und die Haut hineinwerfen, und blieb selber dabei, bis sie ganz zu Asche verbrannt war. Weil er aber sehen wollte wie sich der Beraubte anstellen würde, blieb er die Nacht über wach und lauschte. Als der Jüngling ausgeschlafen hatte, beim ersten Morgenschein, stand er auf und wollte die Eselshaut anziehen, aber sie war nicht zu finden. Da erschrak er und sprach voll Trauer und Angst »nun muss ich sehen dass ich entfliehe.« Wie er hinaustrat, stand aber der König da und sprach »mein Sohn, wohin so eilig, was hast du im Sinn? Bleib hier, du bist ein so schöner Mann, du sollst nicht wieder von mir. Ich gebe dir jetzt mein Reich halb, und nach meinem Tod bekommst du es ganz.« »So wünsch ich dass der gute Anfang auch ein gutes

Ende nehme« sprach der Jüngling, »ich bleibe bei euch.«
Da gab ihm der Alte das halbe Reich, und als er nach einem
Jahr starb, hatte er das ganze, und nach dem Tod seines Va-
ters noch eins dazu, und lebte in aller Herrlichkeit.

145.

Der undankbare Sohn.

Es saß einmal ein Mann mit seiner Frau vor der Haustür,
und sie hatten ein gebraten Huhn vor sich stehen und wollten das zusammen verzehren. Da sah der Mann wie sein alter Vater daher kam, geschwind nahm er das Huhn und versteckte es, weil er ihm nichts davon gönnte. Der Alte kam,
tat einen Trunk und gieng fort. Nun wollte der Sohn das gebratene Huhn wieder auf den Tisch tragen, aber als er danach griff, war es eine große Kröte geworden, die sprang
ihm ins Angesicht und saß da, und gieng nicht wieder weg;
und wenn sie jemand wegtun wollte, sah sie ihn giftig an, als
wollte sie ihm ins Angesicht springen, so dass keiner sie anzurühren getraute. Und die Kröte musste der undankbare
Sohn alle Tage füttern, sonst fraß sie ihm aus seinem Angesicht; und also gieng er ohne Ruhe in der Welt hin und her.

146.

Die Rübe.

Es waren einmal zwei Brüder, die dienten beide als Soldaten, und war der eine reich, der andere arm. Da wollte der
Arme sich aus seiner Not helfen, zog den Soldatenrock aus
und ward ein Bauer. Also grub und hackte er sein Stück-

chen Acker und säte Rübsamen. Der Same gieng auf, und
es wuchs da eine Rübe, die ward groß und stark und zuse-
hends dicker und wollte gar nicht aufhören zu wachsen, so
dass sie eine Fürstin aller Rüben heißen konnte, denn nimmer war so eine gesehen und wird auch nimmer wieder gesehen werden. Zuletzt war sie so groß, dass sie allein einen
ganzen Wagen anfüllte, und zwei Ochsen daran ziehen
mussten, und der Bauer wusste nicht was er damit anfangen
sollte und ob's sein Glück oder sein Unglück wäre. Endlich
dachte er »verkaufst du sie, was wirst du großes dafür bekommen, und willst du sie selber essen, so tun die kleinen
Rüben denselben Dienst: am besten ist, du bringst sie dem
König und machst ihm eine Verehrung damit.« Also lud er
sie auf den Wagen, spannte zwei Ochsen vor, brachte sie an
den Hof und schenkte sie dem König. »Was ist das für ein
seltsam Ding?« sagte der König, »mir ist viel Wunderliches
vor die Augen gekommen, aber so ein Ungetüm noch
nicht; aus was für Samen mag die gewachsen sein? oder dir
gerät's allein und du bist ein Glückskind.« »Ach nein«, sagte der Bauer, »ein Glückskind bin ich nicht, ich bin ein armer Soldat, der, weil er sich nicht mehr nähren konnte, den
Soldatenrock an den Nagel hieng und das Land baute. Ich
habe noch einen Bruder, der ist reich, und Euch, Herr König, auch wohl bekannt, ich aber, weil ich nichts habe, bin
von aller Welt vergessen.« Da empfand der König Mitleid
mit ihm und sprach »deiner Armut sollst du überhoben
und so von mir beschenkt werden, dass du wohl deinem
reichen Bruder gleich kommst.« Da schenkte er ihm eine
Menge Gold, Äcker, Wiesen und Herden, und machte ihn
steinreich, so dass des andern Bruders Reichtum gar nicht
konnte damit verglichen werden. Als dieser hörte was sein
Bruder mit einer einzigen Rübe erworben hatte, beneidete
er ihn und sann hin und her wie er sich auch ein solches
Glück zuwenden könnte. Er wollt's aber noch viel gescheiter anfangen, nahm Gold und Pferde und brachte sie dem
König und meinte nicht anders, der würde ihm ein viel grö-

ßeres Gegengeschenk machen«, denn hätte sein Bruder so viel für eine Rübe bekommen, was würde es ihm für so schöne Dinge nicht alles tragen. Der König nahm das Geschenk und sagte er wüsste ihm nichts wieder zu geben, das seltener und besser wäre als die große Rübe. Also musste der Reiche seines Bruders Rübe auf einen Wagen legen und nach Haus fahren lassen. Daheim wusste er nicht an wem er seinen Zorn und Ärger auslassen sollte, bis ihm böse Gedanken kamen und er beschloss seinen Bruder zu töten. Er gewann Mörder, die mussten sich in einen Hinterhalt stellen, und darauf gieng er zu seinem Bruder und sprach »lieber Bruder, ich weiß einen heimlichen Schatz, den wollen wir mit einander heben und teilen.« Der andere ließ sich's auch gefallen und gieng ohne Arg mit. Als sie aber hinauskamen, stürzten die Mörder über ihn her, banden ihn und wollten ihn an einen Baum hängen. Indem sie eben darüber waren, erscholl aus der Ferne lauter Gesang und Hufschlag, dass ihnen der Schrecken in den Leib fuhr und sie über Hals und Kopf ihren Gefangenen in den Sack steckten, am Ast hinaufwanden und die Flucht ergriffen. Er aber arbeitete oben bis er ein Loch im Sack hatte, wodurch er den Kopf stecken konnte. Wer aber des Wegs kam, war nichts als ein fahrender Schüler, ein junger Geselle, der fröhlich sein Lied singend durch den Wald auf der Straße daher ritt. Wie der oben nun merkte dass einer unter ihm vorbei gieng, rief er »sei mir gegrüßt, zu guter Stunde.« Der Schüler guckte sich überall um, wusste nicht, wo die Stimme herschallte, endlich sprach er »wer ruft mir?« Da antwortete es aus dem Wipfel »erhebe deine Augen, ich sitze hier oben im Sack der Weisheit: in kurzer Zeit habe ich große Dinge gelernt, dagegen sind alle Schulen ein Wind: um ein Weniges, so werde ich ausgelernt haben, herabsteigen und weiser sein als alle Menschen. Ich verstehe die Gestirne und Himmelszeichen, das Wehen aller Winde, den Sand im Meer, Heilung der Krankheit, die Kräfte der Kräuter, Vögel und Steine. Wärst du einmal darin, du würdest fühlen was für

Herrlichkeit aus dem Sack der Weisheit fließt.« Der Schüler, wie er das alles hörte, erstaunte und sprach »gesegnet sei die Stunde, wo ich dich gefunden habe, könnt ich nicht auch ein wenig in den Sack kommen?« Oben der antwortete, als tät er's nicht gerne, »eine kleine Weile will ich dich wohl hinein lassen für Lohn und gute Worte, aber du musst doch noch eine Stunde warten, es ist ein Stück übrig, das ich erst lernen muss.« Als der Schüler ein wenig gewartet hatte, war ihm die Zeit zu lang und er bat dass er doch möchte hineingelassen werden, sein Durst nach Weisheit wäre gar zu groß. Da stellte sich der oben als gäbe er endlich nach und sprach »damit ich aus dem Haus der Weisheit heraus kann, musst du den Sack am Strick herunterlassen, so sollst du eingehen.« Also ließ der Schüler ihn herunter, band den Sack auf und befreite ihn, dann rief er selber »nun zieh mich recht geschwind hinauf«, und wollt geradstehend in den Sack einschreiten. »Halt!« sagte der andere, »so geht's nicht an«, packte ihn beim Kopf, steckte ihn umgekehrt in den Sack, schnürte zu, und zog den Jünger der Weisheit am Strick baumwärts, dann schwengelte er ihn in der Luft und sprach »wie steht's, mein lieber Geselle? siehe, schon fühlst du dass dir die Weisheit kommt und machst gute Erfahrung, sitze also fein ruhig, bis du klüger wirst.« Damit stieg er auf des Schülers Pferd, ritt fort, schickte aber nach einer Stunde jemand, der ihn wieder herablassen musste.

147.

Das junggeglühte Männlein.

Zur Zeit da unser Herr noch auf Erden gieng, kehrte er eines Abends mit dem heiligen Petrus bei einem Schmied ein und bekam willig Herberge. Nun geschah's, dass ein armer Bettelmann, von Alter und Gebrechen hart gedrückt, in dieses Haus kam und vom Schmied Almosen forderte. Des erbarmte sich Petrus und sprach »Herr und Meister, so dir's gefällt, heil ihm doch seine Plage, dass er sich selbst sein Brot möge gewinnen.« Sanftmütig sprach der Herr »Schmied, leih mir deine Esse und lege mir Kohlen an, so will ich den alten kranken Mann zu dieser Zeit verjüngen.« Der Schmied war ganz bereit, und St. Petrus zog die Bälge, und als das Kohlenfeuer auffunkte, groß und hoch, nahm unser Herr das alte Männlein, schob's in die Esse, mitten ins rote Feuer, dass es drin glühte wie ein Rosenstock, und Gott lobte mit lauter Stimme. Nachdem trat der Herr zum Löschtrog, zog das glühende Männlein hinein, dass das Wasser über ihm zusammenschlug, und nachdem er's fein sittig abgekühlt, gab er ihm seinen Segen: siehe, zuhand sprang das Männlein heraus, zart, gerade, gesund, und wie von zwanzig Jahren. Der Schmied, der eben und genau zugesehen hatte, lud sie alle zum Nachtmahl. Er hatte aber eine alte halb blinde bucklichte Schwieger die machte sich zum Jüngling hin und forschte ernstlich ob ihn das Feuer hart gebrennet habe. Nie sei ihm besser gewesen antwortete jener, er habe da in der Glut gesessen wie in einem kühlen Tau.

Was der Jüngling gesagt hatte, das klang die ganze Nacht in den Ohren der alten Frau, und als der Herr frühmorgens die Straße weiter gezogen war und dem Schmied wohl gedankt hatte, meinte dieser er könnte seine alte Schwieger auch jung machen, da er fein ordentlich alles mit angesehen habe, und es in seine Kunst schlage. Rief sie deshalb an, ob sie auch wie ein Mägdlein von achtzehn Jahren in Sprüngen daher wollte gehen. Sie sprach »von ganzem Herzen«, weil es dem Jüngling auch so sanft angekommen war. Machte also der Schmied große Glut und stieß die Alte hinein, die sich hin und wieder bog und grausames Mordgeschrei anstimmte. »Sitz still, was schreist und hüpfst du, ich will erst weidlich zublasen.« Zog damit die Bälge von neuem bis ihr alle Haderlumpen brannten. Das alte Weib schrie ohne

Ruhe, und der Schmied dachte »Kunst geht nicht recht zu«, nahm sie heraus und warf sie in den Löschtrog. Da schrie sie ganz überlaut, dass es droben im Haus die Schmiedin und ihre Schnur hörten: die liefen beide die Stiegen herab, und sahen die Alte heulend und maulend ganz zusammen geschnurrt im Trog liegen, das Angesicht gerunzelt, gefaltet und ungeschaffen. Darob sich die zwei, die beide mit Kindern giengen, so entsetzten, dass sie noch dieselbe Nacht zwei Junge gebaren, die waren nicht wie Menschen geschaffen, sondern wie Affen, liefen zum Wald hinein; und von ihnen stammt das Geschlecht der Affen her.

148.

Des Herrn und des Teufels Getier.

Gott der Herr hatte alle Tiere erschaffen und sich die Wölfe zu seinen Hunden auserwählet: bloß der Geiß hatte er vergessen. Da richtete sich der Teufel an, wollte auch schaffen und machte die Geiße mit feinen langen Schwänzen. Wenn sie nun zur Weide giengen, blieben sie gewöhnlich mit ihren Schwänzen in den Dornhecken hängen, da musste der Teufel hineingehen und sie mit vieler Mühe losknüpfen. Das verdross ihn zuletzt war her und biss jeder Geiß den Schwanz ab, wie noch heut des Tags an den Stümpfen zu sehen ist.

Nun ließ er sie zwar allein weiden, aber es geschah, dass Gott der Herr zusah wie sie bald einen fruchtbaren Baum benagten, bald die edeln Reben beschädigten, bald andere zarte Pflanzen verderbten. Das jammerte ihn, so dass er aus Güte und Gnaden seine Wölfe dran hetzte, welche die Geiße, die da giengen, bald zerrissen. Wie der Teufel das vernahm, trat er vor den Herrn und sprach »dein Geschöpf hat mir das meine zerrissen.« Der Herr antwortete »was hattest du es zu Schaden erschaffen!« Der Teufel sagte »ich musste das: gleichwie selbst mein Sinn auf Schaden geht, konnte was ich erschaffen keine andere Natur haben, und musst mir's teuer zahlen.« »Ich zahl dir's sobald das Eichenlaub abfällt, dann komm, dein Geld ist schon gezählt.« Als das Eichenlaub abgefallen war, kam der Teufel und forderte seine Schuld. Der Herr aber sprach »in der Kirche zu Constantinopel steht eine hohe Eiche, die hat noch alles ihr Laub.« Mit Toben und Fluchen entwich der Teufel und wollte die Eiche suchen, irrte sechs Monate in der Wüstenei, ehe er sie befand, und als er wieder kam, waren derweil wieder alle andere Eichen voll grüner Blätter. Da musste er seine Schuld fahren lassen, stach im Zorn allen übrigen Geißen die Augen aus und setzte ihnen seine eigenen ein.

Darum haben alle Geiße Teufelsaugen und abgebissene Schwänze, und er nimmt gern ihre Gestalt an.

149.

Der Hahnenbalken.

Es war einmal ein Zauberer, der stand mitten in einer großen Menge Volks und vollbrachte seine Wunderdinge. Da ließ er auch einen Hahn einherschreiten, der hob einen schweren Balken und trug ihn als wäre er federleicht. Nun war aber ein Mädchen, das hatte eben ein vierblättriges Kleeblatt gefunden und war dadurch klug geworden, so dass kein Blendwerk vor ihm bestehen konnte, und sah dass der Balken nichts war als ein Strohhalm. Da rief es »ihr Leute, seht ihr nicht, das ist ein bloßer Strohhalm und kein Balken, was der Hahn da trägt.« Alsbald verschwand der Zauber, und die Leute sahen was es war und jagten den Hexenmeister mit Schimpf und Schande fort. Er aber, voll innerlichen Zornes, sprach »ich will mich schon rächen.«

Nach einiger Zeit hielt das Mädchen Hochzeit, war geputzt und gieng in einem großen Zug über das Feld nach dem Ort, wo die Kirche stand. Auf einmal kamen sie an einen stark angeschwollenen Bach, und war keine Brücke und kein Steg, darüber zu gehen. Da war die Braut flink, hob ihre Kleider auf und wollte durchwaten. Wie sie nun eben im Wasser so steht, ruft ein Mann, und das war der Zauberer, neben ihr ganz spöttisch »ei! wo hast du deine Augen, dass du das für ein Wasser hältst?« Da giengen ihr die Augen auf, und sie sah dass sie mit ihren aufgehobenen Kleidern mitten in einem blaublühenden Flachsfeld stand. Da sahen es die Leute auch allesamt und jagten sie mit Schimpf und Gelächter fort.

150.

Die alte Bettelfrau.

Es war einmal eine alte Frau, du hast wohl ehe eine alte Frau sehn betteln gehn? diese Frau bettelte auch, und wann sie etwas bekam, dann sagte sie »Gott lohn euch.« Die Bettelfrau kam an die Tür, da stand ein freundlicher Schelm von Jungen am Feuer und wärmte sich. Der Junge sagte freundlich zu der armen alten Frau, wie sie so an der Tür stand und zitterte, »kommt, Altmutter, und erwärmt euch.« Sie kam herzu, gieng aber zu nahe ans Feuer stehn, dass ihre alten Lumpen anfiengen zu brennen, und sie ward's nicht gewahr. Der Junge stand und sah das, er hätt's doch löschen sollen? Nicht wahr, er hätte löschen sollen? Und wenn er kein Wasser gehabt hätte, dann hätte er alles Wasser in seinem Leibe zu den Augen herausweinen sollen, das hätte so zwei hübsche Bächlein gegeben zu löschen.

Die drei Faulen.

Ein König hatte drei Söhne, die waren ihm alle gleich lieb, und er wusste nicht welchen er zum König nach seinem Tode bestimmen sollte. Als die Zeit kam, dass er sterben wollte, rief er sie vor sein Bett und sprach »liebe Kinder, ich habe etwas bei mir bedacht, das will ich euch eröffnen: welcher von euch der Faulste ist, der soll nach mir König werden.« Da sprach der älteste »Vater, so gehört das Reich mir, denn ich bin so faul, wenn ich liege und will schlafen, und es fällt mir ein Tropfen in die Augen, so mag ich sie nicht zutun, damit ich einschlafe.« Der zweite sprach »Vater, das Reich gehört mir, denn ich bin so faul, wenn ich beim Feuer sitze mich zu wärmen, so ließ ich mir eher die Fersen verbrennen, eh ich die Beine zurück zöge.« Der dritte sprach »Vater, das Reich ist mein, denn ich bin so faul, sollt ich aufgehenkt werden, und hätte den Strick schon um den Hals, und einer gäbe mir ein scharf Messer in die Hand, damit ich den Strick zerschneiden dürfte, so ließ ich mich eher aufhenken, eh ich meine Hand erhübe zum Strick.« Wie der Vater das hörte sprach er »du hast es am weitesten gebracht und sollst der König sein.«

151.*

Die zwölf faulen Knechte.

Zwölf Knechte, die den ganzen Tag nichts getan hatten, wollten sich am Abend nicht noch anstrengen, sondern legten sich ins Gras und rühmten sich ihrer Faulheit. Der erste sprach »was geht mich eure Faulheit an, ich habe mit meiner eigenen zu tun. Die Sorge für den Leib ist meine

Hauptarbeit: ich esse nicht wenig und trinke desto mehr. Wenn ich vier Mahlzeiten gehalten habe, so faste ich eine kurze Zeit bis ich wieder Hunger empfinde, das bekommt mir am besten. Früh aufstehn ist nicht meine Sache, wenn es gegen Mittag geht, so suche ich mir schon einen Ruheplatz aus. Ruft der Herr, so tue ich als hätte ich es nicht gehört, und ruft er zum zweitenmal, so warte ich noch eine Zeitlang bis ich mich erhebe und gehe auch dann recht langsam. So lässt sich das Leben ertragen.« Der zweite sprach »ich habe ein Pferd zu besorgen, aber ich lasse ihm das Gebiss im Maul, und wenn ich nicht will, so gebe ich ihm kein Futter und sage es habe schon gefressen. Dafür lege ich mich in den Haferkasten und schlafe vier Stunden. Hernach strecke ich wohl einen Fuß heraus und fahre damit dem Pferd ein paarmal über den Leib, so ist es gestriegelt und geputzt; wer wird da viel Umstände machen? Aber der Dienst ist mir doch noch zu beschwerlich.« Der dritte sprach »wozu sich mit Arbeit plagen? dabei kommt nichts heraus. Ich legte mich in die Sonne und schlief. Es fieng an zu tröpfeln, aber weshalb aufstehen? ich ließ es in Gottes Namen fortregnen. Zuletzt kam ein Platzregen und zwar so heftig, dass er mir die Haare vom Kopf ausriss und wegschwemmte, und ich ein Loch in den Schädel bekam. Ich legte ein Pflaster darauf und damit war's gut. Schaden der Art habe ich schon mehr gehabt.« Der vierte sprach »soll ich eine Arbeit angreifen, so dämmere ich erst eine Stunde herum, damit ich meine Kräfte spare. Hernach fange ich ganz gemächlich an und frage ob nicht andere da wären, die mir helfen könnten. Die lasse ich dann die Hauptarbeit tun, und sehe eigentlich nur zu: aber das ist mir auch noch zu viel.« Der fünfte sprach »was will das sagen! denkt euch, ich soll den Mist aus dem Pferdestall fortschaffen und auf den Wagen laden. Ich lasse es langsam angehen, und habe ich etwas auf die Gabel genommen, so hebe ich es nur halb in die Höhe und ruhe erst eine Viertelstunde bis ich es vollends hinauf werfe. Es ist übrig genug, wenn ich des Tags ein Fuder hinaus fahre. Ich habe keine Lust mich tot zu arbeiten.« Der sechste sprach »schämt euch, ich erschrecke vor keiner Arbeit, aber ich lege mich drei Wochen hin und ziehe nicht einmal meine Kleider aus. Wozu Schnallen an die Schuhe? die können mir immerhin von den Füßen abfallen, es schadet nichts. Will ich eine Treppe ersteigen, so ziehe ich einen Fuß nach dem andern langsam auf die erste Stufe herauf, dann zähle ich die übrigen, damit ich weiß wo ich ruhen muss.« Der siebente sprach »bei mir geht das nicht: mein Herr sieht auf meine Arbeit, nur ist er den ganzen Tag nicht zu Haus. Doch versäume ich nichts, ich laufe so viel das möglich ist, wenn man schleicht. Soll ich fortkommen, so müssten mich vier stämmige Männer mit allen Kräften fortschieben. Ich kam dahin, wo auf einer Pritsche sechs neben einander lagen und schliefen: ich legte mich zu ihnen und schlief auch. Ich war nicht wieder zu wecken, und wollten sie mich heim haben, so mussten sie mich wegtragen.« Der achte sprach »ich sehe wohl dass ich allein ein munterer Kerl bin, liegt ein Stein vor mir, so gebe ich mir nicht die Mühe meine Beine aufzuheben und darüber hinweg zu schreiten, ich lege mich auf die Erde nieder, und bin ich nass, voll Kot und Schmutz, so bleibe ich liegen bis mich die Sonne wieder ausgetrocknet hat: höchstens drehe ich mich so, dass sie auf mich scheinen kann.« Der neunte sprach »das ist was rechts! heute lag das Brot vor mir, aber ich war zu faul danach zu greifen, und wäre fast Hungers gestorben. Auch ein Krug stand dabei, aber so groß und schwer dass ich ihn nicht in die Höhe heben mochte und lieber Durst litt. Mich nur umzudrehen, war mir zu viel, ich blieb den ganzen Tag liegen wie ein Stock.« Der zehnte sprach »mir hat die Faulheit Schaden gebracht, ein gebrochenes Bein und geschwollene Waden. Unser drei lagen auf einem Fahrweg und ich hatte die Beine ausgestreckt. Da kam jemand mit einem Wagen und die Räder giengen mir darüber. Ich hätte die Beine freilich zurückziehen können, aber ich hörte den Wagen nicht kommen: die Mücken

summten mir um die Ohren, krochen mir zu der Nase herein und zu dem Mund wieder heraus; wer will sich die
Mühe geben das Geschmeiß weg zu jagen.« Der elfte
sprach »gestern habe ich meinen Dienst aufgesagt. Ich hatte
keine Lust meinem Herrn die schweren Bücher noch länger
herbei zu holen und wieder weg zu tragen: das nahm den
ganzen Tag kein Ende. Aber die Wahrheit zu sagen, er gab
mir den Abschied und wollte mich auch nicht länger behalten, denn seine Kleider, die ich im Staub liegen ließ, waren
von den Motten zerfressen; und das war recht.« Der zwölfte sprach »heute musste ich mit dem Wagen über Feld fahren, ich machte mir ein Lager von Stroh darauf und schlief
richtig ein. Die Zügel rutschten mir aus der Hand, und als
ich erwachte, hatte sich das Pferd beinahe los gerissen, das
Geschirr war weg, das Rückenseil, Kummet, Zaum und
Gebiss. Es war einer vorbei gekommen, der hatte alles fortgetragen. Dazu war der Wagen in eine Pfütze geraten und
stand fest. Ich ließ ihn stehen und streckte mich wieder aufs
Stroh. Der Herr kam endlich selbst und schob den Wagen
heraus, und wäre er nicht gekommen, so läge ich nicht hier,
sondern dort und schliefe in guter Ruh.«

152.

Das Hirtenbüblein.

Es war einmal ein Hirtenbübchen, das war wegen seiner
weisen Antworten, die es auf alle Fragen gab, weit und
breit berühmt. Der König des Landes hörte auch davon,
glaubte es nicht und ließ das Bübchen kommen. Da sprach
er zu ihm »kannst du mir auf drei Fragen, die ich dir vorlegen will, Antwort geben, so will ich dich ansehen wie mein
eigen Kind, und du sollst bei mir in meinem königlichen
Schloss wohnen.« Sprach das Büblein »wie lauten die drei

Fragen?« Der König sagte »die erste lautet wieviel Tropfen Wasser sind in dem Weltmeer?« Das Hirtenbüblein antwortete »Herr König, lasst alle Flüsse auf der Erde verstopfen, damit kein Tröpflein mehr daraus ins Meer läuft, das ich nicht erst gezählt habe, so will ich euch sagen, wie viel Tropfen im Meere sind.« Sprach der König »Die andere Frage lautet wie viel Sterne stehen am Himmel?« Das Hirtenbübchen sagte »gebt mir einen großen Bogen weiß Papier«, und dann machte es mit der Feder so viel feine Punkte darauf, dass sie kaum zu sehen und fast gar nicht zu zählen waren und einem die Augen vergiengen, wenn man darauf blickte. Darauf sprach es »so viel Sterne stehen am Himmel, als hier Punkte auf dem Papier zählt sie nur.« Aber niemand war dazu im Stand. Sprach der König »die dritte Frage lautet wie viel Sekunden hat die Ewigkeit?« Da sagte das Hirtenbüblein »in Hinterpommern liegt der Demantberg, der hat eine Stunde in die Höhe, eine Stunde in die Breite und eine Stunde in die Tiefe; dahin kommt alle hundert Jahre ein Vögelein und wetzt sein Schnäblein daran, und wenn der ganze Berg abgewetzt ist, dann ist die erste Sekunde von der Ewigkeit vorbei.«

Sprach der König »du hast die drei Fragen aufgelöst wie ein Weiser und sollst fortan bei mir in meinem königlichen Schlosse wohnen, und ich will dich ansehen wie mein eigenes Kind.«

153.

Die Sterntaler.

Es war einmal ein kleines Mädchen, dem war Vater und Mutter gestorben, und es war so arm, dass es kein Kämmerchen mehr hatte darin zu wohnen und kein Bettchen mehr darin zu schlafen und endlich gar nichts mehr als die Kleider auf dem Leib und ein Stückchen Brot in der Hand, das ihm ein mitleidiges Herz geschenkt hatte. Es war aber gut und fromm. Und weil es so von aller Welt verlassen war, gieng es im Vertrauen auf den lieben Gott hinaus ins Feld. Da begegnete ihm ein armer Mann, der sprach »ach, gib mir etwas zu essen, ich bin so hungerig.« Es reichte ihm das ganze Stückchen Brot und sagte »Gott segne dir's« und gieng weiter. Da kam ein Kind das jammerte und sprach »es friert mich so an meinem Kopfe, schenk mir etwas, womit ich ihn bedecken kann.« Da tat es seine Mütze ab und gab sie ihm. Und als es noch eine Weile gegangen war, kam wieder ein Kind und hatte kein Leibchen an und fror: da gab es ihm seins: und noch weiter, da bat eins um ein Röcklein, das gab es auch von sich hin. Endlich gelangte es in einen Wald, und es war schon dunkel geworden, da kam noch eins und bat um ein Hemdlein, und das fromme Mädchen dachte »es ist dunkle Nacht, da sieht dich niemand du kannst wohl dein Hemd weg geben«, und zog das Hemd ab und gab es auch noch hin. Und wie es so stand und gar nichts mehr hatte, fielen auf einmal die Sterne vom Himmel, und waren lauter harte blanke Taler: und ob es gleich sein Hemdlein weg gegeben, so hatte es ein neues an und das war vom allerfeinsten Linnen. Da sammelte es sich die Taler hinein und war reich für sein Lebtag.

154.

Der gestohlene Heller.

Es saß einmal ein Vater mit seiner Frau und seinen Kindern Mittags am Tisch, und ein guter Freund, der zum Besuch gekommen war, aß mit ihnen. Und wie sie so saßen, und es zwölf Uhr schlug, da sah der Fremde die Tür aufgehen und ein schneeweiß gekleidetes, ganz blasses Kindlein hereinkommen. Es blickte sich nicht um und sprach auch nichts,

sondern gieng geradezu in die Kammer neben an. Bald darauf kam es zurück und gieng eben so still wieder zur Türe
hinaus. Am zweiten und am dritten Tag kam es auf eben
diese Weise. Da fragte endlich der Fremde den Vater wem
das schöne Kind gehörte das alle Mittag in die Kammer
gienge. »Ich habe es nicht gesehen«, antwortete er, »und
wüsste auch nicht wem es gehören könnte.« Am andern
Tage, wie es wieder kam, zeigte es der Fremde dem Vater,
der sah es aber nicht, und die Mutter und die Kinder alle
sahen auch nichts. Nun stand der Fremde auf, gieng zur
Kammertüre, öffnete sie ein wenig und schaute hinein. Da
sah er das Kind auf der Erde sitzen und emsig mit den Fingern in den Dielenritzen graben und wühlen; wie es aber
den Fremden bemerkte, verschwand es. Nun erzählte er
was er gesehen hatte und beschrieb das Kind genau, da erkannte es die Mutter und sagte »ach, das ist mein liebes
Kind, das vor vier Wochen gestorben ist.« Sie brachen die
Dielen auf und fanden zwei Heller, die hatte einmal das
Kind von der Mutter erhalten, um sie einem armen Manne
zu geben, es hatte aber gedacht »dafür kannst du dir einen
Zwieback kaufen«, die Heller behalten und in die Dielenritzen versteckt; und da hatte es im Grabe keine Ruhe gehabt, und war alle Mittage gekommen um nach den Hellern
zu suchen. Die Eltern gaben darauf das Geld einem Armen,
und nachher ist das Kind nicht wieder gesehen worden.

155.

Die Brautschau.

Es war ein junger Hirt, der wollte gern heiraten und kannte
drei Schwestern, davon war eine so schön wie die andere,
dass ihm die Wahl schwer wurde und er sich nicht entschließen konnte einer davon den Vorzug zu geben. Da

fragte er seine Mutter um Rat, die sprach »lad alle drei ein
und setz ihnen Käs vor und hab acht wie sie ihn anschnei-
den.« Das tat der Jüngling, die erste aber verschlang den
Käs mit der Rinde: die zweite schnitt in der Hast die Rinde
vom Käs ab, weil sie aber so hastig war, ließ sie noch viel
Gutes daran und warf das mit weg: die dritte schälte ordentlich die Rinde ab, nicht zu viel und nicht zu wenig.
Der Hirt erzählte das alles seiner Mutter, da sprach sie
»nimm die dritte zu deiner Frau.« Das tat er und lebte zufrieden und glücklich mit ihr.

156.

Die Schlickerlinge.

Es war einmal ein Mädchen, das war schön, aber faul und
nachlässig. Wenn es spinnen sollte, so war es so verdrießlich dass wenn ein kleiner Knoten im Flachs war, es gleich
einen ganzen Haufen mit herausriss und neben sich zur
Erde schlickerte. Nun hatte es ein Dienstmädchen, das war
arbeitsam, suchte den weggeworfenen Flachs zusammen,
reinigte ihn, spann ihn fein und ließ sich ein hübsches Kleid
daraus weben. Ein junger Mann hatte um das faule Mädchen geworben, und die Hochzeit sollte gehalten werden.
Auf dem Polterabend tanzte das fleißige in seinem schönen
Kleide lustig herum, da sprach die Braut

»ach, wat kann dat Mäken springen
in minen Slickerlingen!«

Das hörte der Bräutigam und fragte die Braut was sie damit
sagen wollte. Da erzählte sie ihm dass das Mädchen ein
Kleid von dem Flachs trüge, den sie weggeworfen hätte.
Wie der Bräutigam das hörte und ihre Faulheit bemerkte
und den Fleiß des armen Mädchens, so ließ er sie stehen,
gieng zu jener und wählte sie zu seiner Frau.

157

Der Sperling und seine vier Kinder.

Ein Sperling hatte vier Junge in einem Schwalbennest. Wie sie nun flügg sind, stoßen böse Buben das Nest ein, sie kommen aber alle glücklich in Windbraus davon. Nun ist dem Alten leid, weil seine Söhne in die Welt kommen, dass er sie nicht vor allerlei Gefahr erst verwarnet, und ihnen gute Lehren fürgesagt habe.

Aufn Herbst kommen in einem Weizenacker viel Sperlinge zusammen, allda trifft der Alte seine vier Jungen an, die führt er voll Freuden mit sich heim. »Ach, meine lieben Söhne, was habt ihr mir den Sommer über Sorge gemacht, dieweil ihr ohne meine Lehre in Winde kamet; höret meine Worte und folget eurem Vater und sehet euch wohl vor: kleine Vöglein haben große Gefährlichkeit auszustehen!« darauf fragte er den älteren wo er sich den Sommer über aufgehalten und wie er sich ernähret hätte. »Ich habe mich in den Gärten gehalten, Räuplein und Würmlein gesucht, bis die Kirschen reif wurden.« »Ach, mein Sohn«, sagte der Vater, »die Schnabelweid ist nicht bös, aber es ist große Gefahr dabei, darum habe fortan deiner wohl Acht, und sonderlich wenn Leut in Gärten umher gehn, die lange grüne Stangen tragen, die inwendig hohl sind und oben ein Löchlein haben.« »Ja, mein Vater, wenn dann ein grün Blättlein aufs Löchlein mit Wachs geklebt wäre?« spricht der Sohn. »Wo hast du das gesehen?« »In eines Kaufmanns Garten« sagte der Junge. »O mein Sohn«, spricht der Vater, »Kaufleut, geschwinde Leut! bist du um die Weltkinder gewesen, so hast du Weltgeschmeidigkeit genug gelernt, siehe und brauch's nur recht wohl und trau dir nicht zu viel.«

Darauf befragt er den andern »wo hast du dein Wesen gehabt?« »Zu Hofe« spricht der Sohn. »Sperling und alberne Vöglein dienen nicht an diesem Ort, da viel Gold, Sammet, Seiden, Wehr, Harnisch, Sperber, Kauzen und Blaufüß sind,

halt dich zum Rossstall, da man den Hafer schwingt, oder
wo man drischet, so kann dir's Glück mit gutem Fried auch
dein täglich Körnlein bescheren.« »Ja, Vater«, sagte dieser
Sohn, »wenn aber die Stalljungen Hebritzen machen und
ihre Maschen und Schlingen ins Stroh binden, da bleibt
auch mancher behenken.« »Wo hast du das gesehen?« sagte
der Alte. »Zu Hof, beim Rossbuben.« »O, mein Sohn,
Hofbuben, böse Buben! bist du zu Hof und um die Herren
gewesen und hast keine Federn da gelassen, so hast du
ziemlich gelernet und wirst dich in der Welt wohl wissen
auszureißen, doch siehe dich um und auf; die Wölfe fressen
auch oft die gescheiten Hündlein.«
Der Vater nimmt den dritten auch vor sich, »wo hast du
dein Heil versucht?« »Auf den Fahrwegen und Landstra-
ßen hab ich Kübel und Seil eingeworfen und da bisweilen
ein Körnlein oder Gräuplein angetroffen.« »Dies ist ja«,
sagt der Vater, »eine feine Nahrung, aber merk gleich wohl
auf die Schanz und siehe fleißig auf, sonderlich wenn sich
einer bücket und einen Stein aufheben will, da ist dir nicht
lang zu bleiben.« »Wahr ist's«, sagt der Sohn, »wenn aber
einer zuvor einen Wand- oder Handstein im Busen oder
Tasche trüge?« »Wo hast du dies gesehn?« »Bei den Berg-
leuten, lieber Vater, wenn sie ausfahren, führen sie gemein-
lich Handsteine bei sich.« »Bergleut, Werkleut, anschlägige
Leut! bist du um Bergburschen gewesen, so hast du etwas
gesehen und erfahren.

Fahr hin und nimm deiner Sachen gleichwohl gut
Acht,
Bergbuben haben manchen Sperling mit Kobold
umbracht.«

Endlich kommt der Vater an [den] jüngsten Sohn, »du mein
liebes Gackennestle, du warst allzeit der alberst und schwä-
chest, bleib du bei mir, die Welt hat viel grober und böser
Vögel, die krumme Schnäbel und lange Krallen haben und
nur auf arme Vöglein lauern und sie verschlucken: halt dich
zu deinesgleichen und lies die Spinnlein und Räuplein von

den Bäumen oder Häuslein, so bleibst du lang zufrieden.«
»Du, mein lieber Vater, wer sich nährt ohn andrer Leut
Schaden, der kommt lang hin, und kein Sperber, Habicht,
Aar oder Weih wird ihm nicht schaden, wenn er zumal sich
und seine ehrliche Nahrung dem lieben Gott all Abend und
Morgen treulich befiehlt, welcher aller Wald- und Dorfvög-
lein Schöpfer und Erhalter ist, der auch der jungen Räblein
Geschrei und Gebet höret, denn ohne seinen Willen fällt
auch kein Sperling oder Schneekünglein auf die Erde.« »Wo
hast du dies gelernt?« Antwortet der Sohn »wie mich der
große Windbraus von dir wegriss, kam ich in eine Kirche,
da las ich den Sommer die Fliegen und Spinnen von den
Fenstern ab und hörte diese Sprüch predigen, da hat mich
der Vater aller Sperlinge den Sommer über ernährt und be-
hütet vor allem Unglück und grimmigen Vögeln.« »Traun!
mein lieber Sohn, fleuchst du in die Kirchen und hilfest
Spinnen und die sumsenden Fliegen aufräumen und zirpst
zu Gott wie die jungen Räblein und befiehlst dich dem
ewigen Schöpfer, so wirst du wohl bleiben, und wenn die
ganze Welt voll wilder tückischer Vögel wäre.

Denn wer dem Herrn befiehlt seine Sach,
schweigt, leidet, wartet, betet, braucht Glimpf, tut
gemach,
bewahrt Glaub und gut Gewissen rein,
dem will Gott Schutz und Helfer sein.«

158.

Das Märchen vom Schlauraffenland.

In der Schlauraffenzeit da gieng ich, und sah an einem kleinen Seidenfaden hieng Rom und der Lateran, und ein fuß-
loser Mann der überlief ein schnelles Pferd und ein bitter-
scharfes Schwert das durchhieb eine Brücke. Da sah ich ei-

nen jungen Esel mit einer silbernen Nase, der jagte hinter
zwei schnellen Hasen her, und eine Linde, die war breit,
auf der wuchsen heiße Fladen. Da sah ich eine alte dürre
Geiß, trug wohl hundert Fuder Schmalzes an ihrem Leibe
und sechzig Fuder Salzes. Ist das nicht gelogen genug? Da
sah ich zackern einen Pflug ohne Ross und Rinder, und ein
jähriges Kind warf vier Mühlensteine von Regensburg bis
nach Trier und von Trier hinein in Straßburg, und ein Habicht schwamm über den Rhein: das tat er mit vollem
Recht. Da hört ich Fische mit einander Lärm anfangen,
dass es in den Himmel hinauf scholl, und ein süßer Honig
floss wie Wasser von einem tiefen Tal auf einen hohen
Berg; das waren seltsame Geschichten. Da waren zwei
Krähen, mähten eine Wiese, und ich sah zwei Mücken an
einer Brücke bauen, und zwei Tauben zerrupften einen
Wolf, zwei Kinder die wurfen zwei Zicklein, aber zwei
Frösche droschen mit einander Getreid aus. Da sah ich
zwei Mäuse einen Bischof weihen, zwei Katzen, die einem
Bären die Zunge auskratzten. Da kam eine Schnecke ge-
rannt und erschlug zwei wilde Löwen. Da stand ein Bart-
scherer, schor einer Frauen ihren Bart ab, und zwei säu-
gende Kinder hießen ihre Mutter stillschweigen. Da sah ich
zwei Windhunde, brachten eine Mühle aus dem Wasser getragen, und eine alte Schindmähre stand dabei, die sprach
es wäre Recht. Und im Hof standen vier Rosse, die droschen Korn aus allen Kräften, und zwei Ziegen, die den
Ofen heizten, und eine rote Kuh schoss das Brot in den
Ofen. Da krähte ein Huhn »kikeriki, das Märchen ist aus-
erzählt, kikeriki.«

159.

Das Diethmarsische Lügenmärchen.

Ich will euch etwas erzählen. Ich sah zwei gebratene Hühner fliegen, folgen schnell und hatten die Bäuche gen Himmel gekehrt, die Rücken nach der Hölle, und ein Amboss und ein Mühlstein schwammen über den Rhein, fein langsam und leise, und ein Frosch saß und fraß eine Pflugschar zu Pfingsten auf dem Eis. Da waren drei Kerle, wollten einen Hasen fangen, giengen auf Krücken und Stelzen, der eine war taub, der zweite blind, der dritte stumm, und der vierte konnte keinen Fuß rühren. Wollt ihr wissen, wie das geschah? Der Blinde der sah zuerst den Hasen über Feld traben, der Stumme der rief dem Lahmen zu, und der Lahme fasste ihn beim Kragen. Etliche die wollten zu Land segeln und spannten die Segel im Wind und schifften über große Äcker hin: da segelten sie über einen hohen Berg, da mussten sie elendig ersaufen. Ein Krebs jagte einen Hasen in die Flucht, und hoch auf dem Dach lag eine Kuh, die war hinauf gestiegen. In dem Lande sind die Fliegen so groß als hier die Ziegen. Mache das Fenster auf, damit die Lügen hinaus fliegen.

160.

Rätselmärchen.

Drei Frauen waren verwandelt in Blumen, die auf dem Felde standen, doch deren eine durfte des Nachts in ihrem Hause sein. Da sprach sie auf eine Zeit zu ihrem Mann, als sich der Tag nahete und sie wiederum zu ihren Gespielen auf das Feld gehen und eine Blume werden musste, »so du heute Vormittag kommst und mich abbrichst, werde ich erlöst und fürder bei dir bleiben«; als dann auch geschah.

Nun ist die Frage, wie sie ihr Mann erkannt habe, so die Blumen ganz gleich und ohne Unterschied waren? Antwort, »dieweil sie die Nacht in ihrem Haus und nicht auf dem Feld war, fiel der Tau nicht auf sie, als auf die andern zwei, dabei sie der Mann erkannte.«

161.

Schneeweißchen und Rosenrot.

Eine arme Witwe, die lebte einsam in einem Hüttchen, und vor dem Hüttchen war ein Garten, darin standen zwei Rosenbäumchen, davon trug das eine weiße, das andere rote Rosen: und sie hatte zwei Kinder, die glichen den beiden Rosenbäumchen, und das eine hieß Schneeweißchen, das andere Rosenrot. Sie waren aber so fromm und gut, so arbeitsam und unverdrossen, als je zwei Kinder auf der Welt gewesen sind: Schneeweißchen war nur stiller und sanfter als Rosenrot. Rosenrot sprang lieber in den Wiesen und Feldern umher, suchte Blumen und fieng Sommervögel: Schneeweißchen aber saß daheim bei der Mutter, half ihr im Hauswesen, oder las ihr vor, wenn nichts zu tun war. Die beiden Kinder hatten einander so lieb, dass sie sich immer an den Händen fassten, so oft sie zusammen ausgiengen: und wenn Schneeweißchen sagte »wir wollen uns nicht verlassen«, so antwortete Rosenrot »so lange wir leben nicht«, und die Mutter setzte hinzu »was das eine hat soll's mit dem andern teilen.« Oft liefen sie im Walde allein umher und sammelten rote Beeren, aber kein Tier tat ihnen etwas zu leid, sondern sie kamen vertraulich herbei: das Häschen fraß ein Kohlblatt aus ihren Händen, das Reh graste an ihrer Seite, der Hirsch sprang ganz lustig vorbei und die Vögel blieben auf den Ästen sitzen und sangen was sie nur wussten. Kein Unfall traf sie: wenn sie sich im Walde verspätet hatten und die Nacht sie überfiel, so legten sie sich nebeneinander auf das Moos und schliefen bis der Morgen kam, und die Mutter wusste das und hatte ihrentwegen keine Sorge. Einmal, als sie im Walde übernachtet hatten und das Morgenrot sie aufweckte, da sahen sie ein schönes Kind in einem weißen glänzenden Kleidchen neben ihrem Lager sitzen. Es stand auf und blickte sie ganz freundlich an, sprach aber nichts und gieng in den Wald hinein. Und als sie sich umsahn, so hatten sie ganz nahe bei einem Abgrunde geschlafen, und wären gewiss hinein gefallen, wenn sie in der Dunkelheit noch ein paar Schritte weiter gegangen wären. Die Mutter aber sagte ihnen das müsste der Engel gewesen sein, der gute Kinder bewache.

Schneeweißchen und Rosenrot hielten das Hüttchen der Mutter so reinlich, dass es eine Freude war hinein zu schauen. Im Sommer besorgte Rosenrot das Haus und stellte der Mutter jeden Morgen, ehe sie aufwachte, einen Blumenstrauß vors Bett, darin war von jedem Bäumchen eine Rose. Im Winter zündete Schneeweißchen das Feuer an und hieng den Kessel an den Feuerhaken, und der Kessel war von Messing, glänzte aber wie Gold, so rein war er gescheuert. Abends, wenn die Flocken fielen, sagte die Mutter »geh, Schneeweißchen, und schieb den Riegel vor«, und dann setzten sie sich an den Herd, und die Mutter nahm die Brille und las aus einem großen Buche vor, und die beiden Mädchen hörten zu, saßen und spannen; neben ihnen lag ein Lämmchen auf dem Boden, und hinter ihnen auf einer Stange saß ein weißes Täubchen und hatte seinen Kopf unter den Flügel gesteckt.

Eines Abends, als sie so vertraulich beisammen saßen, klopfte jemand an die Türe, als wollte er eingelassen sein. Die Mutter sprach »geschwind, Rosenrot, mach auf, es wird ein Wanderer sein, der Obdach sucht.« Rosenrot gieng und schob den Riegel weg und dachte es wäre ein armer Mann, aber der war es nicht, es war ein Bär, der seinen dicken schwarzen Kopf zur Türe herein streckte. Rosenrot schrie laut und sprang zurück: das Lämmchen blökte, das Täubchen flatterte auf und Schneeweißchen versteckte sich hinter der Mutter Bett. Der Bär aber fieng an zu sprechen und sagte »fürchtet euch nicht, ich tue euch nichts zu leid, ich bin halb erfroren und will mich nur ein wenig bei euch wärmen.« »Du armer Bär«, sprach die Mutter, »leg dich ans Feuer, und gib nur acht dass dir dein Pelz nicht brennt.« Dann rief sie »Schneeweißchen, Rosenrot, kommt hervor, der Bär tut euch nichts, er meint's ehrlich.« Da kamen sie beide heran, und nach und nach näherten sich auch das Lämmchen und Täubchen und hatten keine Furcht vor ihm. Der Bär sprach »ihr Kinder, klopft mir den Schnee ein wenig aus dem Pelzwerk«, und sie holten den Besen und kehrten dem Bär das Fell rein: er aber streckte sich ans Feuer und brummte ganz vergnügt und behaglich. Nicht lange, so wurden sie ganz vertraut und trieben Mutwillen mit dem unbeholfenen Gast. Sie zausten ihm das Fell mit den Händen, setzten ihre Füßchen auf seinen Rücken und walgerten ihn hin und her, oder sie nahmen eine Haselrute und schlugen auf ihn los, und wenn er brummte, so lachten sie. Der Bär ließ sich's aber gerne gefallen, nur wenn sie's gar zu arg machten, rief er »lasst mich am Leben, ihr Kinder:

    Schneeweißchen, Rosenrot,
    schlägst dir den Freier tot.«

Als Schlafenszeit war und die andern zu Bett giengen, sagte die Mutter zu dem Bär »du kannst in Gottes Namen da am Herde liegen bleiben, so bist du vor der Kälte und dem bösen Wetter geschützt.« Sobald der Tag graute, ließen ihn die beiden Kinder hinaus, und er trabte über den Schnee in den Wald hinein. Von nun an kam der Bär jeden Abend zu der bestimmten Stunde, legte sich an den Herd und erlaubte den Kindern Kurzweil mit ihm zu treiben, so viel sie wollten; und sie waren so gewöhnt an ihn, dass die Türe nicht eher zugeriegelt ward, als bis der schwarze Gesell angelangt war.

Als das Frühjahr herangekommen und draußen alles grün
war, sagte der Bär eines Morgens zu Schneeweißchen »nun
muss ich fort und darf den ganzen Sommer nicht wieder
kommen.« »Wo gehst du denn hin, lieber Bär?« fragte
Schneeweißchen. »Ich muss in den Wald und meine Schätze
vor den bösen Zwergen hüten: im Winter, wenn die Erde
hart gefroren ist, müssen sie wohl unten bleiben und können sich nicht durcharbeiten, aber jetzt, wenn die Sonne die
Erde aufgetaut und erwärmt hat, da brechen sie durch, steigen herauf, suchen und stehlen; was einmal in ihren Händen ist und in ihren Höhlen liegt, das kommt so leicht
nicht wieder an des Tages Licht.« Schneeweißchen war
ganz traurig über den Abschied und als es ihm die Türe
aufriegelte, und der Bär sich hinaus drängte, blieb er an
dem Türhaken hängen und ein Stück seiner Haut riss auf,
und da war es Schneeweißchen, als hätte es Gold durch-
schimmern gesehen: aber es war seiner Sache nicht gewiss.
Der Bär lief eilig fort und war bald hinter den Bäumen verschwunden.

Nach einiger Zeit schickte die Mutter die Kinder in den
Wald, Reisig zu sammeln. Da fanden sie draußen einen großen Baum, der lag gefällt auf dem Boden, und an dem
Stamme sprang zwischen dem Gras etwas auf und ab, sie
konnten aber nicht unterscheiden was es war. Als sie näher
kamen, sahen sie einen Zwerg mit einem alten verwelkten
Gesicht und einem ellenlangen schneeweißen Bart. Das
Ende des Bartes war in eine Spalte des Baums eingeklemmt,
und der Kleine sprang hin und her wie ein Hündchen an einem Seil und wusste nicht wie er sich helfen sollte. Er
glotzte die Mädchen mit seinen roten feurigen Augen an
und schrie »was steht ihr da! könnt ihr nicht herbei gehen
und mir Beistand leisten?« »Was hast du angefangen, kleines Männchen?« fragte Rosenrot. »Dumme neugierige
Gans«, antwortete der Zwerg, »den Baum habe ich mir
spalten wollen, um kleines Holz in der Küche zu haben; bei
den dicken Klötzen verbrennt gleich das bisschen Speise,

das unser einer braucht, der nicht so viel hinunter schlingt als ihr, grobes, gieriges Volk. Ich hatte den Keil schon glücklich hinein getrieben, und es wäre alles nach Wunsch gegangen, aber das verwünschte Holz war zu glatt und sprang unversehens heraus, und der Baum fuhr so geschwind zusammen, dass ich meinen schönen weißen Bart nicht mehr herausziehen konnte; nun steckt er drin, und ich kann nicht fort. Da lachen die albernen glatten Milchgesichter! pfui, was seid ihr garstig!« Die Kinder gaben sich alle Mühe, aber sie konnten den Bart nicht heraus ziehen, er steckte zu fest. »Ich will laufen und Leute herbei holen« sagte Rosenrot. »Wahnsinnige Schafsköpfe«, schnarrte der Zwerg, »wer wird gleich Leute herbeirufen, ihr seid mir schon um zwei zu viel; fällt euch nicht besseres ein?« »Sei nur nicht ungeduldig«, sagte Schneeweißchen, »ich will schon Rat schaffen«, holte sein Scherchen aus der Tasche und schnitt das Ende des Bartes ab. Sobald der Zwerg sich frei fühlte, griff er nach einem Sack, der zwischen den Wurzeln des Baums steckte und mit Gold gefüllt war, hob ihn heraus und brummte vor sich hin »ungehobeltes Volk, schneidet mir ein Stück von meinem stolzen Barte ab! lohn's euch der Guckuck!« damit schwang er seinen Sack auf den Rücken und gieng fort ohne die Kinder nur noch einmal anzusehen.

Einige Zeit danach wollten Schneeweißchen und Rosenrot ein Gericht Fische angeln. Als sie nahe bei dem Bach waren, sahen sie dass etwas wie eine große Heuschrecke nach dem Wasser zu hüpfte, als wollte es hinein springen. Sie liefen heran und erkannten den Zwerg. »Wo willst du hin?« sagte Rosenrot, »du willst doch nicht ins Wasser?« »Solch ein Narr bin ich nicht«, schrie der Zwerg, »seht ihr nicht, der verwünschte Fisch will mich hinein ziehen?« Der Kleine hatte da gesessen und geangelt, und unglücklicher Weise hatte der Wind seinen Bart mit der Angelschnur verflochten: als gleich darauf ein großer Fisch anbiss, fehlten dem schwachen Geschöpf die Kräfte ihn herauszuziehen: der

Fisch behielt die Oberhand und riss den Zwerg zu sich hin. Zwar hielt er sich an allen Halmen und Binsen, aber das half nicht viel, er musste den Bewegungen des Fisches folgen, und war in beständiger Gefahr ins Wasser gezogen zu werden. Die Mädchen kamen zu rechter Zeit, hielten ihn fest und versuchten den Bart von der Schnur loszumachen, aber vergebens, Bart und Schnur waren fest in einander verwirrt. Es blieb nichts übrig als das Scherchen her vor zuholen und den Bart abzuschneiden, wobei ein kleiner Teil desselben verloren gieng. Als der Zwerg das sah, schrie er sie an, »ist das Manier, ihr Lorche, einem das Gesicht zu schänden? nicht genug, dass ihr mir den Bart unten abgestutzt habt, jetzt schneidet ihr mir den besten Teil davon ab: ich darf mich vor den Meinigen gar nicht sehen lassen. Dass ihr laufen müsstet und die Schuhsohlen verloren hättet!« Dann holte er einen Sack Perlen, der im Schilfe lag, und ohne ein Wort weiter zu sagen, schleppte er ihn fort und verschwand hinter einem Stein.

Es trug sich zu, dass bald hernach die Mutter die beiden Mädchen nach der Stadt schickte, Zwirn Nadeln Schnüre und Bänder einzukaufen. Der Weg führte sie über eine Heide, auf der hier und da mächtige Felsenstücke zerstreut lagen. Da sahen sie einen großen Vogel in der Luft schweben, der langsam über ihnen kreiste, sich immer tiefer herab senkte und endlich nicht weit bei einem Felsen niederstieß. Gleich darauf hörten sie einen durchdringenden, jämmerlichen Schrei. Sie liefen herzu und sahen mit Schrecken dass der Adler ihren alten Bekannten, den Zwerg, gepackt hatte und ihn forttragen wollte. Die mitleidigen Kinder hielten gleich das Männchen fest und zerrten sich so lange mit dem Adler herum, bis er seine Beute fahren ließ. Als der Zwerg sich von dem ersten Schrecken erholt hatte, schrie er mit seiner kreischenden Stimme »konntet ihr nicht säuberlicher mit mir umgehen? gerissen habt ihr an meinem dünnen Röckchen dass es überall zerfetzt und durchlöchert ist, unbeholfenes und täppisches

Gesindel, das ihr seid!« Dann nahm er einen Sack mit Edelsteinen und schlüpfte wieder unter den Felsen in seine Höhle. Die Mädchen waren an seinen Undank schon gewöhnt, setzten ihren Weg fort und verrichteten ihr Geschäft in der Stadt. Als sie beim Heimweg wieder auf die Heide kamen, über raschten sie den Zwerg, der auf einem reinlichen Plätzchen seinen Sack mit Edelsteinen ausgeschüttet und nicht gedacht hatte dass so spät noch jemand daher kommen würde. Die Abendsonne schien über die glänzenden Steine, sie schimmerten und leuchteten so prächtig in allen Farben, dass die Kinder stehenblieben und sie betrachteten. »Was steht ihr da und habt Maulaffen feil!« schrie der Zwerg, und sein aschgraues Gesicht ward zinnoberrot vor Zorn. Er wollte mit seinen Scheltworten fortfahren, als sich ein lautes Brummen hören ließ und ein schwarzer Bär aus dem Walde herbei trabte. Erschrocken sprang der Zwerg auf, aber er konnte nicht mehr zu seinem Schlupfwinkel gelangen, der Bär war schon in seiner Nähe. Da rief er in Herzensangst »lieber Herr Bär, verschont mich, ich will euch alle meine Schätze geben, sehet, die schönen Edelsteine, die da liegen. Schenkt mir das Leben, was habt ihr an mir kleinen schmächtigen Kerl? ihr spürt mich nicht zwischen den Zähnen: da, die beiden gottlosen Mädchen packt, das sind für euch zarte Bissen, fett wie junge Wachteln, die fresst in Gottes Namen.« Der Bär kümmerte sich um seine Worte nicht, gab dem boshaften Geschöpf einen einzigen Schlag mit der Tatze, und es regte sich nicht mehr.

Die Mädchen waren fortgesprungen, aber der Bär rief ihnen nach »Schneeweißchen und Rosenrot, fürchtet euch nicht, wartet ich will mit euch gehen.« Da erkannten sie seine Stimme und blieben stehen, und als der Bär bei ihnen war, fiel plötzlich die Bärenhaut ab, und er stand da als ein schöner Mann, und war ganz in Gold gekleidet. »Ich bin eines Königs Sohn«, sprach er, »und war von dem gottlosen Zwerg, der mir meine Schätze gestohlen hatte, verwünscht als ein wilder Bär in dem Walde zu laufen, bis ich durch seinen Tod erlöst würde. Jetzt hat er seine wohlverdiente Strafe empfangen.«

Schneeweißchen ward mit ihm vermählt und Rosenrot mit seinem Bruder und sie teilten die großen Schätze mit einander, die der Zwerg in seine Höhle zusammen getragen hatte. Die alte Mutter lebte noch lange Jahre ruhig und glücklich bei ihren Kindern. Die zwei Rosenbäumchen aber nahm sie mit, und sie standen vor ihrem Fenster und trugen jedes Jahr die schönsten Rosen, weiß und rot.

162.

Der kluge Knecht.

Wie glücklich ist der Herr, und wie wohl steht es mit seinem Hause, wenn er einen klugen Knecht hat, der auf seine Worte zwar hört, aber nicht danach tut und lieber seiner eigenen Weisheit folgt. Ein solcher kluger Hans ward einmal von seinem Herrn ausgeschickt, eine verlorene Kuh zu suchen. Er blieb lange aus, und der Herr dachte »der treue Hans, er lässt sich in seinem Dienste doch keine Mühe verdrießen.« Als er aber gar nicht wiederkommen wollte, befürchtete der Herr es möchte ihm etwas zugestoßen sein, machte sich selbst auf und wollte sich nach ihm umsehen. Er musste lange suchen, endlich erblickte er den Knecht, der im weiten Feld auf und ab lief. »Nun lieber Hans«, sagte der Herr, als er ihn eingeholt hatte, »hast du die Kuh gefunden, nach der ich dich ausgeschickt habe?« »Nein, Herr«, antwortete er, »die Kuh habe ich nicht gefunden, aber auch nicht gesucht.« »Was hast du denn gesucht, Hans?« »Etwas Besseres und das habe ich auch glücklich gefunden.« »Was ist das, Hans?« »Drei Amseln« antwortete der Knecht. »Und wo sind sie?« fragte der Herr. »Eine sehe ich, die andere höre ich und die dritte jage ich« antwortete der kluge Knecht.

Nehmt euch daran ein Beispiel, bekümmert euch nicht um euern Herrn und seine Befehle, tut lieber was euch einfällt und wozu ihr Lust habt, dann werdet ihr eben so weise handeln, wie der kluge Hans.

163.

Der gläserne Sarg.

Sage niemand dass ein armer Schneider es nicht weit bringen und nicht zu hohen Ehren gelangen könne, es ist weiter gar nichts nötig als dass er an die rechte Schmiede kommt und, was die Hauptsache ist, dass es ihm glückt. Ein solches artiges und behendes Schneiderbürschchen gieng einmal seiner Wanderschaft nach und kam in einen großen Wald, und weil es den Weg nicht wusste, verirrte es sich. Die Nacht brach ein, und es blieb ihm nichts übrig als in dieser schauerlichen Einsamkeit ein Lager zu suchen. Auf dem weichen Moose hätte er freilich ein gutes Bett gefunden, allein die Furcht vor den wilden Tieren ließ ihm da keine Ruhe, und er musste sich endlich entschließen auf einem Baume zu übernachten. Er suchte eine hohe Eiche, stieg bis in den Gipfel hinauf und dankte Gott dass er sein Bügeleisen bei sich trug, weil ihn sonst der Wind, der über die Gipfel der Bäume wehete, weggeführt hätte.

Nachdem er einige Stunden in der Finsternis, nicht ohne Zittern und Zagen, zugebracht hatte, erblickte er in geringer Entfernung den Schein eines Lichtes; und weil er dachte dass da eine menschliche Wohnung sein möchte, wo er sich besser befinden würde als auf den Ästen eines Baums, so stieg er vorsichtig herab und gieng dem Lichte nach. Es leitete ihn zu einem kleinen Häuschen, das aus Rohr und Binsen geflochten war. Er klopfte mutig an, die Türe öffnete

sich, und bei dem Scheine des herausfallenden Lichtes sah
er ein altes eisgraues Männchen, das ein von buntfarbigen
Lappen zusammengesetztes Kleid an hatte. »Wer seid ihr,
und was wollt ihr?« fragte es mit einer schnarrenden Stimme. »Ich bin ein armer Schneider«, antwortete er, »den die
Nacht hier in der Wildnis überfallen hat, und bitte euch inständig mich bis Morgen in eurer Hütte aufzunehmen.«
»geh deiner Wege«, erwiderte der Alte mit mürrischem
Tone, »mit Landstreichern will ich nichts zu schaffen haben; suche dir anderwärts ein Unterkommen.« Nach diesen
Worten wollte er wieder in sein Haus schlüpfen, aber der
Schneider hielt ihn am Rockzipfel fest und bat so beweg-
lich, dass der Alte, der so böse nicht war als er sich anstell-
te, endlich erweicht ward und ihn mit in seine Hütte nahm,
wo er ihm zu essen gab und dann in einem Winkel ein ganz
gutes Nachtlager anwies.

Der müde Schneider brauchte keines Einwiegens, sondern
schlief sanft bis an den Morgen, würde auch noch nicht an
das Aufstehen gedacht haben, wenn er nicht von einem lauten Lärm wäre aufgeschreckt worden. Ein heftiges Schreien
und Brüllen drang durch die dünnen Wände des Hauses.
Der Schneider, den ein unerwarteter Mut überkam, sprang
auf, zog in der Hast seine Kleider an und eilte hinaus. Da
erblickte er nahe bei dem Häuschen einen großen schwarzen Stier und einen schönen Hirsch, die in dem heftigsten
Kampfe begriffen waren. Sie giengen mit so großer Wut
aufeinander los, dass von ihrem Getrampel der Boden erzitterte, und die Luft von ihrem Geschrei erdröhnte. Es
war lange ungewiss, welcher von beiden den Sieg davon
tragen würde: endlich stieß der Hirsch seinem Gegner das
Geweih in den Leib, worauf der Stier mit entsetzlichem
Brüllen zur Erde sank, und durch einige Schläge des Hirsches völlig getötet ward.

Der Schneider, welcher dem Kampfe mit Erstaunen zugesehen hatte, stand noch unbeweglich da, als der Hirsch in
vollen Sprüngen auf ihn zu eilte und ihn, ehe er entfliehen

konnte, mit seinem großen Geweihe geradezu aufgabelte. Er konnte sich nicht lange besinnen, denn es gieng schnellen Laufes fort über Stock und Stein, Berg und Tal, Wiese und Wald. Er hielt sich mit beiden Händen an die Enden des Geweihes fest und überließ sich seinem Schicksal. Es kam ihm aber nicht anders vor als flöge er davon. Endlich hielt der Hirsch vor einer Felsenwand still und ließ den Schneider sanft herabfallen. Der Schneider, mehr tot als lebendig, bedurfte längerer Zeit, um wieder zur Besinnung zu kommen. Als er sich einigermaßen erholt hatte, stieß der Hirsch, der neben ihm stehen geblieben war, sein Geweih mit solcher Gewalt gegen eine in dem Felsen befindliche Türe, dass sie aufsprang. Feuerflammen schlugen heraus, auf welche ein großer Dampf folgte, der den Hirsch seinen Augen entzog. Der Schneider wusste nicht was er tun und wohin er sich wenden sollte, um aus dieser Einöde wieder unter Menschen zu gelangen. Indem er also unschlüssig stand, tönte eine Stimme aus dem Felsen, die ihm zurief »tritt ohne Furcht herein, dir soll kein Leid widerfahren.« Er zauderte zwar, doch, von einer heimlichen Gewalt angetrieben, gehorchte er der Stimme und gelangte durch die eiserne Tür in einen großen geräumigen Saal, dessen Decke, Wände und Boden aus glänzend geschliffenen Quadratsteinen bestanden, auf deren jedem ihm unbekannte Zeichen eingehauen waren. Er betrachtete alles voll Bewunderung und war eben in Begriff wieder hinaus zu gehen, als er abermals die Stimme vernahm, welche ihm sagte »tritt auf den Stein, der in der Mitte des Saales liegt, und dein wartet großes Glück.«

Sein Mut war schon so weit gewachsen, dass er dem Befehle Folge leistete. Der Stein begann unter seinen Füßen nachzugeben und sank langsam in die Tiefe hinab. Als er wieder feststand, und der Schneider sich umsah, befand er sich in einem Saale, der an Umfang dem vorigen gleich war. Hier aber gab es mehr zu betrachten und zu bewundern. In die Wände waren Vertiefungen eingehauen, in welchen Gefäße von durchsichtigem Glase standen, die mit farbigem Spiritus oder mit einem bläulichen Rauche angefüllt waren. Auf dem Boden des Saales standen, einander gegenüber, zwei große gläserne Kasten, die sogleich seine Neugierde reizten. Indem er zu dem einen trat, erblickte er darin ein schönes Gebäude, einem Schlosse ähnlich, von Wirtschafts-gebäuden, Ställen und Scheuern und einer Menge anderer artigen Sachen umgeben. Alles war klein, aber überaus sorgfältig und zierlich gearbeitet, und schien von einer kunstreichen Hand mit der höchsten Genauigkeit ausge-schnitzt zu sein.

Er würde seine Augen von der Betrachtung dieser Selten-heiten noch nicht abgewendet haben, wenn sich nicht die Stimme abermals hätte hören lassen. Sie forderte ihn auf sich umzukehren und den gegenüberstehenden Glaskasten zu beschauen. Wie stieg seine Verwunderung als er darin ein Mädchen von größter Schönheit erblickte. Es lag wie im Schlafe, und war in lange blonde Haare wie in einen kost-baren Mantel eingehüllt. Die Augen waren fest geschlossen, doch die lebhafte Gesichtsfarbe und ein Band, das der Atem hin und her bewegte, ließen keinen Zweifel an ihrem Leben. Der Schneider betrachtete die Schöne mit klopfen-dem Herzen, als sie plötzlich die Augen aufschlug und bei seinem Anblick in freudigem Schrecken zusammenfuhr. »Gerechter Himmel«, rief sie, »meine Befreiung naht! ge-schwind, geschwind, hilf mir aus meinem Gefängnis: wenn du den Riegel an diesem gläsernen Sarg wegschiebst, so bin ich erlöst.« Der Schneider gehorchte ohne Zaudern, alsbald hob sie den Glasdeckel in die Höhe, stieg heraus und eilte in die Ecke des Saals, wo sie sich in einen weiten Mantel verhüllte. Dann setzte sie sich auf einen Stein nieder, hieß den jungen Mann heran gehen, und nachdem sie einen freundlichen Kuss auf seinen Mund gedrückt hatte, sprach sie »mein lang ersehnter Befreier, der gütige Himmel hat dich zu mir geführt und meinen Leiden ein Ziel gesetzt. An demselben Tage, wo sie endigen, soll dein Glück beginnen.

Du bist der vom Himmel bestimmte Gemahl, und sollst, von mir geliebt und mit allen irdischen Gütern überhäuft, in ungestörter Freud dein Leben zubringen. Sitz nieder und höre die Erzählung meines Schicksals.

Ich bin die Tochter eines reichen Grafen. Meine Eltern starben als ich noch in zarter Jugend war und empfahlen mich in ihrem letzten Willen meinem ältern Bruder, bei dem ich auferzogen wurde. Wir liebten uns so zärtlich und waren so übereinstimmend in unserer Denkungsart und unsern Neigungen, dass wir beide den Entschluss fassten uns niemals zu verheiraten, sondern bis an das Ende unseres Lebens beisammen zu bleiben. In unserm Hause war an Gesellschaft nie Mangel: Nachbarn und Freunde besuchten uns häufig, und wir übten gegen alle die Gastfreundschaft in vollem Maße. So geschah es auch eines Abends, dass ein Fremder in unser Schloss geritten kam und, unter dem Vorgeben den nächsten Ort nicht mehr erreichen zu können, um ein Nachtlager bat. Wir gewährten seine Bitte mit zuvorkommender Höflichkeit, und er unterhielt uns während des Abendessens mit seinem Gespräche und eingemischten Erzählungen auf das anmutigste. Mein Bruder hatte ein so großes Wohlgefallen an ihm, dass er ihn bat ein paar Tage bei uns zu verweilen, wozu er nach einigem Weigern einwilligte. Wir standen erst spät in der Nacht vom Tische auf, dem Fremden wurde ein Zimmer angewiesen, und ich eilte, ermüdet wie ich war, meine Glieder in die weichen Federn zu senken. Kaum war ich ein wenig eingeschlummert, so weckten mich die Töne einer zarten und lieblichen Musik. Da ich nicht begreifen konnte woher sie kamen, so wollte ich mein im Nebenzimmer schlafendes Kammermädchen rufen, allein zu meinem Erstaunen fand ich dass mir, als lastete ein Alp auf meiner Brust, von einer unbekannten Gewalt die Sprache benommen und ich unvermögend war den geringsten Laut von mir zu geben. Indem sah ich bei dem Schein der Nachtlampe den Fremden in mein durch zwei Türen fest verschlossenes Zimmer eintreten. Er näherte

sich mir und sagte dass er durch Zauberkräfte, die ihm zu
Gebote ständen, die liebliche Musik habe ertönen lassen
um mich aufzuwecken, und dringe jetzt selbst durch alle
Schlösser in der Absicht, mir Herz und Hand anzubieten.
Mein Widerwille aber gegen seine Zauberkünste war so
groß, dass ich ihn keiner Antwort würdigte. Er blieb eine
Zeit lang unbeweglich stehen, wahrscheinlich in der Absicht einen günstigen Entschluss zu erwarten, als ich aber
fortfuhr zu schweigen, erklärte er zornig dass er sich rächen und Mittel finden werde meinen Hochmut zu bestrafen, worauf er das Zimmer wieder verließ. Ich brachte die
Nacht in höchster Unruhe zu und schlummerte erst gegen
Morgen ein. Als ich erwacht war, eilte ich zu meinem Bruder, um ihn von dem was vorgefallen war zu benachrich-
tigen, allein ich fand ihn nicht auf seinem Zimmer, und der
Bediente sagte mir dass er bei anbrechendem Tage mit dem
Fremden auf die Jagd geritten sei.
Mir ahnete gleich nichts gutes. Ich kleidete mich schnell an,
ließ meinen Leibzelter satteln und ritt, nur von einem Diener begleitet, in vollem Jagen nach dem Walde. Der Diener
stürzte mit dem Pferde und konnte mir, da das Pferd den
Fuß gebrochen hatte, nicht folgen. Ich setzte, ohne mich
aufzuhalten, meinen Weg fort, und in wenigen Minuten sah
ich den Fremden mit einem schönen Hirsch, den er an der
Leine führte, auf mich zukommen. Ich fragte ihn wo er
meinen Bruder gelassen habe und wie er zu diesem Hirsche
gelangt sei, aus dessen großen Augen ich Tränen fließen
sah. Anstatt mir zu antworten fieng er an laut aufzulachen.
Ich geriet darüber in höchsten Zorn, zog eine Pistole und
drückte sie gegen das Ungeheuer ab, aber die Kugel prallte
von seiner Brust zurück und fuhr in den Kopf meines Pferdes. Ich stürzte zur Erde, und der Fremde murmelte einige
Worte, die mir das Bewusstsein raubten.
Als ich wieder zur Besinnung kam fand ich mich in dieser
unterirdischen Gruft in einem gläsernen Sarge. Der
Schwarzkünstler erschien nochmals, sagte dass er meinen

Bruder in einen Hirsch verwandelt, mein Schloss, mit allem Zubehör, verkleinert, in den andern Glaskasten eingeschlossen, und meine in Rauch verwandelten Leute in Glasflaschen gebannt hätte. Wolle ich mich jetzt seinem Wunsche fügen, so sei ihm ein leichtes, alles wieder in den vorigen Stand zu setzen: er brauche nur die Gefäße zu öffnen, so werde alles wieder in die natürliche Gestalt zurückkehren. Ich antwortete ihm so wenig als das erste Mal. Er verschwand und ließ mich in meinem Gefängnisse liegen, in welchem mich ein tiefer Schlaf befiel. Unter den Bildern, welche an meiner Seele vorübergiengen, war auch das tröstliche, dass ein junger Mann kam und mich befreite, und als ich heute die Augen öffne, so erblicke ich dich und sehe meinen Traum erfüllt. Hilf mir vollbringen was in jenem Gesichte noch weiter geschah. Das erste ist dass wir den Glaskasten, in welchem mein Schloss sich befindet, auf jenen breiten Stein heben.«

Der Stein, sobald er beschwert war, hob sich mit dem Fräulein und dem Jüngling in die Höhe, und stieg durch die Öffnung der Decke in den obern Saal, wo sie dann leicht ins Freie gelangen konnten. Hier öffnete das Fräulein den Deckel, und es war wunderbar anzusehen, wie Schloss, Häuser und Gehöfte sich ausdehnten und in größter Schnelligkeit zu natürlicher Größe heranwuchsen. Sie kehrten darauf in die unterirdische Höhle zurück und ließen die mit Rauch gefüllten Gläser von dem Steine herauftragen. Kaum hatte das Fräulein die Flaschen geöffnet, so drang der blaue Rauch heraus und verwandelte sich in lebendige Menschen, in welchen das Fräulein ihre Diener und Leute erkannte. Ihre Freude ward noch vermehrt als ihr Bruder, der den Zauberer in dem Stier getötet hatte, in menschlicher Gestalt aus dem Walde heran kam, und noch denselben Tag reichte das Fräulein, ihrem Versprechen gemäß, dem glücklichen Schneider die Hand am Altare.

164

Der faule Heinz.

Heinz war faul, und obgleich er weiter nichts zu tun hatte, als seine Ziege täglich auf die Weide zu treiben, so seufzte er dennoch, wenn er nach vollbrachtem Tagewerk Abends nach Hause kam. »Es ist in Wahrheit eine schwere Last«, sagte er, »und ein mühseliges Geschäft, so eine Ziege Jahr aus Jahr ein bis in den späten Herbst ins Feld zu treiben. Und wenn man sich noch dabei hinlegen und schlafen könnte! aber nein, da muss man die Augen auf haben, damit sie die jungen Bäume nicht beschädigt, durch die Hecke in einen Garten dringt oder gar davon läuft. Wie soll da einer zur Ruhe kommen, und seines Lebens froh werden!« Er setzte sich, sammelte seine Gedanken und überlegte wie er seine Schultern von dieser Bürde frei machen könnte. Lange war alles Nachsinnen vergeblich, plötzlich fiel's ihm wie Schuppen von den Augen. »Ich weiß was ich tue«, rief er aus, »ich heirate die dicke Trine, die hat auch eine Ziege, und kann meine mit austreiben, so brauche ich mich nicht länger zu quälen.«

Heinz erhob sich also, setzte seine müden Glieder in Bewegung, gieng quer über die Straße, denn weiter war der Weg nicht, wo die Eltern der dicken Trine wohnten, und hielt um ihre arbei[t]same und tugendreiche Tochter an. Die Eltern besannen sich nicht lange, »gleich und gleich gesellt sich gern« meinten sie und willigten ein. Nun ward die dicke Trine Heinzens Frau und trieb die beiden Ziegen aus. Heinz hatte gute Tage und brauchte sich von keiner andern Arbeit zu erholen, als von seiner eigenen Faulheit. Nur dann und wann gieng er mit hinaus und sagte »es geschieht bloß damit mir die Ruhe hernach desto besser schmeckt: man verliert sonst alles Gefühl dafür.«

Aber die dicke Trine war nicht minder faul. »Lieber Heinz«, sprach sie eines Tages, »warum sollen wir uns das

Leben ohne Not sauer machen und unsere beste Jugendzeit
verkümmern? Ist es nicht besser, wir geben die beiden Ziegen, die jeden Morgen einen mit ihrem Meckern im besten
Schlafe stören, unserm Nachbar und der gibt uns einen Bienenstock dafür? den Bienenstock stellen wir an einen sonnigen Platz hinter das Haus und bekümmern uns weiter
nicht darum. Die Bienen brauchen nicht gehütet und nicht
ins Feld getrieben zu werden: sie fliegen aus, finden den
Weg nach Haus von selbst wieder und sammeln Honig
ohne dass es uns die geringste Mühe macht.« »Du hast wie
eine verständige Frau gesprochen« antwortete Heinz, »deinen Vorschlag wollen wir ohne Zaudern ausführen: außer-
dem schmeckt und nährt der Honig besser als die Ziegen-
milch und lässt sich auch länger aufbewahren.«
Der Nachbar gab für die beiden Ziegen gerne einen Bienenstock. Die Bienen flogen unermüdlich vom frühen
Morgen bis zum späten Abend aus und ein, und füllten den
Stock mit dem schönsten Honig, so dass Heinz im Herbst
einen ganzen Krug voll heraus nehmen konnte.
Sie stellten den Krug auf ein Brett, das oben an der Wand in
ihrer Schlafkammer befestigt war, und weil sie fürchteten er
könnte ihnen gestohlen werden oder die Mäuse könnten
darüber geraten, so holte Trine einen starken Haselstock
herbei und legte ihn neben ihr Bett, damit sie ihn, ohne un-
nötigerweise aufzustehen, mit der Hand erreichen und die
ungebetenen Gäste von dem Bette aus verjagen könnte.
Der faule Heinz verließ das Bett nicht gerne vor Mittag:
»wer früh aufsteht«, sprach er, »sein Gut verzehrt.« Eines
Morgens als er so am hellen Tage noch in den Federn lag
und von dem langen Schlaf ausruhte, sprach er zu seiner
Frau »die Weiber lieben die Süßigkeit, und du naschest von
dem Honig, es ist besser, ehe er von dir allein ausgegessen
wird, dass wir dafür eine Gans mit einem jungen Gänslein
erhandeln.« »Aber nicht eher«, erwiderte Trine, »als bis wir
ein Kind haben, das sie hütet. Soll ich mich etwa mit den
jungen Gänsen plagen und meine Kräfte dabei unnötiger-

weise zusetzen?« »Meinst du«, sagte Heinz, »der Junge
werde Gänse hüten? heutzutage gehorchen die Kinder
nicht mehr: sie tun nach ihrem eigenen Willen, weil sie sich
klüger dünken als die Eltern, gerade wie jener Knecht, der
die Kuh suchen sollte, und drei Amseln nachjagte.« »Oh«,
antwortete Trine, »dem soll es schlecht bekommen, wenn
er nicht tut was ich sage. Einen Stock will ich nehmen und
mit ungezählten Schlägen ihm die Haut gerben. Siehst du,
Heinz«, rief sie in ihrem Eifer und fasste den Stock, mit
dem sie die Mäuse verjagen wollte, »siehst du, so will ich
auf ihn losschlagen.« Sie holte aus, traf aber unglücklicher-
weise den Honigkrug über dem Bette. Der Krug sprang wider die Wand und fiel in Scherben herab, und der schöne
Honig floss auf den Boden. »Da liegt nun die Gans mit
dem jungen Gänslein«, sagte Heinz, »und braucht nicht gehütet zu werden. Aber ein Glück ist es, dass mir der Krug
nicht auf den Kopf gefallen ist, wir haben alle Ursache mit
unserm Schicksal zufrieden zu sein.« Und da er in einer
Scherbe noch etwas Honig bemerkte, so langte er danach
und sprach ganz vergnügt »das Restchen, Frau, wollen wir
uns noch schmecken lassen und dann nach dem gehabten
Schrecken ein wenig ausruhen, was tut's, wenn wir etwas
später als gewöhnlich aufstehen, der Tag ist doch noch lang
genug.« »Ja« antwortete Trine, »man kommt immer noch
zu rechter Zeit. Weißt du, die Schnecke war einmal zur
Hochzeit eingeladen, machte sich auf den Weg, kam aber
zur Kindtaufe an. Vor dem Haus stürzte sie noch über den
Zaun und sagte ›Eilen tut nicht gut.‹«

165

Der Vogel Greif.

's isch einisch e Chönig gsi, woner gregiert hat und wiener gheiße hat weiß i nümme. De het kei Sohn gha, nummene einzige Tochter, die isch immer chrank gsi, und kei Dokter het se chönne heile. Do isch em Chönig profizeit worde si Tochter werd se an Öpfle gsund ässe. Do lot er dur sis ganz Land bchant mache wer siner Tochter Öpfel bringe, dass se gsund dar chönn ässe, de müesse zur Frau und Chönig wärde. Das het au ne Pur verno, de drei Söhn gha het. Do säit er zum elste »gang ufs Gade ufe, nimm e Chratte (Handkorb) voll vo dene schöne Öpfle mit rote Bagge und träg se a Hof; villicht cha se d' Chönigstochter gsund dra esse und de darfsche hürote und wirsch Chönig.« De Kärle het's e so gmacht und der Weg under d' Füeß gno. Woner e Zitlang gange gsi isch, begegnet es chlis isigs Manndle, das frogt ne was er do e dem Chratte häig, do seit der Uele, denn so het er gheiße, »Fröschebäi.« Das Manndle säit druf »no es sölle si und blibe« und isch witer gange. Ändle chunt der Uele fürs Schloss un lot se amelde, er hob Öpfel, die d' Tochter gsund mache, wenn se dervo ässe tue. Das het der Chönig grüsele gfreut und lot der Uele vor se cho, aber, o häie! woner ufdeckt, so het er anstatt Öpfel Fröschebäi e dem Chratte, die no zapled händ. Drob isch der Chönig bös worde, und lot ne zum Hus us jage. Woner häi cho isch, so verzelter dem Ätte wie's em gange isch. Do schickt der Ätte der noelst So[h]n, de Säme gheiße het; aber dem isch es ganz glich gange wie im Uele. Es isch em halt au es chlis isigs Manndle begegnet und das het ne gfrogt was er do e dem Chratte häig, der Säme säit: »Seüborst«, und das isigs Manndle säit »no es söll si und blibe.« Woner do vor es Chönigsschloss cho isch, und säit er heb Öpfel, a dene se d' Chönigstochter gsund chönn ässe, so händ se ne nid welle ine lo, und händ gsäit es sig scho eine do gsi und

heb se füre Nare gha. Der Säme het aber aghalte, er heb
gwüss dere Öpfel, se solle ne nume ine lo. Ändle händ sem
glaubt, und füre ne vor der Chönig. Aber woner er si
Chratte ufdeckt, so het er halt Seüborst. Das het der Chönig gar schröckele erzürnt, so dass er der Säme us em Hus
het lo peütsche. Woner häi cho isch, so het er gsäit wie's em
gange isch. Do chunt der jüngst Bueb, dem händse nume
der dumm Hans gsäit, und frogt der Ätte ob er au mit Öpfel goh dörf. »Jo«, säit do der Ätte, »du wärst der rächt
Kerle derzue, wenn die gschite nüt usrichte, was wettest
denn du usrichte.« Der Bueb het aber nit no glo: »e woll,
Ätte, i will au goh.« »Gang mer doch ewäg, du dumme
Kerle, du muest warte bis gschiter wirsch« säit druf der
Ätte und chert em der Rügge. Der Hans aber zupft ne hin-
de am Chittel, »e woll, Ätte, i will au goh.« »No minetwä-
ge, so gang, de wirsch woll wieder ome cho« gitt der Ätte
zur Antwort eme nidige Ton. Der Bueb hat se aber grüsele
gfreut und isch ufgumpet. »Jo, tue jetz no wiene Nar, du
wirsch vo äim Tag zum andere no dümmer« säit der Ätte
wieder. Das het aber im Hans nüt gmacht und het se e siner
Freud nid lo störe. Wil's aber gli Nacht gsi isch, so het er
dänkt er well warte bis am Morge, er möcht hüt doch nümme na Hof gcho. Z' Nacht im Bett het er nid chönne
schloffe, und wenn er au ne ihli igschlummert isch, so he's
em traumt vo schöne Jumpfere, vo Schlössern, Gold und
Silber und allerhand dere Sache meh. Am Morge früe
macht er se uf der Wäg, und gli druse bchuntem es chlis
mutzigs Manndle, eme isige Chläidle, un frogt ne was er do
e dem Chratte häig. Der Hans gitt em zur Antwort er heb
Öpfel, a dene d' Chönigstochter se gsund ässe sött. »No«,
säit das Manndle, »es sölle söttige (solche) si und blibe.«
Aber am Hof händ se der Hans partu nit welle ine lo, denn
es sige scho zwee do gsi und hebe gsäit se bringe Öpfel und
do heb äine Fröschebäi und der ander Seüborst gha. Der
Hans het aber gar grüsele aghalte, er heb gewöss kene Fröschebäi, sondern von de schönste Öpfel, die im ganze Chö-

nigreich wachse. Woner de so ordele gredt het, so dänke d'
Törhüeter de chönn nid lüge und lönde ine, und se händ au
rächt gha, denn wo der Hans si Chratte vor em Chönig ab-
deckt, so sind goldgäle Öpfel füre cho. De Chönig het se
gfreut und lot gli der Tochter dervo bringe, und wartet jetz
e banger Erwartig bis menem der Bericht bringt, was se für
Würkig to hebe. Aber nid lange Zit vergot, so bringt em
öpper Bricht: aber was meineder wer isch das gsi? d' Tochter selber isch es gsi. So bald se vo dene Öpfel ggässe gha
het, isch e gsund us em Bett gsprunge. Wie der Chönig e
Freud gha het, chame nid beschribe. Aber jetz het er d'
Tochter dem Hans nid welle zur Frau ge un säit er müess
em zerst no ne Wäidlig (Nachen) mache, de ufem drochne
Land wäidliger geu as im Wasser. Der Hans nimmt de Be-
tingig a und got häi und verzelt's wie's eme gangen seig. Do
schickt der Atte der Uele is Holz um e söttige Wäidlig z'
mache. Er hat flißig gewärret (gearbeitet) und derzue gpfif-
fe. Z' Mittag, wo d' Sunne am höchste gstande isch, chunt
es chlis isigs Manndle und frogt was er do mach. Der Uele
gitt em zur Antwort »Chelle (hölzernes Gerät).« Das isig
Manndle säit »no es sölle si und blibe.« Z' Obe meint der
Uele er heb jetz e Wäidlig gmacht, aber woner het welle
isitze, so sind's alles Chelle gsi. Der anner Tag got der Säme
e Wald, aber 's isch em ganz gliche gange wie im Uele. Am
dritte Tag got der dumm Hans. Er schafft rächt fliß, dass
es im ganze Wald tönt vo sine chräftige Schläge, derzue
singt er und pfift er rächt lustig. Da chunt wieder das chli
Manndle z' Mittag, wo's am heißeste gsi isch, und frogt was
er do mach. »E Wäidlig, de uf em drochne Land wäidliger
got as uf em Wasser«, un wenn er dermit fertig seig, so
chom er d' Chönigstochter zur Frau über. »No«, säit das
Manndle, »es söll e so äine ge und blibe.« Z' Obe, wo d'
Sunne aber z' Gold gange isch, isch der Hans au fertig gsi
mit sim Wäidlig und Schiff und Gscher. Er sitzt i und rue-
deret der Residenz zue. Der Wäidlig isch aber so gschwind
gange wie der Wind. Der Chönig het's von witen gseh, will

aber im Hans si Tochter nonig ge und säit er müess zerst no
hundert Hase hüete vom Morge früeh bis z' Obe spot, und
wenn em äine furt chömm, so chömm er d' Tochter nit
über. Der Hans isch e des z' friede gsi, und gli am andere
Tag got er mit siner Heerd uf d' Wäid und passt verwändt
uf dass em keine dervo laufe. Nid mänge Stund isch ver-
gange, so chunt e Magd vom Schloss und säit zum Hans er
söll ere gschwind e Has ge, so hebe Wisite über cho. Der
Hans hett aber woll gemerkt wo das use will und säit er
gäb e keine, der Chönig chön denn morn siner Wisite mit
Hasepfäffer ufwarte. D' Magd het aber nid no glo: und am
Änd fot so no a resniere. Do säit der Hans wenn d' Chö-
nigtochter selber chömm, so woll er ene Has ge. Das het
d' Magd im Schloss gsäit, und d' Tochter isch selber gange.
Underdesse isch aber zum Hans das chli Manndle wieder
cho und frogt der Hans was er do tüej. He, do müess er
hundert Hase hüete, dass em kaine dervo lauf, und denn
dörf er d' Chönigstochter hürote und wäre Chönig.
»Guet«, säit das Manndle, »do hesch es Pfifle, und wenn
der äine furtlauft, so pfif nume, denn chunt er wieder
ume.« Wo do d' Tochter cho isch, so gitt ere der Hans e
Has is Fürtüchle. Aber wo se öppe hundert Schritt wit gsi
isch, so pfift der Hans, und de Has springt ere us em
Schäubele use und, was gisch was hesch, wieder zu der
Herd. Wo's Obe gsi isch, so pfift de Hasehirt no emol und
luegt ob alle do sige und treibt se do zum Schloss. Der
Chönig het se verwunderet wie au der Hans im Stand gsi
seig hundert Hase z' hüete, dass em käine dervo glofe isch;
er will em aber d' Tochter äine weg no nig ge, und säit er
müss em no ne Fädere us d' Vogelgrife Stehl bringe. Der
Hans macht se grad uf der Wäg und marschiert räckt handle vorwärts. Z' Obe chunt er zu neme Schloss, do frogt er
umenes Nachtlager, denn sälbesmol het me no käine Wirts-
hüser gha, das säit em der Herr vom Schloss mit vele Freude zue und frogt ne woner he well. Der Hans git druf zur
Antwort »zum Vogelgrif.« »So, zum Vogelgrif, me säit ame

er wuss alles, und i hane Schlössel zue nere isige Gäldchiste
verlore: ehr chöntet doch so guet si und ne froge woner
seig.« »Jo frile«, säit der Hans, »das will i scho tue.« Am
Morgen früe isch er do witer gange, und chunt unterwägs
zue mene andere Schloss, i dem er wieder übernacht blibt.
Wo d' Lüt drus verno händ dass er zum Vogelgrif well, so
säge se es sig im Hus ne Tochter chrank, und se hebe scho
alle Mittel brucht, aber es well kais aschlo, er söll doch so
guet si und der Vogelgrif froge was die Tochter wieder
chön gsund mache. Der Hans säit das weller gärn tue und
goht witer. Do chunt er zue emne Wasser, und anstatt eme
Feer isch e große große Ma do gsi, de all Lüt het müesse
übere träge. De Ma het der Hans gfrogt wo si Räis ane geu.
»Zum Vogelgrif« säit der Hans. »No, wenn er zue ume
chömet«, säit do de Ma, »sö froget ne an worum i all Lüt
müess über das Wasser träge.« Do säit der Hans »jo, min
Gott jo, das will i scho tue.« De Ma het ne do uf d' Achsle
gno und übere trät. Ändle chunt do der Hans zum Hus
vom Vogelgrif, aber do isch nume d' Frau dehäime gsi und
der Vogelgrif sälber nid. Do frogt ne d' Frau was er well.
Do het ere der Hans alles verzelt, dass ere Fädere sött ha us
's Vogelgrife Stehl, und denn hebe se emene Schloss der
Schlüssel zue nere Gäldchiste verlore, und er sött der Vogelgrif froge wo der Schlüssel seig; denn seig eme andere
Schloss e Tochter chrank, und er söt[t] wüsse was die Tochter chönt gsund mache; denn seig nig wid vo do es Wasser
und e Ma derbi, de d' Lüt müess übere träge, und er möcht
au gern wüsse worum de Ma all Lüt müess übere träge. Do
säit die Frau »ja lueget, mi guete Fründ, 's cha käi Christ
mit em Vogelgrif rede, er frisst se all; wenn er aber wänd, so
chön neder under sis Bett undere ligge, und z' Nacht, wenn
er rächt fest schloft, so chönneder denn use länge und em e
Fädere usem Stehl risse; und wäge dene Sache, die ner wüsse söttet, will i ne sälber froge. Der Hans isch e das alles z'
friede gsi und lit unders Bett undere. Z' Obe chunt der Vogelgrif häi, und wiener i d' Stube chunt, so säit er »Frau, i

schmöke ne Christ.« »Jo«, säit do d' Frau, »'s isch hüt äine do gsi, aber er isch wieder furt«; und mit dem het der Vogelgrif nüt me gsäit. Z' mitzt e der Nacht, wo der Vogelgrif rächt geschnarchlet het, so längt der Hans ufe und risst em e Fädere usem Stehl. Do isch der Vogelgrif plötzle ufgjuckt und säit »Frau, i schmöcke ne Christ, und 's isch mer, 's heb me öpper am Stehl zehrt.« De säit d' Frau »de hesch gwüss traumet, und i ho der jo hüt scho gsäit, 's isch e Christ do gsi, aber isch wieder furt. Do het mer allerhand Sache verzellt. Si hebe ime Schloss der Schlüssel zue nere Gäldchiste verlore und chönnene nümme finde.« »O di Nare«, säit der Vogelgrif, »de Schlüssel lit im Holzhus hinder der Tör undere Holzbig.« »Und denn het er au gsäit imene Schloss seig e Tochter chrank und se wüsse kais Mittel für se gsund z' mache.« »O di Nare«, säit der Vogelgrif, »under der Chällerstäge het e Chrot es Näscht gmacht von ere Hoore, und wenn se die Hoor wieder het, so wer se gsund.« »Und denn het er au no gsäit 's sig amene Ort es Wasser un e Ma derbi, der müess all Lüt übere träge.« »O de Nar«, säit de Vogelgrif, »täter nome emol äine z' mitzt dri stelle, er müesst denn käine me übere träge.« Am Morge frue isch der Vogelgrif uf gstande und isch furt gange. Do chunt der Hans underem Bett füre und het e schöne Fädere gha; au het er ghört was der Vogelgrif gsäit het wäge dem Schlüssel und der Tochter und dem Ma. D' Frau vom Vogelgrif het em do alles no nemol verzellt, dass er nüt vergässe, und denn isch er wieder häi zue gange. Zerst chunt er zum Ma bim Wasser, de frogt ne gli was der Vogelgrif gsäit heb, do säit der Hans er söll ne zerst übere träge, er well em's denn däne säge. Do träit ne der Ma übere. Woner däne gsi isch, so säit em der Hans er söllt nume äinisch äine z' mitzt dri stelle, er müess denn käine me übere träge. Do het se de Ma grüsele gfreut und säit zum Hans er well ne zum Dank none mol ume und äne trage. Do säit der Hans näi, er well em di Müeh erspare, er seig sust mit em z'friede, und isch witer gange. Do chunt er zue dem Schloss, wo die Tochter

chrank gsi isch, die nimmt er do uf d' Achsle, denn se het
nit chönne laufe, und trait se d' Chellerstäge ab und nimmt
das Chrotenäst unter dem underste Tritt füre und git's der
Tochter i d' Händ, und die springt em ab der Achsle abe
und vor im d' Stäge uf, und isch ganz gsund gsi. Jetz händ
der Vater und d' Mueter e grüsliche Freud gha und händ
dem Hans Gschänke gmacht vo Gold und Silber: und was
er nume het welle, das händ se 'm gge. Wo do der Hans is
an der Schloss cho isch, isch er gli is Holzhus gange, und
het hinder der Tör under der Holzbige de Schlüssel richtig
gfunde, und het ne do dem Herr brocht. De het se au nid
wenig gfreut und het dem Hans zur Belohnig vill vo dem
Gold gge, das e der Chiste gsi isch, und sust no aller derhand für Sache, so Chüe und Schoof und Gäiße. Wo der
Hans zum Chönig cho isch mit deme Sache alle, mit dem
Gäld und dem Gold und Silber und dene Chüene, Schoofe
und Gäiße, so frogt ne der Chönig, woner au das alles
übercho heb. Do säit der Hans der Vogelgrif gäb äin so vill
me well. Do dänkt der Chönig er chönt das au bruche und
macht se au uf der Weg zum Vogelgrif, aber woner zue dem
Wasser cho isch, so isch er halt der erst gsi, der sid em Hans
cho isch, und de Ma stellt e z' mitzt ab und goht furt, und
der Chönig isch ertrunke. Der Hans het do d' Tochter ghü-
rotet und isch Chönig worde.

166.

Der starke Hans.

Es war einmal ein Mann und eine Frau, die hatten nur ein
einziges Kind, und lebten in einem abseits gelegenen Tale
ganz allein. Es trug sich zu, dass die Mutter einmal ins
Holz gieng, Tannenreiser zu lesen, und den kleinen Hans,
der erst zwei Jahr alt war, mitnahm. Da es gerade in der

Frühlingszeit war und das Kind seine Freude an den bunten Blumen hatte, so gieng sie immer weiter mit ihm in den Wald hinein. Plötzlich sprangen aus dem Gebüsch zwei Räuber hervor, packten die Mutter und das Kind und führten sie tief in den schwarzen Wald, wo Jahr aus Jahr ein kein Mensch hinkam. Die arme Frau bat die Räuber inständig sie mit ihrem Kinde frei zu lassen, aber das Herz der Räuber war von Stein: sie hörten nicht auf ihr Bitten und Flehen und trieben sie mit Gewalt an weiter zu gehen. Nachdem sie etwa zwei Stunden durch Stauden und Dörner sich hatten durcharbeiten müssen, kamen sie zu einem Felsen, wo eine Türe war, an welche die Räuber klopften, und die sich alsbald öffnete. Sie mussten durch einen langen dunkelen Gang und kamen endlich in eine große Höhle, die von einem Feuer, das auf dem Herd brannte, erleuchtet war. An der Wand hiengen Schwerter, Säbel und andere Mordgewehre, die in dem Lichte blinkten, und in der Mitte stand ein schwarzer Tisch, an dem vier andere Räuber saßen und spielten, und oben an saß der Hauptmann. Dieser kam, als er die Frau sah, herbei, redete sie an und sagte sie sollte nur ruhig und ohne Angst sein, sie täten ihr nichts zu Leid, aber sie müsste das Hauswesen besorgen, und wenn sie alles in Ordnung hielte, so sollte es nicht schlimm bei ihnen haben. Darauf gaben sie ihr etwas zu essen und zeigten ihr ein Bett, wo sie mit ihrem Kinde schlafen könnte.

Die Frau blieb viele Jahre bei den Räubern, und Hans ward groß und stark. Die Mutter erzählte ihm Geschichten und lehrte ihn in einem alten Ritterbuch, das sie in der Höhle fand, lesen. Als Hans neun Jahr alt war, machte er sich aus einem Tannenast einen starken Knüttel und versteckte ihn hinter das Bett: dann gieng er zu seiner Mutter und sprach »liebe Mutter, sage mir jetzt einmal wer mein Vater ist, ich will und muss es wissen.« Die Mutter schwieg still und wollte es ihm nicht sagen, damit er nicht das Heimweh bekäme: sie wusste auch dass die gottlosen Räu-

ber den Hans doch nicht fortlassen würden; aber es hätte
ihr fast das Herz zersprengt, dass Hans nicht sollte zu seinem Vater kommen. In der Nacht, als die Räuber von ihrem Raubzug heimkehrten, holte Hans seinen Knüttel hervor, stellte sich vor den Hauptmann und sagte »jetzt will
ich wissen wer mein Vater ist, und wenn du mir's nicht
gleich sagst, so schlag ich dich nieder.« Da lachte der
Hauptmann und gab dem Hans eine Ohrfeige, dass er unter den Tisch kugelte. Hans machte sich wieder auf,
schwieg und dachte »ich will noch ein Jahr warten und es
dann noch einmal versuchen, vielleicht geht's besser.« Als
das Jahr herum war, holte er seinen Knüttel wieder hervor,
wischte den Staub ab, betrachtete ihn und sprach »es ist ein
tüchtiger wackerer Knüttel.« Nachts kamen die Räuber
heim, tranken Wein, einen Krug nach dem anderen, und
fiengen an die Köpfe zu hängen. Da holte der Hans seinen
Knüttel herbei, stellte sich wieder vor den Hauptmann und
fragte ihn wer sein Vater wäre. Der Hauptmann gab ihm
abermals eine so kräftige Ohrfeige, dass Hans unter den
Tisch rollte, aber es dauerte nicht lange, so war er wieder
oben und schlug mit seinem Knüttel auf den Hauptmann
und die Räuber, dass sie Arme und Beine nicht mehr regen
konnten. Die Mutter stand in einer Ecke und war voll Verwunderung über seine Tapferkeit und Stärke. Als Hans mit
seiner Arbeit fertig war, gieng er zu seiner Mutter und sagte »jetzt ist mir's Ernst gewesen, aber jetzt muss ich auch
wissen wer mein Vater ist.« »Lieber Hans«, antwortete die
Mutter, »komm wir wollen gehen und ihn suchen bis wir
ihn finden.« Sie nahm dem Hauptmann den Schlüssel zu
der Eingangstüre ab, und Hans holte einen großen Mehl-
sack, packte Gold, Silber und was er sonst noch für schöne
Sachen fand, zusammen, bis er voll war, und nahm ihn
dann auf den Rücken. Sie verließen die Höhle, aber was tat
Hans die Augen auf, als er aus der Finsternis heraus in das
Tageslicht kam, und den grünen Wald, Blumen und Vögel
und die Morgensonne am Himmel erblickte. Er stand da

und staunte alles an, als wenn er nicht recht gescheit wäre. Die Mutter suchte den Weg nach Haus, und als sie ein paar Stunden gegangen waren, so kamen sie glücklich in ihr einsames Tal und zu ihrem Häuschen. Der Vater saß unter der Türe, er weinte vor Freude als er seine Frau erkannte und hörte dass Hans sein Sohn war, die er beide längst für tot gehalten hatte. Aber Hans, obgleich erst zwölf Jahr alt, war doch einen Kopf größer als sein Vater. Sie giengen zusammen in das Stübchen, aber kaum hatte Hans seinen Sack auf die Ofenbank gesetzt, so fieng das ganze Haus an zu krachen, die Bank brach ein und dann auch der Fußboden, und der schwere Sack sank in den Keller hinab. »Gott behüte uns«, rief der Vater »was ist das? jetzt hast du unser Häuschen zerbrochen.« »Lasst euch keine graue Haare darüber wachsen, lieber Vater«, antwortete Hans, »da in dem Sack steckt mehr als für ein neues Haus nötig ist.« Der Vater und Hans fiengen auch gleich an ein neues Haus zu bauen, Vieh zu erhandeln und Land zu kaufen und zu wirtschaften. Hans ackerte die Felder, und wenn er hinter dem Pflug gieng und ihn in die Erde hinein schob, so hatten die Stiere fast nicht nötig zu ziehen. Den nächsten Frühling sagte Hans »Vater, behaltet alles Geld und lasst mir einen zentnerschweren Spazierstab machen, damit ich in die Fremde gehen kann.« Als der verlangte Stab fertig war, verließ er seines Vaters Haus, zog fort und kam in einen tiefen und finstern Wald. Da hörte er etwas knistern und knastern, schaute um sich und sah eine Tanne, die von unten bis oben wie ein Seil gewunden war: und wie er die Augen in die Höhe richtete, so erblickte er einen großen Kerl, der den Baum gepackt hatte und ihn wie eine Weidenrute umdrehte. »He!« rief Hans, »was machst du da droben?« Der Kerl antwortete »ich habe gestern Reiswellen zusammen getragen und will mir ein Seil dazu drehen.« »Das lass ich mir gefallen«, dachte Hans, »der hat Kräfte«, und rief ihm zu, »lass du das gut sein und komm mit mir.« Der Kerl kletterte von oben herab, und war einen ganzen

Kopf größer als Hans, und der war doch auch nicht klein.
»Du heißest jetzt Tannendreher« sagte Hans zu ihm. Sie
giengen darauf weiter und hörten etwas klopfen und häm-
mern, so stark dass bei jedem Schlag der Erdboden zitterte.
Bald darauf kamen sie zu einem mächtigen Felsen, vor dem
stand ein Riese und schlug mit der Faust große Stücke davon ab. Als Hans fragte was er da vor hätte, antwortete er
»wenn ich Nachts schlafen will, so kommen Bären, Wölfe
und anderes Ungeziefer der Art, die schnuppern und
schnuffeln an mir herum und lassen mich nicht schlafen, da
will ich mir ein Haus bauen und mich hinein legen, damit
ich Ruhe habe.« »Ei ja wohl«, dachte Hans, »den kannst
du auch noch brauchen« und sprach zu ihm »lass das
Hausbauen gut sein und geh mit mir, du sollst der Felsenklipperer heißen.« Er willigte ein, und sie strichen alle drei
durch den Wald hin und wo sie hinkamen, da wurden die
wilden Tiere aufgeschreckt und liefen vor ihnen weg.
Abends kamen sie in ein altes verlassenes Schloss, stiegen
hinauf und legten sich in den Saal schlafen. Am andern
Morgen gieng Hans hinab in den Garten, der war ganz
verwildert und stand voll Dörner und Gebüsch. Und wie
er so herum gieng, sprang ein Wildschwein auf ihn los: er
gab ihm aber mit seinem Stab einen Schlag dass es gleich
niederfiel. Dann nahm er es auf die Schulter und brachte es
hinauf; da steckten sie es an einen Spieß, machten sich einen Braten zurecht und waren guter Dinge. Nun verabredeten sie dass jeden Tag, der Reihe nach zwei auf die Jagd
gehen sollten und einer daheim bleiben und kochen, für jeden neun Pfund Fleisch. Den ersten Tag blieb der Tannendreher daheim und Hans und der Felsenklipperer giengen
auf die Jagd. Als der Tannendreher beim Kochen beschäftigt war, kam ein kleines altes zusammengeschrumpeltes
Männchen zu ihm auf das Schloss, und forderte Fleisch.
»Pack dich, Duckmäuser«, antwortete er, »du brauchst
kein Fleisch.« Aber wie verwunderte sich der Tannendreher, als das kleine unscheinbare Männlein an ihm hinauf

sprang und mit Fäusten so auf ihn losschlug, dass er sich
nicht wehren konnte, zur Erde fiel und nach Atem
schnappte. Das Männlein gieng nicht eher fort, als bis es
seinen Zorn völlig an ihm ausgelassen hatte. Als die zwei
andern von der Jagd heimkamen, sagte ihnen der Tannendreher nichts von dem alten Männchen und den Schlägen,
die er bekommen hatte und dachte »wenn sie daheim bleiben, so können sie's auch einmal mit der kleinen Kratz-
bürste versuchen«, und der bloße Gedanke machte ihm
schon Vergnügen. Den folgenden Tag blieb der Steinklip-
perer daheim, und dem gieng es gerade so wie dem Tannendreher, er ward von dem Männlein übel zugerichtet,
weil er ihm kein Fleisch hatte geben wollen. Als die andern
Abends nach Haus kamen, sah es ihm der Tannendreher
wohl an was er erfahren hatte, aber beide schwiegen still
und dachten »der Hans muss auch von der Suppe kosten.«
Der Hans, der den nächsten Tag daheim bleiben musste,
tat seine Arbeit in der Küche, wie sich's gebührte, und als
er oben stand und den Kessel abschaumte, kam das Männchen und forderte ohne weiteres ein Stück Fleisch. Da
dachte Hans »es ist ein armer Wicht, ich will ihm von meinem Anteil geben, damit die andern nicht zu kurz kommen« und reichte ihm ein Stück Fleisch. Als es der Zwerg
verzehrt hatte, verlangte er nochmals Fleisch, und der gutmütige Hans gab es ihm und sagte da wäre noch ein schönes Stück, damit sollte er zufrieden sein. Der Zwerg forderte aber zum drittenmal. »Du wirst unverschämt« sagte
Hans und gab ihm nichts. Da wollte der boshafte Zwerg
an ihm hinaufspringen und ihn wie den Tannendreher und
Felsenklipperer behandeln, aber er kam an den unrechten.
Hans gab ihm, ohne sich anzustrengen, ein paar Hiebe,
dass er die Schlosstreppe hinabsprang. Hans wollte ihm
nachlaufen, fiel aber, so lang er war, über ihn hin. Als er
sich wieder aufgerichtet hatte, war ihm der Zwerg voraus.
Hans eilte ihm bis in den Wald nach und sah wie er in eine
Felsenhöhle schlüpfte. Hans kehrte nun heim, hatte sich

aber die Stelle gemerkt. Die beiden andern, als sie nach Haus kamen, wunderten sich dass Hans so wohl auf war. Er erzählte ihnen was sich zugetragen hatte, und da verschwiegen sie nicht länger wie es ihnen ergangen war. Hans lachte und sagte »es ist euch ganz recht, warum seid ihr so geizig mit eurem Fleisch gewesen, aber es ist eine Schande, ihr seid so groß und habt euch von dem Zwerge Schläge geben lassen.« Sie nahmen darauf Korb und Seil und giengen alle drei zu der Felsenhöhle, in welche der Zwerg geschlüpft war, und ließen den Hans mit seinem Stab im Korb hinab. Als Hans auf dem Grund angelangt war, fand er eine Türe, und als er sie öffnete, saß da eine bildschöne Jungfrau, nein so schön, dass es nicht zu sagen ist, und neben ihr saß der Zwerg und grinste den Hans an wie eine Meerkatze. Sie aber war mit Ketten gebunden und blickte ihn so traurig an, dass Hans großes Mitleid empfand und dachte »du musst sie aus der Gewalt des bösen Zwerges erlösen«, und gab ihm einen Streich mit seinem Stab, dass er tot niedersank. Alsbald fielen die Ketten von der Jungfrau ab, und Hans war wie verzückt über ihre Schönheit. Sie erzählte ihm, sie wäre eine Königstochter, die ein wilder Graf aus ihrer Heimat geraubt und hier in den Felsen eingesperrt hätte, weil sie nichts von ihm hätte wissen wollen: den Zwerg aber hätte der Graf zum Wächter gesetzt und er hätte ihr Leid und Drangsal genug angetan. Darauf setzte Hans die Jungfrau in den Korb und ließ sie hinauf ziehen. Der Korb kam wieder herab, aber Hans traute den beiden Gesellen nicht und dachte »sie haben sich schon falsch gezeigt und dir nichts von dem Zwerg gesagt, wer weiß was sie gegen dich im Schild führen.« Da legte er seinen Stab in den Korb, und das war sein Glück, denn als der Korb halb in der Höhe war, ließen sie ihn fallen, und hätte Hans wirklich darin gesessen, so wäre es sein Tod gewesen. Aber nun wusste er nicht wie er sich aus der Tiefe herausarbeiten sollte und wie er hin und her dachte, er fand keinen Rat. »Es ist doch traurig«, sagte er

»dass du da unten verschmachten sollst.« Und als er so auf und abgieng, kam er wieder zu dem Kämmerchen, wo die Jungfrau gesessen hatte, und sah dass der Zwerg einen Ring am Finger hatte, der glänzte und schimmerte. Da zog er ihn ab und steckte ihn an, und als er ihn am Finger umdrehte, so hörte er plötzlich etwas über seinem Kopf rauschen. Er blickte in die Höhe und sah da Luftgeister schweben, die sagten er wäre ihr Herr und fragten was sein Begehren wäre. Hans war anfangs ganz verstummt, dann aber sagte er sie sollten ihn hinauf tragen. Augenblicklich gehorchten sie, und es war nicht anders als flöge er hinauf. Als er aber oben war, so war kein Mensch mehr zu sehen, und als er in das Schloss gieng, so fand er auch dort niemand. Der Tannendreher und der Felsenklipperer waren fortgeeilt und hatten die schöne Jungfrau mit geführt. Aber Hans drehte den Ring, da kamen die Luftgeister und sagten ihm die zwei wären auf dem Meer. Hans lief und lief in einem fort bis er zu dem Meeresstrand kam, da erblickte er weit weit auf dem Wasser ein Schiffchen, in welchem seine treulosen Gefährten saßen. Und im heftigen Zorn sprang er, ohne sich zu besinnen, mit samt seinem Stab ins Wasser und fieng an zu schwimmen, aber der zentnerschwere Stab zog ihn tief hinab, dass er fast ertrunken wäre. Da drehte er noch zu rechter Zeit den Ring, alsbald kamen die Luftgeister und trugen ihn, so schnell wie der Blitz, in das Schiffchen. Da schwang er seinen Stab und gab den bösen Gesellen den verdienten Lohn und warf sie hinab ins Wasser; dann aber ruderte er mit der schönen Jungfrau, die in den größten Ängsten gewesen war und die er zum zweiten Male befreit hatte, heim zu ihrem Vater und ihrer Mutter, und ward mit ihr verheiratet, und haben alle sich gewaltig gefreut.

167.

Das Bürle im Himmel.

's isch emol es arms fromms Bürle gstorbe, und chunt do vor d' Himmelspforte. Zur gliche Zit isch au e riche riche Herr do gsi und het au i Himmel welle. Do chunt der heilige Petrus mit em Schlüssel und macht uf und lot der Herr ine; das Bürle het er aber, wie's schint, nid gseh und macht d' Pforte ämel wieder zue. Do het das Bürle vorusse ghört wie de Herr mit alle Freude im Himmel uf gno worde isch, und wie se drin musiziert und gsunge händ. Ändle isch es do wider still worde, und der heilig Petrus chunt, macht d' Himmelspforte uf un lot das Bürle au ine. 's Bürle het do gmeint 's werd jetzt au musiziert und gsunge, wenn es chöm, aber do isch alles still gsi; me het's frile mit aller Liebe ufgno, und d' Ängele sind em egäge cho, aber gsunge het niemer (niemand). Do frogt das Bürle der heilig Petrus worum das me be em nid singe wie be dem riche Herr, 's geu, schint's, do im Himmel au parteiisch zue wie uf der Erde. Do säit der heilig Petrus »nai wäger, du bisch is so lieb wie alle andere und muesch alle himmlische Freude gnieße wie de rich Herr, aber lueg, so arme Bürle, wie du äis bisch, chömme alle Tag e Himmel, so ne riche Herr aber chunt nume alle hundert Johr öppe äine.«

168.

Die hagere Liese.

Ganz anders als der faule Heinz und die dicke Trine, die sich von nichts aus ihrer Ruhe bringen ließen, dachte die hagere Liese. Sie äscherte sich ab von Morgen bis Abend und lud ihrem Mann, dem langen Lenz, so viel Arbeit auf, dass er schwerer zu tragen hatte als ein Esel an drei Säcken. Es war aber alles umsonst, sie hatten nichts und kamen zu nichts. Eines Abends, als sie im Bette lag und vor Müdigkeit kaum ein Glied regen konnte, ließen sie die Gedanken doch nicht einschlafen. Sie stieß ihren Mann mit dem Ellenbogen in die Seite und sprach »hörst du, Lenz, was ich gedacht habe? wenn ich einen Gulden fände, und einer mir geschenkt würde, so wollte ich einen dazu borgen, und du solltest mir auch noch einen geben: so bald ich dann die vier Gulden beisammen hätte, so wollte ich eine junge Kuh kaufen.« Dem Mann gefiel das recht gut, »ich weiß zwar nicht«, sprach er, »woher ich den Gulden nehmen soll, den du von mir willst geschenkt haben, aber wenn du dennoch das Geld zusammenbringst, und du kannst dafür eine Kuh kaufen, so tust du wohl, wenn du dein Vorhaben ausführst. Ich freue mich«, fügte er hinzu, »wenn die Kuh ein Kälbchen bringt, so werde ich doch manchmal zu meiner Erquickung einen Trunk Milch erhalten.« »Die Milch ist nicht für dich«, sagte die Frau, »wir lassen das Kalb saugen, damit es groß und fett wird, und wir es gut verkaufen können.« »Freilich«, antwortete der Mann, »aber ein wenig Milch nehmen wir doch, das schadet nichts.« »Wer hat dich gelehrt mit Kühen umgehen?« sprach die Frau, »es mag schaden oder nicht, ich will es nicht haben: und wenn du dich auf den Kopf stellst, du kriegst keinen Tropfen Milch. Du langer Lenz, weil du nicht zu ersättigen bist, meinst du du wolltest verzehren was ich mit Mühe erwerbe.« »Frau«, sagte der Mann, »sei still, oder ich hänge dir eine Maultasche an.« »Was«, rief sie, »du willst mir drohen, du Nimmersatt, du Strick, du fauler Heinz.« Sie wollte ihm in die Haare fallen, aber der lange Lenz richtete sich auf, packte mit der einen Hand die dürren Arme der hageren Liese zusammen, mit der andern drückte er ihr den Kopf auf das Kissen, ließ sie schimpfen und hielt sie so lange bis sie vor großer Müdigkeit eingeschlafen war. Ob sie am andern Morgen beim Erwachen fortfuhr zu zanken, oder ob sie ausgieng den Gulden zu suchen, den sie finden wollte, das weiß ich nicht.

169.
Das Waldhaus.

Ein armer Holzhauer lebte mit seiner Frau und drei Töchtern in einer kleinen Hütte an dem Rande eines einsamen Waldes. Eines Morgens, als er wieder an seine Arbeit wollte, sagte er zu seiner Frau, »lass mir mein Mittagsbrot von dem ältesten Mädchen hinaus in den Wald bringen, ich werde sonst nicht fertig. Und damit es sich nicht verirrt«, setzte er hinzu, »so will ich einen Beutel mit Hirsen mitnehmen und die Körner auf den Weg streuen.« Als nun die Sonne mitten über dem Walde stand, machte sich das Mädchen mit einem Topf voll Suppe auf den Weg. Aber die Feld- und Waldsperlinge, die Lerchen und Finken, Amseln und Zeisige hatten den Hirsen schon längst aufgepickt, und das Mädchen konnte die Spur nicht finden. Da gieng es auf gut Glück immer fort, bis die Sonne sank und die Nacht einbrach. Die Bäume rauschten in der Dunkelheit, die Eulen schnarrten, und es fieng an ihm angst zu werden. Da erblickte es in der Ferne ein Licht, das zwischen den Bäumen blinkte. »Dort sollten wohl Leute wohnen«, dachte es, »die mich über Nacht behalten«, und gieng auf das Licht zu. Nicht lange so kam es an ein Haus, dessen Fenster erleuchtet waren. Es klopfte an, und eine rauhe Stimme rief von innen »herein.« Das Mädchen trat auf die dunkle Diele, und pochte an der Stubentür. »Nur herein« rief die Stimme, und als es öffnete, saß da ein alter eisgrauer Mann an dem Tisch, hatte das Gesicht auf die beiden Hände gestützt, und sein weißer Bart floss über den Tisch herab fast bis auf die Erde. Am Ofen aber lagen drei Tiere, ein Hühnchen, ein Hähnchen und eine buntgescheckte Kuh. Das Mädchen erzählte dem Alten sein Schicksal und bat um ein Nachtlager. Der Mann sprach

»schön Hühnchen,
schön Hähnchen,

und du schöne bunte Kuh,
was sagst du dazu?«

»duks!« antworteten die Tiere: und das musste wohl heißen
»wir sind es zufrieden«, denn der Alte sprach weiter »hier
ist Hülle und Fülle, geh hinaus an den Herd und koch uns
ein Abendessen.« Das Mädchen fand in der Küche Überfluss an allem und kochte eine gute Speise, aber an die Tiere
dachte es nicht. Es trug die volle Schüssel auf den Tisch,
setzte sich zu dem grauen Mann, aß und stillte seinen Hunger. Als es satt war, sprach es »aber jetzt bin ich müde, wo
ist ein Bett, in das ich mich legen und schlafen kann?« Die
Tiere antworteten

»du hast mit ihm gegessen,
du hast mit ihm getrunken,
du hast an uns gar nicht gedacht,
nun sieh auch wo du bleibst die Nacht.«

Da sprach der Alte »steig nur die Treppe hinauf, so wirst
du eine Kammer mit zwei Betten finden, schüttle sie auf
und decke sie mit weißem Linnen so will ich auch kommen
und mich schlafen legen.« Das Mädchen stieg hinauf, und
als es die Betten geschüttelt und frisch gedeckt hatte, legte
es sich in das eine, ohne weiter auf den Alten zu warten.
Nach einiger Zeit aber kam der graue Mann, beleuchtete
das Mädchen mit dem Licht und schüttelte mit dem Kopf.
Und als er sah dass es fest eingeschlafen war, öffnete er eine
Falltüre und ließ es in den Keller sinken.
Der Holzhauer kam am späten Abend nach Haus und
machte seiner Frau Vorwürfe, dass sie ihn den ganzen Tag
habe hungern lassen. »Ich habe keine Schuld« antwortete
sie, »das Mädchen ist mit dem Mittagsessen hinausgegan-
gen, es muss sich verirrt haben: morgen wird es schon wiederkommen.« Vor Tag aber stand der Holzhauer auf, wollte in den Wald und verlangte die zweite Tochter sollte ihm
diesmal das Essen bringen. »Ich will einen Beutel mit Linsen mitnehmen«, sagte er, »die Körner sind größer als Hirsen, das Mädchen wird sie besser sehen und kann den Weg

nicht verfehlen.« Zur Mittagszeit trug auch das Mädchen die Speise hinaus, aber die Linsen waren verschwunden: die Waldvögel hatten sie, wie am vorigen Tag, aufgepickt und keine übrig gelassen. Das Mädchen irrte im Walde umher bis es Nacht ward, da kam es ebenfalls zu dem Haus des Alten, ward hereingerufen, und bat um Speise und Nachtlager. Der Mann mit dem weißen Barte fragte wieder die Tiere

>schön Hühnchen,

schön Hähnchen,

und du schöne bunte Kuh,

was sagst du dazu?«

Die Tiere antworteten abermals »duks«, und es geschah alles wie am vorigen Tag. Das Mädchen kochte eine gute Speise, aß und trank mit dem Alten und kümmerte sich nicht um die Tiere. Und als es sich nach seinem Nachtlager erkundigte, antworteten sie

»du hast mit ihm gegessen,

du hast mit ihm getrunken,

du hast an uns gar nicht gedacht,

nun sieh auch wo du bleibst die Nacht.«

Als es eingeschlafen war, kam der Alte, betrachtete es mit Kopfschütteln und ließ es in den Keller hinab.

Am dritten Morgen sprach der Holzhacker zu seiner Frau »schicke mir heute unser jüngstes Kind mit dem Essen hinaus, das ist immer gut und gehorsam gewesen, das wird auf dem rechten Weg bleiben und nicht wie seine Schwestern, die wilden Hummeln, herum schwärmen.« Die Mutter wollte nicht und sprach »soll ich mein liebstes Kind auch noch verlieren?« »Sei ohne Sorge«, antwortete er, »das Mädchen verirrt sich nicht, es ist zu klug und verständig; zum Überfluss will ich Erbsen mitnehmen, und ausstreuen, die sind noch größer als Linsen und werden ihm den Weg zeigen.« Aber als das Mädchen mit dem Korb am Arm hinaus kam, so hatten die Waldtauben die Erbsen schon im Kropf, und es wusste nicht wohin es sich wenden sollte. Es

war voll Sorgen und dachte beständig daran wie der arme
Vater hungern und die gute Mutter jammern würde, wenn
es ausbliebe. Endlich als es finster ward, erblickte es das
Lichtchen und kam an das Waldhaus. Es bat ganz freundlich sie möchten es über Nacht beherbergen, und der Mann
mit dem weißen Bart fragte wieder seine Tiere

>>schön Hühnchen,
schön Hähnchen,
und du schöne bunte Kuh,
was sagst du dazu?<<

>>duks<< sagte sie. Da trat das Mädchen an den Ofen, wo die
Tiere lagen, und liebkoste Hühnchen und Hähnchen, indem
es mit der Hand über die glatten Federn hinstrich, und die
bunte Kuh kraute es zwischen den Hörnern. Und als es auf
Geheiß des Alten eine gute Suppe bereitet hatte und die
Schüssel auf dem Tisch stand, so sprach es >>soll ich mich sättigen und die guten Tiere sollen nichts haben? Draußen ist
die Hülle und Fülle, erst will ich für sie sorgen.<< Da ging es,
holte Gerste und streute sie dem Hühnchen und Hähnchen
vor, und brachte der Kuh wohlriechendes Heu einen ganzen
Arm voll. >>Lassts euch schmecken, ihr lieben Tiere<<, sagte
es, >>und wenn ihr durstig seid, sollt ihr auch einen frischen
Trunk haben.<< Dann trug es einen Eimer voll Wasser herein,
und Hühnchen und Hähnchen sprangen auf den Rand,
steckten den Schnabel hinein und hielten den Kopf dann in
die Höhe wie die Vögel trinken, und die bunte Kuh tat auch
einen herzhaften Zug. Als die Tiere gefüttert waren, setzte
sich das Mädchen zu dem Alten an den Tisch und aß was er
ihm übrig gelassen hatte. Nicht lange so fieng Hühnchen
und Hähnchen an das Köpfchen zwischen die Flügel zu stecken, und die bunte Kuh blinzelte mit den Augen. Da sprach
das Mädchen >>sollen wir uns nicht zur Ruhe begeben?

schön Hühnchen,
schön Hähnchen,
und du schöne bunte Kuh,
was sagst du dazu?<<

Die Tiere antworteten »duks,

    du hast mit uns gegessen,

    du hast mit uns getrunken,

    du hast uns alle wohl bedacht,

    wir wünschen dir eine gute Nacht.«

Da gieng das Mädchen die Treppe hinauf, schüttelte die Federkissen und deckte frisches Linnen auf, und als es fertig war, kam der Alte und legte sich in das eine Bett, und sein weißer Bart reichte ihm bis an die Füße. Das Mädchen legte sich in das andere, tat sein Gebet und schlief ein.

Es schlief ruhig bis Mitternacht, da ward es so unruhig in dem Hause, dass das Mädchen erwachte. Da fieng es an in den Ecken zu knittern und zu knattern, und die Türe sprang auf und schlug an die Wand: die Balken dröhnten, als wenn sie aus ihren Fugen gerissen würden, und es war als wenn die Treppe herab stürzte, und endlich krachte es als wenn das ganze Dach zusammen fiele. Da es aber wieder still ward und dem Mädchen nichts zu Leid geschah, so blieb es ruhig liegen und schlief wieder ein. Als es aber am Morgen bei hellem Sonnenschein aufwachte, was erblickten seine Augen? Es lag in einem großen Saal, und rings umher glänzte alles in königlicher Pracht: an den Wänden wuchsen auf grün seidenem Grund goldene Blumen in die Höhe, das Bett war von Elfenbein und die Decke darauf von rotem Samt, und auf einem Stuhl daneben standen ein paar mit Perlen gestickte Pantoffel. Das Mädchen glaubte es wäre ein Traum, aber es traten drei reichgekleidete Diener herein und fragten was es zu befehlen hätte. »Geht nur«, antwortete das Mädchen, »ich will gleich aufstehen und dem Alten eine Suppe kochen und dann auch schön Hühnchen, schön Hähnchen und die schöne bunte Kuh füttern.« Es dachte der Alte wäre schon aufgestanden und sah sich nach seinem Bette um, aber er lag nicht darin, sondern ein fremder Mann. Und als es ihn betrachtete und sah dass er jung und schön war, erwachte er, richtete sich auf und sprach »ich bin ein Königssohn, und war von einer bösen

Hexe verwünscht worden als ein alter eisgrauer Mann in
dem Wald zu leben: niemand durfte um mich sein als meine
drei Diener in der Gestalt eines Hühnchens eines Hähn-
chens und einer bunten Kuh. Und nicht eher sollte die Ver-
wünschung aufhören, als bis ein Mädchen zu uns käme, so
gut von Herzen, dass es nicht gegen die Menschen allein,
sondern auch gegen die Tiere sich liebreich bezeigte, und
das bist du gewesen, und heute um Mitternacht sind wir
durch dich erlöst und das alte Waldhaus ist wieder in meinen königlichen Palast verwandelt worden.« Und als sie
aufgestanden waren, sagte der Königssohn den drei Dienern sie sollten hinfahren und Vater und Mutter des Mädchens zur Hochzeitsfeier herbei holen. »Aber wo sind meine zwei Schwestern?« fragte das Mädchen. »Die habe ich in
den Keller gesperrt, und Morgen sollen sie in den Wald geführt werden und sollen bei einem Köhler so lange als
Mägde dienen, bis sie sich gebessert haben und auch die armen Tiere nicht hungern lassen.«

170.

Lieb und Leid teilen.

Es war einmal ein Schneider, der war ein zänkischer
Mensch, und seine Frau, die gut, fleißig und fromm war,
konnte es ihm niemals recht machen. Was sie tat, er war
unzufrieden, brummte, schalt, raufte und schlug sie. Als die
Obrigkeit endlich davon hörte, ließ sie ihn vorfordern und
ins Gefängnis setzen, damit er sich bessern sollte. Er saß
eine Zeitlang bei Wasser und Brot, dann wurde er wieder
freigelassen, musste aber geloben seine Frau nicht mehr zu
schlagen, sondern friedlich mit ihr zu leben, Lieb und Leid
zu teilen, wie sich's unter Eheleuten gebührt. Eine Zeitlang
gieng es gut, dann aber geriet er wieder in seine alte Weise,

war mürrisch und zänkisch. Und weil er sie nicht schlagen durfte, wollte er sie bei den Haaren packen und raufen. Die Frau entwischte ihm und sprang auf den Hof hinaus, er lief aber mit der Elle und Schere hinter ihr her, jagte sie herum und warf ihr die Elle und Schere, und was ihm sonst zur Hand war, nach. Wenn er sie traf, so lachte er, und wenn er sie fehlte, so tobte und wetterte er. Er trieb es so lange bis die Nachbaren der Frau zu Hilfe kamen. Der Schneider ward wieder vor die Obrigkeit gerufen und an sein Versprechen erinnert. »Liebe Herrn«, antwortete er, »ich habe gehalten was ich gelobt habe, ich habe sie nicht geschlagen, sondern Lieb und Leid mit ihr geteilt.« »Wie kann das sein«, sprach der Richter, »da sie abermals so große Klage über Euch führt?« »Ich habe sie nicht geschlagen, sondern ihr nur, weil sie so wunderlich aussah, die Haare mit der Hand kämmen wollen: sie ist mir aber entwichen und hat mich böslich verlassen. Da bin ich ihr nachgeeilt und habe, damit sie zu ihrer Pflicht zurückkehre, als eine gutgemeinte Erinnerung nachgeworfen was mir eben zur Hand war. Ich habe auch Lieb und Leid mit ihr geteilt, denn so oft ich sie getroffen habe, ist es mir lieb gewesen und ihr leid: habe ich sie aber gefehlt, so ist es ihr lieb gewesen, mir aber leid.« Die Richter waren aber mit dieser Antwort nicht zufrieden, sondern ließen ihm seinen verdienten Lohn auszahlen.

171.

Der Zaunkönig.

In den alten Zeiten da hatte jeder Klang noch Sinn und Bedeutung. Wenn der Hammer des Schmieds ertönte, so rief er »smiet mi to! smiet mi to!« Wenn der Hobel des Tischlers schnarrte, so sprach er »dor häst! dor, dor häst!« Fieng das Räderwerk der Mühle an zu klappern, so sprach es

»help, Herr Gott! help, Herr Gott!« und war der Müller
ein Betrüger, und ließ die Mühle an, so sprach sie hoch-
deutsch und fragte erst langsam »wer ist da? wer ist da?«
dann antwortete sie schnell »der Müller! der Müller!« und
endlich ganz geschwind »stiehlt tapfer, stiehlt tapfer, vom
Achtel drei Sechter.«

Zu dieser Zeit hatten auch die Vögel ihre eigene Sprache, die
jedermann verstand, jetzt lautet es nur wie ein Zwitschern,
Kreischen und Pfeifen, und bei einigen wie Musik ohne
Worte. Es kam aber den Vögeln in den Sinn, sie wollten
nicht länger ohne Herrn sein und einen unter sich zu ihrem
König wählen. Nur einer von ihnen, der Kibitz, war dagegen: frei hatte er gelebt und frei wollte er sterben, und angstvoll hin und her fliegend rief er »wo bliew ick? wo bliew
ick?« Er zog sich zurück in einsame und unbesuchte Sümpfe
und zeigte sich nicht wieder unter Seinesgleichen.

Die Vögel wollten sich nun über die Sache besprechen, und
an einem schönen Maimorgen kamen sie alle aus Wäldern
und Feldern zusammen, Adler und Buchfinke, Eule und
Krähe, Lerche und Sperling, was soll ich sie alle nennen?
selbst der Kuckuck kam und der Wiedehopf, sein Küster,
der so heißt, weil er sich immer ein paar Tage früher hören
lässt; auch ein ganz kleiner Vogel, der noch keinen Namen
hatte, mischte sich unter die Schar. Das Huhn, das zufällig
von der ganzen Sache nichts gehört hatte, verwunderte sich
über die große Versammlung. »Wat, wat, wat is den dar to
don?« gackerte es, aber der Hahn beruhigte seine liebe
Henne und sagte »luter riek Lüd«, erzählte ihr auch was sie
vor hätten. Es ward aber beschlossen dass der König sein
sollte, der am höchsten fliegen könnte. Ein Laubfrosch, der
im Gebüsche saß, rief, als er das hörte, warnend »natt, natt,
natt! natt, natt, natt!« weil er meinte es würden deshalb viel
Tränen vergossen werden. Die Krähe aber sagte »Quark
ok!«, es sollte alles friedlich abgehen.

Es ward nun beschlossen, sie wollten gleich an diesem
schönen Morgen aufsteigen, damit niemand hinterher sagen

könnte »ich wäre wohl noch höher geflogen, aber der Abend kam, da konnte ich nicht mehr.« Auf ein gegebenes Zeichen erhob sich also die ganze Schar in die Lüfte. Der Staub stieg da von dem Felde auf, es war ein gewaltiges Sausen und Brausen und Fittichschlagen, und es sah aus als wenn eine schwarze Wolke dahin zöge. Die kleinern Vögel aber blieben bald zurück, konnten nicht weiter und fielen wieder auf die Erde. Die größern hielten's länger aus, aber keiner konnte es dem Adler gleich tun, der stieg so hoch dass er der Sonne hätte die Augen aushacken können. Und als er sah dass die andern nicht zu ihm herauf konnten, so dachte er »was willst du noch höher fliegen, du bist doch der König«, und fieng an sich wieder herab zu lassen. Die Vögel unter ihm riefen ihm alle gleich zu »du musst unser König sein, keiner ist höher geflogen als du.« »Ausgenommen ich« schrie der kleine Kerl ohne Namen, der sich in die Brustfedern des Adlers verkrochen hatte. Und da er nicht müde war, so stieg er auf und stieg so hoch, dass er Gott auf seinem Stuhle konnte sitzen sehen. Als er aber so weit gekommen war, legte er seine Flügel zusammen, sank herab und rief unten mit feiner durchdringender Stimme »König bün ick! König bün ick!«

»Du unser König?« schrien die Vögel zornig, »durch Ränke und Listen hast du es dahin gebracht.« Sie machten eine andere Bedingung, der sollte ihr König sein, der am tiefsten in die Erde fallen könnte. Wie klatschte da die Gans mit ihrer breiten Brust wieder auf das Land! Wie scharrte der Hahn schnell ein Loch! Die Ente kam am schlimmsten weg, sie sprang in einen Graben, verrenkte sich aber die Beine und watschelte fort zum nahen Teiche mit dem Ausruf »Pracherwerk! Pracherwerk!« Der Kleine ohne Namen aber suchte ein Mäuseloch, schlüpfte hinab und rief mit seiner feinen Stimme heraus »König bün ick! König bün ick!«

»Du unser König?« riefen die Vögel noch zorniger, »meinst du deine Listen sollten gelten?« Sie beschlossen ihn in seinem Loch gefangen zu halten und auszuhungern. Die Eule ward als Wache davor gestellt: sie sollte den Schelm nicht heraus lassen, so lieb ihr das Leben wäre. Als es aber Abend geworden war und die Vögel von der Anstrengung beim Fliegen große Müdigkeit empfanden, so giengen sie mit Weib und Kind zu Bett. Die Eule allein blieb bei dem Mäuseloch stehen und blickte mit ihren großen Augen unverwandt hinein. Indessen war sie auch müde geworden und dachte »ein Auge kannst du wohl zu tun, du wachst ja noch mit dem andern, und der kleine Bösewicht soll nicht aus seinem Loch heraus.« Also tat sie das eine Auge zu und schaute mit dem andern steif auf das Mäuseloch. Der kleine Kerl guckte mit dem Kopf heraus und wollte wegwitschen, aber die Eule trat gleich davor, und er zog den Kopf wieder zurück. Dann tat die Eule das eine Auge wieder auf und das andere zu, und wollte so die ganze Nacht abwechseln. Aber als sie das eine Auge wieder zu machte, vergaß sie das andere aufzutun, und sobald die beiden Augen zu waren, schlief sie ein. Der Kleine merkte das bald und schlüpfte weg.

Von der Zeit an darf sich die Eule nicht mehr am Tage sehen lassen, sonst sind die andern Vögel hinter ihr her und zerzausen ihr das Fell. Sie fliegt nur zur Nachtzeit aus, hasst aber und verfolgt die Mäuse, weil sie solche böse Löcher machen. Auch der kleine Vogel lässt sich nicht gerne sehen, weil er fürchtet es gienge ihm an den Kragen, wenn er erwischt würde. Er schlüpft in den Zäunen herum, und wenn er ganz sicher ist, ruft er wohl zuweilen »König bün ick!« und deshalb nennen ihn die andern Vögel aus Spott *Zaunkönig*.

Niemand aber war froher als die Lerche, dass sie dem Zaunkönig nicht zu gehorchen brauchte. Wie sich die Sonne blicken lässt, steigt sie in die Lüfte und ruft »ach, wo ist dat schön! schön is dat! schön! schön! ach, wo is dat schön!«

172.

Die Scholle.

Die Fische waren schon lange unzufrieden dass keine Ordnung in ihrem Reich herrschte. Keiner kehrte sich an den
andern, schwamm rechts und links, wie es ihm einfiel, fuhr
zwischen denen durch, die zusammenbleiben wollten, oder
sperrte ihnen den Weg, und der stärkere gab dem schwä-
cheren einen Schlag mit dem Schwanz, dass er weit weg
fuhr, oder er verschlang ihn ohne weiteres. »Wie schön
wäre es, wenn wir einen König hätten, der Recht und Ge-
rechtigkeit bei uns übte« sagten sie, und vereinigten sich
den zu ihrem Herren zu wählen, der am schnellsten die
Fluten durchstreichen und dem Schwachen Hilfe bringen
könnte.

Sie stellten sich also am Ufer in Reihe und Glied auf, und
der Hecht gab mit dem Schwanz ein Zeichen, worauf sie
alle zusammen aufbrachen. Wie ein Pfeil schoss der Hecht
dahin und mit ihm der Hering, der Gründling, der Barsch,
die Karpfe, und wie sie alle heißen. Auch die Scholle
schwamm mit und hoffte das Ziel zu erreichen.

Auf einmal ertönte der Ruf »der Hering ist vor! der Hering
ist vor.« »Wen is vör?« schrie verdrießlich die platte miss-
günstige Scholle, die weit zurückgeblieben war, »wen is
vör?« »Der Hering, der Hering« war die Antwort. »De
nackte Hiering?« rief die neidische, »de nackte Hiering?«
Seit der Zeit steht der Scholle zur Strafe das Maul schief.

173.

Rohrdommel und Wiedehopf.

»Wo weidet ihr eure Herde am liebsten?« fragte einer einen
alten Kuhhirten. »Hier, Herr, wo das Gras nicht zu fett ist
und nicht zu mager; es tut sonst kein gut.« »Warum nicht?«
fragte der Herr. »Hört ihr dort von der Wiese her den
dumpfen Ruf?« antwortete der Hirt, »das ist der Rohrdommel, der war sonst ein Hirte und der Wiedehopf war es
auch. Ich will euch die Geschichte erzählen.
Der Rohrdommel hütete seine Herde auf fetten grünen Wiesen, wo Blumen im Überfluss standen, davon wurden seine
Kühe mutig und wild. Der Wiedehopf aber trieb das Vieh
auf hohe dürre Berge, wo der Wind mit dem Sand spielt, und
seine Kühe wurden mager und kamen nicht zu Kräften.
Wenn es Abend war und die Hirten heimwärts trieben,
konnte Rohrdommel seine Kühe nicht zusammenbringen,
sie waren übermütig und sprangen ihm davon. Er rief ›bunt,
herüm‹ (bunte Kuh, herum), doch vergebens, sie hörten
nicht auf seinen Ruf. Wiedehopf aber konnte sein Vieh nicht
auf die Beine bringen, so matt und kraftlos war es geworden.
›Up, up, up!‹ schrie er, aber es half nicht, sie blieben auf dem
Sand liegen. So geht's wenn man kein Maß hält. Noch heute,
wo sie keine Herde mehr hüten, schreit Rohrdommel ›bunt,
herüm‹, und der Wiedehopf ›up, up, up!‹«

174.

Die Eule.

Vor ein paar hundert Jahren, als die Leute noch lange nicht
so klug und verschmitzt waren, als sie heutzutage sind, hat
sich in einer kleinen Stadt eine seltsame Geschichte zuge-

tragen. Von Ungefähr war eine von den großen Eulen, die man Schuhu nennt, aus dem benachbarten Walde bei nächtlicher Weile in die Scheuer eines Bürgers geraten und wagte sich, als der Tag anbrach, aus Furcht vor den andern Vögeln, die wenn sie sich blicken lässt, ein furchtbares Geschrei erheben, nicht wieder aus ihrem Schlupfwinkel heraus. Als nun der Hausknecht Morgens in die Scheuer kam um Stroh zu holen, erschrak er bei dem Anblick der Eule, die da in einer Ecke saß, so gewaltig, dass er fortlief und seinem Herrn ankündigte ein Ungeheuer, wie er Zeit seines Lebens keins erblickt hätte, säße in der Scheuer, drehte die Augen im Kopf herum und könnte einen ohne Umstände verschlingen. »Ich kenne dich schon«, sagte der Herr, »einer Amsel im Felde nachzujagen, dazu hast du Mut genug, aber wenn du ein totes Huhn liegen siehst, so holst du dir erst einen Stock, ehe du ihm nahe kommst. Ich muss nur selbst einmal nachsehen was das für ein Ungeheuer ist« setzte der Herr hinzu, gieng ganz tapfer zur Scheuer hinein und blickte umher. Als er aber das seltsame und greuliche Tier mit eigenen Augen sah, so geriet er in nicht geringere Angst als der Knecht. Mit ein paar Sätzen sprang er hinaus, lief zu seinen Nachbarn und bat sie flehentlich ihm gegen ein unbekanntes und gefährliches Tier Beistand zu leisten; ohnehin könnte die ganze Stadt in Gefahr kommen, wenn es aus der Scheuer, wo es säße, herausbräche. Es entstand großer Lärm und Geschrei in allen Straßen: die Bürger kamen mit Spießen Heugabeln Sensen und Äxten bewaffnet herbei als wollten sie gegen den Feind ausziehen: zuletzt erschienen auch die Herrn des Rats mit dem Bürgermeister an der Spitze. Als sie sich auf dem Markt geordnet hatten, zogen sie zu der Scheuer und umringten sie von allen Seiten. Hierauf trat einer der beherztesten hervor und gieng mit gefälltem Spieß hinein, kam aber gleich darauf mit einem Schrei und totenbleich wieder heraus gelaufen, und konnte kein Wort hervor bringen. Noch zwei andere wagten sich hinein, es ergieng ihnen aber nicht besser. Endlich

trat einer hervor, ein großer starker Mann, der wegen seiner
Kriegstaten berühmt war, und sprach »mit bloßen Ansehen
werdet ihr das Ungetüm nicht vertreiben, hier muss Ernst
gebraucht werden, aber ich sehe dass ihr alle zu Weibern
geworden seid und keiner den Fuchs beißen will.« Er ließ
sich Harnisch Schwert und Spieß bringen, und rüstete sich.
Alle rühmten seinen Mut, obgleich viele um sein Leben besorgt waren. Die beiden Scheuertore wurden aufgetan, und
man erblickte die Eule, die sich indessen in die Mitte auf einen großen Querbalken gesetzt hatte. Er ließ eine Leiter
herbeibringen, und als er sie anlegte und sich bereitete hin-
aufzusteigen, so riefen ihm alle zu er solle sich männlich
halten, und empfahlen ihn dem heiligen Georg, der den
Drachen getötet hatte. Als er bald oben war, und die Eule
sah dass er an sie wollte, auch von der Menge und dem Geschrei des Volks verwirrt war und nicht wusste wohinaus,
so verdrehte sie die Augen, sträubte die Federn, sperrte die
Flügel auf, gnappte mit dem Schnabel und ließ ihr schuhu,
schuhu mit rauher Stimme hören. »Stoß zu, stoß zu!« rief
die Menge draußen dem tapfern Helden zu. »Wer hier stände, wo ich stehe«, antwortete er, »der würde nicht ›Stoß zu‹
rufen.« Er setzte zwar den Fuß noch eine Staffel höher,
dann aber fieng er an zu zittern und machte sich halb ohnmächtig auf den Rückweg.
Nun war keiner mehr übrig, der sich in die Gefahr hätte
begeben wollen. »Das Ungeheuer«, sagten sie, »hat den
stärksten Mann, der unter uns zu finden war, durch sein
Gnappen und Anhauchen allein vergiftet und tödlich ver-
wundet, sollen wir andern auch unser Leben in die Schanze
schlagen?« Sie ratschlagten was zu tun wäre, wenn die ganze Stadt nicht sollte zu Grunde gehen. Lange Zeit schien alles vergeblich, bis endlich der Bürgermeister einen Ausweg
fand. »Meine Meinung geht dahin«, sprach er, »dass wir aus
gemeinem Säckel diese Scheuer samt allem, was darin liegt,
Getreide Stroh und Heu, dem Eigentümer bezahlen und
ihn schadlos halten, dann aber das ganze Gebäude und mit

ihm das fürchterliche Tier abbrennen, so braucht doch niemand sein Leben daran zu setzen. Hier ist keine Gelegenheit zu sparen, und Knauserei wäre übel angewendet.« Alle stimmten ihm bei. Also ward die Scheuer an vier Ecken angezündet, und mit ihr die Eule jämmerlich verbrannt. Wer's nicht glauben will, der gehe hin und frage selbst nach.

175.

Der Mond.

Vorzeiten gab es ein Land, wo die Nacht immer dunkel und der Himmel wie ein schwarzes Tuch darüber gebreitet war, denn es gieng dort niemals der Mond auf, und kein Stern blinkte in der Finsternis. Bei Erschaffung der Welt hatte das nächtliche Licht nicht ausgereicht. Aus diesem Land giengen einmal vier Bursche auf die Wanderschaft und gelangten in ein anderes Reich, wo Abends, wenn die Sonne hinter den Bergen verschwunden war, auf einem Eichbaum eine leuchtende Kugel stand, die weit und breit ein sanftes Licht ausgoss. Man konnte dabei alles wohl sehen und unterscheiden, wenn es auch nicht so glänzend wie die Sonne war. Die Wanderer standen still und fragten einen Bauer, der da mit seinem Wagen vorbei fuhr, was das für ein Licht sei. »Das ist der Mond«, antwortete dieser, »unser Schultheiß hat ihn für drei Taler gekauft und an den Eichbaum befestigt. Er muss täglich Öl aufgießen und ihn rein erhalten, damit er immer hell brennt. Dafür erhält er von uns wöchentlich einen Taler.«

Als der Bauer weggefahren war, sagte der eine von ihnen »diese Lampe könnten wir brauchen, wir haben daheim einen Eichbaum, der eben so groß ist, daran können wir sie hängen. Was für eine Freude, wenn wir Nachts nicht in der Finsternis herum tappen!« »Wisst ihr was?« sprach der

zweite, »wir wollen Wagen und Pferde holen und den
Mond wegführen. Sie können sich hier einen andern kaufen.« »Ich kann gut klettern«, sprach der dritte, »ich will
ihn schon herunter holen.« Der vierte brachte einen Wagen
mit Pferden herbei, und der dritte stieg den Baum hinauf,
bohrte ein Loch in den Mond, zog ein Seil hindurch und
ließ ihn herab. Als die glänzende Kugel auf dem Wagen lag,
deckten sie ein Tuch darüber, damit niemand den Raub bemerken sollte. Sie brachten ihn glücklich in ihr Land und
stellten ihn auf eine hohe Eiche. Alte und junge freuten
sich, als die neue Lampe ihr Licht über alle Felder leuchten
ließ und Stuben und Kammern damit erfüllte. Die Zwerge
kamen aus den Felsenhöhlen hervor, und die kleinen Wich-
telmänner tanzten in ihren roten Röckchen auf den Wiesen
den Ringeltanz.

Die vier versorgten den Mond mit Öl, putzten den Docht
und erhielten wöchentlich ihren Taler. Aber sie wurden alte
Greise, und als der eine erkrankte und seinen Tod voraus
sah, verordnete er dass der vierte Teil des Mondes als sein Eigentum ihm mit in das Grab sollte gegeben werden. Als er
gestorben war, stieg der Schultheiß auf den Baum und
schnitt mit der Heckenschere ein Viertel ab, das in den Sarg
gelegt ward. Das Licht des Mondes nahm ab, aber noch nicht
merklich. Als der zweite starb, ward ihm das zweite Viertel
mitgegeben und das Licht minderte sich. Noch schwächer
ward es nach dem Tod des dritten, der gleichfalls seinen Teil
mitnahm, und als der vierte ins Grab kam, trat die alte Finsternis wieder ein. Wenn die Leute Abends ohne Laterne ausgiengen, stießen sie mit den Köpfen zusammen.

Als aber die Teile des Monds in der Unterwelt sich wieder
vereinigten, so wurden dort, wo immer Dunkelheit ge-
herrscht hatte, die Toten unruhig und erwachten aus ihrem
Schlaf. Sie erstaunten als sie wieder sehen konnten: das
Mondlicht war ihnen genug, denn ihre Augen waren so
schwach geworden, dass sie den Glanz der Sonne nicht ertragen hätten. Sie erhoben sich, wurden lustig und nahmen

ihre alte Lebensweise wieder an. Ein Teil gieng zum Spiel und Tanz, andere liefen in die Wirtshäuser, wo sie Wein forderten, sich betranken, tobten und zankten, und endlich ihre Knüttel aufhoben und sich prügelten. Der Lärm ward immer ärger und drang endlich bis in den Himmel hinauf.

Der heil. Petrus, der das Himmelstor bewacht, glaubte die Unterwelt wäre in Aufruhr geraten und rief die himmlischen Heerscharen zusammen, die den bösen Feind, wenn er mit seinen Gesellen den Aufenthalt der Seligen stürmen wollte, zurück jagen sollten. Da sie aber nicht kamen, so setzte er sich auf sein Pferd und ritt durch das Himmelstor hinab in die Unterwelt. Da brachte er die Toten zur Ruhe, hieß sie sich wieder in ihre Gräber legen und nahm den Mond mit fort, den er oben am Himmel aufhieng.

176.

Die Lebenszeit.

Als Gott die Welt geschaffen hatte und allen Kreaturen ihre Lebenszeit bestimmen wollte, kam der Esel und fragte »Herr, wie lange soll ich leben?« »Dreißig Jahre«, antwortete Gott, »ist dir das recht?« »Ach Herr«, erwiderte der Esel, »das ist eine lange Zeit. Bedenke mein mühseliges Dasein: von Morgen bis in die Nacht schwere Lasten tragen, Kornsäcke in die Mühle schleppen, damit andere das Brot essen, mit nichts als mit Schlägen und Fußtritten ermuntert und aufgefrischt zu werden! erlass mir einen Teil der langen Zeit.« Da erbarmte sich Gott und schenkte ihm achtzehn Jahre. Der Esel gieng getröstet weg und der Hund erschien. »Wie lange willst du leben?« sprach Gott zu ihm, »dem Esel sind dreißig Jahre zu viel, du aber wirst damit zufrieden sein.« »Herr«, antwortete der Hund, »ist das dein Wille? bedenke was ich laufen muss, das halten meine Füße so lange nicht aus; und habe ich erst die Stimme zum Bellen verloren und die Zähne zum Beißen, was bleibt mir übrig als aus einer Ecke in die andere zu laufen und zu knurren?« Gott sah dass er recht hatte und erließ ihm zwölf Jahre. Darauf kam der Affe. »Du willst wohl gerne dreißig Jahre leben?« sprach der Herr zu ihm, »du brauchst nicht zu arbeiten, wie der Esel und der Hund, und bist immer guter Dinge.« »Ach Herr«, antwortete er, »das sieht so aus, ist aber anders. Wenn's Hirsenbrei regnet, habe ich keinen Löffel. Ich soll immer lustige Streiche machen, Gesichter schneiden damit die Leute lachen, und wenn sie mir einen Apfel reichen und ich beiße hinein, so ist er sauer. Wie oft steckt die Traurigkeit hinter dem Spaß! Dreißig Jahre halte ich das nicht aus.« Gott war gnädig und schenkte ihm zehn Jahre.

Endlich erschien der Mensch, war freudig, gesund und frisch und bat Gott ihm seine Zeit zu bestimmen. »Dreißig Jahre sollst du leben«, sprach der Herr, »ist dir das genug?« »Welch eine kurze Zeit!« rief der Mensch, »wenn ich mein Haus gebaut habe, und das Feuer auf meinem eigenen Herde brennt: wenn ich Bäume gepflanzt habe, die blühen und Früchte tragen, und ich meines Lebens froh zu werden gedenke, so soll ich sterben! o Herr, verlängere meine Zeit.« »Ich will dir die achtzehn Jahre des Esels zulegen« sagte Gott. »Das ist nicht genug« erwiderte der Mensch. »Du sollst auch die zwölf Jahre des Hundes haben.« »Immer noch zu wenig.« »Wohlan«, sagte Gott, »ich will dir noch die zehn Jahre des Affen geben, aber mehr erhältst du nicht.« Der Mensch gieng fort, war aber nicht zufrieden gestellt.

Also lebt der Mensch siebenzig Jahr. Die ersten dreißig sind seine menschlichen Jahre, die gehen schnell dahin; da ist er gesund heiter, arbeitet mit Lust und freut sich seines Daseins. Hierauf folgen die achtzehn Jahre des Esels, da wird ihm eine Last nach der andern aufgelegt: er muss das Korn tragen, das andere nährt, und Schläge und Tritte sind der

Lohn seiner treuen Dienste. Dann kommen die zwölf Jahre des Hundes, da liegt er in den Ecken, knurrt und hat keine Zähne mehr zum Beißen. Und wenn diese Zeit vorüber ist, so machen die zehn Jahre des Affen den Beschluss. Da ist der Mensch schwachköpfig und närrisch, treibt alberne Dinge und wird ein Spott der Kinder.

177.

Die Boten des Todes.

Vor alten Zeiten wanderte einmal ein Riese auf der großen Landstraße, da sprang ihm plötzlich ein unbekannter Mann entgegen und rief »halt! keinen Schritt weiter!« »Was«, sprach der Riese, »du Wicht, den ich zwischen den Fingern zerdrücken kann, du willst mir den Weg vertreten? Wer bist du, dass du so keck reden darfst?« »Ich bin der Tod«, erwiderte der andere, »mir widersteht niemand, und auch du musst meinen Befehlen gehorchen.« Der Riese aber weigerte sich und fieng an mit dem Tode zu ringen. Es war ein langer heftiger Kampf, zuletzt behielt der Riese die Oberhand und schlug den Tod mit seiner Faust nieder, dass er neben einen Stein zusammensank. Der Riese gieng seiner Wege, und der Tod lag da besiegt und war so kraftlos, dass er sich nicht wieder erheben konnte. »Was soll daraus werden«, sprach er, »wenn ich da in der Ecke liegen bleibe? es stirbt niemand mehr auf der Welt, und sie wird so mit Menschen angefüllt werden, dass sie nicht mehr Platz haben neben einander zu stehen.« Indem kam ein junger Mensch des Wegs, frisch und gesund, sang ein Lied und warf seine Augen hin und her. Als er den halbohnmächtigen erblickte, gieng er mitleidig heran, richtete ihn auf, flößte ihm aus seiner Flasche einen stärkenden Trank ein und wartete bis er wieder zu Kräften kam. »Weißt du auch«, fragte der Fremde, indem er sich aufrichtete, »wer ich bin, und wem du wieder auf die Beine geholfen hast?« »Nein«, antwortete der Jüngling, »ich kenne dich nicht.« »Ich bin der Tod«, sprach er, »ich verschone niemand und kann auch mit dir keine Ausnahme machen. Damit du aber siehst dass ich dankbar bin, so verspreche ich dir dass ich dich nicht unversehens überfalle sondern dir erst meine Boten senden will, bevor ich komme und dich abhole.« »Wohlan«, sprach der Jüngling, »immer ein Gewinn, dass ich weiß wann du kommst und so lange wenigstens sicher vor dir bin.« Dann zog er weiter, war lustig und guter Dinge und lebte in den Tag hinein. Allein Jugend und Gesundheit hielten nicht lange aus, bald kamen Krankheiten und Schmerzen, die ihn bei Tag plagten und ihm Nachts die Ruhe wegnahmen. »Sterben werde ich nicht«, sprach er zu sich selbst, »denn der Tod sendet erst seine Boten, ich wollte nur die bösen Tage der Krankheit wären erst vorüber.« Sobald er sich gesund fühlte, fieng er wieder an in Freuden zu leben. Da klopfte ihn eines Tages jemand auf die Schulter: er blickte sich um, und der Tod stand hinter ihm und sprach »folge mir, die Stunde deines Abschieds von der Welt ist gekommen.« »Wie«, antwortete der Mensch, »willst du dein Wort brechen? hast du mir nicht versprochen dass du mir, bevor du selbst kämest, deine Boten senden wolltest? ich habe keinen gesehen.« »Schweig«, erwiderte der Tod, »habe ich dir nicht einen Boten über den andern geschickt? kam nicht das Fieber, stieß dich an, rüttelte dich und warf dich nieder? hat der Schwindel dir nicht den Kopf betäubt? zwickte dich nicht die Gicht in allen Gliedern? brauste dir's nicht in den Ohren? nagte nicht der Zahnschmerz in deinen Backen? ward dir's nicht dunkel vor den Augen? Über das alles, hat nicht mein leiblicher Bruder, der Schlaf, dich jeden Abend an mich erinnert? lagst du nicht in der Nacht, als wärst du schon gestorben?« Der Mensch wusste nichts zu erwidern, ergab sich in sein Geschick und gieng mit dem Tode fort.

178

Meister Pfriem.

Meister Pfriem war ein kleiner hagerer aber lebhafter Mann, der keinen Augenblick Ruhe hatte. Sein Gesicht, aus dem nur die aufgestülpte Nase vorragte, war pockennarbig und leichenblass, sein Haar grau und struppig, seine Augen klein, aber sie blitzten unaufhörlich rechts und links hin. Er bemerkte alles, tadelte alles, wusste alles besser und hatte in allem Recht. Gieng er auf der Straße, so ruderte er heftig mit beiden Armen, und einmal schlug er einem Mädchen, das Wasser trug, den Eimer so hoch in die Luft, dass er selbst davon begossen ward. »Schafskopf«, rief er ihr zu indem er sich schüttelte, »konntest du nicht sehen dass ich hinter dir herkam?« Seines Handwerks war er ein Schuster, und wenn er arbeitete, so fuhr er mit dem Draht so gewaltig aus, dass er jedem, der sich nicht weit genug in der Ferne hielt, die Faust in den Leib stieß. Kein Geselle blieb länger als einen Monat bei ihm, denn er hatte an der besten Arbeit immer etwas auszusetzen. Bald waren die Stiche nicht gleich, bald war ein Schuh länger, bald ein Absatz höher als der andere, bald war das Leder nicht hinlänglich geschlagen. »Warte« sagte er zu dem Lehrjungen, »ich will dir schon zeigen wie man die Haut weich schlägt«, holte den Riemen und gab ihm ein paar Hiebe über den Rücken. Faulenzer nannte er sie alle. Er selber brachte aber doch nicht viel vor sich, weil er keine Viertelstunde ruhig sitzen blieb. War seine Frau frühmorgens aufgestanden und hatte Feuer angezündet, so sprang er aus dem Bett und lief mit bloßen Füßen in die Küche. »Wollt ihr mir das Haus anzünden?« schrie er, »das ist ja ein Feuer, dass man einen Ochsen dabei braten könnte! oder kostet das Holz etwa kein Geld?« Standen die Mägde am Waschfass, lachten und erzählten sich was sie wussten, so schalt er sie aus, »da stehen die Gänse und schnattern und vergessen über dem Ge-

schwätz ihre Arbeit. Und wozu die frische Seife? heillose
Verschwendung und obendrein eine schändliche Faulheit:
sie wollen die Hände schonen und das Zeug nicht ordentlich reiben.« Er sprang fort, stieß aber einen Eimer voll
Lauge um, so dass die ganze Küche überschwemmt ward.
Richtete man ein neues Haus auf, so lief er ans Fenster und
sah zu. »Da vermauern sie wieder den roten Sandstein«,
rief er, »der niemals austrocknet; in dem Haus bleibt kein
Mensch gesund. Und seht einmal wie schlecht die Gesellen
die Steine aufsetzen. Der Mörtel taugt auch nichts: Kies
muss hinein, nicht Sand. Ich erlebe noch dass den Leuten
das Haus über dem Kopf zusammenfällt.« Er setzte sich
und tat ein paar Stiche, dann sprang er wieder auf, hakte
sein Schurzfell los und rief »ich will nur hinaus und den
Menschen ins Gewissen reden.« Er geriet aber an die Zim-
merleute. »Was ist das?« rief er, »ihr haut ja nicht nach der
Schnur. Meint ihr die Balken würden gerad stehen? es
weicht einmal alles aus den Fugen.« Er riss einem Zimmer-
mann die Axt aus der Hand und wollte ihm zeigen wie er
hauen müsste, als aber ein mit Lehm beladener Wagen her-
angefahren kam, warf er die Axt weg und sprang zu dem
Bauer, der neben her gieng. »Ihr seid nicht recht bei Trost«,
rief er, »wer spannt junge Pferde vor einen schwer beladenen Wagen? die armen Tiere werden euch auf dem Platz
umfallen.« Der Bauer gab ihm keine Antwort, und Pfriem
lief vor Ärger in seine Werkstätte zurück. Als er sich wieder zur Arbeit setzen wollte, reichte ihm der Lehrjunge einen Schuh. »Was ist das wieder?« schrie er ihn an, »habe
ich euch nicht gesagt ihr solltet die Schuhe nicht so weit
ausschneiden? wer wird einen solchen Schuh kaufen an
dem fast nichts ist als die Sohle? ich verlange dass meine
Befehle unmangelhaft befolgt werden.« »Meister«, antwortete der Lehrjunge, »ihr mögt wohl Recht haben, dass der
Schuh nichts taugt, aber es ist derselbe, den ihr zugeschnit-
ten und selbst in Arbeit genommen habt. Als ihr vorhin
aufgesprungen seid, habt ihr ihn vom Tisch herabgeworfen,

und ich habe ihn nur aufgehoben. Euch könnte es aber ein Engel vom Himmel nicht recht machen.«

Meister Pfriem träumte in einer Nacht er wäre gestorben und befände sich auf dem Weg nach dem Himmel. Als er anlangte, klopfte er heftig an die Pforte: »es wundert mich«, sprach er, »dass sie nicht einen Ring am Tor haben, man klopft sich die Knöchel wund.« Der Apostel Petrus öffnete und wollte sehen wer so ungestüm Einlass begehrte. »Ach, ihr seid's, Meister Pfriem«, sagte er, »ich will euch wohl einlassen, aber ich warne euch dass ihr von eurer Gewohnheit ablasst und nichts tadelt, was ihr im Himmel seht: es könnte euch übel bekommen.« »Ihr hättet euch die Ermahnung sparen können«, erwiderte Pfriem, »ich weiß schon was sich ziemt, und hier ist, Gott sei Dank, alles vollkommen und nichts zu tadeln, wie auf Erden.« Er trat also ein und gieng in den weiten Räumen des Himmels auf und ab. Er sah sich um, rechts und links, schüttelte aber zuweilen mit dem Kopf oder brummte etwas vor sich hin. Indem erblickte er zwei Engel, die einen Balken wegtrugen. Es war der Balken, den einer im Auge gehabt hatte, während er nach dem Splitter in den Augen anderer suchte. Sie trugen aber den Balken nicht der Länge nach, sondern quer. »Hat man je eine solchen Unverstand gesehen?« dachte Meister Pfriem; doch schwieg er und gab sich zufrieden: »es ist im Grunde einerlei, wie man den Balken trägt, gerade aus oder quer, wenn man nur damit durchkommt, und wahrhaftig ich sehe sie stoßen nirgend an.« Bald hernach erblickte er zwei Engel, welche Wasser aus einem Brunnen in ein Fass schöpften, zugleich bemerkte er, dass das Fass durchlöchert war und das Wasser von allen Seiten herauslief. Sie tränkten die Erde mit Regen. »Alle Hagel!« platzte er heraus, besann sich aber glücklicherweise und dachte »vielleicht ist's bloßer Zeitvertreib; macht's einem Spaß, so kann man dergleichen unnütze Dinge tun, zumal hier im Himmel, wo man, wie ich schon bemerkt habe, doch nur faulenzt.« Er gieng weiter und sah einen Wagen, der in einem tiefen Loch stecken geblieben war. »Kein Wunder«, sprach er zu dem Mann, der dabei stand, »wer wird so unvernünftig aufladen? was habt ihr da?« »Fromme Wünsche«, antwortete der Mann, »ich konnte damit nicht auf den rechten Weg kommen, aber ich habe den Wagen noch glücklich herauf geschoben, und hier werden sie mich nicht stecken lassen.« Wirklich kam ein Engel und spannte zwei Pferde vor. »Ganz gut«, meinte Pfriem, »aber zwei Pferde bringen den Wagen nicht heraus, viere müssen wenigstens davor.« Ein anderer Engel kam und führte noch zwei Pferde herbei, spannte sie aber nicht vorn sondern hinten an. Das war dem Meister Pfriem zu viel. »Talpatsch«, brach er los, »was machst du da? hat man je, so lange die Welt steht, auf diese Weise einen Wagen herausgezogen? Da meinen sie aber in ihrem dünkelhaften Übermut alles besser zu wissen.« Er wollte weiter reden, aber einer von den Himmelsbewohnern hatte ihn am Kragen gepackt und schob ihn mit unwiderstehlicher Gewalt hinaus. Unter der Pforte drehte der Meister noch einmal den Kopf nach dem Wagen und sah wie er von vier Flügelpferden in die Höhe gehoben ward.

In diesem Augenblick erwachte Meister Pfriem. »Es geht freilich im Himmel etwas anders her, als auf Erden«, sprach er zu sich selbst, »und da lässt sich manches entschuldigen, aber wer kann geduldig mit ansehen dass man die Pferde zugleich hinten und vorn anspannt? freilich sie hatten Flügel, aber wer kann das wissen? Es ist übrigens eine gewaltige Dummheit Pferden, die vier Beine zum Laufen haben, noch ein paar Flügel anzuheften. Aber ich muss aufstehen, sonst machen sie mir im Haus lauter verkehrtes Zeug. Es ist nur ein Glück, dass ich nicht wirklich gestorben bin.«

179

Die Gänsehirtin am Brunnen.

Es war einmal ein steinaltes Mütterchen, das lebte mit seiner Herde Gänse in einer Einöde zwischen Bergen und hatte da ein kleines Haus. Die Einöde war von einem großen Wald umgeben, und jeden Morgen nahm die Alte ihre Krücke und wackelte in den Wald. Da war aber das Mütterchen ganz geschäftig, mehr als man ihm bei seinen hohen Jahren zugetraut hätte, sammelte Gras für seine Gänse, brach sich das wilde Obst ab, so weit es mit den Händen reichen konnte, und trug alles auf seinem Rücken heim. Man hätte meinen sollen die schwere Last müsste sie zu Boden drücken, aber sie brachte sie immer glücklich nach Haus. Wenn ihr jemand begegnete, so grüßte sie ganz freundlich, »guten Tag, lieber Landsmann, heute ist schönes Wetter. Ja, ihr wundert euch dass ich das Gras schleppe, aber jeder muss seine Last auf den Rücken nehmen.« Doch die Leute begegneten ihr nicht gerne und nahmen lieber einen Umweg, und wenn ein Vater mit seinem Knaben an ihr vorübergieng, so sprach er leise zu ihm »nimm dich in Acht vor der Alten, die hat's faustdick hinter den Ohren: es ist eine Hexe.«

Eines Morgens gieng ein hübscher junger Mann durch den Wald. Die Sonne schien hell, die Vögel sangen, und ein kühles Lüftchen strich durch das Laub, und er war voll Freude und Lust. Noch war ihm kein Mensch begegnet, als er plötzlich die alte Hexe erblickte, die am Boden auf den Knien saß und Gras mit einer Sichel abschnitt. Eine ganze Last hatte sie schon in ihr Tragtuch geschoben, und daneben standen zwei Körbe, die mit wilden Birnen und Äpfeln angefüllt waren. »Aber, Mütterchen«, sprach er, »wie kannst du das alles fortschaffen?« »Ich muss sie tragen, lieber Herr«, antwortete sie, »reicher Leute Kinder brauchen es nicht. Aber beim Bauer heißt's

    schau dich nicht um,
    dein Buckel ist krumm.«
»Wollt ihr mir helfen?« sprach sie, als er bei ihr stehen
blieb, »ihr habt noch einen geraden Rücken und junge Beine, es wird euch ein leichtes sein. Auch ist mein Haus nicht
so weit von hier: hinter dem Berge dort steht es auf einer
Heide. Wie bald seid ihr da hinaufgesprungen.« Der junge
Mann empfand Mitleiden mit der Alten, »zwar ist mein Vater kein Bauer«, antwortete er, »sondern ein reicher Graf,
aber damit ihr seht dass die Bauern nicht allein tragen können, so will ich euer Bündel aufnehmen.« »Wollt ihr's versuchen«, sprach sie, »so soll mir's lieb sein. Eine Stunde
weit werdet ihr freilich gehen müssen, aber was macht euch
das aus! Dort die Äpfel und Birnen müsst ihr auch tragen.«
Es kam dem jungen Grafen doch ein wenig bedenklich vor,
als er von einer Stunde Wegs hörte, aber die Alte ließ ihn
nicht wieder los, packte ihm das Tragtuch auf den Rücken
und hieng ihm die beiden Körbe an den Arm. »Seht ihr, es
geht ganz leicht«, sagte sie. »Nein es geht nicht leicht« antwortete der Graf und machte ein schmerzliches Gesicht,
»der Bündel drückt ja so schwer, als wären lauter Wackersteine darin, und die Äpfel und Birnen haben ein Gewicht,
als wären sie von Blei; ich kann kaum atmen.« Er hatte
Lust alles wieder abzulegen, aber die Alte ließ es nicht zu.
»Seht einmal«, sprach sie spöttisch, »der junge Herr will
nicht tragen was ich alte Frau schon so oft fortgeschleppt
habe. Mit schönen Worten sind sie bei der Hand, aber
wenn's Ernst wird, so wollen sie sich aus dem Staub machen. Was steht ihr da«, fuhr sie fort, »und zaudert, hebt
die Beine auf. Es nimmt euch niemand den Bündel wieder
ab.« So lange er auf ebener Erde gieng, war's noch auszuhalten, aber als sie an den Berg kamen und steigen mussten,
und die Steine hinter seinen Füßen hinabrollten, als wären
sie lebendig, da gieng's über seine Kräfte. Die Schweißtropfen standen ihm auf der Stirne und liefen ihm bald heiß
bald kalt über den Rücken hinab. »Mütterchen«, sagte er,

»ich kann nicht weiter, ich will ein wenig ruhen.« »Nichts da«, antwortete die Alte, »wenn wir angelangt sind, so könnt ihr ausruhen, aber jetzt müsst ihr vorwärts. Wer weiß wozu euch das gut ist.« »Alte, du wirst unverschämt«, sagte der Graf und wollte das Tragtuch abwerfen, aber er bemühte sich vergeblich: es hieng so fest an seinem Rücken, als wenn es angewachsen wäre. Er drehte und wendete sich, aber er konnte es nicht wieder los werden. Die Alte lachte dazu und sprang ganz vergnügt auf ihrer Krücke herum. »Erzürnt euch nicht, lieber Herr«, sprach sie, »ihr werdet ja so rot im Gesicht, wie ein Zinshahn. Tragt euern Bündel mit Geduld, wenn wir zu Hause angelangt sind, so will ich euch schon ein gutes Trinkgeld geben.« Was wollte er machen? er musste sich in sein Schicksal fügen und geduldig hinter der Alten herschleichen. Sie schien immer flinker zu werden und ihm seine Last immer schwerer. Auf einmal tat sie einen Satz, sprang auf das Tragtuch und setzte sich oben darauf; wie zaundürre sie war, so hatte sie doch mehr Gewicht als die dickste Bauerndirne. Dem Jünglinge zitterten die Knie, aber wenn er nicht fortgieng, so schlug ihn die Alte mit einer Gerte und mit Brennesseln auf die Beine. Unter beständigem Ächzen stieg er den Berg hinauf und langte endlich bei dem Haus der Alten an, als er eben niedersinken wollte. Als die Gänse die Alte erblickten, streckten sie die Flügel in die Höhe und die Hälse voraus, liefen ihr entgegen und schrien ihr »wulle, wulle«. Hinter der Herde mit einer Rute in der Hand gieng eine bejahrte Trulle, stark und groß, aber hässlich wie die Nacht. »Frau Mutter«, sprach sie zur Alten, »ist euch etwas begegnet? ihr seid so lange ausgeblieben.« »Bewahre, mein Töchterchen«, erwiderte sie, »mir ist nichts Böses begegnet, im Gegenteil der liebe Herr da hat mir meine Last getragen; denk dir, als ich müde war, hat er mich selbst noch auf den Rücken genommen. Der Weg ist uns auch gar nicht lang geworden, wir sind lustig gewesen und haben immer Spaß miteinander gemacht.« Endlich rutschte die Alte herab, nahm dem jungen Mann den Bündel vom Rücken und die Körbe vom Arm, sah ihn ganz freundlich an und sprach »nun setzt euch auf die Bank vor die Türe und ruht euch aus. Ihr habt euern Lohn redlich verdient, der soll auch nicht ausbleiben.« Dann sprach sie zu der Gänsehirtin »geh du ins Haus hinein, mein Töchterchen, es schickt sich nicht dass du mit einem jungen Herrn allein bist, man muss nicht Öl ins Feuer gießen; er könnte sich in dich verlieben.« Der Graf wusste nicht ob er weinen oder lachen sollte. »Solch ein Schätzchen«, dachte er, »und wenn es dreißig Jahre jünger wäre, könnte doch mein Herz nicht rühren.« Indessen hätschelte und streichelte die Alte ihre Gänse wie Kinder und gieng dann mit ihrer Tochter in das Haus. Der Jüngling streckte sich auf die Bank unter einem wilden Apfelbaum. Die Luft war lau und mild: rings umher breitete sich eine grüne Wiese aus, die mit Himmelsschlüsseln, wildem Thymian und tausend andern Blumen übersät war: mitten durch rauschte ein klarer Bach, auf dem die Sonne glitzerte: und die weißen Gänse giengen auf und ab spazieren oder pudelten sich im Wasser. »Es ist recht lieblich hier«, sagte er, »aber ich bin so müde, dass ich die Augen nicht aufbehalten mag: ich will ein wenig schlafen. Wenn nur kein Windstoß kommt und bläst mir meine Beine vom Leib weg, denn sie sind mürb wie Zunder.«

Als er ein Weilchen geschlafen hatte, kam die Alte, und schüttelte ihn wach. »Steh auf«, sagte sie, »hier kannst du nicht bleiben. Freilich habe ich dir's sauer genug gemacht, aber das Leben hat's doch nicht gekostet. Jetzt will ich dir deinen Lohn geben, Geld und Gut brauchst du nicht, da hast du etwas anderes.« Damit steckte sie ihm ein Büchslein in die Hand, das aus einem einzigen Smaragd geschnitten war. »Bewahr's wohl«, setzte sie hinzu, »es wird dir Glück bringen.« Der Graf sprang auf, und da er fühlte dass er ganz frisch und wieder bei Kräften war, so dankte er der Alten für ihr Geschenk und machte sich auf den Weg ohne nach dem schönen Töchterchen auch nur einmal umzubli-

cken. Als er schon eine Strecke weg war, hörte er noch aus
der Ferne das lustige Geschrei der Gänse.

Der Graf musste drei Tage in der Wildnis herum irren, ehe
er sich heraus finden konnte. Da kam er in eine große
Stadt, und weil ihn niemand kannte, ward er in das königliche Schloss geführt, wo der König und die Königin auf
dem Thron saßen. Der Graf ließ sich auf ein Knie nieder,
zog das smaragdene Gefäß aus der Tasche und legte es der
Königin zu Füßen. Sie hieß ihn aufstehen und er musste ihr
das Büchslein hinauf reichen. Kaum aber hatte sie es geöffnet und hinein geblickt, so fiel sie wie tot zur Erde. Der
Graf ward von den Dienern des Königs festgehalten und
sollte in das Gefängnis geführt werden, da schlug die Königin die Augen auf und rief sie sollten ihn frei lassen, und jedermann sollte hinaus gehen, sie wollte insgeheim mit ihm
reden.

Als die Königin allein war, fieng sie bitterlich an zu weinen
und sprach »was hilft mir Glanz und Ehre, die mich umgeben, jeden Morgen erwache ich mit Sorgen und Kummer.
Ich habe drei Töchter gehabt, davon war die jüngste so
schön, dass sie alle Welt für ein Wunder hielt. Sie war so
weiß wie Schnee, so rot wie Apfelblüte, und ihr Haar so
glänzend wie Sonnenstrahlen. Wenn sie weinte, so fielen
nicht Tränen aus ihren Augen, sondern lauter Perlen und
Edelsteine. Als sie fünfzehn Jahr alt war, da ließ der König
alle drei Schwestern vor seinen Thron kommen. Da hättet
Ihr sehen sollen was die Leute für Augen machten, als die
jüngste eintrat, es war als wenn die Sonne aufgieng. Der
König sprach ›meine Töchter, ich weiß nicht wann mein
letzter Tag kommt, ich will heute bestimmen was eine jede
nach meinem Tode erhalten soll. Ihr alle habt mich lieb,
aber welche mich von euch am liebsten hat, die soll das
beste haben.‹ Jede sagte sie hätte ihn am liebsten. ›Könnt
ihr mir's nicht ausdrücken‹, erwiderte der König, ›wie lieb
ihr mich habt? daran werde ich's sehen wie ihr's meint.‹ Die
älteste sprach ›ich habe den Vater so lieb wie den süßesten

Zucker.‹ Die zweite ›ich habe den Vater so lieb wie mein
schönstes Kleid.‹ Die jüngste aber schwieg. Da fragte der
Vater ›und du, mein liebstes Kind, wie lieb hast du mich?‹
›Ich weiß es nicht‹, antwortete sie, ›und kann meine Liebe
mit nichts vergleichen.‹ Aber der Vater bestand darauf, sie
müsste etwas nennen. Da sagte sie endlich ›die beste Speise
schmeckt mir nicht ohne Salz, darum habe ich den Vater so
lieb wie Salz.‹ Als der König das hörte, geriet er in Zorn
und sprach ›wenn du mich so liebst als Salz, so soll deine
Liebe auch mit Salz belohnt werden.‹ Da teilte er das Reich
zwischen den beiden ältesten, der jüngsten aber ließ er einen Sack mit Salz auf den Rücken binden, und zwei
Knechte mussten sie hinaus in den wilden Wald führen.
Wir haben alle für sie gefleht und gebeten«, sagte die Königin, »aber der Zorn des Königs war nicht zu erweichen.
Wie hat sie geweint, als sie uns verlassen musste! der ganze
Weg ist mit Perlen besät worden, die ihr aus den Augen geflossen sind. Den König hat bald hernach seine große Härte
gereut und hat das arme Kind in dem ganzen Wald suchen
lassen, aber niemand konnte sie finden. Wenn ich denke
dass sie die wilden Tiere gefressen haben, so weiß ich mich
vor Traurigkeit nicht zu fassen; manchmal tröste ich mich
mit der Hoffnung, sie sei noch am Leben und habe sich in
einer Höhle versteckt oder bei mitleidigen Menschen
Schutz gefunden. Aber stellt euch vor, als ich euer Sma-
ragdbüchslein aufmachte, so lag eine Perle darin, gerade der
Art, wie sie meiner Tochter aus den Augen geflossen sind,
und da könnt ihr euch vorstellen wie mir der Anblick das
Herz bewegt hat. Ihr sollt mir sagen wie ihr zu der Perle
gekommen seid.« Der Graf erzählte ihr dass er sie von der
Alten im Walde erhalten hätte, die ihm nicht geheuer vor-
gekommen wäre, und eine Hexe sein müsste; von ihrem
Kinde aber hätte er nichts gehört und gesehen. Der König
und die Königin fassten den Entschluss die Alte aufzusuchen; sie dachten, wo die Perle gewesen wäre, da müssten
sie auch Nachricht von ihrer Tochter finden.

Die Alte saß draußen in der Einöde bei ihrem Spinnrad und
spann. Es war schon dunkel geworden, und ein Span, der
unten am Herd brannte, gab ein sparsames Licht. Auf einmal ward's draußen laut, die Gänse kamen heim von der
Weide und ließen ihr heiseres Gekreisch hören. Bald hernach trat auch die Tochter herein. Aber die Alte dankte ihr
kaum und schüttelte nur ein wenig mit dem Kopf. Die
Tochter setzte sich zu ihr nieder, nahm ihr Spinnrad und
drehte den Faden so flink wie ein junges Mädchen. So saßen beide zwei Stunden, und sprachen kein Wort mit einander. Endlich raschelte etwas am Fenster und zwei feurige
Augen glotzten herein. Es war eine alte Nachteule, die
dreimal uhu schrie. Die Alte schaute nur ein wenig in die
Höhe, dann sprach sie »jetzt ist's Zeit, Töchterchen, dass
du hinaus gehst, tu deine Arbeit.«
Sie stand auf und gieng hinaus. »Wo ist sie denn hingegangen?« über die Wiesen immer weiter bis in das Tal. Endlich
kam sie zu einem Brunnen, bei dem drei alte Eichbäume
standen. Der Mond war indessen rund und groß über dem
Berg aufgestiegen, und es war so hell, dass man eine Steck-
nadel hätte finden können. Sie zog eine Haut ab, die auf ihrem Gesicht lag, bückte sich dann zu dem Brunnen und
fieng an sich zu waschen. Als sie fertig war, tauchte sie auch
die Haut in das Wasser, und legte sie dann auf die Wiese,
damit sie wieder im Mondschein bleichen und trocknen
sollte. Aber wie war das Mädchen verwandelt! So was habt
ihr nie gesehen! Als der graue Zopf abfiel, da quollen die
goldenen Haare wie Sonnenstrahlen hervor und breiteten
sich, als wär's ein Mantel, über ihre ganze Gestalt. Nur die
Augen blitzten heraus so glänzend wie die Sterne am Himmel, und die Wangen schimmerten in sanfter Röte wie die
Apfelblüte.
Aber das schöne Mädchen war traurig. Es setzte sich nieder
und weinte bitterlich. Eine Träne nach der andern drang
aus seinen Augen und rollte zwischen den langen Haaren
auf den Boden. So saß es da und wäre lang sitzen geblieben,

wenn es nicht in den Ästen des nahe stehenden Baumes ge-
knittert und gerauscht hätte. Sie sprang auf wie ein Reh, das
den Schuss des Jägers vernimmt. Der Mond ward gerade
von einer schwarzen Wolke bedeckt, und im Augenblick
war das Mädchen wieder in die alte Haut geschlüpft, und
verschwand wie ein Licht, das der Wind ausbläst.

Zitternd wie ein Espenlaub lief sie zu dem Haus zurück.
Die Alte stand vor der Türe, und das Mädchen wollte ihr
erzählen was ihm begegnet war, aber die Alte lachte
freundlich und sagte »ich weiß schon alles.« Sie führte es in
die Stube und zündete einen neuen Span an. Aber sie setzte
sich nicht wieder zu dem Spinnrad, sondern sie holte einen
Besen, und fieng an zu kehren und zu scheuern. »Es muss
alles rein und sauber sein« sagte sie zu dem Mädchen.
»Aber, Mutter«, sprach das Mädchen, »warum fangt ihr in
so später Stunde die Arbeit an? was habt ihr vor?« »Weißt
du denn welche Stunde es ist?« fragte die Alte. »Noch nicht
Mitternacht«, antwortete das Mädchen, »aber schon elf
Uhr vorbei.« »Denkst du nicht daran«, fuhr die Alte fort,
»dass du heute vor drei Jahren zu mir gekommen bist? Deine Zeit ist aus, wir können nicht länger beisammen bleiben.« Das Mädchen erschrak und sagte »ach, liebe Mutter,
wollt ihr mich verstoßen? wo soll ich hin? ich habe keine
Freunde und keine Heimat, wohin ich mich wenden kann.
Ich habe alles getan was ihr verlangt habt, und ihr seid immer zufrieden mit mir gewesen: schickt mich nicht fort.«
Die Alte wollte dem Mädchen nicht sagen was ihm bevor-
stand. »Meines Bleibens ist nicht länger hier«, sprach sie zu
ihm, »wenn ich aber ausziehe, muss Haus und Stube sauber
sein: darum halt mich nicht auf in meiner Arbeit. Deinet-
wegen sei ohne Sorgen, du sollst ein Dach finden, unter
dem du wohnen kannst, und mit dem Lohn, den ich dir geben will, wirst du auch zufrieden sein.« »Aber sagt mir nur
was ist vor?« fragte das Mädchen weiter. »Ich sage dir
nochmals störe mich nicht in meiner Arbeit. Rede kein
Wort weiter, geh in deine Kammer, nimm die Haut vom

Gesicht und zieh das seidene Kleid an, das du trugst als du
zu mir kamst, und dann harre in deiner Kammer, bis ich
dich rufe.«

Aber ich muss wieder von dem König und der Königin erzählen, die mit dem Grafen ausgezogen waren und die Alte
in der Einöde aufsuchen wollten. Der Graf war Nachts in
dem Walde von ihnen abgekommen, und musste allein weiter gehen. Am andern Tag kam es ihm vor, als befände er
sich auf dem rechten Weg. Er gieng immer fort, bis die
Dunkelheit einbrach, da stieg er auf einen Baum und wollte
da übernachten, denn er war besorgt er möchte sich verirren. Als der Mond die Gegend erhellte, so erblickte er eine
Gestalt, die den Berg herabwandelte. Sie hatte keine Rute
in der Hand, aber er konnte doch sehen dass es die Gänsehirtin war, die er früher bei dem Haus der Alten gesehen
hatte. »Oho!« rief er, »da kommt sie, und habe ich erst die
eine Hexe, so soll mir die andere auch nicht entgehen.« Wie
erstaunte er aber, als sie zu dem Brunnen trat, die Haut ab-
legte und sich wusch, als die goldenen Haare über sie her-
abfielen, und sie so schön war, wie er noch niemand auf der
Welt gesehen hatte. Kaum dass er zu atmen wagte, aber er
streckte den Hals zwischen dem Laub so weit vor, als er
nur konnte, und schaute sie mit unverwandten Blicken an.
Ob er sich zu weit überbog, oder was sonst Schuld war,
plötzlich krachte der Ast, und in demselben Augenblick
schlüpfte das Mädchen in die Haut, sprang wie ein Reh davon, und da der Mond sich zugleich bedeckte, so war sie
seinen Blicken entzogen.

Kaum war sie verschwunden, so stieg der Graf von dem
Baum herab und eilte ihr mit behenden Schritten nach. Er
war noch nicht lange gegangen, so sah er in der Dämmerung zwei Gestalten über die Wiese wandeln. Es war der
König und die Königin, die hatten aus der Ferne das Licht
in dem Häuschen der Alten erblickt und waren drauf zu
gegangen. Der Graf erzählte ihnen was er für Wunderdinge
bei dem Brunnen gesehen hätte, und sie zweifelten nicht

dass das ihre verlorene Tochter gewesen wäre. Voll Freude
giengen sie weiter und kamen bald bei dem Häuschen an:
die Gänse saßen rings herum, hatten den Kopf in die Flügel
gesteckt und schliefen, und keine regte sich nicht. Sie
schauten zum Fenster hinein, da saß die Alte ganz still und
spann, nickte mit dem Kopf und sah sich nicht um. Es war
ganz sauber in der Stube, als wenn da die kleinen Nebel-
männlein wohnten, die keinen Staub auf den Füßen tragen.
Ihre Tochter aber sahen sie nicht. Sie schauten das alles eine
Zeitlang an, endlich fassten sie ein Herz und klopften leise
ans Fenster. Die Alte schien sie erwartet zu haben, sie stand
auf und rief ganz freundlich »nur herein, ich kenne euch
schon.« Als sie in die Stube eingetreten waren, sprach die
Alte »den weiten Weg hättet ihr euch sparen können, wenn
ihr euer Kind, das so gut und liebreich ist, nicht vor drei
Jahren ungerechter Weise verstoßen hättet. Ihr hat's nichts
geschadet, sie hat drei Jahre lang die Gänse hüten müssen:
sie hat nichts Böses dabei gelernt sondern ihr reines Herz
behalten. Ihr aber seid durch die Angst, in der ihr gelebt
habt, hinlänglich gestraft.« Dann gieng sie an die Kammer
und rief »komm heraus, mein Töchterchen.« Da gieng die
Türe auf, und die Königstochter trat heraus in ihrem seidenen Gewand mit ihren goldenen Haaren und ihren leuch-
tenden Augen, und es war als ob ein Engel vom Himmel
käme.
Sie gieng auf ihren Vater und ihre Mutter zu, fiel ihnen um
den Hals und küsste sie: es war nicht anders, sie mussten
alle vor Freude weinen. Der junge Graf stand neben ihnen,
und als sie ihn erblickte, ward sie so rot im Gesicht wie
eine Moosrose; sie wusste selbst nicht warum. Der König
sprach »liebes Kind, mein Königreich habe ich verschenkt,
was soll ich dir geben?« »Sie braucht nichts«, sagte die Alte,
»ich schenke ihr die Tränen, die sie um euch geweint hat,
das sind lauter Perlen, schöner als sie im Meer gefunden
werden, und sind mehr wert als euer ganzes Königreich.
Und zum Lohn für ihre Dienste gebe ich ihr mein Häus-

chen.« Als die Alte das gesagt hatte, verschwand sie vor ihren Augen. Es knatterte ein wenig in den Wänden, und als
sie sich umsahen, war das Häuschen in einen prächtigen
Palast verwandelt, und eine königliche Tafel war gedeckt,
und die Bedienten liefen hin und her.

Die Geschichte geht noch weiter, aber meiner Großmutter,
die sie mir erzählt hat, war das Gedächtnis schwach geworden: sie hatte das übrige vergessen. Ich glaube immer die
schöne Königstochter ist mit dem Grafen vermählt worden, und sie sind zusammen in dem Schloss geblieben und
haben da in aller Glückseligkeit gelebt so lange Gott wollte.
Ob die schneeweißen Gänse, die bei dem Häuschen gehütet
wurden, lauter Mädchen waren (es braucht's niemand übel
zu nehmen), welche die Alte zu sich genommen hatte, und
ob sie jetzt ihre menschliche Gestalt wieder erhielten, und
als Dienerinnen bei der jungen Königin blieben, das weiß
ich nicht genau, aber ich vermute es doch. So viel ist gewiss, dass die Alte keine Hexe war, wie die Leute glaubten,
sondern eine weise Frau, die es gut meinte. Wahrscheinlich
ist sie es auch gewesen, die der Königstochter schon bei der
Geburt die Gabe verliehen hat Perlen zu weinen statt der
Tränen. Heutzutage kommt das nicht mehr vor, sonst
könnten die Armen bald reich werden.

180.

Die ungleichen Kinder Evas.

Als Adam und Eva aus dem Paradies vertrieben waren, so
mussten sie auf unfruchtbarer Erde sich ein Haus bauen
und im Schweiße ihres Angesichts ihr Brot essen. Adam
hackte das Feld und Eva spann Wolle. Eva brachte jedes
Jahr ein Kind zur Welt, die Kinder waren aber ungleich, einige schön, andere hässlich. Nachdem eine geraume Zeit

verlaufen war, sendete Gott einen Engel an die beiden und ließ ihnen entbieten dass er kommen und ihren Haushalt schauen wollte. Eva, freudig dass der Herr so gnädig war, säuberte emsig ihr Haus, schmückte es mit Blumen und streute Binsen auf den Estrich. Dann holte sie ihre Kinder herbei, aber nur die schönen. Sie wusch und badete sie, kämmte ihnen die Haare, legte ihnen neugewaschene Hemder an und ermahnte sie in der Gegenwart des Herrn sich anständig und züchtig zu betragen. Sie sollten sich vor ihm sittig neigen, die Hand darbieten und auf seine Fragen bescheiden und verständig antworten. Die hässlichen Kinder aber sollten sich nicht sehen lassen. Das eine verbarg sie unter das Heu, das andere unter das Dach, das dritte in das Stroh, das vierte in den Ofen, das fünfte in den Keller, das sechste unter eine Kufe, das siebente unter das Weinfass, das achte unter ihren alten Pelz, das neunte und zehnte unter das Tuch, aus dem sie ihnen Kleider zu machen pflegte, und das elfte und zwölfte unter das Leder, aus dem sie ihnen die Schuhe zuschnitt. Eben war sie fertig geworden, als es an die Haustüre klopfte. Adam blickte durch eine Spalte und sah dass es der Herr war. Ehrerbietig öffnete er und der himmlische Vater trat ein. Da standen die schönen Kinder in der Reihe, neigten sich, boten ihm die Hände dar und knieten nieder. Der Herr aber fieng an sie zu segnen, legte auf den ersten seine Hände und sprach »du sollst ein gewaltiger König werden« ebenso zu dem zweiten »du ein Fürst«, zu dem dritten »du ein Graf« zu dem vierten »du ein Ritter« zu dem fünften »du ein Edelmann« zu dem sechsten »du ein Bürger« zum siebenten »du ein Kaufmann« zu dem achten »du ein gelehrter Mann«. Er erteilte ihnen also allen seinen reichen Segen. Als Eva sah dass der Herr so mild und gnädig war, dachte sie »ich will meine ungestalten Kinder herbeiholen, vielleicht dass er ihnen auch seinen Segen gibt.« Sie lief also und holte sie aus dem Heu, Stroh, Ofen, und wo sie sonst hin versteckt waren, hervor. Da kam die ganze grobe, schmutzige, grindige und rußige Schar. Der Herr lächelte, betrachtete sie alle und sprach »auch diese will ich segnen.« Er legte auf den ersten die Hände und sprach zu ihm »du sollst werden ein Bauer«, zu dem zweiten »du ein Fischer«, zu dem dritten »du ein Schmied«, zu dem vierten »du ein Lohgerber«, zu dem fünften »du ein Weber«, zu dem sechsten »du ein Schuhmacher«, zu dem siebenten »du ein Schneider«, zu dem achten »du ein Töpfer«, zu dem neunten »du ein Karrenführer«, zu dem zehnten »du ein Schiffer«, zu dem elften »du ein Bote«, zu dem zwölften »du ein Hausknecht dein Lebelang.«

Als Eva das alles mit angehört hatte, sagte sie »Herr, wie teilst du deinen Segen so ungleich! Es sind doch alle meine Kinder, die ich geboren habe: deine Gnade sollte über alle gleich ergehen.« Gott aber erwiderte »Eva, das verstehst du nicht. Mir gebührt und ist not dass ich die ganze Welt mit deinen Kindern versehe: wenn sie alle Fürsten und Herrn wären, wer sollte Korn bauen, dreschen, mahlen und backen? wer schmieden, weben, zimmern, bauen, graben, schneiden und nähen? Jeder soll seinen Stand vertreten, dass einer den andern erhalte und alle ernährt werden wie am Leib die Glieder.« Da antwortete Eva »ach, Herr, vergib, ich war zu rasch, dass ich dir einredete. Dein göttlicher Wille geschehe auch an meinen Kindern.«

181.

Die Nixe im Teich.

Es war einmal ein Müller, der führte mit seiner Frau ein vergnügtes Leben. Sie hatten Geld und Gut, und ihr Wohlstand nahm von Jahr zu Jahr noch zu. Aber Unglück kommt über Nacht: wie ihr Reichtum gewachsen war, so schwand er von Jahr zu Jahr wieder hin, und zuletzt konnte der Müller kaum noch die Mühle, in der er saß, sein Eigentum nennen. Er war voll Kummer, und wenn er sich nach der Arbeit des Tags nieder legte, so fand er keine Ruhe, sondern wälzte sich voll Sorgen in seinem Bett. Eines Morgens stand er schon vor Tagesanbruch auf, gieng hinaus ins Freie und dachte es sollte ihm leichter ums Herz werden. Als er über dem Mühldamm dahin schritt, brach eben der erste Sonnenstrahl hervor, und er hörte in dem Weiher etwas rauschen. Er wendete sich um und erblickte ein schönes Weib, das sich langsam aus dem Wasser erhob. Ihre langen Haare, die sie über den Schultern mit ihren zarten Händen gefasst hatte, flossen an beiden Seiten herab und bedeckten ihren weißen Leib. Er sah wohl dass es die Nixe des Teichs war und wusste vor Furcht nicht ob er davon gehen oder stehen bleiben sollte. Aber die Nixe ließ ihre sanfte Stimme hören, nannte ihn bei Namen und fragte warum er so traurig wäre. Der Müller war anfangs verstummt, als er sie aber so freundlich sprechen hörte, fasste er sich ein Herz und erzählte ihr dass er sonst in Glück und Reichtum gelebt hätte, aber jetzt so arm wäre, dass er sich nicht zu raten wüsste. »Sei ruhig«, antwortete die Nixe, »ich will dich reicher und glücklicher machen als du je gewesen bist, nur musst du mir versprechen dass du mir geben willst was eben in deinem Hause jung geworden ist.« »Was kann das anders sein«, dachte der Müller, »als ein junger Hund oder ein junges Kätzchen?« und sagte ihr zu was sie verlangte. Die Nixe stieg wieder in das Wasser hinab, und er eilte getröstet und gutes Mutes nach seiner Mühle. Noch hatte er sie nicht erreicht, da trat die Magd aus der Haustüre und rief ihm zu er sollte sich freuen, seine Frau hätte ihm einen kleinen Knaben geboren. Der Müller stand wie vom Blitz gerührt, er sah wohl dass die tückische Nixe das gewusst und ihn betrogen hatte. Mit gesenktem Haupt trat er zu dem Bett seiner Frau, und als sie ihn fragte »warum freust du dich nicht über den schönen Knaben?« so erzählte er ihr was ihm begegnet war und was für ein Versprechen er der Nixe gegeben hatte. »Was hilft mir Glück und Reichtum«, fügte er hinzu, »wenn ich mein Kind verlieren soll? aber was kann ich tun?« Auch die Verwandten, die herbeigekommen waren, Glück zu wünschen, wussten keinen Rat.

Indessen kehrte das Glück in das Haus des Müllers wieder ein. Was er unternahm gelang, es war als ob Kisten und Kasten von selbst sich füllten und das Geld im Schrank über Nacht sich mehrte. Es dauerte nicht lange, so war sein Reichtum größer als je zuvor. Aber er konnte sich nicht ungestört darüber freuen: die Zusage, die er der Nixe getan hatte, quälte sein Herz. So oft er an dem Teich vorbei kam, fürchtete er sie möchte auftauchen und ihn an seine Schuld mahnen. Den Knaben selbst ließ er nicht in die Nähe des Wassers: »hüte dich«, sagte er zu ihm, »wenn du das Wasser berührst, so kommt eine Hand heraus, hascht dich und zieht dich hinab.« Doch als Jahr auf Jahr vergieng, und die Nixe sich nicht wieder zeigte, so fieng der Müller an sich zu beruhigen.

Der Knabe wuchs zum Jüngling heran und kam bei einem Jäger in die Lehre. Als er ausgelernt hatte und ein tüchtiger Jäger geworden war, nahm ihn der Herr des Dorfes in seine Dienste. In dem Dorf war ein schönes und treues Mädchen, das gefiel dem Jäger, und als sein Herr das bemerkte, schenkte er ihm ein kleines Haus; die beiden hielten Hochzeit, lebten ruhig und glücklich und liebten sich von Herzen.

Einsmals verfolgte der Jäger ein Reh. Als das Tier aus dem Wald in das freie Feld ausbog, setzte er ihm nach und streckte es endlich mit einem Schuss nieder. Er bemerkte nicht dass er sich in der Nähe des gefährlichen Weihers befand, und gieng, nachdem er das Tier ausgeweidet hatte, zu dem Wasser, um seine mit Blut befleckten Hände zu waschen. Kaum aber hatte er sie hinein getaucht, als die Nixe emporstieg, lachend mit ihren nassen Armen ihn umschlang und so schnell hinabzog, dass die Wellen über ihm zusammenschlugen.

Als es Abend war und der Jäger nicht nach Haus kam, so
geriet seine Frau in Angst. Sie gieng aus ihn zu suchen, und
da er ihr oft erzählt hatte dass er sich vor den Nachstellun-
gen der Nixe in Acht nehmen müsste und nicht in die Nähe
des Weihers sich wagen dürfte, so ahnte sie schon was geschehen war. Sie eilte zu dem Wasser, und als sie am Ufer
seine Jägertasche liegen fand, da konnte sie nicht länger an
dem Unglück zweifeln. Wehklagend und händeringend rief
sie ihren Liebsten mit Namen, aber vergeblich: sie eilte hinüber auf die andere Seite des Weihers, und rief ihn aufs
neue: sie schalt die Nixe mit harten Worten, aber keine
Antwort erfolgte. Der Spiegel des Wassers blieb ruhig, nur
das halbe Gesicht des Mondes blickte unbeweglich zu ihr
herauf.
Die arme Frau verließ den Teich nicht. Mit schnellen
Schritten, ohne Rast und Ruhe, umkreiste sie ihn immer
von neuem, manchmal still, manchmal einen heftigen Schrei
ausstoßend, manchmal in leisem Wimmern. Endlich waren
ihre Kräfte zu Ende: sie sank zur Erde nieder und verfiel in
einen tiefen Schlaf. Bald überkam sie ein Traum.
Sie stieg zwischen großen Felsblöcken angstvoll aufwärts;
Dornen und Ranken hakten sich an ihre Füße, der Regen
schlug ihr ins Gesicht und der Wind zauste ihr langes Haar.
Als sie die Anhöhe erreicht hatte, bot sich ein ganz anderer
Anblick dar. Der Himmel war blau, die Luft mild, der Boden senkte sich sanft hinab und auf einer grünen, bunt be-
blümten Wiese stand eine reinliche Hütte. Sie gieng darauf
zu und öffnete die Türe, da saß eine Alte mit weißen Haaren, die ihr freundlich winkte. In dem Augenblick erwachte
die arme Frau. Der Tag war schon angebrochen, und sie
entschloss sich gleich dem Traum Folge zu leisten. Sie stieg
mühsam den Berg hinauf, und es war alles so, wie sie es in
der Nacht gesehen hatte. Die Alte empfieng sie freundlich
und zeigte ihr einen Stuhl, auf den sie sich setzen sollte.
»Du musst ein Unglück erlebt haben«, sagte sie, »weil du
meine einsame Hütte aufsuchst.« Die Frau erzählte ihr un-

ter Tränen was ihr begegnet war. »Tröste dich«, sagte die
Alte, »ich will dir helfen: da hast du einen goldenen Kamm.
Harre bis der Vollmond aufgestiegen ist, dann geh zu dem
Weiher, setze dich am Rand nieder und strähle dein langes
schwarzes Haar mit diesem Kamm. Wenn du aber fertig
bist, so lege ihn am Ufer nieder, und du wirst sehen was geschieht.«

Die Frau kehrte zurück, aber die Zeit bis zum Vollmond
verstrich ihr langsam. Endlich erschien die leuchtende
Scheibe am Himmel, da gieng sie hinaus an den Weiher,
setzte sich nieder und kämmte ihre langen schwarzen Haare mit dem goldenen Kamm, und als sie fertig war, legte sie
ihn an den Rand des Wassers nieder. Nicht lange, so brauste es aus der Tiefe, eine Welle erhob sich, rollte an das Ufer
und führte den Kamm mit sich fort. Es dauerte nicht länger
als der Kamm nötig hatte, auf den Grund zu sinken, so teilte sich der Wasserspiegel und der Kopf des Jägers stieg in
die Höhe. Er sprach nicht, schaute aber seine Frau mit
traurigen Blicken an. In demselben Augenblick kam eine
zweite Welle herangerauscht und bedeckte das Haupt des
Mannes. Alles war verschwunden, der Weiher lag so ruhig
wie zuvor und nur das Gesicht des Vollmondes glänzte
darauf.

Trostlos kehrte die Frau zurück, doch der Traum zeigte ihr
die Hütte der Alten. Abermals machte sie sich am nächsten
Morgen auf den Weg und klagte der weisen Frau ihr Leid.
Die Alte gab ihr eine goldene Flöte, und sprach »harre bis
der Vollmond wieder kommt, dann nimm diese Flöte, setze
dich an das Ufer, blas ein schönes Lied darauf, und wenn
du damit fertig bist, so lege sie auf den Sand; du wirst sehen
was geschieht.«

Die Frau tat wie die Alte gesagt hatte. Kaum lag die Flöte auf
dem Sand, so brauste es aus der Tiefe: eine Welle erhob sich,
zog heran, und führte die Flöte mit sich fort. Bald darauf
teilte sich das Wasser und nicht bloß der Kopf auch der
Mann bis zur Hälfte des Leibes stieg hervor. Er breitete voll

Verlangen seine Arme nach ihr aus, aber eine zweite Welle rauschte heran, bedeckte ihn und zog ihn wieder hinab.

»Ach, was hilft es mir«, sagte die Unglückliche, »dass ich meinen Liebsten nur erblicke, um ihn wieder zu verlieren.« Der Gram erfüllte aufs neue ihr Herz, aber der Traum führte sie zum drittenmal in das Haus der Alten. Sie machte sich auf den Weg, und die weise Frau gab ihr ein goldenes Spinnrad, tröstete sie und sprach »es ist noch nicht alles vollbracht, harre bis der Vollmond kommt, dann nimm das Spinnrad, setze dich an das Ufer und spinn die Spule voll, und wenn du fertig bist, so stelle das Spinnrad nahe an das Wasser und du wirst sehen was geschieht.«

Die Frau befolgte alles genau. Sobald der Vollmond sich zeigte, trug sie das goldene Spinnrad an das Ufer und spann emsig bis der Flachs zu Ende und die Spule mit dem Faden ganz angefüllt war. Kaum aber stand das Rad am Ufer, so brauste es noch heftiger als sonst in der Tiefe des Wassers, eine mächtige Welle eilte herbei und trug das Rad mit sich fort. Alsbald stieg mit einem Wasserstrahl der Kopf und der ganze Leib des Mannes in die Höhe. Schnell sprang er ans Ufer, fasste seine Frau an der Hand und entfloh. Aber kaum hatten sie sich eine kleine Strecke entfernt, so erhob sich mit entsetzlichem Brausen der ganze Weiher und strömte mit reißender Gewalt in das weite Feld hinein. Schon sahen die Fliehenden ihren Tod vor Augen, da rief die Frau in ihrer Angst die Hilfe der Alten an, und in dem Augenblick waren sie verwandelt, sie in eine Kröte, er in einen Frosch. Die Flut, die sie erreicht hatte, konnte sie nicht töten, aber sie riss sie beide von einander und führte sie weit weg.

Als das Wasser sich verlaufen hatte und beide wieder den trocknen Boden berührten, so kam ihre menschliche Gestalt zurück. Aber keiner wusste wo das andere geblieben war; sie befanden sich unter fremden Menschen, die ihre Heimat nicht kannten. Hohe Berge und tiefe Täler lagen zwischen ihnen. Um sich das Leben zu erhalten mussten beide die Schafe hüten. Sie trieben lange Jahre ihre Herden durch Feld und Wald und waren voll Trauer und Sehnsucht.

Als wieder einmal der Frühling aus der Erde hervorgebrochen war, zogen beide an einem Tag mit ihren Herden aus und der Zufall wollte dass sie einander entgegen zogen. Er erblickte an einem fernen Bergesabhang eine Herde und trieb seine Schafe nach der Gegend hin. Sie kamen in einem Tal zusammen, aber sie erkannten sich nicht, doch freuten sie sich dass sie nicht mehr so einsam waren. Von nun an trieben sie jeden Tag ihre Herde neben einander: sie sprachen nicht viel, aber sie fühlten sich getröstet. Eines Abends, als der Vollmond am Himmel schien und die Schafe schon ruhten, holte der Schäfer die Flöte aus seiner Tasche und blies ein schönes aber trauriges Lied. Als er fertig war, bemerkte er dass die Schäferin bitterlich weinte. »Warum weinst du?« fragte er. »Ach«, antwortete sie, »so schien auch der Vollmond als ich zum letztenmal dieses Lied auf der Flöte blies und das Haupt meines Liebsten aus dem Wasser hervorkam.« Er sah sie an und es war ihm als fiele eine Decke von den Augen, er erkannte seine liebste Frau: und als sie ihn anschaute und der Mond auf sein Gesicht schien, erkannte sie ihn auch. Sie umarmten und küssten sich, und ob sie glückselig waren braucht keiner zu fragen.

182.

Die Geschenke des kleinen Volkes.

Ein Schneider und ein Goldschmied wanderten zusammen und vernahmen eines Abends, als die Sonne hinter die Berge gesunken war, den Klang einer fernen Musik, die immer deutlicher ward; sie tönte ungewöhnlich aber so anmutig, dass sie aller Müdigkeit vergaßen und rasch weiter schritten.

Der Mond war schon aufgestiegen, als sie zu einem Hügel gelangten, auf dem sie eine Menge kleiner Männer und Frauen erblickten, die sich bei den Händen gefasst hatten, und mit größter Lust und Freudigkeit im Tanze herum wirbelten: sie sangen dazu auf das lieblichste; und das war die Musik, die die Wanderer gehört hatten. In der Mitte saß ein Alter, der etwas größer war als die übrigen, der einen buntfarbigen Rock trug, und dem ein eisgrauer Bart über die Brust herabhieng. Die beiden blieben voll Verwunderung stehen und sahen dem Tanz zu. Der Alte winkte, sie sollten eintreten, und das kleine Volk öffnete bereitwillig seinen Kreis. Der Goldschmied, der einen Höcker hatte und wie alle Buckeligen keck genug war, trat herzu: der Schneider empfand zuerst einige Scheu und hielt sich zurück, doch als er sah wie es so lustig hergieng, fasste er sich ein Herz und kam nach. Alsbald schloss sich der Kreis wieder und die Kleinen sangen und tanzten in den wildesten Sprüngen weiter, der Alte aber nahm ein breites Messer, das an seinem Gürtel hieng, wetzte es und als es hinlänglich geschärft war, blickte er sich nach den Fremdlingen um. Es ward ihnen angst, aber sie hatten nicht lange Zeit sich zu besinnen, der Alte packte den Goldschmied und schor in der größten Geschwindigkeit ihm Haupthaar und Bart glatt hinweg; ein gleiches geschah hierauf dem Schneider. Doch ihre Angst verschwand als der Alte nach vollbrachter Arbeit beiden freundlich auf die Schulter klopfte, als wollte er sagen, sie hätten es gut gemacht dass sie ohne Sträuben Alles willig hätten geschehen lassen. Er zeigte mit dem Finger auf einen Haufen Kohlen, der zur Seite lag, und deutete ihnen durch Gebärden an dass sie ihre Taschen damit füllen sollten. Beide gehorchten, obgleich sie nicht wussten wozu ihnen die Kohlen dienen sollten, und giengen dann weiter, um ein Nachtlager zu suchen. Als sie ins Tal gekommen waren, schlug die Glocke des benachbarten Klosters zwölf Uhr: augenblicklich verstummte der Gesang, Alles war verschwunden und der Hügel lag in einsamem Mondschein.

Die beiden Wanderer fanden eine Herberge und deckten sich auf dem Strohlager mit ihren Röcken zu, vergaßen aber wegen ihrer Müdigkeit die Kohlen zuvor heraus zu nehmen. Ein schwerer Druck auf ihren Gliedern weckte sie früher als gewöhnlich. Sie griffen in die Taschen und wollten ihren Augen nicht trauen, als sie sahen dass sie nicht mit Kohlen, sondern mit reinem Gold angefüllt waren; auch Haupthaar und Bart war glücklich wieder in aller Fülle vorhanden. Sie waren nun reiche Leute geworden, doch besaß der Goldschmied, der seiner habgierigen Natur gemäß die Taschen besser gefüllt hatte, nocheinmal so viel als der Schneider. Ein Habgieriger, wenn er viel hat, verlangt noch mehr, der Goldschmied machte dem Schneider den Vorschlag, noch einen Tag zu verweilen, am Abend wieder hinaus zu gehen, um sich bei dem Alten auf dem Berge noch größere Schätze zu holen. Der Schneider wollte nicht und sagte »ich habe genug und bin zufrieden: jetzt werde ich Meister, heirate meinen angenehmen Gegenstand (wie er seine Liebste nannte) und bin ein glücklicher Mann.« Doch wollte er, ihm zu Gefallen, den Tag noch bleiben. Abends hieng der Goldschmied noch ein paar Taschen über die Schulter, um recht einsacken zu können, und machte sich auf den Weg zu dem Hügel. Er fand, wie in der vorigen Nacht, das kleine Volk bei Gesang und Tanz, der Alte schor ihn abermals glatt und deutete ihm an Kohlen mitzunehmen. Er zögerte nicht einzustecken was nur in seine Taschen gehen wollte, kehrte ganz glückselig heim und deckte sich mit dem Rock zu. »Wenn das Gold auch drückt«, sprach er, »ich will das schon ertragen«, und schlief endlich mit dem süßen Vorgefühl ein, Morgen als steinreicher Mann zu erwachen. Als er die Augen öffnete, erhob er sich schnell, um die Taschen zu untersuchen, aber wie erstaunte er als er nichts herauszog als schwarze Kohlen, so oft hinein greifen als er wollte. »Noch bleibt mir das Gold, das ich die Nacht vorher gewonnen habe« dachte er und holte es herbei, aber wie erschrak er, als er sah dass es

ebenfalls wieder zu Kohle geworden war. Er schlug sich
mit der schwarzbestäubten Hand an die Stirne, da fühlte er
dass der ganze Kopf kahl und glatt war wie der Bart. Aber
sein Missgeschick war noch nicht zu Ende, er merkte erst
jetzt dass ihm zu dem Höcker auf dem Rücken noch ein
zweiter eben so großer vorn auf der Brust gewachsen war.
Da erkannte er die Strafe seiner Habgier und begann laut
zu weinen. Der gute Schneider, der davon aufgeweckt
ward, tröstete den Unglücklichen so gut es gehen wollte
und sprach »du bist mein Geselle auf der Wanderschaft gewesen, du sollst bei mir bleiben und mit von meinem
Schatz zehren.« Er hielt Wort, aber der arme Goldschmied
musste sein Lebtag die beiden Höcker tragen und seinen
kahlen Kopf mit einer Mütze bedecken.

183.

Der Riese und der Schneider.

Einem Schneider, der ein großer Prahler war, aber ein
schlechter Zahler, kam es in den Sinn ein wenig auszugehen
und sich in dem Wald umzuschauen. Sobald er nur konnte,
verließ er seine Werkstatt,

> wanderte seinen Weg,
> über Brücke und Steg,
> bald da, bald dort,
> immer fort und fort.

Als er nun draußen war, erblickte er in der blauen Ferne einen steilen Berg und dahinter einen himmelhohen Turm, der
aus einem wilden und finstern Wald hervorragte. »Potz
Blitz!« rief der Schneider, »was ist das?« und weil ihn die
Neugierde gewaltig stach, so gieng er frisch darauf los. Was
sperrte er aber Maul und Augen auf, als er in die Nähe kam,
denn der Turm hatte Beine, sprang in einem Satz über den

steilen Berg und stand als ein großmächtiger Riese vor dem
Schneider. »Was willst du hier, du winziges Fliegenbein«,
rief der mit einer Stimme, als wenn's von allen Seiten don-
nerte. Der Schneider wisperte »ich will mich umschauen, ob
ich mein Stückchen Brot in dem Wald verdienen kann.«
»Wenn's um die Zeit ist«, sagte der Riese, »so kannst du ja
bei mir im Dienst eintreten.« »Wenn's sein muss, warum das
nicht? was krieg ich aber für einen Lohn?« »Was du für einen Lohn kriegst?« sagte der Riese, »das sollst du hören.
Jährlich dreihundert und fünf und sechzig Tage, und wenn's
ein Schaltjahr ist, noch einen obendrein. Ist dir das recht?«
»Meinetwegen«, antwortete der Schneider und dachte in seinem Sinn »man muss sich strecken nach seiner Decke. Ich
such mich bald wieder los zu machen.«
Darauf sprach der Riese zu ihm »geh, kleiner Halunke, und
hol mir einen Krug Wasser.« »Warum nicht lieber gleich
den Brunnen mitsamt der Quelle?« fragte der Prahlhans
und gieng mit dem Krug zu dem Wasser. »Was? den Brunnen mitsamt der Quelle?« brummte der Riese, der ein bisschen tölpisch und albern war, in den Bart hinein und fieng
an sich zu fürchten, »der Kerl kann mehr als Äpfel braten:
der hat einen Alraun im Leib. Sei auf deiner Hut, alter
Hans, das ist kein Diener für dich.« Als der Schneider das
Wasser gebracht hatte, befahl ihm der Riese in dem Wald
ein paar Scheite Holz zu hauen und heim zu tragen. »Warum nicht lieber den ganzen Wald mit einem Streich,

      den ganzen Wald
      mit jung und alt,
      mit allem, was er hat,
      knorzig und glatt?«

fragte das Schneiderlein, und gieng das Holz zu hauen.
»Was?

      den ganzen Wald
      mit jung und alt,
      mit allem, was er hat,
      knorzig und glatt?

und den Brunnen mit samt der Quelle?« brummte der leichtgläubige Riese in den Bart und fürchtete sich noch mehr, »der Kerl kann mehr als Äpfel braten, der hat einen Alraun im Leib. Sei auf deiner Hut, alter Hans, das ist kein Diener für dich.« Wie der Schneider das Holz gebracht hatte, befahl ihm der Riese zwei oder drei wilde Schweine zum Abendessen zu schießen. »Warum nicht lieber gleich tausend auf einen Schuss und die alle hierher?« fragte der hoffärtige Schneider. »Was?« rief der Hasenfuß von einem Riesen und war heftig erschrocken, »lass es nur für heute gut sein und lege dich schlafen.«

Der Riese fürchtete sich so gewaltig, dass er die ganze Nacht kein Auge zutun konnte und hin und her dachte, wie er's anfangen sollte, um sich den verwünschten Hexenmeister von Diener je eher je lieber vom Hals zu schaffen. Kommt Zeit, kommt Rat. Am andern Morgen giengen der Riese und der Schneider zu einem Sumpf, um den ringsherum eine Menge Weidenbäume standen. Da sprach der Riese »hör einmal, Schneider, setz dich auf eine von den Weidenruten, ich möchte um mein Leben gern sehen, ob du im Stand bist sie herabzubiegen.« Husch, saß das Schneiderlein oben, hielt den Atem ein und machte sich schwer, so schwer dass sich die Gerte niederbog. Als er aber wieder Atem schöpfen musste, da schnellte sie ihn, weil er zum Unglück kein Bügeleisen in die Tasche gesteckt hatte, zu großer Freude des Riesen, so weit in die Höhe, dass man ihn gar nicht mehr sehen konnte. Wenn er nicht wieder herunter gefallen ist, so wird er wohl noch oben in der Luft herum schweben.

184.

Der Nagel.

Ein Kaufmann hatte auf der Messe gute Geschäfte gemacht, alle Waren verkauft und seine Geldkatze mit Gold und Silber gespickt. Er wollte jetzt heimreisen und vor Einbruch der Nacht zu Haus sein. Er packte also den Mantelsack mit dem Geld auf sein Pferd und ritt fort. Zu Mittag rastete er in einer Stadt: als er weiter wollte, führte ihm der Hausknecht das Ross vor, sprach aber »Herr, am linken Hinterfuß fehlt im Hufeisen ein Nagel.« »Lass ihn fehlen«, erwiderte der Kaufmann, »die sechs Stunden, die ich noch zu machen habe, wird das Eisen wohl fest halten. Ich habe Eile.« Nachmittags als er wieder abgestiegen war und dem Ross Brot geben ließ, kam der Knecht in die Stube, und sagte »Herr, euerm Pferd fehlt am linken Hinterfuß ein Hufeisen. Soll ich's zum Schmied führen?« »Lass es fehlen«, erwiderte der Herr, »die paar Stunden, die noch übrig sind, wird das Pferd wohl aushalten. Ich habe Eile.« Er ritt fort, aber nicht lange, so fieng das Pferd zu hinken an. Es hinkte nicht lange, so fieng es an zu stolpern, und es stolperte nicht lange, so fiel es nieder und brach ein Bein. Der Kaufmann musste das Pferd liegen lassen, den Mantelsack abschnallen, auf die Schulter nehmen und zu Fuß nach Haus gehen, wo er erst spät in der Nacht anlangte. »An allem Unglück«, sprach er zu sich selbst, »ist der verwünschte Nagel Schuld.« Eile mit Weile.

185

Der arme Junge im Grab.

Es war einmal ein armer Hirtenjunge, dem war Vater und Mutter gestorben, und er war von der Obrigkeit einem reichen Mann in das Haus gegeben, der sollte ihn ernähren und erziehen. Der Mann aber und seine Frau hatten ein böses Herz, waren bei allem Reichtum geizig und missgünstig, und ärgerten sich wenn jemand einen Bissen von ihrem Brot in den Mund steckte. Der arme Junge mochte tun was er wollte, er erhielt wenig zu essen, aber desto mehr Schläge.

Eines Tages sollte er die Glucke mit ihren Küchlein hüten. Sie verlief sich aber mit ihren Jungen durch einen Heckenzaun: gleich schoss der Habicht herab und entführte sie durch die Lüfte. Der Junge schrie aus Leibeskräften »Dieb, Dieb, Spitzbub.« Aber was half das? der Habicht brachte seinen Raub nicht wieder zurück. Der Mann hörte den Lärm, lief herbei, und als er vernahm dass seine Henne weg war, so geriet er in Wut und gab dem Jungen eine solche Tracht Schläge, dass er sich ein paar Tage lang nicht regen konnte. Nun musste er die Küchlein ohne die Henne hüten, aber da war die Not noch größer, das eine lief dahin, das andere dorthin. Da meinte er es klug zu machen, wenn er sie alle zusammen an eine Schnur bände, weil ihm dann der Habicht keins wegstehlen könnte. Aber weit gefehlt. Nach ein paar Tagen, als er von dem Herumlaufen und vom Hunger ermüdet einschlief, kam der Raubvogel und packte eins von den Küchlein, und da die andern daran fest hiengen, so trug er sie alle mit fort, setzte sich auf einen Baum und schluckte sie hinunter. Der Bauer kam eben nach Haus und als er das Unglück sah, erboste er sich und schlug den Jungen so unbarmherzig, dass er mehrere Tage im Bette liegen musste.

Als er wieder auf den Beinen war, sprach der Bauer zu ihm »du bist mir zu dumm, ich kann dich zum Hüter nicht

brauchen, du sollst als Bote gehen.« Da schickte er ihn zum
Richter, dem er einen Korb voll Trauben bringen sollte,
und gab ihm noch einen Brief mit. Unterwegs plagte Hunger und Durst den armen Jungen so heftig, dass er zwei von
den Trauben aß. Er brachte dem Richter den Korb, als dieser aber den Brief gelesen und die Trauben gezählt hatte, so
sagte er »es fehlen zwei Stück.« Der Junge gestand ganz
ehrlich dass er, von Hunger und Durst getrieben, die fehlenden verzehrt habe. Der Richter schrieb einen Brief an
den Bauer und verlangte noch einmal so viel Trauben. Auch
diese musste der Junge mit einem Brief hintragen. Als ihn
wieder so gewaltig hungerte und durstete, so konnte er sich
nicht anders helfen, er verzehrte abermals zwei Trauben.
Doch nahm er vorher den Brief aus dem Korb, legte ihn
unter einen Stein und setzte sich darauf, damit der Brief
nicht zusehen und ihn verraten könnte. Der Richter aber
stellte ihn doch der fehlenden Stücke wegen zur Rede.
»Ach«, sagte der Junge, »wie habt ihr das erfahren? der
Brief konnte es nicht wissen, denn ich hatte ihn zuvor unter einen Stein gelegt.« Der Richter musste über die Einfalt
lachen, und schickte dem Mann einen Brief, worin er ihn
ermahnte den armen Jungen besser zu halten und es ihm an
Speis und Trank nicht fehlen zu lassen; auch möchte er ihn
lehren was Recht und Unrecht sei.
»Ich will dir den Unterschied schon zeigen«, sagte der harte Mann; »willst du aber essen, so musst du auch arbeiten,
und tust du etwas Unrechtes, so sollst du durch Schläge
hinlänglich belehrt werden.« Am folgenden Tag stellte er
ihn an eine schwere Arbeit. Er sollte ein paar Bund Stroh
zum Futter für die Pferde schneiden; dabei drohte der
Mann, »in fünf Stunden«, sprach er, »bin ich wieder zurück, wenn dann das Stroh nicht zu Häcksel geschnitten
ist, so schlage ich dich so lange bis du kein Glied mehr regen kannst.« Der Bauer gieng mit seiner Frau dem Knecht
und der Magd auf den Jahrmarkt und ließ dem Jungen
nichts zurück als ein kleines Stück Brot. Der Junge stellte

sich an den Strohstuhl und fieng an aus allen Leibeskräften
zu arbeiten. Da ihm dabei heiß ward, so zog er sein Röcklein aus und warf's auf das Stroh. In der Angst nicht fertig
zu werden schnitt er immer zu, und in seinem Eifer zerschnitt er unvermerkt mit dem Stroh auch sein Röcklein.
Zu spät ward er das Unglück gewahr, das sich nicht wieder
gut machen ließ. »Ach«, rief er, »jetzt ist es aus mit mir.
Der böse Mann hat mir nicht umsonst gedroht, kommt er
zurück und sieht was ich getan habe, so schlägt er mich tot.
Lieber will ich mir selbst das Leben nehmen.«

Der Junge hatte einmal gehört wie die Bäuerin sprach »unter dem Bett habe ich einen Topf mit Gift stehen.« Sie hatte
es aber nur gesagt, um die Näscher zurückzuhalten, denn
es war Honig darin. Der Junge kroch unter das Bett, holte
den Topf hervor und aß ihn ganz aus. »Ich weiß nicht«,
sprach er, »die Leute sagen der Tod sei bitter, mir schmeckt
er süß. Kein Wunder dass die Bäuerin sich so oft den Tod
wünscht.« Er setzte sich auf ein Stühlchen und war gefasst
zu sterben. Aber statt dass er schwächer werden sollte,
fühlte er sich von der nahrhaften Speise gestärkt. »Es muss
kein Gift gewesen sein«, sagte er, »aber der Bauer hat einmal gesagt in seinem Kleiderkasten läge ein Fläschchen mit
Fliegengift, das wird wohl das wahre Gift sein und mir den
Tod bringen.« Es war aber kein Fliegengift, sondern Ungarwein. Der Junge holte die Flasche heraus und trank sie
aus. »Auch dieser Tod schmeckt süß«, sagte er, doch als
bald hernach der Wein anfieng ihm ins Gehirn zu steigen
und ihn zu betäuben, so meinte er sein Ende nahte sich heran. »Ich fühle dass ich sterben muss«, sprach er, »ich will
hinaus auf den Kirchhof gehen, und ein Grab suchen.« Er
taumelte fort, erreichte den Kirchhof und legte sich in ein
frisch geöffnetes Grab. Die Sinne verschwanden ihm immer
mehr. In der Nähe stand ein Wirtshaus, wo eine Hochzeit
gefeiert wurde: als er die Musik hörte, däuchte er sich
schon im Paradies zu sein, bis er endlich alle Besinnung
verlor. Der arme Junge erwachte nicht wieder, die Glut des

heißen Weins und der kalte Tau der Nacht nahmen ihm das Leben, und er verblieb in dem Grab, in das er sich selbst gelegt hatte.

Als der Bauer die Nachricht von dem Tod des Jungen erhielt, erschrak er und fürchtete vor das Gericht geführt zu werden: ja die Angst fasste ihn so gewaltig, dass er ohnmächtig zur Erde sank. Die Frau, die mit einer Pfanne voll Schmalz am Herde stand, lief herzu um ihm Beistand zu leisten. Aber das Feuer schlug in die Pfanne, ergriff das ganze Haus, und nach wenigen Stunden lag es schon in Asche. Die Jahre, die sie noch zu leben hatten, brachten sie, von Gewissensbissen geplagt, in Armut und Elend zu.

186.

Die wahre Braut.

Es war einmal ein Mädchen, das war jung und schön, aber seine Mutter war ihm früh gestorben, und die Stiefmutter tat ihm alles gebrannte Herzeleid an. Wenn sie ihm eine Arbeit auftrug, sie mochte noch so schwer sein, so gieng es unverdrossen daran und tat was in seinen Kräften stand. Aber es konnte damit das Herz der bösen Frau nicht rühren, immer war sie unzufrieden, immer war es nicht genug. Je fleißiger es arbeitete, je mehr ward ihm aufgelegt, und sie hatte keinen andern Gedanken, als wie sie ihm eine immer größere Last aufbürden und das Leben recht sauer machen wollte.

Eines Tags sagte sie zu ihm »da hast du zwölf Pfund Federn, die sollst du abschleißen, und wenn du nicht heute Abend damit fertig bist, so wartet eine Tracht Schläge auf dich. Meinst du, du könntest den ganzen Tag faulenzen?« Das arme Mädchen setzte sich zu der Arbeit nieder, aber die Tränen flossen ihm dabei über die Wangen herab, denn

es sah wohl dass es unmöglich war mit der Arbeit in einem
Tage zu Ende zu kommen. Wenn es ein Häufchen Federn
vor sich liegen hatte und es seufzte oder schlug in seiner
Angst die Hände zusammen, so stoben sie aus einander
und es musste sie wieder auflesen und von neuem anfangen.
Da stützte es einmal die Ellbogen auf den Tisch, legte sein
Gesicht in beide Hände, und rief »ist denn niemand auf
Gottes Erdboden, der sich meiner erbarmt?« Indem hörte
es eine sanfte Stimme, die sprach »tröste dich, mein Kind,
ich bin gekommen dir zu helfen.« Das Mädchen blickte
auf, und eine alte Frau stand neben ihm. Sie fasste das Mädchen freundlich an der Hand, und sprach »vertraue mir nur
an was dich drückt.« Da sie so herzlich sprach, so erzählte
ihr das Mädchen von seinem traurigen Leben, dass ihm eine
Last auf die andere gelegt würde und es mit den aufgegebe-
nen Arbeiten nicht mehr zu Ende kommen könnte. »Wenn
ich mit diesen Federn heute Abend nicht fertig bin, so
schlägt mich die Stiefmutter; sie hat mir's angedroht, und
ich weiß sie hält Wort.« Ihre Tränen fiengen wieder an zu
fließen, aber die gute Alte sprach »sei unbesorgt, mein
Kind, ruhe dich aus, ich will derweil deine Arbeit verrichten.« Das Mädchen legte sich auf sein Bett und schlief bald
ein. Die Alte setzte sich an den Tisch bei die Federn, hu!
wie flogen sie von den Kielen ab, die sie mit ihren dürren
Händen kaum berührte. Bald war sie mit den zwölf Pfund
fertig. Als das Mädchen erwachte, lagen große schneeweiße
Haufen aufgetürmt, und alles war im Zimmer reinlich auf-
geräumt, aber die Alte war verschwunden. Das Mädchen
dankte Gott und saß still bis der Abend kam. Da trat die
Stiefmutter herein und staunte über die vollbrachte Arbeit.
»Siehst du, Trulle«, sprach sie, »was man ausrichtet, wenn
man fleißig ist? hättest du nicht noch etwas anderes vornehmen können? aber da sitzest du und legst die Hände in
den Schoß.« Als sie hinausgieng, sprach sie, »die Kreatur
kann mehr als Brot essen, ich muss ihr schwerere Arbeit
auflegen.«

Am andern Morgen rief sie das Mädchen und sprach »da hast du einen Löffel, damit schöpfe mir den großen Teich aus, der bei dem Garten liegt. Und wenn du damit Abends nicht zu Rand gekommen bist, so weißt du was erfolgt.« Das Mädchen nahm den Löffel und sah dass er durchlöchert war, und wenn er es auch nicht gewesen wäre, es hätte nimmermehr damit den Teich ausgeschöpft. Es machte sich gleich an die Arbeit, kniete am Wasser, in das seine Tränen fielen, und schöpfte. Aber die gute Alte erschien wieder, und als sie die Ursache von seinem Kummer erfuhr, sprach sie »sei getrost, mein Kind, geh in das Gebüsch und lege dich schlafen, ich will deine Arbeit schon tun.« Als die Alte allein war, berührte sie nur den Teich: wie ein Dunst stieg das Wasser in die Höhe und vermischte sich mit den Wolken. Allmählig ward der Teich leer, und als das Mädchen vor Sonnenuntergang erwachte und herbeikam, so sah es nur noch die Fische, die in dem Schlamm zappelten. Es gieng zu der Stiefmutter und zeigte ihr an dass die Arbeit vollbracht wäre. »Du hättest längst fertig sein sollen«, sagte sie und ward blass vor Ärger, aber sie sann etwas Neues aus.

Am dritten Morgen sprach sie zu dem Mädchen »dort in der Ebene musst du mir ein schönes Schloss bauen und zum Abend muss es fertig sein.« Das Mädchen erschrak und sagte »wie kann ich ein so großes Werk vollbringen?« »Ich dulde keinen Widerspruch«, schrie die Stiefmutter, »kannst du mit einem durchlöcherten Löffel einen Teich ausschöpfen, so kannst du auch ein Schloss bauen. Noch heute will ich es beziehen, und wenn etwas fehlt, sei es das geringste in Küche oder Keller, so weißt du was dir bevorsteht.« Sie trieb das Mädchen fort, und als es in das Tal kam, so lagen da die Felsen über einander aufgetürmt; mit aller seiner Kraft konnte es den kleinsten nicht einmal bewegen. Es setzte sich nieder und weinte, doch hoffte es auf den Beistand der guten Alten. Sie ließ auch nicht lange auf sich warten, kam und sprach ihm Trost ein, »lege dich nur

dort in den Schatten, und schlaf, ich will dir das Schloss
schon bauen. Wenn es dir Freude macht, so kannst du
selbst darin wohnen.« Als das Mädchen weggegangen war,
rührte die Alte die grauen Felsen an. Alsbald regten sie
sich, rückten zusammen und standen da, als hätten Riesen
die Mauer gebaut: darauf erhob sich das Gebäude, und es
war als ob unzählige Hände unsichtbar arbeiteten und Stein
auf Stein legten. Der Boden dröhnte, große Säulen stiegen
von selbst in die Höhe und stellten sich neben einander in
Ordnung. Auf dem Dach legten sich die Ziegeln zurecht,
und als es Mittag war, drehte sich schon die große Wetter-
fahne wie eine goldene Jungfrau mit fliegendem Gewand
auf der Spitze des Turms. Das Innere des Schlosses war bis
zum Abend vollendet. Wie es die Alte anfieng, weiß ich
nicht, aber die Wände der Zimmer waren mit Seide und
Sammet bezogen, buntgestickte Stühle standen da und
reichverzierte Armsessel an Tischen von Marmor, kristallne
Kronleuchter hiengen von der Bühne herab und spiegelten
sich in dem glatten Boden: grüne Papageien saßen in goldenen Käfigen und fremde Vögel, die lieblich sangen: überall
war eine Pracht, als wenn ein König da einziehen sollte.
Die Sonne wollte eben untergehen, als das Mädchen erwachte und ihm der Glanz von tausend Lichtern entgegen
leuchtete. Mit schnellen Schritten kam es heran und trat
durch das geöffnete Tor in das Schloss. Die Treppe war mit
rotem Tuch belegt und das goldene Geländer mit blühen-
den Bäumen besetzt. Als es die Pracht der Zimmer erblickte, blieb es wie erstarrt stehen. Wer weiß wie lang es so gestanden hätte, wenn ihm nicht der Gedanke an die Stiefmutter gekommen wäre. »Ach«, sprach es zu sich selbst,
»wenn sie doch endlich zufrieden gestellt wäre und mir das
Leben nicht länger zur Qual machen wollte.« Das Mädchen
gieng und zeigte ihr an dass das Schloss fertig wäre.
»Gleich will ich einziehen« sagte sie und erhob sich von ihrem Sitz. Als sie in das Schloss eintrat, musste sie die Hand
vor die Augen halten, so blendete sie der Glanz. »Siehst

du«, sagte sie zu dem Mädchen, »wie leicht dir's geworden ist, ich hätte dir etwas Schwereres aufgeben sollen.« Sie gieng durch alle Zimmer und spürte in allen Ecken ob etwas fehlte oder mangelhaft wäre, aber sie konnte nichts auffinden. »Jetzt wollen wir hinabsteigen«, sprach sie und sah das Mädchen mit boshaften Blicken an, »Küche und Keller muss noch untersucht werden, und hast du etwas vergessen, so sollst du deiner Strafe nicht entgehen.« Aber das Feuer brannte auf dem Herd, in den Töpfen kochten die Speisen, Kluft und Schippe waren angelehnt, und an den Wänden das blanke Geschirr von Messing aufgestellt. Nichts fehlte, selbst nicht der Kohlenkasten und die Wassereimer. »Wo ist der Eingang zum Keller?« rief sie, »wo der nicht mit Weinfässern reichlich angefüllt ist, so wird dir's schlimm ergehen.« Sie hob selbst die Falltüre auf und stieg die Treppe hinab, aber kaum hatte sie zwei Schritte getan, so stürzte die schwere Falltüre, die nur angelehnt war, nieder. Das Mädchen hörte einen Schrei, hob die Türe schnell auf, um ihr zu Hilfe zu kommen, aber sie war hinabgestürzt und es fand sie entseelt auf dem Boden liegen.

Nun gehörte das prächtige Schloss dem Mädchen ganz allein. Es wusste sich in der ersten Zeit gar nicht in seinem Glück zu finden, schöne Kleider hiengen in den Schränken, die Truhen waren mit Gold und Silber oder mit Perlen und Edelsteinen angefüllt, und es hatte keinen Wunsch, den es nicht erfüllen konnte. Bald gieng der Ruf von der Schönheit und dem Reichtum des Mädchens durch die ganze Welt. Alle Tage meldeten sich Freier, aber keiner gefiel ihr. Endlich kam auch der Sohn eines Königs, der ihr Herz zu rühren wusste, und sie verlobte sich mit ihm. In dem Schlossgarten stand eine grüne Linde, darunter saßen sie eines Tages vertraulich zusammen, da sagte er zu ihr »ich will heimziehen und die Einwilligung meines Vaters zu unserer Vermählung holen; ich bitte dich harre mein hier unter dieser Linde, in wenigen Stunden bin ich wieder zurück.« Das Mädchen küsste ihn auf den linken Backen und sprach

»bleib mir treu, und lass dich von keiner andern auf diesen Backen küssen. Ich will hier unter der Linde warten bis du wieder zurückkommst.«

Das Mädchen blieb unter der Linde sitzen, bis die Sonne untergieng, aber [er] kam nicht wieder zurück. Sie saß drei Tage von Morgen bis Abend, und erwartete ihn, aber vergeblich. Als er am vierten Tag noch nicht da war, so sagte sie »gewiss ist ihm ein Unglück begegnet, ich will ausgehen und ihn suchen und nicht eher wiederkommen als bis ich ihn gefunden habe.« Sie packte drei von ihren schönsten Kleidern zusammen, eins mit glänzenden Sternen gestickt, das zweite mit silbernen Monden, das dritte mit goldenen Sonnen, band eine Hand voll Edelsteine in ihr Tuch und machte sich auf. Sie fragte aller Orten nach ihrem Bräutigam, aber niemand hatte ihn gesehen, niemand wusste von ihm. Weit und breit wanderte sie durch die Welt, aber sie fand ihn nicht. Endlich vermietete sie sich bei einem Bauer als Hirtin, und vergrub ihre Kleider und Edelsteine unter einem Stein.

Nun lebte sie als eine Hirtin, hütete ihre Herde, war traurig und voll Sehnsucht nach ihrem Geliebten. Sie hatte ein Kälbchen, das gewöhnte sie an sich, fütterte es aus der Hand, und wenn sie sprach

»Kälbchen, Kälbchen, knie nieder,
vergiss nicht deine Hirtin wieder,
wie der Königssohn die Braut vergaß,
die unter der grünen Linde saß«,

so kniete das Kälbchen nieder und ward von ihr gestreichelt.

Als sie ein paar Jahre einsam und kummervoll gelebt hatte, so verbreitete sich im Lande das Gerücht, dass die Tochter des Königs ihre Hochzeit feiern wollte. Der Weg nach der Stadt gieng an dem Dorf vorbei, wo das Mädchen wohnte, und es trug sich zu, als sie einmal ihre Herde austrieb, dass der Bräutigam vorüber zog. Er saß stolz auf seinem Pferd und sah sie nicht an, aber als sie ihn ansah, so erkannte sie

ihren Liebsten. Es war als ob ihr ein scharfes Messer in das
Herz schnitte. »Ach«, sagte sie, »ich glaubte er wäre mir
treu geblieben, aber er hat mich vergessen.«

Am andern Tag kam er wieder des Wegs. Als er in ihrer
Nähe war, sprach sie zum Kälbchen,

>   »Kälbchen, Kälbchen, knie nieder,
>   vergiss nicht deine Hirtin wieder,
>   wie der Königssohn die Braut vergaß,
>   die unter der grünen Linde saß.«

Als er die Stimme vernahm, blickte er herab und hielt sein
Pferd an. Er schaute der Hirtin ins Gesicht, hielt dann die
Hand vor die Augen, als wollte er sich auf etwas besinnen,
aber schnell ritt er weiter und war bald verschwunden.
»Ach«, sagte sie, »er kennt mich nicht mehr«, und ihre
Trauer ward immer größer.

Bald darauf sollte an dem Hofe des Königs drei Tage lang
ein großes Fest gefeiert werden, und das ganze Land ward
dazu eingeladen. »Nun will ich das Letzte versuchen«
dachte das Mädchen, und als der Abend kam, gieng es zu
dem Stein, unter dem es seine Schätze vergraben hatte. Sie
holte das Kleid mit den goldenen Sonnen hervor, legte es an
und schmückte sich mit den Edelsteinen. Ihre Haare, die
sie unter einem Tuch verborgen hatte, band sie auf, und sie
fielen in langen Locken an ihr herab. So gieng sie nach der
Stadt und ward in der Dunkelheit von niemand bemerkt.
Als sie in den hell erleuchteten Saal trat, wichen alle voll
Verwunderung zurück, aber niemand wusste wer sie war.
Der Königssohn gieng ihr entgegen, doch er erkannte sie
nicht. Er führte sie zum Tanz und war so entzückt über
ihre Schönheit dass er an die andere Braut gar nicht mehr
dachte. Als das Fest vorüber war, verschwand sie im Ge-
dränge und eilte vor Tagesanbruch in das Dorf, wo sie ihr
Hirtenkleid wieder anlegte.

Am andern Abend nahm sie das Kleid mit den silbernen
Monden heraus und steckte einen Halbmond von Edelsteinen in ihre Haare. Als sie auf dem Fest sich zeigte, wende-

ten sich alle Augen nach ihr, aber der Königssohn eilte ihr
entgegen, und ganz von Liebe erfüllt tanzte er mit ihr allein
und blickte keine andere mehr an. Ehe sie wegging, musste sie ihm versprechen den letzten Abend nochmals zum
Fest zu kommen.

Als sie zum drittenmal erschien, hatte sie das Sternenkleid
an, das bei jedem ihrer Schritte funkelte, und Haarband
und Gürtel waren Sterne von Edelsteinen. Der Königssohn
hatte schon lange auf sie gewartet und drängte sich zu ihr
hin. »Sage mir nur wer du bist«, sprach er, »mir ist als wenn
ich dich schon lange gekannt hätte.« »Weißt du nicht«, antwortete sie, »was ich tat, als du von mir schiedest?« Da trat
sie zu ihm heran und küsste ihn auf den linken Backen: in
dem Augenblick fiel es wie Schuppen von seinen Augen
und er erkannte die wahre Braut. »Komm«, sagte er zu ihr,
»hier ist meines Bleibens nicht länger«, reichte ihr die Hand
und führte sie hinab zu dem Wagen. Als wäre der Wind
vorgespannt, so eilten die Pferde zu dem Wunderschloss.
Schon von weitem glänzten die erleuchteten Fenster. Als sie
bei der Linde vorbei fuhren, schwärmten unzählige Glüh-
würmer darin, sie schüttelte ihre Äste und sendete ihre
Düfte herab. Auf der Treppe blühten die Blumen, aus dem
Zimmer schallte der Gesang der fremden Vögel, aber in
dem Saal stand der ganze Hof versammelt und der Priester
wartete um den Bräutigam mit der wahren Braut zu vermählen.

187.

Der Hase und der Igel.

Disse Geschicht is lögenhaft to vertellen, Jungens, aver
wahr is se doch, denn mien Grootvader, van den ick se hew,
plegg jümmer, wenn he se mie vortüerde (mit Behaglichkeit
vortrug), dabi to seggen »wahr mutt se doch sien, mien

Söhn, anners kunn man se jo nich vertellen.« De Geschicht
hett sick aber so todragen.

Et wöör an enen Sündagmorgen tor Harvesttied, jüst as de
Bookweeten bloihde: de Sünn wöör hellig upgaen am Hewen, de Morgenwind güng warm över de Stoppeln, de Lar-
ken süngen inn'r Lucht (Luft), de Immen sumsten in den
Bookweeten un de Lühde güngen in ehren Sündagsstaht
nah t' Kerken, un alle Kreatur wöör vergnögt, un de Swinegel ook.

De Swinegel aver stünd vör siener Döhr, harr de Arm ün-
nerslagen, keek dabi in den Morgenwind hinut un quinke-
leerde en lütjet Leedken vör sick hin, so good un so slecht
as nu eben am leewen Sündagmorgen en Swinegel to singen
pleggt. Indem he nu noch so half liese vör sick hin sung,
füll em up eenmal in he künn ook wol, mittelwiel sien Fro
de Kinner wüsch un antröcke, en beeten in't Feld spazeeren
un tosehen wie sien Stähkröwen stünden. De Stähkröwen
wöören aver de nöchsten bi sienem Huuse, un he pleggte
mit siener Familie davon to eten, darüm sahg he se as de
sienigen an. Gesagt, gedahn. De Swinegel makte de Huus-
döör achter sick to un slög den Weg nah 'n Felde in. He
wöör noch nich gans wiet von Huuse un wull jüst um den
Slöbusch, (Schlehenbusch), de dar vörm Felde liggt, nah
den Stähkröwenacker hinup dreien, as em de Haas bemött,
de in ähnlichen Geschäften uutgahn wöör, nämlich um sienen Kohl to besehn. As de Swinegel den Haasen ansichtig
wöör, so böhd he em en fründlichen go'n Morgen. De Haas
aver, de up siene Wies en vörnehmer Herr was, un grau-
sahm hochfahrtig dabi, antwoorde nicks up den Swinegel
sienen Gruß, sondern seg[g]te tom Swinegel, wobi he en
gewaltig höhnische Miene annöhm, »wie kummt et denn,
dat du hier all bi so fröhem Morgen im Felde rumlöppst?«
»Ick gah spazeeren« seg[g]t de Swinegel. »Spazeeren?«
lachte de Haas, »mi ducht du kunnst de Been ook wol to
betern Dingen gebruuken.« Disse Antwoord verdrööt den
Swinegel ungeheuer, denn alles kunn he verdregen, aver up

siene Been laet he nicks komen, eben weil se von Natuhr scheef wöören. »Du bildst di wol in«, seggt nu de Swinegel tom Haasen, »as wenn du mit diene Beene mehr utrichten kunnst?« »Dat denk ick« seggt de Haas. »Dat kummt up 'n Versöök an«, meent de Swinegel, »ick pareer, wenn wi in de Wett loopt, ick loop di vörbi.« »Dat is tum Lachen, du mit diene scheefen Been«, seggt de Haas, »aver mienetwegen mach't sien, wenn du so övergroote Lust hest. Wat gilt de Wett?« »En goldne Lujedor un 'n Buddel Branwien« seggt de Swinegel. »Angenahmen«, spröök de Haas, »sla in, un denn kann't gliek los gahn.« »Nä, so groote Ihl hett et nich«, meen de Swinegel, »ick bün noch gans nüchdern; eerst will ick to Huus gahn un en beeten fröhstücken: inner halwen Stünd bün ick wedder hier upp'n Platz.«

Damit güng de Swinegel, denn de Haas wöör et tofreeden. Ünnerweges dachte de Swinegel bi sick »de Haas verlett sick up siene langen Been, aver ick will em wol kriegen. He is zwar ehn vörnehm Herr, aber doch man 'n dummen Keerl, un betahlen sall he doch.« As nu de Swinegel to Huuse ankööm, spröök he to sien Fro »Fro, treck di gau (schnell) an, du must mit mi nah 'n Felde hinuut.« »Wat givt et denn?« seggt sien Fro. »Ick hew mit 'n Haasen wett't üm 'n golden Lujedor un 'n Buddel Branwien, ick will mit em in Wett loopen un da salst du mit dabi sien.« »O mien Gott, Mann«, füng nu den Swinegel sien Fro an to schreen, »büst du nich klook, hest du denn ganz den Verstand verlaaren? Wie kannst du mit den Haasen in de Wett loopen wollen?« »Holt dat Muul, Wief«, seggt de Swinegel, »dat is mien Saak. Resonehr nich in Männergeschäfte. Marsch, treck di an un denn kumm mit.« Wat sull den Swinegel sien Fro maken? se musst wol folgen, se mugg nu wollen oder nich.

As se nu mit eenander ünnerwegs wöören, spröök de Swinegel to sien Fro »nu pass up, wat ick seggen will. Sühst du, up den langen Acker dar wüll wi unsen Wettloop maken. De Haas löppt nemlich in der eenen Föhr (Furche) un ick inner andern, un von baben (oben) fang wi an to loopen.

Nu hast du wieder nicks to dohn as du stellst di hier unnen in de Föhr, un wenn de Haas up de andere Siet ankummt, so röpst du em entgegen ›ick bün all (schon) hier.‹«

Damit wöören se bi den Acker anlangt, de Swinegel wiese siener Fro ehren Platz an un gung nu den Acker hinup. As he baben ankööm, wöör de Haas all da. »Kann et losgahn?« seggt de Haas. »Ja wol« seggt de Swinegel. »Denn man to!« Un damit stellde jeder sick in siene Föhr. De Haas tellde (zählte) »hahl een, hahl twee, hahl dree« un los güng he wie en Stormwind den Acker hindahl (hinab). De Swinegel aver lööp ungefähr man dree Schritt, dann duhkde he sick dahl (herab) in de Föhr un bleev ruhig sitten.

As nu de Haas in vullen Loopen ünnen am Acker ankööm, rööp em den Swinegel sien Fro entgegen »ick bün all hier.« De Haas stutzd un verwunderde sick nich wenig: he menede nich anders als et wöör de Swinegel sülvst, de em dat toröp, denn bekanntlich süht den Swinegel sien Fro jüst so uut wie ehr Mann.

De Haas aver meende »datt geiht nich to mit rechten Dingen.« He rööp »nochmal geloopen, wedder üm!« Un fort güng he wedder wie en Stormwind, datt em de Ohren am Koppe flögen. Den Swinegel sien Fro aver blev ruhig up ehren Platze. As nu de Haas baben ankööm, rööp em de Swinegel entgegen »Ick bün all hier.« De Haas aver, ganz unter sick vör Ihwer (Ärger), schreede »nochmal geloopen, wedder üm!« »Mi nich to schlimm«, antwoorde de Swinegel, »mienetwegen so oft as du Lust hest.« So löp de Haas noch dreeunsöbentigmal, un de Swinegel höhl (hielt) et ümmer mit em uut. Jedesmal, wenn de Haas ünnen oder baben ankööm, seggten de Swinegel oder sien Fro »ick bün all hier.«

Tum veerunsöbentigstenmal aver köm de Haas nich mehr to ende. Midden am Acker stört he tor Eerde, datt Blohd flög em ut 'n Halse un he bleev doot up 'n Platze. De Swinegel aver nöhm siene gewunnene Lujedor un den Buddel Branwien, rööp siene Fro uut der Föhr aff, un beide gün-

gen vergnögt mit eenanner nah Huus; un wenn se nich
storben sünd, lewt se noch.

So begev et sick, dat up der Buxtehuder Heid de Swinegel
den Haasen dodt lopen hett, un sied jener Tied hatt et sick
keen Haas wedder infallen laten mit 'n Buxtehuder Swinegel in de Wett to lopen.

De Lehre aver uut disser Geschicht is erstens, datt keener,
un wenn he sick ook noch so vörnehm düücht, sick sall bi-
kommen laten, övern geringen Mann sick lustig to maken,
un wöört ook man 'n Swinegel. Un tweetens, datt et gerah-
den is, wenn eener freet, datt he sick ne Fro uut sienem
Stande nimmt, un de jüst so uutsüht as he sülwst. Wer also
en Swinegel is, de mutt tosehn datt siene Fro ook en Swinegel is, un so wieder.

188.

Spindel, Weberschiffchen und Nadel.

Es war einmal ein Mädchen, dem starb Vater und Mutter,
als es noch ein kleines Kind war. Am Ende des Dorfes
wohnte in einem Häuschen ganz allein seine Pate, die sich
von Spinnen Weben und Nähen ernährte. Die Alte nahm
das verlassene Kind zu sich, hielt es zur Arbeit an und er-
zog es in aller Frömmigkeit. Als das Mädchen fünfzehn
Jahr alt war, erkrankte sie, rief das Kind an ihr Bett und
sagte »liebe Tochter, ich fühle dass mein Ende herannaht,
ich hinterlasse dir das Häuschen, darin bist du vor Wind
und Wetter geschützt, dazu Spindel, Weberschiffchen und
Nadel, damit kannst du dir dein Brot verdienen.« Sie legte
noch die Hände auf seinen Kopf, segnete es und sprach
»behalt nur Gott in dem Herzen, so wird dir's wohl gehen.« Darauf schloss sie die Augen, und als sie zur Erde bestattet wurde, gieng das Mädchen bitterlich weinend hinter
dem Sarg und erwies ihr die letzte Ehre.

Das Mädchen lebte nun in dem kleinen Haus ganz allein, war fleißig, spann, webte und nähte, und auf allem, was es tat, ruhte der Segen der guten Alten. Es war als ob sich der Flachs in der Kammer von selbst mehrte, und wenn sie ein Stück Tuch oder einen Teppich gewebt, oder ein Hemd genäht hatte, so fand sich gleich ein Käufer, der es reichlich bezahlte, so dass sie keine Not empfand und andern noch etwas mitteilen konnte.

Um diese Zeit zog der Sohn des Königs im Land umher und wollte sich eine Braut suchen. Eine arme sollte er nicht wählen und eine reiche wollte er nicht. Da sprach er »die soll meine Frau werden, die zugleich die ärmste und die reichste ist.« Als er in das Dorf kam, wo das Mädchen lebte, fragte er, wie er überall tat, wer in dem Ort die reichste und ärmste wäre. Sie nannten ihm die reichste zuerst: die ärmste, sagten sie, wäre das Mädchen, das in dem kleinen Haus ganz am Ende wohnte. Die Reiche saß vor der Haustür in vollem Putz, und als der Königssohn sich näherte, stand sie auf, gieng ihm entgegen und neigte sich vor ihm. Er sah sie an, sprach kein Wort und ritt weiter. Als er zu dem Haus der Armen kam, stand das Mädchen nicht an der Türe, sondern saß in seinem Stübchen. Er hielt das Pferd an und sah durch das Fenster, durch das die helle Sonne schien, das Mädchen an dem Spinnrad sitzen und emsig spinnen. Es blickte auf, und als es bemerkte dass der Königssohn hereinschaute, ward es über und über rot, schlug die Augen nieder und spann weiter; ob der Faden diesmal ganz gleich ward, weiß ich nicht, aber es spann so lange bis der Königssohn wieder weggeritten war. Dann trat es ans Fenster, öffnete es und sagte »es ist so heiß in der Stube«, aber es blickte ihm nach so lange es noch die weißen Federn an seinem Hut erkennen konnte.

Das Mädchen setzte sich wieder in seine Stube zur Arbeit und spann weiter. Da kam ihm ein Spruch in den Sinn, den die Alte manchmal gesagt hatte, wenn es bei der Arbeit saß, und es sang so vor sich hin

>Spindel, Spindel, geh du aus,
bring den Freier in mein Haus.«

Was geschah? Die Spindel sprang ihm augenblicklich aus
der Hand und zur Türe hinaus; und als es vor Verwunderung aufstand und ihr nachblickte, so sah es dass sie lustig
in das Feld hinein tanzte und einen glänzenden goldenen
Faden hinter sich herzog. Nicht lange, so war sie ihm aus
den Augen entschwunden. Das Mädchen, da es keine Spindel mehr hatte, nahm das Weberschiffchen in die Hand,
setzte sich an den Webstuhl und fieng an zu weben.
Die Spindel aber tanzte immer weiter, und eben als der Faden zu Ende war, hatte sie den Königssohn erreicht. »Was
sehe ich?« rief er, »die Spindel will mir wohl den Weg zeigen?« drehte sein Pferd um und ritt an dem goldenen Faden zurück. Das Mädchen aber saß an seiner Arbeit und
sang

>Schiffchen, Schiffchen, webe fein,
führ den Freier mir herein.«

Alsbald sprang ihr das Schiffchen aus der Hand und sprang
zur Türe hinaus. Vor der Türschwelle aber fieng es an, einen Teppich zu weben, schöner als man je einen gesehen
hat. Auf beiden Seiten blühten Rosen und Lilien und in der
Mitte auf goldenem Grund stiegen grüne Ranken herauf,
darin sprangen Hasen und Kaninchen: Hirsche und Rehe
streckten die Köpfe dazwischen: oben in den Zweigen saßen bunte Vögel; es fehlte nichts als dass sie gesungen hätten. Das Schiffchen sprang hin und her, und es war als
wüchse alles von selber.
Weil das Schiffchen fortgelaufen war, hatte sich das Mädchen zum Nähen hingesetzt: es hielt die Nadel in der Hand
und sang

>Nadel, Nadel, spitz und fein,
Mach das Haus dem Freier rein.«

Da sprang ihr die Nadel aus den Fingern und flog in der
Stube hin und her, so schnell wie der Blitz. Es war nicht
anders als wenn unsichtbare Geister arbeiteten, alsbald

überzogen sich Tisch und Bänke mit grünem Tuch, die Stühle mit Sammet, und an den Fenstern hiengen seidene Vorhänge herab. Kaum hatte die Nadel den letzten Stich getan, so sah das Mädchen schon durch das Fenster die weißen Federn von dem Hut des Königssohns, den die Spindel an dem goldenen Faden herbei geholt hatte. Er stieg ab, schritt über den Teppich in das Haus herein, und als er in die Stube trat, stand das Mädchen da in seinem ärmlichen Kleid, aber es glühte darin wie eine Rose im Busch. »Du bist die Ärmste und auch die Reichste«, sprach er zu ihr, »komm mit mir, du sollst meine Braut sein.« Sie schwieg, aber sie reichte ihm die Hand. Da gab er ihr einen Kuss, führte sie hinaus, hob sie auf sein Pferd und brachte sie in das königliche Schloss, wo die Hochzeit mit großer Freude gefeiert ward. Spindel, Weberschiffchen und Nadel wurden in der Schatzkammer verwahrt und in großen Ehren gehalten.

189.
Der Bauer und der Teufel.

Es war einmal ein kluges und verschmitztes Bäuerlein, von dessen Streichen viel zu erzählen wäre: die schönste Geschichte ist aber doch, wie er den Teufel einmal dran gekriegt und zum Narren gehabt hat.

Das Bäuerlein hatte eines Tages seinen Acker bestellt und rüstete sich zur Heimfahrt als die Dämmerung schon eingetreten war. Da erblickte er mitten auf seinem Acker einen Haufen feuriger Kohlen, und als er voll Verwunderung hinzugieng, so saß oben auf der Glut ein kleiner schwarzer Teufel. »Du sitzest wohl auf einem Schatz?« sprach das Bäuerlein. »Ja wohl«, antwortete der Teufel, »auf einem Schatz, der mehr Gold und Silber enthält als du dein Lebtag gesehen hast.« »Der Schatz liegt auf meinem Feld und gehört mir«

sprach das Bäuerlein. »Er ist dein« antwortete der Teufel, »wenn du mir zwei Jahre lang die Hälfte von dem gibst, was dein Acker hervorbringt: Geld habe ich genug, aber ich trage Verlangen nach den Früchten der Erde.« Das Bäuerlein gieng auf den Handel ein. »Damit aber kein Streit bei der Teilung entsteht«, sprach es, »so soll dir gehören was über der Erde ist und mir was unter der Erde ist.« Dem Teufel gefiel das wohl, aber das listige Bäuerlein hatte Rüben gesät. Als nun die Zeit der Ernte kam, so erschien der Teufel und wollte seine Frucht holen, er fand aber nichts als die gelben welken Blätter, und das Bäuerlein, ganz vergnügt, grub seine Rüben aus. »Einmal hast du den Vorteil gehabt«, sprach der Teufel, »aber für das nächstemal soll das nicht gelten. Dein ist was über der Erde wächst und mein was darunter ist.« »Mir auch recht« antwortete das Bäuerlein. Als aber die Zeit zur Aussaat kam, säte das Bäuerlein nicht wieder Rüben, sondern Weizen. Die Frucht ward reif, das Bäuerlein gieng auf den Acker und schnitt die vollen Halme bis zur Erde ab. Als der Teufel kam, fand er nichts als die Stoppeln und fuhr wütend in eine Felsenschlucht hinab. »So muss man die Füchse prellen« sprach das Bäuerlein, gieng hin und holte sich den Schatz.

190.

Die Brosamen auf dem Tisch.

Der Güggel het einisch zue sine Hüendlene gseit »chömmet weidli i dStuben ufe goh Brotbrösmeli zämmebicke ufem Tisch: euse Frau isch ußgange goh ne Visite mache.« Do säge do dHüendli »nei nei, mer chömme nit: weist dFrau balget amme mit is.« Do seit der Güggel »se weiß jo nüt dervo, chömmet er nume: se git is doch au nie nit guets.« Do säge dHüendli wider »nei nei, sisch uß und verby, mer gönd nit ufe.« Aber der Güggel het ene kei ruei

glo, bis se endlig gange sind und ufe Tisch, und do Brotbrösmeli zämme gläse hend in aller Strenge. Do chunt jus-
tement dFrau derzue und nimmt gschwind e Stäcke und
steubt se abe und regiert gar grüseli mit ene. Und wo se do
vor em hus unde gsi sind, so säge do dHüendli zum Güggel
»gse gse gse gse gse gse gsehst aber?« Do het der Güggel
glachet und numme gseit »ha ha han is nit gwüsst?« do
händ se chönne goh.

191.

Das Meerhäschen.

Es war einmal eine Königstochter, die hatte in ihrem
Schloss hoch unter der Zinne einen Saal mit zwölf Fenstern, die giengen nach allen Himmelsgegenden, und wenn
sie hinaufstieg und umher schaute, so konnte sie ihr ganzes
Reich übersehen. Aus dem ersten sah sie schon schärfer als
andere Menschen, in dem zweiten noch besser, in dem dritten noch deutlicher und so immer weiter bis in dem zwölften, wo sie alles sah, was über und unter der Erde war und
ihr nichts verborgen bleiben konnte. Weil sie aber stolz
war, sich niemand unterwerfen wollte und die Herrschaft
allein behalten, so ließ sie bekannt machen, es sollte niemand ihr Gemahl werden, der sich nicht so vor ihr verstecken könnte dass es ihr unmöglich wäre ihn zu finden. Wer
es aber versuche und sie entdecke ihn, so werde ihm das
Haupt abgeschlagen und auf einen Pfahl gesteckt. Es standen schon sieben und neunzig Pfähle mit toten Häuptern
vor dem Schloss, und in langer Zeit meldete sich niemand.
Die Königstochter war vergnügt und dachte »ich werde
nun für mein Lebtag frei bleiben.« Da erschienen drei Brüder vor ihr und kündigten ihr an dass sie ihr Glück versuchen wollten. Der älteste glaubte sicher zu sein, wenn er in
ein Kalkloch krieche, aber sie erblickte ihn schon aus dem

ersten Fenster, ließ ihn herausziehen und ihm das Haupt
abschlagen. Der zweite kroch in den Keller des Schlosses,
aber auch diesen erblickte sie aus dem ersten Fenster, und
es war um ihn geschehen: sein Haupt kam auf den neun
und neunzigsten Pfahl. Da trat der jüngste vor sie hin und
bat sie möchte ihm einen Tag Bedenkzeit geben, auch so
gnädig sein es ihm zweimal zu schenken, wenn sie ihn entdecke: misslinge es ihm zum drittenmal, so wolle er sich
nichts mehr aus seinem Leben machen. Weil er so schön
war und so herzlich bat, so sagte sie »ja, ich will dir das bewilligen, aber es wird dir nicht glücken.«
Den folgenden Tag sann er lange nach wie er sich verstecken wollte, aber es war vergeblich. Da ergriff er seine
Büchse und gieng hinaus auf die Jagd. Er sah einen Raben
und nahm ihn aufs Korn; eben wollte er losdrükken, da rief
der Rabe »schieß nicht, ich will dir's vergelten!« Er setzte
ab, gieng weiter und kam an einen See, wo er einen großen
Fisch überraschte, der aus der Tiefe herauf an die Oberflä-
che des Wassers gekommen war. Als er angelegt hatte, rief
der Fisch »schieß nicht, ich will dir's vergelten!« Er ließ ihn
untertauchen, gieng weiter und begegnete einem Fuchs der
hinkte. Er schoss und verfehlte ihn, da rief der Fuchs
»komm lieber her und zieh mir den Dorn aus dem Fuß.«
Er tat es zwar, wollte aber dann den Fuchs töten und ihm
den Balg abziehen. Der Fuchs sprach »lass ab, ich will dir's
vergelten!« Der Jüngling ließ ihn laufen, und da es Abend
war, kehrte er heim.
Am andern Tag sollte er sich verkriechen, aber wie er sich
auch den Kopf darüber zerbrach, er wusste nicht wohin. Er
gieng in den Wald zu dem Raben und sprach »ich habe dich
leben lassen, jetzt sage mir wohin ich mich verkriechen soll,
damit mich die Königstochter nicht sieht.« Der Rabe senkte den Kopf und bedachte sich lange. Endlich schnarrte er
»ich hab's heraus!« Er holte ein Ei aus seinem Nest, zerleg-
te es in zwei Teile und schloss den Jüngling hinein: dann
machte er es wieder ganz und setzte sich darauf. Als die

Königstochter an das erste Fenster trat, konnte sie ihn nicht entdecken, auch nicht in den folgenden, und es fieng an ihr bange zu werden, doch im elften erblickte sie ihn. Sie ließ den Raben schießen, das Ei holen und zerbrechen, und der Jüngling musste heraus kommen. Sie sprach »einmal ist es dir geschenkt, wenn du es nicht besser machst, so bist du verloren.«

Am folgenden Tag gieng er an den See, rief den Fisch herbei und sprach »ich habe dich leben lassen, nun sage wohin soll ich mich verbergen, damit mich die Königstochter nicht sieht.« Der Fisch besann sich, endlich rief er »ich hab's heraus! ich will dich in meinen Bauch verschließen.« Er verschluckte ihn und fuhr hinab auf den Grund des Sees. Die Königstochter blickte durch ihre Fenster, auch im elften sah sie ihn nicht, und war bestürzt, doch endlich im zwölften entdeckte sie ihn. Sie ließ den Fisch fangen und töten, und der Jüngling kam zum Vorschein. Es kann sich jeder denken wie ihm zu Mut war. Sie sprach »zweimal ist dir's geschenkt, aber dein Haupt wird wohl auf den hundertsten Pfahl kommen.«

An dem letzten Tag gieng er mit schwerem Herzen aufs Feld und begegnete dem Fuchs. »Du weißt alle Schlupfwinkel zu finden«, sprach er, »ich habe dich leben lassen, jetzt rat mir wohin ich mich verstecken soll, damit mich die Königstochter nicht findet.« »Ein schweres Stück«, antwortete der Fuchs, und machte ein bedenkliches Gesicht. Endlich rief er »ich hab's heraus!« Er gieng mit ihm zu einer Quelle, tauchte sich hinein und kam als ein Marktkrämer und Tierhändler heraus. Der Jüngling musste sich auch in das Wasser tauchen, und ward in ein kleines Meerhäschen verwandelt. Der Kaufmann zog in die Stadt und zeigte das artige Tierchen. Es lief viel Volk zusammen um es anzusehen. Zuletzt kam auch die Königstochter, und weil sie großen Gefallen daran hatte, kaufte sie es und gab dem Kaufmann viel Geld dafür. Bevor er es ihr hinreichte, sagte er zu ihm »wenn die Königstochter ans Fenster geht, so krieche schnell unter ihren Zopf.« Nun kam die Zeit, wo sie ihn suchen sollte. Sie trat nach der Reihe an die Fenster vom ersten bis zum elften und sah ihn nicht. Als sie ihn auch bei dem zwölften nicht sah, war sie voll Angst und Zorn und schlug es so gewaltig zu, dass das Glas in allen Fenstern in tausend Stücke zersprang und das ganze Schloss erzitterte.

Sie gieng zurück und fühlte das Meerhäschen unter ihrem Zopf, da packte sie es, warf es zu Boden und rief »fort mir aus den Augen!« Es lief zum Kaufmann und beide eilten zur Quelle, wo sie sich untertauchten und ihre wahre Gestalt zurück erhielten. Der Jüngling dankte dem Fuchs und sprach »der Rabe und der Fisch sind blitzdumm gegen dich, du weißt die rechten Pfiffe, das muss wahr sein!«

Der Jüngling gieng geradezu in das Schloss. Die Königstochter wartete schon auf ihn und fügte sich ihrem Schicksal. Die Hochzeit ward gefeiert und er war jetzt der König und Herr des ganzen Reichs. Er erzählte ihr niemals, wohin er sich zum drittenmal versteckt und wer ihm geholfen hatte, und so glaubte sie, er habe alles aus eigener Kunst getan und hatte Achtung vor ihm, denn sie dachte bei sich »der kann doch mehr als du!«

192.

Der Meisterdieb.

Eines Tages saß vor einem ärmlichen Hause ein alter Mann mit seiner Frau, und wollten von der Arbeit ein wenig ausruhen. Da kam auf einmal ein prächtiger, mit vier Rappen bespannter Wagen herbeigefahren, aus dem ein reichgekleideter Herr stieg. Der Bauer stand auf, trat zu dem Herrn, und fragte, was sein Verlangen wäre und worin er ihm dienen könnte. Der Fremde reichte dem Alten die Hand und sagte »ich wünsche nichts als einmal ein ländliches Gericht

zu genießen. Bereitet mir Kartoffel, wie ihr sie zu essen
pflegt, dann will ich mich zu euerm Tisch setzen, und sie
mit Freude verzehren.« Der Bauer lächelte und sagte »ihr
seid ein Graf oder Fürst, oder gar ein Herzog, vornehme
Herrn haben manchmal solch ein Gelüsten; euer Wunsch
soll aber erfüllt werden.« Die Frau gieng in die Küche und
sie fieng an Kartoffel zu waschen und zu reiben und wollte
Klöße daraus bereiten, wie sie die Bauern essen. Während
sie bei der Arbeit stand, sagte der Bauer zu dem Fremden
»kommt einstweilen mit mir in meinen Hausgarten, wo ich
noch etwas zu schaffen habe.« In dem Garten hatte er Löcher gegraben und wollte jetzt Bäume einsetzen. »Habt ihr
keine Kinder«, fragte der Fremde, »die euch bei der Arbeit
behilflich sein könnten?« »Nein« antwortete der Bauer;
»ich habe freilich einen Sohn gehabt«, setzte er hinzu,
»aber der ist schon seit langer Zeit in die weite Welt gegangen. Es war ein ungeratener Junge, klug und verschlagen,
aber er wollte nichts lernen und machte lauter böse Streiche; zuletzt lief er mir fort, und seitdem habe ich nichts von
ihm gehört.« Der Alte nahm ein Bäumchen, setzte es in ein
Loch und stieß einen Pfahl daneben: und als er Erde hin-
eingeschaufelt und sie festgestampft hatte, band er den
Stamm unten, oben und in der Mitte mit einem Strohseil
fest an den Pfahl. »Aber sagt mir«, sprach der Herr, »warum bindet ihr den krummen knorrichten Baum, der dort in
der Ecke fast bis auf den Boden gebückt liegt, nicht auch an
einen Pfahl, wie diesen, damit er strack wächst?« Der Alte
lächelte und sagte »Herr, ihr redet wie ihr's versteht: man
sieht wohl dass ihr euch mit der Gärtnerei nicht abgegeben
habt. Der Baum dort ist alt und verknorzt, den kann niemand mehr gerad machen: Bäume muss man ziehen, so lange sie jung sind.« »Es ist wie bei euerm Sohn«, sagte der
Fremde, »hättet ihr den gezogen, wie er noch jung war, so
wäre er nicht fortgelaufen; jetzt wird er auch hart und
knorzig geworden sein.« »Freilich«, antwortete der Alte,
»es ist schon lange seit er fortgegangen ist; er wird sich ver-

ändert haben.« »Würdet ihr ihn noch erkennen, wenn er
vor euch träte?« fragte der Fremde. »Am Gesicht schwer-
lich«, antwortete der Bauer, »aber er hat ein Zeichen an
sich, ein Muttermal auf der Schulter, das wie eine Bohne
aussieht.« Als er das gesagt hatte, zog der Fremde den Rock
aus, entblößte seine Schulter und zeigte dem Bauer die
Bohne. »Herr Gott«, rief der Alte, »du bist wahrhaftig
mein Sohn«, und die Liebe zu seinem Kind regte sich in
seinem Herzen. »Aber«, setzte er hinzu, »wie kannst du
mein Sohn sein, du bist ein großer Herr geworden und
lebst in Reichtum und Überfluss? auf welchem Weg bist du
dazu gelangt?« »Ach, Vater«, erwiderte der Sohn, »der junge Baum war an keinen Pfahl gebunden und ist krumm gewachsen: jetzt ist er zu alt; er wird nicht wieder gerad. Wie
ich das alles erworben habe? ich bin ein Dieb geworden.
Aber erschreckt euch nicht, ich bin ein Meisterdieb. Für
mich gibt es weder Schloss noch Riegel: wonach mich ge-
lüstet, das ist mein. Glaubt nicht dass ich stehle wie ein ge-
meiner Dieb, ich nehme nur vom Überfluss der Reichen.
Arme Leute sind sicher: ich gebe ihnen lieber als dass ich
ihnen etwas nehme. So auch was ich ohne Mühe List und
Gewandtheit haben kann, das rühre ich nicht an.« »Ach,
mein Sohn«, sagte der Vater, »es gefällt mir doch nicht, ein
Dieb bleibt ein Dieb; ich sage dir es nimmt kein gutes
Ende.« Er führte ihn zu der Mutter, und als sie hörte dass
es ihr Sohn war, weinte sie vor Freude, als er ihr aber sagte
dass er ein Meisterdieb geworden wäre, so flossen ihr zwei
Ströme über das Gesicht. Endlich sagte sie »wenn er auch
ein Dieb geworden ist, so ist er doch mein Sohn, und meine
Augen haben ihn noch einmal gesehen.«

Sie setzten sich an den Tisch, und er aß mit seinen Eltern
wieder einmal die schlechte Kost, die er lange nicht gegessen hatte. Der Vater sprach »wenn unser Herr, der Graf
drüben im Schlosse, erfährt wer du bist und was du treibst,
so nimmt er dich nicht auf die Arme und wiegt dich darin,
wie er tat, als er dich am Taufstein hielt, sondern er lässt

dich am Galgenstrick schaukeln.« »Seid ohne Sorge, mein Vater, er wird mir nichts tun, denn ich verstehe mein Handwerk. Ich will heute noch selbst zu ihm gehen.« Als die Abendzeit sich näherte, setzte sich der Meisterdieb in seinen Wagen und fuhr nach dem Schloss. Der Graf empfieng ihn mit Artigkeit, weil er ihn für einen vornehmen Mann hielt. Als aber der Fremde sich zu erkennen gab, so erbleichte er und schwieg eine Zeitlang ganz still. Endlich sprach er »du bist mein Pate, deshalb will ich Gnade für Recht ergehen lassen und nachsichtig mit dir verfahren. Weil du dich rühmst ein Meisterdieb zu sein, so will ich deine Kunst auf die Probe stellen wenn du aber nicht bestehst, so musst du mit des Seilers Tochter Hochzeit halten, und das Gekrächze der Raben soll deine Musik dabei sein.« »Herr Graf«, antwortete der Meister, »denkt euch drei Stücke aus, so schwer ihr wollt, und wenn ich eure Aufgabe nicht löse, so tut mit mir wie euch gefällt.« Der Graf sann einige Augenblicke nach, dann sprach er »wohlan, zum ersten sollst du mir mein Leibpferd aus dem Stalle stehlen, zum andern sollst du mir und meiner Gemahlin, wenn wir eingeschlafen sind, das Bettuch unter dem Leib wegnehmen, ohne dass wir's merken, und dazu meiner Gemahlin den Trauring vom Finger: zum dritten und letzten sollst du mir den Pfarrer und Küster aus der Kirche wegstehlen. Merke dir alles wohl, denn es geht dir an den Hals.«

Der Meister begab sich in die zunächst liegende Stadt. Dort kaufte er einer alten Bauerfrau die Kleider ab, und zog sie an. Dann färbte er sich das Gesicht braun und malte sich noch Runzeln hinein, so dass ihn kein Mensch wieder erkannt hätte. Endlich füllte er ein Fässchen mit altem Ungarwein, in welchen ein starker Schlaftrunk gemischt war. Das Fässchen legte er auf eine Kötze, die er auf den Rücken nahm, und gieng mit bedächtigen, schwankenden Schritten zu dem Schloss des Grafen. Es war schon dunkel als er anlangte: er setzte sich in dem Hof auf einen Stein, fieng an zu husten, wie eine alte brustkranke Frau und rieb die

Hände, als wenn er fröre. Vor der Türe des Pferdestalls lagen Soldaten um ein Feuer: einer von ihnen bemerkte die Frau und rief ihr zu »komm näher, altes Mütterchen, und wärme dich bei uns. Du hast doch kein Nachtlager und nimmst es an, wo du es findest.« Die Alte trippelte herbei, bat ihr die Kötze vom Rücken zu heben und setzte sich zu ihnen ans Feuer. »Was hast du da in deinem Fässchen, du alte Schachtel?« fragte einer. »Einen guten Schluck Wein«, antwortete sie, »ich ernähre mich mit dem Handel, für Geld und gute Worte gebe ich euch gerne ein Glas.« »Nur her damit«, sagte der Soldat, und als er ein Glas gekostet hatte, rief er »wenn der Wein gut ist, so trink ich lieber ein Glas mehr«, ließ sich nochmals einschenken, und die andern folgten seinem Beispiel. »Heda, Kameraden«, rief einer denen zu, die in dem Stall saßen, »hier ist ein Mütterchen, das hat Wein, der so alt ist wie sie selber, nehmt auch einen Schluck, der wärmt euch den Magen noch besser als unser Feuer.« Die Alte trug ihr Fässchen in den Stall. Einer hatte sich auf das gesattelte Leibpferd gesetzt, ein anderer hielt den Zaum in der Hand, ein dritter hatte den Schwanz gepackt. Sie schenkte ein so viel verlangt ward, bis die Quelle versiegte. Nicht lange so fiel dem einen der Zaum aus der Hand, er sank nieder und fieng an zu schnarchen, der andere ließ den Schwanz los, legte sich nieder und schnarchte noch lauter. Der welcher im Sattel saß, blieb zwar sitzen, bog sich aber mit dem Kopf fast bis auf den Hals des Pferdes, schlief und blies mit dem Mund wie ein Schmiedebalg. Die Soldaten draußen waren schon längst eingeschlafen, lagen auf der Erde und regten sich nicht, als wären sie von Stein. Als der Meisterdieb sah dass es ihm geglückt war, gab er dem einen statt des Zaums ein Seil in die Hand, und dem andern, der den Schwanz gehalten hatte, einen Strohwisch; aber was sollte er mit dem, der auf dem Rücken des Pferdes saß, anfangen? Herunter werfen wollte er ihn nicht, er hätte erwachen und ein Geschrei erheben können. Er wusste aber guten Rat, er schnallte die

Sattelgurt auf, knüpfte ein paar Seile, die in Ringen an der Wand hiengen, an den Sattel fest, und zog den schlafenden Reiter mit dem Sattel in die Höhe, dann schlug er die Seile um den Pfosten und machte sie fest. Das Pferd hatte er bald von der Kette los gebunden, aber wenn er über das steinerne Pflaster des Hofs geritten wäre, so hätte man den Lärm im Schloss gehört. Er umwickelte ihm also zuvor die Hufen mit alten Lappen, führte es dann vorsichtig hinaus, schwang sich auf und jagte davon.

Als der Tag angebrochen war, sprengte der Meister auf dem gestohlenen Pferd zu dem Schloss. Der Graf war eben aufgestanden und blickte aus dem Fenster. »Guten Morgen, Herr Graf«, rief er ihm zu, »hier ist das Pferd, das ich glücklich aus dem Stall geholt habe. Schaut nur, wie schön eure Soldaten da liegen und schlafen, und wenn ihr in den Stall gehen wollt, so werdet ihr sehen, wie bequem sich's eure Wächter gemacht haben.« Der Graf musste lachen, dann sprach er »einmal ist dir's gelungen, aber das zweitemal wird's nicht so glücklich ablaufen. Und ich warne dich, wenn du mir als Dieb begegnest, so behandle ich dich auch wie einen Dieb.« Als die Gräfin Abends zu Bette gegangen war, schloss sie die Hand mit dem Trauring fest zu, und der Graf sagte »alle Türen sind verschlossen und verriegelt, ich bleibe wach und will den Dieb erwarten; steigt er aber zum Fenster ein, so schieße ich ihn nieder.« Der Meisterdieb aber gieng in der Dunkelheit hinaus zu dem Galgen, schnitt einen armen Sünder, der da hieng, von dem Strick ab und trug ihn auf dem Rücken nach dem Schloss. Dort stellte er eine Leiter an das Schlafgemach, setzte den Toten auf seine Schultern und fieng an hinauf zu steigen. Als er so hoch gekommen war, dass der Kopf des Toten in dem Fenster erschien, drückte der Graf, der in seinem Bett lauerte, eine Pistole auf ihn los: alsbald ließ der Meister den armen Sünder herab fallen, sprang selbst die Leiter herab, und versteckte sich in eine Ecke. Die Nacht war von dem Mond so weit erhellt, dass der Meister deutlich sehen

konnte wie der Graf aus dem Fenster auf die Leiter stieg,
herabkam und den Toten in den Garten trug. Dort fieng er
an ein Loch zu graben, in das er ihn legen wollte. »Jetzt«,
dachte der Dieb, »ist der günstige Augenblick gekommen«,
schlich behende aus seinem Winkel und stieg die Leiter
hinauf, geradezu ins Schlafgemach der Gräfin. »Liebe
Frau«, fieng er mit der Stimme des Grafen an, »der Dieb
ist tot, aber er ist doch mein Pate und mehr ein Schelm als
ein Bösewicht gewesen: ich will ihn der öffentlichen
Schande nicht preis geben; auch mit den armen Eltern habe
ich Mitleid. Ich will ihn, bevor der Tag anbricht, selbst im
Garten begraben, damit die Sache nicht ruchtbar wird. Gib
mir auch das Betttuch, so will ich die Leiche einhüllen und
ihn wie einen Hund verscharren.« Die Gräfin gab ihm das
Tuch. »Weißt du was«, sagte der Dieb weiter, »ich habe
eine Anwandlung von Großmut, gib mir noch den Ring;
der Unglückliche hat sein Leben gewagt, so mag er ihn ins
Grab mitnehmen.« Sie wollte dem Grafen nicht entgegen
sein, und obgleich sie es ungern tat, so zog sie doch den
Ring vom Finger und reichte ihn hin. Der Dieb machte
sich mit beiden Stücken fort und kam glücklich nach Haus,
bevor der Graf im Garten mit seiner Totengräberarbeit fertig war.
Was zog der Graf für ein langes Gesicht, als am andern
Morgen der Meister kam und ihm das Betttuch und den
Ring brachte. »Kannst du hexen?« sagte er zu ihm, »wer
hat dich aus dem Grab geholt, in das ich selbst dich gelegt
habe, und hat dich wieder lebendig gemacht?« »Mich habt
ihr nicht begraben«, sagte der Dieb, »sondern den armen
Sünder am Galgen« und erzählte ausführlich wie es zugegangen war; und der Graf musste ihm zugestehen dass er
ein gescheiter und listiger Dieb wäre. »Aber noch bist du
nicht zu Ende«, setzte er hinzu, »du hast noch die dritte
Aufgabe zu lösen, und wenn dir das nicht gelingt, so hilft
dir alles nichts.« Der Meister lächelte und gab keine Antwort.

Als die Nacht eingebrochen war, kam er mit einem langen
Sack auf dem Rücken, einem Bündel unter dem Arm, und
einer Laterne in der Hand zu der Dorfkirche gegangen. In
dem Sack hatte er Krebse, in dem Bündel aber kurze
Wachslichter. Er setzte sich auf den Gottesacker, holte einen Krebs heraus und klebte ihm ein Wachslichtchen auf
den Rücken; dann zündete er das Lichtchen an, setzte den
Krebs auf den Boden und ließ ihn kriechen. Er holte einen
zweiten aus dem Sack, machte es mit diesem ebenso und
fuhr fort bis auch der letzte aus dem Sacke war. Hierauf
zog er ein langes schwarzes Gewand an, das wie eine
Mönchskutte aussah und klebte sich einen grauen Bart an
das Kinn. Als er endlich ganz unkenntlich war, nahm er
den Sack, in dem die Krebse gewesen waren, gieng in die
Kirche und stieg auf die Kanzel. Die Turmuhr schlug eben
zwölf: als der letzte Schlag verklungen war, rief er mit lauter gellender Stimme »hört an, ihr sündigen Menschen, das
Ende aller Dinge ist gekommen, der jüngste Tag ist nahe:
hört an, hört an. Wer mit mir in den Himmel will, der krieche in den Sack. Ich bin Petrus, der die Himmelstüre öffnet
und schließt. Seht ihr draußen auf dem Gottesacker wandeln die Gestorbenen und sammeln ihre Gebeine zusammen. Kommt, kommt und kriecht in den Sack, die Welt
geht unter.« Das Geschrei erschallte durch das ganze Dorf.
Der Pfarrer und der Küster, die zunächst an der Kirche
wohnten, hatten es zuerst vernommen, und als sie die Lichter erblickten, die auf dem Gottesacker umher wandelten,
merkten sie dass etwas Ungewöhnliches vorgieng und traten sie in die Kirche ein. Sie hörten der Predigt eine Weile
zu, da stieß der Küster den Pfarrer an und sprach »es wäre
nicht übel, wenn wir die Gelegenheit benutzten und zusammen vor dem Einbruch des jüngsten Tags auf eine
leichte Art in den Himmel kämen.« »Freilich«, erwiderte
der Pfarrer, »das sind auch meine Gedanken gewesen; habt
ihr Lust, so wollen wir uns auf den Weg machen.« »Ja«,
antwortete der Küster, »aber ihr, Herr Pfarrer, habt den

Vortritt, ich folge nach.« Der Pfarrer schritt also vor und
stieg auf die Kanzel, wo der Meister den Sack öffnete. Der
Pfarrer kroch zuerst hinein, dann der Küster. Gleich band
der Meister den Sack fest zu, packte ihn am Bausch und
schleifte ihn die Kanzeltreppe hinab: so oft die Köpfe der
beiden Toren auf die Stufen aufschlugen, rief er »jetzt geht's
schon über die Berge.« Dann zog er sie auf gleiche Weise
durch das Dorf, und wenn sie durch Pfützen kamen, rief er
»jetzt geht's schon durch die nassen Wolken«, und als er sie
endlich die Schlosstreppe hinaufzog, so rief er »jetzt sind
wir auf der Himmelstreppe und werden bald im Vorhof
sein.« Als er oben angelangt war, schob er den Sack in den
Taubenschlag, und als die Tauben flatterten, sagte er »hört
ihr wie die Engel sich freuen und mit den Fittichen schlagen.« Dann schob er den Riegel vor und gieng fort.
Am andern Morgen begab er sich zu dem Grafen, und sagte ihm dass er auch die dritte Aufgabe gelöst und den Pfarrer und Küster aus der Kirche weggeführt hätte. »Wo hast
du sie gelassen?« fragte der Herr. »Sie liegen in einem Sack
oben auf dem Taubenschlag und bilden sich ein sie wären
im Himmel.« Der Graf stieg selbst hinauf und überzeugte
sich dass er die Wahrheit gesagt hatte. Als er den Pfarrer
und Küster aus dem Gefängnis befreit hatte, sprach er »du
bist ein Erzdieb, und hast deine Sache gewonnen. Für diesmal kommst du mit heiler Haut davon, aber mache dass du
aus meinem Land fortkommst, denn wenn du dich wieder
darin betreten lässt, so kannst du auf deine Erhöhung am
Galgen rechnen.« Der Erzdieb nahm Abschied von seinen
Eltern, gieng wieder in die weite Welt, und niemand hat
wieder etwas von ihm gehört.

193

Der Trommler.

Eines Abends gieng ein junger Trommler ganz allein auf dem Feld und kam an einen See, da sah er an dem Ufer drei Stückchen weiße Leinewand liegen. »Was für feines Leinen« sprach er, und steckte eines davon in die Tasche. Er gieng heim, dachte nicht weiter an seinen Fund und legte sich zu Bett. Als er eben einschlafen wollte, war es ihm als nennte jemand seinen Namen. Er horchte und vernahm eine leise Stimme, die ihm zurief »Trommeler, Trommeler, wach auf.« Er konnte, da es finstere Nacht war, niemand sehen, aber es kam ihm vor als schwebte eine Gestalt vor seinem Bett auf und ab. »Was willst du?« fragte er. »Gib mir mein Hemdchen zurück«, antwortete die Stimme, »das du mir gestern Abend am See weggenommen hast.« »Du sollst es wieder haben«, sprach der Trommler, »wenn du mir sagst wer du bist.« »Ach«, erwiderte die Stimme, »ich bin die Tochter eines mächtigen Königs, aber ich bin in die Gewalt einer Hexe geraten, und bin auf den Glasberg gebannt. Jeden Tag muss ich mich mit meinen zwei Schwestern im See baden, aber ohne mein Hemdchen kann ich nicht wieder fort fliegen. Meine Schwestern haben sich fort gemacht, ich aber habe zurück bleiben müssen. Ich bitte dich gib mir mein Hemdchen wieder.« »Sei ruhig, armes Kind«, sprach der Trommler, »ich will dir's gerne zurückgeben.« Er holte es aus seiner Tasche, und reichte es ihr in der Dunkelheit hin. Sie erfasste es hastig, und wollte damit fort. »Weile einen Augenblick«, sagte er »vielleicht kann ich dir helfen.« »Helfen kannst du mir nur, wenn du auf den Glasberg steigst und mich aus der Gewalt der Hexe befreist. Aber zu dem Glasberg kommst du nicht, und wenn du auch ganz nahe daran wärst, so kannst du nicht hinauf.« »Was ich will, das kann ich«, sagte der Trommler, »ich habe Mitleid mit dir und ich fürchte mich vor nichts. Aber ich

weiß den Weg nicht, der nach dem Glasberge führt:« »Der
Weg geht durch den großen Wald, in dem die Menschenfresser hausen«, antwortete sie, »mehr darf ich dir nicht sagen.« Darauf hörte er wie sie fortschwirrte.
Bei Anbruch des Tags machte sich der Trommler auf, hieng
seine Trommel um und gieng ohne Furcht geradezu in den
Wald hinein. Als er ein Weilchen gegangen war und keinen
Riesen erblickte, so dachte er »ich muss die Langeschläfer
aufwecken«, hieng die Trommel vor und schlug einen Wir-
bel, dass die Vögel aus den Bäumen mit Geschrei aufflogen.
Nicht lange so erhob sich auch ein Riese in die Höhe, der
im Gras gelegen und geschlafen hatte, und war so groß wie
eine Tanne. »Du Wicht«, rief er ihm zu, »was trommelst du
hier und weckst mich aus dem besten Schlaf?« »Ich tromm-
le«, antwortete er, »weil viele tausende hinter mir herkommen, damit sie den Weg wissen.« »Was wollen die hier in
meinem Wald?« fragte der Riese. »Sie wollen dir den Garaus machen und den Wald von einem Ungetüm, wie du
bist, säubern.« »Oho«, sagte der Riese, »ich trete euch wie
Ameisen tot.« »Meinst du, du könntest gegen sie etwas ausrichten?« sprach der Trommler, »wenn du dich bückst, um
einen zu packen, so springt er fort und versteckt sich: wie
du dich aber niederlegst und schläfst, so kommen sie aus allen Gebüschen herbei, und kriechen an dir hinauf. Jeder hat
einen Hammer von Stahl am Gürtel stecken, damit schlagen sie dir den Schädel ein.« Der Riese ward verdrießlich
und dachte »wenn ich mich mit dem listigen Volk befasse,
so könnte es doch zu meinem Schaden ausschlagen. Wölfen
und Bären drücke ich die Gurgel zusammen, aber vor den
Erdwürmen kann ich mich nicht schützen.« »Hör, kleiner
Kerl«, sprach er, »zieh wieder ab, ich verspreche dir, dass
ich dich und deine Gesellen in Zukunft in Ruhe lassen will,
und hast du noch einen Wunsch, so sag's mir, ich will dir
wohl etwas zu Gefallen tun.« »Du hast lange Beine«,
sprach der Trommler, »und kannst schneller laufen als ich,
trag mich zum Glasberge, so will ich den Meinigen ein Zei-

chen zum Rückzug geben, und sie sollen dich diesmal in Ruhe lassen.« »Komm her, Wurm«, sprach der Riese, »setz dich auf meine Schulter, ich will dich tragen wohin du verlangst.« Der Riese hob ihn hinauf, und der Trommler fieng oben an nach Herzenslust auf der Trommel zu wirbeln. Der Riese dachte »das wird das Zeichen sein, dass das andere Volk zurückgehen soll.« Nach einer Weile stand ein zweiter Riese am Weg, der nahm den Trommler dem ersten ab und steckte ihn in sein Knopfloch. Der Trommler fasste den Knopf, der wie eine Schüssel groß war, hielt sich daran und schaute ganz lustig umher. Dann kamen sie zu einem dritten, der nahm ihn aus dem Knopfloch und setzte ihn auf den Rand seines Hutes; da gieng der Trommler oben auf und ab und sah über die Bäume hinaus, und als er in blauer Ferne einen Berg erblickte, so dachte er »das ist gewiss der Glasberg«, und er war es auch. Der Riese tat nur noch ein paar Schritte, so waren sie an dem Fuß des Bergs angelangt, wo ihn der Riese absetzte. Der Trommler verlangte er sollte ihn auch auf die Spitze des Glasberges tragen, aber der Riese schüttelte mit dem Kopf, brummte etwas in den Bart und gieng in den Wald zurück.

Nun stand der arme Trommler vor dem Berg, der so hoch war, als wenn drei Berge aufeinander gesetzt wären, und dabei so glatt wie ein Spiegel, und wusste keinen Rat um hinauf zu kommen. Er fieng an zu klettern, aber vergeblich, er rutschte immer wieder herab. »Wer jetzt ein Vogel wäre« dachte er, aber was half das Wünschen, es wuchsen ihm keine Flügel. Indem er so stand, und sich nicht zu helfen wusste, erblickte er nicht weit von sich zwei Männer, die heftig miteinander stritten. Er gieng auf sie zu und sah dass sie wegen eines Sattels uneins waren, der vor ihnen auf der Erde lag und den jeder von ihnen haben wollte. »Was seid ihr für Narren«, sprach er, »zankt euch um einen Sattel und habt kein Pferd dazu.« »Der Sattel ist wert dass man darum streitet«, antwortete der eine von den Männern, »wer darauf sitzt und wünscht sich irgend wohin, und wär's am Ende der

Welt, der ist im Augenblick angelangt, wie er den Wunsch ausgesprochen hat. Der Sattel gehört uns gemeinschaftlich, die Reihe darauf zu reiten ist an mir, aber der andere will es nicht zulassen.« »Den Streit will ich bald austragen«, sagte der Trommler, gieng eine Strecke weit und steckte einen weißen Stab in die Erde. Dann kam er zurück und sprach »jetzt lauft nach dem Ziel, wer zuerst dort ist, der reitet zuerst.« Beide setzten sich in Trab, aber kaum waren sie ein paar Schritte weg, so schwang sich der Trommler auf den Sattel, wünschte sich auf den Glasberg, und ehe man die Hand umdrehte, war er dort. Auf dem Berg oben war eine Ebne, da stand ein altes steinernes Haus, und vor dem Haus lag ein großer Fischteich, dahinter aber ein finsterer Wald. Menschen und Tiere sah er nicht, es war alles still, nur der Wind raschelte in den Bäumen, und die Wolken zogen ganz nah über seinem Haupt weg. Er trat an die Türe und klopfte an. Als er zum drittenmal geklopft hatte, öffnete eine Alte mit braunem Gesicht und roten Augen die Türe; sie hatte eine Brille auf ihrer langen Nase und sah ihn scharf an, dann fragte sie was sein Begehren wäre. »Einlass, Kost und Nachtlager« antwortete der Trommler. »Das sollst du haben«, sagte die Alte, »wenn du dafür drei Arbeiten verrichten willst.« »Warum nicht?« antwortete er, »ich scheue keine Arbeit, und wenn sie noch so schwer ist.« Die Alte ließ ein, gab ihm Essen und Abends ein gutes Bett. Am Morgen als er ausgeschlafen hatte, nahm die Alte einen Fingerhut von ihrem dürren Finger, reichte ihn dem Trommler hin, und sagte »jetzt geh an die Arbeit und schöpfe den Teich draußen mit diesem Fingerhut aus: aber ehe es Nacht wird musst du fertig sein, und alle Fische, die in dem Wasser sind, müssen nach ihrer Art und Größe ausgesucht und nebeneinander gelegt sein.« »Das ist eine seltsame Arbeit«, sagte der Trommler, gieng aber zu dem Teich und fieng an zu schöpfen. Er schöpfte den ganzen Morgen, aber was kann man mit einem Fingerhut bei einem großen Wasser ausrichten, und wenn man tausend Jahre schöpft? Als es Mittag war, dachte er »es ist alles umsonst, und ist einerlei ob ich arbeite oder nicht«, hielt ein, und setzte sich nieder. Da kam ein Mädchen aus dem Haus gegangen, stellte ihm ein Körbchen mit Essen hin, und sprach »du sitzest da so traurig, was fehlt dir?« Er blickte es an und sah dass es wunderschön war. »Ach«, sagte er, »ich kann die erste Arbeit nicht vollbringen, wie wird es mit den andern werden? Ich bin ausgegangen eine Königstochter zu suchen, die hier wohnen soll, aber ich habe sie nicht gefunden; ich will weiter gehen.« »Bleib hier«, sagte das Mädchen, »ich will dir aus deiner Not helfen. Du bist müde, lege deinen Kopf in meinen Schoß und schlaf. Wenn du wieder aufwachst, so ist die Arbeit getan.« Der Trommler ließ sich das nicht zweimal sagen. Sobald ihm die Augen zufielen, drehte sie einen Wunschring und sprach »Wasser herauf, Fische heraus.« Alsbald stieg das Wasser wie ein weißer Nebel in die Höhe und zog mit den andern Wolken fort, und die Fische schnalzten, sprangen ans Ufer, und legten sich nebeneinander, jeder nach seiner Größe und Art. Als der Trommler erwachte, sah er mit Erstaunen dass alles vollbracht war. Aber das Mädchen sprach »einer von den Fischen liegt nicht bei seinesgleichen, sondern ganz allein. Wenn die Alte heute Abend kommt, und sieht dass alles geschehen ist, was sie verlangt hat, so wird sie fragen ›was soll dieser Fisch allein?‹ Dann wirf ihr den Fisch ins Angesicht und sprich ›der soll für dich sein, alte Hexe.‹« Abends kam die Alte, und als sie die Frage getan hatte, so warf er ihr den Fisch ins Gesicht. Sie stellte sich als merkte sie es nicht und schwieg still, aber sie blickte ihn mit boshaften Augen an. Am andern Morgen sprach sie »gestern hast du es zu leicht gehabt, ich muss dir schwerere Arbeit geben. Heute musst du den ganzen Wald umhauen, das Holz in Scheite spalten und in Klaftern legen, und am Abend muss alles fertig sein.« Sie gab ihm eine Axt, einen Schläger und zwei Keile. Aber die Axt war von Blei, der Schläger und die Keile waren von Blech. Als er anfieng zu hauen, so legte sich die Axt um, und Schläger und Keile drückten sich zusammen. Er wusste sich

nicht zu helfen, aber Mittags kam das Mädchen wieder mit
dem Essen und tröstete ihn. »Lege deinen Kopf in meinen
Schoß«, sagte sie, »und schlaf, wenn du aufwachst, so ist die
Arbeit getan.« Sie drehte ihren Wunschring, in dem Augenblick sank der ganze Wald mit Krachen zusammen, das
Holz spaltete sich von selbst, und legte sich in Klaftern zusammen; es war als ob unsichtbare Riesen die Arbeit voll-
brächten. Als er aufwachte, sagte das Mädchen »siehst du
das Holz ist geklaftert und gelegt: nur ein einziger Ast ist
übrig, aber wenn die Alte heute Abend kommt und fragt
was der Ast solle, so gib ihr damit einen Schlag und sprich
›der soll für dich sein, du Hexe.‹« Die Alte kam, »siehst du«,
sprach sie, »wie leicht die Arbeit war: aber für wen liegt der
Ast noch da?« »Für dich, du Hexe« antwortete er und gab
ihr einen Schlag damit. Aber sie tat als fühlte sie es nicht,
lachte höhnisch und sprach »Morgen früh sollst du alles
Holz auf einen Haufen legen, es anzünden und verbrennen.« Er stand mit Anbruch des Tages auf und fieng an das
Holz herbei zu holen, aber wie kann ein einziger Mensch einen ganzen Wald zusammen tragen? die Arbeit rückte nicht
fort. Doch das Mädchen verließ ihn nicht in der Not: es
brachte ihm Mittags seine Speise, und als er gegessen hatte,
legte er seinen Kopf in den Schoß und schlief ein. Bei seinem
Erwachen brannte der ganze Holzstoß in einer ungeheuern
Flamme, die ihre Zungen bis in den Himmel ausstreckte.
»Hör mich an«, sprach das Mädchen, »wenn die Hexe
kommt, wird sie dir allerlei auftragen: tust du ohne Furcht
was sie verlangt, so kann sie dir nichts anhaben: fürchtest du
dich aber, so packt dich das Feuer und verzehrt dich. Zuletzt, wenn du alles getan hast, so packe sie mit beiden Händen, und wirf sie mitten in die Glut.« Das Mädchen gieng
fort, und die Alte kam herangeschlichen, »hu! mich friert«,
sagte sie, »aber das ist ein Feuer, das brennt, das wärmt mir
die alten Knochen, da wird mir wohl. Aber dort liegt ein
Klotz, der will nicht brennen, den hol mir heraus. Hast du
das noch getan, so bist du frei, und kannst ziehen wohin du

willst. Nur munter hinein.« Der Trommler besann sich nicht lange sprang mitten in die Flammen, aber sie taten ihm nichts, nicht einmal die Haare konnten sie ihm versengen. Er trug den Klotz heraus und legte ihn hin. Kaum aber hatte das Holz die Erde berührt, so verwandelte es sich, und das schöne Mädchen stand vor ihm, das ihm in der Not geholfen hatte: und an den seidenen goldglänzenden Kleidern, die es anhatte, merkte er wohl dass es die Königstochter war. Aber die Alte lachte giftig und sprach »du meinst du hättest sie, aber du hast sie noch nicht.« Eben wollte sie auf das Mädchen losgehen, und es fortziehen, da packte er die Alte mit beiden Händen, hob sie in die Höhe, und warf sie den Flammen in den Rachen, die über ihr zusammenschlugen, als freuten sie sich dass sie eine Hexe verzehren sollten.

Die Königstochter blickte darauf den Trommler an, und als sie sah dass es ein schöner Jüngling war und bedachte dass er sein Leben daran gesetzt hatte, um sie zu erlösen, so reichte sie ihm die Hand und sprach »du hast alles für mich gewagt, aber ich will auch für dich alles tun. Versprichst du mir deine Treue, so sollst du mein Gemahl werden. An Reichtümern fehlt es uns nicht, wir haben genug an dem, was die Hexe hier zusammen getragen hat.« Sie führte ihn in das Haus, da standen Kisten und Kasten, die mit ihren Schätzen angefüllt waren. Sie ließen Gold und Silber liegen und nahmen nur die Edelsteine. Sie wollte nicht länger auf dem Glasberg bleiben, da sprach er zu ihr »setze dich zu mir auf meinen Sattel, so fliegen wir hinab wie Vögel.« »Der alte Sattel gefällt mir nicht«, sagte sie, »ich brauche nur an meinem Wunschring zu drehen, so sind wir zu Haus.« »Wohlan«, antwortete der Trommler, »so wünsch uns vor das Stadttor.« Im Nu waren sie dort, der Trommler aber sprach »ich will erst zu meinen Eltern gehen und ihnen Nachricht geben, harre mein hier auf dem Feld, ich will bald zurück sein.« »Ach«, sagte die Königstochter, »ich bitte dich, nimm dich in Acht, küsse deine Eltern bei deiner Ankunft nicht auf die rechte Wange, denn sonst wirst du

alles vergessen, und ich bleibe hier allein und verlassen auf
dem Feld zurück.« »Wie kann ich dich vergessen?« sagte er
und versprach ihr in die Hand recht bald wieder zu kommen. Als er in sein väterliches Haus trat, wusste niemand
wer er war, so hatte er sich verändert, denn die drei Tage,
die er auf dem Glasberg zugebracht hatte, waren drei lange
Jahre gewesen. Da gab er sich zu erkennen, und seine Eltern fielen ihm vor Freude um den Hals, und er war so bewegt in seinem Herzen, dass er sie auf beide Wangen küsste
und an die Worte des Mädchens nicht dachte. Wie er ihnen
aber den Kuss auf die rechte Wange gegeben hatte, verschwand ihm jeder Gedanke an die Königstochter. Er leerte
seine Taschen aus und legte Händevoll der größten Edelsteine auf den Tisch. Die Eltern wussten gar nicht was sie
mit dem Reichtum anfangen sollten. Da baute der Vater ein
prächtiges Schloss, von Gärten, Wäldern und Wiesen umgeben, als wenn ein Fürst darin wohnen sollte. Und als es
fertig war, sagte die Mutter »ich habe ein Mädchen für dich
ausgesucht, in drei Tagen soll die Hochzeit sein.« Der Sohn
war mit allem zufrieden, was die Eltern wollten.

Die arme Königstochter hatte lange vor der Stadt gestanden
und auf die Rückkehr des Jünglings gewartet. Als es Abend
ward, sprach sie »gewiss hat er seine Eltern auf die rechte
Wange geküsst, und hat mich vergessen.« Ihr Herz war voll
Trauer, sie wünschte sich in ein einsames Waldhäuschen
und wollte nicht wieder an den Hof ihres Vaters zurück.
Jeden Abend gieng sie in die Stadt, und gieng an seinem
Haus vorüber: er sah sie manchmal, aber er kannte sie nicht
mehr. Endlich hörte sie wie die Leute sagten »morgen wird
seine Hochzeit gefeiert.« Da sprach sie »ich will versuchen
ob ich sein Herz wieder gewinne.« Als der erste Hochzeits-
tag gefeiert ward, da drehte sie ihren Wunschring und
sprach »ein Kleid so glänzend wie die Sonne.« Alsbald lag
das Kleid vor ihr und war so glänzend, als wenn es aus lauter Sonnenstrahlen gewebt wäre. Als alle Gäste sich versammelt hatten, so trat sie in den Saal. Jedermann wunderte

sich über das schöne Kleid, am meisten die Braut, und da
schöne Kleider ihre größte Lust waren, so gieng sie zu der
Fremden und fragte ob sie es ihr verkaufen wollte. »Für
Geld nicht«, antwortete sie, »aber wenn ich die erste Nacht
vor der Türe verweilen darf, wo der Bräutigam schläft, so
will ich es hingeben.« Die Braut konnte ihr Verlangen nicht
bezwingen und willigte ein, aber sie mischte dem Bräutigam einen Schlaftrunk in seinen Nachtwein, wovon er in
tiefen Schlaf verfiel. Als nun alles still geworden war, so
kauerte sich die Königstochter vor die Türe der Schlafkammer, öffnete sie ein wenig und rief hinein

> »Trommler, Trommler, hör mich an,
> hast du mich denn ganz vergessen?
> hast du auf dem Glasberg nicht bei mir gesessen?
> habe ich vor der Hexe nicht bewahrt dein Leben?
> hast du mir auf Treue nicht die Hand gegeben?
> Trommler, Trommler, hör mich an.«

Aber es war alles vergeblich, der Trommler wachte nicht
auf, und als der Morgen anbrach, musste die Königstochter
unverrichteter Dinge wieder fortgehen. Am zweiten Abend
drehte sie ihren Wunschring und sprach »ein Kleid so sil-
bern als der Mond.« Als sie mit dem Kleid, das so zart war,
wie der Mondschein, bei dem Fest erschien, erregte sie wieder das Verlangen der Braut und gab es ihr für die Erlaubnis auch die zweite Nacht vor der Türe der Schlafkammer
zubringen zu dürfen. Da rief sie in nächtlicher Stille

> »Trommler, Trommler, hör mich an,
> hast du mich denn ganz vergessen?
> hast du auf dem Glasberg nicht bei mir gesessen?
> habe ich vor der Hexe nicht bewahrt dein Leben?
> hast du mir auf Treue nicht die Hand gegeben?
> Trommler, Trommler, hör mich an.«

Aber der Trommler, von dem Schlaftrunk betäubt, war
nicht zu erwecken. Traurig gieng sie den Morgen wieder
zurück in ihr Waldhaus. Aber die Leute im Haus hatten die
Klage des fremden Mädchens gehört und erzählten dem

Bräutigam davon: sie sagten ihm auch dass es ihm nicht möglich gewesen wäre etwas davon zu vernehmen, weil sie ihm einen Schlaftrunk in den Wein geschüttet hätten. Am dritten Abend drehte die Königstochter den Wunschring und sprach »ein Kleid flimmernd wie Sterne.« Als sie sich darin auf dem Fest zeigte, war die Braut über die Pracht des Kleides, das die andern weit übertraf, ganz außer sich und sprach »ich soll und muss es haben.« Das Mädchen gab es, wie die andern, für die Erlaubnis die Nacht vor der Türe des Bräutigams zuzubringen. Der Bräutigam aber trank den Wein nicht, der ihm vor dem Schlafengehen gereicht wurde, sondern goss ihn hinter das Bett. Und als alles im Haus still geworden war, so hörte er eine sanfte Stimme, die ihn anrief

»Trommler, Trommler, hör mich an,
hast du mich denn ganz vergessen?
hast du auf dem Glasberg nicht bei mir gesessen?
habe ich vor der Hexe nicht bewahrt dein Leben?
hast du mir auf Treue nicht die Hand gegeben?
Trommler, Trommler, hör mich an.«

Plötzlich kam ihm das Gedächtnis wieder. »Ach«, rief er, »wie habe ich so treulos handeln können, aber der Kuss, den ich meinen Eltern in der Freude meines Herzens auf die rechte Wange gegeben habe, der ist Schuld daran, der hat mich betäubt.« Er sprang auf, nahm die Königstochter bei der Hand und führte sie zu dem Bett seiner Eltern. »Das ist meine rechte Braut«, sprach er, »wenn ich die andere heirate, so tue ich großes Unrecht.« Die Eltern, als sie hörten wie alles sich zugetragen hatte, willigten ein. Da wurden die Lichter im Saal wieder angezündet, Pauken und Trompeten herbei geholt, die Freunde und Verwandten eingeladen wieder zu kommen, und die wahre Hochzeit ward mit großer Freude gefeiert. Die erste Braut behielt die schönen Kleider zur Entschädigung und gab sich zufrieden.

194

Die Kornähre.

Vorzeiten, als Gott noch selbst auf Erden wandelte, da war die Fruchtbarkeit des Bodens viel größer als sie jetzt ist: damals trugen die Ähren nicht funfzig- oder sechzigfältig, sondern vier- bis fünfhundertfältig. Da wuchsen die Körner am Halm von unten bis oben hinauf: so lang er war, so lang war auch die Ähre. Aber wie die Menschen sind, im Überfluss achten sie des Segens nicht mehr, der von Gott kommt, werden gleichgültig und leichtsinnig. Eines Tages gieng eine Frau an einem Kornfeld vorbei, und ihr kleines Kind, das neben ihr sprang, fiel in eine Pfütze und beschmutzte sein Kleidchen. Da riss die Mutter eine Hand voll der schönen Ähren ab und reinigte ihm damit das Kleid. Als der Herr, der eben vorüberkam, das sah, zürnte er und sprach »fortan soll der Kornhalm keine Ähre mehr tragen: die Menschen sind der himmlischen Gabe nicht länger wert.« Die Umstehenden, die das hörten, erschraken, fielen auf die Knie und flehten, dass er noch etwas möchte an dem Halm stehen lassen: wenn sie selbst es auch nicht verdienten, doch der unschuldigen Hühner wegen, die sonst verhungern müssten. Der Herr, der ihr Elend voraus sah, erbarmte sich und gewährte die Bitte. Also blieb noch oben die Ähre übrig, wie sie jetzt wächst.

195.

Der Grabhügel.

Ein reicher Bauer stand eines Tags in seinem Hof und schaute nach seinen Feldern und Gärten: das Korn wuchs kräftig heran und die Obstbäume hiengen voll Früchte. Das

Getreide des vorigen Jahrs lag noch in so mächtigen Haufen auf dem Boden, dass es kaum die Balken tragen konnten. Dann gieng er in den Stall, da standen die gemästeten Ochsen, die fetten Kühe und die spiegelglatten Pferde. Endlich gieng er in seine Stube zurück und warf seine Blicke auf die eisernen Kasten, in welchen sein Geld lag. Als er so stand, und seinen Reichtum übersah, klopfte es auf einmal heftig bei ihm an. Es klopfte aber nicht an die Türe seiner Stube, sondern an die Türe seines Herzens. Sie tat sich auf und er hörte eine Stimme, die zu ihm sprach »hast du den Deinigen damit wohl getan? hast du die Not der Armen angesehen? hast du mit den Hungrigen dein Brot geteilt? war dir genug was du besaßest oder hast du noch immer mehr verlangt?« Das Herz zögerte nicht mit der Antwort »ich bin hart und unerbittlich gewesen und habe den Meinigen niemals etwas Gutes erzeigt. Ist ein Armer gekommen, so habe ich mein Auge weg gewendet. Ich habe mich um Gott nicht bekümmert, sondern nur an die Mehrung meines Reichtums gedacht. Wäre alles mein eigen gewesen, was der Himmel bedeckte, dennoch hätte ich nicht genug gehabt.« Als er diese Antwort vernahm, erschrak er heftig: die Knie fiengen an ihm zu zittern und er musste sich niedersetzen. Da klopfte es abermals an, aber es klopfte an die Türe seiner Stube. Es war sein Nachbar, ein armer Mann, der ein Häufchen Kinder hatte, die er nicht mehr sättigen konnte. »Ich weiß«, dachte der Arme, »mein Nachbar ist reich, aber er ist ebenso hart: ich glaube nicht dass er mir hilft, aber meine Kinder schreien nach Brot, da will ich es wagen.« Er sprach zu dem Reichen »Ihr gebt nicht leicht etwas von dem eurigen weg, aber ich stehe da wie einer, dem das Wasser bis an den Kopf geht: meine Kinder hungern, leiht mir vier Malter Korn.« Der Reiche sah ihn lange an, da begann der erste Sonnenstrahl der Milde einen Tropfen von dem Eis der Habsucht abzuschmelzen. »Vier Malter will ich dir nicht leihen«, antwortete er, »sondern achte will ich dir schenken, aber eine Bedingung

musst du erfüllen.« »Was soll ich tun?« sprach der Arme.
»Wenn ich tot bin, sollst du drei Nächte an meinem Grabe
wachen.« Dem Bauer ward bei dem Antrag unheimlich zu
Mut, doch in der Not, in der er sich befand, hätte er alles
bewilligt: er sagte also zu und trug das Korn heim.
Es war, als hätte der Reiche vorausgesehen was geschehen
würde, nach drei Tagen fiel er plötzlich tot zur Erde; man
wusste nicht recht wie es zugegangen war, aber niemand
trauerte um ihn. Als er bestattet war, fiel dem Armen sein
Versprechen ein: gerne wäre er davon entbunden gewesen,
aber er dachte »er hat sich gegen dich doch mildtätig erwie-
sen, du hast mit seinem Korn deine hungrigen Kinder gesättigt, und wäre das auch nicht, du hast einmal das Versprechen gegeben und musst du es halten.« Bei einbrechender
Nacht gieng er auf den Kirchhof und setzte sich auf den
Grabhügel. Es war alles still, nur der Mond schien über die
Grabhügel und manchmal flog eine Eule vorbei und ließ
ihre kläglichen Töne hören. Als die Sonne aufgieng, begab
sich der Arme ungefährdet heim und ebenso gieng die zweite Nacht ruhig vorüber. Den Abend des dritten Tags empfand er eine besondere Angst, es war ihm als stände noch etwas bevor. Als er hinaus kam, erblickte er an der Mauer des
Kirchhofs einen Mann, den er noch nie gesehen hatte. Er
war nicht mehr jung, hatte Narben im Gesicht und seine
Augen blickten scharf und feurig umher. Er war ganz von
einem alten Mantel bedeckt und nur große Reiterstiefeln
waren sichtbar. »Was sucht ihr hier?« redete ihn der Bauer
an, »gruselt euch nicht auf dem einsamen Kirchhof?« »Ich
suche nichts«, antwortete er, »aber ich fürchte auch nichts.
Ich bin wie der Junge, der ausgieng das Gruseln zu lernen,
und sich vergeblich bemühte, der aber bekam die Königstochter zur Frau und ich mit ihr große Reichtümer, und ich bin
immer arm geblieben. Ich bin nichts als ein abgedankter Soldat und will hier die Nacht zubringen, weil ich sonst kein
Obdach habe.« »Wenn ihr keine Furcht habt«, sprach der
Bauer, »so bleibt bei mir und helft mir dort den Grabhügel

bewachen.« »Wacht halten ist Sache des Soldaten« antwortete er, »was uns hier begegnet, Gutes oder Böses, das wollen wir gemeinschaftlich tragen.« Der Bauer schlug ein und sie setzten sich zusammen auf das Grab.

Alles blieb still bis Mitternacht, da ertönte auf einmal ein schneidendes Pfeifen in der Luft, und die beiden Wächter erblickten den Bösen, der leibhaftig vor ihnen stand. »Fort, ihr Halunken«, rief er ihnen zu, »der in dem Grab liegt, ist mein: ich will ihn holen, und wo ihr nicht weg geht, dreh ich euch die Hälse um.« »Herr mit der roten Feder«, sprach der Soldat, »ihr seid mein Hauptmann nicht, ich brauch euch nicht zu gehorchen, und das Fürchten hab ich noch nicht gelernt. Geht eurer Wege, wir bleiben hier sitzen.« Der Teufel dachte »mit Gold fängst du die zwei Haderlumpen am besten«, zog gelindere Saiten auf und fragte ganz zutraulich ob sie nicht einen Beutel mit Gold annehmen und damit heim gehen wollten. »Das lässt sich hören«, antwortete der Soldat, »aber mit *Einem* Beutel voll Gold ist uns nicht gedient: wenn ihr so viel Gold geben wollt, als da in einen von meinen Stiefeln geht, so wollen wir Euch das Feld räumen und abziehen.« »So viel habe ich nicht bei mir«, sagte der Teufel, »aber ich will es holen: in der benachbarten Stadt wohnt ein Wechsler, der mein guter Freund ist, der streckt mir gerne so viel vor.« Als der Teufel verschwunden war, zog der Soldat seinen linken Stiefel aus und sprach »dem Kohlenbrenner wollen wir schon eine Nase drehen: gebt mir nur euer Messer, Gevatter.« Er schnitt von dem Stiefel die Sohle ab und stellte ihn neben den Hügel in das hohe Gras an den Rand einer halb überwachsenen Grube. »So ist alles gut« sprach er, »nun kann der Schornsteinfeger kommen.«

Beide setzten sich und warteten, es dauerte nicht lange, so kam der Teufel und hatte ein Säckchen Gold in der Hand. »Schüttet es nur hinein«, sprach der Soldat und hob den Stiefel ein wenig in die Höhe, »das wird aber nicht genug sein.« Der Schwarze leerte das Säckchen, das Gold fiel durch und

der Stiefel blieb leer. »Dummer Teufel«, rief der Soldat, »es
schickt nicht: habe ich es nicht gleich gesagt? kehrt nur wieder um und holt mehr.« Der Teufel schüttelte den Kopf,
gieng und kam nach einer Stunde mit einem viel größeren
Sack unter dem Arm. »Nur eingefüllt«, rief der Soldat, »aber
ich zweifle, dass der Stiefel voll wird.« Das Gold klingelte als
es hinab fiel, und der Stiefel blieb leer. Der Teufel blickte mit
seinen glühenden Augen selbst hinein und überzeugte sich
von der Wahrheit. »Ihr habt unverschämt starke Waden« rief
er und verzog den Mund. »Meint ihr«, erwiderte der Soldat,
»ich hätte einen Pferdefuß wie ihr? seit wann seid ihr so
knauserig? macht dass ihr mehr Gold herbeischafft, sonst
wird aus unserm Handel nichts.« Der Unhold trollte sich
abermals fort. Diesmal blieb er länger aus, und als er endlich
erschien, keuchte er unter der Last eines Sackes, der auf seiner Schulter lag. Er schüttete ihn in den Stiefel, der sich aber
so wenig füllte als vorher. Er ward wütend und wollte dem
Soldat den Stiefel aus der Hand reißen, aber in dem Augenblick drang der erste Strahl der aufgehenden Sonne am Himmel herauf und der böse Geist entfloh mit lautem Geschrei.
Die arme Seele war gerettet.

Der Bauer wollte das Gold teilen, aber der Soldat sprach
»gib den Armen was mir zufällt: ich ziehe zu dir in deine
Hütte und wir wollen mit dem übrigen in Ruhe und Frieden zusammen leben, so lange es Gott gefällt.«

196.

Oll Rinkrank.

Dar war mal 'n König wän, un de har 'n Dochter hat: un de
har 'n glasen Barg maken laten, un har segt de dar över lopen kun, an to vallen, de schull sin Dochter to 'n Fro hebben. Do is dar ok en, de mag de Königsdochter so gärn li-

den, de vragt den König of he sin Dochter nich hebben
schal? »Ja«, segt de König, »wenn he dar över den Barg lopen kan, an dat he valt, den schal he är hebben.« Do segt de
Königsdochter den wil se dar mit hüm över lopen un wil
hüm hollen, wen he war vallen schul. Do lopt se dar mit
'nanner över, un as se dar miden up sünt, do glit de Königsdochter ut un valt, un de Glasbarg de deit sick apen, un se
schütt darin hendal: un de Brögam de kan nich sen war se
herdör kamen is, den de Barg het sick glick wär to dan. Do
jammert un went he so väl, un de König is ok so trorig un
let den Barg dar wedder weg bräken un ment he wil är
wedder ut krigen, man se könt de Stä ni finnen wär se hendal vallen is. Unnertüsken is de Königsdochter ganz dep in
de Grunt in 'n gröte Höl kamen. Do kumt är dar 'n ollen
Kärl mit 'n ganzen langen grauen Bart to möt, un de segt
wen se sin Magd wäsen wil un all don wat he bevelt, den
schal se läven bliven, anners wil he är ümbringen. Do deit
se all wat he är segt. 's Morgens den kricht he sin Ledder ut
de Task un legt de an den Barg un sticht darmit to 'n Barg
henut: un den lukt he de Ledder na sick ümhoch mit sick
henup. Un den mut se sin Äten kaken und sin Bedd maken
un all sin Arbeit don, un den, wen he wedder in Hus kumt,
den bringt he alltit 'n Hüpen Golt un Sülver mit. As se al
väl Jaren bi em wäsen is un al ganz olt wurden is, do het he
är Fro *Mansrot*, un se möt hüm *oll Rinkrank* heten. Do is
he ok ins enmal ut, do makt se hüm sin Bedd un waskt sin
Schöttels, un do makt se de Dören un Vensters all dicht to,
un do is dar so 'n Schuf wäsen, war 't Lecht herin schint
het, dat let se apen. As d' oll Rinkrank do wedder kumt, do
klopt he an sin Dör un röpt »Fro Mansrot, do mi d' Dör
apen.« »Na«, segt se, »ik do di, oll Rinkrank, d' Dör nich
apen.« Do segt he

> »hir sta ik arme Rinkrank
> up min söventein Benen lank
> up min en vergüllen Vot,
> Fro Mansrot, wask mi d' Schöttels.«

»'k heb din Schöttels al wusken« segt se. Do segt he wedder
>»hir sta ik arme Rinkrank
up min söventein Benen lank,
up min en vergüllen Vot,
Fro Mansrot, mak mi 't Bedd.«
»'k heb din Bedd al makt« segt se. Do segt he wedder
»hir sta ik arme Rinkrank
up min söventein Benen lank,
up min en vergüllen Vot,
Fro Mansrot, do mi d' Dör apen.«
Do löpt he all runt üm sin Hus to un süt, dat de lütke Luk
dar apen is, do denkt he »du schast doch ins tosen wat se
dar wol makt, warüm dat se mi d' Dör wol nich apen don
wil.« Do wil he dar dör kiken un kan den Kop dar ni dör
krigen van sin langen Bart. Do stekt he sin Bart dar erst dör
de Luk, un as he de dar hendör het, do geit Fro Mansrot bi
un schuft de Luk grad to mit 'n Bant, de se dar an bunnen
het, un de Bart blift darin vast sitten. Do fangt he so jam-
merlik an to kriten, dat deit üm so sär: un do bidd't he är se
mag üm wedder los laten. Do segt se er nich as bet he är de
Ledder deit, war he mit to 'n Barg herut sticht. Do mag he
willen oder nich, he mot är seggen war de Ledder is. Do
bint se 'n ganzen langen Bant dar an de Schuf, un do legt se
de Ledder an un sticht to 'n Barg herut: un as se baven is,
do lukt se de Schuf apen. Do geit se na är Vader hen un ver-
telt wo dat är all gan is. Do freut de König sick so un är
Brögam is dar ok noch, un do gat se hen un gravt den Barg
up un finnt den ollen Rinkrank mit all sin Golt un Sülver
darin. Do let de König den ollen Rinkrank dot maken, un
all sin Sülver un Golt nimt he mit. Do kricht de Königsdochter den ollen Brögam noch ton Mann, un se lävt recht
vergnögt un herrlich un in Freuden.

197

Die Kristallkugel.

Es war einmal eine Zauberin, die hatte drei Söhne, die sich brüderlich liebten: aber die Alte traute ihnen nicht und dachte sie wollten ihr ihre Macht rauben. Da verwandelte sie den ältesten in einen Adler, der musste auf einem Felsengebirge hausen und man sah ihn manchmal am Himmel in großen Kreisen auf und nieder schweben. Den zweiten verwandelte sie in einen Walfisch, der lebte im tiefen Meer, und man sah nur wie er zuweilen einen mächtigen Wasserstrahl in die Höhe warf. Beide hatten nur zwei Stunden jeden Tag ihre menschliche Gestalt. Der dritte Sohn, da er fürchtete sie möchte ihn auch in ein reißendes Tier verwandeln, in einen Bären oder einen Wolf, so gieng er heimlich fort. Er hatte aber gehört dass auf dem Schloss der goldenen Sonne eine verwünschte Königstochter säße, die auf Erlösung harrte: es müsste aber jeder sein Leben daran wagen, schon drei und zwanzig Jünglinge wären eines jämmerlichen Todes gestorben und nur noch einer übrig, dann dürfte keiner mehr kommen. Und da sein Herz ohne Furcht war, so fasste er den Entschluss das Schloss von der goldenen Sonne aufzusuchen. Er war schon lange Zeit herum gezogen, und hatte es nicht finden können, da geriet er in einen großen Wald und wusste nicht wo der Ausgang war. Auf einmal erblickte er in der Ferne zwei Riesen, die winkten ihm mit der Hand, und als er zu ihnen kam, sprachen sie »wir streiten um einen Hut, wem er zugehören soll, und da wir beide gleich stark sind, so kann keiner den andern überwältigen: die kleinen Menschen sind klüger als wir, daher wollen wir dir die Entscheidung überlassen.« »Wie könnt ihr euch um einen alten Hut streiten?« sagte der Jüngling. »Du weißt nicht was er für Eigenschaften hat, es ist ein Wünschhut, wer den aufsetzt, der kann sich hinwünschen wohin er will, und im Augenblick ist er dort.«

»Gebt mir den Hut« sagte der Jüngling, »ich will ein Stück Wegs gehen, und wenn ich euch dann rufe, so lauft um die Wette, und wer am ersten bei mir ist, dem soll er gehören.« Er setzte den Hut auf und gieng fort, dachte aber an die Königstochter, vergaß die Riesen und gieng immer weiter. Einmal seufzte er aus Herzensgrund und rief, »ach, wäre ich doch auf dem Schloss der goldenen Sonne!« und kaum waren die Worte über seine Lippen, so stand er auf einem hohen Berg vor dem Tor des Schlosses.

Er trat hinein und gieng durch alle Zimmer, bis er in dem letzten die Königstochter fand. Aber wie erschrak er, als er sie anblickte: sie hatte ein aschgraues Gesicht voll Runzeln, trübe Augen und rote Haare. »Seid ihr die Königstochter, deren Schönheit alle Welt rühmt?« rief er aus. »Ach«, erwiderte sie, »das ist meine Gestalt nicht, die Augen der Menschen können mich nur in dieser Hässlichkeit erblicken, aber damit du weißt wie ich aussehe, so schau in den Spiegel, der lässt sich nicht irre machen, der zeigt dir mein Bild, wie es in Wahrheit ist.« Sie gab ihm den Spiegel in die Hand, und er sah darin das Abbild der schönsten Jungfrau, die auf der Welt war, und sah wie ihr vor Traurigkeit die Tränen über die Wangen rollten. Da sprach er »wie kannst du erlöst werden? ich scheue keine Gefahr.« Sie sprach »wer die kristallne Kugel erlangt und hält sie dem Zauberer vor, der bricht damit seine Macht, und ich kehre in meine wahre Gestalt zurück. Ach«, setzte sie hinzu, »schon so mancher ist darum in seinen Tod gegangen, und du junges Blut, du jammerst mich, wenn du dich in die großen Gefährlichkeiten begiebst.« »Mich kann nichts abhalten« sprach er, »aber sage mir was ich tun muss.« »Du sollst alles wissen«, sprach die Königstochter, »wenn du den Berg auf dem das Schloss steht, hinabgehst, so wird unten an einer Quelle ein wilder Auerochs stehen, mit dem musst du kämpfen. Und wenn es dir glückt ihn zu töten, so wird sich aus ihm ein feuriger Vogel erheben, der trägt in seinem Leib ein glühendes Ei, und in dem Ei steckt als Dotter die Kris-

tallkugel. Er lässt aber das Ei nicht fallen, bis er dazu gedrängt wird, fällt es aber auf die Erde, so zündet es und
verbrennt alles in seiner Nähe, und das Ei selbst zer-
schmilzt und mit ihm die kristallne Kugel, und all deine
Mühe ist vergeblich gewesen.«
Der Jüngling stieg hinab zu der Quelle, wo der Auerochse
schnaubte und ihn anbrüllte. Nach langem Kampf stieß er
ihm sein Schwert in den Leib und er sank nieder. Augenblicklich erhob sich aus ihm der Feuervogel und wollte fort
fliegen, aber der Adler, der Bruder des Jünglings, der zwischen den Wolken daher zog, stürzte auf ihn herab, jagte
ihn nach dem Meer hin und stieß ihn mit seinem Schnabel
an, so dass er in der Bedrängnis das Ei fallen ließ. Es fiel
aber nicht in das Meer, sondern auf eine Fischerhütte, die
am Ufer stand, und die fieng gleich an zu rauchen und
wollte in Flammen aufgehen. Da erhoben sich im Meer
haushohe Wellen, strömten über die Hütte und bezwangen
das Feuer. Der andere Bruder, der Walfisch, war heran geschwommen und hatte das Wasser in die Höhe getrieben.
Als der Brand gelöscht war, suchte der Jüngling nach dem
Ei und fand es glücklicher Weise: es war noch nicht ge-
schmolzen, aber die Schale war von der plötzlichen Abküh-
lung durch das kalte Wasser zerbröckelt und er konnte die
Kristallkugel unversehrt heraus nehmen.
Als der Jüngling zu dem Zauberer gieng und sie ihm vor-
hielt, so sagte dieser »meine Macht ist zerstört und du bist
von nun an der König vom Schloss der goldenen Sonne.
Auch deinen Brüdern kannst du die menschliche Gestalt
damit zurück geben.« Da eilte der Jüngling zu der Königstochter, und als er in ihr Zimmer trat, so stand sie da in vollem Glanz ihrer Schönheit, und beide wechselten voll Freude ihre Ringe mit einander.

198

Jungfrau Maleen.

Es war einmal ein König, der hatte einen Sohn, der warb um die Tochter eines mächtigen Königs, die hieß Jungfrau Maleen und war wunderschön. Weil ihr Vater sie einem andern geben wollte, so ward sie ihm versagt. Da sich aber beide von Herzen liebten, so wollten sie nicht von einander lassen, und die Jungfrau Maleen sprach zu ihrem Vater »ich kann und will keinen andern zu meinem Gemahl nehmen.« Da geriet der Vater in Zorn und ließ einen finstern Turn bauen, in den kein Strahl von Sonne oder Mond fiel. Als er fertig war, sprach er »darin sollst du sieben Jahre lang sitzen, dann will ich kommen und sehen ob dein trotziger Sinn gebrochen ist.« Für die sieben Jahre ward Speise und Trank in den Turn getragen, dann ward sie und ihre Kammerjungfer hinein geführt und eingemauert, und also von Himmel und Erde geschieden. Da saßen sie in der Finsternis, wussten nicht wann Tag oder Nacht anbrach. Der Königssohn gieng oft um den Turn herum und rief ihren Namen, aber kein Laut drang von außen durch die dicken Mauern. Was konnten sie anders tun als jammern und klagen? Indessen gieng die Zeit dahin und an der Abnahme von Speise und Trank merkten sie dass die sieben Jahre ihrem Ende sich näherten. Sie dachten der Augenblick ihrer Erlösung wäre gekommen, aber kein Hammerschlag ließ sich hören und kein Stein wollte aus der Mauer fallen: es schien als ob ihr Vater sie vergessen hätte. Als sie nur noch für kurze Zeit Nahrung hatten und einen jämmerlichen Tod voraus sahen, da sprach die Jungfrau Maleen »wir müssen das letzte versuchen und sehen ob wir die Mauer durchbrechen.« Sie nahm das Brotmesser, grub und bohrte an dem Mörtel eines Steins, und wenn sie müd war, so löste sie die Kammerjungfer ab. Nach langer Arbeit gelang es ihnen einen Stein heraus zu nehmen, dann einen zweiten und dritten, und nach drei Tagen fiel der erste Lichtstrahl in ihre Dunkelheit, und endlich war die Öffnung so groß dass sie hinaus schauen konnten. Der Himmel war blau, und eine frische Luft wehte ihnen entgegen, aber wie traurig sah rings umher alles aus: das Schloss ihres Vaters lag in Trümmern, die Stadt und die Dörfer waren, so weit man sehen konnte, verbrannt, die Felder weit und breit verheert: keine Menschenseele ließ sich erblicken. Als die Öffnung in der Mauer so groß war, dass sie hindurchschlüpfen konnten, so sprang zuerst die Kammerjungfer herab und dann folgte die Jungfrau Maleen. Aber wo sollten sie sich hinwenden? Die Feinde hatten das ganze Reich verwüstet, den König verjagt und alle Einwohner erschlagen. Sie wanderten fort um ein anderes Land zu suchen, aber sie fanden nirgend ein Obdach oder einen Menschen, der ihnen einen Bissen Brot gab, und ihre Not war so groß dass sie ihren Hunger an einem Brennnesselstrauch stillen mussten. Als sie nach langer Wanderung in ein anderes Land kamen, boten sie überall ihre Dienste an, aber wo sie anklopften wurden sie abgewiesen, und niemand wollte sich ihrer erbarmen. Endlich gelangten sie in eine große Stadt und giengen nach dem königlichen Hof. Aber auch da hieß man sie weiter gehen, bis endlich der Koch sagte sie könnten in der Küche bleiben und als Aschenputtel dienen.

Der Sohn des Königs, in dessen Reich sie sich befanden, war aber gerade der Verlobte der Jungfrau Maleen gewesen. Der Vater hatte ihm eine andere Braut bestimmt, die ebenso hässlich von Angesicht als bös von Herzen war. Die Hochzeit war festgesetzt und die Braut schon angelangt, bei ihrer großen Hässlichkeit aber ließ sie sich vor niemand sehen und schloss sich in ihre Kammer ein, und die Jungfrau Maleen musste ihr das Essen aus der Küche bringen. Als der Tag heran kam, wo die Braut mit dem Bräutigam in die Kirche gehen sollte, so schämte sie sich ihrer Hässlichkeit und fürchtete wenn sie sich auf der Straße zeigte, würde sie von den Leuten verspottet und ausge-

lacht. Da sprach sie zur Jungfrau Maleen »dir steht ein
großes Glück bevor, ich habe mir den Fuß vertreten und
kann nicht gut über die Straße gehen: du sollst meine
Brautkleider anziehen und meine Stelle einnehmen: eine
größere Ehre kann dir nicht zu Teil werden.« Die Jungfrau
Maleen aber schlug es aus und sagte »ich verlange keine
Ehre, die mir nicht gebührt.« Es war auch vergeblich dass
sie ihr Gold anbot. Endlich sprach sie zornig »wenn du
mir nicht gehorchst, so kostet es dir dein Leben: ich brauche nur ein Wort zu sagen, so wird dir der Kopf vor die
Füße gelegt.« Da musste sie gehorchen und die prächtigen
Kleider der Braut samt ihrem Schmuck anlegen. Als sie in
den königlichen Saal eintrat erstaunten alle über ihre große
Schönheit und der König sagte zu seinem Sohn »das ist die
Braut, die ich dir ausgewählt habe und die du zur Kirche
führen sollst.« Der Bräutigam erstaunte und dachte »sie
gleicht meiner Jungfrau Maleen, und ich würde glauben sie
wäre es selbst, aber die sitzt schon lange im Turn gefangen
oder ist tot.« Er nahm sie an der Hand und führte sie zur
Kirche. An dem Wege stand ein Brennnesselbusch, da
sprach sie

> »Brennnettelbusch,
> Brennnettelbusch so klene,
> wat steist du hier allene?
> ik hef de Tyt geweten
> da hef ik dy ungesaden
> ungebraden eten.«

»Was sprichst du da?« fragte der Königssohn. »Nichts«,
antwortete sie, »ich dachte nur an die Jungfrau Maleen.« Er
verwunderte sich dass sie von ihr wusste, schwieg aber still.
Als sie an den Steg vor dem Kirchhof kamen sprach sie

> »Karkstegels, brik nich,
> Bün de rechte Brut nich.«

»Was sprichst du da?« fragte der Königssohn. »Nichts«,
antwortete sie, »ich dachte nur an die Jungfrau Maleen.«
»Kennst du die Jungfrau Maleen?« »Nein«, antwortete sie,

»wie sollt ich sie kennen, ich habe nur von ihr gehört.« Als
sie an die Kirchtüre kamen, sprach sie abermals

>Karkendär, brik nich,
bün de rechte Brut nich.«

»Was sprichst du da?« fragte er. »Ach«, antwortete sie, »ich
habe nur an die Jungfrau Maleen gedacht.« Da zog er ein
kostbares Geschmeide hervor, legte es ihr an den Hals und
hakte die Kettenringe in einander. Darauf traten sie in die
Kirche und der Priester legte vor dem Altar ihre Hände in
einander und vermählte sie. Er führte sie zurück, aber sie
sprach auf dem ganzen Weg kein Wort. Als sie wieder in
dem königlichen Schloss angelangt waren, eilte sie in die
Kammer der Braut, legte die prächtigen Kleider und den
Schmuck ab, zog ihren grauen Kittel an und behielt nur das
Geschmeide um den Hals, das sie von dem Bräutigam empfangen hatte.

Als die Nacht heran kam und die Braut in das Zimmer des
Königssohns sollte geführt werden, so ließ sie den Schleier
über ihr Gesicht fallen, damit er den Betrug nicht merken
sollte. Sobald alle Leute fortgegangen waren, sprach er zu
ihr »was hast du doch zu dem Brennnesselbusch gesagt, der
an dem Weg stand?« »Zu welchem Brennnesselbusch?«
fragte sie, »ich spreche mit keinem Brennnesselbusch.«
»Wenn du es nicht getan hast, so bist du die rechte Braut
nicht« sagte er. Da half sie sich und sprach

>mut herut na myne Maegt,
de my myn Gedanken draegt.«

Sie gieng hinaus und fuhr die Jungfrau Maleen an, »Dirne,
was hast du zu dem Brennnesselbusch gesagt?« »Ich sagte
nichts als

Brennnettelbusch,
Brennnettelbusch so klene,
wat steist du hier allene?
Ik hef de Tyt geweten,
da hef ik dy ungesaden
ungebraden eten.«

Die Braut lief in die Kammer zurück und sagte »jetzt weiß ich was ich zu dem Brennnesselbusch gesprochen habe«, und wiederholte die Worte, die sie eben gehört hatte. »Aber was sagtest du zu dem Kirchensteg, als wir darüber giengen?« fragte der Königssohn. »Zu dem Kirchensteg?« antwortete sie, »ich spreche mit keinem Kirchensteg.« »Dann bist du auch die rechte Braut nicht.« Sie sagte wiederum

»mut herut na myne Maegt,
de my myn Gedanken draegt.«

Lief hinaus und fuhr die Jungfrau Maleen an, »Dirne, was hast du zu dem Kirchsteg gesagt?« »Ich sagte nichts als

Karkstegels, brik nich,
bün de rechte Brut nich.«

»Das kostet dich dein Leben« rief die Braut, eilte aber in die Kammer und sagte »jetzt weiß ich was ich zu dem Kirchsteg gesprochen habe« und wiederholte die Worte. »Aber was sagtest du zur Kirchentür?« »Zur Kirchentür?« antwortete sie, »ich spreche mit keiner Kirchentür.« »Dann bist du auch die rechte Braut nicht.« Sie gieng hinaus, fuhr die Jungfrau Maleen an »Dirne, was hast du zu der Kirchentür gesagt?« »Ich sagte nichts als

Karkendär, brik nich,
bün de rechte Brut nich.«

»Das bricht dir den Hals« rief die Braut und geriet in den größten Zorn, eilte aber zurück in die Kammer und sagte »jetzt weiß ich was ich zu der Kirchentür gesprochen habe«, und wiederholte die Worte. »Aber, wo hast du das Geschmeide, das ich dir an der Kirchentür gab?« »Was für ein Geschmeide«, antwortete sie, »du hast mir kein Geschmeide gegeben.« »Ich habe es dir selbst um den Hals gelegt und selbst eingehakt: wenn du das nicht weißt, so bist du die rechte Braut nicht.« Er zog ihr den Schleier vom Gesicht, und als er ihre grundlose Hässlichkeit erblickte, sprang er erschrocken zurück und sprach »wie kommst du hierher? wer bist du?« »Ich bin deine verlobte Braut, aber weil ich fürchtete die Leute würden mich verspotten, wenn sie mich draußen erblickten, so habe ich dem Aschenputtel befohlen meine Kleider anzuziehen und statt meiner zur Kirche zu gehen.« »Wo ist das Mädchen« sagte er, »ich will es sehen, geh und hol es hierher.« Sie gieng hinaus und sagte den Dienern das Aschenputtel sei eine Betrügerin, sie sollten es in den Hof hinabführen und ihm den Kopf abschlagen. Die Diener packten es und wollten es fortschleppen, aber es schrie so laut um Hilfe, dass der Königssohn seine Stimme vernahm, aus seinem Zimmer herbei eilte und den Befehl gab das Mädchen augenblicklich loszulassen. Es wurden Lichter herbei geholt und da bemerkte er an ihrem Hals den Goldschmuck den er ihm vor der Kirchentür gegeben hatte. »Du bist die rechte Braut« sagte er, »die mit mir zur Kirche gegangen ist: komm mit mir in meine Kammer.« Als sie beide allein waren, sprach er »du hast auf dem Kirchgang die Jungfrau Maleen genannt, die meine verlobte Braut war: wenn ich dächte es wäre möglich, so müsste ich glauben sie stände vor mir: du gleichst ihr in allem.« Sie antwortete »ich bin die Jungfrau Maleen, die um dich sieben Jahre in der Finsternis gefangen gesessen, Hunger und Durst gelitten und so lange in Not und Armut gelebt hat: aber heute bescheint mich die Sonne wieder. Ich bin dir in der Kirche angetraut und bin deine rechtmäßige Gemahlin.« Da küssten sie einander und waren glücklich für ihr Lebtag. Der falschen Braut ward zur Vergeltung der Kopf abgeschlagen. Der Turn, in welchem die Jungfrau Maleen gesessen hatte, stand noch lange Zeit, und wenn die Kinder vorüber giengen, so sangen sie

»kling klang kloria,
wer sitt in dissen Toria?
Dar sitt en Königsdochter in,
die kann ik nich to seen krygn.
De Muer de will nich bräken,
De Steen de will nich stechen.
Hänschen mit de bunte Jak,
kumm unn folg my achterna.«

199

Der Stiefel von Büffelleder.

Ein Soldat, der sich vor nichts fürchtet, kümmert sich auch
um nichts. So einer hatte seinen Abschied erhalten, und da
er nichts gelernt hatte und nichts verdienen konnte, so zog
er umher und bat gute Leute um ein Almosen. Auf seinen
Schultern hieng ein alter Wettermantel, und ein paar Reiterstiefeln von Büffelleder waren ihm auch noch geblieben.
Eines Tages gieng er, ohne auf Weg und Steg zu achten, immer ins Feld hinein und gelangte endlich in einen Wald. Er
wusste nicht wo er war, sah aber auf einem abgehauenen
Baumstamm einen Mann sitzen, der gut gekleidet war und
einen grünen Jägerrock trug. Der Soldat reichte ihm die
Hand, ließ sich neben ihm auf das Gras nieder und streckte
seine Beine aus. »Ich sehe du hast feine Stiefel an, die glänzend gewichst sind« sagte er zu dem Jäger, »wenn du aber
herum ziehen müsstest wie ich, so würden sie nicht lange
halten. Schau die meinigen an, die sind von Büffelleder und
haben schon lange gedient, gehen aber durch dick und
dünn.« Nach einer Weile stand der Soldat auf und sprach
»ich kann nicht länger bleiben, der Hunger treibt mich fort.
Aber, Bruder Wichsstiefel, wohinaus geht der Weg?« »Ich
weiß es selber nicht« antwortete der Jäger, »ich habe mich
in dem Wald verirrt.« »So geht dir's ja, wie mir« sprach der
Soldat, »gleich und gleich gesellt sich gern, wir wollen bei
einander bleiben und den Weg suchen.« Der Jäger lächelte
ein wenig, und sie giengen zusammen fort immer weiter,
bis die Nacht einbrach. »Wir kommen aus dem Wald nicht
heraus« sprach der Soldat, »aber ich sehe dort in der Ferne
ein Licht schimmern, da wird's etwas zu essen geben.« Sie
fanden ein Steinhaus, klopften an die Türe und ein altes
Weib öffnete. »Wir suchen ein Nachtquartier« sprach der
Soldat, »und etwas Unterfutter für den Magen, denn der
meinige ist so leer wie ein alter Tornister.« »Hier könnt ihr

nicht bleiben«, antwortete die Alte, »das ist ein Räuberhaus, und ihr tut am klügsten dass ihr euch fortmacht, bevor sie heim kommen, denn finden sie euch, so seid ihr verloren.« »Es wird so schlimm nicht sein«, antwortete der Soldat, »ich habe seit zwei Tagen keinen Bissen genossen, und es ist mir einerlei ob ich hier umkomme oder im Wald vor Hunger sterbe. Ich gehe herein.« Der Jäger wollte nicht folgen, aber der Soldat zog ihn am Ärmel mit sich: »komm, Bruderherz, es wird nicht gleich an den Kragen gehen.« Die Alte hatte Mitleiden und sagte »kriecht hinter den Ofen, wenn sie etwas übrig lassen und eingeschlafen sind, so will ich's euch zustecken.« Kaum saßen sie in der Ecke, so kamen zwölf Räuber herein gestürmt, setzten sich an den Tisch, der schon gedeckt war, und forderten mit Ungestüm das Essen. Die Alte trug einen großen Braten herein, und die Räuber ließen sich's wohl schmecken. Als der Geruch von der Speise dem Soldaten in die Nase stieg, sagte er zum Jäger »ich halt's nicht länger aus, ich setze mich an den Tisch und esse mit.« »Du bringst uns ums Leben« sprach der Jäger und hielt ihn am Arm. Aber der Soldat fieng an laut zu husten. Als die Räuber das hörten, warfen sie Messer und Gabel hin, sprangen auf und entdeckten die beiden hinter dem Ofen. »Aha, ihr Herrn«, riefen sie, »sitzt ihr in der Ecke? was wollt ihr hier? seid ihr als Kundschafter ausgeschickt? wartet, ihr sollt an einem dürren Ast das Fliegen lernen.« »Nur manierlich« sprach der Soldat, »mich hungert, gebt mir zu essen, hernach könnt ihr mit mir machen was ihr wollt.« Die Räuber stutzten und der Anführer sprach »ich sehe du fürchtest dich nicht, gut, Essen sollst du haben, aber hernach musst du sterben.« »Das wird sich finden« sagte der Soldat, setzte sich an den Tisch und fieng an tapfer in den Braten einzuhauen. »Bruder Wichsstiefel, komm und iss«, rief er dem Jäger zu, »du wirst hungrig sein, so gut als ich, und einen bessern Braten kannst du zu Haus nicht haben«; aber der Jäger wollte nicht essen. Die Räuber sahen dem Soldaten mit Erstaunen zu und sagten

»der Kerl macht keine Umstände.« Hernach sprach er »das Essen wäre gut, nun schafft auch einen guten Trunk herbei.« Der Anführer war in der Laune sich das auch noch gefallen zu lassen und rief der Alten zu »hol eine Flasche aus dem Keller und zwar von dem besten.« Der Soldat zog den Propfen heraus dass es knallte, gieng mit der Flasche zu dem Jäger und sprach »gib acht, Bruder, du sollst dein blaues Wunder sehen: jetzt will ich eine Gesundheit auf die ganze Sippschaft ausbringen.« Dann schwenkte er die Flasche über den Köpfen der Räuber, rief »ihr sollt alle leben, aber das Maul auf und die rechte Hand in der Höhe« und tat einen herzhaften Zug. Kaum waren die Worte heraus, so saßen sie alle bewegungslos als wären sie von Stein, hatten das Maul offen und streckten den rechten Arm in die Höhe. Der Jäger sprach zu dem Soldaten »ich sehe du kannst noch andere Kunststücke, aber nun komm und lass uns heim gehen.« »Oho, Bruderherz, das wäre zu früh abmarschiert, wir haben den Feind geschlagen und wollen erst Beute machen. Die sitzen da fest und sperren das Maul vor Verwunderung auf: sie dürfen sich aber nicht rühren bis ich es erlaube. Komm iss und trink.« Die Alte musste noch eine Flasche von dem besten holen, und der Soldat stand nicht eher auf als bis er wieder für drei Tage gegessen hatte. Endlich als der Tag kam, sagte er »nun ist Zeit dass wir das Zelt abbrechen, und damit wir einen kurzen Marsch haben, so soll die Alte uns den nächsten Weg nach der Stadt zeigen.« Als sie dort angelangt waren, gieng er zu seinen alten Kameraden und sprach »ich habe draußen im Wald ein Nest voll Galgenvögel aufgefunden, kommt mit, wir wollen es ausheben.« Der Soldat führte sie an und sprach zu dem Jäger »du musst wieder mit zurück und zusehen wie sie flattern, wenn wir sie an den Füßen packen.« Er stellte die Mannschaft rings um die Räuber herum, dann nahm er die Flasche, trank einen Schluck, schwenkte sie über ihnen her und rief »ihr sollt alle leben!« Augenblicklich hatten sie ihre Bewegung wieder, wurden aber nieder-

geworfen und an Händen und Füßen mit Stricken gebunden. Dann hieß sie der Soldat wie Säcke auf einen Wagen
werfen und sagte »fahrt sie nur gleich vor das Gefängnis.«
Der Jäger aber nahm einen von der Mannschaft bei Seite
und gab ihm noch eine Bestellung mit.

»Bruder Wichsstiefel«, sprach der Soldat, »wir haben den
Feind glücklich überrumpelt und uns wohl genährt, jetzt
wollen wir als Nachzügler in aller Ruhe hinter her marschieren.« Als sie sich der Stadt näherten, so sah der Soldat
wie sich eine Menge Menschen aus dem Stadttor drängten,
lautes Freudengeschrei erhuben und grüne Zweige in der
Luft schwangen. Dann sah er dass die ganze Leibwache
herangezogen kam. »Was soll das heißen?« sprach er ganz
verwundert zu dem Jäger. »Weißt du nicht« antwortete er,
»dass der König lange Zeit aus seinem Reich entfernt war,
heute kehrt er zurück, und da gehen ihm alle entgegen.«
»Aber wo ist der König« sprach der Soldat, »ich sehe ihn
nicht.« »Hier ist er«, antwortete der Jäger »ich bin der König und habe meine Ankunft melden lassen.« Dann öffnete
er seinen Jägerrock, dass man die königlichen Kleider sehen konnte. Der Soldat erschrak, fiel auf die Knie und bat
ihn um Vergebung dass er ihn in der Unwissenheit wie seines Gleichen behandelt und ihn mit solchem Namen angeredet habe. Der König aber reichte ihm die Hand und
sprach »du bist ein braver Soldat und hast mir das Leben
gerettet. Du sollst keine Not mehr leiden, ich will schon
für dich sorgen. Und wenn du einmal ein Stück guten Braten essen willst, so gut als in dem Räuberhaus, so komm
nur in die königliche Küche. Willst du aber eine Gesundheit ausbringen, so sollst du erst bei mir Erlaubnis dazu
holen.«

200.

Der goldene Schlüssel.

Zur Winterszeit, als einmal ein tiefer Schnee lag, musste ein armer Junge hinausgehen und Holz auf einem Schlitten holen. Wie er es nun zusammengesucht und aufgeladen hatte, wollte er, weil er so erfroren war, noch nicht nach Haus gehen, sondern erst Feuer anmachen und sich ein bisschen wärmen. Da scharrte er den Schnee weg, und wie er so den Erdboden aufräumte, fand er einen kleinen goldenen Schlüssel. Nun glaubte er wo der Schlüssel wäre, müsste auch das Schloss dazu sein, grub in der Erde und fand ein eisernes Kästchen. »Wenn der Schlüssel nur passt!« dachte er, »es sind gewiss kostbare Sachen in dem Kästchen.« Er suchte, aber es war kein Schlüsselloch da, endlich entdeckte er eins, aber so klein dass man es kaum sehen konnte. Er probierte und der Schlüssel passte glücklich. Da drehte er einmal herum, und nun müssen wir warten bis er vollends aufgeschlossen und den Deckel aufgemacht hat, dann werden wir erfahren was für wunderbare Sachen in dem Kästchen lagen.

Kinderlegenden.

1.

Der heilige Joseph im Walde.

Es war einmal eine Mutter, die hatte drei Töchter, davon war die älteste unartig und bös, die zweite schon viel besser, obgleich sie auch ihre Fehler hatte, die jüngste aber war ein frommes gutes Kind. Die Mutter war aber so wunderlich, dass sie gerade die älteste Tochter am liebsten hatte und die jüngste nicht leiden konnte. Daher schickte sie das arme Mädchen oft hinaus in einen großen Wald, um es sich vom Hals zu schaffen, denn sie dachte es würde sich verirren und nimmermehr wieder kommen. Aber der Schutzengel, den jedes fromme Kind hat, verließ es nicht, sondern brachte es immer wieder auf den rechten Weg. Einmal indessen tat das Schutzenglein als wenn es nicht bei der Hand wäre, und das Kind konnte sich nicht wieder aus dem Walde herausfinden. Es gieng immer fort bis es Abend wurde, da sah es in der Ferne ein Lichtchen brennen, lief darauf zu und kam vor eine kleine Hütte. Es klopfte an, die Türe gieng auf, und es gelangte zu einer zweiten Türe, wo es wieder anklopfte. Ein alter Mann, der einen schneeweißen Bart hatte und ehrwürdig aussah, machte ihm auf, und das war niemand anders als der heilige Joseph. Er sprach ganz freundlich »komm, liebes Kind, setze dich ans Feuer auf mein Stühlchen und wärme dich, ich will dir klar Wässerchen holen, wenn du Durst hast; zu essen aber hab ich hier im Walde nichts für dich als ein paar Würzelcher, die musst du dir erst schaben und kochen.« Da reichte ihm der heil. Joseph die Wurzeln: das Mädchen schrappte sie säuberlich ab, dann holte es ein Stückchen Pfannkuchen, und das Brot, das ihm seine Mutter mitgegeben hatte, und tat alles zusammen in einem Kesselchen bei's Feuer, und kochte sich ein Mus. Als das fertig war, sprach der heil. Joseph »ich bin so hungrig, gib mir etwas von deinem Essen.« Da war das Kind bereitwillig und gab ihm mehr als es für sich behielt, doch war Gottes Segen dabei, dass es satt ward. Als sie nun gegessen hatten, sprach der heil. Joseph »nun wollen wir zu Bett gehen: ich habe aber nur *Ein* Bett, lege du dich hinein, ich will mich ins Stroh auf die Erde legen.« »Nein«, antwortete es, »bleib du nur in deinem Bett, für mich ist das Stroh weich genug.« Der heil. Joseph aber nahm das Kind auf den Arm und trug es ins Bettchen, da tat es sein Gebet und schlief ein. Am andern Morgen, als es aufwachte, wollte es dem heil. Joseph guten Morgen sagen, aber es sah ihn nicht. Da stand es auf und suchte ihn, konnte ihn aber in keiner Ecke finden: endlich gewahrte es hinter der Tür einen Sack mit Geld, so schwer, als es ihn nur tragen konnte, darauf stand geschrieben das wäre für das Kind, das heute Nacht hier geschlafen hätte. Da nahm es den Sack und sprang damit fort und kam auch glücklich zu seiner Mutter, und weil es ihr alle das Geld schenkte, so konnte sie nicht anders, sie musste mit ihm zufrieden sein. Am folgenden Tag bekam das zweite Kind auch Lust in den Wald zu gehen. Die Mutter gab ihm ein viel größeres Stück Pfannkuchen und Brot mit. Es ergieng ihm nun gerade wie dem ersten Kinde. Abend[s] kam es in das Hüttchen des heil. Joseph, der ihm Wurzeln zu einem Mus reichte. Als das fertig war, sprach er gleichfalls zu ihm »ich bin so hungerig, gib mir etwas von deinem Essen.« Da antwortete das Kind »iss als mit.« Als ihm danach der heil. Joseph sein Bett anbot und sich aufs Stroh legen wollte, antwortete es »nein, leg dich als mit ins Bett, wir haben ja beide wohl Platz darin.« Der heil. Joseph nahm es auf den Arm, legte es ins Bettchen und legte sich ins Stroh. Morgens, als das Kind aufwachte und den heil. Joseph suchte, war er verschwunden, aber hinter der Türe fand es ein Säckchen mit Geld, das war händelang, und darauf stand geschrieben es wäre für das Kind, das heute Nacht hier geschlafen hätte. Da nahm es das Säckchen und lief damit heim, und brachte es seiner Mutter, doch behielt es heimlich ein paar Stücke für sich.

Nun war die älteste Tochter neugierig und wollte den folgenden Morgen auch hinaus in den Wald. Die Mutter gab ihr Pfannkuchen mit, so viel sie wollte, Brot und auch Käse dazu. Abends fand sie den heil. Joseph in seinem Hüttchen gerade so, wie ihn die zwei andern gefunden hatten. Als das Mus fertig war und der heil. Joseph sprach »ich bin so hungerig, gib mir etwas von deinem Essen«, antwortete das Mädchen »warte, bis ich satt bin, was ich dann übrig lasse, das sollst du haben.« Es aß aber beinah alles auf und der heil. Joseph musste das Schüsselchen ausschrappen. Der gute Alte bot ihm hernach sein Bett an und wollte auf dem Stroh liegen, das nahm es ohne Widerrede an, legte sich in das Bettchen und ließ dem Greis das harte Stroh. Am andern Morgen, wie es aufwachte, war der heil. Joseph nicht zu finden, doch darüber machte es sich keine Sorgen: es suchte hinter der Türe nach einem Geldsack. Es kam ihm vor als läge etwas auf der Erde, doch weil es nicht recht unterscheiden konnte, was es war, bückte es sich und stieß mit seiner Nase daran. Aber es blieb an der Nase hangen, und wie es sich aufrichtete, sah es zu seinem Schrecken, dass es noch eine zweite Nase war, die an der seinen festhieng. Da hub es an zu schreien und zu heulen, aber das half nichts, es musste immer auf seine Nase sehen, wie die so weit hinausstand. Da lief es in einem Geschrei fort, bis es dem heil. Joseph begegnete, dem fiel es zu Füßen und bat so lange, bis er aus Mitleid ihm die Nase wieder abnahm und noch zwei Pfennige schenkte. Als es daheim ankam, stand vor der Türe seine Mutter und fragte »was hast du geschenkt kriegt?« Da log es und antwortete »einen großen Sack voll Gelds, aber ich habe ihn unterwegs verloren.« »Verloren!« rief die Mutter, »o den wollen wir schon wieder finden«, nahm es bei der Hand und wollte mit ihm suchen. Zuerst fieng es an zu weinen und wollte nicht mit gehen, endlich aber gieng es mit, doch auf dem Wege kamen so viel Eidechsen und Schlangen auf sie beide los, dass sie sich nicht zu retten wussten; sie stachen auch endlich das böse Kind tot, und die Mutter stachen sie in den Fuß, weil sie es nicht besser erzogen hatte.

2.

Die zwölf Apostel.

Es war dreihundert Jahre vor des Herrn Christi Geburt, da lebte eine Mutter, die hatte zwölf Söhne, war aber so arm und dürftig, dass sie nicht wusste womit sie ihnen länger das Leben erhalten sollte. Sie betete täglich zu Gott, er möchte doch geben dass alle ihre Söhne mit dem verheißenen Heiland auf Erden zusammen wären. Als nun ihre Not immer größer ward, schickte sie einen nach dem andern in die Welt, um sich ihr Brot zu suchen. Der älteste hieß Petrus, der gieng aus, und war schon weit gegangen, eine ganze Tagreise, da geriet er in einen großen Wald. Er suchte einen Ausweg, konnte aber keinen finden und verirrte sich immer tiefer; dabei empfand er so großen Hunger dass er sich kaum aufrecht erhalten konnte. Endlich ward er so schwach, dass er liegen bleiben musste und glaubte dem Tode nahe zu sein. Da stand auf einmal neben ihm ein kleiner Knabe, der glänzte und war so schön und freundlich wie ein Engel. Das Kind schlug seine Händchen zusammen, dass er aufschauen und es anblicken musste. Da sprach es »warum sitzest du da so betrübt?« »Ach«, antwortete Petrus, »ich gehe umher in der Welt und suche mein Brot, damit ich noch den verheißenen lieben Heiland sehe; das ist mein größter Wunsch.« Das Kind sprach »komm mit, so soll dein Wunsch erfüllt werden.« Es nahm den armen Petrus an der Hand und führte ihn zwi-

schen Felsen zu einer großen Höhle. Wie sie hineinkamen,
so blitzte alles von Gold Silber und Kristall, und in der Mitte
standen zwölf Wiegen neben einander. Da sprach das Englein »lege dich in die erste und schlaf ein wenig, ich will dich
wiegen.« Das tat Petrus, und das Englein sang ihm und
wiegte ihn so lange bis er eingeschlafen war. Und wie er
schlief, kam der zweite Bruder, den auch sein Schutzenglein
herein führte, und ward wie der erste in den Schlaf gewiegt,
und so kamen die andern nach der Reihe, bis alle zwölfe da
lagen in den goldenen Wiegen und schliefen. Sie schliefen
aber dreihundert Jahre, bis in der Nacht, worin der Weltheil-
land geboren ward. Da erwachten sie und waren mit ihm auf
Erden und wurden die zwölf Apostel genannt.

3.

Die Rose.

Et was mal eine arme Frugge, de hadde twei Kinner; dat
jungeste moste olle Dage in en Wald gohn un langen (holen) Holt. Asset nu mal ganz wiet söken geit, kam so en
klein Kind, dat was awerst ganz wacker, to em und holp
(half) flietig Holt lesen un drog et auck bis für dat Hus;
dann was et awerst, eh en Augenschlägsken (Augenblick)
vergienk, verswunnen. Dat Kind vertelde et siner Moder,
de wul et awerst nig glöven. Up et lest brochte et en Rause
(Rose) mit un vertelde dat schöne Kind hädde em deise
Rause gieven un hädde em sägt wenn de Rause upblöhet
wär, dann wull et wier kummen. De Moder stellde dei Rause in't Water. Einen Morgen kam dat Kind gar nig ut dem
Bedde, de Moder gink to dem Bedde hen un fund dat Kind
daude (tot); et lag awerst ganz anmotik. Un de Rause was
den sulftigen Morgen upblöhet.

Armut und Demut führen zum Himmel.

Es war einmal ein Königssohn, der gieng hinaus in das Feld und war nachdenklich und traurig. Er sah den Himmel an, der war so schön rein und blau, da seufzte er und sprach »wie wohl muss einem erst da oben im Himmel sein!« Da erblickte er einen armen greisen Mann, der des Weges daher kam, redete ihn an und fragte »wie kann ich wohl in den Himmel kommen?« Der Mann antwortete »durch Armut und Demut. Leg an meine zerrissenen Kleider, wandere sieben Jahre in der Welt und lerne ihr Elend kennen: nimm kein Geld, sondern wenn du hungerst, bitt mitleidige Herzen um ein Stückchen Brot, so wirst du dich dem Himmel nähern.« Da zog der Königssohn seinen prächtigen Rock aus und hieng dafür das Bettlergewand um, gieng hinaus in die weite Welt und duldete groß Elend. Er nahm nichts als ein wenig Essen, sprach nichts, sondern betete zu dem Herrn dass er ihn einmal in seinen Himmel aufnehmen wollte. Als die sieben Jahre herum waren, da kam er wieder an seines Vaters Schloss, aber niemand erkannte ihn. Er sprach zu den Dienern »geht und sagt meinen Eltern dass ich wiedergekommen bin.« Aber die Diener glaubten es nicht, lachten und ließen ihn stehen. Da sprach er »geht und sagt's meinen Brüdern, dass sie herab kommen, ich möchte sie so gerne wieder sehen.« Sie wollten auch nicht, bis endlich einer von ihnen hingieng und es den Königskindern sagte, aber diese glaubten es nicht und bekümmerten sich nicht darum. Da schrieb er einen Brief an seine Mutter, und beschrieb ihr darin all sein Elend, aber er sagte nicht dass er ihr Sohn wäre. Da ließ ihm die Königin aus Mitleid einen Platz unter der Treppe anweisen und ihm täglich durch zwei Diener Essen bringen. Aber der eine war bös und sprach »was soll dem Bettler das gute Essen!« behielt's für sich oder gab's den Hunden und brachte dem Schwachen, Abgezehrten nur Wasser; doch der andere war ehrlich und brachte ihm was er für ihn bekam. Es war wenig, doch konnte er davon eine Zeit lang leben; dabei war er ganz geduldig, bis er immer schwächer ward. Als aber seine Krankheit zunahm, da begehrte er das heil. Abendmahl zu empfangen. Wie es nun unter der halben Messe ist, fangen von selbst alle Glocken in der Stadt und in der Gegend an zu läuten. Der Geistliche geht nach [d]er Messe zu dem armen Mann unter der Treppe, so liegt er da tot, in der einen Hand eine Rose, in der andern eine Lilie, und neben ihm ein Papier, darauf steht seine Geschichte aufgeschrieben. Als er begraben war, wuchs auf der einen Seite des Grabes eine Rose, auf der andern eine Lilie heraus.

5.

Gottes Speise.

Es waren einmal zwei Schwestern, die eine hatte keine Kinder und war reich, die andere hatte fünf Kinder und war eine Witwe und war so arm, dass sie nicht mehr Brot genug hatte, sich und ihre Kinder zu sättigen. Da gieng sie in der Not zu ihrer Schwester, und sprach »meine Kinder leiden mit mir den größten Hunger, du bist reich, gib mir einen Bissen Brot.« Die steinreiche war auch steinhart, sprach »ich habe selbst nichts in meinem Hause« und wies die Arme mit bösen Worten fort. Nach einiger Zeit kam der Mann der reichen Schwester heim, und wollte sich ein Stück Brot schneiden, wie er aber den ersten Schnitt in den Laib tat, floss das rote Blut heraus. Als die Frau das sah, erschrak sie und erzählte ihm was geschehen war. Er eilte hin und wollte helfen, wie er aber in die Stube der Witwe trat, so fand er sie betend; die beiden jüngsten Kinder hatte sie auf den Armen, die drei ältesten lagen da und waren gestor-

ben. Er bot ihr Speise an, aber sie antwortete »nach irdi-
scher Speise verlangen wir nicht mehr; drei hat Gott schon
gesättigt, unser Flehen wird er auch erhören.« Kaum hatte
sie diese Worte ausgesprochen, so taten die beiden Kleinen
ihren letzten Atemzug, und darauf brach ihr auch das Herz
und sie sank tot nieder.

6.

Die drei grünen Zweige.

Es war einmal ein Einsiedler, der lebte in einem Walde an
dem Fuße eines Berges und brachte seine Zeit in Gebet
und guten Werken zu, und jeden Abend trug er noch zur
Ehre Gottes ein paar Eimer Wasser den Berg hinauf. Manches Tier wurde damit getränkt und manche Pflanze damit
erquickt, denn auf den Anhöhen weht beständig ein harter
Wind, der die Luft und die Erde austrocknet, und die wilden Vögel, die vor den Menschen scheuen, kreisen dann
hoch und suchen mit ihren scharfen Augen nach einem
Trunk. Und weil der Einsiedler so fromm war, so gieng ein
Engel Gottes, seinen Augen sichtbar, mit ihm hinauf, zählte seine Schritte und brachte ihm, wenn die Arbeit vollendet war, sein Essen, so wie jener Prophet auf Gottes Geheiß von den Raben gespeiset ward. Als der Einsiedler in
seiner Frömmigkeit schon zu einem hohen Alter gekommen war, da trug es sich zu, dass er einmal von weitem sah
wie man einen armen Sünder zum Galgen führte. Er sprach
so vor sich hin »jetzt widerfährt diesem sein Recht.«
Abends, als er das Wasser den Berg hinauftrug, erschien
der Engel nicht, der ihn sonst begleitete und brachte ihm
auch nicht seine Speise. Da erschrak er, prüfte sein Herz
und bedachte womit er wohl könnte gesündigt haben, weil
Gott also zürne, aber er wusste es nicht. Da aß und trank
er nicht, warf sich nieder auf die Erde und betete Tag und

Nacht. Und als er einmal in dem Walde so recht bitterlich
weinte, hörte er ein Vöglein, das sang so schön und herrlich, da ward er noch betrübter und sprach »wie singst du
so fröhlich! dir zürnt der Herr nicht: ach, wenn du mir sagen könntest womit ich ihn beleidigt habe, damit ich Buße
täte, und mein Herz auch wieder fröhlich würde!« Da
fieng das Vöglein an zu sprechen und sagte »du hast unrecht getan, weil du einen armen Sünder verdammt hast,
der zum Galgen geführt wurde, darum zürnt dir der Herr;
er allein hält Gericht. Doch wenn du Buße tun und deine
Sünde bereuen willst, so wird er dir verzeihen.« Da stand
der Engel neben ihm und hatte einen trockenen Ast in der
Hand und sprach »diesen trockenen Ast sollst du so lange
tragen, bis drei grüne Zweige aus ihm hervorsprießen, aber
Nachts, wenn du schlafen willst, sollst du ihn unter dein
Haupt legen. Dein Brot sollst du dir an den Türen erbitten
und in demselben Hause nicht länger als eine Nacht verweilen. Das ist die Buße, die dir der Herr auflegt.«
Da nahm der Einsiedler das Stück Holz und gieng in die
Welt zurück, die er so lange nicht gesehen hatte. Er aß und
trank nichts, als was man ihm an den Türen reichte; manche Bitte aber ward nicht gehört, und manche Türe blieb
ihm verschlossen, also dass er oft ganze Tage lang keinen
Krumen Brot bekam. Einmal war er vom Morgen bis
Abend von Türe zu Türe gegangen, niemand hatte ihm etwas gegeben, niemand wollte ihn die Nacht beherbergen,
da gieng er hinaus in einen Wald, und fand endlich eine an-
gebaute Höhle, und eine alte Frau saß darin. Da sprach er
»gute Frau, behaltet mich diese Nacht in euerm Hause.«
Aber sie antwortete »nein, ich darf nicht, wenn ich auch
wollte. Ich habe drei Söhne, die sind bös und wild, wenn
sie von ihrem Raubzug heim kommen und finden euch, so
würden sie uns beide umbringen.« Da sprach der Einsiedler
»lasst mich nur bleiben, sie werden euch und mir nichts
tun«, und die Frau war mitleidig und ließ sich bewegen. Da
legte sich der Mann unter die Treppe und das Stück Holz

unter seinen Kopf. Wie die Alte das sah, fragte sie nach der
Ursache, da erzählte er ihr dass er es zur Buße mit sich herum trage und Nachts zu einem Kissen brauche. Er habe
den Herrn beleidigt, denn als er einen armen Sünder auf
dem Gang nach dem Gericht gesehen, habe er gesagt diesem widerfahre sein Recht. Da fieng die Frau an zu weinen
und rief »ach, wenn der Herr ein einziges Wort also be-
straft, wie wird es meinen Söhnen ergehen, wenn sie vor
ihm im Gericht erscheinen.«

Um Mitternacht kamen die Räuber heim, lärmten und tobten. Sie zündeten ein Feuer an, und als das die Höhle er-
leuchtete und sie einen Mann unter der Treppe liegen sahen, gerieten sie in Zorn und schrien ihre Mutter an, »wer
ist der Mann? haben wir's nicht verboten irgend jemand
aufzunehmen?« Da sprach die Mutter »lasst ihn, es ist ein
armer Sünder der seine Schuld büßt.« Die Räuber fragten
»was hat er getan?« »Alter«, riefen sie, »erzähl uns deine
Sünden.« Der Alte erhob sich und sagte ihnen wie er mit
einem einzigen Wort schon so gesündigt habe, dass Gott
ihm zürne, und er für diese Schuld jetzt büße. Den Räubern ward von seiner Erzählung das Herz so gewaltig gerührt, dass sie über ihr bisheriges Leben erschraken, in sich
giengen und mit herzlicher Reue ihre Buße begannen. Der
Einsiedler, nachdem er die drei Sünder bekehrt hatte, legte
sich wieder zum Schlafe unter die Treppe. Am Morgen aber
fand man ihn tot, und aus dem trocknen Holz, auf welchem sein Haupt lag, waren drei grüne Zweige hoch empor
gewachsen. Also hatte ihn der Herr wieder in Gnaden zu
sich aufgenommen.

7.

Muttergottesgläschen.

Es hatte einmal ein Fuhrmann seinen Karren, der mit Wein schwer beladen war, festgefahren, so dass er ihn trotz aller Mühe nicht wieder losbringen konnte. Nun kam gerade die Mutter Gottes des Weges daher, und als sie die Not des armen Mannes sah, sprach sie zu ihm »ich bin müd und durstig, gib mir ein Glas Wein, und ich will dir deinen Wagen frei machen.« »Gerne«, antwortete der Fuhrmann, »aber ich habe kein Glas, worin ich dir den Wein geben könnte.« Da brach die Mutter Gottes ein weißes Blümchen mit roten Streifen ab, das Feldwinde heißt und einem Glase sehr ähnlich sieht, und reichte es dem Fuhrmann. Er füllte es mit Wein, und die Mutter Gottes trank ihn, und in dem Augenblick ward der Wagen frei und der Fuhrmann konnte weiter fahren. Das Blümchen heißt noch immer Muttergottesgläschen.

8.

Das alte Mütterchen.

Es war in einer großen Stadt ein altes Mütterchen, das saß Abends allein in seiner Kammer: es dachte so darüber nach wie es erst den Mann, dann die beiden Kinder, nach und nach alle Verwandte, endlich auch heute noch den letzten Freund verloren hätte und nun ganz allein und verlassen wäre. Da ward es in tiefstem Herzen traurig, und vor allem schwer war ihm der Verlust der beiden Söhne, dass es in seinem Schmerz Gott darüber anklagte. So saß es still und in sich versunken, als es auf einmal zur Frühkirche läuten hörte. Es wunderte sich dass es die ganze Nacht also in Leid durchwacht hätte, zündete seine Leuchte an und gieng zur Kirche. Bei seiner Ankunft war sie schon erhellt, aber nicht, wie gewöhnlich, von Kerzen, sondern von einem dämmernden Licht. Sie war auch schon angefüllt mit Menschen, und alle Plätze waren besetzt, und als das Mütterchen zu seinem gewöhnlichen Sitz kam, war er auch nicht mehr ledig, sondern die ganze Bank gedrängt voll. Und wie es die Leute ansah, so waren es lauter verstorbene Verwandten, die saßen da in ihren altmodischen Kleidern aber mit blassem Angesicht. Sie sprachen auch nicht und sangen nicht, es gieng aber ein leises Summen und Wehen durch die Kirche. Da stand eine Muhme auf, trat vor, und sprach zu dem Mütterlein »dort sieh nach dem Altar, da wirst du deine Söhne sehen.« Die Alte blickte hin und sah ihre beiden Kinder, der eine hieng am Galgen, der andere war auf das Rad geflochten. Da sprach die Muhme »siehst du, so wär es ihnen ergangen, wären sie im Leben geblieben und hätte sie Gott nicht als unschuldige Kinder zu sich genommen.« Die Alte gieng zitternd nach Haus und dankte Gott auf den Knieen dass er es besser mit ihr gemacht hätte als sie hätte begreifen können; und am dritten Tag legte sie sich und starb.

9.

Die himmlische Hochzeit.

Es hörte einmal ein armer Bauernjunge in der Kirche wie der Pfarrer sprach »wer da will ins Himmelreich kommen, muss immer gerad aus gehen.« Da machte er sich auf, und gieng immer zu, immer gerade ohne abzuweichen, über Berg und Tal. Endlich führte ihn sein Weg in eine große Stadt, und mitten in die Kirche, wo eben Gottesdienst gehalten wurde. Wie er nun all die Herrlichkeit sah, meinte er nun wäre er im Himmel angelangt, setzte sich hin und war von Herzen froh. Als der Gottesdienst vorbei war und der

Küster ihn hinausgehen hieß, antwortete er »nein, ich gehe nicht wieder hinaus, ich bin froh dass ich endlich im Himmel bin.« Da gieng der Küster zum Pfarrer und sagte ihm es wäre ein Kind in der Kirche, das wollte nicht wieder heraus, weil es glaubte es wäre im Himmelreich. Der Pfarrer sprach »wenn es das glaubt, so wollen wir es darin lassen.« Darauf gieng er hin und fragte ob es auch Lust hätte zu arbeiten. »Ja«, antwortete der Kleine, ans Arbeiten wäre er gewöhnt, aber aus dem Himmel gienge er nicht wieder heraus. Nun blieb er in der Kirche, und als er sah wie die Leute zu dem Muttergottesbild mit dem Jesuskind, das aus Holz geschnitten war, kamen, knieten und beteten, dachte er »das ist der liebe Gott« und sprach »hör einmal, lieber Gott, was bist du mager! gewiss lassen dich die Leute hungern: ich will dir aber jeden Tag mein halbes Essen bringen.« Von nun an brachte er dem Bilde jeden Tag die Hälfte von seinem Essen, und das Bild fieng auch an die Speise zu genießen. Wie ein paar Wochen herum waren, merkten die Leute dass das Bild zunahm, dick und stark ward, und wunderten sich sehr. Der Pfarrer konnt es auch nicht begreifen, blieb in der Kirche und gieng dem Kleinen nach, da sah er wie der Knabe sein Brot mit der Mutter Gottes teilte und diese es auch annahm.

Nach einiger Zeit wurde der Knabe krank und kam acht Tage lang nicht aus dem Bett; wie er aber wieder aufstehen konnte, war sein erstes dass er seine Speise der Mutter Gottes brachte. Der Pfarrer gieng ihm nach und hörte wie er sprach »lieber Gott, nimm's nicht übel, dass ich dir so lange nichts gebracht habe: ich war aber krank und konnte nicht aufstehen.« Da antwortete ihm das Bild und sprach »ich habe deinen guten Willen gesehen, das ist mir genug; nächsten Sonntag sollst du mit mir auf die Hochzeit kommen.« Der Knabe freute sich darüber und sagte es dem Pfarrer, der bat ihn hinzugehen und das Bild zu fragen ob er auch dürfte mitkommen. »Nein«, antwortete das Bild, »du allein.« Der Pfarrer wollte ihn erst vorbereiten und ihm das

Abendmahl geben, das war der Knabe zufrieden; und nächsten Sonntag, wie das Abendmahl an ihn kam, fiel er um, und war tot und war zur ewigen Hochzeit.

10.

Die Haselrute.

Eines Nachmittags hatte sich das Christkind in sein Wiegenbett gelegt und war eingeschlafen, da trat seine Mutter heran, sah es voll Freude an und sprach »hast du dich schlafen gelegt, mein Kind? schlaf sanft, ich will derweil in den Wald gehen und eine Handvoll Erdbeeren für dich holen; ich weiß wohl, du freust dich darüber, wenn du aufgewacht bist.« Draußen im Wald fand sie einen Platz mit den schönsten Erdbeeren, als sie sich aber herabbückt um eine zu brechen, so springt aus dem Gras eine Natter in die Höhe. Sie erschrickt, lässt die Beere stehen und eilt hinweg. Die Natter schießt ihr nach, aber die Mutter Gottes, das könnt ihr denken, weiß guten Rat, sie versteckt sich hinter eine Haselstaude und bleibt da stehen, bis die Natter sich wieder verkrochen hat. Sie sammelt dann die Beeren, und als sie sich auf den Heimweg macht, spricht sie »wie die Haselstaude diesmal mein Schutz gewesen ist, so soll sie es auch in Zukunft andern Menschen sein.« Darum ist seit den ältesten Zeiten ein grüner Haselzweig gegen Nattern, Schlangen und was sonst auf der Erde kriecht, der sicherste Schutz.

Anhang

In der Ausgabe letzter Hand (1856/57)
nicht mehr enthaltene Märchen früherer Auflagen

Von der Nachtigall und der Blindschleiche.

Es waren einmal eine Nachtigall und eine Blindschleiche, die hatten jede nur ein Aug' und lebten zusammen in einem Haus lange Zeit in Frieden und Einigkeit. Eines Tags aber wurde die Nachtigall auf eine Hochzeit gebeten, da sprach sie zur Blindschleiche: »ich bin da auf eine Hochzeit gebeten und mögte nicht gern so mit einem Aug' hingehen, sei doch so gut und leih mir deins dazu, ich bring dir's Morgen wieder.« Und die Blindschleiche tat es aus Gefälligkeit.

Aber den andern Tag, wie die Nachtigall nach Haus gekommen war, gefiel es ihr so wohl, dass sie zwei Augen im Kopf trug und zu beiden Seiten sehen konnte, dass sie der armen Blindschleiche ihr geliehenes Aug' nicht wiedergeben wollte. Da schwur die Blindschleiche, sie wollte sich an ihr, an ihren Kindern und Kindeskindern rächen. »Geh nur«, sagte die Nachtigall, »und such einmal:

  ich bau mein Nest auf jene Linden,
  so hoch, so hoch, so hoch, so hoch,
  da magst du's nimmermehr finden!«

Seit der Zeit haben alle Nachtigallen zwei Augen und alle Blindschleichen keine Augen. Aber wo die Nachtigall hinbaut, da wohnt unten auch im Busch eine Blindschleiche, und sie trachtet immer hinaufzukriechen, Löcher in die Eier ihrer Feindin zu bohren oder sie auszusaufen.

Anhang Nr. 2

Die Hand mit dem Messer.

Es war ein kleines Mädchen, das hatte drei Brüder, die galten bei der Mutter alles, und es wurde überall zurückgesetzt, hart angefahren und musste tagtäglich Morgens früh ausgehen, Torf zu graben auf dürrem Heidegrund, den sie zum Kochen und Brennen brauchten. Noch dazu bekam es ein altes und stumpfes Gerät, womit es die sauere Arbeit verrichten sollte.

Aber das kleine Mädchen hatte einen Liebhaber, der war ein Elfe und wohnte nahe an ihrer Mutter Haus in einem Hügel, und so oft es nun an dem Hügel vorbei kam, streckte er seine Hand aus dem Fels, und hielt darin ein sehr scharfes Messer, das von sonderlicher Kraft war und alles durchschnitt. Mit diesem Messer schnitt sie den Torf bald heraus, ging vergnügt mit der nötigen Ladung heim, und wenn sie am Felsen vorbei kam, klopfte sie zweimal dran, so reichte die Hand heraus und nahm das Messer in Empfang.

Als aber die Mutter merkte, wie geschwind und leicht sie immer den Torf heimbrachte, erzählte sie den Brüdern, es müsste ihr gewiss jemand anders dabei helfen, sonst wäre es nicht möglich. Da schlichen ihr die Brüder nach und sahen, wie sie das Zaubermesser bekam, holten sie ein und drangen es ihr mit Gewalt ab. Darauf kehrten sie zurück, schlugen an den Felsen, als sie gewohnt war zu tun, und wie der gute Elf die Hand herausstreckte, schnitten sie sie ihm ab mit seinem selbeigenen Messer. Der blutende Arm zog sich zurück, und weil der Elf glaubte seine Geliebte hätte es aus Verrat getan, so wurde er seitdem nimmermehr gesehen.

Wie Kinder Schlachtens
miteinander gespielt haben.

I

In einer Stadt, Franecker genannt, gelegen in Westfriesland, da ist es geschehen, dass junge Kinder, fünf- und sechsjährige, Mägdlein und Knaben, mit einander spielten. Und sie ordneten ein Büblein an, das solle der Metzger sein, ein anderes Büblein, das solle Koch sein, und ein drittes Büblein, das solle eine Sau sein. Ein Mägdlein, ordneten sie, solle Köchin sein, wieder ein anderes, das solle Unterköchin sein; und die Unterköchin solle in einem Geschirrlein das Blut von der Sau empfahen, dass man Würste könne machen. Der Metzger geriet nun verabredetermaßen an das Büblein, das die Sau sollte sein, riss es nieder und schnitt ihm mit einem Messerlein die Gurgel auf, und die Unterköchin empfing das Blut in ihrem Geschirrlein. Ein Ratsherr, der von ungefähr vorübergeht, sieht dies Elend: er nimmt von Stund an den Metzger mit sich und führt ihn in des Obersten Haus, welcher sogleich den ganzen Rat versammeln ließ. Sie saßen all über diesen Handel und wussten nicht, wie sie ihm tun sollten, denn sie sahen wohl, dass es kindlicher Weise geschehen war. Einer unter ihnen, ein alter weiser Mann, gab den Rat, der oberste Richter solle einen schönen roten Apfel in eine Hand nehmen, in die andere einen rheinischen Gulden, solle das Kind zu sich rufen und beide Hände gleich gegen dasselbe ausstrecken: nehme es den Apfel, so soll' es ledig erkannt werden, nehme es aber den Gulden, so solle man es töten. Dem wird gefolgt, das Kind aber ergreift den Apfel lachend, wird also aller Strafe ledig erkannt.

II

Einstmals hat ein Hausvater ein Schwein geschlachtet, das haben seine Kinder gesehen; als sie nun Nachmittag mit einander spielen wollen, hat das eine Kind zum andern gesagt: »du sollst das Schweinchen und ich der Metzger sein«; hat darauf ein bloß Messer genommen, und es seinem Brüderchen in den Hals gestoßen. Die Mutter, welche oben in der Stube saß und ihr jüngstes Kindlein in einem Zuber badete, hörte das Schreien ihres anderen Kindes, lief alsbald hinunter, und als sie sah, was vorgegangen, zog sie das Messer dem Kind aus dem Hals und stieß es im Zorn, dem andern Kind, welches der Metzger gewesen, ins Herz. Darauf lief sie alsbald nach der Stube und wollte sehen, was ihr Kind in dem Badezuber mache, aber es war unterdessen in dem Bad ertrunken; deswegen dann die Frau so voller Angst ward, dass sie in Verzweifelung geriet, sich von ihrem Gesinde nicht wollte trösten lassen, sondern sich selbst erhängte. Der Mann kam vom Felde und als er dies alles gesehen, hat er sich so betrübt, dass er kurz darauf gestorben ist.

Anhang Nr. 4

Der Tod und der Gänshirt.

Es ging ein armer Hirt an dem Ufer eines großen und ungestümen Wassers, hütend einen Haufen weißer Gänse. Zu diesem kam der Tod über Wasser, und wurde von dem Hirten gefragt, wo er herkomme, und wo er hin wolle? Der Tod antwortete, dass er aus dem Wasser komme und aus der Welt wolle. Der arme Gänshirt fragte ferners: wie man doch aus der Welt kommen könne? Der Tod sagte, dass man über das Wasser in die neue Welt müsse, welche jenseits gelegen. Der Hirt sagte, dass er dieses Lebens müde, und bate den Tod, er sollte ihn mit über nehmen. Der Tod sagte, dass es noch nicht Zeit, und hätte er jetzt sonst zu verrichten. Es war aber unferne davon ein Geizhals, der trachtete bei Nachts auf seinem Lager, wie er doch mehr Geld und Gut zusammenbringen mögte, den führte der Tod zu dem großen Wasser und stieß ihn hinein. Weil er aber nicht schwimmen konnte, ist er zu Grunde gesunken, bevor er an das Ufer kommen. Seine Hunde und Katzen, so ihm nachgelaufen, sind auch mit ihm ersoffen. Etliche Tage hernach kam der Tod auch zu dem Gänshirten, fand ihn fröhlich singen und sprach zu ihm: »willst du nun mit?« Er war willig und kam mit seinen weißen Gänsen wohl hinüber, welche alle in weiße Schafe verwandelt worden. Der Gänshirt betrachtete das schöne Land und hörte, dass die Hirten der Orten zu Königen würden, und indem er sich recht umsahe, kamen ihm die Erzhirten Abraham, Isaac und Jacob entgegen, setzten ihm eine königliche Krone auf, und führten ihn in der Hirten Schloss, allda er noch zu finden.

Anhang Nr. 5

Der gestiefelte Kater.

mill

Ein Müller hatte drei Söhne, seine Mühle, einen Esel und einen Kater; die Söhne mussten mahlen, der Esel Getreide holen und Mehl forttragen und die Katz die Mäuse wegfangen. Als der Müller starb, teilten sich die drei Söhne in die Erbschaft, der älteste bekam die Mühle, der zweite den Esel, der dritte den Kater, weiter blieb nichts für ihn übrig. Da war er traurig und sprach zu sich selbst: »ich hab es doch am allerschlimmsten kriegt, mein ältster Bruder kann mahlen, mein zweiter kann auf seinem Esel reiten, was kann ich mit dem Kater anfangen? lass ich mir ein paar Pelzhandschuhe aus seinem Fell machen, so ist's vorbei.« »Hör«,

fing der Kater an, der alles verstanden hatte, was er gesagt,
»du brauchst mich nicht zu töten, um ein paar schlechte
Handschuh aus meinem Pelz zu kriegen, lass mir nur ein
paar Stiefel machen, dass ich ausgehen kann und mich unter
den Leuten sehen lassen, dann soll dir bald geholfen sein.«
Der Müllerssohn verwunderte sich, dass der Kater so
sprach, weil aber eben der Schuster vorbeiging, rief er ihn
herein und ließ ihm ein Paar Stiefel anmessen. Als sie fertig
waren, zog sie der Kater an, nahm einen Sack, machte den
Boden desselben voll Korn, oben aber eine Schnur daran,
womit man ihn zuziehen konnte, dann warf er ihn über
den Rücken und ging auf zwei Beinen, wie ein Mensch, zur
Tür hinaus.

Dazumal regierte ein König in dem Land, der aß die Rebhühner so gern: es war aber eine Not, dass keine zu kriegen
waren. Der ganze Wald war voll, aber sie waren so scheu,
dass kein Jäger sie erreichen konnte. Das wusste der Kater
und gedacht seine Sache besser zu machen; als er in den
Wald kam, tät er den Sack auf, breitete das Korn auseinander, die Schnur aber legte er ins Gras und leitete sie hinter
eine Hecke. Da versteckte er sich selber, schlich herum und
lauerte. Die Rebhühner kamen bald gelaufen, fanden das
Korn und eins nach dem andern hüpfte in den Sack hinein.
Als eine gute Anzahl darin war, zog der Kater den Strick
zu, lief herzu und drehte ihnen den Hals um; dann warf er
den Sack auf den Rücken und ging geradeswegs nach des
Königs Schloss. Die Wache rief: »halt! wohin.« »Zu dem
König«, antwortete der Kater kurzweg. »Bist du toll, ein
Kater zum König?« »Lass ihn nur gehen«, sagte ein anderer, »der König hat doch oft lange Weil, vielleicht macht
ihm der Kater mit seinem Brummen und Spinnen Vergnügen.« Als der Kater vor den König kam, machte er einen
Reverenz und sagte: »mein Herr, der Graf«, dabei nannte er
einen langen und vornehmen Namen, »lässt sich dem
Herrn König empfehlen und schickt ihm hier Rebhühner,
die er eben in Schlingen gefangen hat.« Der König erstaun-

te über die schönen fetten Rebhühner, wusste sich vor
Freude nicht zu lassen, und befahl dem Kater, so viel Gold
aus der Schatzkammer in den Sack zu tun, als er tragen
könne: »das bring deinem Herrn und dank ihm noch viel-
mal für sein Geschenk.«

Der arme Müllerssohn aber saß zu Haus am Fenster, stützte den Kopf auf die Hand und dachte, dass er nun sein letztes für die Stiefeln des Katers weggegeben, und was werde
ihm der großes dafür bringen können. Da trat der Kater
herein, warf den Sack vom Rücken, schnürte ihn auf und
schüttete das Gold vor den Müller hin: »da hast du etwas
vor die Stiefeln, der König lässt dich auch grüßen und dir
viel Dank sagen.« Der Müller war froh über den Reichtum,
ohne dass er noch recht begreifen konnte, wie es zugegangen war. Der Kater aber, während er seine Stiefel auszog,
erzählte ihm alles, dann sagte er: »du hast zwar jetzt Geld
genug, aber dabei soll es nicht bleiben, morgen zieh ich
meine Stiefel wieder an, du sollst noch reicher werden, dem
König hab ich auch gesagt, dass du ein Graf bist.« Am andern Tag ging der Kater, wie er gesagt hatte, wohl gestiefelt
wieder auf die Jagd, und brachte dem König einen reichen
Fang. So ging es alle Tage, und der Kater brachte alle Tage
Gold heim, und ward so beliebt wie einer bei dem König,
dass er aus- und eingehen durfte und im Schloss herum-
streichen, wo er wollte. Einmal stand der Kater in der Küche des Königs beim Herd und wärmte sich, da kam der
Kutscher und fluchte: »ich wünsch', der König mit der
Prinzessin wär beim Henker! ich wollt ins Wirtshaus gehen
und einmal trinken und Karte spielen, da soll ich sie spazieren fahren an den See.« Wie der Kater das hörte, schlich er
nach Haus und sagte zu seinem Herrn: »wenn du willst ein
Graf und reich werden, so komm mit mir hinaus an den
See und bad dich darin.« Der Müller wusste nicht, was er
dazu sagen sollte, doch folgte er dem Kater, ging mit ihm,
zog sich splinternackend aus und sprang ins Wasser. Der
Kater aber nahm seine Kleider, trug sie fort und versteckte

sie. Kaum war er damit fertig, da kam der König dahergefahren; der Kater fing sogleich an, erbärmlich zu lamentieren: »ach! allergnädigster König! mein Herr, der hat sich hier im See gebadet, da ist ein Dieb gekommen und hat ihm die Kleider gestohlen, die am Ufer lagen, nun ist der Herr Graf im Wasser und kann nicht heraus, und wenn er länger darin bleibt wird er sich verkälten und sterben.« Wie der König das hörte, ließ er Halt machen, und einer von seinen Leuten musste zurückjagen und von des Königs Kleidern holen. Der Herr Graf zog die prächtigsten Kleider an, und weil ihm ohnehin der König wegen der Rebhühner, die er meinte von ihm empfangen zu haben, gewogen war, so musste er sich zu ihm in die Kutsche setzen. Die Prinzessin war auch nicht bös darüber, denn der Graf war jung und schön, und er gefiel ihr recht gut.

Der Kater aber war vorausgegangen und zu einer großen Wiese gekommen, wo über hundert Leute waren und Heu machten. »Wem ist die Wiese, ihr Leute?« fragte der Kater. »Dem großen Zauberer.« »Hört, jetzt wird der König bald vorbeifahren, wenn der fragt, wem die Wiese gehört, so antwortet: dem Grafen; und wenn ihr das nicht tut, so werdet ihr alle totgeschlagen.« Darauf ging der Kater weiter und kam an ein Kornfeld, so groß, dass es niemand übersehen konnte, da standen mehr als zweihundert Leute und schnitten das Korn. »Wem ist das Korn ihr Leute?« »Dem Zauberer.« »Hört, jetzt wird der König vorbeifahren, wenn er frägt, wem das Korn gehört, so antwortet: dem Grafen; und wenn ihr das nicht tut, so werdet ihr alle totgeschlagen.« Endlich kam der Kater an einen prächtigen Wald, da standen mehr als dreihundert Leute, fällten die großen Eichen und machten Holz. »Wem ist der Wald, ihr Leute?« »Dem Zauberer.« »Hört, jetzt wird der König vorbeifahren, wenn er frägt, wem der Wald gehört, so antwortet: dem Grafen; und wenn ihr das nicht tut, so werdet ihr alle umgebracht.« Der Kater ging noch weiter, die Leute sahen ihm alle nach und weil er so wunderlich aussah, und wie

ein Mensch in Stiefeln daherging, fürchteten sie sich vor
ihm. Er kam bald an des Zauberers Schloss, trat kecklich
hinein und vor ihn hin. Der Zauberer sah ihn verächtlich
an, und fragte ihn, was er wolle. Der Kater machte einen
Reverenz und sagte: »ich habe gehört, dass du in jedes Tier
nach deinem Gefallen dich verwandeln könntest; was einen
Hund, Fuchs oder auch Wolf betrifft, da will ich es wohl
glauben, aber von einem Elefant, das scheint mir ganz unmöglich, und deshalb bin ich gekommen um mich selbst zu
überzeugen.« Der Zauberer sagte stolz: »das ist mir eine
Kleinigkeit«, und war in dem Augenblick in einen Elefant
verwandelt; »das ist viel, aber auch in einen Löwen?« »Das
ist auch nichts«, sagte der Zauberer und stand als ein Löwe
vor dem Kater. Der Kater stellte sich erschrocken und rief:
»das ist unglaublich und unerhört, dergleichen hätt ich mir
nicht im Traume in die Gedanken kommen lassen; aber
noch mehr, als alles andere, wär es, wenn du dich auch in
ein so kleines Tier, wie eine Maus ist, verwandeln könntest,
du kannst gewiss mehr, als irgendein Zauberer auf der Welt,
aber das wird dir doch zu hoch sein.« Der Zauberer ward
ganz freundlich von den süßen Worten und sagte: »o ja, liebes Kätzchen, das kann ich auch« und sprang als eine Maus
im Zimmer herum. Der Kater war hinter ihm her, fing die
Maus mit einem Sprung und fraß sie auf.
Der König aber war mit dem Grafen und der Prinzessin
weiter spazieren gefahren, und kam zu der großen Wiese.
»Wem gehört das Heu?« fragte der König. »dem Herrn
Grafen« riefen alle, wie der Kater ihnen befohlen hatte.
»Ihr habt da ein schön Stück Land, Herr Graf«, sagte er.
Darnach kamen sie an das große Kornfeld. »Wem gehört
das Korn, ihr Leute?« »Dem Herrn Grafen.« »Ei! Herr
Graf! große, schöne Ländereien!« Darauf zu dem Wald:
»wem gehört das Holz, ihr Leute?« »Dem Herrn Grafen.«
Der König verwunderte sich noch mehr und sagte: »Ihr
müsst ein reicher Mann sein, Herr Graf, ich glaube nicht,
dass ich einen so prächtigen Wald habe.« Endlich kamen sie

an das Schloss, der Kater stand oben an der Treppe, und als der Wagen unten hielt, sprang er herab, machte die Türe auf und sagte: »Herr König, Ihr gelangt hier in das Schloss meines Herrn, des Grafen, den diese Ehre für sein Lebtag glücklich machen wird.« Der König stieg aus und verwunderte sich über das prächtige Gebäude, das fast größer und schöner war als sein Schloss; der Graf aber führte die Prinzessin die Treppe hinauf in den Saal, der ganz von Gold und Edelsteinen flimmerte.

Da ward die Prinzessin mit dem Grafen versprochen, und als der König starb, ward er König, der gestiefelte Kater aber erster Minister.

Anhang Nr. 6

Von der Serviette, dem Tornister, dem Kanonenhütlein und dem Horn.

Es waren drei Brüder aus dem Schwarzenfelsischen, von Haus sehr arm, die reisten nach Spanien, da kamen sie an einen Berg, der ganz von Silber umgeben war. Der älteste Bruder machte sich bezahlt, nahm so viel als er nur tragen konnte, und ging mit seiner Beute nach Haus. Die andern zwei reisten weiter fort und kamen zu einem Berg, wo nichts als Gold zu sehen war. Nun sprach der eine zu dem andern: »wie sollen wir es machen?« und der zweite nahm sich auch soviel Gold als er nur tragen konnte und ging nach Haus; der dritte aber wollte sein Glück noch besser versuchen und ging weiter fort. Nach drei Tagen kam er in einen ungeheuren Wald, da hatte er sich müd gegangen, Hunger und Durst plagten ihn, und er konnte nicht aus dem Wald heraus. Da stieg er auf einen hohen Baum und wollte sehen, ob er Waldes Ende finden mögte, er sah aber nichts als Baumspitzen; da wünschte er nur noch einmal seinen Leib zu sättigen und begab sich, von dem Baum herunter zu steigen. Als er herunter kam, erblickte er unter dem Baum einen Tisch mit vielerlei Speise besetzt, da ward er vergnügt, nahte sich dem Tisch und aß sich satt. Und als er fertig gegessen hatte, nahm er die Serviette mit sich und ging weiter, und wenn ihn wieder Hunger und Durst ankam, so deckte er die Serviette auf und was er wünschte, das stund darauf. Nach einer Tagreise kam er zu einem Köhler, der brannte Kohlen und kochte Kartoffeln. Der Köhler bat ihn zu Gast, er sagte aber: »ich will nicht bei dir essen, aber ich will dich zu Gast bitten,« der Köhler fragte: »wie ist das möglich, ich sehe ja nicht, dass du etwas bei dir hast.« – »Das tut nichts, setz dich nur her« damit deckte er seine Serviette auf, da stand alles, was zu wünschen war. Der Köhler ließ sich's gut schmecken und hatte großen Gefallen an der Serviette und als sie abgegessen hatten sagte er: »tausch mit mir, ich geb dir für die Serviette einen alten Soldatentornister wenn du mit der Hand darauf klopfst, kommt jedesmal ein Gefreiter und sechs Mann Soldaten mit Ober- und Untergewehr heraus, die können mir im Wald nichts helfen, aber die Serviette wär mir lieb.« Der Tausch ging vor sich, der Köhler behielt die Serviette, der Schwarzenfelser nahm den Tornister mit. Kaum war er aber ein Stück Wegs gegangen, so schlug er darauf, da kamen die Kriegshelden heraus: »was verlangt mein Herr?« – »Ihr marschiert hin und holet bei dem Köhler meine Serviette, die ich dort gelassen.« Also gingen sie zurück und brachten ihm die Serviette wieder. Abends kam er zu einem andern Kohlenbrenner, der lud ihn wiederum zum Abendessen ein und hatte desgleichen Kartoffeln ohne Fett. Der Schwarzenfelser aber deckte seine Serviette auf und bat ihn zu Gast, da war alles nach Wunsch. Als die Mahlzeit vorbei war, hielt auch dieser Köhler um den Tausch an, er gab für die Serviette einen Hut, drehte man den auf dem Kopf herum, so gingen die Kanonen, als stünd eine Batterie auf dem Flecken. Als der Schwarzenfelser ein Stück Wegs fort war, klopfte er wieder auf seinen alten Ranzen, und der Gefreite

mit sechs Mann musste ihm die Serviette wieder holen.
Nun ging es weiter fort in dem nämlichen Wald und er kam
Abends zu dem dritten Köhler, der lud ihn, wie die andern,
auf ungeschmälzte Kartoffeln, erhielt aber von ihm ein
Traktament und vertauschte ihm die Serviette für ein Hörnchen, wenn man darauf blies, fielen alle Städte und Dorf-
schaften, wie auch alle Festungswerke übern Haufen. Der
Köhler behielt aber die Serviette nicht länger als die andern,
denn der Gefreite mit sechs Mann kam bald und holte sie
ab. Wie nun der Schwarzenfelser alles beisammen hatte,
kehrte er um nach Haus, und wollt seine beiden Brüder besuchen. Diese waren reich von ihrem vielen Gold und Silber und wie er nun kam, einen alten zerrissenen Rock an-
habend, da wollten sie ihn nicht für ihren Bruder erkennen.
Alsobald schlug er auf seinen Tornister und ließ 150 Mann
aufmarschieren, die mussten seinen Brüdern die Hucke
(den Buckel) recht vollschlagen. Das ganze Dorf kam zu
Hülfe, aber sie richteten wenig aus bei der Sache; da ward
es dem König gemeldet, der schickte ein militärisch Kommando ab, diese Soldaten gefangen zu nehmen; aber der
Schwarzenfelser schlug in einem hin auf seinen Ranzen und
ließ Infanterie und Kavallerie aufmarschieren, die schlugen
das militärische Kommando wieder zurück an seinen Ort.
Am andern Tag ließ der König noch viel mehr Volk aus-
marschieren um den alten Kerl in Ruh zu setzen. Der aber
schlug auf seinen Ranzen so lang bis eine ganze Armee her-
ausgekommen, dazu drehte er seinen Hut ein paar mal, da
gingen die Kanonen und der Feind ward geschlagen und in
die Flucht gejagt. Da ward Friede geschlossen und er zum
Vizekönig gemacht, wie auch die Prinzessin ihm zur Gemahlin gegeben.
Der Prinzessin aber lag es beständig im Sinn, dass sie so einen alten Kerl zum Gemahl nehmen müssen und wünschte
nichts mehr, als dass sie ihn wieder los werden könnte. Sie
forschte täglich in welchen Vorteilen seine Macht bestehe,
er war auch so treu und entdeckte ihr alles. Da schwätzte

sie ihm seinen Ranzen ab und verstieß ihn, und als darauf
Soldaten gegen ihn marschierten, war sein Volk verloren,
aber noch hatte er sein Hütgen, da griff er daran und ließ
die Kanonen gehen, so schlug er den Feind und ward wieder Friede gemacht. Darnach aber ließ er sich wieder betrügen und die Prinzessin schwätzte ihm sein Hütchen ab.
Und als nun der Feind auf ihn eindrang, hatte er nichts als
sein Hörnchen, da blies er darauf, alsbald fielen Dörfer,
Städte und alle Festungswerke übern Haufen. Da war er
König allein und blieb, bis er gestorben ist.

Anhang Nr. 7

Die wunderliche Gasterei.

Auf eine Zeit lebte eine Blutwurst und eine Leberwurst in
Freundschaft, und die Blutwurst bat die Leberwurst zu
Gast. Wie es Essenszeit war, ging die Leberwurst auch ganz
vergnügt zu der Blutwurst, als sie aber in die Haustüre trat,
sah sie allerlei wunderliche Dinge, auf jeder Stiege der
Treppe, deren viele waren, immer etwas anderes, da war
etwa ein Besen und eine Schippe, die sich miteinander
schlugen, dann ein Affe mit einer großen Wunde am Kopf
und dergleichen mehr.
Die Leberwurst war ganz erschrocken und bestürzt darüber, doch nahm sie sich ein Herz, trat in die Stube und
wurde von der Blutwurst freundschaftlich empfangen. Die
Leberwurst hub an, sich nach den seltsamen Dingen zu er-
kundigen, die draußen auf der Treppe wären, die Blutwurst
tat aber, als hörte sie es nicht, oder als sei es nicht der Mühe
wert davon zu sprechen, oder sie sagte etwa von der Schippe und dem Besen »es wird meine Magd gewesen sein, die
auf der Treppe mit jemand geschwätzt hat«, und brachte
die Rede auf etwas anderes.

Die Blutwurst ging darauf hinaus und sagte, sie müsse in der Küche nach dem Essen sehen, ob alles ordentlich angerichtet werde, und nichts in die Asche geworfen. Wie die Leberwurst derweil in der Stube auf und ab ging und immer die wunderlichen Dinge im Kopf hatte, kam jemand, ich weiß nicht, wer's gewesen ist, herein und sagte »ich warne dich, Leberwurst, du bist in einer Blut- und Mörderhöhle, mach dich eilig fort, wenn dir dein Leben lieb ist.« Die Leberwurst besann sich nicht lang, schlich zur Tür hinaus und lief, was sie konnte; sie stand auch nicht eher still, bis sie aus dem Haus mitten auf der Straße war. Da blickte sie sich um, und sah die Blutwurst oben im Bodenloch stehen mit einem langen, langen Messer, das blinkte, als wär's frisch gewetzt, und damit drohte sie, und rief herab:

»hätt ich dich, so wollt ich dich!«

Anhang Nr. 8

Hans Dumm.

Es war ein König, der lebte mit seiner Tochter, die sein einziges Kind war, vergnügt: auf einmal aber brachte die Prinzessin ein Kind zur Welt, und niemand wusste, wer der Vater war; der König wusste lang nicht, was er anfangen sollte, am Ende befahl er, die Prinzessin solle mit dem Kind in die Kirche gehen, da sollte ihm eine Zitrone in die Hand gegeben werden, und wem es die reiche, solle der Vater des Kinds und Gemahl der Prinzessin sein. Das geschah nun, doch war der Befehl gegeben, dass niemand als schöne Leute in die Kirche sollten eingelassen werden. Es war aber in der Stadt ein kleiner, schiefer und buckelichter Bursch, der nicht recht klug war, und darum der Hans Dumm hieß, der drängte sich ungesehen zwischen den andern auch in die Kirche, und wie das Kind die Zitrone austeilen sollte, so reichte es sie dem Hans Dumm. Die Prinzessin war erschrocken, der König war so aufgebracht, dass er sie und das Kind mit dem Hans Dumm in eine Tonne stecken und aufs Meer setzen ließ. Die Tonne schwamm bald fort, und wie sie allein auf dem Meere waren, klagte die Prinzessin und sagte: »du garstiger, buckelichter, naseweiser Bub, bist an meinem Unglück Schuld, was hast du dich in die Kirche gedrängt, das Kind ging dich nichts an.« »O ja«, sagte Hans Dumm, »das ging mich wohl etwas an, denn ich habe es einmal gewünscht, dass du ein Kind bekämst, und was ich wünsche, das trifft ein.« »Wenn das wahr ist, so wünsch uns doch, was zu essen hierher.« »Das kann ich auch«, sagte Hans Dumm, wünschte sich aber eine Schüssel recht voll Kartoffel, die Prinzessin hätte gern etwas Besseres gehabt, aber weil sie so hungrig war, half sie ihm die Kartoffel essen. Nachdem sie satt waren, sagte Hans Dumm: »nun will ich uns ein schönes Schiff wünschen!« und kaum hatte er das gesagt, so saßen sie in einem prächtigen Schiff, darin war alles zum Überfluss, was man nur verlangen konnte. Der Steuermann fuhr grad ans Land, und als sie ausstiegen, sagte Hans Dumm: »nun soll ein Schloss dort stehen!« Da stand ein prächtiges Schloss und Diener in Goldkleidern kamen und führten die Prinzessin und das Kind hinein, und als sie mitten in dem Saal waren, sagte Hans Dumm: »nun wünsch ich, dass ich ein junger und kluger Prinz werde!« Da verlor sich sein Buckel, und er war schön und gerad und freundlich, und er gefiel der Prinzessin gut und ward ihr Gemahl.

So lebten sie lange Zeit vergnügt; da ritt einmal der alte König aus, verirrte sich, und kam zu dem Schloss. Er verwunderte sich darüber, weil er es noch nie gesehen und kehrte ein. Die Prinzessin erkannte gleich ihren Vater, er aber erkannte sie nicht, er dachte auch, sie sei schon längst im Meer ertrunken. Sie bewirtete ihn prächtig, und als er wieder nach Haus wollte, steckte sie ihm heimlich einen goldenen Becher in die Tasche. Nachdem er aber fortgeritten war, schickte sie ein paar Reuter nach, die mussten ihn anhalten und untersuchen, ob er den goldenen Becher nicht gestohlen, und wie sie ihn in seiner Tasche fanden, brachten sie ihn mit zurück. Er schwur der Prinzessin, er habe ihn nicht gestohlen, und wisse nicht, wie er in seine Tasche gekommen sei, »darum«, sagte sie, »muss man sich hüten, jemand gleich für schuldig zu halten«, und gab sich als seine Tochter zu erkennen. Da freute sich der König und sie lebten vergnügt zusammen, und nach seinem Tod ward Hans Dumm König.

Anhang Nr. 9

Blaubart.

In einem Walde lebte ein Mann, der hatte drei Söhne und eine schöne Tochter. Einmal kam ein goldener Wagen mit sechs Pferden und einer Menge Bedienten angefahren, hielt vor dem Haus still, und ein König stieg aus und bat den Mann, er möchte ihm seine Tochter zur Gemahlin geben. Der Mann war froh, dass seiner Tochter ein solches Glück widerfuhr, und sagte gleich ja; es war auch an dem Freier gar nichts auszusetzen, als dass er einen ganz blauen Bart hatte, so dass man einen kleinen Schrecken kriegte, so oft man ihn ansah. Das Mädchen erschrak auch anfangs davor, und scheute sich ihn zu heiraten, aber auf Zureden ihres Vaters, willigte es endlich ein. Doch weil es so eine Angst fühlte, ging es erst zu seinen drei Brüdern, nahm sie allein und sagte: »liebe Brüder, wenn Ihr mich schreien hört, wo ihr auch seid, so lasst alles stehen und liegen und kommt mir zu Hülfe.« Das versprachen ihm die Brüder und küssten es, »leb wohl, liebe Schwester, wenn wir deine Stimme hören, springen wir auf unsere Pferde, und sind bald bei dir.« Darauf setzte es sich in den Wagen zu dem Blaubart, und fuhr mit ihm fort. Wie es in sein Schloss kam, war alles prächtig, und was die Königin nur wünschte, das geschah, und sie wären recht glücklich gewesen, wenn sie sich nur an den blauen Bart des Königs hätte gewöhnen können, aber immer, wenn sie den sah, erschrak sie innerlich davor. Nachdem das einige Zeit gewährt, sprach er: »ich muss eine große Reise machen, da hast du die Schlüssel zu dem ganzen Schloss, du kannst überall aufschließen und alles besehen, nur die Kammer, wozu dieser kleine goldene Schlüssel gehört, verbiet ich dir; schließt du die auf, so ist dein Leben verfallen.« Sie nahm die Schlüssel, versprach ihm zu gehorchen, und als er fort war, schloss sie nach einander die Türen auf, und sah so viel Reichtümer und Herrlichkeiten, dass sie meinte aus der ganzen Welt wären sie hier zusammen gebracht. Es war nun nichts mehr übrig, als die verbotene Kammer, der Schlüssel war von Gold, da gedachte sie, in dieser ist vielleicht das allerkostbarste verschlossen; die Neugierde fing an sie zu plagen, und sie hätte lieber all das andere nicht gesehen, wenn sie nur gewusst, was in dieser wäre. Eine Zeit lang widerstand sie der Begierde, zuletzt aber ward diese so mächtig, dass sie den Schlüssel nahm und zu der Kammer hinging: »wer wird es sehen, dass ich sie öffne«, sagte sie zu sich selbst, »ich will auch nur einen Blick hineintun.« Da schloss sie auf, und wie die Türe aufging, schwomm ihr ein Strom Blut entgegen, und an den Wänden herum sah sie tote Weiber hängen, und von einigen waren nur die Gerippe noch übrig. Sie erschrak so heftig, dass sie die Türe gleich wieder zuschlug, aber der Schlüssel sprang dabei heraus und fiel in das Blut. Geschwind hob sie ihn auf, und wollte das Blut abwischen, aber es war umsonst, wenn sie es auf der einen Seite abgewischt, kam es auf der andern wieder zum Vorschein; sie setzte sich den ganzen Tag hin und rieb daran, und versuchte alles Mögliche, aber es half nichts, die Blutflecken waren nicht herabzubringen; endlich am Abend legte sie ihn ins Heu, das sollte in der Nacht das Blut ausziehen. Am andern Tag kam der Blaubart zurück, und das erste war, dass er die Schlüssel von ihr forderte; ihr Herz schlug, sie brachte die andern und hoffte, er werde es nicht bemerken, dass der goldene fehlte. Er aber zählte sie alle, und wie er fertig war, sagte er: »wo ist der zu der heimlichen Kammer?« dabei sah er ihr in das Gesicht. Sie ward blutrot und antwortete: »er liegt oben, ich habe ihn verlegt, morgen will ich ihn suchen.« »Geh lieber gleich, liebe Frau, ich werde ihn noch heute brauchen.« »Ach ich will dir's nur sagen, ich habe ihn im Heu verloren, da muss ich erst suchen.« »Du hast ihn nicht verloren«, sagte der Blaubart zornig, »du hast ihn dahin gesteckt, damit die Blutflecken herausziehen sollen, denn du hast mein Gebot übertreten, und bist in der Kammer gewesen, aber jetzt sollst du hinein, wenn du auch nicht willst.« Da musste sie den Schlüssel holen, der war noch voller Blutflecken. »Nun bereite dich zum Tode, du sollst noch heute sterben«, sagte der Blaubart, holte sein großes Messer und führte sie auf den Hausehrn. »Lass mich nur noch vor meinem Tod mein Gebet tun«, sagte sie; »So geh, aber eil dich, denn ich habe keine Zeit lang zu warten.« Da lief sie die Treppe hinauf, und rief so laut sie konnte zum Fenster hinaus: »Brüder, meine lieben Brüder, kommt, helft mir!« Die Brüder saßen im Wald beim kühlen Wein, da sprach der jüngste: »mir ist als hätt ich unserer Schwester Stimme gehört; auf! wir müssen ihr zu Hülfe eilen!« da sprangen sie auf ihre Pferde und ritten, als wären sie der Sturmwind. Ihre Schwester aber lag in Angst auf den Knieen; da rief der Blaubart unten: »nun, bist du bald fertig?« dabei hörte sie, wie er auf der untersten Stufe sein Messer wetzte; sie sah hinaus, aber sie sah nichts, als von Ferne einen Staub, als käm eine Herde gezogen. Da schrie sie noch einmal: »Brüder, meine lieben Brüder! kommt, helft mir!« und ihre Angst ward immer größer. Der Blaubart aber rief: »wenn du nicht bald kommst, so hol ich dich, mein Messer ist gewetzt!« Da sah sie wieder hinaus, und sah ihre drei Brüder durch das Feld reiten, als flögen sie wie Vögel in der Luft, da schrie sie zum drittenmal in der höchsten Not und aus allen Kräften: »Brüder, meine lieben Brüder! kommt, helft mir!« und der jüngste war schon so nah, dass sie seine Stimme hörte: »tröste dich, liebe Schwester, noch einen Augenblick, so sind wir bei dir!« Der Blaubart aber rief: »nun ist's genug gebetet, ich will nicht länger warten, kommst du nicht, so hol ich dich!« »Ach! nur noch für meine drei lieben Brüder lass mich beten.« Er hörte aber nicht, kam die Treppe heraufgegangen und zog sie hinunter, und eben hatte er sie an den Haaren gefasst, und wollte ihr das Messer in das Herz stoßen, da schlugen die drei Brüder an die Haustüre, drangen herein und rissen sie ihm aus der Hand, dann zogen sie ihre Säbel und hieben ihn nieder. Da ward er in die Blutkammer aufgehängt zu den andern Weibern, die er getötet, die Brüder aber nahmen ihre liebste Schwester mit nach Haus, und alle Reichtümer des Blaubarts gehörten ihr.

Anhang Nr. 10

Hurleburlebutz.

Ein König verirrte sich auf der Jagd, da trat ein kleines weißes Männchen vor ihn: »Herr König, wenn ihr mir eure jüngste Tochter geben wollt, so will ich euch wieder aus dem Wald führen.« Der König sagte es in seiner Angst zu, das Männchen brachte ihn auf den Weg, nahm dann Abschied und rief noch nach: »in acht Tagen komm ich und hol meine Braut.« Daheim aber war der König traurig über sein Versprechen, denn die jüngste Tochter hatte er am liebsten; das sahen ihm die Prinzessinnen an, und wollten wissen, was ihm Kummer mache. Da musst er's endlich gestehen, er habe die jüngste von ihnen einem kleinen weißen Waldmännchen versprochen, und das komme in acht Tagen und hole sie ab. Sie sprachen aber, er solle gutes Muts sein, das Männchen wollten sie schon anführen. Darnach als der Tag kam, kleideten sie eine Kuhhirtstochter mit ihren Kleidern an, setzten sie in ihre Stube und befahlen ihr: »wenn jemand kommt, und will dich abholen, so gehst du mit!« sie selber aber gingen alle aus dem Hause fort. Kaum waren sie weg, so kam ein Fuchs in das Schloss, und sagte zu dem Mädchen: »setz dich auf meinen rauhen Schwanz, Hurleburlebutz! hinaus in den Wald!« Das Mädchen setzte sich dem Fuchs auf den Schwanz, und so trug er es hinaus in den Wald; wie sie aber auf einen schönen grünen Platz kamen, wo die Sonne recht hell und warm schien, sagte der Fuchs: »steig ab und laus mich!« Das Mädchen gehorchte, der Fuchs legte seinen Kopf auf ihren Schoß und ward gelaust; bei der Arbeit sprach das Mädchen: »gestern um die Zeit war's doch schöner in dem Wald!« »Wie bist du in den Wald gekommen?« fragte der Fuchs. »Ei, da hab ich mit meinem Vater die Kühe gehütet.« »Also bist du nicht die Prinzessin! setz dich auf meinen rauhen Schwanz, Hurleburlebutz! zurück in das Schloss!« Da trug sie der Fuchs zurück und sagte zum König: »du hast mich betrogen, das ist eine Kuhhirtstochter, in acht Tagen komm ich wieder und hol mir deine.« Am achten Tage aber kleideten die Prinzessinnen eine Gänsehirtstochter prächtig an, setzten sie hin und gingen fort. Da kam der Fuchs wieder und sprach: »setz dich auf meinen rauhen Schwanz, Hurleburlebutz! hinaus in den Wald!« Wie sie in dem Wald auf den sonnigen Platz kamen, sagte der Fuchs wieder: »steig ab und laus mich.« Und als das Mädchen den Fuchs lauste, seufzte es und sprach: »wo mögen jetzt meine Gänse sein!« »Was weißt du von Gänsen?« »Ei, die hab ich alle Tage mit meinem Vater auf die Wiesen getrieben.« »Also bist du nicht des Königs Tochter! setz dich auf meinen rauhen Schwanz, Hurleburlebutz! zurück in das Schloss!« Der Fuchs trug sie zurück und sagte zum König: »du hast mich wieder betrogen, das ist eine Gänsehirtstochter, in acht Tagen komm ich noch einmal, und wenn du mir dann deine Tochter nicht giebst, so soll dir's übel gehen.« Dem König ward Angst, und wie der Fuchs wieder kam, gab er ihm die Prinzessin. »Setz dich auf meinen rauhen Schwanz, Hurleburlebutz! hinaus in den Wald!« Da musste sie auf dem Schwanz des Fuchses hinausreiten, und als sie auf den Platz im Sonnenschein kamen, sprach er auch zu ihr: »steig ab und laus mich!« als er ihr aber seinen Kopf auf den Schoß legte, fing die Prinzessin an zu weinen und sagte: »ich bin eines Königs Tochter und soll einen Fuchs lausen, säß ich jetzt daheim in meiner Kammer, so könnt ich meine Blumen im Garten sehen!« Da hörte der Fuchs, dass er die rechte Braut hatte, verwandelte sich in das kleine, weiße Männchen, und das war nun ihr Mann, bei dem musst sie in einer kleinen Hütte wohnen, ihm kochen und nähen, und es dauerte eine gute Zeit. Das Männchen aber tat ihr alles zu Liebe.

Einmal sagte das Männchen zu ihr: »ich muss fortgehen, aber es werden bald drei weiße Tauben geflogen kommen, die werden ganz niedrig über die Erde hinstreifen, davon fang die mittelste, und wenn du sie hast, schneid ihr gleich den Kopf ab, hüt dich aber, dass du keine andere ergreifst, als die mittelste, sonst entsteht ein groß Unglück daraus.« Das Männchen ging fort; es dauerte auch nicht lang, so kamen drei weiße Tauben daher geflogen. Die Prinzessin gab Acht, ergriff die mittelste, nahm ein Messer und schnitt ihr den Kopf ab. Kaum aber lag der auf dem Boden, so stand ein schöner junger Prinz vor ihr und sprach: »mich hat eine Fee verzaubert, sieben Jahr lang sollt ich meine Gestalt verlieren, und sodann als eine Taube an meiner Gemahlin vorbeifliegen, zwischen zwei andern, da müsse sie mich fangen und mir den Kopf abhauen, und fange sie mich nicht, oder eine unrechte, und ich sei einmal vorbeigeflogen, so sei alles vorbei und keine Erlösung mehr möglich: darum hab ich dich gebeten, ja Acht zu haben, denn ich bin das graue Männlein und du meine Gemahlin.« Da war die Prinzessin vergnügt, und sie gingen zusammen zu ihrem Vater, und als der starb, erbten sie das Reich.

Der Okerlo.

Eine Königin setzte ihr Kind in einer goldenen Wiege aufs Meer, und ließ es fortschwimmen; es ging aber nicht unter, sondern schwamm zu einer Insel, da wohnten lauter Menschenfresser. Wie nun so die Wiege geschwommen kam, stand gerade die Frau des Menschenfressers am Ufer, und als sie das Kind sah, welches ein wunderschönes Mädchen war, beschloss sie, es groß zu ziehen für ihren Sohn, der sollte es einmal zur Frau haben. Doch hatte sie große Not damit, dass sie es sorgfältig vor ihrem Mann, dem alten Okerlo versteckte, denn hätte er es zu Gesicht bekommen, so wäre es mit Haut und Haar aufgefressen worden.

Als nun das Mädchen groß geworden war, sollte es mit dem jungen Okerlo verheiratet werden, es mochte ihn aber gar nicht leiden, und weinte den ganzen Tag. Wie es so einmal am Ufer saß, da kam ein junger, schöner Prinz geschwommen, der gefiel ihm und es gefiel ihm auch, und sie versprachen sich miteinander; indem aber kam die alte Menschenfresserin, die wurde gewaltig bös, dass sie den Prinzen bei der Braut ihres Sohnes fand, und kriegte ihn gleich zu packen: »wart nun, du sollst zu meines Sohnes Hochzeit gebraten werden!«

Der junge Prinz, das Mädchen und die drei Kinder des Okerlo schliefen aber alle in einer Stube zusammen, wie es nun Nacht wurde, kriegte der alte Okerlo Lust nach Menschenfleisch, und sagte: »Frau, ich habe nicht Lust bis zur Hochzeit zu warten, gieb mir den Prinzen nur gleich her!« Das Mädchen aber hörte alles durch die Wand, stand geschwind auf, nahm dem einen Kind des Okerlo die goldene Krone ab, die es auf dem Haupte trug, und setzte sie dem Prinzen auf. Die alte Menschenfresserin kam gegangen, und weil es dunkel war, so fühlte sie an den Häuptern, und das, welches keine Krone trug, brachte sie dem Mann, der es au-

genblicklich aufaß. Indessen wurde dem Mädchen himmel-
angst, es dachte: »bricht der Tag an, so kommt alles heraus,
und es wird uns schlimm gehen.« Da stand es heimlich auf
und holte einen Meilenstiefel, eine Wünschelrute und einen
Kuchen mit einer Bohne, die auf alles Antwort gab.

Nun ging sie mit dem Prinzen fort, sie hatten den Meilenstiefel an, und mit jedem Schritt machten sie eine Meile.
Zuweilen frugen sie die Bohne:

»Bohne, bist du auch da?«

»ja«, sagte die Bohne, »da bin ich, eilt euch aber, denn die
alte Menschenfresserin kommt nach im andern Meilenstie-
fel, der dort geblieben ist!« Da nahm das Mädchen die
Wünschelrute und verwandelte sich in einen Schwan, den
Prinzen in einen Teich, worauf der Schwan schwimmt. Die
Menschenfresserin kam und lockte den Schwan ans Ufer,
allein es gelang ihr nicht, und verdrießlich ging sie heim.
Das Mädchen und der Prinz setzten ihren Weg fort:

»Bohne, bist du da?«

»ja«, sprach die Bohne, »hier bin ich, aber die alte Frau
kommt schon wieder, der Menschenfresser hat ihr gesagt,
warum sie sich habe anführen lassen.« Da nahm das Mädchen den Stab, und verwandelte sich und den Prinzen in
eine Staubwolke, wodurch die Frau Okerlo nicht dringen
kann, also kehrte sie unverrichteter Sache wieder um, und
die andern setzten ihren Weg fort.

»Bohne, bist du da?«

»ja, hier bin ich, aber ich sehe die Frau Okerlo noch einmal
kommen, und gewaltige Schritte macht sie.« Das Mädchen
nahm zum drittenmal den Wünschelstab und verwandelte
sich in einen Rosenstock und den Prinzen in eine Biene, da
kam die alte Menschenfresserin, erkannte sie in dieser Ver-
wandelung nicht und ging wieder heim.

Allein nun konnten die zwei ihre menschliche Gestalt nicht
wieder annehmen, weil das Mädchen das letztemal in der
Angst den Zauberstab zu weit weggeworfen; sie waren aber
schon so weit gegangen, dass der Rosenstock in einem Gar-

ten stand, der gehörte der Mutter des Mädchens. Die Biene saß auf der Rose, und wer sie abbrechen wollte, den stach sie mit ihrem Stachel. Einmal geschah es, dass die Königin selber in ihren Garten ging und die schöne Blume sah, worüber sie sich so verwunderte, dass sie sie abbrechen wollte. Aber Bienchen kam und stach sie so stark in die Hand, dass sie die Rose musste fahren lassen, doch hatte sie schon ein wenig eingerissen. Da sah sie, dass Blut aus dem Stengel quoll, ließ eine Fee kommen, damit sie die Blume entzauberte. Da erkannte die Königin ihre Tochter wieder, und war von Herzen froh und vergnügt. Es wurde aber eine große Hochzeit angestellt, eine Menge Gäste gebeten, die kamen in prächtigen Kleidern, tausend Lichter flimmerten im Saal, und es wurde gespielt und getanzt bis zum hellen Tag.

»Bist du auch auf der Hochzeit gewesen?« »ja wohl bin drauf gewesen:

mein Kopfputz war von Butter, da kam ich in die Sonne,
und er ist mir abgeschmolzen;
mein Kleid war von Spinnweb, da kam ich durch Dornen,
die rissen es mir ab;
meine Pantoffel waren von Glas, da trat ich auf einen Stein,
da sprangen sie entzwei.«

Anhang Nr. 12

Prinzessin Mäusehaut.

Ein König hatte drei Töchter; da wollte er wissen, welche ihn am liebsten hätte, ließ sie vor sich kommen und fragte sie. Die älteste sprach, sie habe ihn lieber, als das ganze Königreich; die zweite, als alle Edelsteine und Perlen auf der

Welt; die dritte aber sagte, sie habe ihn lieber als das Salz. Der König ward aufgebracht, dass sie ihre Liebe zu ihm mit einer so geringen Sache vergleiche, übergab sie einem Diener und befahl, er solle sie in den Wald führen und töten. Wie sie in den Wald gekommen waren, bat die Prinzessin den Diener um ihr Leben; dieser war ihr treu, und würde sie doch nicht getötet haben, er sagte auch, er wolle mit ihr gehen, und ganz nach ihren Befehlen tun. Die Prinzessin verlangte aber nichts, als ein Kleid von Mausehaut, und als er ihr das geholt, wickelte sie sich hinein und ging fort. Sie ging geradezu an den Hof eines benachbarten Königs, gab sich für einen Mann aus, und bat den König, dass er sie in seine Dienste nehme. Der König sagte es zu, und sie solle bei ihm die Aufwartung haben: Abends musste sie ihm die Stiefel ausziehen, die warf er ihr allemal an den Kopf. Einmal fragte er, woher sie sei? »Aus dem Lande, wo man den Leuten die Stiefel nicht um den Kopf wirft.« Der König ward da aufmerksam, endlich brachten ihm die andern Diener einen Ring; Mausehaut habe ihn verloren, der sei zu kostbar, den müsse er gestohlen haben. Der König ließ Mausehaut vor sich kommen und fragte, woher der Ring sei? da konnte sich Mausehaut nicht länger verbergen, sie wickelte sich von der Mausehaut los, ihre goldgelben Haare quollen hervor, und sie trat heraus so schön, aber auch so schön, dass der König gleich die Krone von seinem Kopf abnahm und ihr aufsetzte, und sie für seine Gemahlin erklärte.

Zu der Hochzeit wurde auch der Vater der Mausehaut eingeladen, der glaubte seine Tochter sei schon längst tot, und erkannte sie nicht wieder. Auf der Tafel aber waren alle Speisen, die ihm vorgesetzt wurden, ungesalzen, da ward er ärgerlich und sagte: »ich will lieber nicht leben als solche Speise essen!« Wie er das Wort ausgesagt, sprach die Königin zu ihm: »jetzt wollt ihr nicht leben ohne Salz, und doch habt ihr mich einmal wollen töten lassen, weil ich sagte, ich hätte euch lieber als Salz!« da erkannt er seine Tochter, und küsste

sie, und bat sie um Verzeihung, und es war ihm lieber als
sein Königreich, und alle Edelsteine der Welt, dass er sie
wiedergefunden.

Anhang Nr. 13

Das Birnli will nit fallen.

Der Herr will das Birnli schüttle,
das Birnli will nit fallen:
der Herr, der schickt das Jockli hinaus,
es soll das Birnli schüttle:
das Jockli schüttelt's Birnli nit,
das Birnli will nit fallen.

Da schickt der Herr das Hündli naus,
es soll das Jockli beißen:
das Hündli beißt das Jockli nit,
das Jockli schüttelt's Birnli nit,
das Birnli will nit fallen.

Da schickt der Herr das Prügeli naus,
es soll das Hündli treffen:
das Prügeli trifft das Hündli nit,
das Hündli beißt das Jockli nit,
das Jockli schüttelt's Birnli nit,
das Birnli will nit fallen.

Da schickt der Herr das Fürli (Feuer) naus,
es soll das Prügeli brennen:
das Fürli brennt, das Prügeli nit,
das Prügeli trifft das Hündli nit,
das Hündli beißt das Jockli nit,
das Jockli schüttelt's Birnli nit,
das Birnli will nit fallen.

Da schickt der Herr das Wässerli naus,
es soll das Fürli löschen:
das Wässerli löscht das Fürli nit,
das Fürli brennt das Prügeli nit,
das Prügeli trifft das Hündli nit,
das Hündli beißt das Jockli nit,
das Jockli schüttelt's Birnli nit,
das Birnli will nit fallen.

Da schickt der Herr das Kälbli naus,
es soll das Wässerli läpple (trinken):
das Kälbli läppelt das Wässerli nit,
das Wässerli löscht das Fürli nit,
das Fürli brennt das Prügeli nit,
das Prügeli trifft das Hündli nit,
das Hündli beißt das Jockli nit,
das Jockli schüttelt's Birnli nit,
das Birnli will nit fallen.

Da schickt der Herr den Metzger naus,
er soll das Kälbli metzle:
der Metzger metzelt's Kälbli nit,
das Kälbli läppelt das Wässerli nit,
das Wässerli löscht das Fürli nit,
das Fürli brennt das Prügeli nit,
das Prügeli trifft das Hündli nit,
das Hündli beißt das Jockli nit,
das Jockli schüttelt's Birnli nit,
das Birnli will nit fallen.

Da schickt der Herr den Schinder naus,
er soll den Metzger hängen:
der Schinder will den Metzger hänge,
der Metzger will das Kälbli metzle,
das Kälbli will das Wässerli läpple,
das Wässerli will das Fürli lösche,

das Fürli will das Prügeli brenne,
das Prügeli will das Hündli treffe,
das Hündli will das Jockli beiße,
das Jockli will das Birnli schüttle,
das Birnli, das will fallen.

Anhang Nr. 14

Das Mordschloss.

Es war einmal ein Schuhmacher, welcher drei Töchter hatte; auf eine Zeit als der Schuhmacher aus war, kam da ein Herr, welcher sehr gut gekleidet war, und welcher eine prächtige Equipage hatte, so dass man ihn für sehr reich hielt, und verliebte sich in eine der schönen Töchter, welche dachte, ihr Glück gemacht zu haben mit so einem reichen Herrn, und machte also keine Schwierigkeit mit ihm zu reiten. Da es Abend ward, als sie unterwegs waren fragte er sie:

»Der Mond scheint so hell
meine Pferdchen laufen so schnell
süß Lieb, reut dich's auch nicht?«

»Nein, warum sollt mich's reuen? ich bin immer bei Euch wohl bewahrt«, da sie doch innerlich eine Angst hatte. Als sie in einem großen Wald waren, fragte sie, ob sie bald da wären? »Ja«, sagte er, »siehst du das Licht da in der Ferne, da ist mein Schloss«; endlich kamen sie da an, und alles war gar schön.

Am andern Tage sagte er zu ihr, er müsst auf einige Tage sie verlassen, weil er wichtige Affären hätte, die notwendig wären, aber er wolle ihr alle Schlüssel lassen, damit sie das ganze Kastell sehen könnte, von was für Reichtum sie all Meister wär. Als er fort war, ging sie durch das ganze Haus, und fand alles so schön, dass sie völlig damit zufrieden war, bis sie endlich an einen Keller kam, wo eine alte Frau saß und Därme schrappte. »Ei Mütterchen, was macht sie da?« »Ich schrapp Därme, mein Kind, morgen schrapp ich eure auch!« Wovon sie so erschrak, dass sie den Schlüssel, welcher in ihrer Hand war, in ein Becken mit Blut fallen ließ, welches nicht gut wieder abzuwaschen war: »Nun ist euer Tod sicher«, sagte das alte Weib, »weil mein Herr sehen kann, dass ihr in der Kammer gewesen seid, wohin außer ihm und mir kein Mensch kommen darf.«

(Man muss aber wissen, dass die zwei vorigen Schwestern auf dieselbe Weise waren umgekommen.)

Da in dem Augenblick ein Wagen mit Heu von dem Schloss wegfuhr, so sagte die alte Frau, es wäre das einzige Mittel, um das Leben zu behalten, sich unter das Heu zu verstecken, und dann da mit weg zu fahren; welches sie auch tät. Da inzwischen der Herr nach Haus kam, fragte er, wo die Mamsell wäre! »Oh«, sagte die alte Frau, »da ich keine Arbeit mehr hatte, und sie morgen doch dran musste, hab ich sie schon geschlachtet, und hier ist eine Locke von ihrem Haar, und das Herz, wie auch was warm Blut, das übrige haben die Hunde alle gefressen, und ich schrapp die Därme.« Der Herr war also ruhig, dass sie tot war.

Sie kommt inzwischen mit dem Heuwagen zu einem nah bei gelegenen Schloss, wo das Heu hin verkauft war, und sie kommt mit aus dem Heu und erzählt die ganze Sache, und wird ersucht, da einige Zeit zu bleiben. Nach Verlauf von einiger Zeit nötigt der Herr von diesem Schloss alle in der Nähe wohnenden Edelleute zu einem großen Fest, und das Gesicht und Kleidung von der fremden Mamsell wird so verändert, dass sie nicht erkannt werden konnte, weil auch der Herr von dem Mord-Kastell dazu eingeladen war.

Da sie alle da waren, musste ein jeder etwas erzählen, da die Reihe an die Mamsell kam, erzählte sie die bewusste Historie, wobei dem sogenannten Herrn Graf so ängstlich ums Herz ward, dass er mit Gewalt weg wollte, aber der gute

Herr von dem adelichen Haus hatte inzwischen gesorgt, dass das Gericht unsern schönen Herrn Grafen in Gefängnis nahm, sein Kastell ausrottete, und seine Güter alle der Mamsell zu eigen gab, die nach der Hand mit dem Sohn des Hauses, wo sie so gut empfangen war, sich verheiratete und lange Jahre lebte.

Anhang Nr. 15

Vom Schreiner und Drechsler.

Ein Schreiner und ein Drechsler sollten ihr Meisterstück machen. Da machte der Schreiner einen Tisch, der konnte von sich selbst schwimmen, der Drechsler Flügel, mit denen man fliegen konnte. Und alle sagten, dass dem Schreiner sein Kunststück besser gelungen wäre, der Drechsler nahm also seine Flügel, tat sie an und flog fort aus dem Land, von Morgen bis zu Abend in einem fort.

In dem Land war ein junger Prinz, der sah ihn fliegen, und bat ihn, er möchte ihm doch seine paar Flügel leihen, er wollt's ihm gut lohnen. Der Prinz bekam also die Flügel und flog, bis er in ein anderes Reich kam, da war ein Turm mit vielen Lichtern erleuchtet, dabei senkte er sich nieder zur Erde, fragte nach der Ursache und hörte, dass hier die allerschönste Prinzessin der Welt wohnte. Nun wurde er höchst neugierig, und als es Abend wurde, flog er in ein offenes Fenster hinein: wie sie aber nicht lange Zeit beisammen waren, wurde die Sache verraten, und der Prinz samt der Prinzessin sollten auf dem Scheiterhaufen sterben.

Der Prinz nahm indessen seine Flügel mit hinauf, und als die Flamme schon zu ihnen heraufschlug, band er sich die Flügel um und entfloh mit der Prinzessin bis in sein Vaterland, da ließ er sich nieder, und weil jedermann über seine Abwesenheit betrübt war, so gab er sich zu erkennen, und wurde zum König erwählt.

Nach einiger Zeit aber ließ der Vater der entführten Prinzessin bekannt machen, dass derjenige das halbe Königreich bekommen sollte, der ihm seine Tochter wiederbringe. Dies erfährt der Prinz, rüstet ein Heer aus und bringt die Prinzessin selbst ihrem Vater zu, den er zwingt, ihm sein Versprechen zu erfüllen.

Anhang Nr. 16

Die drei Schwestern.

Es war einmal ein reicher König, der war so reich, dass er glaubte sein Reichtum könne gar nicht all werden, da lebte er in Saus und Braus, spielte auf goldenem Brett und mit silbernen Kegeln, und als das eine Zeit lang gewährt hatte, da nahm sein Reichtum ab und darnach verpfändete er eine Stadt und ein Schloss nach dem andern, und endlich blieb nichts mehr übrig, als ein altes Waldschloss. Dahin zog er nun mit der Königin und den drei Prinzessinnen und sie mussten sich kümmerlich erhalten und hatten nichts mehr als Kartoffeln, die kamen alle Tage auf den Tisch. Einmal wollte der König auf die Jagd, ob er etwa einen Hasen schießen könnte, steckte sich also die Tasche voll Kartoffeln und ging aus. Es war aber in der Nähe ein großer Wald, in den wagte sich kein Mensch, weil fürchterliche Dinge erzählt wurden, was einem all darin begegne: Bären, die die Menschen auffräßen, Adler, die die Augen aushackten, Wölfe, Löwen und alle grausamen Tiere. Der König aber fürchtete sich kein bisschen und ging geradezu hinein. Anfangs sah er gar nichts, große mächtige Bäume standen da, aber es war alles still darunter; als er so eine Weile herumgegangen und hungrig geworden war, setzte er sich unter einen Baum und wollte seine Kartoffeln essen, da kam auf einmal aus dem Dickicht ein Bär hervor, trabte gerade auf ihn los und brummte: »was unterstehst du dich bei meinem Honigbaum zu sitzen? das sollst du mir teuer bezahlen!« der König erschrak, reichte dem Bären seine Kartoffeln, und wollte ihn damit besänftigen. Der Bär aber fing an zu sprechen und sagte »deine Kartoffeln, mag ich nicht, ich will dich selber fressen und davon kannst du dich nicht anders erretten, als dass du mir deine älteste Tochter giebst, wenn du das aber tust, geb ich dir noch obendrein einen Zentner Gold.« Der König in der Angst, gefressen zu werden, sagte, »die sollst du haben, lass mich nur in Frieden.« Da wies ihm der Bär den Weg, und brummte noch hintendrein: »in sieben Tagen komm ich und hol meine Braut.« Der König aber ging getrost nach Haus und dachte, der Bär wird doch nicht durch ein Schlüsselloch kriechen können, und weiter soll gewiss nichts offen bleiben. Da ließ er alle Tore verschließen, die Zugbrücken aufziehen, und hieß seine Tochter gutes Muts sein, damit sie aber recht sicher vor dem Bärenbräutigam war, gab er ihr ein Kämmerlein hoch unter der Zinne, darin sollte sie versteckt bleiben, bis die sieben Tage herum wären. Am siebenten Morgen aber ganz früh, wie noch alles schlief, kam ein prächtiger Wagen mit sechs Pferden bespannt und von vielen goldgekleideten Reutern umringt nach dem Schloss gefahren, und wie er davor war, ließen sich die Zugbrücken von selber herab und die Schlösser sprangen ohne Schlüssel auf. Da fuhr der Wagen in den Hof und ein junger schöner Prinz stieg heraus, und wie der König von dem Lärm aufwachte und zum Fenster hinaus sah, sah er, wie der Prinz schon seine älteste Tochter oben aus dem verschlossenen Kämmerlein geholt und eben in den Wagen hob, und er konnte ihr nur noch nachrufen:

> »Ade! du Fräulein traut,
> Fahr hin, du Bärenbraut!«

Sie winkte ihm mit ihrem weißen Tüchlein noch aus dem Wagen, und dann ging's fort, als wär der Wind vorgespannt, immer in den Zauberwald hinein. Dem König aber war's recht schwer ums Herz, dass er seine Tochter an einen Bären hingegeben hatte, und weinte drei Tage mit der Königin, so traurig war er. Am vierten Tag aber als er sich ausgeweint hatte, dachte er, was geschehen, ist einmal nicht zu ändern, stieg hinab in den Hof, da stand eine Kiste von Ebenholz und war gewaltig schwer zu heben, alsbald fiel ihm ein, was ihm der Bär versprochen hatte, und machte sie auf, da lag ein Zentner Goldes darin und glimmerte und flimmerte.

Wie der König das Gold erblickte, ward er getröstet und löste seine Städte und sein Reich ein, und fing das vorige Wohlleben von vorne an. Das dauerte so lang als der Zentner Gold dauerte, darnach musste er wieder alles verpfänden und auf das Waldschloss zurückziehen und Kartoffeln essen. Der König hatte noch einen Falken, den nahm er eines Tags mit hinaus auf das Feld und wollte mit ihm jagen, damit er etwas Besseres zu essen hätte. Der Falk stieg auf, und flog nach dem dunkeln Zauberwald zu, in den sich der König nicht mehr getraute, kaum aber war er dort, so schoss ein Adler hervor und verfolgte den Falken, der zum König floh. Der König wollte mit seinem Spieß den Adler abhalten, der Adler aber packte den Spieß und zerbrach ihn wie ein Schilfrohr, dann zerdrückte er den Falken mit einer Kralle, die andern aber hackte er dem König in die Schulter und rief: »warum störst du mein Luftreich, dafür sollst du sterben oder du giebst mir deine zweite Tochter zur Frau!« der König sagte: »ja die sollst du haben, aber was giebst du mir dafür?« »Zwei Zentner Gold« sprach der Adler, »und in sieben Wochen komm ich, und hol sie ab«; dann ließ er ihn los und flog fort in den Wald.

Der König war betrübt, dass er seine zweite Tochter auch einem wilden Tiere verkauft hatte und getraute sich nicht ihr etwas davon zu sagen. Sechs Wochen waren herum, in der siebenten ging die Prinzessin hinaus auf einen Rasenplatz vor der Burg und wollte ihre Leinwand begießen, da kam auf einmal ein prächtiger Zug von schönen Rittern und zuvorderst ritt der allerschönste, der sprang ab und rief:

»schwing, schwing dich auf, du Fräulein traut,
komm mit, du schöne Adlerbraut!«

und eh sie ihm antworten konnte, hatte er sie schon aufs
Ross gehoben und jagte mit ihr in den Wald hinein als flög
ein Vogel: Ade! Ade!!

In der Burg warteten sie lang auf die Prinzessin aber die
kam nicht und kam nicht, da entdeckte der König endlich
dass er einmal in der Not sie einem Adler versprochen, und
der werde sie geholt haben. Als aber bei dem König die
Traurigkeit ein wenig herum war, fiel ihm das Versprechen
des Adlers ein und er ging hinab, und fand auf dem Rasen
zwei goldne Eier, jedes einen Zentner schwer. Wer Gold
hat, ist fromm genug, dachte er, und schlug sich alle schweren Gedanken aus dem Sinn! Da fing das lustige Leben von
neuem an, und währte so lang, bis die zwei Zentner Gold
auch durchgebracht waren, dann kehrte der König wieder
ins Waldschloss zurück, und die Prinzessin, die noch übrig
war, musste die Kartoffeln sieden.

Der König wollte keine Hasen im Wald und keine Vögel in
der Luft mehr jagen, aber einen Fisch hätt er gern gegessen.
Da musste die Prinzessin ein Netz stricken, damit ging er
zu einem Teich, der nicht weit von dem Wald lag. Weil ein
Nachen darauf war, setzte er sich ein, und warf das Netz,
da fing er auf einen Zug eine Menge schöner rotgefleckter
Forellen. Wie er aber damit ans Land wollte, stand der Nachen fest und er konnte ihn nicht los kriegen, er mochte
sich stellen wie er wollte. Da kam auf einmal ein gewaltiger
Walfisch daher geschnaubt: »was fängst du mir meine Un-
tertanen weg, das soll dir dein Leben kosten.« dabei sperrte
er seinen Rachen auf, als wollte er den König samt dem
Nachen verschlingen. Wie der König den entsetzlichen Rachen sah, verlor er allen Mut, da fiel ihm seine dritte Tochter ein und er rief: »schenk mir das Leben und du sollst
meine jüngste Tochter haben.« »Meintwegen« brummte der
Walfisch, »ich will dir auch etwas dafür geben; Gold hab
ich nicht, das ist mir zu schlecht, aber der Grund meines

Sees ist mit Zahlperlen gepflastert, davon will ich dir drei Säcke voll geben: im siebenten Mond komm ich und hol meine Braut.« Dann tauchte er unter.

Der König trieb nun ans Land und brachte seine Forellen heim, aber als sie gebacken waren, wollt er keine davon essen, und wenn er seine Tochter ansah, die einzige die ihm noch übrig war und die schönste und liebste von allen, war's ihm, als zerschnitten tausend Messer sein Herz. So gingen sechs Monat herum, die Königin und die Prinzessin wussten nicht, was dem König fehle, der in all der Zeit keine vergnügte Miene machte. Im siebenten Mond stand die Prinzessin gerade im Hof vor einem Röhrbrunnen und ließ ein Glas voll laufen, da kam ein Wagen mit sechs weißen Pferden und ganz silbernen Leuten angefahren, und aus dem Wagen stieg ein Prinz, so schön, dass sie ihr Lebtag keinen schönern gesehen hatte, und bat sie um ein Glas Wasser. Und wie sie ihm das reichte, das sie in der Hand hielt, umfasste er sie und hob sie in den Wagen, und dann ging's wieder zum Tor hinaus, über das Feld nach dem Teich zu.

»Ade, du Fräulein traut,

fahr hin, du schöne Walfischbraut!«

Die Königin stand am Fenster und sah den Wagen noch in der Ferne, und als sie ihre Tochter nicht sah, fiel's ihr schwer aufs Herz, und sie rief und suchte nach ihr allenthalben; sie war aber nirgends zu hören und zu sehen. Da war es gewiss und sie fing an zu weinen und der König entdeckte ihr nun: ein Walfisch werde sie geholt haben, dem hab er sie versprechen müssen, und darum wäre er immer so traurig gewesen; er wollte sie auch trösten, und sagte ihr von dem großen Reichtum, den sie dafür bekommen würden, die Königin wollt aber nichts davon wissen und sprach, ihr einziges Kind sei ihr lieber gewesen, als alle Schätze der Welt. Während der Walfischprinz die Prinzessin geraubt, hatten seine Diener drei mächtige Säcke in das Schloss getragen, die fand der König an der Tür stehen, und als er sie aufmachte, waren sie voll schöner großer Zahlperlen, so groß, wie die dicksten

Erbsen. Da war er auf einmal wieder reich und reicher, als er
je gewesen; er löste seine Städte und Schlösser ein, aber das
Wohlleben fing er nicht wieder an, sondern war still und
sparsam und wenn er daran dachte, wie es seinen drei lieben
Töchtern bei den wilden Tieren ergehen mögte, die sie vielleicht schon aufgefressen hätten, verging ihm alle Lust.
Die Königin aber wollt sich gar nicht trösten lassen und
weinte mehr Tränen um ihre Tochter, als der Walfisch Perlen dafür gegeben hatte. Endlich ward's ein wenig stiller,
und nach einiger Zeit ward sie wieder ganz vergnügt, denn
sie brachte einen schönen Knaben zur Welt und weil Gott
das Kind so unerwartet geschenkt hatte, ward es Reinald,
das Wunderkind, genannt. Der Knabe ward groß und stark,
und die Königin erzählte ihm oft von seinen drei Schwestern, die in dem Zauberwald von drei Tieren gefangen gehalten würden. Als er sechszehn Jahr alt war verlangte er
von dem König Rüstung und Schwert, und als er es nun erhalten, wollte er auf Abenteuer ausgehen, gesegnete seine
Eltern, und zog fort.
Er zog aber geradezu nach dem Zauberwald und hatte
nichts anders im Sinn als seine Schwestern zu suchen. Anfangs irrte er lange in dem großen Walde herum, ohne einem Menschen oder einem Tiere zu begegnen. Nach drei
Tagen aber sah er vor einer Höhle eine junge Frau sitzen
und mit einem jungen Bären spielen: einen andern, ganz
jungen, hatte sie auf ihrem Schoß liegen: Reinald dachte,
das ist gewiss meine älteste Schwester, ließ sein Pferd zurück, und ging auf sie zu: »liebste Schwester, ich bin dein
Bruder Reinald und bin gekommen dich zu besuchen.« Die
Prinzessin sah ihn an, und da er ganz ihrem Vater glich,
zweifelte sie nicht an seinen Worten, erschrak und sprach:
»ach liebster Bruder, eil und lauf fort, was du kannst, wenn
dir dein Leben lieb ist, kommt mein Mann, der Bär, nach
Haus und findet dich, so frisst er dich ohne Barmherzigkeit.« Reinald aber sprach: »ich fürchte mich nicht und
weiche auch nicht von dir, bis ich weiß, wie es um dich

steht.« Wie die Prinzessin sah, dass er nicht zu bewegen war, führte sie ihn in ihre Höhle, die war finster und wie eine Bärenwohnung; auf der einen Seite lag ein Haufen Laub und Heu, worauf der Alte und seine Jungen schliefen, aber auf der andern Seite stand ein prächtiges Bett, von rotem Zeug mit Gold, das gehörte der Prinzessin. Unter das Bett hieß sie ihn kriechen, und reichte ihm etwas hinunter zu essen. Es dauerte nicht lang so kam der Bär nach Haus: »ich wittre, wittre Menschenfleisch« und wollte seinen dicken Kopf unter das Bett stecken. Die Prinzessin aber rief: »sei ruhig, wer soll hier hineinkommen!« »Ich hab ein Pferd im Wald gefunden und gefressen« brummte er, und hatte noch eine blutige Schnauze davon, »dazu gehört ein Mensch und den riech ich« und wollte wieder unter das Bett. Da gab sie ihm einen Fußtritt in den Leib, dass er einen Burzelbaum machte, auf sein Lager ging, die Tatze ins Maul nahm und einschlief.

Alle sieben Tage war der Bär in seiner natürlichen Gestalt und ein schöner Prinz, und seine Höhle ein prächtiges Schloss und die Tiere im Wald, waren seine Diener. An einem solchen Tage hatte er die Prinzessin abgeholt; schöne junge Frauen kamen ihr vor dem Schloss entgegen, es war ein herrliches Fest und sie schlief in Freuden ein, aber als sie erwachte, lag sie in einer dunkeln Bärenhöhle und ihr Gemahl war ein Bär geworden und brummte zu ihren Füßen, nur das Bett und alles was sie angerührt hatte, blieb in seinem natürlichen Zustand unverwandelt. So lebte sie sechs Tage in Leid aber am siebenten ward sie getröstet, und da sie nicht alt ward und nur der eine Tag ihr zugerechnet wurde, so war sie zufrieden mit ihrem Leben. Sie hatte ihrem Gemahl zwei Prinzen geboren, die waren auch sechs Tage lang Bären und am siebenten in menschlicher Gestalt. Sie steckte sich jedesmal ihr Bettstroh voll von den köstlichsten Speisen Kuchen und Früchten, davon lebte sie die ganze Woche, und der Bär war ihr auch gehorsam und tat, was sie wollte.

Als Reinald erwachte, lag er in einem seidenen Bett, Diener kamen ihm aufzuwarten und ihm die reichsten Kleider anzutun, denn es war gerade der siebente Tag eingefallen. Seine Schwester mit zwei schönen Prinzen und sein Schwager Bär traten ein, und freuten sich seiner Ankunft. Da war alles in Pracht und Herrlichkeit und der ganze Tag voll Lust und Freude; am Abend aber sagte die Prinzessin: »lieber Bruder, nun mach dass du fort kommst, mit Tages Anbruch nimmt mein Gemahl wieder Bärengestalt an, und findet er dich morgen noch hier, kann er seiner Natur nicht widerstehen und frisst dich auf.« Da kam der Prinz Bär und gab ihm drei Bärenhaare, und sagte; »wenn du in Not bist so reib daran, und ich will dir zu Hülfe kommen.« Darauf küssten sie sich und nahmen Abschied, und Reinald stieg in einen Wagen mit sechs Rappen bespannt und fuhr fort. So ging's über Stock und Stein, Berg auf, Berg ab, durch Wüsten und Wälder, Horst und Hecke, ohne Ruh und Rast, bis gegen Morgen, als der Himmel anfing grau zu werden, da lag Reinald auf einmal auf der Erde und Ross und Wagen war verschwunden, und beim Morgenrot erblickte er sechs Ameisen, die galoppierten dahin und zogen eine Nussschale.

Reinald sah dass er noch in dem Zauberwald war, und wollte seine zweite Schwester suchen. Wieder drei Tage irrte er umsonst in der Einsamkeit, am vierten aber hörte er einen großen Adler daher rauschen, der sich auf ein Nest niederließ. Reinald stellte sich ins Gebüsch und wartete bis er wieder wegflog, nach sieben Stunden hob er sich auch wieder in die Höhe. Da kam Reinald hervor, trat vor den Baum und rief: »liebste Schwester bist du droben, so lass mich deine Stimme hören, ich bin Reinald dein Bruder, und bin gekommen dich zu besuchen!« Da hörte er es herunter rufen, »bist du Reinald mein liebster Bruder, den ich noch nicht gesehen habe, so komm herauf zu mir.« Reinald wollte hinauf klettern aber der Stamm war zu dick und glatt, dreimal versuchte er's, aber umsonst, da fiel eine seidene Strickleiter hinab, auf der stieg er bald zu dem Adlernest, das war stark und fest, wie eine Altane auf einer Linde. Seine Schwester saß unter einem Thronhimmel von rosenfarbener Seide und auf ihrem Schoß lag ein Adlerei, das hielt sie warm und wollt es ausbrüten. Sie küssten sich und freuten sich, aber nach einer Weile sprach die Prinzessin: »nun eil, liebster Bruder, dass du fort kommst, sieht dich der Adler, mein Gemahl, so hackt er dir die Augen aus und frisst dir das Herz ab, wie er dreien deiner Diener getan, die dich im Walde suchten.« Reinald sagte, »nein, ich bleibe hier, bis dein Gemahl verwandelt wird.« »Das geschieht erst in sechs Wochen, doch wenn du es aushalten kannst, steck dich in den Baum, der inwendig hohl ist, ich will dir alle Tage Essen hinunter reichen.« Reinald kroch in den Baum, die Prinzessin ließ ihm alle Tage Essen hinunter, und wenn der Adler wegflog, kam er herauf zu ihr. Nach sechs Wochen geschah die Umwandlung, da erwachte Reinald wieder in einem Bett, wie bei seinem Schwager Bär, nur dass alles noch prächtiger war, und er lebte sieben Tage bei dem Adlerprinz in aller Freude. Am siebenten Abend nahmen sie Abschied, der Adler gab ihm drei Adlerfedern und sprach: »wenn du in Not bist, so reib daran, und ich will dir zu Hülfe kommen.« Dann gab er ihm Diener mit, ihm den Weg zu zeigen, als aber der Morgen kam, waren sie auf einmal fort, und Reinald in einer furchtbaren Wildnis auf einer hohen Felsenwand allein.

Reinald blickte um sich her, da sah er in der Ferne den Spiegel einer großen See, auf dem eben die ersten Sonnenstrahlen glänzten. Er dachte an seine dritte Schwester, und dass sie dort sein werde. Da fing er an hinabzusteigen, und arbeitete sich durch die Büsche und zwischen den Felsen durch; drei Tage verbrachte er damit, und verlor oft den See aus den Augen, aber am vierten Morgen gelangte er hin. Er stellte sich an das Ufer und rief: »liebste Schwester bist du darin, so lass mich deine Stimme hören, ich bin Reinald

dein Bruder und bin gekommen dich zu besuchen«; aber es
antwortete niemand, und war alles ganz still. Er bröselte
Brotkrumen ins Wasser und sprach zu den Fischen: »ihr
lieben Fische, geht hin zu meiner Schwester und sagt ihr,
dass Reinald das Wunderkind da ist und zu ihr will.« Aber
die rotgefleckten Forellen schnappten das Brot auf, und
hörten nicht auf seine Worte. Da sah er einen Nachen, alsbald warf er seine Rüstung ab, und behielt nur sein blankes
Schwert in der Hand, sprang in das Schiff und ruderte fort.
So war er lang geschwommen, als er einen Schornstein von
Bergkristall über dem Wasser ragen sah, aus dem ein ange-
nehmer Geruch hervor stieg. Reinald ruderte darauf hin
und dachte, da unten wohnt gewiss meine Schwester, dann
setzte er sich in den Schornstein und rutschte hinab. Die
Prinzessin erschrak recht als sie auf einmal ein paar Men-
schenbeine im Schornstein zappeln sah, bald kam ein ganzer Mann herunter, und gab sich als ihren Bruder zu erkennen. Da freute sie sich von Herzen, dann aber ward sie betrübt und sagte: »der Walfisch, hat gehört, dass du mich
aufsuchen willst, und hat geklagt, wenn du kämst und er sei
Walfisch, könne er seiner Begierde dich zu fressen nicht widerstehen, und würde mein kristallenes Haus zerbrechen,
und dann würde ich auch in den Wasserfluten umkom-
men.« »Kannst du mich nicht so lang verbergen, bis die
Zeit kommt wo der Zauber vorbei ist?« »Ach nein wie sollte das gehen, siehst du nicht die Wände sind alle von Kristall und ganz durchsichtig«, doch sann sie und sann, endlich fiel ihr die Holzkammer ein, da legte sie das Holz
so künstlich dass von außen nichts zu sehen war und da-
hinein versteckte sie das Wunderkind. Bald darauf kam
der Walfisch und die Prinzessin zitterte wie Espenlaub, er
schwamm ein paarmal um das Kristallhaus und als er ein
Stückchen von Reinalds Kleid aus dem Holz hervorgucken
sah, schlug er mit dem Schwanz, schnaubte gewaltig und
wenn er mehr gesehen, hätte er gewiss das Haus eingeschlagen. Jeden Tag kam er einmal und schwamm darum, bis

endlich im siebenten Monat der Zauber aufhörte. Da befand sich Reinald in einem Schloss, das an Pracht gar des Adlers seines übertraf, und mitten auf einer schönen Insel stand; nun lebte er einen ganzen Monat mit seiner Schwester und Schwager in aller Lust, als der aber zu Ende war, gab ihm der Walfisch drei Schuppen und sprach: »wenn du in Not bist, so reib daran und ich will dir zu Hülfe kommen« und ließ ihn wieder ans Ufer fahren, wo er noch seine Rüstung fand.

Das Wunderkind zog darauf sieben Tage in der Wildnis weiter und sieben Nächte schlief es unter freiem Himmel, da erblickte es ein Schloss mit einem Stahltor und einem mächtigen Schloss daran. Vorn aber ging ein schwarzer Stier mit funkelnden Augen und bewachte den Eingang. Reinald ging auf ihn los und gab ihm auf den Hals einen gewaltigen Streich aber der Hals war von Stahl und das Schwert zerbrach darauf, als wäre es Glas. Er wollte seine Lanze brauchen, aber die zerknickte wie ein Strohhalm und der Stier fasste ihn mit den Hörnern und warf ihn in die Luft, dass er auf den Ästen eines Baums hängen blieb. Da besann sich Reinald in der Not auf die drei Bärenhaare, rieb sie in der Hand und in dem Augenblick kam ein Bär daher getrabt, kämpfte mit dem Stier und zerriss ihn. Aber aus dem Bauch des Stiers flog ein Entvogel in die Höhe und eilig weiter; da rieb Reinald die drei Adlerfedern, alsbald kam ein mächtiger Adler durch die Luft und verfolgte den Vogel, der gerade nach einem Weiher floh, schoss auf ihn herab, und zerfleischte ihn; aber Reinald hatte gesehen, wie er noch ein goldnes Ei hatte ins Wasser fallen lassen. Da rieb er die drei Fischschuppen in der Hand, gleich kam ein Walfisch geschwommen, verschluckte das Ei und spie es ans Land. Reinald nahm es und schlug es mit einem Stein auf, da lag ein kleiner Schlüssel darin, und das war der Schlüssel, der die Stahltür öffnete. Und wie er sie nur damit berührte, sprang sie von selber auf, und er trat ein, und vor den andern Türen schoben sich die Riegel von sel-

ber zurück, und durch ihrer sieben trat er in sieben prächtige hellerleuchtete Kammern, und in der letzten Kammer
lag eine Jungfrau auf einem Bett und schlief. Die Jungfrau
war aber so schön, dass er ganz geblendet davon ward, er
wollte sie aufwecken, das war aber vergebens, sie schlief
so fest als wäre sie tot. Da schlug er vor Zorn auf eine
schwarze Tafel, die neben dem Bett stand; in dem Augenblick erwachte die Jungfrau, fiel aber gleich wieder in den
Schlaf zurück, da nahm er die Tafel und warf sie auf den
steinernen Boden, dass sie in tausend Stücken zersprang.
Kaum war das geschehen, so schlug die Jungfrau die Augen hell auf, und der Zauber war gelöst. Sie war aber die
Schwester von den drei Schwägern Reinalds, und weil sie
einem gottlosen Zauberer ihre Liebe versagt, hatte er sie in
den Todesschlaf gesenkt, und ihre Brüder in Tiere verwandelt, und das sollte so lang währen, als die schwarze Tafel
unversehrt blieb.

Reinald führte die Jungfrau heraus und wie er vor das Tor
kam, da ritten von drei Seiten seine Schwäger heran und
waren nun erlöst, und mit ihnen ihre Frauen und Kinder,
und die Adlerbraut hatte das Ei ausgebrütet und ein schönes Fräulein auf dem Arm; da zogen sie alle zu dem alten
König und der alten Königin, und das Wunderkind brachte
seine drei Schwestern mit nach Haus, und bald vermählte
es sich mit der schönen Jungfrau; da war Freude und Lust
in allen Ecken; und die Katz läuft nach Haus, mein Märchen ist aus.

Fragmente.

a) Schneeblume.

Eine junge Königstochter hieß Schneeblume, weil sie weiß, wie der Schnee war, und im Winter geboren. Eines Tags war ihre Mutter krank geworden, und sie ging in den Wald und wollte heilsame Kräuter brechen, wie sie nun an einem großen Baum vorüber ging, flog ein Schwarm Bienen heraus und bedeckten ihren ganzen Leib von Kopf bis zu Füßen. Aber sie stachen sie nicht und taten ihr nicht weh, sondern trugen Honig auf ihre Lippen, und ihr ganzer Leib strahlte ordentlich von Schönheit.

b) Vom Prinz Johannes.

Von seinem Wandeln in Sehnen und Wehmut, von seinem Flug mit der Erscheinung, von der roten Burg, von den vielen herzbewegenden Prüfungen, bis ihm der einzigste Anblick der schönen Sonnenprinzessin gewährt wurde.

c) Der gute Lappen.

Zwei Nähtersmädchen hatten nichts geerbt, als einen guten alten Lappen, der machte alles zu Gold, was man hineinwickelte, damit hatten sie genug und nähten dabei noch zu kleinem Verdienst. Die eine Schwester war sehr klug, die andere sehr dumm. Eines Tags, war die älteste in die Kirche gegangen, da kam ein Jude die Straße her und rief: »schöne, neue Lappen zu verkaufen oder zu vertauschen gegen alte, nichts zu handeln?« Wie die dumme das hörte, lief sie hin und vertauschte ihren guten alten Lappen für einen neuen;

das wollte der Jud gerad, denn er kannte die Tugend des alten gar wohl. Als die älteste nun heimkam, sprach sie: »mit dem Nähverdienst geht's schlecht, ich muss uns ein bisschen Geld schaffen, wo ist unser Lappen?« »Desto besser«, sprach die dumme, »ich hab auch während du aus warst einen neuen und frischen dafür eingehandelt für den alten.« – (Nachher wird der Jude ein Hund, die zwei Mädchen Hühner, die Hühner aber endlich Menschen, und prügeln den Hund zu Tode.)

Anhang Nr. 18

Die treuen Tiere.

Es war einmal ein Mann, der hatte gar nicht viel Geld, und mit dem wenigen, was ihm übrig geblieben war, zog er in die weite Welt. Da kam er in ein Dorf, wo die Jungen zusammen liefen, schrien und lärmten. »Was habt ihr vor, ihr Jungen?« fragte der Mann. »Ei«, antworteten sie, »da haben wir eine Maus, die muss uns tanzen, seht einmal was das für ein Spaß ist, wie die herumtrippelt!« Den Mann aber dauerte das arme Tierchen und er sprach »lasst die Maus laufen, ihr Jungen, ich will euch auch Geld geben.« Da gab er ihnen Geld, und sie ließen die Maus los, und das arme Tier lief, was es konnte, in ein Loch hinein. Der Mann ging fort und kam in ein anderes Dorf, da hatten die Jungen einen Affen, der musste tanzen und Purzelbäume machen, und sie lachten darüber und ließen dem Tier keine Ruh. Da gab ihnen der Mann auch Geld, damit sie den Affen los ließen. Danach kam der Mann in ein drittes Dorf, da hatten die Jungen einen Bären an der Kette, der musste sich aufrecht setzen und tanzen, und wenn er dazu brummte, war's ihnen eben recht. Da kaufte ihn der Mann auch los, und der Bär war froh dass er wieder auf seine vier Beine kam, und trabte fort.

Der Mann aber hatte nun sein bisschen übriges Geld ausgegeben und hatte keinen roten Heller mehr in der Tasche.
Da sprach er zu sich selber »der König hat so viel in seiner
Schatzkammer, was er nicht braucht: Hungers kannst du
nicht sterben, du willst da etwas nehmen, und wenn du
wieder zu Geld kommst, kannst du's ja wieder hinein legen.« Also machte er sich über die Schatzkammer und
nahm sich ein wenig davon, allein beim Herausschleichen
ward er von den Leuten des Königs erwischt. Sie sagten er
wäre ein Dieb und führten ihn vor Gericht, und weil er
Unrecht getan hatte, ward er verurteilt, dass er in einem
Kasten sollte aufs Wasser gesetzt werden. Der Kastendeckel
war voll Löcher: damit Luft hinein konnte: auch ward ihm
ein Krug Wasser und ein Laib Brot mit hinein gegeben. Wie
er nun so auf dem Wasser schwamm und recht in Angst
war hörte er was krabbeln am Schloss, nagen und schnauben: auf einmal springt das Schloss auf, und der Deckel
fährt in die Höhe, und stehen da Maus, Affe und Bär, die
hatten's getan; weil er ihnen geholfen hatte, wollten sie ihm
wieder helfen. Nun wussten sie aber nicht was sie noch
weiter tun sollten und ratschlagten mit einander. Indem
kam ein weißer Stein in dem Wasser daher gerollt, der sah
aus wie ein rundes Ei. Da sagte der Bär »der kommt zu
rechter Zeit, das ist ein Wunderstein: wem der eigen ist, der
kann sich wünschen, wozu er nur Lust hat.« Da holte der
Mann den Stein herauf, und wie er ihn in der Hand hielt,
wünschte er sich ein Schloss mit Garten und Marstall, und
kaum hatte er den Wunsch ausgesprochen, so saß er in dem
Schloss mit dem Garten und dem Marstall, und war alles so
schön und prächtig, dass er sich nicht genug verwundern
konnte.
Nach einer Zeit zogen Kaufleute des Wegs vorbei. »Sehe einer«, riefen sie, »was da für ein herrliches Schloss steht, und
das letztemal, wie wir vorbei kamen, lag da noch schlechter
Sand.« Weil sie nun neugierig waren, giengen sie hinein und
erkundigten sich bei dem Mann wie er alles so geschwind

hätte bauen können. Da sprach er »das hab ich nicht getan, sondern mein Wunderstein.« »Was ist das für ein Stein?« fragten sie. Da gieng er hin, holte ihn herbei und zeigte ihn den Kaufleuten. Sie hatten große Lust dazu und fragten ob er nicht zu erhandeln wäre, auch boten sie ihm alle ihre schönen Waren dafür. Dem Manne stachen die Waren in die Augen, und weil das Herz unbeständig ist und sich nach neuen Dingen sehnt, so ließ er sich betören, und meinte die schönen Waren wären mehr wert, als sein Wunderstein und gab ihn hin. Kaum aber hatte er ihn aus den Händen gegeben, da war auch alles Glück dahin, und er saß auf einmal wieder in dem verschlossenen Kasten auf dem Fluss und hatte nichts als einen Krug Wasser und einen Laib Brot. Die treuen Tiere, Maus, Affe und Bär, wie sie sein Unglück sahen, kamen wieder herbei und wollten ihm helfen, aber sie konnten nicht einmal das Schloss aufsprengen, weil's viel fester war als das erstemal. Da sprach der Bär »wir müssen den Wunderstein wieder schaffen, oder es ist alles umsonst.« Weil nun die Kaufleute in dem Schloss geblieben waren und da wohnten, so giengen die Tiere mit einander da hin, und wie sie nahe dabei kamen, sagte der Bär »Maus, guck einmal durchs Schlüsselloch und sieh was anzufangen ist; du bist klein, dich merkt kein Mensch.« Die Maus war willig, kam aber wieder und sagte »es geht nicht, ich habe hineingeguckt, der Stein hängt unter dem Spiegel an einem roten Bändchen, und hüben und drüben sitzen ein paar große Katzen mit feurigen Augen, die sollen ihn bewachen.« Da sagten die andern »geh nur wieder hinein und warte bis der Herr im Bett liegt und schläft, dann schleich dich durch ein Loch hinein und kriech aufs Bett und zwick ihn an der Nase und beiß ihm seine Haare ab.« Die Maus kroch wieder hinein und tat wie die andern gesagt hatten. Der Herr wachte auf, rieb sich die Nase, war ärgerlich und sprach »die Katzen taugen nichts sie lassen die Mäuse herein, die mir die Haare vom Kopf abbeißen«, und jagte sie alle beide fort. Da hatte die Maus gewonnen Spiel.

Wie nun der Herr die andere Nacht wieder eingeschlafen war, machte sich die Maus hinein, knuperte und nagte an dem roten Band, woran der Stein hieng, so lange bis es entzwei war und der Stein herunter fiel: dann schleifte sie ihn bis zur Haustür. Das ward aber der armen kleinen Maus recht sauer, und sie sprach zum Affen, der schon auf der Lauer stand »zieh ihn mit deiner Pfote vollends heraus.« Das war dem Affen ein Leichtes, er nahm den Stein in die Hand, und sie giengen mit einander bis zum Fluss. Da sagte der Affe »wie sollen wir nun zu dem Kasten kommen?« Der Bär antwortete »das ist bald geschehen, ich gehe ins Wasser und schwimme: Affe, setz du dich auf meinen Rücken, halt dich aber mit deinen Händen fest und nimm den Stein ins Maul: Mäuschen, du kannst dich in mein rechtes Ohr setzen.« Also taten sie und schwammen den Fluss hinab. Nach einiger Zeit gieng's dem Bären zu still her, er fieng an zu schwätzen und sagte »hör, Affe, wir sind doch brave Kameraden, was meinst du?« Der Affe aber antwortete nicht und schwieg still. »Ist das Manier?« sagte der Bär, »willst du deinem Kameraden keine Antwort geben? ein schlechter Kerl, der nicht antwortet!« Da konnte sich der Affe nicht länger zurückhalten, er ließ den Stein ins Wasser fallen und rief »dummer Kerl, wie konnt ich mit dem Stein im Mund dir antworten? jetzt ist er verloren, und daran bist du Schuld.« »Zank nur nicht«, sagte der Bär, »wir wollen schon etwas erdenken.« Da beratschlagten sie sich und riefen die Laubfrösche, Unken und alles Getier, das im Wasser lebt, zusammen und sagten »es wird ein gewaltiger Feind über euch kommen, macht dass ihr Steine zusammen schafft, so viel ihr könnt, so wollen wir euch eine Mauer bauen, die euch schützt.« Da erschraken die Tiere und brachten Steine von allen Seiten herbeigeschleppt, endlich kam auch ein alter dicker Quakfrosch aus dem Grund heraufgerudert und hatte das rote Band mit dem Wunderstein im Mund. Da war der Bär froh, nahm dem Frosch seine Last ab, sagte es wäre alles gut, sie könnten wieder nach

Hause gehen, und machte einen kurzen Abschied. Darauf
fuhren die drei den Fluss hinab zu dem Mann im Kasten,
sprengten den Deckel mit Hülfe des Steins, und waren zu
rechter Zeit gekommen, denn er hatte das Brot schon aufgezehrt und das Wasser getrunken, und war schon halb
verschmachtet. Wie er aber den Wunderstein wieder in die
Hände bekam, wünschte er sich eine gute Gesundheit und
versetzte sich in sein schönes Schloss mit dem Garten und
Marstall; da lebte er vergnügt, und die drei Tiere blieben
bei ihm und hatten's gut ihr Lebelang.

Anhang Nr. 19

Die Krähen.

Es hatte ein rechtschaffener Soldat etwas Geld verdient und
zusammengespart, weil er fleißig war, und es nicht, wie die
andern, in den Wirtshäusern durchbrachte. Nun waren
zwei von seinen Kameraden, die hatten eigentlich ein falsches Herz, und wollten ihn um sein Geld bringen, sie
stellten sich aber äußerlich ganz freundschaftlich an. Auf
eine Zeit sprachen sie zu ihm »hör, was sollen wir hier in
der Stadt liegen, wir sind ja eingeschlossen darin, als wären
wir Gefangene, und gar einer wie du, der könnte sich daheim was ordentliches verdienen, und vergnügt leben.« Mit
solchen Reden setzten sie ihm auch so lange zu, bis er endlich einwilligte, und mit ihnen ausreißen wollte; die zwei
andern hatten aber nichts anders im Sinn, als ihm draußen
sein Geld abzunehmen. Wie sie nun ein Stück Wegs fortgegangen waren, sagten die zwei »wir müssen uns da rechts
einschlagen, wenn wir an die Grenze kommen wollen.«
»Nein«, antwortete er, »da geht's gerade wieder in die Stadt
zurück, links müssen wir uns halten.« »Was, du willst dich
mausig machen?« riefen die zwei, drangen auf ihn ein,

schlugen ihn bis er niederfiel, und nahmen ihm sein Geld aus den Taschen; das war aber noch nicht genug, sie stachen ihm die Augen aus, schleppten ihn zum Galgen, und banden ihn daran fest. Da ließen sie ihn, und giengen mit dem gestohlenen Geld in die Stadt zurück.

Der arme Blinde wusste nicht an welchem schlechten Ort er war, fühlte um sich, und merkte dass er unter einem Balken Holz saß. Da meinte er es wäre ein Kreuz, sprach »es ist doch gut von ihnen, dass sie mich wenigstens unter ein Kreuz gebunden haben, Gott ist bei mir«, und fieng an recht zu Gott zu beten. Wie es ungefähr Nacht werden mochte, hörte er etwas flattern; das waren aber drei Krähen, die ließen sich auf dem Balken nieder. Danach hörte er wie eine sprach »Schwester, was bringt ihr Gutes? ja, wenn die Menschen wüssten, was wir wissen! die Königstochter ist krank, und der alte König hat sie demjenigen versprochen, der sie heilt; das kann aber keiner, denn sie wird nur gesund, wenn die Kröte in dem Teich dort zu Asche verbrannt wird, und sie die Asche mit Wasser trinkt.« Da sprach die zweite »ja, wenn die Menschen wüssten, was wir wissen! heute Nacht fällt ein Tau vom Himmel, so wunderbar und heilsam, wer blind ist, und bestreicht seine Augen damit, der erhält sein Gesicht wieder.« Da sprach auch die dritte »ja, wenn die Menschen wüssten, was wir wissen! Die Kröte hilft nur einem, und der Tau hilft nur wenigen, aber in der Stadt ist große Not, da sind alle Brunnen vertrocknet, und niemand weiß dass der große viereckige Stein auf dem Markt muss weggenommen und darunter gegraben werden, dort quillt das schönste Wasser.« Wie die drei Krähen das gesagt hatten, hörte er es wieder flattern, und sie flogen da fort. Er machte sich allmählig von seinen Banden los, und dann bückte er sich, und brach ein paar Gräserchen ab, und bestrich seine Augen mit dem Tau, der darauf gefallen war. Alsbald ward er wieder sehend und waren Mond und Sterne am Himmel, und sah er dass er neben dem Galgen stand. Danach suchte er Scherben, und sammelte von dem köstlichen Tau, so viel er zusammen bringen konnte, und wie das geschehen war, gieng er zum Teich, grub das Wasser davon ab, holte die Kröte heraus, und verbrannte sie zu Asche. Mit der Asche gieng er an des Königs Hof, und ließ die Königstochter davon einnehmen, und als sie gesund war, verlangte er sie, wie es versprochen war, zur Gemahlin. Dem König aber gefiel er nicht, weil er so schlechte Kleider an hatte, und er sprach wer seine Tochter haben wollte, der müsste der Stadt erst Wasser verschaffen, und hoffte ihn damit los zu werden. Er aber gieng hin, hieß die Leute den viereckigen Stein auf dem Markt wegheben, und darunter nach Wasser graben. Kaum hatten sie angefangen zu graben, so kamen sie schon zu einer Quelle, aus der ein mächtiger Wasserstrahl hervor sprang. Der König konnte ihm nun seine Tochter nicht länger verweigern, er wurde mit ihr vermählt, und lebten sie in einer vergnügten Ehe.

Auf eine Zeit, als er durchs Feld spazieren gieng, begegneten ihm seine beiden ehemaligen Kameraden, die so treulos an ihm gehandelt hatten. Sie kannten ihn nicht, er aber erkannte sie gleich, gieng auf sie zu und sprach »seht, das ist euer ehemaliger Kamerad, dem ihr so schändlich die Augen ausgestochen habt, aber der liebe Gott hat mir's zum Glück gedeihen lassen.« Da fielen sie ihm zu Füßen, und baten um Gnade, und weil er ein gutes Herz hatte, erbarmte er sich ihrer, und nahm sie mit sich, gab ihnen auch Nahrung und Kleider. Er erzählte ihnen danach wie es ihm ergangen, und wie er zu diesen Ehren gekommen wäre. Als die zwei das vernahmen, hatten sie keine Ruhe, und wollten sich eine Nacht unter den Galgen setzen, ob sie vielleicht auch etwas Gutes hörten. Wie sie nun unter dem Galgen saßen, flatterte auch bald etwas über ihren Häuptern, und kamen die drei Krähen. Die eine sprach zur andern »hört, Schwestern, es muss uns jemand behorcht haben, denn die Königstochter ist gesund, die Kröte ist fort aus dem Teich, ein Blinder ist sehend geworden, und in der Stadt haben sie einen frischen Brunnen gegraben, kommt, lasst uns den Horcher suchen, und ihn bestrafen.« Da flatterten sie herab, und fanden die beiden, und eh sich die helfen konnten, saßen ihnen die Raben auf den Köpfen, und hackten ihnen die Augen aus, und hackten weiter so lange ins Gesicht, bis sie ganz tot waren. Da blieben sie liegen unter dem Galgen. Als sie nun ein paar Tage nicht wieder kamen, dachte ihr ehemaliger Kamerad »wo mögen die zwei herumirren«, und gieng hinaus sie zu suchen. Da fand er aber nichts mehr, als ihre Gebeine, die trug er vom Galgen weg, und legte sie in ein Grab.

Anhang Nr. 20

Der Faule und der Fleißige.

Es waren einmal zwei Handwerkspursche, die wanderten zusammen und gelobten bei einander zu halten. Als sie aber in eine große Stadt kamen, ward der eine ein Bruder Liederlich, vergaß sein Wort, verließ den andern und zog allein fort, hin und her; wo's am tollsten zuging war's ihm am liebsten. Der andere hielt seine Zeit aus, arbeitete fleißig und wanderte hernach weiter. Da kam er in der Nacht am Galgen vorbei, ohne dass er's wusste, aber auf der Erde sah er unten einen liegen und schlafen, der war dürftig und bloß, und weil es sternenhell war, erkannte er seinen ehemaligen Gesellen. Da legte er sich neben ihn, deckte seinen Mantel über ihn und schlief ein. Es dauerte aber nicht lang, so wurde er von zwei Stimmen aufgeweckt, die sprachen mit einander, das waren zwei Raben, die saßen oben auf dem Galgen. Der eine sprach: »Gott ernährt!« der andere: »tu darnach!« und einer fiel nach den Worten matt herab zur Erde, der andere blieb bei ihm sitzen und wartete bis es Tag war, da holte er etwas Gewürm und Wasser, erfrischte ihn damit und erweckte ihn vom Tod. Wie die beiden

Handwerksburschen das sahen, verwunderten sie sich und fragten den einen Raben, warum der andere so elend und krank wäre, da sprach der kranke: »weil ich nichts tun wollte und glaubte, die Nahrung käm doch vom Himmel.« Die beiden nahmen die Raben mit sich in den nächsten Ort, der eine war munter und suchte sich sein Futter, alle Morgen badete er sich und putzte sich mit dem Schnabel, der andere aber hockte in den Ecken herum, war verdrießlich und sah immerfort struppig aus. Nach einer Zeit hatte die Tochter des Hausherrn, die ein schönes Mädchen war, den fleißigen Raben gar lieb, nahm ihn von dem Boden auf, streichelte ihn mit der Hand, endlich drückte sie ihn einmal ans Gesicht und küsste ihn vor Vergnügen. Der Vogel fiel zur Erde, wälzte sich und flatterte und ward zu einem schönen jungen Mann. Da erzählte er, der andere Rabe wär sein Bruder und sie hätten beide ihren Vater beleidigt, der hätte sie dafür verwünscht und gesagt: »fliegt als Raben umher, so lang, bis ein schönes Mädchen euch freiwillig küsst.« Also war der eine erlöst, aber den andern trägen wollte niemand küssen und er starb als Rabe. – Bruder Liederlich nahm sich das zur Lehre, ward fleißig und ordentlich und hielt sich bei seinem Gesellen.

Anhang Nr. 21

Der Löwe und der Frosch.

Es war ein König und eine Königin, die hatten einen Sohn und eine Tochter, die hatten sie herzlich lieb. Der Prinz ging oft auf die Jagd und blieb manchmal lange Zeit außen im Wald, einmal aber kam er gar nicht wieder. Darüber weinte sich seine Schwester fast blind, endlich, wie sie's nicht länger aushalten konnte, ging sie fort in den Wald und wollte ihren Bruder suchen. Als sie nun lange Wege gegangen war, konnte sie vor Müdigkeit nicht weiter und wie sie sich umsah, da stand ein Löwe neben ihr, der tat ganz freundlich und sah so gut aus. Da setzte sie sich auf seinen Rücken und der Löwe trug sie fort und streichelte sie immer mit seinem Schwanze und kühlte ihr die Backen. Als er nun ein gut Stück fortgelaufen war, kamen sie vor eine Höhle, da trug sie der Löwe hinein und sie fürchtete sich nicht und wollte auch nicht herabspringen, weil der Löwe so freundlich war. Also ging's durch die Höhle, die immer dunkler war und endlich ganz stockfinster, und als das ein Weilchen gedauert hatte, kamen sie wieder an das Tagslicht in einen wunderschönen Garten. Da war alles so frisch und glänzte in der Sonne, und mittendrin stand ein prächtiger Palast. Wie sie ans Tor kamen, hielt der Löwe und die Prinzessin stieg von seinem Rücken herunter. Da fing der Löwe an zu sprechen und sagte: »in dem schönen Haus sollst du wohnen und mir dienen, und wenn du alles erfüllst was ich fordere, so wirst du deinen Bruder wiedersehen.«

Da diente die Prinzessin dem Löwen und gehorchte ihm in allen Stücken. Einmal ging sie in dem Garten spazieren, darin war es so schön und doch war sie traurig, weil sie so allein und von aller Welt verlassen war. Wie sie so auf und ab ging, ward sie einen Teich gewahr und auf der Mitte des Teichs war eine kleine Insel mit einem Zelt. Da sah sie, dass unter dem Zelt ein grasgrüner Laubfrosch saß und hatte ein Rosenblatt auf dem Kopf statt einer Haube. Der Frosch guckte sie an und sprach: »warum bist du so traurig?« »Ach«, sagte sie, »warum sollte ich nicht traurig sein?« und klagte ihm da recht ihre Not. Da sprach der Frosch ganz freundlich: »wenn du was brauchst, so komm nur zu mir, so will ich dir mit Rat und Tat zur Hand gehen.« »Wie soll ich dir das aber vergelten?« »Du brauchst mir nichts zu vergelten«, sprach der Quakfrosch, »bring mir nur alle Tage ein frisches Rosenblatt zur Haube.« Da ging nun die Prinzessin wieder zurück und war ein Bisschen getröstet und so oft der Löwe etwas verlangte, lief sie zum Teich, da sprang

der Frosch herüber und hinüber und hatte ihr bald herbeigeschafft, was sie brauchte. Auf eine Zeit sagte der Löwe:
»heut Abend äß ich gern eine Mückenpastete, sie muss aber
gut zubereitet sein.« Da dachte die Prinzessin, wie soll ich
die herbei schaffen, das ist mir ganz unmöglich, lief hinaus
und klagte es ihrem Frosch. Der Frosch aber sprach: »mach
dir keine Sorgen, eine Mückenpastete will ich schon herbeischaffen.« Darauf setzte er sich hin, sperrte rechts und links
das Maul auf, schnappte zu und fing Mücken, so viel er
brauchte. Darauf hüpfte er hin und her, trug Holzspäne zusammen und blies ein Feuer an. Wie's brannte, knetete er
die Pastete und setzte sie über Kohlen, und es währte keine
zwei Stunden, so war sie fertig und so gut als einer nur
wünschen konnte. Da sprach er zu dem Mädchen: »die
Pastete kriegst du aber nicht eher, als bis du mir versprichst, dem Löwen, sobald er eingeschlafen ist, den Kopf
abzuschlagen mit einem Schwert, das hinter seinem Lager
verborgen ist.« »Nein«, sagte sie, »das tue ich nicht, der
Löwe ist doch immer gut gegen mich gewesen.« Da sprach
der Frosch: »wenn du das nicht tust, wirst du nimmermehr
deinen Bruder wiedersehen, und dem Löwen selber tust du
auch kein Leid damit an.« Da fasste sie Mut, nahm die Pastete und brachte sie dem Löwen. »Die sieht ja recht gut
aus«, sagte der Löwe, schnupperte daran und fing gleich an
einzubeißen, aß sie auch ganz auf. Wie er nun fertig war,
fühlte er eine Müdigkeit und wollte ein wenig schlafen; also
sprach er zur Prinzessin: »komm und setz dich neben mich
und krau mir ein Bisschen hinter den Ohren, bis ich eingeschlafen bin.« Da setzt sie sich neben ihn, kraut ihn mit der
Linken und sucht mit der Rechten nach dem Schwert, welches hinter seinem Bette liegt. Wie er nun eingeschlafen ist,
so zieht sie es hervor, drückt die Augen zu und haut mit einem Streich dem Löwen den Kopf ab. Wie sie aber wieder
hinblickt, da war der Löwe verschwunden und ihr lieber
Bruder stand neben ihr, der küsste sie herzlich und sprach:
»du hast mich erlöst, denn ich war der Löwe und war ver-

wünscht es so lang zu bleiben, bis eine Mädchenhand aus Liebe zu mir dem Löwen den Kopf abhauen würde.« Darauf gingen sie miteinander in den Garten und wollten dem Frosch danken, wie sie aber ankamen, sahen sie, wie er nach allen Seiten herumhüpfte und kleine Späne suchte und ein Feuer anmachte. Als es nun recht hell brannte, hüpfte er selber hinein und da brennt's noch ein Bisschen und dann geht das Feuer aus, und steht ein schönes Mädchen da, das war auch verwünscht worden und die Liebste des Prinzen. Da ziehen sie miteinander heim zu dem alten König und der Frau Königin und wird eine große Hochzeit gehalten und wer dabei gewesen, der ist nicht hungrig nach Haus gegangen.

Anhang Nr. 22

Der Soldat und der Schreiner.

Es wohnten in einer Stadt zwei Tischler, deren Häuser stießen aneinander und jeder hatte einen Sohn; die Kinder waren immer beisammen, spielten miteinander und hießen darum das *Messerchen* und *Gäbelchen*, die auch immer nebeneinander auf den Tisch gelegt werden. Als sie nun beide groß waren, wollten sie auch von einander nicht weichen, der eine war aber mutig und der andere furchtsam, da ward der eine Soldat, der andere lernte das Handwerk. Wie die Zeit kam, dass dieser wandern musste, wollt ihn der Soldat nicht verlassen und gingen sie zusammen aus. Sie kamen nun in eine Stadt, wo der Tischler bei einem Meister in die Arbeit ging, der Soldat wollte da auch bleiben und verdingte sich bei demselben Meister als Hausknecht. Das wär gut gewesen, aber der Soldat hatte keine Lust am Arbeiten, lag auf der Bärenhaut und es dauerte nicht lang, so wurde er vom Meister weggeschickt; der fleißige wollt ihn aus Treue nun nicht allein lassen, sagte dem Meister auf und zog mit ihm weiter. So ging's aber immer fort; hatten sie Arbeit, so dauerte es nicht lang, weil der Soldat faul war und fortgeschickt wurde, der andere aber ohne ihn nicht bleiben wollte. Einmal kamen sie in eine große Stadt, weil aber der Soldat keine Hand regen wollte, ward er am Abend schon verabschiedet und sie mussten dieselbe Nacht wieder hinaus. Da führte sie der Weg vor einen unbekannten großen Wald; der Furchtsame sprach: »ich geh nicht hinein, darin springen Hexen und Gespenster herum.« Der Soldat aber antwortete: »ei was! davor fürcht ich mich noch nicht!« ging voran, und der Furchtsame, weil er doch nicht von ihm lassen wollte, ging mit. In kurzer Zeit hatten sie den Weg verloren und irrten in der Dunkelheit durch die Bäume, endlich sahen sie ein Licht. Das suchten sie auf und kamen zu einem schönen Schloss, das hell erleuchtet war, und haußen lag ein schwarzer Hund und auf einem Teich neben saß ein roter Schwan; als sie aber hineintraten, sahen sie nirgends einen Menschen, bis sie in die Küche kamen, da saß noch eine graue Katze bei einem Topf am Feuer und kochte. Sie gingen weiter und fanden viele prächtige Zimmer, die waren alle leer, in einem aber stand ein Tisch mit Essen und Trinken reichlich besetzt. Weil sie nun großen Hunger hatten, machten sie sich daran und ließen sich's gut schmecken. Darnach sprach der Soldat: »wenn du gegessen hast und satt worden bist, sollst du schlafen gehen!« machte eine Kammer auf, darin standen zwei schöne Betten. Sie legten sich, aber als sie eben einschlafen wollten, fiel dem Furchtsamen ein, dass sie noch nicht gebetet hätten, da stand er auf und sah in der Wand einen Schrank, den schloss er auf und war da ein Kruzifix mit zwei Gebetbüchern dabei. Gleich weckte er den Soldaten, dass er aufstehen musste und sie knieten beide nieder und taten ihr Gebet; darnach schliefen sie ruhig ein. Am andern Morgen kriegte der Soldat einen heftigen Stoß, dass er in die Höhe fuhr: »du, was schlägst du mich« rief er dem andern zu, der aber hatte auch einen Stoß gekriegt und sprach: »was stößt du mich, ich stoß dich nicht!« Da sagte der Soldat: »es wird wohl ein Zeichen sein, dass wir hervor sollen.« Wie sie nun herauskamen, stand schon ein Frühstück auf dem Tisch, der Furchtsame sprach aber: »eh wir es anrühren, wollen wir erst nach einem Menschen suchen.« »Ja«, sagte der Soldat, »ich mein auch immer, die Katze hätt's gekocht und eingebrockt, da vergeht mir alle Lust.«

Sie gingen also wieder von unten bis oben durchs Schloss, fanden aber keine Seele, endlich sagte der Soldat: »wir wollen auch in den Keller steigen.« Wie sie die Treppe herunter waren, sahen sie vor dem ersten Keller eine alte Frau sitzen; sie redeten sie an und sprachen: »guten Tag! hat sie uns das gute Essen gekocht?« »Ja, Kinder, hat's euch geschmeckt?« Da gingen sie weiter und kamen zum zweiten Keller, davor saß ein Jüngling von 14 Jahren, den grüßten sie auch, er gab ihnen aber keine Antwort. Endlich kamen sie in den dritten Keller, davor saß ein Mädchen von zwölf Jahren, das antwortete ihnen auch nicht auf ihren Gruß. Sie gingen noch weiter durch alle Keller, fanden aber weiter niemand. Wie sie nun wieder zurückkamen, war das Mädchen von seinem Sitz aufgestanden, da sagten sie zu ihm: »willst du mit uns hinaufgehen?« Es sprach aber: »ist der *rote Schwan* noch oben auf dem Teich?« »Ja, wir haben ihn beim Eingang gesehen.« »Das ist traurig, so kann ich nicht mitgehen.« Der Jüngling war auch aufgestanden und als sie zu ihm kamen, fragten sie ihn: »willst du mit uns hinauf gehen?« Er aber sprach: »ist der *schwarze Hund* noch auf dem Hof?« »Ja, wir haben ihn beim Eingang gesehen.« »Das ist traurig, so kann ich nicht mit euch gehen.« Als sie zu der alten Frau kamen, hatte sie sich auch aufgerichtet: »Mütterchen«, sprachen sie, »wollt ihr mit uns hinaufgehen?« »Ist die *graue Katze* noch oben in der Küche?« »Ja, sie sitzt auf dem Herd bei einem Topf und kocht.« »Das ist traurig, eh ihr nicht den roten Schwan, den schwarzen Hund und die graue Katze tötet, können wir nicht aus dem Keller heraus.«

Als die zwei Gesellen wieder oben in die Küche kamen,
wollten sie die Katze streicheln, sie machte aber feurige
Augen und sah ganz wild aus. Nun war noch eine kleine
Kammer übrig, in der sie nicht gewesen waren, wie sie die
aufmachten, war sie ganz leer, nur an der Wand ein Bogen
und Pfeil, ein Schwert und eine Eisen-Zange. Über Bogen
und Pfeil standen die Worte: »das tötet den roten Schwan«,
über dem Schwert: »das haut dem schwarzen Hund den
Kopf herunter«, und über der Zange: »das kneift der grau-
en Katze den Kopf ab«. »Ach«, sagte der Furchtsame, »wir
wollen fort von hier«, der Soldat aber: »nein, wir wollen
die Tiere aufsuchen.« Sie nahmen die Waffen von der Wand
und gingen in die Küche, da standen die drei Tiere, der
Schwan, der Hund und die Katze beisammen, als hätten sie
was Böses vor. Wie der Furchtsame das sah, lief er wieder
fort; der Soldat sprach ihm ein Herz ein, er hingegen wollte
erst etwas essen; wie er gegessen hatte, sagte er: »in einem
Zimmer hab ich Harnische gesehen, da will ich einen zuvor
anlegen.« Als er in dem Zimmer war, wollt er sich forthelfen und sprach: »es ist besser, wir steigen zum Fenster hinaus, was kümmern uns die Tiere!« Wie er aber zum Fenster
trat, war ein stark Eisen-Gitter davor. Nun konnt er's nicht
länger verreden, ging zu den Harnischen und wollte einen
anziehen, aber sie waren alle zu schwer. Da sagte der Soldat: »ei was, lass uns so gehen, wie wir sind.« »Ja«, sprach
der andere, »wenn unser noch drei wären.« Wie er die Worte sprach, da flatterte eine weiße Taube außen ans Fenster
und stieß daran, der Soldat machte ihr auf und wie sie herein war, stand ein schöner Jüngling vor ihnen, der sprach:
»ich will bei euch sein und euch helfen« und nahm Bogen
und Pfeil. Der Furchtsame sprach zu ihm, er hätt's am besten, mit dem Bogen und Pfeil, nach dem Schuss wär's gut
und er könnte hingehen, wohin er Lust hätte, sie aber
müssten mit ihren Waffen den Zauber-Tieren näher auf den
Leib. Da gab der Jüngling ihm den Bogen und Pfeil und
nahm das Schwert.

Da gingen alle drei zur Küche, wo die Tiere noch beisammen standen, und der Jüngling hieb dem schwarzen Hund den Kopf ab, und der Soldat packte die graue Katze mit der Zange und der Furchtsame stand hinten und schoss den roten Schwan tot. Und wie die drei Tiere niederfielen, in dem Augenblick kam die Alte und ihre zwei Kinder mit großem Geschrei aus dem Keller gelaufen: »ihr habt meine liebsten Freunde getötet, ihr seid Verräter«, drangen auf sie und wollten sie ermorden. Aber die drei überwältigten sie und töteten sie mit ihren Waffen und wie sie tot waren, fing auf einmal ein wunderliches Gemurmel rings herum an und kam aus allen Ecken. Der Furchtsame sprach: »wir wollen die drei Leichen begraben, es waren doch Christen, das haben wir am Kruzifix gesehen.« Sie trugen sie also hinaus auf den Hof, machten drei Gräber und legten sie hinein. Während der Arbeit nahm aber das Gemurmel im Schloss immer zu, ward immer lauter und wie sie fertig waren, hörten sie ordentlich Stimmen darin, und einer rief: »wo sind sie? wo sind sie?« Und weil der schöne Jüngling nicht mehr da war, ward ihnen Angst und sie liefen fort. Als sie ein wenig weg waren, sagte der Soldat: »ei, das ist Unrecht, dass wir so fortgelaufen sind, wir wollen umkehren und sehen, was dort ist.« »Nein«, sagte der andere, »ich will mit dem Zauberwesen nichts zu tun haben und mein ehrliches Auskommen in der Stadt suchen.« Aber der Soldat ließ ihm keine Ruhe, bis er mit ihm zurückging. Wie sie vors Schloss kamen, war alles voll Leben, Pferde sprangen durch den Hof und Bediente liefen hin und her. Da gaben sie sich für zwei arme Handwerker aus und baten um ein wenig Essen. Einer aus dem Haufen sprach: »ja, kommt nur herein, heut wird allen Gutes getan.« Sie wurden in ein schönes Zimmer geführt und ward ihnen Speise und Wein gegeben. Darnach wurden sie gefragt, ob sie nicht zwei junge Leute von der Burg hätten kommen sehen. »Nein«, sagten sie. Als aber einer sah, dass sie Blut an den Händen hatten, fragte er, woher das Blut käme? Da sprach der Soldat: »ich habe mich in den Finger geschnitten.« Der Diener aber sagte es dem Herrn, der kam selber und wollt es sehen, es war aber der schöne Jüngling, der ihnen beigestanden hatte und wie er sie mit Augen sah, rief er: »das sind sie, die das Schloss errettet haben!« Da empfing er sie mit Freuden und erzählte, wie es zugegangen wäre: »Im Schloss war eine Haushälterin mit ihren zwei Kindern, die war eine heimliche Hexe und als sie einmal von der Herrschaft gescholten wurde, geriet sie in Bosheit und verwandelte alles, was Leben hatte im Schloss, zu Steinen, nur über drei andere böse Hofbediente, die auch Zauberei verstanden, hatte sie keine rechte Gewalt und konnte sie nur in Tiere verwandeln, die nun oben im Schloss ihr Wesen trieben, dabei fürchtete sie sich vor ihnen und flüchtete mit ihren Kindern in den Keller. Auch über mich hatte sie nur soviel Gewalt gehabt, dass sie mich in eine weiße Taube außerhalb des Schlosses verwandeln konnte. Wie ihr zwei ins Schloss kamt, da solltet ihr die Tiere töten, damit sie frei würde und zum Lohn wollte sie euch wieder umbringen, aber Gott hat es besser gemacht, das Schloss ist erlöst und die Steine sind wieder lebendig geworden in dem Augenblick, wo die gottlose Hexe mit ihren Kindern getötet wurde und das Gemurmel, das ihr gehört, das waren die ersten Worte, welche die frei gewordenen sprachen.« Darauf führte er die zwei Gesellen zu dem Hausherrn, der hatte zwei schöne Töchter, die wurden ihnen gegeben, und sie lebten vergnügt ihr Lebelang, als große Ritter.

Anhang Nr. 23

De wilde Mann.

Et was emoel en wilden Mann, de was verwünsket, un genk bie de Bueren in de Goren (Garten), un in't Korn, un moek alles to Schande. Do klagden se an eeren Gutsheeren se können eere Pacht nig mehr betalen, un do leit de Gutsheer alle

Jägers bie ene kummen: we dat Dier fangen könne, de soll ne
graute Belohnung hebben. Do kümmt do en ollen Jäger an,
de segd he wüll dat Dier wull fangen. Do mött se em ne Pulle met Fusel (Branntwein), un ne Pulle met Wien, un ne Pulle met Beer gierwen (geben), de settet he an dat Water, wo
sick dat Dier, alle Dage wäskt. Un do geiht he achter en
Baum stohn, do kümmt dat Dier un drinket ut de Pullen, do
leckt et alle de Mund, un kickt herüm ov dat auck well süht.
Do werd et drunken, un do geit et liegen un schlöpd. Do geit
de Jäger to, un bind et an Händen un Föten, do weckt he et
wier up, un segd »du wilde Mann, goh met, söck sast du alle
Dage drinken.« Do nimmt he et mit noh dat adlicke Schloss,
do settet se et in den Thornt, un de Heer geit to andre No-
bers, de söllt seihn (sehen) wat he för 'n Dier fangen hed. Do
spierlt ene von den jungen Heerens met'n Ball, un let de in
den Thornt fallen, un dat Kind segd »wilde Mann, schmiet
mie den Ball wier to.« Do segd de wilde Mann »den Ball
most du sölvst wier hahlen.« »Je«, segd dat Kind, »ick heve
kinen Schlürtel.« »Dann mack du dat du die dien Mooer
eere Tasken kümmst, un stehl eer den Schlürtel.« Da schlüt
dat Kind den Thornt orpen, un de wilde Mann löpd derut.
Do fänk dat Kind an to schreien »o wilde Mann, bliev doch
hier, ick kriege süs Schläge.« Do niermt de wilde Mann dat
Kind up de Nacken, un lopd dermet de Wildnis herin; de
wilde Mann was weg, dat Kind was verloren. De wilde
Mann de tüt dat Kind en schlechten Kiel (Kittel) an, un
schickt et noh den Görner an den Kaisers Hof, do mot et
frogen ov de kinen Görnersjungen van dohn (nötig) hed. Do
segd de he wöre so schmeerig antrocken, de annern wullen
nig bie em schlopen. Do seg[d] he he wull int Strauh liegen,
un geit alltied des Morgens fröh in den Goren, do kümmt
em de wilde Mann entgiergen, do seg[d] he, »nu waske die,
nu kämme die.« Un de wilde Mann mackt den Goren so
schön, dat de Görner et sölvst nig so gut kann. Un de Prinzessin süt alle Morgen den schönen Jungen, do seg[d] se to
den Görner de kleine Lehrjunge söll eer een Busk Blomen

brengen. Un se fróg dat Kind van wat fór Stand dat et wóre,
do seg[d] et ja dat wüs et nig; do giv se em en broden Hohn
vull Ducoeten. Es he in kümmt, giv he dat Geld sinen Heeren, un segd »wat sall ick do met dohn, dat bruckt ji men.«
Un he moste eer noh enen Busk Blomen brengen, do giv se
em ne Aant (Ente) vull Ducoeten, de giv he wier an sinen
Heeren. Un do noh enmoel, do giv se em ne Gans vull Ducoeten, de giv de Junge wier an sinen Heeren. Do ment de
Prinzessin he hev Geld, un he hev nix, un do hierothet se em
in't geheem, un do weeret ehre Óldern so beise, un setten se
in dat Brauhuse, do mot se sick met spinnen ernähren, un he
geit in de Kücke, un helpt den Kock de Broden dreien, un
steld manxden (zuweilen) en Stück Fleesk, un bringd et an
sine Frau.
Do kümmt so 'n gewoltigen Krieg in Engelland, wo de
Kaiser hin mott un alle de grauten Heerens, do segd de junge Mann he wull do auck hen, ov se nig no en Perd in Stall
hedden, un se saden se hedden noh ent, dat gónk up drei
Beenen, dat wór em gut genog. He settet sick up dat Perd,
dat Perd dat geit alle husepus husepus. Do kümmt em de
wilde Mann in de móte (entgegen), do döt sick so 'n grauten Berg up, do sind wull dusend Regimenter Soldaten un
Offzeers in, do dät he schöne Kleeder an, un krigd so 'n
schön Perd. Do tüt (zieht) he met alle sin Volk in den Krieg
noh Engelland de Kaiser enfänk en so fröndlick, un begerd
en he móg em doh biestoen. He gewinnt de Schlacht, un
verschleit alles. Do dät sick de Kaiser so bedanken vör em,
un frägd wat he fór 'n Heer wöre, he segd »dat froget mie
men nig, dat kann ick ju nig seggen.« He ritt met sin Volk
wier ut Engelland, do kümmt em de wilde Mann wier entgiergen, un döt alle dat Volk wier in den Berg, un he geit
wier up sien dreibeenige Perd sitten. Do seg[g]et de Luide
»do kümmet usse Hunkepus wier an met dat dreibeenige
Perd«, un se froget »wo hest du achter de Hierge (Hecke)
lägen, un hest schlopen?« »Je«, segd he, »wenn ick der nig
wör west, dann hädde et in Engelland nig gut gohn.« Se

segget »Junge, schwieg stille, süs giv die de Heer wat up d'Jack.« Un so genk et noh tweenmoel, un ton derdenmoel gewient he alles; do kreeg he en Stick in den Arm, do niermt de Kaiser sinen Dock (Tuch), un verbind em de Wunden. Do neidigt (nötigt) se em he mög do bie ihnen blieven, »ne, ick blieve nig bie ju, un wat ick sin, geit ju nig an.« Do kümmet em de wilde Mann wier entgiergen, un deih alle dat Volk wier in den Berg, un he genk wier up sin Perd sitten, un genk wier noh Hues. Do lachten de Luide, un segden »do kümmt usse Hunkepus wier an, wo hest du doh lägen un schlopen?« He segd »ick heve förwohr nig slopen, nu is ganz Engelland gewunnen, un et is en wohren Frerden (Frieden).«

Do segde de Kaiser von den schönen Ritter, de em hev biestohen; do segd de junge Mann to en Kaiser »wöre ick nig bie ju west, et wöre nig guet gahen.« Do will de Kaiser em wat upn Buckel gierwen, »ji«, segd he, »wenn ji dat nig gleiwen willt, will ick ju minen Arm wiesen.« Un asse he den Arm wiest, un asse de Kaiser de Wunde süt, do werr he gans verwündert, un segd »viellicht büst du Gott sölvst ader en Engel, den mie Gott toschickt hev«, un bat em üm Verzeihnüs, dat he so grov met em handelt hädde, un schenket em sin ganse Kaisersgut. Un de wilde Mann was erlöset, un stund ase en grauten Künig för em, un vertelde em de ganse Sacke, un de Berg was en gans Künigsschloss, un he trock met sine Fru derup, un lerweten vergnögt bis an eeren Daud.

Anhang Nr. 24

Die Kinder in Hungersnot.

Es war einmal eine Frau mit ihren zwei Töchtern in solche Armut geraten, dass sie auch nicht ein Bisschen Brot mehr in den Mund zu stecken hatten. Wie nun der Hunger bei ihnen so groß ward, dass die Mutter ganz außer sich und in

[handwritten note: despair]

Verzweiflung geriet, sprach sie zu der ältesten: »ich muss dich töten, damit ich etwas zu essen habe.« Die Tochter sagte: »ach, liebe Mutter, schont meiner, ich will ausgehen und sehen, dass ich etwas zu essen kriege ohne Bettelei.« Da ging sie aus, kam wieder, und hatte ein Stückchen Brot eingebracht, das aßen sie miteinander, es war aber zu wenig, um den Hunger zu stillen. Darum hub die Mutter zur andern Tochter an: »so musst du daran.« Sie antwortete aber: »ach, liebe Mutter, schont meiner, ich will gehen und unbemerkt etwas zu essen anderswo ausbringen.« Da ging sie hin, kam wieder und hatte zwei Stückchen Brot eingebracht; das aßen sie mit einander, es war aber zu wenig, um den Hunger zu stillen. Darum sprach die Mutter nach etlichen Stunden abermals zu ihnen: »ihr müsset doch sterben, denn wir müssen sonst verschmachten.« Darauf antworteten sie: »liebe Mutter, wir wollen uns niederlegen und schlafen, und nicht eher wieder aufstehen, als bis der jüngste Tag kommt.« Da legten sie sich hin und schliefen einen tiefen Schlaf, aus dem sie niemand erwecken konnte, die Mutter aber ist weggekommen und weiß kein Mensch, wo sie geblieben ist.

[handwritten note: languish]

[handwritten note: der Jüngste Tag = day of judgement]

Anhang Nr. 25

Die heilige Frau Kummernis.

Es war einmal eine fromme Jungfrau, die gelobte Gott, nicht zu heiraten, und war wunderschön, so dass es ihr Vater nicht zugeben und sie gern zur Ehe zwingen wollte. In dieser Not flehte sie Gott an, dass er ihr einen Bart wachsen lassen sollte, welches alsogleich geschah; aber der König ergrimmte und ließ sie ans Kreuz schlagen, da ward sie eine Heilige.

Nun geschah es, dass ein gar armer Spielmann in die Kirche kam, wo ihr Bildnis stand, kniete davor nieder, da freute es die

Heilige, dass dieser zuerst ihre Unschuld anerkannte, und das Bild, das mit güldnen Pantoffeln angetan war, ließ einen davon los- und herunterfallen, damit er dem Pilgrim zu gut käme. Der neigte sich dankbar und nahm die Gabe.

Bald aber wurde der Goldschuh in der Kirchen vermisst, und geschah allenthalben Frage, bis er zuletzt bei dem armen Geigerlein gefunden, auch es als ein böser Dieb verdammt und ausgeführt wurde, um zu hangen. Unterwegs aber ging der Zug an dem Gotteshaus vorbei, wo die Bildsäule stand, begehrte der Spielmann hineingehen zu dürfen, dass er zu guter Letzt Abschied nähme mit seinem Geiglein und seiner Guttäterin die Not seines Herzens klagen könnte. Dies wurde ihm nun erlaubt. Kaum aber hat er den ersten Strich getan, siehe, so ließ das Bild auch den andern güldnen Pantoffel herabfallen, und zeigte damit, dass er des Diebstahls unschuldig wäre. Also wurde der Geiger der Eisen und Bande ledig, zog vergnügt seiner Straßen, die heil. Jungfrau aber hieß Kummernis.

Anhang Nr. 26

Das Unglück.

Wen das Unglück aufsucht, der mag sich aus einer Ecke in die andere verkriechen oder ins weite Feld fliehen, es weiß ihn dennoch zu finden. Es war einmal ein Mann so arm geworden, dass er kein Scheit Holz mehr hatte, um das Feuer auf seinem Herde zu erhalten. Da gieng er hinaus in den Wald und wollte einen Baum fällen, aber sie waren alle zu groß und stark: er gieng immer tiefer hinein, bis er einen fand, den er zu bezwingen dachte. Als er eben die Axt aufgehoben hatte, sah er aus dem Dickicht eine Schar Wölfe hervorbrechen und mit Geheul auf ihn eindringen. Er warf die Axt hin, floh und erreichte eine Brücke. Das tiefe Wasser aber hatte die Brücke unterwühlt, und in dem Augenblick, wo er darauf treten wollte, krachte sie und fiel zusammen. Was sollte er tun? Blieb er stehen und erwartete die Wölfe, so zerrissen sie ihn. Er wagte in der Not einen Sprung in das Wasser, aber da er nicht schwimmen konnte, sank er hinab. Ein paar Fischer, die an dem jenseitigen Ufer saßen, sahen den Mann ins Wasser stürzen, schwammen herbei und brachten ihn ans Land. Sie lehnten ihn an eine alte Mauer, damit er sich in der Sonne erwärmen und wieder zu Kräften kommen sollte. Als er aber aus der Ohnmacht erwachte, den Fischern danken und ihnen sein Schicksal erzählen wollte, fiel das Gemäuer über ihm zusammen und erschlug ihn.

Anhang Nr. 27

Die Erbsenprobe.

Es war einmal ein König, der hatte einen einzigen Sohn, der wollte sich gern vermählen, und bat seinen Vater um eine Frau. »Dein Wunsch soll erfüllt werden, mein Sohn«, sagte der König, »aber es will sich nicht schicken dass du eine andere nimmst als eine Prinzessin, und es ist gerade in der Nähe [k]eine zu haben. Indessen will ich es bekannt machen lassen, vielleicht meldet sich eine aus der Ferne.« Es ging also ein offenes Schreiben aus, und es dauerte nicht lange, so meldeten sich Prinzessinnen genug. Fast jeden Tag kam eine, wenn aber nach ihrer Geburt und Abstammung gefragt wurde, so ergab sich's dass es keine Prinzessin war, und sie musste unverrichteter Sache wieder abziehen. »Wenn das so fortgeht«, sagte der Prinz, »so bekomm ich am Ende gar keine Frau.« »Beruhige dich, mein Söhnchen«, sagte die Königin, »eh du dich's versiehst, so ist eine da; das Glück steht oft vor der Türe, man braucht sie nur aufzumachen.« Es war wirklich so, wie die Königin gesagt hatte.

Bald hernach, an einem stürmischen Abend, als Wind und Regen ans Fenster schlugen, ward heftig an das Tor des königlichen Palastes geklopft. Die Diener öffneten, und ein wunderschönes Mädchen trat herein, das verlangte gleich vor den König geführt zu werden. Der König wunderte sich über den späten Besuch, und fragte sie woher sie käme, wer sie wäre und was sie begehre. »Ich komme aus weiter Ferne«, antwortete sie, »und bin die Tochter eines mächtigen Königs. Als eure Bekanntmachung mit dem Bildnis eures Sohnes in meines Vaters Reich gelangte, habe ich heftige Liebe zu ihm empfunden und mich gleich auf den Weg gemacht, in der Absicht seine Gemahlin zu werden.« »Das kommt mir ein wenig bedenklich vor«, sagte der König, »auch siehst du mir gar nicht aus wie eine Prinzessin. Seit wann reist eine Prinzessin allein ohne alles Gefolge und in so schlechten Kleidern?« »Das Gefolge hätte mich nur aufgehalten«, erwiderte sie, »die Farbe an meinen Kleidern ist in der Sonne verschossen, und der Regen hat sie vollends herausgewaschen. Glaubt ihr nicht dass ich eine Prinzessin bin, so sendet nur eine Botschaft an meinen Vater.« »Das ist mir zu weitläufig«, sagte der König, »eine Gesandtschaft kann nicht so schnell reisen, wie du. Die Leute müssen die nötige Zeit dazu haben; es würden Jahre vergehen, ehe sie wieder zurück kämen. Kannst du nicht auf andere Art beweisen, dass du eine Prinzessin bist, so blüht hier dein Weizen nicht, und du tust besser je eher je lieber dich wieder auf den Heimweg zu machen.« »Lass sie nur bleiben«, sagte die Königin, »ich will sie auf die Probe stellen, und will bald wissen ob sie eine Prinzessin ist.«

Die Königin stieg selbst den Turm hinauf, und ließ in einem prächtigen Gemach ein Bett zurecht machen. Als die Matratze herbeigebracht war, legte sie drei Erbsen darauf, eine oben hin, eine in die Mitte und eine unten hin, dann wurden noch sechs weiche Matratzen darüber gebreitet,

Linnentücher und eine Decke von Eiderdunen. Wie alles fertig war, führte sie das Mädchen hinauf in die Schlafkammer. »Nach dem weiten Weg wirst du müde sein, mein Kind«, sagte sie, »schlaf dich aus: Morgen wollen wir weiter sprechen.«

Kaum war der Tag angebrochen, so stieg die Königin schon den Turm hinauf in die Kammer. Sie dachte das Mädchen noch in tiefem Schlaf zu finden, aber es war wach. »Wie hast du geschlafen, mein Töchterchen?« fragte sie. »Erbärmlich«, antwortete die Prinzessin, »ich habe die ganze Nacht kein Auge zugetan.« »Warum? mein Kind, war das Bett nicht gut?« »In einem solchen Bett hab ich mein Lebtag noch nicht gelegen, hart vom Kopf bis zu den Füßen; es war als wenn ich auf lauter Erbsen läge.« »Ich sehe wohl«, sagte die Königin, »du bist eine echte Prinzessin. Ich will dir königliche Kleider schicken, Perlen und Edelsteine: schmücke dich wie eine Braut. Wir wollen noch heute die Hochzeit feiern.«

Anhang Nr. 28

Der Räuber und seine Söhne.

Es war einmal ein Räuber, der hauste in einem großen Walde und lebte mit seinen Gesellen in Schluchten und Felsenhöhlen, und wenn Fürsten, Herrn und reiche Kaufleute auf der Landstraße zogen, so lauerte er ihnen auf und raubte ihnen Geld und Gut. Als er zu Jahren kam, so gefiel ihm das Handwerk nicht mehr und es gereute ihn dass er so viel Böses getan hatte. Er hub also an ein besseres Leben zu führen, lebte als ein ehrlicher Mann, und tat Gutes wo er konnte. Die Leute wunderten sich dass er sich so schnell bekehrt hatte, aber sie freuten sich darüber. Er hatte drei Söhne, als die herangewachsen waren: rief er sie vor sich und sprach »liebe Kinder, sagt mir was für ein Handwerk wollt ihr er-wählen, womit ihr euch ehrlich ernähren könnt?« Die Söhne besprachen sich mit einander und gaben ihm dann zur Antwort »der Apfel fällt nicht weit vom Stamm, wir wollen uns ernähren, wie ihr euch ernährt habt: wir wollen Räuber werden. Ein Handwerk, wobei wir von Morgen bis Abend uns abarbeiten und doch wenig Gewinn und ein mühseliges Leben haben, das gefällt uns nicht.« »Ach, liebe Kinder«, antwortete der Vater, »warum wollt ihr nicht ruhig leben und mit wenigem zufrieden sein; ehrlich währt am längsten. Die Räuberei ist eine böse und gottlose Sache, die zu einem schlimmen Ende führt: an dem Reichtum, den ihr zusammenbringt, habt ihr keine Freude: ich weiß ja wie es mir dabei zu Mut gewesen ist. Ich sage euch es nimmt einen schlechten Ausgang: der Krug geht so lange zu Wasser bis er bricht; ihr werdet zuletzt ergriffen, und an den Galgen gehenkt.« Die Söhne aber achteten nicht auf seine Ermahnungen und blieben bei ihrem Vorsatz.

Nun wollten die drei Jünglinge gleich ihr Probestück machen. Sie wussten dass die Königin in ihrem Stall ein schönes Pferd hatte, das von großem Wert war: das wollten sie ihr stehlen. Sie wussten auch dass das Pferd kein ander Futter fraß als ein saftiges Gras, das allein in einem feuchten Wald wuchs. Sie giengen also hinaus, schnitten das Gras ab und machten einen großen Bündel daraus, in welchen die beiden ältesten den jüngsten und kleinsten so geschickt versteckten, dass er nicht konnte gesehen werden, und trugen den Bündel auf den Markt. Der Stallmeister der Königin kaufte das Futter, ließ es zu dem Pferd in den Stall tragen und hinwerfen. Als es Mitternacht war und jedermann schlief, machte sich der Kleine aus dem Grasbündel heraus, band das Pferd ab, zaumte es mit dem goldenen Zaum und legte ihm das goldgestickte Reitzeug an: und die Schellen, die daran hiengen, verstopfte er mit Wachs, damit sie keinen Klang gäben. Dann öffnete er die verschlossene Pforte und ritt auf dem Pferd in aller Eile fort nach dem Ort, wohin ihn seine Brüder beschieden hatten. Allein die Wächter in der Stadt bemerkten den Dieb, eilten ihm nach, und als sie ihn draußen mit seinen Brüdern fanden, nahmen sie alle drei gefangen und führten sie in das Gefängnis.

Am andern Morgen wurden sie vor die Königin geführt, und als diese sah dass es drei schöne Jünglinge waren, so forschte sie nach ihrer Herkunft und vernahm dass es die Söhne des alten Räubers wären, der seine Lebensweise geändert und als ein gehorsamer Untertan gelebt hatte. Sie ließ sie also wieder in das Gefängnis zurückführen und bei dem Vater anfragen ob er seine Söhne lösen wollte. Der Alte kam und sagte »meine Söhne sind nicht wert dass ich sie mit einem Pfennig löse.« Da sprach die Königin zu ihm »du bist ein weitbekannter, verrufener Räuber gewesen, erzähle mir das merkwürdigste Abenteuer aus deinem Räuberleben, so will ich dir deine Kinder wiedergeben.«

Als der Alte das vernahm, hub er an »Frau Königin, hört meine Rede, ich will euch ein Ereignis erzählen, was mich mehr erschreckt hat als Feuer und Wasser. Ich brachte in Erfahrung dass in einer wilden Waldschlucht zwischen zwei Bergen, zwanzig Meilen von den Menschen entfernt, ein Riese lebte, der einen großen Schatz viel tausend Mark Silber und Gold besäße. Ich wählte also aus meinen Gesellen so viele aus, dass unser hundert waren und wir zogen hin. Es war ein langer mühsamer Weg zwischen Felsen und Abgründen. Wir fanden den Riesen nicht zu Haus, waren froh darüber, und nahmen von dem Gold und Silber, so viel wir tragen konnten. Als wir damit uns auf den Heimweg machen wollten, und ganz sicher zu sein glaubten, da kam der Riese mit zehn andern Riesen unversehens daher und nahm uns alle gefangen. Sie teilten uns unter sich aus: jeder erhielt zehn von uns, und ich fiel mit neun meiner Gesellen dem Riesen zu, dem wir seinen Schatz genommen hatten. Er band uns die Hände auf den Rücken und trieb uns wie Schafe in seine Felsenhöhle. Wir waren bereit uns mit Geld und Gut zu lösen, er aber antwortete ›eure Schätze brauche ich nicht, ich will euch behalten und euer Fleisch verzehren, das ist mir lieber.‹ Dann befühlte er uns alle, wählte einen aus und sprach ›der ist der fetteste, mit dem will ich den Anfang machen.‹ Dann schlug er ihn nieder, warf das zerschnittene Fleisch in einen Kessel mit Wasser, den er über das Feuer setzte, und als es gesotten war, hielt er seine Mahlzeit. So aß er jeden Tag einen von uns, und weil ich der magerste war, so sollte ich der letzte sein. Als nun meine neun Gesellen aufgezehrt waren, und die Reihe an mich kam, so besann ich mich auf eine List. ›Ich sehe wohl dass du böse Augen hast‹, sprach ich zu ihm, ›und am Gesicht leidest: ich bin ein Arzt, und bin in meiner Kunst wohl erfahren, ich will dir deine Augen heilen, wenn du mir mein Leben lassen willst.‹ Er sicherte mir mein Leben zu, wenn ich das vermöchte. Er gab mir alles was ich dazu verlangte. Ich tat Öl in einen Kessel, mengte Schwefel, Pech, Salz, Arsenik und andere verderbliche Dinge hinein, und stellte den Kessel über das Feuer, als wollte ich ein Pflaster für seine Augen bereiten. Sobald das Öl im Sieden war, musste der Riese sich niederlegen, und ich goss ihm alles, was im Kessel war, auf die Augen, über den Hals und den Leib, so dass er das Gesicht völlig verlor und die Haut am ganzen Leib verbrannte und zusammenschrumpfte. Er fuhr mit entsetzlichem Geheul in die Höhe, warf sich wieder zur Erde, wälzte sich hin und her, und schrie und brüllte dabei wie ein Löwe oder ein Ochse. Dann sprang er in Wut auf, packte eine große Keule, und in dem Haus umher laufend, schlug er auf die Erde und gegen die Wand und dachte mich zu treffen. Entfliehen konnte ich nicht, denn das Haus war überall von hohen Mauern umgeben, und die Türen waren mit eisernen Riegeln verschlossen. Ich sprang aus einem Winkel in den andern, endlich wusste ich mir nicht anders zu helfen, ich stieg auf eine Leiter bis zu dem Dach, und hieng mich mit beiden Händen an den Hahnenbalken. Da hieng ich einen Tag und eine Nacht als ich es aber nicht länger aushalten konnte, so stieg ich wieder herab und mischte mich unter die Schafe. Da musste ich behend sein, und immer mit den Tieren zwischen seinen Beinen hindurchlaufen ohne dass er mich gewahr ward. Endlich fand ich in einer Ecke unter den Schafen die Haut eines Widders liegen, ich schlüpfte hinein und wusste es so zu machen, dass mir die Hörner des Tiers gerade auf dem Kopf standen. Der Riese hatte die Gewohnheit, wenn die Schafe hinaus auf die Weide gehen sollten, so ließ er sie vorher durch seine Beine laufen. Da zählte er sie, und welches am feistesten war, das packte er, kochte es und hielt damit seine Mahlzeit. Ich wäre bei dieser Gelegenheit gerne davon gelaufen und drängte mich durch seine Beine, wie die Schafe taten: als er mich aber packte und merkte dass ich schwer war, so sprach er ›du bist feist, du sollst mir heute meinen Bauch füllen.‹ Ich tat einen Satz und entsprang ihm aus den Händen, aber er ergriff mich wieder. Ich entkam nochmals, aber er packte mich aufs neue, und so gieng es siebenmal. Da ward er zornig und sprach ›lauf hin, die Wölfe mögen dich fressen, du hast mich genug genarrt.‹ Als ich draußen war, warf ich die Haut ab, rief ihm spöttisch zu dass ich ihm doch entsprungen wäre und höhnte ihn. Er zog einen Ring vom Finger und sprach ›nimm diesen goldenen Ring als eine Gabe von mir, du hast ihn wohl verdient. Es ziemt sich nicht, dass ein so listiger und behender Mann unbeschenkt von mir gehe.‹ Ich nahm den Ring und steckte ihn an meinen Finger, aber ich wusste nicht dass ein Zauber darin lag. Von dem Augenblick an, wo er mir am Finger saß, musste ich unaufhörlich rufen ›hier bin ich! hier bin ich!‹, ich mochte wollen oder nicht. Da der Riese daran merken konnte wo ich mich befand, so lief er mir in den Wald nach. Dabei rannte er, weil er blind war, jeden Augenblick gegen einen Ast oder einen Stamm und fiel nieder wie ein mächtiger Baum: aber er erhob sich schnell wieder, und da er lange Beine hatte und große Schritte machen konnte, so holte er mich immer wieder ein, und war mir schon ganz nahe, denn ich rief ohne Unterlass ›hier bin ich! hier bin ich‹. Ich merkte wohl dass der Ring

die Ursache meines Geschreies war und wollte ihn abziehen, aber ich vermochte es nicht. Da blieb mir nichts anderes übrig, ich biss mir mit meinen Zähnen den Finger ab. In
dem Augenblick hörte ich auf zu rufen, und entlief glücklich dem Riesen. Zwar hatte ich meinen Finger verloren,
aber ich hatte doch mein Leben behalten.«

»Frau Königin«, sprach der Räuber, »ich habe euch diese
Geschichte erzählt, um einen meiner Söhne zu erlösen,
jetzt will ich, um den zweiten zu befreien, berichten was
sich weiter zutrug. Als ich den Händen des Riesen entronnen war, irrte ich in der Wildnis umher und wusste nicht
wo ich mich hinwenden sollte. Ich stieg auf die höchsten
Tannen und auf die Gipfel der Berge, aber wohin ich blickte, weit und breit war kein Haus, kein Acker, keine Spur
von menschlichem Dasein, überall nichts als eine schreckliche Wildnis. Ich stieg von himmelhohen Bergen herab in
Täler, die den tiefsten Abgründen zu vergleichen waren.
Mir begegneten Löwen, Bären, Büffel, Waldesel, giftige
Schlangen und scheußliches Gewürm; ich sah wilde, behaarte Waldmenschen, Leute mit Hörnern und Schnäbeln,
so entsetzlich, dass mir noch jetzt schaudert, wenn ich daran zurückdenke. Ich zog immer weiter, Hunger und Durst
quälten mich, und ich musste jeden Augenblick befürchten
vor Müdigkeit umzusinken. Endlich, eben als die Sonne
untergehen wollte, kam ich auf einen hohen Berg, da sah
ich in einem öden Tal einen Rauch aufsteigen, wie aus einem angezündeten Backofen. Ich lief so schnell ich konnte
den Berg herab nach dem Rauch zu: als ich unten ankam,
sah ich drei tote Männer, die waren an dem Ast eines Baumes aufgehängt. Ich erschrak, denn ich dachte ich würde in
die Gewalt eines anderen Riesen kommen, und war um
mein Leben besorgt. Doch fasste mir ein Herz, gieng
weiter, und fand ein kleines Haus, dessen Türe weit offen
stand: bei dem Feuer des Herds saß da eine Frau mit ihrem
Kinde. Ich trat ein, grüßte sie, und fragte warum sie hier so
allein säße und wo ihr Mann sich befände; ich fragte auch

ob es noch weit bis dahin wäre, wo Menschen wohnten. Sie
antwortete mir, das Land, wo Menschen wohnten, das läge
in weiter Ferne, und erzählte mit weinenden Augen in vori-
ger Nacht wären die wilden Waldungeheuer gekommen
und hätten sie und das Kind von der Seite ihres Mannes
weggeraubt und in diese Wildnis gebracht. Dann wären sie
am Morgen wieder ausgezogen und hätten ihr geboten das
Kind zu töten und zu kochen, weil sie es, wenn sie zurück-
kämen, aufessen wollten. Als ich das gehört hatte, empfand
ich großes Mitleid mit der Frau und dem Kinde und beschloss sie aus ihrer Not zu erlösen. Ich lief fort zu dem
Baum, an welchem die drei Diebe aufgehängt waren, nahm
den Mittelsten, der wohlbeleibt war, herab und trug ihn in
das Haus. Ich zerteilte ihn in Stücke und sagte der Frau sie
sollte ihn den Riesen zu essen geben. Das Kind aber nahm
ich, und versteckte es in einen hohlen Baum, dann verbarg
ich mich selbst hinter das Haus, so dass ich bemerken
konnte wo die wilden Menschen herkämen und ob es Not
wäre, der Frau selbst zu Hilfe zu eilen. Als die Sonne untergehen wollte, sah ich die Ungeheuer von dem Berge her-
ablaufen: sie waren gräulich und furchtbar anzusehen, den
Affen an Gestalt ähnlich. Sie schleppten einen toten Leib
hinter sich her, aber ich konnte nicht sehen wer es war. Als
sie in das Haus kamen, zündeten sie ein großes Feuer an,
zerrissen den blutigen Leib mit ihren Zähnen und verzehr-
ten ihn. Darnach nahmen sie den Kessel, in dem das Fleisch
des Diebes gekocht war, vom Feuer, und zerteilten die Stücke unter sich zum Abendessen. Als sie fertig waren, fragte
einer, der ihr Oberhaupt zu sein schien, die Frau ob das,
was sie gegessen hätten, das Fleisch ihres Kindes gewesen
wäre. Die Frau sagte ›ja‹. Da sprach das Ungeheuer ›ich
glaube du hast dein Kind versteckt und uns einen von den
Dieben gekocht, die an dem Ast hängen.‹ Er ließ drei von
seinen Gesellen hinlaufen und ihm von einem jeden der
drei Diebe ein Stück Fleisch bringen, damit er sähe dass sie
noch alle dort wären. Als ich das hörte lief ich schnell vor-

aus und hieng mich mit meinen Händen, mitten zwischen die zwei Diebe, an das Seil, von dem ich den dritten abgenommen hatte. Als nun die Ungeheuer kamen, schnitten sie einem jeden ein Stück Fleisch aus den Lenden. Auch mir schnitten sie ein Stück heraus, aber ich duldete es ohne einen Laut von mir zu geben. Ich habe zum Zeugnis noch die Narbe an meinem Leib.«

Hier schwieg der Räuber einen Augenblick und sprach dann »Frau Königin, ich habe euch dies Abenteuer erzählt für meinen zweiten Sohn, jetzt will ich euch für den dritten den Schluss der Geschichte berichten. Als das wilde Volk mit den drei Stücken Fleisch fortgelaufen war, so ließ ich mich wieder herab und verband meine Wunde mit Streifen von meinem Hemd so gut ich konnte; doch das Blut ließ sich nicht stillen, sondern strömte an mir herab. Aber ich achtete nicht darauf, sondern dachte nur wie ich der Frau mein Versprechen halten, und sie und das Kind retten wollte. Ich eilte also wieder zu dem Haus zurück, hielt mich verborgen, und horchte auf das was geschah, aber ich konnte mich nur mit Mühe aufrecht erhalten: mich schmerzte die Wunde, und ich war von Hunger und Durst ganz abgemattet. Indessen versuchte der Riese die drei Stücke Fleisch, die ihm gebracht waren, und als er das gekostet hatte, welches mir ausgeschnitten und noch blutig war, so sprach er ›lauft hin und bringt mir den mittelsten Dieb, sein Fleisch ist noch frisch und behagt mir.‹ Als ich das hörte, eilte ich zurück zu dem Galgen und hieng mich wieder an das Seil zwischen die zwei Toten. Bald darauf kamen die Ungeheuer nahmen mich von dem Galgen herab und schleiften mich über Dornen und Distel zu dem Haus, wo sie mich auf den Boden hinstreckten. Sie schärften ihre Zähne, wetzten ihre Messer über mir und bereiteten sich mich zu schlachten und zu essen. Eben wollten sie Hand anlegen, als plötzlich ein solches Ungewitter mit Blitz, Donner und Wind sich erhob, dass die Ungeheuer selbst in Schrecken gerieten und mit grässlichem Geschrei zu den

Fenstern, Türen und zum Dach hinausfuhren und mich auf dem Boden liegen ließen. Nach drei Stunden begann es Tag zu werden, und die klare Sonne stieg empor. Ich machte mich mit der Frau und dem Kinde auf, wir wanderten vierzig Tage durch die Wildnis und hatten keine andere Nahrung als Wurzeln Beeren und Kräuter, die im Walde wachsen. Endlich kam ich wieder unter Menschen und brachte die Frau mit dem Kinde zu ihrem Mann zurück: wie groß seine Freude war, kann sich jeder leicht denken.

Damit war die Geschichte des Räubers zu Ende. »Du hast durch die Befreiung der Frau und des Kindes viel Böses wieder gut gemacht«, sprach die Königin zu ihm, »ich gebe dir deine drei Söhne frei.«